Miguel de Cervantes

Don Quixote

A New Translation by Edith Grossman

INTRODUCTION
BY HAROLD BLOOM

ecco
An Imprint of HarperCollinsPublishers

HarperCollins books may be purchased for educational, business, or sales promotional use. For information, please write: Special Markets Department, HarperCollins Publishers Inc., 10 East 53rd Street, New York, NY 10022.

FIRST EDITION

Designed by Cassandra J. Pappas

Library of Congress Cataloging-in-Publication Data

Cervantes Saavedra, Miguel de, 1547–1616
[Don Quixote. English]
Don Quixote / Miguel de Cervantes Saavedra ; translated by Edith Grossman ; with an introduction by Harold Bloom.—1st ed.
p. cm.
ISBN 0-06-018870-7 (alk. paper)
I. Grossman, Edith, 1936–   II. Bloom, Harold.   III. Title.
PQ6329.A2 2003b
863'.3—dc21
2003045216

Contents

FIRST PART OF THE INGENIOUS GENTLEMAN
DON QUIXOTE OF LA MANCHA

Part Two of the Ingenious Gentleman Don Quixote of La Mancha

Part Three of the Ingenious Gentleman
Don Quixote of La Mancha

Part Four of the Ingenious Gentleman Don Quixote of La Mancha

Second Part of the Ingenious Gentleman Don Quixote of La Mancha

Translator's Note to the Reader

In the author's prologue to what is now called part I of *Don Quixote* (part II appeared ten years later, in 1615, following the publication of a continuation of the knight's adventures written by someone using the pseudonym "Avellaneda"), Cervantes said this about his book and the need to write a preface for it:

> I wanted only to offer it to you plain and bare, unadorned by a prologue or the endless catalogue of sonnets, epigrams, and laudatory poems that are usually placed at the beginning of books. For I can tell you that although it cost me some effort to compose, none seemed greater than creating the preface you are now reading. I picked up my pen many times to write it, and many times I put it down again because I did not know what to write; and once, when I was baffled, with the paper in front of me, my pen behind my ear, my elbow propped on the writing table and my cheek resting in my hand, pondering what I would say, a friend of mine . . . came in, and seeing me so perplexed he asked the reason, and I . . . said I was thinking about the prologue I had to write for the history of Don Quixote. . . .

Cervantes's fictional difficulty was certainly my factual one as I contemplated the prospect of writing even a few lines about the wonderfully utopian task of translating the first—and probably the greatest—modern novel. Substitute keyboard and monitor for pen and paper, and my dilemma and posture were the same; the dear friend who helped me solve the problem was really Cervantes himself, an embodied spirit who emerged out of the shadows and off the pages when I realized I could begin this note by quoting a few sentences from his prologue.

I call the undertaking utopian in the sense intended by Ortega y Gasset when he deemed translations utopian but then went on to say that all human efforts to communicate—even in the same language— are equally utopian, equally luminous with value, and equally worth the doing. Endeavoring to translate artful writing, particularly an indispensable work like *Don Quixote*, grows out of infinite optimism as the translator valiantly, perhaps quixotically, attempts to enter the mind of the first writer through the gateway of the text. It is a daunting and inspiring enterprise.

I have never kept a translating journal, though I admire those I have read. Keeping records of any kind is not something I do easily, and after six or seven hours of translating at the computer, the idea of writing about what I have written looms insurmountably, as does the kind of self-scrutiny required: the actuality of the translation is in the translation, and having to articulate how and why I have just articulated the text seems cruelly redundant. Yet there are some general considerations that may be of interest to you. I hesitated over the spelling of the protagonist's name, for instance, and finally opted for an *x*, not a *j*, in Quixote (I wanted the connection to the English "quixotic" to be immediately apparent); I debated the question of footnotes with myself and decided I was obliged to put some in, though I had never used them before in a translation (I did not want the reader to be put off by references that may now be obscure, or to miss the layers of intention and meaning those allusions create); I wondered about consulting other translations and vowed not to—at least in the beginning—in order to keep my ear clear and the voice of the translation free of outside influences (I kept the vow for the first year, and then, from time to time, I glanced at other people's work); I chose to use Martín de Riquer's edition of *Don Quixote*, which is based on the first printing of the book (with all its historic slips and errors) and has useful notes that include discussions of problematic words and phrases based on Riquer's comparisons of the earliest seventeenth-century translations into English, French, and Italian. Finally, I assure you that I felt an ongoing, unstoppable rush of exhilaration and terror, for perfectly predictable and transparent reasons, at undertaking so huge and so important a project.

Every translator has to live with the kind of pedantic critic who is always ready to pounce at an infelicitous phrase or misinterpreted word in a book that can be hundreds of pages long. I had two or three soul-searing nightmares about rampaging hordes laying waste to my translation of the work that is not only the great monument of literature in Spanish but a pillar of the entire Western literary tradition. The extraordinary significance and influence of this novel were reaffirmed, once again, in 2002, when one hundred major writers from fifty-four countries voted *Don Quixote* the best work of fiction in the world. One reason for the exalted position it occupies is that Cervantes's book contains within itself, in germ or full-blown, practically every imaginative technique and device used by subsequent fiction writers to engage their readers and construct their works. The prospect of translating it was stupefying.

Shortly before I began work, while I was wrestling with the question of what kind of voice would be most appropriate for the translation of a book written some four hundred years ago, I mentioned my fears to Julián Ríos, the Spanish novelist. His reply was simple and profound and immensely liberating. He told me not to be afraid; Cervantes, he said, was our most modern writer, and what I had to do was to translate him the way I translated everyone else—that is, the contemporary authors whose works I have brought over into English. Julián's characterization was a revelation; it desacralized the project and allowed me, finally, to confront the text and find the voice in English. For me this is the essential challenge in translation: hearing, in the most profound way I can, the text in Spanish and discovering the voice to say (I mean, to write) the text again in English. Compared to that, lexical difficulties shrink and wither away.

I believe that my primary obligation as a literary translator is to recreate for the reader in English the experience of the reader in Spanish. When Cervantes wrote *Don Quixote*, it was not yet a seminal masterpiece of European literature, the book that crystallized forever the making of literature out of life *and* literature, that explored in typically ironic fashion, and for the first time, the blurred and shifting frontiers between fact and fiction, imagination and history, perception and physical reality, or that set the stage for all Hispanic studies and all serious discussions of the history and nature of the novel. When Cervantes wrote *Don Quixote*, his language was not archaic or quaint. He wrote in a crackling, up-to-date Spanish that was an intrinsic part of his time (this is instantly apparent when he has Don Quixote, in transports of knightly madness, speak in the old-fashioned idiom of the novels of chivalry), a modern language that both reflected and helped to shape the way people experienced the world. This meant that I did not need to find a special, anachronistic, somehow-seventeenth-century voice but could translate his astonishingly fine writing into contemporary English.

And his writing is a marvel: it gives off sparks and flows like honey. Cervantes's style is so artful it seems absolutely natural and inevitable; his irony is sweet-natured, his sensibility sophisticated, compassionate, and humorous. If my translation works at all, the reader should keep turning the pages, smiling a good deal, periodically bursting into laughter, and impatiently waiting for the next synonym (Cervantes delighted in accumulating synonyms, especially descriptive ones, within the same phrase), the next mind-bending coincidence, the next variation on the structure of Don Quixote's adventures, the next incomparable conversation between the knight and his squire. To quote again from Cervantes's prologue: "I do not want to charge you too much for the service I have performed in introducing you to so noble and honorable a knight; but I do want you to thank me for allowing you to make the acquaintance of the famous Sancho Panza, his squire. . . ."

I began the work in February 2001 and completed it two years later, but it is important for you to know that "final" versions are determined more by a publisher's due date than by any sense on my part that the work is actually finished. Even so, I hope you find it deeply amusing and truly compelling. If not, you can be certain the fault is mine.

EDITH GROSSMAN
March 2003
New York

Introduction:
Don Quixote, Sancho Panza, and
Miguel de Cervantes Saavedra

BY HAROLD BLOOM

1

What is the true object of Don Quixote's quest? I find that unanswerable. What are Hamlet's authentic motives? We are not permitted to know. Since Cervantes's magnificent Knight's quest has cosmological scope and reverberation, no object seems beyond reach. Hamlet's frustration is that he is allowed only Elsinore and revenge tragedy. Shakespeare composed a poem unlimited, in which only the protagonist is beyond all limits.

Cervantes and Shakespeare, who died almost simultaneously, are the central Western authors, at least since Dante, and no writer since has matched them, not Tolstoi or Goethe, Dickens, Proust, Joyce. Context cannot hold Cervantes and Shakespeare: the Spanish Golden Age and the Elizabethan-Jacobean era are secondary when we attempt a full appreciation of what we are given.

W. H. Auden found in Don Quixote a portrait of the Christian saint, as opposed to Hamlet, who "lacks faith in God and in himself." Though Auden *sounds* perversely ironic, he was quite serious and, I think, wrongheaded. Against Auden I set Miguel de Unamuno, my favorite critic of *Don Quixote*. For Unamuno, Alonso Quixano is the Christian saint, while Don Quixote is the originator of the actual Spanish religion, Quixotism.

Herman Melville blended Don Quixote and Hamlet in Captain Ahab (with a touch of Milton's Satan added for seasoning). Ahab desires to avenge himself upon the white whale, while Satan would destroy God, if only he could. Hamlet is death's ambassador to us, according to G. Wilson Knight. Don Quixote says that his quest is to destroy injustice. The final injustice is death, the ultimate bondage. To set captives free is the knight's pragmatic way of battling against death.

Though there have been many valuable English translations of *Don Quixote*, I would commend Edith Grossman's version for the extraordinarily high quality of her prose. The Knight and Sancho are so eloquently rendered by Grossman that the vitality of their characterization is more clearly conveyed than ever before. There is also an astonishing contextualization of Don Quixote and Sancho in Grossman's translation that I believe has not been achieved before. The spiritual atmosphere of a Spain already in steep decline can be felt throughout, thanks to the heightened quality of her diction.

Grossman might be called the Glenn Gould of translators, because she, too, articulates every note. Reading her amazing mode of finding equivalents in English for Cervantes's darkening vision is an entrance into a further understanding of why this great book contains within itself all the novels that have followed in its sublime wake. Like Shakespeare, Cervantes is inescapable for all writers who have come after him. Dickens and Flaubert, Joyce and Proust reflect the narrative procedures of Cervantes, and their glories of characterization mingle strains of Shakespeare and Cervantes.

2

You cannot locate Shakespeare in his own works, not even in the sonnets. It is this near invisibility that encourages the zealots who believe that almost anyone wrote Shakespeare, except Shakespeare himself. As far as I know, the Hispanic world does not harbor covens who labor to prove that Lope de Vega or Calderón de la Barca composed *Don Quixote*. Cervantes inhabits his great book so pervasively that we need to see that it has three unique personalities: the Knight, Sancho, and Cervantes himself.

Yet how sly and subtle is the presence of Cervantes! At its most hilarious, *Don Quixote* is immensely somber. Shakespeare again is the illuminating analogue: Hamlet at his most melancholic will not cease his punning or his gallows humor, and Falstaff's boundless wit is tormented by intimations of rejection. Just as Shakespeare wrote in no genre, *Don Quixote* is tragedy as well as comedy. Though it stands forever as the birth of the novel out of the prose romance, and is still the best of all novels, I find its sadness augments each time I reread it and does make it "the Spanish Bible," as Unamuno termed this greatest of all narratives. Novels are written by George Eliot and Henry James, by Balzac and Flaubert, or by the Tolstoi of *Anna Karenina. Don Quixote* may not be a scripture, but it so contains us that, as with Shakespeare, we cannot get out of it, in order to achieve perspectivism. We are inside the vast book, privileged to hear the superb conversations between the Knight and his squire, Sancho Panza. Sometimes we are fused with Cervantes, but more often we are invisible wanderers who accompany the sublime pair in their adventures and debacles.

If there is a third Western author with universal appeal from the Renaissance on, it could only be Dickens. Yet Dickens purposely does not give us "man's final lore," which Melville found in Shakespeare and presumably in Cervantes also. *King Lear*'s first performance took place as part I of *Don Quixote* was published. Contra Auden, Cervantes, like Shakespeare, gives us a secular transcendence. Don Quixote does regard himself as God's knight, but he continuously follows his own capricious will, which is gloriously idiosyncratic. King Lear appeals to the skyey heavens for aid, but on the personal grounds that they and he are old. Battered by realities that are even more violent than he is, Don Quixote resists yielding to the authority of church and state. When he ceases to assert his autonomy, there is nothing left except to be Alonso Quixano the Good again, and no action remaining except to die.

I return to my initial question: the Sorrowful Knight's object. He is at war with Freud's reality principle, which accepts the necessity of dying. But he is neither a fool nor a madman, and his vision always is at least double: he sees what we see, yet he sees something else also, a possible glory that he desires to appropriate or at least share. Unamuno names this transcendence as literary fame, the immortality of Cervantes and Shakespeare. Certainly that is part of the Knight's quest; much of part II turns upon his and Sancho's delightful apprehension that their adventures in part I are recognized everywhere. Perhaps Unamuno underestimated the complexities involved in so grand a disruption in the aesthetics of representation. *Hamlet* again is the best analogue: from the entrance of the players in act II through the close of the performance of

The Mousetrap in act III, all the rules of normative representation are tossed away, and everything is theatricality. Part II of *Don Quixote* is similarly and bewilderingly advanced, since the Knight, Sancho, and everyone they encounter are acutely conscious that fiction has disrupted the order of reality.

3

We need to hold in mind as we read *Don Quixote* that we cannot condescend to the Knight and Sancho, since together they know more than we do, just as we never can catch up to the amazing speed of Hamlet's cognitions. Do we know exactly who we are? The more urgently we quest for our authentic selves, the more they tend to recede. The Knight and Sancho, as the great work closes, know exactly who they are, not so much by their adventures as through their marvelous conversations, be they quarrels or exchanges of insights.

Poetry, particularly Shakespeare's, teaches us how to talk to ourselves, but not to others. Shakespeare's great figures are gorgeous solipsists: Shylock, Falstaff, Hamlet, Iago, Lear, Cleopatra, with Rosalind the brilliant exception. Don Quixote and Sancho really listen to each other and change through this receptivity. Neither of them *overhears* himself, which is the Shakespearean mode. Cervantes or Shakespeare: they are rival teachers of how we change and why. Friendship in Shakespeare is ironic at best, treacherous more commonly. The friendship between Sancho Panza and his Knight surpasses any other in literary representation.

We do not have *Cardenio*, the play Shakespeare wrote, with John Fletcher, after reading Thomas Shelton's contemporaneous translation of *Don Quixote*. Therefore we cannot know what Shakespeare thought of Cervantes, though we can surmise his delight. Cervantes, an unsuccessful dramatist, presumably never heard of Shakespeare, but I doubt that he would have valued Falstaff and Hamlet, both of whom chose the self's freedom over obligations of any kind. Sancho, as Kafka remarked, is a free man, but Don Quixote is metaphysically and psychologically bound by his dedication to knight errantry. We can celebrate the Knight's endless valor, but not his literalization of the romance of chivalry.

4

But does Don Quixote altogether believe in the reality of his own vision? Evidently he does not, particularly when he (and Sancho) is surrendered by Cervantes to the sadomasochistic practical jokes—indeed, the vicious and humiliating cruelties—that afflict the Knight and squire in part II. Nabokov is very illuminating on this in his *Lectures on Don Quixote*, published posthumously in 1983:

> Both parts of *Don Quixote* form a veritable encyclopedia of cruelty. From that viewpoint it is one of the most bitter and barbarous books ever penned. And its cruelty is artistic.

To find a Shakespearean equivalent to this aspect of *Don Quixote*, you would have to fuse *Titus Andronicus* and *The Merry Wives of Windsor* into one work, a grim prospect because they are, to me, Shakespeare's weakest plays. Falstaff's dreadful humiliation by the merry wives is unacceptable enough (even if it formed the basis for Verdi's sublime *Falstaff*). Why does Cervantes subject Don Quixote to the physical abuse of part I and the psychic tortures of part II? Nabokov's answer is aesthetic: The cruelty is vitalized by Cervantes's characteristic artistry. That seems to me something of an evasion. *Twelfth Night* is comedy unsurpassable, and on the stage we are consumed by hilarity at Malvolio's terrible humiliations. When we reread the play, we become uneasy, because Malvolio's socioerotic fantasies echo in virtually all of us. Why are we not made at least a little dubious by the torments, bodily and socially, suffered by Don Quixote and Sancho Panza?

Cervantes himself, as a constant if disguised presence in the text, is the answer. He was the most battered of eminent writers. At the great naval battle of Lepanto, he was wounded and so at twenty-four permanently lost the use of his left hand. In 1575, he was captured by Barbary pirates and spent five years as a slave in Algiers. Ransomed in 1580, he served Spain as a spy in Portugal and Oran and then returned to Madrid, where he attempted a career as a dramatist, almost invariably failing after writing at least twenty plays. Somewhat desperately, he became a tax collector, only to be indicted and imprisoned for supposed malfeasance in 1597. A fresh imprisonment came in 1605; there is a tradition that he began to compose *Don Quixote* in jail. Part I, written at incredible speed, was published in 1605. Part II, spurred by a false continuation of *Don Quixote* by one Avellaneda, was published in 1615.

Fleeced of all royalties of part I by the publisher, Cervantes would have died in poverty except for the belated patronage of a discerning nobleman, in the last three years of his life. Though Shakespeare died at just fifty-two (why, we do not know), he was an immensely successful dramatist and became quite prosperous by shareholding in the actors' company that played at the Globe Theater. Circumspect, and only too aware of the government-inspired murder of Christopher Marlowe, and their torture of Thomas Kyd, and branding of Ben Jonson, Shakespeare kept himself nearly anonymous, in spite of being the reigning dramatist of London. Violence, slavery, and imprisonment were the staples of Cervantes's life. Shakespeare, wary to the end, had an existence almost without a memorable incident, as far as we can tell.

The physical and mental torments suffered by Don Quixote and Sancho Panza had been central to Cervantes's endless struggle to stay alive and free. Yet Nabokov's observations are accurate: cruelty is extreme throughout *Don Quixote*. The aesthetic wonder is that this enormity fades when we stand back from the huge book and ponder its shape and endless range of meaning. No critic's account of Cervantes's masterpiece agrees with, or even resembles, any other critic's impressions. *Don Quixote* is a mirror held up not to nature, but to the reader. How can this bashed and mocked knight errant be, as he is, a universal paradigm?

5

Hamlet does not need or want our admiration and affection, but Don Quixote does, and he receives it, as Hamlet generally does also. Sancho, like Falstaff, is replete with self-delight, though Sancho does not rouse moralizing critics to wrath and disapproval, as the sublime Falstaff does. Much more has been written about the Halmet/Don Quixote contrast than about Sancho/Falstaff, two vitalists in aesthetic contention as masters of reality. But no critic has called Don Quixote a murderer or Sancho an immoralist. Hamlet is responsible for eight deaths, his own included, and Falstaff is a highwayman, a warrior averse to battle, and a fleecer of everyone he encounters. Yet Hamlet and Falstaff are victimizers, not victims, even if Hamlet dies properly fearing a wounded name and Falstaff is destroyed by Hal/Henry V's rejection. It does not matter. The fascination of Hamlet's intellect and of Falstaff's wit is what endures. Don Quixote and Sancho are victims, but both are extraordinarily resilient, until the Knight's final defeat and dying into the identity of

Quixano the Good, whom Sancho vainly implores to take to the road again. The fascination of Don Quixote's endurance and of Sancho's loyal wisdom always remains.

Cervantes plays upon the human need to withstand suffering, which is one reason the Knight awes us. However good a Catholic he may (or may not) have been, Cervantes is interested in heroism and not in sainthood. Shakespeare, I think, was not interested in either, since none of his heroes can endure close scrutiny: Hamlet, Othello, Antony, Coriolanus. Only Edgar, the recalcitrant survivor who inherits the nation, most unwillingly, in *King Lear,* abides our skepticism, and at least one prominent Shakespeare critic weirdly has called Edgar "weak and murderous." The heroism of Don Quixote is by no means constant: he is perfectly capable of flight, abandoning poor Sancho to be beaten up by an entire village. Cervantes, a hero at Lepanto, wants Don Quixote to be a new kind of hero, neither ironic nor mindless, but one who wills to be himself, as José Ortega y Gasset accurately phrased it.

Hamlet subverts the will, while Falstaff satirizes it. Don Quixote and Sancho Panza both exalt the will, though the Knight transcendentalizes it, and Sancho, the first postpragmatic, wants to keep it within limits. It is the transcendent element in Don Quixote that ultimately persuades us of his greatness, partly because it is set against the deliberately coarse, frequently sordid context of the panoramic book. And again it is important to note that this transcendence is secular and literary, and not Catholic. The Quixotic quest is erotic, yet even the eros is literary. Crazed by reading (as so many of us still are), the Knight is in quest of a new self, one that can overgo the erotic madness of Orlando (Roland) in Ariosto's *Orlando Furioso* or of the mythic Amadís of Gaul. Unlike Orlando's or Amadís's, Don Quixote's madness is deliberate, self-inflicted, a traditional poetic strategy. Still, there is a clear sublimation of the sexual drive in the Knight's desperate courage. Lucidity keeps breaking in, reminding him that Dulcinea is his own supreme fiction, transcending an honest lust for the peasant girl Aldonza Lorenzo. A fiction, believed in even though you know it is a fiction, can be validated only by sheer will.

Erich Auerbach argued for the book's "continuous gaiety," which is not at all my own experience as a reader. But *Don Quixote,* like the best of Shakespeare, will sustain any theory you bring to it, as well or as badly as any other. The Sorrowful Knight is more than an enigma: he seeks an undying name, literary immortality, and finds it, but only through being all but dismantled in part I and all but teased into real madness in part II:

Cervantes performs the miracle, nobly Dante-like, of presiding over his creation like a Providence, but also subjecting himself to the subtle changes brought about both in the Knight and in Sancho Panza by their wonderful conversations, in which a shared love manifests itself by equality and grumpy disputes. They are brothers, rather than father and son. To describe the precise way that Cervantes regards them, whether with ironic love or loving irony, is an impossible critical task.

6

Harry Levin shrewdly phrased what he called "Cervantes' formula":

> This is nothing more nor less than a recognition of the difference between verses and reverses, between words and deeds, *palabras* and *hechos*—in short, between literary artifice and that real thing which is life itself. But literary artifice is the only means that a writer has at his disposal. How else can he convey his impression of life? Precisely by discrediting those means, by repudiating that air of bookishness in which any book is inevitably wrapped. When Pascal observed that the true eloquence makes fun of eloquence, he succinctly formulated the principle that could look to Cervantes as its recent and striking exemplar. It remained for La Rochefoucauld to restate the other side of the paradox: some people would never have loved if they had not heard of love.

It is true that I cannot think of any other work in which the relations between words and deeds are as ambiguous as in *Don Quixote*, except (once again) for *Hamlet*. Cervantes's formula is also Shakespeare's, though in Cervantes we feel the burden of the experiential, whereas Shakespeare is uncanny, since nearly all of his experience was theatrical. Still, the ironizing of eloquence characterizes the speeches of both Hamlet and Don Quixote. One might at first think that Hamlet is more word-conscious than is the Knight, but part II of Cervantes's dark book manifests a growth in the Sorrowful Face's awareness of his own rhetoricity.

I want to illustrate Don Quixote's development by setting him against the wonderful trickster Ginés de Pasamonte, whose first appearance is as a galley-bound prisoner in part I, chapter XXII, and who pops up again in part II, chapters XXV–XXVII, as Master Pedro, the divinator and puppeteer. Ginés is a sublime scamp and picaroon confidence man, but also a picaresque romance writer in the model of *Lazarillo de Tormes* (1533), the anonymous masterpiece of its mode (see W. S. Merwin's beautiful translation, in 1962). When Ginés reappears as Master Pedro in part II, he has become a satire upon Cervantes's hugely successful rival, Lope de Vega, the "monster of literature" who turned out a hit play nearly every week (whereas Cervantes had failed hopelessly as a dramatist).

Every reader has her or his favorite episodes in *Don Quixote*; mine are the two misadventures the Knight inaugurates in regard to Ginés/Master Pedro. In the first, Don Quixote gallantly frees Ginés and his fellow prisoners, only to be beaten nearly to death (with poor Sancho) by the ungrateful convicts. In the second, the Knight is so taken in by Master Pedro's illusionism that he charges at the puppet show and cuts the puppets to pieces, in what can be regarded as Cervantes's critique of Lope de Vega. Here first is Ginés, in the admirable new translation by Edith Grossman:

"He's telling the truth," said the commissary. "He wrote his own history himself, as fine as you please, and he pawned the book for two hundred *reales* and left it in prison."

"And I intend to redeem it," said Ginés, "even for two hundred *ducados*."

"Is it that good?" said Don Quixote.

"It is so good," responded Ginés, "that it's too bad for *Lazarillo de Tormes* and all the other books of that genre that have been written or will be written. What I can tell your grace is that it deals with truths, and they are truths so appealing and entertaining that no lies can equal them."

"And what is the title of the book?" asked Don Quixote.

"The Life of Ginés de Pasamonte," he replied.

"And is it finished?" asked Don Quixote.

"How can it be finished," he responded, "if my life isn't finished yet? What I've written goes from my birth to the moment when they sentenced me to the galleys this last time."

"Then you have been there before?" said Don Quixote.

"To serve God and the king, I've already spent four years on the galleys, and I know the taste of the hardtack and the overseer's whip," responded Ginés. "And I'm not too sorry to go there, because I'll have time to finish my book, for I still have lots of things to say, and on the galleys of Spain there's more leisure than I'll need, though I don't need much for what I have to write because I know it by heart."

Ginés, admirable miscreant, is a demonic parody of Cervantes himself, who had served five years in Algerian slavery and whose total *Don Quixote* became nearly unfinishable. The death of Cervantes came only a year after the publication of the second part of the great saga. Doubtless, Cervantes regarded Lope de Vega as his own demonic shadow, which is made clearer in the magnificent assault upon Master Pedro's puppet show. The picaroon Ginés follows the general law of part II, which is that everyone of consequence either has read part I or is aware that he was a character in it. Master Pedro evades identity with Ginés, but at the high cost of witnessing another furious assault by the Knight of the Woeful Face. But this comes just after Master Pedro is strongly identified with Lope de Vega:

> The interpreter said nothing in reply but went on, saying:
>
> "There was no lack of curious eyes, the kind that tend to see everything, to see Melisendra descend from the balcony and mount the horse, and they informed King Marsilio, who immediately gave orders to sound the call to arms; and see how soon this is done, and how the city is flooded with the sound of the bells that ring from all the towers of the mosques."
>
> "No, that is wrong!" said Don Quixote. "Master Pedro is incorrect in the matter of the bells, for the Moors do not use bells but drums and a kind of flute that resembles our flageolet, and there is no doubt that ringing bells in Sansueña is a great piece of nonsense."
>
> This was heard by Master Pedro, who stopped the ringing and said:
>
> "Your grace should not concern yourself with trifles, Señor Don Quixote, or try to carry things so far that you never reach the end of them. Aren't a thousand plays performed almost every day that are full of a thousand errors and pieces of nonsense, and yet are successful productions that are greeted not only with applause but with admiration? Go on, boy, and let them say what they will, for as long as I fill my purse, there can be more errors than atoms in the sun."
>
> "That is true," replied Don Quixote.

When Don Quixote assaults the puppet show, Cervantes assaults the popular taste that had preferred the theater of Lope de Vega to his own:

> And Don Quixote, seeing and hearing so many Moors and so much clamor, thought it would be a good idea to assist those who were fleeing; and rising to his feet, in a loud voice he said:

"I shall not consent, in my lifetime and in my presence, to any such offense against an enamored knight so famous and bold as Don Gaiferos. Halt, you lowborn rabble; do not follow and do not pursue him unless you wish to do battle with me!"

And speaking and taking action, he unsheathed his sword, leaped next to the stage, and with swift and never before seen fury began to rain down blows on the crowd of Moorish puppets, knocking down some, beheading others, ruining this one, destroying that one, and among many other blows he delivered so powerful a downstroke that if Master Pedro had not stooped, crouched down, and hunched over, he would have cut off his head more easily than if it had been so much marzipan. Master Pedro cried out, saying:

"Your grace must stop, Señor Don Quixote, and realize that the ones you are overthrowing, destroying, and killing are not real Moors but only pasteboard figures. Sinner that I am, you are destroying and ruining everything I own!"

But this did not keep Don Quixote from raining down slashes, two-handed blows, thrusts, and backstrokes. In short, in less time than it takes to tell about it, he knocked the puppet theater to the floor, all its scenery and figures cut and broken to pieces: King Marsilio was badly wounded, and Emperor Charlemagne's head and crown were split in two. The audience of spectators was in a tumult, the monkey ran out the window and onto the roof, the cousin was fearful, the page was frightened, and even Sancho Panza was terrified, because, as he swore when the storm was over, he had never seen his master in so wild a fury. When the general destruction of the puppet theater was complete, Don Quixote calmed down somewhat and said:

"At this moment I should like to have here in front of me all those who do not believe, and do not wish to believe, how much good knights errant do in the world: if I had not been here, just think what would have happened to the worthy Don Gaiferos and the beauteous Melisendra; most certainly, by this time those dogs would have overtaken them and committed some outrage against them. In brief, long live knight errantry, over and above everything in the world today!"

This gorgeous, mad intervention is also a parable of the triumph of Cervantes over the picaresque and of the triumph of the novel over the romance. The downward stroke that nearly decapitates Ginés/Master Pedro is a metaphor for the aesthetic power of *Don Quixote*. So subtle is Cervantes that he needs to be read at as many levels as Dante. Perhaps

the Quixotic can be accurately defined as the literary mode of an absolute reality, not as impossible dream but rather as a persuasive awaken-
ing into mortality.

                                  7

The aesthetic truth of Don Quixote is that, again like Dante and Shakespeare, it makes us confront greatness directly. If we have difficulty fully
understanding Don Quixote's quest, its motives and desired ends, that is
because we confront a reflecting mirror that awes us even while we yield
to delight. Cervantes is always out ahead of us, and we can never quite
catch up. Fielding and Sterne, Goethe and Thomas Mann, Flaubert and
Stendhal, Melville and Mark Twain, Dostoevsky: these are among Cervantes's admirers and pupils. Don Quixote is the only book that Dr. Johnson desired to be even longer than it already was.

    Yet Cervantes, although a universal pleasure, is in some respects even
more difficult than are Dante and Shakespeare upon their heights. Are
we to believe everything that Don Quixote says to us? Does *he* believe it?
He (or Cervantes) is the inventor of a mode now common enough, in
which figures, within a novel, read prior fictions concerning their own
earlier adventures and have to sustain a consequent loss in the sense of
reality. This is one of the beautiful enigmas of Don Quixote: it is simultaneously a work whose authentic subject is literature and a chronicle of a
hard, sordid actuality, the declining Spain of 1605–1615. The Knight is
Cervantes's subtle critique of a realm that had given him only harsh
measures in return for his own patriotic heroism at Lepanto. Don
Quixote cannot be said to have a double consciousness; his is rather the
multiple consciousness of Cervantes himself, a writer who knows the
cost of confirmation. I do not believe that the Knight can be said to tell
lies, except in the Nietzschean sense of lying against time and time's
grim "It was." To ask what it is that Don Quixote himself believes is to
enter the visionary center of his story.

    It is the superb descent of the Knight into the Cave of Montesinos
(part II, chapters XXII–XXIII) that constitutes Cervantes's longest reach
toward hinting that the Sorrowful Face is aware of its self-enchantment.
Yet we never will know if Hamlet ever touched clinical madness, or if
Don Quixote was himself persuaded of the absurd wonders he beheld in
the Cave of Enchantment. The Knight too is mad only north-northwest,
and when the wind blows from the south he is as canny as Hamlet,
Shakespeare, and Cervantes.

By descending to the cave, Don Quixote parodies the journey to the underworld of Odysseus and Aeneas. Having been lowered by a rope tied around him, the Knight is hauled up less than an hour later, apparently in deep slumber. He insists that he has sojourned below for several days and describes a surrealistic world, for which the wicked enchanter Merlin is responsible. In a crystal palace, the celebrated knight Durandarte lies in a rather vociferous state of death, while his beloved, Belerma, marches by in tears, with his heart in her hands. We scarcely can apprehend this before it turns into outrageous comedy. The enchanted Dulcinea, supposedly the glory sought by Don Quixote's quest, manifests as a peasant girl, accompanied by two other girls, her friends. Seeing the Knight, the immortal Dulcinea runs off yet sends an emissary to her lover, requesting immediate financial aid:

but of all the grievous things I saw and noted, the one that caused me most sorrow was that as Montesinos was saying these words to me, one of the companions of the unfortunate Dulcinea approached me from the side, without my seeing her, and with her eyes full of tears, in a low, troubled voice, she said to me:

"My lady Dulcinea of Toboso kisses the hands of your grace, and implores your grace to let her know how you are; and, because she is in great need, she also entreats your grace most earnestly to be so kind as to lend her, accepting as security this new cotton underskirt that I have here, half a dozen *reales* or whatever amount your grace may have, and she gives her word to return them to you very soon."

I was astounded and amazed at this message, and turning to Señor Montesinos, I asked:

"Is it possible, Señor Montesinos, that distinguished persons who are enchanted suffer from need?" To which he responded:

"Your grace can believe me, Señor Don Quixote of La Mancha, that what is called need is found everywhere, and extends to all places, and reaches everyone, and does not excuse even those who are enchanted; and since Señora Dulcinea of Toboso has sent someone to ask you for six *reales*, and the pledge is good, it seems, then you must give them to her, for she undoubtedly is in very great difficulty."

"Her security, I shall not take," I responded, "nor shall I give her what she asks, because I have no more than four *reales*."

I gave these to her (they were the ones that you, Sancho, gave me the other day so that I could give alms to the poor whom I met along the road) . . .

This curious blend of the sublime and the bathetic does not come again until Kafka, another pupil of Cervantes, would compose stories like "The Hunter Gracchus" and "A Country Doctor." To Kafka, Don Quixote was Sancho Panza's daemon or genius, projected by the shrewd Sancho into a book of adventure unto death:

> Without making any boast of it, Sancho Panza succeeded in the course of years, by devouring a great number of romances of chivalry and adventure in the evening and night hours, in so diverting from him his demon, whom he later called Don Quixote, that his demon thereupon set out in perfect freedom on the maddest exploits, which, however, for the lack of a preordained object, which should have been Sancho Panza himself, harmed nobody. A free man, Sancho Panza philosophically followed Don Quixote on his crusades, perhaps out of a sense of responsibility, and had of them a great and edifying entertainment to the end of his days.

In Kafka's marvelous interpretation, the authentic object of the Knight's quest is Sancho Panza himself, who as an auditor refuses to believe Don Quixote's account of the cave. So I circle back to my question: Does the Knight believe his own story? It makes little sense to answer either "yes" or "no," so the question must be wrong. We cannot know what Don Quixote and Hamlet believe, since they do not share in our limitations. Don Quixote knows who he is, even as the Hamlet of act V comes to know what can be known.

Cervantes stations his Knight quite close to us, while Hamlet always is remote and requires mediation. Ortega y Gasset remarks of Don Quixote: "Such a life is a perpetual suffering," which holds also for Hamlet's existence. Though Hamlet tends to accuse himself of cowardice, he is as courageous, metaphysically and in action, as Don Quixote: they compete as literary instances of moral valor. Hamlet does not believe the will and its object can be brought together: "Our thoughts are ours, their ends none of our own." That is the Player-King enacting *The Mousetrap*, Hamlet's revision of the (nonexistent) *Murder of Gonzago*. Don Quixote refuses such despair yet nevertheless suffers it.

Thomas Mann loved *Don Quixote* for its ironies, but then Mann could have said, at any time: "Irony of ironies, all is irony." We behold in Cervantes's vast scripture what we already are. Dr. Samuel Johnson, who could not abide Jonathan Swift's ironies, easily accepted those of Cervantes; Swift's satire corrodes, while Cervantes's allows us some hope. Johnson felt that we required some illusions, lest we go mad. Is that part of Cervantes's design?

Mark Van Doren, in a very useful study, *Don Quixote's Profession*, is haunted by the analogues between the Knight and Hamlet, which to me seem inevitable. Here are the two characters, beyond all others, who seem always to know what they are doing, though they baffle us whenever we try to share their knowledge. It is a knowledge unlike that of Sir John Falstaff and Sancho Panza, who are so delighted at being themselves that they bid knowledge to go aside and pass them by. I would rather be Falstaff or Sancho than a version of Hamlet or Don Quixote, because growing old and ill teaches me that being matters more than knowing. The Knight and Hamlet are reckless beyond belief; Falstaff and Sancho have some awareness of discretion in matters of valor.

We cannot know the object of Don Quixote's quest unless we ourselves are Quixotic (note the capital Q). Did Cervantes, looking back upon his own arduous life, think of it as somehow Quixotic? The Sorrowful Face stares out at us in his portrait, a countenance wholly unlike Shakespeare's subtle blandness. They match each other in genius, because more even than Chaucer before them, and the host of novelists who have blended their influences since, they gave us personalities more alive than ourselves. Cervantes, I suspect, would not have wanted us to compare him to Shakespeare or to anyone else. Don Quixote says that all comparisons are odious. Perhaps they are, but this may be the exception. We need, with Cervantes and Shakespeare, all the help we can get in regard to ultimates, yet we need no help at all to enjoy them. Each is as difficult and yet available as is the other. To confront them fully, where are we to turn except to their mutual power of illumination?

First Part of the Ingenious Gentleman Don Quixote of La Mancha

Prologue

IDLE READER: Without my swearing to it, you can believe that I would like this book, the child of my understanding, to be the most beautiful, the most brilliant, and the most discreet that anyone could imagine. But I have not been able to contravene the natural order; in it, like begets like. And so what could my barren and poorly cultivated wits beget but the history of a child who is dry, withered, capricious, and filled with inconstant thoughts never imagined by anyone else, which is just what one would expect of a person begotten in a prison, where every discomfort has its place and every mournful sound makes its home?[1] Tranquility, a peaceful place, the pleasant countryside, serene skies, murmuring fountains, a calm spirit, are a great motivation for the most barren muses to prove themselves fertile and produce offspring that fill the world with wonder and joy. A father may have a child who is ugly and lacking in all the graces, and the love he feels for him puts a blindfold over his eyes so that he does not see his defects but considers them signs of charm and intelligence and recounts them to his friends as if they were clever and witty. But though I seem to be the father, I am the stepfather of Don Quixote, and I do not wish to go along with the common custom and implore you, almost with tears in my eyes, as others do, dearest reader, to forgive or ignore the faults you may find in this my child, for you are neither his kin nor his friend, and you have a soul in your body and a will as free as anyone's, and you are in your own house, where you are lord, as the sovereign is master of his revenues, and you know the old saying: under

---

1. Cervantes was imprisoned in Seville in 1597 and in 1602.

cover of my cloak I can kill the king. Which exempts and excuses you from all respect and obligation, and you can say anything you desire about this history without fear that you will be reviled for the bad things or rewarded for the good that you might say about it.

I wanted only to offer it to you plain and bare, unadorned by a prologue or the endless catalogue of sonnets, epigrams, and laudatory poems that are usually placed at the beginning of books. For I can tell you that although it cost me some effort to compose, none seemed greater than creating the preface you are now reading. I picked up my pen many times to write it, and many times I put it down again because I did not know what to write; and once, when I was baffled, with the paper in front of me, my pen behind my ear, my elbow propped on the writing table, and my cheek resting in my hand, pondering what I would say, a friend of mine, a man who is witty and wise, unexpectedly came in and seeing me so perplexed asked the reason, and I hid nothing from him and said I was thinking about the prologue I had to write for the history of Don Quixote, and the problem was that I did not want to write it yet did not want to bring to light the deeds of so noble a knight without one.

"For how could I not be confused at what that old legislator, the public, will say when it sees that after all the years I have spent asleep in the silence of obscurity, I emerge now, carrying all my years on my back,[2] with a tale as dry as esparto grass, devoid of invention, deficient in style, poor in ideas, and lacking all erudition and doctrine, without notes in the margins or annotations at the end of the book, when I see that other books, even if they are profane fictions, are so full of citations from Aristotle, Plato, and the entire horde of philosophers that readers are moved to admiration and consider the authors to be well-read, erudite, and eloquent men? Even more so when they cite Holy Scripture! People are bound to say they are new St. Thomases and other doctors of the Church; and for this they maintain so ingenious a decorum that in one line they depict a heartbroken lover and in the next they write a little Christian sermon that is a joy and a pleasure to hear or read. My book will lack all of this, for I have nothing to note in the margin or to annotate at the end, and I certainly don't know which authors I have followed so that I can mention them at the beginning, as everyone else does, in alphabetical order, beginning with Aristotle and ending with Xenophon, and with Zoilus and Zeuxis, though one was a slanderer and the other a painter. My book will also lack sonnets at the beginning, especially sonnets whose authors are

---

2. *La Galatea* appeared in 1585 and the first part of *Don Quixote* in 1605; Cervantes published nothing in the intervening twenty years. He was fifty-eight years old in 1605.

dukes, marquises, counts, bishops, ladies, or celebrated poets, though if I asked two or three officials who are friends of mine, I know they would give me a few that would be more than the equal of ones by writers who are more famous in our Spain. In short, my friend," I continued, "I have decided that Don Quixote should remain buried in the archives of La Mancha until heaven provides someone who can adorn him with all the things he lacks; for I find myself incapable of correcting the situation because of my incompetence and my lack of learning, and because I am by nature too lazy and slothful to go looking for authors to say what I know how to say without them. This is the origin of the perplexity and abstraction in which you found me: the reasons you have heard from me are enough reason for my being in this state."

On hearing this, my friend clapped his hand to his forehead, burst into laughter, and said:

"By God, brother, now I am disabused of an illusion I have lived with for all the time I have known you, for I always considered you perceptive and prudent in everything you do. But now I see that you are as far from having those qualities as heaven is from earth. How is it possible that things so trivial and so easy to remedy can have the power to perplex and absorb an intelligence as mature as yours, and one so ready to demolish and pass over much greater difficulties? By my faith, this does not have its origins in lack of skill but in an excess of laziness and a paucity of reasoning. Do you want to see if what I say is true? Then listen carefully and you will see how in the blink of an eye I confound all your difficulties and remedy all the problems that you say bewilder you and make you fearful to bring to light the history of your famous Don Quixote, the paragon and model of all knights errant."

"Tell me," I replied, listening to what he was saying. "How do you intend to fill the void of my fear and bring clarity to the chaos of my confusion?"

To which he said:

"First, to solve the question of the sonnets, epigrams, or laudatory poems by distinguished and titled people, which you need at the beginning, you must make a certain effort and write them yourself, and then you can baptize them with any name you want, attributing them to Prester John of the Indies[3] or to the emperor of Trebizond,[4] both of whom, I have

---

3. A legendary medieval Christian king and priest supposed to have ruled in a variety of places, including Ethiopia and the Far East.

4. One of the four divisions of the Greek empire in the Middle Ages, it was frequently cited in novels of chivalry.

heard, were famous poets; and if they were not, and certain pedants and university graduates backbite and gossip about the truth of the attributions, you should not give two *maravedís*[5] for what they say, because even if they prove the lie, they won't cut off the hand you used to write with. As for citing in the margins the books and authors that were the source of the sayings and maxims you put into your history, all you have to do is insert some appropriate maxims or phrases in Latin, ones that you know by heart or, at least, that won't cost you too much trouble to look up, so that if you speak of freedom and captivity, you can say:

Non bene pro toto libertas venditur auro.[6]

And then, in the margin, you cite Horace or whoever it was who said it. If the subject is the power of death, you can use:

Pallida mors aequo pulsat pede pauperum tabernas,
Regumque turres.[7]

If it's the friendship and love that God commands us to have for our enemies, you turn right to Holy Scripture, which you can do with a minimum of effort, and say the words of God Himself: *Ego autem dico vobis: diligite inimicos vestros.*[8] If you mention evil thoughts, go to the Gospel: *De corde exeunt cogitationes malae.*[9] If the topic is the fickleness of friends, Cato's there, ready with his couplet:

Done eris felix, multos numerabis amicos,
Tempora si fuerint nubila, solus eris.[10]

And with these little Latin phrases and others like them, people will think you are a grammarian; being one is no small honor and advantage these days. As for putting annotations at the end of the book, certainly

---

5. An ancient Spanish coin introduced by the Moors; its precise value is difficult to determine, since it changed over time.

6. The line ("Liberty cannot be bought for gold") comes from a collection of Aesop's fables.

7. The line ("Pale death comes both to the hovel of the poor wretch and the palace of the mighty king") is from Horace.

8. Matthew 1:4 ("But I say unto you, Love your enemies").

9. Matthew 15:19 ("For out of the heart proceed evil thoughts").

10. These lines are from Ovid, not Cato, and they translate roughly as "Nobody knows you when you're down and out."

you can do it this way: if you name some giant in your book, make him the giant Goliath, and just by doing that, which is almost no trouble at all, you have a nice long annotation, because then you can write: *The giant Goliath, or Goliat, was a Philistine whom the shepherd David slew with a stone in the valley of Terebint, as recounted in the Book of Kings,* and you can easily find the chapter. After this, to show that you are a scholar in humane letters and a cosmographer, be sure to mention the Tajo River in your history, and you'll have another worthy annotation if you write: *The Tajo River received its name from a king of all the Spains; it is born in that place and dies in the Ocean Sea, kissing the walls of the famous city of Lisbon, and it is thought that its sands are of gold, etc.* If you mention thieves, I will tell you the history of Cacus, which I know by heart; if the subject is prostitutes, there's the Bishop of Mondoñedo, who will provide you with Lamia, Laida, and Flora, and citing him will be a credit to you;[11] if you refer to cruelty, Ovid will give you Medea; enchanters and sorcerers, and you have Homer's Calypso; valiant captains, and none other than Julius Caesar will give you himself in his *Commentaries,* and Plutarch will provide you with a thousand Alexanders. If you write about love, with the couple of ounces of Tuscan that you know you'll run right into León Hebreo,[12] who will inflate your meters. And if you don't care to travel to foreign lands, right at home you have Fonseca's *Del amor de Dios,*[13] which summarizes everything that you or the most ingenious writer might wish to know about the subject. In short, all you have to do is to name the names or touch on the histories that I have mentioned, and leave it to me to put in annotations and notes; I swear to you that I'll fill up the margins and use four quartos of paper at the end. Let's turn now to the citation of authors, found in other books and missing in yours. The solution to this is very simple, because all you have to do is find a book that cites them all from A to Z, as you put it. Then you'll put that same alphabet in your book, and though the lie is obvious it doesn't matter, since you'll have little need to use them; perhaps someone will be naive enough to believe you have consulted all of them in your plain and simple history; if it serves no other purpose, at least a lengthy catalogue of authors will give the book an unexpected authority. Furthermore, no

11. Fray Antonio de Guevara, a sixteenth-century writer, was, among other things, the bishop of Mondoñedo. The irony lies in the fact that his books were well-known for their inaccuracies.

12. Author of *Dialoghi d'amore* (*Dialogues of Love*), his theories of love influenced Cervantes in the writing of his pastoral novel, *La Galatea*.

13. The reference is to *Tratado del amor de Dios* (*Treatise on the Love of God*), published by Cristóbal de Fonseca in 1592.

one will try to determine if you followed them or did not follow them, having nothing to gain from that. Besides, if I understand it correctly, this book of yours has no need for any of the things you say it lacks, because all of it is an invective against books of chivalry, which Aristotle never thought of, and St. Basil never mentioned, and Cicero never saw, and whose unbelievable absurdities do not enter into the calculations of factual truth, or the observations of astrology;[14] geometrical measurements are of no importance to them, and neither is the refutation of arguments used in rhetoric; there is no reason for your book to preach to anyone, weaving the human with the divine, which is a kind of cloth no Christian intelligence should wear. It only has to make use of mimesis in the writing, and the more precise that is, the better the writing will be. And since this work of yours intends only to undermine the authority and wide acceptance that books of chivalry have in the world and among the public, there is no reason for you to go begging for maxims from philosophers, counsel from Holy Scripture, fictions from poets, orations from rhetoricians, or miracles from saints; instead you should strive, in plain speech, with words that are straightforward, honest, and well-placed, to make your sentences and phrases sonorous and entertaining, and have them portray, as much as you can and as far as it is possible, your intention, making your ideas clear without complicating and obscuring them. Another thing to strive for: reading your history should move the melancholy to laughter, increase the joy of the cheerful, not irritate the simple, fill the clever with admiration for its invention, not give the serious reason to scorn it, and allow the prudent to praise it. In short, keep your eye on the goal of demolishing the ill-founded apparatus of these chivalric books, despised by many and praised by so many more, and if you accomplish this, you will have accomplished no small thing."

In deep silence I listened to what my friend told me, and his words made so great an impression on me that I did not dispute them but acknowledged their merit and wanted to use them to write this prologue in which you will see, gentle reader, the cleverness of my friend, my good fortune in finding the adviser I needed in time, and your own relief at finding so sincere and uncomplicated a history as that of the famous Don Quixote of La Mancha, who is thought by all the residents of the district of Montiel[15] to have been the most chaste lover and most valiant knight

14. In contemporary terms, Cervantes is referring here to the science of astronomy.

15. A town in La Mancha, in the province of Ciudad Real.

seen in those environs for many years. I do not want to charge you too much for the service I have performed in introducing you to so noble and honorable a knight; but I do want you to thank me for allowing you to make the acquaintance of the famous Sancho Panza, his squire, in whom, in my opinion, I have summarized for you all the squirely wit and charm scattered throughout the great mass of inane books of chivalry. And having said this, may God grant you health and not forget me. *Vale*.[16]

16. "Farewell" in Latin.

TO THE BOOK OF DON QUIXOTE
OF LA MANCHA

URGANDA THE UNRECOGNIZED[16]

If to reach goodly read-
oh book, you proceed with cau-,
you cannot, by the fool-,
be called a stumbling nin-.
But if you are too impa-
and pull the loaf untime-
from the fire and go careen-
into the hands of the dim-
you'll see them lost and puzz-
though they long to appear learn-.

And since experience teach-
that 'neath a tree that's stur-
the shade is the most shelt-
in Béjar your star so luck-
unto you a royal tree off-,
its fruit most noble prin-;
there a generous duke does flow-,
like a second Alexand-:

---

16. Urganda was a sorceress in *Amadís of Gaul* who could change her appearance at will.

In this form of humorous poetic composition, called *versos de cabo roto* ("lines with unfinished endings"), the syllables following the last stressed syllable in the final word of each line are dropped.

seek out his shade, for bold-
is favored by Dame Fort-.[17]

You will recount the advent-
of a gentleman from La Manch-
whose idle reading of nov-
caused him to lose his reas-:
fair maidens, arms, and chiv-
spurred him to imita-
of Orlando Furio-,[18]
exemplar of knightly lov-;
by feats of his arm so might-
he won the lady of Tobo-.

Do not inscribe indiscre-
on your shield, or hieroglyph-;
for when your hand lacks face-
with deuces and treys you wag-.
Be humble in your dedica-
and you will hear no deri-;
"What? Don Alvaro de la Lu-,[19]
and great Hannibal of Carth-,
and in Spain, King Francis-
all lamenting his misfor-!"

Since it's not the will of hea-
for you to be quite as cle-
as Juan Latin the Afri-,[20]
avoid Latin words and phra-.
Don't pretend to erudi-,
or make claims to philo-;
when you commence the fak-
and twist your mouth in decep-
those who are truly the learn-
will call your tricks into ques-.

Don't mind the business of oth-,

17. These lines are a homage to the Duke of Béjar, Cervantes's patron.

18. A reference to Ariosto's *Orlando furioso* (*Roland Gone Mad*).

19. Don Alvaro de la Luna (1388?–1453), lord high constable (*Condestable*) of Castilla under Juan II, was considered the most powerful man of his time.

20. An allusion to a black servant of the duchess of Terranova, who knew so much Latin that he was given this nickname.

and don't engage in gos-;
it's a sign of utmost wis-:
ignore the faults of your broth-.
Those who speak much too glib-
often fail in their inten-;
your only goal and ambi-
should be a good reputa-;
the writer who stoops to fol-
gains nothing but constant cen-.

    Be careful: it is impru-
if your walls are made of crys-
to pick up stones and peb-
and throw them at your neigh-.
Let the mature man of reas-
in the works that he compo-
place his feet with circumspec-;
if his writing's too lightheart-,
meant for young girls' sheer amuse-,
he writes only for the sim-.

AMADÍS OF GAUL[21] TO DON QUIXOTE
OF LA MANCHA

A Sonnet

You, who mimicked the tearful life of woe
that I, in isolation, scorned by love,
led on the lofty heights of Peña Pobre,[22]
when all my joy did shrink to penitence,

    you, to whom your eyes did give to drink
abundant waters, though briny with salt tears,
and, removing for your sake its min'ral wealth,
earth did give of the earth for you to eat,

    be certain that for all eternity,
as long, at least, as golden-haired Apollo

---

21. Amadís of Gaul was the hero of the most famous of the Renaissance novels of chivalry. He was the prototype of the perfect knight and perfect chivalric lover.

22. *Peña Pobre* ("Mount Mournful") is where Amadís carried out his penance of love, later imitated by Don Quixote.

drives steeds across the fourth celestial sphere,
you will enjoy renown as a valiant knight;
your kingdom will be first among all realms;
and your wise chronicler, unique on earth.

DON BELIANÍS OF GREECE[23] TO DON QUIXOTE
OF LA MANCHA

A Sonnet

I bruised, and fought, and cut, and said, and did
more than any knight errant who e'er lived;
I was deft, I was valiant, I was proud;
I avenged a thousand wrongs and righted more.
    To Lady Fame I gave eternal deeds;
I was a lover courtly and discreet;
to me great giants were no more than dwarves,
and I answered every challenge with a duel.
    I had Dame Fortune prostrate at my feet;
my prudence seized on Chance and never failed
to turn her to me, pulling with both hands.
    And yet, though my good fortunes ever soared
as high as the hornéd moon that sails the sky,
I envy, O Quixote, your great feats!

LADY ORIANA[24] TO DULCINEA OF TOBOSO

A Sonnet

Oh, if only, beauteous Dulcinea,
for greater ease and peace I had my castle,
Miraflores, in Toboso; could change
its London for the comforts of your town!
    Oh, if only your desire and your dress
adorned my soul and body, I could see
the famous knight you made so fortunate
in unequal combat with his enemies!

23. Another fictional knight from the literature of chivalry.
24. Oriana was the lady-love of Amadís.

Oh, if only I chastely might escape
Sir Amadís, as you did Don Quixote,
that courteous and noble errant knight!
  Then I'd be the envied, not the envying,
and melancholy time would turn to joy,
and I'd delight in pleasures without end.

GANDALÍN, SQUIRE TO AMADÍS OF GAUL,
TO SANCHO PANZA,
SQUIRE TO DON QUIXOTE

A Sonnet

Oh hail, famed man, when our good Lady Fortune
brought you to this our squirely vocation,
she carried out her plan with so much care,
that you ne'er suffered grief or dire disgrace.
  Now the hoe and the scythe do not repel
knight errantry; now it is common custom
to find a simple squire, and so I denounce
the pride that sets its sights upon the moon.
  I envy you your donkey and your name,
I envy you as well the saddlebags
that proved your forethought and sagacity.
  Hail once again, O Sancho! So good a man,
that only you, when the Ovid of our Spain
bows to kiss your hand, smack him on the head.

FROM DONOSO, AN ECLECTIC POET,
TO SANCHO PANZA
AND ROCINANTE

I am the squire, Sancho Pan-,
of the Manchegan Don Quixo-;
I often turned, oft retreat-,
and lived; the better part's discre-;
that wise man called Villadie-[25]

---

25. An allusion to the idiom "to imitate Villadiego," meaning to run away.

summarized his long life's mot-
in a single word: withdraw-.
That's the view in *Celesti-*,[26]
a book that'd be divine, I reck-,
if it embraced more of the hum-.

To Rocinante

I am famous Rocinan-,
great-grandson of Babie-,[27]
for the sin of being skin-
I belonged to Don Quixo-.
I ran races like a slack-
but was never late for sup-.
I learned this from Lazari-.[28]
to empty out the blind man's wine-
you must use a straw: how cle-.

ORLANDO FURIOSO TO DON QUIXOTE
OF LA MANCHA

A *Sonnet*

If you are not a peer, then you've had none:
for you would have no peer among a thousand;
nor could there be a peer where you are found,
unconquerable conqueror, ne'er conquered.
    I am Orlando who, Quixote, undone
by fair Angelica, saw distant seas,
and offered on the altars of Lady Fame
the valor that respected oblivion.
    I cannot be your equal; I am humbled
by your prowess, your noble deeds, your fame,
for you, like me, have gone and lost your mind.

---

26. First published in 1499, the book commonly known as *La Celestina* is one of the great monuments of Renaissance literature in Spain.

27. Babieca was the name of the horse belonging to El Cid.

28. In *Lazarillo de Tormes*, the first picaresque novel (1554), Lazarillo manages to steal wine from his blind master, who refuses to allow him to drink, by surreptitiously inserting a straw into the jug of wine.

But my equal you will be if you defeat
the haughty Moor, the charging beast; today
we are called equal in ill-fated love.

The Knight of Phoebus[29] to Don Quixote
of La Mancha

A Sonnet

This my sword was no equal to your own,
O Spanish Phoebus, courtly paragon,
nor to your heights of valor this my hand
though it flashed where the day is born and dies.
    I turned down empires, refused the monarchy
that red-lit Orient offered me in vain
so I could look upon the sovereign visage
of Claridiana, my most beauteous dawn.
    I loved her by a miracle rare and strange,
and, absent in misfortune, she came to fear
this arm of mine that tamed her raging scorn.
    But you, noble Quixote, high and brave,
your lady's made you eternal in this world,
and through you she is famous, good, and wise.

From Solisdán[30] to Don Quixote
of La Mancha

A Sonnet

Well may it be, Quixote, that sheer folly
hath overturned thy reason and thy wit,
but ne'er wilt thou be assailed by any man
as one who hath wrought actions vile and base.
    These thy great feats will judge this to be truth,
for thou, knight errant, hath righted many wrongs

---

29. Another fictional hero of chivalric literature.

30. The name may be an invention of Cervantes's or a misprint for Solimán, the emperor of Trebizond.

and wreaked thy vengeance on a thousand varlets
for dastardly assaults and villainies.

  And if thy lady-love, fair Dulcinea,
treateth thee with harsh and rigorous scorn,
and looketh not with pity on thy grief,

    in such affliction let thy comfort be
that Sancho Panza wast no go-between,
a fool he, she of stone, and thou no lover.

DIALOGUE BETWEEN BABIECA AND ROCINANTE

A Sonnet

B. Why is it, Rocinante, that you're so thin?
R. Too little food, and far too much hard labor.
B. But what about your feed, your oats and hay?
R. My master doesn't leave a bite for me.
B. Well, Señor, your lack of breeding shows
    because your ass's tongue insults your master.
R. He's the ass, from the cradle to the grave.
    Do you want proof? See what he does for love.
B. Is it foolish to love?   R. It's not too smart.
B. You're a philosopher.   R. I just don't eat.
B. And do you complain of the squire?   R. Not enough.
    How can I complain despite my aches and pains
if master and squire, or is it majordomo,
are nothing but skin and bone, like Rocinante?

Part One of the Ingenious Gentleman Don Quixote of La Mancha

CHAPTER I

Which describes the condition and profession of the famous gentleman Don Quixote of La Mancha

Somewhere in La Mancha, in a place whose name I do not care to remember, a gentleman lived not long ago, one of those who has a lance and ancient shield on a shelf and keeps a skinny nag and a greyhound for racing. An occasional stew, beef more often than lamb, hash most nights, eggs and abstinence on Saturdays, lentils on Fridays, sometimes squab as a treat on Sundays—these consumed three-fourths of his income.[1] The rest went for a light woolen tunic and velvet breeches and hose of the same material for feast days, while weekdays were honored with dun-colored coarse cloth. He had a housekeeper past forty, a niece not yet twenty, and a man-of-all-work who did everything from saddling the horse to pruning the trees. Our gentleman was approximately fifty years old; his complexion was weathered, his flesh scrawny, his face gaunt, and he was a very early riser and a great lover of the hunt. Some claim that his family name was Quixada, or Quexada, for there is a certain amount of disagreement among the authors who write of this mat-

1. Cervantes describes typical aspects of the ordinary life of the rural gentry. The indications of reduced circumstances include the foods eaten by Don Quixote: beef, for example, was less expensive than lamb.

ter, although reliable conjecture seems to indicate that his name was Quexana. But this does not matter very much to our story; in its telling there is absolutely no deviation from the truth.

And so, let it be said that this aforementioned gentleman spent his times of leisure—which meant most of the year—reading books of chivalry with so much devotion and enthusiasm that he forgot almost completely about the hunt and even about the administration of his estate; and in his rash curiosity and folly he went so far as to sell acres of arable land in order to buy books of chivalry to read, and he brought as many of them as he could into his house; and he thought none was as fine as those composed by the worthy Feliciano de Silva,[2] because the clarity of his prose and complexity of his language seemed to him more valuable than pearls, in particular when he read the declarations and missives of love, where he would often find written: *The reason for the unreason to which my reason turns so weakens my reason that with reason I complain of thy beauty.* And also when he read: *. . . the heavens on high divinely heighten thy divinity with the stars and make thee deserving of the deserts thy greatness deserves.*

With these words and phrases the poor gentleman lost his mind, and he spent sleepless nights trying to understand them and extract their meaning, which Aristotle himself, if he came back to life for only that purpose, would not have been able to decipher or understand. Our gentleman was not very happy with the wounds that Don Belianís gave and received, because he imagined that no matter how great the physicians and surgeons who cured him, he would still have his face and entire body covered with scars and marks. But, even so, he praised the author for having concluded his book with the promise of unending adventure, and he often felt the desire to take up his pen and give it the conclusion promised there; and no doubt he would have done so, and even published it, if other greater and more persistent thoughts had not prevented him from doing so. He often had discussions with the village priest—who was a learned man, a graduate of Sigüenza[3]—regarding who had been the greater knight, Palmerín of England or Amadís of Gaul; but Master Nicolás, the village barber, said that none was the equal of the Knight of Phoebus, and if any could be compared to him, it was Don Galaor, the brother of Amadís of Gaul, because he was moderate in

2. The author of several novels of chivalry; the phrases cited by Cervantes are typical of the language in these books that drove Don Quixote mad.

3. The allusion is ironic: Sigüenza was a minor university, and its graduates had the reputation of being not very well educated.

everything: a knight who was not affected, not as weepy as his brother, and incomparable in questions of courage.

In short, our gentleman became so caught up in reading that he spent his nights reading from dusk till dawn and his days reading from sunrise to sunset, and so with too little sleep and too much reading his brains dried up, causing him to lose his mind. His fantasy filled with everything he had read in his books, enchantments as well as combats, battles, challenges, wounds, courtings, loves, torments, and other impossible foolishness, and he became so convinced in his imagination of the truth of all the countless grandiloquent and false inventions he read that for him no history in the world was truer. He would say that El Cid Ruy Díaz[4] had been a very good knight but could not compare to Amadís, the Knight of the Blazing Sword, who with a single backstroke cut two ferocious and colossal giants in half. He was fonder of Bernardo del Carpio[5] because at Roncesvalles[6] he had killed the enchanted Roland by availing himself of the tactic of Hercules when he crushed Antaeus, the son of Earth, in his arms. He spoke highly of the giant Morgante because, although he belonged to the race of giants, all of them haughty and lacking in courtesy, he alone was amiable and well-behaved. But, more than any of the others, he admired Reinaldos de Montalbán,[7] above all when he saw him emerge from his castle and rob anyone he met, and when he crossed the sea and stole the idol of Mohammed made all of gold, as recounted in his history. He would have traded his housekeeper, and even his niece, for the chance to strike a blow at the traitor Guenelon.[8]

The truth is that when his mind was completely gone, he had the strangest thought any lunatic in the world ever had, which was that it seemed reasonable and necessary to him, both for the sake of his honor and as a service to the nation, to become a knight errant and travel the world with his armor and his horse to seek adventures and engage in everything he had read that knights errant engaged in, righting all manner of wrongs and, by seizing the opportunity and placing himself in danger and ending those wrongs, winning eternal renown and everlasting fame. The poor man imagined himself already wearing the crown, won by

4. A historical figure (eleventh century) who has passed into legend and literature.

5. A legendary hero, the subject of ballads as well as poems and plays.

6. The site in the Pyrenees, called Roncesvaux in French, where Charlemagne's army fought the Saracens in 778.

7. A hero of the French *chansons de geste*; in some Spanish versions, he takes part in the battle of Roncesvalles.

8. The traitor responsible for the defeat of Charlemagne's army at Roncesvalles.

the valor of his arm, of the empire of Trebizond at the very least; and so it was that with these exceedingly agreeable thoughts, and carried away by the extraordinary pleasure he took in them, he hastened to put into effect what he so fervently desired. And the first thing he did was to attempt to clean some armor that had belonged to his great-grandfathers and, stained with rust and covered with mildew, had spent many long years stored and forgotten in a corner. He did the best he could to clean and repair it, but he saw that it had a great defect, which was that instead of a full sallet helmet with an attached neckguard, there was only a simple headpiece; but he compensated for this with his industry, and out of pasteboard he fashioned a kind of half-helmet that, when attached to the headpiece, took on the appearance of a full sallet. It is true that in order to test if it was strong and could withstand a blow, he took out his sword and struck it twice, and with the first blow he undid in a moment what it had taken him a week to create; he could not help being disappointed at the ease with which he had hacked it to pieces, and to protect against that danger, he made another one, placing strips of iron on the inside so that he was satisfied with its strength; and not wanting to put it to the test again, he designated and accepted it as an extremely fine sallet.

Then he went to look at his nag, and though its hooves had more cracks than his master's pate and it showed more flaws than Gonnella's horse, that *tantum pellis et ossa fuit*,[9] it seemed to him that Alexander's Bucephalus and El Cid's Babieca were not its equal. He spent four days thinking about the name he would give it; for—as he told himself—it was not seemly that the horse of so famous a knight, and a steed so intrinsically excellent, should not have a worthy name; he was looking for the precise name that would declare what the horse had been before its master became a knight errant and what it was now; for he was determined that if the master was changing his condition, the horse too would change its name to one that would win the fame and recognition its new position and profession deserved; and so, after many names that he shaped and discarded, subtracted from and added to, unmade and remade in his memory and imagination, he finally decided to call the horse *Rocinante*,[10] a name, in his opinion, that was noble, sonorous, and reflective of what it had been when it was a nag, before it was what it was now, which was the foremost nag in all the world.

9. Pietro Gonnella, the jester at the court of Ferrara, had a horse famous for being skinny. The Latin translates as "was nothing but skin and bones."

10. *Rocín* means "nag"; *ante* means "before," both temporally and spatially.

Having given a name, and one so much to his liking, to his horse, he wanted to give one to himself, and he spent another eight days pondering this, and at last he called himself *Don Quixote*,[11] which is why, as has been noted, the authors of this absolutely true history determined that he undoubtedly must have been named Quixada and not Quexada, as others have claimed. In any event, recalling that the valiant Amadís had not been content with simply calling himself Amadís but had added the name of his kingdom and realm in order to bring it fame, and was known as Amadís of Gaul, he too, like a good knight, wanted to add the name of his birthplace to his own, and he called himself *Don Quixote of La Mancha*,[12] thereby, to his mind, clearly stating his lineage and country and honoring it by making it part of his title.

Having cleaned his armor and made a full helmet out of a simple headpiece, and having given a name to his horse and decided on one for himself, he realized that the only thing left for him to do was to find a lady to love; for the knight errant without a lady-love was a tree without leaves or fruit, a body without a soul. He said to himself:

"If I, because of my evil sins, or my good fortune, meet with a giant somewhere, as ordinarily befalls knights errant, and I unseat him with a single blow, or cut his body in half, or, in short, conquer and defeat him, would it not be good to have someone to whom I could send him so that he might enter and fall to his knees before my sweet lady, and say in the humble voice of surrender: 'I, lady, am the giant Caraculiambro, lord of the island Malindrania, defeated in single combat by the never sufficiently praised knight Don Quixote of La Mancha, who commanded me to appear before your ladyship, so that your highness might dispose of me as you chose'?"

Oh, how pleased our good knight was when he had made this speech, and even more pleased when he discovered the one he could call his lady! It is believed that in a nearby village there was a very attractive peasant girl with whom he had once been in love, although she, apparently, never knew or noticed. Her name was Aldonza Lorenzo,[13] and he thought it a good idea to call her the lady of his thoughts, and, searching for a name that would not differ significantly from his and would suggest

11. *Quixote* means the section of armor that covers the thigh.

12. La Mancha was not one of the noble medieval kingdoms associated with knighthood.

13. Aldonza, considered to be a common, rustic name, had comic connotations.

and imply that of a princess and great lady, he decided to call her *Dulcinea of Toboso*,[14] because she came from Toboso, a name, to his mind, that was musical and beautiful and filled with significance, as were all the others he had given to himself and everything pertaining to him.

CHAPTER II

Which tells of the first sally that the ingenious Don Quixote made from his native land

And so, having completed these preparations, he did not wish to wait any longer to put his thought into effect, impelled by the great need in the world that he believed was caused by his delay, for there were evils to undo, wrongs to right, injustices to correct, abuses to ameliorate, and offenses to rectify. And one morning before dawn on a hot day in July, without informing a single person of his intentions, and without anyone seeing him, he armed himself with all his armor and mounted Rocinante, wearing his poorly constructed helmet, and he grasped his shield and took up his lance and through the side door of a corral he rode out into the countryside with great joy and delight at seeing how easily he had given a beginning to his virtuous desire. But as soon as he found himself in the countryside he was assailed by a thought so terrible it almost made him abandon the enterprise he had barely begun; he recalled that he had not been dubbed a knight, and according to the law of chivalry, he could not and must not take up arms against any knight; since this was the case, he would have to bear blank arms, like a novice knight without a device on his shield, until he had earned one through his own efforts. These thoughts made him waver in his purpose; but, his madness being stronger than any other faculty, he resolved to have himself dubbed a knight by the first person he met, in imitation of many others who had done the same, as he had read in the books that had brought him to this state. As for his arms being blank and white,[1] he planned to

14. Her name is based on the word *dulce* ("sweet").
1. The wordplay is based on the word *blanco*, which can mean both "blank" and "white."

clean them so much that when the dubbing took place they would be whiter than ermine; he immediately grew serene and continued on his way, following only the path his horse wished to take, believing that the virtue of his adventures lay in doing this.

And as our new adventurer traveled along, he talked to himself, saying: "Who can doubt that in times to come, when the true history of my famous deeds comes to light, the wise man who compiles them, when he begins to recount my first sally so early in the day, will write in this manner: 'No sooner had rubicund Apollo spread over the face of the wide and spacious earth the golden strands of his beauteous hair, no sooner had diminutive and bright-hued birds with dulcet tongues greeted in sweet, mellifluous harmony the advent of rosy dawn, who, forsaking the soft couch of her zealous consort, revealed herself to mortals through the doors and balconies of the Manchegan horizon, than the famous knight Don Quixote of La Mancha, abandoning the downy bed of idleness, mounted his famous steed, Rocinante, and commenced to ride through the ancient and illustrious countryside of Montiel.' "

And it was true that this was where he was riding. And he continued: "Fortunate the time and blessed the age when my famous deeds will come to light, worthy of being carved in bronze, sculpted in marble, and painted on tablets as a remembrance in the future. O thou, wise enchanter, whoever thou mayest be, whose task it will be to chronicle this wondrous history! I implore thee not to overlook my good Rocinante, my eternal companion on all my travels and peregrinations."

Then he resumed speaking as if he truly were in love:

"O Princess Dulcinea, mistress of this captive heart! Thou hast done me grievous harm in bidding me farewell and reproving me with the harsh affliction of commanding that I not appear before thy sublime beauty. May it please thee, Señora, to recall this thy subject heart, which suffers countless trials for the sake of thy love."

He strung these together with other foolish remarks, all in the manner his books had taught him and imitating their language as much as he could. As a result, his pace was so slow, and the sun rose so quickly and ardently, that it would have melted his brains if he had had any.

He rode almost all that day and nothing worthy of note happened to him, which caused him to despair because he wanted an immediate encounter with someone on whom to test the valor of his mighty arm. Some authors say his first adventure was the one in Puerto Lápice; others claim it was the adventure of the windmills; but according to what I have been able to determine with regard to this matter, and what I have discovered written in the annals of La Mancha, the fact is that he rode all that day, and at dusk he and his horse found themselves exhausted and half-dead with hunger; as he looked all around to see if he could find some castle or a sheepfold with shepherds where he might take shelter and alleviate his great hunger and need, he saw an inn not far from the path he was traveling, and it was as if he had seen a star guiding him not to the portals, but to the inner towers of his salvation. He quickened his pace and reached the inn just as night was falling.

At the door there happened to be two young women, the kind they call ladies of easy virtue, who were on their way to Sevilla with some muledrivers who had decided to stop at the inn that night, and since everything our adventurer thought, saw, or imagined seemed to happen according to what he had read, as soon as he saw the inn it appeared to him to be a castle complete with four towers and spires of gleaming silver, not to mention a drawbridge and deep moat and all the other details depicted on such castles. He rode toward the inn that he thought was a castle, and when he was a short distance away he reined in Rocinante and waited for a dwarf to appear on the parapets to signal with his trumpet that a knight was approaching the castle. But when he saw that there was some delay, and that Rocinante was in a hurry to get to the stable, he rode toward the door of the inn and saw the two profligate wenches standing there, and he thought they were two fair damsels or two gracious ladies taking their ease at the entrance to the castle. At that moment a swineherd who was driving his pigs—no excuses, that's what they're called—out of some mudholes blew his horn, a sound that pigs respond to, and it immediately seemed to Don Quixote to be just what he had desired, which was for a dwarf to signal his arrival; and so with extreme joy he rode up to the inn, and the ladies, seeing a man armed in that fashion, and carrying a lance and shield, became frightened and were about to retreat into the inn, but Don Quixote, inferring their fear from their flight, raised the pasteboard visor, revealing his dry, dusty face, and in a gallant manner and reassuring voice, he said to them:

"Flee not, dear ladies, fear no villainous act from me; for the order of chivalry which I profess does not countenance or permit such deeds to be committed against any person, least of all highborn maidens such as yourselves."

The women looked at him, directing their eyes to his face, hidden by the imitation visor, but when they heard themselves called maidens, something so alien to their profession, they could not control their laughter, which offended Don Quixote and moved him to say:

"Moderation is becoming in beauteous ladies, and laughter for no reason is foolishness; but I do not say this to cause in you a woeful or dolorous disposition, for mine is none other than to serve you."

The language, which the ladies did not understand, and the bizarre appearance of our knight intensified their laughter, and his annoyance increased and he would have gone even further if at that moment the innkeeper had not come out, a man who was very fat and therefore very peaceable, and when he saw that grotesque figure armed with arms as incongruous as his bridle, lance, shield, and corselet, he was ready to join the maidens in their displays of hilarity. But fearing the countless difficulties that might ensue, he decided to speak to him politely, and so he said:

"If, Señor, your grace seeks lodging, except for a bed (because there is none in this inn), a great abundance of everything else will be found here."

Don Quixote, seeing the humility of the steward of the castle-fortress, which is what he thought the innkeeper and the inn were, replied:

"For me, good castellan, anything will do, for

> my trappings are my weapons,
> and combat is my rest,"[2]

The host believed he had called him castellan because he thought him an upright Castilian, though he was an Andalusian from the Sanlúcar coast,[3] no less a thief than Cacus and as malicious as an apprentice page, and so he responded:

"In that case, your grace's beds must be bare rocks, and your sleep a constant vigil; and this being true, you can surely dismount, certain of finding in this poor hovel more than enough reason and reasons not to sleep in an entire year, let alone a single night."

And having said this, he went to hold the stirrup for Don Quixote, who dismounted with extreme difficulty and travail, like a man who had not broken his fast all day long.

Then he told his host to take great care with his horse, because it was the best mount that walked this earth. The innkeeper looked at the horse and did not think it as good as Don Quixote said, or even half as good; after leading it to the stable, he came back to see what his guest might de-

2. These lines are from a well-known ballad; the first part of the innkeeper's response quotes the next two lines.

3. In Cervantes's time, this was known as a gathering place for criminals.

sire, and the maidens, who by this time had made peace with him, were divesting him of his armor; although they removed his breastplate and back-piece, they never knew how or were able to disconnect the gorget or remove the counterfeit helmet, which was tied on with green cords that would have to be cut because the ladies could not undo the knots; but he absolutely refused to consent to this, and so he spent all night wearing the helmet and was the most comical and curious figure anyone could imagine; as they were disarming him, and since he imagined that those well-worn and much-used women were illustrious ladies and damsels from the castle, he said to them with a good deal of grace and verve:

> "Never was a knight
> so well-served by ladies
> as was Don Quixote
> when he first sallied forth:
> fair damsels tended to him;
> princesses cared for his horse,[4]

or Rocinante, for this is the name, noble ladies, of my steed, and Don Quixote of La Mancha is mine; and although I did not wish to disclose my name until the great feats performed in your service and for your benefit would reveal it, perforce the adaptation of this ancient ballad of Lancelot to our present purpose has been the cause of your learning my name before the time was ripe; but the day will come when your highnesses will command, and I shall obey, and the valor of this my arm will betoken the desire I have to serve you."

The women, unaccustomed to hearing such high-flown rhetoric, did not say a word in response; they only asked if he wanted something to eat.

"I would consume any fare," replied Don Quixote, "because, as I understand it, that would be most beneficial now."

It happened to be a Friday, and in all the inn there was nothing but a few pieces of a fish that in Castilla is called cod, and in Andalucía codfish, and in other places salt cod, and elsewhere smoked cod. They asked if his grace would like a little smoked cod, for there was no other fish to serve him.

"Since many little cod," replied Don Quixote, "all together make one large one, it does not matter to me if you give me eight *reales*[5] in coins or

4. Don Quixote paraphrases a ballad about Lancelot.

5. *Real* was the name given to a series of silver coins, no longer in use, which were roughly equivalent to thirty-four *maravedís*, or one-quarter of a *peseta*.

in a single piece of eight. Moreover, it well might be that these little cod are like veal, which is better than beef, and kid, which is better than goat. But, in any case, bring it soon, for the toil and weight of arms cannot be borne if one does not control the stomach."

They set the table at the door of the inn to take advantage of the cooler air, and the host brought Don Quixote a portion of cod that was badly prepared and cooked even worse, and bread as black and grimy as his armor; but it was a cause for great laughter to see him eat, because, since he was wearing his helmet and holding up the visor with both hands, he could not put anything in his mouth unless someone placed it there for him, and so one of the ladies performed that task. But when it was time to give him something to drink, it was impossible, and would have remained impossible, if the innkeeper had not hollowed out a reed, placing one end in the gentleman's mouth and pouring some wine in the other; and all of this Don Quixote accepted with patience in order not to have the cords of his helmet cut. At this moment a gelder of hogs happened to arrive at the inn, and as he arrived he blew on his reed pipe four or five times, which confirmed for Don Quixote that he was in a famous castle where they were entertaining him with music, and that the cod was trout, the bread soft and white, the prostitutes ladies, the innkeeper the castellan of the castle, and that his decision to sally forth had been a good one. But what troubled him most was not being dubbed a knight, for it seemed to him he could not legitimately engage in any adventure if he did not receive the order of knighthood.

CHAPTER III

Which recounts the amusing manner in which Don Quixote was dubbed a knight

And so, troubled by this thought, he hurried through the scant meal served at the inn, and when it was finished, he called to the innkeeper and, after going into the stable with him, he kneeled before him and said:

"Never shall I rise up from this place, valiant knight, until thy courtesy grants me a boon I wish to ask of thee, one that will redound to thy glory and to the benefit of all humankind."

The innkeeper, seeing his guest at his feet and hearing these words, looked at him and was perplexed, not knowing what to do or say; he insisted that he get up, but Don Quixote refused until the innkeeper declared that he would grant the boon asked of him.

"I expected no less of thy great magnificence, my lord," replied Don Quixote. "And so I shall tell thee the boon that I would ask of thee and thy generosity has granted me, and it is that on the morrow thou wilt dub me a knight, and that this night in the chapel of thy castle I shall keep vigil over my armor, and on the morrow, as I have said, what I fervently desire will be accomplished so that I can, as I needs must do, travel the four corners of the earth in search of adventures on behalf of those in need, this being the office of chivalry and of knights errant, for I am one of them and my desire is disposed to such deeds."

The innkeeper, as we have said, was rather sly and already had some inkling of his guest's madness, which was confirmed when he heard him say these words, and in order to have something to laugh about that night, he proposed to humor him, and so he told him that his desire and request were exemplary and his purpose right and proper in knights who were as illustrious as he appeared to be and as his gallant presence demonstrated; and that he himself, in the years of his youth, had dedicated himself to that honorable profession, traveling through many parts of the world in search of adventures, to wit the Percheles in Málaga, the Islas of Riarán, the Compás in Sevilla, the Azoguejo of Segovia, the Olivera of Valencia, the Rondilla in Granada, the coast of Sanlúcar, the Potro in Córdoba, the Ventillas in Toledo,[1] and many other places where he had exercised the light-footedness of his feet and the light-fingeredness of his hands, committing countless wrongs, bedding many widows, undoing a few maidens, deceiving several orphans, and, finally, becoming known in every court and tribunal in almost all of Spain; in recent years, he had retired to this castle, where he lived on his property and that of others, welcoming all knights errant of whatever category and condition simply because of the great fondness he felt for them, so that they might share with him their goods as recompense for his virtuous desires.

He also said that in this castle there was no chapel where Don Quixote could stand vigil over his arms, for it had been demolished in order to rebuild it, but, in urgent cases, he knew that vigils could be kept

---

1. These were all famous underworld haunts.

anywhere, and on this night he could stand vigil in a courtyard of the castle; in the morning, God willing, the necessary ceremonies would be performed, and he would be dubbed a knight, and so much of a knight there could be no greater in all the world.

He asked if he had any money; Don Quixote replied that he did not have a copper *blanca*,[2] because he never had read in the histories of knights errant that any of them ever carried money. To this the innkeeper replied that he was deceived, for if this was not written in the histories, it was because it had not seemed necessary to the authors to write down something as obvious and necessary as carrying money and clean shirts, and if they had not, this was no reason to think the knights did not carry them; it therefore should be taken as true and beyond dispute that all the knights errant who fill so many books to overflowing carried well-provisioned purses for whatever might befall them; by the same token, they carried shirts and a small chest stocked with unguents to cure the wounds they received, for in the fields and clearings where they engaged in combat and were wounded there was not always someone who could heal them, unless they had for a friend some wise enchanter who instantly came to their aid, bringing through the air, on a cloud, a damsel or a dwarf bearing a flask of water of such great power that, by swallowing a single drop, the knights were so completely healed of their injuries and wounds that it was as if no harm had befallen them. But in the event such was not the case, the knights of yore deemed it proper for their squires to be provisioned with money and other necessities, such as linen bandages and unguents to heal their wounds; and if it happened that these knights had no squire—which was a rare and uncommon thing—they themselves carried everything in saddlebags so finely made they could barely be seen on the haunches of their horse, as if they were something of greater significance, because, except in cases like these, carrying saddlebags was not well-favored by knights errant; for this reason he advised, for he could still give Don Quixote orders as if he were his godson, since that is what he soon would be, that from now on he not ride forth without money and the provisions he had described, and then he would see how useful and necessary they would be when he least expected it.

Don Quixote promised to do as he advised with great alacrity, and so it was arranged that he would stand vigil over his arms in a large corral to

2. An ancient copper coin whose value varied over the years; it eventually was worth half a *maravedí*.

one side of the inn; and Don Quixote gathered all his armor together and placed it on a trough that was next to a well, and, grasping his shield, he took up his lance and with noble countenance began to pace back and forth in front of the trough, and as he began his pacing, night began to fall.

The innkeeper told everyone in the inn about the lunacy of his guest, about his standing vigil over his armor and his expectation that he would be dubbed a knight. They marveled at so strange a form of madness and went to watch him from a distance, and saw that with a serene expression he sometimes paced back and forth; at other times, leaning on his lance, he turned his eyes to his armor and did not turn them away again for a very long time. Night had fallen, but the moon was so bright it could compete with the orb whose light it reflected, and therefore everything the new knight did was seen clearly by everyone. Just then it occurred to one of the muledrivers in the inn to water his pack of mules, and for this it was necessary to move Don Quixote's armor, which was on the trough; our knight, seeing him approach, said in a booming voice:

"O thou, whosoever thou art, rash knight, who cometh to touch the armor of the most valiant knight who e'er girded on a sword! Lookest thou to what thou dost and toucheth it not, if thou wanteth not to leave thy life in payment for thy audacity."

The muleteer cared nothing for these words—and it would have been better for him if he had, because it meant caring for his health and well-being; instead, he picked up the armor by the straps and threw it a good distance away. And seeing this, Don Quixote lifted his eyes to heaven and, turning his thoughts—or so it seemed to him—to his lady Dulcinea, he said:

"Help me, Señora, in this the first affront aimed at this thy servant's bosom; in this my first challenge letteth not thy grace and protection fail me."

And saying these and other similar phrases, and dropping his shield, he raised his lance in both hands and gave the muledriver so heavy a blow on the head that he knocked him to the ground, and the man was so badly battered that if the first blow had been followed by a second, he would have had no need for a physician to care for his wounds. Having done this, Don Quixote picked up his armor and began to pace again with the same tranquility as before. A short while later, unaware of what had happened—for the first muledriver was still in a daze—a second approached, also intending to water his mules, and when he began to remove the armor to allow access to the trough, without saying a word or asking for anyone's favor, Don Quixote again dropped his shield and again raised his lance, and did not shatter it but instead broke the head of the second muledriver into more than three pieces because he cracked his skull in at least four places. When they heard the noise, all the people in the inn hurried over, among them the innkeeper. When he saw this, Don Quixote took up his shield, placed his hand on his sword, and said:

"O beauteous lady, strength and vigor of my submissive heart! This is the moment when thou needs must turn the eyes of thy grandeur toward this thy captive knight, who awaiteth so great an adventure."

And with this he acquired, it seemed to him, so much courage that if all the muledrivers in the world had charged him, he would not have taken one step backward. The wounded men's companions, seeing their friends on the ground, began to hurl stones at Don Quixote from a distance, and he did what he could to deflect them with his shield, not daring to move away from the trough and leave his armor unprotected. The innkeeper shouted at them to stop because he had already told them he was crazy, and that being crazy he would be absolved even if he killed them all. Don Quixote shouted even louder, calling them perfidious traitors and saying that the lord of the castle was a varlet and a discourteous knight for allowing knights errant to be so badly treated, and that if he had already received the order of chivalry, he would enlighten him as to the full extent of his treachery.

"But you, filthy and lowborn rabble, I care nothing for you; throw, approach, come, offend me all you can, for you will soon see how perforce you must pay for your rash insolence."

He said this with so much boldness and so much courage that he instilled a terrible fear in his attackers, and because of this and the persuasive arguments of the innkeeper, they stopped throwing stones at him, and he allowed the wounded men to withdraw and resumed his vigil over his armor with the same serenity and tranquility as before.

The innkeeper did not think very highly of his guest's antics, and he decided to cut matters short and give him the accursed order of chivalry then and there, before another misfortune occurred. And so he approached and begged his pardon for the impudence these lowborn knaves had shown, saying he had known nothing about it but that they had been rightfully punished for their audacity. He said he had already told him there was no chapel in the castle, nor was one necessary for what remained to be done, because according to his understanding of the ceremonies of the order, the entire essence of being dubbed a knight consisted in being struck on the neck and shoulders, and that could be accomplished in the middle of a field, and he had already fulfilled every-thing with regard to keeping a vigil over his armor, for just two hours of vigil satisfied the requirements, and he had spent more than four. Don Quixote believed everything and said he was prepared to obey him, and that he should conclude matters with as much haste as possible, because if he was attacked again and had already been dubbed a knight, he did not intend to leave a single person alive in the castle except for those the castellan ordered him to spare, which he would do out of respect for him.

Forewarned and fearful, the castellan immediately brought the book in which he kept a record of the feed and straw he supplied to the muledrivers, and with a candle end that a servant boy brought to him, and the two aforementioned damsels, he approached the spot where Don Quixote stood and ordered him to kneel, and reading from his book as if he were murmuring a devout prayer, he raised his hand and struck him on the back of the neck, and after that, with his own sword, he de-livered a gallant blow to his shoulders, always murmuring between his teeth as if he were praying. Having done this, he ordered one of the ladies to gird Don Quixote with his sword, and she did so with a good deal of refinement and discretion, and a good deal was needed for them not to burst into laughter at each moment of the ceremony, but the great feats they had seen performed by the new knight kept their laughter in check. As she girded on his sword, the good lady said:

"May God make your grace a very fortunate knight and give you good fortune in your fights."

Don Quixote asked her name, so that he might know from that day forth to whom he was obliged for the benison he had received, for he desired to offer her some part of the honor he would gain by the valor of his arm. She answered very humbly that her name was Tolosa, and that she was the daughter of a cobbler from Toledo who lived near the stalls of the Sancho Bienaya market, and no matter where she might be she would serve him and consider him her master. Don Quixote replied that for the sake of his love, would she have the kind-ness to henceforth ennoble herself and call herself Doña Tolosa.[3] She promised she would, and the other girl accoutred him with his knightly spurs, and he had almost the same conversation with her as with the

3. The unwarranted use of the honorifics *don* and *doña* was often satirized in the literature of the Re-naissance.

one who girded on his sword. He asked her name, and she said she was called Molinera, the miller's girl, and that she was the daughter of an honorable miller from Antequera, and Don Quixote also implored her to ennoble herself and call herself Doña Molinera, offering her more services and good turns.

And so, these never-before-seen ceremonies having been performed at a gallop, in less than an hour Don Quixote found himself a knight, ready to sally forth in search of adventures, and he saddled Rocinante and mounted him, and, embracing his host, he said such strange things to him as he thanked him for the boon of having dubbed him a knight that it is not possible to adequately recount them. The innkeeper, in order to get him out of the inn, replied with words no less rhetorical but much more brief, and without asking him to pay for the cost of his lodging, he allowed him to leave at an early hour.

CHAPTER IV

Concerning what happened to our knight when he left the inn

It must have been dawn when Don Quixote left the inn so contented, so high-spirited, so jubilant at having been dubbed a knight that his joy almost burst the cinches of his horse. But calling to mind the advice of his host regarding the necessary provisions that he had to carry with him, especially money and shirts, he resolved to return to his house and outfit himself with everything, including a squire, thinking he would take on a neighbor of his, a peasant who was poor and had children but was very well suited to the chivalric occupation of squire. With this thought he guided Rocinante toward his village, and the horse, as if he could see his stall, began to trot with so much eagerness that his feet did not seem to touch the ground.

Don Quixote had not gone very far when it seemed to him that from a dense wood on his right there emerged the sound of feeble cries, like those of a person in pain, and as soon as he heard them he said:

"I give thanks to heaven for the great mercy it has shown in so quickly placing before me opportunities to fulfill what I owe to my profession, allowing me to gather the fruit of my virtuous desires. These cries, no doubt, belong to some gentleman or lady in need who requires my assistance and help."

And, pulling on the reins, he directed Rocinante toward where he thought the cries were coming from. And after he had taken a few steps into the wood, he saw a mare tied to an oak, and tied to another was a boy about fifteen years old, naked from the waist up, and it was he who was crying out, and not without cause, for with a leather strap a robust peasant was whipping him and accompanying each lash with a reprimand and a piece of advice. For he was saying:

"Keep your tongue still and your eyes open."

And the boy replied:

"I won't do it again, Señor; by the Passion of Christ I won't do it again, and I promise I'll be more careful from now on with the flock."

And when Don Quixote saw this, he said in an angry voice:

"Discourteous knight, it is not right for you to do battle with one who cannot defend himself; mount your horse and take up your lance"—for a lance was leaning against the oak where the mare was tied—"and I shall make you understand that what you are doing is the act of a coward."

The peasant, seeing a fully armed figure ready to attack and brandishing a lance in his face, considered himself a dead man, and with gentle words he replied:

"Señor Knight, this boy I'm punishing is one of my servants, and his job is to watch over a flock of sheep I keep in this area, and he's so careless that I lose one every day, and when I punish his carelessness, or villainy, he says I do it out of miserliness because I don't want to pay him his wages, and by God and my immortal soul, he lies."

"You dare to say 'He lies' in my presence, base varlet?"[1] said Don Quixote. "By the sun that shines down on us, I am ready to run you through with this lance. Pay him now without another word; if you do not, by the God who rules us I shall exterminate and annihilate you here and now. Untie him immediately."

The peasant lowered his head and, without responding, he untied his servant, and Don Quixote asked the boy how much his master owed him. He said wages for nine months, at seven *reales* a month. Don Quixote calculated the sum and found that it amounted to seventy-three *reales*,[2] and he told the peasant to take that amount from his purse unless

---

1. It was considered insulting to call someone a liar in front of others without first begging their pardon.

2. Martín de Riquer, the editor of the Spanish text, speculates that the error in arithmetic may be an intentional, ironic allusion to Cervantes's three imprisonments for faulty accounts.

he wanted to die on their account. The terrified farmer replied that by the danger in which he found himself and the oath he had sworn—and so far he had sworn to nothing—the total was not so high, because from that amount one had to subtract and take into account three pairs of shoes that he had given his servant and a *real* for the two bloodlettings he had provided for him when he was sick.

"All of that is fine," said Don Quixote, "but the shoes and bloodlettings should compensate for the blows you have given him for no reason, for if he damaged the hide of the shoes you paid for, you have damaged the hide of his body, and if the barber drew blood when he was sick, you have drawn it when he was healthy; therefore, by this token, he owes you nothing."

"The difficulty, Señor Knight, is that I have no money here: let Andrés come with me to my house, and I'll pay him all the *reales* he deserves."

"Me, go back with him?" said the boy. "Not me! No, Señor, don't even think of it; as soon as we're alone he'll skin me alive, just like St. Bartholomew."

"No, he will not," replied Don Quixote. "It is enough for me to command and he will respect me, and if he swears to me by the order of chivalry that he has received, I shall let him go free, and I shall guarantee the payment."

"Señor, your grace, think of what you are saying," said the boy. "For this master of mine is no knight and he's never received any order of chivalry; he's Juan Haldudo the rich man, and he lives in Quintanar."

"That is of no importance," replied Don Quixote. "For there can be knights among Haldudos, especially since each man is the child of his deeds."

"That's true," said Andrés, "but what deeds is this master of mine the son of if he denies me my wages and my sweat and my labor?"

"I don't deny them, Andrés, my brother," answered the farmer. "Be so kind as to come with me, and I swear by all the orders of chivalry in the world that I'll pay you, as I've said, one *real* after another, and they'll be perfumed by my goodwill and pleasure."

"I absolve you from perfumes," said Don Quixote. "Just pay him in *reales*, and that will satisfy me, and be sure you fulfill what you have sworn; if you do not, by that same vow I vow that I shall return to find and punish you, and find you I shall, even if you conceal yourself like a wall lizard. And if you wish to know who commands you to do this, so that you have an even greater obligation to comply, know that I am the valiant Don

Quixote of La Mancha, the righter of wrongs and injustices, and now go
with God, and do not even think of deviating from what you have promised and sworn, under penalty of the penalty I have indicated to you."

And having said this, he spurred Rocinante and soon left them behind. The farmer followed him with his eyes, and when he saw that he
had crossed the wood and disappeared from view, he turned to his servant Andrés and said:

"Come here, my son; I want to pay you what I owe you, as that righter
of wrongs has ordered me to do."

"I swear," said Andrés, "that your grace better do the right thing and
obey the commands of that good knight, may he live a thousand years;
for, as he's a valiant man and a fair judge, heaven be praised, if you don't
pay me he'll come back and do what he said!"

"I swear, too," said the farmer, "but because I love you so much, I
want to increase the debt so I can increase the payment."

And seizing him by the arm, he tied the boy to the oak tree again and
gave him so many lashes that he left him half-dead.

"Now, Señor Andrés," said the farmer, "you can call the righter of
wrongs; you'll see how he can't undo this one. Though I don't think it's
over yet, because I feel like skinning you alive, just as you feared."

But at last he untied him and gave him permission to go in search of
his judge so that he could carry out the sentence. Andrés left in a fairly
gloomy frame of mind, swearing he would find the valiant Don Quixote
of La Mancha and tell him, point by point, what had happened, and that
his master would have to pay a fine and damages. Even so, the boy left
weeping and his master stayed behind to laugh.

In this way the valiant Don Quixote righted a wrong, and exceedingly
pleased with what had occurred, for it seemed to him that he had given a
happy and noble beginning to his chivalric adventures, he was very satisfied with himself as he rode to his village, saying in a quiet voice:

"Well mayest thou call thyself the most fortunate of ladies in the
world today, O most beauteous of all the beauteous, Dulcinea of Toboso!
For it is thy portion to have as vassal and servant to thy entire will and
disposition so valiant and renowned a knight as Don Quixote of La
Mancha is and will be, for he, as all men know, received the order of
chivalry yesterday and today he has righted the greatest wrong and injustice that iniquity e'er devised and cruelty e'er committed: today he removed the whip from the hand of a merciless enemy who, without
reason, did flog that delicate child."

Saying this, he arrived at a road that divided in four, and immediately there came to his imagination the crossroads where knights errant would begin to ponder which of those roads they would follow, and in order to imitate them, he remained motionless for a time, and after having thought very carefully, he loosened the reins and subjected his will to Rocinante's, and the horse pursued his initial intent, which was to head back to his own stall.

And having gone about two miles, Don Quixote saw a great throng of people who, as he subsequently discovered, were merchants from Toledo on their way to Murcia to buy silk. There were six of them, holding sunshades, and four servants on horseback, and three boys on foot leading the mules. No sooner had Don Quixote seen them than he imagined this to be a new adventure; and in order to imitate in every way possible the deeds he had read in his books, this seemed the perfect opportunity for him to perform one that he had in mind. And so, with gallant bearing and great boldness, he set his feet firmly in the stirrups, grasped his lance, brought the shield up to his chest, and, stopping in the middle of the road, he waited until those knights errant, for that is what he deemed and considered them to be, had reached him; and when they had come close enough to see and hear him, Don Quixote raised his voice and, in an imperious manner, he said:

"Halt, all of you, unless all of you confess that in the entire world there is no damsel more beauteous than the empress of La Mancha, the peerless Dulcinea of Toboso."

The merchants stopped when they heard these words and saw the strange appearance of the one who said them, and because of his appearance and words, they soon saw the madness of the man, but they wished to see at their leisure the purpose of the confession he was demanding, and one of them, who was something of a jokester and clever in the extreme, said:

"Señor Knight, we do not know this good lady you have mentioned; show her to us, for if she is as beautiful as you say, we will gladly and freely confess the truth you ask of us."

"If I were to show her to you," replied Don Quixote, "where would the virtue be in your confessing so obvious a truth? The significance lies in not seeing her and believing, confessing, affirming, swearing, and defending that truth; if you do not, you must do battle with me, audacious and arrogant people. And whether you come one by one, as the order of chivalry demands, or all at once, in the vicious manner of those of your ilk, here I am, ready and waiting for you, certain of the rightness of my claim."

"Señor Knight," replied the merchant, "in the name of all these princes, of whom I am one, and in order not to burden our consciences with the confession of something we have never seen or heard, and which, moreover, is so prejudicial to the empresses and queens of Alcarria and Extremadura, I implore your grace to have the goodness to show us a portrait of this lady, even if it is no larger than a grain of wheat; for with a single thread one has the entire skein, and we will be satisfied and certain, and your grace will be recompensed and requited, and although I believe we are so partial to your position that even if her portrait shows us that she is blind in one eye and that blood and brimstone flow from the other, despite all that, to please your grace, we will praise her in everything you might wish."

"Nothing flows from her, vile rabble," replied Don Quixote, burning with rage. "Nothing flows from her, I say, but amber and delicate musk; and she is not blind or humpbacked but as upright as a peak of the Guadarramas. But you will pay for how you have blasphemed against beauty as extraordinary as that of my lady!"

And, having said this, he lowered his lance and charged the man who had spoken, with so much rage and fury that if, to the daring merchant's good fortune, Rocinante had not tripped and fallen on the way, things would have gone badly for him. Rocinante fell, and his master rolled some distance on the ground, and when he tried to get up, he could not: he was too burdened by lance, shield, spurs, helmet, and the weight of his ancient armor. And as he struggled to stand, and failed, he said:

"Flee not, cowards; wretches, attend; for it is no fault of mine but of my mount that I lie here."

One of the muledrivers, who could not have been very well intentioned, heard the poor man on the ground making these insolent statements, and he could not stand by without giving him his response in the ribs. And walking up to him, he took the lance, broke it into pieces, and with one of them he began to beat our knight so furiously that notwithstanding and in spite of his armor, he thrashed Don Quixote as if he were threshing wheat. His masters shouted for him to stop and let him be, but by now the muledriver's blood was up and he did not want to leave the game until he had brought into play the last of his rage, and having recourse to the other pieces of the lance, he shattered them all on the wretched man on the ground, who, despite that storm of blows raining down on him, did not once close his mouth but continued to rail against heaven and earth and these wicked knaves, which is what they seemed to him.

The muledriver tired, and the merchants continued on their way, taking with them stories to tell about the beaten man for the rest of the journey. And he, when he found himself alone, tried again to see if he could stand, but if he could not when he was hale and healthy, how could he when he was beaten almost to a pulp? And still he considered himself fortunate, for it seemed to him that this was the kind of mishap that befell knights errant, and he attributed it all to his horse's misstep, but his body was so bruised and beaten it was not possible for him to stand.

CHAPTER V

In which the account of our knight's misfortune continues

Seeing, then, that in fact he could not move, he took refuge in his usual remedy, which was to think about some situation from his books, and his madness made him recall that of Valdovinos and the Marquis of Mantua, when Carloto left him wounded in the highlands,[1] a history known to children, acknowledged by youths, celebrated, and even believed by the old, and, despite all this, no truer than the miracles of Mohammed. This is the tale that seemed to him perfectly suited for the situation in which he found himself, and so, with displays of great emotion, he began to roll about on the ground and to say with faint breath exactly what people say was said by the wounded Knight of the Wood:

> "Where art thou, my lady,
> that thou weepest not for my ills?
> Dost not know of them, lady,
> Or art thou truly false?"

And in this way he continued reciting the ballad until the lines that say:

---

1. These characters appear in the well-known ballad that Don Quixote recites.

> "O noble Marquis of Mantua,
> mine uncle and natural lord!"

And as luck would have it, when he reached this line, a farmer from his village happened to pass by, a neighbor of his on the way home after taking a load of wheat to the mill; the farmer, seeing a man lying there, approached and asked who he was and what the trouble was that made him complain so pitifully. Don Quixote no doubt thought the farmer was the Marquis of Mantua, his uncle, and so the only answer he gave was to go on with the ballad, recounting his misfortune and the love of the emperor's son for his wife, all of it just as it is told in the ballad.

The farmer was astounded when he heard these absurdities, and after removing the visor, which had been shattered in the beating, he wiped the fallen man's face, which was covered in dust, and as soon as he had wiped it he recognized him and said:

"Señor Quijana!"—for this must have been his name when he was in his right mind and had not yet changed from a quiet gentleman into a knight errant—"Who has done this to your grace?"

But Don Quixote went on reciting his ballad in response to every question. Seeing this, the good man, as carefully as he could, removed the breastplate and backpiece to see if he was wounded but did not see blood or cuts of any kind. He managed to lift him from the ground and with a good deal of effort put him on his own donkey, because he thought it a steadier mount. He gathered up his arms, even the broken pieces of the lance, and tied them on Rocinante, and leading the horse by the reins and the jackass by the halter, he began to walk toward his village, very dispirited at hearing the nonsense that Don Quixote was saying; Don Quixote was no less dispirited, for he was so beaten and broken that he could barely keep his seat on the burro, and from time to time he would raise his sighs to heaven, which obliged the farmer to ask him again to tell him what was wrong; one cannot help but think that the devil made Don Quixote recall stories suited to the events that had occurred, because at that point, forgetting about Valdovinos, he remembered the Moor Abindarráez, when the governor of Antequera, Rodrigo de Narváez, captured him and brought him back to his domain as his prisoner.[2] So when the farmer asked him again how he felt and what was wrong, he answered with the same words and phrases that the captive

2. The story is included in book IV of Jorge de Montemayor's *Diana* (1559?), the first of the Spanish pastoral novels; it is one of the volumes in Don Quixote's library.

scion of the Abencerraje family said to Rodrigo de Narváez, just as he had read them in the history of *Diana*, by Jorge de Montemayor, where they are written, and he did this so deliberately that as the farmer walked along he despaired at hearing such an enormous amount of foolishness; in this way he realized that his neighbor was mad, and he hurried to reach the village in order to rid himself of the impatience Don Quixote provoked in him with his long-winded harangue. When it was concluded, Don Quixote went on to say:

"Your grace should know, Don Rodrigo de Narváez, that this beautiful Jarifa I have mentioned to you is now the lovely Dulcinea of Toboso, for whose sake I have performed, perform now, and shall perform in the future the most famous feats of chivalry the world has seen, sees now, and will ever see."

To this the farmer replied:

"Look, your grace, poor sinner that I am, I'm not Don Rodrigo de Narváez or the Marquis of Mantua, but Pedro Alonso, your neighbor, and your grace isn't Valdovinos or Abindarráez, but an honorable gentleman, Señor Quijana."

"I know who I am," replied Don Quixote, "and I know I can be not only those I have mentioned but the Twelve Peers of France[3] as well, and even all the nine paragons of Fame,[4] for my deeds will surpass all those they performed, together or singly."

Having these exchanges and others like them, they reached the village as night was falling, but the farmer waited until it grew a little darker, so that no one would see what a poor knight the beaten gentleman was. When he thought the right time had come, he entered the village and came to Don Quixote's house, which was in an uproar; the priest and barber, who were great friends of Don Quixote, were there, and in a loud voice his housekeeper was saying to them:

"What does your grace think, Señor Licentiate Pero Pérez"—for this was the priest's name—"of my master's misfortune? Three days and no sign of him, or his horse, or his shield, or his lance, or his armor. Woe is me! Now I know, and it's as true as the death I owe God, that those accursed books of chivalry he's always reading have driven him crazy; and now I remember hearing him say time and time again, when he was talking to

3. Knights chosen by the king of France and called peers because they were equal in skill and courage. They appear in *The Song of Roland*.

4. The nine were Joshua, David, Judah Macabee, Hector, Alexander, Julius Caesar, King Arthur, Charlemagne, and Godfrey of Bouillon (commander of the First Crusade).

himself, that he wanted to become a knight errant and go out in the wide world in search of adventures. Those books should go straight to Satan and Barrabas, for they have ruined the finest mind in all of La Mancha."

His niece said the same and even added:

"You should know, Master Nicolás"—for this was the name of the barber—"that it often happened that my dear uncle would read these cruel books of adventures for two days and nights without stopping, and when he was finished he would toss away the book and pick up his sword and slash at the walls, and when he was very tired he would say that he had killed four giants as big as four towers, and the sweat dripping from him because of his exhaustion he would say was blood from the wounds he had received in battle, and then he would drink a whole pitcher of cold water and become cured and calm again, saying that the water was a precious drink brought to him by Esquife the Wise, a great wizard and a friend of his. But I am to blame for everything because I didn't let your graces know about the foolishness of my dear uncle so that you could help him before it went this far, and burn all these wicked books, and he has many that deserve to be burned, just as if they belonged to heretics."

"That is what I say, too," said the priest, "and by my faith, no later than tomorrow we will have a public proceeding, and they will be condemned to the flames so that they do not give occasion to whoever reads them to do what my good friend must have done."

The farmer and Don Quixote heard all of this, which allowed the farmer to understand finally what his neighbor's sickness was, and so he called out:

"Your graces, open to Señor Valdovinos and to Señor Marquis of Mantua, who is badly wounded, and to Señor the Moor Abindarráez, captive of the valiant Rodrigo de Narváez, governor of Antequera."

At the sound of his voice they all came out, and since some recognized their friend, and others their master and uncle, who had not yet dismounted from the donkey because he could not, they ran to embrace him, and he said:

"Stop, all of you, for I have been sorely wounded on account of my horse. Take me to my bed and call, if such is possible, Uganda the Wise, that she may heal and tend to my wounds."

"Look, all of you," said the housekeeper, "in what an evil hour my heart knew exactly what was wrong with my master. Your grace can go up and rest easy, because without that gander woman coming here, we'll know how to cure you. And I say that these books of chivalry should be cursed another hundred times for bringing your grace to such a pass!"

They led him to his bed and looked for his wounds but could find none, and he said it was simple bruising because he had taken a great fall with Rocinante, his horse, as they were doing battle with ten of the most enormous and daring giants one could find anywhere in the world.

"Tut, tut!" said the priest. "So there are giants at the ball? By the Cross, I shall burn them before nightfall tomorrow."

They asked Don Quixote a thousand questions, but the only answer he gave was that they should give him something to eat and let him sleep, which was what he cared about most. They did so, and the priest questioned the farmer at length regarding how he had found Don Quixote. He told the priest everything, including the nonsense Don Quixote had said when he found him and brought him home, giving the licentiate an even greater desire to do what he did the next day, which was to call on his friend, the barber Master Nicolás, and go with him to the house of Don Quixote,

CHAPTER VI

Regarding the beguiling and careful examination carried out by the priest and the barber of the library of our ingenious gentleman

who was still asleep. The priest asked the niece for the keys to the room that contained the books responsible for the harm that had been done, and she gladly gave them to him. All of them went in, including the housekeeper, and they found more than a hundred large volumes, very nicely bound, and many other smaller ones; and as soon as the housekeeper saw them, she hurried out of the room and quickly returned with a basin of holy water and a hyssop and said to the priest:

"Take this, Señor Licentiate, and sprinkle this room, so that no enchanter, of the many in these books, can put a spell on us as punishment for wanting to drive them off the face of the earth."

The licentiate had to laugh at the housekeeper's simplemindedness, and he told the barber to hand him the books one by one so that he could see what they contained, for he might find a few that did not deserve to be punished in the flames.

"No," said the niece, "there's no reason to pardon any of them, because they all have been harmful; we ought to toss them out the windows into the courtyard, and make a pile of them and set them on fire; or better yet, take them to the corral and light the fire there, where the smoke won't bother anybody."

The housekeeper agreed, so great was the desire of the two women to see the death of those innocents; but the priest was not in favor of doing that without even reading the titles first. And the first one that Master Nicolás handed him was *The Four Books of Amadís of Gaul*,[1] and the priest said:

"This one seems to be a mystery, because I have heard that this was the first book of chivalry printed in Spain,[2] and all the rest found their origin and inspiration here, and so it seems to me that as the proponent of the doctrine of so harmful a sect, we should, without any excuses, condemn it to the flames."

"No, Señor," said the barber, "for I've also heard that it is the best of all the books of this kind ever written, and as a unique example of the art, it should be pardoned."

"That's true," said the priest, "and so we'll spare its life for now. Let's see the one next to it."

"It is," said the barber, "the *Exploits of Esplandián*,[3] who was the legitimate son of Amadís of Gaul."

"In truth," said the priest, "the mercy shown the father will not help the son. Take it, Señora Housekeeper, open that window, throw it into the corral, and let it be the beginning of the pile that will fuel the fire we shall set."

The housekeeper was very happy to do as he asked, and the good Esplandián went flying into the corral, waiting with all the patience in the world for the fire that threatened him.

"Next," said the priest.

"This one," said the barber, "is *Amadís of Greece*,[4] and I believe that all these over here come from the line of Amadís."

"Well, let them all go into the corral," said the priest. "For the sake of burning Queen Pintiquiniestra, and the shepherd Darinel and all his

---

1. Published in their complete version in 1508, these are the first in the long series of novels of chivalry devoted to the exploits of Amadís, a prototypical knight, and his descendants.

2. The Catalan novel *Tirant lo Blanc* was published in 1490; Cervantes probably knew only the translation into Castilian, which was not published until 1511.

3. This is the fifth book of the Amadís series and was published in 1521.

4. Published by Feliciano de Silva in 1535, it is the ninth book of the Amadís series.

eclogues, and the perverse and complicated language of their author, I would burn along with them the father who sired me if he were to appear in the form of a knight errant."

"I'm of the same opinion," said the barber.

"And so am I," added the niece.

"Well, then," said the housekeeper, "hand them over and into the corral with them."

They handed them to her, and there were a good many of them, and she saved herself a trip down the stairs and tossed them all out the window.

"Who's that big fellow?" asked the priest.

"This," replied the barber, "is *Don Olivante of Laura*."[5]

"The author of that book," said the priest, "was the same one who composed *Garden of Flowers*, and the truth is I can't decide which of the two is more true or, I should say, less false; all I can say is that this one goes to the corral, because it is silly and arrogant."

"This next one is *Felixmarte of Hyrcania*,"[6] said the barber.

"Is Sir Felixmarte there?" the priest responded. "Well, by my faith, into the corral with him quickly, despite his strange birth and resounding adventures, for the harshness and dryness of his style allow no other course of action. Into the corral with him and this other one, Señora Housekeeper."

"With pleasure, Señor," she replied, and with great joy she carried out her orders.

"This one is *The Knight Platir*,"[7] said the barber.

"That's an old book," said the priest, "and I don't find anything in it that would warrant forgiveness. Let it join the others, with no defense."

And that is what happened. Another book was opened and they saw that its title was *The Knight of the Cross*.[8]

"Because of the holy name this book bears one might pardon its stupidity, but as the saying goes, 'The devil can hide behind the cross.' Into the fire."

Picking up another book, the barber said:

---

5. Published by Antonio de Torquemada in 1564. In 1600, his *Jardín de flores* (*Garden of Flowers*) was translated into English as *The Spanish Mandeville*.

6. Published by Lenchor Ortega de Ubeda in 1556.

7. Published anonymously in 1533, this is the fourth book of the series about Palmerín, another fictional knight.

8. Published anonymously, it has two parts, which appeared in 1521 and 1526, respectively.

"This is *The Mirror of Chivalry.*"[9]

"I already know his grace," said the priest. "There you'll find Reinaldos de Montalbán and his friends and companions, greater thieves than Cacus, and the Twelve Peers along with that true historian Turpín,[10] and the truth is I'm inclined to condemn them to no more than perpetual exile, if only because they contain part of the invention of the famous Matteo Boiardo, from which the cloth was woven by the Christian poet Ludovico Ariosto,[11] who, if I find him here, speaking in some language not his own, I will have no respect for him at all; but if he speaks in his own language, I bow down to him."

"Well, I have him in Italian," said the barber, "but I don't understand it."

"There's no reason you should," replied the priest, "and here we would pardon the captain if he had not brought it to Spain and translated it into Castilian, for he took away a good deal of its original value, which is what all who attempt to translate books of poetry into another language will do as well: no matter the care they use and the skill they show, they will never achieve the quality the verses had in their first birth. In fact, I say that this book, and all those you find that deal with the matter of France, should be thrown into a dry well and kept there until we can agree on what should be done with them, except for a *Bernardo del Carpio* that's out there, and another called *Roncesvalles*,[12] for these, on reaching my hands, will pass into the housekeeper's and then into the fire, with no chance of a pardon."

All this the barber seconded, and thought it right and proper, for he understood that the priest was so good a Christian and so loved the truth that he would not speak a falsehood for anything in the world. And opening another book, he saw that it was *Palmerín of the Olive*,[13] and with it was another called *Palmerín of England*, and seeing this, the priest said:

9. An unfaithful prose translation of Boiardo's *Orlando innamorato* (*Roland in Love*), it was published in three parts in 1533, 1536, and 1550, respectively. The first two are attributed to López de Santa Catalina and the third to Pedro de Reynosa.

10. The archbishop of Reims, whose *Fables* (1527) are a fictional Carolingian chronicle. He is constantly cited for his veracity in *The Mirror of Chivalry*.

11. Matteo Boiardo was the author of *Orlando innamorato*; Ludovico Ariosto, who wrote *Orlando furioso*, referred only to the Christian God in his work. Cervantes disliked the Spanish translations of Ariosto, including the one by Captain Jerónimo de Urrea (1549), which he refers to in the next paragraph.

12. The references are to two poems, the first by Agustín Alonso (1585) and the second by Francisco Garrido Vicena (1555).

13. The first of the Palmerín novels, published in 1511, is of uncertain authorship. The *Palmerín of England* was the third novel in the series; it was written in Portuguese by Francisco Moraes Cabral and translated into Castilian by Luis Hurtado (1547).

"The olive branch should be cut up immediately and burned until there's nothing left but ashes, but the palm branch of England should be kept and preserved as something unique; a chest should be made for it like the one Alexander found among the spoils of Darius and which he designated for preserving the works of the poet Homer. This book, my friend, has authority for two reasons: one, because it is very good in and of itself, and two, because it is well-known that it was composed by a wise and prudent king of Portugal. All the adventures in the castle of Miraguarda are excellent and very artful; the language is courtly and clear, for it takes into account and respects the decorum of the person speaking with a good deal of exactness and understanding. I say, therefore, that unless you are of another mind, Master Nicolás, this one and *Amadís of Gaul* should escape the fire, and all the rest, without further investigation or inquiry, should perish."

"No, my friend," the barber responded, "for the one I have here is the renowned *Don Belianís.*"[14]

"Well, that one," replied the priest, "and its second, third, and fourth parts need a little dose of rhubarb to purge their excess of choler, and it would be necessary to remove everything about the castle of Fame and other, more serious impertinences, and therefore they are given a delayed sentence, and the degree to which they are emended will determine if mercy or justice are shown to them; in the meantime, my friend, keep them in your house, but permit no one to read them."

"It will be my pleasure," replied the barber.

And not wishing to tire himself further with the perusal of books of chivalry, he ordered the housekeeper to take all the large ones to the corral. This was not said to a foolish woman or a deaf one, but to a person who would rather burn the books than weave a piece of cloth, no matter how large or fine it might be, and she seized almost eight at a time and threw them out the window. Because she took so many together, one of them fell at the feet of the barber, who wanted to see which one it was and saw that it said: *History of the Famous Knight Tirant lo Blanc*.[15]

"God help me!" said the priest with a great shout. "Here is Tirant lo Blanc. Let me have it, friend, for I state here and now that in it I have found a wealth of pleasure and a gold mine of amusement. Here is Don

14. Written by Jerónimo Fernández and published in 1547.

15. As indicated earlier, this was first published in 1490; composed in Catalan by Johanot Martorell and continued by Martí Johan de Galba, the anonymous Castilian translation was published in 1511.

Quirieleisón of Montalbán, that valiant knight, and his brother Tomás of Montalbán, and the knight Fonseca, not to mention the battle that the brave Tirant waged against the Alani, and the witticisms of the damsel Placerdemivida, and the loves and lies of the widow Reposada, and the lady Emperatriz, beloved of Hipólito, her squire. I tell you the truth, my friend, when I say that because of its style, this is the best book in the world: in it knights eat, and sleep, and die in their beds, and make a will before they die, and do everything else that all the other books of this sort leave out. For these reasons, since the author who composed this book did not deliberately write foolish things but intended to entertain and satirize, it deserves to be reprinted in an edition that would stay in print for a long time.[16] Take it home and read it, and you'll say that everything I've said about it is true."

"I'll do that," answered the barber. "But what shall we do with these small books that remain?"

"These," said the priest, "are probably not about chivalry; they must be poetry."

And opening one, he saw that it was *Diana*, by Jorge de Montemayor,[17] and he said, believing that all the others were of the same genre:

"These do not deserve to be burned like the rest, because they do not and will not cause the harm that books of chivalry have, for they are books of the understanding and do no injury to anyone."

"Oh, Señor!" said the niece. "Your grace should send them to be burned, just like all the rest, because it's very likely that my dear uncle, having been cured of the chivalric disease, will read these and want to become a shepherd and wander through the woods and meadows singing and playing, and, what would be even worse, become a poet, and that, they say, is an incurable and contagious disease."

"What the girl says is true," said the priest, "and it would be a good idea to remove from the path of our friend this obstacle and danger. And, to begin with Montemayor's *Diana*, I am of the opinion that it should not be burned, but that everything having to do with the wise Felicia and the enchanted water, and almost all the long verses, should be excised, and let it happily keep all the prose and the honor of being the first of such books."

---

16. In the translation of this sentence, which has been called the most obscure in the entire novel, I have followed the interpretation offered by Martín de Riquer. One of the problematic issues in Spanish is the word *galeras*, or "galleys," which can mean either ships or publisher's proofs.

17. As indicated earlier, this was the first pastoral novel in Spanish.

"This next one," said the barber, "is called *Diana the Second, by the Salamancan,* and here's another one with the same name, whose author is Gil Polo."[18]

"The one by the Salamancan," replied the priest, "should join and add to the number of those condemned in the corral, and the one by Gil Polo should be preserved as if it were by Apollo himself; and move on, my friend, and let's hurry; it's growing late."

"This book," said the barber, opening another one, "is *The Ten Books of Fortune in Love,* composed by Antonio de Lofraso, a Sardinian poet."[19]

"By the orders I received," said the priest, "since Apollo was Apollo, and the muses muses, and poets poets, no book as amusing or nonsensical has ever been written, and since, in its way, it is the best and most unusual book of its kind that has seen the light of day, anyone who has not read it can assume that he has never read anything entertaining. Give it to me, friend, for I value finding it more than if I were given a cassock of rich Florentine cloth."

He set it aside with great delight, and the barber continued, saying:

"These next ones are *The Shepherd of Iberia, Nymphs of Henares,* and *Deceptions of Jealousy.*"[20]

"Well, there's nothing else to do," said the priest, "but turn them over to the secular arm of the housekeeper; and don't ask me why, for I'd never finish."

"This one is *The Shepherd of Fílida.*"[21]

"He isn't a shepherd," said the priest, "but a very prudent courtier; keep that as if it were a precious jewel."

"This large one here," said the barber, "is called *Treasury of Various Poems.*"[22]

"If there weren't so many," said the priest, "they would be more highly esteemed; this book needs a weeding and clearing out of certain base things contained among all its grandeurs. Keep it, because its author

---

18. A very poor continuation by Alonso Pérez, a Salamancan physician, printed in 1564; also published in 1564 is the highly esteemed *Diana enamorada (Diana in Love)* by Gil Polo.

19. Published in 1573; according to Martín de Riquer, Cervantes's praise is ironic, since he mocked the book in his *Viaje del Parnaso (Voyage from Parnassus).*

20. The first, by Bernardo de la Vega, was published in 1591; the second, by Bernardo González de Bobadilla, was published in 1587; the third, by Bartolomé López de Encino, was published in 1586.

21. Published in 1582 by Luis Gálvez de Montalvo.

22. Published in 1580 by Pedro de Padilla.

is a friend of mine, and out of respect for other, more heroic and elevated works that he has written."

"This," said the barber, "is *The Songbook* by López Maldonado."[23]

"The author of that book," replied the priest, "is also a great friend of mine, and when he recites his verses they amaze anyone who hears them, and the delicacy of his voice when he sings them is enchanting. He's somewhat long-winded in the eclogues, but you can't have too much of a good thing: keep it with the chosen ones. But what's that book next to it?"

"*La Galatea*, by Miguel de Cervantes,"[24] said the barber.

"This Cervantes has been a good friend of mine for many years, and I know that he is better versed in misfortunes than in verses. His book has a certain creativity; it proposes something and concludes nothing. We have to wait for the second part he has promised; perhaps with that addition it will achieve the mercy denied to it now; in the meantime, keep it locked away in your house, my friend."

"Gladly," the barber responded. "And here are three all together: *La Araucana*, by Don Alonso de Ercilla, *La Austríada*, by Juan Rufo, a magistrate of Córdoba, and *El Monserrate*, by Cristóbal de Virués, a Valencian poet."[25]

"All three of them," said the priest, "are the best books written in heroic verse in the Castilian language, and they can compete with the most famous from Italy: keep them as the richest gems of poetry that Spain has."

The priest wearied of seeing more books, and so, without further reflection, he wanted all the rest to be burned; but the barber already had one open, and it was called *The Tears of Angelica*.[26]

"I would shed them myself," said the priest when he heard the name, "if I had sent such a book to be burned, because its author was one of the famous poets not only of Spain but of the world, and he had great success translating some fables by Ovid."

---

23. Published in 1586 by Gabriel López Maldonado and his collaborator, Miguel de Cervantes.

24. This pastoral novel was the first work published by Cervantes, in 1585; the often promised second part was never published and has been lost.

25. Epic poems of the Spanish Renaissance, they were published in 1569, 1584, and 1588, respectively.

26. Published in 1586 by Luis Barahona de Soto.

CHAPTER VII

Regarding the second sally of our good knight Don Quixote of La Mancha

At this point, Don Quixote began to shout, saying:

"Here, here, valiant knights; here each must show the might of his valiant arm, for the courtiers are winning the tourney."

Because of their response to this noise and uproar, the examination of the remaining books went no further; and so, it is believed that into the flames, without being seen or heard, went *La Carolea* and *The Lion of Spain*, along with *The Deeds of the Emperor*, composed by Don Luis de Ávila,[1] which no doubt were among the remaining books; perhaps, if the priest had seen them, they would not have suffered so harsh a sentence.

When they reached Don Quixote, he was already out of bed, still shouting and engaging in senseless acts, slashing forehand and backhand with his sword and as awake as if he had never slept. They seized him and forced him back to bed, and after he had calmed down somewhat, he turned to speak to the priest and said:

"In truth, Señor Archbishop Turpín, it is a great discredit to those of us called the Twelve Peers to do nothing more and allow the courtier knights victory in this tourney, when we, the knights who seek adventures, have won glory on the three previous days."

"Be still, my friend," said the priest, "for it is God's will that fortune changes, and that what is lost today is won tomorrow; your grace should tend to your health now, for it seems to me your grace must be fatigued, if not badly wounded."

1. The first two are epic poems by Jerónimo Sempere (1560) and Pedro de la Vecilla Castellanos (1586); the third work is not known, although Luis de Ávila did write a prose commentary on Spain's wars with the German Protestants. Martín de Riquer believes that Cervantes intended to cite the poem *Carlo famoso* (1566) by Luis Zapata.

"Not wounded," said Don Quixote, "but bruised and broken, there is no doubt about that, for the ignoble Don Roland beat me mercilessly with the branch of an oak tree, all on account of envy, because he sees that I alone am his rival in valorous deeds. But my name would not be Reinaldos de Montalbán if, upon rising from this bed, I did not repay him in spite of all his enchantments; for now, bring me something to eat, since I know that is what I need most at present, and leave my revenge to me."

They did as he asked: they gave him food, and he went back to sleep, and they marveled at his madness.

That night, the housekeeper burned and consigned to the flames all the books that were in the corral and in the house, and some must have been in the fire that should have been preserved in perpetual archives; but their destiny, and the sloth of the examiner, did not permit this, and so, as the proverb says, at times the just must pay for sinners.

One of the remedies that the priest and the barber devised for their friend's illness was to wall up and seal off the room that held the books, so that when he got up he would not find them—perhaps by removing the cause, they would end the effect—and they would say that an enchanter had taken the books away, along with the room and everything in it; and this is what they did, with great haste. Two days later Don Quixote got out of bed, and the first thing he did was to go to see his books, and since he could not find the library where he had left it, he walked back and forth looking for it. He went up to the place where the door had been, and he felt it with his hands, and his eyes looked all around, and he did not say a word; but after some time had passed, he asked his housekeeper what had become of the library and his books. The housekeeper, who had been well-instructed in how she should respond, said:

"What library and what anything is your grace looking for? There's no more library and no more books in this house, because the devil himself took them away."

"It wasn't a devil," replied the niece, "but an enchanter who came on a cloud one night, after the day your grace left here, and he dismounted from the serpent he was riding and entered the library, and I don't know what he did inside, but after a little while he flew up through the roof and left the house full of smoke; and when we had the presence of mind to see what he had done, we could find no books and no library; the only thing the housekeeper and I remember very clearly is that as the evil old man was leaving, he shouted that because of the secret enmity he felt for the owner of the books and the room, he had done damage in the house, which we would see soon enough. He also said he was called Muñatón the Wise."

"He must have said Frestón,"[2] said Don Quixote.

"I don't know," the housekeeper replied, "if he was called Frestón or Fritón; all I know is that his name ended in *tón*."

"That is true," said Don Quixote. "He is a wise enchanter, a great enemy of mine who bears me a grudge because he knows through his arts and learning that I shall, in time, come to do battle in single combat with a knight whom he favors and whom I am bound to vanquish, and he will not be able to stop it, and for this reason he attempts to cause me all the difficulties he can; but I foresee that he will not be able to contravene or avoid what heaven has ordained."

"Who can doubt it?" said the niece. "But, Señor Uncle, who has involved your grace in those disputes? Wouldn't it be better to stay peacefully in your house and not wander around the world searching for bread made from something better than wheat, never stopping to think that many people go looking for wool and come back shorn?"

"Oh, my dear niece," replied Don Quixote, "how little you understand! Before I am shorn I shall have plucked and removed the beard of any man who imagines he can touch even a single hair of mine."

The two women did not wish to respond any further because they saw that he was becoming enraged.

So it was that he spent two very quiet weeks at home, showing no signs of wanting to repeat his initial lunacies, and during this time he had lively conversations with his two friends the priest and the barber, in which he said that what the world needed most were knights errant and that in him errant chivalry would be reborn. The priest at times contradicted him, and at other times he agreed, because if he did not maintain this ruse, he would not have been able to talk to him.

During this time, Don Quixote approached a farmer who was a neighbor of his, a good man—if that title can be given to someone who is poor—but without much in the way of brains. In short, he told him so much, and persuaded and promised him so much, that the poor peasant resolved to go off with him and serve as his squire. Among other things, Don Quixote said that he should prepare to go with him gladly, because it might happen that one day he would have an adventure that would gain him, in the blink of an eye, an ínsula,[3] and he would make him its governor. With these promises and others like

2. The enchanter Frestón is the alleged author of *Don Belianís of Greece*, a chivalric novel.

3. A Latinate word for "island" that appeared frequently in novels of chivalry; Cervantes uses it throughout for comic effect.

them, Sancho Panza,[4] for that was the farmer's name, left his wife and children and agreed to be his neighbor's squire.

Then Don Quixote determined to find some money, and by selling one thing, and pawning another, and undervaluing everything, he managed to put together a reasonable sum. He also acquired a round shield, which he borrowed from a friend, and doing the best he could to repair his broken helmet, he informed his squire of the day and time he planned to start out so that Sancho could supply himself with whatever he thought he would need. He ordered him in particular to bring along saddlebags, and Sancho said he certainly would bring them and also planned to take along a donkey he thought very highly of because he wasn't one for walking any great distance. As for the donkey, Don Quixote had to stop and think about that for a while, wondering if he recalled any knight errant who had with him a squire riding on a donkey, and none came to mind, yet in spite of this he resolved to take Sancho along, intending to obtain a more honorable mount for him at the earliest opportunity by appropriating the horse of the first discourteous knight he happened to meet. He furnished himself with shirts and all the other things he could, following the advice the innkeeper had given him; and when this had been accomplished and completed, without Panza taking leave of his children and wife, or Don Quixote of his housekeeper and niece, they rode out of the village one night, and no one saw them, and they traveled so far that by dawn they were certain they would not be found even if anyone came looking for them.

Sancho Panza rode on his donkey like a patriarch, with his saddlebags, and his wineskin, and a great desire to see himself governor of the ínsula his master had promised him. Don Quixote happened to follow the same direction and route he had followed on his first sally, which was through the countryside of Montiel, and he rode there with less difficulty than he had the last time, because at that hour of the morning the sun's rays fell obliquely and did not tire them. Then Sancho Panza said to his master:

"Señor Knight Errant, be sure not to forget what your grace promised me about the ínsula; I'll know how to govern it no matter how big it is."

To which Don Quixote replied:

"You must know, friend Sancho Panza, that it was a very common custom of the knights errant of old to make their squires governors of the ínsulas or kingdoms they won, and I have resolved that so amiable a usage will not go unfulfilled on my account; on the contrary, I plan to

4. *Panza* means "belly" or "paunch."

improve upon it, for they sometimes, and perhaps most times, waited until their squires were old, and after they had had their fill of serving, and enduring difficult days, and nights that were even worse, they would grant them the title of count, or perhaps even marquis, of some valley or province of greater or smaller size; but if you live and I live, it well might be that before six days have passed I shall win a kingdom that has others allied to it, and that would be perfect for my crowning you king of one of them. And do not think this is any great thing; for events and eventualities befall knights in ways never seen or imagined, and I might well be able to give you even more than I have promised."

"If that happens," replied Sancho Panza, "and I became king through one of those miracles your grace has mentioned, then Juana Gutiérrez,[5] my missus, would be queen, and my children would be princes."

"Well, who can doubt it?" Don Quixote responded.

"I doubt it," Sancho Panza replied, "because in my opinion, even if God rained kingdoms down on earth, none of them would sit well on the head of Mari Gutiérrez. You should know, Señor, that she isn't worth two *maravedís* as a queen; she'd do better as a countess, and even then she'd need God's help."

"Leave it to God, Sancho," said Don Quixote, "and He will give what suits her best; but do not lower your desire so much that you will be content with anything less than the title of captain general."

"I won't, Señor," Sancho replied, "especially when I have a master as distinguished as your grace, who will know how to give me everything that's right for me and that I can handle."

---

5. Presumably through an oversight on the part of Cervantes, Sancho's wife has several other names, including Mari Gutiérrez, Juana Panza, Teresa Cascajo, and Teresa Panza.

CHAPTER VIII

*Regarding the good fortune of the valorous Don Quixote in the fearful and
never imagined adventure of the windmills, along with other events worthy of
joyful remembrance*

As they were talking, they saw thirty or forty of the windmills found in
that countryside, and as soon as Don Quixote caught sight of them, he
said to his squire:

"Good fortune is guiding our affairs better than we could have desired, for there you see, friend Sancho Panza, thirty or more enormous giants with whom I intend to do battle and whose lives I intend to take,
and with the spoils we shall begin to grow rich, for this is righteous warfare, and it is a great service to God to remove so evil a breed from the
face of the earth."

"What giants?" said Sancho Panza.

"Those you see over there," replied his master, "with the long arms;
sometimes they are almost two leagues long."

"Look, your grace," Sancho responded, "those things that appear
over there aren't giants but windmills, and what looks like their arms
are the sails that are turned by the wind and make the grindstone
move."

"It seems clear to me," replied Don Quixote, "that thou art not well-
versed in the matter of adventures: these are giants; and if thou art
afraid, move aside and start to pray whilst I enter with them in fierce and
unequal combat."

And having said this, he spurred his horse, Rocinante, paying no attention to the shouts of his squire, Sancho, who warned him that, beyond any doubt, those things he was about to attack were windmills and
not giants. But he was so convinced they were giants that he did not

hear the shouts of his squire, Sancho, and could not see, though he was very close, what they really were; instead, he charged and called out:

"Flee not, cowards and base creatures, for it is a single knight who attacks you."

Just then a gust of wind began to blow, and the great sails began to move, and, seeing this, Don Quixote said:

"Even if you move more arms than the giant Briareus,[1] you will answer to me."

And saying this, and commending himself with all his heart to his lady Dulcinea, asking that she come to his aid at this critical moment, and well-protected by his shield, with his lance in its socket, he charged at Rocinante's full gallop and attacked the first mill he came to; and as he thrust his lance into the sail, the wind moved it with so much force that it broke the lance into pieces and picked up the horse and the knight, who then dropped to the ground and were very badly battered. Sancho Panza hurried to help as fast as his donkey could carry him, and when he reached them he discovered that Don Quixote could not move because he had taken so hard a fall with Rocinante.

"God save me!" said Sancho. "Didn't I tell your grace to watch what you were doing, that these were nothing but windmills, and only somebody whose head was full of them wouldn't know that?"

"Be quiet, Sancho my friend," replied Don Quixote. "Matters of war, more than any others, are subject to continual change; moreover, I think, and therefore it is true, that the same Frestón the Wise who stole my room and my books has turned these giants into windmills in order to deprive me of the glory of defeating them: such is the enmity he feels for me; but in the end, his evil arts will not prevail against the power of my virtuous sword."

"God's will be done," replied Sancho Panza.

He helped him to stand, and Don Quixote remounted Rocinante, whose back was almost broken. And, talking about their recent adventure, they continued on the road to Puerto Lápice,[2] because there, said Don Quixote, he could not fail to find many diverse adventures since it was a very heavily trafficked place; but he rode heavyhearted because he did not have his lance; and expressing this to his squire, he said:

"I remember reading that a Spanish knight named Diego Pérez de Var-

1. A monstrous giant in Greek mythology who had fifty heads and a hundred arms.

2. An entrance to the mountains of the Sierra Morena, between La Mancha and Andalucía.

gas, whose sword broke in battle, tore a heavy bough or branch from an
oak tree and with it did such great deeds that day, and thrashed so many
Moors, that he was called Machuca, the Bruiser, and from that day forward
he and his descendants were named Vargas y Machuca.[3] I have told you
this because from the first oak that presents itself to me I intend to tear off
another branch as good as the one I have in mind, and with it I shall do
such great deeds that you will consider yourself fortunate for deserving to
see them and for being a witness to things that can hardly be believed."

"It's in God's hands," said Sancho. "I believe everything your grace
says, but sit a little straighter, it looks like you're tilting, it must be from
the battering you took when you fell."

"That is true," replied Don Quixote, "and if I do not complain about
the pain, it is because it is not the custom of knights errant to complain
about any wound, even if their innards are spilling out because of it."

"If that's true, I have nothing to say," Sancho responded, "but God
knows I'd be happy if your grace complained when something hurt you.
As for me, I can say that I'll complain about the smallest pain I have, unless what you said about not complaining also applies to the squires of
knights errant."

Don Quixote could not help laughing at his squire's simplemindedness; and so he declared that he could certainly complain however and
whenever he wanted, with or without cause, for as yet he had not read
anything to the contrary in the order of chivalry. Sancho said that it was
time to eat. His master replied that he felt no need of food at the moment, but that Sancho could eat whenever he wished. With this permission, Sancho made himself as comfortable as he could on his donkey,
and after taking out of the saddlebags what he had put into them, he
rode behind his master at a leisurely pace, eating and, from time to time,
tilting back the wineskin with so much gusto that the most self-
indulgent tavern-keeper in Málaga might have envied him. And as he
rode along in that manner, taking frequent drinks, he did not think
about any promises his master had made to him, and he did not consider
it work but sheer pleasure to go around seeking adventures, no matter
how dangerous they might be.

In short, they spent the night under some trees, and from one of them
Don Quixote tore off a dry branch to use as a lance and placed on it the
iron head he had taken from the one that had broken. Don Quixote did
not sleep at all that night but thought of his lady Dulcinea, in order to

3. A historical figure of the thirteenth century.

conform to what he had read in his books of knights spending many sleepless nights in groves and meadows, turning all their thoughts to memories of their ladies. Sancho Panza did not do the same; since his stomach was full, and not with chicory water, he slept the entire night, and if his master had not called him, the rays of the sun shining in his face and the song of numerous birds joyfully greeting the arrival of the new day would have done nothing to rouse him. When he woke he made another pass at the wineskin and found it somewhat flatter than it had been the night before, and his heart grieved, for it seemed to him they were not likely to remedy the lack very soon. Don Quixote did not wish to eat breakfast because, as has been stated, he meant to live on sweet memories. They continued on the road to Puerto Lápice, and at about three in the afternoon it came into view.

"Here," said Don Quixote when he saw it, "we can, brother Sancho Panza, plunge our hands all the way up to the elbows into this thing they call adventures. But be advised that even if you see me in the greatest danger in the world, you are not to put a hand to your sword to defend me, unless you see that those who offend me are baseborn rabble, in which case you certainly can help me; but if they are gentlemen, under no circumstances is it licit or permissible for you, under the laws of chivalry, to help me until you are dubbed a knight."

"There's no doubt, Señor," replied Sancho, "that your grace will be strictly obeyed in this; besides, as far as I'm concerned, I'm a peaceful man and an enemy of getting involved in quarrels or disputes. It's certainly true that when it comes to defending my person I won't pay much attention to those laws, since laws both human and divine permit each man to defend himself against anyone who tries to hurt him."

"I agree," Don Quixote responded, "but as for helping me against gentlemen, you have to hold your natural impulses in check."

"Then that's just what I'll do," replied Sancho, "and I'll keep that precept as faithfully as I keep the Sabbath on Sunday."

As they were speaking, there appeared on the road two Benedictine friars mounted on two dromedaries, for the two mules they rode on were surely no smaller than that. They wore their traveling masks and carried sunshades. Behind them came a carriage, accompanied by four or five men on horseback, and two muledrivers on foot. In the carriage, as was learned later, was a Basque lady going to Sevilla, where her husband was preparing to sail for the Indies to take up a very honorable post. The friars were not traveling with her, although their route was the same, but as soon as Don Quixote saw them, he said to his squire:

"Either I am deceived, or this will be the most famous adventure ever seen, because those black shapes you see there must be, and no doubt are, enchanters who have captured some princess in that carriage, and I needs must do everything in my power to right this wrong."

"This will be worse than the windmills," said Sancho. "Look, Señor, those are friars of St. Benedict, and the carriage must belong to some travelers. Look carefully, I tell you, look carefully at what you do, in case the devil is deceiving you."

"I have already told you, Sancho," replied Don Quixote, "that you know very little about the subject of adventures; what I say is true, and now you will see that it is so."

And having said this, he rode forward and stopped in the middle of the road that the friars were traveling, and when they were close enough so that he thought they could hear what he said, he called to them in a loud voice:

"You wicked and monstrous creatures, instantly unhand the noble princesses you hold captive in that carriage, or else prepare to receive a swift death as just punishment for your evil deeds."

The friars pulled on the reins, taken aback as much by Don Quixote's appearance as by his words, and they responded:

"Señor, we are neither wicked nor monstrous, but two religious of St. Benedict who are traveling on our way, and we do not know if there are captive princesses in that carriage or not."

"No soft words with me; I know who you are, perfidious rabble," said Don Quixote.

And without waiting for any further reply, he spurred Rocinante, lowered his lance, and attacked the first friar with so much ferocity and courage that if he had not allowed himself to fall off the mule, the friar would have been thrown to the ground and seriously injured or even killed. The second friar, who saw how his companion was treated, kicked his castle-size mule and began to gallop across the fields, faster than the wind.

Sancho Panza, who saw the man on the ground, quickly got off his donkey, hurried over to the friar, and began to pull off his habit. At this moment, two servants of the friars came over and asked why he was stripping him. Sancho replied that these clothes were legitimately his, the spoils of the battle his master, Don Quixote, had won. The servants had no sense of humor and did not understand anything about spoils or battles, and seeing that Don Quixote had moved away and was talking to the occupants of the carriage, they attacked Sancho and knocked him down, and leaving no hair in his beard unscathed, they kicked him breathless and senseless and left him lying on the ground. The friar, frightened and terrified and with no color in his face, did not wait another moment but got back on his mule, and when he was mounted, he rode off after his companion, who was waiting for him a good distance away, wondering what the outcome of the attack would be; they did not wish to wait to learn how matters would turn out but continued on their way, crossing themselves more than if they had the devil at their backs.

Don Quixote, as has been said, was talking to the lady in the carriage, saying:

"O beauteous lady, thou canst do with thy person as thou wishest, for the arrogance of thy captors here lieth on the ground, vanquished by this my mighty arm; and so that thou mayest not pine to know the name of thy emancipator, know that I am called Don Quixote of La Mancha, knight errant in search of adventures, and captive of the beauteous and peerless Doña Dulcinea of Toboso, and as recompense for the boon thou hast received from me, I desire only that thou turnest toward Toboso, and on my behalf appearest before this lady and sayest unto her what deeds I have done to gain thy liberty."

One of the squires accompanying the carriage was a Basque, who listened to everything that Don Quixote was saying; and seeing that he would not allow the carriage to move forward but said it would have to go to Toboso, the squire approached Don Quixote and, seizing his lance, in bad Castilian and even worse Basque, he said:

"Go on, mister, you go wrong; by God who make me, if don't let carriage go, as I be Basque I kill you."

Don Quixote understood him very well and replied with great serenity:

"If you were a gentleman, as you are not, I would already have punished your foolishness and audacity, unhappy creature."

To which the Basque replied:

"Not gentleman me? As Christian I make vow to God you lie. Throw away lance and pull out sword and soon see which one make horse drink. Basque by land, noble by sea, noble by devil, if say other thing you lie."

"Now you will see, said Agrajes,"[4] replied Don Quixote.

And after throwing his lance to the ground, he drew his sword, grasped his shield, and attacked the Basque, determined to take his life.

4. Agrajes, a character in *Amadís of Gaul*, would say these words before doing battle; it became a proverbial expression used at the beginning of a fight.

The Basque, who saw him coming at him in this manner, wanted to get off the mule, which, being one of the inferior ones for hire, could not be trusted, but all he could do was draw his sword; it was his good fortune, however, to be next to the carriage, and he seized one of the pillows and used it as a shield, and the two of them went at each other as if they were mortal enemies. The rest of the people tried to make peace between them but could not, because the Basque said in his tangled words that if they did not allow him to finish his fight, he himself would kill his mistress and everyone else who got in his way. The lady in the carriage, stunned and fearful at what she saw, had the coachman drive some distance away, and from there she watched the fierce contest, in the course of which the Basque went over Don Quixote's shield and struck a great blow with his sword to his shoulder, and if it had not been protected by armor, he would have opened it to the waist. Don Quixote, who felt the pain of that enormous blow, gave a great shout, saying:

"O lady of my soul, Dulcinea, flower of beauty, come to the aid of this thy knight, who, for the sake of thy great virtue, finds himself in grave peril!"

Saying this, and grasping his sword, and protecting himself with his shield, and attacking the Basque were all one, for he was determined to venture everything on the fortune of a single blow.

The Basque, seeing him attack in this fashion, clearly understood the courage in this rash act and resolved to do the same as Don Quixote. And so he waited for him, shielded by his pillow, and unable to turn the mule one way or the other, for the mule, utterly exhausted and not made for such foolishness, could not take another step.

As has been said, Don Quixote was charging the wary Basque with his sword on high, determined to cut him in half, and the Basque, well-protected by his pillow, was waiting for him, his sword also raised, and all the onlookers were filled with fear and suspense regarding the outcome of the great blows they threatened to give to each other, and the lady in the carriage and all her maids were making a thousand vows and offerings to all the images and houses of devotion in Spain so that God would deliver the squire and themselves from the great danger in which they found themselves.

But the difficulty in all this is that at this very point and juncture, the author of the history leaves the battle pending, apologizing because he found nothing else written about the feats of Don Quixote other than what he has already recounted. It is certainly true that the second author[5] of this work did not want to believe that so curious a history would be subjected to the laws of oblivion, or that the great minds of La Mancha possessed so little interest that they did not have in their archives or writing tables a few pages that dealt with this famous knight; and so, with this thought in mind, he did not despair of finding the conclusion to this gentle history, which, with heaven's help, he discovered in the manner that will be revealed in part two.[6]

Part Two of the Ingenious Gentleman Don Quixote of La Mancha

CHAPTER IX

In which the stupendous battle between the gallant Basque and the valiant Manchegan is concluded and comes to an end

In part one of this history, we left the brave Basque and the famous Don Quixote with their swords raised and unsheathed, about to deliver two downstrokes so furious that if they had entirely hit the mark, the combatants would have been cut and split in half from top to bottom and opened like pomegranates; and at that extremely uncertain point, the delectable history stopped and was interrupted, without the author giving us any information as to where the missing parts could be found.

This caused me a good deal of grief, because the pleasure of having read so small an amount was turning into displeasure at the thought of the difficult road that lay ahead in finding the large amount that, in my opinion, was missing from so charming a tale. It seemed impossible and

5. The "second author" is Cervantes (that is, the narrator), who claims, in the following chapter, to have arranged for the translation of another (fictional) author's book. This device was common in novels of chivalry.

6. Cervantes originally divided the 1605 novel (commonly called the "first part" of *Don Quixote*) into four parts. The break in the narrative action between parts was typical of novels of chivalry.

completely contrary to all good precedent that so good a knight should have lacked a wise man who would assume the responsibility of recording his never-before-seen deeds, something that never happened to other knights errant,

> the ones, that people say
> go searching for adventures,[1]

because each of them had one or two wise men whose purpose was not only to record their deeds, but to depict their slightest thoughts and fancies, no matter how secret they might be; and so good a knight could not be so unfortunate as to lack what Platir and others like him had in abundance.[2] And therefore I was not inclined to believe that so gallant a history had been left maimed and crippled, and I blamed the malignity of Time, the devourer and consumer of all things, who had either hidden it away or consumed it.

On the other hand, it seemed to me that since works as modern as *Deceptions of Jealousy* and *Nymphs and Shepherds of Henares*[3] had been found among Don Quixote's books, his history also had to be modern, and though it might not be written down, it had to live on in the memories of people from his village and from other villages nearby. This thought left me disconcerted and longing to know, really and truly and in its entirety, the life and miracles of our famous Spaniard Don Quixote of La Mancha, the model and paragon of Manchegan chivalry, and the first in our age and in these calamitous times to take up the exercise and profession of chivalric arms, righting wrongs, defending widows, and protecting those maidens who rode, with whips and palfreys, and bearing all their virginity on their backs, from mountain to mountain and valley to valley; and unless some villain, or some farmer with hatchet and pitchfork, or some enormous giant forced her, a maiden could, in days of yore, after eighty years of never once sleeping under a roof, go to her grave as pure as the day her mother bore her. I say, then, that for these and many other reasons, our gallant Don Quixote is deserving of continual and memorable praise, as am I, on account of the toil and effort I have put into finding the conclusion of this amiable history, though I know very well that if heaven, cir-

---

1. These lines, probably taken from a ballad, appeared in Alvar Gómez's Spanish translation of Petrarch's *Trionfi*, although nothing comparable is in the Italian original.

2. A commonplace in chivalric fiction was that the knight's adventures (Platir's, for example) had been recorded by a wise man and then translated, the translation being the novel.

3. Published in 1586 and 1587, respectively.

cumstances, and fortune do not assist me, the world will be deprived of the almost two hours of entertainment and pleasure the attentive reader may derive from it. This is how I happened to find it:

One day when I was in the Alcaná market in Toledo, a boy came by to sell some notebooks and old papers to a silk merchant; as I am very fond of reading, even torn papers in the streets, I was moved by my natural inclinations to pick up one of the volumes the boy was selling, and I saw that it was written in characters I knew to be Arabic. And since I recognized but could not read it, I looked around to see if some Morisco[4] who knew Castilian, and could read it for me, was in the vicinity, and it was not very difficult to find this kind of interpreter, for even if I had sought a speaker of a better and older language,[5] I would have found him. In short, fortune provided me with one, and when I told him what I wanted and placed the book in his hands, he opened it in the middle, read for a short while, and began to laugh.

I asked him why he was laughing, and he replied that it was because of something written in the margin of the book as an annotation. I told him to tell me what it was, and he, still laughing, said:

"As I have said, here in the margin is written: 'This Dulcinea of Toboso, referred to so often in this history, they say had the best hand for salting pork of any woman in all of La Mancha.' "

When I heard him say "Dulcinea of Toboso," I was astounded and filled with anticipation, for it occurred to me that those volumes contained the history of Don Quixote. With this thought in mind, I urged him to read the beginning, which he did, extemporizing a translation of the Arabic into Castilian and saying that it said: *History of Don Quixote of La Mancha. Written by Cide Hamete Benengeli,*[6] *an Arab Historian.* I needed a good deal of cleverness to hide the joy I felt when the title of the book reached my ears; moving more quickly than the silk merchant, I bought all the papers and notebooks from the boy for half a *real*, but if he had been astute and known how much I wanted them, he certainly could have demanded and received more than six *reales* for their purchase. I immediately went with the Morisco to the cloister of the main church and asked him to render the journals, all those that dealt with Don Quixote, into the Castilian language, without taking away or

4. A Moor who had been converted to Christianity.

5. An allusion to Hebrew, spoken by the Jews who were merchants in the Alcaná.

6. *Cide* is the equivalent of *señor*; *Hamete* is the Arabic name *Hamid*; *Benengeli* (*berenjena* in Spanish) means "eggplant," a favorite food of Spanish Moors and Jews. In chapter II of the second volume (1615), the "first author" is, in fact, referred to as Cide Hamete Berenjena.

adding anything to them, offering him whatever payment he might desire. He was satisfied with two *arrobas* of raisins and two *fanegas* of wheat,[7] and he promised to translate them well and faithfully and very quickly. But to facilitate the arrangement and not allow such a wonderful find out of my hands, I brought him to my house, where, in a little more than a month and a half, he translated the entire history, just as it is recounted here.

In the first notebook there was a very realistic depiction of the battle of Don Quixote with the Basque, both in the postures recounted in the history, their swords raised, one covered by his round shield, the other by his pillow, and the Basque's mule so lifelike that at the distance of a crossbow shot one could see that it was a mule for hire. At the mule's feet was a caption that read: *Don Sancho de Azpetia*, which, no doubt, was the Basque's name; and at the feet of Rocinante was another that said: *Don Quixote*. Rocinante was so wonderfully depicted, so long and lank, so skinny and lean, with so prominent a backbone, and an appearance so obviously consumptive, that it was clear with what foresight and accuracy he had been given the name Rocinante. Next to him was Sancho Panza, holding the halter of his donkey, and at its feet was another caption that said: *Sancho Zancas*,[8] and as the picture showed, he must have had a big belly, short stature, and long shanks, and for this reason he was given the name Panza as well as Zancas, for from time to time the history calls him by both these surnames. A few other details were worthy of notice, but they are of little importance and relevance to the true account of this history, for no history is bad if it is true.

If any objection can be raised regarding the truth of this one, it can only be that its author was Arabic, since the people of that nation are very prone to telling falsehoods, but because they are such great enemies of ours, it can be assumed that he has given us too little rather than too much. So it appears to me, for when he could and should have wielded his pen to praise the virtues of so good a knight, it seems he intentionally passes over them in silence; this is something badly done and poorly thought out, since historians must and ought to be exact, truthful, and absolutely free of passions, for neither interest, fear, rancor, nor affection should make them deviate from the path of the truth, whose mother is history, the rival of time, repository of great deeds, witness to the past, example and adviser to the present, and forewarning to the future. In

7. Two *arrobas* is approximately fifty pounds; two *fanegas* is a little more than three bushels.

8. *Zancas* means "shanks"; *panza*, as indicated earlier, means "belly" or "paunch."

this account I know there will be found everything that could be rightly desired in the most pleasant history, and if something of value is missing from it, in my opinion the fault lies with the dog who was its author rather than with any defect in its subject. In short, its second part, according to the translation, began in this manner:

With the sharp-edged swords of the two valiant and enraged combatants held and raised on high, they seemed to threaten heaven, earth, and the abyss: such was their boldness and bearing. The first to strike a blow was the choleric Basque, and he delivered it with so much force and fury that if his sword had not turned on its way down, that single blow would have been enough to end this fierce combat and all the adventures of our knight; but good fortune, which had greater things in store for Don Quixote, twisted the sword of his adversary, so that although it struck his left shoulder, it did no more than tear through the armor along that side, taking with it as it passed a good part of his helmet and half an ear, both of which, in fearful ruin, fell to the ground, leaving him in a very sad state.

Lord save me, who can accurately tell of the rage that now filled the heart of our Manchegan when he saw himself so mistreated! Suffice it to say it was so great that he stood again in the stirrups, and grasping his sword in both hands, he struck his opponent with so much fury, hitting him square on his pillow and his head, that despite those good defenses, and as if a mountain had fallen on him, the Basque began to bleed from his nose, mouth, and ears and to show signs of falling off the mule, and he would have fallen, no doubt, if he had not thrown his arms around the animal's neck, but even so his feet slipped out of the stirrups and his arms loosened, and the mule, terrified by the awful blow, began to run across the field and, after bucking a few times, threw his rider to the ground.

Don Quixote watched very calmly, and when he saw him fall, he leaped from his horse, raced over to him, placed the tip of his sword between the Basque's eyes, and ordered him to surrender or else he would cut off his head. The Basque was so stunned he could not say a word, and he would have come to a bad end, given Don Quixote's blind rage, if the ladies in the carriage, who until that moment had watched the battle with great dismay, had not approached him and implored him most earnestly that he do them the favor and grant them the boon of sparing the life of their squire. To which Don Quixote responded with pride and gravity:

"Certainly, beauteous ladies, I am very happy to do as you ask; but it must be with a condition and a stipulation, and it is that this knight must promise to go to Toboso and present himself on my behalf to the peerless Doña Dulcinea, so that she may do with him as she pleases."

The frightened and distressed ladies, without considering what Don Quixote was demanding, and without asking who Dulcinea was, promised that the squire would do everything he was ordered to do.

"With confidence in that promise, I shall do him no more harm, although he so richly deserves it."

CHAPTER X

Concerning what further befell Don Quixote with the Basque and the danger in which he found himself with a band of Galicians from Yanguas[1]

By this time Sancho Panza, rather badly treated by the servants of the friars, had gotten to his feet and was paying close attention to the battle waged by his master and imploring God, in his heart, that it would be His will to grant Don Quixote a victory in which he would win an ínsula and make Sancho the governor, as he had promised. Seeing, then, that the combat had ended and his master was about to remount Rocinante, he came to hold the stirrups for him, and before Don Quixote mounted, Sancho fell to his knees before him, and grasping his hand, he kissed it and said:

"May it please your grace, Señor Don Quixote, to give me the governorship of the ínsula that you have won in this fierce combat; for no matter how big it may be, I feel I have the ability to govern it just as well as anyone else who has ever governed ínsulas in this world."

To which Don Quixote responded:

"Let me point out, brother Sancho, that this adventure and those like it are adventures not of ínsulas but of crossroads, in which nothing is won but a broken head or a missing ear. Have patience, for adventures will present themselves in which you can become not only a governor, but perhaps even more."

1. Cervantes apparently divided this portion of the text into chapters after he had written it, and he did so in haste: the adventure with the Basque is concluded, and the Galicians do not appear for another five chapters.

Sancho thanked him profusely, and after kissing his hand again, and the skirt of his cuirass, he helped him to mount Rocinante, and then he mounted his donkey and began to follow his master, who, at a rapid pace, without saying goodbye or speaking any further with the ladies in the carriage, rode into a nearby wood. Sancho followed as fast as his jackass would go, but Rocinante moved so quickly that the squire, seeing himself left behind, was obliged to call to his master to wait for him. Don Quixote did so, pulling on Rocinante's reins until his weary squire caught up to him, and when he did, Sancho said:

"It seems to me, Señor, that it would be a good idea for us to take refuge in some church; for that man you fought was so badly injured that it won't be long before he tells the Holy Brotherhood[2] what happened, and they'll arrest us, and by my faith, if they do, before we get out of prison they'll put us through a terrible time."

"Be quiet," said Don Quixote. "Where have you ever seen or read that a knight errant has been brought before the law no matter how many homicides he may have committed?"

"I don't know anything about omecils,"[3] replied Sancho, "and I never did bear one in my life; all I know is that the Holy Brotherhood takes care of people who fight in the countryside, and I don't want anything to do with that."

"Well, do not trouble yourself, my friend," Don Quixote responded, "for I shall save you from the hands of the Chaldeans, not to mention those of the Brotherhood. But tell me as you value your life: have you ever seen a more valiant knight than I anywhere on the face of the earth? Have you read in histories of another who has, or ever had, more spirit in attacking, more courage in persevering, more dexterity in wounding, or more ingenuity in unhorsing?"

"The truth is," replied Sancho, "that I never read any history because I don't know how to read or write, but I'll wager that in all my days I've never served a bolder master than your grace, and may it please God that all this boldness isn't paid for in the place I said. What I beg of your grace is that we treat your wounds; a lot of blood is coming out of that ear; and I have some lint[4] and a little white salve here in the saddlebags."

"None of that would be needed," replied Don Quixote, "if I had re-

2. The *Santa Hermandad*, or Holy Brotherhood, was an armed force that policed the countryside and the roads.

3. Sancho confuses *homicidios* ("homicides") and *omecillos* ("grudges").

4. Lint was used in much the same way that absorbent cotton is used in modern medicine.

membered to prepare a flask of the balm of Fierabrás,[5] for just one drop saves both time and medicines."

"What flask and what balm is that?" asked Sancho Panza.

"It is a balm," replied Don Quixote, "the recipe for which I have memorized, and with it one need not fear death, nor think that one will die of any wound. When I prepare it and give it to you, all you need do, when you see in some battle that they have cut my body in two (as is wont to happen), is to pick up the part of my body that has fallen to the ground, and very artfully, and with great cunning, before the blood congeals, place it on top of the other half still in the saddle, being careful to fit them together precisely and exactly. Then you will give me only two mouthfuls to drink of the balm I have mentioned, and you will see me sounder than an apple."

"If that is true," said Panza, "I renounce here and now the governorship of the ínsula you have promised and want nothing else in payment for my many good services but that your grace give me the recipe for this marvelous potion, for I think an ounce of it will bring more than two *reales* anywhere, and I don't need more than that to live an easy and honorable life. But what I'd like to know now is if it costs a lot to make."

"With less than three *reales* you can make more than six *azumbres*,"[6] replied Don Quixote.

"Poor sinner that I am!" said Sancho. "What is your grace waiting for, why don't you make it and show me how it's done?"

"Be quiet, my friend," Don Quixote responded, "for I intend to show you greater secrets and do you greater good turns; for now, let us treat these wounds, for my ear hurts more than I should like."

Sancho took lint and salve out of the saddlebags. But when Don Quixote saw that his helmet had been broken, he thought he would go mad, and placing his hand on his sword and lifting his eyes to heaven, he said:

"I make a vow to the Creator of all things, and to the four Holy Gospels in the fullness of all their writing, that I shall lead the life led by the great Marquis of Mantua when he swore to avenge the death of his nephew Valdovinos, which was to eat no bread at the table, nor to lie with his wife, and other things which I do not remember but I consider

---

5. Mentioned in a twelfth-century chanson de geste that was translated into Spanish prose in 1525 and became very popular, the balm could heal the wounds of anyone who drank it.

6. An *azumbre* was the equivalent of a little more than two liters.

them stated here, until I take my entire revenge on the one who has done me so great a wrong."

On hearing this, Sancho said:

"Look, your grace, Señor Don Quixote, if the gentleman did what you ordered him to and went to present himself to my lady Dulcinea of Toboso, then he has already done what he had to do and doesn't deserve another punishment if he doesn't commit another crime."

"You have spoken very well and to the point," Don Quixote responded, "and so I revoke the part of the vow that deals with wreaking new vengeance on him, but I make it and confirm it again with regard to leading the life I mentioned until such time that I take by force another helmet just as good as this one from some other knight. And do not think, Sancho, that I do this without reflection, for I have a good model to emulate; the same thing happened in exactly the same way with regard to the helmet of Mambrino, which cost Sacripante[7] so dearly."

"Your grace should send such vows to the devil, Señor," replied Sancho, "for they are very dangerous to your health and very damaging to your conscience. If not, then tell me: if for many days we don't happen to run into a man armed with a helmet, what will we do? Must we keep the vow in spite of so many inconveniences and discomforts, like sleeping in our clothes, and sleeping in the open, and a thousand other acts of penance contained in the vow of that crazy old man the Marquis of Mantua, which your grace wants to renew now? Look, your grace, no armed men travel along these roads, only muledrivers and wagondrivers, and they not only don't have helmets, but maybe they haven't even heard of them in all their days."

"In this you are deceived," said Don Quixote, "because in less than two hours' time at these crossroads we shall see more armed men than those who besieged Albracca,[8] when Angelica the Fair was defeated."

"All right, then; so be it," said Sancho, "and may it please God that all goes well with us and the time comes soon when we win this ínsula that is costing me so dear, and then I can die."

"I have already told you, Sancho, that you should have no care in that regard; if an ínsula is lacking, there is always the kingdom of Den-

7. Loosely based on an episode in Ariosto's *Orlando furioso*, in which Reinaldos de Montalbán takes the enchanted helmet of the Moorish king Mambrino from Dardinel (not Sacripante) and kills him in the process.

8. A reference to an episode in Boiardo's *Orlando innamorato*, in which Agricane's army, consisting of "twenty-two hundred thousand knights," laid siege to Albracca.

mark, or that of Soliadisa,[9] which will fit you like the ring on your finger, and because they are on terra firma you ought to rejoice even more. But all of this in due course; look and see if you have anything to eat in those saddlebags, and then we shall go in search of a castle where we can stay the night and prepare the balm I told you of, because I swear before God that my ear is hurting a good deal."

"I have here an onion, and a little cheese, and I don't know how many crusts of bread," said Sancho, "but these are not victuals suitable for a knight as valiant as your grace."

"How little you understand!" Don Quixote responded. "I shall tell you, Sancho, that it is a question of honor for knights errant not to eat for a month, and when they do eat, it is whatever they find near at hand, and you would know the truth of this if you had read as many histories as I; although there are many of them, in none have I found it written that knights errant ever ate, unless perhaps at some sumptuous banquet offered in their honor; the rest of the time they all but fasted. Although it is understood that they could not live without eating or doing all the other necessities of nature because, in fact, they were men like ourselves, it must also be understood that because they spent most of their lives in the open, unpopulated countryside, without a cook, their most common food would be rustic viands, like those which you offer me now. And so, Sancho my friend, do not concern yourself with what may or may not be to my taste. You should not try to make the world over again or change the nature of errant chivalry."

"Forgive me, your grace," said Sancho. "Since I don't know how to read or write, as I told you before, I don't know and am not aware of the rules of the chivalric profession; from now on I'll stock the saddlebags with all kinds of dried fruit for your grace, since you are a knight, and for me, since I'm not, I'll fill them with other things that have wings and are more substantial."

"I am not saying, Sancho," replied Don Quixote, "that it is necessary for knights errant not to eat anything other than those fruits you mention, but simply that their most ordinary sustenance consisted of them and of certain plants found in the fields, which were known to them, and to me as well."

"It's a great virtue," Sancho responded, "to know those plants, for I'm thinking that one day we'll need to use that knowledge."

9. This name appears in a novel of chivalry, *Clamades y Clarmonda* (1562); in later editions of *Don Quixote* it was changed to "Sobradisa," a kingdom mentioned in *Amadís of Gaul*.

He took out the things he said he was carrying, and they ate in peace and good companionship. But they wanted to find a place to sleep that night, and they quickly finished their dry and meager meal. Then they climbed back on their mounts and hurried to reach a village before dark, but the sun set, along with the hope of achieving their desire, when they were near the huts of some goatherds, and so they decided to spend the night there; as much as it grieved Sancho not to be in a town, it pleased his master to sleep outdoors, for it seemed to him that each time this occurred it was another act of certification that helped to prove his claim to knighthood.

CHAPTER XI

Regarding what befell Don Quixote with some goatherds

He was welcomed cheerfully by the goatherds, and Sancho, having done his best to tend to Rocinante and his donkey, followed the aroma coming from certain pieces of dried goat meat that were bubbling over the fire in a pot, and though he wished at that very moment to test if they were ready to be transferred from the pot to his stomach, he did not, because the goatherds removed them from the fire, spread some sheepskins on the ground, quickly prepared their rustic table, and with displays of goodwill invited them both to share what they had. The six of them, which was the number in their flock, sat down around the skins, having first with artless ceremony asked Don Quixote to sit on a small wooden trough that they turned upside down and set out for him. Don Quixote sat down, and Sancho remained standing to serve him and fill his cup, which was made of horn. His master saw him standing and said:

"So that you may see, Sancho, the virtue contained in knight errantry, and how those who practice any portion of it always tend to be honored and esteemed in the world, I want you to sit here at my side and in the company of these good people, and be the same as I, who am your natural lord and master; eat from my plate and drink where I drink, for one may say of knight errantry what is said of love: it makes all things equal."

"You're too kind!" said Sancho. "But I can tell your grace that as long as I have something good to eat, I'll eat it just as well or better standing and all alone as sitting at the height of an emperor. Besides, if truth be told, what I eat, even if it's bread and onion, tastes much better to me in my corner without fancy or respectful manners, than a turkey would at other tables where I have to chew slowly, not drink too much, wipe my mouth a lot, not sneeze or cough if I feel like it, or do other things that come with solitude and freedom. And so, Señor, these honors that your grace wants to grant me for being a servant and follower of knight errantry, which I am, being your grace's squire, you should turn into other things that will be of greater comfort and benefit to me; these, though I am grateful for them, I renounce now and forever."

"Despite all that, you will sit down, for God exalts the man who humbles himself."

And seizing him by the arm, he obliged Sancho to sit next to him.

The goatherds did not understand their nonsensical talk about squires and knights errant, and they simply ate and were silent and looked at their guests, who, with a good deal of grace and eagerness, devoured pieces of goat meat as big as their fists. When the meat course was over, the goatherds spread out on the unshorn sheepskins a great quantity of dried acorns, along with half a cheese that was harder than mortar. In all this time the horn was not idle, for it made the rounds so often—sometimes full, sometimes empty, like the bucket at a well—that one of the two wineskins in evidence was emptied with no difficulty. After Don Quixote had satisfied his stomach, he picked up a handful of acorns, and, regarding them attentively, he began to speak these words:

"Fortunate the age and fortunate the times called golden by the ancients, and not because gold, which in this our age of iron is so highly esteemed, could be found then with no effort, but because those who lived in that time did not know the two words *thine* and *mine*. In that blessed age all things were owned in common; no one, for his daily sustenance, needed to do more than lift his hand and pluck it from the sturdy oaks that so liberally invited him to share their sweet and flavorsome fruit. The clear fountains and rushing rivers offered delicious, transparent waters in magnificent abundance. In the fissures of rocks and the hollows of trees diligent and clever bees established their colonies, freely offering to any hand the fertile harvest of their sweet labor.

Noble cork trees, moved only by their own courtesy, shed the wide, light bark with which houses, supported on rough posts, were covered as a protection, but only against the rain that fell from heaven. In that time all was peace, friendship, and harmony; the heavy curve of the plowshare had not yet dared to open or violate the merciful womb of our first mother, for she, without being forced, offered up, everywhere across her broad and fertile bosom, whatever would satisfy, sustain, and delight the children who then possessed her. In that time simple and beautiful shepherdesses could wander from valley to valley and hill to hill, their hair hanging loose or in braids, wearing only the clothes needed to modestly cover that which modesty demands, and has always demanded, be covered, and their adornments were not those used now, enveloping the one who wears them in the purple dyes of Tyre, and silk martyrized in countless ways, but a few green burdock leaves and ivy vines entwined, and in these they perhaps looked as grand and elegant as our ladies of the court do now in the rare and strange designs which idle curiosity has taught them. In that time amorous concepts were recited from the soul simply and directly, in the same way and manner that the soul conceived them, without looking for artificial and devious words to enclose them. There was no fraud, deceit, or malice mixed in with honesty and truth. Justice stood on her own ground, and favor or interest did not dare disturb or offend her as they so often do now, defaming, confusing, and persecuting her. Arbitrary opinions formed outside the law had not yet found a place in the mind of the judge, for there was nothing to judge, and no one to be judged. Maidens in their modesty wandered, as I have said, wherever they wished, alone and mistresses of themselves, without fear that another's boldness or lascivious intent would dishonor them, and if they fell it was through their own desire and will.

But now, in these our detestable times, no maiden is safe, even if she is hidden and enclosed in another labyrinth like the one in Crete; because even there, through chinks in the wall, or carried by the air itself, with the zealousness of accursed solicitation the amorous pestilence finds its way in and, despite all their seclusion, maidens are brought to ruin. It was for their protection, as time passed and wickedness spread, that the order of knights errant was instituted: to defend maidens, protect widows, and come to the aid of orphans and those in need. This is the order to which I belong, my brother goatherds, and I thank you for the kindness and hospitality you have shown to me and my squire. For, although by natural law all men are obliged to favor knights errant, still, because I know that without knowing this obligation you welcomed me and treated me so generously, I wish, with all my goodwill, to thank you for yours."[1]

This long harangue—which could very easily have been omitted—

---

1. Don Quixote's soliloquy incorporates all the elements traditionally associated with the classical idea of the Golden Age.

was declaimed by our knight because the acorns served to him brought to mind the Golden Age, and with it the desire to make that foolish speech to the goatherds, who, stupefied and perplexed, listened without saying a word. Sancho too was silent, and ate acorns, and made frequent trips to the second wineskin, which had been hung from a cork tree to cool the wine.

Don Quixote spent more time speaking than it took to finish supper, but when it was concluded, one of the goatherds said:

"So that your grace, Señor Knight, can say even more truly that we welcomed you with a ready goodwill, we want to give you joy and pleasure by having a friend of ours sing for you; he'll be here very soon; he's a smart lad, and very much in love, and above all, he knows how to read and write and is so good a musician on the rebec[2] that you couldn't ask for anything better."

No sooner had the goatherd said this than the sound of the rebec reached their ears, and a short while later the one playing it appeared, a good-looking boy no more than twenty-two years of age. His friends asked if he had eaten, and when he answered that he had, the one who had made the offer said:

"That means, Antonio, that you could do us the favor of singing a little, and this gentleman, our guest, can see that in the woods and forests we also have somebody who knows about music. We told him about your talents and we want you to show them and prove we told the truth, and so I ask you please to sit down and sing the ballad about your love that your uncle the vicar composed for you, the one the people in the village liked so much."

"I'd be happy to," the boy replied.

And without having to be asked a second time, he sat on the trunk of a fallen oak and, after tuning his rebec, with great charm he soon began to sing these words:

ANTONIO

I know, Olalla, that you adore me
though you haven't told me so,
not even with your eyes,
in the silent language of love.

---

2. A precursor of the violin, mentioned frequently in pastoral novels.

Since I know that you are clever,
that you love me I do claim;
for love was ne'er unrequited
if it has been proclaimed.

It is true that once or twice
Olalla, you've made it known
that your soul is made of bronze
and your white bosom of stone.

But hiding behind your reproaches
and your virtuous rebukes
hope may reveal a glimpse of
the hemmed edge of her cloak.

My faith is firm and steadfast,
its eager response ne'er wanes
because not called, ne'er waxes
because it has been chosen.

If love is courtesy, then
yours lets me conclude
that the outcome of my hopes
will be just as I assume.

And if service plays a part
in making a bosom kind,
then those that I have rendered
will help to sway your mind.

For if you think about it,
more than once have I worn
the same clothes on a Monday
that honored Sunday morn.

For love and finery
always walk hand in hand,
and in your eyes I wish
always to seem gallant.

Speak not of my dances for you,
the songs that I bestow
so late into the night
and before the rooster's crow.

Speak not of my praises of you,
that I tell to all the world;
though they have earned for me
the displeasure of many a girl.

I was singing your praises,
and Teresa del Berrocal said:
"He thinks he adores an angel,
and he loves a monkey instead.

Thanks to all her trinkets,
her dyes and wigs and falls,
the god of Love is deceived
by beauty that is false."

I said she lied; she grew angry;
her cousin came to her aid
and challenged me; you know
what he and I did and said.

I love no one but you, yet
I don't court you sinfully;
though I beseech and woo you
there's more virtue in my plea.

Mother Church has chains
whose links are made of silk;
I will join you there
if you bend your neck to the yoke.

If not, I make this vow
by the blessed saintly choir
not to leave these mountains
except as a Capuchin friar.

Here the goatherd ended his song, and although Don Quixote asked him to sing something else, Sancho Panza did not concur because he was readier for sleep than for hearing songs. And so he said to his master:

"Your grace ought to decide now where you're going to spend the night; the work these good men do all day doesn't allow them to spend their nights singing."

"I understand you very well, Sancho," Don Quixote responded. "It is clear to me that your visits to the wineskin ask to be repaid with sleep rather than music."

"It tasted good to all of us, thanks be to God," replied Sancho.

"I do not deny that," Don Quixote responded. "But you can settle down wherever you like, for those of my profession prefer standing vigil to sleeping. Even so, Sancho, it would be good if you tended this ear again, for it is hurting more than is necessary."

Sancho did as he was ordered, and when one of the goatherds saw the wound, he told him not to worry, for he would give him a remedy that would heal it right away. And after picking some rosemary leaves, which grew there in abundance, he chewed them and mixed them with a little salt, and applied them to Don Quixote's ear and bandaged it carefully, assuring him that no other medicine was needed, which was the truth.

CHAPTER XII

Regarding what a goatherd recounted to those who were with Don Quixote

At this moment another young man approached, one of those who brought the goatherds provisions from the village, and he said:

"Friends, do you know what has happened in town?"

"How could we know?" one replied.

"Well, then, I'll tell you," the young man continued. "This morning the famous student shepherd named Grisóstomo died, and they say he died of love for that accursed girl Marcela, the daughter of Guillermo the rich man, the same girl who dresses up like a shepherdess and wanders around the wild, empty places."

"Marcela, did you say?" asked one of them.

"The same," replied the goatherd. "And the strange thing is that in his will he said he wanted to be buried in the countryside, like a Moor, and that his grave should be at the bottom of the rocky hill where the spring at the cork tree is, because everybody knows, and they say he said so himself, that this is where he saw her for the first time. And he also asked for some other things that the abbots in the village say shouldn't be done, that it isn't right to do them because they seem heathenish. And to all of this that great friend of his, Ambrosio, the student who dresses up like a shepherd, too, says that everything Grisóstomo wanted has to be done just the way he asked, with nothing left out, and the whole village is in an uproar over this, but people are saying that in the end, they'll do what Ambrosio and his shepherd friends want; tomorrow they'll come to bury him with great ceremony in the place I said, and I think it will be something worth seeing; at least, I'll be sure to go and see it, even though I'm supposed to go back to town tomorrow."

"We'll all do the same," the goatherds responded, "and we'll draw straws to see who has to stay behind and watch all the goats."

"Good idea, Pedro," said one, "but you won't have to draw straws; I'll stay here for all of you. And don't think it's because I'm good or not very curious, it's just that the sharp branch I stepped on the other day makes it hard for me to walk."

"Even so, we all thank you," Pedro replied.

And Don Quixote asked Pedro to tell him about the dead man and the shepherdess, to which Pedro responded that all he knew was that the dead man was a rich gentleman, a resident of a nearby village, who had been a student in Salamanca for many years and then had returned home with a reputation for being very learned and well-read.

"Mainly people said he knew the science of the stars and what happens up there in the sky with the sun and the moon, because he would always tell us when there'd be a clips of the sun and the moon."

"It is called an *eclipse*, my friend, not a *clips*, when those two great heavenly bodies darken," said Don Quixote.

But Pedro, paying little attention to such trifles, continued with his story, saying:

"And he also could tell when the land would produce and when it would be bairn."

"You mean *barren*, my friend," said Don Quixote.

"*Barren* or *bairn*," responded Pedro, "it's all the same in the end. And what I'm saying is that because of what he told them, his father and his friends, who believed him, became very rich because they listened when he said: 'This year plant barley, not wheat; and this year you can plant chickpeas and not barley; next year there'll be a good olive oil harvest, but for the next three you won't get a drop.'"

"This science is called astrology," said Don Quixote.

"I don't know what it's called," Pedro replied, "but I do know he knew all that, and even more. Finally, not many months after he came home from Salamanca, he suddenly appeared one day dressed like a shepherd, with a staff and sheepskin jacket instead of the long gown he wore as a scholar, and a close friend of his named Ambrosio, who had studied with him in Salamanca, dressed up like a shepherd, too. I forgot to say that Grisóstomo, the dead man, was a great one for writing verses; in fact, he wrote the carols for the night of Our Lord's Birth, and the plays for Corpus Christi that the lads from our village put on, and everybody said they were wonderful. When the people in the village saw the two scholars suddenly dressed like shepherds, they were really surprised and couldn't guess the reason why they'd made so odd a change. At about this time his father died, and Grisóstomo inherited a big estate, goods as well as lands, no small amount of livestock both large and small, and a large amount of money; the boy became lord and master of all of this, and the truth is he deserved it all, for he was a very good companion and a charitable man and a friend of good people, and his face was like a blessing. Later on, people began to understand that the change in the way he dressed had been for no other reason than to go wandering through these wild places, following after that shepherdess Marcela our lad mentioned before, because our poor dead Grisóstomo had fallen in love with her. And I want to tell you now who this girl is, because you ought to know; maybe, and maybe there's no maybe about it, you won't hear anything like it in all your born days, even if you live to be as old as my mouth sores."

"You mean *Methuselah*," replied Don Quixote, unable to tolerate the goatherd's confusion of words.

"My mouth sores last a good long time," Pedro responded, "and if, Señor, you keep correcting every word I say, we won't finish in a year."

"Forgive me, my friend," said Don Quixote. "I mentioned it only because there is such a great difference between *my mouth sores* and *Methuselah*; but you answered very well, since *my mouth sores* live longer than *Methuselah*; go on with your story, and I shall not contradict you again in anything."

"Well, Señor, as I was saying," said the goatherd, "in our village there was a farmer even richer than Grisóstomo's father, and his name was Guillermo, and God gave him not only great wealth but also a daughter, whose mother died giving birth to her, and her mother was the most respected woman in this whole district. It seems to me I can see her now, with that face of hers shining like the sun on one side and the moon on the other; more than anything else, she was a hardworking friend to the poor, and for this reason I believe that right this minute her spirit is enjoying God in the next world. Her husband, Guillermo, died of grief at the death of such a good woman, and their daughter, Marcela, was left a very rich girl, in the care of an uncle who was a priest, the vicar of our village. The girl grew, and her beauty reminded us of her mother's, which was very great, though people thought the daughter's would be even greater. And it was, for when she reached the age of fourteen or fifteen, no man could look at her and not bless God for making her so beautiful, and most fell madly in love with her. Her uncle kept her carefully and modestly secluded, but even so, word of her great beauty spread so that for her own sake, and because of her great fortune, not only the men of our village but those for many miles around, the best among them, asked, begged, and implored her uncle for her hand in marriage. But he, a good and honest Christian, though he wanted to arrange her marriage as soon as she was of age, didn't want to do it without her consent, and didn't even care about the profit and gain from the girl's estate that he would enjoy if he delayed her marriage. And by my faith, there was many a gossip in the village who said this in praise of the good priest. For I want you to know, Señor Knight, that in these small hamlets people talk and gossip about everything, and you can be sure, as I am, that a priest must be better than good if his parishioners have to speak well of him, especially in a village."

"That is true," said Don Quixote, "and please continue; the story is very good, and you, my good Pedro, tell it with a good deal of grace."

"May God's grace be with me, that's the one that matters. As for the rest, you should know that even though the uncle suggested names to his niece, and told her the qualities of each of the many suitors begging for her hand, and asked her to choose and marry a man she liked, she never said anything except that she didn't want to marry just then, and since she was so young she didn't feel able to bear the burdens of matrimony. Hearing these excuses, which seemed so reasonable, the uncle stopped asking and waited for her to get a little older, when she would be able to choose a husband she liked. Because he said, and rightly so, that parents shouldn't force their children into marriage against their will.

But then one day, to everybody's surprise, the finicky Marcela appeared dressed like a shepherdess, and paying no attention to her uncle or to all the villagers, who warned her not to do it, she started to go out to the countryside with the other shepherdesses and to watch over her own flock. And as soon as she appeared in public and her beauty was seen in the open, I can't tell you how many rich young men, noblemen and farmers, began to dress up like Grisóstomo and to court her in these fields. One of them, as I've said, was our dead man, who, people said, had stopped loving her and begun to worship her. And don't think that just because Marcela took on the liberty of a life that's so free, with so little seclusion, or none at all, she gave any sign or suggestion that would damage her modesty and virtue; instead, she watches over her honor with so much vigilance that of all the men who woo and court her, not one has boasted or could truthfully claim that she's given him any hope of achieving his desire. For though she doesn't run from or avoid the company and conversation of the shepherds, and treats them with courtesy and friendship, if any of them reveals his desire to her, even one as honest and holy as matrimony, she hurls it away from her like a stone in a catapult. And by living this way, she does more harm in this land than the plague, because her affability and beauty attract the hearts of those who try to woo her and love her, but her disdain and reproaches drive them to despair so that they don't know what to say about her except to call her cruel and ungrateful and other names that plainly show the nature of her disposition. And if you spent one day here, Señor, you'd hear these mountains and valleys echoing with the lamentations of the disappointed men who follow her.

Not very far from here is a place where there are almost two dozen tall beech trees, and there's not one that doesn't have the name of Marcela carved and written on its smooth bark, and at the top of some there's a crown carved into the tree, as if the lover were saying even more clearly that Marcela wears and deserves the crown more than any other human beauty. Here a shepherd sighs, there another moans, over yonder amorous songs are heard, and farther on desperate lamentations. One spends all the hours of the night sitting at the foot of an oak tree or a rocky crag, not closing his weeping eyes, and the sun finds him in the morning absorbed and lost in his thoughts; another gives no respite or rest to his sighs, and in the middle of the burning heat of the fiercest summer afternoon, lying on the burning sand, he sends his complaints up to merciful heaven. And over this one, that one, and all of them, the beautiful Marcela, free and self-assured, triumphs, and those of us who know her are waiting to see where her haughtiness will end and who will be the fortunate man to conquer so difficult a nature and enjoy such extreme beauty.

Since everything I've told you is the absolute truth, I take it for granted that what our lad said about what people were saying about the reason for Gristóstomo's death is also true. And so my advice, Señor, is that tomorrow you be sure to attend his burial, which will be something worth seeing, because Grisóstomo has a lot of friends, and it's no more than half a league from here to the place where he wanted to be buried."

"I shall be certain to," said Don Quixote, "and I thank you for the pleasure you have given me with the narration of so delightful a story."

"Oh!" replied the goatherd. "I still don't know the half of what's hap-

pened to the lovers of Marcela, but it may be that tomorrow we'll meet
some shepherd on the way who'll tell us about them. For now, it would
be a good idea if you slept under a roof, because the night air might hurt
your wound, though the medicine you've put on it is so good there's no
reason to fear any trouble."

Sancho Panza, who by this time was cursing the goatherd's endless
talk, also asked his master to go into Pedro's hut to sleep. He did so, and
spent the rest of the night thinking of his lady Dulcinea, in imitation of
Marcela's lovers. Sancho Panza settled down between Rocinante and his
donkey and slept, not like a scorned lover, but like a man who had been
kicked and bruised.

CHAPTER XIII

*In which the tale of the shepherdess Marcela is concluded, and other events
are related*

But no sooner had day begun to appear on the balconies of the east than
five of the six goatherds got up and went to wake Don Quixote and tell
him that if he was still of a mind to go to see the famous burial of Grisóstomo, they would accompany him. Don Quixote, who desired nothing
else, got up and ordered Sancho to saddle and prepare the mounts immediately, which he did very promptly, and just as promptly they all set out.
And they had gone less than a quarter of a league when, at an intersec-
tion with another path, they saw coming toward them approximately six
shepherds, dressed in black sheepskin jackets, their heads crowned with
wreaths of cypress and bitter oleander. Each carried a heavy staff of holly
in his hand. With them rode two gentlemen on horseback, very well
equipped for traveling and accompanied by three servants on foot. As
the two groups drew close they exchanged courteous greetings, asked
where the other was going, discovered they were all heading for the burial site, and so began to travel together.

One of the men on horseback, speaking to his companion, said:

"It seems to me, Señor Vivaldo, that we must consider our lingering
to see this extraordinary funeral as time well spent, for it most certainly

will be extraordinary, according to the strange tales these shepherds have told us not only about the dead shepherd, but about the murderous shepherdess."

"I think so, too," responded Vivaldo. "And I would have been willing to linger not merely one day but four in order to see it."

Don Quixote asked what they had heard about Marcela and Grisóstomo. The traveler replied that early that morning they had encountered the shepherds and, seeing them in such mournful dress, had asked the reason for their going about in that manner, and one of them had recounted the strange behavior and beauty of a shepherdess named Marcela, and the love so many suitors had for her, and the death of Grisóstomo, to whose burial they were going. In short, he related everything that Pedro had told Don Quixote.

This conversation ended and another began when the traveler called Vivaldo asked Don Quixote the reason for his going about armed in that manner when the land was so peaceful. To which Don Quixote replied:

"The exercise of my profession does not allow or permit me to go about in any other manner. Tranquility, luxury, and repose were invented for pampered courtiers, but travail, tribulation, and arms were invented and created only for those whom the world calls knights errant, and I, although unworthy, am the least of that number."

As soon as they heard this, they considered him mad, and to learn more and see what sort of madness this was, Vivaldo asked him the meaning of knights errant.

"Have your graces not read," responded Don Quixote, "the annals and histories of England, in which are recounted the famous deeds of King Arthur, whom, in our Castilian ballads, we continuously call King Artús? According to an ancient and widespread tradition throughout the kingdom of Great Britain, this king did not die but, through the art of enchantment, was turned into a crow and in time will return to rule and recover his kingdom and scepter; for this reason, it can be demonstrated that no Englishman has ever killed a crow from that time to this. Well, it was in the days of this good king that the famous chivalric order of the Knights of the Round Table was instituted, and, in these same chronicles, in the minutest detail, there is also a recounting of the love between Sir Lancelot of the Lake and Queen Guinevere, their intermediary and confidante being the highly honored Duenna Quintañona, and here was born that well-known ballad, so praised in our Spain:

> Never was a knight
> so well served by ladies
> as was Lancelot when
> he from Brittany came;

followed by the sweet and gentle tale of his feats of love and of valor. Since that time, from one generation to the next, the order of chivalry has extended and spread through many different parts of the world, and among its members, famous and known for their great deeds, were the valiant Amadís of Gaul and all his sons and grandsons unto the fifth generation, and the valorous Felixmarte of Hyrcania, and the never-sufficiently-praised Tirant lo Blanc, and in our own time we have almost seen and communicated with and heard the invincible and valiant knight Don Belianís of Greece. This, then, gentlemen, is what it means to be a knight errant, and the order of chivalry is just as I have said, and in it, as I have also said, I, though a sinner, have taken my vows, professing exactly what was professed by the knights I have mentioned. And therefore I wander these solitary and desolate places in search of adventures, determined to bring my arm and my person to the most dangerous that fortune may offer, in defense of the weak and helpless."

These words fully persuaded the travelers that Don Quixote had lost his reason, and they realized the nature of the madness that controlled him and felt the same astonishment that was felt by all who came to know it. Vivaldo, who was a very clever person with a merry disposition, wanted to give Don Quixote the opportunity to go on with his nonsense and entertain them for the short distance that remained before they reached the burial site. And so he said:

"It seems to me, Señor Knight Errant, that your grace has taken a vow to follow one of the most austere professions in the world; in my opinion, not even Carthusian friars have one so austere."

"Theirs may be as austere," responded our Don Quixote, "but I have some doubt that it is just as necessary in the world. Because, if truth be told, the soldier, when he carries out his captain's orders, does no less than the captain who issues the orders. I mean to say that the religious, in absolute peace and tranquility, ask heaven for the well-being of the world, but we soldiers and knights effect what they ask, defending the world with the valor of our good right arms and the sharp edge of our swords, not protected by a roof but under the open sky, subject to the unbearable rays of the sun in summer and the icy blasts of winter. In this way we are ministers of God on earth, the arms by which His justice is put into effect on earth. And since the deeds of war and all things concerned with and related to war cannot be effected except with toil, perspiration, and travail, it follows that those whose profession it is undoubtedly face greater difficulties than those who in tranquil peace and repose pray to God to favor those who cannot help themselves. I do not mean to say, nor has it even passed through my mind, that the state of a knight errant is as virtuous as that of a cloistered religious; I wish only to suggest, given what I must suffer, that it is undoubtedly more toilsome and more difficult, more subject to hunger and thirst, more destitute, straitened, and impoverished, for there can be no doubt that knights errant in the past endured many misfortunes in the course of their lives. And if some rose to be emperors through the valor of their mighty right arms, by my faith, it cost them dearly in the quantities of blood and sweat they shed, and if those who rose to such great heights had not had enchanters and wise men to help them, they would have been thwarted in their desires and deceived in their hopes."

"I am of the same opinion," replied the traveler, "but there is one thing, among many others, concerning knights errant that seems objectionable to me, and it is that when they find themselves about to embark on a great and perilous adventure, in which there is a manifest danger that they will lose their lives, never at the moment of undertaking it do they think of commending themselves to God, as every Christian is obliged to do at times of danger; instead, they commend themselves to their ladies with as much zeal and devotion as if those ladies were their God, and to me this seems to have a somewhat heathenish smell."

"Señor," responded Don Quixote, "under no circumstances can they do any less, and the knight errant who did otherwise would fall into disrepute, for it is tradition and custom in knight errantry that the knight errant who is about to embark on some great feat of arms and has his lady before him must gently and lovingly turn his eyes toward her as if asking her to favor and protect him in the fearful battle he is undertaking; even if no one is there to hear him, he is obliged to murmur a few words under his breath in which, with all his heart, he commends himself to her; we have countless examples of this in the histories. But one should not assume, therefore, that they fail to commend themselves to God, for they have the time and place to do that in the course of combat."

"Even so," replied the traveler, "I still have a misgiving, and it is that I have often read that words are exchanged between two knights errant, and one word leads to another, their anger rises, they turn their horses and ride off a good distance to the far ends of the field, and then, without further ado, they ride at full tilt toward each other, and in the middle of the charge they commend themselves to their ladies, and what usually happens after their encounter is that one falls from his horse, run through by his opponent's lance, and the same thing happens to the other as well, for unless he holds on to his horse's mane, he cannot help but fall to the ground, too. And I don't know how the one who is dead had time to commend himself to God in the course of so swift a combat. It would be better if the words he used during the charge to commend himself to his lady had been used instead to do what he ought to have done and was obliged to do as a Christian. Furthermore, I don't believe that all the knights errant have ladies to whom they can commend themselves because not all of them are in love."

"That cannot be," responded Don Quixote. "I mean, there cannot be a knight errant without a lady, because it is as fitting and natural for them to be in love as for the sky to have stars, and, just as certainly, you have never seen a history in which you find a knight errant without a love, for if he had none, he would not be deemed a legitimate knight but a bastard who entered the fortress of chivalry not through the door but over the walls, like a robber and a thief."

"Even so," said the traveler, "it seems to me that if I remember correctly, I have read that Don Galaor, brother of the valorous Amadís of Gaul, never had a specific lady to whom he could commend himself, and despite this he was not held in any less esteem, and was a very valiant and famous knight."

To which our Don Quixote responded:

"Señor, one swallow does not a summer make. Furthermore, I happen to know that this knight was secretly very much in love, even though his courting all the lovely ladies he found attractive was a natural inclination that he could not resist. However, it is clearly demonstrated that there was one lady whom he had made mistress of his will, and to her he commended himself very frequently and very secretly, because he prided himself on being a secretive knight."

"Well then, if it is essential that every knight errant has to be in love," said the traveler, "we most certainly can suppose that your grace is as well, since you are a member of the profession. And unless your grace prides himself on being as secretive as Don Galaor, I most earnestly implore you, in the name of all this company and on my own behalf, to tell us the name, the kingdom, the condition, and the beauty of your lady; for she would think herself fortunate if all the world knew she was loved and served by the sort of knight your grace appears to be."

Whereupon Don Quixote heaved a great sigh and said:

"I cannot declare whether my sweet enemy would be pleased or not if the world were to know that I serve her; I can only state, responding to what you so courteously ask, that her name is Dulcinea, her kingdom, Toboso, which is in La Mancha, her condition must be that of princess, at the very least, for she is my queen and lady, and her beauty is supernatural, for in it one finds the reality of all the impossible and chimerical aspects of beauty which poets attribute to their ladies: her tresses are gold, her forehead Elysian fields, her eyebrows the arches of heaven, her eyes suns, her cheeks roses, her lips coral, her teeth pearls, her neck alabaster, her bosom marble, her hands ivory, her skin white as snow, and the parts that modesty hides from human eyes are such, or so I believe and understand, that the most discerning consideration can only praise them but not compare them."

"We would like to know her lineage, ancestry, and family," replied Vivaldo.

To which Don Quixote responded:

"She is not of the ancient Roman families of Curtius, Gaius, and Scipio, nor of the more modern Colonnas and Ursinos, nor of the Moncadas and Requesenes of Cataluña, nor even the Rebellas and Villanovas of Valencia, the Palafoxes, Nuzas, Rocabertís, Corellas Lunas, Alagones, Urreas, Foces, and Gurreas of Aragón, the Cerdas, Manriques, Mendozas, and Guzmanes of Castilla, the Alencastros, Pallas, and Meneses of Portugal; but she is of the family of Toboso of La Mancha, a lineage so fine, although modern, that it can give a generous beginning to the most illustrious families of centuries to come. And I shall brook no reply to this except under the conditions inscribed by Cervino beneath Orlando's victorious arms, which said:

> Let no one move them
> who cannot prove his worth against Roland."[1]

"Although my lineage is the Cachopines of Laredo," responded the traveler, "I won't dare compare it to that of Toboso of La Mancha, for, to tell the truth, that name has not reached my ears until now."

"Is it possible that so notable a thing has not reached them?" replied Don Quixote.

All the others had been listening with great attention to their con-

---

1. The lines are from *Orlando furioso*. "Roland" is the English (and French) for "Orlando." The Spanish version of the name is "Roldán."

versation, and even the goatherds and shepherds realized that Don Quixote was not in his right mind. Only Sancho Panza, knowing who he was and having known him since he was born, thought that everything his master said was true, but he did have some doubts concerning the beauteous Dulcinea of Toboso, because he had never heard of that name or that princess, even though he lived so close to Toboso.

As they were conversing, they saw that coming down the pass formed by two high mountains were about twenty shepherds, all wearing black wool jackets and crowned with wreaths that, as they saw later, were made either of yew or cypress. Six were carrying a bier covered with a great variety of flowers and branches. When one of the goatherds saw this, he said:

"Those men there are carrying the body of Grisóstomo, and the foot of that mountain is the place where he said he should be buried."

For this reason they hurried to reach the spot, which they did as the bearers were setting the bier on the ground, and, with sharp picks, four of them began digging the grave to one side of a rugged crag.

They exchanged courteous greetings, and then Don Quixote and those who had accompanied him began to look at the bier, and on it, covered with flowers, they saw a dead body, apparently thirty years of age, dressed as a shepherd, and although he was dead, he showed signs of having had a handsome face and a gallant disposition when he was alive. Around him on the bier were bound volumes and many papers, both opened and closed. And those who were watching, and the men who were digging the grave, and everyone else who was present maintained a wondrous silence, until one of those who had been carrying the dead man said to another:

"Look carefully, Ambrosio, to see if this is the place Grisóstomo mentioned, since you want everything he asked for in his will to be carried out to the letter."

"It is," Ambrosio responded, "for here my unhappy friend often told me the history of his misfortune. Here, he said, he first saw that mortal enemy of the human race, and here was also where he first declared to her his desire, as honest as it was amorous, and here was where Marcela finally disillusioned and disdained him for the last time, putting an end to the tragedy of his wretched life. Here, in memory of so much affliction, he wanted to be consigned to the depths of eternal oblivion."

And turning to Don Quixote and the travelers, he went on to say:

"This body, Señores, that you look at with pitying eyes, was the depository of a soul in which heaven placed an infinite number of its gifts. This is the body of Grisóstomo, who was unique in intelligence, unequaled in courtesy, inimitable in gallantry, peerless in friendship, faultless in generosity, serious without presumption, merry without vulgarity, and, finally, first in everything it means to be good and second to none in everything it means to be unfortunate. He loved deeply and was rejected; he adored and was scorned; he pleaded with a wild beast, importuned a piece of marble, pursued the wind, shouted in the desert, served ingratitude, and his reward was to fall victim to death in the middle of his life, which was ended by a shepherdess whom he attempted to immortalize so that she would live on in memory, which could have been clearly shown in those papers you see there if he had not ordered them committed to the fire when his body had been committed to the earth."

"You would use greater harshness and cruelty with them," said Vivaldo, "than their own master, for it is neither just nor correct to carry out the will of someone whose orders go against all reasonable thought. You would not think so highly of Caesar Augustus if he had agreed to carry out what the divine Mantuan had ordered in his will.[2] And so, Señor Ambrosio, although you surrender your friend's body to the ground, do not surrender his writings to oblivion; if he gave the order as an aggrieved man, it is not proper for you to carry it out like a foolish one. Rather, by giving life to these papers, you can have Marcela's cruelty live on as an example to those who live in future days so that they can flee and run from similar dangers; I and my companions know the history of your loving and desperate friend, and the reason for his death, and what he ordered to be done when his life was over; from this lamentable history one can learn how great was the cruelty of Marcela, the love of Grisóstomo, and the steadfastness of your friendship, as well as the final destination of those who madly gallop along the path that heedless love places in front of them. Last night we learned of Grisóstomo's death and that he would be buried in this place; and filled with curiosity and pity, we halted our journey and decided to come and see with our own eyes what had saddened us so much when we heard it. And as recompense for this sorrow, and the desire born in us to alleviate it if we could, we beg you—at least, I implore you—O most discreet Ambrosio, not to burn these papers, and to allow me to have some of them."

And not waiting for the shepherd to respond, he stretched out his

2. Virgil requested that the *Aeneid* be burned at his death.

hand and took some of the papers closest to him; seeing this, Ambrosio said:

"Out of courtesy I consent to your keeping, Señor, the ones you already have, but to think that I won't burn those that remain is to think vain thoughts."

Vivaldo, who wanted to see what the papers said, immediately opened one of them and saw that it had as a title "Song of Despair." When Ambrosio heard the title, he said:

"This is the last paper the unfortunate man wrote; and so that you may see, Señor, the lengths to which his misfortunes had driven him, read it aloud so that all may hear, for the time it will take to dig the grave will be more than enough time for you to read it."

"I will do that gladly," said Vivaldo.

And since all those present had the same desire, they came to stand around him, and Vivaldo, reading in a clear voice, saw that it said:

CHAPTER XIV

In which are found the desperate verses of the deceased shepherd, along with other unexpected occurrences

GRISÓSTOMO'S SONG

Since you, most cruel, wish all tongues to proclaim,
all men to know the harsh power of your will,
I will have hell itself teach a mournful song
to my grieving breast; then add to that discord
with the stridency of this my tuneless voice.
And, companion to my desire as it strives
to tell of my sorrow and your heartless deeds,
that fearful voice will resound; worse torment,
it will carry pieces of my wretched heart.
Listen, then, to no harmonious song
but to the clangor rising from the depths
of my embittered breast, and borne by frenzy,
sounding to my delight and your displeasure.

The roar of the lion, the fearful howling
of the savage wolf, the terrible hisses
of the scaly serpent, the ghastly shrieks of
monsters, the portents of the raven's croak,
the din of winds battling unsettled seas,
the great bull's vengeful bellow in defeat,
the widowed turtledove's heartbroken call,
the grief-stricken hooting of the envied owl, and
the cries of all the souls in darkest hell,
let these join with my spirit in its grief,
blending in song, confounding all the senses,
for the merciless anguish I endure
demands new modes, new styles, for its recounting.

    The wailing echoes of this dissonance
will not be heard on sands of Father Tajo,
or in the Andalusian olive groves:
my heartless agony will be carried by
a dead man's tongue, in words that will survive him,
to craggy heights, or bottomless ravines,
to darkened valleys, to some hostile shore
bare of human commerce, or to places where
the sunlight ne'er was seen, or to the hordes of
ravening toxic beasts that live and thrive
on the Libyan plain; for though in desert wastes
the hoarse, uncertain echoes of my ills
may sound with unmatched harshness, like your own,
as a privilege of my destiny cut short,
they will be carried all around the world.

    Disdain can kill, suspicions true or false
can bring down patience; and jealousy slays
with grim ferocity; long absence can
confound a life; feared oblivion defeats
the surest hope for a life of happiness.
In all this, certain death cannot be fled;
but I—O wondrous miracle!—I live on
jealous, absent, disdained, and certain of
suspicions that fell me, forgotten by one
for whom I burn with ever hotter flame,
and in so much torment I can never see
even the shadow of hope that, in despair,

I do not attempt to find; rather, to carry
my woe to the furthest extreme, I vow
eternally to live bereft of hope.

    Can one feel hope and at the same time fear,
or is it wise to do so when the reasons
for fear are so much stronger? Must I then
close these eyes when flint-hard jealousy
appears before them, only to watch it tear
a thousand open wounds deep in my soul?
Who would not open wide the door to despair
when he sees disdain undisguised, laid bare,
when he sees all his suspicions, oh bitter
transformation, converted into truths,
and honest truth transmuted into lies?
O jealousy, in the kingdom of love
a pitiless tyrant, place these my hands
in chains. And condemn me, disdain,
to be bound in twisted rope. But woe is me
when in your memory, O cruelest triumph,
my suffering is smothered and erased.

    I die, I die; and so that I may never
hope for a good end in my death or life
I will be steadfast in my vagaries,
say that true love is bound to succeed, say
the soul most enslaved to the ancient tyranny
of love, lives most free. Say that my enemy
is beautiful in body and in soul, that
I bear the blame for her forgetting me,
that love inflicts these sorrows and these ills
to keep his realm in order and at peace.
With this thought and a merciless cruel scourge
I will slash and cut the brief time left to me
by your disdain, and offer to the winds
this soul and body, uncrowned by the palm
or laurel of future bliss and joy to come.

    You, whose unreason shows the reason clear
that forces me to end this weary life
grown hateful to me, can see the patent signs
of the fatal wound that cuts this heart in two,

and how I bend, submissive, to your will,
and if, by chance, you learn that I deserve
to have clouds fill the fair sky of your eyes
when you hear of my death, forbid it, for I
want you unrepentant, without remorse, when
I hand to you the ruins of my soul.
And then your laughter at that grievous time
will show my end was cause for your rejoicing;
what lack of wit to caution you in this,
when I know your brightest glory lies in seeing
that my life draws so quickly to its close.

 Come, it is time for Tantalus to rise
with all his thirst from the abysmal deeps;
let Sisyphus come, bearing the awful weight
of that dread stone; let Tityus bring the vultures,
let Ixion hasten on the remorseless wheel,
and the grim sisters ceaseless at their toil;
may they pass their mortal torments to my breast,
and in hushed voices let them sadly chant
—if one in despair deserves such obsequies—
songs to a body not yet in its shroud.
And the three-faced guardian of the gates
of hell, chimeras, monsters by the thousands,
let them intone the dolorous counterpoint;
for there can be no better funeral rite
than this, I think, for one who dies of love.

 Song of despair, do not weep at leaving me;
since that will swell the joy of one who is
the reason for your birth and my misfortune,
do not grieve for me even in the grave.

Those who had listened to Grisóstomo's song thought it was very good, though the one who read it said he did not think it conformed to the accounts he had heard of Marcela's virtue and modesty, because in it Grisóstomo complained of jealousy, suspicions, and absence, all to the detriment of Marcela's good name and reputation. To which Ambrosio, as the one who knew best the most hidden thoughts of his friend, replied:

"Señor, so that you may free yourself of this doubt, you ought to know that when the unfortunate man wrote this song he was absent from Marcela; he had absented himself from her voluntarily, to see if absence would have its customary effects on him, and since there is nothing that does not vex the absent lover, and no fear that does not overwhelm him, Grisóstomo was as vexed by the jealousy he imagined and the suspicions he feared as if they had been real. And with this the truth of Marcela's reputation for virtue remains unshaken; for aside from her being cruel, and somewhat arrogant, and very disdainful, envy itself cannot or should not find any fault in her."

"That is true," responded Vivaldo.

He wanted to read another of the papers he had rescued from the fire but was stopped by a marvelous vision—this is what it seemed to him— that suddenly appeared before his eyes; at the top of the crag where the grave was being dug, there came into view the shepherdess Marcela, whose beauty far surpassed her fame for beauty. Those who had not seen her before looked at her in amazement and silence, and those who were already accustomed to seeing her were no less thunderstruck than those who had not seen her until then. But no sooner had he seen her than Ambrosio, showing signs of outrage, said to her:

"Do you come, O savage basilisk of these mountains, to see if with your presence blood spurts from the wounds of this wretched man whose life was taken by your cruelty?[1] Or do you come to gloat over the cruelties of your nature, or to watch from that height, like another heartless Nero, the flames of burning Rome, or, in your arrogance, to tread on this unfortunate corpse, as the ungrateful daughter of Tarquinus[2] did to the body of her father? Tell us quickly why you have come, or what it is you want most, for since I know that Grisóstomo's thoughts never failed to obey you in life, I shall see to it that even though he is dead, those who called themselves his friends will obey you as well."

"I do not come, O Ambrosio, for any of the causes you have mentioned," Marcela responded, "but I return here on my own behalf to explain how unreasonable are those who in their grief blame me for the death of Grisóstomo, and so I beg all those present to hear me, for there will be no need to spend much time or waste many words to persuade discerning men of the truth. Heaven made me, as all of you say, so beautiful that you cannot resist my beauty and are compelled to love me, and be-

---

1. According to a medieval legend, the wounds of a murder victim would bleed in the presence of the killer.

2. The reference is to Tulia, the wife, not the daughter, of the Roman king Tarquinus the Proud.

cause of the love you show me, you claim that I am obliged to love you in return. I know, with the natural understanding that God has given me, that everything beautiful is lovable, but I cannot grasp why, simply because it is loved, the thing loved for its beauty is obliged to love the one who loves it. Further, the lover of the beautiful thing might be ugly, and since ugliness is worthy of being avoided, it is absurd for anyone to say: 'I love you because you are beautiful; you must love me even though I am ugly.' But in the event the two are equally beautiful, it does not mean that their desires are necessarily equal, for not all beauties fall in love; some are a pleasure to the eye but do not surrender their will, because if all beauties loved and surrendered, there would be a whirl of confused and misled wills not knowing where they should stop, for since beautiful subjects are infinite, desires would have to be infinite, too.

According to what I have heard, true love is not divided and must be voluntary, not forced. If this is true, as I believe it is, why do you want to force me to surrender my will, obliged to do so simply because you say you love me? But if this is not true, then tell me: if the heaven that made me beautiful had made me ugly instead, would it be fair for me to complain that none of you loved me? Moreover, you must consider that I did not choose the beauty I have, and, such as it is, heaven gave it to me freely, without my requesting or choosing it. And just as the viper does not deserve to be blamed for its venom, although it kills, since it was given the venom by nature, I do not deserve to be reproved for being beautiful, for beauty in the chaste woman is like a distant fire or sharp-edged sword: they do not burn or cut the person who does not approach them. Honor and virtue are adornments of the soul, without which the body is not truly beautiful, even if it seems to be so. And if chastity is one of the virtues that most adorn and beautify both body and soul, why should a woman, loved for being beautiful, lose that virtue in order to satisfy the desire of a man who, for the sake of his pleasure, attempts with all his might and main to have her lose it?

I was born free, and in order to live free I chose the solitude of the countryside. The trees of these mountains are my companions, the clear waters of these streams my mirrors; I communicate my thoughts and my beauty to the trees and to the waters. I am a distant fire and a far-off sword. Those whose eyes forced them to fall in love with me, I have discouraged with my words. If desires feed on hopes, and since I have given no hope to Grisóstomo or to any other man regarding those desires, it is correct to say that his obstinacy, not my cruelty, is what killed him. And if you claim that his thoughts were virtuous, and for this reason I was obliged to respond to them, I say that when he revealed to me the virtue of his desire, on the very spot where his grave is now being dug, I told him that mine was to live perpetually alone and have only the earth enjoy the fruit of my seclusion and the spoils of my beauty; and if he, despite that discouragement, wished to persist against all hope and sail into the wind, why be surprised if he drowned in the middle of the gulf of his folly? If I had kept him by me, I would have been false; if I had gratified him, I would have gone against my own best intentions and purposes. He persisted though I discouraged him, he despaired though I did not despise him: tell me now if it is reasonable to blame me for his grief! Let the one I deceived complain, let the man despair to whom I did not grant a hope I had promised, or speak if I called to him, or boast if I accepted him; but no man can call me cruel or a murderer if I do not promise, deceive, call to, or accept him. Until now heaven has not ordained that I love, and to think that I shall love of my own accord is to think the impossible.

Let this general discouragement serve for each of those who solicit me for his own advantage; let it be understood from this day forth that if anyone dies because of me, he does not die of jealousy or misfortune, because she who loves no one cannot make anyone jealous, and discouragement should not be taken for disdain. Let him who calls me savage basilisk avoid me as he would something harmful and evil; let him who calls me ungrateful, not serve me, unapproachable, not approach me, cruel, not follow me; let him not seek out, serve, approach, or follow in any way this savage, ungrateful, cruel, unapproachable basilisk. For if his impatience and rash desire killed Grisóstomo, why should my virtuous behavior and reserve be blamed? If I preserve my purity in the company of trees, why should a man want me to lose it if he wants me to keep it in the company of men? As you know, I have wealth of my own and do not desire anyone else's; I am free and do not care to submit to another; I do not love or despise anyone. I do not deceive this one or solicit that one; I do not mock one or amuse myself with another. The honest conversation of the shepherdesses from these hamlets, and tending to my goats, are my entertainment. The limits of my desires are these mountains, and if they go beyond here, it is to contemplate the beauty of heaven and the steps whereby the soul travels to its first home."

And having said this, and not waiting to hear any response, she turned her back and entered the densest part of a nearby forest, leaving all those present filled with admiration as much for her intelligence as for her beauty. And some—those who were pierced by the powerful arrow of the light in her beautiful eyes—gave indications of wishing to follow her, disregarding the patent discouragement they had heard. Seeing this, Don Quixote thought it an appropriate time to put his chivalry into practice by coming to the aid of a maiden in distress, and he placed his hand on the hilt of his sword, and in a loud, clear voice he said:

"Let no person, whatever his circumstance or condition, dare to follow the beautiful Marcela lest he fall victim to my fury and outrage. She has shown with clear and sufficient reasons that she bears little or no blame in the death of Grisóstomo, and she has also shown how far she is from acquiescing to the desires of any who love her, and therefore it is just that rather than being followed and persecuted, she should be honored and esteemed by all good people in the world, for she has shown herself to be the only woman in it who lives with so virtuous a desire."

Whether it was because of Don Quixote's warnings, or because Ambrosio said they should conclude what they owed to their good friend, none of the shepherds left or moved away from the place until, when the grave was dug and Gristóstomo's papers had been burned, they placed his body in the ground, not without those present shedding many tears. They closed the grave with a heavy boulder until such time as the stone was finished that, Ambrosio said, he planned to have made, with an epitaph that would read:

> Here lies the sad cold
> body of a lover,
> a shepherd destroyed
> by an icy heart.
> The pitiless hand
> of cruel beauty killed him,
> extending the power
> of love's tyranny.

Then they scattered many flowers and branches over the grave, offered their condolences to his friend Ambrosio, and took their leave of him. Vivaldo and his companion said goodbye, and Don Quixote bade farewell to his hosts and to the two travelers, who asked him to accompany them to Sevilla because it was a place so well-suited to finding adventures, since more were to be found there on every street and around every corner than in any other city. Don Quixote thanked them for the information and their clear desire to favor him, but he said that for the moment he should not nor did he wish to go to Sevilla, until he had emptied those mountains that were full, it was said, of villainous thieves. Seeing his firm determination, the travelers did not wish to importune him, and saying goodbye again, they left him and continued their journey, during which they had much to talk about, from the history of Marcela and Grióstomo to the madness of Don Quixote. Our knight resolved to seek out the shepherdess Marcela and offer to serve her in any way he could. But matters did not turn out as he expected, as is recounted in the course of this true history, the second part of which concludes here.

Part Three of the Ingenious Gentleman Don Quixote of La Mancha

CHAPTER XV

In which is recounted the unfortunate adventure that Don Quixote happened upon when he happened upon some heartless Yanguesans

The learned Cide Hamete Benengeli tells us that as soon as Don Quixote took his leave of his hosts and all the others who had been present at the burial of the shepherd Grisóstomo, he and his squire entered the same forest the shepherdess Marcela had entered; and having ridden more than two hours, looking for her everywhere and not finding her, they decided to stop in a meadow full of new grass where a cool, gentle stream ran, so welcoming that it invited and obliged one to spend the hottest hours of the day there, for the rigors of the afternoon were just beginning.

Don Quixote and Sancho dismounted and, leaving the donkey and

Rocinante free to graze on the abundant grass that grew there, pillaged the saddlebags, and without any ceremony, in peace and harmony, master and servant companionably ate what they found in them.

Sancho had not bothered to hobble Rocinante, certain that he knew him to be so meek and so little given to lustful thoughts that all the mares of the pastures of Córdoba could not tempt him to go astray. As luck and the devil, who is not always sleeping, would have it, grazing in that valley was a herd of Galician ponies tended by some drovers from Yanguas,[1] whose custom it is to take a siesta with their animals in grassy, well-watered places and sites, and the spot where Don Quixote happened to find himself served the Yanguesans' purposes very well.

As it happened, Rocinante felt the desire to pleasure himself with the ladies, and as soon as he picked up their scent he abandoned his natural ways and customs, did not ask permission of his owner, broke into a brisk little trot, and went off to communicate his need to them. But the ponies, who apparently had more desire to graze than anything else, greeted him with hooves and teeth, so that in a short while his cinches broke and he was left naked, without a saddle. But what he must have regretted most was that the drovers, seeing the violence being done to their mares, hurried over with their staffs and hit him so many times that they knocked him to the ground, badly injured.

By now Don Quixote and Sancho, who had seen Rocinante's beating, had run up, panting heavily; and Don Quixote said to Sancho:

"From what I can see, Sancho my friend, these are not knights but base people of low breeding. I say this because you can certainly assist me in taking the proper revenge for the offense that has been done to Rocinante before our very eyes."

"What the devil kind of revenge are we supposed to take," Sancho responded, "if there are more than twenty of them and only two of us, or maybe only one and a half?"

"I am worth a hundred," Don Quixote replied.

And without making more speeches, he grasped his sword and rushed at the Yanguesans, and Sancho Panza, incited and moved by his master's example, did the same. To begin with, Don Quixote landed a blow on one drover that slashed open a leather tunic he was wearing, as well as a good part of his shoulder.

---

1. There is a Yanguas in the modern province of Soria and another in the province of Segovia; in the first edition, however, Cervantes calls the drovers "Galicians." For the sake of clarity, I have called them "Yanguesans," which is how they are referred to in part II.

The Yanguesans, who saw themselves attacked by only two men when there were so many of them, had recourse to their staffs, and surrounding the two men, they began to rain blows down on them with great zeal and eagerness. The truth is that with the second blow they knocked Sancho to the ground, and the same thing happened to Don Quixote, and all his skill and courage were of no use to him; as luck would have it, he fell at the feet of Rocinante, who had not yet stood up, which proves what furious beatings staffs can administer when wielded by angry rustic hands.

When the Yanguesans saw the damage they had done, they loaded their animals as quickly as they could and continued on their way, leaving the two adventurers looking bad and feeling worse.

The first to stir was Sancho Panza; finding himself next to his master, in a weak, plaintive voice he said:

"Señor Don Quixote! Ah, Señor Don Quixote!"

"What do you want, brother Sancho?" replied Don Quixote in a voice as feeble and pitiful as Sancho's.

"What I want, if it's possible," replied Sancho Panza, "is for your grace to give me two swigs of that drink of Fearsome Blas,[2] if your grace happens to have any on hand. Maybe it's as good for broken bones as it is for wounds."

"Ah, woe is me, if I had it here, what else would we need?" Don Quixote responded. "But I swear to you, Sancho Panza, by my faith as a knight errant, that in two days' time, if fortune does not ordain otherwise, I shall have it in my possession, unless my hands fail me."

"And how many days does your grace think we'll need before we can move our legs?" Sancho Panza replied.

"As for me," said a beaten and exhausted Don Quixote, "I do not know how many days it will be. But I hold myself responsible for everything; I should not have raised my sword against men who were not dubbed knights like myself; and therefore I believe that as a punishment for having trespassed against the laws of chivalry, the god of battles has allowed me to be injured in this way. Therefore, Sancho Panza, it is fitting that you heed carefully what I shall say to you now, because it is important to the well-being of both of us, and it is that when you see rabble like this offending us in some way, do not wait for me to raise my sword against them, because I shall not do that; instead, you must seize your

---

2. Sancho misremembers the name (Fierabrás) associated with the healing potion.

sword and punish them as you like, and if knights come to their aid and defense, I shall know how to defend you and offend them with all my power, for you have seen in a thousand demonstrations and experiences the extent of the valor of this my mighty arm."

This was how arrogant the poor gentleman was after his defeat of the valiant Basque. But his master's advice did not seem very good to Sancho, and he had to respond, saying:

"Señor, I'm a peaceful, mild, and quiet man, and I know how to conceal any insult because I have a wife and children to support and care for. So let your grace be advised as well, since I can't give an order, that under no circumstances will I raise my sword against either lowborn or gentry, and from now until the day I appear before God, I forgive all offenses that have been done or will be done to me, whether they were done, are being done, or will be done by a person high or low, rich or poor, noble or common, without exception, and regardless of rank or position."

Hearing which, his master responded:

"I wish I had enough breath to speak with less effort and that the pain I feel in this rib would ease just a little, so that I could make clear to you, Panza, how wrong you are. Come closer, you sinner: if the winds of fortune, until now so contrary, blow again in our favor, filling the sails of our desire and carrying us safely and with no sudden changes of direction to port on one of the ínsulas which I have promised you, what would happen when I, having won it, make you its ruler? Will you render that impossible because you are not a knight, and do not wish to be one, and do not have the courage or desire to avenge offenses and defend your realm? Because you must know that in newly conquered kingdoms and provinces, the spirits of the inhabitants are never so peaceful or so favorable to their new ruler that he need not fear they will do something unexpected to disturb things and, as they say, try their luck again; and so it is necessary for the new ruler to have the intelligence to know how to govern and the valor to go on the offensive and defend himself under any circumstances."

"In this circumstance that has just happened to us," Sancho responded, "I would have liked to have the intelligence and valor your grace has mentioned; but I swear to you, by my faith as a poor man, that I need a poultice more than I need talk. Your grace, see if you can stand, and we'll help Rocinante, though he doesn't deserve it, because he's the main reason for this beating. I never would have believed it of Rocinante; I always thought he was a person as chaste and peaceable as I am. Well, like they say, you need a long time to know a person, and nothing in this life is certain. Who would have thought that hard on the heels and so soon after those mighty blows struck by your grace's sword against that unfortunate knight errant, this great storm of a beating would rain down on our backs?"

"Yours, at least, Sancho," replied Don Quixote, "must be accustomed to such cloudbursts; but mine, brought up on cambric and fine Dutch linen, of course will feel more deeply the pain of this misfortune. And if it were not because I imagine . . . did I say imagine? . . . because I know for a fact that all these discomforts are an integral part of the practice of arms, I would let myself die here of sheer annoyance."

To which the squire replied:

"Señor, since these misfortunes are the harvest reaped by chivalry, tell me, your grace, if they happen very often or come only at certain times, because it seems to me that after two harvests like this one, we'll be useless for the third if God, in His infinite mercy, doesn't come to our aid."

"You should know, Sancho my friend," responded Don Quixote, "that the lives of knights errant are subject to a thousand dangers and disasters, and by the same token they are just as likely to become kings and emperors at any moment, as demonstrated by the experience of many different and diverse knights whose histories I know thoroughly and completely. And I could tell you now, if the pain I feel would allow, of some who, by the sheer valor of their mighty arm, have risen to the high estates I have mentioned to you, and yet, both before and afterward, these same knights have borne all manner of calamities and miseries. For the valorous Amadís of Gaul found himself in the power of his mortal enemy the enchanter Arcalaus, who, as has been verified, tied him to a column in a courtyard and gave him more than two hundred lashes with the reins of his horse. And there is even a little-known author, but a very creditable one, who says that in a certain castle the Knight of Phoebus was caught in a certain trapdoor that opened beneath his feet, and he fell and found himself in a deep pit under the earth, tied hand and foot, and there he was given one of those things called an enema, composed of melted snow and sand, which almost killed him, and if he had not been helped in those dire straits by a wise man who was a great friend of his, things would have gone very badly for the poor knight. And I may certainly suffer along with so many virtuous knights, for they endured greater affronts than the ones we are suffering now. For I want you to know, Sancho, that injuries inflicted by the tools one happens to be holding are not offenses; this is expressly stated in the law of dueling: if the cobbler hits another with the last he holds in his hand, although it really is made of wood, it cannot be said that the one he struck has been clubbed. I say this so that you will not think, although we have been cudgeled in this dispute, that we have been offended, because the weapons those men were carrying, the ones they used to hit us, were simply their staffs, and none of them, if I remember correctly, had a rapier, a sword, or a poniard."

"They didn't give me a chance," Sancho responded, "to look at them so carefully, because as soon I put my hand on my sword they made the sign of the cross on my shoulders with their pinewood, so that they took the sight from my eyes and the strength from my feet, knocking me down where I'm lying now, where it doesn't hurt at all to think about whether the beating they gave me with their staffs was an offense or not, unlike the pain of the beating, which will make as much of an impression on my memory as it has on my back."

"Even so, I want you to know, brother Sancho," replied Don Quixote, "that there is no memory that time does not erase, no pain not ended by death."

"Well, what misfortune can be greater," replied Panza, "than waiting for time to end it and death to erase it? If this misfortune of ours was the kind that could be cured with a couple of poultices, it wouldn't be so bad, but I can see that all the poultices in a hospital won't be enough to set us straight again."

"Stop that now and find strength in weakness, Sancho," Don Quixote responded, "and I shall do the same, and let us see how Rocinante is, because it seems to me the poor animal may have gotten the worst of this misfortune."

"There's no reason to be surprised at that," Sancho responded, "since he's such a good knight errant; what does surprise me is that my donkey walked away without any costs while we were left without any ribs."[3]

"Fortune always leaves a door open in adversity so that it can be remedied," said Don Quixote. "I say this because the beast can make up for the lack of Rocinante and carry me from here to some castle where

---

3. The humor here stems from wordplay based on *costas* ("costs") and *costillas* ("ribs").

my wounds may be cured. Further, I shall not consider such a mount a dishonor, because I remember reading that when Silenus, the good old tutor and teacher of the merry god of laughter,[4] entered the city of one hundred gates,[5] he rode very happily mounted on a beautiful jackass."

"It may be true that he rode mounted, as your grace says," Sancho responded, "but there's a big difference between riding mounted and riding slung across the animal's back like a sack of trash."

To which Don Quixote replied:

"The wounds received in battles bestow honor, they do not take it away; and so, Panza my friend, do not answer me any further, but as I have already told you, stand the best you can and put me any way you choose on the back of your donkey, and let us leave before night falls upon us in this deserted place."

"I've heard your grace say," said Panza, "that it's very common for knights errant to sleep in deserted places and wastelands most of the year, and that they consider it good fortune."

"That is so," said Don Quixote, "when it cannot be helped or when they are in love; and this is so true that there have been knights who stayed on a rocky crag, in sun and in shadow and in all kinds of weather, for two years, and their ladies never learned of it. One of these was Amadís when, calling himself Beltenebros, he lived on Peña Pobre, I do not know if it was for eight years or eight months: I am not absolutely certain regarding the length of time; it is enough to know that he was there doing penance for some sorrow or other that his lady Oriana had caused him. But let us talk no more of this, Sancho, and hurry, before the donkey suffers a misfortune like the one that befell Rocinante."

"That would be the devil's work, too," said Sancho.

And emitting thirty groans and sixty sighs, and hurling a hundred twenty curses and blasphemies at the one who had brought him there, Sancho struggled to his feet, remaining bent double like a Turkish arch when he was halfway up, unable to stand straight; with great difficulty he saddled his donkey, who with that day's excessive liberty had also become somewhat inattentive. Then he helped Rocinante to his feet, and if the horse had had a tongue with which to complain, he certainly would not have been outdone by Sancho and his master.

In short, Sancho settled Don Quixote on the back of the donkey and

4. The "merry god" is Bacchus.

5. Cervantes erroneously describes the city entered by Silenus as having one hundred gates, which refers to Egyptian Thebes; Silenus rode into Thebes in Boeotia, which had seven gates.

tied Rocinante behind, in single file, and leading the jackass by the halter, he walked more or less in the direction of where he thought the king's highway might be. And luck, going from good to better, guided his steps, and in less than a league it led him to the highway, where he discovered an inn that, to his sorrow and Don Quixote's joy, had to be a castle. Sancho insisted it was an inn, and his master said no, it was a castle, and the dispute lasted so long that before it was settled they had come to the inn, which Sancho and his retinue entered without further inquiry.

CHAPTER XVI

Regarding what befell the ingenious gentleman in the inn that he imagined to be a castle

The innkeeper, who saw Don Quixote lying across the donkey, asked Sancho what was wrong with him. Sancho responded that it was not serious, that he had fallen off a crag and bruised his ribs slightly. The innkeeper's wife was a woman whose disposition was unlike the one usually found in those of her trade, for she was naturally charitable and took pity on the calamities of others, and so she hurried to tend Don Quixote and had her daughter, a very pretty young girl, help her care for her guest. Working as a servant in the inn was an Asturian girl with a broad face, a back of the head that was flat, a nose that was snubbed, and one eye that was blind, while the other was not in very good condition. The truth is that the charm of her body made up for her other faults: she measured less than seven spans[1] from her feet to the top of her head, and her back, which weighed somewhat heavily on her, forced her to look down at the ground more than she would have wished. This engaging creature helped the innkeeper's daughter, and the two of them made up a very uncomfortable bed for Don Quixote in an attic that gave clear signs of having been a hayloft for a long time, many years ago. Also staying at the inn was a muledriver whose bed was just past the bed of Don

1. A span is approximately eight inches.

Quixote. And though it was composed of his mules' packsaddles and blankets, it was far superior to Don Quixote's, which consisted only of four rough boards laid across two benches of not very equal height, and a pallet so thin it resembled a bedspread and was filled with lumps that felt like pebbles to the touch, though some holes revealed they were merely tufts of wool; there were two sheets made of shield leather, and a blanket so worn that every thread could be counted without missing a single one.

Don Quixote lay down on this wretched bed, and the innkeeper's wife and her daughter applied poultices from head to toe, while Maritornes, which was the Asturian girl's name, held a light for them, and as she applied the plasters, the innkeeper's wife saw Don Quixote so bruised and black and blue in so many parts that she said it looked more like a beating than a fall.

"It wasn't a beating," said Sancho, "it's just that the rock had lots of sharp points and edges, and each one left its bruise." He also said: "Señora, see if your grace can arrange to have a few pieces of cloth left over, since there's somebody else who'll need them; my ribs are hurting a little, too."

"So that means," responded the innkeeper's wife, "you must have fallen, too."

"I didn't fall," said Sancho Panza, "but it gave me a great start to see my master fall, and because of that my body hurts so much it feels as if somebody beat me a thousand times with a stick."

"That well could be," said the daughter. "It's often happened to me that I dream I'm falling off a tower but never reach the ground, and when I wake up from the dream I find myself as bruised and sore as if I really had fallen."

"That's my point, Señora," Sancho Panza responded. "I didn't dream anything, but was as wide awake as I am now, and I have almost as many bruises as my master, Don Quixote."

"What's this gentleman's name?" asked Maritornes the Asturian.

"Don Quixote of La Mancha," replied Sancho Panza, "and he is an adventuring knight, and one of the best and strongest the world has seen in a long time."

"What's an adventuring knight?" the servant asked.

"Are you so new to the world that you don't know?" replied Sancho Panza. "Well, let me tell you, my sister, in just a few words, that an adventuring knight is someone who's beaten and then finds himself emperor. Today he's the most unfortunate creature in the world, and the poorest, and tomorrow he'll have the crowns of two or three kingdoms to give to his squire."

"How is it, then, since you serve so good a master," said the innkeeper's wife, "that you, or so it seems, don't even have a countship yet?"

"It's still early," Sancho responded, "because it's only been a month[2] that we've been seeking adventures, and so far we haven't come across anything that even resembles one. Maybe you go looking for one thing and find another. The truth is that if my master, Don Quixote, is healed of his wounds, or his fall, and I'm not crippled by mine, I wouldn't trade my hopes for the best title in Spain."

Don Quixote had been listening very attentively to this entire conversation, and sitting up the best he could in his bed, and grasping the hand of the innkeeper's wife, he said:

"Believe me, beauteous lady, thou canst call thyself fortunate for having welcomed into this thy castle my person, which I do not praise because, as it is said, self-praise is self-debasement, but my squire wilt tell thee who I am. I say only that I shall keep eternally written in my memory the service that thou hast rendered me, so that I may thank thee for it as long as I shall live; and if it were not the will of heaven that love held me captive and subject to its laws and to the eyes of that thankless beauty whose name I murmur before battle, then those of this fair damsel would surely be the masters of my liberty."

The innkeeper's wife, and her daughter, and the good Maritornes were perplexed when they heard the words of the wandering knight, for they understood no more of them than if he had been speaking Greek, although they did realize that all were intended as compliments and flattery; because they were unaccustomed to such language, they looked at him in astonishment, and he seemed to them a different kind of man from the ones they were used to, and, after thanking him in their own innlike words for his compliments, they left him, and Maritornes the Asturian tended to Sancho, who had no less need of healing than his master.

The muledriver had arranged with Maritornes that they would take their pleasure that night, and she had given her word that when all the guests were quiet and her master and mistress asleep, she would come to him and satisfy his desire in any way he asked. It was said of this good ser-

2. Sancho is mistaken (or lying): he and Don Quixote have been traveling for three days.

vant that she never gave her word without keeping it, even if she gave it on a mountain with no witnesses, for she prided herself on being very wellborn and did not consider it an affront to be a servant in the inn because, she said, misfortunes and bad luck had brought her to that state.

The hard, narrow, cramped, and precarious bed of Don Quixote was the first in line in that starlit stall, and then next to it Sancho made his, which consisted only of a rush mat and a blanket that was more coarse burlap than wool. Past these two beds was that of the muledriver, made, as we have said, of the packsaddles and all the trappings of the two best mules in his train, although there were twelve of them, shiny, fat, and famous, because he was one of the wealthy muledrivers of Arévalo, according to the author of this history, who makes particular mention of this muledriver because he knew him very well; there are even some who say he was a distant relation.[3] In any case, Cide Hamete Benengeli was a very careful historian, and very accurate in all things, as can be clearly seen in the details he relates to us, for although they are trivial and inconsequential, he does not attempt to pass over them in silence; his example could be followed by solemn historians who recount actions so briefly and succinctly that we can barely taste them, and leave behind in the inkwell, through carelessness, malice, or ignorance, the most substantive part of the work. A thousand blessings on the author of *Tablante de Ricamonte*[4] and on the author of that other book that tells of the deeds of Count Tomillas,[5] for they describe everything in minute detail!

Well then, after the muledriver had seen to his train of mules and given them their second ration of feed, he lay down on the packsaddles to wait for the punctual Maritornes. Sancho was already poulticed and in his bed, and although he tried to sleep, the pain in his ribs would not allow it, and Don Quixote's ribs hurt so much that his eyes were as wide open as a hare's. The entire inn was quiet, and the only light came from a lamp hanging in the middle of the main entrance.

This wondrous silence, and the thoughts of our knight, which always were turned to the events constantly recounted in the books responsible for his misfortune, brought to his mind as strange a bit of madness as anyone could imagine, and it was that he thought he had come to a famous castle—for, as has been said, it seemed to him that all the inns where he

---

3. According to Martín de Riquer, muledrivers were usually Moriscos, and Cervantes is suggesting a connection between this character and Cide Hamete Benengeli.

4. A book of chivalry based on an earlier French poem and published in Spanish in 1513.

5. A figure who appeared in ballads and in a novel of chivalry published in 1498.

stayed were castles—and that the innkeeper's daughter was the daughter of the lord of the castle, and that she, conquered by his gentle bearing, had fallen in love with him and had promised to steal away from her parents that night and come and lie with him for a time; and since he considered this entire fantasy, which he had invented, as solid and true, he became distressed as he began to think of the dangerous predicament in which his virtue would find itself, and he resolved in his heart not to betray his lady Dulcinea of Toboso even if Queen Guinevere herself, along with her duenna Quintañona, were to appear before him.

As he was thinking about this foolishness, the time and hour arrived—and for Don Quixote it was an unfortunate one—when the Asturian was to come in, and wearing her chemise, with bare feet and her hair tied back in a cotton snood, with silent, cautious steps she entered the room where the three men were lying, looking for the muledriver. But as soon as she walked through the door, Don Quixote heard her, and sitting up in his bed, despite the poultices and the pain in his ribs, he extended his arms to welcome his fair damsel. The Asturian, who, tentatively and quietly, was holding her hands out in front of her and looking for her beloved, collided with Don Quixote's arms; he seized her by the wrist and, pulling her to him, while she did not dare to say a word, forced her to sit on the bed. Then he touched her chemise, and though it was made of burlap, to him it seemed the finest and sheerest silk. On her wrists she wore glass beads, but he imagined them to be precious pearls of the Orient. Her tresses, which were rather like a horse's mane, he deemed strands of shining Arabian gold whose brilliance made the sun seem dim. And her breath, which undoubtedly smelled of yesterday's stale salad, seemed to him a soft, aromatic scent wafting from her mouth; in short, he depicted her in his imagination as having the form and appearance of another princess he had read about in his books who, overcome by love and endowed with all the charms stated here, came to see the badly wounded knight. And the blind illusions of the poor gentleman were so great that neither her touch, nor her breath, nor any other of the good maiden's attributes could discourage him, though they were enough to make any man who was not a muledriver vomit; on the contrary, it seemed to him that he clasped in his arms the goddess of beauty. And holding her close, in a low, amorous voice he began to say:

"Would that I were able, O beauteous and exalted lady, to repay the great boon thou hast granted me with the sight of thy sublime beauty, but Fortune, which never wearies of pursuing the virtuous, hath chosen to place me in this bed, where I lie so bruised and broken that even if I, with all my heart, desired to satisfy thine own desires, I could not. Further, added to this impossibility is another even greater, which is the promise of faithfulness that I have sworn to the incomparable Dulcinea of Toboso, the sole mistress of my most hidden thoughts; if this great obstacle did not loom between us, I would not be so foolish a knight as to turn away from so gladsome an opportunity as this that thy great kindness affords me."

Maritornes, extremely agitated and perspiring freely at finding herself held so firmly by Don Quixote, and not understanding or paying much attention to what he was saying, attempted, without saying a word, to break free. The good muledriver, whose sinful desires had kept him awake, heard his bawd come through the door and listened attentively to everything Don Quixote was saying; jealous at the thought that the Asturian had broken her word for the sake of another man, he moved closer and closer to Don Quixote's bed and stood there in silence to see what that talk, which he could not understand, would lead to. But when he saw the girl struggling to free herself and Don Quixote endeavoring to hold on to her, and thinking that the joke had gone far enough, the muledriver raised his arm on high and delivered such a terrible blow to the narrow jaws of the enamored knight that he bathed his whole mouth in blood; not content with this, he jumped on his ribs, and with his feet moving faster than a trot, he stomped them all from one end to the other.

The bed, which was rather flimsy and not on a very firm base, could not support the addition of the muledriver and collapsed, and the great crash woke the innkeeper, who imagined that Maritornes must be involved in some dispute, because he had called for her and she had not responded. With this suspicion in mind he got up, lit a small oil lamp, and went to the place where he had heard the disturbance. The girl, seeing that her master was coming and was in a terrible rage, became so fearful and distressed that she took refuge in the bed of Sancho Panza, who was still asleep, and there she hid, curling up into a little ball. The innkeeper came in, saying:

"Where are you, you whore? I know this is your doing."

At this point Sancho awoke and, feeling that bulk almost on top of him, thought it was a nightmare, and he began to throw punches in all directions, and I don't know how many of them struck Maritornes, but she, feeling the pain and tossing all modesty aside, hit back at Sancho so many times that he lost all desire to sleep; seeing himself treated in this way, and not knowing by whom, he struggled to his feet, threw his arms around Maritornes, and the two of them began the fiercest and most laughable scuffle the world has ever seen.

By the light of the innkeeper's lamp, the muledriver saw what was happening to his lady, and leaving Don Quixote, he hurried to give her the help she needed. The innkeeper also approached, but with a different purpose, because he went to her to punish the girl, believing, no doubt, that she alone was the reason for so much harmony. And, as the old saying goes, the cat chased the rat, the rat chased the rope, the rope chased the stick: the muledriver hit Sancho, Sancho hit the girl, the girl hit Sancho, the innkeeper hit the girl, and all of them acted so fast and furiously that they did not let up for an instant; then, the best part was that the innkeeper's lamp went out, and since they were in darkness, everyone hit everyone with so little mercy that wherever their hands landed they left nothing whole and sound.

It so happened that staying in the inn that night was an officer of what is called the old Holy Brotherhood of Toledo, and he, hearing the noise of the fight, seized his staff of office and the tin box that held his documents and entered the darkened room, saying:

"Stop in the name of the law! Stop in the name of the Holy Brotherhood!"

And the first one he came across was a badly beaten Don Quixote, who lay face-up and senseless on his collapsed bed; and groping in the dark until he had grasped Don Quixote's beard, the officer did not stop saying:

"You must assist the law!"

But seeing that the man he had seized did not move or stir, he assumed he was dead and that those in the room were his killers, and with this suspicion he shouted even louder, saying:

"Lock the door of the inn! Make sure no one leaves, a man's been killed here!"

This shout startled all of them, and they abandoned the fight at the point where they had heard the voice. The innkeeper withdrew to his room, the muledriver to his packsaddles, the girl to her cot; only the unfortunate Don Quixote and Sancho could not move from where they were lying. The officer let go of Don Quixote's beard and went to find a light so that he could look for and arrest the criminals, but he did not find one because the innkeeper had intentionally put out the lamp when he went to his bedroom, and the officer was obliged to turn to the fireplace, where, with great difficulty and after a good deal of time, he managed to light another oil lamp.

CHAPTER XVII

Which continues the account of the innumerable difficulties that the brave Don Quixote and his good squire, Sancho Panza, experienced in the inn that, to his misfortune, he thought was a castle

By this time Don Quixote had recovered from his swoon, and in the same tone of voice he had used the day before to call to his squire when he was lying in the vale of staffs,[1] he began to call to him now, saying:

"Sancho my friend, are you sleeping? Are you sleeping, friend Sancho?"

"How could I sleep, oh woe is me," responded Sancho, full of sorrow and despair, "when it seems that all the devils in hell had their way with me tonight?"

"You undoubtedly are correct about that," Don Quixote responded, "because either I understand little, or this castle is enchanted. For you must know . . . But what I wish to tell you now you must swear to keep secret until after my death."

"I swear," Sancho responded.

"I say this," replied Don Quixote, "because I do not wish to take away anyone's honor."

"I say that I swear," Sancho said again, "to keep quiet about it until your grace has reached the end of your days, and God willing, I'll be able to reveal it tomorrow."

"Have I acted so badly with you, Sancho," Don Quixote responded, "that you wish to see me dead so soon?"

"That's not the reason," Sancho replied, "but I don't like keeping secrets, and I wouldn't want them to spoil because I kept them too long."

1. The phrase recalls the opening of a traditional ballad about El Cid.

"Whatever the reason may be," said Don Quixote, "I have great confidence in your love and courtesy, and so you must know that tonight I have had one of the strangest adventures one could ever imagine; to make the story brief, I shall tell you that a short while ago the daughter of the lord of this castle came to me, and she is one of the most elegant and beauteous damsels to be found anywhere on earth. What can I say of the grace of her person, the nobility of her understanding, the other hidden things which, in order to keep the faith I owe to my lady Dulcinea of Toboso, I shall keep inviolate and pass over in silence? I wish only to say that heaven, envious of the good that Fortune had placed in my hands, or perhaps, and this is more likely, the castle, as I have said, being enchanted, as I was engaged in sweet and amorous conversation with her, without my seeing or knowing whence it came, a hand attached to the arm of some monstrous giant came down and struck me so hard a blow on the jaws that they were bathed in blood, and then beat me so badly that I feel worse than I did yesterday when the Yanguesans, because of Rocinante's audacity, committed the offense against us which you already know. And from this I conjecture that the treasure of this maiden's beauty must be guarded by some enchanted Moor and is not intended for me."

"Not for me either," responded Sancho, "because more than four hundred Moors gave me such a beating that the attack by the staffs was like cakes and icing. But tell me, Señor, how can you call this a good and singular adventure if it left us the way it left us? Not so bad for your grace, because you had between your hands that incomparable beauteousness you mentioned; but what did I have except the worst cudgeling I'll ever get in my life? Woe is me and the mother who bore me: I'm not a knight errant and don't ever plan to be one, and so I get the worst of all our calamities!"

"Then, you have been beaten as well?" responded Don Quixote.

"Didn't I just tell you I was, to the sorrow of me and my whole family?" said Sancho.

"Do not be distressed, my friend," said Don Quixote, "for I shall now prepare the precious balm with which we shall be healed in the wink of an eye."

By now the officer of the Holy Brotherhood had lit the lamp, and he came in to see the man he thought was dead; as soon as Sancho saw him come in wearing his nightshirt and nightcap and holding a lamp in his hand and with a very grim expression on his face, he asked his master:

"Señor, can this by any chance be the enchanted Moor, come back to hit us some more in case there's anything left in the inkwell?"

"He cannot be the Moor," responded Don Quixote, "because those who are enchanted do not permit themselves to be seen by anyone."

"If they don't permit themselves to be seen, they do permit themselves to be felt," said Sancho, "as my back can tell you."

"As could mine," Don Quixote responded, "but that is not sufficient evidence for believing that the man you see is the enchanted Moor."

The officer was perplexed when he discovered them engaged in so peaceable a conversation. It is certainly true that Don Quixote still lay on his back, but he was unable to move simply because he was so badly beaten and so covered with poultices. The officer came up to him and said:

"Well, how goes it, my good man?"

"I would speak with more courtesy," responded Don Quixote, "if I were you. Is it the custom in this land to speak in that manner to knights errant, you dolt?"

Finding himself treated so abusively by someone whose appearance was so unprepossessing, the officer could not bear it; he raised the lamp filled with oil, brought it down on Don Quixote's head, and dealt him a serious blow; since everything was now in darkness, he left immediately, and Sancho Panza said:

"There's no doubt, Señor, that this man is the enchanted Moor, who must be guarding the treasure for others, but for us he only has fists and blows with lamps."

"That is true," responded Don Quixote, "and one must not take notice of such matters in enchantments, nor is there reason to become angry or enraged at them, for, as these beings are invisible and magical, we shall find no one on whom to take our revenge no matter how much we try. Get up, Sancho, if you can, and summon the warder of this fortress, and persuade him to give me some oil, wine, salt, and rosemary so that I may prepare the health-giving balm; for, in truth, I believe I have great need of it now, since I am losing a good deal of blood from the wound this phantom has inflicted on me."

Sancho stood, all his bones aching, and began to walk in the darkness to find the innkeeper, but he encountered the officer, who had been listening to hear what his adversary would do, and Sancho said to him:

"Señor, whoever you may be, do us the kindness and favor of giving us a little rosemary, oil, salt, and wine; they are needed to heal one of the

best knights errant on the face of the earth, lying in that bed badly
wounded at the hands of the enchanted Moor who's in this inn."

When the officer heard this, he thought Sancho was out of his mind,
but since day was beginning to break, he opened the door of the inn,
called to the innkeeper, and told him what the good man wanted. The
innkeeper gave him what he asked for, and Sancho carried it to Don
Quixote, who was holding his head in his hands and moaning at the pain
of the blow from the lamp, which had done him little harm other than
the raising of two rather large bumps; what he thought was blood was
nothing but the sweat pouring out of him because of the distress he had
experienced in the tempest that had just passed.

In short, he took his simples and made a compound of them, mixing
them all together and cooking them for a while until it seemed to him
they were ready. Then he asked for a flask to pour the potion into, but
since there was none in the inn, he decided to put it into a cruet or oil
container made of tinplate, which the innkeeper gave to him at no
charge. Then, over the cruet, he said more than eighty Pater Nosters and
an equal number of Ave Marías, Salves, and Credos, and he accompanied each word with the sign of the cross, in a kind of blessing, all of
which was witnessed by Sancho, the innkeeper, and the officer; the
muledriver, in the meantime, had quietly gone out to tend to his animals.

Having completed this, Don Quixote himself wanted to test the
virtue of what he imagined to be the precious balm, and so he drank it
down, and the portion that could not fit into the cruet and was left in the
pot where it had cooked amounted to almost a liter; as soon as he finished drinking it, he began to vomit until nothing was left in his stomach, and with the nausea and agitation of vomiting, he broke into a
copious sweat, for which reason he ordered them to wrap him up well
and leave him alone. This they did, and he slept for more than three
hours, and when he woke his body felt much relieved and so much better
after his beating that he considered himself cured; he truly believed he
had found the balm of Fierabrás, and that with this remedy he could
from now on, and with no fear whatsoever, engage in any combat, battle,
or contest no matter how perilous it might be.

Sancho Panza, who also deemed the improvement in his master a
miracle, requested the portion that remained in the pot, which was no
small quantity. Don Quixote agreed, and Sancho picked up the pot in
both hands, and with a good amount of trust and even greater optimism,

he gulped the potion down thirstily, swallowing only a little less than his master had. It seems, however, that poor Sancho's stomach was not as delicate as his master's, and so, before he vomited, he endured so much nausea and felt so sick to his stomach, and sweated so much and felt so faint, that he really and truly thought it was his final hour, and finding himself in so much pain and anguish, he cursed the balm and the villain who had given it to him. Seeing him in this state, Don Quixote said:

"I believe, Sancho, that this affliction has befallen you because you have not been dubbed a knight, for I am of the opinion that this potion is not suitable for those who are not knights."

"Curse me and all my kin! If your grace knew that," replied Sancho, "why did you let me taste it?"

At this point the concoction took effect, and the poor squire began to erupt from both channels, and with so much force that the reed mat on which he lay, and the canvas blanket that covered him, could not be used again. He was perspiring and sweating and suffering such paroxysms and mishaps that not only he but everyone else thought his life was coming to an end. This tempest of affliction lasted almost two hours, at the end of which he was left not as his master had been, but so bruised and battered he could barely stand.

Don Quixote, however, who, as we have said, felt cured and healthy, wanted to leave immediately to seek adventures, it being his opinion that the time he spent in that place meant he was depriving the world, and all those in it who were in need, of his help and assistance, especially now when he had so much trust and confidence in the balm. And so, impelled by this desire, he himself saddled Rocinante, and put the packsaddle on his squire's donkey, and helped Sancho to dress and climb on the animal. Then he mounted his horse, and as he rode past a corner of the inn, he picked up a pike he found there to use as a lance.

All those in the inn, amounting to more than twenty people, were watching him; the innkeeper's daughter looked at him as well, and he did not take his eyes off her, either, and from time to time he heaved a sigh that seemed to come from the bottom of his soul, and everyone thought this must have been on account of the pain he felt in his ribs; at least, those who had seen him covered with poultices the night before thought so.

When he and Sancho were both mounted and standing at the entrance to the inn, he called to the innkeeper, and in a very calm and serious voice he said:

"Many and great are the kindnesses, Señor Warder, which I have received in this thy castle, and it is my deepest obligation to show thee my gratitude for all the days of my life. If I can repay thee by taking vengeance upon some arrogant villain who may have offended thee, know that my profession is none other than to defend those who are defenseless, and to avenge those who are wronged, and to punish malfeasance. Search thy memory, and if thou findest anything of this nature to entrust to me, thou hast only to say it, for I promise, by the order of chivalry which I received, to give thee as much satisfaction and redress as thou mayest desire."

The innkeeper responded with the same calm:

"Señor Knight, I have no need for your grace to avenge any offense, because I know how to take the revenge I think fit when I am offended. All I need from your grace is that you pay for the night you spent in the inn: straw and feed for your two animals, and your supper and your beds."

"Then, this is an inn?" replied Don Quixote.

"And a very honorable one," the innkeeper responded.

"Then I have been deceived all along," responded Don Quixote, "for in truth I thought this was a castle, and not a bad one; however, since it is not a castle but an inn, what you can do now is forgive the debt, for I cannot contravene the order of knights errant, about whom I know it is true, not having read anything to the contrary, that they never paid for their lodging or anything else in any inn where they stayed, because whatever welcome they receive is owed to them as their right and privilege in return for the unbearable hardships they suffer as they seek adventures by night and by day, in winter and in summer, on foot and on horseback, suffering thirst and hunger, heat and cold, and exposed to all the inclemencies of heaven and all the discomforts on earth."

"That has nothing to do with me," responded the innkeeper. "Pay me what you owe me, and leave off your stories and chivalries; I don't care about anything but earning my living."

"You are a fool and a bad innkeeper," responded Don Quixote.

And spurring Rocinante, and grasping his pike, he left the inn and no one stopped him, and he, not looking to see if his squire was following, rode for a fair distance.

The innkeeper, who saw him leave without paying, turned for payment to Sancho Panza, who said that since his master had not wanted to pay, he would not pay, either, for as the squire of a knight errant, the same rule and law applied to him as to his master with regard to not paying anything in hostelries and inns. This greatly displeased the innkeeper, who warned him that if he did not pay, he would collect his money in a way Sancho would regret. To which Sancho replied that by the law of chivalry his master had received, he would not pay a *coronado*[2] even if it cost him his life; for the virtuous and ancient customs of knights errants would not be brought down by him, nor would the squires of future knights have reason to complain of him or reproach him for breaking so just a law.

It was unhappy Sancho's misfortune that among the people staying at the inn were four wool carders from Segovia, three needlemakers from El Potro in Córdoba, and two residents of La Feria in Sevilla, people who were good-natured, well-intentioned, rough-mannered, and playful, and they, almost as if impelled and moved by the same spirit, approached Sancho and pulled him off his donkey, while one of them went to get the blanket from the innkeeper's bed, and, after placing him on it, they looked up and saw that the roof was a little too low for the work they had in mind, and they decided to go out into the corral, where the sky was the limit. And there, with Sancho in the middle of the blanket, they began to toss him and make merry with him as if he were a dog at Carnival.[3]

The shouts of the wretch being tossed in the blanket were so loud and so many that they reached the ears of his master, who, deciding to listen carefully, believed some new adventure was under way, until it became clear that the man who was shouting was his squire; after he turned his horse around and reached the inn at a laborious gallop, and found it closed, he rode around it to see if he could find a way in, but as soon as he came to the walls of the corral, which were not very high, he saw the bad turn being done to his squire. He saw him going up and down in the air with so much grace and speed that if his wrath had permitted it, I think he would have laughed. He attempted to climb from his horse to the top of the wall, but he was so bruised and stiff he could not dismount; and so, standing in his stirrups, he began to call those who were tossing Sancho in the blanket more insults and abusive names than it is possible to write down, but this did not stop them from laughing and doing their work, nor did the flying Sancho leave off his complaints, sometimes mixed with threats and sometimes with pleas; none of it did much good, however, until the men stopped from sheer weariness. Then they brought Sancho his donkey and placed him on it and his overcoat on him. And the compassionate Maritornes, seeing him so exhausted, thought it

2. A coin of little value, worth about one-sixth of a *maravedí*.

3. Tossing a dog in a blanket was a Carnival diversion.

would be a good idea to help him with a pitcher of water, and so she brought him one from the well because the water there was colder. Sancho took the pitcher, raised it to his mouth, and stopped when he heard his master call to him, saying:

"Sancho my son, do not drink water! My son, do not drink it, for it will kill you! Do you see? Here I have the blessed balm"—and he showed him the cruet filled with the potion—"and if you drink only two drops, you surely will be healed."

At these words Sancho looked at him askance and said in an even louder voice:

"Has your grace by chance forgotten that I'm not a knight, or do you want me to finish vomiting up whatever guts I have left from last night? You can keep your potion or send it to the devil; just leave me alone."

And saying this and beginning to drink were all one, but at the first swallow he saw that it was water and did not wish to continue, and he asked Maritornes to bring him wine; she did so very willingly and paid for it with her own money, because it can truly be said of her that though she followed the trade that she did, she bore a remote resemblance to a Christian woman.

As soon as Sancho finished drinking, he dug his heels into his donkey, and the gate of the inn was opened wide for him, and he left, very pleased at not paying anything and having his way, though it had been at the expense of his usual guarantor, which was his back. The truth is that the innkeeper had kept his saddlebags as payment, but Sancho was so distracted when he left that he did not miss them. The innkeeper wanted to bar the gate as soon as he saw them outside, but the blanket tossers did not agree, for they were people who would not have cared an *ardite*[4] even if Don Quixote really had been one of the knights errant of the Round Table.

4. An ancient Spanish coin of very little value.

CHAPTER XVIII

*Which relates the words that passed between Sancho Panza and his master,
Don Quixote, and other adventures that deserve to be recounted*

When Sancho reached his master, he was so weak and enfeebled that he
could not even prod his donkey. Seeing him in this state, Don Quixote
said:

"Now I am convinced, my good Sancho, that this castle or inn is undoubtedly enchanted, because what else could those who so brutally
took their amusement with you be but phantoms or beings from the next
world? And I can attest to this because I saw, when I was at the wall of
the corral watching the events in your sad tragedy, that it was not possible for me to climb over the wall or even to dismount Rocinante, and
therefore they must have enchanted me, for I swear to you, by who I am,
that if I could have climbed over or dismounted, I should have avenged
you in a way that would have made those varlets and knaves remember
the experience for the rest of their days, even though by so doing I
should have contravened the laws of chivalry, which, as I have told you
so often, do not permit a knight to raise a hand against one who is not a
knight, except in defense of his own life and person in circumstances of
urgent and great necessity."

"I would have taken my revenge, too, if I could have, knight or no
knight, but I couldn't, though in my opinion the ones who had so much
fun with me weren't phantoms or enchanted beings, as your grace says,
but men of flesh and blood, like us; and all of them, as I heard when
they were making me turn somersaults, had names, and one was Pedro
Martínez, and the other Tenorio Hernández, and I heard that the
innkeeper's name was Lefthanded Juan Palomeque. And so, Señor, your
not being able to get over the corral wall or off your horse was due to

something besides enchantments. And what's clear to me in all this is that in the long run, these adventures we're looking for will bring us so many misadventures that we won't know our right foot from our left. And the better and smarter thing, to the best of my poor understanding, would be for us to go back home now that it's harvesttime, and tend to our own affairs, and stop going from pillar to post and from bad to worse, as they say."

"How little you know, Sancho," Don Quixote responded, "about the matter of chivalry! Be quiet and have patience, for the day will come when you will see with your own eyes how honorable a thing it is to exercise this profession. If not, then tell me: what greater joy can there be in the world, what pleasure can equal that of conquering in battle and defeating one's enemy? None, most certainly there is none."

"That must be true," responded Sancho, "though I don't know anything about it; all I know is that ever since we've been knights errant, or your grace has been one (because there's no reason to include me in so honorable a company), we haven't won a single battle except for the one with the Basque, and even there your grace came out missing half an ear and half a shield; since then it's been nothing but cudgels and more cudgels, beatings and more beatings, and for me the extra advantage of being tossed in a blanket by enchanted beings, but I can't take my revenge on them so I'll never know how great the pleasure is of defeating my enemy, as your grace says."

"That is my sorrow, and it surely is yours as well, Sancho," responded Don Quixote, "but from this moment on I shall try to have at hand some sword so artfully made that whosoever carries it will be immune to any kind of enchantment; it well might be that fortune will grant me the one Amadís had when he was called *The Knight of the Blazing Sword*,[1] that being one of the best swords any knight in the world ever had, because, in addition to the virtue I have already mentioned, it cut like a razor, and no armor, no matter how strong or enchanted, could withstand it."

"I'm so lucky," said Sancho, "that when that happens and your grace finds such a sword, it'll be exactly like the balm and only work for and benefit dubbed knights, while squires can just swallow their sorrows."

"Do not be afraid, Sancho," said Don Quixote, "for heaven will deal more kindly with you than that."

As Don Quixote and his squire were having this conversation, Don

---

1. The reference is to Amadís of Greece, the great-grandson of Amadís of Gaul.

Quixote saw a large, thick cloud of dust coming toward them along the road they were traveling, and when he saw it, he turned to Sancho and said:

"This is the day, O Sancho, when the good fortune that destiny has reserved for me will be revealed! This is the day, I say, when, as much as on any other, the valor of this my arm will be proved, and I shall perform deeds that will be inscribed in the book of Fame for all time to come. Do you see that cloud of dust rising there, Sancho? Well, it conceals a vast army, composed of innumerable and diverse peoples, which is marching toward us."

"If that's the case, there must be two," said Sancho, "because over in the opposite direction there's another cloud of dust just like it."

Don Quixote turned to look, and he saw that it was true; he was overjoyed, thinking, no doubt, that these were two armies coming to attack and fight each other in the middle of that broad plain. Because at all times and at every moment his fantasy was filled with the battles, enchantments, feats, follies, loves, and challenges recounted in books of chivalry, and everything he said, thought, or did was directed toward such matters. The dust clouds he saw had been raised by two large flocks of ewes and rams traveling along the same road from opposite directions, which could not be seen through the dust until they were very close. But Don Quixote insisted so fervently they were armies that Sancho believed him and said:

"Señor, then what should we do?"

"Do?" said Don Quixote. "Defend and protect the needy and helpless. You must know, Sancho, that the army in front of us is led and directed by the great Emperor Alifanfarón, lord of the great Ínsula Trapobane;[2] the other, marching behind us, belongs to his enemy, the king of the Garamantes, Pentapolín of the Tucked-up Sleeve, so-called because he always enters into battle with a bare right arm."

"Why do these two gentlemen hate each other so much?" asked Sancho.

"They hate each other," responded Don Quixote, "because this Alifanfarón, a fierce pagan, is in love with Pentapolín's daughter, an exceedingly beauteous and charming lady, and a Christian, whose father does

---

2. The Greek and Roman name for Sri Lanka. The names of the warriors in this section are parodies of the kinds of grandiloquent names typical of novels of chivalry (*Alifanfarón* is roughly equivalent to "Alibombast," *Pentapolín* to "Pentaroller"). The listing of combatants appears to be a brief detour by Cervantes into the world of the epic poem.

not wish to give her to the pagan king unless he first renounces the law of his false prophet Mohammed and turns to her faith."

"By my beard," said Sancho, "Pentapolín is doing just the right thing, and I'm bound to help him any way I can!"

"In this you would be doing just as you should, Sancho," said Don Quixote, "because to enter into battles such as these it is not required to be dubbed a knight."

"That's good enough for me," responded Sancho, "but where will we put this donkey so we're sure to find him when the fight's over? Because I don't believe that riding into battle on this kind of animal has been the custom up to now."

"That is true," said Don Quixote. "What you can do is let him find his own adventures, regardless of whether he is lost or not, because we shall have so many horses when we emerge victorious that even Rocinante runs the risk of being exchanged for another. But listen to me, and look, for I want to name for you the most eminent knights riding in these two armies. And so that you may see and mark them more clearly, let us withdraw to that hillock, where we should be able to perceive both armies."

This they did, riding to the top of a hill from which there would have been a clear view of the two flocks that Don Quixote took for armies if the clouds of dust they raised had not confused and blurred the sight of anyone looking at them, but despite this, in his imagination he saw what he did not see and what was not there, and in a loud voice he began to say:

"That knight you see there in the gold-colored armor, who bears on his shield a crowned lion kneeling at the feet of a damsel, is the valiant Laurcalco,[3] lord of the Bridge of Silver; the other in armor with flowers of gold, who bears on his shield three crowns of silver on a blue field, is the redoubtable Micocolembo, grand duke of Quirocia; the one on his right with the gigantic limbs is the never fearful Brandabarbarán de Boliche, lord of the three Arabias, whose armor is a snakeskin and whose shield is a door rumored to be one of those from the temple demolished by Samson when, with his death, he wreaked vengeance on his enemies. Now turn your eyes in the other direction, and you will see in front of

3. The names in this section suggest ludicrous associations: *Laurcalco,* "Laurelfacsimile"; *Micocolembo,* "Monkeywedge"; *Brandabarbarán de Boliche,* "Brandabarbarian of Ninepins"; *Timonel de Carcajona,* "Helmsman of Guffawjona"; *Nueva Vizcaya,* "New Basqueland"; *Miulina,* "Mewlina"; *Alfeñiquén del Algarbe,* "Mollycoddle of Babble"; *Pierres Papín,* "Pierres Bonbon"; *Espartafilardo del Bosque,* "Esparragrass of the Forest."

and at the head of the other army the ever victorious and never defeated Timonel of Carcajona, prince of Nueva Vizcaya, who wears his armor quartered—blue, green, white, and yellow—and who bears on his shield a cat of gold on a tawny field, with a legend that reads: Meow, which is the beginning of the name of his lady who, they say, is the peerless Miulina, daughter of Duke Alfeñiquén of Algarbe; this other, who weighs down and oppresses the back of that powerful mare, whose armor is snowy white and whose shield is blank and lacking all devices, is a novice knight of the French nation, named Pierres Papín, lord of the baronies of Utrique; that one, who with armored heels is kicking the flanks of that colorful swift zebra and whose armor bears blue vairs,[4] is the powerful duke of Nervia, Espartafilardo del Bosque, who bears as a device on his shield a bed of asparagus, with a legend in Castilian that reads: Follow my fate."[5]

And in this fashion he named many knights from the two hosts, which he was imagining, and for all of them he improvised armor, colors, legends, and devices, carried along by the imagination of his unheard-of madness, and without pausing he continued, saying:

"This host facing us is made up and composed of people from diverse nations: here are those who drink the sweet waters of the famous Xanthus;[6] the mountain folk who tread the Massilian plain; those who sift fine gold nuggets in Arabia Felix; those who enjoy the famous cool shores of the crystalline Thermodon; those who drain by many diverse means the golden Pactolus; and Numidians, untrustworthy in their promises; Persians, those notable archers; Parthians and Medes, who fight as they flee; Arabians, with movable houses; Scythians, as cruel as they are white-skinned; Ethiopians, with pierced lips; and an infinite number of other nations, whose faces I recognize and see, although I do not recall their names. In this other host come those who drink the crystalline currents of the olive-bearing Betis; those who shine and burnish their faces with the liquid of the forever rich and golden Tajo; those who enjoy the beneficial waters of the divine Genil; those who tread Tartessian fields, with their abundant pastures; those who take pleasure in the

4. In heraldry, these are blue and white cups, or bells, that fit together perfectly.

5. The legend, Rastrea mi Suerte, is ambiguous and can be interpreted in several ways, including "Look into my fate," "Delve into my fate," "My fate creeps along," and "Follow [the trail of] my fate."

6. Don Quixote begins his description with ancient and foreign references; in the second half of his evocation, beginning with "In this other host . . ." he alludes, for the most part, to Iberian rivers.

Elysian meadows of Jerez; Manchegans, rich and crowned with yellow spikes of wheat; those clad in iron, ancient relics of Gothic blood; those who bathe in the Pisuerga, famous for the gentleness of its current; those who graze their cattle on the extensive pasturelands of the sinuous Guadiana, celebrated for its hidden currents; those who tremble in the cold of the wooded Pyrenees and the white peaks of the high Apennines; in short, all those contained and sheltered in the entirety of Europe."

Lord save me! What a number of provinces he mentioned and nations he named, attributing to each one, with marvelous celerity, the characteristics that belonged to it, so absorbed and immersed was he in his lying books!

Sancho Panza hung on his words but said none of his own, and from time to time he turned his head to see if he could see the knights and giants his master was naming; since he could not make out any of them, he said:

"Señor, may the devil take me, but no man, giant, or knight of all those your grace has mentioned can be seen anywhere around here; at least, I don't see them; maybe it's all enchantment, like last night's phantoms."

"How can you say that?" responded Don Quixote. "Do you not hear the neighing of the horses, the call of the clarions, the sound of the drums?"

"I don't hear anything," responded Sancho, "except the bleating of lots of sheep."

And this was the truth, because the two flocks were drawing near.

"It is your fear, Sancho," said Don Quixote, "that keeps you from seeing or hearing properly, because one of the effects of fear is to cloud the senses and make things appear other than they are; if you are so frightened, withdraw somewhere and leave me alone; alone I suffice to give victory to the army to whom I shall proffer my assistance."

And having said this, he spurred Rocinante, fixed his lance in its socket, and rode down the side of the hill like a flash of lightning. Sancho called to him, saying:

"Your grace, come back, Señor Don Quixote, I swear to God you're charging sheep! Come back, by the wretched father who sired me! What madness is this? Look and see that there are no giants or knights, no cats or armor or shields either parted or whole, no blue vairs or bedeviled ones, either. Poor sinner that I am in the sight of God, what are you doing?"

But none of this made Don Quixote turn back; instead, in a loud voice, he cried:

"Come, you knights who follow and serve under the banners of the valiant Emperor Pentapolín of the Tucked-up Sleeve, follow me, all of you, and you will see how easily I give you revenge upon your enemy Alifanfarón of Trapobane!"

Saying this, he rode into the midst of the host of sheep and began to run at them with his lance as fearlessly and courageously as if he really were attacking his mortal enemies. The shepherds and herdsmen guarding the flock came running, shouting for him to stop, but seeing that this had no effect, they unhooked their slings and began to greet his ears with stones as big as fists. Don Quixote took no notice of the stones; instead, he rode back and forth, crying:

"Where art thou, haughty Alifanfarón? Come here to me, for I am only one knight who wishes, in single combat, to try thy strength and take thy life as forfeit for the wrong thou hast done to the valiant Pentapolín Garamanta."

At that moment, a small round pebble[7] came flying and hit him in the side, entombing two ribs inside his body. Seeing himself so battered, he undoubtedly believed he was dead or gravely wounded, and remembering his potion, he took out the cruet, put it to his mouth, and began to pour the potion into his stomach, but before he had finished swallowing what seemed to him a sufficient quantity, another almond came flying and hit his hand, striking the cruet so squarely that it broke into pieces, taking along three or four teeth and molars from his mouth and smashing two of his fingers.

The first blow was so hard, as well as the second, that the poor knight could not help falling from his horse. The shepherds came running and thought they had killed him, and so they hurriedly gathered their flocks together, picked up the dead animals, which numbered more than seven, and left without further inquiry.

All this time Sancho was on the hill, watching the lunatic actions of his master, and he tore at his beard, cursing the hour and the moment when fortune had allowed him to make his acquaintance. When he saw that Don Quixote was lying on the ground and that the shepherds had gone, he came down the slope and went over to his master and found

7. The Spanish word *peladilla* can mean either "pebble" or "sugared almond." In the next sentence, Cervantes confirms the wordplay by using *almendra*, directly equivalent to "almond."

him in a very bad way, although he had not lost consciousness, and he said to him:

"Didn't I tell you, Señor Don Quixote, to come back, that it wasn't armies you were attacking but flocks of sheep?"

"This is how that thieving wise man, who is my enemy, can make things disappear and seem to be what they are not. You should know, Sancho, that it is very easy for those like him to make us see whatever they wish, and this villain who pursues me, envious of the glory that he saw I would achieve in this battle, has turned the contending armies into flocks of sheep. And if you do not believe me, by my life you can do something, Sancho, to be undeceived and see the truth of what I am telling you: mount your donkey and follow them, with some cunning, and you will see how, when they have moved a certain distance away, they resume their original form and are no longer sheep but real, complete men, just as I first described them to you. . . . But do not go now, for I have need of your help and assistance; come here and see how many molars and teeth I have lost, because it seems to me I do not have a single one left in my mouth."

Sancho came so close that his eyes were almost in his master's mouth; by this time the balm had taken effect in Don Quixote's stomach, and just as Sancho looked into his mouth, he threw up, more vigorously than if he were firing a musket, everything he had inside, and all of it hit the compassionate squire in the face.

"Mother of God!" said Sancho. "What's happened? Surely this poor sinner is mortally wounded, for he's vomiting blood from his mouth."

But looking a little more closely, he realized by the color, taste, and smell that it was not blood but the balm from the cruet, which he had seen him drink, and he was so disgusted by this that his stomach turned over and he vomited his innards all over his master, and the two of them were left as splendid as pearls. Sancho went to his donkey to find something in the saddlebags with which to clean himself and heal his master, and when he did not see the saddlebags he almost lost his mind. He cursed his fate again and resolved in his heart to leave his master and return home even if he lost his wages for the time he had worked, along with his hopes for the governorship of the promised ínsula.

Then Don Quixote rose to his feet, placed his left hand over his mouth so that no more teeth would fall out, and grasped Rocinante's reins with the other, for the horse had not moved from his master's side—that is how loyal and well-disposed he was—and walked to where his squire was standing, leaning against his donkey and resting his cheek in his hand, in the manner of a man deep in thought. And seeing him like this, showing signs of so much sadness, Don Quixote said:

"You should know, Sancho, that a man is not worth more than any other if he does not do more than any other. All these squalls to which we have been subjected are signs that the weather will soon improve and things will go well for us, because it is not possible for the bad or the good to endure forever; from this it follows that since the bad has lasted so long a time, the good is close at hand. Therefore you must not grieve for the misfortunes that befall me, for you have no part in them."

"What do you mean, no part?" responded Sancho. "By some chance was the man tossed in a blanket yesterday anybody but my father's son? And the saddlebags that are missing today, along with all my valuable goods, do they belong to anybody else but me?"

"Did you say that the saddlebags are missing, Sancho?" said Don Quixote.

"Yes, they're missing," responded Sancho.

"Then we have nothing to eat today," replied Don Quixote.

"That would be true," responded Sancho, "if these fields didn't have the wild plants your grace says you know about, the ones that unfortunate knights errant such as your grace use to make up for shortages like this one."

"Despite that," Don Quixote responded, "now I would rather have a ration of bread or a large loaf and a couple of sardine heads than all the plants described by Dioscorides or commented on by Dr. Laguna.[8] But be that as it may, mount your donkey, my good Sancho, and follow me, for God, who provides all things, will not fail us, especially since we are so much in His service, when He does not fail the gnats in the air, or the grubs in the earth, or the tadpoles in the water; He is so merciful that He makes His sun to shine on the good and the evil and His rain to fall on the unjust and the just."

"Your grace would do better," said Sancho, "as a preacher than as a knight errant."

"Knights errant knew and must know about everything, Sancho," said Don Quixote, "because there were knights errant in past times who would stop to give a sermon or a talk in the middle of the field of battle just as if they were graduates of the University of Paris, from which one can infer that the lance never blunted the pen, nor the pen the lance."

8. Andrés Laguna, an eminent sixteenth-century physician, translated and commented on the medical treatise by Dioscorides, a Greek physician of the first century C.E.

"Fine, whatever your grace says," responded Sancho, "but let's leave now and find a place to spend the night, and, God willing, there won't be any blankets, or people who toss blankets, or phantoms, or enchanted Moors, and if there are, I'll send the whole pack of them to the devil."

"God's will be done, my son," said Don Quixote, "and lead the way, for this time I want you to select the place where we shall sleep. But first give me your hand, and feel with your finger, and see how many teeth and molars I am missing here on the right side of my upper jaw, for that is where I feel the pain."

Sancho put his fingers in his master's mouth, and as he was feeling inside, he said:

"How many molars did your grace have on this side?"

"Four," responded Don Quixote, "and except for the wisdom tooth, all of them sound and healthy."

"Señor, your grace should think carefully about what you're saying," Sancho responded.

"I say four, or perhaps five," responded Don Quixote, "because never in my life have I had a tooth or molar pulled, nor has one ever fallen out, or been eaten by decay, or afflicted by any abscess."

"Well, in this lower part," said Sancho, "your grace has no more than two and a half molars, and in the upper part, none at all, not even a half; it's all as smooth as the palm of your hand."

"Woe is me!" said Don Quixote when he heard the sad news from his squire. "I should rather have lost an arm, as long as it was not the one that wields my sword. For I must tell you, Sancho, that a mouth without molars is like a mill without a millstone, and dentation is to be valued much more than diamonds. But we who profess the arduous order of chivalry are subject to all of this. Mount, my friend, and lead the way, for I shall follow you along any path you choose."

Sancho did so and headed in the direction where he thought they might find lodging without leaving the king's highway, which was very well traveled in that area.

They rode very slowly because the pain in Don Quixote's jaws gave him no peace and did not allow him to go any faster; Sancho wanted to divert and distract him by talking to him, and among other things, he said what will be related in the next chapter.

CHAPTER XIX

Regarding the discerning words that Sancho exchanged with his master, and the adventure he had with a dead body, as well as other famous events

"It seems to me, Señor, that all these misfortunes we've had recently are surely a punishment for the sin your grace committed against your order of chivalry, since you didn't keep the vow you made not to eat bread from a tablecloth or to lie with the queen, and everything else that comes afterward and that your grace swore to fulfill, including taking that helmet of Malandrino[1] or whatever the Moor's name is, I don't remember exactly."

"You are certainly correct, Sancho," said Don Quixote, "but to tell you the truth, it had slipped my mind; and you can also be sure your negligence in not reminding me of it in time is the reason you had the incident with the blanket, but I shall rectify that for you, for in the order of chivalry there are means to grant dispensations for everything."

"But when did I ever swear to anything?" responded Sancho.

"It does not matter that you have not made a vow," said Don Quixote. "It is enough for me to understand that you are not completely free of complicity, and so, just in case, it would be a good idea for us to settle on a remedy."

"Well, if that's true," said Sancho, "your grace should be sure not to forget about it the way you forgot your vow; maybe the phantoms will feel like having fun with me again, or even with your grace, if they see you being so persistent."

They were engaged in this and other conversations when night

1. Sancho does not remember the name "Mambrino" and confuses it with *malandrín* ("scoundrel" or "rascal").

found them still on the road, not having found a place to sleep; even worse, they were perishing of hunger, for the loss of the saddlebags meant the loss of all their provisions and supplies. And as a final confirmation of their misfortune, they had an adventure that, without any kind of contrivance, really did seem to be one. And so night fell, bringing some darkness with it, but despite this they continued on, for Sancho believed that since the road was the king's highway, in one or two leagues it was likely they would find an inn.

They were riding along, then, the night dark, the squire hungry, and the master with a desire to eat, when they saw coming toward them, on the same road they were traveling, a great multitude of lights that looked like nothing so much as moving stars. Sancho was frightened when he saw them, and Don Quixote felt uneasy; one tugged on his donkey's halter, and the other pulled at the reins of his skinny horse, and they came to a halt, looking carefully to see what those lights might be, and they saw them approaching, and the closer they came the bigger they seemed; seeing this, Sancho began to tremble like a jack-in-the-box, and the hairs on Don Quixote's head stood on end; then, taking heart, he said:

"This, Sancho, is undoubtedly an exceedingly great and dangerous adventure, in which it will be necessary for me to demonstrate all my valor and courage."

"Woe is me!" Sancho responded. "If this adventure has anything to do with phantoms, which is how it's looking to me, who has the ribs that can stand it?"

"Whether they are phantoms or not," said Don Quixote, "I shall not permit any of them to touch even a thread of your garments, for if they had their fun with you the last time, it was because I could not get over the wall of the corral, but now we are in open country, where I shall be able to wield my sword as I choose."

"And if they enchant you and stop you from moving the way they did the last time," said Sancho, "what difference will it make if you're in open country or not?"

"Despite everything," replied Don Quixote, "I beg you, Sancho, to have courage, for experience will allow you to understand the extent of mine."

"I will, may it please God," responded Sancho.

And the two of them moved to the side of the road and began again to look closely to see what those traveling lights might be, and it was not long before they were able to make out a good number of shirted men,[2] and at that fearful sight Sancho completely lost his courage, and his teeth began to chatter as if he had quartain fever, and the clatter of his teeth grew louder when they could make out clearly what this was, because they saw some twenty shirted men, all of them mounted and carrying burning torches in their hands, and behind them came a litter covered in mourning, followed by another six mounted men draped in mourning down to the hooves of their mules, for the calm gait made it clear that these were not horses. The shirted men were talking quietly among themselves in low, sorrowful voices. This strange vision, at that hour and in so deserted a place, was more than enough to instill fear in Sancho's heart, and even in his master's, and if that was true for Don Quixote, then Sancho had already lost whatever courage he had. But the opposite happened to his master, for in his vivid imagination this appeared to be another adventure from his books.

It seemed to him that the litter was a bier carrying a gravely wounded or dead knight, and that it was reserved for him alone to take revenge on his behalf, and so, without another word, he couched his lance, positioned himself in the saddle, and with a gallant spirit and bearing stopped in the middle of the road along which the shirted men necessarily had to pass; when he saw that they were near, he raised his voice and said:

"Halt, O knights, or whomsoever you may be, and give an account of yourselves: from whence you come, whither you are going, and whom you carry on that bier; for by all indications either you have committed an offense or one has been committed against you, and it is needful and proper that I know of it, either to punish you for your evil deeds or to avenge the wrong that has been done to you."

"We're in a hurry," responded one of the shirted men, "and the inn is far, and we can't stop to give the accounting you ask for."

And spurring his mule, he rode forward. Don Quixote took great offense at this reply, and seizing the mule's bridle, he said:

"Halt, and be more courteous, and give the accounting for which I have asked; otherwise, all of you must do battle with me."

The mule was skittish, and when his bridle was seized he became so frightened that he bucked and threw his rider to the ground. A servant who was on foot, seeing the shirted man fall, began to insult Don Quixote, who was angry by now, and without waiting to hear more, he couched his lance, attacked one of the mourners, wounded him, and

---

2. The reference is to soldiers who wore shirts of a specific color over their armor during night battles so they would not be mistaken for the enemy.

knocked him to the ground; when he turned to face the rest of them, it was wonderful to see how quickly he charged and routed them, for at that moment Rocinante moved with such speed and arrogance, it seemed as if he had sprouted wings.

All the shirted men were timorous and unarmed, and at the first opportunity they immediately left the fray and began to run across the fields, holding their burning torches, and they looked like nothing so much as the figures in masks who run about on nights of revels and celebrations. The men in mourning, caught up and swaddled in their soutanes and cassocks, could not move; and so, in complete safety, Don Quixote struck them all and drove them away against their will, for they all thought he was not a man but a devil from hell who had come to take the dead body they were carrying on the litter.

Sancho saw it all, amazed at his master's boldness, and he said to himself:

"No doubt about it, this master of mine is as courageous and brave as he says."

A torch was burning on the ground next to the first man who had been thrown by his mule, and in its light Don Quixote could see him; and coming over to him, he put the point of his lance to his face, telling him to yield; if not, he would kill him. To which the fallen man responded:

"I have yielded and then some; I can't move because my leg is broken; I beg your grace, if you are a Christian gentleman, not to kill me, for you would commit a great sacrilege: I am a licentiate and have taken my first vows."

"Then what the devil has brought you here," said Don Quixote, "being a man of the Church?"

"What, Señor?" replied the fallen man. "My misfortune."

"An even greater one awaits you," said Don Quixote, "if you do not answer to my satisfaction everything I asked you earlier."

"Your grace will easily have your satisfaction," responded the licentiate, "and so your grace should know that even though I said before that I was a licentiate, I am only a bachelor, and my name is Alonso López; I'm a native of Alcobendas, and I have come from the city of Baeza, with eleven other priests, the men who fled with the torches; we are going to the city of Segovia, escorting the dead body that lies in that litter, a gentleman who died in Baeza, where he was originally interred, and now, as I've said, we are carrying his bones to his grave in Segovia, his native city."

"Who killed him?" asked Don Quixote.

"God, by means of a pestilential fever," responded the bachelor.

"In that case," said Don Quixote, "Our Lord has relieved me of the task which I was going to undertake to avenge his death, if anyone else had killed him; but since he was killed by the One who killed him, there is no other recourse but to be silent and shrug one's shoulders, which is what I should do if He had killed me. And I want your reverence to know that I am a knight from La Mancha, named Don Quixote, and it is my occupation and profession to wander the world righting wrongs and rectifying injuries."

"I don't know how you can speak of righting wrongs," said the bachelor, "for you have certainly wronged me and broken my leg, which won't ever be right again; and in rectifying my injuries, you have injured me so much that I'll go on being injured for the rest of my life; it was a great misadventure for me to run across a man who is seeking adventures."

"Not all things," responded Don Quixote, "happen in precisely the same way. The harm, Señor Bachelor Alonso López, lay in all of you coming as you did, at night, dressed in those surplices, holding burning torches, and praying, and draped in mourning, for you indeed appeared to be evil beings from the next world; as a consequence, I could not fail to fulfill my obligation and attack you, and I should have attacked even if I had known for a fact you were all demons from hell, which is what I deemed and considered you to be."

"Since this is what fate had in store for me," said the bachelor of arts, "I implore your grace, Señor Knight Errant (who has treated me with such errancy), to help me out from under this mule, for my leg is caught between the stirrup and the saddle."

"I might have talked until morning!" said Don Quixote. "How long would you have waited to tell me of your plight?"

Then he called to Sancho Panza, who took no notice, because he was busy going through the provisions on a pack mule that belonged to those good gentlemen and was well-supplied with things to eat. Sancho made a sack out of his coat, gathered up as much as he could fit into that pouch, loaded it onto his donkey, and then responded to his master's calls and helped to remove the weight of the mule from the bachelor. After placing him on the animal's back, Sancho handed him his torch, and Don Quixote told him to follow after his companions and, on his behalf, to beg their pardon for the offense against them, which it had not been in his power to avoid committing. Sancho also said to him:

"If, by chance, those gentlemen would like to know who the valiant man is who offended them, your grace can say he is the famous Don Quixote of La Mancha, also known as *The Knight of the Sorrowful Face*."

At this the bachelor rode off, and Don Quixote asked Sancho what had moved him to call him *The Knight of the Sorrowful Face* at that moment and at no other.

"I'll tell you," responded Sancho. "I was looking at you for a while in the light of the torch that unlucky man was carrying, and the truth is that your grace has the sorriest-looking face I've seen recently, and it must be on account of your weariness after this battle, or the molars and teeth you've lost."

"It is not that," responded Don Quixote, "but rather that the wise man whose task it will be to write the history of my deeds must have thought it would be a good idea if I took some appellative title as did the knights of the past: one was called *The Knight of the Blazing Sword*; another, *The Knight of the Unicorn*; yet another, *The Knight of the Damsels*; this one, *The Knight of the Phoenix*; that one, *The Knight of the Griffon*; the other, *The Knight of Death*;[3] and by these names and insignias they were known all around the world. And so I say that the wise man I have already mentioned must have put on your tongue and in your thoughts the idea of calling me *The Knight of the Sorrowful Face*, which is what I plan to call myself from now on; and so that this name may be even more fitting, I resolve to have depicted on my shield, when there is time, a very sorrowful face."

"There's no reason to waste time and money making that face," said Sancho. "What your grace should do instead is uncover yours and show it to those who are looking at you, and right away, without any images or shields, they'll call you *The Knight of the Sorrowful Face*; believe me, I'm telling you the truth, because I promise your grace, Señor, and I'm only joking, that hunger and your missing teeth give you such a sorry-looking face that, as I've said, you can easily do without the sorrowful picture."

Don Quixote laughed at Sancho's witticism, but even so, he resolved to call himself by that name as soon as his shield, or buckler, could be painted as he had imagined.

Then the bachelor returned and said to Don Quixote:

"I forgot to say that your grace should be advised that you have been

---

3. All of these are fictional except for the Knight of the Griffon, a count who lived during the reign of Philip II.

excommunicated for having laid violent hands on something sacred, *juxta illud: Si quis suadente diabolo*, etc."[4]

"I do not understand those Latin words," Don Quixote responded, "but I do know very well that I did not use my hands but this lance; furthermore, I did not think I was attacking priests or things of the Church, which I respect and adore as the Catholic and faithful Christian I am, but phantoms and apparitions of the next world. Even so, I remember what happened to El Cid Ruy Díaz when he broke the chair of the king's ambassador before his holiness the pope, for which he was excommunicated, and on that day good Rodrigo de Vivar showed himself to be a very honored and valiant knight."[5]

On hearing this, the bachelor left without saying a word in reply. Don Quixote wanted to see if the body on the litter was actually bones or not, but Sancho did not agree, saying:

"Señor, your grace has come to the end of this dangerous adventure more safely than all the others I have seen; these people, though they've been defeated and routed, may realize that only one man defeated them and be ashamed and embarrassed by that, and they may rally and look for us, and give us something we won't forget. The donkey is carrying what it should, the mountains are nearby, hunger is pressing, and there's nothing else to do but withdraw as fast as we can and, as they say, let the dead go to the grave and the living to the loaf of bread."

And riding ahead on his donkey, he asked his master to follow him, and since it seemed to Don Quixote that Sancho was right, he followed him without another word. After riding a short while between two hills, they found themselves in a broad, secluded valley, where they dismounted, and Sancho lightened the donkey's load, and they stretched out on the green grass, and with hunger as their sauce, they had breakfast, lunch, dinner, and supper all at once, satisfying their stomachs with more than one of the comestibles that the dead man's priests—who rarely permit themselves to go hungry—carried in their saddlebag of provisions.

But they suffered another misfortune, which Sancho considered the worst of all, and it was that they had no wine to drink or even water to put to their lips; troubled by thirst, Sancho, seeing that the meadow where they were sitting was full of abundant green grass, said what will be recounted in the next chapter.

4. This is part of a phrase established by the Council of Trent for excommunicating those who committed violence against a member of the clergy.

5. The incident is narrated in several ballads about El Cid (Rodrigo de Vivar, also called Ruy Díaz).

CHAPTER XX

Regarding the most incomparable and singular adventure ever concluded with less danger by a famous knight, and which was concluded by the valiant Don Quixote of La Mancha

"It's not possible, Señor, for this grass not to be a sign that somewhere nearby there's a spring or brook that waters these plants, and so it would be a good idea for us to go a little farther until we find a place where we can quench this terrible thirst that's plaguing us and is, no doubt about it, harder to bear than hunger."

This seemed good advice to Don Quixote, and after packing away the remains of their supper on the donkey, he led Rocinante by the reins, and Sancho held his donkey's halter, and they began to walk to the top of the meadow, feeling their way because the dark of night did not allow them to see anything at all; but they had not gone two hundred paces when a sound of crashing reached their ears, as if water were hurtling over large, high cliffs. The sound made them very happy, and they stopped to hear where it was coming from, when they suddenly heard another exceedingly loud noise that watered down their joy at finding water, especially Sancho's, for he was naturally fearful and not very brave. I say that they heard the sound of rhythmic pounding, along with a certain clanking of irons and chains that, accompanied by the clamorous fury of the water, would have put terror in any heart other than Don Quixote's.

The night, as we have said, was dark, and they happened to walk under some tall trees whose leaves, moved by the gentle breeze, made a muffled, frightening sound; in short, the solitude, the place, the darkness, the noise of the water, and the murmur of the leaves all combined to cause panic and consternation, especially when they saw that the pounding did not stop, the wind did not cease, and morning did not come; added to this was their not knowing where they were. But Don Quixote, accompanied by his intrepid heart, leaped onto Rocinante, and, holding his shield, he grasped his lance and said:

"Sancho, my friend, know that I was born, by the will of heaven, in this our iron age, to revive the one of gold, or the Golden Age, as it is called. I am he for whom are reserved dangers, great deeds, valiant feats. I am, I repeat, he who is to revive the Knights of the Round Table, the Twelve Peers of France, the Nine Worthies, he who is to make the world forget the Platirs, Tablants, Olivants, and Tirants, the Phoebuses and Belianises, and the entire horde of famous knights errant of a bygone age, by performing in this time in which I find myself such great and extraordinary deeds and feats of arms that they will overshadow the brightest they ever achieved. Note well, my faithful and loyal squire, the darkness of this night, its strange silence, the indistinct and confused sound of these trees, the fearful clamor of the water we came seeking, which seems to be falling and crashing from the high mountains of the moon, and the unceasing noise of pounding that wounds and pains our ears; all these things, taken together and separately, are enough to instill fear, terror, and dread in the bosom of Mars himself, not to mention one who is unaccustomed to such occurrences and adventures. But these things I have described for you are inspiration and encouragement to my valor, which makes my heart almost burst in my bosom with the desire to embark on this adventure, no matter how difficult it may prove to be. And so, tighten the cinches on Rocinante, and God be with you, and wait for me here no more than three days, and if I have not come back by then, you may return to our village, and from there, as a boon and good deed for my sake, you will go to Toboso and tell my peerless lady Dulcinea that her captive knight died performing deeds that would make him worthy of being called her own."

When Sancho heard his master's words, he began to cry with the greatest tenderness in the world, and he said:

"Señor, I don't know why your grace wants to embark on this fearful adventure; it's night, nobody can see us here, we can turn around and get away from the danger, even if we don't drink anything for three days, and since there's nobody here to see us, there's nobody to call us cowards; besides, I've heard the sermons of our village priest, and your grace knows him very well, and he says that whoever goes looking for danger perishes; so it isn't a good idea to tempt God by undertaking something so terrible that you can't get out of it except through some miracle, and heaven has done enough of them for your grace, letting you escape being tossed in the blanket, like I was, and letting you come out victorious, free, and unharmed, over so many enemies who were escorting the dead man. And if all this doesn't touch or soften your hard heart, let it be moved by thinking and believing that as soon as your grace has left this place, fear will make me give up my soul to anybody who wants to take it. I left my home and my children and my wife to serve your grace, thinking I would be better off, not worse; but just as greed makes the sack burst, it has torn my hopes apart when they were brightest for getting that wretched, ill-starred ínsula your grace has promised me so often; I see that as payment and reward you want to leave me now in a desolate place far from all other human beings. By the One God, Señor, you must not wrong me so, and if your grace absolutely refuses to think again about embarking on this deed, at least put it off until morning, for the lore I learned when I was a shepherd tells me it's less than three hours till dawn, because the mouth of the Horn is over my head and midnight's in line with my left arm."[1]

"How can you, Sancho," said Don Quixote, "see where that line is, or where the mouth of any Horn or any head is, if the night is so dark there is not a single star visible in all the sky?"

"That's true," said Sancho, "but fear has many eyes and can see things under the ground, let alone high in the sky; even so, it stands to reason that it won't be long until daylight."

"However long it may be," responded Don Quixote, "let no one say of me, now or ever, that tears and pleas turned me from doing what I, as a knight, was obliged to do; and so I beg you, Sancho, to be quiet, for God, who has placed in my heart the desire to embark on this incomparable and most fearsome adventure, will surely look after my well-being and console you in your grief. What you must do is tighten Rocinante's cinches and remain here; I shall soon return, either alive or dead."

Sancho, seeing his master's firm resolve, and how little he accomplished with tears, advice, and pleas, decided to take advantage of his task and do what he could to make Don Quixote wait until day, and so, as he was tightening the horse's cinches, he very cunningly and quietly tied Rocinante's forelegs together with his donkey's halter, and when

---

1. The Horn is the constellation of Ursa Minor; Sancho refers to a method of telling the time by the stars in which the person would extend his arms in the shape of a cross and calculate the hour by determining the position of the Horn in relationship to his arms.

Don Quixote tried to leave he could not because his horse could not move except by hops and jumps. Seeing the success of his deception, Sancho Panza said:

"Oh, Señor, heaven, moved by my tears and prayers, has willed Rocinante not to move, and if you persist, and spur and urge him on, that will anger Fortune, and it will be, as they say, like kicking at thorns."

At this Don Quixote grew desperate, for no matter how hard he spurred his horse, he could not make him move; then, not realizing that the animal's legs had been tied, he thought it a good idea to be calm and wait, either for the dawn or until Rocinante could move forward, believing, no doubt, that this situation was caused by something other than Sancho's labors, and so he said to him:

"Well, Sancho, since Rocinante cannot move, I am content to wait until dawn smiles upon us, although I weep at how long she will take to arrive."

"There's no reason to cry," responded Sancho. "I'll entertain your grace by telling you stories until daylight, unless you want to dismount and sleep a little on the green grass, in the manner of knights errant, so that you'll be rested when day comes, and ready to embark on the unrivaled adventure that awaits you."

"What do you mean, dismount and sleep?" said Don Quixote. "Am I, perchance, one of those knights who take their rest in the midst of dangers? You sleep, for you were born to sleep, or do whatever you wish, and I shall do what I deem most becoming to my profession."

"Señor, your grace shouldn't be angry," responded Sancho, "I didn't mean anything by it."

And, going up to him, Sancho placed one hand on the front of the saddle and the other on the rear, so that he stood with his arms around his master's left thigh, not daring to move a finger's breadth away from him, so great was the fear he had of the pounding, which continued to sound rhythmically. Don Quixote told him to recount some story to amuse him, as he had promised, to which Sancho replied that he would, if his terror at what he was hearing allowed him to.

"But, even so, I'll make an effort to tell a story, and if I manage to tell it and my fear doesn't stop me, it's the best of all stories; and your grace should pay careful attention, because here I go. 'Once upon a time, and may good come to all and evil to him who seeks it . . .' And, Señor, your grace should notice that the beginnings the ancients gave to their tales didn't come out of nowhere; this was a maxim of the Roman Cato Nonsensor,[2] and it says: 'Evil to him who seeks it,' which fits here like the ring on your finger and means that your grace should stay put and not go looking for evil anywhere, and we should take another route, nobody's forcing us to continue on this one with so many frightening things to scare us."

"You go on with your story, Sancho," said Don Quixote, "and leave the route we shall follow to me."

"Well, I'll tell you," Sancho continued, "that somewhere in Extremadura there was a goatherd, I mean to say the man tended goats, and this goatherd I was telling you about in my story was named Lope Ruiz, and this Lope Ruiz was in love with a shepherdess named Torralba, and this shepherdess named Torralba was the daughter of a rich herder, and this rich herder—"

"If you tell your story this way, Sancho," said Don Quixote, "repeating everything you say two times, you will not finish in two days; tell it in a continuous way, and speak like a man of understanding, or do not say anything at all."

"The way I'm telling it," responded Sancho, "is how tales are told in my village, and I don't know any other way to tell it, and it isn't right for your grace to ask me to do things in new ways."

"Tell it however you wish," responded Don Quixote. "Fate has willed that I cannot help listening to you, and so continue."

"And so it was, Señor of my soul," Sancho continued, "that, as I've already said, this goatherd was in love with Torralba, the shepherdess, who was a stout girl, and wild, and a little mannish because she had something of a mustache; it's as if I could see her now."

"Then, did you know her?" said Don Quixote.

"I didn't know her," responded Sancho. "But the man who told me this story said it was so true and correct that I certainly could, when I told it to somebody else, affirm and swear that I had seen it all. And so, as the days came and went, the devil, who never sleeps and is always stirring up trouble, turned the love that the goatherd had for the shepherdess into hate and ill will, and the reason was, the gossips said, a certain amount of jealousy that she made him feel, and it went too far, into forbidden areas, and then the goatherd hated her so much that in order not to see her he wanted to leave his home and go where he would never lay eyes on her again. Torralba, when she found herself rejected

2. Sancho is alluding to Cato the Censor, or *Cato Censorino*, who was popularly considered to be a source of proverbs and sayings; in the process, he mispronounces his title, calling him *zonzorino*, which suggests "simpleminded."

by Lope, began to love him dearly, though she had never loved him before."

"That is the nature of women," said Don Quixote. "They reject the
man who loves them and love the man who despises them. Go on,
Sancho."

"It so happened," said Sancho, "that the goatherd put his plan into
effect, and, driving his goats ahead of him, he set out through the countryside of Extremadura, heading for the kingdom of Portugal. Torralba,
who found this out, went after him, and followed him at a distance,
walking barefoot, with a staff in her hand and some saddlebags around
her neck, and in them she was carrying, people say, a piece of mirror, and
a broken comb, and some kind of paint for her face; but, whatever it was
that she was carrying, I don't want to take the trouble to find out about
it, so I'll just say that people say that the goatherd and his flock came to
the Guadiana River, and at that time of year it was rising and almost
flooding its banks, and at the part he came to there wasn't any boat or
barge or anybody to ferry him and his flock to the other side, and this
caused him a lot of grief because he saw that Torralba was coming closer
and closer and would bother him with her pleading and her tears; but he
kept looking around until he saw a fisherman with a boat, one so small
that only one person and one goat could fit in it; even so, he talked to
him and they arranged for the fisherman to ferry him and his three hundred goats across the river. The fisherman got into the boat and ferried
across a goat; he came back, and ferried another one; he came back
again, and again he ferried one across. Your grace has to keep count of
the goats the fisherman ferries across, because if you miss one the story
will be over and it won't be possible to say another word. And so I'll go
on and say that the landing on the other side was very muddy and slip-
pery, and it took the fisherman a long time to go back and forth. Even so,
he came back for another goat, and another, and another—"

"Just say he ferried them all," said Don Quixote. "If you keep going
back and forth like that, it will take you a year to get them across."

"How many have gone across so far?" said Sancho.

"How the devil should I know?" responded Don Quixote.

"That's just what I told your grace to do: to keep a good count. Well,
by God, the story's over, and there's no way to go on."

"How can that be?" responded Don Quixote. "Is it so essential to the
story to know the exact number of goats that have crossed that a mistake
in the count means you cannot continue the tale?"

"No, Señor, I can't," responded Sancho, "because as soon as I asked your grace to tell me how many goats had crossed, and you said you didn't know, at that very moment I forgot everything I had left to say, and, by my faith, it was very interesting and pleasing."

"Do you mean to say that the story is finished?" said Don Quixote.

"As finished as my mother," said Sancho.

"I tell you truthfully," responded Don Quixote, "that you have told one of the strangest tales, stories, or histories that anyone in the world ever thought of, and this manner of telling it and then stopping it is something I shall never see, and have never seen, in my life, although I expected nothing else from your intellect; but I am not surprised, for perhaps the sound of the pounding, which has not ceased, has clouded your understanding."

"That may be," responded Sancho, "but I know that in my story, there's nothing else to say: it ended right where you lost count of the number of goats that had crossed."

"Then let it end where it will," said Don Quixote, "and now let us see if Rocinante can move."

He spurred him again, and Rocinante hopped again and then stood still: that is how well he was tied.

At this moment it seems that either because of the cold of the morning, which was approaching, or because Sancho had eaten something laxative for supper, or because it was in the natural order of things—which is the most credible—he felt the urge and desire to do what no one else could do for him, but his heart was so overwhelmed by fear that he did not dare to move a nail paring away from his master. But not doing what he desired to do was not possible, either, and so what he did as a compromise was to free his right hand, which was clutching the back of the saddle, and with it, cunningly and without making a sound, he loosened the slip knot that was the only thing holding up his breeches, and when he did they came down and settled around his ankles like leg irons. After this he lifted his shirt the best he could and stuck out both buttocks, which were not very small. Having done this—which he thought was all he had to do to escape that terrible difficulty and anguish—he was overcome by an even greater distress, which was that it seemed to him he could not relieve himself without making some noise and sound, and he began to clench his teeth and hunch his shoulders, holding his breath as much as he could, but despite all his efforts, he was so unfortunate that he finally made a little noise quite different from the one that had caused him so much fear. Don Quixote heard it and said:

"What sound is that, Sancho?"

"I don't know, Señor," he responded. "It must be something new; adventures and misadventures never begin for no reason."

He tried his luck again, and things went so smoothly that with no more noise or disturbance than the last time, he found himself rid of the burden that had caused him so much grief. But since Don Quixote had a sense of smell as acute as his hearing, and Sancho was joined so closely to him, and the vapors rose up almost in a straight line, some unavoidably reached his nostrils, and as soon as they did he came to the assistance of his nostrils and squeezed them closed between two fingers, and in a somewhat nasal voice, he said:

"It seems to me, Sancho, that you are very frightened."

"Yes, I am," responded Sancho, "but what makes your grace see that now more than ever?"

"Because you smell now more than ever, and not of amber," responded Don Quixote.

"That might be," said Sancho, "but it's not my fault, it's your grace's for choosing the most ungodly times to put me through the strangest paces."

"Take three or four of them back, friend," said Don Quixote without removing his fingers from his nose, "and from now on be more mindful of your person and of what you owe to mine; engaging in so much conversation with you has caused this lack of respect."

"I'll wager," replied Sancho, "that your grace thinks I've done something with my person I shouldn't have."

"The less said the better, Sancho my friend," responded Don Quixote.

Master and servant passed the night in these exchanges and others like them. But Sancho, seeing that morning would soon be upon them, very carefully unhobbled Rocinante and tied up his breeches. When Rocinante found himself free, though he was not by nature highspirited, it seems he felt offended and began to paw the ground because—and for this I beg his pardon—he could not prance. Don Quixote, seeing that Rocinante was moving again, took this as a favorable sign and believed it meant he should embark on the fearful adventure. By this time dawn finally had made its presence known and changed the appearance of things, and Don Quixote saw that he was under some tall trees; they were chestnuts and cast a very dark shadow. He also heard that the pounding had not stopped, but he did not see who could be causing it, and so, with no further delay, he made Rocinante feel his spurs, and, turning to take his leave of Sancho, he ordered him to wait no more than three days, as he had already told him, and if at the end of that time he had not returned, Sancho could be certain it had been God's will that his master's days come to an end in that perilous adventure. Don Quixote told him again about the message and communication he was to take to his lady Dulcinea; as for payment for his services, Sancho should not be concerned because Don Quixote had made his will before leaving home, and in it the squire would find himself recompensed for everything relating to his salary, the amount prorated according to the length of time he had been in his service, but if God allowed him to emerge from this danger safe and sound and unharmed, then Sancho could be more than certain of the promised ínsula.

Sancho began to cry again when he heard the sorrowful words of his good master, and he resolved not to leave him until the final conclusion and end of that affair.

These tears and Sancho Panza's honorable decision lead the author of this history to conclude that he must have been wellborn and, at the very least, an Old Christian;[3] the sentiment softened his master somewhat, but not enough for him to demonstrate any weakness; instead, dissimulating as much as he could, he began to ride toward the place where it seemed to him the sound of the water and the pounding originated.

Sancho followed on foot, leading by the halter, as was his custom, the donkey who was his constant companion in good fortune and bad; having traveled some distance through those somber chestnut trees, they came upon a small meadow at the foot of some high crags over which a great rush of water fell. At the foot of the crags were some dilapidated hovels that looked more like ruins than houses, and they realized that the noise and din of the pounding, which had not ceased, was coming from these structures.

Rocinante became agitated by the clamor of the water and the pounding, and Don Quixote, calming him, gradually approached the hovels, commending himself with all his heart to his lady, imploring that she favor him in this fearsome circumstance and undertaking, and he also commended himself to God, praying that He not forget him. Sancho did not leave his side, craning his neck and peering between the legs of Rocinante to see if he could see what it was that had so frightened and perplexed him.

They must have gone another hundred paces when, as they turned a

---

3. A term used to describe those who had no Jewish or Muslim ancestors, as opposed to more recent converts (the "New Christians"); being an "Old Christian" was considered a significant attribute following the forced conversions of the fifteenth and sixteenth centuries.

corner, there appeared, clear and plain, the unmistakable cause of the terrible-sounding and, for them, terrifying noise that had kept them frightened and perplexed the whole night. And it was—if you have not already guessed, O reader, in sorrow and anger!—six wooden fulling hammers that with their alternating strokes were responsible for the clamor.

When Don Quixote saw this he fell silent and sat as if paralyzed from head to toe. Sancho looked at him and saw that his head hung down toward his chest, indicating that he was mortified. Don Quixote also looked at Sancho and saw that his cheeks were puffed out and his mouth full of laughter, clear signs that he soon would explode, and Don Quixote's melancholy was not so great that he could resist laughing at the sight of Sancho, and when Sancho saw that his master had begun, the floodgates opened with such force that he had to press his sides with his fists to keep from bursting with laughter. Four times he calmed down, and four times his laughter returned as powerfully as before; by now Don Quixote was sending him to the devil, especially when he heard him say, in a derisive tone:

" 'Sancho my friend, know that I was born, by the will of heaven, in this our iron age, to revive the one of gold, or the Golden Age. I am he for whom are reserved dangers, great deeds, valiant feats . . .' "

And in this fashion he repeated all or most of the words that Don Quixote had said when they first heard the fearful pounding.

Don Quixote, seeing that Sancho was mocking him, became so wrathful and angry that he raised his lance and struck him twice, blows so hard that if he had received them on his head instead of his back, his master would have been freed of the obligation of paying his salary, unless it was to his heirs. Sancho, seeing that his jokes were taken so seriously and fearing that his master would go even further, said to him very humbly:

"Your grace should calm down; by God, I'm only joking."

"Well, you may be joking, but I am not,"[4] responded Don Quixote. "Come here, you merry man; do you think that if these were not fulling hammers but a dangerous adventure, I would not have displayed the courage needed to undertake and conclude it? Am I obliged, perchance, being, as I am, a knight, to recognize and differentiate sounds, and know which are fulling hammers and which are not? Moreover, it well might be, as is the case, that I have never seen them in my life, though you must have, being the lowborn peasant you are, and reared and born

---

4. For the next few sentences, Don Quixote uses a more formal mode of address with Sancho (a change that cannot be rendered in modern English) to indicate extreme displeasure and his desire for distance between them.

among them. If not, pretend that these six fulling hammers are six giants, and turn them on me one by one, or all together, and if I do not knock them all to the ground, you can mock me in any way you choose."

"No more, Señor," replied Sancho. "I confess that I have gone a little too far with my joking. But tell me, your grace, now that we're at peace (and may God bring you as safe and sound through all the adventures you have as He has brought you through this one), wasn't it laughable how frightened we were, and wouldn't it make a good story? At least, how frightened I was, for I already know that your grace doesn't know what fright is or understand the meaning of fear or terror."

"I do not deny," responded Don Quixote, "that what happened to us is deserving of laughter, but it does not deserve to be told, for not all persons are wise enough to put things in their proper place."

"At least," responded Sancho, "your grace knew how to place the lance, aiming for my head and hitting me on the back, thanks be to God and the care I took to move to the side. Well, well, it all comes out in the end, for I've heard people say: 'The one who hurts you is the one who loves you,' and I've also heard that great gentlemen, after speaking harshly to a servant, give him breeches, though I don't know what they give after beating him with a lance, unless knights errant give ínsulas after a beating, or kingdoms on dry land."

"The dice may fall," said Don Quixote, "so that everything you say turns out to be true; forgive what happened, for you are clever and know that first impulses are not ours to control, but be advised of one thing: from now on you are to refrain and abstain from speaking too much to me, for in all the books of chivalry I have read, which are infinite in number, I have never found any squire who talks as much with his master as you do with yours. In truth I consider it a great fault, both on your part and on mine: on yours, because you do not have a high opinion of me; on mine, because I do not allow a higher opinion. For instance, Gandalín, the squire of Amadís of Gaul, became count of Ínsula Firme, yet one reads of him that he always spoke to his master with hat in hand, bending his head and bowing his body, *more turquesco*.[5] And what shall we say of Gasabal, the squire of Don Galaor, who was so silent that in order to declare to us the excellence of his wondrous silence, his name is mentioned only once in the course of that history, as great as it is true? From everything I have said you must infer, Sancho, that it is necessary to distinguish between master and minion, gentleman and servant, knight and squire. Therefore, from this

5. Latin for "in the Turkish manner."

day forward, we must treat each other with more respect and refrain from mockery, because no matter why I lose my temper with you, it will be bad for the pitcher.[6] The rewards and benefits that I have promised you will come in time, and if they do not, your wages, at least, will not be lost, as I have already told you."

"Everything your grace says is fine," said Sancho. "But I'd like to know, if the time for rewards happens not to come and it's necessary to fall back on wages, how much the squire of a knight errant earned in those days, and if he was paid by the month or by the day, like a mason's helpers."

"I do not believe," Don Quixote responded, "that those squires ever received wages, but only favors. And if I have mentioned you in the last will and testament that I left in my house, it was because of what might happen, for I do not yet know the standing of chivalry in these our calamitous times, and I should not want my soul to suffer in the next world on account of trivial details. Because I want you to know, Sancho, that there is no profession more dangerous than that of adventuring knight."

"That's true," said Sancho, "for just the noise of the fulling hammers could upset and disturb the heart of an adventuring knight errant as valiant as your grace. But you can be sure that from now on my lips will not open to joke about your grace's affairs, but only to honor you as my master and natural lord."

"In that way," replied Don Quixote, "you will live long on the face of the earth, for after parents, masters must be respected as if they were progenitors."

CHAPTER XXI

Which relates the high adventure and rich prize of the helmet of Mambrino, as well as other things that befell our invincible knight

At this point a light rain began to fall, and Sancho would have liked for them to take shelter in the fulling mill, but Don Quixote had acquired such an aversion to it because of the insufferable deception that under no circumstances did he wish to go inside, and so, turning to the right,

6. This is the second half of a proverb: "It doesn't matter if the pitcher hits the stone or the stone hits the pitcher: it will be bad for the pitcher."

they came upon another road similar to the one they had followed on the previous day.

A short while later, Don Quixote caught sight of a man riding toward them and wearing on his head something that glistened as if it were made of gold, and no sooner had he seen him than he turned to Sancho and said:

"It seems to me, Sancho, that there is no proverb that is not true, because all of them are judgments based on experience, the mother of all knowledge, in particular the one that says: 'One door closes and another opens.' I say this because if last night fortune closed the door on what we were seeking, deceiving us with fulling hammers, now she opens wide another that will lead to a better and truer adventure; if I do not succeed in going through this door, the fault will be mine, and I shall not be able to blame my ignorance of fulling hammers or the dark of night. I say this because, unless I am mistaken, coming toward us is a man who wears on his head the helmet of Mambrino,[1] concerning which, as you well know, I have made a vow."

"Your grace, be careful what you say, and more careful what you do," said Sancho, "for you wouldn't want this to be more fulling hammers that end up hammering and battering our senses."

"The devil take the man!" replied Don Quixote. "What does a helmet have to do with fulling hammers?"

"I don't know anything about that," responded Sancho, "but by my faith, if I could talk as much as I used to, maybe I could say some things that would make your grace see that you were mistaken in what you said."

"How can I be mistaken in what I say, you doubting traitor?" said Don Quixote. "Tell me, do you not see that knight coming toward us, mounted on a dappled gray and wearing on his head a helmet of gold?"

"What I see and can make out," responded Sancho, "is just a man riding a donkey that's gray like mine, and wearing something shiny on his head."

"Well, that is the helmet of Mambrino," said Don Quixote. "Move aside and let me face him alone; you will see that without speaking a word so as not to waste time, I shall bring this adventure to a conclusion and acquire the helmet I have so long desired."

"I'll be sure to move aside," replied Sancho, "but may it please God," he continued, "that it turns out to be oregano and not fulling hammers."[2]

---

1. An enchanted helmet worn by Reinaldos de Montalbán.

2. Sancho is citing part of a proverb—"May it please God that this is oregano and not caraway"—which warns against fool's gold (oregano was considered more valuable than caraway).

"I have already told you, brother, not to mention or even think about mentioning those fulling hammers to me," said Don Quixote, "or I swear . . . I shall say no more, but I shall hammer and full your soul."

Sancho fell silent, fearful his master might carry out the vow, as roundly categorical as a ball, that he had hurled at him.

This is the truth concerning the helmet, the horse, and the knight that Don Quixote saw: in that area there were two villages, one of them so small it did not have an apothecary or a barber, but the other, which was nearby, did, and so the barber in the larger one served the smaller, where a man happened to be sick and needed to be bled, and another needed to have his beard trimmed, and consequently the barber was traveling there, carrying a brass basin; as luck would have it, as he was traveling it began to rain, and to keep his hat from being stained, for it must have been new, he put the basin on his head, and since it was clean, at a distance of half a league, it glistened. He was riding a gray donkey, as Sancho had said, which gave rise to Don Quixote's thinking that he saw a dappled gray, a knight, and a gold helmet, for everything he saw he very easily accommodated to his chivalric nonsense and errant thoughts. And when he saw the poor gentleman approaching, without saying a word to him, and with Rocinante at full gallop, he attacked with lowered pike, intending to run him through, but when he drew near, without stopping the fury of his charge, he cried:

"Defend yourself, base creature, or hand over to me of your own free will what is so rightly mine!"

The barber, who never imagined or feared such a thing when he saw that apparition bearing down on him, had no other choice, in order to protect himself from the lance, than to fall off his donkey; and as soon as he touched the ground, he leaped up as nimbly as a deer and began to run across the plain, so fast the wind could not catch him. He left the basin on the ground, which satisfied Don Quixote, who said that the heathen had behaved with discretion and imitated the beaver, which, finding itself pursued by hunters, bites and tears off the thing for which he knows, by natural instinct, he is being hunted down.[3] He told Sancho to pick up the helmet, and the squire, lifting the basin in his hands, said:

"By God, this is a good basin and must be worth eight *reales* if it's worth a *maravedí*."

And he gave it to his master, who then put it on his head, turning it

---

3. Castor, a strong-smelling secretion of the beaver's sexual glands, was used in making perfume.

around from one side to the other, looking for the visor; and since he did not find it, he said:

"No doubt the heathen for whom this famous sallet helmet was first forged must have had an extremely large head; worst of all, half of it is missing."

When Sancho heard the basin called a sallet, he could not contain his laughter, but then he recalled his master's wrath, and he broke off in the middle.

"Why are you laughing, Sancho?" said Don Quixote.

"It makes me laugh," he responded, "to think of the big head on that heathen owner of this old helmet, which looks exactly like a barber's basin."

"Do you know what I imagine, Sancho? This famous piece of the enchanted helmet, by some strange accident, must have fallen into the hands of one who could not recognize or estimate its value, and not knowing what he was doing, and seeing that it was made of purest gold, he must have melted down one half to take advantage of its high price, and from the other half he made this, which resembles a barber's basin, as you say. Be that as it may, I recognize it, and its transmutation does not matter to me, for I shall repair it in the first village that has a blacksmith, and in a manner that will leave far behind the one made and forged by the god of smithies for the god of war;[4] in the meantime, I shall do the best I can to wear it, for something is better than nothing, especially since it will serve quite well to protect me from any stones that people may throw at me."

"It will," said Sancho, "if they're not using a slingshot like they did in the battle of the two armies, when they made the sign of the cross over your grace's molars and broke the cruet that held the blessed potion that made me vomit up my innards."

"Losing it does not grieve me greatly, for you know, Sancho," said Don Quixote, "that I have the recipe committed to memory."

"So do I," responded Sancho, "but if I ever make it or taste it again in my life, let this be my final hour. Besides, I don't intend to put myself in the position of needing it, because I plan to use all my five senses to keep from being wounded or wounding anybody else. As for being tossed in a blanket again, I won't say another word, for such misfortunes are difficult to foresee, and if they come, all you can do is shrug your shoulders, hold

4. Vulcan made armor for Mars, but not a helmet.

your breath, close your eyes, and let yourself go where luck and the blanket take you."

"You are a bad Christian, Sancho," said Don Quixote when he heard this, "because you never forget an injury once it has been done to you, but you should know that noble and generous bosoms do not pay attention to trifles. Were you left with a lame foot, a cracked rib, a broken skull? Is that why you never can forget the jest? For, if the matter is viewed correctly, it was merely a jest and a diversion; if I did not understand it in this way, I should have returned and, in avenging you, inflicted more harm than the Greeks did because of the abducted Helen, who, if she had lived in this time, or my Dulcinea lived in hers, could be certain of not enjoying the reputation for beauty she has now."

Whereupon he heaved a sigh and sent it heavenward. And Sancho said:

"Let it pass as a joke, since it can't be avenged in reality, but I know what this reality and this joke mean, and I also know they won't fall away from my memory any more than they'll fade from my back. But, leaving that aside, your grace should tell me what we're going to do with this dappled gray horse that looks like a gray donkey and was left behind by that Martino[5] who was toppled by your grace, because seeing how he took to his heels and ran like Villadiego,[6] he has no intention of ever coming back for it. By my beard, this dappled gray is a good one!"

"It has never been my practice," said Don Quixote, "to plunder those I conquer, nor is it a knightly custom to deprive them of their horses and leave them on foot, unless the victor has lost his mount in the battle; in such cases, it is licit to take that of the conquered knight as the spoils of legitimate combat. Therefore, Sancho, leave this horse, or donkey, or whatever you say it is, for when its owner sees that we have departed, he will return for it."

"God knows I'd like to take it," replied Sancho, "or at least exchange it for this one of mine, because I don't think it's as good. Really, the laws of chivalry are strict if they can't be stretched to let you trade one donkey for another; I'd like to know if I could at least swap the trappings."

"I am not certain about that," responded Don Quixote. "In case of doubt, until I am better informed, I should say that you may exchange them if you are in dire need of them."

5. Sancho means "Mambrino."

6. An idiom, used earlier, that means to flee an unexpected danger.

"So dire," responded Sancho, "that if they were for my own person I couldn't need them more."

Then, on the basis of that permission, he executed a *mutatio capparum*[7] and decked out his donkey, showing him off to great advantage.

Having done this, they ate the remains of the food that had been taken from the pack mule and drank from the stream where the fulling hammers were, not turning their faces to look at them, so great was their loathing because of how much they had frightened them.

Having pacified their hunger and tempered their melancholy, they remounted, and with no fixed destination, since it was very much in the tradition of knights errant not to follow a specific route, they began to ride wherever Rocinante's will took them; behind his will came his master's, and even the donkey's, who always followed wherever the horse led, in virtuous love and companionship. And so they returned to the king's highway and followed it with no set plan or purpose in mind.

As they were riding along, Sancho said to his master:

"Señor, does your grace wish to give me leave to talk a little? After you gave me that harsh order of silence, more than a few things have been spoiling in my stomach, and one that I have now on the tip of my tongue I wouldn't want to go to waste."

"Say it," Don Quixote said, "and be brief, for no speech is pleasing if it is long."

"What I have to say, Señor," responded Sancho, "is that for the past few days I've been thinking how little gain or profit there is in looking for the adventures that your grace looks for in these deserted places and crossroads, because even when you conquer and conclude the most dangerous, there's nobody to see them or know about them, and so they remain in perpetual silence, which isn't your grace's intention or what they deserve. And so it seems to me it would be better, unless your grace thinks otherwise, if we went to serve some emperor or other great prince who's involved in some war, and in his service your grace could demonstrate the valor of your person, your great strength, and even greater understanding; and when the lord we serve sees this, he'll have to reward us, each according to his merits, and there's sure to be somebody there who'll put into writing your grace's great deeds so they can be remembered forever. About mine I don't say anything, for they won't go beyond squirely limits, though I can say that if it's customary in chivalry to write about the deeds of squires, I don't think mine will be forgotten."

7. A ritual in which cardinals change their hoods on Easter Sunday.

"You speak sensibly, Sancho," responded Don Quixote, "but before one reaches that point, it is necessary to wander the world as a kind of test, seeking adventures, so that by concluding some of them, the knight acquires a reputation and fame, and when he goes to the court of some great monarch he is known by his deeds, and as soon as the boys see him ride through the gate of the city, they all follow and surround him, shouting and saying: 'Here is the Knight of the Sun,' or of the Serpent, or of some other device under which he accomplished great feats. 'Here is,' they will say, 'the one who conquered in singular combat the gigantic Brocabruno the Mighty; the one who freed the Great Mameluke of Persia from the long enchantment he suffered for almost nine hundred years.'

In this manner, news of his deeds passes from person to person, and then, to the cheers of the boys and the rest of the populace, the king of the land will appear at the windows of his royal palace, and as soon as he sees the knight, knowing him by his armor or the device on his shield, he perforce will say: 'Hark, look lively! Go forth, my knights, all who are in my court, to greet the flower of chivalry who now comes riding!' At this command all will go forth, and the king will come halfway down the stairs, and embrace the knight warmly, and bid him welcome, kissing him on the face, and then he will lead him by the hand to the chamber of my lady the queen, where the knight will find her with the princess, their daughter, who is, beyond any doubt, one of the most beauteous and perfect damsels that one could find anywhere in the known regions of the earth. After this she will very chastely turn her eyes to the knight, and he will turn his eyes to hers, and each will seem to the other more divine than human, and without knowing how or why, they will be captured and caught in the intricate nets of love, with great affliction in their hearts because they do not know how they will speak and reveal to one another their yearnings and desires.

Then he will no doubt be taken to a sumptuously appointed room in the palace, where, having removed his armor, they will bring him a rich scarlet cloak and drape it around him; and if he looked comely in armor, he looks just as comely and even more so in his quilted doublet. When night falls, he will have supper with the king, queen, and princess, and he will never take his eyes off the maiden, his looks hidden from the rest, and she will do the same with the same sagacity because, as I have said, she is a very discreet damsel. The tables will be cleared and then suddenly, through the door of the chamber, an ugly dwarf will enter, followed by a beauteous duenna between two giants, who tells of a certain adventure devised by an extremely ancient wise man, and whosoever brings it to a conclusion will be deemed the greatest knight in the world. Then the king will command all those present to attempt it, and none will end or finish it except the knight who is his guest, which will add greatly to his fame and make the princess extremely happy, and she will think of herself as exceedingly well-rewarded and compensated for having placed her affections so high. And the fortunate part is that this king, or prince, or whatever he is, is waging a fierce war with another as powerful as he, and the knight who is his guest asks him (after spending a few days in his court) for permission to serve him in that war. The king will give it willingly, and the knight will courteously kiss his hands in gratitude for the boon he has granted him.

And that night he will take his leave of his lady the princess through the grillework at the window of the bedchamber where she sleeps, which overlooks a garden, and through this grillework he has already spoken to her many times, their go-between and confidante being a lady-in-waiting greatly trusted by the princess. He will sigh, she will swoon, the lady-in-waiting will bring water, sorely troubled because morning is coming and, for the sake of her lady's honor, she does not wish them to be discovered. Finally the princess will regain consciousness and pass her white hands through the grillework to the knight, who will kiss them over and over again and bathe them in his tears. The two of them will agree on the manner in which they will keep each other informed of their fortunes and misfortunes, and the princess will beg him to tarry as little as possible; he will promise, making many vows; he will kiss her hands one more time and say goodbye with so much emotion that his life will almost come to an end. Then he goes to his room, throws himself on the bed, cannot sleep because of the pain of their parting, arises very early in the morning, and goes to take his leave of the king, the queen, and the princess; they tell him, when he has bade farewell to the first two, that her highness the princess is indisposed and cannot receive visitors; the knight thinks it is because of her sorrow at his leaving, his heart is wounded, and it is all he can do not to show clear signs of his suffering. The lady-in-waiting, their confidante, is present, and she will take note of everything and recount it all to her lady, who receives her in tears and tells her that one of her greatest griefs is not knowing who her knight is, or if he is of royal lineage; the lady-in-waiting assures her that the degree of courtesy, gallantry, and valor displayed by her knight can exist only in a royal and illustrious person; the suffering princess consoles herself with this; she attempts to find consolation so as not to appear in a bad light before her parents, and after two days she appears in public.

The knight has already gone; he does battle in the war, conquers the king's enemy, takes many cities, emerges victorious from many combats, returns to court, sees his lady in the customary place, and they agree that he will ask her father for her hand in marriage in return for his services. The king does not wish to grant his request because he does not know who the knight is, but despite this, either because he abducts her or by some other means, the princess becomes his wife, and her father comes to consider this his great good fortune because he learns that this knight is the son of a valiant king, ruler of some kingdom I am not certain of because I do not believe it is on the map. The father dies, the princess inherits the kingdom, the knight, in a word, becomes king, and this is where his granting favors to his squire and to all those who helped him rise to so high an estate, comes in: he marries his squire to one of the princess's ladies-in-waiting, the one, no doubt, who acted as mediator in his love affair, and who is the daughter of a very prominent duke."[8]

"That's what I want, honestly," said Sancho, "and that's what I'm counting on, and everything will happen exactly to the letter because now your grace calls yourself *The Knight of the Sorrowful Face*."

"Do not doubt it, Sancho," replied Don Quixote. "For in the same manner and by the same means as I have recounted, knights errant rise and have risen to be kings and emperors. All we need do now is to see which king of Christians or heathens is waging a war and has a beautiful daughter; but there will be time to think about this, for, as I have told you, first one must win fame elsewhere before arriving at court. There is also something else: in the event we find a king at war who has a beautiful daughter, and I have won incredible fame throughout the universe, I do not know how it can be discovered that I am of royal lineage, or, at least, a second cousin to the emperor; the king will not wish to give me his daughter's hand in marriage unless he is very certain of this first, no matter how meritorious my famous deeds; as a consequence, for this reason, I fear I shall lose what my arm so justly deserves. It is certainly true that I am a gentleman of known lineage, with proprietary rights to an ancestral home, and entitlement to a payment of five hundred *sueldos*,[9]

8. It should be noted that Don Quixote's tale is a perfect plot summary of a novel of chivalry.

9. Under certain circumstances, it was a privilege of the gentry to collect five hundred *sueldos* as recompense for damages or injuries.

and it well might be that the wise man who writes my history can elucidate my parentage and ancestry in such a way that I shall find myself to
be a descendant, five or six times removed, of a king. Because I want you
to know, Sancho, that there are two kinds of lineage in the world: some
who trace and derive their ancestry from princes and monarchs, which
time has gradually undone, and in the end they finish in a point, like a
pyramid turned upside down; others have their origin in lowborn people,
and they rise by degrees until they become great lords. Which means
that the difference between them is that some were and no longer are,
and others are what they once were not; I might be one of these, and it
might turn out that I had a great and famous beginning, which ought to
satisfy the king, my future father-in-law; if it does not, the princess will
love me so much despite her father that he, knowing full well that I am
the son of a water-carrier, will accept me as her lord and husband; if he
does not, this is where abducting her and taking her wherever I choose
comes in, for either time or death will put an end to her parents' anger."

"And that's where something else comes in, too," said Sancho, "because some wicked people say: 'Don't ask as a favor what you can take by
force,' though what fits even better is: 'Escaping punishment is worth
more than the pleading of good men.' I say this because if my lord the
king, your grace's father-in-law, does not agree to giving you my lady the
princess, there's nothing else to do, like your grace says, but abduct her
and hide her away. But the trouble with that is that until you make peace
and calmly enjoy the kingdom, the poor squire may be starving for favors. Unless the go-between lady-in-waiting, who will be his wife, es-
capes with the princess, and he suffers misfortunes with her until heaven
wills otherwise, because it well may be, I think, that his master will give
her to him as his legitimate wife."

"No one can deny him that," said Don Quixote.

"Well, since that's the case," responded Sancho, "the best thing is to
commend ourselves to God and let fate take us wherever it chooses."

"May God grant," replied Don Quixote, "what I desire and what you,
Sancho, need, and let him be base who thinks himself base."

"God's will be done," said Sancho, "for I am an Old Christian, and
that alone is enough for me to be a count."

"More than enough," said Don Quixote, "and even if you were not, it
would not change anything, because when I am king I can certainly
grant you nobility without your buying it or serving me in any way. Because when you are made a count, you will find that you are a gentleman,

too, and no matter what people say, they will have to call you lord, even if they do not wish to."

"And by my faith, I'll know how to carry off that tittle!" said Sancho.

"You mean *title*, not *tittle*," said his master.

"Whatever it is," responded Sancho Panza. "I say that I'll know very well how to manage it, because, by my faith, once I was the beadle of a brotherhood, and the beadle's outfit looked so good on me that everybody said I looked like I could be the steward of the brotherhood. Well, what will happen when I put a duke's cape on my back, or dress in gold and pearls, like a foreign count? I think they'll be coming to see me for a hundred leagues around."

"You will look fine," said Don Quixote, "but it will be necessary for you to shave your beard often; yours is so heavy, tangled, and unkempt that unless you shave with a razor at least every other day, people will see what you are from as far away as you can shoot a flintlock."

"That's easy," said Sancho. "All I have to do is hire a barber and keep him in my house. And if I need to, I can have him follow along behind me, like a grandee's groom."

"But, how do you know," asked Don Quixote, "that grandees have their grooms follow them?"

"I'll tell you," responded Sancho. "Years ago I spent a month not far from court, and there I saw a very small gentleman walking, and people said he was a grandee, and a man rode behind him no matter how many turns he made, and he looked like he was his tail. I asked why the man didn't catch up but always came behind him. They told me he was the groom, and it was the custom of grandees to have their grooms follow behind. And since then I've know it so well that I've never forgotten it."

"I say that you are correct," said Don Quixote, "and in the same way you can have your barber follow behind you, for not all customs came into use or were invented at the same time, and you may be the first count to have his barber follow behind him, for you need greater confidence in the man who shaves you than in the one who saddles your horse."

"Just leave the barber to me," said Sancho, "and your grace can take care of becoming a king and making me a count."

"That is what I shall do," responded Don Quixote.

And looking up, he saw what will be recounted in the next chapter.

CHAPTER XXII

Regarding the liberty that Don Quixote gave to many unfortunate men who,
against their wills, were being taken where they did not wish to go

It is recounted by Cide Hamete Benengeli, the Arabic and Manchegan author, in this most serious, high-sounding, detailed, sweet, and inventive history, that following the conversation between the famous Don Quixote of La Mancha and Sancho Panza, his squire, which is referred to at the end of chapter XXI, Don Quixote looked up and saw coming toward him on the same road he was traveling approximately twelve men on foot, strung together by their necks, like beads on a great iron chain, and all of them wearing manacles. Accompanying them were two men on horseback and two on foot; the ones on horseback had flintlocks, and those on foot carried javelins and swords; as soon as Sancho Panza saw them, he said:

"This is a chain of galley slaves, people forced by the king to go to the galleys."

"What do you mean, forced?" asked Don Quixote. "Is it possible that the king forces anyone?"

"I'm not saying that," responded Sancho, "but these are people who, because of their crimes, have been condemned to serve the king in the galleys, by force."

"In short," replied Don Quixote, "for whatever reason, these people are being taken by force and not of their own free will."

"That's right," said Sancho.

"Well, in that case," said his master, "here it is fitting to put into practice my profession: to right wrongs and come to the aid and assistance of the wretched."

"Your grace shouldn't forget," said Sancho, "that justice, which is the king himself, does not force or do wrong to such people, but sentences them as punishment for their crimes."

By now the chain of galley slaves had reached them, and Don Quixote, with very courteous speech, asked those who were guarding them to be so kind as to inform him and tell him the reason or reasons those people were being taken away in that fashion.

One of the mounted guards responded that they were galley slaves, His Majesty's prisoners who were condemned to the galleys, and there was nothing more to say and nothing else he had to know.

"Even so," replied Don Quixote, "I should like to know the particular reason for each one's misfortune."

To these words he added others so civil and discreet to persuade them to tell him what he wished to hear that the other mounted guard said:

"Although we have the record and certificate of sentence of each of these wretched men, this is not the proper time to stop and take them out and read them; your grace may approach and question the prisoners, and they will tell you themselves if they wish to, and they will, because these are people who take pleasure in doing and saying false and wicked things."

With this authorization, which Don Quixote would have taken even if it had not been granted to him, he approached the chain and asked the first man what sins he had committed to be taken away in so unpleasant a manner. He responded that it was on account of his being a lover.

"Is that all?" replied Don Quixote. "If they throw men in the galleys for being lovers, I should have been rowing in one long ago."

"It isn't the kind of love your grace is thinking about," said the galley slave. "Mine was a great love for a laundry basket filled with linen, and I loved it so much and embraced it so tightly that if the law hadn't taken it from me by force, to this day I wouldn't have let go of it willingly. I was caught red-handed, there was no need for torture, the trial concluded, they kissed my back a hundred times, gave me three in the gurapas, and that was the end of that."[1]

"What are gurapas?" asked Don Quixote.

"Gurapas are galleys," responded the galley slave.

He was a young man, about twenty-four years old, who said he was a native of Piedrahíta. Don Quixote asked the same question of the sec-

---

1. The speech of the galley slaves is peppered with underworld slang. Here, for example, the convict says that his sentence was a hundred lashes plus a term of three years in the galleys.

ond man, who was so downcast and melancholy he did not say a word, but the first prisoner responded for him and said:

"This man, Señor, is being taken away for being a canary, I mean a musician and singer."

"What?" Don Quixote repeated. "Men also go to the galleys for being musicians and singers?"

"Yes, Señor," responded the galley slave, "because there's nothing worse than singing when you're in difficulty."

"But I have heard it said," said Don Quixote, "that troubles take wing for the man who can sing."

"Here just the opposite is true," said the galley slave. "Warble once, and you weep the rest of your days."

"I do not understand," said Don Quixote.

But one of the guards told him:

"Señor, among these *non sancta* people, singing when you're in difficulty means confessing under torture. They tortured this sinner and he confessed his crime, which was rustling, or stealing livestock, and because he confessed he was sentenced to six years in the galleys, plus two hundred lashes, which he already bears on his back; he's always very downhearted and sad because the rest of the thieves, the ones he left behind and the ones who are traveling with him, abuse and humiliate and insult him, and think very little of him, because he confessed and didn't have the courage to say his nos. Because they say *no* has even fewer letters than *yes*, and a criminal is very lucky when his life or death depends on his own words and not on those of witnesses, or on evidence, and in my opinion, they're not too far off the mark."

"That is my understanding as well," responded Don Quixote.

He passed on to the third prisoner and asked the question he had asked the others, and the man responded immediately, with great assurance, and said:

"I'm going to my ladies the gurapas for five years because I didn't have ten gold *ducados*."

"I should gladly give twenty," said Don Quixote, "to free you from this sorrowful burden."

"That seems to me," responded the galley slave, "like a man who has money in the middle of the ocean and is dying of hunger and doesn't have a place where he can buy what he needs. I say this because if I'd had those twenty *ducados* your grace is offering me now at the right time, I'd have greased the quill of the clerk and sharpened the wits of my attorney, and today I'd be in the middle of the Plaza de Zocodover in Toledo and not on this road, chained up like a greyhound; but God is great: all you need is patience."

Don Quixote passed on to the fourth prisoner, a man of venerable countenance with a white beard that hung down to his chest; hearing himself asked the reason for his being there, he began to weep and did not say a word in reply; but the fifth prisoner served as his interpreter and said:

"This honest man is going to the galleys for four years, having been paraded through the usual streets in robes of state and on horseback."[2]

"That, it seems to me," said Sancho Panza, "means he was shamed in public."

"That's true," replied the galley slave. "And the crime he was punished for was trading in ears, and even in entire bodies. In other words, I mean that this gentleman is going to the galleys for being a go-between,[3] and for having a hint and a touch of the sorcerer about him."

"If you had not added that hint and touch," said Don Quixote, "for simply being an honest go-between, he does not deserve to be sent to the galleys to row, but to lead and command. Because the position of go-between is not for just anyone; it is an office for the discreet, one that is very necessary in a well-ordered nation and should not be practiced except by the wellborn; there should be supervisors and examiners of go-betweens, as there are for other professions, with a fixed number of known appointees, similar to brokers on the exchange, and in this way many evils would be avoided which are caused because this practice and profession is filled with idiotic and dim-witted people, such as foolish women, pages, and rascals with few years and little experience; when the occasion demands that they find a solution to an important problem, they allow the crumbs to freeze between their hand and their mouth and do not know their right hand from their left. I should like to continue and give reasons why it is appropriate to choose carefully those who fulfill so necessary a function in the nation, but this is not the proper place: one day I shall speak about it to someone who can remedy the situation. For now I shall say only that the sorrow caused in me at seeing this old white head and venerable face in so much distress for being a go-between is mitigated by his being a sorcerer, although I know very well there is no sorcery in the world that can move and compel our desires, as

2. The allusion is to the public flogging and humiliation of convicted criminals.

3. There is a certain intentional confusion or ambiguity regarding "go-between" in the ensuing dialogue, where it alternately implies "matchmaker" and "procurer."

some simpleminded folk believe; our will is free, and there is no herb or
spell that can force it. What certain foolish women and lying scoundrels
do is prepare concoctions and poisons with which they drive men mad,
claiming they have the power to make one person love another, when, as
I say, it is impossible to compel desire."

"That's true," said the old man, "and in fact, Señor, in the matter of
sorcery I was innocent; in the matter of being a go-between, I could not
deny it. But I never thought I was doing wrong: my entire intention was
for everybody to be happy and to live in peace and harmony, without discord or distress; but this virtuous desire did not prevent me from being
sent to a place from which I do not expect to return, given the burden
of my years and a urinary problem that does not give me a moment's
peace."

And here he began to weep again, as he had earlier, and Sancho felt
so much compassion for him that he took a four-*real* coin from inside his
shirt and gave it to him as alms.

Don Quixote moved on and asked another prisoner his crime, and he
responded with not less but much more spirit and wit than the previous
man:

"I'm here because I made too merry with two girls who were cousins of
mine, and with two other sisters who weren't mine; in short, I made so
merry with all of them, and the merriment complicated my family relations so much, that not even the devil can straighten it out. The case was
proved, nobody showed me favor, I had no money, I almost had my gullet
in a noose, they sentenced me to six years in the galleys, and I agreed: it's
a punishment for my crime; I'm young; just let me stay alive, because
where there's life there's hope. If your grace, Señor, has something to help
these poor men, God will reward you in heaven, and here on earth we'll
be sure to ask God in our devotions that the life and well-being of your
grace be as long-lasting and as fine as your meritorious person deserves."

He was dressed as a student, and one of the guards said he was a great
talker and clever in Latin.

Behind all of them came a man of about thirty who was very good-
looking except that one eye tended to veer slightly toward the other. He
was shackled differently from the rest, because around his foot was a
chain so large it encircled his entire body, and there were two fetters
around his neck, one attached to the chain and the other, the kind
called a keeper or a brace,[4] from which there hung two irons that

4. A kind of metal collar placed under the chin, which prevented a prisoner from lowering his head.

reached to his waist, and on these were two manacles holding his hands and locked with a heavy padlock, so that he could not raise his hands to his mouth or lower his head to his hands. Don Quixote asked why that man wore so many more shackles than the others. The guard responded that it was because he alone had committed more crimes than all the rest combined, and was so daring and such a great villain that even though he was bound in this way, they still did not feel secure about him and were afraid he would escape.

"What crimes can they be," said Don Quixote, "if they have deserved no greater punishment than his being sent to the galleys?"

"He's going for ten years," replied the guard, "which is like a civil death. All you need to know is that this is the famous Ginés de Pasamonte, also known as Ginesillo de Parapilla."

"Señor Commissary," the galley slave said, "just take it easy and let's not go around dropping all kinds of names and surnames. My name is Ginés, not Ginesillo, and my family is from Pasamonte, not Parapilla, as you've said; and if each man looks to his own affairs, he'll have plenty to tend to."

"Keep a civil tongue," replied the commissary, "you great thief, unless you want me to shut you up in a way you won't like."

"It certainly seems," responded the galley slave, "that man proposes and God disposes, but one day somebody will know whether or not my name is Ginesillo de Parapilla."

"Well, don't they call you that, you liar?" said the guard.

"They do," responded Ginés, "but I'll make sure they don't, or I'll tear out their hair and they know where. Señor, if you have anything to give us, give it and go with God; your wanting to know so much about other people's lives is becoming irritating, but if you want to know about mine, know that I'm Ginés de Pasamonte, whose life has been written by these very fingers."[5]

"He's telling the truth," said the commissary. "He wrote his own history himself, as fine as you please, and he pawned the book for two hundred *reales* and left it in prison."

"And I intend to redeem it," said Ginés, "even for two hundred *ducados*."

"Is it that good?" said Don Quixote.

5. Cervantes is alluding to the picaresque novel in Ginés's discussion of his book, just as he suggests the pastoral in the story of Marcela. These genres, along with novels of chivalry, were the most popular forms of prose fiction in Spain during the sixteenth century.

"It's so good," responded Ginés, "that it's too bad for *Lazarillo de Tormes* and all the other books of that genre that have been or will be written. What I can tell your grace is that it deals with truths, and they are truths so appealing and entertaining that no lies can equal them."

"And what is the title of the book?" asked Don Quixote.

"The Life of Ginés de Pasamonte," Ginés replied.

"And is it finished?" asked Don Quixote.

"How can it be finished," he responded, "if my life isn't finished yet? What I've written goes from my birth to the moment when they sentenced me to the galleys this last time."

"Then you have been there before?" said Don Quixote.

"To serve God and the king, I've already spent four years on the galleys, and I know the taste of the hardtack and the overseer's whip," responded Ginés. "And I'm not too sorry to go there, because I'll have time to finish my book, for I still have lots of things to say, and on the galleys of Spain there's more leisure than I'll need, though I don't need much for what I have to write because I know it by heart."

"You seem clever," said Don Quixote.

"And unfortunate," responded Ginés, "because misfortunes always pursue the talented."

"They pursue villains," said the commissary.

"I've already told you, Señor Commissary," responded Pasamonte, "to take it easy; those gentlemen didn't give you that staff of office for you to abuse us poor wretches but to lead and guide us to wherever His Majesty commands. If not, by the life of . . . Enough! One day those dark stains at the inn may come to light, so let's all hold our tongues, and live well, and speak better, and keep walking; the joke's gone on too long."

The commissary raised his staff to strike Pasamonte in response to his threats, but Don Quixote placed himself between them and asked that he not abuse the prisoner, for it was not surprising that a man whose hands were so tightly bound would have a rather loose tongue. And turning to all those on the chain, he said:

"From everything you have said to me, dear brothers, I deduce that although you are being punished for your faults, the penalties you are about to suffer are not to your liking, and you go to them unwillingly and involuntarily; it might be that the lack of courage this one showed under torture, that one's need of money, another's lack of favor, and finally, the twisted judgment of the judge, have been the reason for your ruination, and for not having justice on your side. All of which is pictured in my mind, and is telling, persuading, and even compelling me to show to all of you the reason that heaven put me in the world and made me profess the order of chivalry, which I do profess, and take the vow I took to favor those in need and those oppressed by the powerful. But, because I know that one of the rules of prudence is that what can be done by good means should not be done by bad, I want to ask these gentlemen, the guards and the commissary, to be so good as to unchain you and let you go in peace; there will be no lack of other men to serve the king under better circumstances, for to me it seems harsh to make slaves of those whom God and nature made free. Furthermore, these poor wretches have done nothing against you gentlemen. Each man must bear his own sin; there is a God in heaven who does not fail to punish the wicked or reward the good, and it is not right for honorable men to persecute other men who have not harmed them. I ask this quietly and calmly because if you comply, I shall have reason to thank you, and if you do not comply willingly, this lance and this sword, and the valor of this my arm, will force you to comply against your will."

"A fine piece of nonsense!" responded the commissary. "He's finally come out with it! He wants us to let the king's prisoners go, as if we had the authority to free them or he had the authority to order us to do so! Your grace, Señor, be on your way, and straighten that basin you're wearing on your head, and don't go around looking for a three-legged cat."[6]

"You are the cat, the rat, and the scoundrel!" responded Don Quixote.

Speaking and acting were all one, and he charged so quickly that he did not give the commissary time to defend himself and knocked him to the ground, wounding him with a thrust of his lance, and it was fortunate for Don Quixote that he did, for this was the man holding the flintlock. The other guards were stunned, overwhelmed by this unexpected turn of events, but they came to their senses, and those on horseback put their hands on their swords, and those on foot grasped their javelins, and they charged Don Quixote, who very calmly waited for them; matters undoubtedly would have gone badly for him if the galley slaves, seeing the opportunity presented to them to obtain their freedom, had not attempted to achieve it by breaking the chain to which they were fettered. So great was the confusion that the guards, turning now to the galley slaves, who were breaking free, and now to Don Quixote, who was attacking them, did nothing of any use.

---

6. A traditional expression that means, "Don't go looking for trouble."

Sancho, for his part, helped to free Ginés de Pasamonte, who was the first to leap into the battle free and unencumbered, and, rushing at the fallen commissary, he took his sword and flintlock, and by pointing it at one and aiming it at another, without ever firing he cleared the field of guards because they all fled from Pasamonte's flintlock and from the shower of stones that the galley slaves, who were free by now, were hurling at them.

This made Sancho very sad, because it seemed to him that those who were fleeing would inform the Holy Brotherhood, who would then come looking for the lawbreakers, sounding the alarm, and he told this to his master and begged that they leave immediately and hide in the mountains, which were not far away.

"That is all very well and good," said Don Quixote, "but I know what must be done now."

And calling to all the galley slaves, who were in a state of frenzy and had stripped the commissary down to his skin, they gathered round to see what he wanted of them, and he said:

"It is customary for wellborn people to give thanks for the benefits they receive, and one of the sins that most offends God is ingratitude. I say this, Señores, because you have already seen and had manifest proof of what you have received from me, and in payment it is my wish and desire that, bearing the chain which I removed from your necks, you immediately set out for the city of Toboso, and there appear before the lady Dulcinea of Toboso, and say that her knight, he of the Sorrowful Face, commends himself to her, and you will tell her, point by point, every detail of this famous adventure, up to the moment when you achieved your desired freedom; having done this, you may go wherever you wish, and may good fortune go with you."

Ginés de Pasamonte responded for all of them, and he said:

"What your grace, our lord and liberator, orders us to do, is absolutely impossible for us to carry out, because we cannot travel the roads together but must go our separate ways, each man on his own, trying to burrow into the bowels of the earth so as not to be found by the Holy Brotherhood, who, beyond any doubt, will come looking for us. What your grace can do, and it is right and proper that you do so, is to change this service and tribute to the lady Dulcinea of Toboso into a certain number of Ave Marías and Credos, which we will say on your grace's behalf, and this is something that can be done night or day, fleeing or at rest, at peace or at war; but to think that we will go back to our miseries in Egypt, I mean to say, that we will take up our chain and set out for

Toboso, is to think that night has fallen now when it is not yet ten in the morning; asking that of us is like asking pears of an elm tree."

"Well, then, I do swear," said Don Quixote, his wrath rising, "Don Whoreson, Don Ginesillo de Paropillo, or whatever your name is, that you will go alone, your tail between your legs, and the entire chain on your back!"

Pasamonte was not a man of great forbearance; already aware that Don Quixote was not very sane, for he had done something so foolish as wanting to give them their freedom, and seeing himself spoken to in this way, he winked at his companions, and, moving a short distance away, they began to throw so many stones at Don Quixote that he could not even manage to protect himself with his shield, and poor Rocinante paid no more attention to his master's spurs than if he had been made of bronze. Sancho hid behind his donkey, protecting himself in this way from the hailstorm of rocks pouring down on them. Don Quixote could not shield himself as well as Sancho, for so many stones found their mark on his body, and with so much force, that they knocked him to the ground; as soon as he had fallen, the student attacked him and took the basin from his head and struck him three or four blows with it on his shoulders and smashed it an equal number of times on the ground until he had shattered it. They took a doublet he wore over his armor and would have taken his hose if the greaves of his leg armor had not prevented them from doing so. From Sancho they took his coat, leaving him in shirtsleeves; then, after dividing among themselves the other spoils of battle, each went his separate way, more concerned with escaping the Brotherhood, which they feared, than with picking up the chain and carrying it to the lady Dulcinea of Toboso.

The donkey and Rocinante, Sancho and Don Quixote, were left alone; the donkey, pensive, with bowed head, twitching his ears from time to time, thinking that the tempest of stones had not yet ended and was still falling around his ears; Rocinante, lying beside his master, for he too had fallen to the ground in the shower of stones; Sancho, in his shirtsleeves and afraid of the Holy Brotherhood; Don Quixote, grief-stricken at seeing himself so injured by the very people for whom he had done so much good.

CHAPTER XXIII

Regarding what befell the famous Don Quixote in the Sierra Morena, which was one of the strangest adventures recounted in this true history

Seeing himself so injured, Don Quixote said to his squire:

"I have always heard, Sancho, that doing good to the lowborn is throwing water into the sea. If I had believed what you told me, I should have avoided this grief, but what is done is done, and so patience, and let it be a lesson for the future."

"Your grace will learn the lesson," responded Sancho, "the same way I'm a Turk; but since you say that if you had believed me this trouble could have been avoided, believe me now and avoid one even greater; I'm telling you that you can't use chivalries with the Holy Brotherhood because they wouldn't give two *maravedís* for all the knights errant in the world; you should also know that their arrows already seem to be buzzing past my ears."

"You are naturally a coward, Sancho," said Don Quixote, "but so that you will not say that I am stubborn and never do as you advise, on this occasion I want to take your advice and withdraw from the ferocity that frightens you so, but it must be on one condition: that never, in life or in death, are you to tell anyone that I withdrew and retreated from this danger out of fear, but only to satisfy your pleas, and if you say otherwise you will be lying, and from now until then, and then until now, I shall deny it and say that you lie, and will lie every time you think or say it. And do not reply, for merely thinking that I am withdrawing and retreating from any danger, especially this one, which seems to carry with it some small shadow of fear, is enough to make me want to remain and wait here alone, not only for the Holy Brotherhood which you have mentioned and fear so much, but for the brothers

of the twelve tribes of Israel, and the seven Maccabees, and Castor and
Pollux, and all the brothers and brotherhoods that there are in the
world."

"Señor," responded Sancho, "withdrawing is not running away, and
waiting is not sensible when danger outweighs hope, and wise men know
to save something for tomorrow and not risk everything in a single day.
And you should know that even though I'm rough and lowborn, I still
know something about what people call proper behavior, and so don't
repent of taking my advice but mount Rocinante if you can, and if not
I'll help you, and follow me, because my brains tell me we need our feet
now more than our hands."

Don Quixote mounted, not saying another word, and with Sancho
leading the way on his donkey, they entered a part of the Sierra Morena
that was close by, it being Sancho's intention to cross the entire range
and come out at Viso, or Almodóvar del Campo, and hide for a few days
in that rugged terrain and not be found if the Brotherhood came looking
for them. He had been encouraged to do so when he saw that the provisions carried on his donkey had escaped the skirmish with the galley
slaves, which he deemed a miracle considering everything else they had
taken away.[1]

As soon as Don Quixote entered those mountains his heart filled
with joy, for it was a landscape that seemed suited to the adventures he
was seeking. What he recalled were the marvelous events that had befallen knights errant in similarly desolate and wild places. He rode along,
thinking of these things, so enthralled and transported that he thought
of nothing else. And Sancho's only care—after deciding that the way
was safe—was to satisfy his stomach with what remained of their clerical
spoils; and so he rode behind his master, sitting sidesaddle on his donkey
as he took things out of a sack and packed them away in his belly, and
did not care at all about finding any greater fortune as long as he could go
along in this fashion.

Then he looked up and saw that his master had stopped and with the
tip of his lance was attempting to lift some kind of bundle lying on
the ground, and therefore he hurried to offer his help, if necessary; he

---

1. Martín de Riquer faithfully follows the first edition of *Don Quixote*, published in 1605; the second
edition, printed a few months later by Juan de la Cuesta, the same printer, introduces a brief passage
here, indicating that Ginés de Pasamonte, who is also in the mountains, steals Sancho's donkey.
The thorny and ambiguous question of why Cervantes does not mention the theft of the donkey in
the first edition (usually attributed to an author's oversight or a printer's error) is alluded to in the
second part of *Don Quixote*, published in 1615.

reached Don Quixote just as he lifted, with the tip of his lance, a saddle cushion with a traveling case attached to it, half rotting, or completely rotting and falling to pieces, but weighing so much that Sancho had to dismount and pick them up, and his master told him to see what was in the traveling case.

Sancho did so very quickly, and although the case was closed with a chain and padlock, it was so worn and rotten that he could see what was inside: four shirts of fine cambric and some other items of linen as curious as they were clean, and in a handkerchief he found a nice pile of gold *escudos*; and when he saw them, he said:

"Glory be to heaven for sending us a profitable adventure!"

And, searching further, he discovered a small diary that was richly decorated. Don Quixote asked for this but told him to keep the money for himself. Sancho kissed his hands in gratitude and emptied the case of its linen, which he packed away in the sack of provisions. All of this was observed by Don Quixote, who said:

"It seems to me, Sancho, and it cannot be otherwise, that some traveler lost his way in these mountains and was set upon by ruffians, who must have killed him and carried him to this remote spot to bury him."

"That can't be right," responded Sancho, "because if they were thieves, they wouldn't have left the money here."

"That is true," said Don Quixote, "and therefore I cannot guess or surmise what this may be; but wait: we shall see if there is something written in this diary that will allow us to investigate and learn what we wish to know."

He opened the book, and the first thing he found there, in a kind of rough draft, though written in a very fine hand, was a sonnet, and reading aloud so that Sancho could hear the poem, he read:

> Either Love has too little understanding,
> or too much cruelty, or else my grief's
> not equal to its cause though it condemns me
> to suffer this, the harshest kind of torment.
>
> But if Love is a god, then logic tells us
> that he is ignorant of nothing, teaches
> that a god's not cruel. Then, who has ordained
> this terrible anguish that I adore?
>
> If I say you, Phyllis, then I am wrong,
> for evil has no place in so much good,

nor does my woe rain down on me from heav'n.
        Soon I must die, of that I can be sure;
    when the cause of the sickness is unknown
    only a miracle can find the cure.

"From this poem," said Sancho, "you can't learn anything, unless that filly there's the one that leads the way out of the tangle."

"What filly?" said Don Quixote.

"It seems to me," said Sancho, "that your grace mentioned some *filly* there."

"I said *Phyllis*," responded Don Quixote, "which is undoubtedly the name of the lady about whom the author of this sonnet is complaining; and, by my faith, he seems a reasonable poet, or I know little of the art."

"Then," said Sancho, "does your grace also know about poems?"

"More than you think," responded Don Quixote, "as you will see when you carry a letter, written in verse from top to bottom, to my lady Dulcinea of Toboso. Because I want you to know, Sancho, that all or most of the knights errant of a bygone day were great troubadours and great musicians; for these two talents, or endowments, I should say, are attributes of enamored knights errant. Although the truth is that the strophes of the knights of long ago have more spirit in them than skill."

"Your grace, read some more," said Sancho, "and soon you'll find something that will satisfy us."

Don Quixote turned the page and said:

"This is prose and seems to be a letter."

"The kind of letter that's a message, Señor, or the legal kind?" asked Sancho.

"It seems at first glance to be a love letter," responded Don Quixote.

"Read it aloud, your grace," said Sancho. "I really like things that have to do with love."

"I should be happy to," said Don Quixote.

And, reading it aloud, as Sancho had requested, he saw that it said:

Your false promise and my certain misfortune have taken me to a place from which news of my death will reach your ears before the words of my lament. You rejected me, O ungrateful lady, for one who has more than I, but not one of greater worth; but if virtue were the wealth that is held in high esteem, I would not envy the fortunes of others or weep for my own misfortunes. What

your beauty erected was demolished by your actions; from the former I under-
stood that you were an angel, and from the latter I know that you are a
woman. Go in peace, cause of my conflict, and may heaven grant that the de-
ceptions of your husband remain forever hidden, so that you need not repent of
what you did, nor I take my revenge for what I do not desire.

When he had finished reading the letter, Don Quixote said:

"Less from this than from the verses, one can assume that the man who wrote it is a scorned lover."

And leafing through almost the entire notebook, he found other verses and letters, some of which he could read and others not; but what they all contained were complaints, laments, suspicions, joys and sorrows, kindnesses and slights, either celebrated or wept over.

While Don Quixote was looking through the book, Sancho looked through the traveling case, and every corner of it and the cushion was searched, scrutinized, and investigated, every seam pulled apart, every tuft of wool untangled, so that nothing would be left behind for want of effort or diligence, for the *escudos* he had discovered, which amounted to more than a hundred, had awakened an enormous appetite in him. And though he did not find more than he had already found, he considered as time well spent the tossing in the blanket, the vomiting of the potion, the blessings of the staffs, the fists of the muledriver, the loss of his saddlebags, the theft of his coat, and all the hunger, thirst, and weariness he had endured in the service of his worthy lord, for it seemed to him he had been more than well-rewarded when his master favored him and presented his find to him as a gift.

The Knight of the Sorrowful Face was left with a great desire to know who the owner of the traveling case might be, supposing, on the basis of the sonnet and letter, the gold coins and excellent shirts, that he must be a wellborn and noble lover driven to some desperate end by his lady's scorn and harsh treatment. But since no person appeared in that desolate and rugged place whom he could question, his only concern was to move on, following no other path than the one chosen by Rocinante, which tended to be the one the horse could travel most easily, and always imagining that there was bound to be some extraordinary adventure waiting for him in the thickets.

Riding along, thinking these thoughts, at the top of a hill that lay ahead of him Don Quixote saw a man leaping from crag to crag and bush to bush with uncommon speed. The man appeared to be half-dressed, and he had a heavy black beard, long disheveled hair, no shoes on his feet, and nothing at all on his calves; his thighs were covered by breeches that seemed to be made of tawny velvet but were so tattered and torn that in many places his skin showed through. His head was bare, and though he moved with the speed we have mentioned, the Knight of the Sorrowful Face saw and noted all these details; he tried to follow him but could not because it was beyond the strength of Rocinante to travel that rugged ground, especially since he was by nature slow-paced and phlegmatic. Then Don Quixote imagined that the man was the owner of the saddle cushion and traveling case, and he resolved to look for him until he found him, even if he was obliged to spend a year in those mountains, and so he ordered Sancho to get off his donkey and go around one part of the mountain, and he would go around the other, and in this way they might encounter the man who had so quickly disappeared from view.

"I can't do that," responded Sancho, "because when I leave your grace I'm filled with fear that plagues me with a thousand different kinds of sudden frights and visions. And I just want to let you know this, so that from now on I won't have to move a finger's width from your presence."

"So be it," said the Knight of the Sorrowful Face. "I am very pleased that you wish to take advantage of my courage, which will not fail you even if your spirit fails your body. Come now, and follow after me slowly, or however you can, and let your eyes be like lanterns; we shall circle round this hillock, and perhaps we shall come across that man we saw who is, beyond any doubt, the owner of what we have found."

To which Sancho responded:

"It would be much better not to look for him, because if we find him and he's the owner of the money, of course I'll have to return it to him, so it would be better not to undertake a useless task, and let me keep it in good faith until its rightful owner appears in a way that's not so strange or troublesome, and maybe by that time I'll have spent it, and then by the king's law I won't have to pay because I'll be a pauper."

"You are mistaken about that, Sancho," responded Don Quixote, "for now that we have begun to suspect who the owner is, and have had him practically in front of us, we are obliged to search for him and return the money, and if we do not search for him, the strong suspicion we have that he is the owner makes us as culpable as if he really were. Therefore, Sancho my friend, do not let the search for him grieve you, for my grief will be taken away if I find him."

And so he spurred Rocinante, and Sancho followed on his customary donkey,[2] and when they had ridden around part of the mountain, they discovered in a stream, lying dead and half-eaten by dogs and pecked at by crows, a mule that was saddled and bridled, which was further confirmation of their suspicion that the fleeing man was the owner of both the mule and the saddle cushion.

As they were looking at the mule, they heard a whistle like that of a shepherd tending his flock, and suddenly, on their left, they saw a good number of goats and, behind the goats, at the top of the mountain, the goatherd, who was a very old man. Don Quixote called to him and asked him to come down. He shouted in response, asking what had brought them to this place that was rarely, if ever, visited except by goats or wolves or the other animals that lived there. Sancho responded that he should come down, and they would give him a good accounting of everything. The goatherd came down, and when he reached Don Quixote, he said:

"I'll wager you're looking at the mule that's lying dead in that gully. By my faith, it's been there for six months. Tell me: have you run across the owner?"

"We have not run across anyone," responded Don Quixote, "but we found a saddle cushion and traveling case not far from here."

"I found them, too," responded the goatherd, "but I never wanted to pick them up or go near them because I was afraid there'd be trouble and they'd say I stole them; the devil's sly, and he puts things under our feet that make us stumble and fall, and we don't know how or why."

"That's just what I say," responded Sancho. "I found them, too, and I didn't want to get within a stone's throw of them: I left them there, and there they remain, just as they were; I don't want a dog with a bell around its neck."[3]

"Tell me, my good man," said Don Quixote, "do you know who the owner of these articles might be?"

"What I can tell you," said the goatherd, "is that there's a sheepfold about three leagues from here, and about six months ago, more or less, a young gentleman came there, very courteous in his manner and bearing, riding on that same mule that's lying there dead, and with the same saddle cushion and traveling case you say you found and didn't touch. He asked us which part of this country was the most rugged and remote; we

---

2. By the third edition of *Don Quixote*, printed by Juan de la Cuesta, the references to Sancho's donkey in the Sierra Morena had been deleted; here, for example, the revised text says that Sancho was on foot and carrying the donkey's load, "thanks to Ginesillo de Pasamonte."

3. A traditional expression that means "I don't want things that can cause trouble."

told him it was here where we are now, and that's the truth, because if you go in just half a league more, maybe you won't be able to find your way out; I'm surprised you even got this far, because there's no road or path that leads to this spot. Anyway, as I was saying, when the young man heard our answer, he turned and rode off to the place we told him about, leaving us all pleased by his good looks and surprised at his question and at how fast we saw him riding back toward the sierra; and then we didn't see him again until a few days later, when he crossed paths with one of our shepherds, and without saying a word he went up to him and began to punch and kick him, and then he went to the donkey with the provisions and took all the bread and cheese it was carrying; and then, with that strange speed of his, he ran back and hid in the sierra.

When some of us goatherds heard about it, we went and looked for him for almost two days in the wildest part of the sierra, and then we found him in the hollow of a huge old cork tree. He came out as gentle as you please, and his clothes were torn and his face was so changed and burned by the sun that we hardly recognized him, but we had seen his clothes before, and even though they were torn, we knew he was the one we were looking for. He greeted us courteously, and in a few polite words he told us not to be surprised at seeing him in that state because he was performing a certain penance that had been imposed on him because of his many sins. We begged him to tell us who he was, but we could never persuade him to. We also asked that whenever he needed food, for he couldn't get along without it, he should let us know where we could find him, and if he didn't like that idea, at least he ought to come and ask the shepherds for food and not take it from them by force. He thanked us for our offer, asked our forgiveness for his earlier attacks, and said that from then on he'd beg food in God's name and not bother anybody at all. As for his dwelling, he said he slept wherever he could find a place when night fell, and when he finished speaking he began to cry so pitifully that even if we'd been made of stone, those of us listening to him would have had to join him, considering how he looked the first time we saw him and how he looked now. Because, as I told you, he was a very handsome and pleasant young man, and his courteous and agreeable words showed that he was wellborn and a gentleman, and though we were country folk, his courtesy was so great that even country folk could recognize it when we heard it.

And then, when he was talking at his best, he stopped, and fell silent, and looked down at the ground for a good long time, while we were all puzzled and didn't say anything, waiting to see how the fit would end, and feeling very sorry to see him like that, because from the way he opened his eyes wide and stared at the ground for so long, not even moving an eyelash, and then closed them, pressed his lips together, and lowered his eyebrows, we knew that some kind of craziness had come over him. He soon let us know that what we thought was true, because in a great fury he jumped up from the ground where he had been lying and attacked the man closest to him, with so much violence and so much anger that if we hadn't pulled him off, he would have beaten and bitten him to death; and as he was doing this he kept saying: 'Ah, false Fernando! Here, here is where you will pay for the wrong you did me: these hands will rip out your heart, where all the evils live and dwell together, especially fraud and deceit!' To these he added other words, and all of them spoke badly of this Fernando and accused him of being a traitor and a liar. We pulled him off, with great difficulty, and without saying another word he left us and ran off into those briars and brambles so that it was impossible for us to follow him.

From this we guessed that his crazy fits came and went, and that somebody named Fernando must have done something bad to him, so bad that it brought him to this state. All of which turned out to be true, since there have been many times when he comes out onto the path, sometimes to ask the shepherds to give him something to eat, and other times to take it from them by force, because when the craziness is on him, even though the shepherds offer food to him willingly, he doesn't accept it but punches them and steals it from them, and when he's in his right mind he asks for the food in God's name, courteously and reasonably, and offers up many thanks for it, and some few tears. And the truth is, Señores," the goatherd continued, "that yesterday four other herders and I, two helpers and two friends of mine, decided that we would look for him until we found him, and after we found him, whether he went willingly or we had to force him, we'd take him to the town of Almodóvar, which is eight leagues from here, and there we'd have him cured, if his sickness has a cure, or find out who he is when he's in his right mind, and if he has kinfolk we can tell about his misfortune. And this, Señores, is all I can tell you about what you asked me, and you should know that the owner of the articles you found is the same half-dressed man you saw running so fast." For Don Quixote had already told him how he had seen the man leaping among the crags of the sierra.

Don Quixote was astonished at what he had heard from the goatherd and more desirous than ever to know who the unfortunate madman was, and he resolved to do what he had already thought about doing: to look for him all over the mountains, searching every corner and cave until he found him. But Fate did what he was planning and hoping to do, and did it better, because at that very instant, in a ravine that led to the place where they were standing, the young man he was seeking appeared, walking and talking to himself and saying things that could not be understood up close, let alone from a distance. His dress was as it has been described, except that as he approached, Don Quixote saw that a torn leather jerkin he was wearing had been tanned with ambergris, which led him to conclude that a person who wore such clothing could not be of low category.

When the young man reached them, he greeted them in a hoarse and rasping voice, but with great courtesy. Don Quixote returned the greetings with no less courtesy, and, after dismounting Rocinante, with a gallant air and presence he went forward to embrace him and held him close for a long while, as if he had known him for some time. The other man, whom we can call *The Ragged One of the Gloomy Face*—as Don Quixote is *He of the Sorrowful One*—allowed himself to be embraced, then stepped back, placed his hands on Don Quixote's shoulders, and stood looking at him as if wanting to see if he knew him, no less astonished, perhaps, at the face, form, and arms of Don Quixote than Don Quixote was at the sight of him. Finally, the first to speak after their embrace was the Ragged One, and he said what will now be recounted.

CHAPTER XXIV

In which the adventure of the Sierra Morena continues

The history says that Don Quixote paid very close attention to what was said by the tattered Knight of the Sierra, who began to speak, saying:

"Most certainly, Señor, whoever you may be, for I do not know you, I thank you for the demonstrations of affection and courtesy which you have shown me, and I wish I were in a position to respond with more than my desire to the goodwill you have displayed in your warm welcome; but my fate does not choose to give me anything with which to reciprocate your kindness except my sincere wish to do so."

"And mine," responded Don Quixote, "is to serve you; indeed, I had resolved not to leave these mountains until I had found you and learned from you if your sorrow, which your strange way of life indicates you are suffering, might have some kind of remedy, and if it did, to seek it with the greatest possible diligence. If your misfortune were one that had all doors closed to any sort of consolation, I intended to help you weep and lament to the best of my ability, for it is still a consolation in affliction to find someone who mourns with you. And if my good intentions deserve to be thanked with some courtesy, I entreat you, Señor, for the sake of the great courtesy I see in you, and I implore you, for the sake of the thing you have loved or do love most in this life, to tell me who you are and the reason that has compelled you to live and die in this desolate place like a wild animal, for you dwell among the beasts estranged from your true self, as demonstrated by your dress and your person. And I swear," Don Quixote added, "by the order of chivalry which I have received, though unworthy and a sinner, and by the profession of knight errantry, that if, Señor, you satisfy me in this, I shall serve you with the devotion to which I am obliged by being the man I am, whether to remedy your misfortune, if it has a remedy, or to help you lament it, as I have promised you I would."

The Knight of the Forest, who heard the Knight of the Sorrowful Face speak in this way, did nothing but look at him, and look at him again, and look at him one more time, from head to toe; and after he had looked at him very carefully, he said:

"If you have any food to give me, then give it to me in the name of God, and after I have eaten, I shall do all you ask, in gratitude for the goodwill you have shown me here."

Then Sancho from his sack and the goatherd from his pouch took out food with which the Ragged One satisfied his hunger, eating what they gave him as if he were stupefied, and so quickly that one mouthful followed immediately on the other, for he gulped them down instead of swallowing them; and while he ate, neither he nor those who were watching him said a word. When he had finished eating, he signaled to them to follow him, which they did, and he led them to a small green meadow just beyond a nearby crag. When he reached it he lay down on the grass, and the others did the same, all of this without a word, until the Ragged One, after settling comfortably in his place, said:

"If, Señores, you wish me to tell you briefly about the immensity of my misfortunes, you must promise not to interrupt the thread of my sad history with any question, or with anything else, because the moment you interrupt will be the moment my narration ends."

These words of the Ragged One brought to Don Quixote's mind the story his squire had told him, when he had not kept an accurate count of the number of goats that had crossed the river, and the story was never finished. But let us return to the Ragged One, who continued:

"I give you this warning because I would like to pass quickly through the tale of my misfortunes, since bringing them to mind only serves to add new ones, and the less you ask me, the sooner I shall finish telling you about them, though I shall not fail to relate anything of importance to the complete satisfaction of your desire."

Don Quixote promised, in the name of all the others, not to interrupt, and with this assurance the Ragged One began, saying:

"My name is Cardenio;[1] my home, one of the finest cities in Andalucía; my family, noble; my parents, wealthy; my misfortune, so great that my parents had to weep and my family grieve, but their wealth could not alleviate it, for worldly possessions can do little to remedy the afflictions sent by heaven. In that same city there lived a heaven, in which love placed all the glory I could desire: such is the beauty of Luscinda, a maiden as noble and as wealthy as I, but more fortunate and less firmly resolved than my honorable intentions merited. I loved Luscinda, I worshiped and adored her from my earliest youth, and she loved me with all the simplicity and innocence of her tender years. Our parents knew of our intentions and were not troubled by them because they saw clearly that, in time, these intentions could have no other end but our marriage, something that was practically guaranteed by the equality of our families and our fortunes. We matured, as did our love, until it seemed to Luscinda's father that, in deference to public opinion, he was obliged to deny me entrance to his house, almost imitating in this regard the parents of that same Thisbe praised so often by poets. And this denial added more flames to the fire and more ardor to our desire, because, although it silenced our tongues, it could not silence our pens, which, with greater freedom than tongues, tend to reveal to the person we love what is hidden in our soul, for often the presence of the beloved confuses and silences the most determined intention and the boldest tongue. O heavens, the letters I wrote to her! The delicate, virtuous responses I received! The songs and love poems I composed, in which I declared my soul and transcribed its sentiments, depicted its burning desires, prolonged its memories, and re-created its yearnings!

1. A lost play by Shakespeare, *The History of Cardenio*, was apparently based on Cardenio's tale. An English translation of the first part of *Don Quixote* appeared only a few years after its initial publication in 1605.

Finally, finding myself in such an agitated state, and seeing that my soul was being consumed with the desire to see her, I resolved to take action and to do in a moment what seemed necessary to achieve the prize I longed for and deserved, which was to ask her father for her hand in marriage; this I did, to which he replied by thanking me for the desire to honor him, which I had demonstrated, and the wish to honor myself with his beloved treasure; but, since my father was alive, it was his rightful duty to make the request, because if it were not wholeheartedly desired and wanted by him, Luscinda was not a woman to be taken or given furtively. I thanked him for his kindness, thinking that he was correct in what he said, and that my father would agree as soon as I told him, and with this purpose in mind, I went immediately to tell my father what I desired. When I entered the room I found him with an open letter in his hand, and before I could say a word he handed it to me and said: 'In this letter you will see, Cardenio, the desire that Duke Ricardo has to favor you.' This Duke Ricardo, Señores, as you probably know, is a grandee of Spain whose lands are the best in Andalucía. I took the letter, and read it, and it was so insistent and complimentary that even I thought it would be incorrect if my father failed to carry out what it requested, which was that he send me immediately to the duke's estate to be a companion, not a servant, to his oldest son, and the duke would be responsible for granting me the rank that would correspond to the esteem in which he held me.

I read the letter and kept silent as I read it, especially when I heard my father say: 'You will leave in two days' time, Cardenio, to do as the duke desires, and you should give thanks to God for opening the way for you to achieve what I know you deserve.' To these words he added others of fatherly advice. The time for my departure approached, I spoke one night to Luscinda and told her everything that had happened, and I did the same with her father, asking him to wait a few days and delay his response until I knew what Ricardo wanted of me; he promised he would, and she confirmed it with a thousand vows and a thousand swoons.

In short, I arrived at the estate of Duke Ricardo. I was so well-received and -treated by him that envy immediately began its work and affected the older retainers, who thought the indications the duke gave of wanting to favor me would work against them. The one who seemed happiest at my arrival was the duke's younger son, named Fernando, a gallant, charming youth, magnanimous and inclined to fall in love, who in a very short time showed so great a desire for my friendship that everyone spoke of it, and although the oldest son was fond of me and favored me, he did not go as far as Don Fernando in his affectionate treatment.

Now, since there are no secrets between friends, and the preference shown by Don Fernando was no longer preference but friendship, he told me all his thoughts, especially one, having to do with love, which was causing him some concern. He was in love with a peasant girl, one of his father's vassals, whose parents were very wealthy, and she was so beautiful, modest, discreet, and virtuous that no one who knew her could decide in which of these she showed greater excellence or distinction. These outstanding traits in the beautiful peasant so intensified the desires of Don Fernando that he had decided, in order to achieve his desires and conquer her integrity, to promise to be her husband;[2] otherwise, he would be striving for the impossible. Under the obligation imposed by his friendship, and using the best arguments I knew and the most vivid examples I could think of, I attempted to dissuade and discourage him from his intention, but seeing that it was to no avail, I resolved to tell Duke Ricardo, his father, of the matter; but Don Fernando, an astute and discerning man, suspected and feared this, for it seemed to him that I was obliged, as a good retainer, not to hide anything that could so damage the honor of my lord the duke; and so, to distract and deceive me, he said he could find no other remedy that would remove from his thoughts the beauty that held him captive than to leave for a few months, and what he desired was for the two of us to go to my father's house, and he would tell the duke that this was an opportunity to see and purchase some of the very good horses in my city, which is mother to the best in the world. As soon as I heard him say this, I was moved by my own affections to approve his plan as one of the most sensible anyone could imagine, and I would have done so even if it had not been as good, because it was an excellent opportunity and occasion for me to see my Luscinda again.

With this thought and desire, I approved his idea and supported his plan, telling him to put it into effect as quickly as possible because, in truth, absence would do its work despite the most resolute thoughts. When he told me of his proposal, he had already, as I learned later, enjoyed the peasant girl by claiming to be her husband, and he was hoping for an opportunity to disclose this at a safe distance, fearful of what his father, the duke, would do when he learned of his foolishness. And it happened that, since love in young men is, for the most part, nothing but appetite, which, having pleasure as its ultimate goal, ends when that

_____

2. A promise of marriage was considered a legally binding contract.

goal is achieved, and what seemed to be love must recede because it can-not go beyond the limits placed on it by nature, such limits not being placed on true love . . . what I mean to say is that as soon as Don Fer-nando had enjoyed the peasant girl, his longings abated and his desires cooled, and if at first he pretended to want to go away in order to remedy them, now he really wanted to leave in order not to act on them. The duke gave his permission and told me to accompany him.

We came to my city, my father gave him a welcome proper to his rank, I saw Luscinda immediately, my desires were rekindled, though they had not been dead or dampened, and, to my sorrow, I spoke of them to Don Fernando, because it seemed to me that, given the great friend-ship he had shown me, I ought not hide anything from him. I praised the beauty, grace, and discretion of Luscinda in such a way that my praise awakened in him a desire to see a maiden adorned with so many virtues. I satisfied his desire, much to my misfortune, and showed her to him one night, by the light of a candle at a window where the two of us would talk. He saw her in a dressing gown, and the sight of her made him forget all the beauty he had seen until then. He fell silent, lost all sense of his surroundings, was entranced, and, finally, fell in love to the degree that you will see in the course of the story of my afflictions.

To further heighten his desire, which he concealed from me and re-vealed only to heaven when he was alone, one day he happened to find one of her letters that asked me to ask her father for her hand, and it was so discreet, so virtuous, and so loving that when he had read it he told me that in Luscinda alone one could find concentrated the gifts of beauty and intelligence that were divided among all the other women in the world. It is certainly true, and I wish to confess now that even though I saw with what just cause Don Fernando praised Luscinda, it troubled me to hear that praise from his mouth, and I began to fear and mistrust him because not a moment went by when he did not wish to speak of Luscinda, and he would initiate the conversation about her with any far-fetched excuse, which awakened in me a certain jealousy, though not because I feared any kind of change in the goodness and good faith of Luscinda; even so, I began to be apprehensive with regard to the very future about which she gave me assurances. Don Fernando always wanted to read the letters I sent to Luscinda and the ones she sent back to me, claiming that he enjoyed the wit we both displayed. It so happened that Luscinda had asked me for a book of chivalry of which she was very fond, which was *Amadís of Gaul*."

As soon as Don Quixote heard him mention a book of chivalry, he said:

"If your grace had told me at the beginning of your history that her grace the lady Luscinda was fond of books of chivalry, no other embellishment would have been necessary to allow me to grasp the elevation of her understanding, for I would not have considered it as fine as you, Señor, have depicted it, if it had lacked the ability to enjoy such delightful reading, and so, as far as I am concerned, there is no need to use more words in declaring her beauty, worth, and understanding; by simply knowing of this fondness, I affirm her to be the most beautiful and discreet woman in the world. I would have liked, Señor, for your grace to have sent her, along with *Amadís of Gaul,* the worthy *Don Rogel of Greece,*[3] for I know that the lady Luscinda would have enjoyed Daraida and Geraya, and the shepherd Darinel's wit, and the admirable bucolic verses sung and represented by him with all charm, discretion, and eloquence. But the time may come when that lack can be corrected, and the correction can be made as soon as your grace has the goodness to return with me to my village, for there I can give you more than three hundred books, which are the joy of my soul and the delight of my life, although it occurs to me that I may no longer have a single one due to the malice of evil and envious enchanters. Your grace, forgive me for having broken our promise not to interrupt your account, but when I hear things having to do with chivalry and knights errant, I can no more not talk of them than the rays of the sun can fail to warm or those of the moon to dampen. And so, forgive me, and continue, which is the most pertinent thing now."

While Don Quixote was saying what has been said, Cardenio had lowered his head to his chest, showing signs of being lost in deep thought. And although Don Quixote asked him twice to go on with his history, he did not raise his head or say a word, but after some time had gone by he did raise his head, saying:

"I cannot help but think, nor is there anyone in the world who can make me change my mind or lead me to believe otherwise, and whoever does not think or believe so is a villain, that the great scoundrel, the surgeon Master Elisabat, was the lover of Queen Madásima."[4]

"No, by my faith!" Don Quixote responded with great wrath and an oath, as was his custom. "That is wicked, or rather, villainous: Queen

3. This is the eleventh of the books about Amadís and his descendants.

4. Queen Madásima, a character in the *Amadís of Gaul,* did not have a romantic relationship with the surgeon Elisabat.

Madásima was a very distinguished lady, and it should not be assumed that so high a princess would become the paramour of a sawbones and a quack, and whoever believes the contrary is lying, like the base scoundrel he is. And this I will make him understand, on foot or mounted, armed or unarmed, by night or by day, or in whatever manner he prefers."

Cardenio looked at him attentively, for a fit of his madness had come over him and he was in no condition to go on with his story; nor was Don Quixote prepared to hear it, so vexed was he by what he had heard about Madásima. How extraordinary, for it enraged him as if she really were his true and natural queen: that is what his perverse books had done to him! And so I say that since Cardenio was mad again, and he heard himself called liar and villain and other similar insults, he did not take it lightly, and he picked up a stone that was lying near him and with it struck such a blow to Don Quixote's chest that it knocked him flat on his back. Sancho Panza, when he saw what had been done to his master, attacked the madman with a clenched fist, and the Ragged One received him in such a way that with one blow he had Sancho lying at his feet, and then he jumped up and down on his ribs with great enthusiasm. The same fate awaited the goatherd, who tried to defend Sancho. And when Cardenio had battered and bruised them all, he left them and went, calmly and peaceably, to take refuge in the mountains.

Sancho got to his feet and was so angry at finding himself beaten for so little cause that he tried to take his revenge on the goatherd, saying it was his fault for not having warned them that the man suffered fits of madness; if they had known this, they would have been prepared and ready to defend themselves. The goatherd responded that he had told them, and if Sancho had not heard him, he was not to blame. Sancho Panza replied, and so did the goatherd, and all the replies ended in each seizing the other's beard and exchanging so many blows that if Don Quixote had not stopped them, they would have beaten each other to a pulp. Sancho said, as he kept hold of the goatherd:

"Your grace, Señor Knight of the Sorrowful Face, let me be, for with this one, who is lowborn like myself and not a knight, I'm free to avenge his offense against me, fighting him hand to hand, like an honorable man."

"That is true," said Don Quixote, "but I know he is not to blame for what has happened."

Saying this, he pacified them, and Don Quixote asked the goatherd again if it would be possible to find Cardenio, because he wanted very much to know the end of his story. The goatherd said what he had said earlier, that he was not certain where he stayed, but if he wandered the area, Don Quixote could not fail to find him, either in his right mind or out of it.

CHAPTER XXV

Which tells of the strange events that befell the valiant knight of La Mancha in the Sierra Morena, and of his imitation of the penance of Beltenebros[1]

Don Quixote took his leave of the goatherd, and mounting Rocinante once again, he told Sancho to follow him, which he did, on his donkey, very unwillingly. Gradually they were entering the most rugged part of the mountains, and Sancho, longing to talk to his master but not wanting to disobey his orders, waited for him to begin the conversation; unable to endure so much silence, however, Sancho said:

"Señor Don Quixote, your grace should give me your blessing and let me leave, because now I want to go back to my house and my wife and children, for with them, at least, I'll talk and speak all I want; your grace wanting me to go with you through these deserted places by day and by night without talking whenever I feel like it is like burying me alive. If animals could still talk the way they did in the days of Guisopete,[2] it wouldn't be so bad because I could talk to my donkey whenever I wanted to, and that would help me bear my misfortunes; it's a hard thing, and not something to be borne patiently, when a man searches his whole life and doesn't find anything but kicks and tossings in a blanket, stones and fists hitting him, and still he has to keep his mouth shut tight, not daring to say what's in his heart, like a mute."

"I understand you very well, Sancho," responded Don Quixote. "You long to have the interdiction which I have placed on your tongue lifted. Consider it lifted and say whatever you wish, on the condition that this

1. The knight's penance is a favorite topic in the books of chivalry. Beltenebros is the name taken by Amadís during his penance; it suggests "Dark Beauty" or "Beautiful Dark."

2. This was the popular name for Aesop among the uneducated.

license lasts no longer than the time we spend traveling through these mountains."

"That's fine," said Sancho. "Let me talk now, for only God knows what will happen later, and I'll begin to enjoy this freedom now and ask why was it that your grace defended so strongly that Queen Magimasa or whatever her name is? And what difference did it make if that abbot[3] was her lover or not? For if your grace had let it pass, since you weren't her judge, I think the madman would have gone on with his story, and we would have avoided stones, and kicks, and more than half a dozen punches."

"By my faith, Sancho," responded Don Quixote, "if you knew, as I do, what an honorable and distinguished lady Queen Madásima was, I know you would say that I showed a good deal of forbearance, for I did not smash the mouth that uttered such blasphemies. Because it is an exceedingly great blasphemy to say or think that a queen would take a surgeon as her lover. The truth of the matter is that Master Elisabat, mentioned by the madman, was a very prudent man and a wise counselor, and he served as tutor and physician to the queen, but to think that she was his mistress is an outrage deserving of the most severe punishment. And so that you may see that Cardenio did not know what he was saying, you should realize that when he said it, he was not in his right mind."

"That's just what I'm saying," said Sancho. "There wasn't any reason to pay attention to the words of a madman, because if luck hadn't been with your grace, and the stone had hit your head the way it hit your chest, then what kind of condition would we have been in to defend that lady, may God confound her! And, by my faith, Cardenio would've been pardoned because he's crazy!"

"Against sane men and madmen, every knight errant is obliged to defend the honor of ladies, no matter who they may be, and especially queens of such high birth and distinction as Queen Madásima, for whom I have a particular regard because of her many virtues; in addition to being beauteous, she was also very prudent and long-suffering in her calamities, of which she had many, and the advice and companionship of Master Elisabat were of great benefit and comfort to her and helped her to endure her travail with prudence and patience. And the vulgar and low-born took advantage of this to say and think that she was his mistress; and I say that all those who say and think such a thing lie, and lie again, and will lie another two hundred times whenever they say or think it."

"I don't say it and I don't think it," responded Sancho. "It's their af-

3. This is Sancho's misunderstanding of the name Elisabat.

fair and let them eat it with their bread; whether or not they were lovers, they've already made their accounting with God; I tend to my vines, it's their business, not mine; I don't stick my nose in; if you buy and lie, your purse wants to know why. Besides, naked I was born, and naked I'll die: I don't lose or gain a thing; whatever they were, it's all the same to me. And many folks think there's bacon when there's not even a hook to hang it on. But who can put doors on a field? Let them say what they please, I don't care."

"Lord save me!" said Don Quixote. "What a lot of foolish things you put on the same thread, Sancho! What does the subject of our conversation have to do with the proverbs you string together like beads? If you value your life, Sancho, be quiet, and from now on tend to spurring your donkey and leave matters alone that do not concern you. And know with all five of your senses that everything I have done, am doing, and shall do follows the dictates of reason and the laws of chivalry, which I know better than all the knights in the world who have ever professed them."

"Señor," responded Sancho, "is it a law of chivalry that we should wander through these mountains with no path or direction, looking for a madman who, when he's found, may feel like finishing what he began, and I don't mean his story but your grace's head and my ribs, and break them completely?"

"I tell you again, Sancho, to be quiet," said Don Quixote, "because you should know that it is not only my desire to find the madman that brings me to these parts, but also my desire to here perform a deed that will bring me perpetual fame and renown throughout the known world; and it will be so great a deed that with it I shall put the crowning touch on all that can make a knight errant perfect and worthy of fame."

"And is this deed very dangerous?" asked Sancho Panza.

"No," responded the Knight of the Sorrowful Face, "although depending on luck and the throw of the dice, our fortunes may be either favorable or adverse, but everything will depend on your diligence."

"On my diligence?" said Sancho.

"Yes," said Don Quixote, "because if you return quickly from the place where I intend to send you, then my suffering will end quickly and my glory will quickly commence. And since it is not right to keep you in suspense, waiting to hear where my words will lead, I want you, Sancho, to know that the famous Amadís of Gaul was one of the most perfect knights errant. I have misspoken: not *one of*, but the sole, the first, the only, the lord of all those in the world during his lifetime. Bad luck and worse fortune for Don Belianís and for anyone else who may claim to be his equal in anything, because, by my troth, they are deceived. I say, too, that when a painter wishes to win fame in his art, he attempts to copy the original works of the most talented painters he knows; this same rule applies to all the important occupations and professions that serve to embellish nations, and it must be, and is, followed when the man who wishes to be known as prudent and long-suffering imitates Ulysses, in whose person and hardships Homer painted a living portrait of prudence and forbearance; Virgil, too, in the person of Aeneas, portrayed for us the valor of a devoted son and the sagacity of a valiant and experienced captain; they were depicted and described not as they were, but as they should have been, to serve as examples of virtue to men who came after them. In the same manner, Amadís was the polestar, the morning star, the sun to valiant, enamored knights, the one who should be imitated by all of us who serve under the banner of love and chivalry. This being true, and it is, then I deduce, friend Sancho, that the knight errant who most closely imitates Amadís will be closest to attaining chivalric perfection. And one of the things in which this knight most clearly showed his prudence, valor, courage, patience, constancy, and love was when, scorned by the Lady Oriana, he withdrew to do penance on the Peña Pobre,[4] calling himself Beltenebros, a name truly significant and suited to the life he voluntarily had chosen. It is, therefore, easier for me to imitate him in this fashion than by cleaving giants in two, beheading serpents, slaying dragons, routing armies, thwarting armadas, and undoing enchantments. And since this terrain is so appropriate for achieving that end, there is no reason not to seize Opportunity by the forelock[5] when it is convenient to do so."

"In fact," said Sancho, "what is it that your grace wants to do in this lonely place?"

"Have I not told you already," responded Don Quixote, "that I wish to imitate Amadís, playing the part of one who is desperate, a fool, a madman, thereby imitating as well the valiant Don Roland when he discovered in a fountain the signs that Angelica the Fair had committed base acts with Medoro, and his grief drove him mad, and he uprooted

---

4. *Peña Pobre* can be translated as "Poor Rock" or "Bare Rock" or, to retain the alliteration, "Mount Mournful."

5. The figure of Opportunity was traditionally represented as bald except for one lock of hair, which, like the proverbial brass ring, one had to grasp and hold on to.

trees, befouled the waters of clear fountains, killed shepherds, destroyed livestock, burned huts, demolished houses, pulled down mares, and did a hundred thousand other unheard-of things worthy of eternal renown and record? And since I do not intend to imitate Roland, or Roldán, or Orlando, or Rotolando (for he had all those names) in every detail of all the mad things he did, said, and thought, I shall, to the best of my ability, sketch an outline of those that seem most essential to me. And it well may be that I shall be content with the imitation solely of Amadís, who, with no harmful mad acts but only outbursts of weeping and grief, achieved as much fame as anyone else."

"It seems to me," said Sancho, "that the knights who did these things were provoked and had a reason to do senseless things and penances; but what reason does your grace have for going crazy? What lady has scorned you, and what signs have you found to tell you that my lady Dulcinea of Toboso has done anything foolish with Moor or Christian?"

"Therein lies the virtue," responded Don Quixote, "and the excellence of my enterprise, for a knight errant deserves neither glory nor thanks if he goes mad for a reason. The great achievement is to lose one's reason for no reason, and to let my lady know that if I can do this without cause, what should I not do if there were cause? Moreover, I have more than enough reason because of my long absence from her who is forever my lady, Dulcinea of Toboso; as you heard the shepherd Ambrosio say, all ills are suffered and feared by one who is absent. And so, friend Sancho, do not waste time advising me to abandon so rare, so felicitous, so extraordinary an imitation. Mad I am and mad I shall remain until you return with the reply to a letter which I intend to send with you to my lady Dulcinea; if it is such as my fidelity warrants, my madness and my penance will come to an end; if it is not, I shall truly go mad and not feel anything. Therefore, no matter her reply, I shall emerge from the struggle and travail in which you leave me, taking pleasure as a sane man in the good news you bring, or, as a madman, not suffering on account of the bad news you bear. But tell me, Sancho, have you kept the helmet of Mambrino safe? For I saw you pick it up from the ground when that ingrate tried to shatter it. But he could not, and in this we can see how finely it is tempered."

To which Sancho responded:

"By God, Señor Knight of the Sorrowful Face, but I lose my patience and can't bear some of the things your grace says; because of them I even imagine that everything you tell me about chivalry, and winning kingdoms and empires, and giving me ínsulas and granting me other favors and honors, as is the custom of knights errant, must be nothing but empty talk and lies, and all a hamburg or a humbug or whatever you call it. Because if anyone heard your grace calling a barber's basin the helmet of Mambrino without realizing the error after more than four days, what could he think but that whoever says and claims such a thing must be out of his mind? I have the basin in the bag, all dented, and I'm taking it along so I can fix it when I get home, and use it to trim my beard, if someday, by the grace of God, I ever find myself with my wife and children again."

"Well, Sancho, by the same oath you swore before, I swear to you," said Don Quixote, "that you have the dimmest wits that any squire in the world has or ever had. Is it possible that in all the time you have traveled with me you have not yet noticed that all things having to do with knights errant appear to be chimerical, foolish, senseless, and turned inside out? And not because they really are, but because hordes of enchanters always walk among us and alter and change everything and turn things into whatever they please, according to whether they wish to favor us or destroy us; and so, what seems to you a barber's basin seems to me the helmet of Mambrino, and will seem another thing to someone else. It was rare foresight on the part of the wise man who favors me to make what is really and truly the helmet of Mambrino seem a basin to everyone else, because it is held in such high esteem that everyone would pursue me in order to take it from me; but since they see it as only a barber's basin, they do not attempt to obtain it, as was evident when that man tried to shatter it, then left it on the ground, not taking it away with him; by my faith, if he had recognized it for what it was he never would have left it behind. Keep it, my friend, since I have no need of it for the moment; rather, I must remove all this armor and be as naked as the day I was born, if I wish in my penance to follow Roland more than Amadís."

As they were conversing, they came to the foot of a high mountain, which, almost like a peak carved out of the rock, stood alone among the many others that surrounded it. At its base there flowed a gentle stream, and all around it lay a meadow so green and luxuriant it brought joy to the eyes that gazed upon it. There were many woodland trees and plants and flowers, making it a peaceful spot. The Knight of the Sorrowful Face chose this place to carry out his penance, and so, as soon as he saw it, he began to say in a loud voice, as if he had lost his reason:

"This is the place I designate and choose, O heavens, to weep for the misfortune to which you have condemned me. This is the place where the humor of my eyes will increase the waters of this small stream, and my continual deep sighs will constantly move the leaves of these untamed trees in testimony to and as proof of the grief that afflicts my troubled heart. And O you rustic gods, whoever you may be, who dwell in this desolate place, hear the laments of this unfortunate lover, brought by long absence and imagined jealousy to this harsh terrain to complain and weep over the unyielding nature of that ungrateful beauty, the culmination and perfection of all human comeliness. O you nymphs and dryads, who are wont to dwell in thickets and forests, loved, although in vain, by wanton and lustful satyrs, may they ne'er disturb your sweet tranquility and may you help me lament my misfortune, or at least not grow weary of hearing it! O Dulcinea of Toboso, day of my night, glory of my grief, guide of my travels, star of my good fortune, may heaven grant all that thou mayest request just as thou considereth the place and plight to which thy absence hath led me and respondeth with the favor merited by my faithfulness! O solitary trees that from this day forth will accompany my solitude, give a sign, with the gentle movement of your branches, that my presence doth not displease you! O thou, my squire, amiable companion of my favorable and adverse adventures, take note and fix in thy mind what thou wilt see me do here, so that thou mayest recount and relate it to the sole cause of all my actions!"

And having said this, he dismounted Rocinante and in an instant removed the bit and saddle, and slapping the horse on the rump, he said:

"Liberty is given to thee by him who hath none, O steed as great in thy deeds as thou art unfortunate in thy destiny! Goest thou whither thou wilt, for on thy forehead it is written that the Hippogryph of Astolfo was not thy equal in speed, nor the renowned Frontino that cost Bradamante so dear."[6]

Seeing this, Sancho said:

"Good luck to whoever spared us the trouble of unsaddling the gray;[7]

6. The hippogryph, a winged horse, and Frontino, the horse of Ruggiero, Bradamante's lover, appear in Ariosto's *Orlando furioso*; Frontino is also mentioned by Boiardo in *Orlando innamorato*.

7. Over the years, the question of exactly when Sancho's donkey was stolen has been a matter of some controversy among Cervantine scholars. According to the first edition, published in 1605, this is the initial indication that a theft has taken place. In the second edition, however, published a few months after the first, a passage inserted in chapter XXIII states that Ginés de Pasamonte, the galley slave, steals the donkey while Sancho is sleeping. Martín de Riquer, editor of the text on which this translation is based, adheres consistently to the first edition, citing the added passage in a footnote but not including it in the body of the text. In brief, then, through an oversight of Cervantes or the printer, Juan de la Cuesta, the first edition does not prepare the reader for the fact that the donkey has been stolen; despite subsequent corrections, in the second part of *Don Quixote*, published in 1615, Cervantes alludes to this omission in chapter III and apparently accepts criticism of the omission as valid.

by my faith, we would have plenty of little slaps to give that donkey, and plenty of things to say in his praise, but if he were here, I wouldn't agree to anybody unsaddling him, because there'd be no reason to; he couldn't be described as a lover or desperate, since his master, who was me so long as God was willing, wasn't those things either. The truth is, Señor Knight of the Sorrowful Face, that if my leaving and your grace's madness are serious, it would be a good idea to saddle Rocinante again and let him take the place of the gray, which would make my going and coming shorter; if I make the trip on foot, I don't know when I'll arrive or when I'll get back, because, to make a long story short, I'm a very poor walker."

"What I say, Sancho," responded Don Quixote, "is that it will be as you wish, for your plan does not seem to be a bad one, and I also say that three days hence you will leave here, because in that time I want you to see what I do and say for her sake, so that you can recount it to her."

"But what else do I have to see," said Sancho, "besides what I've seen already?"

"How little you know!" responded Don Quixote. "Now I have to tear my clothes, toss aside my armor, and hit my head against these rocks, along with other things of that nature, all of which will astonish you."

"For the love of God," said Sancho, "your grace should be careful how you go around hitting your head, because you might come up against a boulder that's so hard that with the first blow you put an end to the whole plan for this penance; in my opinion, if your grace believes that hitting your head is necessary and you can't do this thing without it, you should be content, since it's all make-believe and fake and a joke, with knocking your head on water or something else that's soft, like cotton; leave the rest to me, and I'll tell my lady that your grace was hitting your head against the sharp edge of a boulder that was harder than a diamond."

"I thank you for your good intentions, friend Sancho," responded Don Quixote, "but I want you to realize that all the things I am doing are not jokes but very real; otherwise, I would be contravening the rules of chivalry that command us never to lie, or else suffer the punishment of those who relapse into sin, and doing one thing instead of another is the same as lying. And so, my head hittings have to be real, solid, and true, with no sophistry or fantasy about them. And it will be necessary for you

to leave me some lint bandages to heal my wounds, since it was our misfortune to lose the balm."

"Losing the donkey was more serious," responded Sancho, "because
when we lost him we lost the bandages and everything else. And I beg
your grace to say no more about that cursed potion; just hearing its name
turns my soul, not to mention my stomach. And I beg something else:
just assume that the three days you gave me to see the mad things you do
have already passed, because as far as I'm concerned, I've seen them, and
judged them, and will tell wonderful things about them to my lady; so
write the letter now and send me on my way, because I have a great desire to come back and take your grace out of this purgatory where I'm
leaving you."

"You call it purgatory, Sancho?" said Don Quixote. "You would do
better to call it hell, and even worse, if anything can be worse."

"Whoever's in hell," responded Sancho, "*nulla es retencio,*[8] or so I've
heard."

"I do not understand what *retencio* means," said Don Quixote.

"*Retencio* means," responded Sancho, "that whoever's in hell never
gets out and can't get out. Which is just the opposite of your grace, unless my feet go the wrong way when I use the spurs to liven up Rocinante; just put me once and for all in Toboso, before my lady Dulcinea,
and I'll tell her such wonders about the foolish things and the crazy
things, because they amount to the same thing, that your grace has done
and is still doing that she'll become softer than a glove even if I find her
harder than a cork tree; with her sweet and honeyed reply I'll come flying back through the air, like a wizard, and I'll take your grace out of this
purgatory that seems like hell but isn't, since there's a hope of getting
out, which, as I said before, the people in hell don't have, and I don't
think your grace will say otherwise."

"That is true," said the Knight of the Sorrowful Face, "but what shall
we use to write the letter?"

"And the order for the donkeys, too,"[9] added Sancho.

"Everything will be included," said Don Quixote, "and it would be a
good idea, since we have no paper, to write it, as the ancients did, on the
leaves of trees, or on some wax tablets, although they would be as diffi-

8. This is Sancho's corruption of a Latin phrase in the service for the dead: *Quia in inferno nulla est
redemptio.*

9. In the passage regarding the theft of the donkey, which was inserted in chapter XXIII in the second edition, Don Quixote offers Sancho his own donkeys as compensation for his loss.

cult to find now as paper. But it occurs to me that it would be good, and even better than good, to write it in the notebook that belonged to Cardenio, and you will take care to have it transcribed onto paper, in a fine hand, in the first town you come to where there is a schoolmaster, or else some sacristan can transcribe it for you, but do not give it to any notary, for their writing is so difficult to read that not even Satan can understand it."

"And what do we do about the signature?" said Sancho.

"The letters of Amadís were never signed," responded Don Quixote.

"That's fine," responded Sancho, "but the order must be signed, and if it's copied they'll say the signature is false, and I won't have my donkeys."

"The order will be written in the same notebook, and it will be signed, and when my niece sees it, there will be no difficulty putting it into effect. As for the love letter, as a signature you will have them put: 'Thine until death, the Knight of the Sorrowful Face.' And it will not matter if it is written in another's hand, because, if I remember correctly, Dulcinea does not know how to read or write, and never in her life has she seen my writing or a letter of mine, because my love and her love have always been platonic, not going beyond a virtuous glance. And even this was so infrequent that I could truly swear that in the twelve years I have loved her more than the light of these eyes that will be consumed by the earth, I have not seen her more than four times; and it well may be that with regard to these four times, she might not have noticed the one time I looked at her; such is the retirement and seclusion in which her father, Lorenzo Corchuelo, and her mother, Aldonza Nogales, have reared her."

"Well, well!" said Sancho. "Are you saying that Lorenzo Corchuelo's daughter, also known as Aldonza Lorenzo, is the lady Dulcinea of Toboso?"

"She is," said Don Quixote, "and she is worthy of being lady and mistress of the entire universe."

"I know her very well," said Sancho, "and I can say that she can throw a metal bar just as well as the brawniest lad in the village. Praise our Maker, she's a fine girl in every way, sturdy as a horse, and just the one to pull any knight errant or about to be errant, who has her for his lady, right out of any mudhole he's fallen into! Damn, but she's strong! And what a voice she has! I can tell you that one day she stood on top of the village bell tower to call some shepherds who were in one of her father's fields, and even though they were more than half a league away, they heard her just as if they were standing at the foot of the tower. And the best thing about her is that she's not a prude. In fact, she's something of a trollop: she jokes with everybody and laughs and makes fun of everything. Now I say, Señor Knight of the Sorrowful Face, that your grace not only can and should do crazy things for her, but with good cause you can be desperate and hang yourself; there won't be anybody who knows about it who won't say you did the right thing, even if the devil carries you off. And I'd like to be on my way, just for the chance to see her; I haven't seen her for a long time, and she must be changed by now, because women's faces become very worn when they're always out in the fields, in the sun and wind. And I confess to your grace, Señor Don Quixote, that till now I lived in great ignorance because I really and truly thought the lady Dulcinea must be a princess your grace was in love with, or the kind of person who deserved the rich presents your grace sent to her, like the Basque and the galley slaves and probably many others, just as many as the victories your grace won in the days before I was your squire. But, thinking it over carefully, what good does it do Aldonza Lorenzo, I mean, the lady Dulcinea of Toboso, if all those vanquished by your grace are sent and will be sent to kneel before her? Because it might be that when they arrive she's out raking flax, or on the threshing floor, and they'll run away when they see her, and she'll laugh and get angry at the present."

"I have already told you many times before now, Sancho," said Don Quixote, "that you talk far too much, and although your wits are dull, your tongue often is sharp; however, so that you may see how foolish you are and how discerning I am, I wish to tell you a brief story. Once there was a widow who was beautiful, free, rich, and above all, easy in her ways, and she fell in love with a lay brother, a sturdy, good-looking boy; his superior learned of this, and one day he said to the good widow, in fraternal reprimand: 'I am amazed, Señora, and with reason, that a woman as distinguished, as beautiful, and as rich as your grace has fallen in love with a man as crude, as base, and as stupid as he, when there are in this house so many masters, so many scholars, so many theologians, among whom your grace could make a selection as if you were choosing pears, saying, I want this one but not the other.' But she responded with a good deal of wit and verve: 'Your grace, Señor, is very much mistaken, and you are thinking in an old-fashioned way if you think I have chosen badly, no matter how stupid he may seem to you; because considering the reason I love and want him, he knows as much philosophy as Aristotle, and even more.' In the same way, Sancho, because of my love for Dulcinea of Toboso, she is worth as much as the highest princess on earth. And yes, not every poet who praises a lady, calling her by another name, really has one. Do you think the Amaryllises, Phyllises, Sylvias, Dianas, Galateas, Alidas, and all the rest that fill books, ballads, barbershops, and theaters are really ladies of flesh and blood who belong to those who celebrate them? No, of course not, for most are imagined in order to provide a subject for their verses, and so that people will think of them as lovers and as men who have the capacity to be lovers. And therefore it is enough for me to think and believe that my good Aldonza Lorenzo is beautiful and virtuous; as for her lineage, it matters little, for no one is going to investigate it in order to give her a robe of office, and I can think she is the highest princess in the world. Because you should know, Sancho, if you do not know already, that two things inspire love more than any other; they are great beauty and a good name, and these two things reach their consummation in Dulcinea, for in beauty, no one is her equal, and as for a good name, few can approach her. And to conclude, I imagine that everything I say is true, no more and no less, and I depict her in my imagination as I wish her to be in beauty and in distinction, and Helen cannot approach her, Lucretia cannot match her, nor can any of the other famous women of past ages, Greek, barbarian, or Latin. Let each man say what he chooses; if because of this I am criticized by the ignorant, I shall not be chastised by the learned."

"I say that your grace is correct in everything," responded Sancho, "and that I am an ass. But I don't know why my mouth says ass, when you shouldn't mention rope in the hanged man's house. But let's have the letter, and I'll say goodbye and be on my way."

Don Quixote took out the notebook, moved off to one side, and very calmly began to write the letter, and when he had finished, he called Sancho and said he wanted to read it to him so that Sancho could commit it to memory in the event he lost it along the way, for his own misfortune was such that it was reasonable to fear the worst. To which Sancho responded:

"Your grace should write it two or three times in the book, and give it to me, and I'll take good care of it, because it's foolish to think I'll commit it to memory; mine is so bad I often forget my own name. But even so, your grace should read it to me, and I'll be very happy to hear it, for it must be perfect."

"Listen, then, for this is what it says," said Don Quixote:

LETTER FROM DON QUIXOTE TO DULCINEA OF TOBOSO

Supreme and most high lady:

He who is sore wounded by the sharp blade of absence, he whose heart-strings are broken, most gentle Dulcinea of Toboso, sendeth thee wishes for the well-being he doth not have. If thy beauty scorneth me, if thy great merit op-poseth me, if thy disdain standeth firm against me e'en though I possess a goodly portion of forbearance, I shall not be able to endure this affliction, which is both grievous and long-lasting. My good squire, Sancho, will recount the entire tale to thee, O ungrateful beauty! O my beloved enemy! regarding the state in which I findeth myself for thy sake: if it be thy desire to succor me, I am thine; if not, do as thou pleaseth, for by ending my life I shall have satis-fied both thy cruelty and mine own desire.

Thine until death,
THE KNIGHT OF THE SORROWFUL FACE

"By my father's life," said Sancho when he heard the letter, "that's the highest thing I've ever heard. Confound it, but how your grace says everything anyone could want, and how well *The Knight of the Sor-rowful Face* fits into the closing! I'm telling the truth when I say your grace is the devil himself, and there's nothing your grace doesn't know."

"Everything is necessary," responded Don Quixote, "for the profes-sion I follow."

"Well, then," said Sancho, "your grace just has to make a note on the other page about the three donkeys, and sign it very clearly so that when they see it they'll know the signature."

"It will be my pleasure," said Don Quixote.

And when he had written it, he read it to Sancho, and it said:

Señora, my niece, your grace will arrange, by means of this order for donkeys, the presentation to Sancho Panza, my squire, of three of the five said animals which I left behind and which are in your grace's charge. These aforemen-tioned three donkeys I hereby order immediately transferred as payment for others herewith received, which shall comprise, by this compensatory writ, full and complete payment thereof. Duly executed in the heart of the Sierra Morena on the twenty-second day of August of the current year.

"That's fine," said Sancho. "Now your grace should sign it."

"It is not necessary to sign it," said Don Quixote. "All I need do is add my mark and flourish, which is the same as a signature and enough for three donkeys, and even for three hundred."

"I trust in your grace," responded Sancho. "Let me go and saddle Rocinante, and let your grace get ready to give me your blessing, for I plan to leave right away without seeing the crazy things your grace is going to do, though I'll say I saw you do more than anyone could wish."

"At least, Sancho, I want, because it is necessary, I say I want you to see me naked and performing one or two dozen mad acts, which will take me less than half an hour, because if you have seen them with your own eyes, you can safely swear to any others you might wish to add, and I assure you that you will not recount as many as I intend to perform."

"For the love of God, Señor, don't let me see your grace naked, for that will make me feel so bad I won't be able to stop crying, and my head's in such a state after the crying I did last night over my gray that I'm in no mood for any more tears; if it's your grace's wish that I see some crazy actions, do them fully dressed, and let them be brief and to the point. Especially because none of this is necessary for me, and like I said before, I want to shorten the time it takes me to get back here with the news your grace desires and deserves. Otherwise, let the lady Dulcinea get ready, and if she doesn't answer the way she should, I make a solemn vow to God that I'll get a good answer out of her stomach if I have to kick her and slap her. Because how can anybody stand for a knight errant as famous as your grace to go crazy, without rhyme or reason, for the sake of a . . . ? And don't let her make me say it, because by God I'll tear everything apart and never look back. And I'm the one who can do it! She doesn't know me! By my faith, if she knew me she'd think twice!"

"Well, Sancho," said Don Quixote, "it seems you are no saner than I."

"I'm not as crazy," responded Sancho, "I just have a more choleric nature. But, leaving that aside, what will your grace eat until I get back? Will you go out to the road, like Cardenio, and take food from the shepherds?"

"Do not concern yourself with that," responded Don Quixote, "because even if I had food, I would eat nothing but the plants and fruits that this meadow and these trees might offer me; for the elegance of my plan lies in not eating and in suffering other comparable hardships. Goodbye, then."

"But, does your grace know what I'm afraid of? That I won't be able to find this place again, it's so out of the way."

"Take careful note of the landmarks, and I shall try not to leave the vicinity," said Don Quixote, "and I shall even be sure to climb up to the highest peaks to watch for your return. Better yet, so that you will not make a mistake and lose your way, you should cut some of the broom that grows in such abundance here, and place the stalks at intervals along the way until you reach level ground, and they will serve as markers and signs, as did the thread of Perseus[10] in the labyrinth, so that you can find me when you return."

"I'll do that," responded Sancho Panza.

And after cutting some stalks of broom, he asked for his master's blessing, and, not without many tears on both their parts, he took his leave. He mounted Rocinante, whom Don Quixote commended to his care, saying he should attend to him as to his own person, and he set out for the plain, scattering stalks of broom at intervals, as his master had advised. And so he left, although Don Quixote was still urging him to watch at least two mad acts. But he had not gone a hundred paces when he turned and said:

"Señor, your grace is right: so that I can swear with a clear conscience that I saw you do crazy things, it would be a good idea for me to see at least one, even though I've already seen a pretty big one in your grace's staying here."

"Did I not tell you so?" said Don Quixote. "Wait, Sancho, and I shall do them before you can say a Credo."

And hastily he pulled off his breeches and was left wearing only his skin and shirttails, and then, without further ado, he kicked his heels twice, turned two cartwheels with his head down and his feet in the air, and revealed certain things; Sancho, in order not to see them again, pulled on Rocinante's reins and turned him around, satisfied and convinced that he could swear his master had lost his mind. And so we shall let him go on his way until his return, which did not take long.

---

10. In an apparent oversight, Cervantes wrote "Perseus" instead of "Theseus."

CHAPTER XXVI

*In which the elegant deeds performed by an enamored Don Quixote in the
Sierra Morena continue*

Returning to the account of what the Knight of the Sorrowful Face did
after he found himself alone, the history relates that when Don Quixote,
with his upper parts clothed and his bottom parts naked, finished his
leaps and turns and saw that Sancho, not wishing to see more mad acts,
had departed, he climbed to the top of a high crag, and there he pondered what he had so often pondered without ever reaching a decision,
which was whether it would be better and more appropriate for him to
imitate Roland in his excessive madness or Amadís in his melancholy,
and talking to himself, he said:

"If Roland was as good and valiant a knight as everyone says, why
should anyone be surprised? After all, he was enchanted, and no one
could kill him except by placing a pin in the bottom of his foot, and he
always wore shoes with seven metal soles, although such stratagems did
him little good against Bernardo del Carpio, who understood them, and
crushed him in his arms at Roncesvalles. But, his valor aside, we come to
the matter of his losing his mind, and it is certain that he lost it because
of the signs to which fortune led him and the news the shepherd gave
him that Angelica had taken more than two siestas with Medoro, a little
curly-haired Moor who was Agramante's page; and if he understood this
to be true, and his lady had committed so great a wrong against him, he
did not do much by going mad; but I, how can I imitate him in his madness if I do not imitate him in its cause? Because I shall go so far as to
swear that my Dulcinea of Toboso has not in all her days seen a single
Moor just as he is, in his own clothing, and that she is today as she was
on the day she was born; and it would be a grievous affront if I, imagining

anything else about her, were to go mad with the type of madness that afflicted Roland in his fury. On the other hand, I see that Amadís of Gaul,
without losing his mind and without performing mad acts, achieved as
much fame as a lover as anyone else; because what he did, according to
his history, was simply that finding himself scorned by his lady Oriana,
who had ordered him not to appear in her presence until she so willed it,
he withdrew to the Peña Pobre, in the company of a hermit, and there
he had his fill of weeping and commending himself to God, until heaven
hearkened to his pleas in the midst of his greatest travail and need. And
if that is true, as it most certainly is, why should I now go to the trouble
of tearing off all my clothes or causing grief to these trees, which have
never done me any harm whatsoever? Nor do I have reason to muddy
the clear waters of these streams, where I may drink whenever I wish.
Long live the memory of Amadís, and let him be imitated in every way
possible by Don Quixote of La Mancha, about whom it will be said, as it
was said of the other, that if he did not achieve great things, he died in
the effort to perform them, and if I am not scorned and disdained by Dulcinea of Toboso, it is enough, as I have said, to be absent from her. Well,
then, to work: let the actions of Amadís come to mind and show me
where I must begin to imitate them. I already know that for the most
part he prayed and commended himself to God, but what shall I use for a
rosary, since I do not have one?"

Then he thought of what he could do, and he tore a long strip from
his shirttails and tied eleven knots in it, one larger than the rest, and this
served as his rosary during the time he was there, when he said a million
Ave Marías.[1] He was greatly troubled at not finding a hermit nearby who
would hear his confession and console him, and so he spent his time
walking through the meadow, writing and scratching on the tree trunks
and in the fine sand many verses, all of them suited to his sorrow and
some of them praising Dulcinea. But the only ones that were found complete, and that could be read after they were discovered, were these:

> O trees, grasses, and plants
> that in this spot do dwell
> so verdant, tall, abundant,
> if you find no joy in my ill
> then hear my honest complaints.

1. This phrase was considered irreverent, and in the second edition it was replaced by "And for a
rosary he took some large galls from a cork tree, which he strung together and used as prayer beads."

Let not my grief alarm you
even when it brings dire fears,
for to pay and recompense you,
Don Quixote here shed tears
for his absent Dulcinea
      of Toboso.

Here in this place, this season,
the truest, most faithful lover
hides his face from his lady,
and has been made to suffer
untold torments without reason.
   Love buffets him about
in merciless battle and quarrel;
and so, till he filled a barrel
Don Quixote here shed tears
for his absent Dulcinea
      of Toboso.

Questing for high adventures
among boulders and rocky tors,
and cursing a heart made of stone,
for in this wild desolation
he finds nought but misadventures,
   love lashed him with a cruel whip,
not with a gentle cordon;
and when it scourged his nape
Don Quixote here shed tears
for his absent Dulcinea
      of Toboso.

A cause of no small laughter in those who discovered these verses
was the *of Toboso* appended to the name of Dulcinea, because they imagined that Don Quixote must have imagined that if, when he named Dulcinea, he did not also say *of Toboso*, the stanza would not be understood,
and this in fact was true, as he later confessed. He wrote many other
stanzas, but, as we have said, no more than these three could be read in
their entirety. He spent his time writing, sighing, and calling on the
fauns and satyrs of the woods, and the nymphs of the rivers, and on

grieving, tearful Echo to answer and console and hear him; he also searched for plants that would sustain him until Sancho returned, and if the squire had taken three weeks instead of three days, the Knight of the Sorrowful Face would have been so altered that not even his own mother would have known him.

It would be a good idea to leave him enveloped in sighs and verses and to recount what befell Sancho Panza as he traveled on his mission. When he came out onto the king's highway, he began to look for the road to Toboso, and the next day he reached the inn where he had suffered the misfortune of the blanket, and no sooner had he seen it than it seemed to him that once again he was flying through the air, and he did not want to go inside even though he had arrived at an hour when he could and should have done so, since it was time to eat and he longed to enjoy something hot, because for many days he had eaten nothing but cold food.

This necessity drove him to approach the inn, still doubtful as to whether he should go in or not, and while he was hesitating, two people came out of the inn and recognized him immediately. And one said to the other:

"Tell me, Señor Licentiate, that man on the horse, isn't he Sancho Panza, the one our adventurer's housekeeper said had left with her master to be his squire?"

"It is," said the licentiate, "and that's the horse of our Don Quixote."

And they knew him so well because they were the priest and barber of his village, the ones who had held a public proceeding and scrutinized the books. As soon as they recognized Sancho Panza and Rocinante, they wished to have news of Don Quixote, and they approached, and the priest called him by name, saying:

"Friend Sancho Panza, where is your master?"

Sancho Panza knew who they were and decided to hide the place and condition in which he had left his master, and so he replied that his master was busy somewhere with something that was very important to him, but by the eyes in his head he could not reveal what it was.

"No, no, Sancho Panza," said the barber, "if you don't tell us where he is, we'll think, and we already do think, that you killed and robbed him, since you're riding his horse. As a matter of fact, you'd better tell us where the horse's owner is or you'll regret it."

"There's no reason to threaten me, I'm not the kind of man who robs or kills anybody: let each man be killed by fate or by God who made him. My master is doing penance in the middle of those mountains, as happy as can be."

And then, in a rush and without stopping, he told them of the state in which he had left him, and the adventures that had befallen him, and how he was carrying a letter to the lady Dulcinea of Toboso, who was the daughter of Lorenzo Corchuelo and the one with whom his master was head over heels in love.

They were both astonished at what Sancho Panza told them, and although they already knew of the madness of Don Quixote, and knew what kind of madness it was, whenever they heard about it they were astonished all over again. They asked Sancho Panza to show them the letter he was carrying to the lady Dulcinea of Toboso. He said it was written in a notebook, and his master had ordered him to have it copied onto paper in the first town he came to; the priest replied that he should show it to him, and he would copy it in a very fine hand. Sancho Panza put his hand in the bosom of his shirt, looking for the notebook, but he did not find it and would not have found it if he had looked for it from then until now, because Don Quixote had kept it and had not given it to him, and he had not remembered to ask for it.

When Sancho saw that he could not find the book, his face turned deathly pale, and quickly patting down his entire body again, he saw again that he could not find it, and without further ado he put both hands to his beard and tore out half of it, and then, very quickly and without stopping, he punched himself half a dozen times on the face and nose until they were bathed in blood. Seeing which, the priest and the barber asked him what had happened to drive him to such lengths.

"What else could have happened," responded Sancho, "except that from one moment to the next, in an instant, I've lost three donkeys, each one as sturdy as a castle?"

"How did that happen?" replied the barber.

"I've lost the notebook," responded Sancho, "that had the letter to Dulcinea, and a document signed by her uncle that told his niece to give me three of the four or five donkeys he has at home."

And he recounted the loss of the gray. The priest consoled him and told him that when they found his master, he would revalidate the order and write the transfer out on paper, as was the usual custom, since the ones written in notebooks were never accepted or executed.

This comforted Sancho, and he said that if this was true, he did not feel too bad about losing the letter to Dulcinea because he knew it almost by heart, and it could be copied wherever and whenever they wished.

"Then tell it to us, Sancho," said the barber, "and we'll copy it later."

Sancho Panza stopped and scratched his head to bring the letter to mind, and he stood now on one foot, now on the other; sometimes he looked at the ground, sometimes at the sky, and after a very long while, when he had gnawed off half a fingertip, keeping those who were waiting for him to speak in suspense, he said:

"By God, Señor Licentiate, may the devil carry away what I remember of the letter, but at the beginning it did say: 'High and sullied lady.' "

"It wouldn't," said the barber, "say *sullied,* but supreme or sovereign lady."

"That's right," said Sancho. "Then, as I recall, it went on to say . . . as I recall: 'This ignorant and sleepless and sore wounded man kisses the hands of your grace, ungrateful and unrecognized beauty,' and then something about health and sickness that he was sending her, and then it just went along until it ended with 'Thine until death, the Knight of the Sorrowful Face.' "

They both derived no small pleasure from Sancho Panza's good memory, and they praised him for it and asked him to repeat the letter two more times so that they too could commit it to memory and copy it at the proper time. Sancho repeated it three more times, and each time he said another three thousand pieces of nonsense. Following this, he recounted other things that had happened to his master but did not say a word about being tossed in the blanket in that same inn which he refused to enter. He also told them how his master, if he brought back a favorable reply promptly from the lady Dulcinea of Toboso, would set out to try to become an emperor, or at least a monarch; that's what the two of them had agreed to, and it was an easy thing for his master to do, given the valor of his person and the strength of his arm; when he had done this, his master would arrange for him to marry, because by then he could not be anything but a widower, and Don Quixote would give him as his wife one of the ladies-in-waiting to the empress, and she would inherit a rich large estate on terra firma, without any insulars or ínsulas, because he didn't want them anymore.

Sancho said this with so much serenity, wiping his nose from time to time, and so little rationality, that the two men were astonished again as they considered how powerful the madness of Don Quixote was, for it had pulled along after it the good sense of this poor man. They did not want to make the effort to disabuse him of the error in which he found himself, for it seemed to them that since it was not injurious to his conscience, it would be better to leave him where he was so that they would have the pleasure of hearing his foolishness. And so they told him to pray to God for the well-being of his master, for it was possible and even probable that with the passage of time he would become an emperor, as he said, or an archbishop, at the very least, or some other equivalent high office. To which Sancho responded:

"Señores, if fortune turns her wheel so that my master decides not to be an emperor but an archbishop, I'd like to know now: what do archbishops errant usually give their squires?"

"Usually," responded the priest, "they give some benefice, a simple one or a parish, or they make him a sacristan, with a very nice fixed income, in addition to other fees that bring in more income."

"For that it would be necessary," replied Sancho, "for the squire not to be married, and to know at least how to assist at Mass, and if that's true, then woe is me, for I'm married and don't know the first letter of the alphabet! What will happen to me if my master decides to be an archbishop and not an emperor, which is the usage and custom of knights errant?"

"Don't worry, friend Sancho," said the barber, "for we'll ask your master, and advise him, and even present it to him as a matter of conscience, that he should become an emperor and not an archbishop, which will be easier for him since he's more soldier than student."

"That's what I think, too," responded Sancho, "though I can say that he has a talent for everything. What I plan to do, for my part, is pray to Our Lord to put him in the place that's best for him and where he can do the most favors for me."

"You speak with good judgment," said the priest, "and will act like a good Christian. But what has to be done now is to arrange to remove your master from that useless penance in which you say he is engaged; in order to think of the best way to do that, and to eat something, since it's time for supper, it would be a good idea for us to go into this inn."

Sancho said that they should go in and he would wait for them outside, and later he would tell them the reason he wasn't going in and why it wouldn't be a good idea if he did, but he asked them to bring out something hot for him to eat, as well as barley for Rocinante. They went inside and left him alone, and a short while later the barber brought him some food. Then, when they had thought carefully about how they would accomplish what they desired, the priest had an idea that would appeal to Don Quixote and achieve what they wanted; he told the barber that what he had thought was that he would dress in the clothes of a wandering maiden, and the barber would look as much like a squire as possible, and they would go to the place where Don Quixote was doing penance, the maiden pretending to be an afflicted damsel in distress who would ask a boon, which, as a valiant knight errant, he could not fail to grant. And the boon would be to follow her wherever she might lead, to undo a great wrong that an evil knight had done unto her; and she would implore him as well not to request that she remove her mask, or ask any other question regarding her estate and fortune until such time as he had righted the injustice so wrongfully done unto her by that base knight; the priest believed beyond any doubt that Don Quixote would comply with everything asked of him in those terms, and in this manner they would take him from that place and bring him home to his village, where they would try to see if there was a cure for his strange madness.

CHAPTER XXVII

Concerning how the priest and the barber carried out their plan, along with other matters worthy of being recounted in this great history

The barber did not think the priest's invention was a bad idea; in fact, it seemed so good that they immediately began to put it into effect. They asked the innkeeper's wife for a skirt and bonnet, giving her as security one of the priest's new cassocks. The barber made a long beard out of a gray or red oxtail where the innkeeper hung his comb. The innkeeper's wife asked why they wanted those things. The priest told her briefly about Don Quixote's madness, and how the disguises were just the thing to get him out of the mountains, which is where he was now. Then the innkeeper and his wife realized that the madman had been their guest, the one who made the balm and was the master of the squire who had been tossed in the blanket, and they recounted to the priest everything that had happened, not keeping silent about the thing Sancho had kept so secret. In short, the innkeeper's wife outfitted the priest in the most remarkable fashion: she dressed him in a woolen skirt with black velvet stripes a hand-span wide, and all of them slashed, and a bodice of green velvet adorned with white satin binding, and both the bodice and the

skirt must have been made in the days of King Wamba.[1] The priest did
not permit his head to be adorned, but he did put on a cap of quilted
linen that he wore to sleep at night, and tied it around the front with a
band of black taffeta, and with another band he fashioned a mask that
covered his beard and face very well; he pulled his broad-brimmed hat
down tightly on his head, and it was so large he could have used it as a
parasol; he wrapped himself in his cape and mounted his mule sidesaddle; the barber, with a beard somewhere between red and white that
hung down to his waist and was made, as we have said, from the tail of a
reddish ox, mounted his mule as well.

They said goodbye to everyone, including the good Maritornes, who
promised to say a rosary, although a sinner, and ask God to grant them
success in so arduous and Christian an enterprise as the one they had undertaken.

But as soon as he had ridden out of the inn, it occurred to the priest
that he was committing an error by dressing in that manner, for it was an
indecent thing for a member of the clergy to do, no matter how important
the end; he told this to the barber and asked him to trade clothes with
him, since it would be better if the barber was the damsel in distress and
the priest played the part of the squire; in this way his office would be less
profaned, but if the barber did not want to make the change, he had decided to go no further, even if the devil made off with Don Quixote.

At this point Sancho approached, and when he saw the two of them
in those clothes, he could not control his laughter. The barber, in fact,
agreed to everything the priest said, and as they traded disguises, the
priest informed him how he should behave and the words he had to say
to Don Quixote in order to move and oblige him to go away with him
and leave the place he had chosen for his useless penance. The barber responded that he had no need of instruction and would do everything
perfectly. He did not want to put on his disguise until they were near the
place where they would find Don Quixote, and so he folded the garments, and the priest adjusted the beard, and they continued their journey, led by Sancho Panza, who recounted what had happened with the
madman they had come across in the sierra, although he did hide the
discovery of the traveling case and everything that was in it, for although he was a fool, the squire was somewhat greedy.

On the following day, they reached the place where Sancho had

1. A Visigoth who ruled Spain in the seventh century (672–680).

made the trail of broom so that he could find the spot where he had left his master; and when he saw this, he said that this was the way into the mountains and they ought to put on their disguises if that was needed to achieve his master's freedom; they had told him earlier that doing what they were doing and dressing in that fashion were crucial to freeing his master from the injudicious life he had chosen, and they had charged him repeatedly that he was not to tell his master who they were, or that he knew them; if his master asked, as he was bound to ask, if he had given the letter to Dulcinea, he was to say yes, and because she did not know how to read she had spoken her reply, saying that she ordered him, under pain of her displeasure, to come to see her immediately, and it was very important because with this, and what they intended to say to him, they were certain they could turn him to a better life and set him on the road to becoming an emperor or a monarch; as for becoming an archbishop, there was no reason to worry about that.

Sancho listened to everything, and noted it carefully in his mind, and thanked them profusely for their intention to advise his master to be an emperor and not an archbishop, because in his opinion, as far as granting favors to their squires was concerned, emperors could do more than archbishops errant. He also said it would be a good idea if he went first and found his master and told him his lady's reply, for that would probably be enough to make him leave the place, saving them a good deal of trouble. What Sancho said seemed reasonable, and they decided to wait until he came back with the news that he had found his master.

Sancho entered the ravines of the sierra, leaving the priest and barber in one where a small, gentle stream ran in the cool, pleasant shade cast by other rocky crags and the trees that grew all around. They had come there on a day in August, and the heat was intense, particularly in that area; the time was three in the afternoon, making the spot even more pleasant, and inviting them to wait until Sancho returned, which is what they did.

While the two men were resting in the shade, a voice unaccompanied by the music of any other instrument reached their ears, and it sounded so sweet and delicate that they were more than a little taken aback, for the place did not seem the kind where there would be anyone who could sing so well. Although it is often said that in the forests and fields one can find shepherds with extremely fine voices, these are more the exaggerations of poets than the truth; they were especially surprised when they realized that they were hearing the verses not of rustic shepherds but of learned courtiers. And in confirmation of this truth, these were the verses they heard:

> Who makes all my joy to wane?
> > Disdain.
> And who prolongs this misery?
> > Jealousy.
> And who assails and tears my patience?
> > Absence.
> And therefore, in my deep-felt sorrow,
> I see no cure on the morrow,
> for I am killed by hope in vain,
> absence, jealousy, and disdain.
>
> Who causes me to sigh and grieve?
> > Love.
> And who deems glory's not my portion?
> > Fortune.
> And who augments my grief by seven?
> > Heaven.
> And therefore, in profound unease
> I fear I'll die of this disease,
> for my enemies, I can prove,
> are heaven, fortune, and love.
>
> Who, then, will improve my fate?
> > Death.
> And who in love claims victory?
> > Perfidy.
> And who can make its ills grow less?
> > Madness.
> And therefore, it's no act of reason
> to attempt to cure this passion
> when the remedies, in truth,
> are madness, perfidy, and death.

The hour, the weather, the solitude, the voice, and the skill of the one who was singing caused both wonder and pleasure in the two who were listening, and they remained quiet, hoping they would hear more;

but seeing that the silence lasted for some time, they resolved to look for the musician who sang with so beautiful a voice. And as they were about to do so, the same voice kept them from moving, for again it reached their ears, singing this sonnet:

SONNET

Most sacred friendship who, with rapid wings,
while your mere semblance stayed here on the ground,
flew, full of joy, up to the vaults of heaven
to mingle with the blessed in paradise,
and there on high, you show us, when you wish,
fair harmony concealed behind a veil
through which, at times, there gleams a fervent zeal
to do good works that ne'er yield ought but ill.
    Leave heaven, friendship, or no more allow
deceit to don the livery of your house
and use it to destroy an earnest will;
    If you take not your semblance from deceit,
the world will soon return to its first strife,
the chaos and dark disquiet of discord.

The song ended with a profound sigh, and the two men waited again, listening attentively for more singing; but seeing that the music had turned to sobs and pitiful laments, they decided to learn who the aggrieved person was who sang so beautifully and wept so mournfully; before they had gone very far, they walked behind a rocky crag and saw a man whose figure and appearance were the same as those described by Sancho Panza when he told them the story of Cardenio, and this man, when he saw them, did not become agitated but remained motionless, his head lowered as if he were lost in thought, and he did not raise his eyes again to look at them after the first glance, when they had appeared so unexpectedly.

The priest, who was a well-spoken man and already knew of Cardenio's misfortune, for he had recognized who he was, approached him, and in brief though very perceptive words implored and exhorted him to leave the wretched life he was pursuing there or else he might lose his life, which would be the greatest of all misfortunes. At that moment

Cardenio was completely rational, free of the fits of madness that so often drove him to fury, and when he saw them dressed in clothing so different from that worn by the men who wandered those desolate places, he could not help but be astonished, especially when he heard his affairs discussed as if they were common knowledge—for the words the priest said led him to this conclusion—and he responded in this manner:

"I see clearly, Señores, whoever you may be, that heaven, watching over the good, and even the bad very often, through no merit of my own has sent me, in this solitary place so far removed from ordinary human commerce, persons who have set before me, with vivid and varied reasons, how lacking in reason I am to live the life I lead, and have attempted to turn me away from this life and toward a better one; but since you do not know that I know that if I leave this evil I fall into another even greater, perhaps you consider me a man whose power of reasoning is weak and, even worse, one who has no judgment at all. It would not be surprising if that were the case, because it is evident to me that in my imagination the power of my afflictions is so intense and contributes so much to my ruination that I am powerless to prevent it and I become like a stone, bereft of all sense and awareness; I become conscious of this truth only when people tell me and show me the evidence of the things I have done while that terrible attack has control over me, and all I can do is lament my fate in vain, and curse it to no avail, and offer as an excuse for my mad acts the recounting of their cause to all who wish to hear it, for if rational men see the cause, they will not be surprised by the effects, and if they cannot help me, at least they will not blame me, and anger at my outbursts will be transformed into pity for my misfortunes. If you, Señores, have come with the same intention that has brought others here, before you go any further in your wise arguments I ask you to hear the as yet unfinished account of my tribulations, because perhaps when you have, you will spare yourselves the trouble of offering consolation for an affliction that is inconsolable."

The two men, who wanted nothing else but to hear from Cardenio's own lips the reason for his ills, asked that he tell it to them and said they would do only what he wished, either to help or to console him; then the aggrieved gentleman began his pitiful history with almost the same words and phrases he had used to relate it to Don Quixote and the goatherd a few days earlier, when, as this history has recounted, because of Master Elisabat and Don Quixote's punctilious defense of chivalric decorum, the tale was not concluded. But now it was their good fortune that the attack of madness was over, giving Cardenio an opportunity to narrate his tale to the end; and so, when he came to the letter Don Fernando had found in the volume of *Amadís of Gaul*, Cardenio said he knew it by heart, and what it said was this:

LUSCINDA TO CARDENIO

Each day I discover in you virtues that oblige and compel me to value you even more; and therefore, if you wished to free me from this debt without attaching my honor, you could do so very easily. I have a father who knows you and loves me, and he, without forcing my will, can meet the obligation of what it is reasonable for you to have, if in fact you value me as you say, and as I believe you do.

This letter moved me to ask for Luscinda's hand, as I have told you; it was the reason Don Fernando considered Luscinda to be one of the most intelligent and prudent women of her time; this letter was the one that filled him with the desire to destroy me before my own desires could be realized. I told Don Fernando what Luscinda's father had said about my father's asking for her hand, which I did not dare mention to my father for fear he would not agree, not because he did not know Luscinda's quality, worth, virtue, and beauty, or that she possessed more than enough excellent traits to ennoble any family in Spain, but because I understood that he did not wish me to marry until he knew what Duke Ricardo had planned for me. In short, I told him I had not risked speaking to my father, for this reason and many others that made me fearful although I did not know precisely what they were, except that it seemed to me that what I desired would never become a reality. To all of this Don Fernando replied that he would assume the responsibility of speaking to my father and persuading him to speak to Luscinda's father.

O ambitious Marius, O cruel Catilina, O wicked Sulla, O lying Galalón, O traitorous Vellido, O vengeful Julián, O greedy Judas! Traitorous, cruel, vengeful, and lying man, what disservice had been done to you by this wretch who so openly revealed to you the secrets and joys of his heart? How did I offend you? What words did I say, what advice did I give that was not intended to increase your honor or your advantage? But woe is me! Why do I complain? Everyone knows that when misfortunes are brought by the course of the stars, hurtling down from on high with fury and violence, no power on earth can stop them, no human effort can prevent them. Who could imagine that Don Fernando, an illustrious and intelligent nobleman under obligation to me for my services, and able to attain whatever his amorous desire might demand no matter where it turned, would, as they say, bother to burden his conscience by taking from me my only sheep, one that I did not yet possess?

But let us put such considerations aside, for they are futile and unprofitable, and take up again the broken thread of my unfortunate history. I shall tell you, then, that Don Fernando thought my presence would be troublesome to him when he put his false and evil idea into effect, and he resolved to send me to his older brother with a request for money to pay for six horses, which he intentionally bought for the sole purpose of having me leave (in order to achieve more easily his reprehensible purpose), and on the same day that he offered to speak to my father he asked me to go for the money. Could I foresee this betrayal? Could I, by some chance, even imagine it? No, of course not; instead, with great pleasure I offered to leave immediately, gratified at the good purchase he had made.

That night I spoke to Luscinda, and told her what I had arranged with Don Fernando, and said she should be confident that our virtuous and honest desires would be realized. She, as unaware as I of Don Fernando's perfidy, told me to try to return home quickly because she believed that the fulfillment of our desires would take no longer than the time it took for my father to speak to her father. I do not know why, but after she said this her eyes filled with tears, and the lump in her throat kept her from speaking another word of the many that, it seemed to me, she was attempting to say. I was taken aback by this uncommon emotion, which I had not seen in her before, because whenever we spoke, on the occasions when good fortune and my diligence permitted it, it was with joy and gladness, and our conversations were not mixed with tears, sighs, jealousies, suspicions, or fears. I would exalt my happiness because heaven had granted me Luscinda as my lady: I exaggerated her beauty and marveled at her virtue and understanding. She returned the favor, praising in me those things that she, as a woman in love, found worthy of praise. We would tell each other a thousand trifles, things that had happened to our neighbors and friends, and the limit of my boldness was to grasp, almost by force, one of her beautiful white hands and raise it to my lips, or as far as the constraints of the grating that divided us would allow. But on the night that preceded the sad day of my departure, she wept, moaned, sighed, and then withdrew, leaving me full of confusion and alarm, apprehensive at having seen such new and melancholy signs of Luscinda's sorrow and grief; in order not to destroy my hopes, I attributed everything to the strength of the love she had for me and the sadness that absence usually causes in those who truly love each other. In short, I set out sad and pensive, my soul filled with imaginings and suspicions, not knowing what I suspected or imagined; these were clear signs of the sad, grievous events that lay ahead of me.

I reached my destination and gave the letters to Don Fernando's brother; I was well-received but not well-dismissed, because much to my displeasure he told me to wait for a week, in a place where his father, the duke, would not see me, because Don Fernando had asked that he send back with me a certain sum of money without his father's knowledge; all of this was an invention of the false Don Fernando, for his brother had enough money to allow me to leave without delay. This was an order and command that I was inclined to disobey because it seemed impossible to endure so many days away from Luscinda, especially since I had left her filled with the sadness I have recounted to you; yet I obeyed, like a good servant, even though I saw that it would be at the cost of my well-being. But four days after my arrival a man came looking for me with a letter, which he gave to me, and by the address I knew it was from Luscinda because the writing was hers. I opened it, fearful and apprehensive, believing that something very important had moved her to write to me when I was far away, for when I was near she did so very rarely.

I asked the man, before I read it, who had given it to him and how long the journey had taken; he said that he happened to be walking down a street in the city at noon, and a very beautiful lady called to him from a window, her eyes filled with tears, and said to him very urgently: 'Brother, if you are a Christian, as you seem to be, for the love of God I beg you to take this letter as quickly as you can to the place and person written here in the address, for both of them are well-known, and by doing this you will do a great service to Our Lord; and so that you can derive some advantage from this, take what is in this handkerchief.'

And then the man said: 'she threw down from the window a knotted handkerchief that contained a hundred *reales* and this gold ring, and the letter that I've given to you. And, without waiting for my reply, she left the window, though first she saw me take the letter and the handkerchief, and signal to her that I would do as she had asked. And so, seeing myself so well-paid for any difficulty I might have in bringing it to you, and knowing by the address that you were the person for whom it intended, because, Señor, I know very well who you are, and being obliged as well by the tears of that beautiful lady, I decided not to trust anyone else and came myself to hand it to you, and I have been traveling for the sixteen hours since it was given to me, and as you know, the distance is eighteen leagues.' While the grateful and novel courier was saying this to me, I hung on his every word, my legs trembling so much I could barely stand. And then I opened the letter and saw that it contained these words:

> *Don Fernando's promise to you that he would speak to your father about speaking to mine has been carried out more to his pleasure than to your bene-fit. Know then, Señor, that he has asked for my hand in marriage, and my fa-ther, carried away by the advantage he thinks Don Fernando has over you, has agreed to everything he wishes, and with so much enthusiasm that in two days' time the betrothal will take place, so secretly and so privately that the only wit-nesses will be heaven and a few of our servants. Imagine the state I am in; if you come, you will see it, and you will know, in the outcome of this business, whether or not I love you dearly. May it please God that this reaches your hands before my hand finds itself joined with that of one who does not know how to keep the faith he promises.*

These, in short, were the words the letter contained, which made me set out immediately, not waiting for any other reply or any other money, for I realized very clearly then that it was the purchase not of horses but of his own pleasure that had moved Don Fernando to send me to his brother. The anger I felt toward Don Fernando, together with my fear of losing the treasure I had earned with so many years of service and devo-tion, gave me wings, for almost as if I had flown, by the next day I reached my city at precisely the right time to go and speak with Lus-cinda. I entered in secret, having left my mule at the house of the good man who had brought me the letter, and as luck would have it, I was for-tunate enough to find Luscinda at the grating that had been witness to our love. Luscinda knew me immediately, and I knew her, but not as she should have known me, and I her. But who in the world can boast that he has penetrated and understood the confused thought and mutable condition of a woman? No one, certainly.

I tell you, then, that as soon as Luscinda saw me, she said: 'Cardenio, I am dressed for the wedding; the traitorous Don Fernando and my avari-cious father are waiting for me in the drawing room, along with other witnesses who will see my death rather than my marriage. Do not be per-turbed, dear friend, but try to be present at this sacrifice, which, since it could not be prevented by my words, my hidden dagger, which could deter even more determined forces, will put an end to my life and a beginning to your knowledge of the love I have had and still have for you.'

I responded urgently and in great agitation, fearful I would not have enough time to answer her: 'May your deeds, Señora, confirm the truth of your words; if you carry a dagger as proof of your sincerity, I am carrying a sword with which to defend you or kill myself, if our luck is unfavorable.' I do not believe she could hear everything I said because I heard them calling to her with some urgency, for the bridegroom was waiting.

With this the night of my sorrow closed over me and the sun of my joy set; I was left with no light in my eyes and no power of reason in my understanding. I could not find the way into her house, I could not even move, but considering how important my presence was to whatever might occur, I did the best I could to rouse myself, and I walked into her house; since I knew all its entrances and exits very well, and especially because of the secret tumult that reigned there, no one saw me; unseen, I was able to hide in the alcove of a window in the drawing room, concealed by two tapestries hanging next to each other, and looking between them; unseen, I could see everything that happened in the drawing room. How can I tell you now about the pounding of my heart as I stood there, or the thoughts that occurred to me, or the deliberations I made? For there were so many and were of such a nature that they cannot and should not be told. It is enough for you to know that the bridegroom entered the drawing room unadorned, wearing the ordinary clothes he usually wore. As best man he had one of Luscinda's first cousins, and in the entire drawing room there was no outsider but only the servants of the house.

A short while later, Luscinda emerged from an antechamber, accompanied by her mother and two of her lady's maids, and she was dressed and adorned as handsomely as her rank and beauty deserved, the very perfection of courtly elegance and charm. My uncertainty and confusion did not permit me to observe and notice the particulars of what she was wearing; I could see only the colors, which were scarlet and white, and the brilliance of the gems and jewels on her headdress and all over her costume, all of it surpassed by the singular beauty of her lovely blond tresses, which, in comparison to the precious stones, and the light from the four flambeaux in the drawing room, offered greater brilliance to the eye. O memory, mortal enemy of my repose! What is the good of picturing for me now the incomparable beauty of my adored enemy? Would it not be better, cruel memory, if you recalled and pictured for me what she did then, so that I, moved by so manifest a wrong, can attempt, if not to avenge it, at least to lose my own life?

Do not be vexed, Señores, at hearing these digressions of mine, for my grief is not the kind that can or should be recounted succinctly and in passing, for each of its circumstances seems to me worthy of a long discourse."

To which the priest responded that not only were they not vexed at listening to him, they were pleased by the details he recounted, for they were of the sort that should not be passed over in silence and deserved the same attention as the principal part of the story.

"Well, then," Cardenio continued, "when we were all in the drawing room, the parish priest came in and took both of them by the hand in order to do what the ceremony requires, and when he said: 'Do you, Señora Luscinda, take Señor Don Fernando, here present, to be your lawful wedded husband, as decreed by Holy Mother Church?' I extended my head and neck between the two tapestries, and with attentive ears and my soul in distress I listened for Luscinda's response, expecting her reply to be either a sentence of death or the affirmation of my life. Oh, if only I had dared to come out then and shout: 'Ah, Luscinda, Luscinda! Think what you are doing; consider what you owe me; remember that you are mine and cannot belong to another! Realize that your saying yes and the end of my life are all one! Ah, you traitor, Don Fernando, thief of my glory, death of my life! What do you want? What are you seeking? Consider that as a Christian you cannot attain the object of your desires because Luscinda is my wife and I am her husband.'

Ah, madman that I am! Now that I am absent and far from danger, I say I should have done what I did not do! Now that I have allowed the theft of my most precious jewel, I curse the thief upon whom I could have wreaked my vengeance if I would have had as much courage for that as I do for my laments! In short, I was a coward and a fool then, and it is no surprise that I am dying now ashamed, repentant, and mad.

The priest was waiting for Luscinda's reply, and she took a long time to give it, and when I thought she would take out the dagger to prove her sincerity, or would loosen her tongue to utter a truth or reproach that would redound to my benefit, I heard her say in a weak, faint voice: 'Yes, I do,' and Don Fernando said the same, and gave her the ring, and they were joined in an indissoluble bond. The groom moved to embrace his bride, and she, placing her hand over her heart, fainted into her mother's arms.

All that remains now is to tell you the state I was in when I saw, in the sound of her *yes*, the mockery of my hopes, the falsity of Luscinda's words and promises, and the impossibility of ever retrieving the treasure I had lost at that instant. I was left with nothing, abandoned, it seemed to me, by all of heaven, the enemy of the earth that sustained me; air denied me breath for my sighs, water denied its humor for my eyes; only fire grew stronger so that my entire being burned with rage and jealousy. Everyone became agitated at Luscinda's swoon, and when her mother loosened her bodice to give her air, a sealed letter was discovered, which Don Fernando immediately took and began to read in the light of one of the flambeaux; when he finished reading it, he sat on a chair and rested his cheek in his hand, like a man lost in thought, and took no part in the remedies administered to his wife to help her recover.

Seeing the agitation of everyone in the house, I dared come out, regardless of whether anyone saw me or not, resolved that if I were seen, I would do something so rash that everyone would understand the righteous determination in my heart to punish the false Don Fernando and even the fickle, swooning traitor; but my fate, which must be saving me for even greater ills, if there can possibly be any, decreed that I would have a surfeit at that moment of the reason I have been lacking ever since; and so, not wishing to take revenge on my greatest enemies, which, since I was so far from their minds, would have been an easy thing to do, I decided to turn my hand and inflict on myself the punishment they deserved, perhaps with even greater severity than if I had killed them then and there, for if death is sudden, the punishment is soon over, but death that is extended by torture goes on killing but does not end life.

In short, I departed that house and went to the one where I had left my mule; I had it saddled, and without saying goodbye to anyone I mounted and left the city, not daring, like a second Lot, to look back; when I found myself alone in the countryside, and the darkness of the night covered me and its silence invited my lamentations, with no misgiving or fear that I would be heard or recognized, I freed my voice and liberated my tongue and hurled curses at Luscinda and Don Fernando as if that would avenge the wrong they had done me. I called her cruel, ungrateful, false, thankless, and above all, greedy, for my enemy's wealth had closed the eyes of her love, taking it from me and giving it to one with whom fortune had been more generous and munificent; in the midst of this rush of curses and vituperations, I excused her, saying it was no surprise that a young girl, cloistered in the house of her parents, accustomed and trained to always obey them, would have wanted to accede to their wishes, since they were giving her as a husband a nobleman who was so distinguished, so wealthy, and so gallant that if she refused, it might be thought that she had no judgment, or that her desire lay elsewhere, something that would do grave harm to her good name and reputation. Then I said the opposite: if she had said I was her husband, they would have seen that in choosing me she had not made so bad a choice that they could not forgive her; before Don Fernando presented himself to them, they could not, if they kept their desires within reason, have wished for a better man than I to be their daughter's husband, and she, before placing herself in the critical position of being compelled to give her hand, could very well have said that I had already pledged her mine, and in that case I would have come forth and agreed to any tale she might have invented. In short, I decided that too little love, too little judgment, too much ambition, and too much desire for wealth had made her forget the words with which she had deceived, encouraged, and sustained me in my firm hopes and virtuous desires.

With these arguments and this disquiet I traveled the rest of the night, and at dawn I came upon a way into these mountains, where I rode for another three days, with no direction or goal of any kind, until I reached some meadows, though I do not know on which side of the mountains they may be, and there I asked some drovers where I could find the harshest terrain in the sierra. They told me it lay in this direction. I traveled here, intending to end my life, and as I was entering these desolate places my mule collapsed, dead of exhaustion and hunger or, what I believe is more likely, to free itself of the useless burden it was carrying. I was left on foot, humbled by nature, broken by hunger, not having, and not planning to look for, anyone to help me. I do not know how long I lay there on the ground, but then I woke, and was not hungry, and there were goatherds with me who undoubtedly were the ones who helped me in my need, because they told me how they had found me, and how I was saying so many foolish things and raving so much that I clearly had lost my reason; from that time on I have felt that I am not always in my right mind, and my reason is so damaged and weak that I do a thousand mad acts, tearing my clothes, shouting in these desolate places, cursing my fate, and repeating in vain the beloved name of my enemy, having no other purpose or intention than to shout my life to an end; when I come back to myself, I am so tired and bruised I can barely move. My most common abode is in the hollow of a cork tree, large enough to shelter this miserable body. The drovers and goatherds who wander these mountains, moved by charity, sustain me, placing food along the paths and around the rocky crags where they know I may pass by and find it; and so, although I may be out of my mind at the time, the demands of nature allow me to recognize sustenance and awaken in me the desire to want it and the will to take it. When I am rational, they tell me that at other times I go out onto the paths and take food by force, though they willingly give it to me, from the shepherds who carry it up from the village to the sheepfolds.

In this manner I spend my miserable and intemperate life until it is heaven's will that it come to an end, or my memory does, so that I cannot remember the beauty and betrayal of Luscinda and the wrong done to me by Don Fernando; if heaven does this without taking my life, I shall turn my thoughts to more reasonable discourse; if not, all I can do is pray that heaven has mercy on my soul, for I do not have the courage or strength to remove my body from this rigorous and difficult place where I have chosen to put it.

This is, Señores, the bitter history of my misfortune: tell me if it is such that it can be heard with less grief than you have seen in me, and do not bother to persuade or counsel me with what reason tells you can be beneficial or helpful to me, for it will profit me as much as the medicine prescribed by a famous physician for a patient who refuses to take it. I do not want health without Luscinda, and since she has chosen to belong to another when she was, or should have been, mine, I choose affliction as my portion when it could have been good fortune. She wanted, with her fickleness, to make my destruction constant; I want, by trying to destroy myself, to satisfy her desire, and it will be an example to those who come after me that I lacked only what all unfortunate men have in abundance, for whom the impossibility of finding any comfort is a consolation, but for me it is reason for even greater griefs and ills, because I think they will not end even with death."

Here Cardenio ended the long recounting of his history, as unfortunate as it was amorous; as the priest was preparing to say some words of consolation to him, he was interrupted by a voice, and they heard it saying in pitiable accents what will be told in the fourth part of this narration, for here the third part was concluded by that wise and judicious historian Cide Hamete Benengeli.

Part Four of the Ingenious Gentleman Don Quixote of La Mancha

CHAPTER XXVIII

Which recounts the novel and agreeable adventure that befell the priest and the barber in the Sierra Morena

Most happy and fortunate were the days when the bold knight Don Quixote of La Mancha sallied forth into the world, since, because of his honorable resolve to resuscitate and return to the world the lost and dying order of knight errantry, we can now enjoy in our own time, which is so in need of joyful entertainment, not only the sweetness of his true history, but also the stories and episodes that appear in it and are, in some ways, no less agreeable and artful and true than the history itself, which, following its tortuous, winding, and meandering thread, recounts that as the priest was preparing to console Cardenio, he was prevented from doing so by a voice that reached his ears and, in melancholy accents, said:

"Oh, God! Let it be true that I have found the place that can serve as the hidden tomb for the heavy burden of this body, which I so unwillingly bear! It is, if the solitude promised by these mountains is not a lie. Oh, woe is me, what agreeble companions these rocks and brambles will be for my purpose: they will allow me, with my laments, to communicate my affliction to heaven, for there is none on earth from whom one can expect counsel for one's doubts, relief for one's complaints, or remedy for one's ills!"

All of these words were heard and heeded by the priest and his companions, and because it seemed to them, as was the case, that they were being said nearby, they went to look for the one who spoke them, and they had not gone twenty paces when, behind a crag, they saw, sitting at the foot of an ash tree, a boy dressed as a peasant, and since his face was lowered as he bathed his feet in the stream that ran there, for the moment they could not see it; they approached so silently that he did not hear them, for he was attentive to nothing else but bathing his feet, which looked exactly like two pieces of white crystal that had been born there among the other stones in the stream. Stunned by the whiteness and beauty of those feet, which, it seemed to them, were not made to walk on clods or follow after a plow and oxen, as suggested by their owner's clothing, and seeing that they had not been detected, the priest, who walked at their head, signaled to the others to crouch down and hide behind some nearby rocks, and all of them did so, looking carefully at what the boy was doing; he wore a short dun-colored jerkin wrapped tightly around his body with white fabric. He also wore breeches and leggings of coarse dun wool and on his head a dun cloth cap. The leggings were raised to the middle of his calves, which, beyond all doubt, seemed like white alabaster. He finished washing his beautiful feet, and then, with a scarf that he took from beneath his cap, he dried them, and as he removed the scarf, he lifted his face, and those who were watching had the opportunity to see an incomparable beauty, so great that Cardenio said to the priest in a low voice:

"This, since it is not Luscinda, is no human being but a divine creature."

The boy removed his cap, shook his head from side to side, and tresses that the rays of the sun might have envied began to loosen and tumble down. With this, they realized that the person who seemed to be a peasant was an exquisite woman, the most beautiful ever seen by the eyes of the priest, the barber, and even Cardenio, if he had not already gazed upon Luscinda; he later affirmed that only Luscinda's beauty could compare with hers. Her long blond hair covered not only her back, but was so abundant and thick that it concealed the rest of her body as well, except for her feet. For a comb she used her hands, and if her feet in the water had looked like pieces of crystal, her hands in her hair seemed like driven snow, all of which further astonished those who were looking at her and made them even more desirous of knowing who she was.

For this reason they resolved to show themselves, and at the sound they made as they rose to their feet the beautiful girl lifted her head, and moving the hair away from her eyes with both hands, she looked at those who were making the sound; as soon as she saw them she leaped up, and, not taking the time to put on her shoes or pin up her hair, she quickly seized a bundle that was beside her and seemed to contain clothes, and attempted to flee, filled with confusion and alarm; but she had not taken six steps when, her delicate feet unable to withstand the jagged rocks, she fell to the ground. When the three men saw this they drew near, and the priest was the first to speak, saying:

"Stop, Señora, whoever you may be; those you see here intend only to serve you: there is no need for so importunate a flight, because your feet will not endure it, and we shall not consent to it."

Frightened and bewildered, she did not say a word in reply. And so they approached her, and the priest, taking her by the hand, continued to speak:

"What your clothes, Señora, deny, your hair reveals: a clear indication that the reasons cannot be inconsequential for disguising your beauty in clothing so unworthy and bringing it to so desolate a place, where it is fortunate we have found you, if not to provide a remedy for your ills, at least to give you counsel; for as long as one has life, no ill can be so worrisome or reach so great an extreme that the one afflicted refuses even to listen to well-intentioned advice. And so, my dear Señora, or Señor, or whatever it is you wish to be, set aside the perturbation that the sight of us has caused you, and recount to us your situation, good or bad; for in all of us together, or in each of us separately, you will find someone to help you lament your misfortunes."

As the priest spoke these words, the disguised girl seemed stupefied, looking at all of them, not moving her lips or saying a word, like a village rustic who is suddenly shown rare and strange things he has never seen before. But the priest continued speaking to the same effect until she heaved a deep sigh, broke her silence, and said:

"Since the solitude of these mountains has not sufficed to hide me, and the loosening of my disheveled hair does not permit my tongue to lie, it would be useless for me to pretend something that you would believe more for the sake of courtesy than for any other reason. Assuming this, I shall say, Señores, that I thank you for the offer you have made, which places me under the obligation to satisfy you in everything you have asked, although I fear that the recounting of my misfortunes will cause you to feel grief as well as compassion, for you will find no remedy to alleviate them or consolation to allay them. Nonetheless, so that you will have no doubts about my honor, and since you have already learned that I am a woman, and have seen that I am alone and dressed in these clothes, things which, together or separately, can overthrow any honest reputation, I shall tell you what I should prefer to keep quiet, if I could."

The one who seemed so beautiful a woman said this without hesitating, and with so fluent a tongue and so gentle a voice that they were astounded as much by her intelligence as her beauty. And repeating their offers, and their pleas that she keep her promise, she did not need to be asked again, but after putting on her shoes with all modesty and pinning up her hair, she settled down on a rock, with the three men gathered around her, and making an effort to hold back the tears that came to her eyes, in a calm, clear voice she began the history of her life in this manner:

"Here in Andalucía there is a place from which a duke takes his title, making him one of those who are called the grandees of Spain.[1] He has two sons: the elder, the heir to his estate and, apparently, to his good character, and the younger, and what he is heir to I do not know other than the treacheries of Vellido and the lies of Galalón. My parents, vassals to this lord, are of humble lineage but so wealthy that if the goods of their natural station were equal to those of their fortune, they would have nothing more to desire nor would I have had any fear of finding myself as wretched as I am now, for perhaps my misfortune is born of theirs because they were not born noble. It is certainly true that they are not so lowborn as to be offended by their state, nor so highborn that they can erase from my imagination the idea that my misfortune comes from their humble station. They, in short, are farmers, simple people with no mixture of any objectionable races, what are called the Oldest of Old Christians, but so rich that their wealth and luxurious way of life are slowly gaining for them the name of gentlefolk, even of nobility. The greatest wealth and nobility that they boasted of, however, was having me as their daughter, and since they had no other heir, daughter or son, and were very loving, I was one of the most pampered daughters ever doted on by her parents. I was the mirror in which they saw their reflection, the staff of their old age, and the object, after heaven, of all their desires; these were virtuous and matched mine precisely. And just as I was mistress of their hearts, I was also mistress of their estate: servants were hired

---

1. This appears to be a reference to the duke of Osuna.

and dismissed by me; the accounts of what was planted and harvested passed through my hands, as did the production of the oil and wine presses, the numbers of livestock, large and small, and the beehives. In short, I kept the accounts of everything that a rich farmer like my father can and does have, and was steward and mistress, with so much care on my part and so much satisfaction on theirs that I cannot express it adequately. My times of leisure, after I had attended to overseers, foremen, and other laborers, I spent in activities both proper and necessary for young women, such as those offered by the needle and pincushion and, at times, the distaff; when I left these activities to refresh my spirit, I would spend the time reading a book of devotions, or playing the harp, for experience had shown me that music soothes unsettled minds and alleviates troubles arising from the spirit. This, then, was the life I led in my parents' house, and if I have recounted it in so much detail, it has not been to boast or to show you that I am rich, but so that you can see how blamelessly I have come from that happy state to the unfortunate one in which I find myself now. The truth is that my life was devoted to so many occupations, and was so cloistered, that it could have been compared to that of a convent, and I was not seen, I thought, by anyone other than the household servants, because on the days I went to Mass it was so early, and I was so well-chaperoned by my mother and by maids, and so modestly covered, that my eyes could barely see more than the ground where I placed my feet; yet the eyes of love, or, rather, of indolence—not even a lynx's eyes are sharper—saw me, and I attracted the attention of Don Fernando, for this is the name of the younger son of the duke I mentioned to you."

As soon as the one telling the tale mentioned Don Fernando, Cardenio turned pale, and began to perspire, and became so agitated that when the priest and the barber looked at him, they feared he would suffer an attack of the madness that, they had been told, overcame him from time to time. But Cardenio did nothing more than perspire and remain very still, staring fixedly at her and imagining who she was, and she, not observing the changes in Cardenio, continued her history, saying:

"No sooner had he seen me than, as he said later, he was smitten with love, as his subsequent actions made clear. But to conclude quickly with the story of my misfortunes, which have no conclusion, I want to pass over in silence the efforts of Don Fernando to declare his desire to me. He bribed all the household servants and gave and offered gifts and favors to my kin. The days were all celebrations and festivals on my street; at night the music prevented everyone from sleeping. The love letters that mysteriously came into my hands were infinite, filled with a lover's words and offers, and more promises and vows than the letters used to write them. All of which not only did not soften my heart, but hardened it as if he were my mortal enemy, and everything he did to turn me to his will had the contrary effect, not because I disliked Don Fernando's gallantry or thought his wooing excessive, for it pleased me somehow to find myself so loved and esteemed by so distinguished a gentleman, nor did it trouble me to see my praises in his letters, for no matter how homely we women may be, it seems to me we always like to hear ourselves called beautiful. But my modesty opposed all this, as did the continual advice offered by my parents, who were well aware of Don Fernando's desire, for by now he did not care at all if everyone knew about it. My parents would tell me that their honor and reputation had been placed for safekeeping in my virtue and chastity, and I should consider the difference in rank between me and Don Fernando, which would allow me to see that his thoughts, although he said otherwise, were directed more toward his pleasure than my benefit, and if I wished to put up some kind of obstacle to make him abandon his unwarranted courtship, they would marry me immediately to whomever I chose from among the most notable men in our town and all the neighboring towns; everything could be hoped for because of their great wealth and my good reputation. With these firm promises, as well as the truth of what my parents were telling me, I strengthened my resolve and refused to say a single word to Don Fernando in reply that might suggest even a distant hope of achieving his desire. All my precautions, which he probably interpreted as disdain, must have been the reason for his lascivious appetite becoming even more inflamed, for that is the name I wish to give to the desire he revealed to me; if it had been what it should have been, you would not know of it now because there would have been no occasion for me to tell you about it.

In short, Don Fernando learned that my parents were about to arrange my marriage in order to deprive him of any hope of possessing me, or, at least, to provide me with more safeguards to protect me, and this news or suspicion was the reason for his doing what you will now hear. One night I was in my bedroom, my sole companion a lady's maid, the doors carefully locked so that my virtue would not be endangered through some oversight; without knowing or imagining how, despite these precautions and preventive measures, and in the solitude of this silent retreat, I found him standing before me; the sight of him perturbed me so much that I lost the sight in my own eyes, and my tongue became mute and I was incapable of crying out, nor do I think he would have allowed me to do so, because he immediately approached and took me in his arms (because, as I have said, I was so distraught I did not have the strength to defend myself), and began to speak in such a manner that I do not know how it is possible for a lie to be so skillful and its words so cleverly arranged that they seem to be the truth. The traitor's tears gave credibility to his words, his sighs confirmed their intention. I, poor girl, alone in the midst of my people, and inexperienced in such matters, began, I do not know how, to think his falsehoods were true, though his tears and sighs could not move me to a compassion that was less than virtuous. And so, as my initial fright faded, I began to recover some of my courage, and with more spirit than I thought I had, I said to him: 'If, Señor, I were in the clutches of a savage lion as I am in your arms now, and I could be sure of freeing myself by doing or saying something to the detriment of my modesty, I could no more do or say it than I could undo the past. Therefore, if you hold my body fast in your arms, my soul is bound by my virtuous desires, which are entirely different from yours, as you will see if you attempt to achieve them by force. I am your vassal, but not your slave; the nobility of your blood does not have nor should it have the power to dishonor and scorn the humbleness of mine; I, a low-born farmer, esteem myself as much as you, a noble lord, esteem yourself. Your force will have no effect on me, your wealth will hold no value for me, your words will not deceive me, and your sighs and tears will not soften me. If I were to see any of the things that I have mentioned in the man to whom my parents were to give me in marriage, I would adjust my will to his, and my will would not deviate from his in any way; as long as I were to keep my honor, even without desire I should willingly give what you, Señor, are now attempting to obtain by force. I have said this because you must not think that a man who is not my legitimate husband can obtain anything from me.'

'If this is all that concerns you, O beautiful Dorotea' (for that is the name of this unfortunate woman), said the traitorous nobleman, 'here and now I offer you my hand to be your husband, and let heaven, which sees all things, and the image of Our Lady that you have here, bear witness to this truth.' ".

When Cardenio heard her say that her name was Dorotea, he became agitated again, confirming the truth of his initial suspicion, but he did not want to interrupt the story, for he wished to see how it turned out, although he almost knew the ending; he said only:

"Then Dorotea is your name, Señora? I have heard of another with the same name whose misfortunes may be equal to your own. Go on, then, and in time I shall tell you things that will cause you both aston- ishment and compassion."

Dorotea listened to Cardenio's words and noticed his strange, ragged clothes and asked that if he knew anything about her affairs, he should tell her so immediately, for if fortune had left her with anything of value, it was the courage to endure any disaster that might occur, since in her opinion nothing could be worse than the one that had already be- fallen her.

"If what I imagine were true, I should lose no time, Señora," re- sponded Cardenio, "in telling you what I think, but now is not the right time, and it is not at all important that you know it."

"Whatever it may be," responded Dorotea, "I shall go on with my story. Don Fernando picked up a holy image that was in the room and called on it to witness our betrothal. With persuasive words and extraor- dinary vows, he promised to be my husband, although before he finished speaking, I told him to think about what he was doing and to consider how angry his father would be to see him married to a peasant, his vassal; he should not allow my beauty, such as it was, to blind him, for it was not great enough for him to find in it an excuse for his mistake; if he wished to do me a good turn for the sake of the love he felt for me, he would let my fate conform to the demands of my rank, for in marriages that are so unequal, the joy with which they begin never lasts very long.

All of these words that I have said now I said to him then, as well as many others that I cannot recall, but they had no effect and could not de- flect him from his purpose, just as a man who has no intention of paying buys in haste, ignoring all the reasons he should not make the purchase. And then I had a brief dialogue with myself, saying: 'Yes, I shall not be the first woman who by way of matrimony has risen from a humble to a noble estate, and Don Fernando will not be the first man moved by beauty, or ir- rational attraction, which is more likely, to take a wife unequal to him in rank. If I am not doing anything that has not been done before, it is a good idea to accept the honor that fate offers me, even if the love he shows me lasts no longer than the satisfaction of his desire, for after all, in the sight of God I shall be his wife. And if I try to reject him with disdain,

I can see that if he does not achieve his ends in the proper way, he will use force, and I shall be dishonored and have no excuse when I am blamed by those who do not know how blamelessly I find myself in this situation. What arguments will be enough to persuade my parents, and others, that this nobleman entered my bedroom without my consent?'

All of these questions and answers I resolved in an instant in my imagination, and even more important, I began to feel inclined to what was, without my knowing it, my perdition, convinced by Don Fernando's vows, the witnesses he called upon, the tears he shed, and, finally, his disposition and gallantry, which, along with so many displays of true love, were enough to vanquish even a heart as unencumbered and chaste as mine. I called my maid so that a witness on earth might join those in heaven; Don Fernando again repeated and confirmed his vows; as witnesses he added new saints to the earlier ones; he called down on himself a thousand future curses if he did not keep his promise to me; tears filled his eyes again and his sighs increased; he clasped me even tighter in his arms, from which he had never released me; then my maid left the room, I ceased to be one, and he became a traitor and a liar.

The day following the night of my misfortune did not come as quickly as I think Don Fernando desired, for when the demands of the appetites are met, the greatest pleasure is to leave the place where one has satisfied them. I say this because Don Fernando hastened to leave me, and through the ingenuity of my maid, the same one who had brought him there, before dawn he found himself on the street. And when he took his leave, he said, though not with the same eagerness and fervor as when he had arrived, that I could be certain that his faith was true and his vows steadfast and unalterable; as further confirmation of his word, he removed a magnificent ring from his finger and put it on mine. Then he left, and I do not know if I was sad or happy; I can say that I was confused and pensive and almost beside myself because of this new turn of events; I did not have the heart, or did not think, to reprimand my maid for her treachery at allowing Don Fernando into my bedroom, because I had not yet decided if what had happened to me was good or bad.

When he left, I told Don Fernando that he could use the same means to visit me on other nights, for now I was his, until such time as he wished to make the matter public. But except for the following night, he did not come again, and I did not see him on the street or in church for more than a month; I tried in vain to communicate with him, for I knew he was in the city and went hunting almost every day; he was an enthusiastic hunter. I can say that for me those days and hours were ominous and filled with shame; and I can say that I began to doubt and even to distrust the good faith of Don Fernando; and I can say that my maid heard then the words she had not heard before, reprimanding her audacity; and I can say that it was necessary for me to contain my tears and control the expression on my face so that my parents would have no reason to ask why I was unhappy, and I would not be obliged to think of a lie to tell them. But all of this came to an abrupt halt when all propriety was trampled, honorable speeches ended, forbearance was lost, and my secret thoughts were made public. And this happened because some days later, the talk was that in a nearby city, Don Fernando had married an extremely beautiful girl, of very distinguished parentage, though not so rich that her dowry would lead her to aspire to so noble a marriage. People said her name was Luscinda, and that certain extraordinary things had happened at the wedding."

Cardenio heard the name of Luscinda and could do nothing but hunch his shoulders, bite his lips, scowl, and then let tears stream from his eyes. But this did not stop Dorotea from continuing her story, and she said:

"This sad news reached my ears, and instead of my heart freezing over when I heard it, it flamed with so much rage and fury that I almost took to the streets to cry out and proclaim how he had betrayed and deceived me. But then my anger began to cool when I thought of a plan that I put into effect that very night, which was to put on these clothes, given to me by one of the men, called shepherd's helpers by farmers, who was a servant of my father's; I told him about my misfortune and asked him to accompany me to the city where I believed my enemy would be found. He, after reprimanding me for my rashness and condemning my decision, saw that I was determined and offered to keep me company, as he called it, to the ends of the earth. I quickly put a dress and some jewels and money into a linen pillowcase, in the event I needed them, and in the silence of the night, without saying anything to my treacherous maid, I left my house, accompanied by my servant and many apprehensions, and started out for the city on foot, although my feet flew with the desire to reach my destination, if not to prevent what I considered already accomplished, at least to ask Don Fernando to tell me how he had had the heart to do it.

I arrived in two and a half days, and as I entered the city I asked for

the house of Luscinda's parents, and the first person I asked responded
with more than I wished to hear. He told me where their house was located, and everything that had occurred at the wedding of their daughter, which was so well-known that people throughout the city were
gathering in groups to talk about it. He told me that on the night Don
Fernando married Luscinda, after she had said her *yes*, she had fallen
into a dead faint, and when her husband came to loosen her bodice and
give her air, he had found a letter written in Luscinda's own hand, which
stated and declared that she could not be Don Fernando's wife because
she was the wife of Cardenio, who was, according to what the man told
me, a very distinguished gentleman from the same city, and if she had
agreed to marry Don Fernando, it was in order not to disobey her parents. In short, he told me that the letter said that she had intended to
kill herself when the ceremony was over, and in the letter she gave her
reasons for taking her life, all of which, they say, was confirmed by a dagger that was found hidden in her clothing. When Don Fernando saw
this, it seemed to him that Luscinda had mocked and scorned and humiliated him, and he threw himself at her while she was still in a swoon,
and with the same dagger tried to stab her, and would have done so if her
parents and the others present had not stopped him. People also said
that Don Fernando left immediately, and Luscinda did not recover from
her swoon until the following day, and then she told her parents that she
was the true wife of this Cardenio whom I have mentioned.

I learned more: people were saying that Cardenio had been present at
the wedding, and when he saw her married, something he never thought
possible, he left the city in despair but first wrote a letter in which he revealed how Luscinda had wronged him, and how he was going to a place
where no one would ever see him again. All of this was widely known
throughout the city, and everyone was talking about it, and talked about
it even more when they learned that Luscinda had disappeared from her
parents' house, and from the city, and was nowhere to be found, and that
her parents were distraught and did not know what to do to find her.
What I heard revived my hopes, and I considered it better not to have
found Don Fernando than to have found him married, for it seemed to
me that the door to my remedy was still not completely closed, assuming
that heaven might have placed that impediment to his second marriage
in order to make him realize what he owed the first, and to remember
that he was a Christian who had a greater obligation to his soul than to
human interests. I resolved all of these things in my imagination and was

consoled without consolation, inventing distant faint hopes in order to live a life which I now despise.

While I was in the city, not knowing what to do since Don Fernando was nowhere to be found, a public proclamation reached my ears, promising a large reward to the person who found me and giving a description of my age and the clothes I was wearing; I heard people saying that I had run off with the servant who accompanied me, and it wounded my very soul to see how my good name had been sullied, besmirched not only by reports of my impetuous departure, but by references to a baseborn person unworthy of my amorous thoughts. As soon as I heard the proclamation, I left the city with my servant, who was already beginning to show signs of wavering in his promise of fidelity to me, and that night we entered a remote part of these mountains, afraid of being discovered. But, as they say, one ill leads to another, and the end of one misfortune tends to be the beginning of another even greater, and that is what happened to me; my good servant, faithful and trustworthy until then, saw me in this desolate place, and inflamed by his own depravity rather than my beauty, attempted to take advantage of the opportunity which, to his mind, this setting offered him; with little shame and less fear of God or respect for me, he tried to persuade me to make love to him, and seeing that I responded with words of censure and rebuke to his outrageous proposals, he set aside the entreaties that he thought at first would succeed and began to use force. But heaven is just, rarely or never failing to regard and favor righteous intentions, and it favored mine, so that with my scant strength, and not too much effort, I pushed him over a precipice, where I left him, not knowing if he was dead or alive; then, with more speed than my fear and exhaustion really allowed, I entered these mountains; my only thought and plan was to hide, to flee my father and those he had sent to look for me.

This was my desire when I came here, I do not know how many months ago; I found a drover who took me on as a servant in a place deep in the sierra, and I have worked as a shepherd's helper all this time, trying always to be out in the fields in order to hide this hair that now, so unexpectedly, has been revealed. But all my effort and care was and has been to no avail, for my master learned that I was not a man, and the same wicked desire was born in him as in my servant; since fortune does not always give remedies along with difficulties, I found no precipice or ravine where I could push the master and save myself, as I had with the servant, and so I thought it less difficult to leave him and take refuge again in these desolate places than to test my strength or my reasoning with him. Therefore, as I said, I took to the wilds again to find the place where, without impediment, I could, with sighs and tears, beg heaven to take pity on my misfortune, and favor me with the ability either to leave that misfortune behind or to lose my life in the wilderness, and to let the memory be erased of this unfortunate woman, who, through no fault of her own, has become the subject of talk and gossip in her own and other lands."

CHAPTER XXIX

Which recounts the amusing artifice and arrangement that was devised for freeing our enamored knight from the harsh penance he had imposed on himself[1]

"This is, Señores, the true history of my tragedy: now deem and judge if the sighs you heard, the words you listened to, and the tears that flowed from my eyes had sufficient reason to appear in even greater abundance; having considered the nature of my misfortune, you will see that consolation would be useless since the remedy is impossible. All I ask of you (this is something you can and should do very easily) is that you advise me where I can spend my life without being overwhelmed by the fear and terror I have of being discovered by those who are searching for me; although I know the great love my parents have for me guarantees that I shall be welcomed by them, I am filled with so much shame when I think that I must appear before them in a state different from the one they had counted upon that it seems better to exile myself forever from their sight rather than see their faces and think that they are looking at mine when it is far removed from the chastity they had a right to expect of me."

She fell silent after she said this, and her face flushed with a color that clearly showed the grief and shame in her soul. The souls of those who had listened to her felt as much compassion as astonishment at her misfortune, and although the priest immediately wanted to console and advise her, Cardenio stepped forward first, saying:

1. In the first edition, this was the epigraph for chapter XXX, while the one for chapter XXIX appeared before chapter XXX. In other words, the epigraphs were reversed.

"So then, Señora, you are the beautiful Dorotea, the only child of the wealthy Clenardo?"

Dorotea was surprised to hear her father's name and to see the wretched condition of the man who named him, for the rags Cardenio wore have already been mentioned, and therefore she said to him:

"And who are you, friend, that you know my father's name? If I am not mistaken, in recounting the story of my misfortune, I have not spoken his name."

"I am, Señora," responded Cardenio, "that luckless man who, as you have told us, Luscinda declared to be her husband. I am the unfortunate Cardenio, and the wicked purpose of the man who has brought you to the condition in which you find yourself has driven me to the one in which you see me now: ragged, naked, bereft of all human consolation, and, what is worse, bereft of reason, except when it pleases heaven to grant it to me for some brief time. I, Dorotea, am the one who witnessed the wrongs committed by Don Fernando, the one who waited until Luscinda spoke the words that made her his wife. I am the one who did not have the courage to see the consequences of her swoon or the outcome of the letter found in her bosom, because my soul could not bear to see so many misfortunes together; and so I abandoned the house, and my forbearance, and gave a letter to the man who was my host, asking him to deliver it into Luscinda's hands, and came to this solitary place where I intended to end my life, which from that moment on I despised as if it were my mortal enemy. But fate has not wished to take it from me, being satisfied with taking my reason, perhaps wanting to preserve me for the good fortune I have had in finding you; for if what you have recounted is true, as I believe it is, it well might be that heaven has in store a more favorable conclusion to our calamities than we can imagine. Since Luscinda cannot marry Don Fernando because she is mine, and Don Fernando cannot marry her because he is yours, and she has openly declared this, we can reasonably hope that heaven will restore to each of us what is ours, for it is still intact, not given away or destroyed. And since we have this consolation, not born of remote hopes, or founded on wild imaginings, I beg you, Señora, to come to another decision in your honorable thoughts, as I intend to do in mine, and prepare to expect better fortune; I give you my vow as a gentleman and a Christian not to abandon you until I see that you are Don Fernando's, and if reason cannot persuade him to recognize his duty to you, then I shall use the prerogative I have as a gentleman to legitimately challenge him and right the wrong he has done you; and I shall not think of the offenses committed against me, vengeance for which I leave to heaven so that here on earth I may attend to those committed against you."

Dorotea was overwhelmed when she heard Cardenio's words, and because she did not know how to express her thanks for so noble an offer, she attempted to kiss his feet, but Cardenio would not permit it, and the licentiate responded for himself and the barber and approved Cardenio's fine speech and in particular asked, advised, and urged them to accompany him to his village, where they could obtain the things they lacked, and decide how to find Don Fernando, or return Dorotea to her parents, or do whatever they thought most appropriate. Cardenio and Dorotea thanked him and accepted his offer of help. The barber, who had reacted to everything with amazement and silence, also made a courteous speech and offered, with no less enthusiasm than the priest, to serve them in any way he could.

He also recounted briefly the reason that had brought them there, the strangeness of Don Quixote's madness, and how they were waiting for his squire, who had gone to find him. Cardenio recalled, as if it had been a dream, his altercation with Don Quixote, and he told the others about it but could not tell them the reason for the dispute.

Then they heard shouting and recognized Sancho Panza's voice, for when he did not find them in the place where he had left them, he began to call their names. They came out to meet him, and when they asked about Don Quixote, he said he had found him naked except for his shirt, thin, yellow, famished, and sighing for his lady Dulcinea; although he had told his master that she had ordered him to leave that place and go to Toboso, where she was waiting for him, Don Quixote had responded that he was resolved not to come before her beauteousness until such time as he had performed such feats as would render him deserving of her grace. And Sancho said that if this went on much longer, Don Quixote ran the risk of not becoming an emperor, as he was obliged to do, or even an archbishop, which was the least he could be. For this reason, they should think about what had to be done to get him out of there.

The licentiate responded that he should not worry, for they would take his master away from there even if he did not wish to go. Then he told Cardenio and Dorotea what they had planned as a remedy for Don Quixote or, at least, as a way to take him home. To which Dorotea replied that she could play the afflicted damsel better than the barber, and, what is more, she had with her the clothes to play the part naturally, and they could trust her to know how to do everything necessary to carry their intention forward, as she had read many books of chivalry and knew very well the style used by damsels in distress when they begged boons of knights errant.

"Well, nothing else is necessary," said the priest, "than to put the plan into effect immediately; Fortune no doubt favors us since she has begun so unexpectedly to open the door to your remedy, my friends, and has provided us with what we needed."

Then Dorotea took from her pillow slip a dress made of a certain fine woolen cloth and a mantilla made of another attractive green fabric, and from a small box she took a necklace and other jewels, and with these she adorned herself and in a moment resembled a rich, great lady. All of this, and more, she said she had removed from her house in the event she needed them, and until now she had not had the opportunity to make use of them. Her extreme grace, charm, and comeliness delighted everyone and confirmed that Don Fernando was a man of limited understanding for having cast aside so much beauty.

But most astonished of all was Sancho Panza, for it seemed to him—and it was true—that never in all his days had he seen so beautiful a creature; and so he asked the priest very eagerly to tell him who the beautiful lady was and what she was doing in this remote place.

"This beautiful lady, brother Sancho," responded the priest, "is, and it is no small thing, the heir by direct male line of the great kingdom of Micomicón, and she has come looking for your master to beg of him a boon, which is that he right a wrong or correct an injustice done to her by an evil giant; and because of the fame your master has throughout the known world as a brave and virtuous knight, this princess has come all the way from Guinea to find him."

"A lucky search and a lucky finding," Sancho Panza said, "especially if my master is fortunate enough to undo that injustice and right that wrong by killing that whoreson of a giant your grace has mentioned; for he surely will kill him if he finds him, unless he's a phantom, because my master has no power at all against phantoms. But one thing I want to beg of your grace, among others, Señor Licentiate, so that my master doesn't take it into his head to be an archbishop, which is what I'm afraid of, is that your grace advise him to marry this princess right away, and then he won't be able to receive archbishopal orders, and he'll come easily into his empire, and I'll finally get the thing I desire; I've thought about it carefully, and as far as I can tell, it does me no good at all if my master becomes an archbishop because I'm useless for the Church since I'm married, and for me to try now to get a dispensation so that I could have an income from the Church, having, as I do, a wife and children, well, there'd be no end to it. And so, Señor, the thing now is for my master to marry this lady right away, and since I don't know her title, I'm not calling her by name."

"Her name," responded the priest, "is the Princess Micomicona; since her kingdom is called Micomicón, of course that is her name."

"No doubt about it," responded Sancho. "I've seen lots of people take the name and lineage of the place where they were born, calling themselves Pedro de Alcalá, Juan de Ubeda, or Diego de Valladolid, and they must have the same custom there in Guinea, so queens take the names of their kingdoms."

"That must be the case," said the priest, "and as for your master marrying, I'll do everything in my power to bring that about."

This made Sancho happy, and the priest was astounded, both by his simplicity and by how his imagination was filled with his master's nonsensical ideas, for Sancho believed beyond the shadow of a doubt that Don Quixote would become an emperor.

By now Dorotea had mounted the priest's mule and the barber had attached the oxtail beard to his face, and they told Sancho to lead them to Don Quixote and warned him not to say that he had recognized the licentiate or the barber, because the whole matter of his master becoming emperor depended on their not being recognized; the priest and Cardenio, however, did not want to accompany them, Cardenio because he did not wish to remind Don Quixote of their dispute and the priest because his presence was no longer needed. And so they allowed the others go ahead while they followed slowly on foot. The priest did not fail to remind Dorotea of what she had to do, to which she replied that there was no need to worry; everything would be done to the letter, exactly as demanded and depicted by the books of chivalry.

They had ridden approximately three-quarters of a league when they caught sight of Don Quixote among some crags, dressed now, but not wearing his armor, and as soon as Dorotea saw him and was informed by Sancho that this was Don Quixote, she applied the whip to her palfrey,[2] followed by the well-bearded barber. And when they reached him, the squire leaped off the mule and took Dorotea in his arms, and she, dismounting very gracefully, went to kneel before Don Quixote; and al-

---

2. The kind of gentle horse normally ridden by women and referred to frequently in novels of chivalry; Cervantes uses the term for comic effect since Dorotea is riding a mule.

though he struggled to lift her up, she, still kneeling, spoke to him in this manner:

"I shall not rise up from this place, O valiant and brave knight, until thy goodness and courtesy grant me a boon, which will redound to the honor and renown of thy person and to the benefit of the most disconsolate and aggrieved damsel e'er seen by the sun. And if it be true that the valor of thy mighty arm correspondeth to the accounts of thy immortal fame, thou needs must favor this unfortunate maiden who hath come from such distant lands, following thy famous name and searching for thee to remedy her afflictions."

"I shall not utter a word, beauteous lady," responded Don Quixote, "nor shall I hearken to thy concerns until thou hast raised thyself from the ground."

"I shall not raise myself, my lord," responded the damsel in distress, "if thy courtesy doth not first grant me the boon I beg of thee."

"I grant and bestow it upon thee," responded Don Quixote, "as long as it doth not harm nor diminish my king, my country, and she who holds the key to my heart and liberty."

"It shall neither harm nor diminish those whom thou sayest, good my lord," responded the mournful maiden.

As they were speaking, Sancho Panza approached and said very quietly into his master's ear:

"Señor, your grace can easily grant the boon she asks, it's nothing, just killing a giant, and the lady who asks it is her highness Princess Micomicona, queen of the great kingdom Micomicón in Ethiopia."

"Whoever she may be," responded Don Quixote, "I shall do what I am obliged to do and what my conscience dictates, in accordance with the order I have professed."

And turning to the damsel, he said:

"Let thy great beauty arise, for I grant whatever boon thou asketh of me."

"Then what I ask," said the damsel, "is that thy magnanimous person cometh with me wheresoever I shall lead thee, and maketh a vow that thou wilt not engage in any other adventure or respond to any other request until thou hast taken revenge for my sake upon a traitor who, counter to all divine and human law, hath usurped my kingdom."

"I say that I do grant it in this wise," responded Don Quixote, "and therefore thou mayest, Señora, from this day forth, cast off the melancholy that afflicts thee and let thy faint hope take on new vigor and strength; for, with the help of God and this my arm, thou wilt soon see thyself restored to thy kingdom and seated on the throne of thy great and ancient state, in spite of and despite the base cowards who wisheth to deny it to thee. And now, to work, for they sayeth that in delay there lieth danger."

The aggrieved maiden struggled insistently to kiss his hands, but Don Quixote, a discreet and courteous knight in all things, would not consent; instead, he helped her to her feet and embraced her with great courtesy and discretion and ordered Sancho to tighten Rocinante's cinches and arm him immediately. Sancho took down the armor, which hung, like a trophy, from a tree, and, after tightening the cinches, he quickly armed his master, who, when he saw himself armed, said:

"Let us leave here, in the name of God, to succor this great lady."

The barber was still on his knees, being very careful to conceal his laughter and to keep his beard from falling off, for if it fell, perhaps they would all fail to achieve their good intentions; and seeing that the boon had been granted, and that Don Quixote was preparing diligently to fulfill it, he rose and took his lady by the other hand, and the two of them lifted her onto the mule. Then Don Quixote mounted Rocinante, and the barber settled onto his animal, and Sancho was left to go on foot, feeling again the loss of his gray, which he needed so much now; but he bore everything with good humor, because it seemed to him that now his master was well on his way and very close to being an emperor, for without a doubt he thought he would marry the princess and become, at the very least, king of Micomicón. The only thing he regretted was the thought that the kingdom was in a country of blacks, and the people who would be given to him as vassals would all be blacks; then, in his imagination, he found a good remedy for this, saying to himself:

"What difference does it make to me if my vassals are blacks? All I have to do is put them on a ship and bring them to Spain, where I can sell them, and I'll be paid for them in cash, and with that money I'll be able to buy some title or office and live on that for the rest of my life. No flies on me! Who says I don't have the wit or ability to arrange things and sell thirty or ten thousand vassals in the wink of an eye? By God, I'll sell them all, large or small, it's all the same to me, and no matter how black they are, I'll turn them white and yellow.[3] Bring them on, then, I'm no fool!"

This made him so eager and happy that he forgot about his sorrow at having to walk.

---

3. In other words, Sancho will turn them into silver and gold.

Cardenio and the priest watched all of this through some brambles, and they did not know what pretext they could use to join the others, but the priest, who was a great plotter, thought immediately of what they could do to achieve their desire, and with a pair of scissors he carried with him in a case, he quickly cut off Cardenio's beard, and dressed him in his gray jacket, and gave him his short black cape, while he was left wearing doublet and breeches, and Cardenio's appearance was so changed from what it had been before that he would not have recognized himself if he had looked in a mirror. When this had been done, although the others had already moved on while they were disguising themselves, they easily reached the king's highway before them, because the thickets and rough terrain in those places makes travel more difficult for those on horseback than for those on foot. In fact, they positioned themselves on the plain at the entrance to the sierra, and as soon as Don Quixote and his companions emerged, the priest began to stare at him, showing signs that he recognized him, and after looking at him for a long time, he went toward him, his arms opened wide, and called out:

"Well met, O paragon of chivalry, my good compatriot Don Quixote of La Mancha, flower of gallantry, protector and defender of the weak, quintessence of knight errantry."

And saying this, he threw his arms around the left knee of Don Quixote, who was stunned at what he saw and heard the man saying and doing and began to look at him carefully; at last he recognized him, and was astonished to see him, and made a great effort to dismount, but the priest would not allow it, for which reason Don Quixote said:

"Your grace, Señor Licentiate, permit me to dismount, for it is not right that I remain on horseback while a reverend person like your grace goes on foot."

"Under no circumstances shall I agree to that," said the priest. "Let your magnificence stay on your horse, for on horseback you perform the greatest deeds and have the greatest adventures that our age has witnessed; as for me, I am only an unworthy priest, and it will be enough for me to climb on the haunches of one of these mules and ride behind one of these gentlefolk traveling with your grace, if they do not consider that an inconvenience. And I shall imagine that I am mounted on Pegasus, or on the zebra or immense horse ridden by that famous Moor Muzaraque, who even now lies enchanted on the slopes of the great Zulema, not far from great Complutum."[4]

---

4. Complutum was the Roman name for Alcalá de Henares, Cervantes's birthplace.

"That did not occur to me, Señor Licentiate," responded Don Quixote, "but I know that my lady the princess is willing, for my sake, to order her squire to give up the saddle on his mule to your grace; he can ride on the haunches, if the animal can carry you both."

"It can, as far as I know," responded the princess, "and I also know it will not be necessary to give any orders to my gentle squire, for he is so courteous and courtly that he will not agree to an ecclesiastical person traveling on foot when he can ride."

"That is true," responded the barber.

And dismounting immediately, he invited the priest to sit on the saddle, and he did so without having to be begged. Unfortunately, when the barber climbed onto its haunches, the mule, which in fact had been hired, which is enough to indicate how bad it was, raised its hindquarters a little and gave two kicks into the air, and if they had landed on Master Nicolás's chest or his head, he would have cursed the day he came after Don Quixote. As it was, they startled him so much that he fell to the ground, paying so little attention to his beard that it fell to the ground as well, and when he found himself without it, all he could do was cover his face with both hands and complain that his teeth had been broken. Don Quixote, when he saw that great clump of beard with no jaw, and no blood, lying far from the face of the fallen squire, said:

"As God lives, what a great miracle this is! His beard has been ripped and torn from his face as if it had been done intentionally!"

The priest, who saw the risk of his deception being discovered, ran to the beard and carried it to where Master Nicolás was still lying on the ground and crying out, and at one stroke he pulled the barber's head down to his chest and put the beard back on, murmuring some words over him, which he said was a special incantation for reattaching beards, as they would soon see; when he had replaced the beard he moved away, and the squire was as well-bearded and undamaged as before; this left Don Quixote dumbfounded, and he asked the priest to teach him the incantation when he had time, because he believed its virtue had to go beyond simply reattaching beards, for it was clear that when the beard was torn off, the skin where it had been attached had to be badly wounded, and since the incantation had cured everything, it was of benefit to more than just beards.

"That is true," said the priest, and he promised to teach it to him at the first opportunity.

They agreed that the priest would mount the mule for the moment, and the three of them would take turns riding until they reached the inn, which was some two leagues away. With three of them riding—that is

Don Quixote, the princess, and the priest—and three of them walking—
to wit, Cardenio, the barber, and Sancho Panza—Don Quixote said to
the damsel:

"Your highness, Señora, lead us wherever you please."

And before she could respond, the licentiate said:

"Toward which kingdom does Your Majesty wish to go? Is it by
chance Micomicón? It must be, or I know little of kingdoms."

She was very sharp-witted and understood what her answer had to
be, and so she said:

"Yes, Señor: I am going to that kingdom."

"If that is true," said the priest, "we have to pass through the center of
my village, and from there your grace will take the road to Cartagena,
where, with good fortune, you can embark, and if there is a favorable
wind, a calm sea, and no storms, in a little less than nine years you can be
in sight of the great Meona,[5] I mean, Meótides Lagoon, which is a little
more than one hundred days' travel from Your Majesty's kingdom."

"Your grace is mistaken, Señor," she said, "because I left there less
than two years ago, and the truth is I never had good weather, and despite all this I have succeeded in seeing the one I longed to see, which is
to say, Señor Don Quixote of La Mancha, news of whom reached my ears
as soon as I set foot in Spain, moving me to seek him in order to commend myself to his courtesy, and entrust my just cause to the valor of his
invincible arm."

"No more: let my praises cease," Don Quixote said then, "because I
am the enemy of any kind of flattery, and even if this is not flattery, such
talk offends my chaste ears. What I can say, my lady, is that whether or
not I possess valor, whatever valor I do or do not possess will be used in
your service until the end of my life; leaving this aside for the moment, I
beg your grace, Señor Licentiate, to tell me the reason that has brought
you to this place, alone, and so lacking in servants, and so lightly clad
that it astounds me."

"I shall reply to that briefly," responded the priest, "because your
grace must know, Señor Don Quixote, that I and Master Nicolás, our
friend and barber, were going to Sevilla to collect a certain sum of money
that a kinsman of mine who went to the Indies many years ago had sent
to me, no small sum since it amounts to more than sixty thousand as-
sayed *pesos*, which are worth twice as much as ordinary ones; yesterday,

5. *Meona* means "urinating frequently" and is often used to describe newborn infants.

as we were traveling through this area, four highwaymen assaulted us and took everything, even our beards; because of that, it suited the barber to put on a false one, and even this young man here"—and he pointed at Cardenio—"they transformed completely. Strangely enough, it is common knowledge all around this area that the men who assaulted us were galley slaves freed, they say, in this very spot, by a man so brave that despite the commissary and the guards, he released them all; there can be no doubt that he was out of his mind, or as great a villain as they, or a man without soul or conscience, for he wanted to set the wolf loose in the midst of the sheep, the fox in the midst of the chickens, the fly in the midst of the honey: he wanted to defraud justice and oppose his king and natural lord, for he opposed his just commands. As I say, he wanted to deprive the galleys of their oars and throw the Holy Brotherhood, which had been at peace for many years, into an uproar; in short, he has committed an act by means of which one loses one's soul and does little good for one's body."

Sancho had told the priest and the barber about the adventure of the galley slaves, which his master had concluded so gloriously, and for this reason the priest was very harsh when he referred to it in order to see what Don Quixote would do or say; he changed color at each word and did not dare say that he had been the liberator of those good people.

"These men, then," said the priest, "were the ones who robbed us. May God in His mercy pardon the man who did not allow them to be taken to the punishment they deserved."

CHAPTER XXX

Which recounts the good judgment of the beautiful Dorotea, along with other highly diverting and amusing matters

No sooner had the priest finished speaking than Sancho said:

"Well, by my faith, Señor Licentiate, the man who did that deed was my master, and don't think I didn't tell him beforehand, and warn him to be careful about what he was doing, and say it was a sin to free them since all of them were there because they were great villains."

"Imbecile," said Don Quixote, "it is not the responsibility or concern of a knight errant to determine if the afflicted, the fettered, and the oppressed whom he meets along the road are in that condition and suffering that anguish because of misdeeds or kind acts. His only obligation is to help them because they are in need, turning his eyes to their suffering and not their wickedness. And I encountered a rosary, a string of disheartened, unfortunate people, and I did for them what my religion[1] asks of me; the rest does not concern me, and I say that whoever thinks this is wrong, excepting the holy dignity of the licentiate and his honored person, knows little of the matter of chivalry, and lies like a lowborn whoreson, and will be taught this by my sword at greater length."

And as he said this, he thrust his feet firmly into the stirrups and set his simple morion helmet firmly on his head, because the barber's basin, which to his mind was the helmet of Mambrino, hung from the forebow of his saddle, waiting for the damage it had received at the hands of the galley slaves to be repaired.

Dorotea, who was quick-witted and very spirited, knew that Don Quixote's reason was impaired and that everyone mocked and deceived him except Sancho Panza; she did not wish to do any less, and seeing him so angry, she said:

"Señor Knight, your grace should remember the boon you have promised me, according to which you cannot become involved in any other adventure no matter how urgent; your grace should calm your spirits, for if the licentiate had known that the galley slaves had been freed by that unvanquished arm, he would have put three stitches across his mouth and even bitten his tongue three times before saying a single word that in any way would redound to your grace's discredit."

"I certainly swear to that," said the priest, "and even would have removed half of my mustache."

"I shall be silent, Señora," said Don Quixote, "and repress the righteous anger that hath welled up in my bosom, and go quietly and peacefully until such time as I have fulfilled the boon I have promised thee; but, as recompense for this virtuous desire, I implore thee to tell me, if it doth not cause thee too much pain, what it is that distresseth thee, and who, what, and how many are the persons on whom I must wreak proper, complete, and entire vengeance."

"I shall be happy to do that," responded Dorotea, "if it doth not trouble thee to hear sorrows and misfortunes."

1. In this context, religion signifies the order of chivalry.

"It troubleth me not, Señora," responded Don Quixote.

To which Dorotea responded:

"If that be so, then your graces should give me your attention."

As soon as she said this, Cardenio and the barber came up beside her, wishing to see how the clever Dorotea would invent her history, and Sancho did the same, for she had misled him as much as she had his master. And she, after making herself comfortable on the saddle and coughing and doing a few other things in preparation, began, with a good deal of vivacity, to speak in the following manner:

"First of all, Señores, I want your graces to know that I am called . . ."

And she paused here for a moment because she had forgotten the name the priest had given her, but he came to the rescue, for he understood why she hesitated, and said:

"It is no surprise, Señora, that your highness becomes confused and distraught when recounting your misfortunes, for they are of the sort that often deprive the afflicted of their memories so that they cannot even remember their own names, and that is what they have done to your most noble person, causing you to forget that your name is Princess Micomicona, legitimate heir to the great kingdom of Micomicón; with this reminder your highness can now easily restore to your aggrieved memory everything you wish to recount."

"That is true," responded the maiden, "and from now on I believe that it will not be necessary to remind me of anything, and that I shall come safely into port with my true history. Which is that the king my father, whose name is Tinacrio the Mage, was very learned in what are called the magical arts, and by means of his knowledge he discovered that my mother, whose name was Queen Jaramilla, would die before him, and that a short while later he too would pass from this life and I would be left an orphan, without father or mother. But he said he was not troubled by this as much as he was confounded by the certain knowledge that a monstrous giant, lord of a large island that almost touches our kingdom, whose name is Pandafilando of the Gloomy Glance (because it is an undisputed fact that although his eyes are in the correct and proper place, he always looks the wrong way round, as if he were cross-eyed, and does this out of malice and to put fear and terror into those he sees); as I say, he knew that this giant, when he heard of my orphaned state, would invade my kingdom with a mighty army and take everything from me and not leave me even a small village where I might take refuge, although I could avoid all this calamity and misfortune if I would agree to marry him; but it was my father's belief that I would not

ever wish to make such an unequal marriage, and in this he told the absolute truth, because it has never entered my mind to marry either that
giant or any other no matter how huge and monstrous he might be. My
father also said that after he was dead, when I saw that Pandafilando was
beginning to invade my kingdom, I should not take the time to set up
defenses because that would mean my destruction, but that I ought to
freely leave my unprotected kingdom if I wished to avoid the death and
total destruction of my good and loyal vassals, because it would not be
possible to defend myself against the devilish power of the giant; instead,
with some of my people, I had to set out immediately for the kingdoms of
Spain, where I would find the remedy for my ills when I found a knight
errant whose fame extended throughout those lands, and whose name, if
I remember correctly, was Don Azote or Don Gigote."[2]

"He must have said Don Quixote," said Sancho Panza, "also known
as the Knight of the Sorrowful Face."

"That is correct," said Dorotea. "He also said that his body would be
tall, his face dry, and that on the right, beneath his left shoulder, or
somewhere near there, he would have a dark mole with certain hairs
growing out of it like bristles."

On hearing this, Don Quixote said to his squire:

"Here, Sancho my son, help me to undress, for I wish to see if I am the
knight foretold by the sage king."

"But why does your grace wish to undress?" said Dorotea.

"To see if I have the mole mentioned by your father," responded Don
Quixote.

"There's no need to undress," said Sancho, "for I know your grace has
a mole like that in the middle of your spine, and it's the sign of a strong
man."

"That is sufficient," said Dorotea, "because among friends one must
not worry over details, and whether it is on the shoulder or the spine is of
little importance: it is enough that there is a mole, and no matter where
it may be, it is all the same flesh; no doubt my good father was correct in
everything, and I was correct in commending myself to Don Quixote, for
he is the one of whom my father spoke: his features match those indicated in the excellent reputation of this knight not only in Spain but in
all of La Mancha, for no sooner had I disembarked in Osuna[3] than I

2. *Azote* means "whip" or "scourge"; *gigote* is "fricassee" or "hash."

3. The humor in Dorotea's statement (comparable to her not being able to recall Don Quixote's
name) lies in the fact that Osuna is landlocked and that La Mancha is part of Spain, and not the reverse, as she implies.

heard of so many of his great deeds that my heart immediately told me he was the one I had come to seek."

"But how could your grace disembark in Osuna, my lady," asked Don Quixote, "if it is not a sea port?"

Before Dorotea could respond, the priest began to speak, saying:

"My lady the princess must mean that after she disembarked in Málaga, the first place she heard of your grace was in Osuna."

"That is just what I meant," said Dorotea.

"And now that is settled," said the priest, "and Your Majesty can continue."

"There is no need to continue," responded Dorotea, "except to say in conclusion that my good fortune has been so great in finding Don Quixote that I already consider and think of myself as queen and mistress of my entire kingdom, for he, in his courtesy and nobility, has promised me the boon of going with me wherever I may lead, and that is nowhere else but to Pandafilando of the Gloomy Glance so that he may kill him and restore to me what the giant has so unjustly usurped; all this will happen exactly as I have said, because this is what Tinacrio the Mage, my good father, prophesied; he also said, and left it written in Chaldean or Greek, neither of which I can read, that if the knight of his prophecy, after cutting off the head of the giant, wished to marry me, I should, immediately and without argument, give myself to him to be his legitimate wife and grant him possession of both my kingdom and my person."

"What do you think, friend Sancho?" said Don Quixote at this point. "Do you hear what is taking place? Did I not tell you? Now see if we have a kingdom to rule and a queen to marry."

"I'll swear we do," said Sancho, "and damn the man who doesn't marry after he slits open the gullet of Señor Pandahilado! Tell me the queen's not a good catch! All the fleas in my bed should be so nice!"

And saying this, he kicked his heels in the air twice, displaying enormous joy, and then he went to grasp the reins of Dorotea's mule, brought it to a halt, and kneeled before her, asking that she give him her hands to kiss as a sign that he had received her as his queen and mistress. Which of those present did not laugh at seeing the madness of the master and the simplemindedness of the servant? Dorotea, in effect, held out her hands for him to kiss and promised to make him a great lord in her kingdom when heaven in its mercy would allow her to recover and enjoy it. Sancho thanked her with words that renewed everyone's laughter.

"This, Señores," continued Dorotea, "is my history; all that remains for me to say is that of the entire entourage I took with me from my kingdom, the only one left is this good bearded squire; the others drowned in a great storm that broke over us when we were in sight of port, and he and I escaped on two planks and reached land as if by miracle; and so the story of my life, as you may have noticed, is one of miracle and mystery. And if I have gone too far in anything, or have not been as accurate as I should have been, blame what the Señor Licentiate said at the beginning of my tale: continual and extraordinary difficulties take away the memory of the one who suffers them."

"Mine will not be taken away, O noble and valiant lady," said Don Quixote, "no matter how great and unprecedented the difficulties I may suffer in serving thee! Therefore I again confirm the boon I have promised, and I vow to go with thee to the ends of the earth until I encounter thy savage enemy whose arrogant head I intend, with the help of God and my strong arm, to cut off with the sharp edge of this . . . I cannot say good sword, thanks to Ginés of Pasamonte, who stole mine from me."[4]

He muttered this last remark between clenched teeth and then continued, saying:

"And after I have cut off his head and placed thee in peaceful possession of thy kingdom, it will be left to thine own will to do with thy person as thou desirest; so long as my memory is filled with, and my will held captive by, and my reason lost because of a certain lady . . . I shall say no more, for it is not possible for me to consider or even think of marrying, although it were with one as unique as the phoenix."

Sancho was so displeased by what his master had said about not wanting to marry that he became very angry, and raising his voice, he said:

"I vow and I swear, Señor Don Quixote, that your grace is not in your right mind. How can your grace have any doubts about marrying a princess as noble as this one? Does your grace think fate will offer you good fortune like this around every corner? Is my lady Dulcinea, by some chance, more beautiful? No, certainly not, not even by half, and I'd go so far as to say she can't even touch the shoes of the lady we have before us. So woe is me, I'll never get the rank I'm hoping for if your grace goes around asking for the moon. Marry, marry right now, Satan take you, and take the kingdom that has dropped into your hands without you lifting a

4. This is the first reference, in either the first or second edition of the novel, to the theft of Don Quixote's sword.

finger, and when you're king make me a marquis or a governor, and then the devil can make off with all the rest."

Don Quixote could not endure hearing such blasphemies said against his lady Dulcinea; he raised his lance, and without saying a word to Sancho, in absolute silence, he struck him twice with blows so hard he knocked him to the ground, and if Dorotea had not called to him and told him to stop, he no doubt would have killed him then and there.

"Do you think,"[5] he said after a while, "base wretch, that you will always be able to treat me with disrespect, that it will always be a matter of your erring and my forgiving you? You are mistaken, depraved villain, something you undoubtedly are since you dare speak ill of the incomparable Dulcinea. Do you not realize, you coarse, contemptible ruffian, that if it were not for the valor she inspires in my arm, I should not have the strength to kill a flea? Tell me, insidious viper's tongue, who do you think has won this kingdom and cut off the head of this giant and made you a marquis, all of which I consider already accomplished, concluded, and finished, if not the valor of Dulcinea, wielding my arm as the instrument of her great deeds? In me she does combat, and in me she conquers, and I live and breathe in her, and have life and being. Oh, foul whoreson! What an ingrate you are, for you see yourself raised from the dust of the earth to be a titled lord, and you respond to this great benefit by speaking ill of the one who performed it for you!"

Sancho was not so badly beaten that he did not hear everything his master said to him, and after getting to his feet in some haste, he went to stand behind Dorotea's palfrey, and from there he said to his master:

"Tell me, Señor: if your grace is determined not to marry this great princess, it's clear the kingdom won't be yours; and if it isn't, what favors can you do for me? That's what I'm complaining about; your grace should marry this queen for now, when we have her here like a gift from heaven, and afterwards you can go back to my lady Dulcinea; there must have been kings in the world who lived with their mistresses. As for beauty, I won't get involved in that; if truth be told, they both seem fine to me, though I've never seen the lady Dulcinea."

"What do you mean, you have not seen her, you blasphemous traitor?" said Don Quixote. "Have you not just brought me a message from her?"

---

5. As indicated earlier, when he is extremely angry Don Quixote changes the way he addresses Sancho, moving from the second person singular to the more distant second person plural. This is the second time he has done so, and he maintains his irate distance until the end of the paragraph.

"I mean I didn't look at her so carefully," said Sancho, "that I could notice her beauty in particular and her good features point by point, but on the whole, she seemed fine to me."

"Now I forgive you," said Don Quixote, "and you must pardon the anger I have shown you; for first impulses are not in the hands of men."

"I can see that," responded Sancho, "just like in me a desire to talk is always my first impulse, and I can never help saying, not even once, what's on my tongue."

"Even so," said Don Quixote, "think about what you say, Sancho, because you can carry the jug to the fountain only so many times . . . and I shall say no more."

"Well," responded Sancho, "God's in His heaven, and He sees all the snares, and He'll be the judge of who does worse: me in not saying the right thing or your grace in not doing it."

"Enough," said Dorotea. "Make haste, Sancho, and kiss your master's hand and beg his pardon, and from now be more careful in your praise and blame, and do not speak ill of that Señora Tobosa, whom I do not know except to serve her, and trust in God that you will not lack an estate where you will live like a prince."

Sancho, with his eyes on the ground, went to ask for his master's hand, and his master gave it to him with a serene bearing, and after Sancho had kissed his hand, Don Quixote gave him his blessing and told him to walk ahead a little, because he had to speak to him and ask him things that were very important. Sancho did so, and the two of them moved ahead of the others, and Don Quixote said:

"Since your return I have not had the occasion or opportunity to ask you many details about the message you carried and the reply you brought back; and now, since fortune has granted us both the time and the place, do not deny me the happiness you can afford me with this good news."

"Your grace can ask whatever you want," responded Sancho, "and I'll finish off each question as easily as it was begun. But, Señor, I beg your grace not to be so vengeful from now on."

"Why do you say that, Sancho?" said Don Quixote.

"I say it," he responded, "because the blows you gave me just now were more because of the dispute the devil started between us the other night than because of what I said against my lady Dulcinea; I love and worship her like a relic, even if she isn't one, just because she belongs to your grace."

"As you value your life, Sancho, do not speak of this again," said Don Quixote, "for it brings me grief; I forgave you then, and you know what they say: a new sin demands a new penance."[6]

While Don Quixote and Sancho were engaged in this conversation, the priest told Dorotea that she had shown great cleverness not only in the story, but in making it so brief and so similar to the tales in books of chivalry. She said she had often spent time reading them but did not know where the provinces or the sea ports were, and that is why she had made the mistake of saying she had disembarked at Osuna.

"I realized that," said the priest, "which is why I hastened to say what I did, and that settled everything. But isn't it strange to see how easily this unfortunate gentleman believes all those inventions and lies simply because they are in the same style and manner as his foolish books?"

"It is," said Cardenio, "and so unusual and out of the ordinary that I don't know if anyone wanting to invent and fabricate such a story would have the wit to succeed."

"Well, there's something else in this," said the priest. "Aside from the foolish things this good gentleman says with reference to his madness, if you speak to him of other matters, he talks rationally and shows a clear, calm understanding in everything; in other words, except if the subject is chivalry, no one would think he does not have a very good mind."

While they were having this conversation, Don Quixote continued his and said to Sancho:

"Panza my friend, let us make peace and forget about our quarrels, and tell me now, without anger or rancor: where, how, and when did you find Dulcinea? What was she doing? What did you say to her? What did she reply? What was her expression when she read my letter? Who transcribed it for you? Tell me everything you saw that is worth knowing, asking, and answering, not exaggerating or falsifying in order to give me pleasure, and not omitting anything, for that will take my pleasure away."

"Señor," responded Sancho, "if truth be told, nobody transcribed the letter for me because I didn't take any letter."

"What you say is true," said Don Quixote. "I found the notebook where I wrote the letter in my possession two days after you left, which caused me great sorrow; I did not know what you would do when you dis-

6. At this point, in the second edition, Ginés de Pasamonte reappears, riding Sancho's donkey. Sancho begins to shout at him, calling him a thief, and Ginés runs away, leaving the donkey behind. Sancho is overjoyed, especially when Don Quixote says that this does not nullify the transfer of the three donkeys he had promised him earlier.

covered that you did not have the letter, and I believed you would return when you realized you did not have it."

"That's what I would have done," responded Sancho, "if I hadn't memorized it when your grace read it to me, and so I told it to a sacristan, and he transcribed it point for point from my memory, and he said that though he'd read many letters of excommunication, in all his days he'd never seen or read a letter as nice as that one."

"And do you still have it in your memory, Sancho?" said Don Quixote.

"No, Señor," responded Sancho, "because after I told it to him, and had no more use for it, I set about forgetting it; if I do remember anything, it's that part about *sullied*, I mean *sovereign lady*, and the last part: *Thine until death, the Knight of the Sorrowful Face*. And between these two things, I put in more than three hundred *souls*, and *lives*, and *eyes of mine*."

CHAPTER XXXI

Regarding the delectable words that passed between Don Quixote and Sancho Panza, his squire, as well as other events

"All this does not displease me; go on," said Don Quixote. "When you arrived, what was that queen of beauty doing? Surely you found her stringing pearls, or embroidering some heraldic device in gold thread for this her captive knight."

"I didn't find her doing anything," responded Sancho, "except winnowing two *fanegas*[1] of wheat in a corral of her house."

"Well, you may be sure," said Don Quixote, "that, touched by her hands, the grains of wheat were pearls. And did you notice, my friend, if it was white wheat or ordinary spring wheat?"

"It was just buckwheat," responded Sancho.

"Well, I assure you," said Don Quixote, "that winnowed by her hands, it undoubtedly made the finest white bread. But go on: when you gave her my letter, did she kiss it? Did she place it on her head?[2] Did she engage in some ceremony worthy of such a letter? What did she do?"

---

1. A *fanega* is approximately 1.6 bushels.

2. As a sign of respect, the recipient of a letter from a person of high station touched it to his or her head before opening it.

"When I was about to give it to her," responded Sancho, "she was in the middle of shaking a good part of the wheat that she had in the sieve, and she said to me: 'Friend, put the letter on that sack; I can't read it until I finish sifting everything I have here.'"

"A wise lady!" said Don Quixote. "That must have been so that she could read it slowly and savor it. Go on, Sancho. And while she was engaged in her task, what discourse did she have with you? What did she ask about me? And you, what did you respond? Come, tell me everything; do not leave even a half-note in the inkwell."

"She didn't ask me anything," said Sancho. "But I told her how your grace, to serve her, was doing penance, naked from the waist up, here in this sierra like a savage, sleeping on the ground, not eating your bread from a cloth or combing your beard, crying and cursing your fate."

"When you said that I cursed my fate, you misspoke," said Don Quixote. "Rather, I bless it and shall bless it all the days of my life for making me worthy of loving so high a lady as Dulcinea of Toboso."

"She's so high," responded Sancho, "that by my faith she's a whole span taller than I am."

"How do you know, Sancho?" said Don Quixote. "Did you measure yourself against her?"

"I measured myself this way," responded Sancho. "When I went over to her to help her load a sack of wheat onto a donkey, we were so close that I could see she was a good span taller than me."

"Well, it is true," replied Don Quixote, "that her great height is accompanied and adorned by a thousand million graces of the soul! But there is one thing you will not deny, Sancho: when you approached her, did you not smell the perfume of Sheba, an aromatic, somehow pleasing fragrance whose name I cannot recall? I mean, an essence or scent as if you were in the shop of some rare glover?"

"What I can say," said Sancho, "is that I smelled a mannish kind of odor, and it must have been that with all that moving around, she was sweaty and sort of sour."

"That could not be," responded Don Quixote. "You must have had a head cold or else you were smelling yourself, because I know very well the fragrance of that rose among thorns, that lily of the field, that delicate liquid ambergris."

"That may be," responded Sancho, "because very often the same smell comes from me, though at the time I thought it was coming from her grace the lady Dulcinea, but there's no reason to be surprised, since one devil looks like another."

"All right, then," Don Quixote went on, "she finished sifting the wheat and sent it to the mill. What did she do when she read the letter?"

"She didn't read the letter," said Sancho, "because she said she didn't know how to read or write; instead, she tore it into tiny pieces, saying that she didn't want to give it to anybody else to read because she didn't want people in the village knowing her secrets, and she was satisfied with what I had told her about the love your grace had for her and the special penance you were doing for her sake. Finally, she told me to tell your grace that she kissed your hands, and had more desire to see you than to write to you, and so she begged and commanded, in view of your letter, that you leave these wild places, and stop doing crazy things, and set out right away for Toboso, if something more important didn't come along, because she wanted to see your grace very much. She laughed a lot when I told her that your grace was called *The Knight of the Sorrowful Face*. I asked her if the Basque we met so long ago had come there, and she said he had, and that he was a very fine man. I also asked her about the galley slaves, but she said that so far she hadn't seen a single one."

"Everything is fine to this point," said Don Quixote. "But tell me: when she said goodbye, what jewel did she give you as a reward for the news of me that you brought to her? Because it is a traditional and ancient custom among knights errant and their ladies to give the squires, maidens, or dwarves who bring the knights news of their ladies, or the ladies news of their knights, the gift of a precious jewel in gratitude for the message."

"That may be true, and I think it's a good custom; but that must have been in the past; nowadays the custom must be just to give a piece of bread and some cheese, for that's what my lady Dulcinea handed me over the corral fence when she said goodbye; and it even looked like the cheese was made of sheep's milk."

"She is liberal in the extreme," said Don Quixote, "and if she did not present you with a jewel of gold, no doubt it was because she did not have one near at hand, but it is never the wrong time for a gift: I shall see her and you will have your reward. Do you know what astounds me, Sancho? It seems to me that you flew there and back, because it has taken you a little more than three days to go to Toboso and come back here again, a distance of more than thirty leagues; which leads me to believe that the wise necromancer who watches over my affairs and is my friend (because perforce there is one, there must be one, else I should not be a good knight errant), I say that he must have helped you on your journey without your realizing it, for there are wise men who pick up a knight errant sleeping in his bed, and without his knowing how or by what means, the knight awakens the following day more than a thousand leagues distant from where he went to sleep. If not for this, knights errant could not help each other when they are in danger, as they do constantly. For one may be doing battle in the mountains of Armenia with a dragon, or a fierce monster, or another knight, and matters are going badly for him and he is on the point of death, and then, when you least expect it, another knight appears on a cloud or in a chariot of fire, a knight who is his friend and was in England just a short while before, and who comes to his aid and saves him from death and that night finds himself at home, enjoying his supper; and the distance between the two places is usually two or three thousand leagues. All of this is accomplished through the skill and wisdom of the wise enchanters who watch over these valiant knights. And so, Sancho my friend, it is not difficult for me to believe that you have traveled back and forth in so short a time between here and Toboso, for, as I have said, some friendly sorcerer must have carried you through the air without your realizing it."

"That must be it," said Sancho, "because, by my faith, Rocinante was galloping like a Gypsy's donkey with quicksilver in its ear."[3]

"And not just quicksilver," said Don Quixote, "but a legion of demons, too, who can run and make others run, without growing tired, whenever they want to! But, leaving that aside, what do you think I ought to do now with regard to my lady commanding that I go to see her? For, although it is clear that I am obliged to obey her command, I am also prevented from doing so by the boon I have promised to the princess who is traveling with us, and the law of chivalry demands that I keep my word before I satisfy my wishes. On the one hand, I am pursued and hounded by the desire to see my lady; on the other, I am stirred and called by the promise I have made and the glory I shall gain in this undertaking. But what I intend to do is to travel swiftly and come without delay to the place where this giant is, and as soon as I arrive I shall cut off his head, and restore the princess peacefully to her kingdom, and immediately return to see the light that illumines my senses, and to her I shall give such excuses that she will come to consider my delay as a good thing, for she will see that it all redounds to her greater glory and fame, for everything I have achieved, achieve now, and shall achieve by force

3. A ruse allegedly used by Gypsies to make their animals run faster.

of arms in this life, comes to me because she favors me, and because I am hers."

"Oh," said Sancho, "those ideas of yours do you so much harm! Tell me, Señor: does your grace intend to make this trip for nothing, and let slip away and lose a marriage as profitable and distinguished as this one, where the dowry is a kingdom? The truth is I've heard it's more than twenty thousand leagues around, and overflowing with all the things needed to sustain human life, and bigger than Portugal and Castilla together. Be quiet, for the love of God, and shame on what you've said, and take my advice, and forgive me, and get married right away in the first town where there's a priest, or else here's our own licentiate, and he'll do a wonderful job. Remember that I'm old enough to give advice, and the advice I'm giving you now is exactly right, and a bird in the hand is better than a vulture in the air, and if you have something good and choose something evil, you can't complain about the good that happens to you."[4]

"Look, Sancho," responded Don Quixote, "if your advice to marry is because I shall become king when I kill the giant and can easily grant you favors and give you what I have promised, you should know that without marrying I shall be able to satisfy your desire, because I shall request as my reward, before I go into battle, that when I emerge victorious, even though I do not marry I shall be given part of the kingdom and then may give it to whomever I wish, and when they have given it to me, to whom shall I give it but to you?"

"That's clear enough," responded Sancho, "but your grace should be sure to choose the part along the coast, because if I'm not happy with the life, I can put my black vassals on a ship and do with them the things I said I would do. Your grace shouldn't take the time to see my lady Dulcinea now; you ought to go and kill the giant, and let's finish up this business, because, by God, it seems to me there's a lot of honor and profit in it."

"I say to you, Sancho," said Don Quixote, "that you are correct, and I shall take your advice with regard to going with the princess before I see Dulcinea. I warn you not to say anything to anyone, not even those who are with us, regarding what we have discussed and deliberated upon, for since Dulcinea is so modest and does not wish her thoughts to be known, it would not be right for me, or anyone speaking for me, to reveal them."

---

4. Sancho confuses the proverb, which ends: ". . . you can't complain about the evil that happens to you."

"Well, if that's true," said Sancho, "why does your grace make all those vanquished by your arm present themselves before my lady Dulcinea, when that's as sure as your signature that you love and serve her? And since they have to fall to their knees in her presence and say that they've been sent by your grace to be her servant, how can her thoughts or yours be hidden?"

"Oh, how foolish and simple you are," said Don Quixote. "Do you not see, Sancho, that all of this redounds to her greater glory? Because you should know that in our style of chivalry, it is a great honor for a lady to have many knights errant who serve her, and whose thoughts go no further than to serve her simply because she is who she is, not hoping for any other reward for their many and virtuous desires but that she be willing to accept them as her knights."

"That's the way," said Sancho, "I've heard it said in sermons, we should love Our Lord: for Himself alone, not because we hope for glory or are afraid of punishment. But I'd rather love and serve Him for what He can do."

"Devil take you for a peasant!" said Don Quixote. "What intelligent things you say sometimes! One would think you had studied."

"By my faith, I don't know how to read," responded Sancho.

At this point, Master Nicolás called to them to wait because the others wanted to stop and drink at a small spring. Don Quixote stopped, much to Sancho's delight; he was tired of telling so many lies and feared that his master would catch him in one, for although he knew that Dulcinea was a peasant from Toboso, he had never seen her in his life.

Cardenio, in the meantime, had put on the clothes worn by Dorotea when they found her, and although they were not very good, they were much better than the ones he discarded. They dismounted beside the spring, and with the food the priest had acquired at the inn, they managed to satisfy to some extent the great hunger they all felt.

As they were eating, a boy traveling along the road happened to pass by, and he began to look very carefully at the people around the spring, and then he ran to Don Quixote, threw his arms around his legs, and burst into tears, saying:

"Oh, Señor! Doesn't your grace know me? Look closely; I'm Andrés, the boy your grace freed from the oak tree where I was tied."

Don Quixote recognized him, and grasping him by the hand, he turned to his companions and said:

"So that your graces may see how important it is that there be knights errant in the world to right the wrongs and offenses committed by the insolent and evil men who live in it, your graces should know that some days ago, as I was passing through a wood, I heard shouts and very pitiful cries that seemed to come from a person in distress and in need; moved by my obligation, I immediately went to the place from which the heartrending cries seemed to come, and there I found this boy tied to an oak, and now you see him before you, which pleases my soul because he will be a witness who will not allow me to lie. I say that he was tied to the oak, naked from the waist up, and a peasant, who I learned later was his master, was beating him with the reins of his mare; as soon as I saw this I asked the reason for so savage a thrashing; the villain replied that he was beating him because he was his servant, and that certain of his careless acts were more a question of thievery than simplemindedness, to which this child said: 'Señor, he's only beating me because I asked for my wages.' The master answered with all kinds of arguments and excuses, which I heard but did not believe. In short, I obliged the peasant to untie him and made him swear that he would take him back with him and pay him one *real* after another, even more than he owed. Is this not true, Andrés my son? Did you not notice how forcefully I commanded him, and how humbly he promised to do everything I ordered him and told him and wanted him to do? Respond; do not be shy or hesitant about anything; tell these gentlefolk what happened, so that they may see and consider the benefit, as I say, of having knights errant wandering the roads."

"Everything that your grace has said is very true," responded the boy, "but the matter ended in a way that was very different from what your grace imagines."

"What do you mean, different?" replied Don Quixote. "Do you mean the peasant did not pay you?"

"He not only didn't pay me," responded the boy, "but as soon as your grace crossed the wood and we were alone, he tied me to the same oak tree again and gave me so many more lashes that I was flayed like St. Bartholomew, and with each lash he mocked you and made a joke about how he had fooled your grace, and if I hadn't been feeling so much pain, I'd have laughed at what he said. But the fact is he raised so many welts that until now I've been in a hospital because of the harm that wicked peasant did to me. Your grace is to blame for everything, because if you had continued on your way and not come when nobody was calling you or mixed into other people's business, my master would have been satisfied with giving me one or two dozen lashes, and then he would have let me go and paid me what he owed me. But your grace dishonored him for no reason, and called him so many names that he lost his temper, and since he couldn't take his revenge on your grace, when we were alone he vented his anger on me, so that it seems to me I won't be the same man again for the rest of my life."

"The mistake," said Don Quixote, "was in my leaving, for I should not have gone until you were paid; I ought to have known, from long experience, that no peasant keeps his word if he sees that it is not to his advantage to do so. But remember, Andrés: I swore that if he did not pay you, I would go in search of him and find him even if he hid in the belly of the whale."

"That's true," said Andrés, "but it didn't do any good."

"Now you will tell me if it does," said Don Quixote.

And having said this, he stood up very quickly and ordered Sancho to put the bridle on Rocinante, who was grazing while they ate.

Dorotea asked what he intended to do. He responded that he wanted to find the peasant, and punish him for behaving so badly, and oblige him to pay Andrés down to the last *maravedí*, in spite of and despite all the peasants in the world. To which she responded that according to the boon he had promised, he could not become involved in any other enterprise until hers was concluded, and since he knew this better than anyone, he must hold his fury in check until he returned from her kingdom.

"That is true," responded Don Quixote, "and it is necessary for Andrés to be patient until my return, as you, Señora, have said; to him I vow and promise again that I shall not rest until I see him avenged and paid."

"I don't believe those vows." said Andrés. "I'd rather have enough to get to Sevilla than all the revenge in the world: if you can spare it, give me some food to take with me, and God bless your grace and all the other knights errant, and I hope they're errant enough to find a punishment as good as the one I got."

Sancho took a piece of bread and some cheese from his bag, and handing them to the boy, he said:

"Take this, brother Andrés, for all of us have a part in your misfortune."

"Which part do you have?" asked Andrés.

"This part, the cheese and bread I'm giving you," responded Sancho, "for God only knows if I'll need it or not, because I'm telling you, my friend, the squires of knights errant are subject to a good deal of hunger and misfortune, and even other things that are felt more easily than said."

Andrés took the bread and cheese, and seeing that no one gave him anything else, he lowered his head and, as they say, seized the road with both hands. It is certainly true that when he left, he said to Don Quixote:

"For the love of God, Señor Knight Errant, if you ever run into me again, even if you see them chopping me to pieces, don't help me and don't come to my aid, but leave me alone with my misfortune; no matter how bad it is, it won't be worse than what will happen to me when I'm helped by your grace, and may God curse you and all the knights errant ever born in this world."

Don Quixote was about to get up to punish him, but Andrés began running so quickly that no one even attempted to follow him. Don Quixote was mortified by Andrés's story, and it was necessary for the others to be very careful not to laugh so as not to mortify him completely.

CHAPTER XXXII

Which recounts what occurred in the inn to the companions of Don Quixote

They finished their meal, saddled their mounts, and without anything worth relating happening to them, on the following day they reached the inn that was the terror and fear of Sancho Panza, but although he would have preferred not to go in, he could not avoid it. The innkeeper's wife, the innkeeper, their daughter, and Maritornes saw Don Quixote and Sancho arriving, and they went out to receive them with displays of great joy; Don Quixote greeted them in a grave and solemn tone and told them to prepare a better bed for him than they had the last time, to which the innkeeper's wife responded that if he paid better than he had the last time, she would provide him with a bed worthy of a prince. Don Quixote said he would, and therefore they prepared a reasonable one for him in the same attic where he had been previously, and he lay down immediately because he felt weakened and dejected.

No sooner had he closed the door than the innkeeper's wife rushed at the barber, seized him by the beard, and said:

"Upon my soul, you can't go on using my oxtail for a beard, and you have to give the tail back to me; it's a shame to see that thing of my husband's on the floor; I mean the comb that I always hung on my nice tail."

The barber refused to give it to her, no matter how hard she pulled, until the licentiate told him to return it, for it was no longer necessary to use the disguise; he could show and reveal himself as he was and tell Don Quixote that when the thieving galley slaves robbed him, he had fled to this inn; if the knight should ask about the princess's squire, they would say she had sent him ahead to inform the people of her kingdom that she was on her way and was bringing their liberator with her. When he heard this, the barber willingly returned the tail to the innkeeper's wife, along with all the other articles they had borrowed for their rescue of Don Quixote. Everyone in the inn was astonished at the beauty of Dorotea and at the fine appearance of young Cardenio. The priest had them prepare whatever food was available at the inn, and the innkeeper, hoping for better payment, quickly prepared a reasonable meal; Don Quixote slept all this time, and they agreed not to wake him because, for the moment, he needed sleep more than food.

During the meal, in the presence of the innkeeper, his wife, their daughter, Maritornes, and the other travelers, they spoke of the strange madness of Don Quixote and the manner in which they had found him. The innkeeper's wife recounted what had happened with him and the muledriver, and after looking around for Sancho, and not seeing him, she told them about his tossing in the blanket, which caused them no small amusement. When the priest said that the books of chivalry that Don Quixote read had made him lose his wits, the innkeeper said:

"I don't know how that can be; the truth is, to my mind, there's no better reading in the world; I have two or three of them, along with some other papers, and they really have put life into me, and not only me but other people, too. Because during the harvest, many of the harvesters gather here during their time off, and there's always a few who know how to read, and one of them takes down one of those books, and more than thirty of us sit around him and listen to him read with so much pleasure that it saves us a thousand gray hairs; at least, as far as I'm concerned, I can tell you that when I hear about those furious, terrible blows struck by the knights, it makes me want to do the same, and I'd be happy to keep hearing about them for days and nights on end."

"The same goes for me," said the innkeeper's wife, "because I never have any peace in my house except when you're listening to somebody read; you get so caught up that you forget about arguing with me."

"That's true," said Maritornes, "and by my faith, I really like to hear those things, too, they're very pretty, especially when they tell about a lady under some orange trees in the arms of her knight, and a duenna's their lookout, and she's dying of envy and scared to death. I think all that's as sweet as honey."

"And you, young lady, what do you think of them?" asked the priest, speaking to the innkeeper's daughter.

"Upon my soul, I don't know, Señor," she responded. "I listen, too, and the truth is that even if I don't understand them, I like to hear them, but I don't like all the fighting that my father likes; I like the laments of the knights when they're absent from their ladies; the truth is that sometimes they make me cry, I feel so sorry for them."

"Then, young lady, would you offer them relief," said Dorotea, "if they were weeping on your account?"

"I don't know what I'd do," the girl responded. "All I know is that some of those ladies are so cruel that their knights call them tigers and lions and a thousand other indecent things. And sweet Jesus, I don't know what kind of people can be so heartless and unfeeling that they don't look at an honorable man, and let him die or lose his mind. I don't know the reason for so much stiffness: if they're so virtuous, let them marry, which is just what their knights want."

"Be quiet, girl," said the innkeeper's wife. "You seem to know a lot about these things, and it's not right for young girls to know or talk so much."

"Since the gentleman asked me," she responded, "I had to answer."

"Well, now," said the priest, "innkeeper, bring me those books; I'd like to see them."

"I'd be glad to," he responded.

He entered his room and brought out an old traveling case, locked with a small chain, and when it was opened, the priest found three large books and some papers written in a very fine hand. He opened the first book and saw that it was *Don Cirongilio of Thrace*;[1] and the second was *Felixmarte of Hyrcania*;[2] and the third, *The History of the Great Captain Gonzalo Hernández de Córdoba, and the Life of Diego García de Paredes*.[3]

1. Written by Bernardo de Vargas, the book was published in 1545.

2. This novel was mentioned in the examination of Don Quixote's library by the priest and the barber.

3. Published in 1580, this chronicle recounts the exploits of one of the most famous and successful officers to serve under the Catholic Sovereigns, Ferdinand and Isabella. Gonzalo Hernández de Córdoba (1453–1515) was called the Great Captain; his aide, Diego García de Paredes, was renowned for his enormous strength.

As soon as the priest read the first two titles, he turned to the barber and said:

"Our friend's housekeeper and his niece are the people we need here now."

"We don't need them," responded the barber. "I also know how to take them to the corral or the hearth, where there's a good fire burning."

"Then your grace wants to burn my books?" said the innkeeper.

"Only these two," said the priest: "*Don Cirongilio* and *Felixmarte*."

"Well," said the innkeeper, "by any chance are my books heretical or phlegmatic, is that why you want to burn them?"

"*Schismatic* is what you mean, friend," said the barber, "not *phlegmatic*."

"That's right," replied the innkeeper. "But if you want to burn one, let it be the one about the Great Captain and that Diego García; I'd rather let a child of mine be burned than either one of the others."

"Dear brother," said the priest, "these two books are false and full of foolishness and nonsense, but this one about the Great Captain is truthful history and tells the accomplishments of Gonzalo Hernández de Córdoba, who, because of his many great feats, deserved to be called *Great Captain* by everyone, a famous and illustrious name deserved by him alone; Diego García de Paredes was a distinguished nobleman, a native of the city of Trujillo, in Extremadura, a very courageous soldier, and so strong that with one finger he could stop a millwheel as it turned; standing with a broadsword at the entrance to a bridge, he brought an immense army to a halt and would not permit them to cross; and he did other comparable things, and he recounts them and writes about them himself, with the modesty of a gentleman writing his own chronicle, but if another were to write about those feats freely and dispassionately, they would relegate all the deeds of Hector, Achilles, and Roland to oblivion."

"Tell those trifles to my old father!" said the innkeeper. "Look at what amazes you: stopping a millwheel! By God, now your grace ought to read what Felixmarte of Hyrcania did, when with one reverse stroke he split five giants down to the waist like the dolls children make out of beans. Another time he attacked a huge, powerful army that had more than a million six hundred thousand soldiers, all of them armed from head to foot, and he routed them like herds of sheep. And what would you say of the good Don Cirongilio of Thrace, who was so valiant and brave, as you can see in the book where it tells us that once when he was sailing down a river a fiery serpent rose up from the water, and as soon as he saw it he attacked it and straddled it, right across its scaly shoulders, and with both hands he squeezed its throat so tight that the serpent, seeing that he was being strangled, could only dive down to the bottom of the river, taking with him the knight who wouldn't let him go. And when they got down there, he found himself in palaces and gardens that were so pretty they were a marvel to see, and then the serpent turned into an old, old man who told him so many things it was really something to hear. Be quiet, Señor, because if you heard this, you'd go mad with pleasure. I don't give two figs for the Great Captain or that Diego García!"

When Dorotea heard this, she said very quietly to Cardenio:

"Our host doesn't have far to go to be a second Don Quixote."

"I agree," responded Cardenio. "According to what he says, he believes that everything these books say really happened just as written, and not even discalced friars could make him think otherwise."

"Listen, my dear brother," the priest said again, "there never was a Felixmarte of Hyrcania in this world, or a Don Cirongilio of Thrace, or any other knights like them that the books of chivalry tell about, because it is all fiction made up by idle minds, composed to create the effect you mentioned, to while away the time, just as your harvesters amuse themselves by reading them. Really, I swear to you, there never were knights like these in the world, and their great deeds, and all that other nonsense, never happened."

"Throw that bone to another dog!" responded the innkeeper. "As if I didn't know how to add two and three or where my shoe pinches! Your grace shouldn't try to treat me like a child, because, by God, I'm not an idiot. That's really something: your grace wants me to think that everything these good books say is foolishness and lies, when they've been printed with the permission of the gentlemen on the Royal Council, as if they were the kind of people who'd allow the printing of so many lies, and so many battles and so many enchantments it could drive you crazy!"

"I have already told you, my friend," replied the priest, "that these books are intended to amuse our minds in moments of idleness; just as in well-ordered nations games such as chess and ball and billiards are permitted for the entertainment of those who do not have to, or should not, or cannot work, the printing of such books is also permitted, on the assumption, which is true, that no one will be so ignorant as to mistake any of these books for true history. If it were correct for me to do so now, and those present were to request it, I would have something to say about the characteristics that books of chivalry ought to have in order to be good books, and perhaps it would be advantageous and even pleasurable for some, but I hope the time will come when I may communicate this to someone who can remedy it; in the meantime, you should believe, Señor Innkeeper, what I have told you, and take your books, and decide on their truths or lies, and much good may they do you; God willing you won't follow in the footsteps of your guest Don Quixote."

"I won't," responded the innkeeper, "because I wouldn't be crazy enough to become a knight errant; I see very well that these days are different from the old days, when they say those famous knights wandered through the world."

Sancho had returned in the middle of this conversation and was left very confused and bewildered when he heard that nowadays there were no more knights errant and that all the books of chivalry were foolish lies, and he resolved in his heart to wait and see the outcome of the journey his master was about to take; if it did not turn out as well as he hoped, he was determined to leave and go back to his wife and his children and his customary work.

The innkeeper picked up the case and the books, but the priest said:

"Wait, I want to see the papers that are written in such a fine hand."

The innkeeper took them out and gave them to him to read, and the priest saw up to eight full sheets of paper written by hand, and at the beginning was the title in large letters: *The Novel of the Man Who Was Recklessly Curious*. The priest read three or four lines to himself and said:

"The title of this novel certainly doesn't seem bad, and I think I would like to read all of it."

To which the innkeeper responded:

"Well, your reverence can certainly read it, and you should know that some guests who read it here liked it very much and asked to have it over and over again, but I wouldn't give it to them, because I plan to return it to the man who left this case here by mistake, along with the books and papers; their owner might come back here one day, and though I know I'll miss the books, by my faith I'm going to give them back; I may be an innkeeper, but I'm still a Christian."

"You are absolutely right, my friend," said the priest, "but even so, if I like the novel, you must allow me to copy it."

"I'll be happy to," responded the innkeeper.

While the two men were conversing, Cardenio had picked up the novel and begun to read it, and being of the same opinion as the priest, he asked him to read it aloud so that all of them could hear it.

"I would gladly read it," said the priest, "but it might be better to spend this time sleeping rather than reading."

"It will be very restful for me," said Dorotea, "to spend the time listening to a story, for my spirit is not yet calm enough to let me sleep at the customary time."

"In that case," said the priest, "I do want to read it, if only out of curiosity; perhaps it will have something both pleasing and unusual."

Master Nicolás made the same request, and so did Sancho; seeing this, and thinking that by reading aloud he would both give and receive pleasure, the priest said:

"Well then, pay careful attention, for this is how the novel begins:"

CHAPTER XXXIII

Which recounts the novel of The Man Who Was Recklessly Curious[1]

In Florence, a rich and famous Italian city in the province called Tuscany, lived two wealthy, eminent gentlemen who were such good friends that they were known by everyone as *the two friends*. They were bachelors, young men who were of the same age and habits, all of which was sufficient cause for both of them to feel a mutual, reciprocal friendship. True, Anselmo was somewhat more inclined to amorous pursuits than Lotario, whose preferred pastime was the hunt, but when the occasion presented itself, Anselmo would leave his pleasures to follow those of Lotario, and Lotario would leave his to pursue those of Anselmo, and in this fashion their desires were so attuned that a well-adjusted clock did not run as well.

Anselmo was deeply in love with a distinguished and beautiful girl from the same city, the daughter of such excellent parents, and so excellent in and of herself, that he decided, with his friend Lotario's agreement, without which he did nothing, to ask her parents for her hand, which he did; his intermediary was Lotario, and he concluded the arrangements so successfully for his friend that in a short time Anselmo

---

1. This is the first of what are called the interpolated novels (in contemporary terms, they are novellas) in the first part of *Don Quixote*; the story is derived from an episode in Canto 43 of Ariosto's *Orlando furioso*. There are indications in the second part of *Don Quixote* that Cervantes was criticized for these "interruptions" of the action.

found himself in possession of what he desired; Camila was so happy at having Anselmo for a husband that she unceasingly gave her thanks to heaven, and to Lotario, through whose intervention so much contentment had come to her. In the first days of the nuptial celebrations, which are always filled with joy, Lotario continued to visit the house of his friend Anselmo as he had before, wishing to honor him, congratulate him, and rejoice with him in every way he could, but when the celebrations were over and the frequency of visits and congratulations had diminished, Lotario carefully began to reduce the number of his visits to Anselmo's house, for it seemed to him—as it reasonably would seem to all discerning people—that one should not visit or linger at the houses of married friends as if both were still single; although good and true friendship cannot and should not be suspect for any reason, the honor of the married man is so delicate that it apparently can be offended even by his own brothers, let alone his friends.

Anselmo noticed Lotario's withdrawal and complained to him bitterly, saying that if he had known that matrimony meant they could not communicate as they once had, he never would have married, and if the good relations the two of them had enjoyed when he was a bachelor had earned them the sweet name of *the two friends,* then he would not, merely for the sake of appearing circumspect and for no other reason, permit so well-known and amiable · a name to be lost; therefore he begged Lotario, if such a term could legitimately be used between them, that he make Anselmo's house his own again, and come and go as he had before, assuring him that his wife, Camila, had no wish or desire other than what he wanted her to have, and she, knowing how truly the two men had loved each other, was bewildered at seeing him so aloof.

To these and the many other arguments that Anselmo used to persuade Lotario to visit his house as he had in the past, Lotario responded with so much prudence, discretion, and discernment that Anselmo was satisfied with his friend's good intentions, and they agreed that twice a week and on feast days Lotario would eat with Anselmo in his house, and although this was their agreement, Lotario resolved to do no more than what he thought would enhance the honor of his friend, whose reputation he valued more than he did his own. He said, and rightly so, that the man to whom heaven has granted a beautiful wife had to be as careful about the friends he brought home as he was about the women with whom his wife associated, because those things not done or arranged on open squares, or in temples, or at public festivals, or on devotional visits to churches—activities that husbands may not always deny to their wives—can be arranged and expedited in the house of her most trusted friend or kinswoman.

Lotario also said that a married man needed to have a friend who would alert him to any negligence in his behavior, since it often happens that because of the great love the husband has for his wife, and his desire not to distress her, he does not warn or tell her to do or not do certain things that could either redound to his honor or cause his censure, but being advised by his friend, he could easily resolve everything. Where could one find a friend as discerning and loyal and true as the one described by Lotario? Certainly I do not know; Lotario alone was the kind of friend who, with utmost care and solicitude, looked after his friend's honor and wished to lessen, reduce, and diminish the number of days he went to his house so that it would not seem amiss to the idle crowd and its wandering, malicious eyes that a wealthy, noble, and wellborn young man, possessing the other good qualities he believed he had, habitually visited the house of a woman as beautiful as Camila; although her virtue and modesty could put a stop to any malicious tongue, he did not want any doubts cast on her good name or his friend's; as a consequence, on most of the visiting days that they had agreed upon, he was occupied and involved in other matters that he claimed were unavoidable, and so a large portion of the time they did spend together was devoted to the complaints of one friend and the excuses of the other.

As it happened, on one of these occasions, when the two men were walking through a meadow outside the city, Anselmo said these words to Lotario:

"Did you think, Lotario my friend, that I cannot respond with gratitude that matches the bounty I have received: the mercies God has shown in making me the son of parents such as mine, and granting me with so generous a hand so many advantages, in what is called nature as well as in fortune, and especially His granting me you as a friend and Camila as my wife, two treasures I esteem, if not as much as I ought to, at least as much as I can? Yet despite all these elements that usually make up the whole that allows men to live happily, I am the most desperate and discontented man in the entire world, because for some days now I have been troubled and pursued by a desire so strange and out of the ordinary that I am amazed at myself, and blame and reprimand myself, and attempt to silence it and hide it away from my thoughts, though I have been no more capable of keeping it secret than if my intention actually had been to reveal it to the entire world. And since, in fact, it must be made public, I want to confide and entrust it to you, certain that with the effort you make, as my true friend, to cure me, I soon shall find myself free of the anguish it causes me, and my joy at your solicitude will be as great as my unhappiness at my own madness."

Anselmo's words left Lotario perplexed, and he did not know where so long an introduction or preamble would lead, and although in his imagination he pondered what the desire could be that was troubling his friend, he never hit the mark of the truth, and in order to quickly end the torment that this uncertainty caused him, Lotario said that it was manifestly insulting to their great friendship for Anselmo to go through so many preliminaries before telling him his most secret thoughts, for he was certain he could promise either the advice that would make them bearable or the remedy that would end them.

"What you say is true," responded Anselmo, "and with that confidence I will tell you, friend Lotario, that the desire that plagues me is my wondering if Camila, my wife, is as good and perfect as I think she is, and I cannot learn the truth except by testing her so that the test reveals the worth of her virtue, as fire shows the worth of gold. Because it seems to me, dear friend, that a woman is not virtuous if she is not solicited, and that she alone is strong who does not bend to promises, gifts, tears, and the constant importunities of lovers who woo her. Why be grateful when a woman is good," he said, "if no one urges her to be bad? Why is it of consequence that she is shy and reserved if she does not have the occasion to lose her restraint and knows she has a husband who, at her first rash act, would take her life? In short, I do not hold the woman who is virtuous because of fear or lack of opportunity in the same esteem as the one who is courted and pursued and emerges wearing the victor's crown. For these reasons, and many others I could mention that support and strengthen this opinion, my desire is for Camila, my wife, to pass through these difficulties, and be refined and prove her value in the fire of being wooed and courted by one worthy of desiring her; and if she emerges, as I believe she will, triumphant from this battle, I shall deem my good fortune unparalleled; I shall be able to say that the cup of my desires is filled to overflowing; I shall say that it fell to me to have a wife strong in virtue, about whom the Wise Man says, 'Who will find her?' And if the outcome is the contrary of what I expect, the pleasure of seeing that I was correct in my opinion will allow me to bear the sorrow that my costly experiment may reasonably cause me. And because you can say many things against my desire but none will succeed in stopping me from realizing it, I want you, my dear friend Lotario, to agree to be the instrument that will effect this plan born of my desire: I shall give you the opportunity to do so, and provide you with everything I think necessary for wooing a woman who is virtuous, honorable, reserved, and not mercenary. Among other reasons, I am moved to entrust you with this arduous undertaking because I know that if Camila is conquered by you, you will not carry the conquest to its conclusion but will do only what has to be done according to our agreement, and I shall not be offended except in desire, and the offense will remain hidden in the virtue of your silence, for I know very well that in any matter having to do with me, it will be as eternal as the silence of death. Therefore, if you want me to have a life that can be called a life, you must enter into this amorous battle, not in a lukewarm or dilatory fashion but with the zeal and diligence that my desire demands, and with the trust assured me by our friendship."

These were the words that Anselmo said to Lotario, who listened so attentively to all of them that, except for those that have been recorded here, none passed his lips until Anselmo had finished; seeing that he had nothing else to say, and after looking at him for a long time as if he were looking at something amazing and terrifying that he had never seen before, Lotario said:

"I cannot persuade myself, O my dear friend Anselmo, that the things you have said are not a joke; if I had thought you were speaking in earnest, I would not have allowed you to go so far, and if I had stopped listening, I would have forestalled your long, impassioned speech. It surely seems to me that you don't know me or I don't know you. But no; I know very well that you are Anselmo, and you know that I am Lotario; the problem is that I think you are not the Anselmo you used to be, and you must have thought I was not the same Lotario, either, because the things you have said to me would not have been said by my friend Anselmo, and what you have asked of me would not have been asked of the Lotario you knew; good friends may test their friends and make use of them, as a poet said, *usque ad aras*,[2] which means that they must not make use of their friendship in things that go against God. If a pagan felt this about friendship, how much more important is it for a Christian to feel the same, for he knows that divine friendship must not be lost for the sake of human friendship. When a friend goes so far as to set aside the demands of

2. Plutarch attributes the phrase to Pericles.

heaven in order to respond to those of his friend, it should not be for vain, trivial things but for those on which the honor and life of his friend depend. Well, Anselmo, tell me now which of these is threatened, so that I can dare oblige you and do something as detestable as what you are asking. Neither one, certainly; rather, if I understand you, you are asking me to attempt and endeavor to take away your honor and your life, and mine as well. Because if I attempt to take away your honor, it is obvious that I take away your life, for the man without honor is worse than dead, and if, as you wish, I become the instrument that inflicts so much evil upon you, do I not lose my honor, and, by the same token, my life? Listen, Anselmo my friend, and have the patience not to respond until I finish telling you what I think of the demands your desire has made of you; there will be time for you to reply and for me to listen."

"Gladly," said Anselmo. "Say whatever you wish."

And Lotario continued, saying:

"It seems to me, my dear Anselmo, that your mind is now in the state in which the Moors have theirs, for they cannot be made to understand the error of their sect with commentaries from Holy Scripture, or arguments that depend on the rational understanding or are founded on articles of faith; instead, they must be presented with palpable, comprehensible, intelligible, demonstrable, indubitable examples, with mathematical proofs that cannot be denied, as when one says, 'If, from two equal parts, we remove equal parts, those parts that remain are also equal'; if they do not understand the words, as in fact they do not, then it must be shown to them with one's hands, and placed before their eyes, yet even after all this, no one can persuade them of the truths of my holy religion. I must use the same terms and methods with you, because the desire that has been born in you is so misguided and so far beyond everything that has a shred of rationality in it that I think it would be a waste of time to try to make you understand your foolishness; for the moment I do not wish to give it another name. I am even tempted to leave you to your folly as punishment for your wicked desire, but my friendship for you does not permit me to be so harsh that I leave you in obvious danger of perdition. And so that you can see it clearly, tell me, Anselmo: haven't you told me that I have to woo a reserved woman, persuade an honest woman, make offers to an unmercenary woman, serve a prudent woman? Yes, you have said that to me. But if you know you have a wife who is reserved, honest, unmercenary, and prudent, what else do you need to know? And if you believe she will emerge victorious from all my assaults, as she undoubtedly will, what designations do you plan to give her afterward that are better than the ones she has now? What will she be afterward that is better than what she is now? Either your opinion of her is not what you say it is, or you do not know what you are asking. If your opinion of her is not what you say it is, why do you want to test her instead of treating her as an unfaithful woman and chastising her as you see fit? But if she is as virtuous as you believe, it would be reckless to experiment with that truth, for when you have done so, it will still have the same value it had before. Therefore we must conclude that attempting actions more likely to harm us than to benefit us is characteristic of rash minds bereft of reason, especially when they are not forced or compelled to undertake them, and when even from a distance it is obvious that the venture is an act of patent madness.

One attempts extremely difficult enterprises for the sake of God, or for the sake of the world, or both; those attempted for God are the ones undertaken by the saints, who endeavor to live the lives of angels in human bodies; those attempted with the world in mind are undertaken by men who endure such infinite seas, diverse climates, and strange peoples in order to acquire great riches. And those ventured for God and the world together are undertaken by valiant soldiers who, as soon as they see in the enemy defenses an opening no larger than the one made by a cannon ball, set aside all fear, do not consider or notice the clear danger that threatens them, and, borne on the wings of their desire to defend their faith, their nation, and their king, hurl themselves boldly into the midst of the thousand possible deaths that await them. These are perilous actions that are ordinarily ventured, and it is honor, glory, and advantage to attempt them despite the many obstacles and dangers. But the one you say you wish to attempt and put into effect will not win you the glory of God, or great riches, or fame among men; even if the outcome is as you desire, you will not be more content, more wealthy, more honored than you are now, and if it is not, you will find yourself in the greatest misery imaginable; then it will be to no avail to think that no one is aware of the misfortune that has befallen you; your knowing will be enough to make you suffer and grieve.

As confirmation of this truth, I want to recite for you a stanza written by the famous poet Luis Tansilo,[3] at the end of the first part of his *The Tears of St. Peter*, which says:

3. An Italian poet of the sixteenth century (1510–1568).

> There grows grief and there grows shame
> in Peter, when the day has dawned,
> and though he sees no one is near
> he feels a deep shame for his sin:
> for a great heart will be moved
> to shame, even if unseen,
> when it transgresses, shame though
> seen by nought but earth and sky.

In similar fashion, you will not escape sorrow even if it is secret; instead, you will weep constantly, if not tears from your eyes, then tears of blood from your heart, like those shed by the simple doctor who, as our poet recounts, agreed to the test of the goblet,[4] while the prudent and more rational Reinaldos refused; although this is poetic fiction, it contains hidden moral truths worthy of being heeded and understood and imitated, especially if, in light of what I am going to say to you now, you come to realize the magnitude of the error you wish to commit.

Tell me, Anselmo: if heaven, or good luck, had made you the possessor and legitimate owner of a fine diamond whose worth and value satisfied every jeweler who saw it, and all of them were of one opinion and said in one voice that in value, size, and purity it was all that such a stone could be, and you believed this as well, having no knowledge to the contrary, would it be reasonable for you to take that diamond, and place it between an anvil and a hammer, and by dint of powerful blows test if it was as hard and fine as they said? Moreover, in the event you did this, and the stone withstood so foolish a test, it would not, for that reason, gain in value or fame, but if it shattered, which is possible, wouldn't everything be lost? Yes, certainly, and its owner would be thought a fool by everyone.

Then understand, Anselmo my friend, that Camila is a fine diamond, both in your estimation and in that of others, and there is no reason to put her at risk of shattering, for even if she remains whole, she cannot become more precious than she is now; and if she fails and does not resist, consider how you would feel without her, and how correctly you would blame yourself for having been the cause of her ruination and your own. For there is no jewel in the world as valuable

4. An allusion to the story, recounted in *Orlando furioso,* of a magic goblet that indicated if the women who drank from it were faithful.

as a chaste and honorable woman, and women's honor consists entirely of the good opinion others have of them; since you know that the good opinion people have of your wife is as high as it can be, why do you want to cast doubt upon this truth? Look, my friend: woman is an imperfect creature, and one should not lay down obstacles where she can stumble and fall; instead, one should remove them and clear all impediments from her path so that she may run easily and quickly to reach the perfection she lacks, which consists in being virtuous.

Naturalists tells us that the ermine is an animal with pure white fur, and when hunters want to trap it, they use this trick: knowing the places where it customarily travels and can be found, they obstruct those places with mud, and then they beat the bushes and drive it toward that spot, and when the ermine reaches the mud it stops and lets itself be captured and caught rather than pass through the mire and risk soiling and losing the whiteness that it values more than liberty and life. The honest and chaste woman is the ermine, and the purity of her virtue is whiter and cleaner than snow; the man who wants her not to lose it but to keep and preserve it must treat her in a manner different from the one used with an ermine; he should not place mud before her—I mean the gifts and wooing of importunate lovers—because perhaps, and there is no perhaps about it, she does not have enough virtue and natural strength to overcome and surmount those obstacles by herself; it is necessary to remove them and place before her the purity of virtue and the beauty that lies in a good reputation.

In similar fashion, the chaste woman is like a mirror of clear, shining glass, liable to be clouded and darkened by any breath that touches it. One must treat the virtuous woman as one treats relics: adore them but not touch them. One must protect and esteem the chaste woman as one protects and esteems a beautiful garden filled with flowers and roses; its owner does not permit people to pass through and handle the flowers; it is enough that from a distance, through the iron bars of the fence, they enjoy its fragrance and beauty.

Finally, I want to recite for you some verses that have just come to mind; I heard them in a modern play, and I think they are relevant to what we are discussing. A prudent old man was advising the father of a young girl to shelter her, protect her, and keep her secluded, and among many other reasons, he mentioned these:

Woman is made of fragile glass;
but do not put her to the test
to see if she will break,
for that might come to pass.

She is too apt to shatter,
and wisdom is surely ended
if what can ne'er be mended
is put in the way of danger.

What I say to you is true,
and let us all agree:
wherever Danae may be,
showers of gold are there, too.[5]

Everything I have said so far, Anselmo, refers to you; now it is time for you to hear something that has to do with me, and if it takes a long time, forgive me, but it is demanded by the labyrinth into which you have walked and from which you wish me to free you. You consider me your friend, yet you wish to take my honor, which is counter to all friendship; not only that, but you want me to try to take yours. It is clear that you want to take mine, for when Camila sees me wooing her, as you are asking me to do, surely she will look upon me as a man without honor or worth because I am attempting and doing something so far removed from the obligations I have as the man I am, and as your friend. There is no doubt that you want me to take your honor, for when Camila sees me wooing her, she will think that I saw in her some looseness of behavior that gave me the audacity to reveal my evil desire, and thinking herself dishonored, her dishonor affects you, for you are part of her. For this reason people commonly say that the husband of an adulterous woman, even though he has no knowledge of wife's adultery and has given her no reason to be what she should not be, and it was not in his power to prevent his misfortune for he was neither negligent nor careless, yet despite all this he is called and characterized by base names that revile him, and in a certain sense those who know of his wife's wickedness look at him with scornful rather than compassionate eyes, even though responsibility for his difficulties lies not with him but with the desires of his unvirtuous wife.

But I want to tell you why it is reasonable and just for the husband of

5. Danae was confined in a tower by her father, King Acrisius, when an oracle stated that her son would kill him. Zeus transformed himself into a shower of gold, visited her, and fathered Perseus.

an immodest woman to be dishonored, even if he does not know about her lack of virtue, and is not responsible for it, and has not been a party to it or given her reason to be unchaste. And do not grow weary of listening to me; everything will redound to your benefit. When God created our first father in the Earthly Paradise, Holy Scripture says that God put Adam to sleep, and as he slept He took a rib out of his left side and from it He formed our mother Eve; when Adam awoke and saw her, he said: 'This is now bone of my bones, and flesh of my flesh,' and God said: 'Therefore shall a man leave his father and his mother, and cleave unto his wife: and they shall be one flesh.' That was when the divine sacrament of marriage was established, with bonds so strong that death alone can undo them. And this miraculous sacrament is so strong and powerful that it makes one flesh of two different people, and in virtuous spouses it does even more, for although they have two souls, they have only one will. And from this it follows that since the flesh of the wife is one with the flesh of the husband, any stain that besmirches her, or any defect that appears in her, redounds to the flesh of the husband even if he has not given her, as I have said, any reason for her wickedness. Just as discomfort in the foot or any other member of the body is felt throughout the entire body because it is all one flesh, and the head feels the ankle's pain although it has not caused it, so the husband participates in his wife's dishonor because he is one with her. And since honors and dishonors in this world are all born of flesh and blood, and those of the unchaste woman are of this kind, it is unavoidable that the husband is party to them and is considered dishonored even if he has no knowledge of them.

Therefore consider, Anselmo, the danger in which you place yourself by wanting to disturb the tranquility in which your virtuous wife lives; think of how, because of a futile and rash inquisitiveness, you wish to disturb the humors that now rest tranquilly in the bosom of your chaste wife; be aware that what you may gain is little, and what you may lose is so great that I will not even mention it because I lack the words to describe it. But if everything I have said is not enough to dissuade you from your evil purpose, then you can find another instrument for your dishonor and misfortune, for I do not intend to be that instrument, even if I lose your friendship, which is the greatest loss I can imagine."

When he had said this, the virtuous and prudent Lotario fell silent, and Anselmo was left so perplexed and pensive that for some time he could not say a word, but at last he said:

"You have seen, Lotario my friend, how attentively I have listened to everything you wanted to say to me, and in your arguments, examples, and comparisons I have seen the great discernment you possess and the far reaches of your true friendship; I also see and confess that if I do not follow your way of thinking but pursue my own, I am fleeing the good and going after the bad. Assuming this, you must consider that I suffer now from the disease that afflicts some women, filling them with the desire to eat earth, plaster, charcoal, and other things that are even worse, and sickening to look at, let alone to eat; therefore it is necessary to use some artifice to cure me, and this could be done with ease if you simply start, even if indifferently and falsely, to woo Camila, who will not be so fragile that your first encounters will bring down her virtue; I will be content with this simple beginning, and you will have fulfilled what you owe to our friendship, not only by giving me back my life, but by persuading me not to lose my honor. You are obliged to do this for only one reason: being determined, as I am, to make this test a reality, you must not allow me to recount my madness to someone else who would endanger the honor that you insist on my not losing; yours not being as high as it should be, in Camila's opinion, while you woo her, matters little or not at all, for in a very short time, when we see in her the integrity we desire, you will be able to tell her the truth of our scheme, and this will return your standing to where it was before. Since you risk so little and can make me so happy by taking that small risk, do not refuse to do it even if greater obstacles are placed before you; as I have said, if you simply begin, I shall consider the matter concluded."

Seeing Anselmo's resolute will, and not knowing what other examples to cite or arguments to present that would dissuade him, and hearing that he threatened to tell someone else about his wicked desire, and wanting to avoid an even greater evil, Lotario decided to agree and do what Anselmo asked; his purpose and intention was to guide the matter in such a way that Camila's thoughts would not be disturbed and Anselmo would be satisfied, and therefore Lotario told Anselmo not to communicate his thought to anyone else and that he would undertake the enterprise and begin whenever his friend wished. Anselmo embraced him tenderly and lovingly and thanked him for his offer as if Lotario had done him a great favor; the two of them agreed that the plan would begin the following day; Anselmo would give Lotario time and opportunity to speak to Camila alone and also provide him with money and jewels to give and present to her. He advised Lotario to play music for her and write verses in her praise, and if he did not wish to take the trouble to do so, Anselmo would write them himself. Lotario agreed to everything, with intentions quite different from what Anselmo believed them to be.

And having come to this understanding, they went back to Anselmo's house, where they found Camila waiting for her husband, troubled and concerned because he came home later than usual that day.

Lotario returned to his house and Anselmo remained in his, and he was as pleased as Lotario was thoughtful, not knowing what course to follow in order to succeed in that rash affair. But that night he thought of how to deceive Anselmo without offending Camila, and the next day he went to eat with his friend and was welcomed by Camila, who always received and treated him warmly, knowing the good opinion her husband had of him.

They finished eating, the table was cleared, and Anselmo asked Lotario to stay with Camila while he went out to tend to a pressing matter; he said he would be back in an hour and a half. Camila asked him not to leave, and Lotario offered to accompany him, but nothing could sway Anselmo; instead, he urged Lotario to wait until he returned because he had to discuss a matter of great importance with him. He also told Camila not to leave Lotario alone while he was out. In short, he knew so well how to feign the necessity or nonsensicality of his absence that no one could have realized it was mere pretense. Anselmo left, and Camila and Lotario remained alone at the table because the servants had gone to have their own meal. Lotario saw himself placed in precisely the dangerous position that his friend desired, facing an enemy who, with no more than her beauty, could conquer an entire squadron of armed knights: Lotario surely had good reason to fear her.

But what he did was to place his elbow on the arm of his chair and rest his cheek on his open hand, and begging Camila's pardon for his rudeness, he said that he wanted to rest for a while until Anselmo returned. Camila responded that he would be more comfortable in the drawing room than in the chair, and she asked him to go in there to sleep. Lotario refused and dozed in the chair until the return of Anselmo, who found Camila in her bedroom and Lotario asleep and thought that since he had come home so late, they had already had the opportunity to talk and even to sleep; he was impatient for Lotario to awaken so that he could go out again with him and ask if he had been successful.

Everything happened as he wished: Lotario awoke, and they left the house together, and Anselmo asked what he wanted to know, and Lotario replied that he had not thought it a good idea to reveal his intentions completely the first time, and so he had done no more than praise Camila for her loveliness, saying that the sole topic of conversation throughout the city was her beauty and discretion; this had seemed to him a good start to winning her over, disposing her to listen to him with pleasure the next time by using the stratagem the devil uses when he wants to deceive someone who is wary and vigilant: he transforms himself into an angel of light, though he is an angel of darkness, and hides behind an appearance of virtue until finally he reveals his identity and achieves his purpose, unless the deception is discovered at the very start. This pleased Anselmo very much, and he said he would provide the same opportunity every day, because even if he did not leave the house, he would occupy himself with other matters, and Camila would not become aware of the ruse.

Many days went by, and though he did not say a word to Camila, Lotario told Anselmo that he was speaking to her but could never elicit from her the slightest interest in anything unchaste or the smallest shred of hope; on the contrary, he said she had warned him that if he did not rid himself of evil thoughts, she would have to tell her husband.

"Good," said Anselmo. "So far Camila has resisted words; it is necessary to see how she resists actions: tomorrow I shall give you two thousand gold *escudos* to offer her, or even give to her, and another two thousand to buy jewels with which to tempt her; for women, no matter how chaste they are, and especially if they are beautiful, tend to be very fond of dressing well and looking elegant; if she resists this temptation, I will be satisfied and trouble you no more."

Lotario responded that since he had begun it, he would see this undertaking through to its conclusion, although he knew that in the end he would be thwarted and defeated. On the following day he received the four thousand *escudos*, and with them four thousand perplexities, because he did not know what new lies he could tell, but finally he decided to tell Anselmo that Camila was as steadfast in her resistance to gifts and promises of gifts as she was to words, and there was no reason to expend any more effort because it was always a waste of time.

But Fate, which arranged matters differently, decreed that Anselmo, having left Lotario and Camila alone as he had done so many other times before, hid in a small antechamber and watched and listened to them through the keyhole, and he saw that in over half an hour Lotario did not speak a word to Camila and would not have spoken to her if he had been there for a century, and Anselmo realized that everything his friend had told him about Camila's responses was a fiction and a lie. To see if this really was true, he walked out of the antechamber and called

Lotario aside, then asked if there was any news and inquired about Camila's mood. Lotario replied that he did not intend to take matters further because her responses had been so harsh and unpleasant; he did not have the heart to say anything else to her.

"Ah," said Anselmo, "Lotario, Lotario, how badly you have fulfilled your duty to me and responded to the trust I put in you! I have been watching through the keyhole of the door to that room, and I have seen that you did not say a word to Camila, which leads me to think you have not said even the first word to her; if this is true, as it undoubtedly is, why have you deceived me, and why do you wish by your actions to take from me the only means I have found to satisfy my desire?"

Anselmo said no more; but what he had said was enough to leave Lotario disconcerted and confused, and taking it almost as a point of honor that he had been discovered in a lie, he swore to Anselmo that from then on he would dedicate himself to satisfying him and not lying to him, as he would see if he were curious enough to spy on him again; Anselmo would not even have to make that effort, however, because Lotario intended to put so much effort into satisfying him that it would eliminate all his suspicions. Anselmo believed him, and in order to give Lotario a more secure and less alarming opportunity, he decided to leave his house for a week and visit a friend who lived in a village not far from the city; Anselmo arranged with this friend to send for him very urgently so that Camila would think there was a reason for his departure.

Oh, Anselmo, how unfortunate and ill-advised! What are you doing? What are you plotting? What are you arranging? Consider that you are acting against yourself, plotting your own dishonor and arranging your own ruination. Camila is a virtuous wife; you possess her in peace and tranquility; no one assails your joy; her thoughts do not go beyond the walls of her house; you are her heaven on earth, the goal of her desires, the fulfillment of her delight, the means by which she measures her will, adjusting it in all things to yours and to that of heaven. If, then, the mine of her honor, beauty, virtue, and modesty gives you, with no effort on your part, all the riches it has, and all that you could wish for, why do you want to dig into the earth and look for more veins of new and unseen treasure, putting yourself in danger of having it all collapse since, after all, it stands on the weak foundations of her frail nature? Remember that if a man seeks the impossible, the possible may justly be denied him; a poet said it better when he wrote:

I search for life in dread death,
in fearful disease for health,
in dark prison for liberty,
escape in a sealed room,
in a traitor, loyalty.
But my own fate from whom
I ne'er hope for the good
has with just heaven ruled:
if the impossible I demand,
for me the possible is banned.

The next day Anselmo left for the village, having told Camila that during the time he was away, Lotario would come to watch over the house and to eat with her, and that she should be sure to treat him as she would himself. Camila, an intelligent and honorable woman, was distressed by her husband's orders and said he ought to be aware that when he was absent, it was not right for anyone to occupy his seat at the table, and if he was doing this because he had no confidence in her ability to manage his house, he should test her this time and learn through his own experience that she was capable of taking on even greater responsibilities. Anselmo replied that this was his pleasure, and her duty was merely to bow her head and obey. Camila said she would, although it was against her will.

Anselmo left, and on the following day Lotario came to the house, where he was received by Camila with an affectionate and virtuous welcome; she never put herself in a position where Lotario would see her alone; she was always accompanied by her servants, both male and female, especially a maid named Leonela, whom she loved dearly because they had grown up together in the house of Camila's parents, and when she married she brought Leonela with her to Anselmo's house. For the first three days Lotario said nothing to her, although he could have when the table was cleared and the servants left to eat their meal—by Camila's orders, a hasty one. Leonela had also been instructed to eat before Camila did and to never leave her side, but the maid, who had her mind on other affairs more to her liking and needed that time and opportunity to tend to her own pleasures, did not always obey her mistress in this; instead, she left them alone, as if that had been her instructions. But Camila's virtuous presence, the gravity of her countenance, and the modesty of her person were so great that they curbed Lotario's tongue.

But the benefit derived from Camila's many virtues imposing silence on Lotario in fact did harm to them both, because if his tongue was silent, his mind was active and had the opportunity to contemplate, one by one, all the exceptional qualities of virtue and beauty in Camila, which were enough to make a marble statue fall in love, let alone a human heart.

Lotario looked at her when he should have been speaking to her; he thought how worthy she was of being loved, and this thought gradually began an assault on the high regard he had for Anselmo; a thousand times over he wanted to leave the city and go to a place where Anselmo would never see him, and where Lotario would never see Camila, but the pleasure he found in looking at her had already become an impediment to his doing so. He contended and struggled with himself to resist and reject the joy he felt when he looked at her. When he was alone he blamed himself for his folly; he called himself a bad friend, even a bad Christian; he reasoned with himself, making comparisons between himself and Anselmo, and he always concluded by saying that Anselmo's madness and trust had been greater than his own scant fidelity, and if this excused him before God as it did before men for what he intended to do, he would not fear punishment for his crime.

In short, the beauty and virtue of Camila, together with the opportunity that her ignorant husband had placed in his hands, overthrew Lotario's loyalty, and without considering anything but what his longing moved him to do, after three days of Anselmo's absence, days when he was in a constant struggle to resist his desires, Lotario began to compliment Camila with so much passion and such amorous words that Camila was stunned, and all she could do was stand and go to her bedroom without saying a word to him. But not even this brusque behavior could weaken Lotario's hope, for hope is always born at the same time as love; instead, he held Camila in even higher esteem. Having seen in Lotario what she never imagined she would see, Camila did not know what to do, but thinking it would not be safe or proper to give him an opportunity to speak to her again, she resolved that very night to send a servant with a letter for Anselmo, which she did, and in it she wrote these words:

CHAPTER XXXIV

In which the novel of The Man Who Was Recklessly Curious *continues*

Just as it is often said that the army without its general seems imperfect, as does the castle without its castellan, I say that the young wife without her husband, when overwhelming reasons do not demand it, seems even worse. I find myself so imperfect without you, and so incapable of enduring this absence, that if you do not return very soon, I shall have to go to the house of my parents for the time you are away, even though I leave yours unguarded, because I believe that the guardian you left for me, if that is what he should be called, is more concerned with his own pleasure than with your interests; since you are clever, I need not say more, nor is it fitting that I do.

Anselmo received this letter and understood that Lotario had begun his suit and that Camila must have reacted just as he wished; extraordinarily happy at the news, he responded by sending a message to Camila, telling her not to leave his house under any circumstances because he would return very shortly. Camila was astonished by Anselmo's reply, which left her more perplexed than she had been earlier: she did not dare either to remain in her house or to go to the house of her parents; if she remained, her virtue would be at risk, and if she left, she would be disobeying her husband.

In short, she made a choice, and chose badly, for she resolved to remain, determined not to flee Lotario's presence and give the servants reason to gossip; she regretted having written what she wrote to her husband, fearful he would think that Lotario had seen some boldness in her that moved him to treat her with less than proper decorum. But, confident of her virtue, she put her trust in God and in her own innocence and planned to resist with silence everything that Lotario said to her, not informing her husband in order to spare him disputes or difficulties. She even tried to think of a way to excuse Lotario to Anselmo when he asked her the reason for writing that letter. With these thoughts, more honorable than accurate or beneficial, she spent another day listening to Lotario, who was so persistent and persuasive that Camila's resolve began to waver, and it was all her virtue could do to attend to her eyes and keep them from showing any sign of the amorous compassion awakened in her bosom by Lotario's tears and words. Lotario noted all of this, and it all set him ablaze.

Finally, it seemed to him that it was necessary, in the time and circumstance allowed by Anselmo's absence, to tighten the siege around the fortress, and so he launched an attack on her conceit with praises of her beauty, because there is nothing more likely to defeat and bring down the haughty towers of beautiful women's vanity than that same vanity, set in words of adulation. In effect, with utmost diligence, he undermined the rock face of her integrity with such effective tools that even if Camila had been made entirely of bronze, she would have fallen. Lotario wept, pleaded, offered, adored, persisted, and deceived with so much emotion and so many signs of sincerity that he brought down Camila's chastity and won the victory he had least expected and most desired.

Camila surrendered; Camila surrendered, but is that any wonder if the friendship of Lotario could not remain standing? A clear example demonstrating that the only way to defeat the amorous passion is to flee it, that no one should attempt to struggle against so powerful an enemy because divine forces are needed to vanquish its human ones. Only Leonela knew of her mistress's frailty, because the two unfaithful friends and new lovers could not hide it from her. Lotario did not want to tell Camila of Anselmo's scheme, or that Anselmo had provided him with the opportunity to come so far: he did not want her to have a low opinion of his love, or to think he had courted her thoughtlessly and by chance rather than intentionally.

A few days later, Anselmo returned to his house and did not notice what was missing, the thing he had treated most contemptuously and valued most highly. He went to see Lotario immediately and found him at home; the two men embraced, and one asked for the news that would give him either life or death.

"The news I can give you, Anselmo my friend," said Lotario, "is that you have a wife worthy of being the model and paragon of all virtuous women. The words I said to her were carried away by the wind; my offers were scorned, my gifts were refused, and a few feigned tears of mine were mocked beyond measure. In short, just as Camila is the sum total of all beauty, she is the treasure house where chastity dwells and discretion and modesty reside, along with all the virtues that make an honorable woman praiseworthy and fortunate. Here is your money, friend; take it back, for I never had need of it; Camila's integrity does not yield to things as low as presents or promises. Be content, Anselmo, and do not attempt more tests; since you have passed through the sea of difficulties and suspicions that one often can have about women, and you have kept your feet dry, do not attempt to return to the deep waters of new dangers, or test, with another pilot, the virtue and strength of the ship that heaven has provided to carry you across the seas of this world; realize instead that you are in a safe harbor; drop the anchors of reason and stay in port until you are asked to pay the debt that no human, no matter how noble, can avoid paying."

Anselmo was made very happy by Lotario's words, and he believed them as if they had been spoken by an oracle. Even so, he asked his friend not to abandon the undertaking, if only for the sake of curiosity and amusement, and even if he no longer brought to it the same zeal and urgency as before; he only wanted Lotario to write some verses in praise of Camila, calling her Clori, and Anselmo would tell her that Lotario was in love with a lady to whom he had given this name so that he could celebrate her with the decorum her modesty required. And if Lotario did not wish to take the trouble of writing the verses, Anselmo would do it.

"That will not be necessary," said Lotario, "for the Muses are not so antagonistic to me that they do not visit me a few times a year. Tell Camila what you said about my fictitious love, and I shall compose the verses, and if they are not as good as the subject deserves, at least they will be the best I can write."

The reckless man and his traitorous friend agreed to this, and when Anselmo returned to his house, he asked what, to Camila's great surprise, he had not asked before, which was that she tell him the reason she had written him the letter. Camila responded that it had seemed Lotario was looking at her somewhat more boldly than when Anselmo was at home, but she had been mistaken and believed it had been her imagination, because now Lotario avoided seeing her and being alone with her. Anselmo said she could be sure of that, because he knew that Lotario was in love with a noble maiden in the city, whom he celebrated under the name of Clori; even if he were not, there was no reason to doubt Lotario's truthfulness or his great friendship for the two of them. If Lotario had not warned Camila that his love for Clori was all pretense, and that he had told Anselmo about it so that he could spend some time writing praises of Camila herself, she undoubtedly would have been caught in the desperate net of jealousy, but she had been forewarned, and this unexpected piece of news did not trouble her.

The next day, when the three of them were sitting at the table after their meal, Anselmo asked Lotario to recite one of the pieces he had composed for his beloved Clori; since Camila did not know her, he surely could say whatever he wished.

"Even if she did know her," responded Lotario, "I would not hide anything, because when a lover praises his lady's beauty and censures her cruelty, he in no way brings dishonor to her good name; but, be that as it may, I can say that yesterday I composed a sonnet to the ingratitude of Clori, and it says:

SONNET

In the deepest quietude of the night,
when gentle sleep embraces mortal men,
I make this poor accounting of my wealth
of woes to heaven, and to Clori mine.
   And at the hour when the sun appears
through rosy-colored portals of the east,
with brokenhearted sighs and halting words
I endlessly renew the old lament.
   And when the sun, from his celestial throne,
hurls burning rays directly down to earth,
my tears flow free and my sobs do increase.
   The night returns; I turn to my sad tale
and once more find, in wearisome complaint,
that heaven is deaf and Clori cannot hear."

Camila liked the sonnet, but Anselmo liked it even more, for he praised it and said that a lady who did not respond to such evident truths was too cruel. To which Camila said:

"Then, everything said by enamored poets is true?"

"Insofar as they are poets, no," responded Lotario, "but insofar as they are enamored, they are always as lost for words as they are truthful."

"There is no doubt about that," replied Anselmo, simply to support and confirm Lotario's opinions before Camila, who was unaware of Anselmo's stratagem and already in love with Lotario.

And so, with the pleasure she derived from everything relating to him, and with the understanding that his desires and his writings were directed to her, and that she was the real Clori, she asked him to recite another sonnet and more verses, if he knew them by heart.

"I do," responded Lotario, "but I do not believe it is as good as—I mean, it is less bad than—the first. But judge for yourself, because it says:

SONNET

I know I die; and if my word is doubted,
my death's more certain; my body lying dead
at your feet, O cruel beauty, is more certain
than my repenting of my love for you.
　　When I am in the land of the forgotten,
deserted by glory, favor, and by life,
there, in my open bosom, you will see,
a sculpted image of your lovely face.
　　I keep this holy relic for the looming
rigors brought on and caused by my persistence,
made stronger by the harshness of your will.
　　Oh, woe to him who sails 'neath darkened skies
across uncharted seas and dangerous routes
where neither port nor polestar lights the way."

Anselmo praised this second sonnet as he had the first, and in this fashion he was adding, link by link, to the chain that bound and fastened him to his dishonor, for the more Lotario dishonored him, the more honored he said Anselmo was, and every step Camila took in her descent to the very center of disgrace was, in the opinion of her husband, an ascent to the pinnacle of her virtue and good name.

It happened that once, when Camila found herself alone with her maid, she said:

"I am mortified, my dear Leonela, to see how lightly I valued myself,

for I did not even oblige Lotario to pay with time for the complete possession of my desire; I gave it to him so quickly, I fear he will judge only
my haste or indiscretion, not taking into account that he urged me so
strongly I could no longer resist him."

"Do not be concerned, Señora," responded Leonela. "Giving quickly
is of little significance, and no reason to lessen esteem, if, in fact, what
one gives is good and in itself worthy of esteem. They even say that by
giving quickly, one gives twice."

"They also say," said Camila, "that what costs less is valued less."

"The argument doesn't apply to you," responded Leonela, "because
love, I've heard it said, sometimes flies and sometimes walks; it runs with
one, and goes slowly with another; it cools some and burns others; some
it wounds, and others it kills; it begins the rush of its desires at one point,
and at the same point it ends and concludes them; in the morning it lays
siege to a fortress, and by nightfall it has broken through, because there
is no power that can resist it. And this being true, why are you concerned
and what do you fear if the same thing must have happened to Lotario,
for love used the absence of my master as the instrument for overcoming
us.[1] It was inevitable that what love had planned would be concluded
before Anselmo could return and prevent the design's completion by his
presence, because love has no better minister for carrying out his desires
than opportunity: he makes use of opportunity in everything he does, especially at the beginning. I know this very well, more from experience
than from hearsay, and one day I'll tell you about it, Señora, for I'm also
young and made of flesh and blood. Besides, Señora Camila, you would
not have given yourself or surrendered so quickly if you had not first seen
in Lotario's eyes, words, sighs, promises, and gifts all his soul, or not seen
in it and its virtues how worthy Lotario was of being loved. If this is true,
do not allow those qualms and second thoughts to assault your imagination, but be assured that Lotario esteems you as you esteem him, and live
contented and satisfied that although you were caught in the snare of
love, it is he who tightens it around you with his admiration and esteem.
He not only has the four Ss[2] that people say good lovers need to have,
but a whole alphabet as well; if you don't believe me, just listen and

---

1. As Martín de Riquer points out, Leonela says "us" because she was complicit in their affair.

2. The four Ss that a lover needed to be were *sabio* ("wise"), *solo* ("alone"), *solícito* ("solicitous"), and *secreto* ("secretive"). This conceit was popular during the Renaissance, as were the ABCs of love cited by many authors. The W is omitted from Leonela's ABC because it is not part of the Spanish alphabet.

you'll see how I can recite it to you by heart. He is, as I see it and in my opinion, Amiable, Benevolent, Courteous, Dignified, Enamored, Firm, Gallant, Honorable, Illustrious, Loyal, Manly, Noble, Openhearted, Pleasing, Quick-witted, Rich, the Ss that everybody knows, and then Truthful, Valiant, X isn't included because it's a harsh letter, Y is the same as I, and Z is Zealous in protecting your honor."

Camila laughed at her maid's alphabet and considered her more experienced in matters of love than she said; in fact, she confessed to this, revealing to Camila her love for a wellborn young man from their city; this troubled Camila, for she feared that here was where her honor could be endangered. She pressed Leonela to find out if their love had gone beyond words. With little shame and a good deal of audacity, she responded that it had. For it is certainly true that negligence in ladies destroys shame in their maids: when they see their mistresses stumble, they do not care if they stumble, too, or if anyone knows about it.

All that Camila could do was to implore Leonela not to say anything about her mistress's affair to the man she said was her lover, and to keep her own secret so that it would not come to the attention of either Anselmo or Lotario. Leonela responded that she would, but she kept her word in a way that affirmed Camila's fear that she would lose her reputation because of her maid, for the immodest and brazen Leonela, when she saw that her mistress's behavior was not what it had once been, dared to bring her lover into the house and keep him there, confident that even if Camila saw him, she would not venture to reveal it; this is one of the many misfortunes caused by the sins of ladies: they become the slaves of their own servants and are obliged to conceal their maids' immodest and base behavior, which is what happened to Camila; although she often saw Leonela with her lover in one of the rooms of her house, she not only did not dare to reprimand her, but provided Leonela with the opportunity to hide him, clearing away every obstacle so that he would not be seen by her husband.

But she could not keep Lotario from seeing him one day as he left the house at dawn; Lotario did not know who he was and at first thought it was a ghost, but when he saw him walk, and muffle his face, and conceal himself with care and caution, he abandoned his simple idea and took up another that would have meant the ruin of them all if Camila had not rectified it. Lotario thought that the man he had seen leaving Anselmo's house at so unusual an hour had not gone there because of Leonela; he did not even remember that there was a Leonela in the world; he believed only that Camila, who had been easy and loose with him, was being just as easy and loose with another man, for the immorality of the immoral woman brings with it this effect: she loses her good name and honor with the very man to whose entreaties and enticements she succumbed; he believes she surrenders more easily to other men and takes as absolute truth any suspicion of the kind that may occur to him. It certainly seems that at this point Lotario lost his good sense and forgot all his skillful reasoning; without a second or even a rational thought, filled with impatience and blinded by the jealous rage gnawing at his entrails and driving him to take his revenge on Camila, who in no way had offended him, he went to see Anselmo, who was still in bed, and said:

"You should know, Anselmo, that for many days I have been struggling with myself, forcing myself not to tell you what it is no longer possible or fair to keep from you. You should know that the fortress of Camila has surrendered and submitted to everything I wished, and if I have delayed in disclosing this to you, it was to see if it was a passing whim, or if she was testing me to see if I was serious about the love I had, with your permission, begun to declare for her. I also believed that if she was as virtuous as she should have been and as we both thought she was, she would already have told you about my solicitations; seeing that she has not, I realize that the promises she has made to me are true, and that the next time you are absent from you house, she will speak to me in the antechamber where you keep your jewels and treasure"—it was true that Camila usually spoke to him there—"but I do not want you to rush off to take your revenge, because the sin has not yet been committed except in thought, and it may be that when the time comes to turn the thought into action, Camila will have changed her mind and replaced the thought with repentance. Therefore, since you have always followed my advice, completely or in part, take the counsel I will give you now, so that prudently forewarned, and with no chance of being deceived, you may be satisfied regarding the best course of action to follow. Pretend that you are leaving for two or three days, as you have in the past, but stay hidden in your antechamber, where there are tapestries and other things that can conceal you very comfortably; then you will see with your own eyes, and I with mine, exactly what Camila wants; and if it is the immorality that may be feared but is not expected, then silently, wisely, and discreetly you can punish the offense committed against you."

Anselmo was bewildered, perplexed, and astonished by Lotario's words, for they came at the moment when he least expected to hear them: he now considered Camila to be victorious over the feigned assaults of Lotario, and he was beginning to enjoy the glory of her triumph. He said nothing for a long time, staring at the floor, not blinking an eye, and then at last he spoke, saying:

"You have done, Lotario, what I expected of your friendship; I shall follow your advice in everything; arrange matters as you wish and keep the secret as it should be kept in so unexpected a circumstance."

Lotario promised he would, and as he left the room, he repented completely for everything he had said, and he saw how foolishly he had behaved, since he could take his own revenge on Camila and not in so cruel and dishonorable a way. He cursed his lack of intelligence, denounced his hasty decision, and did not know by what means he could undo what he had done or give it a more reasonable outcome. Finally, he decided to tell Camila everything, and since there was no lack of opportunity, he found her alone that same day, and as soon as she saw that she could speak freely, she said to him:

"You should know, friend Lotario, that my heart aches so much it seems it is about to break inside my bosom, and it will be a miracle if it does not, for Leonela's shamelessness has grown so great that she brings her lover into this house every night, and is with him until daybreak, putting my reputation at the greatest risk if anyone were to see him leaving my house at that hour. What troubles me is that I cannot punish or reprimand her: she is privy to our affair, and that has curbed my speech and forced me to be silent about hers, and I am afraid this will give rise to some misfortune."

When Camila first began to speak, Lotario believed it was a ruse to convince him that the man he had seen was Leonela's lover, not hers, but when he saw her weep, and grieve, and ask for his help, he believed the truth and then felt completely bewildered and remorseful. Despite this, however, he told Camila not to worry, saying he would devise a plan to put an end to Leonela's insolence. He also told her what, in his jealous rage, he had said to Anselmo, and how it had been agreed that Anselmo would hide in the antechamber and see her lack of fidelity for himself. He begged her forgiveness for this act of madness and asked her advice on how to repair the damage he had done and emerge safely from the intricate labyrinth into which his foolish talk had led them.

Camila was horrified to hear what Lotario was saying, and with a good deal of anger and many well-chosen words, she reproached him, denouncing his wicked thoughts and the simpleminded and wrong-headed decision he had made; but since a woman naturally has a quicker wit for both good and evil than a man, though it tends to fail her when she embarks on any kind of deliberate reasoning, Camila soon found a way to repair the apparently irreparable situation, and she told Lotario to have Anselmo hide the next day in the place he had mentioned, because from his concealment she intended to derive an advantage that would allow the two of them to take their pleasure from then on with no fear of being surprised; not telling him all of her idea, she warned Lotario to be sure, when Anselmo was hidden, to come in as soon as Leonela called him and respond to everything she said as he would if he did not know Anselmo was listening. Lotario insisted she tell him her plan so that he would do everything he needed to do with greater certainty and care.

"I tell you," said Camila, "that there is nothing for you to do except answer the questions I ask you." Camila did not want to tell him before-hand what she planned to do, fearful he would not go along with what she thought was a very good plan but instead would follow or look for others that could not possibly be as good.

At this, Lotario left the house; the next day, using the excuse that he was going to the village where his friend lived, Anselmo went away and then came back to hide, which he did with no trouble since Camila and Leonela had arranged to give him the opportunity.

And so Anselmo hid, feeling, as one can imagine, the agitation of a man who expected to see with his own eyes the very heart of his honor exposed and to lose the supreme treasure he had thought he possessed in his beloved Camila. When Camila and Leonela were absolutely sure and certain that Anselmo was hiding, they walked into the antechamber, and as soon as Camila stepped in, she heaved a great sigh and said:

"Oh Leonela, my friend! Before I carry out my plan, which I do not want you to know about in the event you attempt to prevent it, would it not be better for you to take Anselmo's dagger, the one I asked you to bring, and with it pierce this ignoble bosom of mine? But no, do not; it would not be reasonable for me to bear responsibility for another's crime. First I want to know what the bold and immoral eyes of Lotario saw in me that gave him the audacity to reveal a desire as wicked as the one he has revealed to me, one that shows disdain for his friend and dishonors me. Go, Leonela, to that window and call him; undoubtedly he is in the street, waiting to put his evil intention into effect. But first I shall carry out mine, as cruel as it is honorable."

"Oh, Señora!" responded the clever and forewarned Leonela. "What is it that you want to do with this dagger? Do you by chance wish to take your own life, or that of Lotario? Either action will discredit your name and reputation. It is better for you to hide the offense; do not give that wicked man the opportunity to enter this house and find us alone. Think, Señora: we are women, and weak, and he is a man, and determined; since he comes with his wicked intention, blind with passion, perhaps before you can put your plan into effect, he'll do the thing that would be worse than taking your life. Confound Señor Anselmo for allowing that insolent knave to do so much evil in his house! And if, Señora, you kill him, as I think you intend to do, what will we do with him when he's dead?"

"What will we do, my friend?" responded Camila. "We will leave him for Anselmo to bury, for he will rightly consider it a restful task to put his own infamy under the ground. Call Lotario, once and for all; the more I delay taking my legitimate revenge for the offense, the more I seem to offend the loyalty I owe my husband."

Anselmo listened to all of this, and each word Camila said changed his thoughts, but when he realized that she had determined to kill Lotario, he wanted to come out and show himself and prevent her from doing that; he was held back, however, by his desire to see the outcome of so gallant and virtuous a resolve, although he intended to come out in time to stop it.

Just then Camila fell into a deep swoon, and laying her down on a bed that was in the chamber, Leonela began to cry very bitterly, saying:

"Oh, woe is me if I am so unfortunate and she dies here in my arms: the flower of the world's modesty, the crown of virtuous women, the exemplar of all chastity . . . !"

She said other things similar to these, and no one who heard her would not have taken her for the most aggrieved and loyal maid in the world and her mistress for a second persecuted Penelope. Camila soon recovered from her swoon, and when she did, she said:

"Why do you not go, Leonela, and call the most loyal friend ever seen by the sun or hidden by night? Go, run, hurry, make haste; do not allow delay to cool the flames of rage that I feel or the righteous vengeance I hope for to dwindle into mere threats and curses."

"I am going now to call him, Señora," said Leonela, "but first you must give me the dagger, so that while I am gone you do not do something that will leave all those who love you weeping for the rest of our lives."

"You may go, Leonela my friend, certain that I shall not," responded

Camila, "because although in your opinion it is rash and foolish of me to defend my honor, I shall not go as far as that Lucretia who, they say, killed herself even though she had done no wrong, and without first killing the one responsible for her misfortune. I shall die, if I must; but I have to take my revenge and exact satisfaction from the man who has brought me to this place to weep over the insolence of his actions, for which I am blameless."

Leonela had to be asked many more times before she went out to call Lotario, but finally she left, and while she was gone, Camila said, as if talking to herself:

"Lord save me! Would it not have been better to reject Lotario, as I have so many times before, rather than give him reason to think, as I have done now, that I am immodest and unchaste, even for this short time that I must wait until I make him aware of his error? No doubt it would have been better, but then I would not be avenged, nor my husband's honor satisfied if, with clean hands, he could walk away so easily from the situation to which his wicked thoughts have brought him. Let the traitor pay with his life for what his lascivious desire attempted to do; let the world know, if it ever does come to light, that Camila not only remained faithful to her husband, but took revenge on the one who dared offend him. Even so, I believe it would have been better to tell Anselmo, but I tried in the letter I wrote to him when he was in the village, and I think his not coming to remedy the harm I pointed out to him must have been because he is so good and trusting, he would not or could not believe that the bosom of so firm a friend could harbor any thoughts detrimental to his honor; not even I believed it afterward, not for many days, and I never would have believed it if his insolence had not grown so great, and if his open offers of gifts and exaggerated promises and constant tears had not made it clear to me. But why do I even think about this now? Does a gallant resolve have need of more counsel? Of course not. Away traitors, come revenge! Let the deceiver enter, let him come, let him arrive, let him die and be finished with, let whatever happens happen! I was pure when I came into possession of the man heaven gave me for my own; I shall be pure when I leave it behind, even if I am bathed in my own chaste blood and the impure blood of the falsest friend that friendship has ever known."

And saying this, she paced the room with the dagger unsheathed, making such disordered and extravagant movements and gestures that she appeared to have lost her mind and seemed not a fragile woman but a desperate ruffian.

Anselmo watched it all, concealed behind the tapestries where he had hidden; he was astonished by everything, and it seemed to him that what he had seen and heard was enough to allay the greatest suspicions, and he would have liked to forego the proofs that would come with Lotario's arrival, fearing some dreadful mishap. He was about to show himself and come out of hiding to embrace and reassure his wife, but he stopped when he saw Leonela return, leading Lotario by the hand, and as soon as Camila saw him she drew a line on the floor with the dagger and said:

"Lotario, listen to what I am saying: if by some chance you dare to cross this line, or even approach it, at the very moment I see what you are attempting, I shall plunge the dagger I am holding into my breast. And before you say a word in response, I want you to listen to a few more of mine, and then you can say whatever you wish. First, I want you to tell me, Lotario, if you know my husband Anselmo, and what opinion you have of him; second, I also want to know if you know me. Answer me this, and do not be confused or think too much about how you will reply, for my questions are not difficult."

Lotario was not so simpleminded that he had not realized what Camila intended from the moment she told him to have Anselmo hide, and he responded so cleverly and so appropriately to her intention that the two of them made the lie appear to be the absolute truth, and so he replied to Camila in this fashion:

"I did not think, O beautiful Camila, that you called me in order to ask me things so far from the intention with which I come here. If you are doing this in order to delay granting me the promised favor, you should have done so from a greater distance, for the nearer we are to the object of our desire, the greater our hope of possessing it; but, so that you cannot say I do not answer your questions, I will say that I know your husband, Anselmo, and he and I have known each other since we were children; I do not want to say what you know all too well about our friendship, so that I do not bear witness to the offense that love, which is a powerful excuse for even greater crimes, forces me to commit against him. I know you and hold you in the same high esteem that he does; otherwise, I would not, for any lesser prize, violate what I owe my own person and the holy laws of true friendship, infringed and broken by me on account of an enemy as powerful as love."

"If you confess to that," responded Camila, "mortal enemy of all that justly deserves to be loved, how do you dare appear before the one who, as you know, is the mirror that reflects him? If you looked in it carefully, you would see how little justification you have for offending him. But oh, woe is me, now I realize what has made you disregard what you owe to yourself: it must have been negligence on my part; I do not wish to call it immodesty, since it did not follow from a deliberate decision but from the sort of careless act that women often commit inadvertently when they think they have no reason to be cautious. Otherwise tell me, O traitor, when did I ever respond to your entreaties with a word or gesture that could have awakened in you even the shadow of a hope of satisfying your base desires? When were your amorous words not rejected and reproached with severity and harshness? When were your many promises and gifts ever believed or accepted? But since it seems to me that no one can persevere in his amorous intention for very long if he is not sustained by some hope, I shall blame myself for your impertinence, for no doubt some negligence on my part has sustained your desire for so long, and therefore I shall impose the punishment and penalty on myself that your crime deserves. And so that you may see that if I am cruel with myself, I could be no less cruel with you, I wanted to bring you here to be a witness to the sacrifice I intend to make to the insulted honor of my honorable husband; you offended him with all possible deliberation, as I offended him by my carelessness in giving you the opportunity, if in fact I gave you one, that would favor and condone your wicked intentions. I say again: the suspicion I have that some carelessness of mine engendered those monstrous thoughts in you troubles me greatly; it is what I desire to punish with my own hands, for if another punished me, perhaps my crime would be made public; but before I do that, I want to kill as I die, and take with me the one who will finally satisfy my desire for the vengeance I hope for, and that I shall have when I see, in the next world, the penalty imposed by a disinterested justice that does not bend before the one who has brought me to such desperate straits."

And having said this, with incredible strength and speed she attacked Lotario with the unsheathed dagger, showing such clear intentions of wanting to plunge it into his bosom that he was not certain if her displays were false or true, for he had to use his skill and strength to keep Camila from stabbing him. She was acting out that strange deception and lie so vividly that in order to give it the appearance of truth, she tried to color it with her own blood; seeing that she could not reach Lotario, or pretending that she could not, she said:

"Fate does not wish to satisfy completely my righteous desire, but it will not be strong enough to keep me from satisfying it in part, at least."

And struggling to free from Lotario's grasp the hand that held the dagger, she finally succeeded, aimed the point at a part of her body that she could wound, but not deeply, and plunged it in above her left armpit, near the shoulder; then she dropped to the floor as if she had fallen into a faint.

Leonela and Lotario were dumbfounded, astonished at what had just happened and still doubting its reality although Camila lay on the floor, bathed in blood. Lotario, horrified and breathless, rushed over to her to pull out the dagger, and when he saw how small the wound was, he stopped being afraid and once again marveled at the great sagacity, prudence, and intelligence of the beautiful Camila; in order to comply with his obligations, he began a long, melancholy lamentation over Camila's body, as if she were dead, and he cursed not only himself but the man who had placed her in that situation. And since he knew that his friend Anselmo was listening, he said things that would move anyone to pity him much more than Camila, even if he did think she was dead.

Leonela took her in her arms and laid her on the bed, pleading with Lotario to go and find someone who would heal Camila in secret; she also asked his advice and opinion regarding what they would tell Anselmo about her mistress's wound in the event he came home before she was healed. He replied that they should say whatever they wanted, for he was not the one to give any useful advice; he would say only that she should try to stop the bleeding because he was going where no one would see him again. Displaying great grief and emotion, he left the house, and when he found himself alone, in a place where no one could see him, he could not stop crossing himself as he marveled at Camila's stratagem and Leonela's clever responses. He considered how certain Anselmo would be that his wife was a second Portia, and he wished he could meet with him so they could both celebrate the most hidden truth and concealed lie that anyone could ever imagine.

Leonela staunched her mistress's blood, which was no more than what was necessary to make the lie believable, and washing the wound with a little wine, she bandaged it the best she could, and as she treated her she said words that would have been enough, even if nothing had been said before, to persuade Anselmo that he had in Camila the very image and example of virtue.

Added to Leonela's words were those of Camila, who called herself a craven coward for not having the courage, when she needed it most, to take her own life, which she despised. She asked her maid if she should tell her dear husband about what had happened; Leonela advised her not to, because that would oblige him to take his revenge on Lotario, which would be very dangerous, and it was the duty of a good wife not to give her husband reasons for disputes but to save him from as many as possible.

Camila responded that her advice seemed very good, and she would follow it, but in any case they ought to decide what they would tell Anselmo about the reason for the wound, which he would be bound to see; to which Leonela replied that she did not know how to lie, even as a joke.

"Well, my friend," replied Camila, "then what shall I do if I would not dare create or sustain a lie even if my life depended on it? If we cannot find our way out of this, it would be better to tell him the unadorned truth rather than have him discover us in a falsehood."

"Don't be sad, Señora; by tomorrow," responded Leonela, "I'll think of what we should say, and perhaps because of where the wound is, you'll be able to hide it and he won't see it, and heaven will be merciful and favor our just and honorable thoughts. Be calm, Señora, and try to stay calm so that my master doesn't find you troubled, and you can leave the rest to me, and to God, who always comes to the aid of virtuous desires."

Anselmo had been very attentive as he heard and watched the performance of the tragedy of the death of his honor, which had been performed with such unusual and convincing effects by the actors that they seemed to have been transformed into the very parts they were playing. He longed for night to fall, when he would be able to leave his house, and go to see his good friend Lotario, and celebrate with him the precious pearl he had discovered in the revelation of his wife's virtue. The two women were careful to give him the opportunity to leave, and he did not miss that opportunity, and he left and went to find Lotario, and when he had found him, it is difficult to recount the number of embraces he gave him, the things he said about his joy, his praises of Camila. Lotario listened to all of this and could give no indications of happiness because he thought of how deceived his friend was and how unjustly he had wronged him. And although Anselmo saw that Lotario was not happy, he thought it was because he had left Camila wounded when he had been the reason for the wound; among other things, he even told him not to grieve over what had happened to Camila, because the wound was surely superficial since the two women had agreed to hide it from him; therefore there was nothing to fear, and from now on Lotario should rejoice and celebrate with him because through his efforts, Anselmo found himself lifted to the highest happiness he could ever desire, and he wanted to do nothing else but write verses in praise of Camila that would make her live forever in the memory of future ages. Lotario praised his decision and said that he, for his part, would help him raise so noble an edifice.

And so Anselmo was the most deliciously deceived man in the world: he himself led into his house the man who was the ruination of his name, believing he had been the instrument of his glory. Camila received him with an apparently crestfallen expression, although her soul rejoiced. This deception lasted some months until Fortune spun her wheel, the wickedness they had concealed with so much skill was made public, and Anselmo's reckless curiosity cost him his life.

CHAPTER XXXV

In which the novel of The Man Who Was Recklessly Curious *is concluded*

Only a little more of the novel remained to be read when a distraught Sancho Panza rushed out of the garret where Don Quixote slept, shouting:

"Come, Señores, come quickly and help my master, who's involved in the fiercest, most awful battle my eyes have ever seen! By God, what a thrust he gave to the giant, the enemy of the Señora Princess Micomicona, when he cut his head right off, just like a turnip!"

"What are you saying, brother?" said the priest, who had stopped reading the novel. "Are you in your right mind, Sancho? How the devil can what you say be true if the giant is two thousand leagues from here?"

Just then they heard a loud noise in the garret and the sound of Don Quixote shouting:

"Hold, thief, scoundrel, coward! I have you now, and your scimitar will be of little use to you!"

And he seemed to be slashing at the walls with his sword. Sancho said:

"Don't stand and listen, go in and stop the fight or help my master, though that won't be necessary because, no doubt about it, the giant must be dead by now and giving an accounting to God of his sinful life; I saw his blood running along the floor, and his head cut off and fallen to one side, a head the size of a big wineskin."

"Strike me dead," said the innkeeper, "if Don Quixote, or Don Devil, hasn't slashed one of the skins of red wine hanging at the head of his bed; the spilled wine must be what this good man thinks is blood."

And then he hurried into the room, and all the rest followed him, and they discovered Don Quixote in the strangest outfit in the world. He was in his shirt, which was not long enough in front to cover his thighs completely, and in back it was shorter by a span of six fingers; his legs were very long and thin, hairy, and not particularly clean; on his head he wore a red, greasy nightcap that belonged to the innkeeper; wrapped around his left arm was the blanket from the bed, toward which Sancho felt some animosity, for reasons he knew only too well; in his right hand he held his unsheathed sword and was slashing with it in all directions and shouting as if he really were fighting a giant. Best of all, his eyes were not open because he was sleeping and dreaming that he was doing battle with the giant, for his imagination of the adventure he was about to undertake was so intense that it made him dream he had already come to the kingdom of Micomicón and was already engaged in combat with his enemy. He had slashed the wineskins so many times with his sword, thinking he was slashing the giant, that the entire room was covered in wine. When he saw this, the innkeeper became so enraged that he threw himself on Don Quixote and began to give him so many blows with his fists that if Cardenio and the priest had not pulled him off, he alone would have ended the conflict with the giant; with it all, the poor knight did not awaken until the barber brought a large pot of cold water from the well and threw it at him all at once, which roused Don Quixote, but not enough for him to realize what he was doing.

Dorotea, who saw how scantily and tenuously he was dressed, did not wish to come in and watch the combat between her defender and her adversary.

Sancho looked everywhere on the floor for the giant's head, and when he did not find it, he said:

"Now I know that everything in this house is enchantment; the last time I stood on the very spot where I'm standing now, I was punched and beaten and I never knew who was doing it, and I never could see any-body, and now the head is nowhere to be found, though I saw it cut off with my very own eyes, and the blood ran out of the body like water from a fountain."

"What blood and what fountain are you talking about, you enemy of God and all his saints?" said the innkeeper. "Don't you see, you thief, that the blood and the fountain are only these slashed wineskins and the red wine flooding this room? I'd like to see the soul of whoever slashed them drowning in the floods of hell!"

"All I know," responded Sancho, "is that if I don't find that head, my luck will turn and my countship will dissolve away like salt in water."

Sancho awake was worse than his master asleep: such was the faith he had in the promises his master had made to him. The innkeeper de-spaired when he saw the slow wits of the squire and the damage done by the master, and he swore it would not be like the last time, when they left without paying; this time they could not claim the privileges of chivalry to keep from paying for both stays at the inn, including the cost of the patches he would have to put on the torn wineskins.

The priest was holding Don Quixote by the hands, and the knight, believing the adventure had been concluded and that he was before the Princess Micomicona, kneeled in front of the priest, saying:

"Now your highness, your noble and illustrious ladyship, may live in the certainty that from this day forth, this lowborn creature can do you no harm, and I, from this day forth, am released from the promise I made to you, for with the help of God on high and the favor of her for whom I live and breathe, I have kept the promise, and with great suc-cess."

"Didn't I tell you?" said Sancho when he heard this. "I told you I wasn't drunk: now you can see if my master hasn't slaughtered and salted that giant! Now it's for sure:[1] my countship's on the way!"

Who would not have laughed at the foolishness of both master and servant? Everyone did except the innkeeper, who cursed his luck; but at last, with no small effort, the barber, Cardenio, and the priest returned Don Quixote to the bed, where he fell asleep, showing signs of great weariness. They left him sleeping and went out to the entrance to the inn to console Sancho Panza for not having found the giant's head, though it was more difficult for them to placate the innkeeper, who was

---

1. The phrase in Spanish, *ciertos son los toros*, is equivalent to "the bulls are certain"—that is, "there's no doubt about the outcome."

in despair at the sudden demise of his wineskins. And the innkeeper's wife said, with great cries and shouts:

"It was an evil moment and a cursed hour when this knight errant came into my house; he costs me so much, I wish I'd never laid eyes on him. The last time, he left without paying the cost of a night, a meal, a bed, straw, and barley, for him and his squire and a horse and a donkey, saying that he was an adventuring knight, may God give him unlucky adventures, him and all the adventurers in the world, and that's why he wasn't obliged to pay anything, according to the tariff regulations of errant knighthood. Then, on his account, this other gentleman comes along and takes away my oxtail, and gives it back with more than two *cuartillos*'[2] worth of damage, with not a hair on it, so it's no good for the thing my husband wanted it for. And then, the finishing touch, he slashes my wineskins and spills my wine, and I only wish it was his blood that was spilled. Well, he won't get away with it! By the bones of my father and my mother's old white head, he'll pay me every *cuarto*[3] he owes or my name isn't what it is, and I'm not my parents' daughter!"

These words and others like them were said in great anger by the innkeeper's wife, and her good maid, Maritornes, assisted her in this. Her daughter said nothing, and from time to time she smiled. The priest restored calm by promising to do everything in his power to compensate them for their loss, the wineskins as well as the wine, and in particular the damage to the oxtail, which they valued so highly. Dorotea consoled Sancho Panza, promising him that as soon as it was certain his master had cut off the giant's head and she was peacefully ruling her kingdom again, she would give him the best countship in all the land. Sancho was comforted by this, and he assured the princess that she could be certain he had seen the head of the giant, who seemed to have a beard that came down to his waist, and if the head could not be found, it was because everything that happened in that house was enchantment, as he had learned the last time he stayed here. Dorotea said she believed him, and he should not worry; everything would be fine and turn out just as he wished.

When everyone was calm, the priest wanted to finish reading the novel because he saw that he had almost reached the end. Cardenio, Dorotea, and all the others asked him to finish it, and the priest, who

---

2. A *cuartillo* is one-fourth of a *real*.

3. A *cuarto*, a coin of very little value, was worth four *maravedís*.

wished to satisfy everyone and wanted to read it as well, continued the story.

And so, because of Anselmo's certainty regarding Camila's virtue, he led a carefree and contented life, and Camila intentionally showed coldness to Lotario so that Anselmo would believe her feelings toward him were the opposite of what they truly were; to give this even more weight, Lotario asked permission not to visit his friend's house anymore since it was clear that the sight of him troubled Camila a great deal, but the deluded Anselmo said that under no circumstances would he allow any such thing; in this way, in a thousand ways, Anselmo constructed his own dishonor, believing that he was creating his own delight.

In the meantime, the delight Leonela took in freely engaging in her love affair went so far that she cared about nothing else and pursued it without restraint, certain that her mistress would conceal what she did and even advise her how to carry on an affair without arousing too much suspicion. Finally, one night, Anselmo heard footsteps in Leonela's bedroom, and when he tried to go in to see whose they were, he found the door closed against him, which gave him an even greater desire to open it; he pushed so hard that it opened, and as he went in he saw a man leaping out the window to the street, and when he tried to hurry out to catch him or see who he was, he could do neither because Leonela threw her arms around him, saying:

"Be calm, Señor, don't be angry, you don't need to follow the man who left here; it really is my affair; in fact, he's my husband."

Anselmo did not believe her; instead, blind with rage, he took out his dagger and tried to stab Leonela, saying that if she did not tell him the truth, he would kill her. She was terrified, and not knowing what she was saying, she cried:

"Don't kill me, Señor, and I'll tell you things that are more important than you can imagine."

"Tell me now," said Anselmo, "or you're a dead woman."

"I can't now," said Leonela, "I'm too upset; wait until tomorrow, and then you'll hear things that will amaze you; but you can be sure that the man who jumped out the window is a young man of this city who has given his promise to marry me."

Anselmo grew calmer and was willing to wait the period of time she requested, for he did not think he would hear anything against Camila, he was so certain and sure of her virtue; so he went out of Leonela's bedroom and left her locked inside, saying she would not leave until she told him what she had to tell him.

Then he went to see Camila, and told her everything that had occurred, and said that her maid had promised to tell him great, important things. It goes without saying that Camila became alarmed, fearing, and with reason, that Leonela would tell Anselmo everything she knew about her infidelity; she did not have the courage to wait and see if her suspicions were true, and that same night, when she thought Anselmo was asleep, she gathered together the most precious jewels she had, and some money, and without being detected by anyone, she left her house and went to Lotario's; she told him what had happened and asked that he hide her, or that the two of them go where they would both be safe from Anselmo. Camila threw Lotario into such confusion that he could not say a word, much less decide what to do.

Finally, he decided to take Camila to a convent where one of his sisters was prioress. Camila agreed, and with the speed the situation demanded, Lotario took her to the convent and left her there, and he himself abandoned the city and told no one of his departure.

At dawn, Anselmo's desire to hear what Leonela wanted to tell him was so great, he did not even notice that Camila was not at his side but got up and went to the room where he had left the maid. He unlocked the door and went in but did not find Leonela there; he found only some sheets knotted together and tied to the window, a clear sign that she had used them to climb down and leave the house. Then he walked back to his own room very mournfully to tell Camila and was stunned not to find her in bed or anywhere in the house. He questioned the servants, but no one could answer his questions.

As he was looking for Camila, he happened to see the open chests and saw too that most of her jewels were missing from them, and this was when he became aware of the calamity and knew that Leonela was not the cause of his affliction. He did not even bother to finish dressing, but just as he was, sad and melancholy, he went to tell his friend Lotario about his misfortune. But when he did not find him, and the servants said Lotario had left in the night and taken with him all the money he had, Anselmo thought he would go mad. As a final blow, when he returned home all of the servants had gone, and his house was empty and deserted.

He did not know what to think, what to say, or what to do, but slowly his judgment began to return. He reflected on what had happened and saw himself deprived, in an instant, of his wife, his friend, and his servants, abandoned, it seemed to him, by heaven, and, above all, bereft of honor, for in Camila's absence he saw his ruination.

Finally he resolved, after a long while, to go to the village where he had stayed with his friend when he gave them the opportunity to devise that misfortune. He locked the doors of his house, mounted his horse, and set out with weakening courage; when he had traveled only half the distance, he was overwhelmed by his thoughts and had to dismount; he tied his horse's reins to a tree and dropped to the ground beneath it, heaving tender, pitiful sighs, and lay there until it was almost dark; then he saw a man on horseback riding toward him from the city, and after greeting him, he asked what the news was in Florence. The citizen responded:

"The strangest heard there in many days, because it is being said publicly that Lotario, the great friend of Anselmo the rich man, who lived near San Giovanni, ran off last night with Camila, Anselmo's wife, and Anselmo is nowhere to be found. All of this was disclosed by one of Camila's maids, who was discovered last night by the governor as she climbed down a sheet hanging from a window in Anselmo's house. The fact is that I don't know exactly how everything turned out; all I know is that the whole city is astonished by what happened, since it was not what anybody expected from their great friendship, for they were so close that people called them *the two friends*."

"Do you know, by any chance," said Anselmo, "where Lotario and Camila went?"

"I have no idea," said the Florentine, "although the governor has made every effort to find them."

"Then God go with you, Señor," said Anselmo.

"And with you," responded the Florentine, and he rode away.

At such calamitous news, Anselmo was on the verge not only of losing his mind but of ending his life. He struggled to his feet and reached the house of his friend, who still knew nothing of his misfortune, but when he saw Anselmo come in looking pallid, exhausted, and drawn, he realized that something very serious had happened. Anselmo immediately asked to be helped to his bed and to be given writing materials. This was done, and he was left lying in bed, the door closed, as he had requested. When he found himself alone, his mind became so burdened with thoughts of his misfortune that he knew his life was coming to an end, and so he decided to leave some explanation of his strange death; he began to write, but before he had finished putting down everything he wanted to say, his breath failed, and he yielded up his life to the grief caused by his reckless curiosity.

The master of the house, seeing that it was late and Anselmo had not called for him, decided to go in to find out if he was feeling better, and he found him facedown, half his body in bed and the other half slumped over the writing desk, the paper he had been writing on unsealed and the pen still in his hand. His host came over to him, having first called his name, and when Anselmo did not answer he grasped his hand, found it cold, and knew that he was dead. Shocked and grief-stricken, his friend summoned the household to see the misfortune that had befallen Anselmo, and finally he read the paper, written by Anselmo's own hand, which said:

A foolish and reckless desire took my life. If news of my death should reach Camila, she must know that I forgive her, for she was not obliged to perform miracles, and I had no need to ask her to; since I constructed my own dishonor, there is no reason to . . .

Anselmo wrote this far, making it clear that before he could end his thought, his life came to an end. The following day, his friend informed Anselmo's kin of his death; they already knew of his misfortune and of the convent where Camila was almost at the point of joining her husband on that inevitable journey, not on account of her husband's death, but because of what she had heard about her absent lover. It was said that although a widow, she did not wish to leave the convent, much less take vows to be a nun; then, a few days later, the news reached her that Lotario had died in the battle between Monsieur de Lautrec and the Great Captain Gonzalo Fernández de Córdoba, which had just taken place in the kingdom of Naples, where Anselmo's friend, repentant too late, had fled;[4] when Camila learned this, she took her vows, and not long afterward her life ended in the pitiless embrace of sorrow and melancholy. This was the end met by the three and born of such rash beginnings.

"This novel seems fine," said the priest, "but I cannot persuade myself that it is true; if it is invented, the author invented badly, because no

4. This appears to refer to the battle of Cerignola, in 1503, when the defeat of the French made the kingdom of Naples a Spanish province.

one can imagine any husband foolish enough to conduct the costly experiment that Anselmo did. If this occurred between a lover and his
lady, it might be plausible, but between a husband and his wife it seems
impossible; as for the manner in which it was told, I did not find it dis-
pleasing."

CHAPTER XXXVI

Which recounts the fierce and uncommon battle that Don Quixote had
with some skins of red wine, along with other unusual events that occurred in
the inn[1]

Just then the innkeeper, who was at the entrance to the inn, said:

"Here comes a beautiful collection of guests: if they stop here, we'll
have some *gaudeamus*."

"What kind of people?" said Cardenio.

"Four men," responded the innkeeper, "on horseback, with short stirrups, lances, and shields, and all of them wearing black masks;[2] with
them is a woman dressed in white, riding sidesaddle, and her face is covered, too, and there are two servants with them, on foot."

"Are they very near?" asked the priest.

"So near," responded the innkeeper, "that they're arriving now."

When Dorotea heard this she covered her face, and Cardenio went
into the room where Don Quixote was sleeping; they almost did not
have time to do so before everyone described by the innkeeper came into
the inn; the four riders, of a very gallant appearance and disposition, dismounted and went to help the woman down from the sidesaddle, and
one of them took her in his arms and sat her in a chair that was near the
door of the room where Cardenio had gone to hide. In all this time, neither she nor the men had removed their masks, or spoken a single word,
but as the woman sat in the chair she sighed deeply and let her arms fall

1. In what seems to be another oversight on the part of Cervantes or his printer, the first part of this
epigraph actually belongs to the previous chapter.

2. These were worn to protect travelers from the sun and dust.

to her sides, as if she were sick and weak. The servants who had come on foot led the horses to the stables.

The priest, seeing this, and longing to know who these people were who dressed in this fashion and kept so silent, walked over to the servants and asked one of them what he wanted to know; the servant responded:

"By my faith, Señor, I can't tell you who these people are: I only know that they seem to be very important, especially the one who took the lady in his arms, and I say this because all the others have respect for him and do only what he orders and commands."

"And the lady, who is she?" asked the priest.

"I don't know that, either," the servant responded, "because during the whole journey I haven't seen her face; I've heard her sigh, very often, and moan, and each time it sounds as if her heart were about to break. It's no surprise we don't know more than this, because my companions and I have been traveling with them for only two days; we met on the road, and they asked us and persuaded us to go with them as far as Andalucía, and they offered to pay us very well."

"Have you heard any of their names?" asked the priest.

"No, we surely haven't," responded the servant, "because it's a wonder how silently they travel; all you hear from them are the sighs and sobs of that poor lady, and we really feel sorry for her; we think she's being forced to go wherever it is that she's going; from what we've seen of her clothes, she's a nun, or she's going to become one, which seems more likely, and maybe she isn't becoming a nun of her own free will, and that's why she seems so melancholy."

"That's possible," said the priest.

And leaving them, he walked back to Dorotea, who, hearing the masked woman sigh, and moved by her natural compassion, approached her and said:

"What troubles you, Señora? If it is an ailment that women know about and can cure, I am happy to offer my services to you."

In response to this the sorrowful lady remained silent, and although Dorotea repeated her offer she maintained her silence, until the masked gentleman, the one the servant said was obeyed by the others, approached and said to Dorotea:

"Do not waste your time, Señora, in offering anything to this woman, since it is her custom never to give thanks for anything that is done for her, and do not encourage her to respond, unless you wish to hear her tell a lie."

"I have never told one," said the woman, who up to this moment had been silent. "Rather, it is because I am so truthful, so lacking in deceptive wiles, that I find myself in this predicament; I call on you as my witness, for the absolute truth I tell turns you into a lying traitor."

Cardenio heard these words clearly and distinctly, for he was very near the one who said them, separated from her only by the door to Don Quixote's room, and when he heard them, he gave a great shout, saying:

"God save me! What is this I hear? Whose voice is this that has reached my ears?"

The lady, in great consternation, turned her head when she heard these shouts, and not seeing the one who was shouting, she rose to her feet and was about to enter the room; the gentleman, seeing this, stopped her and did not allow her to take a step. She was so distraught and agitated that the cloth covering her face slipped off, revealing an incomparably beautiful face, though one that was pale and frightened, as her eyes looked all around her, darting back and forth with so much urgency that she seemed a person who had lost her reason; these gestures and movements, though Dorotea did not know why she was making them, filled her and all who looked upon the lady with great pity. The gentleman held her tightly by the shoulders, and because he was so involved in holding her back, he could not keep his own mask raised, and it too slipped off; Dorotea, who had put her arms around the lady, looked up and saw that the man also holding the lady was her husband, Don Fernando; no sooner had she recognized him than from the bottom of her heart there rose a long, mournful *ay!* and she fell backward in a swoon, and if the barber had not been close by and had not caught her in his arms, she would have fallen to the floor.

The priest hurried over and removed Dorotea's veil so that he could sprinkle her face with water, and as soon as her face was uncovered, Don Fernando recognized her, for it was he who held the other woman, and he turned deathly pale when he saw her; even so, he did not release Luscinda, for it was she who was struggling to free herself from his arms, having recognized Cardenio's voice, as he had recognized hers. When Cardenio heard the *ay!* that came from Dorotea when she fainted, he thought it had come from his Luscinda, and he rushed out of the room, terrified, and the first thing he saw was Don Fernando with his arms around Luscinda. Don Fernando also recognized Cardenio, and the three of them, Luscinda, Cardenio, and Dorotea, were left speechless with astonishment, barely knowing what had happened to them.

All were silent as they all looked at one another: Dorotea at Don Fernando, Don Fernando at Cardenio, Cardenio at Luscinda, and Luscinda at Cardenio. But the first one to break the silence was Luscinda, who spoke to Don Fernando in this manner:

"Let me go, Don Fernando, for the sake of what you owe to your person, since you will not do so for any other reason, and let me cling to the wall on which I am the ivy, the support from which you have not been able to tear me despite your solicitations, threats, promises, and gifts. See how heaven, in its miraculous, mysterious way, has brought my true husband before me. And you know very well, after a thousand costly efforts, that only death is strong enough to wipe him from my memory. Therefore let this clear discouragement persuade you to turn love into rage, desire into disgust, and then put an end to my life; if I lose it in the presence of my dear husband, it will be well lost, for perhaps with my death, he will be convinced that I kept faith with him until the very end."

In the meantime, Dorotea had recovered from her swoon; she heard everything Luscinda said and realized who she was, and seeing that Don Fernando still had not freed her or responded to her words, Dorotea used all her strength to stand; then she fell to her knees in front of him, and shedding a great quantity of beautiful, heartrending tears, she began to speak to him, saying:

"If, Señor, the rays from this sun that you hold eclipsed in your arms have not clouded and darkened the light in your own eyes, then you will have seen that she who kneels at your feet is Dorotea, luckless and unfortunate until you will otherwise. I am that humble peasant whom you, out of kindness or for the sake of your own pleasure, wished to elevate to the height where she could call herself yours. I am the one who, secluded and surrounded by virtue, lived a happy life until, heeding your urgent words and what seemed to be fitting and loving sentiments, opened the doors of her modesty and handed you the keys to her freedom, a gift so little valued by you that I have been obliged to come to the place where you find me now, and see you in the manner in which I now see you. Even so, I would not want you to think that my dishonor has directed my steps, when I have been brought here only by the sorrow and grief of being forgotten by you.

You wanted me to be yours, and you wanted it in such a manner that even though you no longer do, it will not be possible for you to stop being mine. Consider, Señor, that the incomparable love I have for you may be recompense for the beauty and nobility for whose sake you have abandoned me. You cannot belong to the beautiful Luscinda because you are mine, and she cannot be yours because she belongs to Cardenio; if you consider it for a moment, it would be easier for you to turn your will to loving one who adores you, rather than trying to force love from one who despises you. You solicited my shame; you pleaded for my integrity; you were not ignorant of my status; you know very well how I surrendered completely to your desire; you have no justification or reason to claim you were deceived. If this is true, and it is, and if you are as much a Christian as you are a gentleman, then why do you go to so much trouble to avoid making me as contented at the end as you did at the beginning? And if you do not love me for what I am, your true and legitimate wife, then at least want me and take me as your slave; if I am possessed by you, I shall think of myself as happy and fortunate. Do not, by leaving and abandoning me, permit my dishonor to become the subject of gossip and rumors; do not ruin the old age of my parents: their loyal service, as good vassals to your family, deserves better. And if it seems to you that you will debase your blood by mixing it with mine, consider that there are few, if any, noble lines in the world that have not taken this path, and that the bloodline on the woman's side is not relevant to an illustrious lineage;[3] furthermore, true nobility consists of virtue, and if you lose yours by denying me what you rightly owe me, then I shall have more noble characteristics than you.

In short, Señor, I say to you for the last time that whether you wish it or not, I am your wife; your words bear witness to that, and they cannot and must not be false, unless you no longer value in yourself what you scorn me for not having; your signature bears witness, as does the heaven you called on to witness what you promised me. And if all this is to no avail, your own conscience cannot help but call to you silently in the midst of all your joys, reminding you of the truth I have told you, and clouding your greatest pleasure and happiness."

The unfortunate Dorotea said these and other words with so much emotion and so many tears that all those present, even the men who accompanied Don Fernando, were moved. Don Fernando listened, not saying a word until she concluded speaking and then began to sob and heave so many sighs that one would have needed a heart of bronze not to be affected by these signs of deep sorrow. Luscinda watched her, as moved by her grief as she was astounded at her great intelligence and beauty, and although she wished to approach her and say some words of comfort, Don Fernando held her tightly in his arms and would not release her. Don Fernando, filled with consternation and confusion, stared at Dorotea for a long time and then lowered his arms, releasing Luscinda, and said:

3. It was believed that nobility was inherited exclusively from the father.

"You have conquered, O beautiful Dorotea, you have conquered, be-cause I do not have the heart to deny so many truths spoken together."

When Don Fernando released her, Luscinda felt so faint she almost fell, but since Cardenio was close to her, standing behind Don Fernando so he would not be recognized,[4] he set aside all fear and defied all danger and hurried to support Luscinda, and taking her in his arms, he said:

"If merciful heaven wishes and desires you to have repose, O loyal, steadfast, and beautiful wife of mine, you will find none more secure than what you have now in these arms that welcome you, and welcomed you in the past, when it was Fortune's will that I call you mine."

At these words Luscinda rested her eyes on Cardenio, and having recognized him, first by hearing his voice and then by seeing him, she was almost mad with joy, and unconcerned about the appearance of modesty, she threw her arms around his neck, and putting her face close to his, she said:

"You indeed, Señor, are the true master of your captive, no matter how Fortune may oppose us or threaten this life of mine, which depends on yours."

This was a strange sight for Don Fernando and for all the others, who marveled at so unusual a turn of events. It appeared to Dorotea that Don Fernando turned pale and seemed ready to take his revenge on Carde-nio, because she saw him move his hand toward his sword, and as soon as this thought occurred to her, she hastened to throw her arms around his knees, kissing them and holding them so close that he could not move, and with her tears still flowing, she said:

"What do you, my sole refuge, intend to do in this unforeseen situa-tion? At your feet you have your wife, and the woman you want instead is in the arms of her husband. Consider if it will be right, or possible, for you to undo what heaven has done, or whether it will be better for you to elevate to your own height one who has been constant in her truth and steadfastness despite all obstacles, and whom you see here before you, bathing the face and bosom of her true husband in amorous tears. I be-seech you for the sake of God, I implore you for your own sake: do not allow this manifest disappointment to increase your anger but diminish it instead, so that, calmly and serenely, you permit these two lovers to enjoy all the time that heaven wishes to grant them, with no hindrance from you; in this you will reveal the generosity of your illustrious and

4. Another apparent oversight: it was indicated earlier in the chapter that the two men had already seen each other.

noble heart, and the world will see that in you, reason is more powerful than appetite."

As Dorotea was saying this, Cardenio held Luscinda in his arms but did not move his eyes away from Don Fernando, determined that if he should see him make any move against him, he would defend himself and attack all those who wished to harm him, even if it cost him his life. But then Don Fernando's friends, and the priest and the barber, who had heard everything, not to mention our good Sancho Panza, approached Don Fernando and surrounded him, imploring him to consider Dorotea's tears, and if what she had said was true, as they believed it undoubtedly was, then he should not allow her to be deprived of her legitimate hopes; he should accept that it was not by chance but the will of divine providence that they all had met in so unlikely a place, and he should be advised—said the priest—that only death could take Luscinda from Cardenio, and even if they were put asunder by a sharp-edged sword, they would consider their death joyous; in the face of bonds as indissoluble as these, it was the height of reason to show his generous heart, overcoming and conquering himself and, by his own free will, permitting the couple to enjoy the happiness already granted them by heaven; he should turn his eyes to the beauty of Dorotea, and he would see that few, if any, women were her equal, let alone her superior, and in addition to her beauty he should consider her humility and her great love for him, and, above all, he should realize that if he valued himself as a gentleman and as a Christian, he could do nothing but keep the promise he had made; by keeping it, he would keep his faith with God and satisfy all discerning people, who know and realize that even in a woman of humble birth, it is a prerogative of beauty, when accompanied by virtue, to rise to any height and be the equal of any highborn man, without in any way lowering the one who raises her and makes her equal to himself, for when the powerful laws of desire hold sway, as long as no sin intervenes, the man who follows them cannot be faulted.

In the end, everyone added their words to these, and they were of such a nature that the valiant heart of Don Fernando—it was, after all, fed by illustrious blood—softened and let itself be vanquished by the truth he could not deny even if he had wished to; the indication that he had surrendered and ceded to the good advice offered to him was that he bent down and embraced Dorotea, saying to her:

"Arise, Señora; it is not right for the woman I have in my heart to kneel at my feet; if, until now, I have not demonstrated what I say, perhaps it was ordained by heaven so that I, seeing the fidelity of your love for me, would esteem you as you deserve to be esteemed. What I ask is that you not reprimand my poor behavior and great negligence, for the same powerful reason that moved me to take you as my own also impelled me to avoid being yours. And to prove to you that this is true, turn and look into the eyes of Luscinda, who is now content, and in them you will find forgiveness for all my errors; since she has found and obtained what she desired, and I have found in you what pleases me, may she live safe and content for many long and happy years with her Cardenio, and I shall pray that heaven allows me to do the same with my Dorotea."

And having said this, Don Fernando embraced Dorotea again and pressed his face to hers with such tender feeling that he had to choke back the tears that were undeniable signs of his love and repentance. But the tears of Luscinda and Cardenio were not held back, nor were those of almost everyone else present, and so many were shed, for one's own joy and for the joy of others, that it seemed as if some calamity had befallen them all. Even Sancho Panza cried, although he later said the reason he cried was his discovery that Dorotea was not, as he had thought, Queen Micomicona, from whom he had hoped to receive innumerable favors. Everyone's bewilderment lasted for some time, at least as long as their weeping, and then Cardenio and Luscinda went to kneel before Don Fernando, thanking him with so much courtesy for the kindness he had shown them that Don Fernando did not know how to respond, and so he raised them up and embraced them, displaying great love and courtesy.

Then he asked Dorotea to tell him how she had come to this place so far from her home. Briefly and discreetly, she recounted everything she had told Cardenio earlier, which pleased Don Fernando and his traveling companions so much that they wanted the story to last longer: such was the charm with which Dorotea recounted her misfortunes. When she had finished, Don Fernando related what had happened to him in the city after the letter was discovered in Luscinda's bodice, the letter in which she declared that she was Cardenio's wife and could not be his. He said he had wanted to kill her and would have done so if her parents had not stopped him; then he, resentful and humiliated, had left the house, determined to have his revenge at a more convenient time; the next day he learned that Luscinda had fled her parents' house, and no one could say where she had gone; after a few months he discovered that she was in a convent, where she desired to remain for the rest of her life if she could not spend it with Cardenio; as soon as he learned this, he chose these three gentlemen to accompany him, and he went to the convent but did not attempt to speak to her, fearful that as soon as it was known that he was there, the convent would be made even more secure. And so he waited for a day when the porter's lodge would be open and left two of his companions to guard the door while he, with the third, entered the convent, looking for Luscinda, whom they found in the cloister talking to a nun; they seized her, not giving her a chance to resist, and brought her to a place where they had prepared everything they would need to abduct her. They had been able to do all of this with impunity because the convent was in the countryside, a good distance from town. He said that as soon as Luscinda found herself in his power, she had fallen into a deep swoon, and when she regained consciousness she had done nothing but weep and sigh and had not spoken a single word; and so, accompanied by silence and tears, they had come to the inn, which for him had been the same as coming to heaven, where all the misfortunes on earth reach their conclusion and end.

CHAPTER XXXVII

In which the history of the famous Princess Micomicona continues, along with other diverting adventures

Sancho listened to all of this with a very sorrowful spirit, for he saw that his hopes for a noble title were disappearing and going up in smoke, and that the lovely Princess Micomicona had turned into Dorotea, and the giant into Don Fernando, and that his master was in a deep, sound sleep, unaware of everything that had happened. Dorotea could not be certain she had not dreamed her great joy, Cardenio was in the same frame of mind, and Luscinda had the same thought. Don Fernando thanked heaven for its mercy in extricating him from the intricate labyrinth in which he had been on the verge of losing both his good name and his soul; in short, all the people in the inn were pleased, rejoicing at the happy outcome of such complex and desperate affairs.

The priest, a judicious man, put the final touch on everything by congratulating them all on the happiness each had achieved; but the one who was happiest and most joyful was the innkeeper's wife, because Cardenio and the priest had promised to pay her for all the damage and all the costs she had incurred on Don Quixote's account. Only Sancho, as we have said, was sorrowful, dejected, and sad, and so, with a melancholy expression, he went in to see his master, who had just awakened, and said:

"Your grace, Señor Sorrowful Face, can sleep all you want to now and not worry about killing any giant or returning the princess to her kingdom; it's all over and done with."

"I certainly believe that," responded Don Quixote, "because with that giant I have had the most uncommon and furious battle I think I shall ever have in all my days, and with a single downstroke—smash!—I knocked his head to the ground, and so much blood poured out of him that it ran in streams along the floor as if it were water."

"As if it were red wine, is what your grace should say," responded Sancho, "because I want your grace to know, in case you don't already, that the dead giant is a slashed wineskin, his blood, the six *arrobas*[1] of red wine contained in its belly, and the head you cut off is the whore who bore me, damn it all to hell!"

"Madman, what are you saying?" replied Don Quixote. "Have you lost your mind?"

"Get up, your grace," said Sancho, "and you'll see what you've won and what we have to pay, and you'll see the queen transformed into an ordinary lady named Dorotea, and other changes that will amaze you, if you can see them for what they are."

"I shall not marvel at any of it," replied Don Quixote, "because, if you remember, the last time we were here I told you that all the things that occurred in this place were works of enchantment, and it would not surprise me if the same were true now."

"I'd believe everything," responded Sancho, "if my tossing in the blanket was that kind of thing, but it wasn't, it was real and true, and I saw the innkeeper who's here today holding a corner of the blanket and tossing me up to the sky with lots of enthusiasm and energy, and as much laughter as strength, and though I'm a simple man and a sinner, as far as I'm concerned, when you can recognize people there's no enchantment at all, just a lot of bruising, and a lot of bad luck."

"Well, then, God will remedy everything," said Don Quixote. "Give me my clothes and let me go out there, for I wish to see the changes and transformations you have mentioned."

---

1. An extremely variable liquid measure, ranging from 2.6 to 3.6 gallons (it is also a dry measure equivalent to twenty-five pounds).

Sancho handed him his clothes, and while he was dressing, the priest told Don Fernando and the others about the madness of Don Quixote, and the stratagem they had used to take him away from Peña Pobre, which is where he imagined he was, brought there by his lady's scorn. He also related almost all the adventures that Sancho had recounted, which both astonished them and made them laugh, for they thought what everyone thought: it was the strangest kind of madness that had ever afflicted an irrational mind. The priest added that the fortunate change in Señora Dorotea's circumstances prevented their plan from going forward, and it would be necessary to devise and invent another so they could take him home. Cardenio offered to continue what they had already begun and have Luscinda act the part played by Dorotea.

"No," said Don Fernando, "by no means: I want Dorotea to go on with the fiction; this good gentleman's village is probably not very far from here, and I would be happy if a cure could be found for him."

"It's no more than two days' travel from here."

"Even if it were more, I would be glad to make the trip for the sake of so good a work."

At this moment Don Quixote came out, leaning on his branch, or lance, and wearing all his armor, the helmet of Mambrino, though battered, on his head, and his shield on his arm. Don Fernando and the others marveled at the strange appearance of Don Quixote, his dry, sallow face that was at least half a league long, his ill-matched weapons, and his solemn demeanor; they remained silent, waiting to see what he would say, and he, very gravely and serenely, turned his eyes toward the beautiful Dorotea, and said:

"I have been informed, O beauteous lady, by this my squire, that your greatness has been annihilated and your person undone, because from the queen and great lady you once were, you have turned into an ordinary damsel. If this has occurred by order of the necromancer king, your father, fearful I would not give you all the assistance you needed and deserved, then I say that he did not and does not know the half of what he should and is not well-versed in chivalric histories; if he had read them as attentively as I, and spent the same amount of time reading them as I, he would have found on every page how knights with less fame than mine had successfully concluded more difficult enterprises, finding it no great matter to kill some insignificant giant, no matter how arrogant; because not many hours ago I found myself with him and . . . I prefer to remain silent, because I do not wish anyone to say that I am lying, but

Time, which reveals all things, will disclose this truth to us when we least expect it."

"You found yourself with two wineskins, not with any giant," said the innkeeper.

Don Fernando ordered him to be quiet and not, under any circumstances, to interrupt Don Quixote; and Don Quixote continued, saying:

"I say, then, O high and disinherited lady, that if for the reason I have mentioned your father has brought about this metamorphosis in your person, then you should place no trust in him because there is no danger on earth through which my sword does not clear a path; with it, in a few short days, I shall send the head of your enemy rolling on the ground and place on yours its rightful crown."

Don Quixote stopped speaking and waited for the princess to respond, and she, knowing Don Fernando's determination that the deception should continue until Don Quixote had been brought home, responded with grace and solemnity:

"Whoever told you, O valiant Knight of the Sorrowful Face, that I had changed and altered my being, did not tell you the truth, because I am today the same woman I was yesterday. It is true that some alteration has been caused in me by certain fortunate events that have given me the best I could desire, but I have not, for that reason, stopped being who I was before, and I still have the same intention I have always had to avail myself of the valor of your valiant and invenerable[2] arm. Therefore, Señor, let your goodness restore honor to the father who sired me, and consider him a wise and prudent man, for with his knowledge he found so easy and true a way to remedy my misfortune that I believe, Señor, if it were not for you, I never would have enjoyed the good fortune I have now; what I say regarding this matter is true, as most of these gentlefolk here present can testify. All that remains is for us to start out tomorrow, because we could not travel very far today, and as for the other good outcomes that I hope to see, I shall leave them to God and to the valor of your heart."

This is what the clever Dorotea said, and when Don Quixote heard it, he turned to Sancho, and showing signs of great anger, he said:

"I say to you now, wretched Sancho, that you are the greatest scoundrel in all of Spain. Tell me, you worthless thief, did you not just say to me that this princess had been transformed into a damsel named

---

2. Martín de Riquer indicates that Dorotea uses this term mockingly.

Dorotea, and that the head I believe I cut off a giant was the whore who bore you, and so much other foolishness that it caused me the greatest confusion I have ever felt in all the days of my life? I swear"—and he looked up to heaven and clenched his teeth—"that I am about to do so much damage to you that from this day forth it will put sense back into the heads of all the lying squires in the world who serve knights errant!"

"Your grace should calm down, Señor," responded Sancho, "because it might be true I made a mistake about the change in the Señora Princess Micomicona, but as for the giant's head, or, I should say, the slashed wineskins, and the blood being red wine, by God I'm not mistaken, because the wounded wineskins are there, at the head of your grace's bed, and the red wine has formed a lake in the room; if you don't believe me, the proof is in the pudding, I mean, you'll have your proof when his grace the innkeeper asks you to pay damages for everything. As for the rest of it, my lady the queen being the same as she was before, that makes me happy because then I'll get what's due me, along with every mother's son."

"I tell you now, Sancho," said Don Quixote, "that you are, forgive me, a dolt, and let us say no more. Enough."

"Enough," said Don Fernando, "let there be no more talk of this; since my lady the princess says she will set out tomorrow because it is too late today, let it be so, and we can spend tonight in pleasant conversation, and when day breaks we shall all accompany Señor Don Quixote, because we want to witness the valiant and extraordinary deeds he will perform in the course of this great enterprise that he has undertaken."

"It is I who should serve and accompany you," responded Don Quixote, "and I am most grateful for the favor you do me and the good opinion you have of me, which I shall strive to make true, or it will cost me my life, and even more, if anything can cost me more."

Many words of praise and many offers of service were exchanged by Don Quixote and Don Fernando, but silence was imposed by a traveler who came into the inn just then; his clothing indicated that he was a Christian recently arrived from Moorish lands, for he was dressed in a short blue woolen tunic with half-sleeves and no collar, breeches of blue linen, and a cap of the same color; he wore ankle boots the color of dates, and a Moorish scimitar hung from a strap across his chest. Then a woman came in after him, riding on a donkey and dressed in the Moorish fashion, her face hidden by a veil; she wore a small brocade cap and a long cloak that covered her from her shoulders to her feet.

The man's appearance was robust and attractive, his age a little over forty, his face rather dark, with a long mustache and a carefully trimmed beard; in short, his bearing revealed that if he had been well-dressed, he would have been deemed noble and highborn.

When he entered he asked for a room, and when he was told there was none in the inn, he seemed troubled; he approached the woman whose dress made her seem Moorish and lifted her down in his arms. Luscinda, Dorotea, the innkeeper's wife, her daughter, and Maritornes, drawn by her clothing, which seemed strange to them, for they had not seen its like before, gathered around the Moorish woman, and Dorotea, who was always charming, courteous, and clever, thought that both she and the man who accompanied her were distressed by the lack of a room, and she said:

"Do not be troubled, Señora, at not finding suitable accommodation here, for it is almost never found in inns; even so, if you would like to stay with us"—and she pointed to Luscinda—"perhaps you will find a better welcome here than elsewhere on your journey."

The veiled lady did not say anything in response, but she rose from the chair where she was sitting, crossed both hands on her bosom, inclined her head, and bowed to show her thanks. From her silence they imagined that she undoubtedly was a Moor and could not speak Christian. Just then the captive,[3] who had been attending to other matters, approached, and seeing that all the women were standing around his companion, but that she did not respond to the statements directed to her, he said:

"Señoras, this maiden barely understands my language and does not know how to speak any other except the one spoken in her own country, and this is why she has not replied and will not reply to the questions you have asked her."

"We have not asked her anything," responded Luscinda, "but we have offered her our companionship for the night, and a place in the room where we will sleep, and as much comfort as it is possible to find here, for we desire and are bound to serve all strangers who need our help, especially if the one in need is a woman."

"On her behalf and on mine," responded the captive, "I kiss your hands, Señora, and I certainly esteem your offer as it deserves to be es-

3. It seems likely that the earlier description of the character as a "Christian recently arrived from Moorish lands" means that he could only be a former prisoner, although the story of his captivity—another interpolated novel—does not begin until chapter XXXIX.

teemed; on an occasion such as this, and from persons such as yourselves, that merit is very high indeed."

"Tell me, Señor," said Dorotea, "is this lady a Christian or a Moor? Her dress and her silence make us think she is what we would rather she was not."

"She is a Moor in her dress and body, but in her soul she is a devout Christian because she has a very strong desire to be one."

"Then, she isn't baptized?" replied Luscinda.

"We have not had the opportunity for that," responded the captive, "since we left Algiers, her home and native land, and until now she has not been in mortal danger that would oblige her to be baptized without first knowing all the ceremonies required by our Holy Mother Church; but God willing, she will soon be baptized with all the decorum her station deserves, for it is higher than that indicated by her attire, or mine."

With these words, he woke everyone's desire to know who the Moorish lady was, and who the captive, but no one wished to ask any questions just then, since it was clearly time to allow them to rest rather than ask about their lives. Dorotea took the stranger by the hand, led her to a seat next to her own, and asked that she remove the veil. The Moorish lady looked at the captive, as if asking him to tell her what was being said and what she should do. He told her, in Arabic, that she was being asked to remove her veil and that she should do so, and she lifted her veil and revealed a face so beautiful that Dorotea thought her more beautiful than Luscinda, and Luscinda thought her more beautiful than Dorotea, and everyone present realized that if any beauty could equal that of those two women, it was the Moorish lady's, and there were even some who thought hers superior in certain details. And since it is the prerogative and charm of beauty to win hearts and attract affection, everyone surrendered to the desire to serve and cherish the beautiful Moor.

Don Fernando asked the captive what her name was, and he replied that it was *Lela*[4] Zoraida, and as soon as the Moor heard this she understood what had been asked, and she hastened to say, with much distress but great charm:

"No! No Zoraida! María, María!" In this way she indicated that her name was María, not Zoraida.

These words, and the great emotion with which the Moorish lady

4. The word means *Señora*, or "Lady."

said them, brought more than one tear to the eyes of some who were listening, especially the women, who are by nature tenderhearted and compassionate. Luscinda embraced her with a good deal of affection, saying:

"Yes, yes! María, María!"

To which the Moor responded:

"Yes, yes, María; Zoraida *macange!*"—a word that means *no.*

By this time night had fallen, and on the orders of those who had accompanied Don Fernando, the innkeeper had been diligent and careful in preparing the best supper he could. When it was time to eat, they all sat at a long refectory table, for there were no round or square ones in the inn, and they gave the principal seat at the head of the table to Don Quixote, although he tried to refuse it, and then he wanted Señora Micomicona at his side, for he was her protector. Then came Luscinda and Zoraida, and facing them Don Fernando and Cardenio, and then the captive and the other gentlemen, and on the ladies' side, the priest and the barber. And in this manner they ate very happily, even more so when Don Quixote stopped eating, moved by a spirit similar to the one that had moved him to speak at length when he ate with the goatherds, and he began by saying:

"Truly, Señores, if one considers it carefully, great and wonderful are the things seen by those who profess the order of knight errantry. For who in this world, coming through the door of this castle and seeing us as we appear now, would judge and believe that we are who we are? Who would say that this lady at my side is the great queen we all know she is, and that I am the Knight of the Sorrowful Face whose name is on the lips of fame? There can be no doubt that this art and profession exceeds all others invented by men, for the more dangerous something is, the more it should be esteemed. Away with those who say that letters are superior to arms,[5] for I shall tell them, whoever they may be, that they do not know what they are saying. The reason usually given by these people, and the one on which they rely, is that the works of the spirit are greater than those of the body, and that arms are professed by the body alone, as if this profession were the work of laborers, for which one needs nothing more than strength, or as if in the profession we call arms, those of us

---

5. The debate between arms and letters (that is, the life of a soldier compared to the life of a cleric or scholar), a frequent literary topic in Europe during the Middle Ages and the Renaissance, was at least as popular as the theme of the Golden Age, the subject of Don Quixote's discourse when he shared a meal with the goatherds.

who practice it do not perform acts of fortitude that demand great intelligence to succeed, or as if the courage of a warrior who leads an army or defends a city under siege does not make use of his spirit as well as his body. If you do not agree, consider that knowing the enemy's intentions, surmising his plans and stratagems, foreseeing difficulties, preventing harm: all of these are actions of mind in which the body plays no part at all. If it is true that arms require spirit, as do letters, let us now see which of the two spirits, that of the lettered man or that of the warrior, is more active; this can be known by the purpose and aim of each, for an intention must be more highly esteemed if it has as its object a nobler end.

The purpose and aim of letters—and I do not speak now of divine letters, whose purpose is to bring and guide souls to heaven; so eternal an end cannot be equaled by any other—I am speaking of human letters, whose purpose is to maintain distributive justice, and give each man what is his, and make certain that good laws are obeyed. A purpose, certainly, that is generous and high and worthy of great praise, but not so meritorious as arms, whose purpose and objective is peace, which is the greatest good that men can desire in this life. And so, the first good news that the world and men received was brought by angels on the night that was our day, when they sang in the air: 'Glory to God in the highest, and on earth peace, goodwill toward men,' and the greeting that the best teacher on earth and in heaven taught His disciples and followers was that when they entered a house they should say: 'Peace be in this house,' and often He said to them: 'My peace I give unto you; my peace I leave with you; peace be with you,' as if it were a precious jewel when given and offered by that hand, a jewel without which there can be no good on earth or in heaven. This peace is the true purpose of war, and saying arms is the same as saying war. Accepting it is true that the purpose of war is peace, which is greater than the purpose of letters, let us turn now to the physical hardships of the lettered man and those of the man who professes arms, and see which are greater."

In this manner, and with these rational arguments, Don Quixote continued his discourse, and no one listening to him at that moment could think of him as a madman; rather, since most were gentlemen engaged in the practice of arms, they were very pleased to listen, and he went on, saying:

"I say, then, that the hardships of the student are these: principally poverty, not because they all are poor, but to make this case as extreme as possible, and having said that he suffers poverty, it seems to me that there is nothing more to say about his bad luck, because the man who is poor has nothing that is good. This poverty is suffered in its various forms, in hunger, cold, and nakedness, and sometimes all of them together; even so, his poverty is not so great that he does not eat, although the meal may be a little later than usual, or may be the leftovers of the rich, and his greatest misery is what students call among themselves *going for soup;*[6] and they do not lack someone else's brazier or hearth, and if it does not warm them, at least it lessens the cold, and at night they sleep under a blanket. I do not wish to discuss other trivial matters, such as a lack of shirts and a shortage of shoes, and clothing that is scant and threadbare, or the relish with which they gorge themselves when fortune offers them a feast. Along this rough and difficult road that I have described, they stumble and fall, pick themselves up and fall again, until they reach the academic title they desire; once this is acquired and they have passed through these shoals, these Scyllas and Charybdises, as if carried on the wings of good fortune, we have seen many who command and govern the world from a chair, their hunger turned into a full belly, their cold into comfort, their nakedness into finery, and their straw mat into linen and damask sheets, the just reward for their virtue. But their hardships, measured against and compared to those of a soldier and warrior, fall far behind, as I shall relate to you now."

CHAPTER XXXVIII

Which tells of the curious discourse on arms and letters given by Don Quixote

Don Quixote continued, saying:

"We began with the student and the forms of his poverty; now let us see if the soldier is richer. And we shall see that no one in his poverty is as poor as he, for he depends on his miserable pay, which comes late or never, or on whatever he can steal with his own hands at great risk to his life and conscience. Sometimes he is so naked that a slashed and torn

6. A phrase that means going to convents and monasteries for the soup that is distributed to the poor.

doublet is both uniform and shirt, and in the middle of winter, in an empty field, the breath from his mouth is his only protection against the inclemencies of heaven, and since that breath comes from an empty place, I consider it certain that it must come out cold, contradicting the laws of nature. But wait for night to fall, when he can make up for all these discomforts in the bed that awaits him, which will never sin by being too narrow unless he makes it so, for he can measure out as many feet of earth as he desires, and toss and turn to his heart's content without fear of wrinkling the sheets. Then, after this, the day and hour arrive when he receives the degree his profession offers: the day of battle; there he will receive his tasseled academic cap, made of bandages to heal a bullet wound, perhaps one that has passed through his temples or will leave him with a ruined arm or leg. If this does not happen, and merciful heaven protects him and keeps him whole and alive, it may be that he will remain in the same poverty as before, and he will have to go through one engagement after another, one battle after another, and emerge victorious from all of them in order to prosper only a little; but these miracles are not seen very often.

But tell me, Señores, if you have considered it: how many more perish in war than profit from it? No doubt you will respond that there is no comparison, that the number of dead cannot be counted, and those who have been rewarded, and survived, can be counted in three digits and never reach a thousand. All of this is the opposite of what happens to lettered men, for with their fees, not to mention the bribes they receive, they have enough to get by, so that even though the hardship of a soldier is greater, his reward is much smaller. But one can respond to this by saying that it is easier to reward two thousand lettered men than thirty thousand soldiers, because the first are rewarded by positions that of necessity must be given to those in their profession, and the latter cannot be rewarded except by the very wealth that belongs to the lord they serve; and this, being impossible, strengthens my argument.

But let us leave this aside, for it is a labyrinth difficult to leave, and return to the preeminence of arms over letters, a question that has not yet been resolved since each side presents its own arguments; among them is the claim that without letters arms could not be sustained, because war also has laws to which it is subject, and laws are subsumed under what are called letters and lettered men. The reply of arms to this is that laws cannot be sustained without arms, because with arms nations are defended, kingdoms maintained, cities defended, roads made secure, seas cleared of pirates; in short, if not for arms, nations, kingdoms, monarchies, cities, roads, and sea lanes would be subject to the hardship and confusion that war brings for as long as it lasts and has the freedom to exercise its privileges and impose its violence. It is a demonstrable truth that whatever costs more is valued, and should be valued, more highly. To become distinguished in letters costs time, sleepless nights, hunger, nakedness, headaches, bouts of indigestion, and other things of this sort, some of which I have already mentioned, but to become a good soldier requires everything required of a student, but to so much higher a degree that there can be no comparison, because at every step the soldier risks losing his life. How can the fear of want and poverty that troubles a student ever equal the fear of the soldier who, finding himself besieged in a fortress, or keeping watch or standing guard at a drawbridge or watch-tower, hears his enemies mining their way toward him, and he cannot leave for any reason or flee the danger that threatens him? All he can do is inform his captain of the situation so that he can remedy it with coun-termines, and he must be quiet, fearing and waiting for the moment when he will suddenly fly up to the clouds without wings or plunge down to the abyss against his will.

And if this seems an insignificant danger, let us see if it is equaled or surpassed when the prows of two galleys collide in the middle of the wide sea, for when they lock and grapple, the soldier is left with no more than two feet of plank on the ram of the ship; despite this, seeing that he has in front of him as many ministers of death threatening him as there are artillery cannons aimed at him from the other side, only a lance's throw away, and seeing that at the first misstep he will visit the deep bosom of Neptune, despite this, with an intrepid heart, carried by the honor that urges him on, he makes himself the target of all their volleys and attempts to cross that narrow passage to the enemy vessel. And the most astounding thing is that no sooner does one man fall, not to rise again until the world comes to an end, than another takes his place, and if he too falls into the sea that waits like an enemy, there is another, and another who follows him, and their deaths come one after the other, without pause: no greater valor and daring can be found in all the perils of war.

Happy were those blessed times that lacked the horrifying fury of the diabolical instruments of artillery, whose inventor, in my opinion, is in hell, receiving the reward for his accursed invention, which allows an ig-noble and cowardly hand to take the life of a valiant knight, so that not knowing how it comes, or from where, a stray shot is fired into the courage and spirit that inflame and animate a brave heart, sent by one who perhaps fled in fear at the bright flare when the damned machine discharged it, and it cuts off and ends in an instant the thoughts and life of one who deserved to enjoy many more long years. When I consider this, I am prepared to say that it grieves my very soul that I have taken up the profession of knight errant in an age as despicable as the one we live in now, for although no danger can cause me to fear, it still fills me with misgivings to think that powder and tin may deprive me of the opportunity to become famous and renowned throughout the known world for the valor of my arm and the sharp edge of my sword. But God's will be done, for I shall be more highly esteemed, if I succeed in my purpose, for having confronted greater dangers than any faced by the knights errant of old."

Don Quixote gave this long discourse while the others were eating, and he forgot to bring a single mouthful of food to his lips, although Sancho Panza told him several times that he should eat and that later there would be time to say all he wanted to say. Those who listened to him were overwhelmed again with pity at seeing that a man who apparently was intelligent and rational in all other matters could lose those faculties completely when it was a question of his accursed and bedeviled chivalry. The priest said that he was correct in everything he had said in favor of arms, and that he, though lettered and a graduate of the university, was of the same opinion.

They finished supper, the table was cleared, and while the innkeeper's wife, her daughter, and Maritornes prepared Don Quixote of La Mancha's garret, for it had been decided that only the women would spend the night there, Don Fernando asked the captive to tell them the story of his life, which was bound to be unusual and interesting, as he had shown by arriving in the company of Zoraida. To which the captive responded that he would gladly do as he asked, though he feared the story would not give them the pleasure he would like; even so, in order to oblige them, he would tell it. The priest and the others thanked him, and again they asked him to begin, and he, seeing himself asked by so many, said that entreaties were not necessary when one request was more than enough.

"And so, let your graces be attentive, and you will hear a true account that could not be equaled by fictions written with so much care and artfulness."

When he said this, they all sat down and became absolutely silent, and seeing that they had stopped talking and were waiting for him to speak, in a calm and pleasant voice he began his story, saying:

CHAPTER XXXIX

In which the captive recounts his life and adventures[1]

"My family had its origins in the mountains of León, where nature was kinder and more generous than fortune, though in the extreme poverty of those villages my father was known as a rich man, and he truly would have been one if he had been as skilled in preserving his wealth as he was in spending it. This propensity for being generous and openhanded came from his having been a soldier in his youth, for soldiering is a school where the stingy man becomes liberal, and the liberal man becomes prodigal, and if there are any soldiers who are miserly, they are, like monsters, very rarely seen. My father exceeded the limits of generosity and bordered on being prodigal, something of little benefit to a man who is married and has children who will succeed to his name and position. My father had three sons, all of an age to choose a profession. Seeing, as he said, that he could not control his own nature, he decided to deprive himself of the means and cause of his being prodigal and a spendthrift by giving up his estate, without which Alexander himself would have seemed a miser. And so one day he called the three of us into a room where we could be alone, and he said something similar to what I will say now:

'My sons, to say that I love you, it is enough to know and say that you are my children, and to understand that I do not love you, it is enough to know that I do not exercise control with regard to preserving your inheritance. So that you may know from now on that I love you as a father, and do not wish to destroy you as if I were your stepfather, I want to do something that I have been thinking about for a long time and, after ma-

1. This is the second of the "interpolated novels." Cervantes himself had been a captive for some five years, and many of the elements in the story may be autobiographical, but it should also be noted, as Martín de Riquer points out, that it was a fairly common practice to insert a romantic tale with Moorish themes into works that otherwise seemed to have little to do with either romance or the Moors.

ture consideration, have resolved to do. You are all of an age to choose a profession or, at least, to select an occupation that will bring you honor and profit when you are older. What I have decided is to divide my fortune into four parts: three I will give to you, each one receiving exactly the same share, and the fourth I will retain to keep me for the time it pleases heaven to grant me life. But after each of you has his share of the estate, I would like you to follow the path I indicate. There is a proverb in our Spain, one that I think is very true, as they all are, for they are brief maxims taken from long, judicious experience; the one I have in mind says: "The Church, the sea, or the royal house"; in other words, whoever wishes to be successful and wealthy should enter the Church, or go to sea as a merchant, or enter the service of kings in their courts, for, as they say: "Better the king's crumbs than the noble lord's favors." I say this because I would like, and it is my desire, that one of you should pursue letters, another commerce, and the third should serve the king in war, for it is very difficult to enter his service at court, and although war does not provide many riches, it tends to bring great merit and fame. In a week's time I shall give each of you his entire share in cash, down to the last *ardite*, as you will see. Tell me now if you wish to follow my opinion and advice in what I have proposed to you.'

And because I was the oldest he ordered me to respond, and after I had told him not to divest himself of his fortune but to spend as much of it as he wished, for we were young and could make one of our own, I concluded by saying I would do as he wished, and my desire was to follow the profession of arms and in that way serve God and my king. The second brother made a similar statement, but he chose to go to the Indies, using his portion to buy goods. The youngest, and, I believe, the wisest, said he wanted to enter the Church and complete the studies he had begun at Salamanca. When we had finished expressing our agreement and choosing our professions, my father embraced us all, and then, in as short a time as he had stated, he put into effect everything he had promised, and gave each of us his share, which, as I remember, amounted to three thousand gold *ducados*[2] (an uncle of ours bought the entire estate so that it would stay in the family, and paid for it in cash).

The three of us said goodbye to our good father on the same day, and on that day, thinking it was inhuman for my father to be left old and bereft of his fortune, I persuaded him to take two thousand of my three

2. An amount worth approximately thirty-three thousand *reales*.

thousand *ducados*, because the remainder would be enough for me to acquire everything I needed to be a soldier. My two brothers, moved by my example, each gave him a thousand *ducados*, so that my father had four thousand in cash and another three thousand that was, apparently, the value of his portion of the estate, which he did not want to sell but kept as land. In short, with a good deal of emotion and many tears from everyone, we took our leave of him and the uncle I have mentioned, who asked us to inform them, whenever possible, about our affairs, whether prosperous or adverse. We promised we would, and they embraced us and gave us their blessing. One of us set out for Salamanca, the other left for Sevilla, and I took the road to Alicante, where I had heard that a Genoese ship was loading on wool, bound for Genoa.

It is twenty-two years since I left my father's house, and in all that time, though I have written several letters, I have not heard anything from him or my brothers. I shall tell you briefly what happened to me in the course of this time. I embarked in Alicante, arrived safely in Genoa, went from there to Milan, where I purchased some arms and soldier's clothing, and from there I decided to go to the Piedmont to enlist; I was already on the road to Alessandria della Paglia[3] when I heard that the great Duke of Alba was on his way to Flanders.[4] I changed my plans, went with him, served in his campaigns, witnessed the deaths of Counts Egmont and Horn,[5] and rose to the rank of ensign under a famous captain from Guadalajara named Diego de Urbina;[6] some time after my arrival in Flanders, we heard news of the alliance that His Holiness Pope Pius V, of happy memory, had made with Venice and Spain to fight our common enemy, the Turks; their fleet had recently conquered the famous island of Cyprus, which had been under the control of the Venetians: a lamentable and unfortunate loss. It was known that the commanding general of this alliance would be His Serene Highness Don Juan of Austria, the natural brother of our good king Don Felipe II. Reports of the great preparations for war that were being made moved my spirit and excited my desire to be part of the expected campaign, and although I had hopes, almost specific promises, that at the first opportunity I would be promoted to captain, I chose to leave it all and go to Italy. And it was my good fortune that Señor Don Juan of Austria

3. A fortified town on the Tenaro River, near Milan.

4. The duke of Alba reached Brussels on August 22, 1567.

5. Belgian noblemen who fought against the French in the Spanish army and were executed by the duke of Alba on June 5, 1568, for rebelling against the Inquisition.

6. Cervantes fought under this captain at the battle of Lepanto, in 1571.

had just arrived in Genoa, on his way to Naples to join the Venetian fleet, as he subsequently did in Messina.[7]

In short, I took part in that glorious battle, having achieved the rank of captain of infantry, an honor due more to my good luck than my merits. And that day, which was so fortunate for Christendom because that was when the world and all the nations realized their error in thinking that the Turks were invincible at sea, on that day, I say, when Ottoman pride and arrogance were shattered, among all the fortunate men who were there (for the Christians who died there were more fortunate than those left alive and victorious), I alone was unfortunate; for, contrary to what I might have expected in Roman times, instead of a naval crown[8] I found myself on the night following so famous a day with chains on my feet and shackles on my hands. This is how it happened.

Uchalí,[9] the king of Algiers, a daring and successful corsair, attacked and defeated the Maltese flagship, leaving only three knights alive, and they were badly wounded; the flagship of Juan Andrea,[10] on which I and my company were sailing, came to her assistance, and doing what needed to be done on such an occasion, I jumped onto the enemy galley that then disengaged from our ship, which had grappled her, preventing my soldiers from following me; and so I found myself alone, surrounded by my enemies, who were so numerous I could not successfully resist them; finally, when I was covered with wounds, they took me prisoner. And, Señores, as you have probably heard, Uchalí escaped with his entire squadron, and I was his captive, the one sad man among so many who rejoiced, the one captive among so many who were free, because on that day fifteen thousand Christians at the oars of the Turkish fleet attained the liberty they longed for. I was taken to Constantinople, where the Great Turk Selim made my master the commanding admiral of the sea because he had done his duty in the battle, having brought back as a trophy of his valor the standard of the Order of Malta. The following year, 1572, I found myself at Navarino, rowing in the flagship that displayed the three lighthouses.[11] There I saw and

7. Cervantes, who was not an officer, apparently joined the fleet in Messina on September 2, 1571; it set sail on September 16, and the battle of Lepanto, the definitive defeat of the Turks by the Christian alliance, took place on October 7.

8. The naval crown, made of gold, was awarded to the first man to board an enemy ship.

9. Uchalí, or Uluch Ali, the viceroy of Algiers in 1570, did in fact take part in the actions described by Cervantes. He commanded the Ottoman fleet from 1571 to 1587 and defeated the flagship of the Order of Malta during the battle of Lepanto.

10. Giovanni Andrea Doria, a Genoese, commanded the Spanish galleys.

11. An insignia that indicated the flagship of an admiral.

noted the chance that was lost to capture the entire Turkish fleet while it was still in port, because all its sailors and janissaries were certain they would be attacked in the harbor itself, and they had their clothing ready, and their *pasamaques*, which are their shoes, so that they could escape immediately by land and not wait to do battle: that was how fearful they had become of our fleet. But heaven ordained otherwise, not through the fault or negligence of the commander of our forces but because of the sins of Christendom, and because it is God's will that there always will be scourges to punish us.

And so Uchalí withdrew to Modón, which is an island near Navarino, and putting his people ashore, he fortified the entrance to the port, and remained there until Señor Don Juan left. On this voyage the galley *La Presa*, whose captain was a son of the famous corsair called Barbarossa, was captured by the flagship of Naples, *La Loba*, under the command of that lightning bolt of war, that father to his soldiers, that victorious and never defeated Don Álvaro de Bazán, the Marquis of Santa Cruz. I want to be sure to tell you what happened in the capture of *La Presa*. The son of Barbarossa was so cruel, and treated his captives so badly, that as soon as those on the oars saw *La Loba* approaching and overtaking them, they all dropped their oars at the same time and seized the captain, who stood at his post and shouted at them to row faster, and they threw him from bench to bench, from stern to bow, biting him so many times that by the time he passed the mast his soul had passed on to hell, so cruel was his treatment of them, as I have said, and so great their hatred of him.

We returned to Constantinople, and the following year, 1573, we heard how Señor Don Juan had conquered Tunis, capturing that kingdom from the Turks and turning it over to Muley Hamet, thereby destroying the hopes of Muley Hamida, the cruelest and most valiant Moor in the world, that he would return to the throne.[12] The Great Turk felt this loss very deeply, and, making use of the sagacity that all those of his house possess, he made peace with the Venetians, who desired it much more than he did, and the following year, which was 1574, he attacked the Goletta[13] and the fort that Señor Don Juan had left partially constructed near Tunis. During all these battles I was at the oar, without any

12. Muley Hamet, or Muley Mohammad, took possession of Tunis in October of 1573; the following year, he was captured by the Turks. His brother, Muley Hamida, or Ahmad-Sultán, attempted to join the attack on Tunis in 1573 by Don Juan of Austria, and died in Palermo in 1575.

13. The fortress that protected Tunis.

hope of freedom; at least, I did not hope to obtain it by means of a ransom, because I had decided not to write the news of my misfortune to my father. In the end, the Goletta was lost, and the fort as well, attacked by seventy-five thousand regular Turkish soldiers and more than four hundred thousand Moors and Arabs from the rest of Africa, and this vast army had so many weapons and supplies, and so many sappers, that they could have picked up earth and covered over the Goletta and the fort using only their bare hands.

The Goletta, until that time considered impregnable, was the first to fall, not because of any fault in its defenders, who did in its defense everything they should have done and all that they could do, but because experience showed how easily earthworks could be built in that desert sand, for at one time water was found at a depth of two spans, but the Turks did not find it at a depth of two *varas*;[14] and so, with countless sacks of sand they built earthworks so high that they rose above the walls of the fort, and their soldiers could fire down on the fort, and no one could stay there or help in its defense. It was the general opinion that our forces should not have closed themselves inside the Goletta but waited for the landing in open country, and those who say this speak from a distance and with little experience of this kind of warfare, because inside the Goletta and the fort there were barely seven thousand soldiers, and how could so small a number, no matter how brave, have gone into open country and defended the forts at the same time against the far larger numbers of the enemy? And how is it possible not to lose a fort when there is no relief, and it is surrounded by so many resolute enemies fighting on their own land? But it seemed to many, and it seemed to me, that it was a special grace and mercy that heaven conferred on Spain when it allowed the destruction of that breeding ground and shelter for wickedness, that voracious, gluttonous devourer of infinite amounts of money spent there to no avail, yet serving no other purpose than to preserve the happy memory of its having been captured by the invincible Carlos V, as if those stones were necessary to make his fame eternal, as it is now and forever will be. The fort was lost, too, but the Turks had to take it a span at a time, because the soldiers who defended it fought so valiantly and fiercely that they killed more than twenty-five thousand of the enemy in twenty-two general assaults. Three hundred of our soldiers survived, every one of them wounded when he was taken prisoner, a sure and cer-

14. A span (*palmo*) is approximately 8 inches; a *vara*, about 2.8 feet.

tain sign of their tenacity and valor and of how well they defended and protected their positions. A small fortress or tower in the middle of the lagoon, commanded by Don Juan Zanoguera, a famous gentleman and soldier from Valencia, surrendered on advantageous terms. They captured Don Pedro Puertocarrero, the general in command of the Goletta, who did everything possible to defend the fortress and felt its loss so deeply that he died of sorrow on the road to Constantinople, where he was being taken as a prisoner. They also captured the general in command of the fort, whose name was Gabrio Cervellón, a Milanese gentleman who was a great engineer and a very courageous soldier.

Many notable men died in those two forts; one was Pagán Doria, a knight of the Order of St. John, an extremely generous man who showed great liberality to his brother, the famous Juan de Andrea Doria; what made his death even sadder was that he died at the hands of some Arabs whom he trusted when he saw that the fort was lost; they offered to take him, dressed as a Moor, to Tabarca, a small port where the Genoese who engage in the coral trade along these shores keep a house; these Arabs cut off his head and took it to the commander of the Turkish fleet, who confirmed for them our Spanish proverb: 'For the treason we are grateful, though we find the traitor hateful.' And so, they say, the commander ordered the two who brought him the present to be hanged because they did not bring the man to him alive. Among the Christians captured in the fort, there was one named Don Pedro de Aguilar, a native of Andalucía, though I do not know the town, who had been an ensign, and a soldier of great note and rare intelligence; he had a special gift for what they call poetry. I say this because his luck brought him to my galley, and my bench, to be the slave of my master, and before we left that port this gentleman composed two sonnets as epitaphs, one for the Goletta and the other for the fort. The truth is I must recite them, because I know them by heart, and I believe they will give you more pleasure than grief."

When the captive named Don Pedro de Aguilar, Don Fernando looked at his companions, and all three of them smiled, and when the captive mentioned the sonnets, one of them said:

"Before your grace continues, I beg you to tell me what happened to this Don Pedro de Aguilar."

"What I do know," responded the captive, "is that after spending two years in Constantinople he escaped, disguised as an Albanian and in the company of a Greek spy, and I do not know if he obtained his freedom, though I believe he did, because a year later I saw the Greek in Constantinople but could not ask if they had been successful."

"Well, they were," responded the gentleman, "for Don Pedro is my brother, and he is now in our home, safe, rich, and married, with three children."

"Thanks be to God," said the captive, "for the mercies he has received; in my opinion, there is no joy on earth equal to that of regaining the freedom one has lost."

"What is more," replied the gentleman, "I know the sonnets my brother wrote."

"Then your grace should recite them," said the captive, "for I am certain you can say them better than I."

"I would be happy to," responded the gentleman. "The one to the Goletta says:

CHAPTER XL

In which the history of the captive continues

Sonnet

O blissful souls, who from the mortal veil
freed and unconfined, flew from this low earth,
borne on the wings of brave and virtuous deeds
to the highest, holiest spheres of glorious heav'n,
ablaze with fury and with righteous zeal,
and summoning all your honor and your strength,
you colored the ocean and the sandy ground
with your own blood, and with the enemy's;
you lost your lives before you lost the valor
of your weary, battling arms; in death,
though you are vanquished, victory is yours.
Your mortal, melancholy fall, between
the ramparts and the attacking horde, brings you
fame in this world, blessed glory in the next."

"That is how I remember it, too," said the captive.

"And the one to the fort, if I remember correctly," said the gentleman, "reads like this:

SONNET

Up from this sterile, devastated ground,
these scattered clods of earth, these ruined stones,
the saintly souls of three thousand warriors
rose, immortal, to their glorious home,
    after wielding, in vain, the emboldened might
of their courageous arms until, at last,
the exhausted few, too few to resist,
gave up their lives to the enemy's sharp blade.
    This is ground that has been the constant home
of a thousand sad, heroic memories
in times long gone and in the present day.
    From its hard bosom no more righteous souls
have risen to the shining gates of heaven,
nor has it held the bodies of braver men."

They liked the sonnets, the captive was glad to hear the news about his comrade, and, continuing with his story, he said:

"Having conquered the Goletta and the fort, the Turks ordered the Goletta to be dismantled, because it had been so damaged there was nothing left to raze, and in order to do this more quickly and easily, they mined it in three places; they could not blow up what had seemed its weakest part, that is, the old walls, but what was left standing of the new fortifications built by El Fratín[1] came down easily. Then the fleet returned to Constantinople, triumphant and victorious, and a few months after that my master, Uchalí, died;[2] he was called *Uchalí Fartax*—in the Turkish language it means "the Renegade with Scabies"—which is, in fact, what he was, for it is customary among the Turks to name people for some fault or virtue that they have, and this is because they have only four family names, and these come from the Ottoman house;[3] the rest, as

1. Nicknamed *El Fratín* ("the Little Friar"), Jacome Paleazzo fortified a number of garrisons for the Spanish monarchy.

2. The historical Uchalí died suddenly on June 21, 1587, in Constantinople.

3. The four Ottoman family names are Muhammat, Mustafa, Murad, and Ali.

I have said, take their first and second names from physical defects or character traits. And this man with scabies rowed in the galleys as a slave of the Great Lord for fourteen years, and when he was past the age of thirty-four he became a renegade because of his fury at a Turk who slapped him while he was rowing: in order to take his revenge, he abandoned his faith; his valor was so great that, without using the vile and devious means that most of the Great Turk's favorites employ in order to succeed, he became king of Algiers and then admiral of the sea, which is the third position in that empire. He came from Calabria, and morally he was a good man who treated his captives very humanely; he had three thousand of them, and after his death they were divided, according to the terms of his will, between the Great Turk, who is the heir of everyone who dies and shares in the inheritance with the dead man's children, and his renegades; I was passed along to a Venetian renegade who had been a cabin boy when he was captured by Uchalí, who was very fond of the boy and pampered him a good deal, yet he became the cruelest renegade anyone has ever seen. His name was Azán Agá, and he became very rich, and he also became king of Algiers;[4] I came there with him from Constantinople, rather happy to be so close to Spain, not because I intended to write to anyone about my misfortunes, but to see if my luck would be better in Algiers than it had been in Constantinople, where I had tried a thousand different ways to escape, and none had been successful; in Algiers I intended to look for other means to achieve what I desired, for the hope of obtaining my freedom never left me, and when what I devised, planned, and attempted did not correspond to my intentions, I did not give up but sought out some other hope to sustain me, no matter how weak and fragile.

This was how I spent my life, locked in a prison or house that the Turks call a *bagnio*, where they hold Christian captives, those that belong to the king as well as some that belong to private individuals, and the ones they call 'stockpiled,' which is like saying 'public prisoners,' who serve the city in public works and in other employment for the general good; these captives find it very difficult to obtain their freedom, because they have no individual master, and there is no one with whom to negotiate their ransom even if a ransom is available. As I have said, some private individuals bring their captives to these *bagnios*, principally when they are ready to be ransomed, because there they can be

---

4. Hasán Bajá, king of Algiers between 1577 and 1578, was born in Venice in 1545; he was captured by the Turks, renounced Christianity, and led the Turkish landings at Cadaqués and Alicante; Cervantes met him during his own captivity.

kept, not working and in safety, until the ransom money arrives. The king's captives who are about to be ransomed do not go out with the work crews, either, unless payment of their ransom is delayed, and then, to make them write more urgently for the money, they are obliged to work and are sent out with the others for wood, which is no easy labor. I was one of those waiting for ransom, for when they learned that I was a captain, though I told them of my limited possibilities and lack of wealth, they put me with the gentlemen and the people awaiting ransom. They put a chain on me, more as a sign that I was to be ransomed than to hold me, and I spent my days in that *bagnio*, with many other gentlemen and people of note who had been selected to be held for ransom. Although hunger and scant clothing troubled us at times, even most of the time, nothing troubled us as much as constantly hearing and seeing my master's remarkably and exceptionally cruel treatment of Christians. Each day he hanged someone, impaled someone, cut off someone's ears, and with so little provocation, or without any provocation at all, that the Turks knew he did it merely for the sake of doing it and because it was in his nature to murder the entire human race. The only one who held his own with him was a Spanish soldier named something de Saavedra,[5] who did things that will be remembered by those people for many years, and all to gain his liberty, yet his master never beat him, or ordered anyone else to beat him, or said an unkind word to him; for the most minor of all the things he did we were afraid he would be impaled, and more than once he feared the same thing; if I had the time, I would tell you something of what that soldier did, which would entertain and amaze you much more than this recounting of my history.

In any case, overlooking the courtyard of our prison were the windows of the house of a wealthy and important Moor, and these, as is true in most Moorish houses, were more slits than windows, yet even these were covered with very heavy and tightly woven jalousies. One day I happened to be on a flat roof in our prison with three companions; we were passing the time by trying to see how far we could jump with our chains on, for we were alone, all the other Christians having gone out to work; by chance I looked up and saw that through one of those narrow little windows I've mentioned a reed appeared, with a handkerchief tied to the end of it, and the reed was moving about, almost as if it were sig-

5. The allusion is to Cervantes himself; his complete surname was Cervantes Saavedra.

naling that we should come and take it. We thought about it, and one of the men who was with me went to stand under the reed to see if it would drop, or what would happen, but as soon as he reached the spot, the reed was raised and moved from side to side, as if shaking its head no. The Christian came back, and again the reed was raised and lowered with the same movements as before. Another of my companions approached, and again the same thing happened. Then the third man approached, the same thing was repeated, and seeing this, I wanted to try my luck, too, and as soon as I placed myself under the reed it was dropped inside the *bagnio* and fell at my feet. I immediately untied the handkerchief, which had a knot in it, and inside were ten *cianíís*, which are coins of base gold used by the Moors, each one worth ten of our *reales*. It goes without saying that I was delighted with this discovery, and my happiness was as great as my amazement at the thought of where that gift had come from, and why it was directed to me, since the signs of not wanting to drop the reed for anyone but me clearly indicated that I was the object of the favor.

I took the money, broke the reed, returned to the roof, looked at the window, and saw an extremely white hand emerge and open and close the window very quickly. With this we understood or imagined that a woman who lived in that house must have done us this kindness, and as a sign that we thanked her for it we made our salaams in the Moorish manner, bending our heads, bowing from the waist, and crossing our arms on our chests. A short while later a small cross made of reeds was dangled from the window and immediately pulled back in. This confirmed that a Christian woman was probably a captive in that house and was the one who had done us the good turn, but the whiteness of her hand and the bracelets we saw on it disabused us of the thought that she was a slave; then we imagined she must be a renegade Christian, for they are often taken as legitimate wives by their masters, who consider this good fortune since the men esteem them more than the women of their own nation. In all our speculations, however, we were very far from the truth of the matter, although from then on we spent all our time looking at the window where our north star of a reed had appeared; but two weeks went by, and we did not see it again, or the hand, or any other signal of any kind.

During this time, although we made every effort to learn who lived in that house, and if there was a renegade Christian woman there, no one would tell us anything except that it belonged to a very prominent and wealthy Moor named Agi Morato,[6] who had been the governor of La Pata,[7] which is a very distinguished position among those people. But when we least expected another shower of *cianiís*, we suddenly saw the reed appear, another handkerchief attached to it that had an even larger knot; this occurred when the *bagnio*, as on the previous occasion, was deserted and empty of people. We made the same test: each of the three men, the same ones who had been with me the last time, went forward before I did, but the reed was not given up to anyone but me, because as soon as I walked forward, it dropped. I untied the knot and found forty Spanish gold *escudos* and a paper written in Arabic, at the bottom of which a large cross had been drawn. I kissed the cross, took the *escudos*, and returned to the roof, where we all made our salaams; the hand appeared again, I signaled that I would read the letter, and the window closed.

We were all astounded and overjoyed at what had happened, but since none of us understood Arabic, our desire to know what the paper said was immense, and the difficulty in finding someone to read it to us was even greater. Finally, I decided to trust a renegade, a native of Murcia, who claimed to be a great friend of mine and made pledges to me obliging him to keep any secrets I confided in him, because certain renegades, when they intend to return to Christian lands, take with them signed statements from important captives testifying, in whatever fashion they can, that the renegade is a moral man, and always has treated Christians well, and desires to escape at the first opportunity. Some obtain these declarations with good intentions; others use them as a possible defense when they come to plunder Christian lands: if they happen to be shipwrecked or are taken prisoner, they show their declarations and say that these papers prove their intention to remain in Christian lands, which was the reason they came on a raid with the Turks. In this way they avoid the initial violence of their captors and reconcile with the Church, and no one does them any harm, and at the first opportunity they return to Barbary to be what they were before. There are others, however, who obtain and use these papers with good intentions and remain in Christian lands.

Well, my friend was one of these renegades, and he had statements from all our comrades attesting in every way possible to his good faith,

6. A historical figure, Agi Morato, or Hajji Murad, the son of Slavic parents, renounced Christianity and became an important personage in Algiers.

7. La Pata is al-Batha, a fortress-city.

and if the Moors had found him with these papers, they would have burned him alive. I had learned that he knew Arabic very well, and could not only speak it but write it, too, but before I told him everything, I asked him to read the paper for me, saying I had found it in a crack in the wall of my cell. He unfolded it and spent a long time looking at it, analyzing it, and murmuring to himself. I asked him if he understood it; he said he understood it very well, and if I wanted him to repeat it word for word, I should give him ink and a pen, which would allow him to do a better job. We soon gave him what he requested, he translated the letter slowly, and when he was finished, he said: 'Everything written here in Spanish is exactly what this Moorish letter contains; you should know that where it says *Lela Marién* it means *Our Lady the Virgin Mary.*' We read the paper, and this is what it said:

> When I was a little girl, my father had a slave woman who taught me in my own language a Christian *zalá*, or prayer, and she told me many things about Lela Marién. The Christian slave died, and I know she did not go to the fire but to Allah, because afterward I saw her two times, and she told me to go to a Christian land to see Lela Marién, who loved me very much. I do not know how to go: I have seen many Christians through this window, and none has seemed as much a gentleman as you. I am very beautiful and young, and I have a good deal of money to take with me; see if you can plan how we can go, and when we are there you can be my husband if you like, and if you do not, it will not matter, because Lela Marién will give me someone to marry. I wrote this; be careful who you ask to read it: do not trust any Moor, because they are all false. I am very worried about that: I wish you would not show it to anybody, because if my father finds out, he will throw me in a well and cover me over with stones. I will put a thread on the reed: tie your answer there, and if you do not have anybody who writes Arabic, give me your answer in signs; Lela Marién will make me understand. May she and Allah protect you, and this cross that I kiss many times, as the captive woman taught me to do.

Consider, Señores, if there was reason for the words of this letter to astound and delight us; our feelings were so intense that the renegade realized the paper had not been found by chance but had really been written to one of us, and he implored us that if what he suspected was true, that we trust him and tell him so, and he would risk his life for our freedom. And saying this, he pulled out from under his shirt a metal crucifix, and with many tears he swore by the God that the image represented, and in whom he, though a sinner, believed completely and faithfully, that he would be loyal to us and keep secret anything we wished to tell him; he thought, and could almost predict, that by means of the woman who had written the letter, he and all of us would obtain our freedom, and he would find himself where he longed to be, which was reunited with the body of Holy Mother Church, from whom, like a rotten limb, he had been separated and severed because of his ignorance and sin. The renegade said this with so many tears and displays of so much repentance that we were all of the same opinion and agreed to tell him the truth, and so we revealed everything to him, hiding nothing. We showed him the narrow window where the reed had appeared, and he took careful note of the house and agreed to take special and particular care to learn who lived in it. We also agreed that it would be a good idea to reply to the Moorish lady's letter; since we now had someone who could do that, the renegade immediately set about writing down the words I told him, which were precisely the ones I shall tell you now, because none of the substantive points of this matter has disappeared from my memory, and none will for as long as I live. This, then, was the response to the Moorish lady:

> May the true Allah keep you, Señora, and the Blessed Marién, the true Mother of God who has given you the desire to go to Christian lands because she loves you dearly. Pray to her and ask how you can accomplish what she commands you to do; she is so good that she will certainly respond to your prayer. On behalf of myself and all these Christians who are with me, I offer to do for you everything that we can until the day of our death. Continue to write to me and tell me what you intend to do, and I shall always reply, for Almighty Allah has given us a Christian captive who can speak and write your language, as you will see by this letter. Therefore, without fear of any kind, you can tell us anything you wish. As for what you have said regarding becoming my wife if you reach Christian lands, I give you my word as a good Christian that you will, and you should know that Christians keep their promises better than Moors. May Allah and His mother, Marién, bless and keep you, Señora.

This letter was written and sealed; I waited two days until I was again alone in the *bagnio*, and then I went to the usual place on the flat roof to see if the reed would appear, and it did in a very short time. As soon as I saw it, though I could not see who was holding it, I displayed my letter as a way of asking that she attach the thread, but she already had, and I tied the letter to it, and a short while later our star appeared again, with the knotted handkerchief, our white flag of peace. She let it drop, and I picked it up, and found in the handkerchief, in a variety of silver and gold coins, more than fifty *escudos*, which increased our joy fifty times over and confirmed our hope of obtaining our freedom. That same night our renegade returned and told us he had learned that a Moor about whom we had already heard, named Agi Morato, lived in the house; he was extremely rich and had one child, a daughter who would inherit his entire estate; it was the general opinion in the city that she was the most beautiful woman in Barbary, and many viceroys had come to ask for her hand, but she never had wanted to marry; he had also learned that she once had a Christian slave woman who had died, all of which agreed with what she had written in her letter. Then we began to consult with the renegade regarding how we could rescue her and escape to Christian lands; finally we decided to wait for a second letter from Zoraida, for this was the name of the lady who now wishes to be called María,[8] because we saw very clearly that she alone would be the means around all our difficulties. After we agreed to this, the renegade told us not to worry, for he would bring us to freedom or die in the attempt.

For four days the *bagnio* was filled with people, which meant that for four days the reed did not appear; then, when the *bagnio* was deserted once more, it appeared as usual, bearing a handkerchief so pregnant that it promised a most fortunate birth. The reed came down to me, and in the handkerchief I found another letter and a hundred gold *escudos* and no other kind of coin. The renegade was there; in our cell we gave him the letter to read, and he said this is what it said:

> *I do not know, Señor, how we shall go to Spain; Lela Marién has not told me, though I have asked her, but what we can do is this: I shall give you many gold coins through the window; use them to ransom yourself and your friends, and one of you go to a Christian land and buy a boat and come back for the others; you will find me on my father's country estate, which is near*

---

8. According to Martín de Riquer, the daughter of Agi Morato (see note 6) was in fact named Za-hara; in 1574 she married Abd al-Malik, who was proclaimed sultan of Morocco in 1576 and died in the battle of Alcazarquivir, against the Portuguese, in 1578. She was remarried, to Hasán Bajá, and after 1580 lived in Constantinople. In other words, some characters in this story of the captive are historical, although the action is fictional.

*the Babazón Gate,[9] close to the ocean, where I must spend the summer
with my father and my servants. At night you could safely take me from
there to the boat; remember that you must marry me, because if you do not,
I shall ask Marién to punish you. If you do not trust anyone else to go for
the boat, pay your own ransom and go yourself; I know you are more likely
to return than any of the others, for you are a gentleman and a Christian.
Try to learn where the estate is, and when you come out to the roof I shall
know the bagnio is empty, and give you a good deal of money. Allah keep
you, Señor.*

This is what the second letter stated and declared; when everyone
had heard it, each man offered to be the one who was ransomed, promising to go and return quickly, and I also made the same offer; this was opposed by the renegade, who said that under no circumstances would he
consent to one man escaping to freedom until all of us could escape together, for experience had taught him how badly free men kept the
promises made in captivity; important prisoners had often used this same
plan, ransoming one man so that he could go to Valencia or Mallorca
with enough money to equip a boat and return for those who had ransomed him, but those men never returned, because, as he said, the freedom they obtained and the fear of losing it again erased from their
memories every obligation they had in the world. As confirmation of the
truth he was telling us, he recounted briefly an incident that had occurred very recently to some Christian gentlemen, the strangest that had
ever happened in that place where astounding and remarkable things
happen every day.

Eventually he said that what we could and should do was to give the
ransom money to him so that he could buy a boat there in Algiers, pretending that he planned to become a merchant and trader in Tetuán and
along the coast; when he was master of the ship, it would be easy to devise a way to get all of us out of the *bagnio* and on board. Especially if the
Moorish lady did as she said and gave us enough money to ransom everyone, for when we were free, it would be extremely easy for us to go
aboard, even in the middle of the day; the greatest difficulty was that the
Moors do not permit any renegade to buy or own a boat, unless it is a
large vessel used for making pirate raids, because they fear that if he buys
a boat, especially if he is a Spaniard, he wants it only to go to Christian

9. Bab Azún, the Gate of Azún, is one of the gates to Algiers.

lands; he would avoid this problem by taking on a *Tagarino*[10] to be his partner in the purchase of the boat and to share in the profits, and by means of this deception he would become master of the ship, and then all the rest would be simple. Although my comrades and I thought it would be better to buy the boat in Mallorca, as the Moorish lady had said, we did not dare contradict him, fearing that if we did not do as he wished, he would betray us and endanger our lives by revealing our dealings with Zoraida, and to protect her life we would certainly have given our own; and so we resolved to put ourselves in the hands of God and the renegade, and we replied to Zoraida, telling her we would do everything she advised because her advice was as good as if Lela Marién had told her what to say, and it was entirely up to her whether the plan should be delayed or put into effect immediately. Again I offered to be her husband, and then, on the following day, the *bagnio* happened to be deserted, and using the reed and the handkerchief several times, she gave me two thousand gold *escudos* and a letter in which she said that next *Jumá*, which is Friday, she was going to her father's country estate, and before she left she would give us more money, and if it was not enough, we should tell her, and she would give us as much as we asked for because her father had so much money he would not miss it, especially since she had the keys to everything.

We gave five hundred *escudos* to the renegade so that he could buy the boat; with eight hundred more I was ransomed, having given the money to a merchant from Valencia who was in Algiers at the time, and who ransomed me from the king by promising to pay the money after the next ship arrived from Valencia; if he paid right away, the king would suspect that my ransom had been in Algiers for some time and the merchant had concealed it for his own profit. Then, too, my master was so suspicious that I did not dare to pay out the money all at once. On the Thursday before the Friday when the beautiful Zoraida was to leave for the estate, she gave us another thousand *escudos*, and informed us that she was leaving, and asked that if I were to be ransomed, I should learn where her father's country estate was and at all costs find a reason for going there and seeing her. I responded with few words, saying that I would, and that she should be sure to commend all of us to Lela Marién with the prayers the slave woman had taught her.

10. This was the name for perfectly bilingual Moors, usually converts to Christianity, who had lived among Christians; they often came from the ancient kingdom of Aragón, which included present-day Aragón, Cataluña, Valencia, and the Balearic Islands.

After this, my three companions were ransomed to facilitate our leaving the *bagnio*, because if they saw me ransomed when they were not, and there was enough money, they might become alarmed and the devil could persuade them to do some harm to Zoraida; even though their being the men they were could have allayed this fear, still, I did not want to endanger the plan in any way, and so I had them ransomed in the same manner that I ransomed myself, giving all the money to the merchant so that he could offer a guaranty for us with confidence and security, but never disclosing our plans and our secret to him because of the danger that would have entailed."

CHAPTER XLI

In which the captive continues his tale

"Before two weeks had passed, our renegade bought a very good boat with room for more than thirty people, and to guarantee the success of his plan and lend it credibility, he wanted to sail to a town called Sargel, some thirty leagues from Algiers in the direction of Oran, where there is a brisk trade in dried figs. He made the trip two or three times, accompanied by the Tagarino he had mentioned. In Barbary they call the Moors from Aragón *Tagarinos* and the ones from Granada *Mudéjares*: in the kingdom of Fez the *Mudéjares* are called *Elches*, and these are the people used most by the king in war.

In any event, each time the renegade passed by in his boat he anchored in a cove not two crossbow shots from the country estate where Zoraida was waiting; there the renegade very purposefully joined the Moors who were at the oars, either to say a *zalá* or to rehearse what he actually intended to do, and so he would go to Zoraida's house and ask for fruit, and her father gave it to him and did not recognize him; although he wanted to speak to Zoraida, as he later told me, and tell her that she should be happy and free of doubt, because he was the man who would take her, on my orders, to a Christian land, it was not possible, because Moorish women do not allow any Moor or Turk to see them unless instructed to do so by their husbands or fathers. They allow Christian captives to spend time with them and talk to them, even more than is reasonable, yet it would have made me unhappy if he had spoken to her, because she might have been alarmed to see that her affairs were being discussed by renegades. God willed otherwise, however, and our renegade did not have the opportunity to carry out his virtuous desire, but he saw that he could go back and forth to Sargel in safety and anchor whenever and however and wherever he chose, and that the Tagarino, his partner, followed his instructions to the letter; I had been ransomed, and all he needed to do was find Christians to man the oars, and so he told me to decide which of the prisoners, besides those who had been ransomed, I wanted to take with me, and to arrange for them to be ready on the following Friday, which he had determined should be the day of our departure.

Consequently I spoke to twelve Spaniards, all of them valiant oarsmen who could leave the city without difficulty; it was no easy task finding so many at that time, because twenty ships were out making raids and had taken all the oarsmen with them, and I would not even have found these if their master had not decided to make no raids that summer in order to finish building a galley that he had in the shipyards. I told them only that on the following Friday, in the afternoon, they were to sneak out one by one, go to the far side of Agi Morato's country estate, and wait for me there. I gave each of them these instructions separately and said that even if they saw other Christians, they were to say nothing except that I had instructed them to wait in that spot.

Having finished this, I still had another task to attend to, which was most important to me: I had to inform Zoraida of the progress we had made so that she would remain observant and alert and not be taken by surprise if we attacked before she thought it possible for the Christian boat to have returned. And so I resolved to go to the estate to see if I could talk to her, and on the pretext of gathering greens, one day before my departure I went there, and the first person I met was her father, who spoke to me in the language used between captives and Moors throughout Barbary, and even in Constantinople; it is not Moorish or Castilian, not the language of any nation, but a mixture of all tongues, and with it we can understand one another; it was in this language that he asked me what I wanted in his garden and whose slave I was. I replied that I belonged to Arnaúte Mamí[1] (I said this because I knew very well that the man was his great friend) and

---

1. This was the name of the pirate who captured Cervantes.

that I was looking for greens to prepare a salad. Then he asked me if I was
for ransom and how much my master was asking for me. As we were exchanging these questions and answers, the beautiful Zoraida, who had not
seen me for some time, came out of the house, and since Moorish women,
as I have said, are in no way reluctant or shy about showing themselves to
Christians, she did not hesitate to approach the spot where her father was
talking to me; in fact, as soon as her father saw that she was walking
toward us, rather slowly, he called to her and asked her to approach.

I cannot begin to describe for you the great beauty and grace, or the
elegance of the rich attire, revealed to me by my beloved Zoraida. I will
say only that more pearls hung from her lovely neck, ears, and tresses
than she had hairs on her head. Around her ankles, which were bare, in
accordance with Moorish custom, she wore two *carcajes* (the Moorish
name for bracelets and bangles for the feet) of purest gold, studded with
so many diamonds that, as she told me later, her father had valued them
at ten thousand *doblas*,[2] and the ones on her wrists were worth the same
amount. She wore a large quantity of very fine pearls, because the greatest pride and joy of Moorish women is to adorn themselves with rich
pearls, both large and small, and so the Moors have more pearls than any
other nation; Zoraida's father was said to own many of the best pearls in
Algiers and to have more than two hundred thousand Spanish *escudos,*
and she who is now mistress of my heart was mistress of all this. If she
looks beautiful now, after her many tribulations, imagine how lovely she
was then, dressed in all her finery. Because it is well-known that the
beauty of some women has its days and its seasons and decreases or in-
creases according to what happens to them, and it is natural for the soul's
passions to heighten or diminish that beauty, although they most commonly destroy it. But at that moment she appeared so richly attired and
so exceedingly beautiful that she seemed the loveliest woman I had ever
seen; furthermore, considering all that I owed her, it seemed to me that I
had before me a heavenly goddess come down to earth to be my joy and
salvation.

As soon as she approached us, her father told her in their language
that I was a slave of his friend Arnaúte Mamí and had come to pick a
salad. She began to speak, and in that mixture of languages I have already mentioned she asked me if I was a gentleman and why I had not
been ransomed. I replied that I had been ransomed, and for a price that

2. A gold coin worth approximately six silver *reales.*

would indicate how much my master valued me, for I had paid fifteen hundred *zoltanís*[3] for myself. To which she responded:

'In truth, if you belonged to my father, I would make certain that he did not ransom you for twice that amount, because you Christians always lie and pretend to be poor in order to deceive the Moors.'

'That may be so, Señora,' I replied, 'but the truth is that I have been honest with my master, as I am and will be with everyone in the world.'

'And when do you leave?' said Zoraida.

'Tomorrow, I believe,' I said, 'because a ship from France is scheduled to sail tomorrow, and I intend to leave on it.'

'Do you think it would be better,' Zoraida replied, 'to wait for a vessel from Spain and sail on that rather than on a ship from France? For the French are not your friends.'

'No,' I responded, 'though if it is true, as I have heard, that a ship is arriving from Spain, I might wait for it, but it is more likely that I shall leave tomorrow, because the desire I have to be in my own country and with the people I love is so great that I cannot endure waiting for another opportunity, even if it is a better one.'

'No doubt you are married in your own country,' said Zoraida, 'and wish to return to your wife.'

'I am not married,' I responded, 'but I have given my word to marry as soon as I return there.'

'And is the lady to whom you gave your word beautiful?' said Zoraida.

'She is so beautiful,' I responded, 'that truthfully, she looks a great deal like you.'

At this her father laughed heartily and said:

'By Allah, Christian, she must be very beautiful if she resembles my daughter, who is the most beautiful woman in this kingdom. If you doubt it, look at her carefully, and you will see that I am telling you the truth.'

Zoraida's father, who was a Ladino,[4] acted as our interpreter for most of this exchange, for although she spoke the debased language that, as I have said, is used there, she tended to declare her meanings more by gestures than by words. As we were conversing, a Moor came running, shouting that four Turks had come over the fence or wall of the estate and were picking the fruit even though it was not ripe. The old man was alarmed, as was Zoraida, because the fear the Moors have of the Turks,

---

3. A coin worth approximately seventeen *reales*.

4. In this context, the word means a Moor who knew a Romance language.

especially the soldiers, is widespread and almost instinctive, for they are so insolent and overbearing in their dealings with the Moors, who are their subjects, that they treat them worse than slaves. And so her father said to Zoraida:

'Daughter, go to the house and lock yourself in, while I speak to these dogs, and you, Christian, look for your salad and leave, and may Allah bring you safely to your home.'

I bowed, and he went to find the Turks, leaving me alone with Zoraida, who began to give indications of following her father's instructions. But as soon as he was hidden by the trees of the garden, she turned to me, her eyes full of tears, and said:

'*Ámexi*, Christian, *ámexi?*' Which means 'Are you leaving, Christian, are you leaving?'

I replied:

'Yes, Señora, but not, under any circumstances, without you; wait for me on *Jumá*, and do not be alarmed when you see us, for there is no doubt that we will go to Christian lands.'

I said this in such a way that she understood very well all the words that had passed between us, and putting her arm around my neck, she began to walk toward the house with faltering steps; as luck would have it, for things could have gone very badly if heaven had not willed otherwise, as we were walking in this fashion, she with her arm around my neck, her father, who had returned from chasing away the Turks, saw us, and we saw that he had seen us; Zoraida, who was intelligent and clever, did not remove her arm but clung even closer and placed her head on my chest, letting her knees go limp and giving clear signs and indications that she was in a swoon, while I, for my part, acted as if I were holding her up against my will. Her father came running over to us, saw his daughter in that condition, and asked her what was wrong; when she did not answer, her father said:

'No doubt her alarm at those dogs coming in here has made her faint.'

And taking her from me, he leaned her head against his chest; she heaved a sigh, and with her eyes still wet with tears, repeated:

'*Ámexi*, Christian, *ámexi*'—'Leave, Christian, leave.'

To which her father replied:

'It does not matter, daughter, if the Christian leaves: he has done you no harm, and the Turks have gone. Do not be afraid, nothing can harm you, I asked the Turks to go and they left the way they came in.'

'Señor, they frightened her, as you have said,' I told her father, 'but since she says I should leave, I do not wish to cause her any distress; peace be with you, and with your permission, I shall return here for greens as they are needed, because according to my master, no estate has better salad greens than this one.'

'Come back as often as you like,' responded Agi Morato. 'My daughter did not say what she did because you or any other Christian troubled her; she became confused, and instead of saying that the Turks should leave she said you should go, or perhaps she thought it was time for you to gather your greens.'

This was when I took my leave of them both; looking as if her heart would break, she went off with her father, while I, pretending to pick salad greens, walked all around the estate, looking carefully at the entrances and exits, and at the house's fortifications, and thinking how all of it could be used to further our scheme. Having done this, I returned to the renegade and my companions and told them everything that had happened, saying that I longed for the moment when I could enjoy without fear the great happiness that fortune had granted me in the person of the lovely and beautiful Zoraida.

Time passed, and finally the day and hour we longed for arrived, and by following the plan and procedure that, after careful consideration and long discussion, we had all agreed upon, we had the good fortune we wished for; on the Friday following the day on which I spoke to Zoraida on the estate, our renegade anchored the boat at nightfall across from the place where the fair Zoraida was staying. The Christians who would row had already been alerted and were hiding in various spots throughout the surrounding area. They were all impatient and excited as they waited for me, and longed to storm the boat that lay before their eyes, for they knew nothing of the renegade's arrangement and thought they would have to win their freedom by force of arms, killing the Moors on board.

As soon as I and my companions showed ourselves, all the other Christians came out of hiding. By now the city gates had been closed, and not a soul was to be seen in the surrounding countryside. Since we were all together, we wondered what we should do first: go for Zoraida or subdue the Moorish oarsmen. As we were discussing this, our renegade approached and asked why we were waiting: the time had come, his Moors were not on their guard, and most were asleep. We told him why we were hesitating, and he said the most important thing was to take over the ship, which could be done very easily and with absolutely no danger, and then we could go for Zoraida. Everything he said seemed to be good advice, and so, without further delay, and with him as our guide, we reached the boat; he boarded it first, held up his scimitar, and said in Moorish: 'None of you move unless you want to lose your life.' By this time almost all the Christians had come on board. The Moors, who were not very courageous, were frightened when they heard their captain speak in that manner, and none of them reached for weapons, for they had very few, if any at all; without a word they allowed the Christians to tie their hands, which they did very quickly, threatening the Moors that if they raised any kind of alarm or called out in any way, they would all be put to the sword.

When this was done, half our men remained on guard, the renegade again acted as our guide, and we went to the estate of Agi Morato; it was our good fortune that when we opened the gate, it opened as easily as if it had never been locked, and so, very quietly and very silently, we approached the house without being detected by anyone. The beautiful Zoraida was waiting for us at a window, and as soon as she heard people moving about, she asked in a quiet voice if we were *Nizarini*, which was the same as asking if we were Christians. I replied that we were and that she should come down. When she recognized my voice she did not hesitate for an instant; without a word she came down, opened the door, and allowed everyone to see her, so beautifully and richly dressed that I am incapable of describing her. As soon as I saw her, I grasped her hand and began to kiss it, and the renegade and my two comrades did the same; the others, who knew nothing of the matter, did what they saw us doing, which seemed to be nothing more than thanking her for our freedom and recognizing her as our lady and mistress. The renegade asked in the Moorish tongue if her father was in the house. She replied that he was and that he was sleeping.

'Then we will have to wake him,' responded the renegade, 'and take him with us, along with everything of value on this beautiful estate.'

'No,' she said, 'my father is not to be touched in any way; in this house there is nothing of value except what I am carrying, and that is so valuable it will make you all rich and happy; just wait a moment and you will see.'

At this, she went back into the house, saying that she would return very soon, and we should be quiet and not make any noise. I asked the renegade what had passed between them, and when he told me, I said that nothing was to be done except what Zoraida wished; then she returned, holding a chest filled with so many gold *escudos* that she could barely carry it. As bad luck would have it, her father awoke and heard the noise outside; he looked out the window, and seeing that all the men there were Christians, he began to shout in an extremely loud voice, crying out in Arabic: "Christians! Christians! Thieves! Thieves!" These shouts caused us all the greatest confusion and fear. Seeing the danger in which we all were and knowing how important it was to complete our business before anyone heard him, the renegade, together with some of our men, hurried up to where Agi Morato was standing, but I did not dare abandon Zoraida, who had fainted into my arms.

In brief, those who ran upstairs had such good luck that in a moment they came down again with Agi Morato, his hands tied and a handkerchief covering his mouth, which did not allow him to say a word; still, they threatened him that if he made a sound, it would cost him his life. When his daughter saw him she covered her eyes so that she would not see him, and her father was horrified, not realizing how willingly she had placed herself in our hands. But just then we had more need of our feet, and cautiously and quickly we boarded the ship; those who had remained on board were waiting in fear that some evil had befallen us. Barely two hours of the evening had passed, and we were all in the boat; Zoraida's father's hands were unbound and the cloth removed from his mouth, and the renegade told him again that if he said a word, he would be killed. But when he saw his daughter there, he began to sigh most piteously, especially when he saw that I held her in a close embrace and that she did not struggle, or protest, or shy away, but remained calm; even so he was silent, fearful the renegade's many threats might be carried out.

When Zoraida came on board and saw that we were ready to put our oars into the water, and that her father and the rest of the Moors were prisoners, she told the renegade to tell me to be so kind as to release those Moors and free her father, because she would throw herself into the ocean rather than see with her own eyes the father who had loved her taken prisoner on her account. The renegade told me what she said, and I responded that I was happy to comply, but he said it was not a good idea; if we left the Moors behind, they would summon the people and alert the city, and they would come after us in fast-moving corvettes and cut us off on land and on sea so that we could not escape; what we could do was set them free in the first Christian land we reached. We all agreed to this, and Zoraida, too, was satisfied when she was told the reasons why we did not wish to comply immediately with her request; then, in contented silence and with joyous effort, our valiant oarsmen picked up their oars and, commending ourselves with all our hearts to God, we began to row toward the islands of Mallorca, the closest Christian land. But because the north wind began to blow and the sea became somewhat rough, it was not possible to stay on course for Mallorca, and we had to follow the coast toward Oran, very fearful that we would be discovered at Sargel, which is about sixty miles along the coast from Algiers. By the same token, we were afraid of running across one of the galleys that ordinarily carry merchandise from Tetuán along that route, though all of us, together and separately, assumed that if we encountered a merchant galley, as long as it was not one of those that make raids, we not only would not be defeated but would capture a ship in which we could finish our voyage more safely.

As we were rowing, Zoraida hid her head in my arms so as not to see her father, and I could hear her calling on Lela Marién to help us. We had gone some thirty nautical miles when dawn found us approximately three harquebus shots from shore, which we saw was uninhabited, with no one who could observe us; even so, we made a great effort to row farther out to sea, which by this time was somewhat calmer; when we had gone almost two leagues, the order was given that only every fourth man should row while the others had something to eat, for the ship was well-provisioned, but the oarsmen said that this was not the time to rest, and those who were not rowing could feed them, for they did not wish to drop oars for any reason whatsoever. This is what we did, but then a quarter wind began to blow, which obliged us to raise sails and stop rowing and head for Oran, since no other direction was possible. All of this was done very quickly, and under sail we traveled at more than eight knots, and our only fear was meeting a pirate ship. We gave our Moorish oarsmen food, and the renegade comforted them by saying they were not prisoners and would be set free at the first opportunity. He said the same thing to Zoraida's father, who responded:

'I might hope and believe nothing else of your liberality and good nature, O Christians! But do not think me so simple as to imagine that you will give me my freedom, for you never would have risked taking it from me only to return it so generously, especially since you know who I am and the profit you can earn by giving it back to me; if you wish to name a

price, here and now I offer you anything you wish for myself and this unfortunate daughter of mine, or if you prefer, for her alone, for she is the
greatest and best part of my soul.'

When he said this, he began to weep so bitterly that he moved us all
to compassion and forced Zoraida to look at him; when she saw him
weep, she felt so much pity that she stood, moved away from me, and
went to embrace her father; she put her face next to his, and the two of
them began so piteous a weeping that many of us wept with them. But
when her father saw her dressed in her finery and wearing so many jewels, he said to her in their language:

'What is this, daughter? Last night, before this terrible misfortune occurred, I saw you wearing your ordinary house-clothes, and now, though
you did not have time to put on these garments and did not receive any
joyful news that had to be celebrated by dressing yourself so elegantly, I
see you wearing the finest clothes I could give you when fortune was
more favorable to us. Answer me, for this is even more disturbing and
surprising to me than the calamity in which I find myself now.'

Everything that the Moor said to his daughter the renegade translated for us, but she did not utter a word in reply. When her father saw at
one side of the ship the small chest where she kept her jewels, which he
knew very well he had left in Algiers and had not brought to his country
estate, he was even more distraught, and he asked her how that chest
had fallen into our hands and what it contained. To which the renegade
replied, not waiting for Zoraida's answer:

'Do not bother, Señor, to ask your daughter, Zoraida, so many questions, because with one answer I can satisfy them all; I want you to know
that she is a Christian and has been the file for our chains and the key to
our prison; she is here voluntarily and, I imagine, is as happy to be here
as one who comes out of darkness into light, out of death into life, out of
suffering into glory.'

'Is what he says true, daughter?' said the Moor.

'It is,' responded Zoraida.

'Then,' replied the old man, 'you really are a Christian and have
placed your father in the hands of his enemies?'

To which Zoraida responded:

'It is true that I am a Christian, but not that I brought you this difficulty, for my desire never was to leave you or to do you harm, but only to
do good for myself.'

'And what good have you done for yourself, daughter?'

'That,' she replied, 'you must ask Lela Marién; she will be able to answer you better than I can.'

As soon as the Moor heard this, he threw himself, with incredible speed, headfirst into the ocean, and he surely would have drowned if the long, heavy clothes he wore had not kept him above water for a while. Zoraida cried that we should rescue him; we all came to his aid, seizing him by his long robe and pulling him out, half-drowned and unconscious, which caused Zoraida so much sorrow that she began to weep over him with heartfelt and mournful tears, as if he were already dead. We turned him facedown, he coughed up a good deal of water, and in two hours he regained consciousness; during that time the wind changed and drove us back toward shore, and we had to use our oars again to keep from running aground, but it was our good fortune to reach a cove beside a small promontory or cape that the Moors call the *Cava Rumía*, which in our language means the 'Wicked Christian Woman'; it is a tradition among the Moors that this is the place where the Cava who caused the loss of Spain lies buried,[5] because *cava* in their language means 'wicked woman,' and *rumía* means 'Christian'; they still take it as an evil omen when a ship is forced to anchor there, because otherwise they would never do so, but for us it was not the shelter of a wicked woman but a safe haven and refuge, for the sea had become very rough. We posted sentries on shore, and not laying down our oars, we ate the food that the renegade had provisioned, and prayed with all our hearts to God and Our Lady that they help and favor us and allow us to bring to a happy conclusion what had begun so auspiciously. At Zoraida's heartfelt request, the order was given for her father and the other Moors, all of whom were bound, to be put ashore, because she did not have the courage and was too tenderhearted to see her father bound and her countrymen prisoners. We promised her that we would when we departed, for there would be no danger to us if we left them in that uninhabited place. Our prayers were not in vain; heaven heard them, and a favorable wind began to blow and the sea grew calm, inviting us to rejoice and resume our voyage. When we saw this we untied the Moors, and one by one we put them ashore, which astounded them, but when it was time for Zoraida's father, who by now was fully conscious, to disembark, he said:

'Christians, why do you think this perverse female wants you to give

5. This is an allusion to the legend of Don Rodrigo, the last Visigothic ruler of Spain, whose illicit love for Florinda, the daughter of Count Julián, caused her father to seek his revenge by betraying Spain to the Moors at the battle of Guadalete, in 711.

me my freedom? Do you think it is because she feels compassion for me? No, of course not, she has done this because my presence will be a hindrance to her when she decides to put her evil desires into effect: do not think she has been moved to change her religion because she believes yours is superior to ours, but only because she knows that in your country there is more lewd behavior than in ours.'

And turning to Zoraida, while I and another Christian held his arms in the event he attempted something rash, he said to her:

'Oh, shameless maiden, misguided girl! Where are you going, blindly and thoughtlessly, in the power of these dogs, our natural enemies? Cursed be the hour I begot you, and cursed be the comfort and luxury in which I reared you!'

But seeing that he did not appear likely to finish any time soon, I hurried to put him ashore, and from there he continued to shout his curses and laments, praying to Mohammed to ask Allah to destroy us, to confound and exterminate us; when we had set sail and could no longer hear his words, we could see his actions: he pulled at his beard and tore out his hair and threw himself on the ground, and once, when he called as loud as he could, we heard him cry:

'Come back, my beloved daughter, come ashore, I forgive everything! Give those men the money, it is already theirs, and come and console your grieving father, who will die on this desolate strand if you leave him!'

Zoraida heard all of this, and she grieved and wept at everything and could only respond:

'Pray to Allah, dear father, that Lela Marién, who is the reason I am a Christian, may console you in your sorrow. Allah knows I could not help doing what I did, and these Christians owe me nothing for my decision, for even if I had chosen not to go with them and to remain in my own house, it would have been impossible for me to do so, given the burning desire in my soul to do this deed that seems as virtuous to me, my beloved father, as it appears wicked to you.'

She said this when her father could not hear her and we could no longer see him; I comforted Zoraida, and we concentrated on our journey, which the wind so favored that we were certain we would be on the coast of Spain by dawn the next day. But since the good rarely, if ever, comes to us pure and simple, but is usually accompanied or followed by some disquieting, disturbing evil, it was our bad fortune, or perhaps the result of the curses the Moor had hurled at his daughter, for a father's curses, no matter who he may be, are always to be feared—in any case, when we were out on the open sea, and almost three hours of the night had gone by, and we were running under full sail and had shipped our oars because the brisk wind meant we did not need them, in the bright moonlight we saw a square-rigged ship very close to us; with all her sails unfurled and heading slightly into the wind, she crossed in front of us, so closely that we were obliged to shorten our sails in order not to ram her, and they had to turn hard on the wheel to give us room to pass. They had gathered on the deck of their vessel to ask us who we were, and where we were going, and where we had come from, but since they asked their questions in French, our renegade said:

'No one should answer them, for they are surely French pirates, and they plunder everything they come across.'

Because of his warning, no one said a word, and when we had moved a little ahead of them, and they were leeward of us, without warning they fired two cannon, apparently loaded with chain shot, for the first cut our mast in two, and it and the sail fell into the sea, and a moment later the second was fired, hitting us amidships so that the entire side of the vessel was blown open, though it suffered no other damage; but we found ourselves sinking, and we all began to shout, calling for help and imploring those on the other ship to rescue us before we drowned. Then they shortened their sails and lowered a skiff, or small boat, into the water, and twelve Frenchmen got in, well-armed with harquebuses and holding flaming torches, and pulled alongside us; seeing how few of us there were and that our ship was sinking, they rescued us, saying that this had happened because of our discourtesy in not answering them. Our renegade picked up the chest of Zoraida's treasure and threw it into the sea without anyone noticing what he was doing.

In short, when we were all on board the French ship, and they had learned everything they wanted to know about us, as if they were our mortal enemies they stole everything we had and stripped Zoraida even of the anklets she wore on her feet. But I was not as perturbed by Zoraida's distress as I was by my own fear that after they had taken her rich and precious jewels they would take her most valuable jewel, the one she prized most highly. But the desires of those people do not go beyond money, for which their lust is never satisfied, and on this occasion it was so inflamed that they would have taken even our captives' attire if it had been of any use to them. Some were of the opinion that they should throw us all overboard, wrapped in a sail, because they intended to trade at certain Spanish ports, claiming to be Bretons, and if they took us with them, they would be punished when their theft of our goods was discovered. But their captain, the man who had robbed my dear Zoraida, said that he was satisfied with the booty he already had and did not wish to go to any Spanish port but only to pass through the Straits of Gibraltar at night, or any way he could, and return to La Rochelle, which was the place he had sailed from; and so they agreed to give us the skiff, and whatever we needed for the short journey that still lay before us, which is what they did the following day when we were within sight of the coast of Spain; at that sight all our sorrows and hardships were forgotten, as if they had never existed, so great is the joy one feels at regaining lost freedom.

It must have been midday when they put us in the boat, giving us two barrels of water and some hardtack, and as the beautiful Zoraida was getting into the skiff, the captain, moved by some sort of mercy, gave her forty gold *escudos* and would not allow his men to take the very clothing she is wearing now. We climbed into the boat and thanked them for their kindness, displaying more gratitude than ill humor; they sailed away, heading for the Straits, and we, with no star other than the land we saw before us, began rowing so quickly that, as the sun began to set, we were so close to shore that we were certain we could touch land before nightfall; but since there was no moon, and the sky looked black, and we did not know precisely where we were, it did not seem safe to rush straight for the coast, as many of us wanted to do, saying that we should go ashore even if there were rocks and we landed in an uninhabited spot, for if we did, we would allay the reasonable fear that we might encounter the ships of pirates out of Teuán, who leave Barbary in the dark, reach the coast of Spain at dawn, make their raids, and return to sleep in their own houses at night; after long discussion we finally decided to approach the coast slowly, and if the sea was calm enough, to put ashore wherever we could. This is what we did, and it must have been just before midnight when we reached the foot of a very high hill set back far enough from the sea so that we had room to land. We ran the boat onto the sand, climbed out onto land, kissed the ground, and with tears of sheer joy gave thanks to the Lord our God for His incomparable goodness to us. We took the provisions out of the skiff, pulled it onto land, then climbed a good way up the hill, for we still were not certain and could not really believe that we were standing on Christian soil.

Day broke more slowly, I thought, than we wished. We climbed to the top of the hill to see if we could discover a village or some shepherds' huts, but though we looked in every direction, we saw no village, person, path, or road. Even so, we resolved to continue inland, for we were bound to meet someone soon who would tell us where we were. What most troubled me was seeing Zoraida walking on that harsh terrain, and though I carried her on my shoulders for a time, she was more wearied by my weariness than rested by the rest I gave her; she would not allow me to take up that burden again, and with a good deal of patience and many displays of joy, and with me leading her by the hand, we must have walked a little less than a quarter of a league when the sound of a small bell reached our ears, a clear sign that a flock was nearby; all of us looked around for it, and at the foot of a cork tree we saw a young shepherd taking his ease and idly whittling a stick with his knife. We called to him, and he looked up and then quickly scrambled to his feet, for, as we learned later, the first people he saw were the renegade and Zoraida, and since they were wearing Moorish clothing, he thought that all of Barbary was attacking, and running with extraordinary speed toward the woods that lay ahead of us, he began to shout at the top of his voice, calling:

'Moors! Moors have landed! Moors, Moors! To arms! To arms!'

His shouts confused us, and we did not know what to do, but assuming that the shepherd's outcry would rouse the countryside, and that the mounted troops who guarded the coast would soon come to investigate, we agreed that the renegade should remove his Turkish jacket and put on a prisoner's coat or tunic that one of us gave to him, though doing so left him in shirtsleeves; and so, commending ourselves to God, we followed the same path the shepherd had taken, expecting the mounted troops to bear down on us at any moment. And we were not wrong, because in less than two hours, when we had come out of the undergrowth and onto a plain, we saw some fifty men on horseback coming toward us at a quick trot; as soon as we saw them we stood still and waited for them, but when they rode up and saw so many poor Christians instead of the Moors they had been searching for, they were perplexed, and one of them asked us if we, by any chance, were the reason a shepherd had sounded the alarm. I said that we were, and as I was about to tell him our story, where we came from and who we were, one of the Christians who was with us recognized the rider who had asked us the question, and without allowing me to utter another word, he said:

'Give thanks to God, Señores, for leading us to so good a place! If I'm not mistaken, we're in Vélez Málaga, and if the years of my captivity haven't erased the memory of this gentleman who is questioning us, you, Señor, are my uncle, Pedro de Bustamante.'

As soon as the Christian captive said this, the rider leaped from his horse and rushed to embrace the lad, saying:

'My dear, dear nephew, I recognize you now, and have wept for your death, as has your mother—my sister—and all your family, those who are still alive, and God has been pleased to give them life so that they can have the pleasure of seeing you: we knew you were in Algiers, and to judge by the clothes you and the rest of this company are wearing, I understand that you've had a miraculous escape.'

'That's true,' said the young man, 'and there will be time to tell you all about it.'

As soon as the horsemen realized that we were Christian captives, they dismounted and each of them invited us to ride his horse into the city of Vélez Málaga, which was a league and a half away. We told them where we had left the skiff, and some went back to bring it into the city; others had us mount behind them, and Zoraida rode with the Christian captive's uncle. The entire city came out to welcome us, for they had been informed of our arrival by a guard who had ridden ahead. They were not surprised to see escaped captives, or captives who were Moors, because all the people along that coast were accustomed to seeing both, but they were astonished by Zoraida's beauty; at that time and moment it was at its height, due to the exertion of the trip and her joy at finding herself in a Christian land, free of the fear that we would be lost; this had brought so much color to her face that unless I was deceived by my affections, I would dare say there was no more beautiful creature in the world, at least none that I had seen. We went directly to the church to thank God for the mercy He had shown us, and as soon as Zoraida entered the church, she said there were faces there that resembled that of Lela Marién. We told her these were images of Lela Marién, and the renegade did the best he could to explain what they meant, so that she could worship them as if each one really were the Lela Marién who had spoken to her. Zoraida, who has a good understanding and a quick, clear intelligence, quickly comprehended everything he said about the images. From the church our companions were taken to various houses in town, but the renegade, Zoraida, and I were taken by the Christian lad to the house of his parents, who were comfortably endowed with material goods and who treated us as lovingly as they did their own son.

We spent six days in Vélez, and at the end of that time the renegade, having made the statement required of him, went to the city of Granada, where, through the mediation of the Holy Inquisition, he would be returned to the blessed fellowship of the Church; each of the freed Christians went wherever he chose; only Zoraida and I remained, with nothing but the *escudos* that the courteous Frenchman had given to her, and with them I bought this animal that she is riding; I have been serving her as father and squire, but not as husband, and we are going to see if my father is still alive or if either of my brothers has been more fortunate than I, although since heaven made me Zoraida's companion, I do not believe I could have any better luck. The patience with which Zoraida endures the hardships that poverty brings, and her desire to at last become a Christian, are both so great that I am amazed and moved to serve her all the rest of my days; yet the pleasure I have in knowing that I am hers and she is mine is troubled and undone by my not knowing if I will find some corner in my own land where I can shelter and protect her, or if time and death will have so altered the fortunes and lives of my father and brothers that if they are gone, I will scarcely find anyone who knows me. There is no more, Señores, of my story to tell you; you can judge for yourselves if it is unusual and interesting; as for me, I can say that though I would have liked to recount it more briefly, fear of tiring you made me omit more than a few details."

CHAPTER XLII

Which recounts further events at the inn as well as many other things worth knowing

Then the captive fell silent, and Don Fernando said:

"Certainly, Señor Captain, the manner in which you have recounted this remarkable tale has been equal to the unusual and marvelous events themselves. The story is rare and strange, full of extraordinary incidents that astonish the listener; we have so liked hearing it that we would enjoy listening to it all over again, even if it took until tomorrow morning."

After he had said this, Cardenio and the others offered to do everything in their power to serve the captain, using words so sincere and language so affectionate that he was certain of their good will, in particular that of Don Fernando, who offered, if he wished to go with him, to have his brother the marquis act as godfather at Zoraida's baptism, while he would provide everything needed so that the captive could return to his own land with the dignity and comfort his person deserved. The captive thanked him very courteously but did not wish to accept any of his generous offers.

Night was falling by this time, and when it grew dark, a carriage arrived at the inn accompanied by some men on horseback. They asked for accommodations, and the innkeeper's wife replied that they did not have an empty place in the whole inn.

"Well, even so," said one of the men on horseback, "you cannot turn away his honor the judge who is approaching now."

When she heard this title, the innkeeper's wife became perturbed and said:

"Señor, the fact is I have no free beds; if his honor the judge has brought his own, as he probably has, then he is welcome, and my husband and I will give up our room in order to accommodate his grace."

"That will be acceptable," said the squire.

By this time a man had descended from the carriage, and his clothing immediately indicated his office and position, for the long robe with shirred sleeves edged in lace showed that he was a judge, as his servant had said. He held the hand of a maiden, approximately sixteen years old, who wore a traveling costume and was so elegant, beautiful, and charming that everyone marveled at the sight of her, and if they had not already seen Dorotea and Luscinda and Zoraida at the inn, they would have thought that beauty comparable to hers would be difficult to find. Don Quixote watched as the judge and the maiden came inside, and when he saw them he said:

"Surely your grace may enter this castle and rest here, for although it is crowded and uncomfortable, there is no place in the world so crowded or uncomfortable that it does not have room for arms and letters, especially if arms and letters are led and guided by comeliness, as the letters of your grace are led by this beauteous damsel, before whom castles must not only open their gates and reveal themselves, but great rocks must split in two and mountains divide and fall in order to give her shelter. I say that your grace should enter this paradise, for here you will find stars and suns to accompany the heaven your grace brings with you: here you will find arms at their most magnificent, and beauty in the extreme."

The judge, astounded at Don Quixote's words, looked at him very carefully and was no less astounded by his appearance, and not finding words with which to respond, he was astounded all over again when he saw Luscinda, Dorotea, and Zoraida, for when the innkeeper's wife told them there were new guests and had described the maiden's beauty, they came out to see and welcome her. Don Fernando, Cardenio, and the priest gave the judge a courteous and more straightforward greeting. His honor, in fact, was somewhat bewildered by what he had seen and heard, but the enchanting women of the inn made the beautiful maiden welcome.

The judge saw clearly that all the people there were gentlefolk, but the figure, face, and bearing of Don Quixote left him perplexed; after the exchange of courteous greetings and a careful consideration of the accommodations offered by the inn, matters were arranged as they had been earlier: all the women would sleep in the previously mentioned garret, and the men would stay outside, as a kind of guard. The judge was content to have the maiden, who was his daughter, go with the ladies, which she did very willingly. With part of the innkeeper's narrow bed, and half of the one the judge had brought with him, they settled in that night more comfortably than they had expected.

From his first glimpse of the judge, the captive's heart had pounded with the certainty that this was his brother, and he asked one of his servants what the judge's name was and if he knew where he was from. The servant responded that his name was Licentiate Juan Pérez de Viedma and that he had heard he came from somewhere in the mountains of León. This information, combined with what he had seen, convinced him that this was his brother, the one who had pursued letters, following his father's advice, and with great excitement and happiness he called aside Don Fernando, Cardenio, and the priest, and told them what had happened, and assured them that the judge was his brother. The servant had told him that his honor was going to the Indies to serve as a judge on the Royal High Court of México, and the captive also learned that the maiden was the judge's daughter, that her mother had died in childbirth, and that he was very wealthy because of the dowry his daughter had inherited. The captive asked their advice as to how he should make himself known, or if he ought to determine first whether his brother would feel humiliated when he saw how poor he was or would welcome him affectionately.

"Let me find out for you," said the priest, "though I am certain, Señor Captain, that you will be very warmly received; your brother's face reveals virtue and good sense, and he gives no sign of being arrogant or ungrateful or ignorant of how to evaluate the adversities of fortune."

"Even so," said the captain, "I would like to reveal myself to him gradually, not all at once."

"And I say," responded the priest, "that I will arrange it in a way that satisfies us all."

By this time supper had been prepared, and they all sat at the table except for the captive and the ladies, who ate by themselves in the garret. In the middle of the meal, the priest said:

"Señor Judge, I had a comrade in Constantinople, where I was held captive for some years, who had the same name as your grace; this comrade was one of the most valiant soldiers and captains in the entire Spanish infantry, but as unfortunate as he was courageous and brave."

"And what was this captain's name, Señor?" asked the judge.

"His name," responded the priest, "was Ruy Pérez de Viedma, and he came from the mountains of León; he told me about something that had happened to him, his father, and his brothers, and if I had not heard it from a man as truthful as he, I would have taken it for one of those old wives' tales told around the fire in winter. Because he said that his father had divided his estate among his three sons and had given them advice that was better than Cato's. And I can say that the counsel he chose to follow, which was to take up arms, served him so well that in a few years, because of his valor and hard work, with no support other than his own great virtue, he rose to the rank of infantry captain and was well on his way to becoming commander of a regiment. But then his luck turned, and just when he could have expected good fortune, he lost it and his freedom on the glorious day when so many won theirs at the battle of Lepanto. I lost my freedom at the Goletta, and then, through a series of circumstances, we became comrades in Constantinople. From there he went to Algiers, where he became involved in one of the strangest stories the world has ever seen."

The priest continued the tale and briefly and succinctly recounted what had happened to the captive and Zoraida; the judge listened more attentively than he had ever listened to evidence in a case. The priest stopped at the moment when the French robbed the Christians in the boat and left his comrade and the beautiful Moorish lady in poverty and want; he said he knew no more about them and did not know if they ever reached Spain or had been carried off to France by the Frenchmen.

The captain listened to everything the priest said, standing a little way off and observing everything his brother did, and the judge, seeing that the priest had come to the end of his tale, heaved a great sigh as his eyes filled with tears and said:

"Oh, Señor, if you only knew what you have just told me! It touches me so deeply I cannot control these tears that stream from my eyes despite all my circumspection and reserve! That brave captain is my older brother, who, being stronger and of more noble thoughts than I or my younger brother, chose the honorable and worthy profession of arms, which was one of the three paths our father proposed to us, as your comrade told you and which you took as nothing but a story. I followed the path of letters, and by the grace of God and my own diligence have reached my present position. My younger brother is in Perú, and so wealthy that with what he has sent home to my father and me he has more than repaid the portion he took, and has even placed in my father's hands the means to satisfy his natural generosity; because of him, I was able to pursue my studies in a decent and suitable manner and achieve my current rank. My father still lives, though dying for news of his oldest son, and he constantly prays to God that death not close his eyes until he can see his son alive. What astonishes me, considering my brother's great intelligence, is that he failed to inform his father of his many hardships and afflictions, or his times of good fortune; if his father or either of his brothers had known, he would have had no need to wait for the miracle of the reeds to obtain his ransom. But my fear now is wondering if those Frenchmen gave him his freedom or killed him to hide their thievery. This means that I shall continue my journey not happily, as I began it, but filled with melancholy and sadness. Oh, my dear brother, if only I knew where you were now! I would go to find you and free you from hardship, even if it meant hardship for me! And bring to our aged father the news that you were alive, even if you were in the deepest dungeons of Barbary, for his wealth, and my brother's and mine, would rescue you! O beautiful and generous Zoraida, if only I could repay your kindness to my brother, and witness the rebirth of your soul, and the marriage that would give all of us so much pleasure!"

The magistrate said these and other words like them, filled with so much emotion at hearing news of his brother that all those present joined him in expressing their sentiments at his sorrow.

The priest, seeing that his plan had worked so well and achieved what the captain desired, did not wish them to be sad any longer, and so he rose from the table, went into the room where Zoraida was staying, and led her out by the hand, followed by Luscinda, Dorotea, and the judge's daughter. The captain was waiting to see what the priest intended to do; he took the captain by the hand as well, and leading both of them, the priest walked to the table where the judge and the other gentlemen were sitting and said:

"Señor Judge, let your tears cease, and your dearest wish will be crowned with all you desire, for here in front of you are your good brother and sister-in-law. This is Captain Viedma, and this is the beautiful Moor who was so kind to him. The Frenchmen, as I said, left them in straitened circumstances, so that you now have the opportunity to show them the liberality of your generous heart."

The captain came forward to embrace his brother, who held him off by placing his hands on his chest so that he could look at him from a slight distance, but when he recognized him he embraced him so closely, shedding so many tears of joy, that the rest of the company were bound to weep, too. The words the two brothers exchanged, the feelings they displayed, can scarcely be imagined, let alone written down. They gave each other a brief accounting of their lives; then they revealed the warmth of their brotherly affections, and the magistrate embraced Zoraida and offered her his entire estate; then he had her embrace his daughter, and the beautiful Christian girl and the beautiful Moorish lady moved them all to tears again.

Don Quixote was very attentive, not saying a word, pondering these strange events and attributing them all to the chimeras of knight errantry. It was agreed that the captain and Zoraida would go with his brother to Sevilla, and they would inform their father that he had been found and was free, and as soon as he could, their father would come to be present at the marriage and baptism of Zoraida, for the judge could not delay his journey; he had been notified that in a month's time the fleet would leave Sevilla for New Spain, and it would have been extremely inconvenient for him not to make the voyage at that time.

In short, everyone was pleased and happy at the captive's good fortune, and since the night was almost two-thirds over, they decided to retire and rest until morning. Don Quixote offered to guard the castle in the event some giant or other nefarious villain decided to attack, greedy for the great treasure of beauty enclosed therein. Those who knew him thanked him, and they told the judge about Don Quixote's strange madness, which amused him more than a little.

Only Sancho Panza was troubled at how late they went to bed, and only he made himself more comfortable than all the rest by lying down on his donkey's harness, which would cost him dearly, as shall be recounted later.

The ladies, then, having withdrawn to their room, and the others having settled down with as little discomfort as possible, Don Quixote stood outside the inn to guard the castle, as he had promised.

It so happened that shortly before dawn, a voice so harmonious and sweet reached the ears of the ladies that they were all obliged to listen carefully, especially Dorotea, who was awake, and beside whom lay Doña Clara de Viedma, which was the name of the judge's daughter. No one could imagine who was singing so beautifully in a voice unaccompanied by any instrument. At times they thought the singing was in the courtyard; other times, it seemed to come from the stable; and as they were listening in bewilderment, Cardenio came to the door and said:

"If anyone is awake, listen, and you will hear the voice of one of the muledrivers' boys; he sings so well that he sounds like an angel."

"We hear him, Señor," replied Dorotea.

And so Cardenio left, and Dorotea, listening very attentively, heard the words that the boy was singing. They were:

CHAPTER XLIII

Which recounts the pleasing tale of the muledriver's boy, along with other strange events that occurred at the inn

> I, a mariner of love,
> sail passion's perilous deeps
> desperate to find a cove
> or harbor, or rest or peace.
>
> Guided by a distant star
> more radiant, more bright,
> though its light shines from afar,
> than any Palinurus spied.
>
> I know not where she leads,
> I sail perplexed, confused,

my soul care-laden, careless,
wanting nothing but to gaze
    Upon her. Uncommon
modesty, rarest virtue,
like clouds hide her fair mien;
I would restore it to view.
    O splendid, luminous star,
cause of my tears and sighs,
when you hide your face entire
then I will surely die!

When the singer had reached this point, it seemed to Dorotea that Clara ought not to miss hearing so fine a voice, and she shook her gently to wake her, saying:

"Forgive me, my dear, for waking you, but I want you to listen to the best voice you may ever have heard in your life."

Clara stirred and was still half-asleep, and at first she did not understand what Dorotea was saying and asked her to repeat it, and when she did, Clara paid close attention. But when she heard barely two lines sung by that voice, she began to tremble as if taken ill in a sudden attack of quartain fever, and throwing her arms around Dorotea, she said:

"Oh, dear lady of my heart and soul! Why did you wake me? The greatest favor that fortune could grant me now would be to close my eyes and ears so that I could not see or hear that unhappy singer."

"What are you saying, my dear? They say that the person singing is a muledriver's boy."

"Oh no, he is the lord of many villages, and of a domain in my heart which he holds so unalterably that unless he chooses to leave it, it will be his forever."

Dorotea was astonished at the girl's deeply felt words, which seemed to her far more discerning than might have been expected from one so young, and so she said to her:

"You speak, Señora Clara, in a way I cannot understand: explain what you mean by heart and domains, and tell me of this musician, whose voice has left you so agitated. But say nothing now, because in the event you become even more perturbed, I do not want to miss the pleasure I derive from his voice; I think he is going to start again, with new lyrics and a new melody."

"By all means," responded Clara.

But in order not to hear him, she covered her ears with her hands, which also astonished Dorotea, who listened carefully, and this is what she heard:

> Oh, sweet hope of mine,
> taming th'impossible, struggling past thorns,
> bravely walking the path
> that you alone have cut, you alone adorn;
> do not despair fair hope
> if each step brings you closer to death's scope.
>   The slothful never win
> laurels of triumph or honored victories;
> since they ne'er contend
> with fate, fortune, and fame they never see,
> but weak in indolence,
> they turn to idle joys of flesh and sense.
>   Love puts a high price
> on its glories; that is just and fair, for
> there's no richer prize
> than one that is esteemed at its true worth,
> and it is surely clear
> that things are not highly valued if not dear.
>   Steadfastness in love
> can often win impossibilities;
> though this may prove
> too harsh a terrain for my tenacity,
> I despise that fear
> and strive to reach my heaven from this sphere.[1]

Here the voice came to an end, and Clara began to sob again, all of which inflamed Dorotea's desire to know the reason for so melodious a song and such piteous weeping. And so she again asked Clara what she had meant earlier, and the girl, fearful that Luscinda would hear her, held Dorotea tightly and placed her mouth so close to Dorotea's ear that she was sure she could speak without being overheard and said:

"The boy who is singing, Señora, is the son of a gentleman from the

---

1. Martín de Riquer indicates that this lyric (and other poems inserted in the text) was composed by Cervantes years before he wrote *Don Quixote* and set to music in 1591 by Salvador Luis, a singer in the chapel choir of Philip II.

kingdom of Aragón who is the lord of two villages, and who had a house across from my father's house in Madrid, and though my father covered the windows of his house with canvas in winter and jalousies in summer,[2] I don't know how it happened, but this young man, as he was going to school, saw me somehow, I don't know if it was in church or somewhere else, and he fell in love with me and let me know it from the windows of his house with so many gestures and so many tears that I had to believe him, and even love him in return without knowing exactly what he wanted of me. One of his gestures was to join his hands, giving me to understand that he would marry me; that would have made me very happy, but as I was alone and motherless and had no one to talk to, I did nothing and did not favor him; but when my father was out of the house, and his father, too, I would raise the canvas or jalousie a little and let him see me full-length, which sent him into such raptures it seemed he would lose his mind.

Then the time came for my father to leave Madrid, and the boy learned about it, but not from me, because I never had the chance to tell him. He was taken ill, as I understand it, with grief, and so the day we were to leave I could not see him to say goodbye, if only with my eyes. But after we had been traveling for two days, as we were entering an inn in a village about a day's travel from here, I saw him in the doorway, dressed in the clothes of a muledriver's boy and looking so natural that if I did not carry his image engraved in my heart, it would have been impossible to recognize him. But I did recognize him, to my amazement and joy; he looked at me without my father's seeing him, and he always hides his face from my father when he passes us on the roads and in the inns where we stay; since I know who he is and believe that it is on account of his love for me that he is traveling on foot and suffering so much hardship, I am dying of sorrow and follow his every step with my eyes. I don't know why he has come here or how he managed to escape his father, who loves him very, very much because he is his only heir, and because he deserves it, as your grace will agree when you see him. And let me tell you something else: everything he sings he makes up in his own head, and I have heard that he's a very fine student and poet. And there's more: whenever I see him or hear him sing, I tremble from head to toe, worried and fearful that my father will recognize him and learn of our feelings and desires. I have never said a

---

2. These were common coverings for windows before glass was in general use.

word to him in my life, and even so, I love him so much I cannot live without him. This, Señora, is all that I can tell you about this musician whose voice has given you so much joy, but it alone says clearly that he is not a muledriver's boy, as you say, but a lord with vassals and lands, as I have told you."

"Say no more, Señora Doña Clara," said Dorotea as she gave her a thousand kisses, "say no more and wait for the new day, for with God's help I hope to arrange this affair so that it has the happy ending such virtuous beginnings deserve."

"Oh, Señora!" said Doña Clara. "What ending can we expect if his father is so distinguished and wealthy that he won't think me good enough to be his son's maid, let alone his wife? Then, too, I would not marry without my father's knowledge for anything in the world. All I want is for this boy to go home and leave me; perhaps if I don't see him, and with the great distance we have to travel, the grief I feel now may begin to fade, though I can say that I don't believe this remedy will do me much good at all. I don't know what the devil this is, or how I ever fell so much in love with him, since I am so young and so is he; I think we're both the same age, I'm almost sixteen, and my father says I'll turn sixteen on Michaelmas Day."

Dorotea could not help laughing when she heard how childishly Doña Clara spoke, and she said:

"Señora, let us sleep for the little bit of night we have left, and tomorrow, with God's help, things will go well for us if I have any skill in such matters."

After this they were silent, and a profound stillness fell over the inn; only the innkeeper's daughter and her maid, Maritornes, were not asleep, for they, knowing the madness that afflicted Don Quixote, who was outside their window, armed, mounted, and on guard, decided to play a trick on him or, at least, to pass the time listening to his foolishness.

It so happened that in all the inn there was no window that opened onto the fields except for a narrow opening in a loft through which they pitched out straw. The two semi-maidens stood at this opening and saw that Don Quixote was on horseback, leaning on his lance, and from time to time heaving sighs so mournful and deep that each one seemed to break his heart in two, and saying in a gentle, tender, and loving voice:

"Oh, Señora Dulcinea of Toboso, pinnacle of all beauty, summit and crest of discernment, archive of grace and wit, depository of virtue, and, finally, ideal of all goodness, modesty, and joy in the world! What can thy grace be doing now? Can thy thoughts be turned to thy captive knight, who hath willingly faced so many dangers for the sake of serving thee? Oh, giveth me news of her, thou three-faced luminary! Perhaps with envy of her brilliance thou art looking at her now, or perhaps she strolleth along a gallery in one of her sumptuous palaces, or leaneth against a balustrade and considereth how, while protecting her modesty and greatness, she canst soften the anguish that this my heart suffereth for her sake, and reward my grief with glory, and lighten my care, and, finally, grant life to my death and recompense for my services. And thou, O sun, who even now must be making haste to saddle thy steeds, and climb the heavens, and see my lady, I pray thee when thou seest her to greet her on my behalf, but be thou certain not to kiss her face when thou seest and greetest her, for then I shall be more envious of thee than thou wert of that fleet ingrate who madest thee to perspire and race across the plains of Thessaly or along the banks of the Peneus, for I do not remember precisely where thou rannest then so envious and enamored."[3]

Don Quixote had reached this point in his piteous lament when the innkeeper's daughter began to attract his attention by saying, "Psst, psst," and calling to him:

"Señor, please come here, if your grace doesn't mind."

Don Quixote heard her voice, turned his head, and saw by the light of the moon, which was then at its brightest, that he was being called from the loft opening that to him seemed a window with grillework of gold, as befits luxurious castles, which is what he imagined the inn to be; then, in an instant, it seemed to him in his mad imagination that once again, as she had in the past, the beauteous damsel, daughter to the chatelaine of that castle, had been overcome by love for him and was soliciting his favors; with this thought in mind, and not wishing to seem discourteous and ungrateful, he pulled on Rocinante's reins and rode to the opening, and when he saw the two young women, he said:

"I am sorely grieved, beauteous lady, that thou hast turned thy amorous thoughts to a place where there is no possibility that they will be returned as thy great worth and nobility deserve; for this thou should'st not blame a wretched knight errant whom love preventeth from giving his heart to any but the one who, when his eyes first saweth her, became the absolute mistress of his soul. Forgive me, good lady, and

---

3. The reference is to Apollo's pursuit of Daphne, the daughter of the river god Peneus.

withdraw to thy chamber, and revealest thou no more of thy desires to me so that I may not appear even more ungrateful; if, in the love thou hast for me, thou findest aught else in me that is not love itself but can make thee content, asketh it of me, for I swear to thee by that sweet and absent enemy of mine that I shall grant it without delay, e'en if thou asketh a lock of the hair of Medusa, which is nought but vipers, or the rays of the sun enclosed in a vial."

"My señora has no need of anything like that, Señor Knight," said Maritornes.

"Then what, O discreet duenna, doth thy señora need?" responded Don Quixote.

"Just one of your beautiful hands," said Maritornes, "so that with it she can ease the great desire that has brought her to this opening at such great risk to her honor, for if my señor, her father, heard her, the least thing he would slice off would be her ear."

"I should like to see him try!" responded Don Quixote. "But surely he will be careful not to do so, unless he wisheth to meet the most calamitous end that any father hath ever met in this world, for laying hands on the delicate appendages of his enamored daughter."

Maritornes, certain that Don Quixote would surely give her the hand she had requested, had decided on what to do, and she climbed down from the opening, went to the stable, took the halter of Sancho Panza's donkey, and hurried back to the opening just as Don Quixote was standing on Rocinante's saddle in order to reach the barred window where he imagined the heartbroken damsel to be; and as he gave her his hand, he said:

"Señora, takest thou this hand, or rather, this scourge of all evildoers in the world; takest thou this hand, I say, untouched by the hand of any woman, not e'en the hand of she who hath entire possession of this my body. I do not give it to thee so that thou mayest kiss it, but so that thou mayest gaze upon the composition of its sinews, the consistency of its muscles, the width and capacity of its veins, and from this conjecture the might of the arm to which such a hand belongeth."

"Now we'll see," said Maritornes.

And after making a slip knot in the halter, she put it around his wrist and climbed down from the opening, then tied the other end of the halter very firmly to the lock on the loft door. Don Quixote, who felt the rough cord around his wrist, said:

"It seemeth to me that thy grace is filing my hand instead of fondling it; treateth it not so harshly, for it is not to blame for the injury my desire hath done thee, nor is it fitting that thou should'st seek vengeance for thy entire displeasure on so small a part of my body. Thou should'st remember, too, that one who loveth sweetly doth not punish severely."

But no one was listening to these words of Don Quixote, because as soon as Maritornes attached the halter to his wrist, she and the innkeeper's daughter went away, convulsed with laughter, and left him so securely tied that it was impossible for him to free himself.

As we have said, he was standing on Rocinante, his entire arm inside the opening and his wrist tied to the lock on the door, extremely uneasy and fearful that if Rocinante moved to one side or the other, he would be left hanging by his arm, and so he did not dare move at all, although considering Rocinante's patience and passivity, one could reasonably expect him to stand for a century without moving.

In short, when Don Quixote discovered that he was bound and the ladies had vanished, he began to imagine that all this was the result of enchantment, as it had been the last time when in that very castle an enchanted Moor of a muledriver had given him a severe beating; to himself he cursed his lack of intelligence and good sense, for after having been hurt so badly in that castle, he had dared enter it a second time, despite the common knowledge among knights errant that when they have embarked on an adventure and have not succeeded, it is a sign that the adventure is meant not for them but for others, and so they have no need to attempt it a second time. Even so, he pulled his arm to see if he could free himself, but he was so securely tied that all his efforts were in vain. It is certainly true that he pulled rather tentatively so that Rocinante would not move, and though he longed to sit down in the saddle, all he could do was remain standing or pull his hand off.

He wished for the sword of Amadís, against which all enchantments were powerless; then he cursed his fate; then he exaggerated how much the world would feel his absence during the time he was under enchantment, and he had no doubt at all that he was enchanted; then he thought again of his beloved Dulcinea of Toboso; then he called for his good squire, Sancho Panza, who, buried in sleep and stretched out on his donkey's saddle, had no thought at that moment even for the mother who bore him; then he called on the sages Lirgandeo and Alquife to help him; then he summoned his good friend Urganda the Wise to come to his aid; finally, morning found him so desperate and perplexed that he was bellowing like a bull, for he had no hope that day would cure his plight because he deemed it eternal, since he was enchanted. This belief was strengthened even further when he saw that Rocinante had hardly moved at all, and he thought that he and his horse would remain in this state, not eating or drinking or sleeping, until the evil influence of the stars had passed or another, wiser enchanter had disenchanted him.

But he was greatly deceived, because just as dawn was breaking, four men on horseback came riding up to the inn, and they were handsomely dressed and well-equipped, with flintlocks resting on their saddlebows. They pounded on the door of the inn, which was still locked, and when this was seen by Don Quixote, who was still guarding the castle from his position at the opening to the loft, he called out to them in a loud and arrogant voice, saying:

"Knights, or squires, or whoever you may be: you have no reason to call at the gates of this castle, for it is more than clear that at this hour those inside are asleep, or are not in the habit of opening their strongholds until the sun is high in the sky. Withdraw, and wait until the day grows bright, and then we shall see if it is proper for them to open to you."

"What the devil kind of stronghold or castle is this," said one, "that we should be obliged to follow such ceremonies? If you're the innkeeper, tell them to open for us; we're travelers and want only to feed our mounts and then move on, because we're in a hurry."

"Does it seem to you, Señores, that I have the appearance of an innkeeper?" responded Don Quixote.

"I don't know what kind of appearance you have," responded another, "but I do know that you talk like a fool when you call this inn a castle."

"It is a castle," replied Don Quixote, "and one of the best in this entire province; there are those inside who have held a scepter in their hands and worn a crown on their heads."

"It would be better the other way round," said the traveler, "with a scepter on their heads and a crown in their hands. It may be that what you mean to say is that there's a company of actors inside, and they often have those crowns and scepters you've mentioned, because I don't believe that people worthy of crowns and scepters would lodge in an inn as small and silent as this one."

"You know little of the world," replied Don Quixote, "for you know nothing of the events that occur in knight errantry."

The questioning traveler's companions grew weary of the conversation he was having with Don Quixote, and they began to pound on the door again with great fury, so loudly that the innkeeper awoke, as did everyone else in the inn, and got up to ask who was at the door. Just then, one of the horses of the four men pounding at the door happened to smell Rocinante, who, melancholy and sad and with drooping ears, stood unmoving as he held his tightly drawn master; and since, after all, he was flesh and blood, though he seemed to be made of wood, he could not help a certain display of feeling as he, in turn, smelled the horse who had come to exchange caresses; as soon as he had moved slightly, Don Quixote's feet, which were close together, slipped from the saddle, and he would have landed on the ground if he had not been hanging by his arm; this caused him so much pain that he believed his hand was being cut off at the wrist or that his arm was being pulled out of its socket; he was left dangling so close to the ground that the tips of his toes brushed the earth, and this made matters even worse, because, since he could feel how close he was to planting his feet firmly on the ground, he struggled all he could to stretch even farther and touch down, just as those sub-jected to the torture of the strappado, whose feet touch, almost touch, the ground, increase their own torment by attempting to extend them-selves to the fullest, deceived in the hope that with just a little more stretching they will reach the ground.

CHAPTER XLIV

In which the remarkable events at the inn continue

Don Quixote cried out so loudly, in fact, that the terrified innkeeper sud-denly threw open the doors of the inn to see who was shouting, and those outside did the same. Maritornes, who had been awakened by those same shouts, guessed what they might be and went to the loft, and without anyone seeing her she untied the halter that held up Don Quixote; he immediately fell to the ground in full view of the innkeeper and the travelers, who went up to him and asked what was wrong and why he was shouting. He, not saying a word in reply, removed the cord from around his wrist, stood up, mounted Rocinante, grasped his shield, couched his lance, and, after riding some distance into the fields, re-turned at a canter, saying:

"Should any sayeth that I have been rightfully enchanted, and if the Señora Princess Micomicona giveth me leave, I shall prove the lie and challenge and charge him in single combat."

The newcomers were astonished at Don Quixote's words, but the innkeeper did away with their astonishment when he told them that this was Don Quixote and there was no need to pay attention to him because he was out of his mind.

They asked the innkeeper if a youth of about fifteen, dressed as a muledriver's boy, had come to the inn, and they described his features, which were the same as those of Doña Clara's lover. The innkeeper responded that with so many people in the inn, he had not noticed the boy about whom they were asking. But when one of them saw the carriage in which the judge had arrived, he said:

"He must be here, no doubt about it, because this is the carriage we were told he was following; one of us should stay at the door while the others go in and look for him, and it might be a good idea if one of us rode around the inn so he doesn't get away over the corral walls."

"That's what we'll do," responded one of the travelers.

And two of them went inside, one stayed at the door, and another rode around the inn; the innkeeper saw all of this and could not imagine why they were taking so many precautions, although he certainly knew they were looking for the boy they had described to him.

By now day had dawned, and because of this, as well as the noise that Don Quixote had made, everyone was awake and out of bed, especially Doña Clara and Dorotea, who had slept very badly that night, one filled with excitement at having her lover so close by, the other with a desire to see him. Don Quixote, who saw that none of the four travelers paid attention to him or responded to his demand, raged and fumed with indignation and fury, and if he had discovered in his laws of chivalry that a knight errant could legitimately take up and embark upon another adventure, having given his word and pledge not to do so until he had completed the one he had promised to undertake, he would have attacked all of them and forced them to respond whether they wished to or not; but since he did not think it correct to begin a new adventure until he had restored Micomicona to her kingdom, he had no choice but to remain silent, saying nothing and waiting to see the outcome of the travelers' efforts; one of them found the lad they were seeking as he slept beside a muledriver's boy, little thinking that anyone was looking for him, let alone that anyone would find him, and seizing the boy by the arm, the man said:

"No doubt, Señor Don Luis, these clothes complement your rank, and this bed in which I find you corresponds to the luxury in which your mother reared you."

The boy tried to rub the sleep out of his eyes and looked for a long moment at the man holding him before he realized that he was one of his father's servants, and this so startled him that he could not say a word for some time, and the servant continued to speak, saying:

"Now, Señor Don Luis, you have no choice but to be patient and return home, unless you wish to see your father and my master in the next world, which is all that can be expected, considering the grief your absence has caused him."

"But how did my father know," said Don Luis, "that I was on this road and wearing these clothes?"

"You disclosed your intentions to a student," responded the servant, "and he was moved by pity at your father's distress when he realized you were gone, and revealed everything, and so your father dispatched four of his servants to look for you, and all of us are here to serve you, happier than you can imagine that we can return quickly and bring you back to the one who loves you so."

"That shall be as I choose or as heaven decrees," responded Don Luis.

"What is there for you to choose or heaven to decree other than your agreeing to return? Nothing else is possible."

The muledriver's boy next to whom Don Luis was lying heard all of this conversation; he got up and went to tell Don Fernando and Cardenio and the others what had happened, for by this time everyone was dressed, and he told them how a man had called the boy *Don*, and about the words that had passed between them, and how they wanted him to return to his father's house but the boy did not want to. And this, in addition to what they already knew about him, which was the beautiful voice that heaven had granted him, filled them all with a great desire to know in detail who he was and even to help him if anyone was forcing him to do something he did not wish to do, and so they went to the place where he was still talking and protesting to his servant.

At this moment Dorotea came out of her room, and behind her was a greatly perturbed Doña Clara; Dorotea called Cardenio aside and briefly told him the tale of the singer and Doña Clara, and Cardenio told her about the arrival of the servants who were looking for the boy, and he did not say this so quietly that Clara could not hear; this so agitated her that if Dorotea had not held her up, she would have fallen to the ground.

Cardenio told Dorotea that she and the girl should return to their room and that he would attempt to resolve everything, and they did as he asked.

The four men who had come looking for Don Luis were all inside the inn and standing around him, trying to persuade him that he should return immediately, and without any delay, to console his father. He responded that under no circumstances could he do so until he had concluded a matter upon which his life, his honor, and his heart depended. Then the servants urged him more insistently, saying that under no circumstances would they return without him and that they would bring him back whether he wished it or not.

"That you will not do," replied Don Luis, "unless you bring me back dead; but no matter how you take me, I shall be without life."

By this time everyone in the inn had come to listen to the dispute, especially Cardenio, Don Fernando, his companions, the judge, the priest, the barber, and Don Quixote, who thought it was no longer necessary to guard the castle. Cardenio, since he already knew the boy's story, asked those who wanted to take him what reason they had to take him against his will.

"What moves us," responded one of the four servants, "is the desire to return life to his father, who is in danger of losing it because of this gentleman's absence."

At this, Don Luis said:

"There is no reason to tell everyone here my business; I am a free man, and I shall return if I wish to, and if I do not, none of you can force me to."

"Reason will force your grace," the man responded, "and if that's not enough, we'll do what we came here to do, and what we are obliged to do."

"Let us hear what is at the bottom of this," said the judge.

But the servant, who recognized him as his master's neighbor, responded:

"Señor Judge, doesn't your grace know this gentleman? He's your neighbor's son, and as your grace can see, he has left his father's house dressed in a manner inappropriate to his station."

Then the judge looked at him more closely, and recognized him, and embraced him, saying:

"What foolishness is this, Señor Don Luis? What reason is so powerful that it has moved you to appear in this manner and in this dress, so unbefitting your rank and station?"

Tears filled the boy's eyes, and he could not say a word in response. The judge told the four men that they could rest assured that everything would be settled, and taking Don Luis by the hand, he drew him aside and asked his reasons for coming to the inn.

As he was asking him this and other questions, there was an outburst of deafening shouts at the door of the inn, and the reason was that two guests who had spent the night there, seeing that everyone was concerned with finding out what the four men were seeking, had attempted to leave without paying what they owed, but the innkeeper, who tended more to his own business than to that of others, laid hands on them as they were leaving and demanded payment, and he cursed them so bitterly for their dishonesty that they were moved to respond with their fists, and they began to beat him so ferociously that the poor innkeeper had to cry out and plead for help. The innkeeper's wife and daughter saw that the only one not too busy to help was Don Quixote, and the daughter said:

"Señor Knight, with the strength God gave your grace, help my poor father, for two wicked men are thrashing him like wheat."

To which Don Quixote responded, very slowly and with great calm:

"O beauteous damsel, the time is not right for thy plea, for I cannot embark upon any adventure until I have brought to a felicitous conclusion one to which I am pledged. But what I can do to serve thee I shall tell thee now: runnest thou to tell thy father to prolong his combat for as long as he can and not allow himself to be defeated, and in the meantime I shall ask leave of the Princess Micomicona to succor him in his plight; if she giveth it to me, thou mayest be certain that I shall save him."

"Poor sinner that I am!" said Maritornes, who was standing nearby. "By the time your grace gets that leave, my master will be in the next world."

"Señora, allowest me only to obtain this leave," responded Don Quixote, "and when I have it, it will not matter at all if he is in the next world, for I shall take him out of there even if that entire world oppose me; at the very least, for thy sake I shall take such revenge on those who sent him there that thou shalt be more than a little satisfied."

And without saying another word, he went to kneel before Dorotea, imploring with knightly and errantly words that her highness be so kind as to give him leave to succor and minister to the castellan of that castle, who had come to a most grievous pass. The princess gave it willingly, and he immediately held up his shield and grasped his sword and hurried to the door of the inn, where the guests were still beating the innkeeper, but as soon as he arrived he stopped and stood perfectly still, although Maritornes and the innkeeper's wife asked why he was stopping and told him to help their master and husband.

"I have stopped," said Don Quixote, "because it is not licit for me to raise my sword against squirely folk; summon my squire, Sancho, for this defense and revenge rightly belong to him."

This took place at the door to the inn, where the punches and blows were reaching their high point, to the detriment of the innkeeper and the fury of Maritornes, the innkeeper's wife, and her daughter, all of whom despaired when they saw not only Don Quixote's cowardice but how badly things were going for their husband, master, and father.

But let us leave the innkeeper here, for someone will help him, and if no one does, let the man who dares more than his strength allows suffer in silence, and we shall go back fifty paces and see how Don Luis responded to the magistrate, whom we had left standing off to one side and asking Don Luis the reason he had arrived on foot, wearing such shabby clothes. And the boy, clasping the judge's hands tightly as a sign that a great sorrow troubled his heart, and shedding an abundance of tears, said:

"Señor, all I can tell you is that from the moment heaven willed, which was facilitated by our being neighbors, that I see Señora Doña Clara, your daughter and my lady, from that very moment I made her mistress of all my desires and wishes; if in your wishes, you who are my true lord and father, there is no objection, on this very day she will be my wife. For her sake I left my father's house, and for her sake I put on these clothes, in order to follow her wherever she might go, as the arrow follows its mark or the sailor his star. She knows nothing of my desires except for what she has been able to deduce when, on occasion and at a distance, she has seen the tears flow from my eyes. Señor, you already know of my parents' wealth and nobility, and also that I am their only heir, and if these seem reason enough for you to venture to make me entirely happy, then accept me as your son, and if my father, moved by his own plans, is not pleased by the great prize I have obtained, time can do more to change and alter things than human desires."

When he had said this, the enamored youth fell silent, and the magistrate was perplexed, confused, and bewildered both by the intelligence and discretion with which Don Luis had revealed his thoughts to him, and by suddenly finding himself in so unsettling and unexpected a situation; he replied only that Don Luis should remain calm for the moment and persuade his servants not to take him back that day, so that there would be time to consider what was best for everyone. Don Luis grasped his hands and kissed them, and even bathed them with tears, which could have softened a heart of marble and not only the magistrate's; he was an intelligent man and already knew how advantageous a marriage this would be for his daughter, although, if possible, he would have preferred it to take place with the approval of Don Luis's father, who, he knew, wanted his son's bride to have a title.

By this time the guests had made peace with the innkeeper, for the persuasion and good arguments of Don Quixote rather than his threats had convinced them to pay all that the innkeeper demanded, and the servants of Don Luis were waiting for the judge to conclude his conversation and for their master to make his decision; at that very moment the devil, who never sleeps, willed the arrival at the inn of the barber from whom Don Quixote had taken the helmet of Mambrino, and Sancho Panza the donkey's gear that he had exchanged for his own; this barber, leading his donkey to the stables, saw Sancho Panza adjusting something on the packsaddle, and as soon as he saw him he recognized him, and he attacked him, saying:

"Ah, Don Thief, I have you now! Give me back my basin and my saddle and all the rest of the harness you stole from me!"

Seeing himself attacked so unexpectedly, and hearing himself insulted so bitterly, Sancho grasped the saddle with one hand and punched the barber with the other, bathing his teeth in blood, but despite this the barber continued to hold on to the saddle and gave so loud a shout that everyone in the inn rushed to the place where they were fighting, and the barber called out:

"Help, help, in the name of the king and of justice! He not only takes my goods, but this thief, this highway robber, is trying to kill me!"

"You lie!" responded Sancho. "I'm no highway robber; my master, Don Quixote, won these spoils in righteous combat!"

Don Quixote was present, very happy to see how well his squire could both defend himself and go on the offensive, and from that moment on he considered Sancho a brave and upright man, and he resolved in his heart to dub him a knight at the first opportunity, for it seemed to him that the order of chivalry would be put to good use in Sancho. One of the things the barber said in the course of their dispute was this:

"Señores, this saddle is as much mine as the death I owe to God, and

I know it as well as if I had given birth to it, and there's my donkey in the stable, and he won't let me lie; just try the saddle on him, and if it isn't a perfect fit, then I'm a villain. And there's more: on the very day they stole it from me, they also took a brand-new brass basin that had never been used and was worth at least an *escudo*."

At this point Don Quixote could not refrain from responding, and placing himself between the two men and separating them, and laying the saddle on the ground where everyone could see it until the truth had been determined, he said:

"Now your graces may clearly and plainly see the error of this good squire, for he calls a basin what was, is, and will be the helmet of Mambrino, which I took from him in righteous combat, thereby becoming its lawful and legitimate owner! I shall not intervene in the matter of the packsaddle, but I can say that my squire, Sancho, asked my permission to remove the trappings from the steed of this vanquished coward; I granted it, he took them, and with regard to those trappings being transformed into a packsaddle, I can give only the ordinary explanation: these are the kinds of transformations seen in matters of chivalry; to confirm this, Sancho my son, run and bring here the helmet that this good man claims is a basin."

"By God, Señor," said Sancho, "if this is the only proof we have of what your grace has said, then the helmet of Malino is as much a basin as this good man's trappings are a packsaddle!"

"Do as I say," replied Don Quixote, "for not everything in this castle must be ruled by enchantment."

Sancho went for the basin and brought it back, and as soon as Don Quixote saw it, he took it in his hands and said:

"Just look, your graces; how does this squire presume to say that this is a basin and not the helmet I say it is? I swear by the order of chivalry which I profess that this helmet is the same one I took from him, and nothing has been added to it or taken away."

"There's no doubt about that," said Sancho, "because from the time my master won it until now, he's fought only one battle wearing it, and that was when he freed the luckless men in chains; if it wasn't for this basihelm,[1] things wouldn't have gone too well for him because there was a lot of stone-throwing in that fight."

---

1. According to Martín de Riquer, Sancho invents the word both as a sarcastic comment on Don Quixote's misperception and in order not to contradict Don Quixote openly.

CHAPTER XLV

In which questions regarding the helmet of Mambrino and the packsaddle are finally resolved, as well as other entirely true adventures

"What do your graces think of what they're saying, Señores?" said the barber. "These gentlefolk are still insisting that this isn't a basin but a helmet."

"And whoever says it is not," said Don Quixote, "if he is a gentleman, I shall show him that he lies, and if he is a squire, that he lies a thousand times over."

Our barber, who was present through all of this, knew Don Quixote's madness so well that he wanted to encourage his lunacies and, by carrying the joke even further, give everyone a good reason to laugh, and so speaking to the second barber, he said:

"Señor Knight, or whoever you may be, you should know that I too follow your trade and have held my certificate[1] for more than twenty years, and know very well all the tools of barbering, without exception; for a time I was even a soldier in my youth, and I also know what a helmet is, and a morion, and a full sallet, and other things related to soldiering, I mean to say, the kinds of weapons that soldiers use; and I say, barring a better opinion and bowing always to better judgment, that this piece in front of us, which this good gentleman is holding in his hands, not only is not a barber's basin, but is as far from being one as white is from black and truth from falsehood; I also say that this, though a helmet, is not a complete helmet."

"No, of course not," said Don Quixote, "for half of it, the visor, is missing."

---

1. Certificates were issued by the trade guilds to indicate a member's skill.

"That is true," said the priest, who had understood the intention of his friend the barber.

And the same was affirmed by Cardenio, Don Fernando, and his companions, and even the judge, if he had not been so involved in the matter of Don Luis, would have taken part in the deception, but he was so preoccupied by the gravity of his thoughts that he paid little or no attention to such amusements.

"Lord save me!" said the barber who was the target of the joke. "Is it possible that so many honorable people are saying that this is not a basin but a helmet? This seems to be something that could astonish an entire university, no matter how learned. Enough: if it's true that this basin is a helmet, then this packsaddle must also be a horse's harness, just as the gentleman said."

"It looks like a saddle to me," said Don Quixote, "but I have already said I shall not intervene in that."

"Whether it is a packsaddle or harness," said the priest, "is for Don Quixote to say, for all these gentlemen and I defer to him in matters of chivalry."

"By God, Señores," said Don Quixote, "so many strange things have happened to me in this castle on the two occasions I have stayed here, that if you were to ask me a question about anything in it, I would not dare give a definitive answer, for I imagine that everything in it is subject to enchantment. The first time I was greatly troubled by an enchanted Moor, and things did not go very well for Sancho at the hands of his companions, and last night I was hung by this arm for almost two hours, not having any idea of how or why I had fallen into that misfortune. Therefore, if I now become involved in so confusing a matter and give my opinion, it would be a rash judgment. As for what has been said regarding this being a basin and not a helmet, I have already responded to that, but as for declaring whether this is a saddle or a harness, I do not dare offer a final opinion: I leave it to the judgment of your graces. Perhaps because you have not been dubbed knights, as I have, the enchantments of this place will not affect your graces, and your minds will be free and able to judge the things in this castle as they really and truly are, and not as they seem to me."

"There is no doubt," responded Don Fernando, "but that Señor Don Quixote has spoken very well today, and it is up to us to decide the case; in order to make our decision a valid one, I shall take the votes of these gentlemen in secret and give a complete and clear report on the outcome."

For those who were aware of Don Quixote's madness, all of this was cause for a good deal of laughter, but for those who were not, it seemed the greatest lunacy in the world, especially the four servants of Don Luis, and Don Luis himself, and another three travelers who had just arrived at the inn and seemed to be members of the Holy Brotherhood, which was, in fact, what they were. But the one who was most confused was the barber, whose basin had been transformed into the helmet of Mambrino before his very eyes and whose packsaddle he undoubtedly thought would be turned into a horse's rich harness; everyone laughed to see Don Fernando going from one to the other and taking his vote, having him whisper it into his ear so that each could declare in secret whether that jewel that had been so fiercely fought over was a packsaddle or a harness. After he had taken the votes of those who knew Don Quixote, he announced in a loud voice:

"The fact is, my good man, that I am weary of hearing so many opinions, because I see that no one whom I ask does not tell me that it is nonsense to say this is a donkey's packsaddle and not the harness of a horse, even a thoroughbred, and so, you will have to be patient because despite you and your donkey, this is a harness and not a packsaddle, and you have presented and proved your case very badly."

"May I never have a place in heaven," said the second barber, "if all of your graces are not deceived, and may my soul appear before God with as much certainty as this appears to be a packsaddle and not a harness, but if you've got the might . . . and I'll say no more; the truth is I'm not drunk, and I haven't broken my fast except to sin."

The barber's simpleminded talk caused no less laughter than the lunacies of Don Quixote, who at this point said:

"All that can be done now is for each man to take what is his, and may St. Peter bless what God has given us."

One of the four servants said:

"Unless this is a trick of some kind, I can't believe that men of intelligence, which is what all of you are, or seem to be, can dare say and affirm that this isn't a basin and that isn't a saddle; but as I see that you do affirm and say it, I suppose there's some mysterious reason why you claim something so contrary to what truth and experience show us, and I swear"—and here he came out with a categorical oath—"that not all the people alive in the world today can make me think that this isn't a barber's basin, and that isn't a jackass's packsaddle."

"It might belong to a jenny," said the priest.

"It doesn't matter," said the servant, "that's not the point, the question is whether it is or isn't a packsaddle, as your graces claim."

Upon hearing this, one of the officers in the Holy Brotherhood who had come in and heard the discussion and dispute said in a fury and a rage:

"If that's not a saddle, then my father's not my father, and whoever says otherwise must be bleary-eyed with drink."

"Thou liest like the base villain thou art," responded Don Quixote.

And raising the lance that had never left his hands, he prepared to strike him so hard on the head that if the man had not dodged the blow, it would have knocked him down. The lance shattered on the ground, and the other officers, seeing their companion so badly treated, shouted for help for the Holy Brotherhood.

The innkeeper, who was a member,[2] went in for his staff and sword and then stood by the side of his comrades; Don Luis's servants surrounded him so that he could not escape during the disturbance; the second barber, seeing everything in a turmoil, seized his packsaddle again, and so did Sancho; Don Quixote drew his sword and charged the officers. Don Luis shouted at his servants to leave him and go to the assistance of Don Quixote, and Cardenio and Don Fernando, who were fighting alongside Don Quixote. The priest shouted, the innkeeper's wife called out, her daughter cried, Maritornes wept, Dorotea was confused, Luscinda distraught, and Doña Clara in a swoon. The barber beat Sancho; Sancho pounded the barber; Don Luis, when one of his servants dared seize him by the arm to keep him from leaving, punched him so hard his mouth was bathed in blood; the judge defended him; Don Fernando had one of the officers under his feet and was trampling him with great pleasure; the innkeeper cried out again, calling for help for the Holy Brotherhood: in short, the entire inn was filled with cries, shouts, yells, confusions, fears, assaults, misfortunes, attacks with knives, fists, sticks, feet, and the spilling of blood. And in the midst of this chaos, this enormous confusion, it passed through the mind of Don Quixote that he had been plunged headlong into the discord in Agramante's camp,[3] and in a voice that thundered throughout the inn, he cried:

"Hold, all of you! All of you sheathe your swords, stop fighting, and listen to me, if you wish to live!"

2. In the sixteenth and seventeenth centuries, it was not unusual for innkeepers to belong to the Holy Brotherhood; the staff was a symbol of authority derived from the king.

3. The dispute, which became proverbial, was described by Ariosto in *Orlando furioso*.

At this great shout everyone stopped, and he continued, saying:

"Did I not tell you, Señores, that this castle was enchanted and that some legion of demons must inhabit it? In confirmation of which I wish you to see with your own eyes what has transpired here and how the discord of Agramante's camp has descended upon us. Look, here they do battle for the sword, there for the horse, over there for the eagle, right here for the helmet, and all of us are fighting and all of us are quarreling.[4] Come then, your grace, Señor Judge, and your grace, Señor Priest; one of you take the part of King Agramante and the other that of King Sobrino and make peace among us, because in the name of God Almighty it is a great wickedness for so many wellborn and distinguished people to kill one another for such trivial reasons."

The officers of the Holy Brotherhood, who did not understand Don Quixote's language and found themselves being mistreated by Don Fernando, Cardenio, and their comrades, did not wish to stop brawling, but the second barber did, since both his beard and his saddle had been damaged in the fracas; Sancho, like a good servant, obeyed every word his master said; and the four servants of Don Luis also stopped, seeing how little they had to gain from doing otherwise. Only the innkeeper insisted that the effronteries of that madman had to be punished, since he was always causing a disturbance at the inn. Finally, the clamor was stilled for the moment, and in the imagination of Don Quixote the saddle remained a harness until Judgment Day, and the basin a helmet, and the inn a castle.

When, at last, persuaded by the judge and the priest, everyone had made peace and become friends, Don Luis's servants began to insist again that he come away with them immediately, and as he was discussing this with them, the judge spoke to Don Fernando, Cardenio, and the priest regarding what should be done in this matter, recounting what Don Luis had said to him. Finally, it was decided that Don Fernando should reveal his identity to Don Luis's servants and tell them it was his wish that Don Luis accompany him to Andalucía, where his brother, the marquis, would welcome him as his great merit deserved, for it was evident that Don Luis would not now return willingly to his father even if he were torn to pieces. When the four men realized both the high rank of Don Fernando and the determination of Don Luis, they decided that three of them would return to report what had happened to his father

---

4. Traditionally, the disputed items in Agramante's camp were a sword, a horse, and a shield emblazoned with an eagle; the helmet is an invention of Don Quixote's.

and one would stay behind to serve Don Luis and not leave him until the other servants returned for him or he had learned what his master's orders were.

In this fashion, a tangle of quarrels was unraveled through the authority of Agramante and the prudence of King Sobrino, but the enemy of harmony and the adversary of peace, finding himself scorned and mocked, and seeing how little he had gained from having thrown them all into so confusing a labyrinth, resolved to try his hand again by provoking new disputes and disagreements.

So it was that the officers stopped fighting when they heard the rank and station of their opponents, and they withdrew from combat because it seemed to them that regardless of the outcome, they would get the worst of the argument; but one of them, the one who had been beaten and trampled by Don Fernando, recalled that among the warrants he was carrying for the detention of certain delinquents, he had one for Don Quixote, whom the Holy Brotherhood had ordered arrested, just as Sancho had feared, because he had freed the galley slaves.

When the officer remembered this, he wanted to certify that the description of Don Quixote in the warrant was correct, and after pulling a parchment from the bosom of his shirt, he found what he was looking for and began to read it slowly, because he was not a very good reader, and at each word he read he raised his eyes to look at Don Quixote, comparing the description in the warrant with Don Quixote's face, and he discovered that there was no question but that this was the person described in the warrant. As soon as he had certified this, he folded the parchment, held the warrant in his left hand, and with his right he seized Don Quixote so tightly by the collar that he could not breathe; in a loud voice he shouted:

"In the name of the Holy Brotherhood! And so everybody can see that I'm serious, read this warrant ordering the arrest of this highway robber."

The priest took the warrant and saw that what the officer said was true and that the features in the description matched those of Don Quixote, who, enraged at his mistreatment by a base and lowborn churl, and with every bone in his body creaking, made a great effort and put his hands around the man's throat, and if his companions had not hurried to his assistance, the officer would have lost his life before Don Quixote released him. The innkeeper, who was obliged to assist his comrade, rushed to his aid. The innkeeper's wife, who saw her husband involved in a dispute again, raised her voice again, and Maritornes and her daughter immediately joined her, imploring the help of heaven and of everyone in the inn. Sancho, when he saw all of this, said:

"Good God! What my master says about enchantments in this castle is true! You can't have an hour's peace here!"

Don Fernando separated the officer and Don Quixote, and to the relief of both he loosened the hands of both men, for one was clutching a collar and the other was squeezing a throat; but this did not stop the officers from demanding that Don Quixote be arrested and that the others assist in binding him and committing him to their authority, as demanded by their duty to the king and the Holy Brotherhood, which once again was asking for their help and assistance in the arrest of this highway robber and roadway thief.

Don Quixote laughed when he heard these words and said very calmly:

"Come, lowborn and filthy creatures, you call it highway robbery to free those in chains, to give liberty to the imprisoned, to assist the wretched, raise up the fallen, succor the needy? Ah, vile rabble, your low and base intelligence does not deserve to have heaven communicate to you the great worth of knight errantry, or allow you to understand the sin and ignorance into which you have fallen when you do not reverence the shadow, let alone the actual presence, of any knight errant. Come, you brotherhood of thieves, you highway robbers sanctioned by the Holy Brotherhood, come and tell me who was the fool who signed an arrest warrant against such a knight as I? Who was the dolt who did not know that knights errant are exempt from all jurisdictional authority, or was unaware that their law is their sword, their edicts their courage, their statutes their will? Who was the imbecile, I say, who did not know that there is no patent of nobility with as many privileges and immunities as those acquired by a knight errant on the day he is dubbed a knight and dedicates himself to the rigorous practice of chivalry? What knight errant ever paid a tax, a duty, a queen's levy, a tribute, a tariff, or a toll? What tailor ever received payment from him for the clothes he sewed? What castellan welcomed him to his castle and then asked him to pay the cost? What king has not sat him at his table? What damsel has not loved him and given herself over to his will and desire? And, finally, what knight errant ever was, is, or will be in the world who does not have the courage to single-handedly deliver four hundred blows to four hundred Brotherhoods if they presume to oppose him?"

CHAPTER XLVI

Regarding the notable adventure of the officers of the Holy Brotherhood, and the great ferocity of our good knight Don Quixote

As Don Quixote was saying this, the priest was attempting to persuade the officers that Don Quixote was not in his right mind, as they could see by his actions and his words, and that they had no need to proceed with the matter, for even if they arrested him and took him away, they would have to release him immediately because he was a madman, to which the officer with the warrant replied that it was not up to him to judge the madness of Don Quixote, but only to do what his commanding officer ordered him to do, and once Don Quixote had been arrested, it was all the same to him if they let him go three hundred times over.

"Even so," said the priest, "this one time you should not take him, and as far as I can tell, he will not allow himself to be taken."

In fact, the priest was so persuasive, and Don Quixote did so many mad things, that the officers would have been crazier than he if they had not recognized Don Quixote's affliction, and so they thought it best not to proceed, and even to intervene and make peace between the barber and Sancho Panza, who still persisted with great rancor in their dispute. In short, as officers of the law, they mediated and arbitrated the matter in a manner that left both parties, if not completely happy, at least somewhat satisfied, because they exchanged saddles but not cinches and headstalls; as for the helmet of Mambrino, the priest secretly, and without Don Quixote's knowing anything about it, paid eight *reales* for the basin, and the barber gave him a receipt promising not to sue for fraud then or forever after, amen.

Having settled these two disputes, which were the most important and most pressing, it remained only for Don Luis's servants to agree that three would return home while one stayed behind to accompany him wherever Don Fernando wished to take him; since good luck had begun to intervene in favor of the lovers and the valiant people at the inn, overcoming all difficulties, a better fortune wished to bring everything to a happy conclusion, and his servants acceded to Don Luis's wishes, which so delighted Doña Clara that no one could look at her face and not know the joy in her heart.

Zoraida, although she did not completely understand all the events she had seen, became sad or happy by turns, depending on what she saw and observed on the faces of other people, especially her Spaniard, on whom her eyes were fixed and her heart and soul depended. The innkeeper, who had not failed to notice the compensatory gift given to the barber by the priest, demanded payment from Don Quixote, including damages to his wineskins and the loss of his wine, swearing that neither Rocinante nor Sancho's donkey[1] would leave the inn unless he was first paid down to the last *ardite*. The priest settled the matter, and Don Fernando paid the bill, although the judge had very willingly offered to pay as well, and everything was so peaceful and serene that the inn no longer resembled the discord in Agramante's camp, as Don Quixote had said, but seemed the very peace and tranquility of the time of Octavian; it was the generally held opinion that thanks for this were owed to the good intentions and great eloquence of the priest and the incomparable liberality of Don Fernando.

When Don Quixote found himself free and clear of so many disputes, his squire's as well as his own, it seemed to him that it would be a good idea to continue the journey he had begun and conclude the great adventure to which he had been called and for which he had been chosen; and so, with resolute determination, he went to kneel before Dorotea, who would not permit him to say a word until he stood, and he, in obedience to her, rose to his feet, and said:

" 'Tis a common proverb, O beauteous lady, that diligence is the mother of good fortune, and in many grave and serious matters experience hath shown that solicitude canst bring a doubtful matter to a successful conclusion, but nowhere is this truth clearer than in questions of war, in which celerity and speed canst disrupt the enemy's plans and achieve victory ere the adversary prepareth his defenses. This I say, most high and exalted lady, because it seemeth that our stay in this castle no

1. In the first edition, this is the first indication that Sancho has recovered his donkey.

longer profiteth us and might even prove harmful, as we may discover one day, for who knoweth if by means of hidden and diligent spies thy enemy the giant hath not learned that I am going to destroy him, and hath taken advantage of our sojourn here to fortify himself in some impregnable castle or bastion against which all my efforts and the might of my tireless arm may be of no avail? And so, Señora, let us, I say, disrupt his designs with our diligence and depart immediately, whilst fortune favoreth us, for to keep it with us, as your highness wisheth, we must delay no longer my encounter with thy adversary."

Don Quixote fell silent and said no more, and waited very calmly for the reply of the beauteous princess, who, with noble bearing, and adapting to the style used by Don Quixote, responded in this fashion:

"I thanketh thee, Señor Knight, for the desire thou hast shown to favor me in my great distress, like a true knight whose profession and preoccupation is to favor orphans and those in need; may heaven grant that thy desire and mine are achieved so that thou mayest see that there are grateful women in the world. As for my departure, let it be immediate, for I have no will other than thine: thou mayest dispose of me as thou pleaseth and chooseth, for she who hath once entrusted to thee the defense of her person and placed in thy hands the restoration of her domains ought not go against what thy prudence ordaineth."

"May it be God's will," said Don Quixote, "for when a lady humbleth herself before me, I do not wish to lose the opportunity to raise her and restore her to her rightful throne. Let us depart now, for the ancient saying that danger lieth in delay spurreth my desire to be on our way. And since heaven hath not created, nor hell seen, any that canst daunt or frighten me, saddle Rocinante, Sancho, and harness thy donkey and the palfrey of the queen, and let us bid farewell to the castellan and these gentlefolk and leave at once."

Sancho, who had been present for this entire exchange, shook his head and said:

"Oh, Señor, Señor, there's more wickedness in the village than they tell you about, begging the pardon of honorable ladies who let themselves be touched."

"What wickedness can there be in any village, or in all the cities of the world, that can discredit me, oh, lowborn knave?"

"If your grace gets angry," responded Sancho, "I'll be quiet and won't say what I'm obliged to say as a good squire, and what a good Christian is obliged to tell his master."

"Say whatever you wish," replied Don Quixote, "as long as your words are not intended to instill fear in me, for if you are afraid, then you are true to the person you are, and if I am not, then I am true to mine."

"That's not it, sinner that I am in the sight of God!" responded Sancho. "It's just that I'm absolutely certain and positive that this lady who says she's the queen of the great kingdom of Micomicón is no more a queen than my mother, because if she was who she says she is, she wouldn't go around hugging and kissing one of the men here at the inn, behind every door and every chance she gets."

Dorotea turned bright red at Sancho's words, because it was true that her husband, Don Fernando, had, on occasion, taken with his lips part of the prize his love had won, which Sancho had witnessed, and such boldness had seemed to him more appropriate to a courtesan than to the queen of so great a kingdom; she could not or would not say a word in response to Sancho, but allowed him to continue, and he did, saying:

"I'm saying this, Señor, because if after having traveled so many highways and byways, and gone through so many bad nights and worse days, the fruit of our labors is being plucked by someone taking his ease in this inn, then there's no reason for me to hurry and saddle Rocinante, and harness the donkey, and prepare the palfrey, because we'd be better off sitting still and doing nothing: let each whore tend to her spinning, and we'll eat."

Oh, Lord save me, but what a rage overcame Don Quixote when he heard his squire's discourteous words! It was so great, I say, that with precipitate voice and stumbling tongue and fire blazing from his eyes, he said:

"Oh, base, lowborn, wretched, rude, ignorant, foul-mouthed, ill-spoken, slanderous, insolent varlet! You have dared to speak such words in my presence and in the presence of these distinguished ladies, dared to fill your befuddled imagination with such vileness and effrontery? Leave my presence, unholy monster, repository of lies, stronghold of falsehoods, storehouse of deceits, inventor of iniquities, promulgator of insolence, enemy of the decorum owed to these royal persons. Go, do not appear before me under pain of my wrath!"

And saying this he scowled, puffed out his cheeks, looked all around him, and stamped his right foot very hard on the ground, all signs of the great anger raging in his heart. These words and furious gestures so frightened and terrified Sancho that he would have been overjoyed if the earth had opened up and swallowed him. And he did not know what to do except to turn and leave the enraged presence of his master. But the perceptive Dorotea, who by this time understood Don Quixote's madness very well, said, in order to pacify his rage:

"Do not be indignant, Señor Knight of the Sorrowful Face, at the foolish things your good squire has said, because it may be that he does not say them without reason, nor can we suspect that his good understanding and Christian conscience allow him to bear false witness against anyone, and so we must believe, beyond the shadow of a doubt, that since, as you have said, Señor Knight, all things in this castle happen and occur through enchantment, it might be, as I say, that Sancho saw, by diabolical means, what he says he saw, which so offends my good name."

"By Almighty God," said Don Quixote, "I swear that your highness has hit the mark, and that some evil illusion appeared before this sinner Sancho, making him see what it would have been impossible to see except by way of enchantment, for I know the goodness and innocence of this unfortunate man too well to think he would bear false witness against anyone."

"That is certainly the case," said Don Fernando, "and therefore, Señor Don Quixote, you ought to pardon him and receive him once more into the bosom of thy grace,[2] *sicut erat in principio*, before these visions affected his judgment."

Don Quixote responded that he would pardon his squire, and the priest went to find Sancho, who came in very humbly, fell to his knees, and begged his master for his hand; Don Quixote gave it to him, allowed him to kiss it, gave him his blessing, and said:

"Now you will know with certainty, Sancho my son, that what I have so often told you is true: everything in this castle occurs by means of enchantment."

"I do believe that," said Sancho, "except for what happened with the blanket, because that really happened by ordinary means."

"Do not believe it," responded Don Quixote, "because if that were true, I would have avenged you then, and even now; but I could not, then or now, and did not see anyone upon whom to wreak my vengeance for the affront to you."

Everyone wanted to know what had happened with the blanket, and the innkeeper told them, in full detail, about Sancho Panza flying

2. The phrase is based on the one used when the excommunicated return to the Church. The Latin that follows is equivalent to "as it was in the beginning."

through the air, which was cause for no small laughter, and Sancho would have been embarrassed to no less a degree if his master had not reassured him again that it had been enchantment; Sancho's foolishness, however, never was so great that he did not believe it was the pure and absolute truth, with no admixture of deception, that he had been tossed in a blanket by flesh-and-blood people, not dreamed or imagined phantoms, as his master believed and affirmed.

The illustrious company had already spent two days at the inn, and thinking it was time to leave, they devised a scheme that would spare Dorotea and Don Fernando the trouble of returning with Don Quixote to his village under the guise of restoring Queen Micomicona to the throne and would allow the priest and barber to take him back with them, as they desired, and treat his madness at home. Their scheme was to arrange with an ox driver who happened to be passing by that he would carry Don Quixote home in this manner: they prepared something like a cage with crisscrossed bars, large enough to hold Don Quixote comfortably, and then Don Fernando and his companions, the servants of Don Luis, the officers of the Brotherhood, and the innkeeper, all of them under the direction and guidance of the priest, covered their faces and disguised themselves in a variety of ways so that Don Quixote would not think they were the people he had seen in the castle.

When they had done this, they silently entered the room where Don Quixote lay sleeping, resting after his recent conflicts. They approached as he slept soundly, suspecting nothing, and seized him firmly and tied his hands and feet tightly, so that when he awoke with a start he could not move or do anything but feel astonishment and wonder at the strange visages he saw before him; he immediately found an explanation in what his delusional imagination continually represented to him, believing that all those figures were phantoms from the enchanted castle and that he, beyond any doubt, had also been enchanted, for he could not move or defend himself, which was exactly what the priest, who had devised the plan, thought would happen. Only Sancho, of all those present, was in his right mind and not pretending to be someone else, and although he was not far from being afflicted by the same disease his master had, he still could recognize who those masked figures were, but he did not dare open his mouth until he saw how far the assault on Don Quixote, and his capture, would go; his master did not say a word either as he waited to see the outcome of this misfortune, and it was that the cage was brought in, Don Quixote was locked inside, and the bars were nailed in so firmly that they could not be quickly broken.

Then they lifted him to their shoulders, and as they left the room a fearful voice was heard, a voice as terrifying as the barber could make it—not the one with the packsaddle, the other one—and it said:

"O Knight of the Sorrowful Face! Grieve not at thy imprisonment, for it is needful in order to more quickly conclude the adventure to which thy great courage hath brought thee. And this will come to an end when the wrathful Manchegan lion shall be joined with the white Tobosan dove, and they have bowed their proud necks to the soft matrimonial yoke, and from their extraordinary union there shall issue forth into the light of the celestial orb brave pups that will imitate the rampant claws of their valiant father. And this shall happen before the pursuer of the fugitive nymph shall twice in his swift and natural course visit the shining images.[3] And thou, O most noble and obedient squire who e'er had a sword in his belt, whiskers on his face, or an odor in his nose! Be not dismayed or saddened at seeing with thine own eyes the flower of chivalry carried away in this fashion; for soon, if it so pleaseth the Maker of the world, thou shalt see thyself so high and exalted, thou wilt not know thyself, nor shall the promises thy good master hath made to thee be broken. And I bring thee assurances from the wise Mentironiana[4] that thy wages wilt be paid thee, as thou shalt soon see; follow the steps of thy valiant and enchanted knight, for it is fitting that thou goest to a place where you both shall be. Now, since it is not licit for me to say more, may God be with thee, and I shall return to the place that I know well."

And as he finished his prophecy, the barber raised his voice to so high a pitch and then lowered it to so quiet a whisper that even those who knew of the deceit almost believed the truth of what they were hearing.

Don Quixote was consoled by the prophecy he had heard, because he quickly grasped its entire meaning and saw that he was being promised a union in holy and sanctified matrimony with his beloved Dulcinea of Toboso, whose happy womb would give birth to pups, which is to say his sons, to the everlasting glory of La Mancha, and believing this firmly and completely, he raised his voice, heaved a great sigh, and said:

"O thou, whoever thou mayest be, who hath foretold such bliss for me! I implore thee that thou asketh the wise enchanter who controlleth

---

3. The allusion is to Apollo pursuing Daphne, as well as to the sun crossing the sky and passing various constellations.

4. The name is based on the verb *mentir*, "to lie."

my affairs not to allow me to perish in this prison where I am now being carried, until the joyous and incomparable promises made to me here hath been fulfilled; if these be true, I shall consider the sorrows of this my prison as glory, and these chains that bindeth me as ease and comfort, and this pallet where they hath lain me as not a hard field of battle but a soft and blissful nuptial bed. As for the consolation of Sancho Panza, my squire, I trusteth in his kindness and goodness and knoweth he will not leave me in good luck or bad; because if it should come to pass, either through his bad fortune or mine, that I canst not give him the ínsula, or other equivalent reward, which I hath promised him, at least his wages shall not be lost; for in my will, which hast already been made, I hath stated what he shall be given, according not to his many good services but to my limited means."

Sancho Panza bowed to him with deep respect and kissed both his hands because he could not kiss only one, since they were tied together.

Then the phantoms lifted the cage to their shoulders and placed it on the oxcart.

CHAPTER XLVII

Regarding the strange manner in which Don Quixote of La Mancha was enchanted, and other notable events

When Don Quixote saw himself caged in that manner and placed on a cart, he said:

"I have read many extremely serious histories of knights errant, but never have I read, or seen, or heard of enchanted knights being carried in this fashion and at the pace promised by these sluggish and dilatory animals; the knights are always transported through the air with remarkable speed, enclosed in a dark and doleful cloud, or riding a chariot of fire, or mounted on a hippogryph or some other similar beast; but being carried now on an oxcart, by God that leaves me in a state of confusion![1] Perhaps in these our modern times, however, chivalry and enchant-

1. It was a mark of great dishonor for a knight to ride in so humble a vehicle; in medieval tales, for example, Lancelot incurred great shame by riding in an oxcart.

ments follow a path different from the one they followed in ancient times. It also might be that since I am a new knight in the world, the first to resuscitate the now forgotten practice of errant chivalry, new kinds of enchantments and new ways of transporting the enchanted have also been devised. What do you think, Sancho my son?"

"I don't know what I think," responded Sancho, "since I'm not as well-read as your grace in errant writings, but even so, I'd say and even swear that these phantoms wandering around here are not entirely Catholic."[2]

"Catholic? By my sainted father!" responded Don Quixote. "How can they be Catholic if they are all demons who have taken on fantastic bodies in order to come here and do this and bring me to this state? And if you wish to see the truth of this, touch them and feel them and you will see that they have no body but are composed of air, and are nothing more than appearance."

"By God, Señor," replied Sancho, "I have touched them, and this devil who's so busy here is stocky and well-fleshed, and has another trait that's very different from what I've heard about demons, because people say all demons stink of sulfur and brimstone and other bad odors, but this one smells of ambergris from half a league away."

Sancho said this about Don Fernando, who, being so noble, must have smelled just as Sancho said.

"Do not be surprised at this, Sancho my friend," responded Don Quixote, "because I can tell you that devils know a great deal, and although they bring odors with them, they themselves do not smell at all because they are spirits, and if they do smell, it cannot be of pleasant things, but only of things that are foul and putrid. The reason is that since they, wherever they may be, carry hell with them and cannot find any kind of relief from their torments, and a pleasant odor is something that brings joy and pleasure, it is not possible for them to have an agreeable smell. And so, if it seems to you that the demon you have mentioned smells of ambergris, either you are mistaken or he wants to deceive you by making you think he is not a demon."

All of these words passed between master and servant; fearing that Sancho would see through their deception, which he had already been very close to doing, Don Fernando and Cardenio decided to make their departure as brief as possible; they called the innkeeper aside and told

2. "Catholic" is used by Sancho metaphorically to mean "trustworthy" or "legitimate," much as we would use "kosher" today; Don Quixote responds to the literal meaning of the word.

him to saddle Rocinante and harness Sancho's donkey, which he did very quickly.

Meanwhile, the priest had reached an arrangement with the officers: they would accompany him to his village, and he would pay them a daily fee. Cardenio hung Don Quixote's shield on one side of Rocinante's saddlebow and the basin on the other; he signaled to Sancho to mount his donkey and lead Rocinante by the reins, and on each side of the cart he placed two officers with their flintlocks. But before the cart began to move, the innkeeper's wife, her daughter, and Maritornes came out to take their leave of Don Quixote, pretending to weep with sorrow at his misfortune, to which Don Quixote said:

"Weepeth not, good ladies, for all such adversities are innate to those who profess what I profess; and if these calamities didst not befall me, I wouldst not deem myself a famous knight errant, for such things ne'er happen to knights of little fame and renown, since there is no one in the world who remembereth them. But they do befall the valiant, for many princes and other knights envieth their virtue and courage, attempting to destroy virtuous knights by wicked means. Despite this, virtue is so powerful that through its own efforts, despite all the necromancy e'er invented by Zoroaster, it shall emerge victorious from every trial and shine its light on the world as the sun shineth down from heaven. Forgive me, beauteous ladies, if I hath offended you inadvertently, for willingly and knowingly I hath never done so to anyone; implore God that He taketh me from this prison where an evil enchanter hath placed me, and if I am freed, I ne'er shall forget the kindnesses you hath shown me in this castle but shall be grateful for them and recognize and repay them according to their merits."

While the ladies of the castle conversed with Don Quixote, the priest and barber took their leave of Don Fernando and his companions, and the captain and his brother, and all the contented ladies, especially Dorotea and Luscinda. Everyone embraced and agreed to send one another their news, and Don Fernando told the priest where he should write to inform him of what happened to Don Quixote, assuring him that nothing would make him happier than to know the outcome; he, in turn, would tell the priest everything that might be to his liking, from his marriage and Zoraida's baptism to Don Luis's fate and Luscinda's return home. The priest promised to do as he requested in the most punctual way. They embraced again, and again they exchanged promises.

The innkeeper came up to the priest and gave him some papers, saying that he had discovered them in the lining of the case that contained the novel of *The Man Who Was Recklessly Curious*, and since the owner had not come back for them, the priest could take them all, because he did not know how to read and did not want them. The priest thanked the innkeeper, and opening the papers, he saw that at the beginning of the manuscript it said *The Novel of Rinconete and Cortadillo*,[3] which led him to assume it was another novel and probably a good one, since *The Man Who Was Recklessly Curious* had also been good, and they might very well be by the same author, and so he kept it, intending to read it as soon as he was able.

The priest mounted his mule, as did his friend the barber, both of them wearing masks so they would not be recognized by Don Quixote, and they began to ride behind the cart. They rode in this order: first came the cart, led by its owner; at each side rode the officers, as we have said, holding their flintlocks; behind the cart came Sancho Panza on his donkey, leading Rocinante by the reins. Bringing up the rear were the priest and the barber on their large mules, their faces covered, as has been mentioned, and riding with a solemn and sober air, their pace no faster than that allowed by the very slow gait of the oxen. Don Quixote sat in the cage, his hands tied, his legs extended, his back leaning against the bars, and with so much silence and patience that he seemed not a man of flesh and blood, but a statue made of stone.

And so, slowly and silently, they rode some two leagues until they reached a valley that the ox driver thought would be a good place to rest and graze the oxen; he communicated this to the priest, but the barber said they should ride on a little farther because he knew that beyond a nearby rise was a valley that had more abundant and better grass than the one where the driver wanted to stop. They followed the barber's advice and continued their journey.

Just then the priest turned his head and saw that six or seven well-dressed and well-mounted men were riding behind them, and they soon overtook them, since they were traveling not at the slow and leisurely pace of the oxen, but like men who were riding on canons' mules and wanted to have their siestas at the inn that could be seen less than a league away. The diligent overtook the slothful, and courteous greetings were exchanged, and one of the newcomers, who was, in fact, a canon from Toledo and the master of those who accompanied him, seeing the

---

3. This is the title of one of the novellas in Cervantes's collection, *Novelas ejemplares* (*Exemplary Novels*), which was published in 1613, eight years after the first part of *Don Quixote*.

orderly procession of the cart, the officers, Sancho, Rocinante, the priest, the barber, and particularly Don Quixote imprisoned in his cage, could not help asking why they were carrying the man in that fashion, although he already knew, seeing the insignia of the officers, that he must be some highway robber or another kind of criminal whose punishment was the responsibility of the Holy Brotherhood. One of the officers, to whom he had directed the question, responded:

"Señor, why this gentleman is being carried this way is something he should say, because we don't know."

Don Quixote heard this exchange and said:

"By chance, Señores, are your graces well-versed and expert in matters pertaining to knight errantry? Because if you are, I shall recount to you my misfortunes, and if not, there is no reason for me to weary myself in the telling."

By this time the priest and the barber, seeing that the travelers were talking to Don Quixote of La Mancha, rode up so that they could respond in a way that would keep their deception from being revealed.

The canon, responding to what Don Quixote had said, replied:

"The truth is, brother, I know more about books of chivalry than I do about Villalpando's *Súmulas*.[4] Therefore, if that is your only concern, you can tell me anything you please."

"May it please God," replied Don Quixote. "I should like you to know, Señor, that I am in this cage because I have been enchanted through the envy and fraud of evil enchanters, for virtue is persecuted by evildoers more than it is loved by good people. I am a knight errant, not one of those whose names were never remembered by Fame or eternalized in her memory, but one who in spite of envy herself, and in defiance of all the magi of Persia, brahmans of India, and gymnosophists of Ethiopia, will have his name inscribed in the temple of immortality so that it may serve as an example and standard to future times, when knights errant can see the path they must follow if they wish to reach the honorable zenith and pinnacle of the practice of arms."

"Señor Don Quixote of La Mancha is telling the truth," said the priest. "He is enchanted, borne in this cart not because of his faults and sins, but on account of the evil intentions of those who are angered by virtue and enraged by valor. This, Señor, is the Knight of the Sorrowful Face, about whom you may have heard, whose valiant deeds and noble

4. A treatise on logic, written by Gaspar Cardillo de Villalpando and used as a text at the University of Alcalá.

feats will be inscribed on everlasting bronze and eternal marble no matter how Envy attempts to hide them or Malice to obscure them."

When the canon heard both the prisoner and the free man speaking in this fashion, he almost crossed himself in astonishment, unable to imagine what had happened, and everyone with him felt the same astonishment. At this point Sancho Panza, who had approached in order to hear the conversation, wanted to put the finishing touches on everything and said:

"Now, Señores, you may love me or hate me for what I say, but the truth of the matter is that my master, Don Quixote, is as enchanted as my mother; he's in his right mind, he eats and drinks and does what he has to do like other men, like he did yesterday before they put him in the cage. If this is true, how can you make me believe he's enchanted? I've heard lots of people say that when you're enchanted you don't eat, or sleep, or talk, and my master, if he isn't held back, will talk more than thirty lawyers."

And turning to look at the priest, he continued, saying:

"Ah Señor Priest, Señor Priest! Did your grace think I didn't know you? Can you think I don't understand and guess where these new enchantments are heading? Well, you should know that I recognize you no matter how you cover your face and understand you no matter how you hide your lies. In short, where envy rules, virtue cannot survive, and generosity cannot live with miserliness. Devil confound it, if it wasn't for your reverence, my master would be married by now to Princess Micomicona and I'd be a count at least, because I expected nothing less from the goodness of my master, the Knight of the Sorrowful Face, and from the greatness of my services! But now I see that what they say is true: the wheel of fortune turns faster than a water wheel, and those who only yesterday were on top of the world today are down on the ground. I grieve for my children and my wife, for when they could and should have expected to see their father come through the door as a governor or viceroy of some ínsula or kingdom, they'll see him come in a stableboy. I've said all this, Señor Priest, just to urge your fathership to take into account the bad treatment my master is receiving, and to be careful that God doesn't demand an accounting from you in the next life for my master's imprisonment, and make you responsible for all the boons and mercies my master, Don Quixote, can't do while he's in the cage."

"I can't believe it!" said the barber. "You, too, Sancho? In the same guild as your master? By God, you've taken in so much of his lunacy and knighthood, it looks like you'll be keeping him company in the cage and be as enchanted as he is! It was an unlucky day for you when he made you pregnant with his promises, an evil hour when you got that ínsula you want so much into your head."

"I'm not pregnant by anybody," responded Sancho, "and I'm not a man who'd let himself get pregnant even by the king, and though I'm poor I'm an Old Christian, and I don't owe anything to anybody, and if I want ínsulas, other people want things that are worse; each man is the child of his actions, and because I'm a man I could be a pope, let alone the governor of an ínsula, especially since my master could win so many he might not have enough people to give them to. Your grace should be careful what you say, Señor Barber, because there's more to life than trimming beards, and there's some difference between one Pedro and the other. I say this because we all know one another, and you can't throw crooked dice with me. As for the enchantment of my master, only God knows the truth, and let's leave it at that, because things get worse when you stir them."

The barber did not want to answer Sancho in case his simplicities uncovered what he and the priest had tried so hard to conceal; because of this same fear, the priest asked the canon to ride ahead with him, and he would explain the mystery of the caged man and tell him other things that he would find amusing. The canon did so, and moving ahead with his servants and with the priest, he listened attentively to everything the priest wished to tell him regarding the condition, life, madness, and customs of Don Quixote, which was a brief account of the origin and cause of his delusions and the series of events that had brought him to that cage, and the scheme they had devised to bring him home to see if they somehow could find a cure for his madness. The canon and his servants were astonished a second time when they heard Don Quixote's remarkable story, and when it was ended, the canon said:

"Truly, Señor Priest, it seems to me that the books called novels of chivalry are prejudicial to the nation, and though I, moved by a false and idle taste, have read the beginning of almost every one that has ever been published, I have never been able to read any from beginning to end, because it seems to me they are all essentially the same, and one is no different from another. In my opinion, this kind of writing and composition belongs to the genre called Milesian tales,[5] which are foolish

---

5. A kind of sensual, supposedly decadent writing associated with the ancient Ionian city of Miletus.

stories meant only to delight and not to teach, unlike moral tales, which delight and teach at the same time. Although the principal aim of these books is to delight, I do not know how they can, being so full of so many excessively foolish elements; for delight conceived in the soul must arise from the beauty and harmony it sees or contemplates in the things that the eyes or the imagination place before it, and nothing that possesses ugliness and disorder can please us. What beauty, what proportion between parts and the whole, or the whole and its parts, can there be in a book or tale in which a boy of sixteen, with one thrust of his sword, fells a giant as big as a tower and splits him in two as if he were marzipan, and, when a battle is depicted, after saying that there are more than a million combatants on the side of the enemy, if the hero of the book fights them, whether we like it or not, of necessity we must believe that this knight achieves victory only through the valor of his mighty arm? What shall we say of the ease with which a hereditary queen or empress falls into the arms of an errant and unknown knight? What mind, unless it is completely barbaric or untutored, can be pleased to read that a great tower filled with knights sails the seas like a ship before a favorable wind, and is in Lombardy at nightfall, and by dawn the next day it is in the lands of Prester John of the Indies, or in others never described by Ptolemy or seen by Marco Polo? If one were to reply that those who compose these books write them as fictions, and therefore are not obliged to consider the fine points of truth, I should respond that the more truthful the fiction, the better it is, and the more probable and possible, the more pleasing. Fictional tales must engage the minds of those who read them, and by restraining exaggeration and moderating impossibility, they enthrall the spirit and thereby astonish, captivate, delight, and entertain, allowing wonder and joy to move together at the same pace; none of these things can be accomplished by fleeing verisimilitude and mimesis, which together constitute perfection in writing. I have seen no book of chivalry that creates a complete tale, a body with all its members intact, so that the middle corresponds to the beginning, and the end to the beginning and the middle; instead, they are composed with so many members that the intention seems to be to shape a chimera or a monster rather than to create a well-proportioned figure. Furthermore, the style is fatiguing, the action incredible, the love lascivious, the courtesies clumsy, the battles long, the language foolish, the journeys nonsensical, and, finally, since they are totally lacking in intelligent artifice, they deserve to be banished, like unproductive people, from Christian nations."

The priest listened with great attention, and thought the canon a man of fine understanding who was correct in everything he said, and so he told him that since he held the same opinion, and felt a good deal of animosity toward books of chivalry, he had burned all of Don Quixote's, of which there were many. He recounted the examination he had made of them, those he had condemned to the flames and those he had saved, and at this the canon laughed more than a little and said that despite all the bad things he had said about those books, he found one good thing in them, which was the opportunity for display that they offered a good mind, providing a broad and spacious field where one's pen could write unhindered, describing shipwrecks, storms, skirmishes, and battles; depicting a valiant captain with all the traits needed to be one, showing him to be a wise predictor of his enemy's clever moves, an eloquent orator in persuading or dissuading his soldiers, mature in counsel, unhesitating in resolve, as valiant in waiting as in the attack; portraying a tragic, lamentable incident or a joyful, unexpected event, a most beautiful lady who is virtuous, discreet, and modest or a Christian knight who is courageous and kind, an insolent barbarian braggart or a prince who is courteous, valiant, and astute; and representing the goodness and loyalty of vassals and the greatness and generosity of lords. The writer can show his conversance with astrology, his excellence as a cosmographer, his knowledge of music, his intelligence in matters of state, and perhaps he will have the opportunity to demonstrate his talents as a necromancer, if he should wish to. He can display the guile of Ulysses, the piety of Aeneas, the valor of Achilles, the misfortunes of Hector, the treachery of Sinon,[6] the friendship of Euryalus,[7] the liberality of Alexander, the valor of Caesar, the clemency and truthfulness of Trajan, the fidelity of Zopyrus,[8] the prudence of Cato, in short, all of those characteristics that make a noble man perfect, sometimes placing them all in one individual, sometimes dividing them among several.

"And if this is done in a pleasing style and with ingenious invention,

6. Sinon persuaded the Trojans to admit the wooden horse, filled with Greek soldiers, into their city, thereby causing the defeat of Troy. According to some accounts, he was a Greek who allowed himself to be taken prisoner by the Trojans; according to others, he was a Trojan in the service of the Greeks.

7. Euryalus was well-known for his friendship with Nisus. They accompanied Aeneas to Italy following the Trojan War and were killed in battle.

8. Zopyrus proved his loyalty to Darius during a revolt by the Babylonians: he mutilated himself severely, then went over to the Babylonian side, claiming to be a victim of Persian cruelty; he gained their confidence, was made leader of their armies, and eventually betrayed Babylon to Darius.

and is drawn as close as possible to the truth, it no doubt will weave a cloth composed of many different and beautiful threads, and when it is finished, it will display such perfection and beauty that it will achieve the greatest goal of any writing, which, as I have said, is to teach and delight at the same time. Because the free writing style of these books allows the author to show his skills as an epic, lyric, tragic, and comic writer, with all the characteristics contained in the sweet and pleasing sciences of poetry and rhetoric; for the epic can be written in prose as well as in verse."

CHAPTER XLVIII

In which the canon continues to discuss books of chivalry, as well as other matters worthy of his ingenuity

"It is just as your grace says, Señor Canon," said the priest, "and for this reason the books of this kind that have been written so far are most worthy of rebuke, their authors caring nothing for solid discourse or the art and rules that could have guided them and made them as famous in prose as the two princes of Greek and Latin poetry are in verse."

"I, at least," replied the canon, "have felt a certain temptation to write a book of chivalry in which I followed all the points I have mentioned, and, to tell the truth, I have already written more than a hundred pages. In order to learn if they correspond to my estimation of them, I have given them to intelligent, learned men who are very fond of this kind of reading, and to other men who are ignorant and care only for the pleasure of hearing nonsense, and from all of them I have received a most agreeable approval; even so, I have not pursued the matter further, for it not only seemed unsuited to my profession, but I also saw that the number of simpleminded men is greater than that of the prudent, and though it is better to be praised by a few wise men and mocked by many fools, I do not wish to subject myself to the confused judgment of the presumptuous mob, who tend to be the ones who read these books. But what most influenced me to put the task of finishing it out of my mind was an argument I had with myself, based on the plays that are produced now, and the argument said:

'If all, or almost all, the plays that are popular now, imaginative works as well as historical ones, are known to be nonsense and without rhyme or reason, and despite this the mob hears them with pleasure and thinks of them and approves of them as good, when they are very far from being so, and the authors who compose them and the actors who perform them say they must be like this because that is just how the mob wants them, and no other way; the plays that have a design and follow the story as art demands appeal to a handful of discerning persons who understand them, while everyone else is incapable of comprehending their artistry; and since, as far as the authors and actors are concerned, it is better to earn a living with the crowd than a reputation with the elite, this is what would happen to my book after I had singed my eyebrows trying to keep the precepts I have mentioned and had become the tailor who wasn't paid.'[1]

And although I have attempted at times to persuade the actors that they are mistaken in thinking as they do and that they would attract a larger audience and gain more renown with artful plays than with non-sensical ones, they are so bound and committed to their opinion that there is no argument or evidence to make them change their minds. I remember that one day I said to one of these stubborn men:

'Tell me, do you remember a few years ago when three tragedies were produced in Spain that were composed by a famous poet from these kingdoms,[2] and they delighted and amazed and enthralled all who heard them, the simple as well as the wise, the mob as well as the elite, and those three plays alone earned more money than thirty of the best plays that have been put on since then?'

'No doubt,' said the author I am telling you about, 'your grace is referring to *Isabela*, *Filis*, and *Alejandra*.'

'Precisely,' I replied, 'and consider whether they followed the precepts of the art, and if following them prevented them from being what they were and pleasing everyone. Which means the fault lies not with the mob, who demands nonsense, but with those who do not know how to produce anything else. For there was no foolishness in *Ingratitude*

---

1. "The tailor who wasn't paid" is the first part of a proverb (the second part usually is not cited) that roughly translates as "The tailor wasn't paid, and had to supply his own braid," meaning that one can lose twice: by not being paid a fee for a service and by not being reimbursed for the expenses incurred in performing the service.

2. The reference is to Lupercio Leonardo de Argensola, who tended to write in the classical style of the early Renaissance (clearly favored by Cervantes) in contrast to the more effusive complexities of the Baroque that were popular in the theater of the time.

Avenged,[3] Numantia[4] had none, none was found in *The Merchant Lover*,[5] or in *The Kindly Enemy*,[6] or in some others composed by certain talented poets who gained fame and renown for themselves and profit for those who produced them.'

I said some other things that I think left him confused, but not persuaded or convinced enough to change his erroneous opinion."

"Your grace has touched on a subject, Señor Canon," said the priest, "that has awakened my long-standing rancor toward the plays that are popular now, one that is equal to my dislike of novels of chivalry; for drama, according to Marcus Tullius Cicero, should be a mirror of human life, an example of customs, and an image of truth, but those that are produced these days are mirrors of nonsense, examples of foolishness, and images of lewdness. For what greater nonsense can there be than for a child to appear in the first scene of the first act in his swaddling clothes, and in the second scene to be a full-grown man with a beard? Or to present to us a valiant old man and a cowardly youth, an eloquent lackey, a wise page, a king who is a laborer, and a princess who is a scullery maid? And what shall I say about their observance of the time in which the actions they represent take place? I have seen plays in which the first act began in Europe, the second in Asia, and the third concluded in Africa, and if there had been four acts, the fourth would have ended in America, making it a play that took place in all four corners of the globe.

And if mimesis is the principal quality a play should have, how can it possibly satisfy anyone of even average intelligence if the action is supposed to occur in the days of King Pepin and Charlemagne, but the central character is the Emperor Heraclius, who entered Jerusalem bearing the cross, and conquered the Holy Sepulchre, like Godfrey of Bouillon, when there is an infinite number of years between one and the other; if the play is based on fictions, historical truths are introduced and parts of others are combined, though they occurred to different people and at different times, and this is done not with any effort at verisimilitude, but with glaring errors that are completely unforgiveable. The worst thing is the ignorant folk who say that this is perfect, and that wanting anything else is pretentious and whimsical. Well then, what shall we say about sa-

---

3. *La ingratitud vengada*, by Lope de Vega.

4. *Numancia*, by Miguel de Cervantes.

5. *El mercader amante*, by Gaspar de Aguilar.

6. *La enemiga favorable*, by Francisco Agustín Tárrega.

cred plays? What a number of false miracles and apocryphal, poorly understood stories they invent, attributing the miracles of one saint to another! And even in their secular plays they dare perform miracles, with no other concern or consideration than thinking that some miracle or stage effect, as they call it, would be a good idea at that point so the ignorant will marvel and come to the theater; all of this is prejudicial to the truth, and damaging to history, and even a discredit to the intelligence of Spaniards, because foreigners, who are punctilious in obeying the rules of drama, think of us as ignorant barbarians, seeing the absurdities and idiocies in the plays we produce.[7]

It would not be a sufficient excuse to say that the principal intention of well-ordered states in allowing the public performance of plays is to entertain the common folk with some honest recreation and distract them from the harmful humors born in idleness, and since this can be achieved with any play, good or bad, there is no reason to impose laws or to oblige those who write and act in them to make plays as they ought to be because, as I have said, any of them can accomplish what they are intended to accomplish. To which I would respond that this purpose would be achieved with unquestionably greater success by good plays rather than bad; for having heard an artful and well-constructed play, the audience would come out amused by the comic portions, instructed by the serious, marveling at the action, enlightened by the arguments, forewarned by the falsehoods, made wiser by the examples, angered at vice, enamored of virtue: a good play can awaken all these responses in the spirit of its audience, no matter how slow and unsophisticated it may be, and it is absolutely impossible for a play with all these qualities not to please, entertain, satisfy, and delight much more than one that lacks them, as do those ordinarily performed these days. The poets who compose them are not responsible for this, because there are some who know very well the errors they are committing, and know extremely well what they ought to do, but since plays have become salable merchandise, they say, and in this they speak the truth, the companies will not buy them if they are not of a certain type, and so the poet attempts to accommodate the requests of the companies that pay him for his work. The truth of this can be seen in the infinite number of plays composed by one of the

---

7. At the time Cervantes wrote this, the classical rules of drama were not followed anywhere in Europe, at least not in Italy, France, or England. Martín de Riquer wonders if Cervantes might actually have been thinking of prescriptive treatises that were widely published but adhered to by no playwright of significance.

most felicitous minds in these kingdoms, which display so much grace and so much charm, such elegant verses and such fine language, such grave thoughts and so eloquent and lofty a style, that his fame is known throughout the world;[8] because these works attempt to accommodate the taste of the theater companies, not all of them have reached, though some have, the necessary degree of perfection. Other poets compose their works so carelessly that after they have been performed, the actors have to flee and go into hiding, fearful that they will be punished, as they often have been, for putting on pieces prejudicial to certain kings and offensive to certain families.

All these difficulties, and many others I will not mention, would cease if there were at court an intelligent and judicious person who would examine each play before it was performed, not only those produced in the capital, but also those put on anywhere in Spain, and without his approval, stamp, and signature, no magistrate anywhere would permit a play to be performed; in this fashion, the players would be careful to send their plays to court, and then they could perform them in safety, and those who write them would consider what they were doing with more thought and care, knowing that their works would have to undergo a rigorous examination by one who understands the art; in this way good plays would be written and their purposes achieved: the entertainment of the common people, the good opinion of creative minds in Spain, the legitimate interests and safety of the actors, and the avoidance of the need to punish them.

And if another official, or this same person, were charged with examining the new books of chivalry that are written, no doubt some with the perfections your grace has mentioned would be published, thereby enriching our language with the pleasing and precious treasure of eloquence, and allowing some of the old books to be obscured by the light of the new ones that would provide virtuous entertainment, not only to the idle but to those who are most occupied, for the bow cannot always be pulled taut, and it is not in the nature of human frailty to endure without honest recreation."

The canon and the priest had reached this point in their conversation when the barber rode up to them and said to the priest:

---

8. The description is of Lope de Vega, who wrote hundreds of *comedias*; the exact number is not known, but a legendary two thousand plays have been attributed to him (not to mention numerous works in other genres). He and Cervantes, his senior by some fifteen years, had a highly competitive relationship. Lope apparently took great offense at this passage.

"This, Señor Licentiate, is the place I mentioned, where we can rest and the oxen can find abundant fresh grass."

"I agree," responded the priest.

He told his companion what they planned to do, and the canon decided to remain with them, for he was drawn by the sight of the beautiful valley that lay before them. In order to enjoy the valley and the conversation of the priest, for whom he had developed a liking, and to learn in more detail the deeds of Don Quixote, the canon ordered some of his servants to go to the inn that was not far away and bring back whatever they could find to eat, enough for everyone, because he had resolved to rest there that afternoon; to which one of his servants responded that the pack mule, which probably had reached the inn already, carried enough provisions so that they would have no need for anything from the inn except barley for the animals.

"If that is true," said the canon, "take all the animals there and bring back the pack mule."

In the meantime, Sancho saw that he could speak to his master without the continual presence of the priest and barber, whom he regarded with suspicion, and he rode up to the cage that carried his master and said to him:

"Señor, I want to relieve my conscience and tell you what is going on in this matter of your enchantment; the fact is that these two riding here with their faces covered are the priest and barber from our village, and I believe they've come up with this way of transporting you out of sheer envy, because your deeds are more famous than theirs. If what I say is true, it means that you're not enchanted but deceived and misled. To prove it, I want to ask you one thing, and if you answer in the way I think you'll answer, you'll put your finger right on the deception and see that you haven't been enchanted but had your wits turned around."

"Ask what you wish, Sancho my son," responded Don Quixote, "for I shall answer and respond as much as you desire. As for your saying that those men riding here with us are the priest and barber, it well may be that they seem to be our compatriots and friends, but you must not believe for a moment that they really and truly are. What you ought to believe and understand is that if they resemble them, as you say, it must be because those who have enchanted me have taken on their appearance and likeness, because it is easy for enchanters to assume whatever semblance they choose; they must have assumed that of our friends in order to give you a reason to think what you think and enter into a labyrinth of imaginings from which not even the cord of Theseus will help you to escape. And they also must have done this so that I would waver in my understanding and not be able to determine the origin of this calamity; if, on one hand, you tell me that I am accompanied by the barber and priest of our village, and if, on the other, I find myself in a cage and know that nothing human but only a supernatural power would be sufficient to put me in a cage, what can I say or think except that the manner of my enchantment exceeds anything I have read in all the histories that deal with knights errant who have been enchanted? Therefore you can rest easy and be assured regarding their being who you say they are, because if they really are, then I am a Turk. As for wanting to ask me something, speak, and I shall respond even if you ask me questions from now until tomorrow."

"By the Blessed Virgin!" responded Sancho with a great shout. "Is it possible that your grace is so thickheaded and so short on brains that you cannot see that what I'm telling you is the absolute truth, and that malice has more to do with your imprisonment and misfortune than enchantment? Even so, I'll prove to you you're not enchanted. Just tell me, when God frees you from this torment and you find yourself in the arms of the Señora Dulcinea when you least expect it—"

"Enough conjuring," said Don Quixote, "and just ask what you wish; I have already told you I shall answer everything completely."

"That's all I ask," replied Sancho, "and what I want to know is for you to tell me, without adding or taking away anything, but truthfully, which is what we expect of all those who profess arms, as your grace professes them, and who call themselves knights errant—"

"I say that I shall not lie in anything," responded Don Quixote. "Ask your question, for the truth is, Sancho, I am growing weary of all your vows and supplications and preambles."

"I say that I'm sure of my master's goodness and truthfulness, and so I'll ask something that goes right to the heart of the matter; speaking with respect, since your grace has been locked in the cage, enchanted, in your opinion, have you had the desire and will to pass what they call major and minor waters?"

"I do not understand what you mean by *passing waters*, Sancho; speak more clearly if you want me to respond in a straightforward way."

"Is it possible that your grace doesn't understand what it means to pass minor or major waters? Even schoolboys know that. Well, what I mean is, have you had the desire to do the thing nobody else can do for you?"

"Ah, now I understand you, Sancho! Yes, I have, quite often, and even do now. Save me from this danger, for not everything is absolutely pristine!"

CHAPTER XLIX

Which recounts the clever conversation that Sancho Panza had with his master, Don Quixote

"Ah!" said Sancho. "I've got you there: that's what I wanted to know with all my heart and soul. Come, Señor, can you deny what people usually say when a person's not feeling well: 'I don't know what's wrong with so-and-so, he doesn't eat, or drink, or sleep, or answer sensibly when you talk to him, he must be enchanted.' From that you can conclude that people who don't eat, or drink, or sleep, or do the natural things I've mentioned are enchanted, but not people who want to do what your grace wants to do, and who drink when someone hands them water, and eat when there's food to be had, and answer every question that's asked of them."

"What you say is true, Sancho," responded Don Quixote, "but I have already told you that there are many forms of enchantment, and it well may be that in the course of time one sort has replaced another, and perhaps in the kinds they use nowadays those who have been enchanted do everything I do, although they did not do so before. In short, one must not argue with or draw conclusions from the custom of the day. I know and believe that I am enchanted, and that suffices to make my conscience easy, for it would weigh heavily on me if I thought I was not enchanted, and in sloth and cowardice had allowed myself to be imprisoned in this cage, depriving the helpless and weak of the assistance I could provide, for at this very moment there must be many in urgent need of my succor and protection."

"Even so," replied Sancho, "for your greater ease and satisfaction, it would be a good idea for your grace to try to get out of this prison, and I promise I'll do everything I can to help get your grace out and back on your good Rocinante, who also seems enchanted, he's so melancholy and sad; and when we've done that, we'll try our luck again and search for more adventures, and if things don't go well for us, we'll still have time to get back to the cage, where I promise, like a good and loyal squire, to lock myself up along with your grace in case your grace is so unfortunate, or I'm so simple, that we can't manage to do what I've said."

"I am happy to do as you say, Sancho my brother," replied Don Quixote, "and when you have the opportunity to effect my liberty, I shall obey you completely in everything, but you will see, Sancho, how mistaken you are in your understanding of my misfortune."

This conversation engaged the knight errant and his erring squire until they reached the spot where the priest, the canon, and the barber, who had already dismounted, were waiting for them. The driver unyoked the oxen from the cart and allowed them to roam free in that green and peaceful place whose freshness was so inviting, if not to persons as enchanted as Don Quixote, then to those as capable and clever as his squire, who pleaded with the priest to allow his master out of the cage for a while, because if they did not let him out, his prison would not be as clean as decency demanded for a knight like his master. The priest understood him and said he would gladly do as he asked if he were not afraid that as soon as his master found himself free, he would do one of those mad things so typical of him, and go away, and never be seen by anyone again.

"I'll guarantee that he won't run away," responded Sancho.

"And I'll guarantee that and more," said the canon, "if he gives me his word as a gentleman and a knight that he will not go away from us until we agree he can."

"I do give it," responded Don Quixote, who was listening to everything, "especially since one who is enchanted, as I am, is not free to do with his person what he might wish, because whoever enchanted him can make him stand stock still and not move from a spot for three centuries, and if he were to flee, he would be flown back through the air."

Since this was true, they could certainly release him, especially because it would be to everyone's benefit, and he protested that if they did not release him, the smell would surely trouble them unless they moved a good distance away.

The canon took one of Don Quixote's hands, although both were tied together, and on the basis of the knight's promise and word, they let him out of the cage, and he was infinitely and immensely happy to find himself free, and the first thing he did was to stretch his entire body, and then he went up to Rocinante, slapped him twice on the haunches, and said:

"I still hope to God and His Blessed Mother, O flower and paragon of horses, that we soon shall see ourselves as we wish to be: you, with your master on your back, and I, mounted on you and exercising the profession for which God put me in this world."

And having said this, Don Quixote moved away with Sancho to a remote spot and returned much relieved and even more desirous of putting his squire's plan into effect.

The canon looked at him, marveling at the strangeness of his profound madness and at how he displayed a very fine intelligence when he spoke and responded to questions, his feet slipping from the stirrups, as has been said many times before, only when the subject was chivalry. And so, after everyone had sat on the green grass to wait for the provisions, the canon, moved by compassion, said to him:

"Is it possible, Señor, that the grievous and idle reading of books of chivalry could have so affected your grace that it has unbalanced your judgment and made you believe that you are enchanted, along with other things of this nature, which are as far from being true as truth is from lies? How is it possible that any human mind could be persuaded that there has existed in the world that infinity of Amadises, and that throng of so many famous knights, so many emperors of Trebizond, so many Felixmartes of Hyrcania, so many palfreys and wandering damsels, so many serpents and dragons and giants, so many unparalleled adventures and different kinds of enchantments, so many battles and fierce encounters, so much splendid attire, so many enamored princesses and squires who are counts and dwarves who are charming, so many love letters, so much wooing, so many valiant women, and, finally, so many nonsensical matters as are contained in books of chivalry? For myself, I can say that when I read them, as long as I do not set my mind to thinking that they are all frivolous lies, I do derive some pleasure from them, but when I realize what they actually are, I throw even the best of them against the wall, and would even toss them in the fire if one were near, and think they richly deserved the punishment, for being deceptive and false and far beyond the limits of common sense, like the founders of new sects and new ways of life, and for giving the ignorant rabble a reason to believe and consider as true all the absurdities they contain.

They are so audacious, they dare perturb the minds of judicious and wellborn gentlemen, as can be plainly seen in what they have done to

your grace, for they have brought you to the point where it has been necessary to lock you in a cage and carry you on an oxcart as if you were a lion
or tiger being transported from town to town so that people could pay to
see you. Come, come, Señor Don Quixote, take pity on yourself! Return
to the bosom of good sense, and learn to use the considerable intelligence
that heaven was pleased to give you, and devote your intellectual talents
to another kind of reading that redounds to the benefit of your conscience and the increase of your honor! And if, following your natural inclination, you still wish to read books about great chivalric deeds, read
Judges in Holy Scripture, and there you will find magnificent truths and
deeds both remarkable and real. Lusitania had a Viriato,[1] Rome had a
Caesar, Carthage a Hannibal, Greece an Alexander, Castilla a Count
Fernán González,[2] Valencia a Cid, Andalucía a Gonzalo Fernández,[3] Extremadura a Diego García de Paredes,[4] Jerez a Garcí Pérez de Vargas,[5]
Toledo a Garcilaso,[6] Sevilla a Don Manuel de León.[7] Reading about their
valorous deeds can entertain, instruct, delight, and astonish the highest
minds. This would certainly be a study worthy of your grace's intelligence,
Señor Don Quixote, and from it you would emerge learned in history, enamored of virtue, instructed in goodness, improved in your customs,
valiant but not rash, bold and not cowardly, and all of this would honor
God, and benefit you, and add to the fame of La Mancha where, I have
learned, your grace has his origin and birthplace."

Don Quixote listened very attentively to the canon's words, and
when he saw that he had concluded, he looked at him for a long time
and said:

"It seems to me, Señor, that the intention of your grace's discourse
has been to persuade me that there have been no knights errant in the

---

1. Viriato led a Lusitanian (Portuguese) rebellion against the Romans.

2. Count Fernán González declared the independence of Castilla from the Moors in the tenth century.

3. Gonzalo Fernández was the Great Captain, so called for his military exploits during the reign of
the Catholic Sovereigns Ferdinand and Isabella.

4. Diego García de Paredes was a military hero who fought with Gonzalo Fernández.

5. Pérez de Vargas, a historical figure mentioned in chapter VIII, broke his sword in battle, then tore
a branch from an oak tree and used it to kill countless Moors.

6. Garcilaso de la Vega, not to be confused with the Renaissance poet of the same name, fought in
the war to capture Granada from the Moors.

7. Don Manuel de León entered a lion's cage to recover a glove that a lady had thrown inside in
order to test his courage. When he returned the glove, he slapped her for endangering the life of a
knight on a whim.

world, and that all the books of chivalry are false, untrue, harmful, and of no value to the nation, and that I have done wrong to read them, and worse to believe them, and worse yet to imitate them by setting myself the task of following the extremely difficult profession of knight errantry which they teach, and you deny that there ever were Amadises in the world, whether of Gaul or of Greece, or any of the other knights that fill the writings."

"That is precisely what I meant; what you have said is absolutely correct," said the canon.

To which Don Quixote responded:

"Your grace also said that these books have done me a good deal of harm, for they turned my wits and put me in a cage, and it would be better for me to alter and change my reading and devote myself to books that are truer and more pleasant and more instructive."

"That is true," said the canon.

"Well, then," replied Don Quixote, "it is my opinion that the one who is deranged and enchanted is your grace, for you have uttered so many blasphemies against something so widely accepted in the world as true that whoever denies it, as your grace has done, deserves the same punishment that your grace says you give to books when you read them and they anger you. Because wanting to convince anyone that there was no Amadís in the world or any of the adventuring knights who fill the histories, is the same as trying to persuade that person that the sun does not shine, ice is not cold, and the earth bears no crops, for what mind in the world can persuade another that the story of Princess Floripes and Guy de Bourgogne is not true, or the tale of Fierabrás and the Bridge of Mantible, which occurred in the time of Charlemagne, and is as true as the fact that it is now day?[8] If that is a lie, it must also be true that there was no Hector, no Achilles, no Trojan War, no Twelve Peers of France, no King Arthur of England who was transformed into a crow and whose return is awaited in his kingdom to this day. Who will go so far as to say that the history of Guarino Mezquino is false,[9] and the search for the Holy Grail, and that the loves of Don Tristan and Queen Iseult, and those of Guinevere and Lancelot, are apocryphal, even though there are

8. The two anecdotes appear in a history of Charlemagne and the Twelve Peers (*La historia del emperador Carlomagno y los doce pares de Francia*) published in Alcalá in 1589.

9. A book entitled *Crónica del nobre caballero Guarino Mezquino* was cited by Juan de Valdés, an important humanist of the early sixteenth century, as being very poorly written and even more absurd than other novels of chivalry.

persons who can almost remember having seen the Duenna Quin-tañona,[10] who was the greatest pourer of wine in Great Britain? And this is so true that I remember my paternal grandmother saying, whenever she saw a lady with a formal headdress: 'My boy, she looks like the Duenna Quintañona.' And from this I argue that she must have known her, or at least seen a portrait of her. And who can deny the truth of the history of Pierres and the beautiful Magalona,[11] for even today one can see in the royal armory the peg, slightly larger than a carriage pole, with which the valiant Pierres directed the wooden horse as he rode it through the air. And next to the peg is the saddle of Babieca, and at Roncesvalles there is Roland's horn, the size of a large rafter, from which one can infer that there were Twelve Peers, and a Pierres, and a Cid, and other knights like them:

the ones that people say
go searching for adventures.[12]

If you deny that, you will also tell me it is not true that the valiant Lusitanian Juan de Merlo[13] was a knight errant who went to Burgundy and fought at the city of Arras with the famous Lord of Charny, called Monseigneur Pierres, and then in the city of Basle with Monseigneur Henri de Remestan, emerging from both undertakings victorious and covered with honor and fame; you will deny the adventures and chal-lenges, also carried out in Burgundy, by the valiant Spaniards Pedro Barba and Gutierre Quijada[14] (from whom I am descended directly through the male line), when they conquered the sons of the Count of San Polo. You will deny as well that Don Fernando de Guevara[15] went to seek adventures in Germany, where he fought with Messire Jorge, a knight in the house of the Duke of Austria; you will say that the jousts of Suero de Quiñones at the Pass were a deception,[16] and you will deny the feats of Monseigneur Luis de Falces against Don Gonzalo de Guzmán, a

10. A figure associated with the Lancelot story who passed into popular ballads and became part of the folk tradition in Spain.

11. The Provençal story of Pierres de Provence and the beautiful Magalona was extremely popular in the sixteenth century; its Spanish translation was published in 1519.

12. These lines were cited previously, in chapter IX.

13. A Castilian knight of Portuguese descent who served under Juan II.

14. The deeds of these two knights, who were cousins, are narrated in chapter 25 of the *Crónica de Juan II* (*The Chronicle of Juan II*).

15. Don Fernando de Guevara was also cited in the *Crónica de Juan II*.

16. In 1434, with the permission of Juan II, Suero Quiñones, for the love of his lady, jousted with sixty-eight challenging knights at what is called the Honorable Pass.

Castilian knight,[17] as well as many other deeds performed by Christian knights from these kingdoms and from foreign ones, deeds so authentic and true that I say again that whoever denies them must be lacking in all reason and good sense."

The canon was astonished when he heard Don Quixote's mixture of truth and falsehood and saw how well-informed he was regarding everything related to and touching on the exploits of knight errantry, and so he responded:

"I cannot deny, Señor Don Quixote, that some of what your grace has said is true, especially with regard to Spanish knights errant; by the same token, I also wish to concede that there were Twelve Peers of France, though I cannot believe they did all those things that Archbishop Turpin writes about them,[18] because the truth of the matter is that they were knights chosen by the kings of France and were called *peers* because they were all equal in worth, nobility, and valor, or at least, if they were not, they should have been; they were like a religious order, similar to the modern orders of Santiago or Calatrava, in which one supposes that those who profess are, or should be, worthy, valiant, and wellborn knights, and just as today one calls a man a Knight of San Juan, or a Knight of Alcántara, in those days one said a Knight of the Twelve Peers, because they were twelve equal knights selected for this military order. As for El Cid, there can be no doubt that he existed, and certainly none about Bernardo del Carpio, but I think it exceedingly doubtful that they performed the deeds people say they did. With regard to the peg of Count Pierres which you mentioned as being next to the saddle of Babieca in the royal armory, I confess my sin: I am so ignorant, or so shortsighted, that although I have seen the saddle, I have never laid eyes on the peg, especially if it is as big as your grace says it is."

"Well, it is there, no doubt about it," replied Don Quixote, "and they also say it is kept in a cowhide sheath to protect it from rust."

"That well may be," responded the canon, "but by the orders I received, I do not remember seeing it. And even if I concede that it is there, I am not therefore obliged to believe the histories of so many Amadises, or those of that throng of knights about whom they tell us stories, nor is it reasonable for an honorable man like your grace, possessed of your qualities and fine understanding, to accept as true the countless absurd exaggerations that are written in those nonsensical books of chivalry."

17. An encounter that was also cited in the *Crónica de Juan II*.

18. Turpin is the fictitious author of a chronicle about Charlemagne.

CHAPTER L

Regarding the astute arguments that Don Quixote had with the canon, as well as other matters

"That is really good!" responded Don Quixote. "Books that are printed with a royal license and with the approval of those officials to whom they are submitted, and read to widespread delight, and celebrated by great and small, poor and rich, educated and ignorant, lowborn and gentry, in short, by all kinds of persons of every rank and station: can they possibly be a lie, especially when they bear so close a resemblance to the truth and tell us about the father, the mother, the nation, the family, the age, the birthplace, and the great deeds, point by point and day by day, of the knight, or knights, in question? Be quiet, your grace, and do not say such blasphemies, and believe me when I tell you what you, as an intelligent man, must do in this matter, which is to read these books, and then you will see the pleasure you derive from them.

If you do not agree, then tell me: is there any greater joy than seeing, before our very eyes, you might say, a great lake of boiling pitch, and in it, swimming and writhing about, there are many snakes, serpents, lizards, and many other kinds of fierce and fearsome creatures, and from the middle of the lake there comes an extremely sad voice, saying: 'Thou, O knight, whosoever thou mayest be, who looketh upon this fearful lake, if thou wishest to grasp the treasure hidden beneath these ebon waters, display the valor of thy mighty heart and throw thyself into the midst of its black and burning liquid, for if thou wilt not, thou canst not be worthy of gazing upon the wondrous marvels contained and enclosed within the seven castles of the seven enchantresses which lieth beneath this blackness.' And no sooner has the knight heard the fearsome voice than without hesitating or stopping to consider the danger he faces, and without even stripping off the weight of his heavy armor, he commends himself to God and his lady and throws himself into the middle of the boiling lake, and when he cannot see or imagine where he will land, he finds himself among flowering meadows even more beautiful than the Elysian Fields. There it seems to him that the sky is more translucent and the sun shines with a new clarity; before him lies a peaceful grove of trees so green and leafy, their verdure brings joy to his eyes, while his ears are charmed by the sweet, untutored song of the infinite number of small, brightly colored birds that fly among the intricate branches. Here he discovers a brook whose cool waters, like liquid crystal, run over fine sand and white pebbles that seem like sifted gold and perfect pearls; there he sees a fountain artfully composed of varicolored jasper and smooth marble; over there he sees another fountain fashioned as a grotto where tiny clamshells and the coiled white-and-yellow houses of the snail are arranged with conscious disorder and mixed with bits of shining glass and counterfeit emeralds, forming so varied a pattern that art, imitating nature, here seems to surpass it. Suddenly, there appears before him a fortified castle or elegant fortress whose walls are made of solid gold, its parapets of diamonds, its doors of sapphires; in short, it is so wonderfully built that although its materials are nothing less than diamonds, carbuncles, rubies, pearls, gold, and emeralds, its workmanship is even finer.

And after this, is there any more marvelous sight than seeing a good number of damsels come out through the gate of the castle, wearing dresses so splendid and sumptuous that if I began now to describe them, as the histories do, I should never finish; and then, the maiden who seems the leader among them takes by the hand the bold knight who threw himself into the boiling lake, and, without saying a word, guides him inside the rich fortress or castle and has him strip as naked as the day as he was born and bathes him in warm water and then smoothes his entire body with sweet-smelling ointments and dresses him in a shirt of finest silk, all fragrant and perfumed, and then another damsel comes and covers his shoulders with a cloak that, they say, is worth at least a city and even more? What better sight, after all this, than when we are told that he is taken to another chamber where he finds tables laid so lavishly, he is stunned and amazed? Observe him as he pours over his hands water that is distilled with ambergris and scented flowers, and see him sit on a chair of ivory, and watch him being served by all the damsels, who maintain a wondrous silence as they bring him so many different foods, so exquisitely prepared that appetite does not know where to place its hands. How marvelous is it to hear the music that plays as he eats, though he does not know who is singing, or where. And when the meal is over and the tables cleared, and the knight is reclining in his chair, perhaps cleaning his teeth with a toothpick, as is the custom,[1] to have another damsel, much more beautiful than any of the others, come in through the chamber door and sit beside the knight and begin to explain to him what castle this is, and that she resides there and is enchanted and many other things that amaze the knight and astound the readers who are reading his history.

I do not wish to go any further with this, for one can gather from what I have said that anyone can read any part of any history of a knight errant and from it derive great pleasure and delight. And your grace should believe me when I tell you, as I already have, to read these books, and you will see how they drive away melancholy if you are so afflicted and improve your spirits if they happen to be low. For myself, I can say that since I became a knight errant I have been valiant, well-mannered, liberal, polite, generous, courteous, bold, gentle, patient, long-suffering in labors, imprisonments, and enchantments, and although only a short while ago I saw myself locked in a cage like a madman, I think that with the valor of my arm, and heaven favoring me, and fortune not opposing me, in a few days I shall find myself the king of some kingdom where I can display the gratitude and liberality of my heart. For by my faith, Señor, the poor man is incapable of displaying the virtue of liberality with anyone, even if he possesses it to the greatest degree, and gratitude that consists of nothing more than desire is a dead thing, as faith without works is dead. For this reason I should like Fortune to offer me without delay an opportunity to become an emperor, so that I can display my heartfelt desire to do good for my friends, especially this poor Sancho Panza, my squire, who is the best man in the world, and I should like to give him a countship, which I promised him many days ago, even though I fear he may not have the ability to govern his estate."

As soon as Sancho heard these last words of his master, he said:

"Your grace, Señor Don Quixote, should work to give me the countship that has been promised by your grace and hoped for by me, and I promise you I'll have no lack of ability to govern it, and if I do, I've heard it said that there are men in the world who farm the estates of gen-

---

1. This detail seems comically incongruous, yet picking one's teeth after a meal was so common during the Renaissance that it was employed as a kind of trope for the necessary deceptions of genteel poverty, for example in *Lazarillo de Tormes,* when the hungry gentleman walks down the street wielding a toothpick to indicate that he has eaten.

tlemen, who pay them so much each year to manage everything, and the gentleman sits with his feet up, enjoying the rent they pay him and not worrying about anything else, and that's what I'll do; I won't haggle over trifles, but I'll turn my back on everything, and enjoy my rent like a duke, and let the others do the work."

"Brother Sancho," said the canon, "that's fine as far as enjoying the rent is concerned, but the administration of justice has to be tended to by the owner of the estate, and this is where ability and good judgment come in, and in particular a real intention to do what is right, for if this is lacking at the beginning, the middle and the end will always be wrong; in this way, God tends to favor the virtuous desires of the simple man and confound the wicked intentions of the intelligent."

"I don't know about these philosophies," responded Sancho Panza, "all I know is that as soon as I have the countship I'll know how to govern it; I have as much soul as any other man, and as much body as the biggest of them, and I'll be as much a king of my estate as any other is of his; and this being true, I'll do what I want, and doing what I want, I'll do what I like, and doing what I like, I'll be happy, and when a man is happy he doesn't wish for anything else, and not wishing for anything else, that'll be the end of it, so bring on my estate, and God willing we'll see, as one blind man said to the other."

"Those aren't bad philosophies, as you call them, Sancho, but even so, there is a good deal to say regarding this matter of countships."

To which Don Quixote replied:

"I do not know if there is more to say; I am guided only by the example of the great Amadís of Gaul, who made his squire count of Ínsula Firme; therefore I can, without scruple or question of conscience, make a count of Sancho Panza, who is one of the best squires a knight errant ever had."

The canon was astounded by the reasoned nonsense spoken by Don Quixote, by the manner in which he had described the adventure of the Knight of the Lake, by the impression that had been made on him by the intentional lies of the books he had read, and, finally, by the simplemindedness of Sancho, who so fervently desired to obtain the countship his master had promised him.

By now the canon's servants had returned from the inn, where they had gone for the pack mule, and making a table of a rug and the meadow's green grass, they sat in the shade of some trees and ate their meal there so that the ox driver could take advantage of the grazing for his animals, as we have already said. While they were eating they suddenly heard a loud noise and the tinkling of a small bell from some nearby brambles and heavy underbrush, and at the same time they saw a beautiful black-, white-, and gray-spotted nanny goat emerge from the thicket. Behind her came a goatherd, calling to her, saying the words that goatherds say to make their animals stop or return to the flock. The fugitive goat, frightened and apprehensive, came up to the company as if asking for their help, and there she stopped. The goatherd ran up, seized her by the horns, and as if she were capable of rational thought and speech, said to her:

"Ah, Spot, my Spot, you're so wild these days, dashing all around! What wolves are scaring you, my girl? Won't you tell me what's wrong, my pretty? What else can it be but that you're a female and can't be quiet, and the devil take your condition and all those females you're imitating! Come back, come back, my friend, and if you're not happy, at least you'll be safer in the fold, or with your companions, and if you, who are supposed to lead and guide them, go astray without a guide, what will happen to them?"

The goatherd's words amused those who were listening, especially the canon, who said to him:

"By your life, brother, calm down a little and do not hurry to return that goat so quickly to her flock, for since she is a female, as you say, she must follow her natural instinct no matter how you may try to prevent it. Eat something, and have a drink to cool your anger, and in the meantime the nanny goat can rest."

And saying this, and handing him a hindquarter of cold rabbit on the tip of a knife, were all one. The goathered accepted it with thanks, he drank and grew calm, and then he said:

"I would not want your graces to think I'm simple just because I talked to this animal sensibly, as if she could understand, for the truth is the words I said are not mysterious. A rustic I may be, but not so rustic that I don't understand how to talk to men and to beasts."

"I certainly believe that," said the priest, "for I already know from experience that mountains breed learned men and shepherds' huts house philosophers."

"At least, Señor," replied the goatherd, "they shelter men who have suffered greatly, and so that you may believe this truth and touch it with your hand, even though I seem to be inviting myself without being asked, if it does not trouble you to do so and if it is your wish, Señores, lend me your ears for a while and I shall tell you a truth that confirms what this gentleman"—and he pointed to the priest—"and I have said."

To which Don Quixote responded:

"Because this matter seems to have some shadow of a knightly adventure, I, for my part, shall hear you very willingly, brother, and all of these gentlemen will do the same, for they are very intelligent and are fond of curious and extraordinary things that amaze, delight, and entertain the senses, as I think your story undoubtedly will. Begin, then, my friend, and all of us shall listen."

"I pass," said Sancho. "I'm going over to that brook with this meat pie, where I plan to eat enough for three days, because I've heard my master, Don Quixote, say that the squire of a knight errant has to eat whenever he can, and as much as he can, because they might go into woods so deep they can't find their way out again for six days, and if the man isn't full, or his saddlebags aren't well-provisioned, he might stay there, as often happens, until his flesh wrinkles and dries like a mummy's."

"You are correct, Sancho," said Don Quixote. "Go where you wish and eat what you can; I am satisfied, and all I need is to nourish my spirit, which I shall do by listening to this good man's story."

"And so shall we all," said the canon.

Then he asked the goatherd to begin the tale he had promised. The goatherd gave the goat, which he was holding by the horns, two slaps on the haunches and said:

"Lie down next to me, Spot, there's time before we have to return to the fold."

The nanny goat seemed to understand him, because when her master sat down, she lay down next to him very calmly and looked into his face, as if letting him know that she was listening to what he was saying, and the goatherd began his history in this fashion:

CHAPTER LI

Which recounts what the goatherd told to all those who were taking Don Quixote home

"Three leagues from this valley is a village that, although small, is one of the richest in the entire region; in it there lived a farmer who was very well respected, so respected, in fact, that although honor tends to go with wealth, he was more honored for his virtue than for the riches he had achieved. But his greatest happiness, as he would say, was having a daughter of such extraordinary beauty and exceptional intelligence, grace, and

virtue, that whoever knew her and saw her marveled to see the unsur-
passed gifts that heaven and nature had granted her. As a child she was
comely, and as she grew so did her loveliness, and at the age of sixteen she
was exceedingly beautiful. The fame of her beauty began to spread to all
the neighboring villages. Why do I say neighboring? It spread to distant
cities, and even entered the royal salons, and came to the attention of all
kinds of people, and as if she were a rare object or a miraculous image,
they came from far and near to see her. Her father watched over her, and
she watched over herself, for there are no locks or bars or bolts that protect a maiden better than her own modesty and virtue.

The father's wealth and the daughter's beauty moved many, from the
village as well as strangers, to ask for her hand, but the farmer, in possession of so rich a jewel, was somewhat perplexed and could not decide to
which of the countless suitors he should give her. I was one of the many
who had this virtuous desire, and I had many great hopes of success
knowing that her father knew who I was, since I came from the same village, and was pure of blood, and in the flower of my youth, and had a rich
estate, and was not lacking in intelligence. Another man from our village, with the same qualifications, had also asked for her hand, causing
her father to hesitate, unable to reach a decision, for it seemed to him
that either one of us would be a good match for his daughter.

In order to resolve the problem, he determined to discuss it with Leandra, which is the name of the wealthy maiden who keeps me in misery,
for he believed that since we were equally qualified, it was a good idea to
allow his beloved daughter to choose to her liking, a course of action
worthy of imitation by all parents who wish their children to marry; I
don't say they should be permitted to choose the base or wicked, but
they should be offered the good and then be allowed to choose freely. I
don't know which of us Leandra chose; I know only that her father put
off both of us with references to his daughter's youth and other general
remarks that did not commit him but did not dismiss us, either. My
rival's name is Anselmo, and I am called Eugenio, so now you know the
names of all the persons who take part in this tragedy, which is not yet
concluded, though it seems clear enough that its end will be calamitous.

At about this time a certain Vicente de la Rosa[1] came to town; he

---

1. In the first edition, the character is called Rosa twice and Roca once; subsequent editions, including many modern ones, call him Roca; in the first English, French, and Italian translations,
which are cited by Martín de Riquer, Shelton calls him "Vincente of the Rose," Oudin calls him
"Vincent de la Roque," and Franciosini calls him "Vincenzio della Rosa."

was the son of a poor farmer from our village and had been a soldier in Italy and in many other places. He had been taken away from our village when he was a boy of twelve by a captain passing through with his troops, and the boy returned twelve years later dressed as a soldier, decked out in a thousand colors and wearing a thousand glass trinkets and thin metal chains. One day he would put on one piece of finery, and the next day another, but all of them were flimsy and garish, lightweight and worthless. Farmers, who by nature are crafty, and who become the very embodiment of craftiness when idleness gives them the opportunity, noticed this, and counted each object and piece of finery, and discovered that he had three outfits, each a different color, with garters and hose to match, but he mixed and combined them so cleverly that if you did not keep count, you would have sworn he had displayed more than ten matched outfits and more than twenty proud plumes. And do not think that what I am saying about his clothes is irrelevant or trivial, because they play an important part in this story.

He would sit on a stone bench that is under a great poplar tree in our village square, and there he would keep us all openmouthed with suspense as he recounted great deeds to us. There was no land anywhere in the world that he had not seen, and no battle in which he had not fought; he had killed as many Moors as live in Morocco and Tunis and had engaged in more single combat than Gante and Luna,[2] Diego García de Paredes, and another thousand men he named, and from all of them he had emerged victorious, without shedding a single drop of blood. On the other hand, he would show us the scars of wounds, and even though we could not make them out, he let us know that they had been caused by shots from flintlocks in various battles and skirmishes. Finally, with unparalleled arrogance, he would address his equals, even those who knew him, as *vos*,[3] saying that his father was his fighting arm, his lineage his deeds, and as a soldier he owed nothing to no man, not even the king. In addition to this arrogance, he was something of a musician who could strum a guitar so well that some said he could make it speak, but his talents did not end here; he also was a poet, and for each trivial event in the village he would compose a ballad at least a league and a half long.

2. The identities of these two men are not known; according to Martín de Riquer, it is possible that the manuscript read "Garci Lasso," who was cited earlier, in chapter XLIX, with García de Paredes.

3. In Spanish, as in many other languages, varying degrees of deference, distance, familiarity, intimacy, and significant class distinctions can be shown by the form of address, either second or third person, singular or plural.

This soldier, then, whom I have just described, this Vicente de la Rosa, this brave gallant, this musician and poet, was often seen and observed by Leandra from a window in her house that overlooked the square. She became infatuated with the glitter of his bright clothes and enchanted by his ballads, for he made twenty copies of each one he composed; she heard of the deeds that he himself attributed to himself, and finally, as the devil must have ordained, she fell in love with him before the presumptuousness of asking for her hand had even occurred to him. And since, in matters of love, no affair is easier to conclude successfully than the one supported by the lady's desire, Leandra and Vicente easily reached an understanding, and before any of her many suitors became aware of her desire, she had satisfied it by leaving the house of her dearly loved father, for she had no mother, and fleeing the village with the soldier, who emerged more triumphant from this undertaking than from the many others he had claimed for himself.

This turn of events astonished the entire village, as well as anyone who even heard about it; I was stunned, Anselmo shocked, her father grief-stricken, her kinfolk humiliated, the law solicitous, and its officers alert; they took to the roads, searched the woods and everything they ran across, and at the end of three days they found the capricious Leandra in a cave in the wild, wearing only her chemise and without the great quantity of money and precious jewels she had taken from her house. They brought her back to her anguished father and questioned her about her misfortune; she confessed willingly that Vicente de la Rosa had deceived her, promising to be her husband and persuading her to leave her father's house, saying that he would take her to the richest and most joyous city in the world, which was Naples; ill-advised and badly deceived, she had believed him and, after robbing her father, had entrusted herself to him on the night she had fled, and he had taken her to a rugged mountain and confined her to the cave where she had been found. She also said that the soldier did not take her honor but robbed her of everything else she had, and left her in that cave, and went away, a series of events that astonished everyone a second time. It was hard for us to believe in the young man's restraint, but she affirmed it so insistently that her disconsolate father found reason to be consoled, caring nothing for the treasure that had been taken from him, for his daughter had preserved the jewel that, once lost, can never be recovered.

On the same day that Leandra appeared, her father removed her from our sight and locked her away in a convent in a town not far from here, hoping that time would dissipate some of the shame that had fallen on his daughter. Leandra's extreme youth helped to excuse some of her inexcusable behavior, at least for those who had nothing to gain from her being either wicked or virtuous; but those who were familiar with her considerable intelligence and perspicacity attributed her sin not to ignorance but to her boldness and the natural inclination of women, which, for the most part, tends to be imprudent and irrational.

With Leandra cloistered, Anselmo's eyes were left sightless, at least they saw nothing that made him happy; mine were darkened, lacking a light that could lead them to any joy; with Leandra's absence our sorrow grew, our patience lessened, and we cursed the soldier's finery and despised her father's lack of foresight. Finally, Anselmo and I agreed to leave the village and come to this valley, where he pastures a large number of sheep that belong to him and I graze a large flock of my goats, and we spend our lives among the trees, proclaiming our passions or together singing the praises of Leandra, or reviling her, or sighing alone and communicating our laments to heaven. In imitation of us, many of Leandra's other suitors have come to these wild mountains to follow our example, and there are so many of them that this place, so crowded with shepherds and sheepfolds, seems to have been transformed into the pastoral Arcadia,[4] and no matter where you go you will hear the name of the beautiful Leandra. One curses her and calls her unpredictable, inconstant, and immodest, another condemns her as forward and flighty; one absolves and pardons her, another judges and censures her; one celebrates her beauty, another denounces her nature; in short, all despise her, and all adore her, and the madness goes so far that there are some who complain of her disdain but never spoke to her, and some even lament their fate and feel the raging disease of jealousy though she never gave anyone reason to feel jealousy because, as I have said, her sin was discovered before her desire. There is no hollow rock, no bank of a stream, no shade of a tree, that is not occupied by a shepherd telling his misfortunes to the air; the echoes repeat the name of Leandra wherever it can be sounded: the mountains ring with the name of Leandra, the streams murmur Leandra, and Leandra has us all bewitched and enchanted, hoping without hope and fearing without knowing what it is we fear.

4. Arcadia was a region of the Peloponnesus where classical and Renaissance authors frequently located their pastoral novels; two important works of this extremely popular genre, by Sannazaro and Lope de Vega, were entitled *La Arcadia*, and Cervantes himself published a pastoral novel called *La Galatea*.

Among all these madmen, the one who shows the least distraction and has the most judgment is my rival Anselmo, who, having so many other things to complain of, complains only of her absence, and to the sound of a rebec, which he plays admirably, and in verses that show his fine intelligence, he sings his complaints. I follow another path, which is easier and, in my opinion, more correct, which is to speak ill of the fickle nature of women, and their inconstancy, their double dealings, their dead promises, their broken vows, and, finally, their irrationality in choosing the objects of their desire and affection. And this was the reason, Señores, for the words and arguments I addressed to this goat when I arrived here, for since she is a female, I hold her in small esteem, though she is the best in my flock. This is the history I promised to tell; if I have gone on too long, I will not give short shrift to serving you: my sheepfold is close by, and there I have fresh milk and delicious cheese and a variety of seasonal fruits as pleasing to the sight as to the taste."

CHAPTER LII

Regarding the quarrel that Don Quixote had with the goatherd, as well as the strange adventure of the penitents, which he brought to a successful conclusion by the sweat of his brow

The tale of the goatherd pleased all who heard it, especially the canon, who, with remarkable curiosity, noted the manner in which he had told it, for he was as far from resembling a rustic goatherd as he was close to seeming an intelligent courtier, and so he said that the priest was absolutely correct when he claimed that the mountains bred educated men. Everyone paid compliments to Eugenio, but the most liberal in doing so was Don Quixote, who said to him:

"There can be no doubt, brother goatherd, that if I were able to embark upon a new adventure, I wouldst begin immediately to bring thine to a happy conclusion, for despite the abbess and all those who might wish to prevent it, I wouldst rescue Leandra from the convent, where she is surely held against her will, and place her in thy hands so that thou couldst do with her as thou wouldst and as it pleaseth thee, always, however, adhering to the laws of the chivalry, which commandeth that no damsel shalt have any offense whatsoever committed against her person, and I trusteth in God Our Lord that the power of an evil enchanter is not so great that it canst not be overcome by that of another enchanter with more virtuous intentions, and when that happeneth I vow to give thee my help and assistance, as I am obliged to do by my profession, which is none other than favoring the weak and helpless."

The goatherd looked at him, and when he saw Don Quixote so badly dressed and looking so shabby, he was taken aback, and he asked the barber, who was not far away:

"Señor, who is this man who looks so peculiar and talks in this fashion?"

"Who would he be," responded the barber, "but the famous Don Quixote of La Mancha, righter of wrongs, redresser of grievances, defender of damsels, scourge of giants, and victor in battle?"

"That sounds to me," responded the goatherd, "like the things one reads in books about knights errant, who did everything your grace says with regard to this man, though it seems to me that either your grace is joking or this gentleman must have a few vacant chambers in his head."

"You are a villain and a scoundrel," said Don Quixote, "and you are the one who is vacant and foolish; I have more upstairs than the whore who bore you ever did."

As he was speaking and saying this, he seized a loaf of bread that was beside him and hit the goatherd with it full in the face with so much fury that he flattened his nose; but the goatherd cared nothing for jokes, and when he saw how badly he was being mistreated, with little regard for the carpet, or the table linen, or those who were eating, he leaped on Don Quixote, and put both hands around his neck, and surely would have choked him if Sancho Panza had not come up just then, seized him by the shoulders, and thrown him down on the makeshift table, breaking plates, shattering cups, and spilling and scattering everything that was on it. Don Quixote, when he found that he was free, threw himself on top of the goatherd, and he, his face covered in blood and bruised where Sancho had kicked him, crawled on all fours, looking for a knife on the table to take his bloody revenge, but was prevented from doing so by the canon and the priest; the barber, however, helped the goatherd to hold Don Quixote down and rain down on him so many blows that the poor knight's face bled as heavily as his adversary's.

The canon and the priest doubled over with laughter, the officers of the Brotherhood jumped up and down with glee, and everyone sicced them on as if they were dogs involved in a fight; only Sancho Panza despaired, because he could not shake free from one of the canon's servants who prevented him from helping his master.

In short, everyone was diverted and amused, except for the two who were flailing away at each other, when they heard a trumpet, a sound so mournful it made them turn toward the place where it seemed to originate, but the one most aroused by the sound was Don Quixote, and though he lay beneath the goatherd, much against his will and more than a little battered, he said to him:

"Brother demon, for it is not possible that you are anything else since you have had sufficient power and strength to overcome mine, I implore you, let us call a truce for no more than an hour, because it seems to me that the dolorous sound of the trumpet reaching our ears summons me to a new adventure."

The goatherd, who by this time was weary of hitting and being hit, released him immediately, and Don Quixote rose to his feet as he turned toward the sound and suddenly saw many men dressed in white, in the manner of penitents, coming down a slope.

In fact, that year the clouds had denied the earth their moisture, and in every village and hamlet in the region there were processions, rogations, and public penances, asking God to open the hands of his mercy and allow it to rain; to this end, the people from a nearby village were coming in procession to a holy hermitage located on one of the hills that formed the valley.

Don Quixote saw the strange dress of the penitents, and not recalling the countless times he must have seen them in the past, he imagined that this was the start of an adventure, and since he was a knight errant, he alone could undertake it, and this idea was confirmed for him when he thought that an image draped in mourning that they were carrying was actually a noble lady carried away against her will by those cowardly and lowborn villains; no sooner had this thought passed through his mind than he rushed over to Rocinante, who was grazing, removed the bridle and shield from the forebow of his saddle, and had the bridle on him in a moment; he asked Sancho for his sword, mounted Rocinante, grasped his shield, and called in a loud voice to all those present:

"Now, my valiant companions, you will see how important it is that there be knights in the world who profess the order of knight errantry; now I say that you will see, in the liberty of that good lady held captive there, how knights errant are to be esteemed."

As he said this, he pressed Rocinante with his thighs because he had no spurs, and at a brisk canter, for nowhere in this true history do we read that Rocinante ran at a full gallop, he rode out to his encounter with the penitents, although the priest, the canon, and the barber did what they could to stop him, to no avail, nor was he stopped by the shouts of Sancho, who cried:

"Where are you going, Señor Don Quixote? What demons in your heart incite you to attack our Catholic faith? Oh, look, devil take me, and see that it's a procession of penitents, and the lady they're carrying on the platform is the holy image of the Blessed Virgin; think, Señor, about what you're doing, because this time it really isn't what you think."

Sancho's efforts were all in vain, because his master was so determined to reach the figures in sheets and to free the lady in mourning that he did not hear a word, and if he had, he would not have turned back, even if the king had ordered him to. And so he reached the procession and reined in Rocinante, who already wanted to rest for a while, and in a hoarse, angry voice he cried:

"O you who keep your faces covered, perhaps because you are evil, attend, and hear what I wish to say to you."

The first to stop were those carrying the image, and one of the four clerics intoning the litanies saw the strange appearance of Don Quixote, the skinniness of Rocinante, and other comic features that he noticed and discovered about the knight, and responded by saying:

"Good brother, if you want to say something, say it quickly, because these brethren are disciplining their flesh and we cannot listen to anything, nor is it right for us to do so, unless it is so brief that it can be said in two words."

"I shall say it in one," replied Don Quixote, "and it is this: you must immediately release that beauteous lady whose tears and melancholy countenance are clear signs that you take her against her will, and have done her some notable wrong, and I, who was born into the world to right such iniquities, shall not consent to your taking another step forward until you give her the freedom she desires and deserves."

When they heard these words, they all realized that Don Quixote had to be a madman, and they began to laugh very heartily; this laughter was like gunpowder thrown into the flames of Don Quixote's wrath, because without saying another word, he drew his sword and charged the procession. One of the men who was carrying the platform let his companions bear his share of the weight and came out to meet Don Quixote, brandishing the forked pole or staff that he used to support the platform while he was resting; Don Quixote struck it a great blow with his sword that broke it in two, leaving the man with the third part in his hand, and with that part he hit Don Quixote so hard on the shoulder, on the same side as his sword, that the knight could not hold up his shield to protect himself from the peasantish attack, and poor Don Quixote fell to the ground in a very sorry state.

Sancho Panza, who came panting close behind him, saw him fall, and he shouted at Don Quixote's attacker not to hit him again because he was a poor enchanted knight who had never harmed anyone in all the days of his life. But what stopped the peasant was not the shouting of Sancho but his seeing that Don Quixote lay without moving hand or foot, and believing that he had killed him, he quickly tucked his penitent's robe up into his belt and fled across the countryside like a deer.

By now all of Don Quixote's companions had reached the spot where he lay; those in the procession who saw them, along with the officers holding their crossbows, running toward them, feared trouble and made a circle around the image; with their pointed hoods[1] raised and their scourges in hand, and the priests clutching their candlesticks, they awaited the assault, determined to defend themselves against their attackers and even go on the offensive if they could. But Fortune arranged matters better than they had expected, because the only thing Sancho did was to throw himself on the body of his master in the belief that he was dead and break into the most woeful and laughable lament in the world.

The priest was recognized by another priest in the procession, and this calmed the fears of both parties. The first priest quickly gave the second a brief accounting of who Don Quixote was, and the second priest, along with the entire crowd of penitents, went to see if the poor knight was dead, and they heard Sancho Panza, with tears in his eyes, saying:

"O flower of chivalry, a single blow with a club has brought your well-spent years to an end! O honor of your lineage, honor and glory of all La Mancha, even of all the world, which, with you absent, will be overrun by evildoers unafraid of being punished for their evil doings! O liberal above all Alexanders, for after a mere eight months of service[2] you have given me the best ínsula ever surrounded and encircled by the sea! O

---

1. Penitents in Spain, for example those still seen today in Holy Week processions, and those brought before the tribunals of the Inquisition, wore sheets and hoods that bear an unfortunate resemblance to the outfits of the Ku Klux Klan.

2. Only seventeen days had passed since Don Quixote's second sally.

humble with the proud and arrogant with the humble, attacker of dangers, endurer of insults, enamored without cause, imitator of the good, scourge of the wicked, enemy of the villainous, in short, O knight errant, which is the finest thing one can say."

Sancho's cries and sobs revived Don Quixote, and the first words he said were:

"He who liveth absent from thee, O dulcet Dulcinea, is subject to greater miseries than these. Help me, friend Sancho, to climb into the enchanted cart; I canst no longer sit in Rocinante's saddle, for my shoulder is shattered."

"I'll do that gladly, Señor," responded Sancho, "and let's return to my village in the company of these gentlefolk, who wish you well, and there we'll arrange to make another sally that will bring us more profit and greater fame."

"Well said, Sancho," responded Don Quixote, "and it will be an act of great prudence to allow the present evil influence of the stars to pass."

The canon and the priest and the barber told Don Quixote that what he intended to do was very wise, and so, having been greatly amused by the simplicities of Sancho Panza, they placed Don Quixote in the cart, just as he had been before. The procession formed once again and continued on its way; the goatherd took his leave of everyone; the officers did not wish to go any farther, and the priest paid them what he owed them. The canon asked the priest to inform him of what happened to Don Quixote, if he was cured of his madness or continued to suffer from it, and with this he excused himself and continued his journey. In short, they parted and went their separate ways, and those remaining were the priest, the barber, Don Quixote, Panza, and the good Rocinante, who endured everything he saw with as much patience as his master.

The driver yoked his oxen and settled Don Quixote on a bundle of hay, and with his customary deliberateness followed the route indicated by the priest, and in six days they reached Don Quixote's village, which they entered in the middle of the day, which happened to be Sunday, when everyone was in the square, and the cart carrying Don Quixote drove right through the middle of it. Everyone hurried to see what was in the cart, and when they recognized their neighbor they were astounded, and a boy ran to give the news to the housekeeper and niece that their uncle and master had arrived, skinny and yellow and lying on a pile of hay in an oxcart. It was a pitiful thing to hear the cries of the two good women, to see how they slapped themselves and cursed once again the accursed books of chivalry, all of which started all over again when they saw Don Quixote come through the door.

At the news of Don Quixote's arrival, Sancho Panza's wife came running, for she had already learned that her husband had gone away with him to serve as his squire, and as soon as she saw Sancho, the first thing she asked was if the donkey was all right. Sancho responded that he was better than his master.

"Thanks be to God," she replied, "for all His mercies; but now tell me, my friend, what have you earned after all your squiring? Have you brought me a new overskirt? Did you bring nice shoes for your children?"

"I didn't bring anything like that, dear wife," said Sancho, "though I do have other things that are more valuable and worthwhile."

"That makes me very happy," she responded. "Show me those things that are more valuable and worthwhile, my friend; I want to see them and gladden this heart of mine, which has been so sad and unhappy during all the centuries of your absence."

"I'll show them to you at home," said Panza, "and for now be happy, because if it's God's will that we go out again in search of adventures, in no time you'll see me made a count, or the governor of an ínsula, and not any of the ones around here, but the best that can be found."

"May it please God, my husband, because we surely need it. But tell me, what's all this about ínsulas? I don't understand."

"Honey's not for the donkey's mouth," responded Sancho. "In time you will, dear wife, and even be amazed to hear yourself called ladyship by all your vassals."

"What are you saying, Sancho, about ladyships, ínsulas, and vassals?" responded Juana Panza, which was the name of Sancho's wife; they were not kin, but in La Mancha wives usually take their husbands' family name.[3]

"Don't be in such a hurry, Juana, to learn everything all at once; it's enough that I'm telling you the truth, so sew up your mouth. I'll just tell you this, in passing: there's nothing nicer in the world for a man than being the honored squire of a knight errant seeking adventures. Even though it's true that most don't turn out as well as the man would like, because out of a hundred that you find, ninety-nine tend to turn out wrong and twisted. I know this from experience, because in some I've been tossed in a blanket, and in others I've been beaten, but even so, it's a fine thing to be out looking for things to happen, crossing moun-

---

3. As indicated in an earlier note in chapter VII, there is a good amount of variation in the name of Sancho's wife.

tains, searching forests, climbing peaks, visiting castles, and staying in inns whenever you please and not paying a devil's *maravedí* for anything."

While Sancho Panza and Juana Panza, his wife, were having this conversation, Don Quixote's housekeeper and niece welcomed him, and undressed him, and put him in his old bed. He stared at them, his eyes transfixed, and did not understand where he was. The priest instructed the niece to look after her uncle with great care and to be very sure she did not allow him to escape again, telling her all that they had been obliged to do to bring him home. At this the two women began to cry out to heaven again, and to renew their curses of books of chivalry, and to ask heaven to throw the authors of so many lies and so much foolishness into the bottomless pit. In short, they were distraught and fearful that they would again find themselves without a master and an uncle at the very moment he showed some improvement, and in fact, it turned out just as they imagined.

But the author of this history, although he has investigated with curiosity and diligence the feats performed by Don Quixote on his third sally, has found no account of them, at least not in authenticated documents; their fame has been maintained only in the memories of La Mancha, which tell us that the third time Don Quixote left home he went to Zaragoza and took part in some famous tourneys held in that city, and there things happened to him worthy of his valor and fine intelligence. Nor could he find or learn anything about Don Quixote's final end, and never would have, if good fortune had not presented him with an ancient physician who had in his possession a leaden box that he claimed to have found in the ruined foundations of an old hermitage that was being renovated; in this box he discovered some parchments on which, in Gothic script, Castilian verses celebrated many of the knight's exploits and described the beauty of Dulcinea of Toboso, the figure of Rocinante, the fidelity of Sancho Panza, and the tomb of Don Quixote, with various epitaphs and eulogies to his life and customs.

Those that were legible and could be transcribed are the ones that the trustworthy author of this new and unparalleled history has set down here. This author does not ask compensation from his readers for the immense labor required to investigate and search all the Manchegan archives in order to bring this history to light; he asks only that they afford it the same credit that judicious readers give to the books of chivalry that are esteemed so highly in the world; with this he will consider himself well-paid and satisfied, and encouraged to seek and publish other histories, if not as true, then at least as inventive and entertaining as this one.

The first words written on the parchment discovered in the lead box were these:

THE ACADEMICIANS OF LA ARGAMASILLA, IN LA MANCHA,
ON THE LIFE AND DEATH OF THE VALIANT
DON QUIXOTE OF LA MANCHA,
Hoc Scripserunt

IGNORAMUS, ACADEMICIAN OF LA ARGAMASILLA,
AT THE TOMB OF DON QUIXOTE

Epitaph

The numbskull who so bravely draped La Mancha
with more rich spoils than Jason brought to Crete,
the mind that deemed the pointed vane to be
needed when something blunter would be meet,
    the arm whose mighty pow'r extends so far
that from Cathay to Italian Gaeta's shore
came the most awesome muse, the most aware
who e'er graved verses on a plaque of bronze,
    he who left each Amadís behind,
who turned his mighty back on Galaor
and vanquished all in valor and in love,
    causing ev'ry Belianis to fall mute,
who mounted Rocinante and went erring,
lies here beneath this cold and marble stone.

BY THE FAWNER, ACADEMICIAN OF LA ARGAMASILLA

In Laudem Dulcineae of Toboso
Sonnet

She with the homely face of a kitchen wench,
her bosom high, her gestures fierce and martial,
is Dulcinea, queen of all Toboso,
beloved of the mighty Don Quixote.
    For her sake he climbed every rugged peak
of the great Sierra, and trod the countryside

from famed Montiel to the green and grassy plain
of Aranjuez, on foot, weary, in pain.

    The fault was Rocinante's. Oh, harsh the fate
of this Manchegan lady and her knight,
errant and unvanquished! In tender youth
    she left her beauty behind her when she died,
and he, though his name's inscribed in snowy marble,
could not escape the piercing toils of love.

BY CAPRICIOUS, THE MOST DISCERNING ACADEMICIAN
OF LA ARGAMASILLA, IN PRAISE OF ROCINANTE,
THE HORSE OF DON QUIXOTE OF
LA MANCHA

Sonnet

Upon the proud and gleaming diamond throne
where mighty Mars leaves footprints marked in blood,
the mad Manchegan plants his noble banner
that flutters still with strength so rare and strange,
    and there he hangs his arms, the sharp-edged steel
that devastates and cleaves and cuts in twain.
New feats of arms! But art must now invent
a new style for this newest paladin.
    And if Gaul boasts and brags of Amadís
whose brave descendants glory brought to Greece
and spread her fame and triumph far and wide,
    today in the chamber where Bellona reigns
she crowns the brave Quixote, and for his sake
La Mancha's honored more than Greece or Gaul.
    Ne'er may these glories bear oblivion's stain,
for even Rocinante, in gallantry,
surpasses Brilladoro and Bayardo.[4]

---

4. These are the horses of Orlando and Reinaldos de Montalbán. It should be noted that this sonnet, the kind called *caudato* in Italian, has an extra tercet.

By Mocker, Argamasillan Academic, to Sancho Panza

Sonnet

This is Sancho Panza, in body small
but great in valor, a miracle most strange!
He was, I swear and certify to you
The simplest squire the world has ever seen.

A hair's breadth away from being a count,
but insolence and insult, a miser's world,
a greedy time, conspired all against him,
for a donkey ne'er is spared that injury.

He rode that ass, and pardon the expression,
a gentle squire behind an even gentler
horse named Rocinante, and his master.

Oh, how we mortals wait and hope in vain!
At first how sweet the promise, then bitterly
it vanishes in shadow, smoke, and dream.

By Devilkin, Academician of La Argamasilla, at the Tomb of Don Quixote

Epitaph

Here lies the famous knight
errant and badly bruised
and borne by Rocinante
down many a primrose path.
Sancho Panza the simple
lies here, too, beside him,
the squire most loyal and true
who ever plied the trade.

By Ticktock, Academician of La Argamasilla,
at the Tomb of Dulcinea of Toboso

Epitaph

Here rests the fair Dulcinea;
once rosy-fleshed and plump,
now turned to dust and ashes
by fearful, hideous death.
    She came of unsullied stock,
with a hint of nobility;
the pure passion of great Quixote,
and the glory of her home.

These were the verses that could be read; in the others, the writing was worm-eaten, and they were given to an academician to be deciphered. Our best information is that he has done so, after many long nights of laborious study, and intends to publish them, hoping for a third sally by Don Quixote.

Forsi altro canterà con miglior plectio.[5]

---

5. The line, from *Orlando furioso*, should read, *Forse altri canterà con miglior plettro* ("Perhaps another will sing in a better style"), and is cited by Cervantes in the first chapter of the second part of the novel.

Second Part of the Ingenious Gentleman Don Quixote of La Mancha

By Miguel de Cervantes Saavedra
Author of the First Part

*Dedicated to Don Pedro Fernández de Castro, Count of Lemos,
Andrade, and Villalba, Marquis of Sarria, Gentleman-in-waiting to
His Majesty, Commander of the jurisdiction of Peñafiel and La Zarza,
member of the Order of Alcántara, Viceroy, Governor, and
Captain General of the Kingdom of Naples, and
President of the Supreme Council of Italy.*

To the Count of Lemos[1]

SOME DAYS AGO, when I sent Your Excellency my plays, printed before they were performed, I said, if I remember correctly, that Don Quixote had his spurs ready to make the journey to kiss Your Excellency's hands, and now I say that he is wearing them, and is on his way, and if he arrives, it seems to me I will have performed a service for Your Excellency, because I have been urged on every side to send him forth in order to alleviate the loathing and disgust caused by another Don Quixote who has traveled the world in the disguise of a second part,[2] and the person who has shown the deepest interest has been the great Emperor of China, who, not more than a month ago, sent an emissary with a letter for me in the Chinese language, asking, or I should say begging, me to send the knight to him, because he wanted to establish a college in which the Castilian language would be read, and the book he wanted the students to read was the history of Don Quixote. He further said that he wanted me to be the rector of the college.

I asked the bearer of the letter if His Majesty had given him anything

---

1. Don Pedro Fernández Ruiz de Castro (1576–1622), seventh count of Lemos, was the viceroy of Naples from 1610 to 1616. He was patron to several writers, including Cervantes, who dedicated to him the *Novelas ejemplares* (*Exemplary Novels*) in 1613, the *Comedias y entremeses* (*Plays and Interludes*) in 1615, the second part of *Don Quixote*, also in 1615, and *Persiles y Sigismunda* (a "Byzantine" novel) in 1616, five days before Cervantes's death.

2. In 1614, what is generally known as the "false *Quixote*" appeared in Tarragona. Its title was *The Second Volume of the Ingenious Gentleman Don Quixote of La Mancha*; its author has never been identified, though the book was published under the name of "Alonso Fernández de Avellaneda, a native of the town of Tordesillas." Cervantes apparently learned of its publication as he was writing chapter LIX of the authentic second part.

that would help me to defray my expenses. He replied that it had not even occurred to him.

"Well, brother," I responded, "you can go back to your China, covering your ten leagues a day, or twenty, or whatever you prefer; because my health is not good enough for me to undertake so long a journey, and not only am I ailing but I am lacking in funds, and emperor for emperor and monarch for monarch, in Naples I have the great Count of Lemos, who, without all the provisos of colleges and rectorships, sustains me and protects me and does me more good turns than I could ever desire."

With this I took my leave of him, and with this I take my leave now, offering to Your Excellency *The Travails of Persiles and Sigismunda*, a book that I will complete in four months, *Deo volente*, and it will be either the worst or best ever composed in our language, I mean, of those written for diversion; I must say I regret having said *the worst*, because in the opinion of my friends it is bound to reach the extremes of possible goodness. May Your Excellency enjoy all the good health we wish for you; *Persiles* will soon be ready to kiss your hands, and I, your feet, being, as I am, the servant of Your Excellency. In Madrid, the last day of October, 1615.

Your Excellency's servant,
MIGUEL DE CERVANTES SAAVEDRA

Prologue to the Reader

LORD SAVE ME, how impatiently you must be waiting for this prologue, illustrious or perhaps plebeian reader, believing you will find in it reprisals, quarrels, and vituperations hurled at the author of the second *Don Quixote*. I mean the one sired in Tordesillas, they say, and born in Tarragona![1] But the truth is I will not give you that pleasure, for although offenses awaken rage in the most humble hearts, in mine this rule must find its exception. You would like me to call him an ass, a fool, an insolent dolt, but the thought has not even entered my mind: let his sin be his punishment, let him eat it with his bread, and let that be an end to it. What I do mind, however, is that he accuses me of being old and one-handed, as if it had been in my power to stop time and halt its passage, or as if I had been wounded in some tavern and not at the greatest event ever seen in past or present times, or that future times can ever hope to see. If my wounds do not shine in the eyes of those who see them, they are, at least, esteemed by those who know where they were acquired; it seems better for a soldier to be dead in combat than safe in flight, and I believe this so firmly that even if I could achieve the impossible now, I would rather have taken part in that prodigious battle than to be free of wounds and not to have been there. The wounds on a soldier's face and bosom are stars that guide others to the heaven of honor and the desire to win glory, and it should be noted that one writes not with gray hairs but with the understanding, which generally improves with the years.

1. Despite his disclaimer, in his prologue Cervantes obviously is responding to the prologue of the "false *Quixote*." The "greatest event" to which Cervantes refers is the battle of Lepanto, where he was wounded.

I am also sorry that he calls me envious and, as if I were an ignorant man, explains to me what envy is, but the fact is that of the two kinds of envy, I know only the one that is holy, noble, and well-intentioned; and this being so, I do not need to persecute any priest, especially one who is a familiar of the Holy Office;[2] if he said this in defense of the person on whose behalf he appears to have said it, he was entirely deceived, for I revere that person's genius and admire his works and continual and virtuous diligence. But I do thank this worthy author for saying that although my novels are more satiric than exemplary, they are good, which they could not be if they were not good in every respect.

I think you will say that I am showing great restraint and am keeping well within the bounds of modesty, knowing that one must not add afflictions to the afflicted, and the affliction of this gentleman is undoubtedly very great, for he does not dare to appear openly in the light of day but hides his name and conceals his birthplace, as if he had committed some terrible act of treason against the crown. If you ever happen to meet him, tell him for me that I do not consider myself offended, for I know very well what the temptations of the devil are, and one of the greatest is to give a man the idea that he can compose and publish a book and thereby win as much fame as fortune, as much fortune as fame; in confirmation of this, I should like you, using all your wit and charm, to tell him this story:

In Sevilla there was a madman who had the strangest, most comical notion that any madman ever had. What he did was to make a tube out of a reed that he sharpened at one end, and then he would catch a dog on the street, or somewhere else, hold down one of its hind legs with his foot, lift the other with his hand, fit the tube into the right place, and blow until he had made the animal as round as a ball, and then, holding it up, he would give the dog two little pats on the belly and let it go, saying to the onlookers, and there were always a good number of them:

"Now do your graces think it's an easy job to blow up a dog?" Now does your grace think it's an easy job to write a book?

And if that story does not please him, my dear reader, you can tell him this one, which is also about a madman and a dog:

In Córdoba there was a madman who was in the habit of carrying on his head a slab of marble, or a stone of no small weight, and when he came across an unwary dog, he would go up to the animal and drop the

---

2. An allusion to Lope de Vega; according to Avellaneda's prologue, Lope was unjustly attacked by Cervantes in the first part of *Don Quixote*; the protestations that follow here are pointedly disingenuous, for despite his being a priest, Lope de Vega's dissolute private life was common knowledge.

weight straight down on it. The dog would go into a panic and, barking and howling, run up three streets without stopping. Now, one of the dogs he dropped the weight on happened to belong to a haberdasher and was much loved by its owner. The stone came down, hit the dog on the head, and the battered animal began to yelp and howl; its master saw and heard this, and he seized a measuring stick, came after the madman, and beat him to within an inch of his life, and with each blow he said:

"You miserable thief, you dog, why did you hurt my hound? Didn't you see, cruel man, that my dog was a hound?"

And repeating the word *hound* over and over again, he beat and pummeled the madman. Chastised, the madman withdrew and was not seen on the street for more than a month, but at the end of this time he returned with the same mad idea and an even heavier weight. He would go up to a dog, stare at it long and hard, and not wanting or daring to drop the stone, he would say:

"This is a hound: watch out!"

In fact, all the dogs he encountered, even if they were mastiffs or little lapdogs, he called hounds, and so he never dropped a stone on one again. Perhaps something similar may happen to this storyteller, who will not dare ever again to set his great talent loose among books, which, when they are bad, are harder than boulders.

Tell him, too, that his threat to deprive me of profits with his book is something I do not care about at all, for in the words of the famous interlude *La Perendenga*,[3] I say long live my Lord High Mayor, and the peace of Christ be with you all. Long live the great Count of Lemos, whose well-known Christianity and liberality keep me standing in spite of all the blows struck by my bad fortune, and long live the supreme charity of His Eminence of Toledo, Don Bernardo de Sandoval y Rojas,[4] even if there were no more printing presses in the world, and even if more books were published against me than there are letters in the verses of Mingo Revulgo.[5] These two princes have not received adulation from me, or flattery, but moved only by their own goodness, they have undertaken to favor me with kindness, and for this I consider myself luckier and richer

3. There seems to be no information about this work, which has probably been lost; there is speculation that an interlude called *La Perendeca*, published in 1663 by Agustín Moreto, may be an adaptation of the one Cervantes had in mind.

4. The Cardinal Archbishop of Toledo, Cervantes's protector.

5. A satirical work in verse written during the reign of Enrique IV (1454–1474), it was widely circulated and immensely popular.

than if fortune had brought me to the heights by any ordinary means. A poor man may have honor, but not a villain; need may cloud nobility, but not hide it completely; if virtue sheds her light, even along the crags and cracks of poverty, it will be esteemed by high, noble spirits, and so be favored.

Say no more to him, and I do not wish to say more to you except to tell you to consider that this second part of *Don Quixote*, which I offer to you now, is cut by the same artisan and from the same cloth as the first, and in it I give you a somewhat expanded Don Quixote who is, at the end, dead and buried, so that no one will dare tell more tales about him, for the ones told in the past are enough, and it is also enough that an honorable man has recounted his clever follies and does not want to take them up again; for abundance, even of things that are good, makes people esteem them less, and scarcity, even of bad things, lends a certain value. I forgot to tell you to expect the *Persiles*, which I am finishing now, and the second part of *Galatea*.[6]

6. This was never published, and if Cervantes in fact wrote it, the work has been lost.

CHAPTER I

Regarding what transpired when the priest and the barber discussed his illness with Don Quixote

Cide Hamete Benengeli tells us in the second part of this history, which recounts the third sally of Don Quixote, that the priest and the barber did not see the knight for almost a month in order not to restore and bring back to his mind events of the past, but this did not stop them from visiting his niece and housekeeper, charging them to be sure to pamper him and give him food to eat that would strengthen and fortify his heart and brain, the source, as they had good reason to think, of all his misfortunes. The two women said that they already were doing so, and would continue to do so, as willingly and carefully as possible, because they could see that there were moments when their lord and master gave signs of being in his right mind; this made the priest and the barber extremely happy, for then it seemed to them that they had done the right thing by bringing him home, enchanted, in the oxcart, as recounted in the final chapter of the first part of this great and accurate history. And so they decided to visit him and see his improvement for themselves, although they considered a complete cure almost impossible, and they agreed not to make any mention at all of knight errantry so as not to run the risk of reopening his wounds, which were still so fresh.

In short, they visited him and found him sitting up in bed, dressed in the green flannel vest he wore under his armor, and a red Toledan cap, and looking so dry and gaunt that he seemed to be a mummy. They received a warm welcome, they asked after his health, and he accounted for himself and the state of his health with very good judgment and in very elegant words, and in the course of their conversation they began to discuss what is called reason of state and ways of governing, correcting

this abuse and condemning that one, reforming one custom and elimi-
nating another, each one of the three becoming a new legislator, a modern Lycurgus, a latter-day Solon,[1] and they so transformed the nation
that it seemed as if they had placed it in the forge and taken out a new
one, and Don Quixote spoke with so much intelligence regarding all the
subjects they touched upon that his two examiners thought there was no
doubt that he was completely well and his sanity restored.

The niece and housekeeper were present at this conversation, and
they never tired of giving thanks to God at seeing their lord and master
with all his wits; the priest, however, changing his earlier intention,
which was not to touch on chivalric matters, wanted a more thorough
test of whether or not Don Quixote's recovery was false or true, and so he
gradually began to recount news of the court, and among other things,
he said it was thought certain that the Turk would come down with a
powerful fleet, but no one knew his plans or where the huge cloud would
burst; this fear, which has us on the alert almost every year, had now affected all of Christendom, and His Majesty had fortified the coasts of
Naples and Sicily and the island of Malta. To which Don Quixote responded:

"His Majesty has behaved like a most prudent warrior by fortifying
his states in good time so that the enemy will not find them unprepared,
but if he were to take my advice, I would counsel him to take a precautionary measure that His Majesty is very far from considering at present."

As soon as the priest heard this, he said to himself:

"May God hold you in his hand, my poor Don Quixote, for it seems
to me you have leaped from the high peak of your madness into the profound abyss of your foolishness!"

But the barber, who had already had the same thought as the priest,
asked Don Quixote to tell him the precautionary measure he thought it
would be good to undertake; perhaps it might be put on the list of the
many impertinent proposals that are commonly offered to princes.

"Mine, Señor Shaver," said Don Quixote, "is not impertinent but
completely pertinent."

"I don't say it isn't," replied the barber, "but experience shows that all
or most of the schemes presented to His Majesty are either impossible, or
absurd, or harmful to the king and his kingdom."

"Well, mine," responded Don Quixote, "is neither impossible nor ab-

1. Famous legislators of ancient Sparta and Athens, respectively.

surd, but is, rather, the easiest, most just, most practical, and shrewdest that has ever occurred to any planner."

"Your grace is slow in telling us what it is, Señor Don Quixote," said the priest.

"I would not want," said Don Quixote, "to state it here and now, and tomorrow have it find its way to the ears of the king's advisers so that another receives the thanks and rewards for my labor."

"As far as I am concerned," said the barber, "I give my word, here and before God, not to repeat what your grace would tell the king or the rook or any man on earth, a vow I learned in the tale of the priest[2] who, in the preface, told the king about the thief who had stolen one hundred *doblas* from him, as well as his mule with the ambling gait."

"I know nothing of stories," said Don Quixote, "but I do know this is a good vow because I know the barber is a trustworthy man."

"Even if he were not," said the priest, "I would vouch for him and guarantee that in this case he will say no more than if he were mute, under pain of sentence by the court."

"And who vouches for your grace, Señor Priest?" said Don Quixote.

"My profession," responded the priest, "which is to keep secrets."

"By my faith!" Don Quixote said then. "What else can His Majesty do but command by public proclamation that on a specific day all the knights errant wandering through Spain are to gather at court, and even if no more than half a dozen were to come, there might be one among them who could, by himself, destroy all the power of the Turk. Your graces should listen carefully and follow what I say. Is it by any chance surprising for a single knight errant to vanquish an army of two hundred thousand men, as if all of them together had but one throat or were made of sugar candy? Tell me, then: how many histories are filled with such marvels? If only—to my misfortune, if not to anyone else's—the famous Don Belianís were alive today, or any one of the countless descendants of Amadís of Gaul! If any of them were here today and confronted the Turk, it would not be to his advantage! But God will look after His people and provide one who, if not as excellent as the knights errant of old, at least will not be inferior to them in courage; God understands me, and I shall say no more."

"Oh!" said the niece at this point. "You can kill me if my uncle doesn't want to be a knight errant again!"

---

2. The reference is to a well-known popular tale.

To which Don Quixote said:

"I shall die a knight errant, and let the Turk come down or go up whenever he wishes and however powerfully he can; once again I say that God understands me."

And then the barber said:

"I beg your graces to give me leave to tell a brief story that occurred in Sevilla; since it is very much to the point here, I should like to tell it now."

Don Quixote gave his permission, and the priest and the others listened carefully, and the barber began in this manner:

"In the madhouse in Sevilla was a man whose relatives had put him there because he had lost his reason. He was a graduate in canon law from Osuna, but even if he had graduated from Salamanca, in the opinion of many he would not have been any less mad. This graduate, after some years of confinement, came to believe that he was sane and in his right mind, and with this thought he wrote to the archbishop earnestly entreating him, in carefully chosen phrases, to have him removed from the misery in which he was living, for through God's mercy he had now recovered his reason, but his relatives, in order to enjoy his share of the estate, were keeping him there, and despite the truth would have wanted him mad until his death. The archbishop, persuaded by his many well-written and well-reasoned letters, ordered one of his chaplains to learn from the superintendent of the madhouse if what the licentiate had written was true, and to speak to the madman as well, and, if it seemed he was in his right mind, to release him and set him free. The chaplain did so, and the superintendent told him that the man was still mad; though he often spoke like a person of great intelligence, he eventually would begin to say countless foolish things, as many and as deeply felt as his earlier rational statements, and this the chaplain could see for himself if he spoke to him. The chaplain agreed, visited the madman, spoke to him for more than an hour, and in all that time the madman never made a confused or foolish statement; rather, he spoke so judiciously that the chaplain was obliged to believe that the madman was sane; one of the things the madman told him was that the superintendent bore him ill will because he did not want to lose the gifts his relatives gave him for saying he was still mad, though with periods of lucidity; the greatest obstacle for him in his misfortune was his wealth, because in order to enjoy it, his enemies were deceptive and denied the mercy Our Lord had shown by turning him from a beast back into a man. In short, what he said depicted the superintendent as suspect, his relatives as greedy and heartless, and himself as so reasonable that the chaplain resolved to take him back so that the archbishop could see and touch the truth of the matter for himself. With this virtuous intention, the good chaplain asked the superintendent to return the clothes the licentiate had been wearing when he was first admitted; again the superintendent told him to think about what he was doing because there was no doubt that the licentiate was still mad. The superintendent's warnings and admonitions were in vain: the chaplain insisted on taking him away; the superintendent obeyed, since it was by order of the archbishop, and the licentiate was dressed in his clothes, which were new and decent, and when he saw himself in the raiment of a sane man and no longer wearing the clothing of a madman, he asked the chaplain to please give him permission to say goodbye to his mad companions. The chaplain said that he wished to accompany him and see the madmen who were in the hospital. And so they went up, along with some other people, and when the licentiate reached a cage that held a raving maniac who was, however, calm and quiet for the moment, he said:

'Brother, see if there is anything you wish to ask of me, for I am going home; God in His infinite goodness and mercy, though I do not deserve it, has been pleased to restore my reason to me: now I am healthy and sane; nothing is impossible for the power of God. Place your hope and trust in Him, for as He has returned me to my earlier state, He will do the same for you if you trust in Him. I will be sure to send you some good things to eat, and eat them you must, for I say that I believe, as one who has experienced it himself, that all our madness comes from having our stomachs empty and our heads full of air. Take heart, take heart: despondency in misfortune lessens one's health and hastens death.'

Another madman who was in a cage facing the cage of the first maniac heard everything the licentiate said, and he got up from an old mat where he had been lying naked and asked in a shout who it was that was leaving healthy and sane. The licentiate responded:

'It is I, brother, who am leaving; I no longer have any need to be here, and for that I give infinite thanks to heaven for the mercy it has shown me.'

'Think about what you are saying, Licentiate, don't let the devil deceive you,' replied the madman. 'Keep your feet still, and stay peacefully in your house, and you'll save yourself the trouble of having to come back.'

'I know I am cured,' replied the licentiate, 'and will not have to do any of this again.'

'You, cured?' said the madman. 'Well, well, time will tell; go with God, but I vow by Jupiter, whose majesty I represent on earth, that on account of the sin that Sevilla commits today by taking you out of this madhouse and calling you sane, I must inflict on her a punishment so severe that its memory will endure for all eternity, amen. And don't you know, you miserable little licentiate, that I can do it? For, as I have said, I am Jupiter the Thunderer, and in my hands I hold the flaming thunderbolts with which I can threaten and destroy the world. But I wish to punish this ignorant city with only one thing: I will not rain on it or its environs for three whole years, which will be counted from the day and hour when the threat was made. You free, and healthy, and sane, while I am mad, and sick, and confined . . . ? I would just as soon rain as hang myself.'

Those who were nearby heard the shouts and the words of the madman, but our licentiate, turning to the chaplain and grasping his hands, said:

'Your grace should not be concerned by or pay attention to what this madman has said, for if he is Jupiter and does not wish to rain, I, who am Neptune, father and god of waters, shall rain whenever I please and whenever it is necessary.'

To which the chaplain replied:

'Even so, Señor Neptune, it would not be a good idea to anger Señor Jupiter; your grace should stay in your house, and another day, when it is more convenient and there is more time, we shall come back for your grace.'

The superintendent and the bystanders all laughed, and their laughter mortified the chaplain; they stripped the licentiate, who remained in the madhouse, and that was the end of the story."

"Well, Señor Barber, this is the story," said Don Quixote, "so much to the point that you had to tell it? Ah, Señor Shaver, Señor Shaver, how blind must one be not to see through a sieve? Is it possible your grace does not know that comparisons of intelligence, or valor, or beauty, or lineage are always hateful and badly received? I, Señor Barber, am not Neptune, the god of waters, nor do I attempt to persuade anyone that I am clever when I am not; I only devote myself to making the world understand its error in not restoring that happiest of times when the order of knight errantry was in flower. But our decadent age does not deserve to enjoy the good that was enjoyed in the days when knights errant took it as their responsibility to bear on their own shoulders the defense of kingdoms, the protection of damsels, the safeguarding of orphans and wards, the punishment of the proud, and the rewarding of the humble. Most knights today would rather rustle in damasks, brocades, and the other rich fabrics of their clothes than creak in chain mail; no longer do knights sleep in the fields, subject to the rigors of heaven, wearing all their armor from head to foot; no longer does anyone, with his feet still in the stirrups and leaning on his lance, catch forty winks, as they say, as the knights errant used to do. No longer does anyone ride out of this forest and into those mountains, and from there tread upon a bare and desolate beach, the sea most often stormy and tempestuous, and find along the shore a small boat without oars, sail, mast, or any kind of rigging, and with intrepid heart climb in and give himself over to the implacable waves of the deepest ocean, which first raise him up to heaven and then toss him into the abyss; and, with his breast turned to the insurmountable storm, when he least expects it he finds himself more than three thousand leagues distant from the place where he embarked, and he leaps out of the boat onto a distant unknown land, and there things occur that are worthy of being written not on parchment, but bronze.

Now, however, sloth triumphs over diligence, idleness over work, vice over virtue, arrogance over valor, and theory over the practice of arms, which lived and shone only in the Golden Age and in the time of the knights errant. If you do not agree, then tell me: who was more virtuous and valiant than the famed Amadís of Gaul? Who more intelligent than Palmerín of England? Who more accommodating and good-natured than Tirant lo Blanc? Who more gallant than Lisuarte of Greece? Who more combative with the sword than Don Belianís? Who more intrepid than Perión of Gaul, or more audacious in the face of danger than Felixmarte of Hyrcania, or more sincere than Esplandián? Who bolder than Don Cirongilio of Thrace? Who more courageous than Rodamonte? Who more prudent than King Sobrino? Who more daring than Reinaldos? Who more invincible than Roland? And who more elegant and courteous than Ruggiero, from whom the modern-day Dukes of Ferrara are descended, according to Turpin in his *Cosmography*? All these knights, and many others I could mention, Señor Priest, were knights errant, the light and glory of chivalry. They, or knights like them, are the ones I would like for my scheme; if they were part of it, His Majesty would be well served and save a good deal of money, and the

Turk would be left tearing his beard; therefore I shall remain in my house, since the chaplain has not taken me out of it, and if his Jupiter, as the barber has said, does not rain, here am I, and I shall rain whenever I please. I say this so that Señor Basin will know I understand him."

"The truth is, Señor Don Quixote," said the barber, "this is not why I told the story, and as God is my witness my intentions were good, and your grace should not be offended."

"I know very well," responded Don Quixote, "whether or not I should be offended."

At this juncture the priest said:

"Although I have hardly said a word until now, I should like to express some misgivings that are gnawing and scratching at my conscience, and were caused by what Señor Don Quixote said here."

"The Señor Priest has permission for many things," responded Don Quixote, "and so he may state his misgivings, for it is not pleasant to have a conscience filled with them."

"Well, having received this approval," responded the priest, "I say that these are my misgivings: I am not at all convinced that this crowd of knights errant to whom your grace, Señor Don Quixote, has referred, were really and truly persons of flesh and blood who lived in the world; rather, I imagine they are all fiction, fable, falsehood—dreams told by men when they are awake, or, I should say, half-asleep."

"That is another error," responded Don Quixote, "into which many have fallen: they do not believe that such knights ever existed in the world, and with a variety of people and on different occasions, I have often attempted to bring this common misconception into the light of truth; sometimes I have not succeeded in my intention, and at other times I have, supporting it on the shoulders of truth, and this truth is so certain I can almost say I have seen Amadís of Gaul with my own eyes: tall, with a pale face and nicely trimmed black beard and a gaze both gentle and severe, he was a man of few words, slow to anger and quick to put aside wrath; and just as I have depicted Amadís, I could, I believe, portray and describe all the knights errant who wander through all the histories in the world, because it is my understanding that they were just as their histories recount, and by means of the deeds they performed and the circumstances in which they lived, and by using sound philosophy, one can deduce their features, their natures, and their stature."

"Then how tall does your grace, Señor Don Quixote," asked the barber, "think the giant Morgante was?"

"In the matter of giants," responded Don Quixote, "there are different opinions as to whether or not they ever existed in the world, but Holy Scripture, which cannot deviate an iota from the truth, shows us that they did by telling us the history of that huge Philistine Goliath, whose stature was seven and a half cubits, which is inordinately tall. And on the island of Sicily, shin bones and shoulder bones have been discovered which are so large that it is clear they belonged to giants as tall as a tall tower; geometry proves this truth beyond any doubt. But despite all this, I could not say with certainty how big Morgante was, though I imagine he was not very tall; I am of this opinion because in his history, when there is particular mention of his deeds, he often was sleeping under a roof, and since he could find a house large enough to hold him, it is obvious his size was not exceptional."

"That is true," said the priest, who enjoyed hearing so much foolishness, and asked his feelings with regard to the appearance of Reinaldos de Montalbán, Don Roland, and the other Twelve Peers of France, for they all had been knights errant.

"With respect to Reinaldos," responded Don Quixote, "I daresay his face was broad and ruddy, his eyes merry and rather prominent, his temperament excessively punctilious and choleric, and that he was a friend of thieves and other dissolute people. With respect to Roland, or Roldán, or Rotolando, or Orlando, for he is called all these names in the histories, I believe and declare that he was of medium height, broadshouldered, somewhat bowlegged, with a dark complexion and a blond beard, a hairy body and a threatening demeanor, a man of few words but very courteous and well-bred."

"If Roland was not more of a gentleman than your grace has indicated," replied the priest, "it is not surprising that Señora Angelica the Fair scorned him and left him for the elegance, spirit, and charm that the downy-cheeked Moorish lad to whom she gave herself must have possessed, and she was wise to fall madly in love with Medoro's gentleness rather than Roland's harshness."

"Angelica, Señor Priest," responded Don Quixote, "was a pleasure-seeker, a gadabout, and a somewhat capricious damsel, and she left the world as full of her impertinences as it was filled with the fame of her beauty: she scorned a thousand brave and intelligent gentlemen, and was satisfied with a little beardless page who had no property or name other than a reputation for gratitude because of his loyalty to a friend. The great singer of her beauty, the famous Ariosto, did not dare or wish to sing what happened to the lady after she so ruinously gave herself to Medoro, for they could not have been overly virtuous things, and he left her at the point where he says:

> And of how she gained the scepter of Cathay,
> perhaps another will sing in a better style.[3]

And no doubt this was a kind of prophecy; poets are called *vates*, which means they are *soothsayers*. This truth can be clearly seen because since then a famous Andalusian poet wept over and sang of her tears, and another famous and unique Castilian poet sang of her beauty."[4]

"Tell me, Señor Don Quixote," said the barber, "among all those who praised her, hasn't there ever been a poet who wrote a satire of this Señora Angelica?"[5]

"I do believe," responded Don Quixote, "that if Sacripante or Roland had been poets, they would already have reprimanded the damsel as she deserved, because it is right and natural for poets who have been scorned and rejected by their imagined ladies, or by the imagined ladies of the characters they have created in their works, whom they have chosen as the mistresses of their thoughts, to take their revenge with satires and attacks, a revenge most certainly unworthy of generous hearts; but until now I have not heard of a single verse attacking Señora Angelica, who turned the world upside down."

"Miraculous!" said the priest.

And at this point they heard the housekeeper and niece, who had already abandoned the conversation, shouting in the courtyard, and they all hurried to the site of the noise.

---

3. The second line, in Italian, closes part I of *Don Quixote*.

4. The first poet is Luis Barahona de Soto, who wrote *Las lágrimas de Angélica* (*The Tears of Angelica*); the second is Lope de Vega, who wrote *La hermosura de Angélica* (*The Beauty of Angelica*).

5. Subsequent to the publication of part II, both Góngora and Quevedo wrote satires of the epic of Charlemagne, including the love of Roland and Angelica, which had been so popular in the early Renaissance.

CHAPTER II

Which deals with the notable dispute that Sancho Panza had with Don Quixote's niece and housekeeper, as well as other amusing topics

Our history recounts that the cries heard by Don Quixote, the priest, and the barber came from the niece and housekeeper and were directed at Sancho Panza, who was struggling to come in to see Don Quixote, while they barred his way, shouting:

"What does this vagabond want in our house? Go back home, brother, for you and nobody else lead our master astray and lure him out of his house and take him to those godforsaken places."

To which Sancho responded:

"Housekeeper from hell, the one who's lured and led astray and taken to godforsaken places is me, not your master; he led me everywhere, and you two are deceived and are blaming the wrong person; he lured me out of my house with tricks and lies, promising me an ínsula that I'm still waiting for."

"I hope you choke on those damned ínsulas, Sancho, you wretch," responded the niece. "And what are ínsulas? Something to eat, you greedy glutton?"

"It's not something to eat," replied Sancho, "but something to govern and rule better than any town council or magistrate in criminal court."

"Even so," said the housekeeper, "you won't come in, you bag of evil and sack of wickedness. Go and govern your own house and work your parcel of land and stop trying to rule ínsulas or ínsulos or whatever you call them."

The priest and the barber were delighted to hear this three-way conversation, but Don Quixote, fearful that Sancho would blurt out and disclose a quantity of malicious nonsense and touch on points that would not redound to his credit, called to him and made the two women be quiet and allow him to enter. Sancho came in, and the priest and the barber took their leave of Don Quixote, in despair over his health, for they saw how fixed his foolish ideas were and how enthralled he was by the nonsense of his calamitously errant chivalry; and so, the priest said to the barber:

"You'll see, compadre, that when we least expect it, our gentleman will leave again and beat the bushes, putting all the birds to flight."

"I have no doubt about that," responded the barber, "but I'm not as astounded by the madness of the knight as I am by the simplicity of the squire, who has so much faith in the story of the ínsula that I don't believe all the disappointments imaginable will ever get it out of his head."

"May God help them," said the priest, "and let us be on the alert: we'll see where all the foolishness in this knight and squire will lead, because it seems as if both were made from the same mold, and that the madness of the master, without the simplicity of the servant, would not be worth anything."

"That's true," said the barber, "and I'd certainly like to know what they're talking about now."

"I assure you," responded the priest, "that the niece or the housekeeper will tell us later, because they're not the kind not to eavesdrop."

In the meantime, Don Quixote had taken Sancho into his room and closed the door, and when they were alone, he said:

"It grieves me, Sancho, that you have said and still say that I lured you away, knowing that I did not remain in my own house; we went out together, we left together, and we traveled together; together we shared a single fortune and a single fate: if you were tossed in a blanket once, I was battered and bruised a hundred times, and that is the one advantage I have over you."

"That was right and proper," responded Sancho, "because, according to your grace, misfortunes afflict knights errant more than their squires."

"You are wrong, Sancho," said Don Quixote. "As the saying goes, *Quando caput dolet*—"

"I don't understand any language but my own," responded Sancho.

"I mean," said Don Quixote, "that when the head aches, all the other members ache, too; since I am your lord and master, I am your head, and you my part, for you are my servant; for this reason, the evil that touches or may touch me will cause you pain, and yours will do the same to me."

"That's how it should be," said Sancho, "but when they tossed me, a member, in the blanket, my head was behind the fence watching me fly through the air and not feeling any pain at all; since the members are obliged to suffer the pains of the head, the head should be obliged to feel their pains, too."

"Do you mean to say, Sancho," responded Don Quixote, "that I felt no pain when you were tossed in the blanket? If that is what you mean, do not say it and do not think it, for at the time I felt more pain in my spirit than you did in your body. But let us put that aside for now; there will be time for us to ponder this and draw the proper conclusion; tell me, Sancho my friend: what are people saying about me in the village? What opinion of me do the commoners have, and the gentlefolk, and the knights? What do they say about my valor, my deeds, and my courtesy? What is the talk with regard to my undertaking to revive and bring back to the world the forgotten order of chivalry? In short, Sancho, I want you to tell me what has reached your ears regarding this, and you must tell me without adding anything to the good or taking anything away from the bad, for it is fitting that loyal vassals tell the exact and unvarnished truth to their lords, not swelling it because of adulation or allowing any other idle considerations to lessen it; and I want you to know, Sancho, that if the naked truth, bare of flattery, were to reach the ears of princes, the times would be different and other ages would be deemed to be of iron when compared to our own, which, I believe, would be considered golden. Heed this warning, Sancho, and with good sense and intentions bring to my ears the truth of what you know in response to what I have asked you."

"I will do that very gladly, Señor," responded Sancho, "on the condition that your grace will not be angry at what I say, since you want me to tell the naked truth and not dress it in any clothes except the ones it was wearing when I heard it."

"Under no circumstances shall I be angry," responded Don Quixote. "You may certainly speak freely, Sancho, without evasions."

"Well, the first thing I'll say," he said, "is that the common people think your grace is a great madman, and that I'm just as great a simpleton. The gentry say you have not stayed within the bounds of being a gentleman and have called yourself *Don*[1] and rushed into being a knight when you have just a vine or two and a couple of fields and nothing but rags on your back. The knights say they wouldn't want the minor gentry

1. The honorific *don* or *doña* was supposed to be used only with specific ranks of nobility, though many people added the title to their names without having any right to it.

to compete with them, especially those squirish gentlefolk who polish their shoes with lampblack and mend their black stockings with green thread."

"That," said Don Quixote, "has nothing to do with me, because I am always well-dressed, and never in patches; my clothes may be frayed, but more by my armor than by time."

"As for your grace's valor, courtesy, deeds, and undertakings," Sancho continued, "there are different opinions. Some say, 'Crazy, but amusing'; others, 'Brave, but unfortunate'; and others, 'Courteous, but insolent'; and they go on and on so much in this vein that they don't leave an untouched bone in your grace's body or mine."

"Look, Sancho," said Don Quixote, "wherever extraordinary virtue resides, there it is persecuted. Very few, if any, of the famous men of the past escaped the slanders of the wicked. Julius Caesar, that most spirited, prudent, and valiant captain, was called ambitious and not particularly clean in his clothing or habits. Alexander, whose feats earned him the title of Great, was said to have been something of a drunkard. Hercules, with all his labors, was called lascivious and soft. Don Galaor, the brother of Amadís of Gaul, was whispered to be more than a little quarrelsome, and his brother was called tearful. And so, dear Sancho, with so many calumnies directed against good men, let them say what they wish about me, as long as there is no more than what you have told me."

"That's the problem, I swear by my father!" replied Sancho.

"Then, there is more?" asked Don Quixote.

"And something much worse," said Sancho. "So far it's been nothing but child's play, but if your grace wants to know all the slander they're saying about you, I'll bring somebody here who will tell you everything and not leave out a crumb; last night Bartolomé Carrasco's son, who's been studying at Salamanca, came home with his bachelor's degree, and I went to welcome him home and he told me that the history of your grace is already in books, and it's called *The Ingenious Gentleman Don Quixote of La Mancha*; and he says that in it they mention me, Sancho Panza, by name, and my lady Dulcinea of Toboso, and other things that happened when we were alone, so that I crossed myself in fear at how the historian who wrote them could have known about them."

"I assure you, Sancho," said Don Quixote, "that the author of our history must be some wise enchanter, for nothing is hidden from them if they wish to write about it."

"Well," said Sancho, "if he was wise and an enchanter, then how is it possible (according to what Bachelor Sansón Carrasco says, for that's the name of the person I was telling you about) that the author of the history is named Cide Hamete Berenjena?"

"That is a Moorish name," responded Don Quixote.

"It must be," responded Sancho, "because I've heard that most Moors are very fond of eggplant."[2]

"You must be mistaken, Sancho," said Don Quixote, "in the last name of this Cide, which in Arabic means *señor*."

"That may be," replied Sancho, "but if your grace would like me to bring Sansón Carrasco here, I'll go find him right away."

"I would like that very much, my friend," said Don Quixote. "What you have told me has left me in suspense, and nothing I eat will taste good until I learn everything."

"Then I'll go for him now," responded Sancho.

And leaving his master, he went to find the bachelor, with whom he returned in a very short while, and the three of them had a most amusing conversation.

CHAPTER III

Regarding the comical discussion held by Don Quixote, Sancho Panza, and Bachelor Sansón Carrasco

Don Quixote was extremely thoughtful as he awaited Bachelor Carrasco, from whom he hoped to hear the news about himself that had been put into a book, as Sancho had said, though he could not persuade himself that such a history existed, for the blood of the enemies he had slain was not yet dry on the blade of his sword and his chivalric exploits were already in print. Even so, he imagined that some wise man, either a friend or an enemy, by the arts of enchantment had printed them: if a friend, in order to elevate them and raise them above the most famous deeds of any knight errant; if an enemy, to annihilate them and place them lower than the basest acts ever attributed to the basest squire, al-

2. See note 6, chapter IX, part I, for a discussion of the Moorish "author's" name.

though—he said to himself—the acts of squires were never written
down; if such a history did exist, because it was about a knight errant it
would necessarily be grandiloquent, noble, distinguished, magnificent,
and true.

This gave him some consolation, but it made him disconsolate to
think that its author was a Moor, as suggested by the name Cide, and one
could not expect truth from the Moors, because all of them are tricksters,
liars, and swindlers. He feared his love had been treated with an inde-
cency that would redound to the harm and detriment of the modesty of
his lady Dulcinea of Toboso; he earnestly hoped there had been a decla-
ration of the fidelity and decorum with which he had always behaved
toward her, disdaining queens, empresses, and maidens of all ranks and
keeping at bay the force of his natural passions; and so, rapt and enrapt
in these and many other thoughts, he was found by Sancho and
Carrasco, whom Don Quixote received with great courtesy.

The bachelor, though his name was Sansón,[1] was not particularly
large, but he was immensely sly; his color was pale, but his intelligence
was very bright; he was about twenty-four years old, with a round face, a
snub nose, and a large mouth, all signs of a mischievous nature and a
fondness for tricks and jokes, which he displayed when, upon seeing Don
Quixote, he kneeled before him and said:

"Your magnificence, Señor Don Quixote of La Mancha, give me your
hands, for by the habit of St. Peter that I wear,[2] though I have taken only
the first four orders, your grace is one of the most famous knights errant
there ever was, or will be, anywhere on this round earth. Blessings on
Cide Hamete Benengeli, who wrote the history of your great deeds, and
double blessings on the inquisitive man who had it translated from Arabic into our vernacular Castilian, for the universal entertainment of all
people."

Don Quixote had him stand, and he said:

"So then, is it true that my history exists, and that it was composed by
a wise Moor?"

"It is so true, Señor," said Sansón, "that I believe there are more than
twelve thousand copies of this history in print today; if you do not think
so, let Portugal, Barcelona, and Valencia tell you so, for they were
printed there; there is even a rumor that it is being printed in Antwerp,

1. *Sansón* is the Spanish equivalent of Samson.

2. The ordinary clothing of the clergy and of scholars; the term is used here mockingly, as if it were
the habit of one of the great military orders, such as the order of Santiago (St. James).

and it is evident to me that every nation or language will have its translation of the book."[3]

"One of the things," said Don Quixote, "that must give the greatest contentment to a virtuous and eminent man is to see, while he is still alive, his good name printed and published in the languages of different peoples. I said *good name*, for if it were the opposite, no death could be its equal."

"In the matter of a good reputation and a good name," said the bachelor, "your grace alone triumphs over all other knights errant, for the Moor in his language and the Christian in his were careful to depict very vividly the gallantry of your grace, your great courage in confronting danger, your patience in adversity, your forbearance in the face of misfortunes and wounds, the virtue and modesty of the Platonic love of your grace and my lady Doña Dulcinea of Toboso."

"Never," said Sancho Panza, "have I heard my lady Dulcinea called *Doña*, just *Señora Dulcinea of Toboso*, and that's where the history's wrong."

"That is not an important objection," responded Carrasco.

"No, of course not," responded Don Quixote, "but tell me, Señor Bachelor: which deeds of mine are praised the most in this history?"

"In that regard," responded the bachelor, "there are different opinions, just as there are different tastes: some prefer the adventure of the windmills, which your grace thought were Briareuses and giants; others, that of the waterwheel; one man favors the description of the two armies that turned out to be two flocks of sheeps; the other praises the adventure of the body that was being carried to Segovia for burial; one says that the adventure of the galley slaves is superior to all the rest; another, that none equals that of the two gigantic Benedictines and the dispute with the valiant Basque."

"Tell me, Señor Bachelor," said Sancho, "is the adventure of the Yanguesans mentioned, when our good Rocinante took a notion to ask for the moon?"

"The wise man," responded Sansón, "left nothing in the inkwell; he

3. Part I had been printed three times in Madrid (twice in 1605, once in 1608), twice in Lisbon (1605), twice in Valencia (1605), twice in Brussels (1607, 1611), and once in Milan (1610) when Cervantes probably wrote these lines. It did not appear in Barcelona until 1617 (when the first and second parts were printed together for the first time) or in Antwerp until 1673 (it is assumed that Cervantes wrote Antwerp instead of Brussels). All of these editions are in Spanish; the first translation of the book (into English, by Thomas Shelton) appeared in London in 1612.

says everything and takes note of everything, even the capering that our good Sancho did in the blanket."

"In the blanket I wasn't capering," responded Sancho, "but I was in the air, and more than I would have liked."

"It seems to me," said Don Quixote, "there is no human history in the world that does not have its ups and downs, especially those that deal with chivalry; they cannot be filled with nothing but successful exploits."

"Even so," responded the bachelor, "some people who have read the history say they would have been pleased if its authors had forgotten about some of the infinite beatings given to Señor Don Quixote in various encounters."

"That's where the truth of the history comes in," said Sancho.

"They also could have kept quiet about them for the sake of fairness," said Don Quixote, "because the actions that do not change or alter the truth of the history do not need to be written if they belittle the hero. By my faith, Aeneas was not as pious as Virgil depicts him, or Ulysses as prudent as Homer describes him."

"That is true," replied Sansón, "but it is one thing to write as a poet and another to write as a historian: the poet can recount or sing about things not as they were, but as they should have been, and the historian must write about them not as they should have been, but as they were, without adding or subtracting anything from the truth."

"Well, if this Moorish gentleman is interested in telling the truth," said Sancho, "then among all the beatings my master received, you're bound to find mine, because they never took the measure of his grace's shoulders without taking it for my whole body; but there's no reason for me to be surprised, because as my master himself says, all the members must share in the head's pain."

"You are very crafty, Sancho," responded Don Quixote. "By my faith, you have no lack of memory when you want to remember."

"When I would like to forget the beatings I've gotten," said Sancho, "the welts won't let me, because they're still fresh on my ribs."

"Be quiet, Sancho," said Don Quixote, "and do not interrupt the bachelor, whom I implore to continue telling me what is said about me in this history."

"And about me," said Sancho. "They also say I'm one of the principal presonages in it."

"*Personages*, not *presonages*, Sancho my friend," said Sansón.

"Another one who corrects my vocabulery?" said Sancho. "Well, both of you keep it up and we'll never finish."

"As God is my witness, Sancho," responded the bachelor, "you are the second person in the history, and there are some who would rather hear you talk than the cleverest person in it, though there are also some who say you were much too credulous when you believed that the governorship of the ínsula offered to you by Señor Don Quixote, here present, could be true."

"The sun has not yet gone down," said Don Quixote, "and as Sancho grows older, with the experience granted by his years he will be more skilled and more capable of being a governor than he is now."

"By God, Señor," said Sancho, "the island that I can't govern at the age I am now I won't be able to govern if I get to be as old as Methuselah. The trouble is that this ínsula is hidden someplace, I don't know where, it's not that I don't have the good sense to govern it."

"Trust in God, Sancho," said Don Quixote, "that everything will turn out well and perhaps even better than you expect; not a leaf quivers on a tree unless God wills it."

"That's true," said Sansón. "If it is God's will, Sancho will have a thousand islands to govern, not just one."

"I have seen some governors," said Sancho, "who, in my opinion, don't come up to the sole of my shoe, and even so they're called lordship and are served their food on silver."

"They aren't governors of ínsulas," replied Sansón, "but of other, more tractable realms; those who govern ínsulas have to know grammar at the very least."

"I can accept the *gram* all right," said Sancho, "but the *mar* I won't go near because I don't understand it. But leaving the question of my being a governor in the hands of God, and may He place me wherever He chooses, I say, Señor Bachelor Sansón Carrasco, that it makes me very happy that the author of the history has spoken about me in such a way that the things said about me do not give offense; for by my faith as a good squire, if things had been said about me that did not suit an Old Christian, which is what I am, even the deaf would have heard us."

"That would be performing miracles," responded Sansón.

"Miracles or no miracles," said Sancho, "each man should be careful how he talks or writes about people and not put down willy-nilly the first thing that comes into his head."

"One of the objections people make to the history," said the bachelor, "is that its author put into it a novel called *The Man Who Was Reck-lessly Curious*, not because it is a bad novel or badly told, but because it is out of place and has nothing to do with the history of his grace Señor Don Quixote."

"I'll bet," replied Sancho, "that the dogson mixed up apples and or-anges."

"Now I say," said Don Quixote, "that the author of my history was no wise man but an ignorant gossip-monger who, without rhyme or reason, began to write, not caring how it turned out, just like Orbaneja, the painter of Úbeda, who, when asked what he was painting, replied: 'Whatever comes out.' Perhaps he painted a rooster in such a fashion and so unrealistically that he had to write beside it, in capital letters: 'This is a rooster.' And that must be how my history is: a commentary will be necessary in order to understand it."

"Not at all," responded Sansón, "because it is so clear that there is nothing in it to cause difficulty: children look at it, youths read it, men understand it, the old celebrate it, and, in short, it is so popular and so widely read and so well-known by every kind of person that as soon as people see a skinny old nag they say: 'There goes Rocinante.' And those who have been fondest of reading it are the pages. There is no lord's an-techamber where one does not find a copy of *Don Quixote*: as soon as it is put down it is picked up again; some rush at it, and others ask for it. In short, this history is the most enjoyable and least harmful entertainment ever seen, because nowhere in it can one find even the semblance of an untruthful word or a less than Catholic thought."

"Writing in any other fashion," said Don Quixote, "would mean not writing truths, but lies, and historians who make use of lies ought to be burned, like those who make counterfeit money; I do not know what moved the author to resort to other people's novels and stories when there was so much to write about mine: no doubt he must have been guided by the proverb that says: 'Straw or hay, it's the same either way.' For the truth is that if he had concerned himself only with my thoughts, my sighs, my tears, my virtuous desires, and my brave deeds, he could have had a volume larger than, or just as large as, the collected works of El Tostado.[4] In fact, as far as I can tell, Señor Bachelor, in order to write histories and books of any kind, one must have great judgment and ma-ture understanding. To say witty things and to write cleverly requires

4. Alonso de Madrigal, bishop of Avila, an immensely prolific writer of the fifteenth century.

great intelligence: the most perceptive character in a play is the fool, because the man who wishes to seem simple cannot possibly be a simpleton. History is like a sacred thing; it must be truthful, and wherever truth
is, there God is; but despite this, there are some who write and toss off
books as if they were fritters."

"There is no book so bad," said the bachelor, "that it does not have
something good in it."

"There is no doubt about that," replied Don Quixote, "but it often
happens that those who had deservedly won and achieved great fame because of their writings lost their fame, or saw it diminished, when they
had their works printed."

"The reason for that," said Sansón, "is that since printed works are
looked at slowly, their faults are easily seen, and the greater the fame of
their authors, the more closely they are scrutinized. Men who are famous
for their talent, great poets, eminent historians, are always, or almost always, envied by those whose particular pleasure and entertainment is
judging other people's writings without ever having brought anything of
their own into the light of day."

"That is not surprising," said Don Quixote, "for there are many theologians who are not good in the pulpit but are excellent at recognizing
the lacks or excesses of those who preach."

"All this is true, Señor Don Quixote," said Carrasco, "but I should
like those censurers to be more merciful and less severe and not pay so
much attention to the motes in the bright sun of the work they criticize,
for if *aliquando bonus dormitat Homerus*,[5] they should consider how often
he was awake to give a brilliant light to his work with the least amount
of shadow possible; and it well may be that what seem defects to them
are birthmarks that often increase the beauty of the face where they appear; and so I say that whoever prints a book exposes himself to great
danger, since it is utterly impossible to write in a way that will satisfy and
please everyone who reads it."

"The one that tells about me," said Don Quixote, "must have pleased
very few."

"Just the opposite is true; since *stultorum infinitus est numerus*,[6] an infinite number of people have enjoyed the history, though some have
found fault and failure in the author's memory, because he forgets to tell

5. A line from Horace's *Ars poetica:* "From time to time even Homer nods."
6. "The number of fools is infinite."

who the thief was who stole Sancho's donkey, for it is never stated and can only be inferred from the writing that it was stolen, and soon after that we see Sancho riding on that same donkey and don't know how it reappears. They also say that he forgot to put in what Sancho did with the hundred *escudos* he found in the traveling case in the Sierra Morena, for it is never mentioned again, and there are many who wish to know what he did with them, or how he spent them, for that is one of the substantive points of error in the work."

Sancho responded:

"I, Señor Sansón, am in no condition now to give accounts or accountings; my stomach has begun to flag, and if I don't restore it with a couple of swallows of mellow wine, I'll be nothing but skin and bone. I keep some at home; my missus is waiting for me; when I finish eating I'll come back and satisfy your grace and anybody else who wants to ask questions about the loss of my donkey or the hundred *escudos*."

And without waiting for a reply or saying another word, he left for his house.

Don Quixote asked and invited the bachelor to stay and eat with him. The bachelor accepted: he stayed, a couple of squab were added to the ordinary meal, chivalry was discussed at the table, Carrasco humored the knight, the banquet ended, they took a siesta, Sancho returned, and their earlier conversation was resumed.

CHAPTER IV

In which Sancho Panza satisfies Bachelor Sansón Carrasco with regard to his doubts and questions, with other events worthy of being known and recounted

Sancho came back to Don Quixote's house, and returning to their earlier discussion, he said:

"As for what Señor Sansón said about people wanting to know who stole my donkey, and how, and when, I can answer by saying that on the same night we were running from the Holy Brotherhood, and entered the Sierra Morena after the misadventurous adventure of the galley slaves, and of the dead man being carried to Segovia, my master and I rode into a stand of trees where my master rested on his lance, and I on my donkey, and battered and tired from our recent skirmishes, we began to sleep as if we were lying on four featherbeds; I was so sound asleep that whoever the thief was could come up to me, and put me on four stakes that he propped under the four sides of my packsaddle, and leave me mounted on them, and take my donkey out from under me without my even knowing it."

"That is an easy thing to do, and nothing new; the same thing happened to Sacripante when he was at the siege of Albraca; with that same trick the famous thief named Brunelo took his horse from between his legs."[1]

"Dawn broke," Sancho continued, "and as soon as I moved, the stakes gave way and I fell to the ground; I looked for the donkey and didn't see him; tears filled my eyes, and I began to lament, and if the author of our history didn't put that in, you can be sure he left out something good. After I don't know how many days, when we were traveling with the Señora Princess Micomicona, I saw my donkey, and riding him, dressed like a Gypsy, was Ginés de Pasamonte, the lying crook that my master and I freed from the chain."

"The error doesn't lie there," replied Sansón, "but in the fact that before the donkey appeared, the author says that Sancho was riding on that same animal."

"I don't know how to answer that," said Sancho, "except to say that either the historian was wrong or the printer made a mistake."

"That must be the case, no doubt about it," said Sansón, "but what happened to the hundred *escudos*? Are they gone?"

"I spent them for myself, and my wife, and my children, and they are the reason my wife patiently puts up with my traveling highways and byways in the service of my master, Don Quixote; if after so much time I came back home without a *blanca* and without my donkey, a black future would be waiting for me; if there's any more to know about me, here I am, and I'll answer the king himself in person, and nobody has any reason to worry about whether I kept them or didn't keep them, spent them or didn't spend them; if the beatings I got on these journeys were paid for in money, even if they didn't cost more than four *maravedís* a piece, another hundred *escudos* wouldn't pay for half of them; so let each man put his hand over his own heart and not start

1. This incident appears in Ariosto's *Orlando furioso*.

judging white as black and black as white; each of us is as God made him, and often much worse."

"I'll be sure," said Carrasco, "to tell the author of the history that if it has a second printing, he should not forget what our good Sancho has said, for that would elevate it a good half-span higher than it is now."

"Is there anything else that needs to be corrected in the book, Señor Bachelor?" asked Don Quixote.

"I'm sure there is," he responded, "but nothing as important as the ones we've already mentioned."

"And by any chance," said Don Quixote, "does the author promise a second part?"

"Yes, he does," responded Sansón, "but he says he hasn't found it and doesn't know who has it, and so we don't know if it will be published or not; for this reason, and because some people say: 'Second parts were never very good,' and others say: 'What's been written about Don Quixote is enough,' there is some doubt there will be a second part; but certain people who are more jovial than saturnine say: 'Let's have more quixoticies: let Don Quixote go charging and Sancho Panza keep talking, and whatever else happens, that will make us happy.'"

"And what does the author say to all of this?"

"He says," responded Sansón, "that as soon as he finds the history, which he is searching for with extraordinary diligence, he will immediately have it printed, for he is more interested in earning his profit than in winning any praise."

Sancho responded to this by saying:

"The author's interested in money and profit? I'd be surprised if he got any, because all he'll do is rush rush rush, like a tailor on the night before a holiday, and work done in a hurry is never as perfect as it should be. Let this Moorish gentleman, or whatever he is, pay attention to what he's doing; my master and I will give him such an abundance of adventures and so many different deeds that he'll be able to write not just a second part, but a hundred more parts. No doubt about it, the good man must think we're asleep here; well, just let him try to shoe us, and he'll know if we're lame or not. What I can say is that if my master would take my advice, we'd already be out in those fields righting wrongs and undoing injustices, which is the habit and custom of good knights errant."

No sooner had Sancho said these words than the sound of Rocinante neighing reached their ears; Don Quixote took this as a very good omen and resolved that in three or four days he would undertake another sally, and after declaring his intention to the bachelor, he asked his advice as to the direction he should take on his journey; the bachelor responded that in his opinion, he ought to go to the kingdom of Aragón and the city of Zaragoza, where in a few days they would be holding solemn jousts for the Festival of San Jorge, and there he could win fame vanquishing all the Aragonese knights, which would be the same as vanquishing all the knights in the world. He praised his determination as being most honorable and brave and warned him to be more cautious about rushing into danger, because his life belonged not to him alone but to all those who needed him to protect and defend them in their misfortunes.

"That's exactly what I hate most, Señor Sansón," said Sancho. "My master goes charging at a hundred armed men like a greedy boy attacking half a dozen melons. Good Lord, Señor Bachelor! There are times to attack and times to retreat, and not everything's 'Charge for Santiago and Spain!'[2] And besides, I've heard it said, I think by my master himself, if I remember correctly, that between the extremes of cowardice and recklessness lies the middle way of valor, and if this is true, I don't want him to run for no reason or attack when the numbers demand something else. But above all, I advise my master that if he wants to take me with him, it has to be on the condition that he'll do all the battles and I won't be obliged to do anything except look after his person in questions of cleanliness and food; as far as this goes, I'll do everything he asks, but to think that I'll raise my sword, even against lowborn scoundrels with their caps and axes, is to think something that will never happen. I, Señor Sansón, don't plan to win fame as a valiant man but as the best and most loyal squire who ever served a knight errant; and if my master, Don Quixote, as a reward for my many good services, wants to give me one of the many ínsulas that his grace says are to be found out there, I'll be very happy to accept it; and if he doesn't give it to me, I'm a human being, and a man shouldn't live depending on anybody but God; besides, bread will taste as good, and maybe even better, whether I'm a governor or not; for all I know, in those governorships the devil could have set a snare for me that will make me stumble and fall and knock out all my teeth. Sancho I was born, and Sancho I plan to die; but even so, if heaven should be so kind as to offer me, without too much trouble or risk, an ínsula or something else like that, I'm not such a fool that I'd turn it down, because, as they say: 'When they give you a heifer, don't

2. The medieval battle cry of Spanish Christians engaged in combat with Muslims.

forget to bring a rope,' and 'When good comes along, lock it in your house.' "

"You, brother Sancho," said Carrasco, "have spoken like a university professor, but still, trust in God and in Señor Don Quixote, who will give you a kingdom, not merely an ínsula."

"Whatever it is, it's all the same to me," responded Sancho, "though I can tell Señor Carrasco that my master won't be tossing that kingdom into a sack with holes in it; I've taken my own pulse and I'm healthy enough to rule kingdoms and govern ínsulas, and this is something I've already told my master."

"Be careful, Sancho," said Sansón, "for offices can alter behavior, and it might be that when you are governor you won't know the mother who bore you."

"That's something that may apply," responded Sancho, "to people of low birth, but not to those who have in their souls a little of the spirit of Old Christians, like me. No, first get to know my character and then tell me if I could be ungrateful to anybody!"

"God willing," said Don Quixote, "we shall see when the governorship comes along, for I seem to see it right before my eyes."

Having said this, he asked the bachelor, if he was a poet, to be so kind as to compose a few verses for him that would deal with the farewell he intended to make to his lady Dulcinea of Toboso, and he said that at the beginning of each line he was to place a letter of her name, so that when one reached the last verse and read all the first letters together, it would say: *Dulcinea of Toboso.*

The bachelor responded that although he was not one of the famous poets of Spain, who, as people said, did not number more than three and a half, he would be sure to write the lines, although he found a great difficulty in their composition because the number of letters in her name was seventeen, and if he made four Castilian stanzas of four octosyllabic lines each, there would be one letter too many, and if he made the stanzas of five octosyllabic lines each, the ones called *décimas* or *redondillas*,[3] there would be three letters too few; despite this, however he would attempt to somehow shrink one letter so that the name Dulcinea of Toboso would fit into four Castilian stanzas.

"It must fit in, however you do it," said Don Quixote, "because if the

3. In Cervantes's day, the *redondilla* was a five-line stanza, and the *décima* was composed of two *redondillas.*

name is not there to see, patent and obvious, no woman will believe that the verses were written for her."

They agreed to this, and to the knight's departing in eight days. Don Quixote asked the bachelor to keep this secret, especially from the priest and Master Nicolás, and from his niece and housekeeper, so that they would not interfere with his honorable and valiant resolve. Carrasco promised he would, and then he took his leave, asking Don Quixote to keep him informed, when possible, of all his successes and failures; and so they said goodbye, and Sancho left to make preparations for their journey.

CHAPTER V

Concerning the clever and amusing talk that passed between Sancho Panza and his wife, Teresa Panza, and other events worthy of happy memory

(When the translator[1] came to write this fifth chapter, he says he thought it was apocryphal, because in it Sancho Panza speaks in a manner different from what one might expect of his limited intelligence, and says things so subtle one would not think it possible that he knew them; but the translator did not wish to omit it, for the sake of his professional obligations, and so he continued, saying:)

Sancho came home so happy and joyful that his wife could see his joy at a distance, which obliged her to ask:

"What's the news, Sancho my friend, that makes you so happy?"

To which he responded:

"My wife, if it were God's will, I'd be delighted not to be as happy as I appear."

"Husband, I don't understand you," she replied, "and I don't know what you mean when you say you'd be delighted, if it were God's will, not to be happy; I may be a fool, but I don't know how anybody can be happy not to be happy."

"Look, Teresa," responded Sancho, "I'm happy because I've decided to serve my master, Don Quixote, again, for he wants to leave a third

1. The original, by Cide Hamete Benengeli, is in Arabic. In part I, a translator was hired in the market in Toledo; his translation is the history of Don Quixote described by the bachelor in part II.

time to seek adventures; and I'll leave with him again, because of my need and the hope, which makes me happy, of thinking that I may find another hundred *escudos* like the ones that have already been spent, though it makes me sad to have to leave you and my children; and if it was God's will to give me food with my feet dry and in my own house, not leading me through wastelands and crossroads, He could do it at very little cost and just by wanting it, then of course my happiness would be firmer and truer, for what I feel now is mixed with the sorrow of leaving you; and so, I was right to say that I would be delighted, if it was God's will, not to be happy."

"Look, Sancho," replied Teresa, "ever since you became a knight errant's servant your talk is so roundabout nobody can understand you."

"It's enough if God understands me, my wife," responded Sancho, "for He understands all things, and say no more about it for now; you should know, Teresa, that you have to take special care of the donkey for the next three days, so that he's ready to carry weapons: double his feed and look over the packsaddle and the rest of the trappings; we're not going to a wedding but to travel the world and have our battles with giants, dragons, and monsters, and hear their hisses, roars, bellows, and shrieks, and none of that would matter very much if we didn't have to contend with Yanguesans and enchanted Moors."

"I do believe, my husband, that squires errant don't get their bread for nothing, and so I'll keep praying that Our Lord delivers you soon from so much misfortune."

"I'll tell you, Teresa," responded Sancho, "that if I didn't expect to be the governor of an ínsula before too much more time goes by, I'd fall down dead right here."

"Not that, my husband," said Teresa, "let the chicken live even if she has the pip; may you live, and let the devil take all the governorships there are in the world; you came out of your mother's womb without a governorship, and you've lived until now without a governorship, and when it pleases God you'll go, or they'll carry you, to the grave without a governorship. Many people in the world live without a governorship, and that doesn't make them give up or not be counted among the living. The best sauce in the world is hunger, and since poor people have plenty of that, they always eat with great pleasure. But look, Sancho: if you happen to find yourself a governor somewhere, don't forget about me and your children. Remember that Sanchico is already fifteen, and he ought to go to school if his uncle the abbot is going to bring him into the Church. And don't forget that our daughter, Mari Sancha, won't die if we marry her; she keeps dropping hints that she wants a husband as much as you want to be a governor, and when all is said and done, a daughter's better off badly married than happily kept."

"By my faith, Teresa," responded Sancho, "if God lets me have any kind of governorship, I'll marry Mari Sancha so high up that nobody will be able to reach her unless they call her Señora."

"Don't do that, Sancho," responded Teresa. "She should marry an equal, that's the best thing; if you raise her from wooden clogs to cork-soled mules, from homespun petticoats to silken hoopskirts and dressing gowns, and from *you, Marica* to *Doña* and *my lady*, the girl won't know who she is, and wherever she turns she'll make a thousand mistakes and show that the threads of her cloth are rough and coarse."

"Quiet, fool," said Sancho, "she just needs to practice for two or three years, and then the nobility and the dignity will be a perfect fit; if not, what difference does it make? Let her be *my lady*, and it won't matter."

"Be content with your station," responded Teresa, "and don't try to go to a higher one; remember the proverb that says: 'Take your neighbor's son, wipe his nose, and bring him into your house.' Sure, it would be very nice to marry our María to some wretch of a count or gentleman who might take a notion to insult her and call her lowborn, the daughter of peasants and spinners! Not in my lifetime, my husband! I didn't bring up my daughter for that! You bring the money, Sancho, and leave her marrying to me; there's Lope Tocho, the son of Juan Tocho, a sturdy, healthy boy, and we know him, and I know for a fact that he doesn't dislike the girl; he's our equal, and she would make a good marriage with him, and we'd always see her, and we'd all be together, parents and children, grandchildren and in-laws, and the peace and blessing of God would be with us; so don't go marrying her in those courts and great palaces where they don't understand her and she won't understand herself."

"Come here, you imbecile, you troublemaker," replied Sancho. "Why do you want to stop me now, and for no good reason, from marrying my daughter to somebody who'll give me grandchildren they'll call *Lord* and *Lady*? Look, Teresa: I've always heard the old folks say that if you don't know how to enjoy good luck when it comes, you shouldn't complain if it passes you by. It wouldn't be a good idea, now that it's come knocking, to shut the door in its face; we should let the favorable wind that's blowing carry us along."

(This manner of speaking, and what Sancho says below, is why the translator of this history considered this chapter apocryphal.)

"Don't you think, you ignorant woman," Sancho continued, "that it will be good for me to come into some profitable governorship that will take us out of poverty? Let Mari Sancha marry the man I choose, and you'll see how they start calling you *Doña Teresa Panza*, and you'll sit in church on a rug with pillows and tapestries, in spite of and regardless of all the gentlewomen in town. But no, not you, you'd rather always stay the same, never changing, like a figure in a wall hanging! And we're not talking about this anymore; Sanchica will be a countess no matter what you say."

"Do you hear what you're saying, husband?" responded Teresa. "Well, even so, I'm afraid that if my daughter becomes a countess it will be her ruin. You'll do whatever you want, whether you make her a duchess or a princess, but I can tell you it won't be with my agreement or consent. Sancho, I've always been in favor of equality, and I can't stand to see somebody putting on airs for no reason. They baptized me Teresa, a plain and simple name without any additions or decorations or trimmings of *Dons* or *Doñas*; my father's name was Cascajo, and because I'm your wife, they call me Teresa Panza, though they really ought to call me Teresa Cascajo. But where laws go kings follow,[2] and I'm satisfied with this name without anybody adding on a *Doña* that weighs so much I can't carry it, and I don't want to give people who see me walking around dressed in a countish or governorish way a chance to say: 'Look at the airs that sow is putting on! Yesterday she was busy pulling on a tuft of flax for spinning, and she went to Mass and covered her head with her skirts instead of a mantilla, and today she has a hoopskirt and brooches and airs, as if we didn't know who she was.' If God preserves my seven senses, or five, or however many I have, I don't intend to let anybody see me in a spot like that. You, my husband, go and be a governor or an insular and put on all the airs you like; I swear on my mother's life that my daughter and I won't set foot out of our village: to keep her chaste, break her leg and keep her in the house; for a chaste girl, work is her fiesta. You go with your Don Quixote and have your adventures, and leave us with our misfortunes, for God will set them right if we're good; I certainly don't know who gave him a *Don*, because his parents and grandparents never had one."

"Now I'll say," replied Sancho, "that you must have an evil spirit in that body of yours. God save you, woman, what a lot of things you've strung together willy-nilly! What do Cascajo, brooches, proverbs, and putting on airs have to do with what I'm saying? Come here, you simple,

---

2. Teresa has the proverb backward. It should be "Where kings go laws follow."

ignorant woman, and I can call you that because you don't understand my words and try to run away from good luck. If I had said that my daughter ought to throw herself off a tower or go roaming around the way the Infanta Doña Urraca wanted to,[3] you'd be right not to go along with me; but if in two shakes and in the wink of an eye I dress her in a *Doña* and put a *my lady* on her back for you, and take her out of the dirt and put her under a canopy and up on a pedestal in a drawing room with more velvet cushions than Moors in the line of the Almohadas of Morroco,[4] why won't you consent and want what I want?"

"Do you know why, Sancho?" responded Teresa. "Because of the proverb that says: 'Whoever tries to conceal you, reveals you!' Nobody does more than glance at the poor, but they look closely at the rich; if a rich man was once poor, that's where the whispers and rumors begin, and the wicked murmurs of gossips who crowd the streets like swarms of bees."

"Look, Teresa," responded Sancho, "and listen to what I want to tell you now; maybe you haven't ever heard it in all the days of your life, and what I'm saying now isn't something I made up on my own; everything I plan to say to you are the judgments of the priest who preached in this village during Lent last year, and if I remember correctly, he said that things which are present and before our eyes appear, are, and remain in our memory much more clearly and sharply than things that are past."

(All the words that Sancho says here are the second of his statements that cause the translator to consider this chapter apocryphal, for they far exceed the capacity of Sancho, who continued, saying:)

"This accounts for the fact that when we see someone finely dressed and wearing rich clothes and with a train of servants, it seems that some force moves and induces us to respect him, although at that moment our memory recalls the lowliness in which we once saw that person; and that shame, whether of poverty or low birth, is in the past and no longer exists, and what is is only what we see in front of us in the present. And if this man, whose earlier lowliness has been erased by the good fortune (these were the very words that the priest said) that has raised him to prosperity, is well-mannered, generous, and courteous with everyone, and does not compete with those who have been noble since ancient times, you can be sure, Teresa, that nobody will remember what he was

3. The allusion is to a ballad about Doña Urraca's desire to go wandering.

4. Sancho confuses *almohada*, the Spanish for "pillow" or "cushion," and Almohade, the name of the Islamic dynasty that ruled North Africa and Spain in the twelfth century.

but will revere him for what he is, unless they are envious, and no good fortune is safe from envy."

"I don't understand you, my husband," replied Teresa, "so do what you want and don't give me any more headaches with your long speeches and fine words. And if you're revolved to do what you say—"

"*Resolved* is what you should say, Teresa," said Sancho, "not *revolved.*"

"Don't start an argument with me, Sancho," responded Teresa. "I talk as God wills, and let's stick to the subject; I say that if you're determined to have a governorship, you should take your son, Sanchico, along so you can teach him how to be a governor; it's a good thing for sons to inherit and learn the trades of their fathers."

"As soon as I have the governorship," said Sancho, "I'll send for him posthaste, and I'll send you some money; I'll have plenty, because there are always plenty of people who lend money to governors when they don't have any; and be sure to dress him so that you hide what he is and he looks like what he'll become."

"You just send the money," said Teresa, "and I'll dress him up as nice as you please."

"So then we agree," said Sancho, "that our daughter will be a countess."

"The day I see her a countess," responded Teresa, "will be the day I'll have to bury her; but again I say that you should do whatever you want; women are born with the obligation to obey their husbands even if they're fools."

And at this she began to cry as piteously as if she already saw Sanchica dead and buried. Sancho consoled her, saying that even if he had to make her a countess, he would delay it as long as he could. This ended their conversation, and Sancho returned to see Don Quixote and arrange for their departure.

CHAPTER VI

Regarding what transpired between Don Quixote and his niece and house-
keeper, which is one of the most important chapters in the entire history

While Sancho Panza and his wife, Teresa Cascajo, were having the incongruous talk that has just been related, Don Quixote's niece and
housekeeper were not idle; a thousand indications had led them to infer
that their uncle and master wished to leave for the third time and return
to the practice of what was, to their minds, his calamitous chivalry, and
they attempted by all means possible to dissuade him from so wicked a
thought, but it was all preaching in the desert and hammering on cold
iron. Even so, in one of the many exchanges they had with him, the
housekeeper said:

"The truth is, Señor, that if your grace doesn't keep your feet firmly
on the ground, and stay quietly in your house, and stop wandering
around the mountains and the valleys like a soul in torment looking for
things that are called adventures but that I call misfortunes, then I'll
have to cry and complain to God and the king and ask them for a
remedy."

To which Don Quixote responded:

"Housekeeper, I do not know how God will respond to your complaints, or His Majesty, either; I know only that if I were king, I should
excuse myself from responding to the countless importunate requests
presented to me each day; one of the greatest burdens borne by kings,
among so many others, is the obligation to listen to all petitions and respond to all of them; consequently, I should not want my affairs to trouble him in any way."

To which the housekeeper said:

"Tell us, Señor, aren't there knights in His Majesty's court?"

"Yes," responded Don Quixote, "quite a few, and it is fitting that there should be, as an adornment to the greatness of princes and to display the stateliness of kings."

"Well, then, couldn't your grace," she replied, "be one of those who stay put to serve their king and lord in court?"

"Look, my friend," responded Don Quixote, "not all knights can be courtiers, and not all courtiers can or should be knights errant: there has to be some of each in the world, and although we are all knights, there is a vast difference between us; courtiers, without leaving their chambers or passing beyond the threshold of the court, travel the entire world by looking at a map, not spending a *blanca* or suffering heat or cold, hunger or thirst; but we, the true knights errant, measure the earth with our own feet, exposed to the sun, the cold, the wind, and the inclemencies of heaven, both night and day, on foot and on horseback; and we know our enemies not only in portraits but in their actual persons, and no matter the danger and regardless of the occasion we do battle with them, not worrying about trifles or the laws governing duels: whether one combatant has or does not have a shorter lance or sword, or has on his person a relic, or some hidden deception, or if the sun is to be apportioned or slashed to bits,[1] and other ceremonies of this nature that are used in private duels between individuals, which you do not know about, but I do. And you should also know something else: the good knight errant may see ten giants whose heads not only touch the clouds but go above them, each with legs that are two immense towers and whose arms resemble the masts of large and powerful ships, each eye like a huge mill wheel burning hotter than a glass furnace, yet he must not be afraid in the slightest, but with a gallant air and an intrepid heart he must charge and attack them and, if possible, defeat and rout them in an instant, even if they are armed with the shells of a certain fish that are, they say, harder than diamonds, and instead of swords they carry sharp knives of Damascene steel, or clubs studded with steel spikes, which I have seen more than a few times. I have said all this, my dear housekeeper, so that you may see the difference between one kind of knight and another, and it would be right and proper for every prince to esteem more highly the second, or I should say the first kind of knights errant, for as we read in their histories, some among them have been the salvation of not only one kingdom, but many."

---

1. "Apportioning the sun" (*partir el sol*) was the arrangement of combatants in a tourney so that the sun would not shine in anyone's eyes; "slashing to bits" is Cervantine wordplay.

"Ah, Señor!" said his niece. "Your grace should remember that everything you say about knights errant is invention and lies, and each of their histories, if it isn't burned, deserves to wear a sanbenito[2] or some other sign that it has been recognized as the infamous ruination of virtuous customs."

"By the God who sustains me," said Don Quixote, "if you were not my lawful niece, the daughter of my own sister, I should punish you so severely for the blasphemy you have uttered that it would be heard all over the world. How is it possible that a mere slip of a girl who barely knows how to manage twelve lace bobbins can dare to speak against and censure the histories of the knights errant? What would Señor Amadís have said if he had heard this? But most certainly he would have pardoned you, because he was the most humble and courteous knight of his time, and a great defender of damsels, but others could have heard you and it would not have gone so well for you, for not all of them are courteous or well-behaved: some are discourteous cowards. Not all those called knights are knights through and through; some are gold, others alchemical, and all appear to be knights, but not all can pass a test by touchstone.[3] There are baseborn men desperate to seem knights, and highborn knights who appear ready to die in order to seem base; the former rise up through ambition or virtue, the latter descend through idleness or vice, and it is necessary for us to use our knowledge and discernment to distinguish between these two kinds of knights, so similar in names, so dissimilar in actions."

"Lord save me!" said the niece. "Your grace knows so much that in an emergency you could stand in the pulpit or preach in the streets, and despite this you have been struck by such great blindness and such obvious foolishness that you try to make us believe that you are valiant when you are old, and strong when you are ailing, that you right wrongs when you are stooped by age, and most of all, that you are a knight when you are not, because though gentlefolk may be knights, poor men never are . . . !"

"You are certainly correct in what you say, my dear niece," responded Don Quixote, "and I could tell you things about lineage that would astonish you, but I shall not say them in order not to mix the human with the divine. Look, my friends, there are four kinds of lineage and, listen

---

2. The stigmatizing hood and robe that those accused by the Inquisition were obliged to wear.

3. A kind of black stone that once was used to test the purity of gold or silver by rubbing the stone with the metal and analyzing the streak left behind.

carefully, all the lineages in the world can be reduced to these: some had humble beginnings, and extended and expanded until they reached the heights of greatness; others had noble beginnings, and preserved them, and still preserve and maintain them just as they were; still others may have had noble beginnings but, like pyramids, they tapered to a point, having diminished and annihilated their origins until they ended in nothingness, as the tip of the pyramid is nothing compared to its base or bottom; finally, there are others, and these are the majority, that did not have a good beginning or a reasonable middle, and therefore in the end they have no name, like the lineages of ordinary plebeians. An example of the first, those who had a humble beginning and rose to the greatness they now possess, is the Ottoman Dynasty, which began with a humble, lowborn shepherd and rose to the pinnacle that we see today. Of the second kind of lineage, which began in greatness and preserved it without increasing it, an example would be the many princes by inheritance who maintain their greatness without increasing or decreasing it, and peacefully stay within the borders of their states. Of those who began great and ended in a point there are thousands of examples: all the pharaohs and Ptolemies of Egypt, the Caesars of Rome, and the entire horde, if that name can be given to them, of countless princes, monarchs, lords, Medes, Assyrians, Persians, Greeks, and Barbarians, all these lineages and nobilities, and those who originated them, have ended in a point, in nothingness, for it would not be possible now to find any of their descendants, and if we did, they would be in a low and humble state. Regarding the plebeian lineages I have nothing to say, except that they serve only to increase the number of the living, and their greatness does not merit any other fame or praise.

From all that I have said I want you to infer, you foolish women, that the confusion surrounding lineages is great, and the only ones that appear distinguished and illustrious are those that display those qualities in their virtue, and in the wealth and generosity of their nobles. I said virtue, wealth, and generosity, because the great man who is vicious will be extremely vicious, and the closefisted rich man will be a miserly beggar, for the person who possesses wealth is not made happy by having it but by spending it, and not spending it haphazardly but in knowing how to spend it well. An impoverished knight has no way to show he is a knight except through his virtue, by being affable, well-mannered, courteous, civil, and diligent, not proud, arrogant, or prone to gossip, and above all, by being charitable, for with two *maravedís* given joyfully to a poor man, he will show that he is as generous as the man who gives alms to the loud ringing of bells; no one who sees a knight adorned with these virtues can fail to judge and consider him to be of good breeding, even if he does not know him, and his not being so would be remarkable; praise was always the reward of virtue, and virtuous men cannot avoid being praised.

There are two roads, my dears, which men can take to become rich and honored: one is that of letters, the other that of arms. I have more arms than letters, and my inclination is toward arms, for I was born under the influence of the planet Mars, and so I am almost compelled to follow his path, and follow it I must despite the rest of the world; it will be useless to try to persuade me that I do not wish what heaven wishes, fortune ordains, reason demands, and, above all, what my will desires; for, knowing as I do the countless travails that accompany knight errantry, I also know the infinite benefits that can be attained through it; I know that the path of virtue is very narrow, and the road of wickedness is broad and spacious; I know that their endings and conclusions are different, because the expansive, spacious road of wickedness ends in death, and the road of virtue, so narrow and difficult, ends in life, not the life that ends, but life everlasting; and I know, as our great Castilian poet[4] says, that

> Along this harsh, rock-strewn terrain we climb
> to the peak, high seat of immortality,
> never reached if these rigors are declined."

"Oh, woe is me," said the niece, "my uncle's a poet, too! He knows everything, he understands everything, and I'd wager that if he wanted to be a mason, he'd know how to build a house as well as a cage."

"I promise you, my niece," responded Don Quixote, "that if these chivalric ideas did not carry with them all my thoughts, there would be nothing I should not make and no curiosity my hands would not create, especially cages and toothpicks."

At that moment there was a knock at the door, and when they asked who was there, Sancho Panza responded that it was he, and as soon as the housekeeper learned who it was she ran to hide, not wanting to see him because she despised him so much. The niece opened the door, and Sancho's master came to greet him with open arms, and the two men shut themselves away in Don Quixote's room, where they had another conversation just as good as the previous one.

---

4. Garcilaso de la Vega (1503–1536), the great Renaissance poet, perfected the Petrarchan style in Spanish.

CHAPTER VII

Regarding the conversation that Don Quixote had with his squire, as well as other exceptionally famous events

When the housekeeper saw that Sancho Panza had shut himself away with her master, she knew what their business was, and imagining that this consultation would result in a determination to embark on a third sally, she put on her cloak and, filled with sorrow and grief, went to find Bachelor Sansón Carrasco, for it seemed to her that because he was well-spoken and a recent friend, he could persuade her master to abandon his mad intentions.

She found him walking in the courtyard of his house, and when she saw him she fell at his feet, perspiring in her distress. When Carrasco saw this display of sorrow and alarm, he said to her:

"What is it, Señora? What has happened? You look as if your heart would break."

"It's nothing, Señor Sansón, except that my master's pushing out, he's pushing out, no doubt about it!"

"And where is he pushing out, Señora?" asked Sansón. "Has he broken any part of his body?"

"He isn't pushing out anywhere," she responded, "except through the door of his madness. I mean, dear Señor Bachelor, that he wants to leave again, and this will be the third time, to search the wide world for what he calls ventures, and I don't understand how he can give them that name.[1] The first time they brought him back to us lying across a donkey,

---

1. The housekeeper's statement is based on her confusing *aventura* ("adventure") with *ventura* ("happiness," "luck," and "fortune" are the relevant meanings). I've translated *ventura* as "venture" in order to establish the connection with "adventure," though a better word would probably be "fortune."

beaten and battered. The second time he came home in an oxcart, locked in a cage and claiming he was enchanted, and the poor man was in such a state that his own mother wouldn't have recognized him: skinny, pale, his eyes sunk right into the top of his head; to bring him back to himself a little, I used more than six hundred eggs; God knows that, and so does everybody else, and my hens, too, and they wouldn't let me lie."

"I certainly can believe that," responded the bachelor, "for they are so good, so plump, and so well-bred that they would not tell a falsehood even if it killed them. In fact, Señora, is there something else, some mishap other than the one you fear Señor Don Quixote plans to undertake?"

"No, Señor," she responded.

"Well then, don't worry," responded the bachelor, "but go home in peace and prepare a hot lunch for me, and on the way say St. Apollonia's prayer,[2] if you know it; I'll be there soon, and then you'll see wonders."

"Lord save us!" replied the housekeeper. "Did your grace say I should say St. Apollonia's prayer? That would work if my master's trouble was in his teeth, but his is in his brain."

"I know what I'm saying, Señora; go now, and don't start arguing with me: you know I'm a bachelor from Salamanca, and there's no better babbler than that,"[3] responded Carrasco.

And at this the housekeeper left, and the bachelor went immediately to find the priest, in order to communicate to him what will be related in due course.

While Don Quixote and Sancho were shut away together, they had a conversation that is recounted in the history with a good deal of accuracy and attention to detail.

Sancho said to his master:

"Señor, I've already conveyanced my wife to let me go with your grace wherever you want to take me."

"*Convinced* is what you mean, Sancho," said Don Quixote, "not *conveyanced*."

"Once or twice," responded Sancho, "if I remember correctly, I've asked your grace not to correct my words if you understand what I mean by them, and when you don't understand, to say: 'Sancho, you devil, I

---

2. This was a prayer to cure toothache.

3. A secondary meaning for *bachiller* (the holder of a bachelor's degree) is "a person who babbles or chatters." Cervantes plays with the two meanings of the word.

don't understand you,' and if I can't explain, then you can correct me; I'm so plaint. . . ."

"I do not understand you, Sancho," said Don Quixote, "because I do not know what *I am so plaint* means."

"So *plaint* means," responded Sancho, *"That's just the way I am."*

"Now I understand you even less," replied Don Quixote.

"Well, if you can't understand me," responded Sancho, "I don't know any other way to say it; that's all I know, and may God protect me."

"Oh, now I have it," responded Don Quixote. "You mean to say that you are *so pliant*, so docile and softhearted, that you will accept what I tell you and learn what I teach you."

"I'll bet," said Sancho, "you knew what I was saying and understood me from the beginning, but wanted to mix me up so you could hear me make another two hundred mistakes."

"That may be," replied Don Quixote. "Tell me, then, what does Teresa say?"

"Teresa says," said Sancho, "that I should keep a sharp eye on you, and there's no arguing against written proof, because if you cut the deck you don't deal, and a bird in hand is worth two in the bush. And I say that a woman's advice is no jewel, and the man who doesn't take it is a fool."

"And I say that as well," responded Don Quixote. "Continue, Sancho my friend, go on, for today you are speaking pearls."

"The fact is," responded Sancho, "that as your grace knows very well, we're all subject to death, here today and gone tomorrow, and the lamb goes as quickly as the sheep, and nobody can promise himself more hours of life in this world than the ones God wants to give him, because death is silent, and when she comes knocking at the door of our life, she's always in a hurry, and nothing will stop her, not prayers or struggles or scepters or miters, and that's something that everybody hears, something they tell us from the pulpit."

"All of that is true," said Don Quixote, "but I do not know where it is taking you."

"It's taking me to this," said Sancho. "Your grace should tell me exactly what salary you'll give me for each month I serve you, and this salary should be paid to me from your estate; I don't want to depend on anybody's favors, which come late, or badly, or never; may God help me to tend to my own business. The point is, I want to know what I'm earning, whether it's a lot or a little; a hen sits on her egg, and a lot of littles make a lot, and as long as you're earning you don't lose a thing. And if it should happen, and I don't believe or expect that it will, that your grace gives me the ínsula you promised, I'm not such an ingrate, and not such a pennypincher, that I won't want the rent from the ínsula to be added up and deducted from my salary pro rat."

"Sancho my friend," responded Don Quixote, "sometimes a rat is as good as a rata."

"I understand," said Sancho. "I'll bet I should have said *rata* and not *rat*, but it doesn't matter at all, because your grace understood me."

"And understood you so well," responded Don Quixote, "that I have penetrated to your most hidden thoughts, and I know the target you are trying to hit with the countless arrows of your proverbs. Look, Sancho: I certainly should have specified a salary for you if I had found in any of the histories of the knights errant an example that would have revealed to me and shown me, by means of the smallest sign, what wages were for a month, or a year, but I have read all or most of their histories, and I do not recall reading that any knight errant ever specified a fixed salary for his squire. I know only that all of them served without pay, and when they least expected it, if things had gone well for their masters, they found themselves rewarded with an ínsula or something comparable; at the very least, they received a title and nobility. If, with these expectations and addenda, you, Sancho, would like to serve me again, then welcome,[4] but if you think I am going to force the ancient usage of knight errantry beyond its limits and boundaries, then you are sadly mistaken. Therefore, my dear Sancho, return to your house and tell your Teresa my intention, and if it pleases her and you to serve me without wages, *bene quidem*,[5] and if not, we shall still be friends, for if the pigeon coop has plenty of feed, it will have plenty of pigeons. And remember, Sancho, that fine hopes are better than miserable possessions, and a good lawsuit better than a bad payment. I am speaking in this manner, Sancho, so you may understand that, like you, I too know how to pour down rainstorms of proverbs. And, finally, I want to tell you, and I do tell you, that if you do not wish to accompany me without pay, and take the same risks I do, then God be with you and turn you into a saint, for I shall have no lack of squires

---

4. With this sentence, Don Quixote again uses a more distant form of address with Sancho in order to indicate his displeasure; he does not return to less formal address until he speaks to Sancho again, following Sansón Carrasco's arrival on the scene.

5. The Latin phrase translates roughly as "Then well and good" or "That's fine with me."

more obedient, more solicitous, less uncouth, and less talkative than you."

When Sancho heard his master's firm resolve, the sky filled with clouds and his heart sank, because he had been certain that his master would not leave without him for all the world's riches, and so he was perplexed and thoughtful when Sansón Carrasco came in, along with the niece,[6] who was eager to hear the arguments he would use to persuade their lord and master not to seek adventures again. Sansón, famous for his sly humor, came up to him, embraced him as he had done the first time, and in a loud voice said to him:

"O flower of errant chivalry! O resplendent light of arms! O honor and paragon of the Spanish nation! May it please Almighty God that the person or persons who impede or hinder your third sally never emerge from the labyrinth of their desires, and never be granted what they most wish for."

And turning to the housekeeper, he said:

"The housekeeper can certainly stop reciting St. Apollonia's prayer, for I know it is the clear decision of the heavenly spheres that Señor Don Quixote should once again put into effect his original and noble thoughts, and it would weigh heavily on my conscience if I did not convey to this knight and persuade him that the strength of his valiant arm and the virtue of his valorous spirit should tarry and be constrained no more, for delay thwarts the righting of wrongs, the defense of orphans, the honoring of damsels, the favoring of widows, the protection of married women, and other things of this nature that touch on, relate to, depend on, and are attached to the order of errant chivalry. O Señor Don Quixote, so fair and brave, let it be today rather than tomorrow that your lofty grace sets out on your way! And if anything is needed to make this a reality, here I am to supply it with my person and my fortune, and if it proves necessary to serve your magnificence as squire, I would consider it a most happy stroke of good fortune!"

At this, Don Quixote turned to Sancho and said:

"Did I not tell you, Sancho, that I would have more than enough squires? Look who is offering to fill the position: none other than the extraordinary Bachelor Sansón Carrasco, perpetual diversion and delight of the courtyards of the Salamancan schools, healthy in body, agile of limb, silent, long-suffering of heat as well as cold, hunger as well as

---

6. The housekeeper, mentioned a few sentences down, clearly comes in now, too, but because of an oversight or an error, by Cervantes or his printer, she is not alluded to here.

thirst, and possessed of all the qualities required to be the squire of a knight errant. But heaven forbid that for the sake of my own pleasure this pillar of letters be weakened, this vessel of sciences broken, this lofty glory of the good and liberal arts cut down. Let this new Samson remain in his native land, and by honoring it may he also honor the white hairs of his aging parents, for I shall be content with any squire at all, since Sancho does not deign to come with me."

"Oh yes, I do, I deign," responded Sancho, deeply moved, his eyes filled with tears, and he continued: "Let nobody say of me, dear master, that when all the bread's eaten he leaves; no, for I don't come from un-grateful stock; everybody knows, especially in my village, what kind of people the Panzas were, and I come from them, and besides, because of your many good actions and even more good words, I know and under-stand your grace's desire to show me favor; if I tried to work out exactly how much my salary would be, it was to please my wife; when she puts her hand to convincing you of something, no mallet can press down the hoops of a barrel the way she can press you to do what she wants, but the truth is, a man must be a man, and a woman a woman, and since I'm a man everywhere, which I cannot deny, I also want to be a man in my own house, no matter who's inside; and so, there's nothing more to do except for your grace to prepare your will and its codicil so it can't be re-soaked, and for us to be on our way soon so that the soul of Señor Sansón doesn't suffer anymore, because he says his conscience demands that he persuade your grace to go out into the world for a third time; and I offer to serve your grace again, faithfully and loyally and as well as and better than all the squires who have ever served knights errant in past or pres-ent times."

The bachelor was astonished to hear the manner and fashion in which Sancho Panza spoke, for although he had read the first history of the knight, he never believed the squire was as amusing as he had been depicted there; but when he heard him say will and codicil that can't be *resoaked* instead of will and codicil that can't be *revoked*, he believed everything about him that he had read, and took him to be one of the most solemn simpletons of our day, and said to himself that two such madmen as this master and servant had never been known in the world before.

Finally, Don Quixote and Sancho embraced and were friends again, and with the approval and blessing of the great Carrasco, who for the moment was his oracle, Don Quixote declared that his departure would take place in three days, which would give him time to prepare what was needed for the journey, and to find a full sallet helmet, which he said he must have at all costs. Sansón offered him one, because he knew that a friend of his who owned one would not refuse to give it to him, though it was darkened by rust and mold rather than having the brightness of polished steel.

The curses that the two women, the housekeeper and the niece, hurled at the bachelor were beyond number; they tore their hair, scratched their faces, and in the manner of professional mourners bewailed the departure of their lord and master as if it were his death. Sansón's plan when he urged Don Quixote to leave again was to do what the history will recount later, and he did it all on the advice of the priest and the barber, with whom he had consulted earlier.

In short, in those three days Don Quixote and Sancho prepared everything they thought necessary, and Sancho having placated his wife, and Don Quixote his niece and his housekeeper, at nightfall, unseen by anyone except the bachelor, who wanted to accompany them half a league from the village, they set out on the road to Toboso, Don Quixote on his good Rocinante and Sancho on his old donkey, his saddlebags supplied with food and provisions, and his purse with money given to him by Don Quixote for any eventualities. Sansón embraced Don Quixote and asked that he keep him informed regarding his good or bad luck, so that he might rejoice over the first or grieve over the second, as the laws of friendship demanded. Don Quixote promised that he would, Sansón returned to the village, and the two men took the road to the great city of Toboso.

CHAPTER VIII

Which recounts what befell Don Quixote as he was going to see his lady Dulcinea of Toboso

"Blessed be almighty Allah!" says Hamete Benengeli at the beginning of the eighth chapter. "Blessed be Allah!" he repeats three times, and says he gives these blessings at seeing that he now has Don Quixote and Sancho in the countryside, and the readers of his amiable history can assume that from this point on, the feats and exploits of Don Quixote and his squire will commence, and he will persuade them to forget the past knightly deeds of the Ingenious Gentleman and set their eyes upon those that are still to come, for they begin now on the road to Toboso, just as the earlier ones began in the fields of Montiel, and what he asks is very little considering all that he promises, and so he continues, saying:

Don Quixote and Sancho were now alone, and as soon as Sansón rode away Rocinante began to neigh and the donkey to snort, and both knight and squire considered this a good sign and a fortunate omen; although, if truth be told, the donkey snorted and brayed more than the horse neighed, and from this Sancho concluded that his good fortune would exceed and go beyond that of his master, and I do not know if he based this on the astrology he may have known, since the history says nothing about that, although he had been heard to say whenever he stumbled or fell that he would have been happy if he had never left his house, because the only thing one got from stumbling or falling was a torn shoe or broken ribs, and though he was a fool, in this he was not far off the mark. Don Quixote said to him:

"Sancho my friend, night is coming on more hurriedly and more darkly than we require if we are to see Toboso at dawn, for I am determined to go there before I embark on another adventure, and there I shall receive the blessing and approval of the peerless Dulcinea, and with this approval I believe and am certain that I shall finish and bring to a happy conclusion every dangerous adventure, for nothing in this life makes knights errant more valiant than finding themselves favored by their ladies."

"I believe that, too," responded Sancho, "but I think it will be difficult for your grace to talk to her or be with her, at least any place where you can receive her blessing, unless she throws it down to you from the fence around the corral where I saw her the first time, when I brought her the letter with news of the foolish and crazy things your grace was doing in the heart of the Sierra Morena."

"Did you imagine they were corral fences, Sancho," said Don Quixote, "which you looked through or over in order to see that never sufficiently praised elegance and beauty? Surely they were galleries, or passageways, or porticoes, or whatever they are called, of rich and regal palaces."

"Anything's possible," responded Sancho, "but they looked like fences to me, unless my memory fails me."

"Despite everything, Sancho, let us go there," replied Don Quixote.

"As long as I see her, it does not matter to me if it is through fences, or windows, or narrow cracks, or the grillework around a garden; any ray of light from the sun of her beauty that reaches my eyes will illuminate my understanding and fortify my heart, so that I shall be unique and incomparable in judgment and valor."

"Well, the truth is, Señor," responded Sancho, "that when I saw the sun of my lady Dulcinea of Toboso, it wasn't bright enough to send out any rays, and it must have been that since her grace was sifting that wheat I told you about, the dust she raised made something like a cloud in front of her face and darkened it."

"Do you still persist, Sancho," said Don Quixote, "in saying, thinking, believing, and insisting that my lady Dulcinea was sifting wheat, when that is a task and a practice far removed from everything that is done and should be done by highborn persons, who are created and intended for other practices and pastimes, which reveal their rank even at a distance . . . ! Oh, Sancho, how badly you remember the verses of our poet[1] in which he depicts for us the labors performed in their crystal dwellings by the four nymphs who raised their heads from their beloved river, the Tajo, and sat in a green meadow to embroider those rich cloths which the ingenious poet describes for us there, all of them intertwined and interwoven with gold, silk thread, and pearls. And the work of my lady must have been of this sort when you saw her, but the envy that an evil enchanter feels toward my affairs alters all things that can give me pleasure, and changes their appearance; I fear that in the history of my deeds, which they say has been published, if the author by chance was some wise man who is my enemy, he will have put in certain things instead of others, mixing a thousand lies with one truth, digressing to recount actions other than those required in the coherent narration of a truthful history. O envy, root of infinite evils and woodworm of virtues! All vices, Sancho, bring with them some kind of delight, but envy brings nothing but vexation, rancor, and rage."

"That's what I say, too," responded Sancho, "and I think that in the legend or history about us that Bachelor Carrasco told us he saw, my good name must be turned upside down and dragged helter-skelter and hither and yon, as they say, through the streets. But by my faith as an honest man, I've never said anything bad about any enchanter, and I

1. Garcilaso de la Vega, in his third eclogue.

don't own enough for anybody to envy me; true, I have some guile in me, and a touch of cunning, but all of it is covered and concealed by the great cloak of my simplicity, which is always natural and never sly. And even if I had nothing else, there is my belief, and I've always believed, firmly and truly, in God and in everything that is thought and believed by the Holy Roman Catholic Church, and there is my being, as I am, a mortal enemy of the Jews, and so the historians ought to take pity on me and treat me well in their writings. But let them say whatever they want; naked I was born, I'm naked now: I haven't lost or gained a thing; as long as I've been put in books and passed from hand to hand out in the world, I don't care what they say about me."

"That reminds me, Sancho," said Don Quixote, "of what happened to a famous poet of our day who, having written a malicious satire against all the courtesans, did not include or mention a certain lady because he was not sure if she was one or not; and this lady, seeing that she was not on the list with the rest, complained to the poet, asking what he had seen in her to make him exclude her from their number, and saying that he ought to lengthen the satire and include her, and if he did not, he would wonder why he had ever been born. The poet did as she asked and said the most vicious things about her, and she was satisfied, for she had become famous, though her fame was infamous. And another tale that is relevant here is one they tell about the shepherd who set fire to and burned the famous Temple of Diana, counted as one of the seven wonders of the world, so that his name would live throughout the centuries; and though it was ordered that no one should name him or mention him in speech or in writing, so that his desire would not be accomplished, yet it was learned that his name was Erostratus. And also to the point is what happened to the great Emperor Charles V and a gentleman in Rome. The emperor wished to see the famous Temple of the Rotunda, which in antiquity was called the Temple of All the Gods, and today is known by the holier name of All Saints, and is the most complete surviving building of all those erected by the gentiles in Rome, and the one that best preserves the fame of its founders for grandeur and magnificence:[2] it has the shape of half an orange and is extremely large, and it is well-lit, though the only light is from a window, or rather, a round skylight at the top, and it was there that the emperor looked down at the building, and at his side was a Roman gentle-

2. The temple, also called the Pantheon, was in fact visited by Charles, who would walk through Rome in disguise; the anecdote told here does not appear in any other text, however, and may be an invention of Cervantes.

man who pointed out the beauties and subtleties of that great structure and its memorable architecture; and when they had come down, he said to the emperor: 'A thousand times, Most Sacred Majesty, I have felt the desire to embrace Your Majesty and then throw myself down from that skylight so my fame in the world will be eternal.' The emperor responded: 'I thank you for not having put so wicked a thought into effect, and from now on I shall not give you occasion to test your loyalty; I command you never to speak to me again or to be anywhere I am.' And with these words he performed a great service for him.

I mean, Sancho, that the desire to achieve fame is extraordinarily active. What do you think made Horatius leap from the bridge, dressed in all his armor, into the depths of the Tiber? What burned the arm and hand of Mutius? What impelled Curtius to throw himself into the deep burning abyss that opened in the center of Rome? What, against all the unfavorable omens that had appeared, drove Caesar to cross the Rubicon? And, with more modern examples, what scuttled the ships and left the valiant Spaniards, led by the gallant Cortés, stranded and isolated in the New World? All these and many other great feats are, were, and will be the works of fame, which mortals desire as a reward and as part of the immortality which their famous deeds deserve, though we as Christians, Catholics, and knights errant must care more for future glory, eternal in the ethereal and celestial spheres, than for the vanity of the fame achieved in this present and transitory world; this fame, no matter how long it may last, must finally come to an end with the world itself, whose end has been determined. And so, O Sancho, our actions must not go beyond the limits placed there by the Christian religion, which we profess. We must slay pride by slaying giants; slay envy with generosity and a good heart; anger with serene bearing and tranquility of spirit; gluttony and sleep by eating little and watching always; lust and lasciviousness by maintaining our fealty toward those whom we have made mistresses of our thoughts; sloth by wandering everywhere in the world, seeking those occasions when we may become famous knights as well as Christians. Here you see, Sancho, the means by which one attains the highest praise that comes with fame and a good name."

"Everything your grace has told me so far," said Sancho, "I have understood very well, but even so, I would like your grace to absolve a doubt that has just come to mind."

"*Resolve* is what you mean, Sancho," said Don Quixote. "Come, tell me, and I shall answer the best I can."

"Tell me, Señor," Sancho continued, "all those Julys or Augusts,[3] and all those brave knights you mentioned, the ones who are dead, where are they now?"

"The gentiles," responded Don Quixote, "are undoubtedly in hell; the Christians, if they were good Christians, are either in purgatory or in heaven."

"That's fine," said Sancho, "but tell me now: the tombs where the bodies of those big important knights are buried, do they have silver lamps burning in front of them, and are the walls of their chapels hung with crutches, shrouds, wigs, and legs and eyes of wax? And if not, how are they decorated?"

To which Don Quixote responded:

"The tombs of the gentiles were, for the most part, sumptuous temples: the ashes of Julius Caesar were placed at the top of an extraordinarily large stone pyramid, which in Rome they now call St. Peter's Needle; the Emperor Hadrian had for his tomb a castle as large as a good-sized village, which was called *Moles Hadriani*, and today is the Castel Santangelo in Rome; Queen Artemisia buried her husband, Mausolus, in a tomb that was considered one of the seven wonders of the world; but none of these tombs, or the many others that the gentiles had, were adorned with shrouds or any of the offerings and signs indicating that those buried there were saints."

"I'm coming to that," replied Sancho. "Now, tell me which is the greater deed, raising a dead man or killing a giant?"

"The answer is self-evident," responded Don Quixote. "It is greater to raise a dead man."

"Then I've got you," said Sancho. "The fame of those who raise the dead, give sight to the blind, heal the lame, and cure the sick, and whose tombs have lamps burning in front of them, and whose chapels are filled with devout people who adore the relics on their knees, that would be a better fame, in this world and the next, than the fame left behind by all the gentile emperors and knights errant who ever lived."

"I admit that this is true," responded Don Quixote.

"Well, this fame, these favors, these prerogatives, or whatever they're called," responded Sancho, "is what the bodies and relics of the saints have, and with the approval and permission of our Holy Mother

3. In this example of Sancho's linguistic and historical confusions, the wordplay is based on the fact that in Spanish *julio* is the month of July, while *Julio* is the equivalent of Julius; *agosto* is the month of August, while *Agosto* is the equivalent of Augustus.

Church, they also have lamps, candles, shrouds, crutches, paintings, wigs, eyes, and legs, and with these they deepen devotion and increase their Christian fame; the bodies of saints or their relics are carried on their shoulders by kings, and they kiss the fragments of their bones, and use them to decorate and adorn their private chapels and their favorite altars."

"What do you wish me to infer, Sancho, from all that you have said?" said Don Quixote.

"I mean," said Sancho, "that we should begin to be saints, and then we'll win the fame we want in a much shorter time; and remember, Señor, that only yesterday or the day before—it happened so recently, it's fair to say that—they canonized or beatified two discalced friars, and the iron chains they used to bind and torture their bodies are now thought to bring great good luck if you kiss and touch them, and are venerated, as I said, more than the sword of Roland in the armory of His Majesty the king, God save him. And so, Señor, it's better to be a humble friar, in any order at all, than a valiant knight errant; two dozen lashings with a scourge have more effect on God than two thousand thrusts with a lance, whether they're aimed at giants, or monsters, or dragons."

"All of that is true," responded Don Quixote, "but we cannot all be friars, and God brings His children to heaven by many paths: chivalry is a religion, and there are sainted knights in Glory."

"Yes," responded Sancho, "but I've heard that there are more friars in heaven than knights errant."

"That is true," responded Don Quixote, "because the number of religious is greater than the number of knights."

"There are many who are errant," said Sancho.

"Many," responded Don Quixote, "but few who deserve to be called knights."

They spent that night and the following day in this and other similar conversations, and nothing worth recounting happened to them, which caused no small sorrow to Don Quixote. Finally, the next day at dusk, they could see the great city of Toboso, a sight that brought joy to Don Quixote's spirit and saddened Sancho's, because he did not know which house was Dulcinea's, for he had never seen it, just as his master had never seen it, so that both were in a state of high agitation, one with his desire to see it, the other because he had not, and Sancho could not imagine what he would do when his master sent him into Toboso. In short, Don Quixote decided to enter the city when night had fallen, and they waited for the hour of darkness in a stand of oaks growing near Toboso, and when the time came they entered the city, where things befell them that certainly were memorable.

CHAPTER IX

Which recounts what will soon be seen

It was on the stroke of midnight,[1] more or less, when Don Quixote and Sancho left the countryside and entered Toboso. The town lay in peaceful silence, because all the residents were in their beds and sleeping like logs, as the saying goes. The night was fairly clear, although Sancho would have preferred it totally dark so that he could find an excuse for his ignorance in the darkness. All that could be heard in the town was the sound of dogs barking, which thundered in Don Quixote's ears and troubled the heart of Sancho. From time to time a donkey brayed, pigs grunted, cats meowed, and the different sounds of their voices seemed louder in the silence of the night, which the enamored knight took as an evil omen; despite this, however, he said to Sancho:

"Sancho, my friend, lead the way to the palace of Dulcinea; perhaps we may find her awake."

"Good God, what palace am I supposed to lead to," responded Sancho, "when the place where I saw her highness was only a very small house?"

"She must have withdrawn, at that time," responded Don Quixote, "to a small apartment in her castle, finding solace alone with her damsels, as is the practice and custom of noble ladies and princesses."

"Señor," said Sancho, "since your grace insists, in spite of what I say, that the house of my lady Dulcinea is a castle, do you think we'll find the door open at this hour? And would it be a good idea for us to knock loud

1. The line is from an old ballad, "El conde Claros" ("Count Claros").

enough for them to hear us and open the door, disturbing everybody with the noise we make? Are we by chance calling at the houses of our kept women, where we can visit and knock at the door and go in any time we want no matter how late it is?"

"Before we do anything else, let us first find the castle," replied Don Quixote, "and then I shall tell you, Sancho, what it would be good for us to do. And listen, Sancho, either I cannot see very well or that large shape and its shadow over there must be the palace of Dulcinea."

"Well, your grace, lead the way," responded Sancho, "and maybe it will be, though even if I saw it with my eyes and touched it with my hands, I'd believe it the way I believe it's daytime now."

Don Quixote led the way, and after some two hundred paces he came to the shape that was casting the shadow, and he saw a high tower, and then he realized that the building was not a castle but the principal church of the town. And he said:

"We have come to the church, Sancho."[2]

"I can see that," responded Sancho. "And may it please God that we don't come to our graves; it's not a good idea to walk through cemeteries at this hour of the night, especially since I told your grace, if I remember correctly, that the lady's house is in a little dead-end lane."

"May God damn you for a fool!" said Don Quixote. "Where have you ever found castles and royal palaces built in little dead-end lanes?"

"Señor," responded Sancho, "each place has its ways: maybe here in Toboso the custom is to build palaces and large buildings in lanes, and so I beg your grace to let me look along these streets and lanes that I see here; maybe at some corner I'll run into that castle, and I hope I see it devoured by dogs for bringing us such a weary long way."

"Speak with respect, Sancho, of the things that pertain to my lady," said Don Quixote, "and let us be patient: we shall not give up."

"I'll control myself," responded Sancho, "but how can I be patient if I saw our lady's house only one time but your grace wants me to know it forever and find it in the middle of the night, when your grace can't find it and you must have seen it thousands of times?"

"You make me despair, Sancho," said Don Quixote. "Come here, you scoundrel: have I not told you a thousand times that in all the days of my

2. This statement is one of the best known in the novel, for it has been interpreted as meaning that Don Quixote and Sancho have "run into" the church in the sense of coming into dangerous conflict with the institution. The sentence is sometimes cited using another verb to underscore that meaning: *topar* (the verb used by Sancho just a few lines down) rather than *dar*. According to Martín de Riquer, this is overinterpretation, and the sentence means only what it says: the building is a church, not Dulcinea's palace.

life I have not seen the peerless Dulcinea, and I have never crossed the threshold of her palace, and I am in love only because I have heard of the great fame she has for beauty and discernment?"

"Now I hear it," responded Sancho, "and I say that just as your grace has not seen her, neither have I."

"That cannot be," replied Don Quixote. "At least you told me that you saw her sifting wheat, when you brought me her answer to the letter I sent with you."

"Don't depend on that, Señor," responded Sancho, "because I want you to know that I only heard about seeing her and bringing you her answer, and I have as much idea who the lady Dulcinea is as I have chances to punch the sky."

"Sancho, Sancho," responded Don Quixote, "there is a time for jokes and a time when jokes are inappropriate and out of place. Simply because I say I have not seen or spoken to the lady of my soul, it does not mean that you must also say you have not spoken to her or seen her, when just the opposite is true, as you well know."

They were engaged in this conversation when they saw a man with two mules coming toward them, and by the noise he made with the plow that was dragging along the ground, they judged him to be a peasant who had gotten up before dawn to begin his labors, which was the truth. As he walked along, the peasant sang the ballad that says:

> A bad day for you, O Frenchmen,
> that defeat at Roncesvalles.

"By heaven, Sancho," said Don Quixote when he heard him, "I doubt anything good will happen to us this night. Do you hear what that laborer is singing?"

"I do," responded Sancho, "but what does the rout at Roncesvalles[3] have to do with us? He could just as easily be singing the ballad of Calaínos, and it wouldn't change whether we have good or bad luck in this business."

By now the laborer had reached them, and Don Quixote asked:

"Can you tell me, my friend, and may God send you good fortune, the location of the palaces of the peerless princess Doña Dulcinea of Toboso?"

"Señor," the young man responded, "I'm a stranger, and I've only

---

3. Sancho quotes a different version of the ballad of Roncesvalles.

been in town a few days, working for a rich farmer in his fields; the priest and the sacristan live in that house in front of us, and either one or both of them will be able to tell your grace about that lady the princess, because they have the list of everybody who lives in Toboso, though it seems to me that no princess lives anywhere around here; but there are lots of ladies, and they're so distinguished that each one could be a princess in her own house."

"Well, friend, the lady I am asking about," said Don Quixote, "must be one of them."

"That might be," responded the young man, "and now goodbye: dawn is breaking."

And prodding his mules, he waited for no more questions. Sancho, seeing his master somewhat baffled and in a bad humor, said:

"Señor, it's almost day and it wouldn't be a good idea to let the sun find us out on the street; it would be better for us to leave the city, and then your grace can wait in some nearby woods, and I'll come back in broad daylight and search every corner of this town for the house, castle, or palace of my lady, and I'll have to be pretty unlucky not to find it; and when I do, I'll talk to her grace and tell her where your grace is waiting for her to give you leave to see her and tell you how you can without doing damage to her honor and good name."

"You have, Sancho," said Don Quixote, "enclosed a thousand wise statements within the circle of a few brief words: the advice you have just given pleases me, and I accept it very willingly. Come, my friend, and let us look for the place where I shall wait while you, as you have said, will come back to find, see, and speak to my lady, from whose intelligence and courtesy I hope for more than wondrous favors."

Sancho was desperate to get his master outside the town so that he would not discover the lie of the response from Dulcinea that he had brought to him in the Sierra Morena, and so he hurried their departure, which took place without delay, and two miles from the town they found a stand of trees or a wood where Don Quixote waited while Sancho returned to the city to speak with Dulcinea; and on this mission things occurred that demand a renewal of both attention and belief.

CHAPTER X

Which recounts Sancho's ingenuity in enchanting the lady Dulcinea, and other events as ridiculous as they are true

When the author of this great history came to recount what is recounted in this chapter, he says he would have preferred to pass over it in silence, fearful it would not be given credence, for the madness of Don Quixote here reached the limits and boundaries of the greatest madnesses that can be imagined, and even passed two crossbow shots beyond them. But finally, despite this fear and trepidation, he wrote down the mad acts just as Don Quixote performed them, not adding or subtracting an atom of truth from the history and not concerning himself about the accusations that he was a liar, which might be made against him; and he was right, because truth may be stretched thin and not break, and it always floats on the surface of the lie, like oil on water.

And so, continuing his history, he says that as soon as Don Quixote had entered the wood, oak grove, or forest near the great Toboso, he ordered Sancho to return to the city and not appear again in his presence without first having spoken on his behalf to his lady, asking her to be so kind as to allow herself to be seen by her captive knight and deign to give him her blessing so that he might hope for a most happy conclusion for all his undertakings and arduous enterprises. Sancho agreed to do everything exactly as ordered and to bring back a reply as good as the one he had brought the first time.

"Go, my friend," replied Don Quixote, "and do not become disconcerted when you find yourself looking at the light emanating from the sun of beauty which you will seek. Oh, you are more fortunate than all the squires in the world! Remember everything and do not miss a detail of how she receives you: if her color changes as you give her my message;

if she becomes agitated or troubled when she hears my name; if she moves about on her pillows, if you happen to find her in the richly furnished antechamber of her rank;[1] if she is standing, look at her to see if she shifts from one foot to another; if she repeats her answer two or three times; if she changes from gentle to severe, from harsh to loving; if she raises her hand to her hair to smooth it, although it is not disarranged; finally, my friend, observe all her actions and movements, because if you relate them to me just as they occurred, I shall interpret what she keeps hidden in the secret places of her heart in response to the fact of my love; for you must know, Sancho, if you do not know it already, that with lovers, the external actions and movements, revealed when the topic of their love arises, are reliable messengers bringing the news of what transpires deep in their souls. Go, my friend, and may better fortune than mine guide you, and may you return with greater success than I dare hope for as I wait in this bitter solitude in which you leave me."

"I'll go and come back very quickly," said Sancho, "and swell that heart of yours, which can't be any bigger now than a hazelnut, and remember what they say: a good heart beats bad luck, and where there is no bacon, there are no stakes,[2] and they also say that a hare leaps out when you least expect it. I'm saying this because if we didn't find my lady's palaces or castles last night, now that it's day I think I'll find them when I least expect to, and once I've found them, just leave everything to me."

"Well, Sancho," said Don Quixote, "you certainly bring in proverbs that suit our affairs perfectly, and I hope God gives me as much good fortune in my desires."

This having been said, Sancho turned away and urged on his donkey, and Don Quixote remained on horseback, resting in the stirrups and leaning on his lance, full of melancholy and confused imaginings, and there we will leave him and go with Sancho Panza, who rode away no less confused and thoughtful than his master; in fact, as soon as he had emerged from the wood he turned his head, and seeing that Don Quixote was nowhere in sight, he dismounted his donkey, sat at the foot of a tree, and began to talk to himself, saying:

"Now, Sancho my brother, let's find out where your grace is going. Are you going to look for some donkey that's been lost?" "No, of course

---

1. Highborn ladies would receive visitors in a special room of the house that had lounging pillows.

2. Sancho misquotes the proverb.

not." "Well, what are you going to look for?" "I'm going to look for a princess—like that was an easy thing to do—who is the sun of beauty and the rest of heaven, too." "And where do you think you'll find all that, Sancho?" "Where? In the great city of Toboso." "All right, for whose sake are you going to look for her?" "For the sake of the famous knight Don Quixote of La Mancha, who rights wrongs, and gives food to the thirsty, and drink to the hungry." "All that's very fine. Do you know where her house is, Sancho?" "My master says it has to be royal palaces or noble castles." "Have you, by chance, ever seen her?" "I've never seen her, and neither has my master." "And do you think it would be the right and proper thing to do, if the people of Toboso found out that you're here intending to coax away their princesses and disturb their ladies, for them to batter your ribs with sticks and break every bone in your body?" "The truth is they'd be right, unless they remembered that I'm following orders, and that

> You are the messenger, my friend,
> and do not deserve the blame."[3]

"Don't rely on that, Sancho, because Manchegans are as quick-tempered as they are honorable, and they don't put up with anything from anybody. By God, if they suspect what you're up to, then I predict bad luck for you." "Get out, you dumb bastard! Let the lighting strike somebody else! Not me, I'm not going to look for trouble to please some-body else! Besides, looking for Dulcinea in Toboso will be like looking for a María in Ravenna or a bachelor in Salamanca. The devil, the devil and nobody else has gotten me into this!"

Sancho held this soliloquy with himself, and the conclusion he drew was that he talked to himself again, saying:

"Well now: everything has a remedy except death, under whose yoke we all have to pass, even if we don't want to, when our life ends. I've seen a thousand signs in this master of mine that he's crazy enough to be tied up, and I'm not far behind, I'm as much a fool as he is because I fol-low and serve him, if that old saying is true: 'Tell me who your friends are and I'll tell you who you are,' and that other one that says, 'Birds of a feather flock together.' Then, being crazy, which is what he is, with the kind of craziness that most of the time takes one thing for another, and

---

3. The lines are from a ballad about Bernardo del Carpio.

thinks white is black and black is white, like the time he said that the windmills were giants, and the friars' mules dromedaries, and the flocks of sheep enemy armies, and many other things of that nature, it won't be very hard to make him believe that a peasant girl, the first one I run into here, is the lady Dulcinea; and if he doesn't believe it, I'll swear it's true; and if he swears it isn't, I'll swear again that it is; and if he insists, I'll insist more; and so I'll always have the last word, no matter what. Maybe I'll be so stubborn he won't send me out again carrying his messages, seeing the bad answers I bring back, or maybe he'll believe, which is what I think will happen, that one of those evil enchanters he says are his enemies changed her appearance to hurt him and do him harm."

When Sancho Panza had this idea his spirit grew calm, and he considered his business successfully concluded, and he stayed there until the afternoon so that Don Quixote would think that he'd had time to go to Toboso and come back; and everything went so well for him that when he stood up to mount the donkey, he saw that coming toward him from the direction of Toboso were three peasant girls on three jackasses, or jennies, since the author does not specify which they were, though it is more likely that they were she-donkeys, for they are the ordinary mounts of village girls, but since not much depends on this, there is no reason to spend more time verifying it. In short: as soon as Sancho saw the peasant girls, he rode back as fast as he could to look for his master, Don Quixote, and found him heaving sighs and saying a thousand amorous lamentations. As soon as Don Quixote saw him, he said:

"What news, Sancho my friend? Shall I mark this day with a white stone or a black?"

"It would be better," responded Sancho, "for your grace to mark it in red paint, like the names of the professors,[4] so that everybody who looks can see it clearly."

"That means," replied Don Quixote, "that you bring good news."

"So good," responded Sancho, "that all your grace has to do is spur Rocinante and ride into the open and you'll see the lady Dulcinea of Toboso, who is coming to see your grace with two of her damsels."

"Holy God! What are you saying, Sancho my friend?" said Don Quixote. "Do not deceive me, or try to lighten my true sorrows with false joys."

"What good would it do me to deceive your grace," responded

4. It was the custom in universities to write on the walls, in red paint, the names of those who had been awarded professorships.

Sancho, "especially since you're so close to discovering that what I say is true? Use your spurs, Señor, and come with me, and you'll see the princess riding toward us, our mistress, all dressed and adorned, like the person she is. She and her damsels are all shining gold, all strands of pearls, all diamonds, all rubies, all brocade cloth ten levels high,[5] their hair, hanging loose down their backs, is like rays of the sun dancing in the wind; best of all, they're riding three piebald pilfers, the prettiest sight you'll ever see."

"You must mean *palfreys*, Sancho."

"There's not much difference," responded Sancho, "between *pilfers* and *palfreys*, but no matter what they're riding, they're the best-looking ladies anybody could want to see, especially my lady the Princess Dulcinea, who dazzles the senses."

"Let us go, Sancho my friend," responded Don Quixote, "and to celebrate this news, as unexpected as it is good, I promise you the best spoils that I shall win in the first adventure I have, and if this does not satisfy you, I promise you the foals that my three mares drop this year, for as you know, they are in the village pasture,[6] ready to give birth."

"I'll take the foals," responded Sancho, "because it's not very certain that the spoils of your first adventure will be any good."

At this point they left the wood and saw the three village girls close by. Don Quixote looked carefully up and down the road to Toboso, and since he saw no one but the three peasants, he was bewildered and asked Sancho if he had left them outside the city.

"What do you mean, outside the city?" he responded. "By any chance are your grace's eyes in the back of your head? Is that why you don't see them riding toward us, shining like the sun at midday?"

"Sancho, I do not see anything," said Don Quixote, "except three peasant girls on three donkeys."

"God save me now from the devil!" responded Sancho. "Is it possible that three snow white palfreys, or whatever they're called, look like donkeys to your grace? God help us, may this beard of mine be plucked out if that's true!"

"Well, I can tell you, friend Sancho," said Don Quixote, "that it is as true that they are jackasses, or jennies, as it is that I am Don Quixote and you Sancho Panza; at least, that is what they seem to be."

5. In the weaving and embroidering of the raised design on brocade, fabric with three levels of handiwork was considered very valuable. Carried away by his fantasy, Sancho exaggerates.

6. Municipalities had community grazing lands for the use of residents.

"Don't speak, Señor," said Sancho, "don't say those things, but clear the mist from your eyes and come and do reverence to the lady of your thoughts, who is almost here."

And having said this, he went forward to receive the three village girls, and after dismounting from his donkey, he grasped the halter of one of the three peasant girls' mounts, fell to his knees, and said:

"Queen and princess and duchess of beauty, may your high mightiness be pleased to receive into your good graces and disposition your captive knight, who is there, turned into marble, confused and struck dumb at finding himself in your magnificent presence. I am Sancho Panza, his squire, and he is the much traveled Don Quixote of La Mancha, also called *The Knight of the Sorrowful Face*."

By this time Don Quixote had kneeled down next to Sancho and looked, with startled eyes and confused vision, at the person Sancho was calling queen and lady, and since he could see nothing except a peasant girl, and one not especially attractive, since she was round-faced and snub-nosed, he was so astounded and amazed that he did not dare open his mouth. The peasant girls were equally astonished at seeing those two men, so different from each other, kneeling and not allowing their companion to continue on her way; but the one who had been stopped was annoyed and angry, and breaking the silence, she said:

"Out of the way, damn it, and let us pass; we're in a hurry!"

To which Sancho responded:

"O princess and universal lady of Toboso! How can your magnanimous heart not soften at seeing the pillar and support of knight errantry on his knees in your sublimal presence?"

Hearing which, another of the girls said:

"Hey, whoa, I'll tan your hide, you miserable donkey! Look at how the gentry are making fun of us country girls now, like we didn't know how to give as good as we get! You go on your way, and let us go on ours, if you want to stay healthy."

"Stand up, Sancho," said Don Quixote, "for I see that Fortune, not satisfied with my sorrows, has captured all the roads by which some joy might come to the wretched spirit that inhabits this flesh. And thou, O highest virtue that can be desired, summit of human courtesy, sole remedy for this afflicted heart that adoreth thee! The wicked enchanter who pursueth me hath placed clouds and cataracts over my eyes, so that for them alone but not for others he hath changed and transformed thy peerless beauty and countenance into the figure of a poor peasant, and if he hath not also turned mine into that of a monster abominable in thy sight, ceaseth not to regard me kindly and lovingly and see in this submission of mine as I kneel before thy deformed beauty, the humility with which my soul adoreth thee."

"You can tell that to my grandpa!" responded the village girl. "I just love listening to crackpated things! Step aside and let us pass, and we'll thank you for it."

Sancho stepped aside and let her pass, delighted to have gotten out of his difficulty so easily.

As soon as the peasant girl who had played the part of Dulcinea was released, she spurred her *pilfer* with a goad that she had on the end of a stick and began to gallop across the meadow. And since the goad irritated the jenny more than usual, she began to buck and threw the lady Dulcinea to the ground; when Don Quixote saw this, he hurried to help her up, and Sancho began to adjust and tighten her packsaddle, which had slipped under the donkey's belly. When the saddle had been put in place, and Don Quixote tried to lift his enchanted lady in his arms and put her back on the donkey, the lady got up from the ground and saved him the trouble, because she moved back, ran a short distance, and, placing both hands on the donkey's rump, jumped right into the saddle, as agile as a hawk and sitting astride as if she were a man; and then Sancho said:

"By St. Roque, our mistress is faster than a falcon, and she could teach the most skilled Cordoban or Mexican how to ride! She was over the hind bow of the saddle in one jump, and without any spurs she makes that palfrey run like a zebra. And her damsels are not far behind; they're all running like the wind."

And it was true, because when Dulcinea was mounted, they all spurred their mounts and fell in behind her and broke into a gallop and did not look back for more than half a league. Don Quixote followed them with his eyes, and when he could no longer see them, he turned to Sancho and said:

"Sancho, what do you think of how the enchanters despise me? Look at the extent of their malice and ill will, for they have chosen to deprive me of the happiness I might have had at seeing my lady in her rightful person. In truth, I was born to be a model of misfortune, the target and mark for the arrows of affliction. And you must also know, Sancho, that it was not enough for these traitors to have changed and transformed my Dulcinea, but they had to transform and change her into a figure as lowborn and ugly as that peasant, and take away something that so rightfully belongs to noble ladies, which is a sweet smell, since they are always surrounded by perfumes and flowers. For I shall tell you, Sancho, that when I came to help Dulcinea onto her palfrey, as you call it, though it looked like a donkey to me, I smelled an odor of raw garlic that almost made me faint and poisoned my soul."

"Oh, you dogs!" shouted Sancho. "Oh, you miserable, evil enchanters, if only I could see you all strung by the gills like sardines on a fisherman's reed! You know so much, and can do so much, and do even more evil. It should have been enough, you villains, to turn the pearls of my lady's eyes into cork-tree galls, and her hair of purest gold into the bristles of a red ox tail, and all her good features into bad, without doing anything to her smell, because from that we could have imagined what was hidden beneath her ugly shell; though to tell you the truth, I never saw her ugliness, only her beauty, which was made even greater by a mole she had on the right side of her lip, like a mustache, with six or seven blond hairs like threads of gold and longer than a span."

"That mole," said Don Quixote, "according to the correspondence that exists between those on the face and those on the body, must be matched by another that Dulcinea has on the broad part of her thigh, on the same side as the one on her face, but the hairs you have mentioned are very long for a mole."

"Well, I can tell your grace," responded Sancho, "that they looked like they'd been born there."

"I can believe it, my friend," replied Don Quixote, "because nature put nothing on Dulcinea that was not perfect and complete, and so, if she had a hundred moles like the one you describe, on her they would not be moles but shining moons and stars. But tell me, Sancho: the saddle that seemed like a packsaddle to me, the one that you adjusted, was it a simple saddle or a sidesaddle?"

"It was," responded Sancho, "just a high-bowed saddle, with a covering so rich it must have been worth half a kingdom."

"And to think I did not see all of that, Sancho!" said Don Quixote. "Now I say it again, and shall say it a thousand more times: I am the most unfortunate of men."

When he heard the foolish things said by his master, who had been so exquisitely deceived, it was all the scoundrel Sancho could do to hide his laughter. Finally, after much more conversation between them, they remounted their animals and followed the road to Zaragoza, where they hoped to arrive in time to take part in the solemn festival held in that celebrated city every year. But before they arrived, certain things happened to them, so numerous, great, and unusual that they deserve to be described and read, as will soon be seen.

CHAPTER XI

Regarding the strange adventure that befell the valiant Don Quixote with the cart or wagon of The Assembly of Death

Don Quixote was thoughtful as he went on his way, considering the awful trick the enchanters had played on him when they turned his lady Dulcinea into the ugly figure of the peasant girl, and he could not imagine what remedy he might have that would return her to her original state; these thoughts distracted him so much that, without realizing it, he dropped the reins, and Rocinante, sensing the freedom that had been given to him, stopped at every step to graze on the green grass that grew so abundantly in those fields. Sancho brought his master back from his preoccupations by saying:

"Señor, sorrows were made not for animals but for men; but if men feel them too much, they turn into animals; your grace should restrain yourself, and come back to yourself, and pick up Rocinante's reins, and liven up and rouse yourself, and show the bravery that knights errant ought to have. What the devil is this? What kind of mood is this? Are we here or in France?[1] Let Satan carry off all the Dulcineas in the world, for the well-being of a single knight errant is worth more than all the enchantments and transformations on earth."

"Be quiet, Sancho," responded Don Quixote in a voice that was not particularly faint. "Be quiet, I say, and do not speak blasphemies against that enchanted lady, for I alone am to blame for her affliction and misfortune: her tribulations were born of the envy those villains have for me."

1. This is a way to say, "Let's behave sensibly and realistically."

"That's what I say, too," responded Sancho. "If you saw her once and see her now, how could your heart not weep?"

"That is something you can rightfully say, Sancho," replied Don Quixote, "for you saw her in the fullness and completeness of her beauty; the enchantment did not go so far as to cloud your sight or hide her beauty from you: it directs the strength of its poison only against me and my eyes. But with it all, Sancho, I have realized something, which is that you described her beauty to me very badly, for if I remember correctly, you said that she had eyes like pearls, and eyes that seem to be of pearl are more appropriate to bream than to a lady; my belief is that Dulcinea's eyes must be like green emeralds and almond-shaped, with two celestial arcs as eyebrows; you should take those pearls from her eyes and move them down to her teeth, for you undoubtedly became confused, Sancho, and said eyes instead of teeth."

"Everything's possible," responded Sancho, "because I was as upset by her beauty as your grace was by her ugliness. But let us leave everything to God, for He knows the things that will happen in this vale of tears, this evil world of ours, where hardly anything's untouched by wickedness, lies, and deception. One thing grieves me, Señor, more than any other, which is to think what should be done when your grace conquers a giant or another knight and orders him to appear before the beauty of the lady Dulcinea: where will this poor giant or this poor wretch of a conquered knight find her? It seems to me I can see them wandering around Toboso like idiots, looking for my lady Dulcinea, and even if they find her in the middle of the street, they won't recognize her any more than they'd know my father."

"Perhaps, Sancho," responded Don Quixote, "the enchantment does not go so far as to take knowledge of Dulcinea from the vanquished giants and knights who appear before her; with one or two of the first ones I vanquish and send to her, we shall determine if they see her or not by commanding them to return and recount to me what happened to them in this regard."

"I'll tell you, Señor," replied Sancho, "that I think what your grace has said is fine, and with this plan we'll find out just what we want to know; and if she's hidden only from your grace, the misfortune is more your grace's than hers; but as long as the lady Dulcinea has health and happiness, we'll resign ourselves and do the best we can, looking for our adventures and letting time do its work, for it's the best doctor for these ailments and others that are even worse."

Don Quixote wanted to respond to Sancho Panza, but he was prevented from doing so by a cart that came out across the road, filled with the most diverse and peculiar personages and figures that one could imagine. The one guiding the mules and serving as the driver of the cart was a hideous demon. The cart was open to the sky, without any covering of canvas or reeds. The first figure that appeared to Don Quixote's eyes was that of Death himself, with a human face; next to him was an angel with large painted wings; to one side was an emperor wearing a crown, apparently of gold, on his head; at the feet of Death was the god called Cupid, without a blindfold but holding his bow, quiver, and arrows. There was a knight in full armor except that he had no helmet or sallet but wore a hat with many plumes of diverse colors; accompanying these persons were others with various outfits and countenances. All of which, seen without warning, agitated Don Quixote somewhat, and put fear in Sancho's heart; but then Don Quixote was glad, believing that a new and dangerous adventure was upon him, and with this thought, and a spirit prepared to face any peril, he stopped in front of the cart, and in a loud, menacing voice he said:

"Cartman, wagon driver, devil, or whatever you are, tell me immediately who you are, and where you are going, and who are the people you are carrying in your wagon, which looks more like Charon's boat than like any ordinary cart."

To which the devil, stopping the cart, gently replied:

"Señor, we are actors in Angulo el Malo's company; this morning, which is the eighth day of Corpus Christi, in a town located behind that hill, we performed the mystery play *The Assembly of Death*,[2] and we are to perform it this afternoon in the town you can see over there, and because it is so close, and to save ourselves the trouble of taking off our costumes and putting them on again, we are dressed in the same clothes we perform in. That young man plays Death; the other one, the Angel; that woman, who is married to the manager, plays the Queen; this one is the Soldier; that one, the Emperor; I play the Demon, and I am one of the principal figures in the play, because in this company I play the leading roles. If your grace wishes to know anything else about us, ask me, and I will respond in every particular; since I am a devil, all things are within my grasp."

"By my faith as a knight errant," responded Don Quixote, "as soon as I saw this wagon I imagined that a great adventure was awaiting me, and now I say that it is necessary to touch appearances with one's hand to

2. This may be a reference to a religious play of the same title (*Las cortes de la muerte*) by Lope de Vega; there was, in fact, a theatrical impresario named Angulo el Malo.

avoid being deceived. Go with God, my good people, and have your festival, and consider if there is any way in which I can be of service to you,
and I shall do it gladly and willingly, because ever since I was a boy I
have enjoyed the theater, and in my youth I was a great lover of plays."

As luck would have it, while they were having this conversation a
member of the company came up to them, and he was dressed as a fool,
wearing a good number of bells, and at the end of a stick he was carrying
there were three inflated cow bladders; this buffoon approached Don
Quixote and began to fence with the stick and hit the ground with the
bladders and leap high into the air, shaking his bells; this terrible sight so
alarmed Rocinante that, without Don Quixote being able to stop him,
he took the bit between his teeth and began to run across the field with
more speed than was ever promised by the bones of his anatomy. Sancho, who considered the danger that Don Quixote would be thrown,
jumped off his donkey and ran as fast as he could to help him, but when
he reached him Don Quixote was already on the ground, and next to
him lay Rocinante, who had fallen along with his master: the usual finale
and conclusion of Rocinante's exuberance and bold exploits.

But as soon as Sancho had left his mount to assist Don Quixote, the
demon dancer jumped on the donkey and began to hit him with the
bladders, and fear and the noise, more than the pain of the blows, made
the donkey fly across the countryside to the town where the festival was
to be held. Sancho looked at his racing donkey and his fallen master and
did not know which of the two problems he should take care of first; but,
in fact, because he was a good squire and a good servant, love for his master won out over affection for his donkey, although each time he saw the
bladders go up in the air and come down on his donkey's rump, he suffered the torments and terrors of death and would rather have had those
blows fall on his own eyes than touch a hair of his donkey's tail. In this
perplexity and tribulation, he reached Don Quixote, who was much
more bruised and battered than he would have wished, and helping him
to mount Rocinante, he said:

"Señor, the devil has made off with my donkey."

"What devil?" asked Don Quixote.

"The one with the bladders," responded Sancho.

"Then I shall get him back," replied Don Quixote, "even if he takes
him down to the deepest and darkest pits of hell. Follow me, Sancho, for
the cart is traveling slowly, and I shall compensate for the loss of the
donkey with the mules."

"There's no need to go to all that trouble, Señor," responded Sancho.

"Your grace should calm your anger, for it seems to me the devil has left the donkey and gone back to his lair."

And this was true, because after the devil had fallen off the donkey in imitation of Don Quixote and Rocinante, the devil went on foot to the town, and the donkey returned to his master.

"Even so," said Don Quixote, "it would be a good idea to punish the discourtesy of that demon by chastising someone in the cart, even the Emperor himself."

"Your grace should put that thought out of your mind," replied Sancho, "and take my advice, which is never to interfere with actors, for they are favored people. I have seen an actor arrested for two deaths and then be released, and no fines. Your grace should know that since they are good-natured and give pleasure to people, everyone favors them, everyone protects and helps and admires them, especially if they're in one of the royal companies with an official license, and all of them, or most of them, look like princes in their costumes and makeup."

"Well, all the same," responded Don Quixote, "the actor demon is not going to exit to applause, even if the entire human race should favor him."

And saying this, he returned to the cart, which by this time was very close to the town. He was shouting as he approached, saying:

"Stop, wait, you happy and cheerful throng, for I want to make you understand how you are supposed to treat the donkeys and animals that serve as mounts to the squires of knights errant."

Don Quixote's shouts were so loud that the people in the cart heard and understood them; and judging by his words the intention of the man who was saying them, in an instant Death jumped out of the cart, and behind him, the Emperor, the Demon cart driver, and the Angel, and the Queen and the god Cupid did not stay behind, and all of them picked up stones and stood in a line, waiting to receive Don Quixote with the sharp edges of their pebbles. Don Quixote, who saw them arranged in so gallant a squadron, their arms raised and ready to throw the stones with great force, pulled on Rocinante's reins and began to think about how he could attack them with less risk to his person. When he stopped, Sancho approached, and seeing him prepared to attack the orderly squadron, he said:

"It would be crazy to attempt this adventure: your grace should consider, Señor, that for pebbles and stones, there's no defensive weapon in the world except to squeeze into a bronze bell and hide there; you should also consider that there is more rashness than courage in a single man attacking an army that has Death in it, and emperors fighting in person, and the help of good and bad angels; and if this doesn't move you to stay put, then remember that among all those people, even though they seem to be kings, princes, and emperors, there's not one knight errant."

"Now, Sancho," said Don Quixote, "you have hit on the point that can and must move me from my determined intention. I cannot and must not draw my sword, as I have told you many times in the past, against anyone who has not been dubbed a knight. It falls to you, Sancho, if you wish to take revenge for the affront committed against your donkey; I shall assist you from here with helpful words and advice."

"There's no need, Señor," responded Sancho, "to take revenge against anyone, since it's not right for good Christians to take revenge for affronts; besides, I'll convince my donkey to let me take care of the insult, and my desire is to live peaceably for all the days of life that heaven will grant me."

"Well, if that is your decision," replied Don Quixote, "good Sancho, wise Sancho, Christian Sancho, sincere Sancho, let us leave these phantoms and again seek better and more appropriate adventures, for I see that this land is the kind that cannot fail to offer many that are quite miraculous."

Then he pulled on the reins and turned Rocinante around, Sancho caught his donkey, Death and all of his flying squadron returned to their cart and continued on their way, and this was the happy conclusion to the fearful adventure of the cart of Death, thanks to the salutary advice that Sancho Panza gave to his master, who the next day had another adventure, no less suspenseful than the previous one, with an enamored knight errant.

CHAPTER XII

Regarding the strange adventure that befell the valiant Don Quixote and the courageous Knight of the Mirrors

Don Quixote and his squire spent the night that followed the day of their encounter with Death beneath some tall shade trees, and Don Quixote, having been persuaded by Sancho, ate some of the provisions carried by the donkey, and during their supper Sancho said to his master:

"Señor, what a fool I would've been if I'd chosen the spoils of the first adventure your grace completed as my reward instead of your three mares' foals! It's true, it's true: a bird in hand is worth two in the bush."

"Even so," responded Don Quixote, "if you, Sancho, had allowed me to attack as I wished to, at the very least you would have had as spoils the gold crown of the Empress and the painted wings of Cupid, for I would have taken them by force and placed them in your hands."

"The scepters and crowns of actor-emperors," responded Sancho Panza, "are never pure gold but only tinsel or tinplate."

"That is true," replied Don Quixote, "because it would not be proper if the finery in plays were really valuable instead of merely illusory and apparent, as the plays themselves are; I want you, Sancho, to think well and to have a good opinion of plays, and to be equally well-disposed toward those who perform them and those who write them, because they are all the instruments whereby a great service is performed for the nation, holding up a mirror to every step we take and allowing us to see a vivid image of the actions of human life; there is no comparison that indicates what we are and what we should be more clearly than plays and players. If you do not agree, then tell me: have you ever seen a play that presents kings, emperors, and pontiffs, knights, ladies, and many other characters? One plays the scoundrel, another the liar, this one the merchant, that one the soldier, another the wise fool, yet another the foolish lover, but when the play is over and they have taken off their costumes, all the actors are equal."

"Yes, I have seen that," responded Sancho.

"Well, the same thing happens in the drama and business of this world, where some play emperors, others pontiffs, in short, all the figures that can be presented in a play, but at the end, which is when life is over, death removes all the clothing that differentiated them, and all are equal in the grave."

"That's a fine comparison," said Sancho, "though not so new that I haven't heard it many times before, like the one about chess: as long as the game lasts, each piece has its particular rank and position, but when the game's over they're mixed and jumbled and thrown together in a bag, just the way life is tossed into the grave."[1]

"Every day, Sancho," said Don Quixote, "you are becoming less simple and more intelligent."

---

1. As Martín de Riquer points out, this kind of comparison was common in Spain, and a frequent subject for sermons, so it is not surprising that Sancho repeats it. Whenever Sancho shows signs of erudition—citing Latin words and phrases, for example—his knowledge, by dint of repetition, has its origin in the Church and consequently does not affect the believability of the character.

"Yes, some of your grace's intelligence has to stick to me," responded Sancho, "for lands that are barren and dry on their own can produce good fruits if you spread manure on them and till them; I mean to say that your grace's conversation has been the manure that has fallen on the barren soil of my dry wits; the time I have served you and talked to you has been the tilling; and so I hope to produce fruits that are a blessing and do not go to seed or stray from the paths of good cultivation that your grace has made in my parched understanding."

Don Quixote laughed at Sancho's pretentious words but thought that what he said about the change in him was true, because from time to time he spoke in a manner that amazed Don Quixote, although almost always, when Sancho wanted to speak in an erudite and courtly way, his words would plummet from the peaks of his simplicity into the depths of his ignorance; the area in which he displayed the most elegance and the best memory was in his use of proverbs, regardless of whether or not they had anything to do with the subject, as has been seen and noted in the course of this history.

They spent a good part of the night in this and other exchanges like it, until Sancho felt the desire to drop the gates of his eyes, as he said when he wanted to sleep, and, after unharnessing the donkey, he allowed him to graze freely on the abundant grass. He did not remove Rocinante's saddle, for his master had expressly ordered that for the time they were out in the countryside or did not sleep under a roof, he should not unharness Rocinante: an ancient custom established and maintained by knights errant was to remove the bit and hang it from the saddlebow, but taking the saddle off the horse? Never! And so this is what Sancho did, and he gave Rocinante the same freedom he had given the donkey, for their friendship was so unusual and so firm that it has been claimed, in a tradition handed down from fathers to sons, that the author of this true history devoted particular chapters to it, but for the sake of maintaining the decency and decorum so heroic a history deserves, he did not include them, although at times he is remiss in his purpose and writes that as soon as the two animals were together they would begin to scratch each other, and then, when they were tired and satisfied, Rocinante would lay his neck across the donkey's—it would extend almost half a meter on the other side—and, staring intently at the ground, the two of them could stand this way for three days or, at least, for as long as they were permitted to do so or were not compelled by hunger to look for food.

I say, then, that it is said that the author wrote that he compared their friendship to that of Nisus and Euryalus, and Pylades and Orestes,[2] and if this is true, we can infer, to widespread admiration, how deep the friendship of these two peaceable animals must have been, to the shame of human beings who do not know how to maintain their friendships. For this reason, it has been said:

> No man is friend to his friend:
> their canes are turned into lances;

and this, that was sung:

> Bedbugs are passed from friend to friend.[3]

No one should think that the author digressed by comparing the friendship of these animals to that of men, for men have learned a good deal from animals and have been taught many important things by them, for example: from storks, the enema,[4] from dogs, vomiting[5] and gratitude; from cranes, vigilance;[6] from ants, foresight; from elephants, chastity; and loyalty from the horse.

Finally Sancho fell asleep at the foot of a cork tree, and Don Quixote dozed under a hardy oak; not too much time had gone by when he was awakened by a noise at his back, and starting to his feet, he began to listen and to look in the direction of the sound, and he saw that there were two men on horseback and that one, dropping to the ground, said to the other:

"Get down, my friend, and unbridle the horses, for it seems to me that this spot has an abundance of grass for them, and the silence and solitude that I require for my amorous thoughts."

Saying this and lying down on the ground were all one, and as he lay down, the armor he was wearing made a noise, a clear sign by which Don Quixote recognized that he must be a knight errant; and going up to

2. Two friendships celebrated in classical mythology, the first Roman, the second Greek.

3. The first citation is from a ballad; the second is a proverb that probably appeared in a song or ballad, as the verb "sung" suggests.

4. Pliny claimed that the ibis could administer an enema to itself by filling its neck with water and using its long beak as a nozzle.

5. A dog returning to its own vomit was cited as a symbol of a backsliding Christian who abandons a vice and then returns to it.

6. Cranes were supposed to post sentinels at night, when the rest of the flock was sleeping, and during the day, when they were feeding. All of these concepts regarding animals were fairly commonplace.

Sancho, who was asleep, he grasped his arm and with no small effort brought him back to consciousness, and in a quiet voice he said:

"Brother Sancho, we have an adventure."

"May God make it a good one," responded Sancho. "And where, Señor, is her grace this lady adventure?"

"Where, Sancho?" replied Don Quixote. "Turn around and look, and there you will see a knight errant lying on the ground, and from what I can deduce he is not very happy, because I saw him get down from his horse and stretch out on the ground showing certain signs of discouragement, and when he lay down I could hear his armor clattering."

"Well, what makes your grace think," said Sancho, "that this is an adventure?"

"I do not mean to say," responded Don Quixote, "that this is a complete adventure, but rather the start of one; this is the way adventures begin. But listen: it seems as if he is tuning a lute or vihuela,[7] and considering how he is spitting and clearing his throat, he must be preparing to sing something."

"By my faith, that's true," responded Sancho, "and so he must be a knight in love."

"There is no knight errant who is not," said Don Quixote. "Let us listen to him, and if he does sing, by following the thread we shall discover the skein of his thoughts, for the tongue speaks from the overflowing abundance of the heart."

Sancho wanted to reply, but the voice of the Knight of the Wood, which was neither very bad nor very good, prevented him from doing so, and the two men listened in amazement as he sang this sonnet:

> Set for me, lady, the line I must pursue,
> created by and matching your sweet will;
> and it shall be so rev'renced by my own,
> that I'll ne'er contravene its slightest whim.
>
> If you wish my voice mute about my ills
> until I die, then here I've reached my end:
> if you desire my woes sung in a fashion
> rare and strange, then love himself will chant them.
>
> A perfect proof of contraries I've become,
> hard as diamond, soft as wax, and yet my soul
> reconciles them, obeying the laws of love.

7. This was an early form of the guitar.

I bare my breast to you, whether soft or hard:
incise there and impress there all you will;
your will, I swear, shall be my eternal rule.

With an *Oh!* torn, apparently, from the very depths of his heart, the Knight of the Wood ended his song, and then, a short while later, in a sad and sorrowful voice, he said:

"O most beautiful and ungrateful woman in the world! How can you, most serene Casildea of Vandalia, allow this your captive knight to be consumed and to perish in continual wanderings and harsh and rigorous labors? Is it not enough that I have obliged all the knights of Navarra, León, Andalucía, Castilla, and La Mancha to confess that you are the most beautiful woman in the world?"

"Oh no," said Don Quixote, "for I am from La Mancha, and I have confessed no such thing, and I could not and ought not confess anything so prejudicial to the beauty of my lady; now you can see, Sancho, that this knight is talking nonsense. But let us listen: perhaps he will say more about himself."

"He's bound to," replied Sancho, "because he seems ready to complain for a month without stopping."

But that did not happen, because the Knight of the Wood, hearing voices speaking nearby, lamented no further but rose to his feet and said in a loud but courteous voice:

"Who is it? Who are you? Do you count yourself among the contented or the afflicted?"

"The afflicted," responded Don Quixote.

"Then approach," responded the Knight of the Wood, "and you shall realize that you are approaching sorrow and affliction personified."

Don Quixote, seeing that his reply was gentle and courteous, approached him, and Sancho did the same.

The lamenting knight grasped Don Quixote's arm, saying:

"Sit here, Señor Knight; for me to understand that you are a knight, and one who professes knight errantry, it is enough to find you in this place, where solitude and the night dews are your companions, the natural couches and proper lodgings of knights errant."

To which Don Quixote responded:

"I am a knight, of the profession you say, and though sorrow, sadness, and misfortune have their own places in my soul, this does not mean that the compassion I feel for other people's afflictions has fled. I gathered from what you sang a little while ago that your woes are amorous, I mean, the result of the love you have for that beautiful ingrate you named in your lamentations."

During this conversation they sat together on the hard ground, in peace and good fellowship, as if at break of day they would not need to break each other's heads.

"By any chance, Señor Knight," the Knight of the Wood asked Don Quixote, "are you in love?"

"Unfortunately I am," responded Don Quixote, "although the adversities born of well-placed thoughts should be considered mercies rather than misfortunes."

"That is true," said the Knight of the Wood, "if too much disdain does not confound our reason and understanding and begin to resemble revenge."

"I never was disdained by my lady," responded Don Quixote.

"No, of course not," said Sancho, who was close to them, "because my lady is as meek as a lamb: she's as soft as butter."

"Is this your squire?" asked the Knight of the Wood.

"Yes, it is," responded Don Quixote.

"I have never seen a squire," replied the Knight of the Wood, "who would dare speak when his master was speaking: at least, there stands mine, as big as his father, and no one can prove he has even moved his lips while I am speaking."

"Well, by my faith," said Sancho, "I have spoken, and can speak, in front of any . . . enough said, we'll let sleeping dogs lie."

The squire of the Knight of the Wood took Sancho by the arm and said:

"Let's go where we can talk in a squirely way about anything we like, and leave these master gentlemen of ours to argue and tell each other stories about their loves; I'll bet they're still at it at dawn, and no closer to finishing."

"All right, then," said Sancho, "and I'll tell your grace who I am, and then you can tell me whether or not I'm a match for any talkative squire."

Saying this, the two squires moved away, and their conversation was as amusing as the one between their masters was solemn.

CHAPTER XIII

*In which the adventure of the Knight of the Wood continues, along with per-
ceptive, unprecedented, and amiable conversation between the two squires*

Knights and squires were separated, the latter recounting their lives and
the former their loves, but the history first relates the conversation of the
servants and then goes on to that of their masters, and so it says that as
they moved a short distance away, the Squire of the Wood said to
Sancho:

"We have a difficult life, Señor, those of us who are squires to knights
errant: the truth is we eat our bread by the sweat of our brow, which is
one of God's curses on our first parents."

"You could also say," added Sancho, "that we eat it in the icy cold of
our bodies, because who suffers more heat and cold than the wretched
squires of knight errantry? If we ate, it would be easier because sorrows
fade with a little bread, but sometimes we can go a day or two with nothing for our breakfast but the wind that blows."

"All of this is made bearable and tolerable," said the Squire of the
Wood, "by our hope of a reward, because if the knight errant is not too
unfortunate, in a little while the squire who serves him will be rewarded
with an attractive governorship of an ínsula or a fine countship."

"I," replied Sancho, "have already told my master that I'll be content
with the governorship of an ínsula, and he's so noble and generous that
he's promised it to me on many different occasions."

"I," said the Squire of the Wood, "will be satisfied with a canonship as
payment for my services, and my master has already set one aside for me,
and what a nice canonship it is!"

"Your grace's master," said Sancho, "must be an ecclesiastical kind of
knight who can do favors like that for his good squires, but mine is a lay

knight, though I do remember when some very wise people, though I think they were malicious, too, advised him to become an archbishop, but he only wanted to be an emperor, and I was trembling at the thought that he'd decide to enter the Church, because I didn't think I was qualified to hold any benefices, because I can tell your grace that even though I look like a man, I'm nothing but an animal when it comes to entering the Church."

"Well, the truth is your grace is mistaken," said the Squire of the Wood, "because not all insular governorships are good. Some are crooked, some are poor, and some are gloomy, and even the proudest and best of them bring a heavy burden of cares and troubles that has to be borne on the shoulders of the unlucky man who happens to be governor. It would be much better for those of us who perform this miserable service to return home and do some easier work, like hunting or fishing, for is there any squire in the world so poor he doesn't have a horse, a couple of greyhounds, and a fishing pole to help him pass the time?"

"I have all those things," responded Sancho. "Well, the truth is I don't have a horse, but my donkey is worth twice as much as my master's nag. May God send me evil days, starting tomorrow, if I'd ever trade with him, even if he threw in four bushelweights of barley. Your grace must think I'm joking about the value I put on my gray, for gray is the color of my donkey. And I wouldn't need greyhounds because there are plenty of them in my village; besides, hunting is much nicer when you do it at somebody else's expense."

"The truth of the matter, Señor Squire," responded the Squire of the Wood, "is that I've decided and resolved to leave the crazy goings-on of these knights and go back to my village and rear my children, for I have three as beautiful as Oriental pearls."

"I have two," said Sancho, "who could be presented to the pope himself, especially the girl, who I'm bringing up to be a countess, God willing, though her mother's against it."

"And how old is this lady who's being brought up to be a countess?" asked the Squire of the Wood.

"Fifteen, give or take a couple of years," responded Sancho, "but she's as tall as a lance, and as fresh as a morning in April, and as strong as a laborer."

"Those are qualities," responded the Squire of the Wood, "for being not only a countess but a nymph of the greenwood. O whoreson, but that damned little whore must be strong!"

To which Sancho replied, rather crossly:

"She isn't a whore, and neither was her mother, and neither of them will ever be one, God willing, as long as I'm alive. And speak more politely; for somebody who's spent time with knights errant, who are courtesy itself, your grace isn't very careful about your words."

"Oh, Señor Squire, how little your grace understands," replied the Squire of the Wood, "about paying a compliment! Can it be that you don't know that when a knight gives the bull in the square a good thrust with the lance, or when anybody does anything well, commoners always say: 'Oh whoreson, but that damned little whoreson did that well!'? And in that phrase, what seems to be an insult is a wonderful compliment, and you should disavow, Señor, any sons or daughters who do not perform deeds that bring their parents that kind of praise."

"I do disavow them," responded Sancho, "and in that sense and for that reason your grace could dump a whole whorehouse on me and my children and my wife, because everything they do and say deserves the best compliments, and I want to see them again so much that I pray God to deliver me from mortal sin, which would be the same as delivering me from this dangerous squirely work that I've fallen into for a second time, tempted and lured by a purse with a hundred *ducados* that I found one day in the heart of the Sierra Morena; and the devil places before my eyes, here, there, not here but over there, a sack filled with *doblones*, and at every step I take I seem to touch it with my hand, and put my arms around it, and take it to my house, and hold mortgages, and collect rents, and live like a prince, and when I'm thinking about that, all the trials I suffer with this simpleton of a master seem easy to bear, even though I know he's more of a madman than a knight."

"That," responded the Squire of the Wood, "is why they say that it's greed that tears the sack, and if we're going to talk about madmen, there's nobody in the world crazier than my master, because he's one of those who say: 'Other people's troubles kill the donkey,' and to help another knight find the wits he's lost, he pretends to be crazy and goes around looking for something that I think will hit him right in the face when he finds it."

"Is he in love, by any chance?"

"Yes," said the Squire of the Wood, "with a certain Casildea of Vandalia, the cruelest lady in the world, and the hardest to stomach, but indigestibility isn't her greatest fault; her other deceits are growling in his belly, and they'll make themselves heard before too many hours have gone by."

"There's no road so smooth," replied Sancho, "that it doesn't have some obstacle or stumbling block; they cook beans everywhere, but in my house they do it by the potful; craziness must have more companions and friends than wisdom. But if what they say is true, that misery loves company, then I can find comfort with your grace, because you serve a master who's as great a fool as mine."

"A fool, but brave," responded the Squire of the Wood, "and more of a scoundrel than foolish or brave."

"Not mine," responded Sancho. "I mean, there's nothing of the scoundrel in him; mine's as innocent as a baby; he doesn't know how to harm anybody, he can only do good to everybody, and there's no malice in him: a child could convince him it's night in the middle of the day, and because he's simple I love him with all my heart and couldn't leave him no matter how many crazy things he does."

"Even so, Señor," said the Squire of the Wood, "if the blind man leads the blind man, they're both in danger of falling into the ditch. Brother, we'd better leave soon and go back where we came from; people who look for adventures don't always find good ones."

Sancho had been spitting often, it seems, a certain kind of sticky, dry saliva, and the charitable woodish squire, seeing and noting this, said:

"I think we've talked so much our tongues are sticking to the roofs of our mouths, but I have an unsticker hanging from my saddlebow, and it's a pretty good one."

And he stood up and came back in a little while carrying a large wineskin and a meat pie half a meter long, and this is not an exaggeration, because it held a white rabbit so large that Sancho, when he touched it, thought it was a goat, and not a kid, either; and when Sancho saw this, he said:

"Señor, did you bring this with you?"

"Well, what did you think?" responded the other man. "Am I by any chance a run-of-the-mill squire? I carry better provisions on my horse's rump than a general does when he goes marching."

Sancho ate without having to be asked twice, and in the dark he wolfed down mouthfuls the size of the knots that hobble a horse. And he said:

"Your grace is a faithful and true, right and proper, magnificent and great squire, as this feast shows, and if you haven't come here by the arts of enchantment, at least it seems that way to me; but I'm so poor and unlucky that all I have in my saddlebags is a little cheese, so hard you could break a giant's skull with it, and to keep it company some four dozen carob beans and the same number of hazelnuts and other kinds of nuts, thanks to the poverty of my master and the idea he has and the rule he keeps that knights errant should not live and survive on anything but dried fruits and the plants of the field."

"By my faith, brother," replied the Squire of the Wood, "my stomach isn't made for thistles or wild pears or forest roots. Let our masters have their knightly opinions and rules and eat what their laws command. I have my baskets of food, and this wineskin hanging from the saddlebow, just in case, and I'm so devoted to it and love it so much that I can't let too much time pass without giving it a thousand kisses and a thousand embraces."

And saying this, he placed the wineskin in Sancho's hands, who tilted it back and put it to his mouth and looked at the stars for a quarter of an hour, and when he had finished drinking, he leaned his head to one side, heaved a great sigh, and said:

"O whoreson, you damned rascal, but that's good!"

"Do you see?" said the Squire of the Wood when he heard Sancho's "whoreson." "You complimented the wine by calling it whoreson."

"And I say," responded Sancho, "that I confess to knowing it's no dishonor to call anybody a whoreson when your intention is to compliment him. But tell me, Señor, by the thing you love most: is this wine from Ciudad Real?"

"Bravo! What a winetaster!" responded the Squire of the Wood. "It's from there and no place else, and it's aged a few years."

"You can't fool me!" said Sancho. "You shouldn't think it was beyond me to know about this wine. Does it surprise you, Señor Squire, that I have so great and natural an instinct for knowing wines that if I just smell one I know where it comes from, its lineage, its taste, its age, and how it will change, and everything else that has anything to do with it? But it's no wonder, because in my family, on my father's side, were the two best winetasters that La Mancha had in many years, and to prove it I'll tell you a story about them. The two of them were asked to taste some wine from a cask and say what they thought about its condition and quality, and whether it was a good or bad wine. One tasted it with the tip of his tongue; the other only brought it up to his nose. The first said that the wine tasted of iron, the second that it tasted more of tanned leather. The owner said the cask was clean and the wine had not been fortified in a way that could have given it the taste of iron or leather. Even so, the two famous winetasters insisted that what they said was true. Time passed, the wine was sold, and when the cask was cleaned, inside it they found a small key on a leather strap. So your grace can see that a man who comes from that kind of family can give his opinion about matters like these."

"That's why I say," said the Squire of the Wood, "that we should stop looking for adventures, and if we have loaves of bread, we shouldn't go around looking for cakes, and we ought to go back home: God will find us there, if He wants to."

"I'll serve my master until he gets to Zaragoza; after that, we'll work out something."

In short, the two good squires spoke so much and drank so much that only sleep could stop their tongues and allay their thirst, for it would have been impossible to take it away altogether; and so, with both of them holding on to the almost empty wineskin, and with mouthfuls of food half-chewed in their mouths, they fell asleep, which is where we shall leave them now in order to recount what befell the Knight of the Wood and the Knight of the Sorrowful Face.

CHAPTER XIV

In which the adventure of the Knight of the Wood continues

Among the many words that passed between Don Quixote and the Knight of the Forest, the history says that the Knight of the Wood said to Don Quixote:

"Finally, Señor Knight, I want you to know that my destiny or, I should say, my own free choice, led me to fall in love with the peerless Casildea of Vandalia. I call her without peer because she has none, in the greatness of her stature or in the loftiness of her rank and beauty. This Casildea, then, whom I am describing to you, repaid my virtuous thoughts and courteous desires by having me, as his stepmother did with Hercules, engage in many different kinds of dangers, promising me at the end of each one that at the end of the next my hopes would be realized; but my labors have been linked together for so long that I have lost count, nor do I know which will be the final one that initiates the satisfaction of my virtuous desires. On one occasion she ordered me to chal-

lenge that famous giantess of Sevilla called La Giralda,[1] who is as valiant
and strong as if she were made of bronze and, without moving from one
spot, is the most changeable and fickle woman in the world. I came, I
saw, I conquered her, and I made her keep still and to the point, because
for more than a week only north winds blew. Another time she ordered
me to weigh the ancient stones of the corpulent Bulls of Guisando,[2] an
undertaking better suited to laborers than to knights. On yet another occasion she ordered me to hurl and fling myself into the abyss of Cabra,[3] a
singular and most fearful danger, and bring her a detailed report of what
lies in its dark depths. I halted the movement of La Giralda, I weighed
the Bulls of Guisando, I threw myself into the chasm and brought to
light what lay hidden there in darkness, and my hopes are deader than
dead, and her commands and disdain are more alive than ever. In short,
most recently she has ordered me to travel through all the provinces of
Spain and have all the knights errant wandering there confess that she
alone is the greatest beauty of all the ladies in the world today, and that I
am the most valiant and most perfectly enamored knight on earth; to
satisfy this request I have already traveled most of Spain and conquered
many knights who dared contradict me. But what gratifies me the most
and makes me proudest is having conquered in single combat that most
famous knight, Don Quixote of La Mancha, and forced him to confess
that my Casildea is more beautiful than his Dulcinea; with this one conquest I consider that I have conquered all the knights in the world, because Don Quixote has conquered them all, and since I conquered him,
his glory, fame, and honor have passed and been transferred to my
person.

> The conqueror enjoys more fame and glory
> the greater the distinction of the vanquished;[4]

and as a consequence, the innumerable deeds of the aforementioned
Don Quixote are mine and redound to my credit."

Don Quixote was stunned at what he heard the Knight of the Wood
say and was about to tell him he was lying a thousand times over, and he

1. The reference is to the weathervane at the top of the tower called La Giralda.

2. Ancient Iberian stone sculptures of bulls discovered outside Guisando, in the province of
Ávila.

3. There is a deep chasm close to Cabra, in the province of Córdoba.

4. These are paraphrased lines from Alonso de Ercilla's epic poem *La Araucana*.

had the *You lie* on the tip of his tongue but did his best to restrain himself in order to have the Knight of the Wood confess his lie with his own mouth, and so, very calmly, he said:

"With regard to your grace, Señor Knight, having vanquished almost all the knights errant in Spain, and even the world, I say nothing; but your having conquered Don Quixote of La Mancha: about that I do have my doubts. It might have been another who resembled him, although there are few men who do."

"What do you mean?" replied the Knight of the Wood. "By the heaven above us, I fought with Don Quixote, and I conquered and defeated him; he is a man of tall stature, a dry face, long, lanky limbs, graying hair, an aquiline, somewhat hooked nose, and a large, black, drooping mustache. He does battle under the name *The Knight of the Sorrowful Face*, and for a squire he has a peasant named Sancho Panza; he sits on the back and holds the reins of a famous horse called Rocinante; finally, the lady of his desire, at one time known as Aldonza Lorenzo, is a certain Dulcinea of Toboso, like my lady, who is named Casildea and comes from Andalucía and therefore is called Casildea of Vandalia. If all this is not enough to validate the truth of what I say, here is my sword, which will oblige incredulity itself to give me credence."

"Be calm, Señor Knight," said Don Quixote, "and hear what I wish to tell you. You should know that this Don Quixote whom you have mentioned is the dearest friend I have in the world; I could even say that I value him as I do my own person, and by the description you have given me, which is detailed and accurate, I can only think that he is indeed the one you have conquered. On the other hand, I see with my eyes and touch with my hands the impossibility of his being the one, and yet there are many enchanters who are his enemies, especially one who ordinarily pursues him, and one of these may have taken on his appearance and allowed himself to be vanquished in order to cheat Don Quixote of the fame that his high chivalric deeds have earned and won for him throughout the known world. And as confirmation of this, I also want you to know that these enchanters, his adversaries, only two days ago transformed the figure and person of the beauteous Dulcinea of Toboso into a foul, lowborn peasant girl, and in the same fashion they must have transformed Don Quixote; if this is not enough to persuade you of the truth of what I say, here is Don Quixote himself, who will sustain it with arms, on foot or on horseback, or in whatever manner pleases you."

And saying this, he rose to his feet and grasped his sword, waiting to see what decision would be made by the Knight of the Wood, who responded in the same tranquil voice, saying:

"The man who pays his debts does not mind guaranties: the man, Señor Don Quixote, who could vanquish you transformed can certainly hope to defeat you in your own person. But since it is not right for knights to engage in feats of arms in the dark, like robbers and thieves, let us wait for day so that the sun may see our deeds. And a condition of our combat must be that the vanquished submits to the will of the victor and does everything he desires as long as his commands respect a knight's virtue."

"I am more than happy with this condition and agreement," responded Don Quixote.

And, having said this, they went to the place where their squires were and found them snoring, in the same positions they were in when sleep overcame them. The knights woke them and ordered them to ready the horses, because as soon as the sun rose, the two of them would have to engage in bloody, single, and unequaled combat; at this news, Sancho was surprised and stunned and fearful for the health of his master because of the brave deeds the Squire of the Wood had attributed to his knight; but, without saying a word, the squires went to find their animals, for by this time all three horses and the donkey had smelled one another and were standing close together.

On the way, the Squire of the Wood said to Sancho:

"You should know, brother, that it's the custom among fighting men in Andalucía, when they are seconds in any dispute, not to stand idly by with their hands folded while the challengers do battle. I say this so you'll know that while our masters are fighting, we have to fight, too, and smash each other to pieces."

"That custom, Señor Squire," responded Sancho, "may be accepted and allowed by the ruffians and fighting men you've mentioned, but for the squires of knights errant it doesn't apply at all. At least, I haven't heard my master mention that custom, and he knows all the rules of knight errantry by heart. No matter how much I'd like it to be true that there's a specific rule that squires have to fight when their masters fight, still, I wouldn't obey it, and I'd pay whatever fine they make peaceable squires pay, and I bet it wouldn't be more than two pounds of wax,[5] and

5. In religious brotherhoods, fines were paid in specific quantities of long wax candles.

I'd be happy to pay those pounds, because I know they'll cost me less than the bandages I'll need to heal my head: I already count it as split and broken in two. And there's something else: it's impossible for me to fight because I don't have a sword, and I've never worn one in my whole life."

"I know a good remedy for that," said the Squire of the Wood. "I have two burlap sacks here, and they're both the same size; you'll take one and I'll take the other, and we'll hit each other with the sacks, and our weapons will be equal."

"Well then, let's do it that way," responded Sancho, "because that kind of fight will dust us off more than it'll hurt us."

"No, it won't be like that," replied the other man, "because we have to put half a dozen nice smooth stones, all of them the same weight, inside the sacks so they don't blow away, and then we can hit each other and not do any harm or damage."

"I swear by my father," responded Sancho, "just think of all the sable pelts or tufts of carded cotton you'll have to put in the sacks so our skulls don't get crushed and our bones ground to dust! But even if you fill them with silk cocoons, let me tell you, Señor, I won't fight; let our masters fight, and welcome to it, and let us drink and live, for time is bound to take our lives, and we don't have to go around looking for reasons to end our lives before their time and season, when they're ripe and ready to fall."

"Even so," replied the Squire of the Wood, "we have to fight for at least half an hour."

"Oh no," responded Sancho, "I'm not discourteous and ungrateful enough to have a quarrel, even a little one, with a man after eating and drinking with him; especially if there's no anger and no insult, who the devil could start a fight just like that?"

"For that," said the Squire of the Wood, "I have just the remedy: before we begin the fight, I'll just come up to your grace and give you three or four slaps in the face that will knock you down, and that'll be enough to wake up your anger even if it's sleeping like a baby."

"Well, I know another move just as good to match that," responded Sancho. "I'll just pick up a stick, and before your grace comes over to wake up my anger, with a few whacks I'll put yours into a sleep that'll last into the next world, where they know I'm not a man to let anybody lay hands on my face. Let each man look out for himself, though the best thing would be to let everybody's anger stay asleep; nobody knows another man's heart, and many who come for wool go home clipped and shorn, and God blessed peace and cursed fights, because if a cat that's hunted and locked up and treated badly turns into a lion, then since I'm a man, God knows what I could turn into, and so from now on I'm letting your grace know, Señor Squire, that all the harm and damage that result from our quarrel will be on your head."

"That's all right," replied the Squire of the Wood. "God's day will dawn and we'll be fine."

By this time a thousand different kinds of brightly colored birds began to warble in the trees, and with their varied and joyous songs they seemed to welcome and greet the new dawn, who, through the doors and balconies of the Orient, was revealing the beauty of her face and shaking from her hair an infinite number of liquid pearls whose gentle liquor bathed the plants that seemed, in turn, to send forth buds and rain down tiny white seed pearls; the willows dripped their sweet-tasting manna, the fountains laughed, the streams murmured, the woods rejoiced, and the meadows flourished with her arrival. But as soon as the light of day made it possible to see and distinguish one thing from another, the first thing that appeared before Sancho Panza's eyes was the nose of the Squire of the Wood, which was so big it almost cast a shadow over the rest of his body. In fact, it is recounted that his nose was outlandishly large, hooked in the middle, covered with warts, and of a purplish color like an eggplant; it came down the width of two fingers past his mouth, and its size, color, warts, and curvature made his face so hideous that when Sancho saw him his feet and hands began to tremble, like a child having seizures, and he decided in his heart to let himself be slapped two hundred times before he would allow his anger to awaken and then fight with that monster.

Don Quixote looked at his opponent and found that his sallet was already lowered, so he could not see his face, but he noticed that his rival was a husky man, though not very tall. Over his armor he wore a kind of long jacket or coat, the cloth apparently made of finest gold, and on it were scattered many small moons of gleaming mirrors, making him look extraordinarily splendid and elegant; waving above his helmet were a large number of green, yellow, and white plumes; his lance, leaning against a tree, was extremely large and thick and plated with more than a span's length of iron.

Don Quixote looked at everything and noted everything and judged from what he had seen and noted that the aforementioned knight must be exceptionally strong, but for that reason he was not, like Sancho Panza, afraid; rather, with gallant courage, he said to the Knight of the Mirrors:

"If, Señor Knight, your great desire to fight does not consume your courtesy, I ask you for courtesy's sake to raise your visor a little so that I may see if the elegance of your face corresponds to that of your accoutrements."

"Regardless of whether you emerge from this undertaking as the vanquished or the victor, Señor Knight," responded the Knight of the Mirrors, "you will have more than enough time and opportunity to see me; and if I do not satisfy your desire now, it is because I think I would give notable offense to the beauteous Casildea of Vandalia if I were to delay the length of time it would take me to raise my visor without first obliging you to confess what you already know I desire."

"Well, as we mount our horses," said Don Quixote, "you can certainly tell me if I am the same Don Quixote you claim to have defeated."

"To that we respond," said the Knight of the Mirrors, "that you resemble the knight I vanquished as much as one egg resembles another; but since you say that enchanters pursue him, I do not dare to state whether you are the aforesaid or not."

"That is enough," responded Don Quixote, "for me to believe you were deceived; however, in order to free you entirely from error, let us mount our steeds; in less time than it would take you to raise your visor, if God, my lady, and my arm come to my aid, I shall see your face, and you will see that I am not the vanquished Don Quixote you think I am."

And with this they cut short their words and mounted their horses, and Don Quixote turned the reins of Rocinante in order to take a position in the field so that he could gallop back and meet his adversary, and the Knight of the Mirrors did the same. But Don Quixote had not gone twenty paces when he heard the Knight of the Mirrors call, and both of them moved off course, and the Knight of the Mirrors said:

"Remember, Señor Knight, that the condition of our combat is that the one vanquished, as I have said before, is subject to the will of the victor."

"I know that," responded Don Quixote, "so long as the things the vanquished is commanded and ordered to perform do not go beyond the limits imposed by chivalry."

"That is understood," responded the Knight of the Mirrors.

At this moment Don Quixote caught a glimpse of the squire's strange nose, and he was no less astounded to see it than Sancho; in fact, he judged him to be some monster or a new kind of man never before seen in the world. Sancho, who saw his master riding off so that he could charge, did not wish to remain alone with the big-nosed man, fearing that a single slap by that nose to his own would be the end of their fight, and he would be knocked to the ground by the blow, or by fright, and so he followed after his master, holding on to a strap hanging from Rocinante's saddle, and when it seemed to him that it was time to return, he said:

"I beg your grace, Señor, that before you turn to charge you help me climb this cork tree, where I'll be able to see better than on the ground the brave encounter your grace is going to have with that knight."

"What I think, Sancho," said Don Quixote, "is that you want to climb up into the stands so you can watch the bullfight in safety."

"To tell the truth," responded Sancho, "the outsize nose of that squire has me so scared and frightened that I don't dare stay anywhere near him."

"It is so large," said Don Quixote, "that if I were not who I am, I would be terrified, too, and so come, I shall help you climb the tree."

While Don Quixote stopped to help Sancho into the cork tree, the Knight of the Mirrors took as much of the field as he thought necessary, and believing that Don Quixote had done the same, and not waiting for the sound of a trumpet or any other warning, he turned the reins of his horse—who was no faster or better looking than Rocinante—and at his full gallop, which was a medium trot, he rode to encounter his enemy, but seeing him occupied with Sancho's climb, he checked the reins and stopped in the middle of the charge, for which the horse was extremely grateful, since he could no longer move. Don Quixote, who thought his enemy was already bearing down on him, swiftly dug his spurs into Rocinante's skinny flanks and goaded him so mercilessly that, the history tells us, this was the only time he was known to have galloped, because on all other occasions he always ran at a pronounced trot, and with this unprecedented fury Rocinante reached the place where the Knight of the Mirrors was digging his spurs all the way into his horse without being able to move him the length of a finger from the spot where he had called a halt to his charge.

At this fortunate time and juncture, Don Quixote found his adversary held back by his horse and hindered by his lance, which he failed to, or did not have a chance to, rest in its socket. Don Quixote, who cared nothing at all for these obstacles, without any risk and with absolutely no danger, charged the Knight of the Mirrors with so much force that almost without intending to he knocked him to the ground, back over the haunches of the horse, causing him so great a fall that without moving feet or hands, he gave every sign of being dead.

As soon as Sancho saw him fall, he slid down from the cork tree and ran as fast as he could to his master, who, dismounting Rocinante, approached the Knight of the Mirrors and, unlacing his helmet to see if he was dead and, if he were alive, to give him some air . . . saw . . . Who can say what he saw without causing amazement, wonder, and fear in his listeners? He saw, says the history, the very face, the very figure, the very appearance, the very physiognomy, the very image, the personification itself of Bachelor Sansón Carrasco, and as soon as he saw him he shouted:

"Come quickly, Sancho, and look at what you will not believe! Hurry, my friend, and see what magic can do, what wizards and enchanters can do!"

Sancho came running, and when he saw the face of Bachelor Carrasco, he began to cross himself a thousand times and to make the sign of the cross a thousand more. During all this time the fallen knight gave no signs of being alive, and Sancho said to Don Quixote:

"It's my opinion, Señor, that to be on the safe side your grace should kneel down and run your sword into the mouth of this man who seems to be Bachelor Sansón Carrasco, and maybe you'll kill one of those enemy enchanters inside him."

"That is not bad advice," said Don Quixote, "because the fewer your enemies, the better."

And as he drew his sword to carry out the advice and counsel of Sancho, the Squire of the Mirrors, now without the nose that had made him so hideous, came up to him and shouted:

"Your grace, Señor Don Quixote, think about what you are doing; that man lying at your feet is your friend Bachelor Sansón Carrasco, and I am his squire."

And Sancho, seeing him free of his earlier ugliness, said:

"What happened to your nose?"

To which he responded:

"I have it here, in my pocket."

And then he put his hand into his right pocket and pulled out a nose made of pasteboard and varnish, a mask, in the shape that has already been described. And Sancho looked at him more and more closely and said in a loud, surprised voice:

"Mother of God! Can this be Tomé Cecial, my neighbor and compadre?"

"Of course it is," responded the denosed squire. "I'm Tomé Cecial, Sancho Panza, my friend and compadre, and I'll tell you later about the secrets and lies and tricks that brought me here; in the meantime, ask and beg your master not to touch, mistreat, wound, or kill the Knight of the Mirrors who is lying at his feet, because beyond any doubt he's the bold but badly advised Bachelor Sansón Carrasco, our neighbor."

At this point the Knight of the Mirrors regained consciousness; Don Quixote, seeing this, held the naked tip of his sword over his face and said:

"Knight, thou art dead if thou dost not confess that the peerless Dulcinea of Toboso is more beauteous than thy Casildea of Vandalia; what is more, if thou wisheth to survive this contest and defeat, thou needs must promise to go to the city of Toboso and appear before her on my behalf, so that she may do with thee whatever she willeth; and if she givest thee leave to go, thou must come back and find me, and the trail of my great deeds will serve thee as a guide that will bring thee to me, and thou must tell me all that transpired with her; these conditions, as we agreed before our combat, do not go beyond the bounds of knight errantry."

"I confess," said the fallen knight, "that the torn and dirty shoe of Señora Dulcinea of Toboso is worth more than the unkempt but clean beard of Casildea, and I promise to go and return from her presence to yours, and to give you a complete and detailed account of whatever you ask."

"Thou must also confess and believe," added Don Quixote, "that the knight whom thou hast vanquished was not, nor could he be, Don Quixote of La Mancha, but another who resembled him, as I confess and believe that although thou resemblest Bachelor Sansón Carrasco, thou art not he but another who resembleth him, and that mine enemies hath placed his figure before me so that I may halt and temper the force of mine anger, and be gentle in how I use the glory of thy defeat."

"I confess, judge, and accept everything that you believe, judge, and accept," responded the knight with the injured back. "Let me get up, I beg you, if my fall will allow that, because it has left me badly battered."

Don Quixote helped him to his feet, as did his squire, Tomé Cecial, and Sancho could not take his eyes off him, asking him questions whose answers were clear indications that he really was the same Tomé Cecial he said he was; but the apprehension created in Sancho by what his mas-

ter had said about the enchanters transforming the figure of the Knight
of the Mirrors into that of Bachelor Carrasco did not permit him to give
credence to the truth he was seeing with his own eyes. In short, both
master and servant were deceived, and the Knight of the Mirrors and his
squire, gloomy and out of sorts, rode away from Don Quixote and
Sancho, intending to find a place where they could plaster and tape the
knight's ribs. Don Quixote and Sancho continued on their way to
Zaragoza, where the history leaves them in order to give an accounting
of who the Knight of the Mirrors and his big-nosed squire were.

CHAPTER XV

*Which recounts and relates the identity of the Knight of the Mirrors and his
squire*

Don Quixote was filled with contentment, pride, and vainglory at having achieved victory over so valiant a knight as he imagined the Knight
of the Mirrors to be, and from his chivalric promise he hoped to learn if
the enchantment of his lady was still in effect, since it was necessary for
the conquered knight to return, under pain of no longer being a knight,
to tell him what had transpired with her. But Don Quixote thought one
thing and the Knight of the Mirrors thought another, for his only
thought then was to find a place where he could apply a plaster, as has already been said.

And so, the history tells us that when Bachelor Sansón Carrasco
advised Don Quixote to return to the chivalric undertakings he had
abandoned, it was because he first had spoken privately with the priest
and the barber regarding the steps that could be taken to prevail upon
Don Quixote to remain quietly and peacefully at home and not be disturbed by ill-fated adventures; and the decision of this meeting was, by
unanimous vote and the particular support of Carrasco, that they
would allow Don Quixote to leave, since it seemed impossible to stop
him, and that Sansón, as a knight errant, would meet him on the road
and engage in combat with him, for there was no lack of reasons to
fight, and he would vanquish him, on the assumption that this would

be an easy thing to do, and it would be agreed and accepted that the vanquished would be at the mercy of the victor, and when Don Quixote had been vanquished, the bachelor-knight would order him to return to his village and his house and not leave again for two years, or until he had commanded otherwise; it was clear that the vanquished Don Quixote would undoubtedly obey in order not to contravene or disrespect the laws of chivalry, and it might be that in the time of his seclusion he would forget his illusions, or a worthwhile remedy would be found to cure his madness.

Carrasco agreed, and Tomé Cecial, Sancho Panza's compadre and neighbor, and a cheerful, lighthearted man, volunteered to be his squire. Sansón armed himself in the manner described, and Tomé Cecial placed on his natural nose the false nose already referred to, so that his compadre would not recognize him when they met; they followed the same route taken by Don Quixote, and they almost arrived in time to take part in the adventure of the cart of Death. Finally, they met in the wood, where everything the prudent reader has just read happened to them, and if it had not been for Don Quixote's extraordinary ideas that led him to believe the bachelor was not the bachelor, Señor Bachelor would have been forever incapable of receiving his licentiate's degree, for he thought he would find birds and did not even find nests.

Tomé Cecial, who saw how badly their plans had turned out and how unfortunately their journey had ended, said to the bachelor:

"Certainly, Señor Sansón Carrasco, we've gotten what we deserved: it's easy enough to think up and begin an enterprise, but most of the time it's hard to end it. Don Quixote's crazy, we're sane, and he walks away healthy and laughing, while your grace is bruised and sad. So tell me now, who's crazier: the man who's crazy because he can't help it or the man who chooses to be crazy?"

To which Sansón responded:

"The difference between those two madmen is that the one who can't help it will always be mad, and the one who chooses can stop whenever he wants to."

"Well, that's true," said Tomé Cecial. "I chose to be crazy when I decided to become your grace's squire, and by the same token I want to stop now and go back home."

"That may be convenient for you," responded Sansón, "but if you think I'll go back to mine before I've given Don Quixote a good beating, then you are sadly mistaken; I'm moved now not by the desire to help him recover his sanity, but by the desire for revenge; the terrible pain in my ribs does not allow me to speak more piously."

The two men conversed in this manner until they reached a village where they happened to find a bonesetter who cured the unfortunate Sansón. Tomé Cecial turned back and left him, and Sansón remained behind to imagine his revenge, and the history speaks of him again at the proper time, but it joyfully returns now to Don Quixote.

CHAPTER XVI

Regarding what befell Don Quixote with a prudent knight of La Mancha

With the joy, contentment, and pride that have already been mentioned, Don Quixote continued his journey, imagining, because of his recent victory, that he was the world's most valiant knight errant of the age; he considered any adventures that might befall him from that time on as already completed and brought to a happy conclusion; he held enchantments and enchanters in contempt; he did not recall the countless beatings he had received in the course of his chivalric exploits, or the stones that had knocked out half his teeth, or the ingratitude of the galley slaves, or the Yanguesans' audacious rainstorm of staffs. In short, he said to himself that if he could find the art, means, or manner to disenchant his lady Dulcinea, he would not envy the greatest good fortune that ever was achieved or could be achieved by the most fortunate knight errant of past times. He was completely lost in these thoughts when Sancho said:

"Isn't it funny, Señor, that I still can see the awful outsize nose of my compadre Tomé Cecial?"

"Do you still believe, Sancho, that the Knight of the Mirrors was Bachelor Carrasco, and your compadre Tomé Cecil was his squire?"

"I don't know what to say about that," responded Sancho. "All I know is that he was the only one who could have told me what he did about my house, my wife, and my children, and except for the nose, his face was the face of Tomé Cecial, just as I have seen it so often in my village and in his house that shares a wall with mine, and the sound of his voice was the same."

"Let us reason about this, Sancho," replied Don Quixote. "Come, does it make sense that Bachelor Sansón Carrasco should appear as a knight errant, armed with offensive and defensive weapons, to do battle with me? Have I, by chance, been his enemy? Have I ever given him reason to bear me ill will? Am I his rival, or does he profess arms, that he would be envious of the fame I have won through their exercise?"

"But what do we say, Señor," responded Sancho, "about that knight, whoever he was, looking so much like Bachelor Carrasco, and his squire looking like my compadre Tomé Cecial? If it's enchantment, like your grace says, weren't there any other men in the world they could have looked like?"

"Everything is artifice and mere appearance," responded Don Quixote, "devised by the evil magicians who pursue me; foreseeing that I would emerge victorious from the battle, they arranged for the defeated knight to show the face of my friend the bachelor, so that the friendship I have for him would be placed between the edges of my sword, and stay the severity of my arm, and temper the righteous anger of my heart, and in this manner the one who was attempting to take my life through trickery and falsehood would save his own. As proof of this you already know, O Sancho, through experience that will not allow you to lie or deceive, how easy it is for enchanters to transform one face into another, making the beautiful ugly and the ugly beautiful; no more than two days ago you saw with your own eyes the beauty and grace of the peerless Dulcinea in all her natural perfection and harmony, and I saw her as an ugly, lowborn peasant girl with cataracts in her eyes and a foul smell in her mouth; further, if the perverse enchanter dared to make so evil a transformation, it is not difficult to believe that he transformed Sansón Carrasco and your compadre in order to steal the glory of conquest right out of my hands. But despite this I am comforted, because in the end, regardless of his shape and appearance, I have conquered my enemy."

"God knows the truth of all things," responded Sancho.

And since he knew that the transformation of Dulcinea had been his own trickery and deception, the chimerical ideas of his master did not satisfy him, but he did not wish to respond so as not to say anything that might reveal his lie.

They were engaged in this conversation when they were overtaken by a man riding behind them on the same road, mounted on a very beautiful dapple mare and wearing a coat of fine green cloth trimmed with tawny velvet and a cap made of the same velvet; the mare's trappings, in the rustic style and with a short stirrup, were also purple and green. He wore a Moorish scimitar hanging from a wide green and gold swordbelt, and his half boots matched his swordbelt; his spurs were not gilt but touched with a green varnish, so glossy and polished that, since they matched the rest of his clothing, they looked better than if they had been made of pure gold. When the traveler reached them he greeted them courteously and spurred his mare in order to pass by, but Don Quixote said:

"Gallant Señor, if your grace is traveling the same road and is not in a hurry, I would be very pleased if we traveled together."

"The truth is," responded the man on the mare, "that I would not ride by so quickly if it were not for my fear that the presence of my mare might disturb your horse."

"Señor," Sancho responded at this point, "you can certainly, certainly tighten your mare's reins, because our horse is the most chaste, best-behaved horse in the world; on similar occasions he has never done anything low or base, and once when he was rude enough to try, my master and I made him pay for it seven times over. I say again that your grace can stop if you want to, because even if she's brought to him on a silver platter, I'm sure our horse won't even look your mare in the face."

The traveler pulled on his reins, marveling at the bearing and face of Don Quixote, who rode without his sallet helmet, which Sancho had hung like a bag over the forebow of the donkey's packsaddle; and if the man in green looked at Don Quixote a great deal, Don Quixote looked even more at the man in green, thinking him a virtuous and judicious person. He seemed to be about fifty, with few gray hairs and an aquiline face; his aspect was both cheerful and grave; in short, his dress and bearing made it clear that he was a man of good qualities.

The judgment of the man in green with regard to Don Quixote of La Mancha was that he had never seen anyone like him in manner or appearance; he was amazed by the length of his horse, his height, his thin, sallow face, his weapons, his bearing and behavior: a form and appearance not seen for many long years in that land. Don Quixote noticed how attentively the traveler was looking at him and read his desires in his astonishment, and since Don Quixote was courteous and wished to please everyone, before the traveler could ask anything he met him halfway, saying:

"Your grace has noticed my appearance, which is so unusual and far removed from what is commonly seen that I am not surprised at your surprise, but your grace will no longer be so when I tell you, as I do now, that I am a knight,

> the kind, as people say,
> who go to seek adventures.

I left my home, mortgaged my estate, left behind my comfort, and threw myself into the arms of Fortune so that she may carry me wherever she chooses. I have desired to revive a long-dead knight errantry, and for many days, stumbling here, falling there, dropping down in one place and standing up in another, I have fulfilled a good part of my desire, helping widows, protecting maidens, favoring married women, orphans, and wards, which is the proper and natural work of knights errant; because of my many worthy Christian deeds, I have deserved to be published in almost all or most of the nations in the world. Thirty thousand copies of my history have been printed, and thirty thousand thousand times more are on their way to being printed if heaven does not intervene. Briefly then, to summarize everything in a few words, or in only one, I say that I am Don Quixote of La Mancha, also known as the Knight of the Sorrowful Face, and although praising oneself is vile, I am obliged perhaps to sing my own praises, which is understandable since there is no one present to do it for me; and so, Señor, neither this horse nor this lance, this shield nor this squire, nor all of my armor, nor my sallow face and extreme thinness: none of this should surprise you now, for I have told you who I am and the profession I follow."

Don Quixote fell silent when he said this, and the man in green took so long to respond that it seemed he did not know what to say, but after some time he said:

"You were correct, Señor Knight, in deducing my desire from my surprise, but you have not taken away the astonishment that seeing you has caused me, for although, Señor, you say my knowing who you are will take it away, that has not happened; rather, now that I know, I am more amazed and astonished than before. How is it possible that there are knights errant in the world today or that there are printed histories of true knightly deeds? I can't convince myself that anyone in the world today favors widows, protects maidens, honors married women, and helps orphans, and I wouldn't believe it if I hadn't seen it in your grace with my own eyes. Heaven be praised! With the history that your grace says has been published about your lofty and true chivalric feats, the countless tales of imaginary knights errant will be forgotten, for they have filled the world, harming good customs and damaging and discrediting good histories."

"There is much to say," responded Don Quixote, "regarding whether the histories of knights errant are imaginary or not."

"Well, who can doubt," said the Man in Green, "that those histories are false?"

"I doubt it," responded Don Quixote, "and let us say no more; if our journey together is a long one, I hope to God to convince your grace that you have erred in going along with those who are certain they are not true."

From this last statement of Don Quixote's, the traveler assumed he must be a simpleton, and he waited to see if any further statements would confirm this, but before they could engage in other conversation, Don Quixote asked him to say who he was, for he had informed him of his circumstances and his life. To which the Man in the Green Coat responded:

"I, Señor Knight of the Sorrowful Face, am a gentleman who is a native of a village where, God willing, we shall have our dinner today. I am more than moderately wealthy, and my name is Don Diego de Miranda; I spend my time with my wife, and my children, and my friends; my pastimes are hunting and fishing, but I keep neither hawk nor greyhounds, only some tame decoy partridges or a few bold ferrets. I have some six dozen books, some in Castilian and some in Latin, some historical and some devotional; books of chivalry have not yet crossed my threshold. I read more profane books than devout ones, as long as the diversion is honest, and the language delights, and the invention amazes and astounds, though there are very few of these in Spain. From time to time I dine with my neighbors and friends, and often I invite them to my table; my meals are carefully prepared and nicely served and in no way meager; I don't like gossip, and I don't allow it in my presence; I don't meddle in other people's lives, and I don't pry into what other people do; I hear Mass every day; I distribute alms to the poor but do not boast of doing good works, so as not to allow hypocrisy and vainglory into my heart, for they are enemies that can easily take possession of the most modest heart; I attempt to bring peace to those whom I know are quarreling; I am devoted to Our Lady, and trust always in the infinite mercy of the Lord our God."

Sancho was very attentive to this recounting of the life and pastimes of the gentleman, and finding it a good and saintly life, and thinking that the man who led it must be able to perform miracles, he quickly dismounted the donkey and hurried to grasp the gentleman's right stirrup, and with a devout heart, and almost in tears, he kissed his feet over and over again. Seeing this, the gentleman asked:

"What are you doing, brother? What is the reason for these kisses?"

"Let me give them to you," responded Sancho, "because I think your grace is the first saint with short stirrups that I've ever seen in my life."

"I'm not a saint," responded the gentleman, "but a great sinner, but you, brother, must be a good man; your simplicity proves it."

Sancho returned to his packsaddle, having moved his master to laughter despite his profound melancholy and causing Don Diego even more amazement. Don Quixote asked how many children he had and said that among the things that ancient philosophers, who lacked a true knowledge of God, considered the highest good were the riches of nature, worldly goods, and having many friends and many good children.

"I, Señor Don Quixote," responded the gentleman, "have a son, and if I didn't have him, perhaps I would consider myself more fortunate than I do, and not because he's bad, but because he isn't as good as I would like him to be. He's eighteen, and has spent the last six years in Salamanca, studying Latin and Greek, and when I wanted him to go on to the study of other areas of knowledge, I found him so enthralled with poetry, if that can be called knowledge, that I can't make him show any enthusiasm for law, which I would like him to study, or for the queen of all study, which is theology. I would like him to be the crown of his lineage, for we live in a time when our kings richly reward good, virtuous letters, for letters without virtue are pearls in the dungheap. He spends the whole day determining if Homer wrote well or badly in a particular line of the *Iliad*; if Martial was indecent in a certain epigram; if specific lines of Virgil are to be understood in this manner or another. In short, all his conversations are about the books of these poets and of Horace, Persius, Juvenal, and Tibullus; he does not think very highly of modern writers, and despite the antipathy he displays toward poetry in the vernacular, his thoughts are now entirely turned to writing a gloss on four lines sent to him from Salamanca, I think for a literary competition."

To which Don Quixote responded:

"Children, Señor, are the very apple of their parents' eyes, and whether they are good or bad, they are loved as we love the souls that

give us life; from the time they are little, it is the obligation of parents to
guide them along the paths of virtue, good breeding, and good Christian
customs, so that when they are grown they will be a support in the old
age of their parents and the glory of their posterity; I do not think it is
wise to force them to study one thing or another, although persuading
them to do so would not be harmful; and when there is no need to study
pane lucrando,[1] if the student is so fortunate that heaven has endowed
him with parents who can spare him that, it would be my opinion that
they should allow him to pursue the area of knowledge to which they
can see he is inclined; although poetry is less useful than pleasurable, it is
not one of those that dishonors the one who knows it. Poetry, Señor, in
my opinion, is like an innocent young maiden who is extremely beautiful, and whom many other maidens, who are the other fields of knowledge, are careful to enrich, polish, and adorn, and she must be served by
all of them, and all of them must encourage her, but this maiden does not
wish to be pawed or dragged through the streets or procalimed at the corners of the squares or in the corners of palaces. Her alchemy is such that
the person who knows how to treat her will turn her into purest gold of
inestimable value; the man who has her must keep her within bounds
and not allow her to turn to indecent satires or cruel sonnets; she should
never be in the marketplace except in heroic poems, heartfelt tragedies,
or joyful, witty comedies; she should not be allowed in the company of
scoundrels or the ignorant mob incapable of knowing or appreciating
the treasures that lie within her. And do not think, Señor, that when I
say mob I mean only humble, plebeian people; for anyone who is ignorant, even a lord and prince, can and should be counted as one of the
mob. And so the man who uses and treats poetry in the requisite ways
that I have mentioned will be famous, and his name esteemed, in all the
civilized nations of the world.

And as for what you have said, Señor, regarding your son's lack of esteem for poetry in the modern languages, it is my understanding that he
is mistaken, for this reason: the great Homer did not write in Latin because he was Greek, and Virgil did not write in Greek because he was
Latin. In short, all the ancient poets wrote in their mother tongues, and
they did not look for foreign languages in order to declare the nobility of
their ideas. And this being true, it is reasonable to extend this custom to
all nations, and not to despise the German poet because he writes in his

---

1. The phrase means "in order to earn one's bread."

own language, or the Castilian, or even the Basque, for writing in his. But I imagine, Señor, that your son does not condemn vernacular poetry but poets who are merely vernacular and do not know other languages or other fields of knowledge, which adorn and awaken and assist their natural impulse; even in this he may be mistaken, because, according to reliable opinion, a poet is born: that is to say, the natural poet is a poet when he comes from his mother's womb, and with that inclination granted to him by heaven, with no further study or artifice he composes things that prove the truthfulness of the man who said: *Est Deus in nobis* . . .[2] I also say that the natural poet who makes use of art will be a much better and more accomplished poet than the one who knows only the art and wishes to be a poet; the reason is that art does not surpass nature but perfects it; therefore, when nature is mixed with art, and art with nature, the result is a perfect poet.

Let me conclude by saying, Señor, that you should allow your son to walk the path to which his star calls him; if he is the good student he should be, and if he has already successfully climbed the first essential step, which is languages, with them he will, on his own, mount to the summit of human letters, which are so admirable in a gentleman with his cape and sword, and adorn, honor, and ennoble him, as mitres do bishops, or robes the learned jurists. Your grace should reprimand your son if he writes satires that damage other people's honor; you should punish him and tear up the poems; but if he composes admonitory sermons in the manner of Horace,[3] in which vices in general are elegantly reproved, then praise him, because it is licit for the poet to write against envy, and to criticize the envious in his verses, and to do the same with the other vices, as long as he does not point out a specific person; but there are poets who, for the sake of saying something malicious, would run the risk of being exiled to the Islands of Pontus.[4] If the poet is chaste in his habits, he will be chaste in his verses as well; the pen is the tongue of the soul: his writings will be like the concepts engendered there; when kings and princes see the miraculous art of poetry in prudent, virtuous, and serious subjects, they honor, esteem, and enrich them, and even crown them with the leaves of the tree that lightning never strikes,[5] as a sign

2. The phrase, "God is in us," is by Ovid.

3. The reference is to the *Satires* of Horace.

4. Augustus exiled Ovid to these islands in the Black Sea.

5. The allusion is to the laurel.

that those whose temples are honored and adorned by such crowns are not to be assaulted by anyone."

The Gentleman in the Green Coat was so amazed at Don Quixote's words that he began to change his mind about his having to be a simpleton. But because it was not very much to his liking, in the middle of this speech Sancho had turned off the road to request a little milk from some shepherds who were milking their sheep nearby, and in the meantime, just as the gentleman was about to resume the conversation, satisfied in the extreme as to Don Quixote's intelligence and good sense, Don Quixote looked up and saw that coming down the road where they had been traveling was a wagon bearing royal banners, and believing that this must be some new adventure, he called to Sancho to bring him his helmet. And Sancho, hearing his shouts, left the shepherds, and spurred his donkey, and rushed to his master, who was about to engage in a terrifying and reckless adventure.

CHAPTER XVII

In which the heights and extremes to which the remarkable courage of Don Quixote could and did go is revealed, along with the happily concluded adventure of the lions

The history recounts that when Don Quixote called to Sancho to bring him his helmet, the squire was in the midst of buying curds from the shepherds, and flustered by his master's great urgency, he did not know what to do with them or where to carry them, and in order not to lose them, since he had already paid for them, he placed them in the helmet. Having made this provision, he went back to see what his master wanted, and as soon as he approached, Don Quixote said:

"Friend, hand me the helmet, for either I know very little about adventures, or what I see there is one that will, and does, oblige me to take up arms."

The Gentleman in the Green Coat heard this, and looked all around, and saw nothing but a wagon coming toward them, with two or three small flags on it, which led him to assume it was carrying currency that belonged to His Majesty, and he told this to Don Quixote, who did not accept what he said, for he always believed and thought that everything that happened to him had to be adventures and more adventures, and so he responded to the gentleman:

"Forewarned is forearmed: nothing is lost by cautioning me, although I know from experience that I have visible and invisible enemies, and I do not know when, or where, or how, or in what guise they will attack me."

And turning to Sancho, he asked for his sallet helmet; Sancho did not have time to take out the curds and was obliged to hand him the helmet just as it was. Don Quixote took it, and without even glancing at what might be inside, he quickly placed it on his head; since the curds were pressed and squeezed together, the whey began to run down Don Quixote's face and beard, which startled him so much that he said to Sancho:

"What can this be, Sancho? It seems as if my head is softening, or my brains are melting, or that I am bathed in perspiration from head to foot. And if I am perspiring, the truth is that it is not because of fear, although I undoubtedly must believe that the adventure about to befall me will be a terrible one. Give me something, if you have it, that I can use to wipe away this copious perspiration, for it is blinding me."

Sancho remained silent and gave him a cloth, and with it he gave his thanks to God that his master had not detected the truth. Don Quixote wiped his face and took off his helmet to see what it was that seemed to be chilling his head, and seeing that white mush inside, he brought the helmet up to his nose, and smelling it, he said:

"By the life of my lady Dulcinea of Toboso, these are curds that you have placed here, you traitorous, shameless, discourteous squire."

To which, with great aplomb and dissimulation, Sancho responded:

"If those are curds, your grace should give them to me and I'll eat them. . . . But let the devil eat them, because he must be the one who put them there. Would I ever dare to dirty your grace's helmet? You must know who the scoundrel is! By my faith, Señor, and the brains God gave me, I must also have enchanters who pursue me, since I'm your grace's servant and one of your members, and they must have put that filth there to turn your patience to anger and move you to beat me around my ribs, as you so often do. But the truth is that this time they're far off the mark, for I trust in the good sense of my master, who will consider that I don't have any curds, or milk, or anything else along those lines, and if I did, I'd put them in my stomach and not in your sallet helmet."

"All things are possible," said Don Quixote.

And the gentleman observed all of this, and all of it amazed him, especially when Don Quixote, after carefully cleaning his head, face, beard, and sallet, steadied his feet in the stirrups, called for his sword, grasped his lance, and said:

"Now come what may, for here I am, ready to do battle with Satan himself."

At this moment the wagon with the flags reached them, and the only people on it were the driver, leading the mules, and a man sitting at the front. Don Quixote stopped in front of the wagon and said:

"Where are you going, brothers? What wagon is this, and what are you carrying in it, and what flags are these?"

To which the driver responded:

"The wagon is mine; inside are two fierce lions in cages that the General of Oran is sending to court as a present for His Majesty; the flags belong to our master, the king, as a sign that what's inside is his."

"And are the lions big?" asked Don Quixote.

"So big," responded the man riding at the door of the wagon, "that no lions bigger, or even as big, have ever been brought over from Africa to Spain; I'm the lion keeper, and I've brought over other lions, but none like these. They're male and female; the male's in this first cage and the female's in the one behind, and they're hungry now because they haven't eaten today, and so, your grace, move out of the way because we have to hurry to the place where we can feed them."

To which Don Quixote, smiling slightly, said:

"You talk of lions to me? To me you speak of these little lions, and at this hour? Well, by God, those gentlemen who sent them here will see if I am a man who is frightened by lions! Get down, my good man, and since you are the lion keeper, open those cages and bring out those beasts, for in the middle of these fields I shall let them know who Don Quixote of La Mancha is, in spite of and in defiance of the enchanters who have sent them to me."

"Well, that proves it!" said the gentleman to himself. "Our good knight has shown exactly who he is: the curds, no doubt, have softened his head and ripened his brains."

At this moment Sancho came up to him and said:

"Señor, for the love of God, your grace, do something to stop my master, Don Quixote, from doing battle with these lions; if he fights them, they'll tear us all to pieces."

"Well, is your master so crazy," responded the gentleman, "that you fear and believe he'll fight with such savage animals?"

"He isn't crazy," responded Sancho, "he's just reckless."

"I'll do what I can to keep him from daring too much," replied the gentleman.

And going up to Don Quixote, who was urging the lion keeper to open the cages, he said:

"Señor Knight, knights errant ought to undertake adventures that promise some hope of success, not those that are completely devoid of hope, for the valor that crosses over into temerity has more to do with madness than courage, particularly because these lions are not attacking your grace, or even dreaming of doing so: they are gifts to His Majesty, and it would not be wise to stop them or interfere with their journey."

"Señor," responded Don Quixote, "your grace should go and see to your tame decoy partridge and your bold ferret, and let each man do his work. This is mine, and I know whether or not these noble lions are attacking me."

And turning to the lion keeper, he said:

"I swear, Don Scoundrel, that if you do not open the cages immediately, I shall pin you to the wagon with this lance!"

The driver, who saw the determination of that armed apparition, said:

"Señor, if it please your grace, I beg you, let me unyoke the mules and take them somewhere safe before the lions show themselves, because if they kill them, I'll be ruined for life; the only thing I own is this wagon and these mules."

"O man of little faith!" responded Don Quixote. "Get down, and unyoke them, and do whatever you wish, for soon you will see that you labored in vain and could have spared yourself the effort."

The driver climbed down and quickly unyoked the mules, and the lion keeper cried out:

"Let all those here present bear witness that I have been forced against my will to open the cages and set free the lions, and that I declare to this gentleman that he is answerable and accountable for all the harm and damage these beasts may do, as well as for my salaries and fees. Your graces should take cover before I let them out, though I'm sure they won't hurt me."

Once again the gentleman tried to persuade him not to commit an act of such madness, for to engage in something so foolish was to tempt God. To which Don Quixote responded that he knew what he was doing. The gentleman responded that he should be careful, for he knew that Don Quixote was deceived.

"Now, Señor," replied Don Quixote, "if your grace does not wish to be a witness to what you believe is going to be a tragedy, use your spurs on the dapple and hurry to safety."

Hearing this, Sancho, with tears in his eyes, begged his master to desist from such an undertaking, compared to which the adventure of the windmills, and that of the waterwheels, and, in short, all the feats he had performed in the entire course of his life had been nothing but child's play.

"Look, Señor," said Sancho, "there's no enchantment here or anything like it; I've seen through the gratings and cracks in the cage the claw of a real lion, and I think the lion that claw belongs to must be bigger than a mountain."

"Your fear, at the very least," responded Don Quixote, "will make it seem bigger to you than half the world. Withdraw, Sancho, and leave me; if I die here, you know our old agreement: you will present yourself to Dulcinea, and I shall say no more to you."

To these words he added others with which he took away all hope that he might not pursue his mad intention. The Gentleman in the Green Coat would have liked to stop him, but he was not as well-armed, and he did not think it prudent to fight with a madman, for by now he thought Don Quixote was completely out of his mind. The knight again began to press the lion keeper and to repeat his threats, which gave the gentleman the opportunity to spur his mare, and Sancho to urge on his donkey, and the driver to hurry his mules, all of them attempting to get as far away from the wagon as they could before the lions were freed.

Sancho wept for the death of his master: this time he believed there was no doubt he would fall into the clutches of the lions; he cursed his luck and called it an evil hour when it had occurred to him to serve his master again, but his weeping and lamentations did not prevent him from kicking the donkey to hurry him away from the wagon. Then the lion keeper, seeing that those who were fleeing had reached safety, pleaded with and warned Don Quixote, using the same pleas and warnings he had used before, and Don Quixote responded that he had heard what he had to say, and he should not trouble himself with more warnings and pleas for they would be to no avail, and what he should do was hurry.

In the time it took the lion keeper to unlock the first cage, Don Quixote was considering if it would be better to do battle on foot or on horseback, and, finally, he decided to do battle on foot, fearing that

Rocinante would become frightened at the sight of the lions. For this reason he leaped from his horse, tossed away his lance, took up his shield, unsheathed his sword, and at a deliberate pace, with marvelous courage and a valiant heart, he went to stand before the wagon, commending himself with all his heart first to God and then to his lady Dulcinea. And it is worth noting that when he reached this point, the author of this true history exclaimed:

"O most valiant and supremely courageous Don Quixote of La Mancha, paragon of all the brave men in the world, a second and new Don Manuel de León,[1] the glory and honor of Spanish knights! What words shall I use to recount this fearsome deed, what phrases will lend it credence in times to come, what phrases can I find that do not suit and befit you even if they are the most hyperbolic of hyperboles? You on foot, you alone, you intrepid and of a noble mind, armed only with a sword, and not one of those with a dog on the blade,[2] and with a shield not made of bright and shining steel, you stand waiting and anticipating the two most savage lions ever born in the African jungle. May your own deeds sing your praises, most valiant Manchegan; I shall leave them here in all their perfection, for I do not have the words with which to extol them."

The aforementioned exclamation of the author ended here, and he moved on, picking up the thread of the history and saying that when the lion keeper saw that Don Quixote was in position, and that he himself could not avoid freeing the male lion without falling into disfavor with the wrathful and audacious knight, he opened wide the first cage, which held, as has been said, the male lion, who appeared to be of extraordinary size and fearsome and hideous aspect. The first thing the lion did was to turn around in the cage where he had been lying and unsheathe his claws and stretch his entire body; then he opened his mouth, and yawned very slowly, and extended a tongue almost two spans long, and cleaned the dust from his eyes and washed his face; when this was finished, he put his head out of the cage and looked all around with eyes like coals, a sight and a vision that could frighten temerity itself. Only Don Quixote looked at him attentively, wanting him to leap from the wagon and come within reach of his hands, for he intended to tear him to pieces.

1. As indicated in note 7, chapter XLIX of part I, Don Manuel de León (*León* is a province of Spain as well as the word that means "lion") retrieved a glove from a lion's cage at the request of a lady and then slapped her for needlessly endangering the life of a knight.

2. Certain fine swords had the image of a dog engraved on the blade.

These are the extremes to which Don Quixote's unprecedented madness took him. But the magnanimous lion, more courteous than arrogant, took no notice of either childishness or bravado, and after looking in both directions, as has been said, he turned his back, and showed his hindquarters to Don Quixote, and with great placidity and calm went back inside the cage. Seeing this, Don Quixote ordered the lion keeper to hit him and provoke him into coming out.

"That I will not do," responded the lion keeper, "because if I instigate him, the first one he'll tear to pieces will be me. Señor, your grace should be content with what you have done, which is all that anyone could ask in the matter of courage, and not tempt fortune a second time. The lion's door is open: it is up to him to come out or not, but if he hasn't come out by now, he won't come out for the rest of the day. The greatness of your grace's heart has been clearly demonstrated: no brave warrior, to my understanding, is obliged to do more than challenge his opponent and wait for him in the field; if his adversary does not appear, the dishonor lies with him, and the one left waiting wins the crown of victory."

"That is true," responded Don Quixote, "and so, friend, close the door and give me the best statement you can regarding what you have seen me do, which is to say, you opened the lion's cage, I waited for him, he did not come out, still I waited for him, and still he did not come out but lay down again. I need do no more, and so away with enchantments, and may God protect justice and truth and true chivalry; close the door, as I have said, while I signal to those who have fled and run away so that they may hear of this great deed from your own lips."

The lion keeper did so, and Don Quixote, attaching to the end of his lance the cloth he had used to wipe away the downpour of curds on his face, began to call those who had not stopped fleeing or looking back at every step, all of them in a mad rush, with the gentleman at their head; but Sancho saw the signal with the white cloth, and he said:

"Strike me dead if my master hasn't defeated the savage beasts, for he's calling us."

Everyone stopped and realized that the one signaling was Don Quixote, and losing some part of their fear, they gradually approached until they could clearly hear Don Quixote calling to them. Finally, they returned to the wagon, and when they arrived Don Quixote said to the driver:

"Yoke your mules again, my friend, and continue on your way, and you, Sancho, give him two gold *escudos*, one for him and one for the lion keeper, in recompense for the delay I have caused them."

"I'll do that gladly," responded Sancho, "but what happened to the lions? Are they dead or alive?"

Then the lion keeper, in great detail and with many pauses, recounted the outcome of the contest, exaggerating to the best of his ability and skill the valor of Don Quixote, the sight of whom made a coward of the lion, who refused and did not dare to leave his cage, although he had kept the door open for some time; and only because he had told the knight that it was tempting God to provoke the lion and force him to come out, which is what he wanted him to do, and despite the knight's wishes and against his will, he had allowed the door to be closed again.

"What do you think of that, Sancho?" said Don Quixote. "Are there any enchantments that can prevail against true courage? Enchanters may deprive me of good fortune, but of spirit and courage, never!"

Sancho gave the men the *escudos*, the driver yoked his team, the lion keeper kissed Don Quixote's hands for the favor received and promised to recount that valiant feat to the king himself when he arrived in court.

"If, by chance, His Majesty asks who performed the deed, tell him it was *The Knight of the Lions;* from this day forth, I want the name I have had until now, *The Knight of the Sorrowful Face*, to be changed, altered, turned, and transformed into this, and in doing so, I follow the ancient usage of knights errant, who changed their names whenever they wished, or whenever it seemed appropriate."

The wagon went on its way, and Don Quixote, Sancho, and the Gentleman of the Green Coat continued on theirs.

In all this time Don Diego de Miranda had not said a word but was careful to observe and note the actions and words of Don Quixote, who seemed to him a sane man gone mad and a madman edging toward sanity. He had not yet heard anything about the first part of Don Quixote's history; if he had read it, he would no longer have been astonished by his actions and words, for he would have known the nature of his madness, but since he did not, he sometimes thought him sane and sometimes mad, because his speech was coherent, elegant, and eloquent and his actions nonsensical, reckless, and foolish. And he said to himself:

"What greater madness can there be than putting on a helmet full of curds and believing that enchanters had softened one's head? And what greater temerity and foolishness than to attempt to do battle with lions?"

Don Quixote drew him away from these thoughts and this soliloquy by saying:

"Who can doubt, Señor Don Diego de Miranda, that in the opinion of your grace I am a foolish and witless man? And it would not be surprising if you did, because my actions do not attest to anything else. Even so, I would like your grace to observe that I am not as mad or as foolish as I must have seemed to you. A gallant knight is pleasing in the eyes of his king when, in the middle of a great plaza, he successfully thrusts his lance into a fierce bull; a knight is pleasing when, dressed in shining armor, he enters the field and contends in lively jousts before the ladies; and all those knights who engage in military exercises, or seem to, entertain and enliven and, if one may say so, honor the courts of their princes; but above and beyond all these, the best seems to be the knight errant, who travels wastelands and desolate places, crossroads and forests and mountains, seeking dangerous adventures and attempting to bring them to a happy and fortunate conclusion, his sole purpose being to achieve glorious and lasting fame. The knight errant who helps a widow in some deserted spot, seems better, I say, than a courtier knight flattering a damsel in the city. All knights have their own endeavors: let the courtier serve the ladies, and lend majesty to the court of his king with livery; let him sustain poor knights with the splendors of his table, arrange jousts, support tourneys, and show himself to be great, liberal, magnanimous, and, above all, a good Christian, and in this manner he will meet his precise obligations. But let the knight errant search all the corners of the world; let him enter into the most intricate labyrinths; attempt the impossible at each step he takes; resist in empty wastelands the burning rays of the sun in summer, and in winter the harsh rigors of freezing winds; let him not be dismayed by lions, or frightened by monsters, or terrified by dragons; searching for these and attacking those and vanquishing them all are his principal and true endeavors.

I, then, since it is my fortune to be counted in the number of knights errant, cannot help but attack all things that seem to me to fall within the jurisdiction of my endeavors; and so, it was my rightful place to attack the lions which I now attacked, although I knew it was exceedingly reckless, because I know very well what valor means; it is a virtue that occupies a place between two wicked extremes, which are cowardice and temerity, but it is better for the valiant man to touch on and climb to the heights of temerity than to touch on and fall to the depths of cowardice; and just as it is easier for the prodigal to be generous than the miser, it is easier for the reckless man to become truly brave than for the coward; and in the matter of undertaking adventures, your grace may believe me, Señor Don Diego, it is better to lose with too many cards than too few, because 'This knight is reckless and daring' sounds better to the ear of those who hear it than 'This knight is timid and cowardly.' "

"Señor Don Quixote," responded Don Diego, "I say that everything your grace has said and done has been balanced on the scale of reason itself, and I understand that if the code and laws of knight errantry were ever lost, they would be found again in your grace's heart as if they were in their own repository and archive. And now let us hurry, for it is getting late; when we reach my village and house, your grace can rest from your recent labors, if not of the body then of the spirit, which can often lead to the body's fatigue."

"I consider your offer a great kindness and favor, Señor Don Diego," responded Don Quixote.

And spurring their mounts more than they had up until then, at about two o'clock they reached the village and house of Don Diego, whom Don Quixote called *The Knight of the Green Coat*.

CHAPTER XVIII

Regarding what befell Don Quixote in the castle or house of the Knight of the Green Coat, along with other bizarre matters

Don Quixote found Don Diego de Miranda's house to be spacious in the rustic manner; his coat of arms, though of rough stone, was above the street door, the storeroom in the courtyard, the wine cellar, the entrance hall, and on many large earthenware jars, which, because they were from Toboso, revived in Don Quixote memories of his enchanted and transformed Dulcinea; and heaving a sigh, and not caring what he said or whom he was with, he said:

> "O sweet treasures, discovered to my sorrow,
> sweet and joyous when God did will them so![1]

O Tobosan vessels, which have brought to mind the sweetest treasure of my deepest grief!"

1. These are verses from one of Garcilaso's sonnets.

He was heard to say this by the student poet, Don Diego's son, who had come out with his mother to receive him, and both mother and son marveled to see the strange figure of Don Quixote, who, dismounting Rocinante, very courteously went up to her and asked to kiss her hands, and Don Diego said:

"Señora, welcome with your customary amiability Señor Don Quixote of La Mancha, whom you have here before you, the most valiant and intelligent knight errant in the world."

The lady, whose name was Doña Cristina, received him with signs of great affection and courtesy, and Don Quixote responded with a number of judicious and courteous phrases. He used almost the same phrases with the student, who, when he heard Don Quixote speak, thought him a man of intelligence and wit.

Here the author depicts all the details of Don Diego's house, portraying for us what the house of a wealthy gentleman farmer contains, but the translator of this history decided to pass over these and other similar minutiae in silence, because they did not accord with the principal purpose of the history, whose strength lies more in its truth than in cold digressions.

They led Don Quixote to a chamber, where Sancho removed his armor, leaving him in pantaloons and a chamois doublet that was stained with the grime of his armor; his collar was wide and soft like a student's, without starch or lace trimming; his tights were date colored and his shoes waxed. He girded on his trusty sword, which hung from a swordbelt made of sealskin, for it is believed that for many years he suffered from a kidney ailment; over this he wore a short cape of good dark cloth; but first of all, with five pots, or perhaps six pots of water, there being some difference of opinion regarding the number, he washed his head and face, and still the water was the color of whey, thanks to Sancho's gluttony and his purchase of the blackhearted curds that turned his master so white. With these adornments, and genteel grace and gallantry, Don Quixote went to another room, where the student was waiting to entertain him while the tables were being laid, for with the arrival of so noble a guest, Señora Doña Cristina wished to show that she knew how and was able to lavish attention on those who visited her house.

While Don Quixote was removing his armor, Don Lorenzo, which was the name of Don Diego's son, had the opportunity to say to his father:

"Señor, who can this knight be whom you have brought to our house?

His name and appearance, and his saying that he is a knight errant, have baffled my mother and me."

"Son, I don't know what to tell you," responded Don Diego. "I can say only that I have seen him do things worthy of the greatest madman in the world, and heard him say things so intelligent that they wipe out and undo his mad acts: speak to him, and explore what he knows, and since you are clever, you'll make a reasonable judgment regarding his cleverness or foolishness, though to tell you the truth, I think he's more mad than sane."

Then Don Lorenzo went in to entertain Don Quixote, as has been said, and among other exchanges that passed between them, Don Quixote said to Don Lorenzo:

"Your grace's father, Señor Don Diego de Miranda, has informed me of the rare ability and subtle ingenuity which your grace possesses, and, in particular, that your grace is a great poet."

"A poet, perhaps," responded Don Lorenzo, "but by no means great. The truth is, I have a predilection for poetry and for reading good poets, but that does not justify calling me great, as my father has done."

"This humility does not seem a bad thing to me," responded Don Quixote, "because there is no poet who is not arrogant and does not think himself the greatest poet in the world."

"Every rule has its exception," responded Don Lorenzo, "and there must be some who are great and do not think so."

"Very few," responded Don Quixote. "But tell me, your grace, what verses are you at work on now? Your father has told me that they have made you somewhat restive and thoughtful. If it is a gloss, I know something about the subject and would like very much to hear it; if the verses are for a literary competition, your grace should try to win second place; first is always won through favor or because of the high estate of the person, second is won because of pure justice, and by this calculation third becomes second, and first becomes third, in the manner of the degrees offered by universities; but, even so, being called *first* carries with it great celebrity."

"So far," said Don Lorenzo to himself, "I can't call you crazy; let's move on."

And to Don Quixote he said:

"It seems to me that your grace has spent time in school: what sciences have you studied?"

"The science of knight errantry," responded Don Quixote, "which is as good as poetry, and perhaps even a little better."

"I don't know that science," replied Don Lorenzo. "I haven't heard of it until now."

"It is a science," replied Don Quixote, "that contains all or most of the sciences in the world, because the man who professes it must be a jurist and know the laws of distributive and commutative justice so that he may give to each person what is his and what he ought to have; he must be a theologian so that he may know how to explain the Christian law he professes, clearly and distinctly, no matter where he is asked to do so; he must be a physician, and principally an herbalist, so that he may know, in the midst of wastelands and deserts, the herbs that have the virtue to heal wounds, for the knight errant cannot always go looking for someone to heal him; he must be an astrologer, so that he can tell by the stars how many hours of the night have passed, and in what part and climate of the world he finds himself; he must know mathematics, because at every step he will have need of them; and leaving aside the fact that he must be adorned with all the theological and cardinal virtues, and descending to the small details, I say that he must know how to swim as well as they say the fishman Nicolás, or Nicolao,[2] could swim; he must know how to shoe a horse and repair a saddle and bridle; and returning to what was said before, he must keep his faith in God and in his lady; he must be chaste in his thoughts, honest in his words, liberal in his actions, valiant in his deeds, long-suffering in his afflictions, charitable with those in need, and, finally, an upholder of the truth, even if it costs him his life to defend it. Of all these great and trivial parts a good knight errant is composed, and so your grace may judge, Señor Don Lorenzo, if the science learned by the knight who studies and professes it is a shallow one, and if it can be compared to the noblest that are taught in colleges and schools."

"If this is true," replied Don Lorenzo, "I say that this science surpasses all of them."

"What do you mean, if this is true?" responded Don Quixote.

"What I mean to say," said Don Lorenzo, "is that I doubt there have ever been knights errant, or that there are any now, who are adorned with so many virtues."

"I have often said what I repeat now," responded Don Quixote.

2. A creature who, like an amphibian, spent as much time in the water as on land. As early as the twelfth century, he was alluded to in troubadour poetry and identified with St. Nicolas of Bari.

"Most of the people in the world are of the opinion that there never have been knights errant, and it seems to me that if heaven does not miraculously reveal to them the truth that they did exist and do exist now, any effort I make must be in vain, as experience has so often shown me, and so I do not wish to take the time now to free your grace from the error you share with many others; what I intend to do is pray that heaven frees you from it, and allows you to understand how beneficial and necessary knights errant were to the world in the past, and how advantageous they could be in the present if they were still in use, but what triumphs now, because of people's sins, are sloth, idleness, gluttony, and self-indulgence."

"Our guest has gotten away from us," said Don Lorenzo to himself, "but even so, he is a gallant madman, and I would be a weak-minded fool if I didn't think so."

Here their conversation came to an end because they were called to the table. Don Diego asked his son what he had deduced regarding their guest's wits, to which he responded:

"Not all the physicians and notaries in the world could make a final accounting of his madness: he is a combination madman who has many lucid intervals."

They went in to eat, and the meal was just the kind that Don Diego had declared on the road that he usually provided for his guests: pure, abundant, and delicious; but what pleased Don Quixote the most was the marvelous silence that reigned throughout the house, which seemed like a Carthusian monastery. And so when the tablecloths had been removed, and thanks given to God, and water poured over hands, Don Quixote most earnestly asked Don Lorenzo to recite his verses for the literary competition, to which he responded that in order not to seem like one of those poets who refuse when they are asked to recite their verses and spew them forth when they aren't asked . . .

". . . I'll recite my gloss, for which I don't expect any prize at all; I've written it only to exercise my wits."

"A wise friend of mine," responded Don Quixote, "was of the opinion that nobody ought to tire of glossing verses, and the reason, he said, was that the gloss never could approach the text, and that many or most times the gloss strayed from the intention and purpose of what the text proposed; moreover, the laws of the gloss were too strict, for they did not allow questions, or *he said* or *I shall say*, or the making of verbs into nouns, or changing the significance, along with other restrictions and regulations that set limits for those who write glosses, as your grace must know."

"Truly, Señor Don Quixote," said Don Lorenzo, "I would like to catch your grace in some foolish mistake, and I can't, because you slip out of my hands like an eel."

"I do not understand," responded Don Quixote, "what your grace says or means to say about my slipping away."

"I'll explain later," responded Don Lorenzo, "but for now your grace should listen to the glossed verses and to the gloss, which read like this:

> If my *was* would be an *is*,
> not waiting for a *will be*,
> or if at last the time would come
> when later is now and here . . .

GLOSS

> At last, since all things pass,
> the good that Fortune gave me
> passed too, though once o'erflowing,
> and never to me returned,
> neither scant nor in abundance.
> Not for centuries, O Fortune,
> have you seen me at your feet;
> make me contented once more;
> my great good fortune will be
> *if my was would be an is*.
>
>   I wish no joy or glory,
> neither honor nor victory,
> no other triumph or conquest,
> but to return to the joy
> that's nothing but grief in memory.
> If you can return me there
> O Fortune, this fiery torment
> will ease; do it now, I pray,
> *not waiting for a will be*.
>
>   What I ask is the impossible,
> for there is no force on earth
> that has the power to turn

back time that has passed us by,
to bring back what once was ours.
Time races, it flies, it charges
past, and will never return,
and only a fool would beg
a halt, or if the time would pass,
or if at last the time would come.

    I live a life of perplexity,
torn between hoping and fear:
this is a death in life for me;
much better to end my sorrow
and die the death of the tomb.
And though my wish is to end
my life, my reason tells me no,
and hands me back my gloomy life
in terror of that after time
when later is now and here."

When Don Lorenzo finished reciting his gloss, Don Quixote rose to his feet, and in a loud voice that was almost a shout, and grasping Don Lorenzo's right hand in his own, he said:

"Praise be to heaven on high, magnanimous youth, for you are the best poet on earth, and you deserve to be crowned with a laurel wreath, not by Cyprus or Gaeta, as a poet once said,[3] may God forgive him, but by the academies of Athens, if they still existed today, and by those that do in Paris, Bologna, and Salamanca! May it please heaven that the judges who would deprive you of first place be pierced by the arrows of Phoebus, and may the Muses never cross the thresholds of their houses! If you please, Señor, tell me some verses in a long line,[4] for I wish to explore your admirable talent thoroughly."

Is it surprising to anyone that Don Lorenzo was extremely happy to be praised by Don Quixote, even though he considered him mad? O Flattery, how powerful you are, how far you extend, how widespread the boundaries of your pleasant domain! Don Lorenzo gave credence to this

---

3. Probably Pedro Liñán de Riaza (1558?–1607), a poet praised by Cervantes.

4. The meter of Spanish poetry is essentially determined by the number of syllables in a line; the short line (*arte menor*) has eight syllables or less; the long line (*arte mayor*) has nine or more syllables. Here the long line is the hendecasyllable—the eleven-syllable line, perfected by Petrarch, which influenced all of European poetry in the Renaissance and is generally associated with the sonnet. Garcilaso de la Vega naturalized this meter in Spanish early in the sixteenth century.

truth by acceding to the request and desire of Don Quixote, and reciting this sonnet on the tale or history of Pyramus and Thisbe:

SONNET

> The wall is breached by the beauteous maid
> who pierced the gallant bosom of Pyramus;
> Love flies from Cyprus, faster than an arrow,
> to see the rift, so prodigious and so narrow.
>
> Silence speaks there, no human voice will dare
> to pass through a cleft so strait and constrained;
> but enamored souls will, for love's sweet speed
> can ease the rigors of that perilous deed.
>
> Desire broke its tether, and the reckless steps
> of th' emboldened damsel seemed to demand
> death as the sole response to longed-for pleasure.
>
> Oh, a rare tale and strange! Both at one moment
> are killed, and interred, and recalled forever:
> one sword, one grave, one memory for two.

"Praise be to God!" said Don Quixote when he had heard Don Lorenzo's sonnet. "Among the infinite number of consumptive poets, Señor, I have seen a consummate poet, which is what your grace is, and what the artfulness of this sonnet leads me to believe."

For four days Don Quixote was wonderfully regaled in the house of Don Diego, and at the end of this time he asked permission to leave, telling his host that he was grateful for the kind and generous treatment he had received in his house, but because it did not seem right for knights errant to devote too many hours to idleness and leisure, he wished to fulfill his obligations and go in search of adventures, for he had heard that this land abounded in them, and this was where he hoped to pass the time until the day of the jousts in Zaragoza, when he would vanquish all adversaries; but first he had to enter the Cave of Montesinos, about which so many marvelous things were recounted in that district, and he would also look into and inquire about the origin and true source of the seven Lakes of Ruidera, as they were commonly called.

Don Diego and his son praised his honorable determination and told him to take from their house and estate everything he wished, for they would serve him most willingly, as they were bound to do because of the worth of his person and the honorable profession he pursued.

At last the day of his departure arrived, as joyful for Don Quixote as it was sad and mournful for Sancho Panza, who was quite content with the abundance in Don Diego's house and opposed this return to the hunger that was customary in forests and wastelands and in the meagerness of his badly provisioned saddlebags. Despite this, he filled them to the top with what he thought most necessary, and as they took their leave, Don Quixote said to Don Lorenzo:

"I do not know if I have already told your grace, and if I have, I shall tell you again, that when your grace wishes to save a good deal of time and trouble in your ascent to the inaccessible summit of the temple of Fame, you need do nothing else but leave the narrow path of poetry and follow the even narrower one of knight errantry, which will suffice to make you an emperor in the blink of an eye."

With these words Don Quixote brought to a close the question of his madness, in particular when he added these, saying:

"God knows I should like to take Señor Don Lorenzo with me, to teach him how one must pardon the meek and subdue and trample the proud, virtues deeply connected to the profession I follow; but since his youth does not ask it, nor his meritorious pursuits consent to it, I shall be content with merely advising your grace that, being a poet, you can achieve fame if you are guided more by other people's opinions than by your own, for no father or mother thinks their children are ugly, and for those born of the understanding, such deception is an even greater danger."

Once again the father and son were astonished by the mixed speech of Don Quixote, sometimes intelligent and sometimes utterly foolish, and by the persistence and perseverance of his complete devotion to the search for his misadventurous adventures, which were the object and goal of all his desires. The compliments and courtesies were repeated, and with the kind permission of the lady of the castle, Don Quixote and Sancho, mounted on Rocinante and the donkey, took their leave.

CHAPTER XIX

Which recounts the adventure of the enamored shepherd, and other truly pleasing matters

Don Quixote had not gone very far from Don Diego's house when he encountered two men who seemed to be clerics or students,[1] and two peasants, each riding a donkeyish mount. One of the students carried as a kind of portmanteau a piece of green buckram, and wrapped in it there were, apparently, a piece of fine scarlet cloth and two pairs of ribbed serge hose; the other carried only two new black fencing foils, with leather tips on the points. The peasants carried other things, which were a sign and indication that they were returning from some large city where they had bought them and were carrying them back to their village; both students and peasants experienced the same astonishment felt by all who saw Don Quixote for the first time, and they longed to know who this man might be who was so different from other men.

Don Quixote greeted them, and after he learned the road they were taking, which was the same one he was following, he offered them his company and asked them to slow their pace because their donkeys walked faster than his horse; and to oblige them, in a few brief words he told them who he was, and his calling and profession, which was to be a knight errant who went seeking adventures everywhere in the world. He told them that his proper name was Don Quixote of La Mancha and that his title was *The Knight of the Lions*. For the peasants, all of this was like speaking to them in Greek or in gibberish, but not for the students, who soon understood the weakness in Don Quixote's mind; even so, they viewed him with admiration and respect, and one of them said:

1. University students and clerics wore the same kind of clothing.

"Señor Knight, if your grace is not following a specific route, as those searching for adventures usually do not, your grace should come with us, and you will see one of the finest and richest weddings ever celebrated in La Mancha, or for many leagues around."

Don Quixote asked him if it was a prince's wedding that he was praising so highly.

"No," responded the student, "not a prince, but the richest farmer in this entire land, and the most beautiful farmgirl men have ever seen. The preparations for the wedding celebration are extraordinary and remarkable, because it will be held in a meadow near the bride's village; she is always called fair Quiteria, and the groom is called rich Camacho; she is eighteen and he is twenty-two; they are equals, though certain inquisitive people who have the lineages of the entire world memorized claim that fair Quiteria's is superior to Camacho's, but nobody thinks about that nowadays: wealth has the power to mend a good many cracks. In fact, Camacho is extremely generous, and he has taken a notion to weave branches into a bower to cover the entire meadow, so that the sun will have great difficulty if it wants to come in to visit the green grass covering the ground. He also has arranged for dances, with swords and with bells, for there are in his village people who are excellent at ringing and shaking them, and I won't say anything about the heel-tappers, for the general opinion is that he has a good number of them ready; but none of the things I've mentioned, or the many others that I've omitted, are what will make this wedding memorable, but rather the things I imagine a desperate Basilio will do. This Basilio is a shepherd from the same village as Quiteria, and his house shared a wall with the house of Quiteria's parents, allowing love the opportunity to renew in the world the long-forgotten loves of Pyramus and Thisbe, because Basilio loved Quiteria from his earliest, tenderest youth, and she responded to his desire with a thousand honest favors, so that in the village the love of the two children, Basilio and Quiteria, was recounted with amusement. As they grew older, Quiteria's father decided to deny Basilio the access to his house that he once had enjoyed, and to spare himself mistrust and endless suspicions, he arranged for his daughter to marry rich Camacho, for it did not seem a good idea to marry her to Basilio, who was better endowed by nature than by fortune; if the truth be told, without envy, he is the most agile youth we know, a great hurler of the bar, an excellent wrestler, a fine pelota player; he runs like a deer, leaps like a goat, and plays bowls as if he were enchanted; he sings like a lark, plays the guitar so well he makes it speak, and, most of all, he can fence with the best of them."

"For that one accomplishment," said Don Quixote, "the youth deserved not only to marry fair Quiteria but Queen Guinevere herself, if she were alive today, in spite of Lancelot and all the others who might wish to prevent it."

"Try telling that to my wife!" said Sancho Panza, who so far had been listening in silence. "The only thing she wants is for everybody to marry their equal, following the proverb that says 'Like goes to like.' What I'd like is for this good Basilio, and I'm growing very fond of him, to marry Señora Quiteria; people who keep people who love each other from marrying should rest in peace, world without end, and I was going to say the opposite."

"If all people who love each other were to marry," said Don Quixote, "it would deprive parents of the right and privilege to marry their children to the person and at the time they ought to marry; if daughters were entitled to choose their own husbands, one would choose her father's servant, and another a man she saw walking on the street, who seemed to her proud and gallant, although he might be a debauchee and a braggart; for love and affection easily blind the eyes of the understanding, which are so necessary for choosing one's estate, and the estate of matrimony is at particular risk of error, and great caution is required, and the particular favor of heaven, in order to choose correctly. If a person wishes to make a long journey, and if he is prudent, before setting out he will find reliable and peaceful companionship for his travels; then why would he not do the same for the journey that takes a lifetime, until it reaches the resting place of death, and especially if his companion will be with him in bed, at the table, everywhere, which is how a wife accompanies her husband? The companionship of one's own wife is not merchandise that, once purchased, can be returned, or exchanged, or altered; it is an irrevocable circumstance that lasts as long as one lives: it is a rope that, if put around one's neck, turns into the Gordian knot, and if the scythe of Death does not cut it, there is no way to untie it. I could say much more with regard to this subject, but I am kept from doing so by my desire to know if the distinguished licentiate has more to tell us of the history of Basilio."

To which the student bachelor, or licentiate, as Don Quixote called him, responded:

"There really is no more for me to say except that ever since the moment Basilio learned that fair Quiteria was marrying rich Camacho, he has not been known to laugh, or to speak coherently, and he always goes about pensive and sad, talking to himself, which are clear and certain signs that he has lost his mind: he eats little and sleeps little, and what he does eat is fruit, and if he does sleep it is in the fields, on the hard ground, like a dumb animal; from time to time he looks up at the sky, at other times he fixes his eyes on the ground and is so entranced that he seems to be a dressed statue whose clothes are moved by the breeze. In short, he gives so many indications of having a heart maddened by love that those of us who know him fear that when fair Quiteria takes her marriage vows tomorrow, it will be his death sentence."

"God will find the cure," said Sancho, "for God gives the malady and also the remedy; nobody knows the future: there's a lot of hours until tomorrow, and in one of them, and even in a moment, the house can fall; I've seen it rain at the same time the sun is shining; a man goes to bed healthy and can't move the next day. And tell me, is there anybody who can boast that he's driven a nail into Fortune's wheel? No, of course not, and I wouldn't dare put the point of a pin between a woman's yes and no, because it wouldn't fit. Tell me that Quiteria loves Basilio with all her heart and all her soul, and I'll give him a sack of good fortune, because I've heard that love looks through spectacles that make copper look like gold, poverty like riches, and dried rheum like pearls."

"Damn you, Sancho, where will you stop?" said Don Quixote. "When you begin to string together proverbs and stories, nobody can endure it but Judas himself, and may Judas himself take you. Tell me, you brute, what do you know of nails, or wheels, or anything else?"

"Oh, well, if none of you understand me," responded Sancho, "it's no wonder my sayings are taken for nonsense. But it doesn't matter: I understand what I'm saying, and I know there's not much foolishness in what I said, but your grace is always sentencing what I say, and even what I do."

"*Censuring* is what you should say," said Don Quixote, "and not *sentencing*, you corrupter of good language, may God confound you!"

"Your grace shouldn't get angry with me," responded Sancho, "because you know I didn't grow up at court or study at Salamanca, so how would I know if I'm adding or taking away letters from my words? God save me! You can't force a Sayagan to talk like a Toledan,[2] and there may be some Toledans who don't talk better than anybody else."

2. People from Sayago (in the modern province of Zamora) spoke with a rustic accent that was often used in the theater for comic effect; natives of Toledo were thought to speak an extremely correct and pure Spanish.

"That's true," said the licentiate, "because those who grew up in Tenerías and in Zocodover cannot speak as well as those who spend almost the entire day strolling in the cloister of the cathedral, and all of them are Toledans. Pure language, appropriate, elegant, and clear, is used by discerning courtiers even if they were born in Majalahonda.[3] I said *discerning*, because there are many who are not, and discernment is the grammar of good language, which is acquired with use. I, Señores, for my sins, have studied canon law at Salamanca and am rather proud of speaking with words that are clear, plain, and meaningful."

"If you hadn't been prouder of how you move those foils you're carrying than of how you wag your tongue," said the other student, whose name was Corchuelo, "maybe you would have placed first for your licentiate instead of last."

"Look, Bachelor," responded the licentiate, "you hold the most erroneous opinion in the world about skill with the sword, since you consider it useless."

"As far as I'm concerned, it's not an opinion but an established truth," replied Corchuelo, "and if you would like me to prove it to you experientially, you're carrying the foils, there's a convenient spot, I have a steady hand, and strength, and together with my courage, which is no small thing, they will make you confess that I am not mistaken. Dismount, and use your changes of posture, your circles, your angles, and your science; I expect to make you see stars at midday with my crude, modern skills, and after God I put my trust in them, and there's no man born who will make me turn away, and none in the world whom I can't force to retreat."[4]

"I won't get involved in questions of turning or not turning away," replied the master swordsman, "though it might be that on the spot where you first set your foot, your grave will open wide: I mean, that you'll be lying dead there on account of the mastery you despise so much."

"Now we'll see," responded Corchuelo.

And he dismounted his donkey with great agility and furiously seized one of the foils that the licentiate was carrying on his animal.

"It should not be this way," said Don Quixote at that moment, "for I

3. A village near Madrid.

4. The dispute between the bachelor and the licentiate is based on the latter's adherence to the elaborately theoretical handbooks on the art and science of fencing that were extremely popular in the sixteenth and seventeenth centuries.

wish to be the master of this duel and the judge of this question so frequently left unresolved."

And after dismounting Rocinante and grasping his lance, he stood in the middle of the road, at the same time that the licentiate, with spirited grace and measured steps, was advancing on Corchuelo, who came toward him, his eyes, as the saying goes, blazing. The two peasants who had accompanied them did not dismount their donkeys, but served as spectators to the mortal tragedy. The innumerable lunges, slashes, downward thrusts, reverse strokes, and two-handed blows executed by Corchuelo were denser than liver and more minute than hail. He attacked like an angry lion but was met with a blow to the mouth by the tip of the licentiate's foil, which stopped him in the middle of his fury, and which he had to kiss as if it were a relic, though not as devotedly as relics should be kissed, and usually are.

Finally, the licentiate's lunges accounted for all the buttons on the short cassock the bachelor was wearing and slashed its skirts into the arms of an octopus; twice he knocked off his hat, and tired him so much that in fury, anger, and rage the bachelor seized his foil by the hilt and threw it into the air with so much force that one of the peasants, who was a notary, went to retrieve it and subsequently testified that it had flown almost three-quarters of a league, and this testimony serves and has served to demonstrate and prove the truth that force is vanquished by art.

Corchuelo sat down, exhausted, and Sancho approached him and said:

"By my faith, Señor Bachelor, if your grace will take my advice, from now on you won't challenge anybody to a duel, but to wrestling or hurling the bar, since you're young enough and strong enough for that, because I've heard that the ones they call *master swordsmen* can put the tip of their sword through the eye of a needle."

"I'm happy," responded Corchuelo, "that I fell off my high horse, and that experience has shown me a truth I refused to acknowledge."

And, standing up, he embraced the licentiate, and they were better friends than before; and not wanting to wait for the notary who had gone after the foil because it seemed it would take too long, they resolved to continue on their way in order to reach Quiteria's village early, for that is where all of them were from.

For the rest of their journey the licentiate told them about the excellencies of the sword, with so many demonstrations and figures and mathematical proofs that all of them were well-informed regarding the virtues of the science, and Corchuelo's obstinacy was overcome.

It was dusk, but before they arrived it seemed to everyone that the village sky was filled with innumerable brilliant stars. They also heard the sweet, confused sounds of various instruments, such as flutes, tambors, psalteries, flageolets, tambourines, and timbrels, and when they came close they saw that a bower of trees, erected at the entrance to the village, was filled with lights, which were not disturbed by the wind that was blowing so gently it did not have the strength to move the leaves on the trees. The musicians were the entertainers at the wedding, and in various bands they wandered around that pleasant spot, some of them dancing, others singing, and still others playing the variety of aforementioned instruments. In fact, it seemed that in the meadow joy was dancing and happiness leaping.

Many other people were busy raising platforms where, on the following day, plays and dances could be comfortably viewed when they were performed in that place dedicated to solemnizing the marriage of rich Camacho and the funeral rites of Basilio. Don Quixote did not want to enter the village, though both the peasant and the bachelor asked him to, but he gave as an excuse, which seemed more than sufficient to him, that it was the custom of knights errant to sleep in fields and forests rather than in towns, even under gilded ceilings; and saying this, he went a little way off the road, much against the will of Sancho, who remembered the fine accommodations he had enjoyed in the castle or house of Don Diego.

CHAPTER XX

Which recounts the wedding of rich Camacho, as well as what befell poor Basilio

No sooner had fair-complexioned dawn allowed bright Phoebus, with the ardor of his burning rays, to dry the liquid pearls of her golden tresses, than Don Quixote, shaking idleness from his limbs, rose to his feet and called to his squire, Sancho, who was still snoring; and Don Quixote saw this, and before he woke him he said:

"O thou, more fortunate than all those who live on the face of the earth, for thou dost not envy nor art thou envied, and thou sleepest with a tranquil spirit, and thou art not pursued by enchanters, nor art thou alarmed by enchantments! Thou sleepest, I say it again and shall say it a hundred times more, without jealousy of thy lady keeping thee continually awake, nor thoughts of how to pay the debts thou owest, nor what thou must do to feed thyself and thy small, anguished family for another day. Ambition doth not disturb thee, nor doth the vain pomp of the world trouble thee, for the limits of thy desires extendeth not beyond caring for thy donkey; thou hast placed care for thine own person on my shoulders, a weight and a burden that nature and custom hath given to masters. The servant sleepeth, and the master standeth watch, thinking of how he may sustain him, and improve him, and grant him favors. The anguish of seeing the sky turning to bronze and not giving succor to the earth with needed dew doth not afflict the servant but the master, who must sustain in barrenness and hunger the one who served in fertility and plenty."

Sancho did not respond to any of this because he was asleep, and he would not have awakened very quickly if Don Quixote, with the blunt end of his lance, had not brought him back to consciousness. He awoke, finally, sleepy and lazy, and turning his head in every direction, he said:

"Coming from the direction of that bower, if I'm not mistaken, there's an aroma that smells much more like a roasted side of bacon than reeds and thyme: by my faith, weddings that begin with smells like this must be plentiful and generous."

"Enough, you glutton," said Don Quixote. "Come, we shall go to this ceremony to see what the scorned Basilio will do."

"No matter what he does, what he'd like," responded Sancho, "is not to be poor and to marry Quiteria. He doesn't have a *cuarto* and he wants to rise up above the clouds? By my faith, Señor, I think a poor man should be content with whatever he finds and not go asking for the moon. I bet an arm that Camacho can bury Basilio in *reales*, and if that's true, as it must be, Quiteria would be a fool to give up the fine gifts and jewels that Camacho must have given her already, and still can give her, for the way Basilio hurls the bar and fences. A good throw and some nice swordplay won't get you a half-liter of wine at the tavern. Talents and skills that can't be sold are fine for Count Dirlos,[1] but

---

1. A figure who appears in traditional ballads.

when those talents fall to somebody who has good money, then that's the life I'd like to have. With a good foundation you can build a good building, and the best foundation and groundwork in the world is money."

"For the love of God, Sancho," said Don Quixote, "that's enough of your harangue. I really believe that if you were allowed to go on with the ones you are constantly beginning, you would not have time to eat or sleep: you would spend all of it talking."

"If your grace had a good memory," replied Sancho, "you'd remember the provisions of our agreement before we left home this last time: one of them was that you'd have to let me talk all I wanted as long as I didn't say anything against my neighbor or your grace's authority, and so far it seems to me I haven't disobeyed that provision."

"I do not remember, Sancho," responded Don Quixote, "any such provision, and since that is so, I want you to be quiet and come along now; the instruments we heard last night again gladden the valleys, and no doubt the wedding will be celebrated in the coolness of the morning, not in the heat of the afternoon."

Sancho did as his master commanded and placed the saddle on Rocinante and the packsaddle on the donkey; the two men mounted, and at an unhurried pace, they rode under the bower.

The first thing that appeared before Sancho's eyes was an entire steer on a roasting spit made of an entire elm; and in the fire where it was to roast, a fair-size mountain of wood was burning, and six pots that were placed around the fire were not made in the common mold of other pots, because these were six huge cauldrons, each one large enough to hold the contents of an entire slaughterhouse: they contained and enclosed entire sheep, which sank out of view as if they were doves; the hares without their skins and the chickens without their feathers that were hanging from the trees, waiting to be buried in the cauldrons, were without number; the various kinds of fowl and game hanging from the trees to cool in the breeze were infinite.

Sancho counted more than sixty wineskins, each one holding more than two *arrobas*,[2] and all of them filled, as was subsequently proven, with excellent wines; there were also mounds of snowy white loaves of bread, heaped up like piles of wheat on the threshing floor; cheeses,

---

2. As indicated earlier, an *arroba* is a dry weight of twenty-five pounds and a variable liquid measure of 2.6 to 3.6 gallons.

crisscrossed like bricks, formed a wall; and two kettles of oil larger than a dyer's vats were used to fry rounds of dough, which were then removed with two strong paddles and plunged into another kettle filled with honey that stood nearby.

The cooks, male and female, numbered more than fifty, all of them devoted, diligent, and contented. Twelve small, tender suckling pigs were sewn into the expanded belly of the steer to give it flavor and make it tender. The various spices seemed to have been bought not by the pound but by the *arroba*, and all of them were clearly visible in a large chest. In short, the provisions for the wedding were rustic, but so abundant they could have fed an army.

Sancho Panza observed everything, and contemplated everything, and felt affection for everything. First, his desire was captivated and conquered by the cauldrons, from which he gladly would have filled a medium-size pot; then his affections were won over by the wineskins; finally, the fruits of the skillet, if one could call the big-bellied kettles skillets; and so, when he could bear it no longer, and it was not in his power to do anything else, he approached one of the diligent cooks and in courteous and hungry terms asked to be allowed to dip a crust of bread into one of those cauldrons. To which the cook responded:

"Brother, thanks to rich Camacho, hunger has no jurisdiction today. Dismount and see if you can find a ladle, and skim off a chicken or two, and hearty appetite to you."

"I don't see one," responded Sancho.

"Wait," said the cook. "Lord save me, but what a squeamish, fussy fellow you must be!"

And having said this, he seized a pot and dipped it into one of the cauldrons, then took out three chickens and two geese and said to Sancho:

"Eat, my friend, and break your fast with these skimmings until it's time to eat."

"I don't have anything to put them in," responded Sancho.

"Then take everything, the pot and all," said the cook, "for the riches and the happiness of Camacho will overlook that."

While Sancho was engaged in these matters, Don Quixote watched as some twelve farmers, dressed in their best holiday clothes and mounted on twelve beautiful mares decked out in rich and colorful rustic trappings, with a good number of bells on the breast straps of their harnesses, rode under the bower; in an orderly troop they galloped not once but many times around the meadow, joyfully crying and shouting:

"Long live Camacho and Quiteria! He's as rich as she's fair, and she's the fairest in the world!"

Hearing which, Don Quixote said to himself:

"It certainly seems that they have not seen my Dulcinea of Toboso, for if they had, they would restrain their praises of Quiteria."

A short while later, many different groups of dancers began to come under the bower, among them one performing a sword dance with twenty-four young men of gallant and spirited appearance, all dressed in thin white linen and wearing head scarves of fine, multicolored silk; one of the men mounted on mares asked their leader, an agile youth, if any of the dancers had been hurt.

"So far, thank God, nobody's been hurt: we're all fine."

And then he began to wind his way among his companions, twisting and turning with so much skill that although Don Quixote had seen many such dances, he had never seen one as good as this.

He also liked another group that came in, composed of beautiful young maidens, none younger than fourteen, none older than eighteen, all dressed in fine green cloth, their hair partly braided and partly hanging loose, and so blond it could compete with the rays of the sun; and in their hair they wore garlands made of jasmine, roses, amaranth, and honeysuckle. They were led by a venerable old man and an ancient matron, more agile and nimble than their years would lead one to expect. Their music was played by a Zamoran bagpipe, and the maidens, with modesty in their eyes and on their faces, and with agility in their feet, showed themselves to be the best dancers in the world.

Behind them came another troop in an ingenious dance, the kind that is called a spoken dance. It consisted of eight nymphs, divided into two lines: at the head of one line was the god Cupid, and at the head of the other, Interest, the former adorned with wings, a bow, and a quiver of arrows, the latter dressed in richly colored silks and gold. The nymphs who followed Love had their names, written on white parchment in large letters, on their backs. *Poetry* was the name of the first, *Discretion* the name of the second, the third was called *Good Lineage*, and the fourth *Valor*. Those who followed Interest were identified in the same fashion: *Liberality* was the name of the first, *Gifts* the name of the second, the third was called *Treasure*, and the fourth

Peaceful Ownership. At the head of all of them came a wooden castle, drawn by four savages dressed in ivy and green-dyed hemp and looking so natural they almost frightened Sancho. On the main facade of the castle, and on all four of its sides, was written *The Castle of Caution*. Their music was played on the timbrel and flute by four skilled musicians.

Cupid began the dance, and having completed two figures, he raised his eyes and shot an arrow at a maiden standing on the parapets of the castle, saying:

> I am a god most powerful
> in the air and on the land
> and the wide, wind-driven sea,
> and in the fiery pit
> and the fearful hell it contains.
> Fear's something I've never known;
> whatever I wish I can do,
> though it may well be impossible;
> in the realm of the possible I rule,
> and give and take away at will.

He finished the strophe, shot an arrow over the castle, and returned to his place. Then Interest came forward and executed another two figures; the timbrels fell silent, and he said:

> I am mightier than Love,
> though it is Love who guides me;
> I am of the finest stock,
> the best known and the noblest,
> that heaven breeds on earth.
> I am Interest, and for my sake
> few men do the deeds they should,
> though deeds *sans* me are miracles;
> I swear my devotion to you
> forever, world without end, amen.

Interest stepped back, Poetry came forward, and after performing her figures as the others had, she turned her eyes toward the maiden of the castle and said:

        In conceits most sweet and high,
    noble, solemn, and discreet,
    gentle Poetry, my lady,
    sends her soul to you in lines
    found in a thousand new sonnets.
    If my pleas and constant prayers
    do not weary you, your fortune,
    envied by so many damsels,
    will be raised on high by me,
    to the Circle of the Moon.

Poetry moved away, and from the side where Interest stood, Liberality stepped forward, performed her figures, and said:

        Liberality is the name
    of giving that shuns th' extremes
    of either prodigality
    or its opposite, th' unwilling
    hand of a miserly soul.
    But, in order to praise you,
    today I shall be prodigal,
    and though a vice, it is honored
    from a heart that is enamored,
    and in giving shows its love.

   In this fashion all the dancers in the two bands came forward and then withdrew, and each one performed her figures and said her verses, some of them elegant and some ridiculous, but Don Quixote could retain in his memory—which was very good—only those that have been cited; then all the dancers mingled, forming pairs and then separating with gentle grace and ease, and when Love passed in front of the castle, he shot his arrows into the air, but Interest broke gilded money boxes against it.

   Finally, after having danced for some time, Interest took out a large bag made of the skin of a big Roman cat,[3] which seemed to be full of coins, and threw it at the castle, and at the impact the boards fell apart and collapsed, leaving the maiden exposed and without any defenses. Interest approached with the dancers in his group, put a long gold chain

---

3. Money bags were made of cat skin; Roman cats had a black-and-gray-striped fur.

around her neck, and pretended to seize and subdue her and make her his prisoner; when Love and his companions saw this, they moved to free her, and all these displays were made to the sound of the timbrels as they danced and twirled in harmony. The savages imposed peace when they quickly set up and put together again the boards of the castle, and the maiden went back inside, concluding the dance that had been watched with great pleasure by the spectators.

Don Quixote asked one of the nymphs who had composed and directed it. She responded that it was a cleric, a beneficiary from the village who had a great talent for these kinds of inventions.

"I would wager," said Don Quixote, "that this beneficiary or bachelor must be more of a friend to Camacho than to Basilio, and that he is more inclined to writing satires than to saying his prayers at vespers. How well he has incorporated into the dance Basilio's skills and Camacho's wealth!"

Sancho Panza, who heard everything, said:

"My cock's king;[4] I'm on Camacho's side."

"In short," said Don Quixote, "it seems clear, Sancho, that you are a peasant, the kind who shouts, 'Long live whoever wins!' "

"I don't know what kind I am," responded Sancho, "but I do know that I'd never get such fine skimmings from Basilio's pots as I've gotten from Camacho's."

And he showed him the pot full of geese and chickens, and seizing one of them, he began to eat with great verve and enthusiasm, saying:

"To hell with Basilio's talents! You're worth what you have, and what you have is what you're worth. There are only two lineages in the world, as my grandmother used to say, and that's the haves and the have-nots, though she was on the side of having; nowadays, Señor Don Quixote, wealth is better than wisdom: an ass covered in gold seems better than a saddled horse. And so I say again that I'm on the side of Camacho, whose pots are overflowing with geese and chickens, hares and rabbits, while Basilio's, if they ever show up, and even if they don't, won't hold anything but watered wine."

"Have you finished your harangue, Sancho?" said Don Quixote.

"I must have," responded Sancho, "because I see that your grace is bothered by it; if you hadn't cut this one short, I could have gone on for another three days."

4. A phrase used to indicate which contender the speaker favored in a cockfight or in any other kind of contest.

"May it please God, Sancho," replied Don Quixote, "that I see you mute before I die."

"At the rate we're going," responded Sancho, "before your grace dies I'll be chewing on mud, and then maybe I'll be so mute I won't say a word till the end of the world or, at least, until Judgment Day."

"Oh, Sancho, even if that should happen," responded Don Quixote, "your silence will never match all that you have said, are saying, and will say in your lifetime! Furthermore, it seems likely in the natural course of events that the day of my death will arrive before yours, and so I think I shall never see you mute, not even when you are drinking, or sleeping, which is what I earnestly desire."

"By my faith, Señor," responded Sancho, "you mustn't trust in the fleshless woman, I mean Death, who devours lamb as well as mutton; I've heard our priest say that she tramples the high towers of kings as well as the humble huts of the poor. This lady is more powerful than finicky; nothing disgusts her, she eats everything, and she does everything, and she crams her pack with all kinds and ages and ranks of people. She's not a reaper who takes naps; she reaps constantly and cuts the dry grass along with the green, and she doesn't seem to chew her food but wolfs it down and swallows everything that's put in front of her, because she's as hungry as a dog and is never satisfied; and though she has no belly, it's clear that she has dropsy and is always thirsty and ready to drink down the lives of everyone living, like somebody drinking a pitcher of cold water."

"Enough, Sancho," said Don Quixote at this point. "Stop now before you fall, for the truth is that what you have said about death, in your rustic terms, is what a good preacher might say. I tell you, Sancho, with your natural wit and intelligence, you could mount a pulpit and go around preaching some very nice things."

"Being a good preacher means living a good life," responded Sancho, "and I don't know any other theologies."

"You do not need them," said Don Quixote, "but I cannot understand or comprehend how, since the beginning of wisdom is the fear of God, you, who fear a lizard more than you fear Him, can know so much."

"Señor, your grace should pass judgment on your chivalries," responded Sancho, "and not start judging other people's fear or bravery, because I fear God as much as the next man. And your grace should let me eat up these skimmings; all the rest is idle words, and we'll have to account for those in the next world."

And saying this, he resumed the assault on his pot with so much gusto that he awoke the appetite of Don Quixote, who no doubt would have helped him if he had not been hindered by what must be recounted below.

CHAPTER XXI

Which continues the account of the wedding of Camacho, along with other agreeable events

While Don Quixote and Sancho were engaged in the conversation described in the previous chapter, loud shouts and a great noise were heard from the men on mares, for with a huge outcry they galloped to receive the bride and groom, who were arriving in the midst of a thousand different kinds of musical instruments and inventions, accompanied by the priest, and their families, and the most distinguished people from the neighboring villages, all of them dressed in their finest clothes. As soon as Sancho saw the bride, he said:

"By my faith, she isn't dressed like a peasant girl but like an elegant lady. By God, as far as I can tell, the medallions[1] she's supposed to be wearing are made of fine coral, and her green cloth from Cuenca is thirty-pile velvet![2] And are the edgings strips of linen? I'd swear they're made of satin! And then, just look at her hands adorned with jet rings! Damn me if they're not rings of gold, and really good gold, and set with pearl as white as curds, each one worth an eye at least. And damn me again for a whoreson, but what hair! If it's not a wig, I've never seen hair longer or blonder in my whole life! No, nobody can say anything about her grace and form except to compare her to a swaying palm tree loaded down with dates, which is just what the jewels look

1. When they married, peasant women usually wore a medallion with religious images on it.

2. Sancho exaggerates to indicate the luxuriousness of the cloth: the warp of velvet normally was two-and-a-half pile.

like hanging from her hair and throat! I swear she's a fine, rosy-cheeked girl who can pass through the banks of Flanders."[3]

Don Quixote laughed at Sancho Panza's rustic praise, though it seemed to him that aside from his lady Dulcinea of Toboso, he had never seen a more beautiful woman. Fair Quiteria seemed somewhat pale, and it must have been because of the sleepless night that brides always experience as they prepare for their wedding on the following day. The wedding party was approaching a stage on one side of the meadow, adorned with carpets and bouquets of flowers, where the marriage would take place and from which they would watch the dances and dramatic inventions, and as they reached this spot, they heard shouts behind them, and one voice cried out, saying:

"Wait a little, you who are as thoughtless as you are hasty."

At these shouts and words, everyone turned around and saw that the one who had called out was a man dressed, apparently, in a black cassock decorated with fiery red strips of cloth. He was crowned—as they later saw—with a wreath of funereal cypress, and in his hands he held a large staff. As he came closer, everyone recognized the gallant Basilio, and everyone was in suspense, waiting to see the outcome of his shouts and his words and fearing the worst from his appearing at that time.

At last he stopped, tired and breathless, before the bride and groom and thrust his staff, which had a steel tip at one end, into the ground; his color changed, he fixed his eyes on Quiteria, and in a hoarse, trembling voice he said:

"You know very well, O forgetful Quiteria, that according to the holy laws which we profess, as long as I am alive you cannot take a husband; and you are not unaware that, as I waited for time and my diligence to improve my fortune, I have not failed to maintain the decorum that your honor demanded; but you, turning your back on all the obligations you owe to my honest desires, wish to make another the lord and master of what is mine, for his riches bring him not only good fortune but even greater happiness. And so, to fill his cup of joy to the brim, not because I think he deserves it but because heaven wishes to grant it to him, I, with my own hands, will take down the obstacle or impediment that may hin-

3. Martín de Riquer explains the reference as follows: Sancho's wordplay alludes to at least three different meanings for the phrase. The first refers to shifting sand banks, making the phrase equivalent to "passing safely between Scylla and Charybdis." The second alludes to the great Flemish banking houses. The third suggests the banks, or benches, made of a wood called Flanders pine, which the poor used as beds in central and southern Spain. Sancho, then, is saying that Quiteria is beautiful enough to pass through any danger, that she is going to marry a very wealthy man, and that she will soon come to her nuptial bed.

der him by removing myself from the scene. Long live rich Camacho, and with the thankless Quiteria may he live many long and happy years, and death, death to poor Basilio, whose poverty cut the wings of his contentment and sent him to the grave!"

And saying this, he seized the staff that he had thrust into the ground, and leaving half of it in the earth, he showed that it served as a sheath for a medium-size sword that was hidden inside; and after placing what could be called the hilt in the ground, with swift agility and resolute purpose he threw himself on it, and in a moment the bloody tip emerged from his back, along with half the steel blade, and the unhappy man lay on the ground, bathed in his own blood and run through by his own weapon.

His friends hurried over to help him, grief-stricken at his misery and his pitiable misfortune; leaving Rocinante, Don Quixote hurried to help him, and took him in his arms, and discovered that he had not yet expired. Some wished to remove the sword, but the priest, who was present, thought it should not be withdrawn until he had heard his confession, because as soon as it was removed he would die. But Basilio began to revive, and in a faint, sorrowful voice, he said:

"If you should wish, O cruel Quiteria, to give me your hand in marriage in my final dying moment, then I think my temerity might find forgiveness, for with it I achieved the good of being yours."

When the priest heard this, he told him to attend to the well-being of his soul rather than to the pleasures of his body and to beg God very sincerely to pardon his sins and his act of despair. To which Basilio replied that under no circumstances would he make his confession until Quiteria gave him her hand in marriage: that joy would strengthen his will and give him the courage to confess.

Don Quixote, hearing the request of the wounded man, said in a loud voice that Basilio was asking for something very fair and reasonable and, moreover, very easy to do, and that Señor Camacho would be just as honored receiving Señora Quiteria as the widow of the valiant Basilio as if he had received her from her father's side:

"Here only one vow will be made, and its only effect will be the saying of it, for the nuptial bed of this marriage will be the grave."

Camacho heard all of this, and all of this confused and baffled him and he did not know what to do or say, but the voices of Basilio's friends were so clamorous, asking him to consent to Quiteria's giving her hand to Basilio so that his soul would not be condemned by leaving this life in despair, that he was moved, perhaps even forced, to say that if Quiteria wished to do so, then he was content, for it meant delaying only for a moment the fulfillment of his desires.

Then they all turned to Quiteria, and some with pleas, and others with tears, and still others with persuasive arguments, urged her to give her hand to poor Basilio; she, as hard as marble and as motionless as a statue, showed that she could not and would not and did not wish to say a word, and she would not have responded at all if the priest had not told her to decide quickly what she was going to do, because Basilio's soul was between his teeth, and there was no time for her to be irresolute or indecisive.

Then fair Quiteria, without saying a word, but perturbed and apparently sad and sorrowful, went toward Basilio, whose eyes were turned up and whose breath was quick and hurried, and who was whispering to himself the name of Quiteria, giving every indication that he would die like a heathen and not like a Christian. Finally, when she reached him, Quiteria fell to her knees and signaled for his hand, not asking for it with words. Basilio rolled down his eyes, and looking at her intently, he said:

"O, Quiteria, you have become merciful at a time when your mercy will serve as the knife that finally ends my life, for I no longer have the strength to bear the glory you have given me by choosing me for your own, or to hold back the pain that so quickly covers my eyes with the fearful shadow of death! What I implore, O my fatal star, is that you not ask for my hand nor give me yours out of a sense of duty, or to deceive me again, but because you confess and admit that of your own free will you give and present it to me as your legitimate husband, for it is not right that you deceive me at a moment like this, or use any pretense with one who has been so truthful with you."

As he said these words he fainted, and all those present thought that each time he fainted his soul would be carried away. Quiteria, filled with modesty and embarrassment, took Basilio's right hand in her own and said:

"No power is strong enough to turn my will, and so, with the freest will I have, I give you my hand as your legitimate wife, and I receive yours, if you give it to me of your own free will, unclouded and unchanged by the calamity your hasty action has brought you to."

"I do," responded Basilio, "not clouded, not confused, but with the clear understanding it has pleased heaven to give to me, and so I give myself and surrender myself to you to be your husband."

"And I give myself to be your wife," responded Quiteria, "whether you live for many long years or are taken now from my arms and carried to your grave."

"For someone who's so badly wounded," said Sancho Panza, "this young man certainly talks a lot; they should make him stop his courting and pay attention to his soul, which in my opinion is more on his tongue than between his teeth."

Then, as Basilio and Quiteria held hands, the priest, tenderhearted and weeping, gave them his blessing and asked heaven to rest the soul of the newly wed husband, who, as soon as he had received the blessing, leaped with great agility to his feet and with remarkable ease pulled out the sword that had been sheathed in his body.

All the onlookers were astonished, and some of them, more simple-minded than inquisitive, began to shout:

"A miracle, a miracle!"

But Basilio replied:

"Not 'a miracle, a miracle,' but ingenuity, ingenuity!"

The priest, confused and bewildered, hurried to touch the wound with both hands, and he discovered that the blade had passed not through the flesh and ribs of Basilio, but through a hollow metal tube filled with blood, which he had carefully placed there; as it was later learned, he had prepared the blood so it would not congeal.

In short, the priest, Camacho, and all the bystanders considered themselves fooled and deceived. The bride showed no signs of regretting the trick; rather, when she heard someone say that the wedding, because it had been deceitful, could not be valid, she said that she confirmed it again; everyone concluded that she had known about and consented to the ruse, and this so angered Camacho and his companions that they took their vengeance into their own hands, unsheathed many swords, and attacked Basilio, and in an instant almost as many swords were drawn in his defense. And at their head rode Don Quixote, who, with his lance at the ready and his shield on his arm, forced everyone to make way for him. Sancho, who never took pleasure or solace from such exploits, took refuge among the cauldrons where he had made his happy skimmings, for he thought the place was sacred and had to be respected. Don Quixote, in a great voice, shouted:

"Hold, Señores, hold, for it is not right to take revenge for the offenses that love commits; you should know that love and war are the same, and just as in war it is legitimate and customary to make use of tricks and stratagems to conquer the enemy, so in the contests and rivalries of love the lies and falsehoods used to achieve a desired end are considered fair, as long as they do not discredit or dishonor the beloved. Quiteria belonged to Basilio and Basilio to Quiteria, by the just and favorable disposition of heaven. Camacho is rich, and can buy whenever, and wherever, and whatever he desires. Basilio has only this sheep, and no man, no matter how powerful, can take her from him; those whom God has joined let no man put asunder, and if any wishes to try, he will first have to pass by the point of this lance."

And saying this, he brandished his lance with so much strength and dexterity that he filled all who did not know him with fear; Quiteria's disdain was fixed so firmly in Camacho's imagination that in an instant he erased her from his memory, and so he was persuaded by the arguments of the priest, a prudent, well-intentioned man, and he and his supporters were calmed and appeased; and to indicate this they returned their swords to their sheathes, blaming Quiteria's complaisance more than Basilio's ingenuity, and Camacho reasoned that if Quiteria truly loved Basilio as a maiden, she would also love him as a married woman, and that he ought to give thanks to heaven for taking her away instead of giving her to him.

Since Camacho and his followers were consoled and appeased, all of Basilio's supporters became calm, and rich Camacho, in order to show that he did not resent the trick or consider it of any importance, decided that the celebration should go on as if he really had been married; but Basilio and his wife and their followers did not wish to attend, and so they went to Basilio's village, for poor men who are virtuous and intelligent can also have people who follow, honor, and assist them, just as the wealthy have those who flatter and accompany them.

They took Don Quixote with them, deeming him a man of great valor and courage. Only Sancho's soul was full of gloom when he found it impossible to stay for Camacho's splendid food and celebrations, which would go on until nightfall; and so, wretched and sad, he followed his master, who was riding away with Basilio's party, and left behind the cauldrons of Egypt, though he carried them in his heart, and his almost entirely consumed and eaten skimmings, which he carried in the pot, represented for him the glory and abundance of the good he was losing; and so, grieving and pensive, though not hungry, and without dismounting the donkey, he followed in Rocinante's footsteps.

CHAPTER XXII

Which recounts the great adventure of the Cave of Montesinos that lies in the heart of La Mancha, which was successfully concluded by the valiant Don Quixote of La Mancha

Great and many were the gifts presented to Don Quixote by the newly-weds, who were indebted to him for the actions he had taken in defense of their cause; they deemed his intelligence equal to his courage, considering him a Cid in arms and a Cicero in eloquence. Our good Sancho had a wonderful time for three days at the couple's expense; from them he learned that the scheme to feign a wound had not been communicated to fair Quiteria but was Basilio's idea; he had hoped to achieve with it exactly what occurred; it is certainly true that he confessed to sharing part of his thinking with some of his friends, so that when it was necessary they would favor his plan and support his deception.

"They cannot and should not be called deceptions," said Don Quixote, "since their purpose was virtuous."

And two lovers marrying was a most excellent purpose, but he warned that the greatest adversary love has is hunger and continual need, because love is all joy, happiness, and contentment, especially when the lover is in possession of the beloved, and its declared enemies are want and poverty; he was saying all of this so that Señor Basilio would stop practicing the skills he knew, for although they brought him fame, they did not bring him money, and attend to acquiring wealth by licit and industrious means, which the prudent and diligent never lack.

"The honorable poor man, if a poor man can be honorable, possesses a jewel when he has a beautiful wife, and when that is taken from him, his honor is taken away and destroyed. The beautiful, honorable woman whose husband is poor deserves to be crowned with laurels and palms of victory and triumph. Beauty, in and of itself, attracts the desires of all who look upon it and recognize it, and royal eagles and high-flying birds swoop down for it as if it were savory bait, but if this beauty is joined to need and want, it is also attacked by crows, kites, and other birds of prey, and the woman who stands firm through so many encounters surely deserves to be called her husband's crown. Look, my clever friend Basilio," added Don Quixote, "it was believed by some wise man or other that there was only one virtuous woman in the entire world, and he advised each man to think and believe that the one virtuous woman was his wife, and in this way he would live contentedly. I am not married, and so far it has not even crossed my mind to marry, and yet I should dare to counsel any man who asks my advice how to find the woman he wishes to marry. First, I should advise him to consider her reputation more than her wealth, because the virtuous woman does not achieve a good reputation simply by being good, but by appearing to be good; women's honor is damaged more by public liberties and acts of boldness than by secret iniquities. If you bring a virtuous woman to your house, it will be easy to maintain and even improve that virtue, but if she is immoral, it will be a formidable task to change her, for it is not very likely that she will pass from one extreme to another. I do not say it is impossible, but I consider it extremely difficult."

Sancho heard this, and to himself he said:

"This master of mine, when I talk about things of pith and substance, usually says that I could take a pulpit in hand and go through the world preaching fine sermons; and I say of him that when he begins to string together judgments and to give advice, he could not only take a pulpit in hand but hang two on each finger, and go through the squares and say exactly the right thing. What a devil of a knight errant you are, and what a lot of things you know! I thought in my heart that he would only know things that had to do with his chivalry, but there's nothing he doesn't pick at or poke his spoon into."

Sancho was mumbling this, and his master heard him and asked:

"What are you mumbling about, Sancho?"

"I'm not saying anything, and I'm not mumbling anything," responded Sancho. "I was just saying to myself that I wish I'd heard what your grace said here before I married; maybe then I'd be saying now: 'The ox who's free can lick where he pleases.' "[1]

---

1. A proverb that extols the joys of liberty.

"Is your Teresa so bad, Sancho?" said Don Quixote.

"She's not very bad," responded Sancho, "but she's not very good, either; at least, she's not as good as I'd like."

"It is wrong of you, Sancho," said Don Quixote, "to speak ill of your wife, who is, in fact, the mother of your children."

"We don't owe each other a thing," responded Sancho, "because she speaks ill of me too whenever she feels like it, especially when she's jealous, and then not even Satan himself can bear her."

In short, they spent three days with the newlyweds and were regaled and entertained as if they were kings. Don Quixote asked the skilled licentiate[2] to give him a guide who would lead him to the Cave of Montesinos,[3] because he had a great desire to enter it and see with his own eyes if the marvels told about it throughout the surrounding area were true. The licentiate said that he would give him one of his cousins, who was a famous student and very fond of reading novels of chivalry, and would be very happy to bring him to the mouth of the cave and show him the Lakes of Ruidera, famous in all of La Mancha, and even in all of Spain; and he said that he would find him pleasant company because he was a lad who knew how to write books that would be printed and how to dedicate them to princes. At last, the cousin arrived on a pregnant donkey, its packsaddle covered by a small striped rug or brightly colored burlap. Sancho saddled Rocinante, readied the donkey, and provisioned his saddlebags that then joined the cousin's, which were also well-stocked, and after commending themselves to God and taking their leave of everyone, they set out on their journey, traveling in the direction of the famous Cave of Montesinos.

On the road, Don Quixote questioned the cousin regarding the character and nature of his activities, his profession, and his studies, to which he responded that his profession was being a humanist, his activities and studies, composing books for publishing, all of them very beneficial and no less diverting for the nation; one was entitled *On Liveries*, in which he depicts seven hundred and three liveries with their colors, devices, and emblems, from which courtier knights could pick and choose the ones they liked for festivals and celebrations and would not have to go begging them from anybody or overtaxing their brains,

2. The reference is to the expert swordsman whom they met on the road at the beginning of chapter XIX and who obviously accompanied them throughout the episode of Camacho's wedding.

3. The cave is near one of the Lakes of Ruidera, the source of the Guadiana River.

as they say, in order to find ones that matched their desires and intentions.

"Because I give to the jealous, the disdained, the forgotten, and the absent the liveries that suit them best and fit them perfectly. I also have another book that I intend to call *Metamorphoses, or the Spanish Ovid,* a new and rare invention, because in it, in a parodic imitation of Ovid, I describe who La Giralda of Sevilla was, and the Angel of the Magdalena,[4] and the Vecinguerra Drainpipe in Córdoba,[5] who the Bulls of Guisando, and the Sierra Morena, and the fountains of Leganitos and Lavapiés, in Madrid, not forgetting the fountains of El Piojo and El Caño Dorado, and the fountain of La Priora,[6] and each has its allegories, metaphors, and transformations that delight, astonish, and instruct, all at the same time. I have another book that I call *Supplement to Virgilio Polidoro,*[7] which deals with the invention of things and is a work of great erudition and scholarship because the things of substance that Polidoro omitted I investigate and write about in an elegant style. Virgilio forgot to tell us who was the first man in the world to have a cold, and the first who used ointments to cure himself of the French disease;[8] I elucidate everything very precisely, citing more than twenty-five authors, and so your grace can see that I have done good work and that the book will be very useful to everyone."

Sancho, who had been very attentive during the cousin's narration, said:

"Tell me, Señor, and may God give you good luck in the printing of your books, would you know, and you must know, because you know everything, but could you tell me who the first man was to scratch his head? To my mind it must have been our father Adam."

"Yes, it must have been," responded the cousin, "because Adam undoubtedly had a head and hair, and this being the case, and Adam being the first man in the world, at some time he must have scratched his head."

---

4. The weathervane on the tower of the Church of the Magdalena in Salamanca was in the shape of an angel.

5. A pipe that carried Córdoba's sewage into the Guadalquivir River.

6. The first two were in the Prado de San Jerónimo and the third in the Plaza de Oriente, in Madrid.

7. The book of the Italian humanist Polidoro Vergilio (1470–1550), *De inventoribus rerum,* which deals with the origin of inventions, was widely read; it was translated into Spanish in 1550.

8. A Spanish term for syphilis.

"I think so, too," responded Sancho, "but now tell me, who was the first acrobat in the world?"

"The truth is, my friend," responded the cousin, "that is something I cannot determine until I study it, and I shall study it as soon as I return to my books, and I shall satisfy your curiosity when next we meet, for this cannot be the last time."

"Well, look, Señor," replied Sancho, "don't go to any trouble, for I just found the answer to the question I asked. Let me say that the first acrobat in the world was Lucifer, when he was tossed or thrown out of heaven and went tumbling down into the pit."

"You're right, my friend," said the cousin.

And Don Quixote said:

"That question and answer are not yours, Sancho; you heard someone else say them."

"Be quiet, Señor," replied Sancho, "for by my faith, if I start asking and answering, I won't finish until tomorrow. As for asking fool questions and giving nonsensical answers, I don't need to go around asking my neighbors for help."

"You have said more, Sancho, than you realize," said Don Quixote, "for there are some who exhaust themselves learning and investigating things that, once learned and investigated, do not matter in the slightest to the understanding or the memory."

The day was spent in this agreeable conversation, and others like it, and at night they stayed in a small village which, the cousin told Don Quixote, was no more than two leagues from the Cave of Montesinos, and if he was determined to go inside, he would need to have ropes so that he could tie them around himself and lower himself into its depths.

Don Quixote said that even if the cave went down into the abyss, he had to see where it ended, and so they bought almost a hundred fathoms of rope, and the next day, at two in the afternoon, they reached the cave, whose mouth is spacious and wide but filled with brambles and box thorn, wild fig trees and briars, so thick and intertwined that they completely cover and hide it. As soon as they saw it, the cousin, Sancho, and Don Quixote dismounted, and the first two tied him very securely with the ropes, and while they were wrapping them around him and tightening them, Sancho said:

"Señor, your grace should think about what you're doing: you don't want to be buried alive, or be in a place where you're like a jar that's hung down a well to cool. Oh yes, it isn't your grace's concern or business to go exploring this place that must be worse than a dungeon."

"Tie the rope and be quiet," responded Don Quixote, "for an undertaking like this, Sancho my friend, was intended only for me."[9]

And then their guide said:

"I beg your grace, Señor Don Quixote, that you observe carefully and scrutinize with a thousand eyes what you find inside: perhaps there are things I can put in my book *Transformations*."

"The tambourine's in just the right hands,"[10] responded Sancho Panza.

This being said, and Don Quixote's ropes having been secured—they were attached not to his armor, but to the doublet he wore underneath—Don Quixote said:

"It was an oversight not to have bought a small cowbell to tie next to me on this rope, for its sound would let you know that I was still descending and still alive; but since that is no longer possible, may the hand of God guide me."

And then he kneeled and said a prayer in a quiet voice, asking God to help him and grant him good fortune in this apparently dangerous new adventure, and then he said aloud:

"O lady of my actions and movements, most illustrious and peerless Dulcinea of Toboso! If it is possible that the prayers and supplications of this thy fortunate lover reach thine ears, for the sake of thy extraordinary beauty I implore thee to hear them, for they beg thee only not to deny me thy favor and protection now that I am in such great need of them. I am going to hurl myself, throw myself, and plunge into the abyss I see here before me, so that the world may know that if thou favorest me, nothing is impossible for me to undertake and bring to a happy conclusion."

And saying this, he approached the chasm; he saw that it was not possible to lower himself or make his way to the entrance except by the strength of his arm or the thrusts of his blade, and so he put his hand to his sword and began to slash and cut the thicket at the mouth of the cave; with the clamor and din, an infinite number of huge crows and rooks flew out of it, and there were so many flying so quickly that they knocked Don Quixote to the ground; if he were as much of a soothsayer as he was a Catholic Christian, he would have taken this as a bad omen and refused to go down into such a place.

9. Don Quixote paraphrases the words of a ballad.
10. The phrase means that matters are being handled by someone competent.

At last he stood, and seeing that no more crows or other nocturnal birds such as bats, which had come out along with the crows, were flying about, and with the cousin and Sancho gradually letting out the rope, he began to lower himself down to the bottom of the fearful cavern; and as he entered, Sancho blessed him and made the sign of a thousand crosses over him, saying:

"May God be your guide, and the Peña de Francia,[11] together with the Trinidad de Gaeta,[12] O flower and cream and skimmings of all knights errant! There you go, the bravest in the world, heart of steel, arms of bronze! Again, may God be your guide and bring you back safe and sound and free to the light of this life that you are leaving to bury yourself in the darkness you are looking for!"

The cousin said almost the same prayers and entreaties.

Don Quixote kept calling out for rope, more rope, and they paid it out slowly; and when his cries, which were channeled out of the cave, could no longer be heard, they had already unwound the hundred fathoms of rope, and it seemed to them that they ought to bring Don Quixote up again since they could not give him more rope. But they waited for about half an hour, and at the end of that time they began to pull up the rope, very easily, and with no weight on it at all, which made them imagine that Don Quixote had remained inside, and because he believed this, Sancho began to cry bitterly and to pull very quickly in order to learn the truth; but when there was a little more than eighty fathoms of rope left, they felt a weight, which made them extremely happy. Finally, when there were ten fathoms remaining, they saw Don Quixote clearly and Sancho began to shout to him, saying:

"A very hearty welcome to your grace, Señor; we thought you were going to stay down there and start a family."

But Don Quixote did not say a word, and when they had pulled him all the way out, they saw that his eyes were closed, as if he were sleeping. They laid him on the ground and untied him, and still he did not awaken, but they turned him this way and that, and shook him and moved him so much, that after a fairly long time he regained consciousness, stretching as if he were waking from a deep and profound sleep, and looking around, as if in alarm, he said:

"May God forgive you, friends, for you have taken me away from the

11. A Dominican monastery between Ciudad Rodrigo and Salamanca.
12. A monastery near Naples that is visible from the sea and invoked by mariners.

sweetest life and most pleasant sights that any human being has ever seen or experienced. In truth, now I realize that all the pleasures of this life pass like shadows and dreams, or wither like the flowers in the field. O unfortunate Montesinos! O gravely wounded Durandarte! O luckless Belerma! O weeping Guadiana, and you unhappy daughters of Ruidera, who show in your waters the number of tears shed by your beautiful eyes!"

The cousin and Sancho listened to the words of Don Quixote, who spoke them as if he were tearing them with great sorrow from the very depths of his being. They begged him to explain what he was saying and to tell them what he had seen in that hell.

"You call it hell?" said Don Quixote. "Do not call it that, for it does not deserve the name, as you shall soon see."

He asked them to give him something to eat, for he was very hungry. They spread the cousin's burlap on the green grass, had recourse to the provisions in the saddlebags, and the three of them sat in companionable friendship and ate both dinner and supper at the same time. When the burlap had been cleared, Don Quixote of La Mancha said:

"Let no one get up, my friends, and listen to me carefully."

CHAPTER XXIII

Regarding the remarkable things that the great Don Quixote said he saw in the depths of the Cave of Montesinos, so impossible and extraordinary that this adventure has been considered apocryphal

It must have been four in the afternoon when the sun, hidden by clouds, its light faint and its rays temperate, gave Don Quixote an opportunity free of oppressive heat to recount what he had seen in the Cave of Montesinos to his two illustrious listeners, and he began in the following manner:

"In this dungeon, at a depth of approximately twelve or fourteen *escudos*,[1] on the right-hand side there is a concavity, a space capable of

---

1. A unit of measurement, roughly seven feet, used to determine height or depth.

holding a large wagon with its mules. A small amount of light comes in through openings in the earth's surface. I saw this concavity and space when I was already weary and tired of hanging and being suspended from the rope as I moved through that dark nether region without a fixed and certain route, and so I decided to go into the space and rest a while. I shouted to you, asking that you not let out more rope until I told you to, but you probably did not hear me. I picked up the rope you sent down, made it into a coil or ring, and sat on it, becoming very thoughtful as I considered how I would reach the bottom without anything to support me; and when I was deep in this thought and confusion, suddenly, and without my wishing it, I was overcome by a profound sleep; and when I least expected it, not knowing how or why, I awoke and found myself in the midst of the most beautiful, pleasant, and charming meadow that nature could create or the most discerning human mind imagine. I opened my eyes wide, rubbed them, and saw that I was not sleeping but really was awake; even so, I felt my head and chest to verify whether it was I myself or some false and counterfeit phantom sitting there, but my sense of touch, my feelings, the reasoned discourse I held with myself, verified for me that, there and then, I was the same person I am here and now. Then there appeared before my eyes a royal and sumptuous palace or castle whose walls and ramparts seemed to be made of clear and transparent crystal; two large doors opened, and I saw that through them there emerged and came toward me a venerable ancient dressed in a long hooded cloak of purple baize that trailed after him on the ground; around his shoulders and chest he wore a scholar's sash and hood of green satin,[2] his head was covered by a black Milanese cap,[3] and a snow white beard reached down below his waist; he carried no weapons of any kind, but held a rosary in his hand, the smaller beads larger than medium-sized walnuts, and the larger ones the size of medium-sized ostrich eggs; his bearing, pace, gravity, and proud demeanor, each one taken separately and all of them taken together, filled me with wonder and amazement. He came up to me, and the first thing he did was to embrace me closely, and then he said:

'For many long years, O valiant knight Don Quixote of La Mancha, we who dwell in this enchanted solitude have waited to see thee, so that thou couldst inform the world of what lies contained and hidden in the

2. This was worn by the holders of doctoral degrees.

3. Round caps that were stiffened by metal bands.

deep cave which thou hast entered, called the Cave of Montesinos: a
feat reserved only for thy invincible heart and wondrous courage. Come
thou with me, illustrious knight, for I wish to show thee the marvels hidden within this transparent castle, of which I am warden and perpetual
chief guardian, for I am the same Montesinos after whom the cave is
named.'

When he told me that he was Montesinos,[4] I asked him if the story
told about him in the world up here was true: that with a small dagger he
had cut out of his chest the heart of his great friend Durandarte[5] and carried it to the lady Belerma, as his friend had commanded when he was at
the point of death. He responded that everything people said was true
except for the dagger, because it was not a dagger and it was not small,
but a blade striated on three sides and sharper than an awl."

"That blade," said Sancho, "must have been made by Ramón de
Hoces, the Sevillan."

"I do not know," continued Don Quixote, "but it probably was not
the work of that knifemaker, since Ramón de Hoces lived yesterday, and
the battle at Roncesvalles, where this misfortune occurred, happened
many years ago; this inquiry is of no importance, for it does not disturb or
confound the truth and validity of the history."

"That is true," responded the cousin. "Your grace should continue,
Señor Don Quixote, for I am listening to you with the greatest pleasure
in the world."

"With no less pleasure do I recount it," responded Don Quixote.
"And so I say that the venerable Montesinos led me into the crystalline
palace, where, in a downstairs chamber that was exceptionally cool and
made all of alabaster, there was a marble sepulcher crafted with great
skill, and on it I saw a knight stretched out to his full length, and made
not of bronze, or marble, or jasper, as is usual on other sepulchers, but of
pure flesh and pure bone. His right hand, which seemed somewhat hairy
and sinewy to me, a sign that its owner was very strong, lay over his
heart, and before I could ask anything of Montesinos, who saw me looking with wonder at the figure on the sepulcher, he said:

'This is my friend Durandarte, the flower and model of enamored and

---

4. Montesinos, an important character in the Spanish ballads that recount the legend of Charlemagne, does not appear in French literature; Don Quixote's adventure is based on the tradition that
has Montesinos marrying Rosaflorida, mistress of the castle of Rocafrida that was identified in the
popular imagination with certain ruins near the Cave of Montesinos.

5. Durandarte, a name originally given to the sword of Roland, became a hero of the Spanish
(though not the French) Carolingian ballad tradition. He was the cousin and close friend of Montesinos, whom he asked, before he was killed at Roncesvalles, to carry his heart to his lady.

valiant knights of his time; here he lies, enchanted, as I and many others are enchanted, by Merlin, the French enchanter who was, people say, the son of the devil; and what I believe is that he was not the son of the devil but knew, as they say, a point or two more than the devil. How and why he enchanted us no one knows, but that will be revealed with the passage of time, and is not too far off now, I imagine. What astonishes me is that I know, as well as I know that it is day, that Durandarte ended the days of his life in my arms, and that when he was dead I removed his heart with my own hands; and the truth is that it must have weighed two pounds, because according to naturalists, the man who has a larger heart has greater courage than the man whose heart is small. If this is the case, and if this knight really died, why does he now moan and sigh from time to time, as if he were alive?'

When this was said, the wretched Durandarte gave a great shout and said:

> 'O my cousin Montesinos!
> The last thing I asked of you
> was, when I had breathed my last
> and my soul had flown away,
> to cut my heart out of my breast
> with a dagger or a blade,
> and bear it as an offering
> to my lady, fair Belerma.'[6]

Hearing this, the venerable Montesinos fell to his knees before the doleful knight and, with tears in his eyes, said to him:

'Oh, Señor Durandarte, my beloved cousin, I did what you commanded on the ill-fated day of our defeat: I removed your heart the best I could, not leaving any fragments behind in your chest; I cleaned it with a lace handkerchief; I took it and hurried away to France, having first placed you in the bosom of the earth, shedding so many tears that they were enough to wash away the blood that covered my hands after I had put them inside your body; and furthermore, my dearest cousin, in the first village I came to after I left Roncesvalles, I sprinkled a little salt on your heart so that it would not smell bad and would be, if not fresh, at least dried and salted, in the presence of the lady Belerma, who, along with you, and me, and Guadiana, your squire, and her lady-in-waiting,

---

6. The poem is composed of lines from several ballads that deal with the subject.

Ruidera, and her seven daughters and two nieces, and many more of your friends and acquaintances the wise Merlin has kept here, enchanted, for many years; and although more than five hundred have passed, none of us has died: the only ones missing are Ruidera and her daughters and nieces, who wept so much that Merlin must have taken pity on them, for he transformed them into lakes, and now, in the world of the living and in the province of La Mancha, they are called the Lakes of Ruidera; seven of them belong to the kings of Spain, and the two nieces belong to the knights of a most holy order called St. John.[7] Guadiana, your squire, also lamented your misfortune and was transformed into a river that bears his name; when he reached the surface of the earth and saw the sun in another sky, the grief he felt at leaving you was so great that he descended again to the bowels of the earth; but since it is not possible to resist the natural course of his current, from time to time he emerges and shows himself where the sun and all people may see him. The lakes I have mentioned provide him with their waters, and with these and many others that flow into him, he enters Portugal with magnificence and grandeur. But despite this, wherever he goes he displays his sadness and melancholy, and does not boast of breeding valuable and highly esteemed fish in his waters, but only ones that are coarse and disagreeable, unlike those found in the golden Tajo; and what I am telling you now, my dear cousin, I have told you many times before; and since you do not respond, I imagine that you do not believe me, or do not hear me, and God knows the grief that causes me. Now I wish to give you some news, and if it does not assuage your sorrow, at least it will not increase it in any way. Know that here in your presence—if you open your eyes you will see him—you have that great knight about whom the wise Merlin has made so many prophecies: I mean Don Quixote of La Mancha, who once again, and to greater advantage than in past times, has revived in the present a long-forgotten knight errantry, and through his mediation and by his favor it may be that the spell over us will be broken, for great deeds are reserved for great men.'

'And if this is not the case,' responded the mournful Durandarte in a low, faint voice, 'if this is not the case, dear cousin, I say have patience and shuffle the deck.'

And turning on his side, he resumed his customary silence and did not utter another word. At this point a great weeping and wailing was heard, along with deep moans and anguished sobs; I turned my head and saw

7. The name of one of the lakes is *del Rey* ("of the King"). All the lakes were the property of the crown except for two, which probably belonged to the Knights of St. John of Jerusalem.

through the crystal walls a procession of two lines of beautiful maidens passing through another chamber, all of them dressed in mourning and wearing white turbans on their heads, in the Turkish fashion. At the very end and conclusion of the two lines came a matron, for her gravity made her seem one, also dressed in black, and wearing a white train so lengthy and long it brushed the ground. Her turban was twice as large as the largest of the others; she was beetle-browed and snub-nosed; her mouth was large, but her lips were red; her teeth, which she may have shown, were few in number and crooked, though as white as peeled almonds; in her hands she carried a delicate cloth, and in it, as far as I could tell, was a heart that had been mummified, it looked so dry and shriveled. Montesinos told me that all the people in the procession were servants of Durandarte and Belerma, enchanted along with their master and mistress, and that the last one, who carried the heart in the cloth, was Señora Belerma herself, who along with her maidens walked in that procession four days a week and sang, or rather wept, dirges over the body and wounded heart of his cousin; and if she had seemed rather ugly, and not as beautiful as her fame proclaimed, the cause was the bad nights and worse days she had spent in that enchantment, as one could see in the deep circles under her eyes and her sickly color.

'And her sallow complexion and deep circles arise not from the monthly distress common in women, because for many months, even years, she has not had it nor has it appeared at her portals, but from the sorrow her heart feels for the one she continually holds in her hands, which always renews and brings to mind the affliction of her unfortunate lover; if this were not the case, then the great Dulcinea of Toboso, so celebrated here and in the rest of the world, would barely be her equal in beauty, grace, and charm.'

'Stop right there, Señor Don Montesinos,' I said then. 'Your grace should recount this history in the proper manner, for you know that all comparisons are odious, and there is no reason to compare anyone to anyone else. The peerless Dulcinea of Toboso is who she is, and Señora Belerma is who she is, and who she was, and no more should be said about it.'

To which he responded:

'Señor Don Quixote, may your grace forgive me, for I confess that I erred and misspoke when I said that Señora Dulcinea would barely be the equal of Señora Belerma, for it was enough for me to have realized, by means of I am not certain what conjectures, that your grace is her knight, and I would rather bite my tongue than compare her to anything but heaven itself.'

With this satisfaction given to me by the great Montesinos, my heart recovered from the shock I had received at hearing my lady compared to Belerma."

"What surprises me," said Sancho, "is that your grace didn't jump on the old man and break every bone in his body and pull out his beard until there wasn't a single hair left."

"No, Sancho my friend," responded Don Quixote, "it would not have been right for me to do that, because we are all obliged to have respect for the old, even if they are not knights, but especially if they are, and are enchanted as well; I know very well that nothing was wanting in the many other questions and answers that passed between us."

At this point the cousin said:

"I don't know, Señor Don Quixote, how your grace could have seen so many things and spoken so much and responded to so much in the short amount of time that you were down there."

"How long ago did I go down?" asked Don Quixote.

"A little more than an hour," responded Sancho.

"That cannot be," replied Don Quixote, "because night fell and day broke while I was there, and they fell and broke three times, and so by my count I have spent three days in those remote regions that are hidden from your eyes."

"My master must be telling the truth," said Sancho. "Since all the things that have happened to him have been by enchantment, maybe what seems like an hour to us seems like three days and nights down there."

"That must be so," responded Don Quixote.

"And, Señor, has your grace eaten in all this time?" asked the cousin.

"Not a mouthful has broken my fast," responded Don Quixote, "nor did the thought of hunger even enter my mind."

"Do the enchanted eat?" said the cousin.

"They do not eat," responded Don Quixote, "nor do they have excretory wastes, although some believe that their nails, beards, and hair all grow."

"And by any chance do the enchanted sleep, Señor?" asked Sancho.

"No, certainly not," responded Don Quixote. "At least, in the three days I have been with them not one of them closed an eye, and neither did I."

"Here," said Sancho, "the proverb fits: birds of a feather flock together; your grace flocks with enchanted people who fast and stay awake, so it's no surprise you don't sleep while you're with them. But, Señor, your grace will forgive me if I tell you that may God take me, and I was going to say the devil, if I believe a single one of all the things you've said here."

"What do you mean?" said the cousin. "Would Señor Don Quixote lie? And even if he wanted to, he hasn't had time to invent and imagine so many millions of lies."

"I don't believe my master is lying," responded Sancho.

"If you do not, then what do you believe?" asked Don Quixote.

"I believe," responded Sancho, "that Merlin, or those enchanters who enchanted that whole crowd your grace says you saw and talked to down there, put into your mind or memory the whole story that you've told us, and the rest that you still have to tell."

"That could be true, Sancho," replied Don Quixote, "but it is not, because what I have recounted I saw with my own eyes and touched with my own hands. But what will you say when I tell you now that among the infinite things and wonders that Montesinos showed to me, which I shall tell you in the course of our journey, slowly and at the proper time so that they are not all recounted here, Montesinos showed me three peasant girls who were leaping and jumping in those pleasant fields like nanny goats, and as soon as I saw them I recognized one of them as the peerless Dulcinea of Toboso, and the other two as those same peasant girls who came with her, the ones we spoke to as we were leaving Toboso. I asked Montesinos if he knew them; he responded that he did not, but he imagined that they must be distinguished ladies who had been enchanted, for they had appeared in those meadows only a few days before, and this should not surprise me because many other ladies from past and present times were there who had been transformed into many strange figures, among whom he recognized Queen Guinevere and her lady-in-waiting, Quintañona, pouring wine for Lancelot,

When he from Brittany came."[8]

When Sancho Panza heard his master say this, he thought he would lose his mind or die laughing; since he knew the truth about the feigned enchantment of Dulcinea, for he had been the enchanter and had invented the story, he recognized beyond the shadow of a doubt that his master was out of his mind and completely mad, and so he said:

8. A line from the ballad about Lancelot that was cited in chapter XIII of the first part.

"It was an evil moment and a worse time and an ill-fated day when your grace went down to the next world, my dear master, and an unlucky meeting that you had with Señor Montesinos, for see how you've come back to us. Your grace was better off up here when you had all your wits, just as God had given them to you, always saying wise things and giving advice, not like now, when you're saying the most foolish things that anybody could imagine."

"Since I know you, Sancho," responded Don Quixote, "I shall ignore your words."

"And I won't pay attention to your grace's," replied Sancho, "not even if you wound me, not even if you kill me on account of the ones I've said to you, or the ones I plan to say if you don't change and correct yours. But tell me, your grace, now that we're at peace: how, and by what signs, did you recognize our lady mistress? If you spoke to her, what did you say, and what did she reply?"

"I knew her," responded Don Quixote, "because she was wearing the same clothing she wore when you showed her to me. I spoke to her, but she did not say a word to me; instead, she turned her back and ran away so quickly that a spear could not have overtaken her. I wanted to follow, and would have done so if Montesinos had not advised me not to bother for it would be in vain, especially since the hour was approaching when I ought to leave the abyss. He also told me that over the course of time he would inform me how the spell on him, and Belerma, and Durandarte, as well as all the others who were there, was to be broken; but of all the grievous things I saw and noted, the one that caused me most sorrow was that as Montesinos was saying these words to me, one of the companions of the unfortunate Dulcinea approached me from the side, without my seeing her, and with her eyes full of tears, and in a low, troubled voice, she said to me:

'My lady Dulcinea of Toboso kisses the hands of your grace, and implores your grace to let her know how you are; and, because she is in great need, she also entreats your grace most earnestly to be so kind as to lend her, accepting as security this new cotton underskirt that I have here, half a dozen *reales* or whatever amount your grace may have, and she gives her word to return them to you very soon.'

I was astounded and amazed at this message, and turning to Señor Montesinos, I asked:

'Is it possible, Señor Montesinos, that distinguished persons who are enchanted suffer from need?' To which he responded:

'Your grace can believe me, Señor Don Quixote of La Mancha, that what is called need is found everywhere, and extends to all places, and reaches everyone, and does not excuse even those who are enchanted; and since Señora Dulcinea of Toboso has sent someone to ask you for six *reales*, and the pledge is good, it seems, then you must give them to her, for she undoubtedly is in very great difficulty.'

'Her security, I shall not take,' I responded, 'nor shall I give her what she asks, because I have no more than four *reales*.'

I gave these to her (they were the ones that you, Sancho, gave me the other day so that I could give alms to the poor whom I met along the road), and I said:

'My friend, tell your mistress that her troubles grieve my heart, and that I should like to be a Fúcar[9] so that I could solve them, and that I want her to know that I cannot and should not enjoy good health as long as I lack the pleasing sight of her, and her discerning conversation, and I entreat her grace as earnestly as I can that she should be so kind as to allow herself to be seen and spoken to by this her captive servant and wandering knight. Tell her too that when she least expects it she will hear that I have made a vow and taken an oath, in the manner of the one taken by the Marquis of Mantua to avenge his nephew Baldovinos when he found him near death in the heart of the mountains,[10] which was not to eat bread at a cloth-covered table, along with the other trifles he mentioned there, until he had avenged him; and I shall do the same, and vow not to rest, and to wander the seven regions of the world more diligently than Don Pedro of Portugal,[11] until I break her enchantment.'

'All this and more your grace owes to my lady,' responded the maiden. And after taking the four *reales*, instead of curtsying she gave a leap and jumped two *varas*[12] into the air."

"Holy God!" shouted Sancho. "Is it possible that there are in the world enchanters and enchantments so strong that they have turned my master's good sense into foolishness and madness? Oh, Señor, Señor, for God's sake think about what you are doing, and take back your honor,

---

9. This is the Spanish version of the name Fugger, the well-known German family of bankers and merchants who were closely associated with Spain.

10. The episode was mentioned in chapter V of the first part.

11. An allusion to the many travels of Pedro of Portugal. There is a traditional tendency to say that he traveled to the seven parts (*partidas*) of the world, rather than the more usual "four corners," perhaps through confusion with the *Siete Partidas*, the treatise on laws compiled by Alfonso the Learned (1221–1284), king of Castilla and León.

12. A *vara* is a Spanish linear measurement (.84 meter).

and don't believe this nonsense that has reduced and lessened your good sense!"

"Since you love me, Sancho, you speak in this fashion," said Don Quixote, "and since you have little experience in the things of this world, all things that are in any way difficult seem impossible to you; but in the course of time, as I have already said, I shall recount to you some of what I have seen down there, which will make you believe what I have recounted here, whose truth admits neither argument nor dispute."

CHAPTER XXIV

In which a thousand trifles are recounted, as irrelevant as they are necessary to a true understanding of this great history

The man who translated this great history from the original composed by its first author, Cide Hamete Benengeli, says that when he reached the chapter concerning the adventure of the Cave of Montesinos, he found in the margin, written in Hamete's own hand, these precise words:

'I cannot believe, nor can I persuade myself, that everything written in the preceding chapter actually happened in its entirety to the valiant Don Quixote: the reason is that all the adventures up to this point have been possible and plausible, but with regard to this one in the cave, I can find no way to consider it true since it goes so far beyond the limits of reason. But it is not possible for me to think that Don Quixote, the truest and most noble knight of his day, would lie, for he would not tell a lie even if he were shot with arrows. Moreover, he recounted and told it in all its circumstances and details, and in so short a time he could not fabricate so enormous a quantity of nonsense; if this adventure seems apocryphal, the fault is not mine, and so, without affirming either its falsity or its truth, I write it down. You, reader, since you are a discerning person, must judge it according to your own lights, for I must not and cannot do more; yet it is considered true that at the time of Don Quixote's passing and death, he is said to have retracted it, saying he had invented it because he thought it was consonant and compatible with the adventures he had read in his histories.'

And then he continues, saying:

The cousin was astounded both by Sancho Panza's boldness and his master's patience, and he assumed that his joy at seeing his lady Dulcinea of Toboso, even though she was enchanted, gave rise to the mildness of disposition he displayed then, for otherwise Sancho's words and phrases would have merited a beating; the cousin, who really thought Sancho had been insolent to his master, said:

"Señor Don Quixote of La Mancha, I consider the journey I have made with your grace very worthwhile, because I have derived four things from it. The first, having met your grace, which I consider a great joy. The second, having learned what is inside the Cave of Montesinos, along with the mutations of Guadiana and the Lakes of Ruidera, which will be of great use to me in the *Spanish Ovid* that I have in hand. The third, having realized the antiquity of cards, which were in use during the time of the Emperor Charlemagne, as one can deduce from the words your grace says Durandarte said when, after that long period of time when Montesinos was talking to him, he awoke and said: 'Have patience and shuffle the deck.' And these words and manner of speaking he could not have learned while he was enchanted but when he was not, in France and at the time of the aforementioned Emperor Charlemagne. And this discovery is just right for another book that I am writing, which is *A Supplement to Virgilio Polidoro, on the Inventions of Antiquity*: I believe that in his book he did not remember to put in the invention of cards, which I shall now include, and it will be of great importance, particularly quoting an authority as serious and reliable as Señor Durandarte. The fourth is having learned the truth regarding the origins of the Guadiana River, unknown to anyone until now."

"Your grace is correct," said Don Quixote, "but I should like to know, if God grants that you receive a license to print your books, which I doubt, to whom you intend to dedicate them."

"There are nobles and grandees in Spain to whom they can be dedicated," said the cousin.

"Not many," responded Don Quixote, "and not because they are not worthy of dedications, but because they do not wish to accept them in order not to be obliged to provide the rewards that the work and courtesy of the authors seem to deserve. I know a prince[1] who can make up for all the others, and with so many advantages that if I dared mention

---

1. The count of Lemos, to whom the second part of the novel is dedicated.

them, I might perhaps awaken envy in more than one generous bosom; but let us put this aside until a more suitable time and find a place where we can spend the night."

"Not far from here," responded the cousin, "is a hermitage where a hermit lives, and people say he once was a soldier, and he is reputed to be a good Christian, and very intelligent, and charitable as well. Beside the hermitage is a small house that he built at his own expense, and although it is little, it can receive guests."

"Does this hermit have chickens, by any chance?" asked Sancho.

"There are few hermits who do not," responded Don Quixote, "because the ones today are not like those in the deserts of Egypt, who dressed in palm leaves and ate roots. And you should not think that because I speak well of earlier hermits, I speak ill of modern ones; I mean to say only that the penances of modern hermits are not as harsh and rigorous as the older ones, but all of them are still good; at least, I judge them to be good; in the worst of circumstances, the hypocrite who pretends to be good does less harm than the public sinner."

While they were conversing, they saw a man coming toward them, walking quickly and using a stick to prod a mule that was loaded down with lances and halberds. When he reached them, he greeted them and passed by. Don Quixote said:

"Stop, my good man, for it seems you are traveling faster than that mule would like."

"I can't stop, Señor," the man responded, "because the weapons you see me carrying must be used tomorrow, and I can't possibly stop, and so go with God. But if you want to know why I'm carrying them, I plan to spend the night at the inn that's past the hermitage, and if you're traveling the same way, you'll find me there, and then I'll tell you some wonderful things. And so again, go with God."

And he prodded his mule so much that Don Quixote did not have the opportunity to ask him what wonderful things he planned to tell them; and since he was rather curious and was always filled with the desire to learn new things, he said that they should leave immediately and go to spend the night at the inn, not stopping at the hermitage where the cousin wanted them to stay.

And so they mounted their animals and all three followed the road that led directly to the inn, where they arrived shortly before nightfall. On the way, the cousin said to Don Quixote that they should stop at the hermitage for something to drink. As soon as Sancho Panza heard this he turned his donkey toward the hermitage, and Don Quixote and the cousin did the same, but as Sancho's bad luck would have it, the hermit was not at home, which is what they were told by an assistant hermit whom they found in the hermitage. They asked for some good wine, and he responded that his master did not have any, but if they wanted some cheap water, he would gladly give it to them.

"If I had a thirst for water," responded Sancho, "there are wells along the road where I could quench it. O wedding of Camacho, O plenty in the house of Don Diego, I miss you so often!"

They left the hermitage and spurred their mounts on to the inn, and in a little while they came upon a boy who was walking, not very quickly, in front of them, and they soon overtook him. He was carrying a sword over his shoulder, and on it there was a bundle or pack, apparently of his clothes, which appeared to be breeches or pantaloons, and a short cape, and a shirt or two, because he was wearing a velvet doublet, with some glimmers of satin, and a shirt hanging out, and his hose was of silk, and his shoes square-toed, in the fashion of the court; he must have been eighteen or nineteen years old, with a joyful face and, it seemed, an agile body. As he walked he sang *seguidillas*[2] to relieve the tedium of the road. When they reached him he had just finished singing one that the cousin committed to memory, and it is said that it said:

> I'm forced to go to the war
> because I'm so poor;
> if I had money, believe
> me I wouldn't leave.

The first to speak to him was Don Quixote, who said:

"Your grace travels very lightly, gallant Señor. Where are you going? Let us know, if you care to tell us."

To which the boy responded:

"My traveling so lightly is because of the heat and poverty; and I am going to war."

"Why poverty?" asked Don Quixote. "The heat is enough of a reason."

"Señor," replied the lad, "in this bundle I'm carrying some velvet pantaloons, companions to this doublet; if I wear them out on the road, I

---

2. A variable Spanish poetic stanza of four to seven lines, its verses alternating between five and seven syllables.

won't be able to honor myself with them in the city, and I don't have the money to buy others; for this reason, and to cool myself, I'll travel this way until I reach the infantry companies that are no more than twelve leagues away, and there I'll enlist, and there will be plenty of wagons that I can ride until we reach the port of embarcation, which they say will be in Cartagena. And I'd rather have the king as my lord and master, and serve him in war, than some fool at court."

"And does your grace have a bonus, by any chance?" asked the cousin.

"If I had served some grandee of Spain, or some distinguished noble-man," the boy responded, "I'd certainly have one, which is what you get when you serve good masters; you leave the servants' table and become an ensign or a captain, or get a good allowance, but I, sad to say, always served office-seekers and upstarts, whose income and revenue were so miserable and sparse that they spent half of it when they paid for the starch in a collar; it would be considered a miracle if a venturesome page were to have any kind of good fortune."

"And tell me, friend, on your life," asked Don Quixote, "is it possible that during the years you served you haven't been able to obtain some livery?"

"I was given two liveries," responded the page, "but like somebody who leaves the church before he takes his vows, and they take away his habit and give him back his clothes, my masters gave me back my own clothes when their business at court was finished, and they went home and took back the liveries they had given just for show."

"That is a noteworthy *spilorceria*,[3] as they say in Italian," said Don Quixote, "but even so, you should consider it good fortune to have left the court with such good intentions, because there is nothing on earth more honorable or beneficial than serving God, first of all, and then your king and natural lord, especially in the practice of arms, by means of which one achieves, if not more wealth, at least more honor than through letters, as I have said so often; although letters have founded more estates than arms, those who pursue arms have I do not know pre-cisely what kind of advantage over those who pursue letters, but I do know what kind of splendor places them above all others. And what I wish to tell you now you should keep in your memory, for it will be of great benefit and consolation to you in your hardships: you must put out

---

3. The word means "miserliness" or "stinginess."

of your mind the adversities that may befall you, for the worst of them is death, and if it is a good death, then dying is the best thing that can happen to you. Julius Caesar, that valiant Roman emperor, was asked what was the best death, and he responded the one that was unexpected, sudden, and unforeseen; and although he responded as a heathen who did not have knowledge of the true God, yet he was correct in view of human feeling, for what does it matter if you are killed in the first battle or skirmish, or are shot by artillery, or blown up by a mine? It is all dying, and the end of the story, and according to Terence, the soldier killed in battle looks better than the one who is safe and sound in flight; and the good soldier achieves as much fame as his obedience to his captains and to those who can command him. And remember, son, that the soldier prefers the smell of gunpowder to the scent of musk, and if old age overtakes you in this honorable profession, even if you are full of wounds, and maimed or crippled, at least when it overtakes you, you will not be without honor, an honor that not even poverty can diminish; furthermore, laws are now being enacted that will protect and assist old and crippled soldiers, because it is not right that they be treated the way blacks are treated who are emancipated and freed when they are old and can no longer serve, and are thrown out of the house and called free men, making them slaves to hunger from which only death can liberate them. And for now I do not wish to say more, except that you should ride behind me on my horse until we reach the inn, and there you will have supper with me, and in the morning you will continue on your way, and may God make it as smooth for you as your desires deserve."

The page did not accept the invitation to ride behind, though he did say yes to eating supper with him in the inn, and at this moment it is said that Sancho said to himself:

"Lord save my master! Is it possible that a man who knows how to say all the many good things that he's said here can say he's seen the impossible foolishness that he says he saw in the Cave of Montesinos? Well now, time will tell."

At this point they reached the inn just as night was falling, and much to Sancho's delight, he saw that his master judged it to be a real inn and not a castle, as he usually did. As soon as they had entered, Don Quixote asked the innkeeper about the man with the lances and halberds, and he responded that the man was in the stable tending to his mule. The cousin and Sancho did the same for their donkeys, giving Rocinante the best manger and stall in the stable.

CHAPTER XXV

In which note is made of the braying adventure and the diverting adventure of the puppet master, along with the memorable divinations of the soothsaying monkey

Don Quixote was on pins and needles, as the saying goes, until he could hear and learn about the marvels promised by the man carrying the weapons. He went to look for him in the place where the innkeeper had said he was, and found him, and said that the man had to tell him now what he would, in any case, tell him later regarding what Don Quixote had asked on the road. To which the man responded:

"The recounting of my marvels has to take place more slowly, and not while we're standing; Señor, your grace must allow me to tend to my animal, and then I shall tell you things that will astound you."

"Do not let that delay you," responded Don Quixote, "for I shall help you with everything."

And he did, sifting the barley for him and cleaning the manger, humble labors that obliged the man to tell him willingly what he had asked, and sitting down on a stone bench, with Don Quixote beside him, and the cousin, the page, Sancho Panza, and the innkeeper as senate and audience, he began to speak in this manner:

"Your graces should know that in a town four and a half leagues from this inn, a councilman lost a donkey through the deceitful efforts of one of his servant girls, but that's a long story, and though the councilman made every effort to find the animal, he could not. According to what everyone says, the donkey had been missing for some two weeks when the councilman who had sustained the loss found himself in the square, and another councilman from the same town said to him:

'You owe me a reward, compadre; your donkey has turned up.'

'I promise you'll get it, compadre,' he responded, 'but where did he turn up?'

'In the woods,' responded the finder. 'I saw him this morning, without a packsaddle or any trappings, and so skinny it made me feel bad just to look at him. I tried to catch him and bring him back to you, but he's so wild and untamed now that when I went up to him, he ran off into the deepest part of the woods. If you want both of us to look for him, just let me take my little jenny home, and I'll be right back.'

'I appreciate that," said the one who had lost his donkey, 'and I'll try to return the favor.'

Everybody who knows the truth of the matter tells the story with the same details, and in the same manner that I'm telling it now. In short, the two councilmen together went on foot into the woods, and they reached the place and the site where they thought they would find the donkey but did not find him there or anywhere nearby no matter how much they searched. Seeing that he was nowhere to be found, the one who had seen the donkey said to the other councilman:

'Look, compadre: I've just had an idea, and there's no doubt that with it we'll be able to find this animal even if he's hiding in the bowels of the earth, let alone the woods; the fact is that I know how to bray wonderfully well, and if you know how even a little, then the matter's settled.'

'Did you say even a little, compadre?' said the other councilman. 'By God, nobody's better than me, not even donkeys.'

'We'll see,' responded the second councilman, 'because I've decided that you should go to one part of the woods and I'll go to the other, so that we'll walk all around it, and every few steps you'll bray and I'll bray, and the donkey will have to hear us and respond if he's in the woods at all.'

To which the owner of the donkey responded:

'Compadre, I say it's an excellent plan and worthy of your great intelligence.'

And separating as they had agreed, it so happened that they both brayed almost at the same time, and each was deceived by the braying of the other and came running, thinking the donkey had returned; and when they saw each other, the one who had lost the donkey said:

'Is it possible, compadre, that it wasn't my donkey who brayed?'

'No, it was me,' responded the other man.

'Then I say, compadre,' said the owner, 'that between you and a jackass there's no difference at all as far as braying is concerned, because never in my life have I seen or heard anything more lifelike.'

'The compliments and flattery,' responded the planner, 'belong and apply to you more than to me, compadre; by the God who made me, you can give a two-bray advantage to the greatest and most expert brayer in the world, because your sound is loud, your voice sustained, with the correct time and rhythm, your inflections numerous and rapid: in short, I admit defeat, and surrender the palm, and hand you the banner for this rare ability.'

'Now I say,' responded the owner, 'that from now on I'll esteem myself more and think better of myself and believe that I know something valuable since I'm graced with this talent; though I thought I could bray well, I never realized I had reached the heights that you say I have.'

'I'll also say now,' responded the second man, 'that there are rare abilities in the world that are lost, and ill-used by those who don't know how to take advantage of them.'

'Except in cases such as the one we're dealing with now,' responded the owner, 'ours are of little use to us, and even here, may it please God that they do us some good.'

Having said this, they separated and returned to their braying, and were constantly being deceived, and came back together again, until they decided on a signal to let them know that they were the ones braying and not the donkey, and it was that they would bray twice, one bray right after the other. In this way, constantly giving two brays in a row, they circled the entire woods, but the lost donkey did not respond, not even with a sign. Yet how could the poor unfortunate respond? For they found him in the deepest part of the woods, devoured by wolves. And when they saw him, his owner said:

'I was surprised at his not responding, because if he hadn't been dead, he would have brayed when he heard us, or wouldn't be a donkey; but as long as I was able to hear you bray so beautifully, compadre, I consider the effort of looking for him well worth the trouble, even though I found him dead.'

'We're a talented pair, compadre,' responded the other, 'because if the abbot sings well, the altar boy's not far behind.'

And so, disconsolate and hoarse, they returned to their village and told their friends, neighbors, and acquaintances what had happened to them in their search for the donkey, each exaggerating the other's talent for braying, all of which was learned and circulated in nearby towns. And the devil, who never sleeps, and loves to sow and plant quarrels and discord wherever he goes, spreading mischief on the wind and creating disputes out of nothing, ordered and arranged matters so that the people from other towns, when they saw someone from our village, would bray, as if throwing the braying of our councilmen back into our faces. The boys joined in, which was like giving it into the hands and mouths of all the demons in hell, and the braying spread from one town to another, so that the natives of a town are known by their braying, just as blacks are known and differentiated from whites; and this unfortunate mockery has gone so far that often the mocked, holding weapons in their hands and marching in formation, have come out to do battle with the mockers, and no one and nothing, neither fear nor shame, can stop it. I believe that tomorrow or the next day the people from my village, who are the people who bray, will go to fight another town that's two leagues away, which is one of those that persecute us the most, and so that they can be well-prepared, I've bought the lances and halberds that you saw. And these are the marvels I said I would tell you, and if they don't seem so to you, I don't know any others."

And saying this, the good man concluded what he had to say, and at that moment a man dressed all in chamois—hose, breeches, and doublet—came through the door of the inn, and in a loud voice he said:

"Señor Innkeeper, is there room at the inn? For the soothsaying monkey is coming here, and a puppet show about the freeing of Melisendra."

"Good Lord!" said the innkeeper. "It's Master Pedro! There's a good night ahead of us."

I forgot to say that this Master Pedro had his left eye and almost half his cheek covered with a patch of green taffeta, a sign that all of that side was probably diseased; the innkeeper continued, saying:

"Your grace is welcome, Señor Master Pedro. Where are the monkey and the puppet stage? I don't see them."

"They're nearby," responded the man in chamois, "but I came on ahead to find out if there's room."

"I'd move out the Duke of Alba himself to make room for Master Pedro," responded the innkeeper. "Bring the monkey and the puppet stage in, because tonight there are people in the inn who will pay to see the show and the monkey's talents."

"That's a stroke of luck," responded the man with the patch. "I'll lower the price, and consider myself well-paid if I cover my costs; now I'll go and bring in the cart that's carrying the monkey and the stage."

And then he left the inn again.

Don Quixote asked the innkeeper about Master Pedro and the puppet show and monkey he was bringing with him. To which the innkeeper responded:

"He's a famous puppet master who's been traveling the Aragonese side of La Mancha for some time, showing a puppet play about Melisendra being freed by the famous Don Gaiferos, which is one of the best and best-acted histories seen in this part of the kingdom for many years. He also has with him a monkey with the rarest talent ever seen among monkeys or imagined among men, because if he's asked something, he pays attention to what he's asked, then jumps onto his master's shoulders and goes up to his ear and tells him the answer to the question, and then Master Pedro says what it is; he has much more to say about past things than about future ones, and even though he isn't right all the time, he's not wrong most of the time, so he makes us think he has the devil in his body. He charges two *reales* for each question if the monkey responds, I mean, if the master responds for him after he's spoken into his ear; people believe that Master Pedro is very rich, a *uomo galante* and a *bon compagno*, as they say in Italy, who leads the best life in the world; he talks more than six men and drinks more than twelve, all paid for by his tongue and his monkey and his puppet show."

At this point Master Pedro returned, and in a cart came the puppet stage and a large tailless monkey with a rump like felt but a face that was nice-looking, and as soon as Don Quixote saw him, he asked:

"Señor Soothsayer, can your grace tell me *che pesce pigliamo?*[1] What will become of us? And here you can see my two *reales*."

And he told Sancho to hand them to Master Pedro, who responded for the monkey, saying:

"Señor, this animal does not respond or give information about things to come; about past things he knows a little, and about present ones, a little more."

"By God," said Sancho, "I wouldn't pay anything to have somebody tell me what's already happened to me! Who knows that better than me? And it would be foolish to pay anybody to tell me what I already know; but since he knows about present things, here's my two *reales* so His Monkeyness can tell me what my wife, Teresa Panza, is doing now, and how she's spending her time."

Master Pedro refused to take the money, saying:

1. This phrase (literally "what fish are we catching?" or "what are we up to, what are we doing?") and others like it, as well as the Italian words spoken by the innkeeper, were introduced into Spain by soldiers returning from Italy.

"I don't wish to receive payment ahead of time, before the service has been provided."

And he hit his left shoulder twice with his right hand, and the monkey leaped onto it, put his mouth up to his ear, clicked his teeth together very quickly, and after doing this for the length of time it takes to say a Credo, gave another leap down to the floor; and when he did this, Master Pedro rushed to kneel in front of Don Quixote, and throwing his arms around his legs, he said:

"I embrace these legs as I would embrace the two Pillars of Hercules, O illustrious revivifier of a now forgotten knight errantry! O never sufficiently praised knight, Don Quixote of La Mancha, courage of the faint-hearted, support of those about to fall, strong arm of those who have fallen, comfort and consolation of all who are unfortunate."

Don Quixote was dumbfounded, Sancho astounded, the cousin baffled, the page stunned, the man who told about the braying stupefied, the innkeeper perplexed, and, in short, all who heard the words of the puppet master were amazed, but he continued, saying:

"And you, O worthy Sancho Panza, the best squire of the best knight in the world, be of good cheer! Your good wife, Teresa, is well, and at this very moment she is carding a pound of flax; to be more specific, on her left is a broken-mouthed jug that holds a good measure of wine, and with it she keeps her spirits up as she works."

"I can believe that," responded Sancho, "because she's a wonderful woman, and except for her being jealous, I wouldn't trade her for the giantess Andandona,[2] who, according to my master, was a very honorable and upright woman; my Teresa is one of those women who won't let themselves fare badly even at the expense of their heirs."

"Now I say," said Don Quixote at this point, "that the man who reads a good deal and travels a good deal, sees a good deal and knows a good deal. I say this because what argument would have been enough to persuade me that there are monkeys in the world who can soothsay, as I have just seen with my own eyes? Because I am the very same Don Quixote of La Mancha mentioned by this good animal, although he has gone a little too far in praising me; but no matter, I give thanks to heaven, who granted me a gentle and compassionate spirit, always inclined to do good to everyone and evil to none."

2. A character in the novel *Amadís of Gaul*.

"If I had money," said the page, "I'd ask this noble monkey what will happen to me on the travels I'm undertaking."

To which Master Pedro, who by this time had risen from the feet of Don Quixote, responded:

"I've already said that this beast does not speak of the future, but if he did, not having money wouldn't matter, because for the sake of serving Señor Don Quixote, here present, I would give up all the profits in the world. And now, because I owe it to him, and to give him pleasure, I would like to set up my puppet stage and delight everyone in the inn, at no charge whatsoever."

When he heard this, the innkeeper, who was overjoyed, indicated the spot where the stage could be placed, and this was done in very short order.

Don Quixote was not very pleased with the monkey's soothsaying, for it did not seem right that a monkey could divine things, whether things of the future or of the past, and so while Master Pedro was arranging the stage, Don Quixote withdrew with Sancho to a corner of the stable where no one could hear them, and he said:

"Look, Sancho, I have considered very carefully the strange talent of this monkey, and in my opinion this Master Pedro, his owner, must have made a pact, either implicit or explicit, with the devil."

"If the pack's split and belongs to the devil," said Sancho, "it must be a very dirty pack, no doubt about it, but what good would that do Master Pedro?"

"You do not understand me, Sancho: I mean only that he must have made some agreement with the devil to grant this talent to the monkey so that Master Pedro could earn his living, and when he is rich the devil will take his soul, which is precisely what the universal enemy wishes. And what makes me believe this is seeing that the monkey replies only to past or present things, which is as far as the devil's knowledge can go; future things cannot be known except through conjecture, and only occasionally, for knowing all times and moments is reserved to God alone, and for Him there is no past or future: everything is present. And this being true, as it is, it is clear that this monkey speaks in the style of the devil, and I am amazed that he has not been denounced to the Holy Office, and examined, and forced to tell by whose power he divines, for it is also clear that this monkey is not an astrologer, and neither he nor his master casts, or knows how to cast, the astrological charts used so widely now in Spain that there's not a fishwife, page, or old cobbler who does not presume to cast a chart as if it were the knave in a pack of cards lying on the floor, corrupting the marvelous truths of science with their lies and ignorance. I know of a lady who asked one of them if a small lapdog she had would become pregnant and give birth, and how many pups she would have and what color they would be. To which our noble astrologer responded that the dog would become pregnant and give birth to three pups, one green, one red, and one spotted, provided that the dog was mounted between eleven and twelve in the morning, or at night, and that it took place on a Monday or a Saturday; and what happened was that two days later the little dog died of indigestion, and the noble prognosticator was credited in the town with being a very accurate caster of charts, a reputation that all or most astrologers have."

"Even so," said Sancho, "I would like your grace to tell Master Pedro to ask his monkey if what happened to your grace in the Cave of Montesinos is true; in my opinion, begging your grace's pardon, it was all deceptions and lies, or at least nothing but dreams."

"Everything is possible," responded Don Quixote, "but I shall do as you advise, although I still have certain scruples in that regard."

As they were speaking, Master Pedro came looking for Don Quixote to tell him that the puppet stage was ready, and that his grace should come to see it because it was worthwhile. Don Quixote told him what he was thinking and implored him to first ask his monkey to tell him if certain things that had occurred in the Cave of Montesinos were dreamed or true, because it seemed to him that they were both. To which Master Pedro, without saying a word, brought back his monkey, and standing in front of Don Quixote and Sancho, he said:

"Look, noble monkey, this knight wishes to know if certain things that happened to him in a cave called Montesinos were false or true."

And after his master had made the usual signal, the monkey jumped onto his left shoulder and spoke to him, apparently, in his ear, and then Master Pedro said:

"The monkey says that some of the things your grace saw, or experienced, in the aforesaid cave are false, and some are true, and this is all he knows, nothing more, with regard to this question, and if your grace should wish to know more, next Friday he will respond to everything you ask of him, but for the moment he has used up his abilities, and they won't return until Friday, as he has said."

"Didn't I say," said Sancho, "that I couldn't believe, Señor, that everything your grace said about what happened in the cave was true, not even half?"

"Events will tell the truth of things, Sancho," responded Don

Quixote, "for time, which reveals all things, brings everything into the light of day even if it is hidden in the bowels of the earth. Enough of that for now; let us go to see the puppet show of our good Master Pedro, for I believe it must hold some surprises."

"What do you mean, some?" responded Master Pedro. "Sixty thousand are contained in this show of mine; I tell your grace, Señor Don Quixote, that it is one of the most spectacular things in the world today, but *operibus credite, et non verbis*.³ and now to work, for it is getting late, and we have much to do and say and show."

Don Quixote and Sancho did as he asked and went to the place where the stage was set up for all to see, and it was filled with the light of little wax candles that made it look colorful and resplendent. As soon as they arrived, Master Pedro went inside the puppet theater, for it was he who would manipulate the figures in the play, and outside stood a boy, a servant of Master Pedro's, to act as interpreter and narrator of the mysteries on stage; in his hand he held a rod with which he pointed to the figures as they came out.

When everyone in the inn was sitting, and some standing, in front of the stage, and Don Quixote, Sancho, the page, and the cousin were settled in the best places, the interpreter began to say what will be heard and seen by those who hear or see the following chapter.

CHAPTER XXVI

In which the diverting adventure of the puppet master continues, along with other things that are really very worthwhile

All fell silent, both Tyrians and Trojans,¹

I mean to say, all those looking at the stage were waiting to hear the words of the narrator regarding its marvels when the sound of a large number of drums and trumpets was heard, and a good deal of artillery firing, then the sound soon ended and the boy raised his voice and said:

---

3. The phrase is based on John 10:38: ". . . though ye believe not me, believe the works."

1. The line is taken from the Spanish translation of the *Aeneid* by Gregorio Hernández de Velasco, 1555.

"This true history, presented here for your graces, is taken literally from the French chronicles and Spanish ballads which are in the mouths of everyone, even children, on our streets. It tells of how Señor Don Gaiferos freed his wife, Melisendra, who was held captive in Spain by the Moors, in the city of Sansueña, which was the name given in those days to the city of Zaragoza;[2] and your graces can see there how Don Gaiferos is playing backgammon, as they sing in the song:

> Don Gaiferos is playing at backgammon,
> his lady Melisendra is forgotten.[3]

And the personage who appears now with a crown on his head and a scepter in his hands is the Emperor Charlemagne, the supposed father of Melisendra, and he, angry at seeing the idleness and neglect of his son-in-law, comes to reprimand him; notice how earnestly and heatedly he reprimands him, as if he wanted to hit him half a dozen times on the head with his scepter, and there are even authors who say that he did hit him, and hit him hard; and after saying many things to him about the danger to his honor because he would not obtain the liberty of his wife, they say that he said to him:

> 'I have said enough: look to it.'[4]

And look, your graces, at how the emperor turns his back and leaves an indignant Don Gaiferos; now see how he, made impatient by anger, tosses away the backgammon board and pieces and quickly asks for his armor, and asks his cousin Don Roland for the loan of his sword, Durindana, and see how Don Roland does not want to lend it to him, offering instead to accompany him in the difficult enterprise he is undertaking; but the angry and valiant knight does not accept, saying that alone he is enough to rescue his wife, even if she is held at the very center of the earth; and now he goes in to put on his armor so that he can set out im-

---

2. The characters and story are taken from Spanish ballads. Gaiferos, Charlemagne's nephew, was about to marry Charlemagne's daughter Melisendra, when she was captured by Moors. For some reason Gaiferos spends seven years in Paris, not thinking of her, until Charlemagne persuades him to free her. Roland lends him weapons and a horse, Gaiferos reaches Sansueña, where Melisendra is being held by King Almanzor, and sees her at a window. He rescues her and they flee, pursued so closely by the Moors that Gaiferos has to dismount and do battle with them; he is victorious, and he and Melisendra return to Paris in triumph.

3. These verses are from a poem on the subject by Miguel Sánchez.

4. The line is from one of the ballads about Gaiferos.

mediately. Your graces, turn your eyes to the tower that you see there; it is one of the towers of Zaragoza's castle-fortress now called La Aljafería; and that lady you see on the balcony, dressed in the Moorish fashion, is the peerless Melisendra, who would often stand there, and look at the road to France, and turn her thoughts to Paris and her husband, finding consolation in her captivity. Look too at what is happening now, perhaps unlike anything you have ever seen before. Don't you see that Moor stealing up behind Melisendra on tiptoe, his finger to his lips? Well, look at how he kisses her right on the mouth, and how quickly she spits and wipes her mouth with the white sleeve of her dress, and how she laments, and in her grief tears at her beautiful hair as if it were to blame for the offense. Look too at that somber Moor in the passageway, King Marsilio of Sansueña, who saw the insolence of the other Moor, had him arrested, though he was a relative and a great favorite, and ordered him to be given two hundred lashes and to be taken through the usual streets of the city,

> With town criers walking before
> and armed bailiffs coming behind;[5]

and see here where they are coming to carry out the sentence so soon after the crime was committed, because the Moors don't have the 'indictment of the accused' and 'remanded to custody' that we do."

"Boy, boy," said Don Quixote in a loud voice, "tell your story in a straight line and do not become involved in curves or transverse lines, for to get a clear idea of the truth, one must have proofs and more proofs."

And from the interior, Master Pedro also said:

"Boy, tend to your business and do what that gentleman says, that's the right thing to do; go on with your plainsong and don't get involved in counterpoints that usually break because they're so refined."

"I will," responded the boy, and he continued, saying:

"This figure who appears here on horseback, wrapped in a Gascony cape, is Don Gaiferos himself, and see his wife, who has been avenged for the insolence of the enamored Moor, looking better and more tranquil as she stands at the window of the tower and talks to her husband, thinking

---

5. The lines are taken from a ballad by Francisco de Quevedo (1580–1645), one of the most brilliant literary figures of the Spanish Golden Age.

he is a passerby, and saying to him all those words and phrases in the ballad that says:

> Señor Knight, if you're bound for France,
> then ask after Don Gaiferos;

I won't recite them now because going on too long gives rise to boredom;
it's enough to see how Don Gaiferos reveals his identity, and through her
joyful gestures Melisendra lets us know that she has recognized him, and
now we see her letting herself down from the balcony in order to sit on
the hindquarters of her good husband's horse. But oh! What misfortune!
The lace of her skirt has caught on some of the wrought iron at the balcony, and she hangs in midair and cannot reach the ground. But see how
merciful heaven sends help at the moment of greatest need, for here
comes Don Gaiferos, and not worrying about tearing the rich skirt, he
grasps her and simply pulls her down to the ground, and then in a leap he
sets her on his horse's hindquarters, astride like a man, and tells her to
hold on tight and places her arms over his shoulders and crosses them on
his chest so that she doesn't fall, since Señora Melisendra was not accustomed to this kind of riding. See too how the neighing of the horse
shows that he is content to be carrying the valiant and beautiful burden
of his lord and lady. See how they turn their backs and leave the city, and
with joy and delight take the road to Paris. Go in peace, O peerless pair
of true lovers! May you arrive safely in your own dear country, and may
fortune place no obstacle in the way of your happy journey! May the eyes
of your friends and relations see you enjoy your days in peace and tranquility, and may those granted you in this life be as many as those of
Nestor!"[6]

At this point Master Pedro once again raised his voice, saying:
"Simplicity, boy, don't be arrogant, all affectation is bad."

The interpreter said nothing in reply but went on, saying:

"There was no lack of curious eyes, the kind that tend to see everything, to see Melisendra descend from the balcony and mount the horse,
and they informed King Marsilio, who immediately gave orders to sound
the call to arms; and see how soon this is done, and how the city is
flooded with the sound of the bells that ring from all the towers of the
mosques."

---

6. A character in the *Iliad* who was extremely old.

"No, that is wrong!" said Don Quixote. "Master Pedro is incorrect in the matter of the bells, for the Moors do not use bells but drums and a kind of flute that resembles our flageolet, and there is no doubt that ringing bells in Sansueña is a great piece of nonsense."

This was heard by Master Pedro, who stopped the ringing and said:

"Your grace should not concern yourself with trifles, Señor Don Quixote, or try to carry things so far that you never reach the end of them. Aren't a thousand plays performed almost every day that are full of a thousand errors and pieces of nonsense, and yet are successful productions that are greeted not only with applause but with admiration? Go on, boy, and let them say what they will, for as long as I fill my purse, there can be more errors than atoms in the sun."

"That is true," replied Don Quixote.

And the boy said:

"Look at the number of brilliant horsemen riding out of the city in pursuit of the two Catholic lovers; look at how many trumpets blare, how many flutes play, how many drums and tabors sound. I am afraid they will overtake them and bring them back tied to the tail of their own horse, which would be an awful sight."

And Don Quixote, seeing and hearing so many Moors and so much clamor, thought it would be a good idea to assist those who were fleeing; and rising to his feet, in a loud voice he said:

"I shall not consent, in my lifetime and in my presence, to any such offense against an enamored knight so famous and bold as Don Gaiferos. Halt, you lowborn rabble; do not follow and do not pursue him unless you wish to do battle with me!"

And speaking and taking action, he unsheathed his sword, leaped next to the stage, and with swift and never before seen fury began to rain down blows on the crowd of Moorish puppets, knocking down some, beheading others, ruining this one, destroying that one, and among many other blows, he delivered so powerful a downstroke that if Master Pedro had not stooped, crouched down, and hunched over, he would have cut off his head more easily than if it had been so much marzipan. Master Pedro cried out, saying:

"Your grace must stop, Señor Don Quixote, and realize that the ones you are overthrowing, destroying, and killing are not real Moors but only pasteboard figures. Sinner that I am, you are destroying and ruining everything I own!"

But this did not keep Don Quixote from raining down slashes, two-handed blows, thrusts, and backstrokes. In short, in less time than it takes to tell about it, he knocked the puppet theater to the floor, all its scenery and figures cut and broken to pieces: King Marsilio was badly wounded, and Emperor Charlemagne's head and crown were split in two. The audience of spectators was in a tumult, the monkey ran out the window and onto the roof, the cousin was fearful, the page was frightened, and even Sancho Panza was terrified, because, as he swore when the storm was over, he had never seen his master in so wild a fury. When the general destruction of the puppet theater was complete, Don Quixote calmed down somewhat and said:

"At this moment I should like to have here in front of me all those who do not believe, and do not wish to believe, how much good knights errant do in the world: if I had not been here, just think what would have happened to the worthy Don Gaiferos and the beauteous Melisendra; most certainly, by this time those dogs would have overtaken them and committed some outrage against them. In brief, long live knight errantry, over and above everything in the world today!"

"Long life and good fortune!" said Master Pedro in a faint voice. "And nothing but death for me, for I am so unfortunate that I can say with King Don Rodrigo:

> Yesterday the lord of all Spain . . .
> today not even a tower
> that I can call my own.[7]

Not half an hour ago, not even half a moment, I was the master of kings and emperors, my stables and coffers and sacks filled with infinite horses and countless treasures, and now I am desolate and dejected, impoverished and a beggar, and worst of all, without my monkey, and by my faith, it will be like pulling teeth to get him back again, and all because of the ill-considered rage of this knight, who, they say, protects orphans, and rights wrongs, and does other charitable works, and in me alone have his generous intentions come to naught, praise be to blessed heaven, where the seats are sublime. In short, the Knight of the Sorrowful Face has certainly brought sorrow to my figures and puppets."

---

7. These lines are from one of the many ballads that deal with Don Rodrigo, the last Visigothic king of Spain, who lost the country to the Moors.

Sancho Panza was deeply affected by the words of Master Pedro, and he said:

"Don't cry, Master Pedro, and don't wail, or you'll break my heart, and let me tell you that my master, Don Quixote, is so Catholic and scrupulous a Christian that if he realizes he's done you any harm, he'll tell you so and want to pay and satisfy you, and with interest."

"If Señor Don Quixote would pay me even in part for the figures he has destroyed, I would be happy, and his grace would satisfy his conscience, because there is no salvation for the man who holds another's property against the will of the owner and does not return it."

"That is true," said Don Quixote, "but until now I did not know that I had anything of yours, Master Pedro."

"What do you mean?" responded Master Pedro. "These relics lying on the hard and sterile ground, what scattered and annihilated them but the invincible strength of that mighty arm? And whose bodies were they but mine? And how did I earn my living except with them?"

"Now I believe," said Don Quixote at this point, "what I have believed on many other occasions: the enchanters who pursue me simply place figures as they really are before my eyes, and then change and alter them into whatever they wish. I tell you really and truly, you gentlemen who can hear me: it seemed to me that everything that happened here was actually happening, that Melisendra was Melisendra, Don Gaiferos Don Gaiferos, Marsilio Marsilio, and Charlemagne Charlemagne; for that reason I was overcome by rage, and to fulfill the obligations of the knight errantry I profess, I wanted to give my help and favor to those who were fleeing, and to this worthy end I did what you have seen; if matters have turned out otherwise, the fault is not mine but lies with the wicked creatures who pursue me; even so, although my error was not the result of malice, I wish to sentence myself to pay the costs: let Master Pedro decide what he wants for the damaged puppets, for I offer to pay him immediately in good, standard Castilian coin."

Master Pedro bowed, saying:

"I expected no less from the extraordinary Christianity of the valiant Don Quixote of La Mancha, a true shelter and protection for all needy and impoverished wanderers; in this the noble innkeeper and the great Sancho will be mediators between your grace and me, and assessors of what the demolished figures are worth, or might have been worth."

The innkeeper and Sancho agreed, and then Master Pedro picked up from the floor King Marsilio of Zaragoza, who was missing his head, and said:

"You can see how impossible it is to return this king to his original state, and so, it seems to me, unless you think otherwise, that for his death, end, and termination I should be given four and a half *reales*."

"Continue!" said Don Quixote.

"Well, for this slash that goes from top to bottom," continued Master Pedro, picking up the two halves of Emperor Charlemagne, "it would not be too much if I asked five and a quarter *reales*."

"That's no small amount," said Sancho.

"Not a large one, either," replied the innkeeper. "Let's settle at five *reales*."

"Give him the entire five and a quarter," said Don Quixote, "for a quarter more or less will not change this notable misfortune in any way; finish quickly, Master Pedro, because it is almost time for supper and I am feeling somewhat hungry."

"For this figure," said Master Pedro, "the beautiful Melisendra, who is missing a nose and one eye, I want, and I think it's fair, two *reales* and twelve *maravedís*."

"It would certainly be the devil's work," said Don Quixote, "if Melisendra and her husband were not already at the French border, at the very least, because the horse they were riding seemed to me to be flying rather than running; and so there is no reason to try to swindle me, showing me a Melisendra without a nose when the other one is at leisure and making merry in France with her husband. May God help each man with his own affairs, Señor Master Pedro, and let all of us proceed in a straightforward way and with honest intentions. Continue."

Master Pedro, who saw that Don Quixote was slipping back into madness and returning to his earlier theme, did not want him to get away, and so he said:

"This can't be Melisendra, it must be one of her maids, and so if you give me sixty *maravedís* for her, I'll consider myself satisfied and well-paid."

In this fashion, prices were set for many other destroyed puppets, which were later modified by the two arbitrating judges to the satisfaction of all parties and reached a total of forty and three-quarters *reales*; in addition to this amount, which Sancho immediately took out of the purse and paid to him, Master Pedro requested two *reales* for the effort of catching the monkey.

"Give them to him, Sancho," said Don Quixote, "not for catching the monkey, but for bending his elbow;[8] and I would give two hundred

8. *Mono* is "monkey," and *mona* is "female monkey." Colloquially, it can also mean "drinking binge" or "hangover." The Spanish reads, ". . . *no para tomar el mono, sino la mona*."

more as a reward to the person who could tell me with certainty that Señora Doña Melisendra and Señor Don Gaiferos were in France now with their people."

"No one could tell us that better than my monkey," said Master Pedro, "but not even the devil can catch him now, though I imagine that affection and hunger will force him to look for me tonight, and God will bring the dawn, and then we'll see."

In short, the storm over the puppet show came to an end, and everyone ate supper in peace and good fellowship, at Don Quixote's expense, for he was generous in the extreme.

Before daybreak the man carrying the lances and halberds left, and shortly after dawn the cousin and the page came to take their leave of Don Quixote: the one to return home and the other to continue his journey, and to help him on his way, Don Quixote gave the page a dozen *reales*. Master Pedro did not wish to engage in further disputes with Don Quixote, whom he knew very well, and so he arose before the sun, and after gathering up the relics of his puppet theater, and his monkey, he also set out to seek adventures. The innkeeper, who did not know Don Quixote, was as astonished by his madness as by his generosity. To conclude, Sancho paid him very well, by order of his master, and when it was almost eight in the morning they said goodbye, left the inn, and took to the road, where we shall leave them, for that will afford us the opportunity to recount other things that are pertinent to the narration of this famous history.

CHAPTER XXVII

In which the identities of Master Pedro and his monkey are revealed, as well as the unhappy outcome of the braying adventure, which Don Quixote did not conclude as he had wished and intended

Cide Hamete, the chronicler of this great history, begins this chapter with the words *I swear as a Catholic Christian . . .* , to which his translator says that Cide Hamete swearing as a Catholic Christian when he was a Moor, which he undoubtedly was, meant only that just as the Catholic

Christian, when he swears, swears or should swear the truth, and tell the truth in everything he says, so too he was telling the truth, as if he were swearing as a Catholic Christian, when he wrote about Don Quixote, especially when he told who Master Pedro was, as well as the sooth-saying monkey who had amazed all those towns and villages with his divinations.

He says, then, that whoever read the first part of this history will re-member very clearly Ginés de Pasamonte, to whom, along with the other galley slaves, Don Quixote gave his freedom in the Sierra Morena, a charitable act that was repaid with ingratitude and thanklessness by those ill-intentioned and badly behaved people. This Ginés de Pasa-monte, whom Don Quixote called Ginesillo de Parapilla, was the man who stole Sancho Panza's donkey; and since the how and when of that theft were not included in the first part through an error of the printers, many have been led to attribute this printing error to the author's defec-tive memory. To be brief, Ginés stole the donkey when Sancho was sleeping on its back, using the same trick and device that Brunelo used when Sacripante was at Albraca and he took the horse out from between his legs, and then Sancho recovered the donkey, as has already been re-counted. This Ginés, fearful of being captured by the officers of the law who were looking for him so that he could be punished for his infinite deceptions and crimes, so numerous and of such a nature that he himself wrote a long book recounting them, decided to cross into the kingdom of Aragón, cover his left eye, and take up the trade of puppet master, for this and sleight of hand were things he knew extremely well.

It so happened that from a group of freed Christians who had come from Barbary he bought the monkey and taught it to jump onto his shoulder at a certain signal and then whisper, or seem to whisper, in his ear. When he had done this, before he would enter any village where he was taking his puppet theater and monkey, he would learn in a nearby village, or from anyone he could, what specific things had happened in the village and to whom; and after he had committed them to memory, the first thing he did was put on his puppet show, sometimes playing one story and sometimes another, but all of them happy, and joyful, and well-known. When the show was over, he proclaimed the abilities of his mon-key, telling the audience that he could see everything past and present, but that he had no skill in divining the future. For the answer to each question he would ask for two *reales*, and for some he lowered the price, depending on the mood of the questioners; on occasion he would stay in houses where he would know certain incidents that had happened to the people who lived there, and even though they did not ask anything because they did not want to pay, he would signal the monkey and then say that the animal had said something that fit perfectly with those incidents. In this fashion he gained remarkable credibility, and everyone came to see him. On other occasions, since he was so intelligent, he responded so that the answers matched the questions, and since no one examined him or pressed him to say how his monkey could be a soothsayer, he made a monkey of them all and filled his pockets.

As soon as he entered the inn he recognized Don Quixote and Sancho, and this made it easy for him to astound Don Quixote and Sancho Panza and everyone at the inn, but it would have cost him dear if Don Quixote had lowered his hand a little when he cut off King Marsilio's head and destroyed all his knights, as related in the previous chapter.

This is what there is to say about Master Pedro and his monkey.

Returning to Don Quixote of La Mancha, I will say that after he left the inn, he decided to first see the banks of the Ebro River and the surrounding region before entering the city of Zaragoza, since he had enough time for everything before the tourney began. This was his intention as he traveled along the road, and he rode on it for two days without anything occurring that was worth writing down, and then on the third day, as he was riding up a hill, he heard the loud sounds of drums and trumpets and the firing of harquebuses. At first he thought a regiment of soldiers was passing through, and in order to see them he spurred Rocinante and rode up the hill, and when he reached the top he saw at the foot of the hill what appeared to be more than two hundred men armed with a variety of weapons, such as pikes, crossbows, battle-axes, halberds, lances, a few harquebuses, and a good number of bucklers. He rode down the hillside and came so close to the squadron that he clearly saw the banners, observing the colors and noting the devices they displayed, especially one, a standard or pennant of white satin on which was painted, in a very lifelike manner, a donkey that seemed to be a small Sardinian,[1] with his head raised, mouth open, and tongue out, as if in the act and posture of braying; around him these two verses were written in large letters:

> Two mayors of two towns:
> they brayed, and not in vain.

---

1. A breed of small donkeys native to Sardinia.

By means of this emblem Don Quixote assumed that these people were from the braying village, and he told Sancho this as he read to him what was written on the banner. He also said that the man who told them about the matter had erred when he said that it had been two councilmen who brayed, because according to the verses on the banner, they had been mayors. To which Sancho Panza responded:

"Señor, that's of no importance, because it well might be that the councilmen who brayed in time became the mayors of their villages, and so can be called by both titles, especially since it doesn't matter to the truth of the history if the brayers were mayors or councilmen, since they really did bray, and a mayor's as good as a councilman for braying."

In short, they realized and concluded that the offended village was coming out to do battle with another that had insulted it more than it was proper and fitting for good neighbors to do.

Don Quixote approached them, to the great sorrow of Sancho, who never liked to find himself involved in these kinds of situations. The men in the squadron welcomed him into their midst, believing he was one of their supporters. Don Quixote, raising his visor, rode with a gallant air and bearing up to the standard with the donkey, where the most distinguished men in the army, astounded with the usual astonishment that struck all those who saw him for the first time, gathered round to see him. Don Quixote, finding them so intent on looking at him, but not saying anything to him or asking any questions, wanted to take advantage of their silence by breaking his, and he raised his voice and said:

"Good sirs, as earnestly as I can I beg you not to interrupt a statement I wish to make, unless you see that it offends and angers you; if this should happen, at the smallest sign from you I shall place a seal on my mouth and a clamp on my tongue."

Everyone told him to say whatever he wished and they would gladly listen to him. With this license, Don Quixote continued, saying:

"I, Señores, am a knight errant whose practice is arms and whose profession is favoring those in need of favor and helping those in distress. Some days ago I learned of your misfortune and the cause that moves you to constantly take up arms and seek revenge against your enemies; and having reflected time and time again on your case, I find that, according to the laws of the duel, you are mistaken in considering yourselves insulted, because no single individual can insult an entire village except by challenging it as a whole with being a traitor, since he does not know who in particular committed the treasonous act. We have an example of this in Don Diego Ordóñez de Lara,[2] who challenged the entire population of Zamora because he did not know that Vellido Dolfos alone had committed the treason of killing his king, and so he challenged them all, and all were entitled to seek revenge and respond, although it is certainly true that Señor Don Diego took it a little too far and even went beyond the limits of the challenge, for he had no reason to challenge the dead, the water, the loaves of bread, those about to be born, or all the other things that are mentioned there;[3] but then, when anger overcomes mother wit, no father, tutor, or restraint can curb the tongue.

Since it is true that a single individual cannot offend an entire kingdom, province, city, nation, or people, it is evident that there is no reason to come out to avenge the challenge of the offense, for it is not one. Imagine if people from the village of the Reloja were constantly killing those who called them by that name,[4] or if the Fusspots, the Eggplant-eaters, the Whalers, the Soapmakers did,[5] or any of the other names and nicknames that are always in the mouths of boys and people of little worth! Imagine if all these noble towns were to take offense and seek vengeance, their swords, like the slide on a sackbut, constantly going in and out in any dispute, no matter how trivial! No, no, God would not permit nor desire that. Prudent men and well-ordered nations take up arms and unsheathe their swords and risk their persons, lives, and fortunes for only four reasons: first, in defense of the Catholic faith; second, in self-defense, which is a natural and divine law; third, in defense of their honor, their family, and their fortune; fourth, to serve their king in a just war; and if we wish to add a fifth, which can be considered the second, it is in defense of their country. To these five capital causes we can add a few others that are just and reasonable and oblige men to take up arms, but anyone who does so for trifles and matters that are more laughable and amusing than insulting seems to lack all good sense; moreover, taking unjust revenge, and no

---

2. The story is based on the cycle of ballads that deals with the struggle for power among the children of Fernando I, and the siege of Zamora, in the eleventh century.

3. The lines in the ballad read: "I challenge you, Zamorans / as false and lying traitors; / I challenge young and old, / I challenge the quick and the dead; / I challenge the plants in the field, / I challenge the river fishes, / I challenge your bread and meat, / and also your water and wine."

4. This was a nickname given to the Andalusian town of Espartinas because, as the story goes, a clock was needed for the church tower, and the priest sent away to Sevilla for a "nice little pregnant female clock" (*reloja* is the nonexistent feminine form of *reloj*, or "clock") so that the baby clocks could subsequently be sold. The same story was also told about other towns.

5. Nicknames given to the residents of Vallodolid, Toledo, Madrid, and Sevilla, respectively.

revenge can be just, is directly contrary to the holy law we profess, which commands us to do good to our enemies and love those who hate us, a commandment that, although it seems somewhat difficult to obey, is not, except for those who care less for God than for the world, and more for the flesh than for the spirit; because Jesus Christ, God and true man, who never lied, nor could He lie, nor can He, being our lawgiver, said that His yoke was gentle and His burden light; and so, He would not command something that was impossible to obey. Therefore, Señores, your graces are obliged by divine and human laws to make peace."

"The devil take me," said Sancho to himself, "if this master of mine isn't a theologian, and if he isn't, then he's as much like one as two peas in a pod."

Don Quixote took a breath, and seeing that they were still listening silently, he wished to continue his speech, and would have if Sancho, with his usual keenness, had not intervened when, seeing that his master had paused, he began to speak, saying:

"My master, Don Quixote of La Mancha, who was once called *The Knight of the Sorrowful Face* and is now called *The Knight of the Lions*, is a very prudent gentleman who knows Latin and Spanish like a bachelor, and in all his dealings and advice he proceeds like a very good soldier, and he knows all the laws and rules about what is called dueling like the back of his hand, and so there's nothing else to do but listen to what he says, and if you're wrong, let it be on my head, especially since they say that it's foolish to lose your temper just because you hear somebody bray; I remember, when I was boy, I used to bray whenever I felt like it, and nobody held me back, and I did it so well and so perfectly that when I brayed all the donkeys in the village brayed, but that didn't stop me from being my parents' son, and they were very honorable people, and even though this talent of mine was envied by more than a few of the conceited boys in my village, I didn't care at all. And so that you can see that I'm telling the truth, wait and listen, because if you know this, it's like knowing how to swim: once you've learned you never forget."

And then he held his nose and began to bray so enthusiastically that all the nearby valleys resonated with the sound. But one of the men who was near him, thinking he was mocking them, raised a long pole that he had in his hand and hit him so hard with it that he knocked Sancho Panza to the ground, senseless. Don Quixote, who saw Sancho so badly treated, turned, his lance in hand, on the man who had hit him, but so many men came between them that it was not possible to avenge his squire; instead, seeing that a storm of stones came raining down on him, and that he was being threatened by a thousand crossbows and a similar number of harquebuses, all of them aimed at him, he turned Rocinante's reins and as fast as his best gallop could carry him, Don Quixote rode away, praying to God with all his heart to save him from that danger, and fearing at each step that a bullet would enter at his back and come out of his chest; at every moment he would take a breath to see if he still could.

But the men in the squadron were content to see him flee, and they did not shoot at him. They put Sancho across his donkey as soon as he came to, and they allowed him to go after his master, not because he was alert enough to guide the animal, but because the donkey followed in Rocinante's footsteps since he did not like being without him. When Don Quixote had gone some distance, he turned his head and saw Sancho and waited for him, for he saw that no one was following him.

The men in the squadron stayed there until nightfall, and since their adversaries had not come out to do battle, they returned to their village joyfully and happily; if they had known about the ancient custom of the Greeks, on that spot and in that place they would have raised a monument to their victory.

CHAPTER XXVIII

Regarding matters that Benengeli says will be known to the reader if he reads with attention

When the brave man flees, trickery is revealed, and the prudent man waits for a better opportunity. This truth was proved in Don Quixote, who yielded to the fury of the village and the evil intent of the enraged squadron and fled, not thinking of Sancho or the danger in which he left him, and rode the distance he thought sufficient to ensure his safety. Sancho followed, lying across his donkey, as has been related. When he had regained consciousness he overtook Don Quixote, and when he did, Sancho dropped off the donkey at Rocinante's feet, perturbed, bruised, and battered. Don Quixote dismounted to tend to the squire's wounds, but since he found him sound from head to foot, with some anger he said:

"It was an evil hour when you learned how to bray, Sancho![1] And when did you decide it would be a good idea to mention rope in the house of the hanged man? When braying is the music, what counterpoint can there be except a beating? Give thanks to God, Sancho, that even though they made the sign of the cross over you with a stick, they did not cut a *per signum crucis*[2] on your face."

"I'm not about to respond," responded Sancho, "because it seems to me I'm talking with my back. Let's mount and leave this place, and I'll silence my braying, but I won't stop saying that knights errant run away and leave their good squires beaten to a pulp or ground up like grain and in the power of their enemies."

"Withdrawal is not flight," responded Don Quixote, "because you should know, Sancho, that valor not founded on the base of prudence is called recklessness, and the deeds of the reckless are attributed more to good fortune than to courage. And so I confess that I withdrew, but not that I fled, and in this I have imitated many valiant men who have waited for a better moment; the histories are full of such cases, but since they would not be to your advantage or my taste, I shall not recount them to you now."

By now Sancho had mounted his donkey, with the assistance of Don Quixote, who then mounted Rocinante, and slowly they rode toward a stand of poplars that appeared about a quarter of a league distant. From time to time Sancho heaved some very deep sighs and mournful groans, and when Don Quixote asked the cause of such bitter feeling, he responded that from the base of his spine to the back of his neck he was in so much pain that it was driving him mad.

"The cause of this pain no doubt must be," said Don Quixote, "that since the staff they used to beat you was long and tall, it hit the length of your back, which is where the parts that pain you are located; if it had hit more of you, more of you would be in pain."

"By God," said Sancho, "your grace has cleared up a great doubt, and said it so nicely, too! Lord save us! Was the cause of my pain so hidden that you had to tell me I hurt where the staff hit me? If my ankles hurt, there might be a reason to try and guess why, but guessing that I hurt where I was beaten isn't much of a guess. By my faith, Señor Master, other people's troubles don't matter very much, and every day I learn something else about how little I can expect from being in your grace's

---

1. As he has done before, an enraged Don Quixote addresses Sancho in more formal terms and does so throughout this paragraph.

2. Latin for "by the sign of the cross."

company, because if you let them beat me this time, then a hundred more times we'll be back to the old tossings in a blanket and other tricks like that, and if it was my back now, the next time it'll be my eyes. I'd be much better off, but I'm an idiot and will never do anything right in my life, but I'd be much better off, and I'll say it again, if I went back home to my wife and children and supported her and brought them up with whatever it pleased God to give me, instead of following after your grace on roads that have no destination, and byways and highways that lead nowhere, drinking badly and eating worse. And sleeping! Brother squire, you can count on seven feet of ground, and if you want more, take another seven, for it's all up to you, and you can stretch out to your heart's content; all I hope is that I can see the first man who put the finishing touches on knight errantry burned and ground into dust, or at least the first one who wanted to be squire to the great fools that all knights errant in the past must have been. I won't say anything about those in the present; since your grace is one of them, I respect them, and I know that your grace knows a point or two more than the devil in all you say and think."

"I would make a wager with you, Sancho,"[3] said Don Quixote. "Now that you are speaking and no one is restraining you, you have no pains anywhere in your body. Speak, my friend, and say everything that comes to your mind and your mouth; in exchange for your not having any pains, I shall consider the irritation your impertinence causes me as pleasure. And if you so fervently desire to return to your house and wife and children, God forbid that I do anything to stop you; you have my money; calculate how long it has been since we left our village this third time, and calculate what you can and should earn each month, and pay yourself a salary."

"When I served Tomé Carrasco," responded Sancho, "the father of Bachelor Sansón Carrasco, and your grace knows him very well, I earned two *ducados* a month, and food besides; with your grace I don't know what I should earn, though I know that the squire of a knight errant has more work than a man who serves a farmer, because when we serve farmers, no matter how much we work during the day, and no matter what bad things happen to us, at night we eat stew and sleep in beds, which I haven't done since I started serving your grace. Except for the short time we were in Don Diego de Miranda's house, and the outing I had with the

---

3. In his anger with Sancho, Don Quixote returns to the more distant form of address, which he uses for the next few paragraphs, until he begins to laugh.

skimmings I took from Camacho's pots, and the way I ate and drank and slept in Basilio's house, all the rest of the time I've slept on the hard ground, outside, exposed to what they call the inclemencies of heaven, eating crumbs of cheese and crusts of bread and drinking water from streams or springs or whatever we find in those out-of-the-way places where we travel."

"I confess," said Don Quixote, "that everything you say, Sancho, is true. In your opinion, how much more should I give you than Tomé Carrasco did?"

"In my opinion," said Sancho, "if your grace added two *reales* more a month, I'd think I was well-paid. This is the salary for my work, but as far as satisfying your grace's word and promise to make me governor of an ínsula, it would be fair to add another six *reales,* and that would be a total of thirty."

"Very well," replied Don Quixote, "and in accordance with the salary you have indicated, it has been twenty-five days since we left our village: calculate, Sancho, the rate times the amount, and see what I owe you, and pay yourself the money, as I have said."

"Oh, Lord," said Sancho, "your grace is very much mistaken in this count, because in the matter of the promise of the ínsula, you have to count from the day your grace promised it to me until this very moment."

"Well, Sancho, how long ago did I promise it to you?" said Don Quixote.

"If I remember correctly," responded Sancho, "it must be more than twenty years, give or take three days."

Don Quixote gave himself a great slap on the forehead and began to laugh very heartily, and he said:

"My travels in the Sierra Morena or in the course of all our sallies took barely two months, and you say, Sancho, that I promised you the ínsula twenty years ago? Now I say that you want to use all my money for your salary, and if this is true, and it makes you happy, I shall give it all to you, and may it do you good; in exchange for finding myself without so bad a squire, I shall enjoy being poor and not having a *blanca.* But tell me, you corrupter of the squirely rules of knight errantry, where have you seen or read that any squire of a knight errant has engaged his master in 'You have to give me this amount plus that amount every month for serving you'? Set sail, set sail, scoundrel, coward, monster, for you seem to be all three, set sail, I say, on the *mare mag-*

num[4] of their histories, and if you find that any squire has said, or even thought, what you have said here, I want you to fasten it to my forehead and then you can pinch my face four times. Turn the reins or halter of your donkey, and go back to your house, because you will not take another step with me. O bread unthanked! O promises misplaced! O man more animal than human! Now, when I intended to place you in a position where, despite your wife, you would be called Señor, now you take your leave? Now you go, when I had the firm and binding intention of making you lord of the best ínsula in the world? In short, as you have said on other occasions, there is no honey . . .[5] You are a jackass, and must be a jackass, and will end your days as a jackass, for in my opinion, your life will run its course before you accept and realize that you are an animal."

Sancho stared at Don Quixote as he was inveighing against him and felt so much remorse that tears came to his eyes, and in a weak and mournful voice he said:

"Señor, I confess that for me to be a complete jackass, all that's missing is my tail; if your grace wants to put one on me, I'll consider it well-placed, and I'll serve you like a donkey for the rest of my days. Your grace should forgive me, and take pity on my lack of experience, and remember that I know very little, and if I talk too much, it comes more from weakness than from malice, and to err is human, to forgive, divine."

"I would be amazed, Sancho, if you did not mix some little proverb into your talk. Well, then, I forgive you as long as you mend your ways and from now on do not show so much interest in your own gain, but attempt to take heart, and have the courage and valor to wait for my promises to be fulfilled, for although it may take some time, it is in no way impossible."

Sancho responded that he would, although it would mean finding strength in weakness.

Saying this, they entered the stand of trees, and Don Quixote settled down at the foot of an elm, and Sancho at the foot of a beech, for these trees, and others like them, always have feet but not hands. Sancho spent a painful night, because he felt the beating more in the night air, and Don Quixote spent the night in his constant memories; even so, their eyes closed in sleep, and at daybreak they continued on their way, looking for the banks of the famous Ebro, where something occurred that will be recounted in the following chapter.

---

4. Latin for "the great sea" or "ocean."

5. "There is no honey without gall" (*No hay miel sin hiel*), or "Nothing is perfect."

CHAPTER XXIX

Regarding the famous adventure of the enchanted boat

At an unhurried and leisurely pace, two days after they left the stand of trees, Don Quixote and Sancho came to the Ebro River, and seeing it brought great joy to Don Quixote because he contemplated and observed the pleasantness of its banks, the clarity of its waters, the gentleness of its current, and the abundance of its liquid crystal, and this happy sight revived in his memory a thousand amorous thoughts. He lingered especially on what he had seen in the Cave of Montesinos; although Master Pedro's monkey had told him that some of those things were true and some a lie, he relied more on the true parts than on the false, unlike Sancho, who considered them all the same lie.

As they proceeded in this fashion, there came into view a small boat that lacked oars or any other kind of gear and was pulled up to shore and tied to the trunk of a tree on the river bank. Don Quixote looked all around and saw no one, and then, without warning, he dismounted Rocinante and told Sancho to do the same with his donkey and to tie both animals very carefully to the trunk of a poplar or willow that was growing there. Sancho asked the reason for this sudden dismounting and tethering of their animals. Don Quixote responded:

"You must know, Sancho, that this boat clearly and beyond any doubt is calling and inviting me to get in it and sail to assist a knight or some other eminent person in need who must be in grave danger, because in the books of chivalric histories this is what is done by the enchanters who become involved and act in them: when a knight is placed in extreme difficulty and cannot be freed except by the hand of another knight, though the second knight may be at a distance of two or three thousand leagues or even more, either they carry him off on a cloud or provide him with a boat which he enters, and in the blink of an eye they move him through the air or over the sea, wherever they wish and wherever his help is needed; and so, O Sancho, this boat has been placed here for the very same purpose, and this is as true as the fact that it is now day; and before this day is over, tie the donkey and Rocinante together, and may the hand of God guide us, for I would not fail to embark even if asked not to by discalced friars."

"Well, if that's true," responded Sancho, "and your grace at every step insists on finding nonsensical things, or whatever you call them, there's nothing I can do but obey, and bow my head, and follow the proverb that says, 'Do what your master tells you and sit with him at the table.' But just to satisfy my conscience, I want to warn your grace that I don't think this boat is one of the enchanted ones; it seems to me it belongs to some fishermen, because the best shad in the world swim this river."

Sancho said this as he was tethering the animals, leaving them, with a grieving heart, in the care and protection of the enchanters. Don Quixote told him not to worry about abandoning the animals, for the enchanter who would take them to such longinquous roads and regions would be sure to care for them.

"I don't understand *logiquos*," said Sancho, "and I don't think I've heard a word like that in all my days."

"*Longinquous*," responded Don Quixote, "means *remote*, and it is no wonder you do not understand it, for you are not obliged to know Latin, as are those who boast of knowing it but do not."

"The animals are tied," replied Sancho. "What do we do now?"

"What?" responded Don Quixote. "Cross ourselves and raise anchor; I mean to say, embark and cut the mooring line that holds this boat."

And after leaping in, with Sancho following him, he cut the rope, and the boat started to move slowly away from shore; when Sancho found himself some two *varas* onto the river he began to tremble, fearing that he was lost; but nothing caused him more grief than the sound of the donkey braying and the sight of Rocinante struggling to break free, and he said to his master:

"The donkey is braying because he is sorry about our absence, and Rocinante is trying to get free so that he can jump in after us. O dearest friends, stay in peace, and let the madness that takes us away from you turn into disappointment and bring us back to you!"

And saying this, he began to cry so bitterly that Don Quixote, displeased and irascible, said:

"What do you fear, coward? Why do you weep, spineless creature?

Who is pursuing you, who is hounding you, heart of a mouse, and what do you lack, beggar in the midst of plenty? Are you perhaps walking barefoot through the mountains of the Rif, or are you sitting on a bench like an archduke and sailing the tranquil current of this pleasant river, from which we shall shortly emerge onto a calm sea? But we must have emerged already, and traveled at least seven hundred or eight hundred leagues; if I had an astrolabe here and could calculate the height of the pole, I could tell you how far we have traveled, although either I know very little, or we have already passed, or will soon pass, the equinoctial line that divides and separates the opposite poles at an equal distance from each."

"And when we reach that lion your grace has mentioned," asked Sancho, "how far will we have traveled?"

"A good distance," replied Don Quixote, "because of the three hundred and sixty degrees of water and earth that the globe contains, according to the computations of Ptolemy, the greatest cosmographer known to man, we shall have traveled half that distance when we reach the line I have mentioned."

"By God," said Sancho, "your grace has brought in a fine witness to testify to what you say, some kind of coast and a raft, and a toll with a meow or something like that."

Don Quixote laughed at the interpretation Sancho had given to the name and computations and calculations of the cosmographer Ptolemy, and he said:

"You should know, Sancho, that the Spaniards and others who embark at Cádiz for the East Indies have a sign to let them know they have passed the equinoctial line, which is that every louse on the ship dies,[1] and not one is left alive, and you could not find a single one on the vessel even if you were paid its weight in gold; and so, Sancho, you can run your hand along your thigh, and if you run across a living thing, our doubts will be resolved, and if you do not, then we have passed the line."

"I don't believe any of that," responded Sancho, "but even so, I'll do what your grace tells me to, though I don't know why we need to make these tests, since I can see with my own eyes that we haven't gone five *varas* from shore, and we haven't moved two *varas* away from the animals because there's Rocinante and the donkey exactly where we left them,

---

1. This was a common belief in Cervantes's time.

and looking carefully, which is what I'm doing now, I swear that we're not even moving or traveling as fast as an ant."

"Sancho, perform the investigation I have told you to, and do not concern yourself with any other, for you know nothing about the colures, lines, parallels, zodiacs, ellipticals, poles, solstices, equinoxes, planets, signs, points, and measurements that compose the celestial and terrestrial spheres; if you knew all these things, or even some of them, you would see clearly which parallels we have cut, how many zodiacal signs we have seen, and how many we have already left behind and are leaving behind now. And I tell you again to probe and go hunting, for in my opinion you are cleaner than a sheet of smooth white paper."

Sancho began to probe, and after extending his hand carefully and cautiously behind his left knee, he raised his head, looked at his master, and said:

"Either the test is false, or we haven't gone as far as your grace says, not by many leagues."

"What is it?" asked Don Quixote. "Have you come across something?"

"More like somethings," responded Sancho.

And shaking his fingers, he washed his entire hand in the river as the boat glided gently along in midstream, moved not by any secret intelligence or hidden enchanter, but by the current of the water itself, which was calm and tranquil then.

At this point they saw two large watermills in the middle of the river, and as soon as Don Quixote saw them, he said in a loud voice to Sancho:

"Do you see? There, my friend, you can see the city, castle, or fortress where some knight is being held captive, or some queen, princess, or noblewoman ill-treated, and I have been brought here to deliver them."

"What the devil kind of city, fortress, or castle is your grace talking about, Señor?" said Sancho. "Can't you see that those are watermills in the river, where they grind wheat?"

"Be quiet, Sancho," said Don Quixote, "for although they seem to be watermills, they are not; I have already told you that enchantments change and alter all things from their natural state. I do not mean to say that they are really altered from one state to another, but that they seem to be, as experience has shown in the transformation of Dulcinea, sole refuge of my hopes."

And then the boat, having entered the middle of the current, began to travel not quite so slowly as it had so far. Many of the millers in the watermills, who saw that the boat was coming down the river and would be swallowed up by the rushing torrent of the wheels, hurried out with long poles to stop it; and since they came out well-floured, their faces and clothes covered in dust from the flour, they were not a pretty sight. They were shouting, saying:

"You devils! Where are you going? Are you crazy? Do you want to drown and be smashed to pieces by those wheels?"

"Did I not tell you, Sancho," said Don Quixote, "that we had come to a place where I would show the valor of my arm? Look at the miscreants and scoundrels who have come out to meet me; look at the number of monsters who oppose me; look at their hideous faces grimacing at us. . . . Well, now you will see, you villains!"

And standing up in the boat, with great shouts he began to threaten the millers, saying:

"Wicked and ill-advised rabble, set free and release the person, high-born or low-, no matter his estate or quality, whom you hold captive in your fortress or prison, for I am Don Quixote of La Mancha, also known as the Knight of the Lions, for whom, by order of the heavens on high, the successful conclusion of this adventure has been reserved."

And saying this, he put his hand on his sword and began to flourish it in the air against the millers, who, hearing but not understanding this nonsense, began to use their poles to stop the boat, which by now was entering the millrace rapids.

Sancho was on his knees, devoutly praying to heaven to save him from so clear a danger, which it did through the efforts and speed of the millers, who pushed against the boat with their poles and stopped it but could not keep it from capsizing and throwing Don Quixote and Sancho into the water; it was fortunate for Don Quixote that he knew how to swim like a goose, although the weight of his armor made him sink twice, and if it had not been for the millers, who jumped into the water and pulled them out, it would have been the end of them both.

When they had been pulled to land, more soaked than dying of thirst, Sancho, on his knees, hands clasped, eyes turned up to heaven, asked God in a long and devout prayer to save him from any future rash desires and acts of his master.

Then the fishermen arrived who owned the boat, which had been shattered by the wheels of the watermills, and seeing that it had been smashed to pieces, they began to strip Sancho and to demand that Don Quixote pay them, and he, very calmly, as if nothing had happened, told the millers and fishermen he would gladly pay for the boat on the condition that they willingly and without reservation turn over to him the person or persons whom they were holding captive in their castle.

"Are you out of your mind? What persons and what castle are you talking about?" responded one of the millers. "Do you want to take the people who come to grind wheat at these mills?"

"Enough!" Don Quixote said to himself. "It will be preaching in the desert to try to convince this rabble to take any virtuous action. In this adventure two valiant enchanters must have had an encounter, and one hinders what the other attempts: one provided me with the boat, and the other threw me out of it. God help us, for the entire world is nothing but tricks and deceptions opposing one another. I can do no more."

And raising his voice and looking at the watermills, he said:

"Friends, whoever you may be, who are captive in this prison, forgive me; to my misfortune, and yours, I cannot free you from your travail. This adventure must be reserved and destined for another knight."

Having said this, he came to an agreement with the fishermen and paid fifty *reales* for the boat, which Sancho gave to them very unwillingly, saying:

"Two more boat trips like this one and everything we own will be at the bottom of the river."

The fishermen and the millers were astonished as they looked at those two figures, apparently so different from other men, and they could not understand the meaning of Don Quixote's words and questions to them; and considering them mad, they left them, the millers returning to their mills and the fishermen to their huts. Don Quixote and Sancho went back to their animals, and to being as foolish as jackasses,[2] and so ended the adventure of the enchanted boat.

2. This phrase is based on the wordplay growing out of *bestia*, which can literally mean "animal" or "beast" as well as "dolt" or "dunce."

CHAPTER XXX

Regarding what befell Don Quixote with a beautiful huntress

Knight and squire returned to their animals feeling rather melancholy and out of sorts, especially Sancho, for whom touching their store of money touched his very soul, since it seemed to him that taking anything away from it meant taking away the apple of his eye. Finally, without saying a word, they mounted and rode away from the famous river, Don Quixote sunk deep in thoughts of love, and Sancho in those of his increased revenues, which at the moment he seemed very far from obtaining; although he was a fool, he understood very well that all or most of his master's actions were mad, and he was looking for an opportunity to tear himself away and go home without engaging his master in explanations or leavetakings, but Fortune ordained that matters should take a turn contrary to his fears.

It so happened, then, that the next day, as the sun was setting and they were riding out of a wood, Don Quixote cast his eye upon a green meadow, and at the far end he saw people, and as he drew near he realized that they were falconers.[1] He came closer, and among them he saw a graceful lady on a snow white palfrey or pony adorned with a green harness and a silver sidesaddle. The lady was also dressed in green, so elegantly and richly that she seemed the very embodiment of elegance. On her left hand she carried a goshawk, which indicated to Don Quixote that she was a great lady and probably the mistress of all the other hunters, which was true, and so he said to Sancho:

"Run, Sancho my friend, and tell the lady with the goshawk, who is on the palfrey, that I, the Knight of the Lions, kiss the hands of her great

1. Hunting with falcons or other birds of prey was a pastime of the upper classes exclusively.

beauty, and if her highness gives me permission to do so, I shall kiss her hands myself and serve her to the best of my ability and to the extent her highness commands. And be careful, Sancho, how you speak, and be careful not to inject any of your proverbs into the message."

"You take me for an injecter!" responded Sancho. "You say that to me! This isn't the first time in my life, you know, that I've carried messages to high and mighty ladies!"

"Except for the one you carried to the lady Dulcinea," replied Don Quixote, "I do not know that you have ever carried another, at least not in my service."

"That is true," responded Sancho, "but if you pay your debts, you don't worry about guaranties, and in a prosperous house supper's soon on the stove; I mean that nobody has to tell me things or give me any advice: I'm prepared for anything, and I know something about everything."

"I believe you, Sancho," said Don Quixote. "Go, then, and may God go with you."

Sancho left at a trot, urging his donkey on to a faster pace than usual, and when he reached the beautiful huntress he dismounted, kneeled before her, and said:

"Beautiful lady, that knight over there, called *The Knight of the Lions*, is my master, and I'm his squire, called Sancho Panza at home. This *Knight of the Lions*, who not long ago was called *The Knight of the Sorrowful Face*, has sent me to ask your highness to have the goodness to give permission for him, with your agreement, approval, and consent, to put his desire into effect, which is, as he says and I believe, none other than to serve your lofty highness and beauty, and by giving it, your ladyship will do something that redounds to your benefit, and from it he'll receive a most notable favor and happiness."

"Indeed, good squire," responded the lady, "you have delivered your message with all the pomp and circumstance that such messages demand. Rise up from the ground; it is not right for the squire of so great a knight as the Knight of the Sorrowful Face, about whom we have heard so much, to remain on his knees: arise, friend, and tell your master that he is very welcome to serve me and my husband, the duke, on a country estate we have nearby."

Sancho stood, amazed by the beauty of the good lady and by her great breeding and courtesy, and especially by her saying that she had heard of his master, the Knight of the Sorrowful Face, and if she did not call him the Knight of the Lions, it must have been because he had taken the name so recently. The duchess, whose title was still unknown, asked him:

"Tell me, my dear squire: this master of yours, isn't he the one who has a history published about him called *The Ingenious Gentleman Don Quixote of La Mancha*, and isn't the mistress of his heart a lady named Dulcinea of Toboso?"

"He's the very one, Señora," responded Sancho, "and that squire of his who is, or ought to be, in that history, the one named Sancho Panza, is me, unless I was changed for another in the cradle, I mean the printing press."

"All of this makes me very happy," said the duchess. "Go, my dear Panza, and tell your master that he is a most welcome visitor to my estates, and that nothing could give me greater joy than to receive him."

Sancho, with this extremely amiable reply, returned to his master with great pleasure and recounted everything that the great lady had said, praising to the skies, in his rustic way, her great beauty, charm, and courtesy. Don Quixote arranged himself in the saddle, set his feet firmly in the stirrups, adjusted his visor, spurred on Rocinante, and with a gallant bearing went to kiss the hands of the duchess, who, sending for the duke, her husband, told him, as Don Quixote was approaching, about his message; and the two of them, because they had read the first part of this history and consequently had learned of Don Quixote's absurd turn of mind, waited for him with great pleasure and a desire to know him, intending to follow that turn of mind and acquiesce to everything he said, and, for as long as he stayed with them, treat him like a knight errant with all the customary ceremonies found in the books of chivalry, which they had read and of which they were very fond.

At this point Don Quixote reached them, with his visor raised, and as he gave signs of dismounting, Sancho hurried to hold the stirrup for him but was so unfortunate that when he dismounted from the donkey he caught his foot in a cord on the packsaddle and could not get free; instead, he was left dangling, with his face and chest on the ground. Don Quixote, who was not in the habit of dismounting without someone to hold the stirrup for him, and thinking that Sancho had already come to do that, went flying off Rocinante and pulled the saddle after him, for its cinches must have been loose, and he and the saddle both fell to the ground, not without great embarrassment to him and a good number of curses that he muttered between his teeth against the luckless Sancho, whose foot was still trammeled.

The duke ordered his hunters to assist the knight and the squire, and they helped up Don Quixote, who was badly bruised from his fall and, limping and hobbling, attempted to kneel before the two nobles, but the duke would not permit it; instead, after dismounting his horse, he went to embrace Don Quixote, saying:

"It grieves me, Señor Knight of the Sorrowful Face, that the first step your grace has taken on my land has turned out so badly, but the carelessness of squires is often the cause of unforeseen events that are even worse."

"The one I experienced when I saw you, most valiant prince," responded Don Quixote, "could not possibly be bad, even if my fall had been to the bottom of the abyss, for the glory of having seen you would lift me and raise me even from the depths. My squire, may God curse him, loosens his tongue to speak mischief better than he fastens the cinches to secure a saddle; but however I may be, fallen or upright, on foot or mounted, I shall always be in your service and in that of my lady the duchess, your most esteemed consort, and most worthy mistress of beauty, and universal princess of courtesy."

"Softly, Señor Don Quixote of La Mancha," said the duke, "for when Señora Doña Dulcinea of Toboso is present, no other beauty should be praised."

By this time Sancho Panza was free of his bonds, and finding himself close by, before his master could respond he said:

"It can't be denied but must be affirmed that my lady Dulcinea of Toboso is very beautiful, but the hare leaps up when you least expect it;[2] I've heard that this thing they call nature is like a potter who makes clay bowls, and if he makes a beautiful bowl, he can also make two, or three, or a hundred: I say this because, by my faith, my lady the duchess is as good-looking as my mistress the lady Dulcinea of Toboso."

Don Quixote turned to the duchess and said:

"Your highness can imagine that no knight errant in the world ever had a squire more talkative or comical than the one I have, and he will prove me truthful if your magnificence should wish to have me serve you for a few days."

To which the duchess responded:

"That our good Sancho is comical is something I esteem greatly, because it is a sign of his cleverness; for wit and humor, Señor Don Quixote, as your grace well knows, do not reside in slow minds, and since our good Sancho is comical and witty, from this moment on I declare him a clever man."

2. An adage that means "Life is full of surprises."

"And a talkative one," added Don Quixote.

"So much the better," said the duke, "for there are many witticisms that cannot be said in only a few words. And in order not to waste time in merely speaking them, let the great Knight of the Sorrowful Face come—"

"Of the Lions is what your highness should say," said Sancho, "because there's no more Sorrowful Face, or Figure: let it be of the Lions."[3]

The duke continued:

"I say that Señor Knight of the Lions should come to a castle of mine that is nearby, and there he will receive the welcome that so distinguished a personage deserves, the kind that the duchess and I are accustomed to offering to all the knights errant who come there."

By this time, Sancho had adjusted Rocinante's saddle and carefully fastened the cinches; Don Quixote mounted, and the duke mounted his beautiful horse, and they rode with the duchess between them and set out for the castle. The duchess told Sancho to ride near her because she took infinite pleasure in hearing the clever things he said. Sancho did not have to be asked twice, and he wove his way in among the three of them and made a fourth in the conversation, to the delight of the duchess and the duke, who considered it their great good fortune to welcome to their castle such a knight errant and so erring a squire.

CHAPTER XXXI

Which deals with many great things

Sancho's joy was great at finding himself, as it seemed to him, so favored by the duchess, because he imagined he would find in her castle what he had found in the house of Don Diego and in the house of Basilio, for he was always very fond of the good life and missed no opportunity to indulge himself whenever one was presented to him.

3. This sentence seems to be a misprint in the first edition; Martín de Riquer indicates in a footnote that two other editors, Cortejón and Schevill, suggest, in his opinion correctly, that it read as follows:

"... there's no more Sorrowful Face or Figure [there is an untranslatable wordplay involving *figura* ("face") and *figuro* (a nonexistent masculine form)]."

"Let it be of the Lions," the duke continued. "I say that . . ."

The history recounts, then, that before they reached the country estate or castle, the duke rode ahead and gave orders to all his servants concerning how they were to treat Don Quixote; as soon as the knight arrived at the gates of the castle with the duchess, two lackeys or grooms immediately came out, dressed in the kind of long, ankle-length gowns that are called at-home robes and were made of very fine crimson satin, and rapidly putting their arms around Don Quixote and taking him down from his horse, almost before he heard or saw them, they said to him:

"Go, your highness, and help my lady the duchess dismount."

Don Quixote did so, and there were extremely courteous exchanges between them regarding this matter, but, in the end, the persistence of the duchess triumphed, and she refused to descend or dismount the palfrey except in the arms of the duke, saying that she did not consider herself worthy of imposing so useless a burden on so great a knight. Finally, the duke came out to help her dismount, and when they had entered a spacious courtyard, two beautiful maidens approached and placed around Don Quixote's shoulders a great mantle of the finest scarlet, and in an instant all the passageways of the courtyard were crowded with the servants, male and female, of those nobles, and the servants were shouting:

"Welcome to the flower of chivalry, the greatest of all knights errant!"

And all, or most of them, sprinkled flagons of perfumed water on Don Quixote and on the duke and duchess, all of which astounded Don Quixote, and this was the first day he really knew and believed he was a true knight errant and not a fantastic one, for he saw himself treated in the same manner in which, he had read, knights were treated in past ages.

Sancho, forsaking his donkey, attached himself to the duchess and entered the castle, and feeling some remorse at leaving the donkey alone, he went up to a reverend duenna,[1] who had come out with other ladies to receive the duchess, and in a quiet voice he said to her:

"Señora González, or whatever your grace's name may be . . ."

"Doña Rodríguez de Grijalba is my name," responded the duenna. "How can I help you, brother?"

To which Sancho responded:

"I would like your grace to please go out of the castle gate, where

---

1. A duenna was an older woman of good family, usually a widow, in the service of a noblewoman. She wore a long headdress and wimple, something like a nun's, which distinguished her from other, usually younger, ladies-in-waiting.

you'll find a donkey of mine, and if your grace would be so kind, have him taken, or take him yourself, to the stable, because the poor thing is a little fearful and doesn't like to be left alone under any circumstances."

"If the master is as clever as his servant," responded the duenna, "then we're certainly sitting pretty! Go on, brother, and may bad luck follow you and whoever brought you here, and take care of your jackass yourself; the duennas in this house are not accustomed to duties of that nature."

"Well, the truth is," responded Sancho, "that I've heard my master, and he knows all about histories, telling the one about Lancelot,

> when he from Britanny came,
> ladies tended to him,
> and duennas cared for his steed;

and in the case of my donkey, I wouldn't trade him for the steed of Señor Lancelot."

"Brother, if you're a jester," replied the duenna, "then keep your jokes for people who like them and pay you for them; you won't get anything but a fig[2] from me."

"That's fine," responded Sancho, "as long as it's nice and ripe, because your grace won't lose the hand if you count years as points."

"Whoreson," said the duenna, in a rage, "if I'm old or not is God's business, not yours, you garlic-stuffed scoundrel!"

And she said this in so loud a voice that the duchess heard her, and turning around and seeing the duenna so agitated, and her eyes ablaze, she asked whom she was berating.

"He's right here," responded the duenna, "this good man who asked me very insistently to go and put a donkey of his at the castle gate into the stable, and brought up as an example that somewhere, I don't know where, some ladies healed somebody named Lancelot and some duennas took care of his horse, and then, for good measure, he called me old."

"I would consider that the worst insult," responded the duchess, "that anyone could say to me."

And speaking to Sancho, she said:

"Be advised, Sancho my friend, that Doña Rodríguez is very young, and wears that headdress more for reasons of authority and custom than because of her years."

---

2. A gesture of contempt or derision made by placing the thumb between the forefinger and middle finger or under the upper front teeth.

"May the ones I have left to live be cursed," responded Sancho, "if I said it for that reason; I said it only because I'm so fond of my donkey that it seemed to me I couldn't entrust him to any person more charitable than Señora Doña Rodríguez."

Don Quixote, who heard all of this, said:

"Is that the kind of talk appropriate to this place?"

"Señor," responded Sancho, "each person must talk of what he needs no matter where he is; here I remembered about my donkey, and here I talked about him; if I remembered about him in the stable, I'd talk about him there."

To which the duke said:

"Sancho is absolutely correct, and there is no reason to blame him for anything; the donkey will be given food to his heart's content, and Sancho need not worry, for the donkey will be treated as if he were Sancho himself."

With these remarks, pleasing to everyone except Don Quixote, they proceeded upstairs and brought Don Quixote into a room adorned with rich tapestries of gold and brocade; six maidens removed his armor and served as pages, all of them instructed and advised by the duke and duchess as to what they were to do and how they were to treat Don Quixote so that he would imagine and believe they were treating him as a knight errant. When his armor had been removed, Don Quixote was left in his narrow breeches and chamois doublet—dry, tall, thin, his jaws kissing each other inside his mouth—and if the maidens who were serving him had not been charged with hiding their laughter, for this was one of the precise orders their mistress and master had given them, they would have split their sides laughing.

They asked that they be allowed to remove his clothing and dress him in a shirt, but he would not give his consent, saying that modesty was as becoming in knights errant as valor. Even so, he said they should give the shirt to Sancho, and after going with his squire into an inner chamber that had a luxurious bed, he stripped and put on the shirt, and finding himself alone with Sancho, he said:

"Tell me, you recent jester and longtime nuisance: does it seem right to you to dishonor and insult a duenna as venerable and worthy of respect as she? Was that the time to remember about your donkey, or would these nobles mistreat animals when they treat their owners so elegantly? For the love of God, Sancho, restrain yourself, and do not reveal your true colors lest they realize that the cloth you are made of is coarse and rustic. Look, sinner that you are: the master is more highly esteemed the more honorable and wellborn his servants are, and one of the greatest advantages princes have over other men is that they are served by men as good as they are. Do you not realize, limited as you are, and unfortunate as I am, that if they see that you are a crude peasant or a comical fool, they will think that I am an imposter or a fraudulent knight? No, no, Sancho my friend, flee, flee these perils, for the man who stumbles into being a talkative fool, at the first obstacle plunges into being an unfortunate buffoon. Curb your tongue; consider and reflect on your words before they leave your mouth, and be aware that we have come to a place from which, by the grace of God and the valor of my arm, we shall emerge with our fame and fortune greatly enhanced."

Sancho promised very earnestly that he would sew up his mouth or bite his tongue before speaking a word that was not fitting and carefully considered, just as his master had ordered, and Don Quixote did not need to worry about that anymore, for never through him would it be discovered who they really were.

Don Quixote dressed, put on his swordbelt and sword, placed the scarlet mantle over his shoulders, put on a green satin cap that the maidens had given him, and in this attire went into the large room, where he found the maidens standing in two equal lines, all of them prepared to pour water over his hands, which they did, with many courtesies and ceremonies.

Then twelve pages and the butler came to take him in to dinner, for the duke and duchess were waiting for him. They placed themselves around him and with great pomp and majesty escorted him to another room, where a rich table was laid with only four place settings. The duchess and duke came to the door of the room to receive him, and with them was a somber ecclesiastic, one of those who guide the houses of princes; one of those who, since they are not born princes, can never successfully teach those who are how to be princes; one of those who want the greatness of the great to be measured by the meanness of their own spirits; one of those who, wishing to show those they guide how to be restrained, make them only miserly; one of those, I say, was the somber cleric who came forward with the duke and duchess to receive Don Quixote. They exchanged a thousand courteous compliments, and finally, with Don Quixote placed between them, they went to take their seats at the table.

The duke invited Don Quixote to sit at the head of the table, and although he refused, the duke urged him so insistently that he had to agree. The ecclesiastic sat across from him, and the duke and the duchess were on either side.

Sancho was present for all of this, stupefied and amazed to see the honor paid his master by those nobles; and seeing the many ceremonies and entreaties that passed between the duke and Don Quixote in order to have him sit at the head of the table, he said:

"If your graces give me permission, I'll tell you a story about this business of seats that happened in my village."

As soon as Sancho said this, Don Quixote began to tremble, no doubt believing he was going to say something foolish. Sancho looked at him, and understood, and said:

"Señor, your grace shouldn't worry that I'll be disrespectful or say something that isn't to the point, for I haven't forgotten the advice your grace gave me just a little while ago about talking a lot or a little, or well or badly."

"I do not recall anything, Sancho," responded Don Quixote. "Say whatever you wish, as long as you say it quickly."

"Well, what I want to say," said Sancho, "is so true that my master, Don Quixote, who is here, won't let me lie."

"As far as I am concerned," replied Don Quixote, "you can lie, Sancho, as much as you wish, and I shall not stop you, but watch your tongue."

"I've watched and rewatched it so much that the bell ringer is safe, as you'll soon see."

"It would be good," said Don Quixote, "if your highnesses were to have this fool taken away from here, for he will make a thousand witless remarks."

"By the life of the duke," said the duchess, "Sancho is not to go even a smidgen away from me; I love him dearly, because I know he is very wise."

"May your holiness live many wise days," said Sancho, "on account of the good opinion you have of me, though I don't deserve it. And the story I want to tell you is this: an invitation was given by a nobleman in my village, very rich and influential because he was one of the Alamos of Medina del Campo, and he married Doña Mencía de Quiñones, who was the daughter of Don Alonso de Marañón, a knight of the Order of Santiago,[3] who drowned at La Herradura,[4] and there was a dispute about

3. A military-religious order founded in the twelfth century; Santiago (St. James) is the patron saint of Spain.

4. A galley ship sank in the port of La Herradura, near Vélez Málaga, in 1562, and more than four thousand people drowned.

him some years ago in our village, and as I understand it, my master, Don Quixote, took part in it, and Tomasillo the Rogue, the son of Balbastro the blacksmith, was wounded. . . . Isn't all of this true, Señor? Say it is, on your life, so that these noble folk won't take me for a lying babbler."

"So far," said the ecclesiastic, "I take you more for a babbler than a liar, but from now on I don't know what I shall take you for."

"You cite so many witnesses, Sancho, and so many particulars, that I cannot help but say that you must be telling the truth. But proceed, and shorten the story, because you are on the way to not concluding for another two days."

"To please me," said the duchess, "he must not shorten it; rather, he must tell it in the fashion that he knows, even if he does not finish in six days, and if it were to take that long, in my opinion they would be the best days I'd ever spent in my life."

"Well, then, Señores," Sancho continued, "I say that this nobleman, and I know him like I know my own hands because it's only the distance of a crossbow shot from my house to his, gave an invitation to a farmer who was poor but honorable."

"Go on, brother," the cleric said at this point. "You're on the way to not finishing your story until you're in the next world."

"I'll stop when I'm less than halfway there, God willing," responded Sancho. "And so, I say that when this farmer came to the house of this nobleman, and may his soul rest in peace because he's dead now, and he died the death of an angel from what people tell me, since I wasn't present at the time because I had gone to Tembleque to work in the harvest—"

"On your life, my son, return quickly from Tembleque, and without burying the nobleman, and unless you want more funerals, finish your story."

"Well, the fact of the matter is," replied Sancho, "that when the two of them were ready to sit down at the table, and it seems to me I can see both of them now as clear as ever . . ."

The duke and duchess greatly enjoyed the annoyance the good cleric was displaying at the delays and pauses used by Sancho in the recounting of his story, but Don Quixote was consumed with rage and fury.

"And so I say," said Sancho, "that, like I said, when the two of them were going to sit down at the table, the farmer insisted that the nobleman should sit at the head of the table, and the nobleman also insisted that the farmer should sit there because in his house his orders had to be followed; but the farmer, who was proud of his courtesy and manners, re-fused to do it, until the nobleman became angry, and putting both hands on his shoulders, he forced him to sit down, saying:

'Sit down, you imbecile; wherever I sit will be the head of the table for you.'

And that's my story, and I don't believe it was out of place here."

Don Quixote turned a thousand different colors that looked like mar-bling on his dark skin, and the duke and duchess, having understood Sancho's sly intent, hid their laughter so that Don Quixote would not lose his temper; and in order to change the subject and keep Sancho from further insolence, the duchess asked Don Quixote what news he had of the lady Dulcinea, and if he had recently sent her any giants or malefactors as presents, for surely he had defeated a good number of them. To which Don Quixote responded:

"Señora, my misfortunes, although they had a beginning, will never have an end. I have vanquished giants, and I have sent villains and malefactors to her, but where can they find her if she has been enchanted and transformed into the ugliest peasant girl anyone can imagine?"

"I don't know," said Sancho Panza. "To me she looks like the most beautiful creature in the world, at least, as far as speed and jumping are concerned, I know that no acrobat could compete with her; by my faith, Señora Duchess, she can leap from the ground onto the back of a donkey just like a cat."

"Have you seen her enchanted, Sancho?" asked the duke.

"Of course I've seen her!" responded Sancho. "Who the devil else but me was the first to catch on to this matter of enchantment? She's as enchanted as my father!"

The ecclesiastic, who heard talk of giants, villains, and enchant-ments, realized that this must be Don Quixote of La Mancha, whose his-tory was the duke's customary reading, for which he had often reprimanded him, saying that it was foolishness to read such foolishness; and knowing that what he suspected was true, he spoke to the duke with a good deal of anger, saying:

"Your Excellency, Señor, must give an accounting to Our Lord for what this good man does. I imagine that this Don Quixote, or Don Half-wit, or whatever his name is, is not so great a fool as Your Excellency wants him to be when you provide him with opportunities to continue his absurdities and nonsense."

And turning to Don Quixote, he said:

"And you, you simpleminded man, whoever put it into your head that you are a knight errant and defeat giants and capture villains? Go now in peace, and in peace I shall say to you: return to your home, and rear your children, if you have any, and tend to your estate, and stop wandering the world and wasting your time and being a laughingstock to all who know you and all who do not. Where the devil did you get the idea that there once were knights errant or that there are any now? Where are there giants in Spain, or malefactors in La Mancha, or enchanted Dulcineas, or any of the endless nonsense that people tell about you?"

Don Quixote listened attentively to the words of that venerable man, and seeing that he had fallen silent, and without regard for the duke and duchess, he rose to his feet, and with an angry countenance and a wrathful face, he said . . .

But this response deserves its own chapter.

CHAPTER XXXII

Regarding the response that Don Quixote gave to his rebuker, along with other events both grave and comical

Don Quixote, then, rose to his feet, and trembling from head to toe like quicksilver, he spoke quickly and with great agitation, saying:

"The place where I am now, and the presence in which I find myself, and the respect I always have had, and have now, for the vocation your grace professes, bind and restrain the censure of my righteous anger; and for the reasons I have said, and because I know that everyone knows that the weapons of men in cassocks are the same as those of women, which is to say, their tongues, I shall with mine enter into equal combat with your grace, from whom one ought to have expected good counsel rather than base vituperation. Holy and well-intentioned rebukes require different circumstances and demand different occasions: at least, your having rebuked me in public, and so harshly, has gone beyond all the bounds of legitimate reproof, which is based more on gentleness than on asperity, nor is it just, having no knowledge of the sin that is being rebuked, so thoughtlessly to call the sinner a simpleton and a fool. Otherwise tell me, your grace: for which of the inanities that you have seen in me do you condemn and revile me, and order me to return to my house and tend to it and my wife and my children, not knowing if I have one or the other? Or is it enough for clerics simply to enter other people's houses willy-nilly to guide the owners, even though some have been brought up in the narrow confines of a boarding school and never have seen more of the world than the twenty or thirty leagues of their district, and then suddenly decide to dictate laws to chivalry and make judgments concerning knights errant? Is it by chance frivolous, or is the time wasted that is spent wandering the world, not seeking its rewards but the asperities by which the virtuous rise to the seat of immortality?

If knights, and the great, the generous, and the highborn considered me a fool, I would take it as an irreparable affront; but that I am thought a simpleton by students who never walked or followed the paths of chivalry does not concern me in the least: a knight I am, and a knight I shall die, if it pleases the Almighty. Some men walk the broad fields of haughty ambition, or base and servile adulation, or deceptive hypocrisy, and some take the road of true religion; but I, influenced by my star, follow the narrow path of knight errantry, and because I profess it I despise wealth but not honor. I have redressed grievances, righted wrongs, punished insolence, vanquished giants, and trampled monsters; I am in love, simply because it is obligatory for knights errant to be so; and being so, I am not a dissolute lover, but one who is chaste and platonic. I always direct my intentions to virtuous ends, which are to do good to all and evil to none; if the man who understands this, and acts on this, and desires this, deserves to be called a fool, then your highnesses, most excellent Duke and Duchess, should say so."

"By God, that's wonderful!" said Sancho. "My lord and master, your grace should say no more on your own behalf, because there's nothing more to say, or to think, or to insist on in this world. Besides, since this gentleman is denying, and has denied, that there ever were knights errant in the world, or that there are any now, is it any wonder he doesn't know any of the things he's talked about?"

"By any chance, brother," said the ecclesiastic, "are you the Sancho Panza to whom, they say, your master has promised an ínsula?"

"I am," responded Sancho, "and I'm the one who deserves it as much as anybody else; I'm a 'Stay close to good men and become one'; and I'm a 'Birds of a feather flock together'; and a 'Lean against a sturdy trunk if you want good shade.' I have leaned against a good master, and traveled with him for many months, and I'll become just like him, God willing; long life to him and to me, and there'll be no lack of empires for him to rule or ínsulas for me to govern."

"No, certainly not, Sancho my friend," said the duke, "for I, in the name of Señor Don Quixote, promise you the governorship of a spare one that I own, which is of no small quality."

"Down on your knees, Sancho," said Don Quixote, "and kiss the feet of His Excellency for the great favor he has done you."

Sancho did so, and when the ecclesiastic saw this he rose from the table in a fury, saying:

"By the habit I wear, I must say that Your Excellency is as much a simpleton as these sinners. Consider that of course they must be mad, since the sane applaud their madness! Stay with them, Your Excellency, and for as long as they are in this house, I shall be in mine, and I exempt myself from reproving what I cannot remedy."

And without saying another word or eating another mouthful, he left, and the pleas of the duke and duchess did nothing to stop him, although the duke was prevented from saying very much by the laughter the ecclesiastic's importunate anger had caused in him. When he finished laughing, he said to Don Quixote:

"Señor Knight of the Lions, your grace has responded so nobly on your own behalf that there is no other satisfaction required, for although this appears to be an insult, it in no way is, because just as women cannot offer an insult, neither can ecclesiastics, as your grace knows better than I."

"That is true," responded Don Quixote, "and the reason is that one who cannot be insulted cannot insult anyone else. Women, children, and ecclesiastics, since they cannot defend themselves even if they have been offended, cannot receive an affront. Because the difference between an insult and an affront, as Your Excellency knows better than I, is that an affront comes from one who can commit it, and does so, and sustains it; an insult can come from anywhere, without being an affront. For example: a man is standing idly in the street; ten men arrive with weapons in their hands and strike him, and he draws his sword to perform his duty, but the number of his adversaries hinders this and does not allow him to carry out his intention, which is to take his revenge; this man has been insulted but not affronted. And another example will confirm the same thing: a man's back is turned, another comes up and strikes him, and having struck him, he flees and does not wait, and the other pursues but cannot overtake him; the one who was struck received an insult but not an affront, because an affront must be sustained. If the one who struck him, even if he did so surreptitiously, had drawn his sword and stood firm, facing his enemy, the man who was struck would be both insulted and affronted: insulted, because he was struck covertly; affronted, because the one who struck him sustained what he had done, not turning his back and standing firm. And so, according to the laws of this accursed dueling, I can be insulted but not affronted, because children are not aware of what they do, and women cannot flee, nor can they be expected to, and the same is true of those who hold positions in holy religion, because these three kinds of people lack both offensive and defensive weapons; consequently, although they naturally may be obliged to defend themselves, they are not capable of offending anyone. And although I said a little while ago that I could be insulted, now I say no, not in any manner, because one who cannot receive an affront is even less capable of committing one; for these reasons I should not be aggrieved, and I am not, by what that good man said to me; I wish only that he had stayed so that I could have convinced him of his error in thinking and saying that there were no knights errant in the world, and that there are none now, for if Amadís or any of his infinite descendants had heard him, I know it would not have gone well for his grace."

"I'll swear to that," said Sancho. "They would have slashed him open from top to bottom like a pomegranate or a very ripe melon. They were the right ones to put up with jokes like that! By my faith, I'm sure if Reinaldos de Montalbán had heard that little man saying those things, he would have slapped him so hard across the mouth he wouldn't have said another word for three years. He should have tried it with them and seen if they'd let him get away!"

The duchess was weak with laughter when she heard Sancho speak, and in her opinion he was more amusing and even crazier than his master, an opinion held by many at the time. Don Quixote at last became calm, and the meal was concluded, and as the table was being cleared, four maidens came in, the first bearing a silver basin, the second a pitcher, also of silver, the third, carrying two very white, very thick towels on her shoulder, and the fourth, with her forearms bared, holding in her white hands—for they undoubtedly were white—a round cake of Neapolitan soap. The one with the basin approached and with charming grace and assurance placed the basin beneath Don Quixote's beard, and he, not saying a word, marveled at such a ceremony but believed that in this land it must be the custom to wash one's beard rather than one's hands, and so he extended his as much as he could, and at that moment the pitcher began to pour, and the maiden with the soap began to rub his beard very quickly, raising flakes of snow no less white than the lather, not only on his beard but all over the face and eyes of the obedient knight, who was obliged to close them.

The duke and duchess, who knew nothing about this, waited to see how so extraordinary a washing would end. The beard-washing maiden, when she had covered him with lather to the depth of a span, pretended there was no more water, and she told the one with the pitcher to go for some because Señor Don Quixote would be waiting. She did so, and Don Quixote was left there, the strangest and most laughable figure that anyone could imagine.

All those present, and there were many, were watching him, and when they saw that he had a neck half a *vara* long, and a complexion more than moderately dark, and closed eyes, and a beard full of soap, it was truly astonishing and a sign of great astuteness that they could hide their laughter; the trickster maidens kept their eyes lowered, not daring to look at their master and mistress, who were torn between anger and laughter and did not know how to respond: to punish the girls for their boldness or reward them for the pleasure they had received at seeing Don Quixote in that condition.

Finally the maiden with the pitcher returned, and they finished washing Don Quixote, and then the girl with the towels very calmly wiped and dried him; then all four of them curtsied, and made obeisance to him at the same time, and attempted to leave, but the duke, to keep Don Quixote from realizing it was a joke, called to the maiden with the basin, saying:

"Come and wash me, and be careful you don't run out of water."

The girl, who was shrewd and diligent, approached and placed the basin beneath the duke's beard as she had with Don Quixote, and they quickly washed and soaped him thoroughly, and having wiped and dried him, they curtsied and left. Later it was learned that the duke had sworn that if they did not wash him as they had Don Quixote, he would punish their daring, but they cleverly changed his mind by soaping him so well.

Sancho paid careful attention to the ceremonies of the washing and said to himself:

"God save me! Can it be the custom in this land to wash the beards of squires as well as knights? Because by my soul I could use it, and even if they shaved me with a razor, I'd think it was a good thing."

"What are you saying, Sancho?" asked the duchess.

"I'm saying, Señora," he responded, "that in the courts of other princes I've always heard that when the tables are cleared they pour water over your hands, but not lather on your beard; and that's why it's good to live a long time, because then you see a lot; though they also say that if you have a long life, you go through a lot of bad times, though going through one of these washings is more pleasure than trouble."

"Don't worry, Sancho my friend," said the duchess. "I'll have my maidens wash you, and even put you in the tub, if necessary."

"Just my beard will satisfy me," responded Sancho, "at least for now; later on, God's will be done."

"Butler," said the duchess, "see to whatever our good Sancho wants, and obey his wishes to the letter."

The butler responded that Señor Sancho would be served in everything, and having said this, he left to eat and took Sancho with him, while the duke and duchess and Don Quixote remained at the table, speaking of many different matters, but all of them touching on the practice of arms and on knight errantry.

The duchess asked Don Quixote to depict and describe, for he seemed to have an excellent memory, the beauty and features of Señora Dulcinea of Toboso, so famous for her beauty that the duchess understood she must be the most beautiful creature in the world, and even in all of La Mancha. Don Quixote sighed when he heard what the duchess had commanded, and he said:

"If I could take out my heart and place it before the eyes of your highness, here on this table, on a plate, it would spare my tongue the effort of saying what can barely be thought, because in it Your Excellency would see her portrayed in detail; but why should I begin now to depict and describe, point by point and part by part, the beauty of the peerless Dulcinea? That is a burden worthy of shoulders other than mine, an enterprise that should be undertaken by the brushes of Parrhasius, Timanthus, and Appelles and the chisels of Lysippus[1] to paint and engrave her on tablets, marble, and bronze, and by Ciceronian and Demosthenian rhetoric to praise her."

"What does *Demosthenian* mean, Señor Don Quixote?" asked the duchess. "That is a word I have never heard before in all my days."

1. These were artists of Greek antiquity.

"*Demosthenian rhetoric*," responded Don Quixote, "is the same as saying the *rhetoric of Demosthenes*, as *Ciceronian* means *of Cicero*, and they were the two greatest rhetoricians in the world."

"That is true," said the duke, "and you must have been confused when you asked the question. But, even so, Señor Don Quixote would give us great pleasure if he would depict her for us, and I am certain that even in the broad strokes of a sketch, she will appear in such a fashion that even the most beautiful women will be envious of her."

"I would do so, most certainly," responded Don Quixote, "if my image of her had not been blurred by the misfortune that befell her recently, one so great that I am better prepared to weep for her than to describe her; because your highnesses must know that not long ago, when I was going to kiss her hands and receive her blessing, approval, and permission for this third sally, I found a person different from the one I was seeking: I found her enchanted, transformed from a princess into a peasant, from beautiful to ugly, from an angel into a devil, from fragrant into foul-smelling, from well-spoken into a rustic, from serene into skittish, from light into darkness, and, finally, from Dulcinea of Toboso into a lowborn farmgirl from Sayago."

"Lord save me!" the duke exclaimed in a loud voice. "Who could have done so much harm to the world? Who has removed from it the beauty that brought it joy, the grace that brought it delight, the virtue that brought it honor?"

"Who?" responded Don Quixote. "Who can it be but some malevolent enchanter, one of the many envious ones who pursue me? An accursed race, born into the world to darken and crush the feats of good men, to shed light on and raise up the deeds of the wicked. Enchanters have pursued me, enchanters pursue me now, and enchanters will pursue me until they throw me and my high chivalric exploits into the profound abyss of oblivion; they harm and wound me in the part where they can see I feel it most, for taking away his lady from a knight errant is taking away the eyes with which he sees, and the sun that shines down on him, and the sustenance that maintains him. I have said it many times before, and now I say it again: the knight errant without a lady is like a tree without leaves, a building without a foundation, a shadow without a body to cast it."

"There is nothing more to say," said the duchess, "but if, despite this, we are to believe the history of Señor Don Quixote that only recently has come into the world to the general applause of all people, we infer from that, if I remember correctly, that your grace has never seen Señora

Dulcinea, and that she does not exist in the world but is an imaginary lady, and that your grace engendered and gave birth to her in your mind, and depicted her with all the graces and perfections that you desired."

"There is much to say about that," responded Don Quixote. "God knows if Dulcinea exists in the world or not, or if she is imaginary or not imaginary; these are not the kinds of things whose verification can be carried through to the end. I neither engendered nor gave birth to my lady, although I contemplate her in the manner proper to a lady who possesses the qualities that can make her famous throughout the world, to wit: she is beautiful without blemish, serious without arrogance, amorous but modest, grateful because she is courteous, courteous because she is well-bred, and, finally, noble because of her lineage, for when coupled with good blood, beauty shines and excels to a greater degree of perfection than in beautiful women of humble birth."

"That is so," said the duke. "But Señor Don Quixote must give me permission to say what I am obliged to say because of the history of his deeds which I have read, and from which one infers that even if it is conceded that Dulcinea exists, in Toboso or outside it, and that she is as exceptionally beautiful as your grace depicts her for us, in the matter of noble lineage she cannot compare with the Orianas, Alastrajareas, Madásimas, or other ladies of that kind who fill the histories which your grace knows so well."

"To that I can say," responded Don Quixote, "that Dulcinea is the child of her actions, and that virtues strengthen the blood, and that a virtuous person of humble birth is to be more highly esteemed and valued than a vice-ridden noble, especially since Dulcinea possesses a quality[2] that can make her a queen with a crown and scepter; for the merits of a beautiful and virtuous woman extend to performing even greater miracles, and in her she carries, virtually if not formally, even greater good fortune."

"Señor Don Quixote," said the duchess, "I say that in everything your grace says you proceed with great caution and, as they say, with the sounding line in your hand; from now on I shall believe, and make my entire household believe, and even my lord the duke, if necessary, that Dulcinea exists in Toboso, and that she lives in our day, and is beautiful, and nobly born, and worthy of having a knight like Señor Don Quixote

2. The word in Spanish, *jirón*, has several meanings and can also signify a heraldic figure called a "gyron," a triangular shape that extends from the border to the center of a coat of arms. The allusion is to Dulcinea's noble blood.

serving her, which is the highest praise I can give, and the highest I know of. But I cannot help having one scruple, and feeling a certain animosity toward Sancho Panza: the scruple is that the aforementioned history says that Sancho Panza found the lady Dulcinea, when he brought her a missive on behalf of your grace, sifting a sack of grain, and, apparently, that it was buckwheat, which makes me doubt the nobility of her lineage."

To which Don Quixote responded:

"Señora, your highness must know that all or almost all the things that befall me go beyond the ordinary scope of things that happen to other knights errant, whether they are directed by the inscrutable will of fate or by the malevolence of some envious enchanter; and since it is well-known about all or almost all the famous knights errant that one has the ability never to be enchanted, and another has impenetrable flesh and cannot be wounded, such as the famous Roland, one of the Twelve Peers of France, of whom it is said that he could not be wounded except on the sole of his left foot, and only with the point of a large pin and not with any other kind of weapon; and so, when Bernardo del Carpio killed him at Roncesvalles, seeing that he could not wound him with his blade, he lifted him off the ground and strangled him, for he had recalled how Hercules killed Antaeus, the fierce giant they say was the child of Earth. I wish to infer from what I have said that I may have one of these abilities; but not the one that keeps me from being wounded, for experience has often shown me that my flesh is weak and not at all impenetrable; and not the one that keeps me from being enchanted, for I have found myself locked in a cage, although the entire world would not have had the strength to put me in there if it were not for enchantments. And since I freed myself from that enchantment, I should like to believe there will not be any other that can harm me; and so these enchanters, seeing that they cannot use their evil craft against my person, wreak their vengeance on the things I love most, and wish to take my life by mistreating Dulcinea, by whose grace I live. And therefore I believe that when my squire carried my message to her, they transformed her into a peasant engaged in labor so menial as sifting grain; but I have already said that the grain was neither buckwheat nor wheat but Oriental pearls; and as proof of this truth I want to tell your highnesses that not long ago, when I was passing through Toboso, I could not find the palaces of Dulcinea, and the next day, Sancho, my squire, saw her real form, which is the most beautiful on earth, but to me she seemed a crude and ugly peasant girl, and in no way well-spoken, although she is the epitome of discernment in the world. And since I am not enchanted, and cannot be, according to sound reasoning, she is the enchanted one, the offended one, the one who is altered, changed, and transformed; through her my enemies have taken their revenge on me, and for her sake I shall live in perpetual tears until I see her restored to her pristine state. I have said this so that no one will pay heed to what Sancho said about Dulcinea's sifting or winnowing; since they altered her for me, it is no wonder they changed her for him. Dulcinea is illustrious and wellborn; of the noble lineages in Toboso, which are numerous, ancient, and very good, the peerless Dulcinea surely possesses more than a small portion, and for her sake the town will be famous and renowned in times to come, as Troy has been for Helen, and Spain for La Cava,[3] although for better reasons and with better fame.

On the other hand, I want your lordship and ladyship to understand that Sancho Panza is one of the most amusing squires who ever served a knight errant; at times his simpleness is so clever that deciding if he is simple or clever is a cause of no small pleasure; his slyness condemns him for a rogue, and his thoughtlessness confirms him as a simpleton; he doubts everything, and he believes everything; when I think that he is about to plunge headlong into foolishness, he comes out with perceptions that raise him to the skies. In short, I would not trade him for any other squire even if I were given a city to do so; consequently, I have some doubt regarding whether sending him to the governorship with which your highness has favored him is the right thing to do, although I see in him a certain aptitude for governing; with just a little refinement of his understanding, he would be as successful with any governorship as the king is with his duties and taxes; moreover, by dint of long experience, we know that neither great ability nor great learning is needed to be a governor, for there are in the world at least a hundred who barely know how to read, and who govern in a grand manner; the essential point is that they have good intentions and the desire always to do the right thing, for they will never lack someone to guide and counsel them in what they must do, like those knightly, unlettered governors who pass judgments with an adviser at their side. I would caution him not to accept bribes, and not to lose sight of the law, and a few other trifles that I

---

3. A major figure in an important early ballad cycle, Florinda, La Cava, the daughter of Count Don Julián, had an illicit and disastrous love affair with King Don Rodrigo; according to legend, the ensuing betrayals and acts of vengeance precipitated the Moorish invasion of 711.

shall not mention now but will come out in due course, to the benefit of Sancho and the advantage of the ínsula which he will govern."

The duke, the duchess, and Don Quixote had reached this point in their conversation when they heard many voices and a clamor of people in the palace, and suddenly a frightened Sancho burst into the room wearing a piece of coarse burlap as a bib, and behind him came a number of young men, that is to say scullery boys and other menials, and one was carrying a tub of water whose color and lack of cleanliness indicated that it was dishwater, and the boy with the tub was following and pursuing Sancho and attempting with all solicitude to place it and put it under his beard, which another rogue showed signs of wanting to wash.

"What is this, my friends?" asked the duchess. "What is this? What do you want from this good man? Haven't you considered that he has been selected governor?"

To which the roguish barber responded:

"This gentleman won't let himself be washed, though that's the custom, in the way the duke my lord was washed, and his own master."

"I will let myself," responded Sancho in a fury, "but I want it to be with cleaner towels, and clearer water, and hands that aren't so dirty, for there's not so much difference between me and my master that they should wash him with angel water and me with the devil's bleach. The customs of different lands and the palaces of princes are good as long as they don't cause any pain, but the custom of washing that they have here is worse than being flagellated. My beard is clean and I don't need any freshening up like this; whoever tries to wash me or touch a hair on my head, I mean, of my beard, with all due respect, I'll hit him so hard that I'll leave my fist embedded in his skull; ceremonies and soapings like these seem more like mockery than hospitality for guests."

The duchess was convulsed with laughter when she saw the anger and heard the words of Sancho, but Don Quixote was not very pleased to see him so badly adorned with the streaked and spotted towel, and so surrounded by so many kitchen scullions; and after making a deep bow to the duke and duchess, as if asking their permission to speak, he spoke to the mob in a tranquil voice, saying:

"Hello, Señores! Your graces must leave the young man alone and return to the place from which you came, or anywhere else you like; my squire is as clean as any other, and those little bowls are for him small and narrow-mouthed vessels. Take my advice and leave him alone, for neither he nor I have any fondness for mockery."

Sancho caught his words as they left his mouth and continued, saying:

"No, let them come and mock the bumpkin, and I'll put up with that the way it's nighttime now! Bring a comb here, or whatever you want, and curry this beard, and if you find anything there that offends cleanliness, then you can shear me willy-nilly."

At this point, the duchess, who was still laughing, said:

"Sancho Panza is correct in everything he has said, and everything he will say: he is clean and, as he says, he has no need of washing; if our custom does not please him, that should be the end of it, especially since you, ministers of cleanliness, have been far too remiss and negligent, and perhaps I should say insolent, in bringing to such a person and such a beard, not basins and pitchers of pure gold, and damask towels, but wooden bowls and pans and cleaning rags. But, after all, you are wicked and base and, like the scoundrels you are, cannot help showing the ill will you bear toward the squires of knights errant."

The roguish ministrants, and even the butler who had come in with them, believed that the duchess was speaking seriously, and so they removed the burlap from Sancho's chest, and disconcerted, and almost embarrassed, they went away and left him alone; and he, seeing himself free of what had seemed to him an extreme danger, went to kneel before the duchess and said:

"From great ladies, great favors are expected; the one your grace has granted me today cannot be repaid unless it is with my desire to see myself dubbed a knight errant so that I can spend all the days of my life serving so high a lady. I am a peasant, my name is Sancho Panza, I am married, I have children, and I serve as a squire; if with any of these things I can be of service to your highness, I will take less time to obey than your ladyship will to command."

"It certainly seems, Sancho," responded the duchess, "that you have learned to be courteous in the school of courtesy itself; it certainly seems, I mean to say, that you have been nurtured in the bosom of Señor Don Quixote, who must be the cream of courtesy and the flower of ceremonies, or *cirimonies*, as you call them. Good fortune to such a master and such a servant, the one for being the polestar of knight errantry, the other for being the star of squirely fidelity. Arise, Sancho my friend, and I shall repay your courtesies by having the duke my lord, as quickly as he can, fulfill the promised favor of a governorship for you."

With this their conversation ended, and Don Quixote went to take his siesta, and the duchess requested that if Sancho had no great desire to sleep, he should come and spend the afternoon with her and her maidens in a room that was cool and pleasant. Sancho replied that although it was true that he was in the habit of taking four- or five-hour siestas in the summer, to respond to her great kindness he would attempt with all his might not to sleep even one that day and would obey her command, and then he left. The duke issued new orders that Don Quixote was to be treated as a knight errant, without deviating in the slightest from the manner in which it has been recounted that knights of old were treated.

CHAPTER XXXIII

Regarding the delightful conversation that the duchess and her ladies had with Sancho Panza, one that is worthy of being read and remembered

Well, the history recounts that Sancho did not sleep that day's siesta but kept his word and came as requested to see the duchess, who derived so much pleasure from listening to him that she had him sit next to her on a low seat, although Sancho, being well-bred, did not wish to sit, but the duchess told him to sit as a governor and speak as a squire, since for both he deserved the ivory seat of El Cid Ruy Díaz Campeador.[1]

Sancho shrugged, obeyed, and sat down, and all the maidens and duennas of the duchess gathered round attentively, in great silence, to hear what he would say; but the duchess was the one who spoke first, saying:

"Now that we are alone, where no one can hear us, I should like you, Señor Governor, to resolve certain doubts I have, which have their origin in the history of the great Don Quixote that has already been published; one of these doubts is that, since our good Sancho never saw Dulcinea, I mean Señora Dulcinea of Toboso, and did not bring her the letter from Señor Don Quixote because it was left in the notebook in the Sierra Morena, how did he dare invent her response and say that he

---

1. An allusion to the throne won by El Cid in Valencia.

found her winnowing grain? This was nothing but a deception and a lie, so harmful to the good name of the peerless Dulcinea, and so inappropriate to the character and fidelity of good squires."

At these words, without saying a single one in response, Sancho got up from the seat, and with silent steps, his body bent, his finger to his lips, he walked around the room lifting all the hangings, and then, when he had done this, he sat down again and said:

"Now that I have seen, Señora, that nobody is hiding and listening to us, except for those present, without fear or sudden fright I'll answer what you have asked me, and anything else you may ask me, and the first thing I'll say is that I believe my master, Don Quixote, is completely crazy, even though sometimes he says things that in my opinion, and in the opinion of everybody who hears him, are so intelligent and well-reasoned that Satan himself couldn't say them better; but even so, truly and without any scruples, it's clear to me that he's a fool. And because I have this idea in mind, I can dare to make him believe anything, even if it makes no sense, like that reply to his letter, or something that happened six or eight days ago that isn't in the history yet, I mean the enchantment of Señora Doña Dulcinea, because I've made him think she's enchanted, and that's as true as a fairy tale."

The duchess asked him to tell her about the enchantment, or deception, and Sancho recounted everything just as it had occurred, from which his listeners derived no small pleasure; and continuing their conversation, the duchess said:

"From what our good Sancho has told me, a certain scruple has leaped into my soul, and a certain whisper reaches my ears, saying:

'Since Don Quixote of La Mancha is a madman, a fool, and a simpleton, and Sancho Panza his squire knows this and still serves him, and follows him, and believes his hollow promises, there can be no doubt that he is more of a madman and a dimwit than his master; and this being the case, and it is, it will not be to your credit, Señora Duchess, if you give this Sancho Panza an ínsula to govern, because if a man cannot govern himself, how will he govern others?' "

"By God, Señora," said Sancho, "that scruple of yours is just what I expected; but your grace should tell it to speak clearly, or however it wants to, because I know it's telling the truth; if I were a clever man, I would have left my master days ago. But this is my fate and this is my misfortune; I can't help it; I have to follow him: we're from the same village, I've eaten his bread, I love him dearly, he's a grateful man, he gave me his donkeys, and more than anything else, I'm faithful; and so it's impossible for anything to separate us except the man with the pick and shovel.[2] And if your highness doesn't want me to have the governorship I've been promised, God made me without it, and maybe not giving it to me will be for the good of my conscience; I may be a fool, but I understand the proverb that says, 'It did him harm when the ant grew wings,' and it might even be that Sancho the squire will enter heaven more easily than Sancho the governor. The bread they bake here is as good as in France, and at night every cat is gray, and the person who hasn't eaten by two in the afternoon has more than enough misfortune, and no stomach's so much bigger than any other that it can't be filled, as they say, with straw and hay,[3] and the little birds of the field have God to protect and provide for them, and four *varas* of flannel from Cuenca will warm you more than four of *limiste*[4] from Segovia, and when we leave this world and go into the ground, the path of the prince is as narrow as the laborer's, and the pope's body doesn't need more room underground than the sacristan's, even if one is higher than the other, because when we're in the grave we all have to adjust and shrink or they make us adjust and shrink, whether we want to or not, and that's the end of it. And I say again that if your ladyship doesn't want to give me the ínsula because I'm a fool, I'll be smart enough not to care at all; I've heard that the devil hides behind the cross, and that all that glitters isn't gold, and that from his oxen, plows, and yokes they took the peasant Wamba to be king of Spain,[5] and from his brocades, entertainments, and riches they took Rodrigo to be eaten by snakes, if the lines from the old ballads don't lie."

"Of course they don't lie!" said Doña Rodríguez the duenna, who was among those listening. "There's a ballad that says they put King Rodrigo alive and kicking into a tomb filled with toads and snakes and lizards, and two days later, from inside the tomb, the king said in a low and mournful voice:

> They're eating me, they're eating me
> in the place where I sinned most;

and so this gentleman is very correct when he says he'd rather be a peasant than a king if vermin are going to eat him."

2. This is an allusion to death.

3. The original proverb is "Straw and hay and hunger's away" (*De paja y de heno, el vientre lleno*).

4. A very fine cloth formerly woven in Segovia.

5. As indicated earlier, Wamba was a Visigothic king of Spain (672–680).

The duchess could not control her laughter when she heard her duenna's simplemindedness, nor could she help but marvel at Sancho's words and proverbs, and she said to him:

"Our good Sancho already knows that what a knight has promised he attempts to fulfill, even if it costs him his life. The duke, my lord and husband, though not a knight errant, is still a knight, and so he will keep his word regarding the promised ínsula, despite the world's envy and malice. Sancho should be of good heart, for when he least expects it he will find himself seated on the throne of his ínsula and of his estate, and he will hold his governorship in his hand and not trade it for another of three-pile brocade.[6] My charge to him is that he attend to how he governs his vassals, knowing that all of them are loyal and wellborn."

"As for governing them well," responded Sancho, "there's no need to charge me with it, because I'm charitable by nature and have compassion for the poor; and if he kneads and bakes, you can't steal his cakes; by my faith, they won't throw me any crooked dice; I'm an old dog and understand every here, boy,[7] and I know how to wake up at the right time, and I don't allow cobwebs in front of my eyes, because I know if the shoe fits: I say this because with me good men will have my hand and a place in my house,[8] and bad men won't get a foot or permission to enter. And it seems to me that in this business of governorships it's all a matter of starting, and it may be that after two weeks of being a governor I'll be licking my lips over the work and know more about it than working in the fields, which is what I've grown up doing."

"You're right, Sancho," said the duchess, "because nobody is born knowing, and bishops are made from men, not stones. But returning to the conversation we had a little while ago about the enchantment of Señora Dulcinea, I consider it true and verified beyond any doubt that the idea Sancho had of tricking his master and leading him to believe that the peasant was Dulcinea, and if his master did not know her, it had to be because she was enchanted, was all an invention of one of the enchanters who pursue Señor Don Quixote, because really and truly, I know from a reliable source that the peasant girl who leaped onto the donkey was and is Dulcinea of Toboso, and that our good Sancho, think-

6. The phrase means "no matter how fine." Brocade of three piles was of the very best quality; in chapter X, Sancho exaggerated by referring to brocade of ten piles.

7. The proverb says, "You don't need here, boy, here, boy, with an old dog" (*A perro viejo no hay tus, tus*).

8. An idiomatic way of saying "trust and confidence." The phrase that follows is Sancho's variation on this and means just the opposite.

ing he was the deceiver, is the deceived; there is no reason to doubt this truth any more than we doubt other things we have never seen, and Señor Sancho Panza should know that we too have enchanters here, and they love us dearly, and tell us what is going on in the world, purely and simply and without plots or complications; let Sancho believe me when I say that the leaping peasant girl was and is Dulcinea of Toboso, who is as enchanted as the mother who bore her; and when we least expect it we shall see her in her true form, and then Sancho will be free of the self-deception in which he lives."

"That may be true," said Sancho Panza, "and now I want to believe what my master says he saw in the Cave of Montesinos, where he says he saw Señora Dulcinea of Toboso in the same dress and garb that I said I had seen her wearing when I enchanted her for my own pleasure; it must all be the reverse, Señora, just like your grace says, because one can't and shouldn't think that in only an instant my poor wits could make up so clever a lie, and I don't believe either that my master is so crazy that with powers of persuasion as weak and thin as mine he would believe something so unbelievable. But, Señora, it wouldn't be right for your highness to consider me a villain because of it, for a dolt like me isn't obliged to fathom the thoughts and evil intentions of wicked enchanters: I made it up to avoid a scolding from my master, Don Quixote, not to offend him, and if it's turned out wrong, God's in heaven and judges men's hearts."

"That is true," said the duchess, "but now tell me, Sancho, what you were saying about the Cave of Montesinos; I'd like to know."

Then Sancho Panza recounted point by point what has already been said about that adventure, and when the duchess heard it, she said:

"From this incident we can infer that since the great Don Quixote says he saw there the same peasant girl Sancho saw on the way out of Toboso, she no doubt is Dulcinea, and very clever and meddlesome enchanters are wandering around here."

"That's what I say," said Sancho Panza. "If my lady Dulcinea of Toboso is enchanted, so much the worse for her, but I, I don't have to take on my master's enemies, and there must be a lot, all of them very wicked. It may be true that the woman I saw was a peasant, and I thought she was a peasant, and judged her to be a peasant; if that was Dulcinea, I'm not to blame, and nobody should hold me responsible; we'll see about that. Picking fights with me all the time: 'Sancho said this, Sancho did that, Sancho turned around, and Sancho went back,' as if Sancho Panza were just anybody and not the same Sancho Panza who's wandering the world now in books, which is what Sansón Carrasco told me, and he's nothing less than a bachelor from Salamanca, and people like him can't lie except if they feel like it or it's very convenient; and so nobody should blame me, and since I have a good reputation, and I've heard my master say that a good name's worth more than great wealth, just let them pass this governorship on to me and they'll see marvels, because whoever's been a good squire will be a good governor."

"Everything said here by our good Sancho," said the duchess, "are Catonian sentences, or, at least, taken from the very heart of Micael Verino himself, *florentibus occidit annis*.[9] Well, well, to say it in his fashion, under a poor cloak you can find a good drinker."

"The truth is, Señora," responded Sancho, "that I never abused drink, though I might have been thirsty, because I'm no hypocrite; I drink when I want to, and when I don't want to, and when somebody offers me a drink so as not to seem finicky or impolite; to toast a friend, whose heart is so like marble that he won't lift a glass? But even if I do, I never dirty it, since the squires of knights errant almost always drink water, because they're always traveling through woods, forests, and meadows, mountains and cliffs, without finding a charitable drop of wine even if they'd give an eye for it."

"I believe that," responded the duchess. "And for now, Sancho should go and rest, and we will speak at length later, and give the order to quickly pass this governorship, as he says, on to him."

Sancho again kissed the hands of the duchess and implored her to be so kind as to take good care of his gray, because he was the light of his eyes.

"What gray is that?" asked the duchess.

"My jackass," responded Sancho, "and so as not to call him by that name, I usually call him the gray, and when I entered this castle I asked this Señora Duenna to take care of him, and she got as angry as if I had called her ugly or old, since it must be more fitting and natural for duennas to give a thought to donkeys than to claim authority in castle halls. Oh, and Lord save me, what a dislike a nobleman from my village had for these ladies!"

"He must have been some peasant," said Doña Rodríguez the duenna, "because if he were noble and wellborn, he would have praised them to the skies."

"Well now," said the duchess, "that's enough: Doña Rodríguez, be

---

9. "Dead in the flower of his youth," a line from a poem by Angelo Poliziano dedicated to Micael Verino, a poet who died at the age of seventeen, during the age of the Medicis. Verino was famous for his Latin couplets, which were very widely known.

still, and Señor Panza, calm down, and let me take care of looking after this gray, for if he is Sancho's jewel, I shall value him more highly than the apple of my eye."

"It's enough if he's in the stable," responded Sancho. "As for being valued more highly than the apple of your highness's eye, he and I aren't worthy of that even for an instant, and I would no more agree to it than to being stabbed; though my master says that in courtesies it's better to lose by a card too many than a card too few, as far as donkeys and apples are concerned, you have to go with your compass in hand, and at a measured pace."

"Let Sancho take him to his governorship," said the duchess, "and there he can treat him as nicely as he wants, and even keep him from hard labor."

"Your grace should not think, Señora Duchess, that you have said anything remarkable," said Sancho, "for I have seen more than two jackasses go into governorships, and if I take mine with me, it won't be anything new."

Sancho's words renewed the duchess's laughter and delight, and after sending him to rest, she went to recount to the duke her conversation with Sancho; and between the two of them, they arranged and planned to play tricks on Don Quixote that would be remarkable and consonant with the chivalric style; and they devised so many, and ones so appropriate and clever, that they are some of the best adventures contained in this great history.

CHAPTER XXXIV

Which recounts the information that was received regarding how the peerless Dulcinea of Toboso was to be disenchanted, which is one of the most famous adventures in this book

The duke and the duchess received great pleasure from Don Quixote's conversation and that of Sancho Panza; they confirmed their intention of playing some tricks that would have the appearance and semblance of adventures, basing their plan on what Don Quixote had already told them about the Cave of Montesinos in order to create for him an adventure that would be famous—though what most astonished the duchess was Sancho's simplemindedness, so great that he had come to believe as an infallible truth that Dulcinea of Toboso was enchanted when he himself had been the enchanter and deceiver in that affair—and so, having given orders to their servants regarding everything they had to do, six days later they took Don Quixote hunting for big game, with so many hunters and trackers that it might have been the party of a crowned king. They gave Don Quixote a hunting outfit, and Sancho another of fine green cloth, but Don Quixote refused to put his on, saying that the next day he would have to return to the harsh profession of arms and could not carry wardrobes and furnishings with him. Sancho, however, accepted what they gave him, intending to sell it at the earliest opportunity.

When the long-awaited day arrived, Don Quixote put on his armor, Sancho donned his outfit, and, riding his donkey, for he did not wish to leave him behind even though they had provided him with a horse, he joined the troop of hunters. The duchess rode out in splendid attire, and Don Quixote, in his courtesy and politeness, took the reins of her palfrey although the duke did not wish to allow it, and finally they reached a forest that lay between two high mountains, where, having set up their posts, their blinds, and their traps, and assigning people to different positions, the hunt began with so great a clamor, so much shouting and calling and barking of dogs and sounding of horns, that they could not hear one another speak.

The duchess dismounted and, holding a sharp javelin in her hands, took up a post where she knew wild boar usually passed by. The duke and Don Quixote also dismounted and stationed themselves on either side of her; Sancho, who was behind them all, did not dismount the donkey, for he did not dare abandon him in the event some mishap befell him. And as soon as they and a good number of other servants had taken their places, then, pursued by the dogs and followed by the trackers, they saw a huge wild boar rushing toward them, grinding its teeth and tusks and foaming at the mouth; when he saw it, Don Quixote grasped his shield and drew his sword and stepped forward to meet it. The duke did the same with his javelin, but the duchess would have gone ahead of all of them if the duke had not stopped her. Only Sancho, when he saw the valiant beast, abandoned his donkey, and began to run as fast as he could, and attempted to climb to the top of a tall oak but failed; instead, when he was halfway up the tree, holding on to a branch as he struggled to reach the top, his luck was so bad and he was so unfortunate that the branch broke, and when it fell to the ground he was still in the air, caught on the stump of a branch and unable to reach the ground. And seeing himself in this situation, and his green tunic tearing, and thinking that if the wild animal ran past it could reach him, he began to give so many shouts and to call for help with so much urgency that everyone who heard him and did not see him believed he was in the jaws of a savage beast.

Finally, the tusked boar was run through by the sharp points of the many javelins it encountered; Don Quixote, turning his head in the direction of Sancho's shouting, for he had realized that the shouts were his, saw him hanging upside down from the oak, his donkey beside him, for the gray did not abandon him in his calamity, and Cide Hamete says he rarely saw Sancho Panza without his donkey, or the donkey without Sancho: such was the friendship and good faith that existed between the two of them.

Don Quixote approached and unhooked Sancho, who, finding himself free and on the ground, looked at how badly torn the hunting tunic was, and it pained him deeply, for he had thought of his outfit as an inheritance. In the meantime, the powerful boar was lain across a mule, covered with sprigs of rosemary and sprays of myrtle, and taken, as a sign of the spoils of victory, to some large field tents that had been pitched in the middle of the wood; there they found the tables prepared and the meal ready, a banquet so sumptuous and large that one could easily see in it the greatness and magnificence of the person who offered it. Sancho, showing the duchess the tears in his ripped tunic, said:

"If this had been a hunt of hares or small birds, my tunic would not have suffered this damage. I don't know what pleasure there is in waiting for an animal that, if it gores you with a tusk, can kill you; I remember hearing an old ballad that says:

> May you be eaten by bears,
> like His Majesty Favila."

"That was a Visigothic king," said Don Quixote, "who went hunting for big game and was devoured by a bear."

"That's what I'm saying," responded Sancho. "I wouldn't want princes and kings to put themselves in that kind of danger in exchange for a pleasure that really shouldn't be one, since it involves killing an animal that hasn't done anything wrong."

"But you're mistaken, Sancho," responded the duke, "because the practice of hunting big game is more appropriate and necessary for kings and princes than any other. Hunting is an image of war: in it there are stratagems, traps, and snares for conquering the enemy safely; one suffers bitter cold and intolerable heat; idleness and sleep are diminished, one's strength is fortified, one's limbs are made agile; in short, it is a practice that harms no one and gives pleasure to many; and the best thing about it is that it is not for everyone, as other forms of hunting are, except for hawking, which also is only for kings and great lords. And so, Sancho, change your opinion, and when you are a governor, devote yourself to hunting and see how it will benefit you a hundred times over."

"No," responded Sancho, "a good governor and a broken leg stay at home.[1] How nice if weary merchants came to see him and he was in the woods enjoying himself! What a misfortune for the governorship! By my faith, Señor, hunting and those pastimes are more for idlers than for governors. What I plan to amuse myself with is playing *triunfo envidado*[2] on feast days and ninepins on Sundays and holidays; all this hunting and hollering[3] doesn't go well with my nature and doesn't sit well with my conscience."

"May it please God, Sancho, because there's many a slip between the cup and the lip."

"That may be so," replied Sancho, "but if you pay your debts, you don't worry about guaranties, and it's better to have God's help than to get up early, and your belly leads your feet, not the other way around; I mean, if God helps me, and I do what I ought to with good intentions, I'll be sure to govern in grand style. Just put a finger in my mouth and see if I bite or not!"

"God and all his saints curse you, wretched Sancho," said Don Quixote, "as I have said so often, will the day ever come when I see you speak an ordinary coherent sentence without any proverbs? Señores, your highnesses should leave this fool alone, for he will grind your souls not between two but two thousand proverbs brought in as opportunely and appropriately as the health God gives him, or me if I wanted to listen to them."

"Sancho Panza's proverbs," said the duchess, "although more numer-

---

1. This is a variation on the adage about a good wife.

2. A card game.

3. The Spanish reads *cazas ni cazos*, a nonsensical wordplay based on *caza*, "the hunt," and *cazo*, "ladle," which seem to be the feminine and masculine forms of the same word but are not.

ous than those of the Greek Commander,[4] because of their brevity are no less estimable. As far as I am concerned, they give me more pleasure than others that may be more fitting and more opportune."

Engaged in this and other amiable conversations, they walked out of the tent and into the forest, and in the collecting of some traps the day passed quickly and night fell, not as clear or as tranquil as it usually was at that time of year, which was the middle of summer, but it did bring a certain chiaroscuro that furthered the plans of the duke and duchess, for as dusk began to turn into night, it suddenly seemed that the entire forest on all four sides was ablaze, and then here and there, this way and that, an infinite number of cornets and other warlike instruments were heard, as if troops of cavalry were riding through the woods. The light of the fires and the sound of martial instruments almost blinded and deafened the eyes and ears of those nearby and even those who were elsewhere in the forest.

Then they heard the sound of infinite *lelelíes*, in the manner of a Moorish battle cry; trumpets and bugles blared, drums sounded, fifes played almost all at the same time, and so continually and so rapidly that one could lose one's senses in the confused din of so many instruments. The duke was stunned, the duchess was astounded, Don Quixote was astonished, Sancho Panza trembled, and even those who knew the cause were frightened. In their fear they fell silent, and a postillion dressed as a demon passed in front of them, and instead of a cornet he was playing a huge, hollow animal horn that emitted a harsh and terrifying sound.

"Hello there, courier!" said the duke. "Who are you, where are you going, and what soldiers are these who seem to be crossing this forest?"

To which the courier, in a dreadful, brash voice, responded:

"I am the devil; I am looking for Don Quixote of La Mancha; the people coming through here are six troops of enchanters who bear the peerless Dulcinea of Toboso on a triumphal carriage. Enchanted, she comes with the gallant Frenchman Montesinos, to instruct Don Quixote as to how the lady is to be disenchanted."

"If you were the devil, as you say and as your figure suggests, you would have known the knight Don Quixote of La Mancha, for you have him here before you."

"By God and my conscience," responded the devil, "I wasn't really thinking; my thoughts are distracted by so many things that I forgot the principal reason for my being here."

4. Hernán Núñez Pinciano, who compiled a famous collection of proverbs (*Refranes y proverbios*) published in 1555.

"There can be no doubt," said Sancho, "that this demon is a decent man and a good Christian, because otherwise he wouldn't swear *by God and my conscience*. Now I think there must be good people even down in hell."

Then the demon, without dismounting, directed his gaze at Don Quixote and said:

"To you, Knight of the Lions (and may I see you in their claws), I am sent by the unfortunate but valiant knight Montesinos, who has ordered me to tell you on his behalf that you should wait for him in the place where I encountered you, because he brings with him the one they call Dulcinea of Toboso, and he will instruct you on what is needed to disenchant her. And since I came here with no other purpose, I need stay no longer: may demons like me be with you, and good angels with these nobles."

And having said this, he blew on the enormous horn, turned his back, and left, not waiting for anyone's reply.

This caused new amazement in everyone, especially in Sancho and Don Quixote: in Sancho, when he saw that despite the truth, people insisted that Dulcinea was enchanted; in Don Quixote, because he could not be certain if what had happened to him in the Cave of Montesinos was true or not. And as he was lost in these thoughts, the duke said to him:

"Does your grace intend to wait, Señor Don Quixote?"

"How could I not?" he responded. "I shall wait here, intrepid and strong, though all of hell were to attack me."

"Well, if I see another devil and hear another horn like that one, I wouldn't wait here any more than I'd wait in Flanders," said Sancho.

By now the night had grown even darker, and a good number of lights began to move through the forest, just as the dry exhalations of the earth move across the sky and to our eyes seem like shooting stars. At the same time a terrifying noise was heard, something like the one made by the solid wheels usually found on oxcarts, from whose harsh and constant screeching, they say, wolves and bears flee if there are any nearby when they pass. To this was added more tumult, another clamor that heightened all the others, which was that it really seemed that in the four corners of the forest four encounters or battles were taking place at the same time, because here the hard thunder of terrifying artillery sounded; there infinite muskets were being fired; the voices of the combatants cried out close by; the Muslim *lelelíes* were repeated in the distance.

Finally, the cornets, the animal horns, the hunting horns, the bugles, the trumpets, the drums, the artillery, the harquebuses, and above all, the awful noise of the carts together formed a sound so confused and horrible that Don Quixote had to summon all his valor to endure it; but Sancho's courage plummeted and sent him, swooning, to the skirts of the duchess, who received him there and quickly ordered that water be thrown in his face. It was, and he regained consciousness just as a cart with screeching wheels arrived at the place where they stood.

It was pulled by four slow oxen draped in black; a great blazing wax torch was tied to each of their horns, and on the cart was a high seat on which a venerable old man was sitting, his beard whiter than the snow, and so long it fell below his waist; he wore a long robe of black buckram, for since the cart was filled with infinite lights, one could clearly see and discern everything it carried. It was driven by two hideous demons dressed in the same buckram, with faces so ugly that Sancho, having seen them once, closed his eyes so as not to see them again. And so the cart reached them, and the venerable old man got up from his high seat, and as he stood there he gave a great shout, saying:

"I am the wise Lirgandeo."[5]

And the cart drove on, and he did not say another word. Behind this one came another cart of the same kind, carrying another old man enthroned, and he, stopping the cart, in a voice no less grave than the other's, said:

"I am the wise Alquife, the great friend of Urganda the Unknown."

And the cart passed on.

Then, in the same manner, another cart arrived, but the one seated on the throne was not an ancient like the others, but a strong, robust, evil-looking man, and as he arrived he rose to his feet, just like the others, and said in a voice that was hoarser and more fiendish:

"I am the enchanter Arcalaus, the mortal enemy of Amadís of Gaul and all his kin."

And he moved on. Not far away from there the three carts halted, and the maddening sound of their wheels stopped, and then something else was heard, not a noise, but the sound made by soft and harmonious music, which made Sancho very happy, and which he took as a good omen; and so, he said to the duchess, from whose side he had moved not one iota:

5. A wizard, the supposed chronicler of the Knight of Phoebus.

"Señora, where there is music, there can be nothing bad."

"Nor where there are lights and brightness," responded the duchess.

To which Sancho replied:

"A flame gives light, and bonfires give brightness, and if we go near them they can burn us, but music is always a sign of cheer and rejoicing."

"We shall see," said Don Quixote, who had heard everything.

And he was correct, as the following chapter shows.

CHAPTER XXXV

In which the information that Don Quixote received regarding the disenchantment of Dulcinea continues, along with other remarkable events

To the rhythm of the pleasant music, they saw coming toward them the kind of cart that is called triumphal, pulled by six gray mules caparisoned in white linen; on each of them rode a penitent of light,[1] also dressed in white and holding a large burning wax torch in his hand. The cart was two or even three times larger than the previous ones, and the sides and front were occupied by twelve other penitents as white as snow, all with their burning torches, a sight that caused both wonder and terror; on a raised throne sat a nymph draped in a thousand veils of silver cloth, and on all of them infinite numbers of gold sequins were sparkling, making her seem if not richly, then at least colorfully dressed. Her face was covered by transparent and delicate sendal,[2] so that despite its folds the very beautiful face of a maiden was revealed, and the many lights made it possible to discern her beauty and her age, which appeared to be no more than twenty and no less than seventeen.

Next to her came a figure dressed in the kind of long robe that is called flowing, with a black veil covering the head; as soon as the cart came face-to-face with the duke and duchess and Don Quixote, the music of the flageolets stopped, followed by the music of the harps and lutes that were playing in the cart; the figure in the robe stood and,

---

1. The name given to those who carried torches or candles in religious processions.

2. A sheer silk fabric.

pulling the robe open and removing the veil, revealed the fleshless, hideous figure of Death itself, causing grief in Don Quixote and dismay in Sancho Panza, while the duke and duchess adopted a semblance of fear. This living Death stood and, in a drowsy voice and with a tongue not fully awake, said:

> "I am Merlin, who, the histories say,
> was sired and fathered by the devil himself
> (a lie made true by the mere passage of time),
> I am the prince of Magic, king and fount
> of Zoroastrian science and lore,
> and enemy to those ages and times
> that attempt to conceal the gallant deeds
> of the brave and courageous errant knights
> whom I so dearly loved, and still do love.
> Although the disposition of enchanters,
> of mages and magicians always is
> flinthearted, harsh, and ruthless, mine alone
> is tender, soft, and loving, wanting no more
> than always to do good to everyone.
>
> Down in the dark mournful caverns of Dis,[3]
> where my soul passed endless time in giving shape
> to certain forms, and characters, and rhomboids,
> the melancholy voice of the beauteous
> and peerless Dulcinea of Toboso
> reached my ears. I learned of her enchantment,
> her misfortune, her transformation from
> highborn lady into a peasant girl;
> my heart was moved, and I encased my spirit
> in the shell of this fierce and fearsome skeleton,
> and pored over a hundred thousand books
> of my diabolic and vicious lore,
> and come now with the remedy to cure
> so grievous a sorrow, so great an ill.
>
> O you, glory and honor of all who don
> tunics of adamant steel and diamond,
> light and lantern, pilot, polestar and guide

---

3. The god of the underworld, associated with Pluto, Orcus, and Hades.

of those who abandon the languor of sleep,
their idle beds, to take up and profess
the unbearable burden and exercise
of blood-drenched and weighty arms, I say to you,
O famous knight, never sufficiently praised,
to you, both valiant and wise, O Don Quixote,
the splendor of La Mancha and star of Spain,
that for the peerless lady Dulcinea
to regain and recover her first state,
your squire, Sancho, needs to give himself
three thousand and three hundred blows upon
both of his broad buttocks, robust and large,
bared to the whip, and struck in such a way
that they turn red, and smart, and give him pain.
This is the decision of all the authors
of her misfortune, woe, and alteration,
and for this I have come, my lords and ladies."

"By my soul!" said Sancho. "I won't talk about three thousand lashes, but I'd as soon give myself three as stab myself three times! To the devil with that kind of disenchanting! I don't know what my backside has to do with enchantments! By God, if Señor Merlin hasn't found any other way to disenchant Señora Dulcinea of Toboso, then she can go to her grave enchanted!"

"I shall take you,"[4] said Don Quixote, "Don Peasant, you churl stuffed with garlic, and I shall tie you to a tree as naked as the day you were born, and I shall give you not three thousand and three hundred, but six thousand and six hundred lashes, and they will go so deep that they will not come off even if you pull them three thousand and three hundred times. And if you say a word to me, I shall tear out your soul."

Hearing which, Merlin said:

"That cannot be, because the lashes our good Sancho is to receive must be by his own will and not by force, and he can take as long as he desires, for there is no fixed time limit; he is also permitted, if he wishes to save himself half the abuse of this whipping, to allow another's hand, even if somewhat heavy, to lash him."

"Not another's, not mine, not heavy, not ready to be weighed,"

---

4. Don Quixote addresses Sancho in a more distant, formal way throughout this paragraph. As always, it indicates extreme anger.

replied Sancho. "No hand at all is going to touch me. Did I, by some chance, give birth to Señora Dulcinea of Toboso? Is that why my back-side has to pay for the sins of her eyes? My master certainly is part of her, for he's always calling her *my life, my soul,* his help and protection, so he can and ought to be lashed for her sake and take the steps he needs to in order to disenchant her, but me whipping myself? I renounce thee!"[5]

No sooner had Sancho said this than the silvered nymph who was next to the spirit of Merlin rose to her feet, removed the sheer veil, and revealed her face, which everyone thought was exceptionally beautiful, and with masculine self-assurance, and a voice not especially feminine, she spoke directly to Sancho Panza, saying:

"O ill-fated squire with your unfeeling soul, torpid heart, stony and flinty nature. If you were commanded, O shameless thief, to throw your-self from a high tower; if you were asked, O enemy of humankind, to eat a dozen toads, two dozen lizards, and three dozen snakes; if you were urged to murder your wife and children with a cruel, sharp scimitar, it would be no surprise if you were reluctant and evasive; but to take notice of three thousand and three hundred lashes, when there's not a boy in catechism class, no matter how puny, who doesn't get that many every month, astounds, alarms, and horrifies all the compassionate natures of those who hear this, and even those who will come to know of it in the course of time. Turn, O wretched and hardhearted beast! Turn, I say, those eyes of a startled owl toward mine, which have been compared to shining stars, and you will see them weep a steady stream—nay, a river— of tears, cutting furrows, tracks, and pathways into the fair fields of my cheeks. Show pity, you crafty and malevolent monster; I am still in my teens—nineteen, not yet twenty—and the flower of my youth is being consumed and withered beneath the coarse hide of a crude peasant girl; and if I do not appear so now, it is a particular favor that Señor Merlin, here present, has done for me, so that my beauty may soften you, for the tears of afflicted beauty can turn crags into cotton and tigers into sheep. Lash, lash that hide, O savage beast, and liberate your energies from the sloth that inclines you only to eating and still more eating; free the smoothness of my flesh, the gentleness of my nature, and the beauty of my face, and if for my sake you do not wish to soften your heart or lessen the time it will take you, then do so for that poor knight there beside

---

5. A formula in the liturgy (*abrenuncio*) used to renounce Satan. Since Merlin is supposed to be the child of the devil, the phrase is strangely appropriate, even though Sancho mispronounces it (*abernuncio*).

you: for your master, I say, whose soul I can see, since it is caught in his throat, not the span of ten fingers from his lips, waiting only for your harsh or gentle response to come out of his mouth or return to his stomach."

Hearing this, Don Quixote felt his throat and said, turning to the duke:

"By God, Señor, what Dulcinea has said is true: here is my soul caught in my throat like the tightening nut on a crossbow."

"What do you say to that, Sancho?" asked the duchess.

"I say, Señora," responded Sancho, "what I have already said: as far as lashes are concerned, I renounce thee."

"*I renounce thee* is what you mean, Sancho; what you said is wrong," said the duke.

"Your highness, leave me alone," responded Sancho, "I'm in no condition now to worry about subtleties or one letter more or less; these lashes that have to be given to me, or that I have to give myself, have me so upset that I don't know what I'm saying or doing. But I'd like to hear from the lady Señora Dulcinea of Toboso where it was that she learned how to ask for things: she comes to ask me to open my flesh with lashes, and she calls me unfeeling soul and savage beast and a whole string of names so bad only the devil could put up with them. By some chance is my flesh made of bronze, or does it matter to me if she's disenchanted or not? What basket of linen, shirts, scarves, gaiters, though I don't use them, does she bring with her to soften me? Nothing but one insult after another, though she must know the proverb that says that a jackass loaded down with gold climbs the mountain fast, and gifts can break boulders, and God helps those who help themselves, and a bird in hand is worth two in the bush. And then my master, who should have coddled me and flattered me so I'd turn as soft as wool and carded cotton, says that if he catches me he'll tie me naked to a tree and double the number of lashes; these noble folk so full of pity should remember that they're not only asking a squire to whip himself, but a governor; like they say, 'That's the finishing touch.' Let them learn, let them learn, damn them, how to beg, and how to ask, and how to have good manners; all times are not the same, and men are not always in a good humor. Here I am, bursting with grief because my green tunic is torn, and they come to ask me to give myself lashes of my own free will, when it's as unwilling to do that as to become an Indian chief."

"Well, the truth is, Sancho my friend," said the duke, "that if you don't become softer than a ripe fig, you won't lay hands on the governorship. It would be a fine thing if I sent my islanders a cruel governor with a heart of flint who does not bow to the tears of damsels in distress or the entreaties of wise, proud, and ancient enchanters and sages! In short, Sancho, either you lash yourself, or let someone else lash you, or you won't be governor."

"Señor," responded Sancho, "can't I have two days to think about what I should do?"

"No, absolutely not," said Merlin. "Here, in this instant and in this place, the matter must be settled: either Dulcinea will return to the Cave of Montesinos and to her earlier condition as a peasant, or now, in her present state, she will be transported to the Elysian Fields, where she will wait until the number of lashes is completed."

"Come now, my good Sancho," said the duchess, "take heart and be grateful to Don Quixote for the bread you have eaten; we all must serve and please him for his virtuous nature and his high acts of chivalry. Say yes, my friend, to this flogging, and let the devil go to the devil and fear to the coward, for a brave heart breaks bad luck, as you know very well."

To this Sancho responded with some foolishness, and speaking to Merlin, he asked:

"Tell me, your grace, Señor Merlin: the devil courier came here and gave my master a message from Señor Montesinos, telling him to wait here because he was going to give him instructions on how to disenchant Señora Doña Dulcinea of Toboso, and so far we haven't seen Montesinos or anybody like him."

To which Merlin responded:

"The devil, Sancho my friend, is ignorant and a great scoundrel: I sent him to look for your master, with a message not from Montesinos but from me, because Montesinos is in his cave, thinking about or, I should say, hoping for his disenchantment, because he still has a long way to go. If he owes you something, or if you have any business to do with him, I'll bring him to you, to whatever place you like. For now, just say yes to this whipping, and believe me when I say that it will be of benefit to your soul and your body: your soul, because of the charity you bring to it, and your body, because I know you have a sanguine temperament, and it won't do you much harm to lose a little blood."

"What a lot of doctors there are in the world: even enchanters are doctors," replied Sancho. "Well, since everybody's telling me to do it, though I can't see it, I say that I'll be happy to give myself three thousand

and three hundred lashes on the condition that I can give them whenever I like, without anybody trying to set the number of days or length of time; and I'll try to wipe out the debt as fast as I can so the world can enjoy the beauty of Señora Doña Dulcinea of Toboso, because though I didn't think so before, it seems she really is beautiful. Another condition has to be that I'm not obliged to draw blood with the whipping, and if some lashes are like the flick of an animal's tail brushing away flies, they still have to be counted. Also, if I make a mistake in the number, Señor Merlin, since he knows everything, has to be responsible for keeping count and letting me know if I have too few or too many."

"No one has to let you know if you have too many," responded Merlin, "because when you reach the correct number, Señora Dulcinea will suddenly be disenchanted and will come, gratefully, to her good Sancho to thank him and even reward him for his good deed. So there is no reason to have any doubt about too many or too few, and heaven forbid that I deceive anybody, even by so much as a hair."

"Well, well, then it's in God's hands," said Sancho. "I consent to my bad fortune; I say that I accept the penance, with the conditions that have been stated."

As soon as Sancho said these words, the music of the flageolets began to sound again, and an infinite number of harquebuses were fired, and Don Quixote threw his arms around Sancho's neck and gave him a thousand kisses on his forehead and cheeks. The duchess and the duke and all those present gave signs of great contentment and joy, and the cart began to move, and as the beautiful Dulcinea passed by, she bowed her head to the duke and duchess and made a deep curtsy to Sancho.

And now a joyful and smiling dawn quickly approached; the flowers of the fields raised their heads and stood erect, and the liquid crystal of the streams, murmuring over smooth white and gray pebbles, hurried to pay tribute to the rivers that awaited them. The joyful earth, the bright sky, the clear air, the serene light, together and separately gave clear indications that the day that came treading on the skirts of the dawn would be calm and bright. And the duke and duchess, satisfied with their hunt and with having achieved their ends so cleverly and successfully, returned to their castle, intending to continue with their deceptions, because for them, there really was nothing that gave them greater pleasure.

CHAPTER XXXVI

*Which recounts the strange and unimaginable adventure of the Dolorous
Duenna, also known as the Countess Trifaldi, as well as a letter that Sancho
Panza wrote to his wife, Teresa Panza*

The duke had a steward, a man with a comic and inventive turn of mind,
who had acted the part of Merlin, prepared all the devices of the previous adventure, composed the verses, and arranged for a page to play
Dulcinea. Then, with the intervention of his master and mistress, he devised another adventure, with the most diverting and strangest con-
trivances anyone could imagine.

The following day, the duchess asked Sancho if he had begun the
task of the penance he was obliged to perform in order to disenchant
Dulcinea. He said yes, that very night he had given himself five lashes.
The duchess asked what implement he had used to administer them. He
responded that he had used his hand.

"That," replied the duchess, "is more like slapping than flogging. It
seems to me that the wise Merlin will not be satisfied with so much gentleness, and that it will be necessary for our good Sancho to use a whip
with metal points or a cat-o'-nine-tails, something he can feel, because a
good teacher never spares the rod, and the freedom of so great a lady as
Dulcinea cannot be gotten cheaply and at so little cost; and be advised,
Sancho, that works of charity performed in a lukewarm and halfhearted
way have no merit and are worth nothing."[1]

To which Sancho responded:

"Your ladyship, give me the right kind of whip or braided rope, and
I'll hit myself with it as long as it doesn't hurt too much; because your

1. This last statement ("and be advised . . . are worth nothing") was suppressed by the Inquisition in
some editions following the *Indice expurgatorio* of 1632.

grace should know that even though I'm a peasant, my flesh is more like cotton than esparto grass, and it wouldn't be right if I did myself harm for somebody else's benefit."

"Let it be all for the best," responded the duchess. "Tomorrow I'll give you a whip that will be perfect for you and suit the tenderness of your flesh as if the two were sisters."

To which Sancho said:

"Señora of my soul, your highness should know that I've written a letter to my wife, Teresa Panza, telling her everything that's happened to me since I left her side; it's here in my shirt, and all that's missing is the address; I'd like your intelligence to read it, because it seems to me it suits a governor, I mean, the way governors ought to write."

"Who dictated it?" asked the duchess.

"Who else would dictate it but me, sinner that I am?" responded Sancho.

"And did you write it?" said the duchess.

"I couldn't do that," responded Sancho, "because I don't know how to read or write, though I can sign my name."

"Let's see it," said the duchess. "I'm sure that in it you display the nature and quality of your wit."

Sancho took an open letter from inside his shirt, and when he gave it to the duchess, she saw that this is what it said:

A LETTER FROM SANCHO PANZA TO TERESA PANZA, HIS WIFE

If they gave me a good whipping, at least I rode a nice donkey;[2] if I have a good governorship, it cost me a good whipping. You won't understand this now, my Teresa, but someday you will. You should know, Teresa, that I've decided you should go around in a carriage, because that's the way it should be; anything else is going around on all fours. You're the wife of a governor, and nobody's going to talk about you behind your back! I'm sending you a green hunting tunic that my lady the duchess gave me; make it into a skirt and bodice for our daughter. I've heard in this land that Don Quixote, my master, is a sane madman and an amusing fool, and that I'm just as good as he is. We've been in the Cave of Montesinos, and the wise Merlin has picked me for the disenchantment of Dulcinea of Toboso, who's called Aldonza Lorenzo

---

2. A person who was whipped publicly was displayed to the crowd mounted on a jackass.

there where you are; with the three thousand and three hundred lashes, less five, that I'll give myself, she'll be as disenchanted as the mother who bore her. Don't tell anybody about this, because if you tell your business in public, some will say it's white, and others that it's black. In a few days I'll leave for the governorship, and I'm going there with a real desire to make money because I've been told that all new governors have this same desire; I'll see how things are there and let you know whether or not you should come to be with me. The gray is fine and sends you his best; I don't plan to leave him even if they make me Grand Turk. My lady the duchess kisses your hands a thousand times; send her back two thousand, because there's nothing that costs less or is cheaper, as my master says, than good manners. It was not God's will to grant me another case with another hundred escudos in it, like before, but don't feel bad about that, Teresa; the man who sounds the alarm is safe, and it'll all come out in the wash of the governorship; what does make me very sad is that they've told me that if I try to take something away from it, I'll go hungry afterwards, and if that's true it won't be very cheap for me, though the maimed and wounded already have their soft job in the alms they beg; so one way or another, you'll be rich and have good luck. God grant you that, if He can, and keep me safe to serve you. From this castle, on the twentieth of July, 1614.

> Your husband the governor,
> SANCHO PANZA

As soon as the duchess finished reading the letter, she said to Sancho:

"There are two things in which the good governor is slightly mistaken: one, when he says or implies that this governorship has been given to him in exchange for the lashes that he'll give himself, when he knows and cannot deny that when my lord the duke promised it to him, nobody even dreamed there were lashes in the world; the other is that he shows himself to be very greedy, and I wouldn't want it to be oregano;[3] greed rips the sack, and a greedy governor dispenses unjust justice."

"I didn't mean it that way, Señora," responded Sancho, "and if your grace thinks the letter isn't the way it should be, there's nothing to do but tear it up and make a new one, though it may be even worse if it's left up to my poor wits."

3. An allusion to the proverb "God grant that it's oregano and not caraway," which expresses the fear that things may not turn out as hoped.

"No, no," replied the duchess, "this is fine, and I want the duke to see it."

Having said this, they went out to a garden where they were to have dinner that day. The duchess showed Sancho's letter to the duke, who derived a good deal of pleasure from it. They ate, and after the table had been cleared, and after amusing themselves for some time with Sancho's delicious talk, they suddenly heard the mournful sound of a fife and a harsh, strident drum. Everyone seemed startled by the confused, martial, and melancholy harmony, especially Don Quixote, who in his agitation could barely keep his seat; regarding Sancho, we need say only that fear carried him to his customary refuge, which was the side or the skirts of the duchess, because, really and truly, the sound they heard was extremely sad and melancholy.

And with all of them in this state of perplexity, they saw two men dressed in mourning come into the garden, their robes so long and flowing that they trailed along the ground; they were playing two large drums that were also covered in black. Beside them a man played the fife, as pitch black and dark as the rest. Following the three men was a personage with a gigantic body, cloaked, rather than dressed, in a deep black, full-length robe whose skirt was also exceptionally long. Girding and encircling the robe was a broad black swordbelt from which there hung an enormous scimitar with a black scabbard and guard. His face was covered by a black transparent veil, through which one could catch glimpses of a very long beard as white as the snow, and he walked, very gravely and serenely, to the beat of the drums. In short, his size, pace, black raiment, and escort could and did astound all those who looked at him but did not know who he was.

The figure approached, then, with the aforementioned slow solemnity, to kneel before the duke, who stood, as did everyone else who was there, to wait for him, but under no circumstances would the duke allow him to speak until he rose to his feet. The prodigiously frightening person obeyed, and when he was standing he raised the veil to reveal the most hideous, longest, whitest, and thickest beard that human eyes had ever seen, and then, from a broad and swelling chest, he forced and coerced a solemn, sonorous voice, and fixing his eyes on the duke, he said:

"Most high and powerful lord, I am called Trifaldín of the White Beard; I am squire to the Countess Trifaldi, also known as the Dolorous Duenna, on whose behalf I bring your highness a message, which is this: may your magnificence have the goodness to give her license and permission to enter and tell you of her affliction, which is one of the strangest and most amazing that the most troubled mind in the world could ever have imagined. And first she wishes to know if the valiant and never vanquished knight Don Quixote of La Mancha is in your castle, for she has come looking for him, on foot, and without breaking her fast, all the way from the kingdom of Candaya to your realm, something that can and ought to be considered a miracle, or else the work of enchantment. She is at the door of this fortress or country house, and awaits only your consent to come in. I have spoken my message."

And then he coughed and stroked his beard with both hands, and with great calm he waited for the duke's response, which was:

"Good Squire Trifaldín of the White Beard, it has been many days since we heard of the misfortune of Señora Countess Trifaldi, obliged by enchanters to be called the Dolorous Duenna; you may certainly, O stupendous squire, tell her to come in, and that the valiant knight Don Quixote of La Mancha is here, and from his generous nature she can surely expect every protection and every assistance; you may also tell her on my behalf that if she finds my favor necessary, she shall have it, for I must give it to her as a knight who is bound and obliged to serve all women, especially widowed, scorned, and afflicted duennas, which is what your mistress must be."

On hearing this, Trifaldín went down on one knee, then signaled the fife and drums to play and walked out of the garden to the same music and at the same pace with which he had entered, leaving everyone stunned by his presence and bearing. And the duke, turning to Don Quixote, said:

"It seems, O famous knight, that the shadows of malice and ignorance cannot cover and obscure the light of valor and virtue. I say this because it is barely six days that your grace has been in this castle, and already the sad and the afflicted come seeking you from distant and remote lands, not in carriages or on dromedaries, but on foot, and fasting, confident they will find in that mighty arm the remedy for their cares and sorrows, for your great deeds are known and admired all over the known world."

"Señor Duke, I wish," responded Don Quixote, "that the blessed religious who displayed at the table the other day so much animosity and ill will toward knights errant were here to see with his own eyes whether such knights are necessary in the world: to touch, at least, with his own hand, the fact that those who are extraordinarily afflicted and disconsolate, in great difficulties and enormous misfortunes, do not go to seek their remedy in the house of the lettered, or the village sacristan, or the knight who has never managed to go beyond the borders of his town, or the idle courtier who would rather seek out news to repeat and recount than perform deeds and great feats so that others can tell about them and write about them; the remedy for difficulties, the help for those in need, the protection of damsels, the consolation of widows, are not found in any persons more clearly than in knights errant, and I give infinite thanks to heaven because I am one, and I welcome any misfortune and travail that may befall me in this honorable exercise. Let the duenna come and make any request she chooses; I shall draw her remedy from the strength of my arm and the intrepid resolve of my courageous spirit."

CHAPTER XXXVII

In which the famous adventure of the Dolorous Duenna continues

The duke and the duchess were exceedingly glad to see how well Don Quixote was responding to their intentions, and at this point Sancho said:

"I wouldn't want this Señora Duenna to put any obstacles in the way of the governorship I've been promised, because I heard a Toledan pharmacist, who could talk the way a goldfinch sings, say that whenever duennas were involved nothing good could happen. God save me, what bad things that pharmacist had to say about them! Which makes me think that since all duennas are annoying and impertinent no matter what their quality and condition may be, what will the dolorous ones be like, I mean this Countess Tres Faldas[1] or Three Skirts or Three Trains? Where I come from, skirts and trains, trains and skirts, are all the same."

"Be quiet, Sancho my friend," said Don Quixote. "Since this duenna has come from such distant lands to find me, she cannot be one of those the pharmacist described, especially since she is a countess, and when countesses serve as duennas, they probably are serving queens and em-

---

1. Sancho hears the name Trifaldi as *tres faldas,* or "three skirts," leading to his comments on skirts and trains.

presses, for in their own houses they are highborn ladies who are served by other duennas."

To which Doña Rodríguez, who was present, responded:

"My lady the duchess has duennas in her service who could be countesses if fortune so desired, but laws go where kings command; let no one speak ill of duennas, in particular those who are old and maidens, for although I am not one of those, I clearly understand and grasp the advantage a maiden duenna has over one who is widowed; and the person who cut us down to size still has the scissors in his hand."

"All the same," replied Sancho, "there's so much to cut in duennas, according to my barber, that it would be better not to stir the rice even if it sticks."

"Squires," responded Doña Rodríguez, "are always our enemies; since they haunt the antechambers and always see us, the times they're not praying, which is most of the time, they spend gossiping about us, digging up our defects and burying our good names. Well, I swear to those fickle dimwits that no matter how much it grieves them, we have to live in the world, and in noble houses, even though we're dying of hunger and cover our delicate or not so delicate flesh with a black mourning habit, just as a person may cover or conceal a dung heap with a tapestry on the day of a procession. By my faith, if I were permitted to, and if the time were right, I'd make people understand, not just those here but everyone in the world, how there is no virtue that cannot be found in a duenna."

"I believe," said the duchess, "that my good Doña Rodríguez is correct, absolutely correct, but she must wait for a more suitable time to defend herself and all other duennas, and so confound the poor opinion of that wicked pharmacist, and tear it out by the roots from the heart of the great Sancho Panza."

To which Sancho responded:

"Ever since I've felt the pride of being a governor I've lost the foolish ideas of a squire, and I don't care a fig for all the duennas in the world."

They would have gone on with the duennaesque conversation if they had not heard the fife and drums begin to play again, leading them to assume that the Dolorous Duenna was coming in. The duchess asked the duke if it would be a good idea to go to receive her, since she was a countess and a distinguished person.

"For the part of her that's a countess," responded Sancho before the duke could respond, "I think it's right for your highnesses to go out to receive her, but for the part that's a duenna, it's my opinion that you shouldn't take a step."

"Who involved you in this, Sancho?" said Don Quixote.

"Who, Señor?" responded Sancho. "I involved myself, and I can involve myself as a squire who has learned the terms of courtesy in the school of your grace, the most courteous and polite knight in all of courtliness; in these things, as I have heard your grace say, you can lose as much for a card too many as for a card too few, and a word to the wise is sufficient."

"What Sancho says is true," said the duke. "Let us see the countess's appearance, and then we can consider the courtesy that is owed her."

Then the drums and fife entered, as they had done earlier.

And here the author concluded this brief chapter and began the next one, following the same adventure, which is one of the most notable in this history.

CHAPTER XXXVIII

Which recounts the tale of misfortune told by the Dolorous Duenna

Behind the mournful musicians a group of duennas, numbering twelve, began to enter the garden in two separate lines, all of them dressed in wide, nunlike habits, apparently of fulled serge, and white headdresses of sheer muslin, which were so long they revealed only the edging of the habits. Behind them came the Countess Trifaldi, led by the hand by the squire Trifaldín of the White Beard, and dressed in very fine black baize without a nap, and if it had been napped, each bit would have been the size of one of the good Martos garbanzos. Her train, or skirt, or whatever it is called, ended in three points, which were held up by the hands of three pages, also dressed in mourning, making an attractive mathematical figure with the three acute angles formed by the three points, leading everyone who saw the acutely pointed skirt to conclude that this was why she was called *The Countess Trifaldi*, as if we had said *The Countess of the Three Skirts*; and this, says Benengeli, was true, for her real name was *The Countess Lobuna*, because there were many wolves in her county,[1] and if there had been foxes instead of wolves, she would have been called *The Countess Zorruna,* because it was the custom in those parts for nobles to take their titles from the thing or things that are most abundant on their lands; but this countess, to favor the novelty of her skirt, abandoned *Lobuna* and adopted *Trifaldi.*

The twelve duennas and their mistress walked at the pace of a procession, their faces covered with black veils, not transparent like Trifaldín's but so heavy that nothing could be seen through them.

As soon as the duennaesque squadron appeared, the duke, the duchess, and Don Quixote rose to their feet, as did everyone who was watching their slow progress. The twelve duennas stopped and opened a path along which the Dolorous One moved forward, still holding Trifaldín's hand; when they saw this, the duke, the duchess, and Don Quixote moved forward some twelve paces to receive her. She fell to her knees and, in a voice more rough and hoarse than subtle and delicate, said:

"May it please your highnesses, you should not show so much courtesy to this your serving man, I mean to say serving woman, because, as I am dolorous, I will not be able to respond as I should since my strange and never-before-seen misfortune has taken away my wits, and I do not know where, it must be a very distant place, because the more I look for them, the less I find them."

"The man would be lacking them," responded the duke, "Señora Countess, who did not discover your worth in your person, and your worth, without any need to see more, deserves all the cream of courtesy and all the flower of polite ceremonies."

And taking her hand, he raised her to her feet and led her to a seat next to the duchess, who also received her with great courtesy.

Don Quixote was silent, and Sancho longed to see the faces of the Countess Trifaldi and some of her many duennas, but that would not be possible until they, of their own free will and desire, uncovered them.

Everyone was quiet and still, waiting to see who would break the silence, and it was the Dolorous Duenna, with these words:

"I am confident, most powerful lord, most beautiful lady, most discerning company, that my most grievous affliction will find in your most valiant bosoms a refuge no less serene than generous and pitying, for it is such that it would be enough to soften marble, and dulcify diamonds,

---

1. *Lobo* is "wolf," and *lobuna* is "wolflike"; in the next phrase, *zorro* is "fox," and *zorruna* is "foxlike."

and bend the steel of the hardest hearts in the world; but before I bring it to your hearing, so as not to say ears, I would be most happy if you would tell me if in this group, circle, and company there is to be found that most unblemished knight Don Quixote of La Manchissima, and his most squirish Panza."

"Panza," said Sancho before anyone else could respond, "is here, and Don Quixotissimo as well, and so, most dolorous duennissima, you can say whatever you wishissima, for we're all ready and most prepared to be your most servantish servantissimos."

At this point Don Quixote rose to his feet, and directing his words to the Dolorous One, he said:

"If your travails, anguished lady, promise some hope of relief through the valor or strength of a knight errant, then here are mine, which, although weak and frail, will be used entirely in your service. I am Don Quixote of La Mancha, whose profession it is to succor all manner of people in need, and this being the case, as it is, it will not be necessary for you, Señora, to win over our benevolence or search for a preamble, but simply and plainly to state your woes, for ears will listen to you that will know, if not how to remedy your troubles, then at least how to feel sorrow for them."

Hearing this, the Dolorous Duenna showed signs of wanting to throw herself at the feet of Don Quixote, which in fact she did, and struggling to embrace them, she said:

"Before these feet and legs I throw myself, O unvanquished knight, for they are the bases and columns of knight errantry! I want to kiss these feet on whose steps all the remedy of my misfortune relies and depends! O courageous errant, whose true deeds leave behind and obscure the extraordinary exploits of Amadís, Esplandián, and Belianis!"

And leaving Don Quixote, she turned to Sancho Panza, and taking his hands, she said:

"O you, the most loyal squire who ever served a knight errant in present or past ages, whose goodness is greater than the beard of Trifaldín, my attendant here present! Well may you boast that by serving the great Don Quixote, you somehow serve the entire troop of knights who have wielded arms in the world. I implore you, for the sake of what you owe your most faithful goodness, to intercede for me with your master so that he may favor this most humble and most unfortunate countess."

To which Sancho responded:

"That my goodness, Señora, is as long and great as the beard of your squire isn't very important to me; just let my soul have a beard and mustache when it leaves this life, which is what matters;[2] I don't worry very much, or at all, about the beards in this world; but without any tricks or entreaties, I'll ask my master (for I know he loves me dearly, especially now when he needs me for a certain piece of business) to favor and help your grace in every way he can. Your grace should unburden yourself, tell us your troubles, and let us take care of it, and we'll all understand one another."

The duke and duchess were bursting with laughter, as were those who realized the nature of this adventure, and to themselves they praised the astute dissembling of Trifaldi, who, taking her seat again, said:

"The famous kingdom of Candaya, which lies between great Trapobana and the Southern Sea, two leagues beyond Cape Comorín,[3] was ruled by Queen Doña Maguncia, widow of King Archipiela, her lord and husband, and in this marriage they conceived and gave birth to Princess Antonomasia,[4] heir to the kingdom; this Princess Antonomasia was brought up and reared under my teaching and tutelage, for I was her mother's oldest and most distinguished duenna. And so the days came and went, and the girl Antonomasia reached the age of fourteen, with a beauty so perfect that nature could do nothing to improve it. And her intelligence was in no way insignificant. She was as intelligent as she was beautiful, and she was the most beautiful girl in the world, and still is if an envious destiny and a hardhearted fate have not already cut the thread of her life. But they can't have, for heaven would not permit so much evil to be done on earth: to pick prematurely a cluster of grapes from the most beautiful vine on the land. Her beauty, which can never be adequately praised by my clumsy tongue, caused an infinite number of princes, both native and foreign, to fall in love with her, and among them an impoverished knight at court dared to lift his thoughts to the heaven of so much beauty, confident of his youth and gallantry, his many talents and abilities, and the ease and liveliness of his wits; because your

2. Sancho's statement is taken from a story about a beardless man, frequently teased because he lacked facial hair, who said, "We have a mustache on our soul; the other kind doesn't matter to us."

3. According to Martín de Riquer, the name Candaya is probably fictional; Trapobana was the old name for Ceylon; Cape Comorín is to the south of Hindustan.

4. *Maguncia* is the Spanish name for the German city Mainz; *Antonomasia* is a rhetorical figure in which a title is used instead of a name (calling a judge "Your Honor") or a proper name instead of a common noun (calling a womanizer "Don Juan"); *Archipiela* seems to be related to *archipiélago*, or "archipelago."

highnesses should know, if you don't find it too tiresome, that he played
the guitar so well he could make it speak, and was a poet besides, and a
fine dancer, and could fashion birdcages so beautiful that in case of necessity he could have earned his living making them; all of these talents
and graces are enough to conquer a mountain, not to mention a delicate
maiden. But all his gallantry and charm, and all his talents and gifts,
would have done little or nothing to defeat my girl's fortress if the brazen
thief had not resorted to defeating me first. First the wicked and heartless
scoundrel tried to win me over and influence my mind so that I, a poor
warden, would hand him the keys to the fortress I was guarding. In short,
he flattered my understanding and overcame my will with all kinds of
trinkets and pendants, but what overpowered me and threw me to the
ground were some verses I heard him sing one night at one of the latticed
windows that faced a lane where he was standing, and if I remember correctly, they said:

> From my enemy sweet and dear
> comes the ill that wounds my soul,
> a greater torment is her hope
> that I suffer with silent tears.[5]

The song seemed like pearls to me, and his voice like honey, and after
that, I mean from that time on, seeing the harm that came to me because
of these and other verses like them, I have believed that from virtuous
and harmonious republics poets must be banished, as Plato advised, at
least the lascivious ones, because they write verses that are not like those
of the Marquis of Mantua, which entertain children and women and
make them weep, but are sharp, like tender thorns that pierce your soul
and, like bolts of lightning, wound you there without tearing your
clothes. And another time he sang:

> Come, death, so secret, so still
> I do not hear your approach,
> so that the pleasure of dying
> does not bring me back to life.[6]

5. The lines, in Spanish translation, are by the Italian poet Serafino dell'Aquila (1466–1500).

6. These lines are by Commander Escrivá, a fifteenth-century poet from Valencia, whose work was
greatly admired by many writers of the Golden Age.

And other little verses and couplets of this kind that charm when they are sung and enthrall when they are read. And when they humbled themselves to compose a kind of verse that was popular in Candaya at the time, which is called *seguidillas?* It meant that souls were leaping, laughter bubbling, bodies restless, and finally, all the senses turned to quicksilver. And so I say, my lords and ladies, that these versifiers very rightly ought to be banished to lizard-infested islands. They, however, are not to blame, but the simpletons who praise them and the foolish women who believe them; and if I were the virtuous duenna I should have been, his hackneyed concepts would not have moved me, nor would I have believed it to be true when he said: 'I live in my dying, I burn in ice, I tremble in fire, I hope without hope, I depart and I stay,' and other impossibilities of this sort that fill their writings. And when they promise the phoenix of Arabia, the crown of Aridiana,[7] the horses of the Sun, the pearls of the South, the gold of Tibar, and the balm of Pancaya?[8] Here is where they most exaggerate with their pens, since it costs them little to promise what they never can nor intend to fulfill. But I digress!

Oh, woe is me, unfortunate woman! What madness or foolishness moves me to recount other people's faults, when I have so much to tell about mine? Oh, woe is me, again, luckless creature! Verses did not defeat me but my own simplemindedness; music did not soften me, but my own flightiness: my great ignorance and small foresight opened the way and cleared the path for the footsteps of Don Clavijo, for that is the name of the aforementioned knight; and so, I acted as intermediary, and he found himself, not once but often, in the chamber of Antonomasia, who was deceived by me, not him, for he claimed to be her true husband; although I am a sinner, without a promise of marriage I would not have consented to his touching the welt on the soles of her slippers. No, no, not that! Matrimony must be the principal thing in any affair of this kind that I am involved in! There was only one difficulty, and that was inequality, Don Clavijo being an impoverished knight and Princess Antonomasia the heiress, as I have said, to the kingdom. For some days this tangle was concealed and hidden by my wise precautions, until it seemed to me that it would soon be revealed by a certain swelling in the belly of Antonomasia, whose fear made the three of us confer, and the

7. This was in the first edition. Martín de Riquer believes it is an intentional corruption of Ariadne, for comic purposes.

8. The last two references in the list were poetic commonplaces.

result was that before this unhappy matter came to light, Don Clavijo would ask for Antonomasia's hand in marriage before the vicar on the basis of a document that the princess had written promising to be his wife, which I had dictated and made so strong that not even the strength of Samson could have broken it. Preparations were made, the vicar saw the document, the same vicar heard the lady's confession, her confession was plain, he ordered her placed in the house of a very honorable bailiff of the court—"

At this point Sancho said:

"So in Candaya there are also bailiffs of the court, poets, and *seguidillas*, which makes me swear that I imagine the whole world's the same. But, Señora Trifaldi, your grace should hurry; it's late, and I'm dying to know how this very long history ends."

"I will," responded the countess.

CHAPTER XXXIX

In which the Countess Trifaldi continues her stupendous and memorable history

Every word that Sancho said pleased the duchess as much as it caused despair in Don Quixote, and ordering him to be quiet, the Dolorous One continued, saying:

"Finally, after many questions and answers, and because the princess never wavered and did not depart from or vary her original statement, the vicar judged in favor of Don Clavijo and gave her to him as his legitimate wife, which so troubled Queen Doña Maguncia, Princess Antonomasia's mother, that in three days' time we buried her."

"No doubt she must have died," said Sancho.

"Of course!" responded Trifaldín. "In Candaya we don't bury the living, only the dead."

"It has been known to happen, Señor Squire," replied Sancho, "that someone in a faint has been buried because people thought he was dead, and it seemed to me that Queen Maguncia ought to have fainted, not died; if you're alive, many things can be remedied, and the princess's recklessness wasn't so great that she had to die over it. If the lady had married one of her pages, or another servant in her house, as many others have done, or so I've heard, there would have been no remedy for the damage; but marrying a knight who was so much the gentleman and so clever, like the one who's been described here, really and truly, even though it was foolish, it wasn't as bad as all that, because according to the rules of my master, who is present and will not let me lie, just as they turn lettered men into bishops, they can turn knights, especially if they're errant, into kings and emperors."

"You are correct, Sancho," said Don Quixote, "because a knight errant, if he has even an iota of luck, is very close to being the greatest lord in the world. But let the Dolorous One continue, for it is clear to me that she still has to recount the bitter part of this history, which so far has been sweet."

"Oh yes, the bitterness is still to come!" responded the countess. "And it is so bitter that in comparison bitter cucumbers are sweet and oleander is delectable. The queen, then, being dead and not in a faint, was buried, and as soon as we had covered her with earth and said our final *vale*,[1] then

Quis talia fando temperet a lacrymis?[2]

over the grave of the queen, seated on a wooden horse, there appeared the giant Malambruno, Maguncia's first cousin, who was both cruel and an enchanter, and with his arts, to avenge the death of his cousin and punish the audacity of Don Clavijo and castigate the excesses of Antonomasia, he left them all enchanted there on the grave; she was turned into a bronze monkey and he into a fearsome crocodile of an unknown metal, and between the two of them stands an inscribed pillar, also of metal, and on it are written some letters in the Syrian language, which, having been translated into Candayan, and now into Castilian, read as follows: *These two daring lovers will not recover their original form until the valiant Manchegan comes to do battle with me in single combat; for his great valor alone have the fates reserved this never-before-seen adventure.*

And having done this, he drew from his scabbard an enormous broad scimitar, and seizing me by the hair, he made as if to slash my throat and

1. "Farewell," in Latin.

2. A line from Virgil's *Aeneid* (II, 6 and 8): "Who, hearing this, can hold back his tears?"

cut off my head at the root. I became distraught; my voice caught in my throat; I was utterly dejected; but, even so, I made the greatest effort I could, and in a trembling and doleful voice I told him a number of different things that made him suspend the execution of so harsh a punishment. Finally, he had all the duennas in the palace brought before him, the same duennas here present, and after having exaggerated our faults and censured the character of duennas, their wicked schemes and even worse intrigues, and laying on them all the blame that I alone deserved, he said that he did not want to inflict capital punishment on us but would impose other more protracted penalties that would cause us an ongoing civil death; and at the very moment and instant that he said this, we all felt the pores on our faces opening, and all over our faces it felt as if we were being punctured by needles. We brought our hands to our faces, and found ourselves in the condition you will see now."

And then the Dolorous One and all the other duennas lifted the veils that concealed them and revealed their faces, which were covered by beards, some blond, some black, some white, some variegated, at the sight of which it was evident that the duke and duchess were amazed, Don Quixote and Sancho stupefied, and all those present astonished.

And the Countess Trifaldi continued:

"In this fashion did the evil and ill-intentioned Malambruno punish us, covering the softness and smoothness of our faces with the harshness of these bristles; if only it had been the will of heaven that he cut off our heads with his huge scimitar rather than darken the light of our faces with this fleece that covers us, because if we consider the matter, my lords and ladies (and what I am going to say now I would like to say with my eyes streaming tears, but thoughts of our misfortune, and the oceans of tears that have poured from them so far, have deprived my eyes of their aqueous humor and made them dry as chaff, and so I'll say it without tears), then, I say, where can a bearded duenna go? What father or mother will take pity on her? Who will help her? For even when her skin is smooth and her face martyrized by a thousand different kinds of potions and cosmetics, she can scarcely find anyone to love her, and so what will she do when she reveals a forest on her face? Oh duennas, my companions, we were born at an unlucky time; in an evil hour did our parents engender us!"

And saying this, she showed signs of falling into a swoon.

CHAPTER XL

Regarding matters that concern and pertain to this adventure and this memorable history

Really and truly, all those who enjoy histories like this one ought to show their gratitude to Cide Hamete, its first author, for his care in telling us its smallest details and clearly bringing everything, no matter how trivial, to light. He depicts thoughts, reveals imaginations, responds to tacit questions, clarifies doubts, resolves arguments; in short, he expresses the smallest points that curiosity might ever desire to know. O celebrated author! O fortunate Don Quixote! O famous Dulcinea! O comical Sancho Panza! Together and separately may you live an infinite number of years, bringing pleasure and widespread diversion to the living.

The history, then, says that as soon as Sancho saw the Dolorous One in a faint, he said:

"I swear by my faith as an honest man, and by the lives of all my Panza forebears, that I have never heard or seen, nor has my master ever told me or even thought about, an adventure like this one. May a thousand Satans keep you, because I wouldn't want to curse you for the enchanter and giant that you are, Malambruno; couldn't you find any other punishment for these sinners except bearding them? Wouldn't it have been better, and more to the point, to take away half their noses from the middle on up, even if they talked with a twang, instead of putting beards on them? I'll wager they don't have enough money to pay for somebody to shave them."

"That is true, Señor," responded one of the twelve, "we don't have the money for a trim, and so some of us, as a frugal measure, are using sticky patches and plasters and applying them to our faces, then pulling them off very quickly, leaving us as smooth and sleek as the bottom of a stone mortar, for although there are women in Candaya who go from house to house to remove body hair, and tweeze eyebrows, and prepare lotions and cosmetics for women, we, the duennas of my lady, never wanted to admit them because most of them smell of being go-betweens since they're no longer in their prime;[1] if Don Quixote cannot bring us relief, we'll go to our graves with beards."

"I would pluck mine out," said Don Quixote, "in a Moorish land if I could not relieve you of yours."

At this point, Countess Trifaldi regained consciousness and said:

"The resonance of that promise, O valiant knight, reached my ears in the midst of my swoon and is the reason I have recovered and returned to all my senses, and so once again I implore you, illustrious knight errant and indomitable lord, to convert your gracious promise into action."

"There will be no delay because of me," responded Don Quixote. "Tell me, then, Señora, what it is that I must do, for my spirit is ready to serve you."

"The fact is," responded the Dolorous One, "that from here to the kingdom of Candaya it is five thousand leagues, give or take a few, if one goes by land, but if one goes by air in a straight line, it is three thousand two hundred twenty-seven leagues. You also should know that Malambruno told me that when fate furnished me with a knight to be our liberator, he would send him a mount infinitely better and less perverse than any hired ones, for it is the same wooden horse on which the valiant Pierres carried off and abducted the fair Magalona,[2] and this horse is controlled by a peg on his forehead, which acts as a harness, and he flies through the air so quickly that he seems to be carried by the devils themselves. This horse, according to an ancient tradition, was built by the wise Merlin, who lent him to Pierres, who was his friend, and with him he made great journeys and abducted, as we have said, the fair Magalona, carrying her off through the air as she sat on the horse's

---

1. The phrase in Spanish (. . . *más oliscan a terceras, habiendo dejado de ser primas* . . .) is based on wordplay that contrasts *terceras* ("go-betweens" or "panders") and *primas* (in this case, "principal party to a love affair"). The humor lies in the connection of the former term to "third" and the latter term to "first."

2. Martín de Riquer points out that the *History of the Fair Magalona, Daughter of the King of Naples, and Pierres, Son of the Count of Provence* (Burgos, 1519) a Provençal novel translated and adapted into almost every European language, has no reference to such a horse, though one does appear in other narrations of this type.

hindquarters, and astounding everyone who was watching them from the ground; Merlin would lend him only to those he loved dearly or who paid him well, and from the time of the great Pierres until now, we don't know if anyone else has mounted him. Malumbruno obtained him through his arts, and has him in his power, and uses him on the journeys that he takes from time to time to different parts of the world: today he is here, and tomorrow in France, and the next day in Potosí; and the good thing is that this horse doesn't eat or sleep or need shoes, and he trots through the air without wings, and his gait is so smooth and even that whoever rides him can hold a cup full of water in his hand without spilling a drop, and for this reason the fair Magalona enjoyed riding him so much."

To which Sancho said:

"My gray's the one for a smooth and even gait, though he doesn't go through the air; but on land I'd put him up against all the trotters in the world."

Everyone laughed, and the Dolorous One continued:

"And this horse, if in fact Malambruno wants to end our misfortune, will be in our presence before the night is half an hour old, because he indicated to me that the sign he would give to let me know I had found the knight I was looking for would be to send me the horse, conveniently and speedily, wherever the knight might be."

"And how many can fit on this horse?" asked Sancho.

The Dolorous One responded:

"Two people: one in the saddle and the other on the hindquarters, and for the most part these two people are knight and squire, when there is no abducted maiden."

"I'd like to know, Señora Dolorous," said Sancho, "what the horse's name is."

"His name," responded the Dolorous One, "is not that of Bellerophon's horse, named Pegasus, or that of Alexander the Great, called Bucephalus, or that of the furious Orlando, dubbed Brillador, much less Bayarte, who belonged to Reinaldos de Montalbán, or Frontino, who was Ruggiero's steed, or Bootes or Pirithous, which, they say, were the names of the horses of the Sun, and his name is not Orelia, like the horse on which the unfortunate Rodrigo, last king of the Visigoths, entered the battle in which he lost his life and his kingdom."

"I'll wager," said Sancho, "that since they didn't give him any of those famous names of well-known horses, they didn't give him the name of my master's, Rocinante, which would suit him better than all those others you've mentioned."

"That is true," responded the bearded countess, "but the name he has fits him, because he is called Clavileño the Fleet,[3] a good name for him because it shows that he's made of wood, and has a peg on his forehead, and moves very quickly; and so, as far as his name is concerned, he can certainly compete with the famous Rocinante."

"I don't dislike the name," replied Sancho, "but what kind of halter or bridle do you use to control him?"

"I've already told you," responded Countess Trifaldi, "that it's done with the peg, and by turning it one way or the other, the rider can make him go wherever he wants, either through the air, or else skimming and almost sweeping along the ground, or following the middle course, which is what one hopes for and must have in all well-regulated actions."

"I'd like to see him," responded Sancho, "but thinking that I'll climb up on him, either in the saddle or on his hindquarters, is asking the elm tree for pears. I can barely stay on my donkey, and that's on a packsaddle softer than silk, and now they want me to sit on hindquarters made of wood, without even a pillow or cushion! By God, I don't plan to bruise myself for the sake of removing anybody's beard: let each person find a way to be shaved, for I don't intend to go with my master on such a long journey. Besides, I don't have anything to do with shaving these beards the way I have something to do with disenchanting Señora Dulcinea."

"Yes, you do, my friend," responded Countess Trifaldi, "so much so that without your presence I understand we won't do anything."

"That's not the king's justice!" said Sancho. "What do squires have to do with the adventures of their masters? Don't they get the fame when they're successful while we get all the work? Good God! If the histories only said: 'Such-and-such a knight concluded such-and-such an adventure, but with the help of so-and-so his squire, and without him it would have been impossible. . . .' But all they write is: 'Don Paralipomenón of the Three Stars concluded the adventure of the six monsters,' and they never mention his squire, who was present for everything, just as if he weren't in the world at all! And so, my lords and ladies, I say again that my master can go alone, and good luck to him; I'll stay here, in the company of my lady the duchess, and it might be that when he gets back he'll

3. *Clavileño*, like *Rocinante*, is a composite name, made up of *clavi* from *clavija* ("peg") and *leño* ("wood").

find the cause of Señora Dulcinea much improved, because in my idle and empty moments I plan to give myself a whole series of lashes, and with a good deal of energy."

"Even so, you'll have to accompany him if it's necessary, my good Sancho, because good people have asked you to; the faces of these ladies should not be left so heavily covered simply because of your foolish fear, for that would certainly be a sad affair."

"That's not the king's justice again!" replied Sancho. "If this act of charity was for some shy maidens, or for girls learning their catechism, a man might risk any undertaking, but to suffer this just to take the beards off duennas, not me, not ever! I'd rather see all of them with beards, from the oldest to the youngest, from the most pretentious to the most affected."

"You have bad feelings toward duennas, Sancho my friend," said the duchess, "and you certainly follow the opinion of the Toledan pharmacist. But, by my faith, you are wrong: there are duennas in my own house who could serve as models for all duennas; here is my Doña Rodríguez, who will not allow me to say another thing."

"Say what you wish, Your Excellency," said Doña Rodríguez, "for God knows the truth of everything, and whether or not we duennas are good or bad, bearded or hairless, our mothers bore us just like all other women, and since God put us into the world, He knows the reason, and I rely on His mercy and not on anybody's beard."

"Well now, Señora Rodríguez," said Don Quixote, "and Señora Trifaldi and company, I trust that heaven will look with kindly eyes upon your afflictions; Sancho will do what I tell him to do, whether Clavileño comes or whether I find myself in combat with Malambruno, for I know there is no razor that could shave your graces more easily than my sword could shave Malambruno's head from his shoulders; God endures the wicked, but not forever."

"Oh!" said the Dolorous One. "May all the stars of the celestial regions look with benevolent eyes upon your greatness, O valiant knight, and infuse your spirit with good fortune and courage to be the shield and protection of the abused and despised duennaesque race, hated by pharmacists, slandered by squires, and deceived by pages; too bad for the wretched girl who in the flower of her youth did not choose to be a nun instead of a duenna! How unfortunate we duennas are! Even if we came directly, through the male line, from Hector the Trojan, our mistresses would still address us as inferiors, as if they thought that would make them queens! O giant Malambruno, even though you are an enchanter, you keep your promises! Send us, then, the peerless Clavileño, so that our misfortune may end, for if the hot weather comes and we still have our beards, then alas, how unfortunate for us!"

Countess Trifaldi said this with so much feeling that she brought tears to the eyes of all those present, and even filled Sancho's to the brim, and he determined in his heart to accompany his master to the ends of the earth if that was required to remove the wool from those venerable faces.

CHAPTER XLI

Regarding the arrival of Clavileño, and the conclusion of this lengthy adventure

By now night had arrived, and with it the moment set for the arrival of the famous horse Clavileño, whose tardiness had begun to trouble Don Quixote, for he thought that since Malambruno had delayed in sending him, either he was not the knight for whom the adventure was intended or Malambruno did not dare to meet him in single combat. But here you will see how four savages suddenly entered the garden, all of them dressed in green ivy and carrying on their shoulders a large wooden horse. They placed his feet on the ground, and one of the savages said:

"Let whoever is brave enough climb onto this machine."

"Well," said Sancho, "I won't climb on because I'm not brave enough and I'm not a knight."

And the savage continued, saying:

"And let his squire, if he has one, sit on the hindquarters and trust in the valiant Malambruno, because unless it is by Malambruno's sword, he will not be harmed by any other sword, or by any other kind of wickedness; all they have to do is turn this peg on his neck, and the horse will carry them through the air to the place where Malambruno is waiting for them, but to prevent the great height and loftiness of the flight from causing them vertigo, they must keep their eyes covered until the horse neighs, which will be a sign that their journey has come to an end."

Having said this, and leaving Clavileño, with a gallant air they returned the way they had come. As soon as she saw the horse, the Dolorous One, almost in tears, said to Don Quixote:

"Valiant knight, the promises of Malambruno have come true: the horse is here, our beards are growing, and all of us, with every hair of our beards, implore you to shave and clip us, for all you have to do is climb onto the horse with your squire and give a joyful beginning to your uncommon journey."

"That I shall do, Señora Countess Trifaldi, very willingly and even more joyfully, not troubling to find a cushion or put on spurs in order not to delay, so great is the desire I have to see you, Señora, and all these duennas, smooth-faced and clean."

"That I shall not do," said Sancho, "by no means, not willingly or any other way; and if this shaving can't be done unless I climb onto those hindquarters, then my master can find another squire to accompany him, and these ladies another way to smooth their faces; I'm not a wizard who likes flying through the air. And what will my insulanos say when they find out that their governor goes traveling on the wind? And one other thing: since it's more than three thousand leagues from here to Candaya, if the horse gets tired or the giant gets angry, it'll take us more than half a dozen years to get back, and by then there won't be any ínsulas or ínsulos left in the world that recognize me; and since it's a common saying that danger lies in delay, and when they give you a heifer you'd better hurry over with the rope, may the beards of these ladies forgive me, but St. Peter's fine in Rome; I mean that I'm fine in this house, where I have received so many favors and where I expect a great benefit from its master, which is being a governor."

To which the duke said:

"Sancho my friend, the ínsula I have promised you is neither movable nor transitory: it has roots growing so deep in the depths of the earth that three pulls will not tear it out or move it from where it is now; and you must know that I know that no position of any distinction is won without some sort of bribe, sometimes more, sometimes less, and the one I want for this governorship is for you to go with your master, Don Quixote, and bring this memorable adventure to an end and a conclusion; regardless of whether you return on Clavileño in the brief time his speed promises, or a contrary fortune returns and brings you back on foot, a pilgrim going from hostelry to hostelry and inn to inn, whenever you return you will find your ínsula where you left it, and your insulanos with the same desire they have always had to welcome you as their governor, and my intention will be the same; have no doubt about the truth of this, Señor Sancho, for that would be a clear affront to the desire I have to serve you."

"No more, Señor," said Sancho. "I'm a poor squire and I can't carry the burden of so many courtesies; let my master climb on, and have them cover these eyes of mine, and commend me to God, and tell me if, when we travel through those heights, I'll be able to commend myself to Our Lord or invoke whatever angels favor me."

To which Trifaldi responded:

"Sancho, you certainly can commend yourself to God or anyone you wish, for Malambruno, though an enchanter, is a Christian, and he does his enchantments with a good deal of wisdom and care, and doesn't interfere with anybody."

"Well then," said Sancho, "may God help me, and the Holy Trinity of Gaeta!"[1]

"Not since the memorable adventure of the waterwheels," said Don Quixote, "have I seen Sancho as fearful as he is now, and if I were as superstitious as others, his pusillanimity would cause my courage to weaken somewhat. But come now, Sancho; with the permission of the duke and duchess, I want to say a few words to you alone."

And leading Sancho to some trees in the garden, and grasping both his hands, he said:

"You see now, friend Sancho, the long journey that awaits us; only God knows when we shall return or what facility and opportunity this business will afford us; therefore, I should like you to withdraw now to your room, as if you were going to find something you needed for the journey, and as quickly as you can give yourself a good measure, perhaps even five hundred, of the three thousand and three hundred lashes you are obliged to receive, and once given you will have them, for well begun is half-done."

"My God!" said Sancho. "Your grace must be out of your mind! Like people say: 'You see I'm in a hurry and you demand virginity!' Now that I have to sit on a bare board, your grace wants me to flog my bottom? Really and truly, your grace is wrong. Let's go now and shave those duennas, and when we get back I promise your grace, like the man I am, to fulfill my obligation so fast it will make your grace happy, and that's all I have to say."

"Then with that promise, my good Sancho, I am comforted, and I believe you will keep it, because in fact, although a simpleton, you are a veridical man."

1. Sancho mentions this same Neapolitan monastery during the adventure of the Cave of Montesinos, when he blesses Don Quixote before his descent (chapter XXII).

"Vertical or horizontal," said Sancho, "I'll keep my word."

And having said this, they returned to mount Clavileño, and as he was mounting, Don Quixote said:

"Put on your blindfold, Sancho, and climb up; the person who sends for us from lands so distant will not deceive us, for there would be little glory in deceiving those who trust him, and even if everything turns out contrary to what I imagine, the glory of having undertaken this deed cannot be obscured by any sort of malevolence."

"Let's go, Señor," said Sancho, "for the beards and tears of these ladies have pierced my heart, and nothing I eat will taste good to me until I see them smooth again. Your grace should mount and put on your blindfold first, because if I have to sit on the hindquarters, the first one to mount has to be the man in the saddle."

"That is true," replied Don Quixote.

And taking a handkerchief from his pocket, he asked the Dolorous One to cover his eyes very carefully, and when she had covered them, he uncovered them again and said:

"If I remember correctly, I have read in Virgil about the Palladium of Troy, a wooden horse the Greeks presented to the goddess Pallas, which was pregnant with armed knights who subsequently caused the total ruin of Troy; and so it would be worthwhile first to see what Clavileño is carrying in his stomach."

"There's no reason to," said the Dolorous One, "for I trust him and know that Malambruno is neither wicked nor a traitor; Señor Don Quixote, your grace can mount without fear, and if anything does happen to you, the fault will be mine."

It seemed to Don Quixote that any reply he might give with regard to his safety would be to the detriment of his valor, and so with no further argument he mounted Clavileño and touched the peg, which turned easily; since he had no stirrups, and his legs hung straight down, he looked exactly like a painted or woven figure in a Flemish tapestry of a Roman triumph. Unwillingly, and very slowly, Sancho finally mounted, and settling himself the best he could on the hindquarters, he found them rather hard and not at all soft, and he asked the duke if it was possible to give him a pillow or cushion, whether from the drawing room couch of his lady the duchess or from the bed of some page, because the hindquarters of that horse seemed more like marble than wood.

To this the Countess Trifaldi said that Clavileño would not tolerate any manner or kind of embellishment on his back, but what Sancho could do was sit sidesaddle, and then he would not feel the hardness quite as much. Sancho did so, and saying, "God help me," he allowed his eyes to be covered, and after they had been covered he uncovered them again, and looking at everyone in the garden tenderly, and with tears in his eyes, he said that they should each help him in his hour of need with some Our Fathers and Hail Marys so that God would provide someone to say them on their behalf when they found themselves in similar danger. To which Don Quixote said:

"You thief, are you by any chance on the gallows, or in the final moments of your life, to plead in that fashion? Are you not, you craven and cowardly creature, in the same spot that was occupied by the fair Magalona, and from which she descended, not into the grave but to be the queen of France, if the histories do not lie? And I, who am at your side, shall I not compare myself to the valiant Pierres, who sat in the same place where I now sit? Cover your eyes, cover your eyes, you frightened animal, and do not allow your fear to escape your lips again, at least not in my presence."

"Blindfold me," responded Sancho, "and since you don't want me to commend myself to God or be commended to Him, is it any wonder I'm afraid that there must be some legion of devils around here who'll carry us off to Peralvillo?"[2]

Both were blindfolded, and Don Quixote, sensing that everything was as it should be, touched the peg, and as soon as he had placed his fingers on it, all the duennas and everyone else present raised their voices, saying:

"May God be your guide, valiant knight!"

"God go with you, intrepid squire!"

"Now, now you are in the air, moving through it faster than an arrow!"

"Now you are beginning to amaze and astonish everyone looking at you from the ground."

"Hold on, valiant Sancho, you're slipping! Be careful you don't fall, because your fall will be worse than that of the daring boy who wanted to drive the chariot of his father, the Sun!"[3]

Sancho heard the voices, and pressing close to his master and putting his arms around him, he said:

"Señor, how can they say we're going so high if we can hear their voices and they seem to be talking right here beside us?"

"Pay no attention to that, Sancho, for since these things and these flights are outside the ordinary course of events, at a distance of a thou-

2. A place where the Holy Brotherhood executed criminals.
3. The reference is to the myth of Phaëthon.

sand leagues you will see and hear whatever you wish. And do not hold me so tightly, for you will throw me off; the truth is I do not know why you are perturbed or frightened; I would dare to avow that in all the days of my life I have never ridden a mount with a smoother gait: it almost seems as if we were not moving at all. Friend, banish your fear, for in fact the matter is proceeding as it should, and we have the wind at our backs."

"That is true," responded Sancho. "On this side the wind's so strong it feels like a thousand bellows blowing on me."

And there were large bellows blowing the air around him, for this adventure had been so well planned by the duke and the duchess and their steward that no element was lacking to make it perfect.

Don Quixote also felt the air blowing, and he said:

"There can be no doubt, Sancho, that we are approaching the second region of air where hail and snow are born; thunder, lightning, and thunderbolts are born in the third region; and if we continue to rise in this fashion, we shall soon come to the region of fire, and I do not know how to adjust the peg to keep us from going so high that we are burned."

Then, with some tow-cloth on a reed that was easy to light and extinguish, their faces were warmed from a distance. Sancho, who felt the heat, said:

"By my soul, we must be in that place of fire already, or very close to it, because a good part of my beard has been singed, and I'm ready, Señor, to take off the blindfold and see where we are."

"Do not," responded Don Quixote. "Remember the true story of Licentiate Torralba,[4] whom the devils carried through the air mounted on a reed, with his eyes closed, and in twelve hours he arrived in Rome and dismounted on the Torre di Nona,[5] which is a street in the city, and saw all the tumult, and the assault and the death of Bourbon,[6] and in the morning he was back in Madrid, where he gave an account of all that he had seen; he himself said that while he was flying through the air, the devil told him to open his eyes, and he opened them, and he saw himself so close, or so it seemed, to the body of the moon that he could have grasped it with his hand, and he did not dare look down at the earth lest he faint. Therefore, Sancho, there is no reason for us to uncover our eyes; the one who is responsible for us will take care of us, and perhaps

4. A reference to an actual person, Dr. Eugenio Torralba, tried by the Inquisition of Cuenca in 1531, about whom it was said that he flew through the air on a reed.

5. The name of a Roman prison.

6. Charles, duke of Bourbon (1490–1527), fighting in the armies of Charles V of Spain, was killed during the sack of Rome.

we are circling and going higher so that we can suddenly swoop down on the kingdom of Candaya, the way a falcon or a hawk, no matter how high it soars, falls on a crane and captures it; and although it seems to us as if we left the garden less than half an hour ago, believe me when I say that we must have gone a great distance."

"I don't know about that," responded Sancho Panza. "All I can say is that if Señora Magallanes[7] or Magalona was happy with these hindquarters, she couldn't have had very tender flesh."

All these exchanges between the two valiant men were heard by the duke and the duchess and those in the garden and gave them extraordinary pleasure; and desiring to conclude the strange and carefully made adventure, they set fire to Clavileño's tail with some tow-cloths, and since the horse was full of fireworks, it suddenly flew into the air with a fearsome noise and threw Don Quixote and Sancho Panza to the ground, half-scorched.

In the meantime, the entire bearded squadron of duennas had disappeared from the garden, including the Countess Trifaldi, and those who were left in the garden lay on the ground as if in a faint. Don Quixote and Sancho, badly bruised, rose to their feet, and looking all around them, they were astonished to find themselves in the same garden from which they had departed and to see such a large number of people lying on the ground; and their stupefaction was even greater when, on one side of the garden, they saw a huge lance driven into the ground and hanging from it by two cords of green silk a smooth white parchment, on which, in large gold letters, the following was written:

The illustrious knight Don Quixote of La Mancha has finished and concluded the adventure of the Countess Trifaldi, also called the Dolorous Duenna, and company, by simply attempting it.

Malambruno considers himself completely satisfied and entirely content; the chins of the duennas are now smooth and clean, and the sovereigns Don Clavijo and Antonomasia are in their pristine state. And when the squirely flogging is completed, the white dove will be free of the foul goshawks that pursue her and in the arms of her beloved suitor;[8] so it has been ordained by the wise Merlin, protoenchanter of all enchanters.

7. *Magallanes*, the Spanish for Magellan, the Portuguese navigator, is used for comic effect to indicate Sancho's ignorance of courtly tales and the names of their protagonists.

8. In this phrase Cervantes takes advantage of two meanings of *arrullador*: "cooing" and "wooing." I have translated it as "suitor," hoping that the idea of billing and cooing is implicit in the word.

When Don Quixote had read the letters on the parchment, he clearly understood that they spoke of the disenchantment of Dulcinea, and giving many thanks to heaven for his having concluded so great an exploit with so little danger, and for returning to their earlier state the faces of the venerable duennas, who were no longer present, he went to where the duke and duchess still lay in a swoon, and grasping the hand of the duke, he said:

"Ah, my good lord, take heart, take heart, for it is all nothing! The adventure is concluded, with no harm to anyone, as the writing on that document clearly demonstrates."

The duke, very slowly, as if waking from a deep sleep, regained consciousness, and in the same fashion so did the duchess and all those who had fallen in the garden, showing signs of so much wonder and astonishment, one could almost believe that what they knew so well how to feign as a joke had really happened. The duke read the statement with half-closed eyes, and then, his arms opened wide, he went to embrace Don Quixote, saying he was the best knight that any age had ever seen.

Sancho kept looking for the Dolorous One to see what kind of face she had without a beard, and if she was as beautiful without one as her gallant disposition promised, but they told him that as soon as Clavileño descended in flames through the air and landed on the ground, the entire squadron of duennas, including Countess Trifaldi, had disappeared, by which time they were already hairless and free of stubble. The duchess asked Sancho how things had gone for him on his long journey, to which Sancho responded:

"Señora, I felt that we were flying, like my master said, through the region of fire, and I wanted to uncover my eyes a little, but my master, who I asked for permission to uncover my eyes, did not agree; but since I have some dab of curiosity in me and want to know what people try to stop me and keep me from knowing, very carefully, without anybody seeing me, right at my nose, I pushed aside just a little bit of the handkerchief that was covering my eyes, and I looked down at the earth, and it seemed to me that it was no larger than a mustard seed, and the men walking on it not much bigger than hazel nuts, so you can see how high we must have been flying then."

To this the duchess said:

"Sancho my friend, think about what you are saying; it seems you did not see the earth but only the men walking on it, for it is clear that if the earth looked to you like a mustard seed and each man like a hazel nut, only one man would have covered the entire earth."

"That's true," responded Sancho, "but even so, I lifted up the blind-fold just a little on one side, and I saw all of it."

"Look, Sancho," said the duchess, "from just one side you can't see all of whatever you may be looking at."

"I don't know about those lookings," replied Sancho. "All I know is that it would be nice if your ladyship would understand that since we were flying by enchantment, by enchantment I could see all the earth and all the men no matter how I looked at them; and if you don't believe me, your grace also won't believe me when I say that moving the blind-fold near my eyebrows, I saw myself so close to the sky that there was less than a span and a half between it and me, and I can swear, Señora, that it's also very big. And as it happened, we were passing by the seven nanny goats,[9] and by God and my immortal soul, since I was a goatherd when I was a boy at home, as soon as I saw them I wanted to spend a lit-tle time with them . . . ! And if I couldn't, I thought I would die. So, quick as you please, what do I do? Without saying anything to anybody, not even my master, very quietly and gently I got down from Clavileño, and I played with the nanny goats, and they're as sweet as gilly flowers, for almost three-quarters of an hour, and Clavileño didn't move from the spot or move forward."

"And while our good Sancho was amusing himself with the goats," asked the duke, "what was Señor Don Quixote doing?"

To which Don Quixote responded:

"Since all these things and all these occurrences lie outside the natu-ral order, it is no surprise that Sancho says what he says. As for myself, I can say that I did not lift the blindfold at the top or the bottom, nor did I see the sky, the earth, the sea, or the sands. It is certainly true that I felt as if I had passed through the region of air, and even touched the region of fire, but I cannot believe we passed beyond that, for since the region of fire lies between the sphere of the moon and the final region of air, we could not reach the sphere of the seven nanny goats that Sancho has mentioned without being burned; and since we are not burned, either Sancho is lying, or Sancho is dreaming."

"I'm not lying and I'm not dreaming," responded Sancho. "And if you don't believe me, just ask me about what those goats look like, and then you'll see if I'm telling the truth or not."

"Tell us, Sancho," said the duchess.

9. The constellation of the Pleiades.

"Two of them," responded Sancho, "are green, two are red, two are blue, and one is a mix."

"That's a new kind of nanny goat," said the duke, "and in our region of the ground they don't have those colors, I mean, goats that are those colors."

"That's very clear," said Sancho. "Yes, that must be the difference between goats in the sky and those on the ground."

"Tell me, Sancho," asked the duke. "Up there with all those nanny goats, did you see any males?"[10]

"No, Señor," responded Sancho, "but I heard that not one of them has passed beyond the horns of the moon."

They did not wish to ask him anything else about his journey, because it seemed to them that Sancho was prepared to wander through all the spheres and give an accounting of everything he had seen there without having moved from the garden.

In short, this was the end of the adventure of the Dolorous Duenna, which gave the duke and duchess reason to laugh, not only then but for the rest of their lives, and Sancho something to talk about for centuries, if he were to live that long; and Don Quixote went up to Sancho, and in his ear he whispered:

"Sancho, just as you want people to believe what you have seen in the sky, I want you to believe what I saw in the Cave of Montesinos. And that is all I have to say."

CHAPTER XLII

Regarding the advice Don Quixote gave to Sancho Panza before he went to govern the ínsula, along with other matters of consequence

The successful and amusing conclusion of the adventure of the Dolorous One so pleased the duke and duchess that they decided to move forward with their deceptions, seeing that they had a very accommodating individual who would accept them as true; and so, having devised their

---

10. The wordplay here does not translate into English. *Cabrón* is both "male goat" and "cuckold"; the sign of the cuckold is horns, as in "the horns of the moon" in the next sentence.

scheme and instructed their servants and vassals as to how they ought to behave toward Sancho in his governorship of the promised ínsula, the next day, which was the one following the flight of Clavileño, the duke told Sancho to prepare and ready himself to leave and be a governor, since his insulanos were waiting for him as if for the showers of May. Sancho kneeled before him and said:

"After I came down from the sky, and after I looked at the earth from that great height and saw how small it was, the burning desire I had to be a governor cooled a little; where's the greatness in ruling a mustard seed, or the dignity or pride in governing half a dozen men the size of hazel nuts? It seemed to me that this was all there was on the whole earth. If your lordship would be kind enough to give me just a tiny part of the sky, something no bigger than half a league, I'd be happier to take that than the best ínsula in the world."

"Look, Sancho my friend," responded the duke, "I can't give anybody a part of the sky, even one no bigger than my nail; those favors and dispensations are reserved for God alone. What I can give I give to you, which is an ínsula, right and true, round and well-proportioned, and exceedingly fertile and bountiful, where, if you know how to manage things, with the riches of the earth you can approach the riches of the sky."

"Well then," responded Sancho, "let's have the ínsula, and I'll do my best to be so good a governor that in spite of rogues and rascals I'll go to heaven; it isn't greed that makes me want to leave my hut or rise to better things, but a desire I have to try it and see what it tastes like to be a governor."

"If you try it once, Sancho," said the duke, "you'll long to eat it again, because it is a very sweet thing to give orders and be obeyed. I'm certain that when your master becomes an emperor, as he undoubtedly will, considering how things are going for him, nobody will be able to tear that away from him, and the time he spent not being one will grieve and sadden him in the very center of his soul."

"Señor," replied Sancho, "I imagine that it's good to command, even if it's only a herd of cattle."

"Let them bury me with you,[1] Sancho, for you know everything," responded the duke, "and I expect you to be the kind of governor your good judgment promises, and let's say no more about it, and be advised

---

1. A formula indicating complete agreement with another person's opinions.

that tomorrow morning you will leave to be governor of the ínsula, and this afternoon you will be outfitted with the proper clothing and all the things necessary for your departure."

"They can dress me," said Sancho, "however they want; no matter what clothes I wear I'll still be Sancho Panza."

"That is true," said the duke, "but clothes must suit the position or profession that one follows, for it would not be correct for a jurist to dress like a soldier, or a soldier like a priest. You, Sancho, will be dressed partly as a lettered man and partly as a captain, because on the ínsula I'm giving you, arms are as necessary as letters and letters as necessary as arms."

"I don't have many letters," responded Sancho, "because I still don't know the ABCs, but it's enough for me to have the *Cristus*[2] in my memory to be a good governor. As for arms, I'll handle the ones I'm given, with God to lead me."

"With so good a memory," said the duke, "Sancho cannot err in any way."

Just then Don Quixote came in, and learning what had happened and how quickly Sancho was to leave for his governorship, with the permission of the duke he took Sancho by the hand and went with him to his room, intending to advise him on how he was to behave as governor.

When they had entered his bedchamber, Don Quixote closed the door behind him and almost forced Sancho to sit down beside him, and in a tranquil voice he said:

"I give infinite thanks to heaven, Sancho my friend, that before and prior to my having found good luck, Fortune has come out to welcome and receive you. I, who had set aside a portion of my success as payment for your services, find myself at the very beginning of my advancement, and you, before it is time and contrary to the law of reasonable discourse, find yourself rewarded with all your desires. Others bribe, importune, solicit, are early risers, plead, persist, and do not achieve what they long for, and another comes along and without knowing how or why finds himself with the office and position that many others strove for; and here the saying certainly applies and is appropriate: aspirations are ruled by good and bad fortune. You, who in my opinion are undoubtedly a dolt, and who, without rising early or staying up late or making any effort whatsoever, with nothing more than the breath of knight errantry that has touched you, without further ado find yourself governor of an ínsula

---

2. The cross that is placed at the beginning of the alphabet in a child's primer.

as if it were of no consequence. I say all this, O Sancho, so that you do not attribute the kindness you have received to your own merits, but give thanks first to heaven for disposing matters so sweetly, and then to the greatness that lies in the profession of knight errantry. Now, with your heart disposed to believe what I have told you, pay heed, my son, to your Cato,[3] who wishes to advise you and be a polestar and guide that sets your course and leads you to a safe port on the tempestuous sea where you are about to set sail, for offices and great responsibilities are nothing more than a deep gulf of confusions.[4] First, my son, you must fear God, because in fearing Him lies wisdom, and if you are wise, you cannot err in anything. Second, you must look at who you are and make an effort to know yourself, which is the most difficult knowledge one can imagine. When you know yourself, you will not puff yourself up like the frog who wanted to be the equal of the ox,[5] and if you can do this, the fact that you kept pigs at home will be like the ugly feet beneath the peacock's tail of your foolishness."

"It's true," responded Sancho, "but that's when I was a boy; later, when I was a little older, it was geese that I kept, not pigs. But this seems beside the point; not everybody who governs comes from the lineage of kings."

"That is true," replied Don Quixote, "and for that reason those who are not of noble origin should bring to the gravity of the position they hold a gentle mildness which, guided by prudence, may save them from the malicious gossip that no station in life can escape. Take pride in the humbleness of your lineage, and do not disdain to say that you come from peasants, for seeing that you are not ashamed of it, no one will attempt to shame you; take more pride in being a humble virtuous man than in being a noble sinner. Innumerable men born of low family have risen to the highest pontifical and imperial dignity, and I could cite so many examples of this truth to you that you would grow weary.

Consider, Sancho: if you take virtue as your means, and pride in per-

---

3. The author of a book of aphorisms, *Disticha Catonis*, which was so popular a text in schools that primers were called "Catos."

4. Don Quixote's advice to Sancho is one of the most famous passages in the novel. Martín de Riquer notes the difficulty of determining Cervantes's exact sources, although he states that the general influence of Erasmus is evident, and he also cites a handful of books on good government, both classical and Renaissance, available in Spanish at the time. Whatever the sources, Don Quixote's remarks to the future governor are clearly the polar opposite of Machiavelli's counsel to the prince.

5. An allusion to a fable by Phaedrus, a Latin fabulist of the first century who wrote in the style of Aesop.

forming virtuous deeds, there is no reason to envy the means of princes and lords, because blood is inherited, and virtue is acquired, and virtue in and of itself has a value that blood does not. This being so, as it is, if one of your relatives comes to see you while you are on your ínsula, do not scorn or insult him; on the contrary, you should welcome, receive, and entertain him; in this way you will satisfy heaven, which does not wish anyone to scorn what it has created, and you will respond as you should to a well-ordered nature. If you bring your wife with you (because it is not a good idea for those who attend to governing for a long time to be without their own spouses), teach her, instruct her, and smooth away her natural roughness, because everything a wise governor acquires can be lost and wasted by a crude and foolish wife. If by chance you are widowed, which is something that can happen, and with your position you wish a better wife, do not take one to serve as your lure and fishing rod, and the hood for your *I don't want it*;[6] because it is true when I tell you that for everything received by the judge's wife her husband will be accountable at the universal reckoning, when he will pay four times over in death for the ledger entries he ignored in life.

Never be guided by arbitrariness in law, which tends to have a good deal of influence on ignorant men who take pride in being clever. Let the tears of the poor find in you more compassion, but not more justice, than the briefs of the wealthy. Try to discover the truth in all the promises and gifts of the rich man, as well as in the poor man's sobs and entreaties. When there can and should be a place for impartiality, do not bring the entire rigor of the law to bear on the offender, for the reputation of the harsh judge is not better than that of the compassionate one. If you happen to bend the staff of justice, let it be with the weight not of a gift, but of mercy. If you judge the case of one of your enemies, put your injury out of your mind and turn your thoughts to the truth of the question. Do not be blinded by your own passion in another's trial, for most of the time the mistakes you make cannot be remedied, and if they can, it will be to the detriment of your good name and even your fortune. If a beautiful woman comes to you to plead for justice, turn your eyes from her tears and your ears from her sobs, and consider without haste the substance of what she is asking if you do not want your reason to be drowned in her weeping and your goodness in her sighs. If you must punish a man with deeds, do not abuse him with words, for the pain of punishment is

6. This is based on a proverb: "I don't want it, I don't want it, just toss it into my hood."

enough for the unfortunate man without the addition of malicious speech. Consider the culprit who falls under your jurisdiction as a fallen man subject to the conditions of our depraved nature, and to the extent that you can, without doing injury to the opposing party, show him compassion and clemency, because although all the attributes of God are equal, in our view mercy is more brilliant and splendid than justice.

If you follow these precepts and rules, Sancho, your days will be long, your fame eternal, your rewards overflowing, your joy indescribable; you will marry your children as you wish, they and your grandchildren will have titles, you will live in peace and harmony with all people, and in the final moments of your life, in a gentle and ripe old age, the moment of your death will come and the tender, delicate hands of your great-great-grandchildren will close your eyes. What I have said to you so far are the teachings that will adorn your soul; now listen to the ones that will serve to adorn your body."

CHAPTER XLIII

Regarding the second set of precepts that Don Quixote gave to Sancho Panza

Who could have heard this past speech of Don Quixote and not taken him for a very wise and well-intentioned person? But, as has been said so often in the course of this great history, he spoke nonsense only with regard to chivalry, and in other conversations he demonstrated a clear and confident understanding, so that his actions constantly belied his judgment, and his judgment belied his actions; but in this matter of the additional advice he gave to Sancho, he showed that he possessed great cleverness and revealed to a very high degree both his intelligence and his madness.

Sancho listened to him very attentively and attempted to commit his advice to memory, like a man who intended to follow it and use it to bring the gestation of his governorship to a successful delivery. And so Don Quixote continued, and he said:

"With regard to how you should govern your person and house, Sancho, the first thing I recommend is that you keep clean, and that you trim your nails and not allow them to grow, as some men do whose ignorance has led them to believe that long nails beautify their hands, as if those superfluous growths that they refuse to cut were nails, when they are actually the claws of a lizard-eating kestrel: a filthy and extraordinary abuse. Do not go around, Sancho, unbelted and negligent; slovenly clothing is an indication of a listless spirit, unless slovenliness and negligence are actually a sign of shrewdness, as was judged to be the case with Julius Caesar. Determine with intelligence the worth of your position, and if it allows you to give your servants livery, let it be modest and useful rather than showy and splendid, and divide it between your servants and the poor: I mean that if you are going to dress six pages, dress three of them and three poor men, and in this way you will have pages both in heaven and on the ground; this unusual manner of giving livery cannot be understood by the vainglorious. Do not eat garlic or onions lest their smell reveal your peasant origins. Walk slowly; speak calmly, but not in a way that makes it seem you are listening to yourself, for all affectation is wrong. Eat sparingly at midday and even less for supper, for the health of the entire body is forged in the workshop of the stomach. Be temperate in your drinking, remembering that too much wine cannot keep either a secret or a promise. Be careful, Sancho, not to chew with your mouth full or to eructate in front of anyone."

"I don't understand *eructate*," said Sancho.

And Don Quixote said:

"*Eructate*, Sancho, means *to belch*, which is one of the crudest words in the Castilian language, although it is very expressive, and so educated people have had recourse to Latin, and instead of *belch* they say *eructate*, and instead of *belches, eructations*; and if some do not understand these terms, it matters very little, for in time their use will be introduced into the language and they will easily be understood; this enriches the language, over which the common people and usage have control."

"Truly, Señor," said Sancho, "one of the pieces of advice and counsel that I plan to carry in my memory will be not to belch, because I tend to do that very often."

"*Eructate*, Sancho, not *belch*," said Don Quixote.

"I'll say *eructate* from now on," responded Sancho, "and by my faith, I won't forget."

"Sancho, you also should not mix into your speech the host of proverbs that you customarily use, for although proverbs are short maxims, the ones you bring in are often so far-fetched that they seem more like nonsense than like maxims."

"God can remedy that," responded Sancho, "because I know more proverbs than a book, and so many of them come into my mouth at one time when I talk that they fight with one another to get out, but my tongue tosses out the first ones it finds, even if they're not to the point. But I'll be careful from now on to say the ones that suit the gravity of my position, because in a well-stocked house, supper is soon cooked; and if you cut the cards, you don't deal; and the man who sounds the alarm is safe; and for giving and keeping, you need some sense."

"Go on, Sancho!" said Don Quixote. "Force the proverbs in, string them together one after another on a thread! No one will stop you! My mother punishes me and I deceive her! I tell you to avoid proverbs, and in an instant you have come out with a litany of them that have as much to do with what we are discussing as the hills of Úbeda. Look, Sancho, I am not saying that an appropriate proverb is wrong, but loading and stringing together proverbs any which way makes your conversation lifeless and lowborn.

When you mount a horse, do not lean your body back over the hind bow of the saddle, or hold your legs stiff and sticking out at an angle from the belly of the horse, or ride so carelessly that it looks as if you were riding your donkey, for riding a horse makes gentlemen of some men and stable boys of others. Be moderate in your sleeping, for the man who does not get up with the sun does not possess the day; and remember, Sancho, that diligence is the mother of good fortune, and sloth, her opposite, never reached the conclusion demanded by good intentions. This final piece of advice that I wish to give you now, although it may not serve for the adornment of the body, I want you to remember very well, for I believe it will be no less useful to you than those I have given you so far, and it is that you should never become involved in arguing about lineages, at least, in comparing one to the other, because of necessity, when they are compared, one has to be better, and you will be despised by the one you place lower, and not rewarded in any way by the one you deem higher. Your dress should be full-length breeches, a long doublet, and a slightly longer cape; absolutely no pantaloons, for they do not become gentlemen or governors. For now, this is what has occurred to me to tell you; time will pass, and my precepts will be appropriate to the occasion, if you are careful to inform me about the circumstances in which you find yourself."

"Señor," responded Sancho, "I see very well that everything your grace has told me is good, holy, and beneficial, but what good will the precepts do if I don't remember a single one? It's true that what you said about not letting my nails grow and getting married again won't slip my mind if I can help it, but those other useless and complicated and troublesome things I don't remember, and I won't remember them any more than I do yesterday's clouds, and so you'll have to write them down for me, and though I don't know how to read or write, I'll give them to my confessor so that he can slip them in and remind me of them whenever it's necessary."

"O, sinner that I am!" responded Don Quixote. "How bad it seems in governors not to be able to read or write! Because you must know, Sancho, that a man not knowing how to read, or being left-handed, means one of two things: either he was the child of parents who were too poor and lowborn, or he was so mischievous and badly behaved himself that he could not absorb good habits or good instruction. This is a great fault in you, and I would like you at least to learn to sign your name."

"I know how to sign my name very well," responded Sancho, "because when I was steward of a brotherhood in my village, I learned to make some letters like the marks on bundles, and they told me that they said my name; better yet, I'll pretend that my right hand has been hurt, and I'll have somebody else sign for me; there's a remedy for everything except death, and since I'll be in charge of everything, I can do whatever I want; then, too, when your father's the magistrate. . . .[1] And being a governor, which is more than being a magistrate, just let them come and they'll see what happens! No, let them make fun of me and speak ill of me: they'll come for wool and go home shorn; and when God loves you, your house knows it; and the rich man's folly passes for good judgment in the world; and since that's what I'll be, being a governor and a very generous one, which is what I plan to be, nobody will notice any faults in me. No, just be like honey and the flies will go after you; you're only worth as much as you have, my grandmother used to say; and you won't get revenge on a well-established man."

"O, may you be accursed, Sancho!" said Don Quixote at this point. "May sixty thousand devils take you and your proverbs! For the past hour you have been stringing them together and with each one giving me a cruel taste of torment. I assure you that one day these proverbs will lead you to the gallows; because of them your vassals will take the governorship away from you, or rise up against you. Tell me, where do you find them, you ignorant man, and how do you apply them, you fool, when to

1. This is the first half of a proverb: "When your father's the magistrate, you're safe when you go to trial."

say only one that is really applicable, I have to perspire and labor like a ditchdigger?"

"By God, my lord and master," replied Sancho, "your grace complains about very small things. Why the devil does it trouble you when I make use of my fortune, when I have no other, and no other wealth except proverbs and more proverbs? And right now four have come to mind that are a perfect fit, like pears in a wicker basket, but I won't say them, because golden silence is what they call Sancho."

"That Sancho is not you," said Don Quixote, "because not only are you not golden silence, you are foolish speech and stubborn persistence, but even so I should like to know which four proverbs came to mind just now that were so to the point, because I have been searching my mind, and I have a good one, and I cannot think of a single proverb."

"Which ones could be better," said Sancho, "than 'Never put your thumbs between two wisdom teeth' and 'There's no answer to get out of my house and what do you want with my wife' and 'Whether the pitcher hits the stone or the stone hits the pitcher, it's bad luck for the pitcher'? They're all just fine. Because nobody should take on his governor or the person in authority because he'll come out of it hurt, like the man who puts his finger between two wisdom teeth, and if they're not wisdom teeth but just plain molars, it doesn't matter; and there's no reply to what the governor says, like the 'Leave my house and what do you want with my wife.' As for the stone and the pitcher, even a blind man can see that. So whoever sees the mote in somebody else's eye has to see the beam in his own, so that nobody can say about him: 'The dead woman was frightened by the one with her throat cut.' And your grace knows very well that the fool knows more in his own house than the wise man does in somebody else's."

"That is not so, Sancho," responded Don Quixote, "for the fool knows nothing whether in his own house or in another's, because on a foundation of foolishness no reasonable building can be erected. Enough of this now, Sancho, for if you govern badly, the fault will be yours and mine the shame; but it consoles me that I did what I had to do and advised you with all the truth and wisdom of which I am capable: now I am relieved of my obligation and my promise. May God guide you, Sancho, and govern you in your governorship, and free me of the misgivings I still have that you will turn the entire ínsula upside down, something I could avoid by revealing to the duke who you are, and telling him that this plump little body of yours is nothing but a sack filled with proverbs and guile."

"Señor," replied Sancho, "if your grace believes I'm not worthy of this governorship, I'll let it go right now, for I care more for a sliver of nail from my soul than I do for my whole body, and just plain Sancho will get by on bread and onions as well as the governor does on partridges and capons; besides, everyone's equal when they sleep, the great and the small, the poor and the rich; and if your grace thinks about it, you'll see that it was you alone who gave me the idea of governing, because I don't know any more about the governorships of ínsulas than a vulture; if you think the devil will carry me off because I'm a governor, I'd rather go to heaven as Sancho than to hell as a governor."

"By God, Sancho," said Don Quixote, "simply because of the last words that you have said I judge you worthy of being the governor of a thousand ínsulas: you have a good nature, and without that no learning is worthwhile; commend yourself to God and try not to wander from your first purpose; I mean that you should always have the firm and steady intention of doing the right thing in everything that happens to you, because heaven always favors virtuous desires. And now let us go to dinner, for I believe the duke and duchess are waiting for us."

CHAPTER XLIV

How Sancho Panza was taken to his governorship, and the strange adventure that befell Don Quixote in the castle

They say that in the actual original of this history, one reads that when Cide Hamete came to write this chapter, his interpreter did not translate what he had written, which was a kind of complaint that the Moor had concerning himself for becoming involved in a history as dry and limited as this one, for it seemed to him he always had to talk of Don Quixote and Sancho, not daring to wander into other digressions and episodes that were more serious and more entertaining; and he said that to have his mind, his hand, and his pen always fixed on writing about a single subject and speaking through the mouths of so few persons was an insupportable hardship whose outcome did not redound to the benefit of the author; in order to circumvent this difficulty, in the first part he had used the device of some novels, such as *The Man Who Was Recklessly*

Curious and *The Captive Captain*, which are, in a sense, separate from the history, although the other matters recounted there are events that occurred to Don Quixote himself, which he could not fail to write down. He also thought, as he says, that many readers, carried away by the attention demanded by the deeds of Don Quixote, would pay none at all to the novels, and pass them over entirely or read them with haste or with annoyance, not realizing the elegance and invention they contain, which would be readily apparent if they came to light on their own, not depending on the madness of Don Quixote or the foolishness of Sancho. And so in this second part he did not wish to introduce any novels, whether detached or attached, but only some episodes born of the very events offered by truth, and even these in a very limited way and using only the words needed to recount them; and so, contained and enclosed within the narrow confines of the narration even though he possesses the ability, competence, and understanding to deal with the entire universe, he asks that his work not be scorned but praised, not for what he has written but for what he has omitted from his writing.

And then the history goes on to say that when Don Quixote had finished dinner on the day he gave advice to Sancho, he also wrote down the precepts so that Sancho could find someone to read them to him, but as soon as Don Quixote gave them to his squire they came and fell into the hands of the duke, who communicated them to the duchess, and the two of them were astonished once more at the madness and intelligence of Don Quixote; and so, going forward with their deceptions, that afternoon they sent Sancho with a large retinue to the village that for him would be an ínsula.

It so happened that the man in charge was one of the duke's stewards, who was very intelligent and very humorous—for there can be no humor where there is no intelligence—and had played the part of Countess Trifaldi with the wit that has already been described; this, and the instructions he had received from the duke and duchess regarding how he was to behave with Sancho, meant that he achieved his purposes wonderfully well. I say, then, that as soon as Sancho saw the steward, he imagined that his face was the same as Countess Trifaldi's, and turning to his master, he said:

"Señor, either the devil will carry me away from where I stand, suddenly and without warning, or your grace has to confess that the face of the duke's steward, here present, is the same as the Dolorous One's."

Don Quixote looked carefully at the steward, and when he had looked, he said to Sancho:

"There is no reason for the devil to carry you off, Sancho, either suddenly or without warning, for I do not know what you mean; the face of the Dolorous One may be that of the steward, but that does not mean the steward is the Dolorous One; if he were, it would imply a very serious contradiction, and this is not the time to make such inquiries, for that would lead us into intricate labyrinths. Believe me, my friend, it is necessary to pray to Our Lord very sincerely to save both of us from evil wizards and wicked enchanters."

"It isn't a joke, Señor," replied Sancho, "because I heard him talking earlier, and it seemed as if the voice of Countess Trifaldi were sounding in my ears. All right: I'll be quiet, but I'll stay on the alert from now on to see if I can find anything else that will prove or disprove what I suspect."

"That is what you must do, Sancho," said Don Quixote, "and keep me informed regarding everything you discover in this matter, and everything that happens to you in your governorship."

At last, accompanied by a good number of people, Sancho set out, dressed in the style of a lettered man, and over that wearing a very wide coat of tawny camel's hair and a cap of the same material, and riding a mule with short stirrups; behind him, by order of the duke, came the gray with new donkey's trappings and a halter made of silk. From time to time Sancho turned his head to look at his jackass, in whose company he felt so content that he would not have traded places with the emperor of Germany.

When he took his leave of the duke and duchess, he kissed their hands and received the blessing of his master, who gave it to him in tears, and which Sancho received with sobs.

Kind reader, let the good Sancho go in peace and good fortune, and expect two bushels of laughter when you learn how he behaved in office, and in the meantime wait and find out what happened to his master that night; and if you do not laugh at this, at least you will spread your lips wide in a monkey grin, because those things that befall Don Quixote have to be celebrated either with astonishment or with laughter.

It is recounted that as soon as Sancho left, Don Quixote felt lonely for him, and if it had been possible for him to revoke the squire's mandate and take the governorship away from him, his master would have done so. The duchess perceived his melancholy and asked him why he was sad, for if it was because of Sancho's absence, there were squires, duennas, and maidens in her house who would serve him to his complete satisfaction.

"It is true, Señora," responded Don Quixote, "that I feel the absence of Sancho, but this is not the principal reason that makes me seem sad; of the many offers Your Excellency has made I accept and choose only the goodwill with which they have been proffered; for the rest, I implore Your Excellency that in my own chamber you allow and permit me to be the only one who serves me."

"In truth," said the duchess, "Señor Don Quixote, that cannot be: you will be served by four of my maidens who are as beautiful as flowers."

"As far as I am concerned," responded Don Quixote, "they will be not like flowers but like thorns piercing my soul. They will no more enter my chamber, or anything like that, than fly. If your highness wishes to proceed to grant me favors I do not deserve, allow me to accept them alone and to serve myself behind my chamber doors; for I place a wall between my desires and my modesty, and I do not wish to lose this custom because of the liberality your highness desires to show me. In short, I would rather sleep in my clothes than allow anyone to undress me."

"Enough, enough, Señor Don Quixote," replied the duchess. "I can tell you that I shall give orders that not even a fly can enter your room, much less a maiden; on no account am I the person to interfere with the propriety of Señor Don Quixote, for it has become clear to me that the most outstanding of his many virtues is modesty. Your grace may undress and dress by yourself, and in your own fashion, however and whenever you wish; there will be none to impede you, for in your chamber you will find the containers required for the needs of one who sleeps with a closed door, so that not even the necessities of nature will oblige you to open it. May the great Dulcinea of Toboso live for a thousand centuries, and may her name be known throughout the world, for she deserved to be the beloved of so valiant and chaste a knight, and may benign heaven fill the heart of Sancho Panza, our governor, with the desire to conclude his whipping quickly so that the world can once again enjoy the beauty of so great a lady."

To which Don Quixote said:

"Your grace has spoken like the person you are, for in the mouths of virtuous ladies there can be nothing that is wicked; Dulcinea will be more fortunate and renowned in the world for your highness's praise than for all the praises of the most eloquent men on earth."

"Well now, Señor Don Quixote," replied the duchess, "it is time to eat supper, and the duke must be waiting; come, your grace, and let us eat, and retire early, for the journey you made yesterday to Candaya was not so short that it has not caused you some weariness."

"I feel none at all, Señora," responded Don Quixote, "for I can swear to Your Excellency that never in my life have I mounted a calmer animal, or one with a better gait, than Clavileño, and I do not know what could have moved Malambruno to destroy so swift and gentle a mount and burn him for no reason at all."

"As for that, I can imagine," responded the duchess, "that he repented of the wrong he had done to Countess Trifaldi and her company, and to other persons, and the many acts of wickedness he must have committed as a wizard and an enchanter, and he wanted to put an end to all the devices of his profession, and since the wooden horse was the principal one that caused him the most concern wandering from country to country, he burned Clavileño so that with those ashes, and the trophy of the scroll, the valor of the great Don Quixote of La Mancha would be made immortal."

Once again Don Quixote thanked the duchess, and when they had eaten supper he withdrew to his chamber alone, not permitting anyone to come in to serve him: so fearful was he of facing situations that would move him or oblige him to lose the decorous modesty that he preserved for his lady Dulcinea, always keeping present in his imagination the virtue of Amadís, flower and model of all knights errant. He closed the door after him, and in the light of two wax candles he undressed, and as he removed his shoes—O misfortune so unworthy of such a person!—there was an eruption, not of sighs or anything else that would discredit the purity of his courtesy, but of some two dozen stitches in a stocking that now looked like latticework. The good gentleman was distraught, and he would have given an ounce of silver for just a small amount of green silk thread; I say green silk because his stockings were green.

Here Benengeli interjected this exclamation, saying:

"O poverty, poverty! I do not know why the great poet of Córdoba[1] was moved to call you

Holy and unwelcome gift!

I, though a Moor, know very well, through the communication I have had with Christians, that holiness consists of charity, humility, faith, obedience, and poverty; but even so, I say that a man must be very close to God if he can be content with being poor, unless it is the kind of

1. Juan de Mena (1411–1456), probably the most historically significant courtly poet of the fifteenth century.

poverty about which one of the greatest saints[2] says: 'Possess all things as if you possessed them not,' and this is called poverty in spirit; but you, the second poverty, the one I am speaking of: why do you wish to crush gentlemen and the wellborn more than other people? Why do you oblige them to patch[3] their shoes, and have some buttons on their doublets that are of silk, and others of horsehair, and others of glass? Why must their collars, for the most part, always be crumpled and not open and smooth?"

And in this one can see that the use of starch and smooth collars is very old. And he continued:

"How wretched is the wellborn man who nurtures his honor by eating badly, behind a closed door, playing the hypocrite with the toothpick he wields when he goes out after not having eaten anything that would oblige him to clean his teeth![4] How wretched is he, I say, who is apprehensive about his honor and thinks that the patch on his shoe, the perspiration on his hat, the darn on his cape, and the hunger in his stomach can be seen from a league away!"

All this was repeated in Don Quixote's thoughts when those stitches tore, but he was consoled at seeing that Sancho had left him a pair of high traveling boots that he intended to wear the next day. Finally he lay down, pensive and melancholy, not only because he missed Sancho, but on account of the irreparable disaster of his stockings, which he would have stitched up, even with silk thread of another color, one of the greatest indications of poverty that a gentleman can give in the course of his wearisome penury. He put out the candles, it was hot and he could not sleep, he got out of bed and opened slightly a jalousied window that overlooked a beautiful garden, and when he opened it he perceived and heard people walking and talking in the garden. He began to listen attentively. Those below him spoke loudly enough for him to hear these words:

"Do not urge me, O Emerencia, to sing, for you know that since the moment the stranger entered this castle and my eyes looked upon him, I can no longer sing but only weep, and besides, my lady is more a light sleeper than a heavy one, and I would not want her to find us here for

2. St. Paul, Corinthians 1.

3. Cervantes uses a phrase, *dar pantalia*, whose exact significance is not clear. It can mean either polishing or repairing shoes (Shelton translates it as "cobble," but the contemporary French and Italian versions differ).

4. The image of the impoverished gentleman who picks his teeth so that everyone will think he has eaten appeared in the anonymous *Lazarillo de Tormes* (1554), the first picaresque novel.

all the riches in the world. And even if she slept and did not awaken, my song would be in vain if this second Aeneas, who has come to my realm only to scorn me and abandon me, should sleep and not awaken."

"Do not be concerned about that, Altisidora my friend," was the reply, "for undoubtedly the duchess and all those in the house are asleep, except for the lord of your heart and the inspiration of your soul, for just now I heard the jalousied window in his room being opened, and no doubt he must be awake; sing, my suffering friend, softly and quietly to the sound of your harp, and if the duchess hears us, we can blame the heat."

"Oh, Emerencia, that isn't the point!" responded Altisidora. "It's just that I wouldn't want to reveal my heart in my song or be judged a capricious and frivolous maiden by those who do not know the power and might of love. But come what may, an embarrassed face is better than a wounded heart."

And then he heard the sound of a harp played very softly. When he heard this, Don Quixote was dumbfounded, because at that instant he remembered an infinite number of adventures similar to this one, with windows, jalousies, gardens, music, amorous compliments, and swoons, which he had read in his delusive books of chivalry. Then he imagined that a maiden of the duchess was in love with him, and that modesty compelled her to keep her desires secret; he feared he might surrender and resolved not to allow himself to be vanquished, and commending himself with all his heart and soul to his lady Dulcinea of Toboso, he decided to listen to the music; to let it be known that he was there, he gave a mock sneeze, which brought no small delight to the maidens, whose sole desire was that Don Quixote should hear them. When she had tuned and adjusted the harp, Altisidora began to sing this ballad:

> O you, who lie in your bed,
> between sheets of Holland linen,
> soundly and deeply asleep
> all night long until the morning,
> O brave knight, the most courageous
> ever born in great La Mancha,
> more modest, more chaste, more blessed
> than the fine gold of Arabia!
> Hear this melancholy maiden,
> so wellborn and so ill-fated:

in the light of your two suns
she feels her soul burst into flames.

    You go in search of adventures
but find the sorrows of others,
inflicting wounds, yet refusing
the remedy that can cure them.

    O tell me, most valiant youth,
—may God make your wishes prosper—
if Libyan sands were your home,
or the craggy peaks of Jaca;

    if you suckled a serpent's milk
or by chance you had for nurses
the harshness of the wild forest
and the horrors of the mountains.

    Well may the fair Dulcinea,
a maiden plump and sturdy,
boast of subduing a tiger,
and vanquishing a fierce beast,

    winning her fame along rivers
from Henares to Jarama,
from Tajo to Manzanares,
from Pisuerga to Arlanza.

    If I could change places with her,
I would give my very best,
my most gaily colored skirt
adorned with trimmings of gold.

    O, if I were but in your arms,
or at least beside your bed,
where I could scratch your dear head
and shake dandruff from your hair!

    I ask for much but am not worthy
of so notable a boon:
I should like to rub your feet;
that's enough for a humble maid.

    O, what fine caps I would give you,
and oh, what gaiters of silver,
and oh, what breeches of damask,
and oh, what short capes of linen!

    And then the most lustrous pearls,
each one as big as a gallnut,

and if they had no companions,
they'd be called *the Only Ones!*[5]

Look not from your Tarpeian Rock[6]
upon the fire that burns me,
Manchegan Nero of the world,
nor fan it with cruelty.

I am a girl, a tender maid,
no more than fifteen years old:
I am fourteen and three months,
I swear by God and my soul.

I am not lame, I do not limp,
I am not deformed or maimed;
my hair is like fairest lilies,
touching the floor when I stand.

And though my mouth is aquiline
and my nose is rather blunt,
I have teeth of topaz, raising
my beauty up to high heaven.

My voice, as you'll see, just listen,
as sweet as the sweetest tone,
and my nature and appearance,
something less than only middling.

All these and my other graces
are the spoils won by your arrows;
I am a maiden of this house;
I am called Altisidora.

Here the song of the afflicted Altisidora came to an end, and here began the astonishment of the fervently wooed Don Quixote, who heaved a great sigh and said to himself:

"Why must I be so unfortunate a knight that no maiden can look upon me without falling in love . . . ! Why must the peerless Dulcinea of Toboso be so unlucky that she cannot be permitted to enjoy my incomparable firmness of purpose . . . ! O queens, what do you wish of her? O empresses, why do you pursue her? O maidens of fourteen to fifteen years old, why do you harass her? Oh, allow her, allow the wretched lady to tri-

5. The allusion is to a pearl that belonged to the Spanish monarchy. Since it had no equal, it was called *La Sola*, "the Only One."

6. According to legend, the place on the Capitoline Hill where Nero stood as he watched Rome burn.

umph and delight and take pride in the good fortune that Love wished to grant her by giving her my heart and presenting her with my soul. Remember, all you enamored ladies, that for Dulcinea alone I am as soft as sugar paste, and for all the rest I am as hard as flint; for her I am honey, and for you, bitter aloe; for me, only Dulcinea is beautiful, wise, modest, gallant, and wellborn, and the rest are ugly, foolish, licentious, and of the worst lineage; to be hers alone, and no other's, nature cast me into the world. Let Altisidora weep or sing; let the lady despair on whose account I was beaten in the castle of the enchanted Moor; for I must belong to Dulcinea, boiled or roasted, clean, wellborn, and chaste, despite all the powers of sorcery in the world."

And with this he slammed the window shut, and as indignant and sorrowful as if some great calamity had befallen him he lay down in his bed, where we shall leave him for now because we are being summoned by the great Sancho Panza, who wishes to begin his famous governorship.

CHAPTER XLV

Regarding how the great Sancho Panza took possession of his ínsula, and the manner in which he began to govern

O perpetual discloser of the Antipodes, torch of the world, eye of heaven, sweet movement of cooling decanters,[1] here Thymbraeus, there Phoebus, here an archer, there a healer. Father of Poetry, Inventor of Music,[2] you who always rise and never set, although you seem to! To you, I say, O Sun, with whose help man engenders man,[3] to you I say that you ought to favor me and illuminate the dimness of my wits so that they may touch upon every point in the narration of the governorship of the great Sancho Panza, for without you I feel weak, fainthearted, and confused.

1. The invocation is to the sun, whose rays make it necessary to move decanters around in a bucket of snow to keep them cool.

2. These are some appellations of Apollo, god of the sun.

3. A phrase from Aristotle's *Physics*, II, 2.

I say, then, that with all his retinue Sancho came to a village with some thousand inhabitants, which was one of the best owned by the duke. They gave him to understand that it was called the Ínsula Barataria, either because the village was named Baratario or because he had been given the governorship at so little cost.⁴ When they reached the gates, for it was a walled town, the village councilmen came out to receive him; the bells were rung, and all the inhabitants displayed general rejoicing, and with a good deal of pomp they brought him to the largest church to give their thanks to God, and then, in a ridiculous ceremony, they presented him with the keys to the village and accepted him as perpetual governor of the Ínsula Barataria.

The clothing, beard, plumpness, and short stature of the new governor surprised all the people who were not privy to the secret, and even all of the many people who were. Finally they led him from the church and brought him to the judge's seat in a courtroom, and seated him upon it, and the duke's steward said to him:

"It is an ancient custom on this ínsula, Señor Governor, that the man who comes to take possession of this famous ínsula is obliged to respond to a question that is somewhat intricate and complicated, and from his response the people can weigh and measure the intelligence of their new governor, and either celebrate or mourn his arrival."

While the steward was telling this to Sancho, Sancho was looking at a number of large letters written on the wall facing his seat, and since he did not know how to read, he asked what was painted there on the wall. The response was:

"Señor, the day on which your lordship took possession of this ínsula is written and noted there, and the inscription says: *Today, on such-and-such a date in such-and-such a year, Señor Don Sancho Panza took possession of this ínsula, and may he enjoy it for many years.*"

"And who are you calling Don Sancho Panza?" asked Sancho.

"Your lordship," responded the steward, "for no other Panza has come to this ínsula except for the one sitting on that seat."

"Well, you should know, brother," said Sancho, "that I don't have a *Don*, and neither did anybody else in my family: my name's Sancho Panza, plain and simple, and my father was named Sancho, and my grandfather was named Sancho, and they were all Panzas, without any

4. The name of the ínsula and the village, and the fact that Sancho did nothing to merit the governorship, are based on the root word *barato*, "cheap."

additions of Don or Doña; I imagine that on this ínsula there must be more Dons than stones, but that's enough of that: God understands me, and it may be that if my governorship lasts a few days, I'll weed out these Dons, because there's so many of them they must be as annoying as gnats. Go on with your question, Señor Steward, and I'll answer the best I can, whether the people go into mourning or not."

At that moment two men entered the courtroom, one wearing the clothes of a peasant and the other dressed as a tailor, for he carried a pair of scissors in his hand, and the tailor said:

"Señor Governor, I and this peasant have come before your grace because this good man came to my shop yesterday (for I, if those present will excuse me, have passed the tailor's examination,[5] God be praised), placed a piece of cloth in my hands, and asked: 'Señor, is there enough cloth here to make me a pointed cap?' I examined the cloth and told him there was; he must have thought, which is what I thought, and thought correctly, that I surely wanted to steal a part of the cloth, basing this on his own wickedness and on the bad reputation of tailors, and he told me to see if there was enough for two; I guessed at what he was thinking, and I told him yes; and he, still riding his earlier wicked intention, kept adding caps, and I kept adding yesses, until we reached five caps; and now he just came for them, and I gave them to him, and he refuses to pay me for my labor but demands that I pay him or return his cloth."

"Is all this true, brother?" asked Sancho.

"Yes, Señor," responded the peasant, "but your grace should have him show you the five caps he made for me."

"Gladly," responded the tailor.

Then, taking his hand out from under his cloak, he showed five caps placed on the five fingertips of his hand, and he said:

"Here are the five caps this good man asked me for, and by God and my conscience, I had no cloth left over, and I'll even show the work to the guild inspectors."

Everyone present laughed at the multitude of caps and the unusual nature of the case. Sancho reflected for a while and said:

"It seems to me that in this case there's no need for long delays, for it can be judged quickly by the judgment of a sensible man, and so my verdict is that the tailor should lose the cost of his labor, and the peasant his

5. In other words, he has been admitted to the tailors guild. He asks to be excused because, at the time, tailors were held in exceptionally bad repute.

cloth, and the caps should be taken to the prisoners in jail, and that's the end of that."

If the subsequent verdict concerning the herder's purse moved the onlookers to amazement, this one provoked their laughter, but in the end, the governor's orders were carried out. The next to come before him were two old men; one carried a length of cane as a walking stick, and the one without a walking stick said:

"Señor, days ago I lent this good man ten gold *escudos* as a kindness and a favor to him, on the condition that he return them to me whenever I asked for them; a good number of days went by without my asking for anything, so that his repayment would not put him in even greater difficulties than when I lent him the money; but because it seemed to me that he was negligent about his debt, I have asked him for repayment over and over again, and not only does he not return my money, but he denies the debt and says I never lent him ten *escudos*, and if I did, he's already returned them to me. There are no witnesses to the loan or to the repayment, because he never repaid me; I would like your grace to take his oath, and if he swears that he's returned the money, I'll forgive the debt here, before God."

"What do you say to this, old man with the walking stick?" said Sancho.

To which the old man said:

"Señor, I confess that he lent me the money, and your grace should lower your staff;[6] and since he leaves it all up to my oath, I'll swear that I have really and truly returned the money and paid the debt."

The governor lowered his staff, and at the same time, as if it were very much in his way, the old man with the walking stick gave his walking stick to the other old man for him to hold while he took his oath, and then he placed his hand on the cross of the staff, saying it was true that the ten *escudos* had been lent to him but that he had paid them into the hands of the other man, who was forgetful and kept asking him for the money. Seeing which the great governor asked the creditor to respond to what his adversary had said, and he said that without any doubt his debtor must be telling the truth, because he considered him an honest man and a good Christian, and he must have forgotten how and when he had returned the money, and from now on he would not ask him for anything. The debtor took back his walking stick, bowed his

6. The judge's staff of office was used to take sworn testimony.

head, and left the courtroom. Sancho, seeing him walk out with no further ado, and seeing too the patience of the claimant, lowered his head to his chest, placed the index finger of his right hand over his eyebrows and nose, sat thoughtfully for a short while, and then raised his head and ordered them to call back the old man with the walking stick, who had already left. They brought him back, and when he saw him, Sancho said:

"My good man, give me that walking stick; I need it."

"Gladly," responded the old man. "Here it is, Señor."

And he placed it in his hand. Sancho took it, gave it to the other old man, and said:

"Go with God, for you have been repaid."

"I, Señor?" responded the old man. "Then is this length of cane worth ten gold *escudos?*"

"Yes," said the governor, "and if not, then I'm the biggest imbecile in the world. And now we'll see if I have the brains to govern a whole kingdom."

And he ordered that there, in front of everyone, the cane should be broken and opened. It was, and in the very center ten gold *escudos* were discovered; everyone was stunned, and they considered their governor to be a second Solomon.

They asked him how he had deduced that the ten *escudos* were inside the cane; he responded that when he had seen the old man who was taking the oath give the walking stick to his adversary to hold while he swore his oath, and then swear that he had really and truly given him the money, and then, when he had finished his oath, ask for his walking stick back again, it occurred to him that the money he was being asked for was inside the cane. From which one can deduce that those who govern, even if they are fools, are occasionally guided by God in their judgments; besides, he had heard the priest in his village tell about another case like this one,[7] and he had such a good memory that if he didn't forget everything he wanted to remember, there wouldn't be another memory like it in all the ínsula. Finally, with one old man mortified and the other repaid, they left, and those present were astounded, and the man writing down the words, deeds, and movements of Sancho could not determine if he should record him as a fool or a wise man.

Then, when this case was concluded, a woman entered the court-

---

7. The story, in fact, dates back to the popular life of the saints called *The Golden Legend* (*Legenda aurea*) by the Italian Dominican Iacopo da Varazze (1228?–1298).

room clutching at a man dressed in the clothes of a rich herder, and as she came in she cried out:

"Justice, Señor Governor, justice, and if I don't find it on earth, I'll go and look for it in heaven! Señor Governor of my soul, this wicked man seized me in the middle of a field, and used my body like a dirty old rag, and, oh woe is me, he took what I had safeguarded for more than twenty-three years, defending it against Moors and Christians, Spaniards and foreigners, and I, always as hard as an oak, kept myself pure like the salamander in the fire, or wool in the brambles, just so this good man would come along now and put his clean hands all over me."

"That's something we have to look into: whether or not this fine fellow has clean hands," said Sancho.

And turning to the man, he told him to answer and respond to the complaint of this woman. The man, greatly agitated, responded:

"Señores, I'm a poor herder of swine, and this morning I left here to sell, you'll forgive my saying so, four pigs, and what with taxes and trickery I let them go for a little less than what they were worth; I was returning to my village, I met this good woman on the way, and the devil, who is always cooking up trouble, made us lie down together; I paid her enough, she wasn't satisfied, she caught hold of me and didn't let go until she brought me here. She says I forced her and she lies, by the oath I swear or plan to swear; this is the whole truth, down to the last crumb."

Then the governor asked him if he was carrying any silver coins; he said he had about twenty *ducados* inside his shirt, in a leather purse. The governor ordered him to take it out and give it, just as it was, to the plaintiff; he did so, trembling; the woman took it, making a thousand obeisances to everyone and praying to God for the life and health of the governor who took such good care of orphans and maidens in need; and with that she left the courtroom, tightly clutching the purse with both hands, although first she looked to see if the coins inside were silver.

As soon as she left, Sancho said to the herder, who was already in tears and whose eyes and heart were following after his purse:

"My good man, go after that woman and take the purse away from her, even if she doesn't want to give it to you, and bring it back here."

And he did not say this to a fool or a deaf man, because the herder ran out like a bolt of lightning to do as he had been ordered. Everyone present was in suspense, waiting to see how the case would end, and in a little while the man and the woman returned holding and clutching each other more tightly than before, she with her skirt tucked up, with the purse thrust inside, and the man struggling to take it away from her, which was not possible because the woman defended it so fiercely, and cried out, saying:

"Justice, God's justice and the world's! Look, your grace, Señor Governor, at how shameless and bold this cruel man is, for in the middle of town and in the middle of the street he has tried to take the purse that your grace ordered him to give to me."

"And did he take it from you?" asked the governor.

"What do you mean, take?" responded the woman. "I'd let them take my life before I'd let them take my purse. Not this girl! You'd have to send someone else after me, not this miserable weakling! Tongs and hammers, mallets and chisels, not even a lion's claws would be enough to tear it out of my hands: first they'd have to get the soul from the very heart of my body!"

"She's right," said the man, "and I'm worn out and confess I don't have the strength to take it from her; I give up."

Then the governor said to the woman:

"Honorable and valiant woman, show me the purse."

She gave it to him immediately, and the governor returned it to the man and said to the forceful and unforced woman:

"If, my dear sister, you had shown the same strength and courage, or even half as much, in defending your body as you showed in defending that purse, the strength of Hercules could not have forced you. Go with God, and a good amount of bad luck, and don't stop anywhere on this ínsula or for six leagues around it, under penalty of two hundred lashes. Leave now, I say, you charlatan and brazen liar!"

The woman was frightened and left, dejected and discontented, and the governor said to the man:

"My good man, go with God to your home with your money, and from now on, if you don't want to lose it, try to hold off your desire to lie with anybody."

The man thanked him in the worst way he knew how and left, and the onlookers were again amazed at the judgments and verdicts of their new governor.[8] All of which, noted by his chronicler, was then written down and sent to the duke, who was eagerly awaiting it.

And let us leave the good Sancho here, for we must quickly return to his master, who has been so disquieted by the music of Altisidora.

8. This story appears in *Norte de los Estados*, by Fr. Francisco de Osuna (Burgos, 1550).

CHAPTER XLVI

Regarding the dreadful belline and feline fright received by Don Quixote in the course of his wooing by the enamored Altisidora

We left the great Don Quixote wrapped in the thoughts that had been caused by the music of the enamored maiden Altisidora. He lay down with them, and, as if they were fleas, they would not let him sleep or rest for a moment, and they joined the ones that plagued him with regard to his stockings; but since time is swift and there is no obstacle that can stop it, the hours raced by and morning soon arrived. Seeing which Don Quixote left the soft featherbed, and, by no means slothful, dressed in his chamois outfit and put on the traveling boots in order to hide the misfortune of his stockings; he threw on his scarlet cloak, and on his head he placed a cap of green velvet adorned with silver trimmings; over his shoulders he hung his swordbelt with his good, sharp blade, picked up a large rosary that he always carried with him, and with great solemnity strode into the antechamber, where the duke and the duchess were already dressed and apparently waiting for him. And as he passed along a gallery, standing there waiting for him were Altisidora and another maiden, and as soon as Altisidora saw Don Quixote she pretended to faint, and her friend held her in her lap and very quickly began to unfasten her bodice. Don Quixote saw this, and going up to them he said:

"I know the reason for these mishaps."

"I don't know what that could be," responded the friend, "because Altisidora is the healthiest maiden in the entire house, and I've never heard even a sigh from her for as long as I've known her; bad luck to all the knights errant in the world if they're all so ungrateful. Your grace should leave, Señor Don Quixote, for this poor girl won't regain consciousness as long as your grace is here."

To which Don Quixote responded:

"Señora, your grace should have a lute placed in my room tonight, and I shall do my best to console this suffering maiden, for at the very beginnings of love, rapid disillusionments are usually considered remedies."

And with this he left, so that he would not attract the attention of anyone who might see him. No sooner had he gone away than the swooning Altisidora came to her senses and said to her companion:

"A lute will have to be placed in his room; no doubt Don Quixote wants to give us some music, and if it's his, it won't be bad."

They went immediately to the duchess to recount what had happened and to tell her about the lute that Don Quixote had requested, and she, with extraordinary pleasure, arranged with the duke and her maidens to play a trick more amusing than harmful; and very happily they waited for the night, which came as quickly as the day, which the duke and duchess spent in delightful conversation with Don Quixote. And that same day, the duchess really and truly dispatched a page—the one who had played the enchanted figure of Dulcinea in the forest—to Teresa Panza, with the letter from her husband, Sancho Panza, and the bundle of clothing he had left behind so that it could be sent to her, and she charged him to bring back a good accounting of everything that passed between them.

Later, when it was eleven o'clock, Don Quixote found a vihuela in his room. He tested it, opened the jalousied window, and heard people walking in the garden; turning the pegs of the vihuela and tuning it the best he knew how, he spat and cleared his throat, and then, in a voice that was husky but in tune, he sang the following ballad, which he had composed that day:

> Often the power of love
> can madden a maiden's soul,
> using as its means, its instrument,
> an unthinking leisure and ease.
>   Fine sewing and needlework,
> constant devotion to labor,
> can be the cure, the antidote,
> to the poison of love's disease.
>   For sheltered and modest maidens
> who aspire to be married,

chastity is the best dowry,
the best voice to sing their praises.

Knights errant who seek adventures
and those knights who stay at court,
woo the free and easy damsels;
they marry the modest maids.

Love can arise in the east,
and be confirmed between guests,
and sink quickly in the west,
because departure is its end.

Love that is recent and new,
that comes today and goes the next,
leaves no image, makes no mark
that endures deep in the soul.

A picture over a picture
is not disclosed nor is it shown;
and where a first beauty exists,
a second won't win the game.

Dulcinea of Toboso:
she is painted on my soul's
tabula rasa, and never
can she ever be erased.

Firm constancy in lovers is
a most precious attribute,
for whose sake Love works miracles
when he raises them on high.

Don Quixote had reached this point in his song, to which the duke
and the duchess, Altisidora, and almost all the people in the castle were
listening, when suddenly, from a gallery that was directly above Don
Quixote's jalousied window, a cord was lowered with more than a hundred cowbells attached to it, and immediately after that a huge sack full
of cats, with smaller bells tied to their tails, was emptied out. The clang-
ing of the bells and the yowling of the cats was so loud that even though
the duke and duchess had contrived the joke, it still startled them, and
Don Quixote was struck dumb with fear. As luck would have it, two or
three of the cats came in the window of his room, and as they raced from
one side to the other, it seemed as if a legion of devils had been set loose
in the chamber. They made the candles that were burning in the room

go out as they looked for a means of escape. The raising and lowering of the cord with the large cowbells on it did not stop; most of the people in the castle, who did not know the truth of what had happened, were amazed and astonished.

Don Quixote rose to his feet, took his sword in hand, and began to thrust it through the jalousy, shouting:

"Away, evil enchanters! Away, base wizards! For I am Don Quixote of La Mancha, against whom your wicked intentions are powerless and of little use!"

And turning to the cats that were racing around the room, he directed many thrusts against them; they ran to the window and went out, although one of them, finding himself so hounded by Don Quixote's sword thrusts, leaped at his face and sank his claws and teeth into his nose, and the pain was so great that Don Quixote began to shout as loudly as he could. The duke and duchess heard this, and considering what it might be, they quickly hurried to his room, and opening the door with a master key, they saw the poor knight struggling with all his might to remove the cat from his face. They came in with lights and saw the unequal battle; the duke attempted to separate them, and Don Quixote shouted:

"No one is to pull him away! Let me fight hand to hand with this demon, this wizard, this enchanter, for I shall teach him, one to one, who Don Quixote of La Mancha is!"

But the cat, caring nothing for these threats, snarled and dug in even deeper; at last the duke uprooted him and tossed him out the window.

Don Quixote's face was covered with scratches and his nose was not very healthy, and he was very indignant because he had not been allowed to finish the battle he had begun with that wicked enchanter. Oil of Aparicio[1] was sent for, and Altisidora herself, with her snow white hands, put bandages over all his wounds, and as she did, in a low voice she said:

"All these misfortunes have occurred, O hardhearted knight, because of the sin of your harshness and obstinacy; may it please God that Sancho your squire forgets to flog himself so that your dearly beloved Dulcinea never is released from her enchantment, and you never enjoy her, or come to your nuptial bed with her, at least as long as I live, for I adore you."

---

1. A medicinal preparation for treating wounds devised in the sixteenth century by Aparicio de Zubia.

To all of this Don Quixote did not respond except to heave a deep sigh, and then he lay down on his bed, thanking the duke and duchess for their kindness, not because he had been afraid of that enchanted feline and belline horde, but because he had realized the good intentions with which they had come to his assistance. The duke and duchess allowed him to rest and left, saddened by the unfortunate outcome of their joke, but they did not believe that the adventure would turn out to be so painful and costly for Don Quixote, who had to spend five days confined to his bed, where another adventure befell him that was more pleasant than the last one, which his historian does not wish to recount now in order to return to Sancho Panza, who was proceeding very diligently and very comically in his governorship.

CHAPTER XLVII

In which the account of how Sancho Panza behaved in his governorship continues

The history recounts that Sancho Panza was taken from the courtroom to a sumptuous palace, where, in a large hall, a royal and extremely clean table was set; as soon as Sancho entered the hall, there was a sound of flageolets, and four pages came out with water to wash his hands, which Sancho received with great solemnity.

The music ceased, and Sancho sat down at the head of the table because that was the only chair and the only place laid on the entire table. A personage, who later proved to be a physician, came to stand at his side, holding a rod of whalebone in his hand. They lifted the fine white cloth that covered the fruit and a wide variety of dishes holding different foods; one man who looked like a student said the blessing, and a page put a bib trimmed in lace on Sancho; another who was performing the duties of a butler placed a dish of fruit in front of him; he had barely eaten a mouthful when the man with the rod used it to touch the dish, and it was taken away with extraordinary speed, but the butler placed another dish of different food in front of him. Sancho was about to try it, but before he could reach it and taste it, the rod had touched it and a page removed it as quickly as the fruit had been taken away. When he saw this, Sancho was perplexed, and looking at everyone, he asked if the dinner was to be eaten like a conjuring trick. To which the man with the rod responded:

"It must be eaten, Señor Governor, according to the traditions and customs of other ínsulas where there are governors. I, Señor, am a physician, and on this ínsula I am paid to tend to its governors, and I care for their health much more than I do my own, studying day and night, and observing the governor's constitution and temperament in order to successfully cure him if he should fall ill; and the principal thing I do is to be present at his dinners and suppers, and allow him to eat what seems appropriate to me, and to take away what I imagine will do him harm and be injurious to his stomach; and so I ordered the dish of fruit removed because it was too damp, and the other dish as well because it was too hot and had a good number of spices, which increase thirst, and if one drinks too much, one destroys and consumes the radical humor, which is to say, life."[1]

"So that means that the dish of roasted partridges over there, nicely seasoned, it seems to me, won't do me any harm."

To which the physician responded:

"The governor will not eat them as long as I am alive."

"But why?" said Sancho.

And the physician responded:

"Because our master Hippocrates, the polestar and light of medicine, says in one of his aphorisms: *Omnis saturatio mala, perdicis autem pessima*. Which means: 'A full stomach is bad, but a stomach full of partridges is very bad.' "[2]

"If that's true," said Sancho, "then see, Señor Doctor, which of the dishes on this table will do me the most good and which the least harm, and let me eat it without you tapping it, because by my life as a governor, and may God allow me to enjoy it, I am dying of hunger, and denying me food, no matter what you tell me, Señor Doctor, means taking my life instead of lengthening it."

"Your grace is correct, Señor Governor," responded the physician, "and so, it is my opinion that your grace should not eat the rabbit stew

---

1. The physician's medical theorizing is based on the idea of the four cardinal humors.

2. A parody of the aphorism *Omnis saturatio mala, panis autem pessima* (i.e., "bread" instead of "partridges").

over there because that is a long-haired animal. You could have tasted the veal, if it hadn't been roasted and marinated, but it's out of the question now."

And Sancho said:

"That big bowl steaming over there looks to me like *olla podrida*,[3] and because those stews have so many different kinds of things in them, I can't help but come across something that I'll like and that will be good for me."

"*Absit!*"[4] said the physician. "May so wicked a thought be far from us: there is nothing in the world less nourishing than an *olla podrida*. Let *ollas podridas* be for canons or rectors of colleges or peasant weddings, and keep them away from the tables of governors, where all things exquisite and elegant should be present; the reason is that simple medicines are always more highly esteemed than compound ones, everywhere and by everyone, because there can be no error in simple medicines, but there can be in compound ones, simply by changing the amounts of the things of which they are compounded; but I know that what the governor must eat now in order to preserve and fortify his health is a hundred rolled wafers and some very thin slices of quince, which will settle his stomach and help his digestion."

Hearing this, Sancho leaned back in his chair and stared fixedly at the physician and in a solemn voice asked him what his name was and where he had studied. To which he responded:

"My name, Señor Governor, is Dr. Pedro Recio de Agüero, and I am a native of a town called Tirteafuera, which is between Caracuel and Almodóvar del Campo, on the right-hand side, and I hold the degree of doctor from the University of Osuna."[5]

To which Sancho, in a rage, responded:

"Well, Señor Doctor Pedro Recio de Mal Agüero,[6] native of Tirteafuera, a village that's on the right as we go from Caracuel to Almodóvar del Campo, graduated from Osuna, get out of my sight, and if you don't, I swear by the sun that I'll take a cudgel, and starting with you, I'll beat all the doctors so hard there won't be a single one left anywhere on the ín-

---

3. A traditional Spanish stew that includes chickpeas, ham, and chicken in addition to the usual meats and vegetables ordinarily found in a stew.

4. "By no means!" in Latin.

5. *Recio* can mean "vigorous," "violent," or "difficult"; *agüero* is "omen"; *tirteafuera* is roughly equivalent to "get the hell out."

6. "Evil omen."

sula, at least the ones I know to be ignorant, because wise, prudent, and intelligent doctors I'll respect and honor as if they were divine. And again I say that you should leave here, Pedro Recio, otherwise I'll take this chair that I'm sitting on and smash it over your head, and they can bring charges against me and I'll clear myself by saying that I did a service for God when I killed a bad doctor, who's the same as an executioner. Now, all of you, give me something to eat, otherwise take your governorship back, because an office that doesn't give a man food to eat isn't worth two beans."

The physician became very agitated when he saw the governor so enraged, and he wanted to do a *tirteafuera* from the hall, but at that moment a post horn sounded in the street, and the butler went to look out the window and then returned, saying:

"A courier has come from my lord the duke; he must be carrying an important dispatch."

The courier came in, perspiring and intimidated, and after taking a sealed letter from inside his shirt, he placed it in the hands of the governor, and Sancho placed it in those of the steward, whom he ordered to read the address, which said: *To Don Sancho Panza, governor of the Ínsula Barataria, to be delivered into his own hands or those of his secretary.* Hearing this, Sancho said:

"Who here is my secretary?"

And one of those present responded:

"I am, Señor, because I know how to read and write, and because I'm Basque."[7]

"With that little addition," said Sancho, "you could be secretary to the emperor himself. Open that letter and see what it says."

The newly born secretary did so, and having read what it said, he said it was a matter that required privacy. Sancho ordered the hall cleared, with only the steward and the butler remaining; all the rest, including the physician, left, and then the secretary read the letter, which said:

It has come to my attention, Señor Don Sancho Panza, that certain enemies of mine and of the ínsula will launch a furious attack, but I do not know on which night; it is advisable to keep watch and stay on guard so that they do not catch you unprepared. I have also learned through trusted spies that four per-

7. Basques were frequently appointed as secretaries because of their reputation for loyalty.

sons in disguise have come to that place to take your life, for they fear your cleverness; keep your eyes open, be aware of who comes to speak to you, and do not eat anything that is offered to you. I shall be sure to come to your aid if you find yourself in difficulty, and in everything you will act with your customary intelligence. From this place, the sixteenth of August, at four in the morning.

Your friend,
THE DUKE

Sancho was astounded, as all the bystanders seemed to be as well, and turning to the steward, he said:

"What has to be done now, and done right away, is to put Dr. Recio in jail, because if anybody's going to kill me, it'll be him, with the slow, painful death that comes from starvation."

"It also seems to me," said the butler, "that your grace shouldn't eat anything that is on this table because it was prepared by nuns, and as the saying goes, behind the cross lurks the devil."

"I don't deny it," responded Sancho, "and for now give me a piece of bread and about four pounds of grapes, because they really can't be poisoned, and I can't get by without eating, and if we have to be ready for those battles that are threatening us, we'll need to be well-fed, because a full belly gives you courage and not the other way around. And you, Secretary, answer my lord the duke and tell him that all his orders will be carried out as ordered, to the letter; and send my lady the duchess a kiss on the hand from me, and say that I beg her not to forget to send a messenger with my letter and my bundle to my wife, Teresa Panza, and I'll be very grateful, and I'll be sure to serve her to the best of my ability; and while you're at it you can include a kiss on the hand for my master, Don Quixote of La Mancha, so that he can see that I'm grateful; and you, like a good secretary and a good Basque, can add anything you want that's to the point. Now clear the table and give me something to eat, and then I'll take on all the spies and killers and enchanters who want to attack me and my ínsula."

At this moment a page came in and said:

"There's a farmer here, a petitioner, who wants to talk to your lordship about a matter that he says is very important."

"It's strange," said Sancho, "about these petitioners. Is it possible they're so foolish they can't see that this isn't the right time of day to come with their petitions? By some chance aren't those of us who are governors and judges men of flesh and blood, too, and don't we need to have time to rest, or do they think we're made of marble? By God and my conscience, if my governorship lasts (and I have an idea it won't), I'll get these petitioners under control. Now tell this good man to come in, but make sure first that he isn't one of those spies, or a killer who wants to murder me."

"No, Señor," responded the page, "because he seems a simple soul, and either I don't know much or he's as good as a piece of bread."

"There's nothing to fear," said the steward. "We're all here."

"Butler, would it be possible," said Sancho, "now that Dr. Pedro Recio isn't here, for me to eat something with a little more weight and substance, even if it's a piece of bread and an onion?"

"Tonight the supper will make up for the defects in your dinner, and your lordship will be well-satisfied and content," said the butler.

"May God grant us that," responded Sancho.

And at this point the farmer came in, a man of very decent appearance, and from a thousand leagues away one could see that he was honest and a good soul. The first thing he said was:

"Which one of you is the governor?"

"Who else would it be," responded the secretary, "except the one who's sitting on the chair?"

"Then I humble myself in his presence," said the farmer.

And going down on his knees, he asked for Sancho's hand to kiss. Sancho refused and ordered him to stand and tell him what he wanted. The farmer complied and said:

"Señor, I'm a farmer, a native of Miguel Turra, a village two leagues from Ciudad Real."

"We have another Tirteafuera!" said Sancho. "Go on, brother, for I can tell you that I know Miguel Turra very well, and it's not very far from my village."

"Well, Señor, the fact is," the farmer continued, "that I, by the grace of God, am married with the blessing and consent of the Holy Roman Catholic Church; I have two sons who are students: the younger is studying for his bachelor's degree and the older one for his licentiate; I'm a widower because my wife died, or I should say, a bad doctor killed her, purging her when she was pregnant, and if it had been God's will for the child to be born, and if it had been a boy, I would have had him study medicine so he wouldn't be envious of his brothers, the bachelor and the licentiate."

"Which means," said Sancho, "that if your wife hadn't died, or hadn't been killed, you wouldn't be a widower now."

"No, Señor, not at all," responded the farmer.

"Well, that's a fine thing!" replied Sancho. "Go on, brother, because now's the time for sleep, not petitions."

"Well, I'll tell you," said the farmer, "that my son who's studying to be a bachelor fell in love with a maiden from our village named Clara Perlerina, the daughter of Andrés Perlerino, a very rich farmer; and this name of Perlerín doesn't come to them from their ancestry or family, but because everyone in this lineage is palsied, and to improve the name they're called Perlerín,[8] though if truth be told, the maiden is like an Oriental pearl, and looked at from the right side she seems a flower of the field; from the left side it's a different story, because she lost that eye when she had smallpox; and though she has many large pockmarks on her face, those who love her dearly say that those aren't pockmarks but the graves where the souls of her suitors are buried. She's so clean that in order not to dirty her face her nose, as they say, is so turned up that it looks like it's running away from her mouth; and still she looks extremely attractive because her mouth is large, and if it weren't missing ten or twelve teeth, it would be counted and considered as one of the best formed. I have nothing to say about her lips, because they're so thin and delicate that if it were usual to wind lips, they could be made into a nice skein, but since their color's different from the one commonly found in lips, they seem miraculous, because they're a mottled blue, green, and purple; and, Señor Governor, please forgive me for painting in so much detail the traits of the woman who, in the long run, is going to be my daughter, because I love her dearly and think she's fine."

"Paint as much as you like," said Sancho, "because I'm enjoying the picture, and if I had eaten, there couldn't be a better dessert for me than your portrait."

"I still have that to serve to you," responded the farmer, "but a time will come when we're ready for it, if we aren't now. And I say, Señor, that if I could paint her elegance and the height of her body, it would be something amazing, but that's impossible, because she's stooped and hunched over, and her mouth is down to her knees, and even so, it's clear to see that if she could stand up, her head would touch the ceiling;

8. The root *perl-* is related to "pearl"; the term Cervantes uses for "palsied" or "paralyzed" is *perlático*, allowing for the wordplay in these lines.

she would have given her hand in marriage to my bachelor by now, but she can't extend it because it's withered, and with it all, by her long grooved nails, you can see how well made and shapely it is."

"That's fine," said Sancho. "You should realize, brother, that now you've painted her from head to toe. What is it that you want? And get to the point without beating around the bush or going around in circles, or taking anything away or adding anything on."

"Señor, I would like," responded the farmer, "for your grace to be so good as to give me a letter of support for her father, asking him kindly to allow this marriage to take place, for we are not unequal in our fortunes or our natures; to tell you the truth, Señor Governor, my son is possessed, and not a day goes by that evil spirits do not torment him; because he fell once into the fire, his face is as wrinkled as parchment, and his eyes are somewhat teary and runny, but he has the disposition of an angel, and if he didn't beat and punch himself, he would be a saint."

"Is there anything else you want, my good man?" replied Sancho.

"I would like something else," said the farmer, "except I don't dare to say it; but, well, after all, whether I get it or not, it shouldn't fester inside. And so, Señor, I would like your grace to give me three hundred or six hundred *ducados* to help with my bachelor's dowry, I mean, to help him set up a house, because, after all, they have to live on their own and not be subject to the interference of in-laws."

"See if there's anything else you want," said Sancho, "and don't be too shy or too embarrassed to say it."

"No, I'm certain, there's nothing else," responded the farmer.

And as soon as he said this, the governor rose to his feet, picked up the chair where he had been sitting, and said:

"I swear, Don Crass and Crude, if you don't leave and get out of my sight right now, I'll break and crack your head open with this chair! Scoundrel and whoreson, the demon's own painter, is this the right time to come and ask me for six hundred *ducados*? Where would I have them, you unbearable pest? And why would I give them to you if I did have them, you shifty fool? And what do I care about Miguel Turra and the lineage of the Perlerín? Get away from me, I say, or by the life of my lord the duke, I'll do what I said! You can't be from Miguel Turra, you must be some sly devil sent here from hell to tempt me. Tell me, you merciless man, I haven't had the governorship for a day and a half yet, and you want me to have six hundred *ducados*?"

The butler signaled to the farmer to leave the hall, which he did, head lowered and apparently fearful that the governor would act on his rage, for the great scoundrel knew his trade very well.

But let us leave Sancho and his rage, dear reader, with no argument or quarrel, and return to Don Quixote, whom we left with his face bandaged and treated for his feline wounds, which did not heal for eight days, and on one of them something happened that Cide Hamete promises to recount as exactly and truthfully as all things in this history are recounted, no matter how trivial they may be.

CHAPTER XLVIII

Regarding what transpired between Don Quixote and Doña Rodríguez, duenna to the duchess, as well as other events worthy of being recorded and remembered forever

A badly wounded Don Quixote, his face bandaged and marked not by the hand of God but by the claws of a cat, was far too dejected and melancholy at the misfortunes inherent in knight errantry. He did not go out in public for six days, and on one of those nights, when he was sleepless and awake, thinking about his misfortunes and his pursuit by Altisidora, he heard someone opening the door of his room with a key, and then he imagined that the enamored maiden was coming to assail his chastity and put him in a situation where he would fall short of the faith he was obliged to keep with his lady Dulcinea of Toboso.

"No," he said in a voice that could be heard, believing what he had just imagined, "the greatest beauty on earth will not influence me to stop adoring the one I have engraved and impressed deep in my heart and at the very center of my being, no matter, my lady, if you are transformed into an uncouth peasant, or a nymph of the golden Tajo weaving cloth of gold and silk, or are being held by Merlin or Montesinos wherever they wish, for wherever you may be, you are mine, and wherever I go, I have been and shall be yours."

The conclusion of these words and the opening of the door were all one. He stood on his bed, wrapped from head to toe in a yellow satin bedspread, a two-cornered beretta on his head, and his face and mustache bandaged: his face on account of the scratches, his mustache so that it would not droop and fall, and in this garb he seemed the most extraordinary phantom that anyone could imagine.

He fixed his eyes on the door, and where he expected to see the overwhelmed and lovesick Altisidora come in, he saw instead a most reverend duenna wearing white veils so long and intricate that they covered and enshrouded her from head to foot. In the fingers of her left hand she carried half a burning candle, and with her right hand she shadowed her face so that the light would not shine in her eyes, which were covered by very large spectacles. She stepped very softly and moved her feet very quietly.

Don Quixote looked down at her from his observation post, and when he saw her manner of dress and noticed her silence, he thought that a witch or a sorceress had come in that attire to commit some villainy against him, and he began very quickly to cross himself. The terrifying vision continued to approach, and when she reached the middle of the chamber, she raised her eyes and saw with what urgency Don Quixote was making the sign of the cross; and if he was fearful at the sight of her figure, she was terrified at seeing his, because as soon as she saw him, so high, and so yellow in the bedspread, and with the bandages that disfigured him, she screamed, saying:

"Jesus! What am I seeing?"

And she was so startled that she dropped the candle, and finding herself in the dark, she turned to leave, and in her fear she tripped on her skirts and fell with a great noise. A fearful Don Quixote began to say:

"I conjure thee, phantom, or whatever thou mayest be, to tell me what thou art and to tell me what it is that thou wantest of me. If thou art a soul in torment, tell me, and I shall do for thee all that is in my power, for I am a Catholic Christian and partial to doing good to everyone; for that reason I took on the order of knight errantry which I profess, whose exercise extends even to doing good to souls in purgatory."

The dumbfounded duenna, who heard herself being conjured, associated Don Quixote's fear with her own, and in a low and grieving voice she responded:

"Señor Don Quixote, if your grace happens to be Don Quixote, I am no phantom or vision or soul in purgatory, as your grace must have thought, but Doña Rodríguez, the duenna-of-honor to my lady the duchess, and I have come to your grace because I am in the sort of need your grace usually remedies."

"Tell me, Señora Doña Rodríguez," said Don Quixote, "by any chance has your grace come to act as a go-between? For I must tell you that I am not available to anyone, thanks to the peerless beauty of my lady Dulcinea of Toboso. In short, Señora Doña Rodríguez, I say that if your grace sets and puts aside all amorous messages, you may light your candle again, and come back, and we shall speak of anything you like and desire, except, as I have said, any invitation to the affections."

"I, serve as anyone's messenger, Señor?" responded the duenna. "Your grace does not know me very well; indeed, I have not yet reached so advanced an age that I resort to such foolishness, for, God be praised, I still have my soul in my body, and all my teeth and molars in my mouth except for a few that were taken by the catarrh, which is so common in this land of Aragón. But wait for me a moment, your grace, and I shall go out to light my candle and return in an instant to tell you of my cares, as if you were the one to remedy all the cares in the world."

And without waiting for a reply, she left the room, where Don Quixote remained, calm and pensive, waiting for her; but then he had a thousand thoughts regarding this new adventure, and it seemed to him that he had behaved incorrectly and shown worse judgment by placing himself in danger of breaking the faith he had promised his lady, and he said to himself:

"Who knows if the devil, who is subtle and cunning, wants to deceive me now with a duenna when he has failed with empresses, queens, duchesses, marquises, and countesses? For I have often heard it said by many wise men that, if he can, he will give you a snub-nosed woman rather than one with an aquiline nose. And who knows whether this solitude, this opportunity, this silence, will awaken my sleeping desires and cause me, at this advanced age, to fall where I never have stumbled? In cases like this, it is better to flee than to wait for the battle. But I cannot be in my right mind, saying and thinking such nonsense, for it is not possible for a duenna in long white veils and spectacles to provoke or stimulate lascivious thoughts in the world's most susceptible bosom. Can there be a duenna on earth whose flesh is chaste? Can there be a duenna on the planet who is not insolent, affected, and pretentious? Be gone, then, duennaesque horde, useless for any human pleasures! Oh, how wise the lady who, they say, had two figures of duennas with their spectacles and pincushions, as if they were doing needlework, at the end of her drawing room couch, and the statues did as much for the authority of the room as real duennas did!"

And saying this, he leaped out of bed, intending to close the door and not allow Señora Rodríguez to enter, but as he was about to close it, Señora Rodríguez returned, holding a lighted candle of white wax, and when she saw Don Quixote more closely, wrapped in the bedspread, with his bandages and his cap or beretta, she became afraid again, took two steps backward, and said:

"Is my safety assured, Señor Knight? Because I do not take it as a sign of modesty that your grace has gotten out of your bed."

"I could very well ask the same question, Señora," responded Don Quixote, "and so I ask if I shall be safe from assault and violation."

"From whom or to whom, Señor Knight, do you ask for that assurance?" responded the duenna.

"From you and to you," responded Don Quixote, "for I am not marble and you are not bronze, and it is not now ten in the morning but midnight, or even a little later, I imagine, and this is a chamber more hidden and secret than the cave where the traitorous and reckless Aeneas enjoyed the beautiful and compassionate Dido. But give me, Señora, your hand, for I wish no greater assurance than that of my own continence and modesty, and that offered by these most reverend veils."

And having said this, he kissed her right hand and held it in his own, and she did the same, with the same ceremony.

Here Cide Hamete offers an aside and says that, by Mohammed, he would give the better cloak of two that he owns to see them holding and grasping each other as they walked from the door to the bed.

Don Quixote at last got into his bed, and Doña Rodríguez sat in a chair at some distance from the bed, not removing her spectacles or setting down the candle. Don Quixote concealed and hid himself completely, leaving only his face uncovered, and when the two had regained their composure, the first to break the silence was Don Quixote, saying:

"Now, Señora Doña Rodríguez, your grace can reveal and disclose all that is in your troubled heart and care-ridden soul, for it will be heard by my chaste ears and remedied by my compassionate deeds."

"I do believe," responded the duenna, "that from your grace's gallant and pleasing presence one could expect only this Christian response. The fact, then, Señor Don Quixote, is that although your grace sees me sitting in this chair, in the middle of the kingdom of Aragón, and in the dress of an exhausted duenna in decline, I am a native of Asturias de

Oviedo,[1] and my lineage is crossed with many of the best in that province, but my bad luck, and the imprudence of my parents who became impoverished too soon, not knowing how or why, brought me to the court, in Madrid, and for their peace of mind and to avoid greater misfortunes, my parents arranged for me to do needlework in the service of a noblewoman; I want your grace to know that no one has ever outdone me in the hemstitch or needlepoint. My parents left me in service and returned home, and in a few years they left there and must have gone to heaven, because they were very good Catholic Christians. I was an orphan, and dependent on the miserable salary and grudging favors that maids like me receive at court; at this time, without any sort of encouragement from me, a squire of the house fell in love with me, a man somewhat advanced in years, bearded and imposing and, above all, as noble as the king because he was from the mountains.[2] Our courtship was not so secret that it did not come to the attention of my lady, who, to avoid gossip and talk, married us with the approval and blessing of our Holy Mother Roman Catholic Church, and from our marriage a daughter was born, putting an end to what good fortune I had, not because I died in childbirth, for I delivered safely and on time, but because not long afterward my husband died of fright, and if I had time now to tell you about it, I know that your grace would be astounded."

And at this she began to cry very piteously and said:

"Señor Don Quixote, your grace must forgive me, but I cannot help it, because every time I remember my poor husband my eyes fill with tears. Lord save me! With what authority did he carry my lady on the hindquarters of a powerful mule, as black as jet itself! For in those days they did not use coaches or saddles, as they do nowadays, and ladies rode behind their squires. This, at least, I must recount, so that you can see the breeding and manners of my good husband. Just as they were entering Calle Santiago in Madrid, which is rather narrow, a court magistrate, with two bailiffs riding in front of him, was coming out, and as soon as my good squire saw him, he turned the reins of the mule, indicating that he would turn back and accompany him.[3] My lady, who was riding on

---

1. There were, at the time, two Asturian provinces: Asturias de Oviedo and Asturias de Santillana.

2. People from the northern mountains were considered to be noble because, compared to other Spaniards, they had relatively few Jewish or Moorish forebears in their family backgrounds.

3. If one came across a distinguished person in the street, it was a sign of respect (though it more often indicated self-interested flattery) to leave one's own route and accompany him.

the hindquarters of the mule, said in a low voice: 'What are you doing, you miserable wretch? Have you forgotten that I am here?' The magistrate, out of courtesy, pulled on the reins of his horse and said: 'Señor, continue on your way: it is I who should accompany Señora Doña Casilda,' for that was the name of my mistress.

My husband still persisted, with hat in hand, in trying to accompany the magistrate, seeing which my lady, full of anger and rage, took a thick needle, or it might have been a long hairpin, from its case, and stuck him in the back, so that my husband gave a great shout and twisted his body around, knocking my lady to the ground. Two of her lackeys hurried to pick her up, as did the magistrate and the bailiffs; the Guadalajara Gate, I mean the shiftless people loitering there, was in an uproar; my mistress left on foot, and my husband went to the house of a barber, saying that his innards had been pierced right through. My husband's courtesy became the subject of so much talk that boys ran after him in the streets, and for that reason, and because he was somewhat shortsighted, my lady the duchess[4] dismissed him, and I have no doubt that his grief over this is what caused his death. I was left a helpless widow, with a daughter to care for, whose beauty was growing like the ocean foam.

Finally, since I was known for fine needlework, my lady the duchess, who had recently married my lord the duke, offered to bring me, as well as my daughter, to this kingdom of Aragón, where the days passed, and my daughter grew and was endowed with all the graces in the world: she sings like a lark, dances court dances like a lightning flash and country dances like a whirlwind, reads and writes like a schoolmaster, and counts like a miser. I say nothing about her purity: running water is not purer, and now, if I remember correctly, she must be sixteen years, five months, and three days old, give or take a few.

In short, the son of a very rich farmer who lives in a village not very far from here, which belongs to my lord the duke, fell in love with my girl. The fact is that I don't know how it happened, but they met, and promising to be her husband, he deceived my daughter, and now he refuses to keep his word; even though my lord the duke knows about it, because I myself have complained to him not once, but many times, and have asked him to order the farmer to marry my daughter, he ignores me and doesn't want to listen to me, and the reason is that since the se-

4. Since there was no earlier indication of the lady's rank, Martín de Riquer believes that the printer confused this noblewoman with Doña Rodríguez's current employer.

ducer's father is so rich and lends him money, and sometimes stands as his guarantor when he gets into difficulties, he doesn't want to anger or trouble him in any way.

And so, Señor, I would like your grace to take responsibility for righting this wrong, either by persuasion or by arms, for according to what everyone says, your grace was born into this world to redress grievances and right wrongs and come to the aid of those in need; your grace should keep in mind that my daughter is an orphan, and well-bred, and young, and possessed of all those gifts that I have mentioned to you, for by God and my conscience, of all the maidens that my mistress has, there is none that can even touch the sole of her shoe, and the one they call Altisidora, the one they consider the most elegant and spirited, can't come within two leagues of my daughter. Because I want your grace to know, Señor, that all that glitters is not gold; this little Altisidora has more vanity than beauty, and more spirit than modesty, and besides, she's not very healthy: she has breath so foul that you can't bear to be near her even for a moment. And then, my lady the duchess . . . But I'd better be quiet, because they say that the walls have ears."

"By my life, what is wrong with my lady the duchess, Señora Doña Rodríguez?" asked Don Quixote.

"With that oath," responded the duenna, "I must respond truthfully to what I have been asked. Señor Don Quixote, has your grace seen the beauty of my lady the duchess, her complexion that resembles a smooth and burnished sword, her two cheeks of milk and carmine, the sun glowing on one and the moon on the other, and the elegance with which she treads, even scorns, the ground, so that it looks as if she were scattering health and well-being wherever she goes? Well, your grace should know that for this she can thank God, first of all, and then the two issues[5] she has on her legs, which drain the bad humors that the doctors say fill her body."

"Holy Mary!" said Don Quixote. "Is it possible that my lady the duchess has those drains? I would not believe it if discalced friars told me so, but since Señora Rodríguez says it, it must be true. But from such issues in such places there must flow not humors but liquid amber. Truly, now I believe that this incising of issues must be important for one's health."

As soon as Don Quixote had finished saying this, the doors of his room banged open, and Doña Rodríguez was so startled that the candle

---

5. An incision cut into the body to allow the discharge of harmful substances.

dropped from her hand, and the room was left like the inside of a wolf's mouth, as the saying goes. Then the poor duenna felt her throat grasped so tightly by two hands that she could not cry out, and another person, with great speed, and without saying a word, raised her skirts, and with what appeared to be a slipper began to give her so many blows that it was pitiful; although Don Quixote was near her, he did not move from the bed, and he did not know what it could be, and he remained still and quiet, even fearing that the thrashing and the blows might be turned on him. And his was not an idle fear, for when they had left the duenna bruised and battered—she did not dare even to moan—the silent scourgers turned on Don Quixote and, stripping him of the sheet and bedspread, pinched him so hard and so often that he could not help but defend himself with his fists, all of this in the most remarkable silence. The battle lasted almost half an hour; the phantoms left, Doña Rodríguez picked up her skirts, and, groaning over her misfortune, went out the door without saying a word to Don Quixote, who, sorrowful and pinched, confused and thoughtful, was left alone, where we shall leave him, desiring to know which perverse enchanter had done this to him. But that will be told in due course, for Sancho Panza is calling us, and the harmonious order of the history requires that we respond.

CHAPTER XLIX

Regarding what befell Sancho Panza as he patrolled his ínsula

We left the great governor angry and annoyed at the sly painter of a farmer who had been instructed by the steward, and the steward by the duke, to ridicule Sancho; but he stood his ground with all of them even though he was foolish, unpolished, and plump, and he said to those who were with him, and to Dr. Pedro Recio, who had come back into the room once the secret matter of the duke's letter was concluded:

"Now I can really understand that judges and governors must be, or should be, made of bronze so they won't feel the demands of petitioners, who at all hours and in every season want them to listen and attend only to their petitions, and to take care of them come what may; and if the poor judge doesn't listen to them and take care of them, either because he can't or because it isn't the time set aside for giving audiences, then they curse him and slander him and gnaw at his bones and even have things to say about his family. Foolish, thoughtless petitioner, don't be in a hurry; wait for the right time and occasion to make your petition; don't come when it's time to eat or sleep, for judges are flesh and blood, and they must give to their natures what they naturally demand, except for me; I don't give mine anything to eat, thanks to our Dr. Pedro Recio Tirteafuera, here present, who wants me to die of hunger, and who claims that this kind of death is life; may God grant the same to him and to all those of his kind: I mean bad doctors; the good ones deserve palms and laurels."

All who knew Sancho Panza were amazed to hear him speak so elegantly, and they did not know how to account for it except for the fact that serious offices and responsibilities either strengthen the mind or make it torpid. Finally, Dr. Pedro Recio de Agüero de Tirteafuera promised to give him supper that night, even if that exceeded all the aphorisms of Hippocrates. This made the governor happy, and he waited very impatiently for night and the supper hour to arrive, and although time, it seemed to him, stood still, not moving from the spot, yet the longed-for moment arrived, and for supper he was served a *salpicón*[1] of beef with onion, and some stewed calves' feet that were a little past their prime. He gave himself up to all of it with more pleasure than if they had served him partridges from Milan, pheasants from Rome, veal from Sorrento, quail from Morón, or geese from Lavajos, and during his supper he turned to the doctor and said:

"Look, Señor Doctor, from now on don't bother about giving me delicate or exquisite things to eat, because that will drive my stomach out of its mind: it's used to goat, beef, bacon, dried meat, turnips, and onions, and if by some chance it's given palace dishes, it gets finicky, and sometimes even sick. What the butler can do is bring me what are called *ollas podridas*,[2] and the more rotten they are, the better they smell, and he can pack them and fill them with anything he likes as long as it's food, and I'll thank him for it and repay him someday; but don't let anybody try to trick me, because we either are or we aren't: let's all live and eat in peace and good friendship, because when God sends the dawn, it's dawn for

---

1. A dish of chopped meat flavored with salt, pepper, vinegar, onion, and sometimes oil and anchovies.

2. As indicated earlier, this is a traditional Spanish stew; *podrida* literally means "rotten" or "putrid."

everybody. I'll govern this ínsula without forsaking the law or taking a bribe, and let everybody keep his eyes open and tend to his own affairs, because I want you to know that the devil makes trouble everywhere, and if you give me a chance, you'll see marvels. And if you turn into honey, the flies will eat you."

"Certainly, Señor Governor," said the butler, "your grace is correct in everything you have said, and I offer, in the name of all the insulanos of this ínsula, to serve your grace with all promptness, love, and benevolence, because the gentle form of governing that your grace has shown from the very beginning does not allow us to do or think anything that would redound to your grace's disservice."

"I believe that," responded Sancho, "and they would be fools if they did or thought anything else. And I say again that care should be taken with my feeding and the feeding of my donkey, which is what matters and is most important in this business; when it's time we'll go on patrol, for it's my intention to clear this ínsula of all kinds of filth, as well as people who are vagrants, idlers, and sluggards, because I want you to know, my friends, that shiftless, lazy people are to the nation what drones are to the hive: they eat the honey that the worker bees produce. I intend to favor those who labor, maintain the privileges of the gentry, reward the virtuous, and, above all, respect religion and the honor of the clergy. What do you think of this, my friends? Have I just said something or am I racking my brains for nothing?"

"Your grace has said so much, Señor Governor," said the steward, "that I'm amazed to see a man as unlettered as your grace, who, I believe, has no letters at all, saying so many things full of wisdom and good counsel, far beyond what was expected of your grace's intelligence by those who sent us here and by those who came here with you. Every day we see new things in the world: deceptions become the truth, and deceivers find themselves deceived."

Night arrived, and the governor had supper with the permission of Dr. Recio. They prepared to go on patrol, and the governor went out with the steward, the secretary, the butler, the chronicler who was charged with recording his deeds, and so many bailiffs and scribes they could have formed a medium-size squadron. Sancho was in the middle of it, holding his staff, and it was a sight to see, and when they had gone down a few streets they heard sounds of a dispute. They hurried to the spot and found only two men fighting; seeing the law approach, the men stood still, and one of them said:

"Here, over here, in the name of God and the king! How can you allow people to be robbed in the middle of town and assaulted in the middle of the street?"

"Calm down, my good man," said Sancho, "and tell me the reason for this fighting, for I am the governor."

The other man said:

"Señor Governor, I'll tell you as briefly as I can. Your grace should know that this gentleman has just won more than a thousand *reales* in the gambling house across the way, God knows how; I happened to be present, and going against the dictates of my conscience, I judged more than one doubtful play in his favor; he left the game with his winnings, and though I expected him to give me at least an *escudo* as a tip, which is usual and customary for important men like me, who determine if things have been done well or badly, and confirm if there has been an injustice, and avoid disputes, he put his money in his pocket and left the house. I came after him, indignant, and with kind and courteous words I asked him to give me even eight *reales*, for he knows I'm an honorable man and have no money and no work because my parents didn't leave me anything or teach me a trade, and this scoundrel, who's a bigger thief than Cacus and a bigger cheat than Andradilla,[3] didn't want to give me more than four *reales*, and now your grace can see, Señor Governor, how little shame he has, and how little conscience! By my faith, if your grace hadn't come by, I would have made him give up his winnings and taught him a good lesson."

"What do you say to this?" asked Sancho.

And the other man responded that what his adversary said was true: he had not wanted to give him more than four *reales* because he had given him that amount many times, and those who expect a tip have to be well-mannered and take what is given to them with a smile, and not demand explanations from the winners unless they know for certain that they are cheats and their winnings are ill-gotten gains; and as a sign that he was an honest man and not a thief, as the other man said, there was no better proof than his not wanting to give him anything, because cheats always have to pay tribute to the onlookers who know them.

"That's true," said the steward. "Señor Governor, your grace will have to decide what ought to be done with these men."

"What ought to be done is this," responded Sancho. "You, the win-

---

3. The identity of Andradilla is not known. A note in Shelton's translation identifies him as "Some famous cheater in Spain," but, as Martín de Riquer says, this clarifies nothing.

ner, good, bad, or indifferent, must give your opponent a hundred *reales*, and another thirty to the poor men in prison; and you who have no money and no work and are not needed on this ínsula, take the hundred *reales* and leave this ínsula by tomorrow; you're banished for ten years, and if you come back before then, you'll finish your sentence in the next life, because I'll hang you from the gallows, or at least the hangman will, on my orders; and let no one reply or he'll feel my hand."

One man paid, the other received, the latter left the ínsula, the former went home, and the governor remained, saying:

"Now, either I'm mistaken or I'm going to close down these gambling houses, because it seems clear to me that they're very harmful."

"Your grace won't be able to close down this one, at least," said a scribe, "because it's owned by a very important person, and what he loses every year at cards is incomparably more than what he wins. Your grace can show your power against other gambling dens of less distinction, which are the ones that do more harm and harbor more outrages; in the houses of highborn gentlemen and nobles, the notorious cheats don't dare to use their tricks, and since the vice of gambling has become so widespread, it's better to gamble in distinguished houses than in those of workmen, where they keep a poor wretch for half the night and skin him alive."

"Now, Scribe," said Sancho, "I know there's a lot to say about this."

At that moment a constable came up to them, holding a young man, and he said:

"Señor Governor, this lad was coming toward us, and as soon as he saw that we were the law, he turned his back and began to run like a deer, a sign that he must be a criminal. I went after him, and if he hadn't tripped and fallen, I never would have caught him."

"Why were you running away?" asked Sancho.

To which the young man responded:

"Señor, to avoid answering all the questions that constables ask."

"What's your trade?"

"A weaver."

"And what do you weave?"

"The iron tips of lances, with your grace's kind permission."

"Are you being funny with me? Are you proud of being a joker? Fine! Where were you going now?"

"Señor, to take the air."

"And where do you take the air on this ínsula?"

"Wherever it blows."

"Good: your answers are right to the point! You're clever, boy, but you should know that I'm the air, and I'm blowing at your back and sending you to prison. You there, seize him and take him away, and I'll make him sleep without any air tonight!"

"By God!" said the young man. "Your grace will make me sleep in prison when you make me king!"

"And why can't I make you sleep in prison?" responded Sancho. "Don't I have the power to arrest you and let you go whenever I want to?"

"No matter how much power your grace has," said the young man, "it won't be enough to make me sleep in prison."

"You think so?" replied Sancho. "Take him right now to the place where he'll see the truth with his own eyes, no matter how much the warden tries to use self-interested generosity with him; I'll fine the warden two thousand *ducados* if he lets you take one step out of prison."

"All this is laughable," responded the young man. "The fact is that every man alive today won't make me sleep in prison."

"Tell me, you demon," said Sancho, "do you have an angel who'll take you out and remove the irons that I plan to put on you?"

"Now, Señor Governor," the young man responded with great charm, "let's use our reason and come to the point. Suppose, your grace, that you order me taken to prison, and there I'm put in irons and chains, and placed in a cell, and the warden will suffer great penalties if he lets me out, and he obeys every order you give him; even so, if I don't want to sleep, and stay awake the whole night without closing my eyes, is all your grace's power enough to make me sleep if I don't want to?"

"No, of course not," said the secretary, "and the man has proven his point."

"Which means," said Sancho, "that you wouldn't sleep simply because it's your will not to, not because you want to go against mine."

"No, Señor," said the young man, "I wouldn't dream of that."

"Well then," said Sancho, "go with God back to your house to sleep, and may God give you a sound sleep, for I don't want to rob you of that, but I do advise that from now on you don't mock the law because you may come across a constable who'll take the joke out of your hide."

The young man left, and the governor continued on his patrol, and in a little while two constables came along holding a man, and they said:

"Señor Governor, this person who looks like a man isn't one, she's a woman, and not an ugly one, and she's dressed in men's clothes."

They raised two or three lanterns up to her eyes, and in their light they saw the face of a woman who seemed to be sixteen years old, or perhaps a little older, with her hair caught up in a net of gold-and-green silk, and as beautiful as a thousand pearls. They looked at her from head to toe and saw that she was wearing stockings of scarlet silk, with garters of white taffeta edged in gold and seed pearls; her breeches were green, made of cloth of gold, as was her jacket or loose coat, under which she wore a doublet of a very fine gold-and-white cloth, and her men's shoes were white. On her belt she did not wear a sword but a richly decorated dagger, and on her fingers there were many precious rings. In short, everyone thought the girl was lovely, and no one recognized her, and the residents of the village said they could not think who she might be, and those who were privy to the tricks that were to be played on Sancho were the ones who were most bewildered, because they had not arranged this incident and discovery, and so they were in doubt, waiting to see how the matter would turn out.

Sancho was amazed at the girl's beauty, and he asked her who she was, where she was going, and what had moved her to dress in those clothes. She, her eyes lowered in modesty and shame, responded:

"I cannot, Señor, say publicly what it has been so important for me to keep secret, but I want one thing understood: I am not a thief or a wicked person, but an unfortunate maiden forced by the power of jealousy to break with the decorum owed to modesty."

Hearing this, the steward said to Sancho:

"Señor Governor, have these other people move away so the lady can say whatever she wishes with less embarrassment."

The governor so ordered, and everyone moved away except the steward, the butler, and the secretary. When they were alone, the maiden continued, saying:

"Señores, I am the daughter of Pedro Pérez Mazorca, the tax collector for wool in this village, who often comes to my father's house."

"This doesn't make sense, Señora," said the steward, "because I know Pedro Pérez very well, and I know he has no children, male or female, and besides, you say he's your father and then you add that he often comes to your father's house."

"I noticed that, too," said Sancho.

"Now, Señores, I'm very upset, and I don't know what I'm saying," responded the maiden, "but the truth is that I'm the daughter of Diego de la Llana, whom all of your graces must know."

"Now that makes sense," responded the steward, "for I know Diego de la Llana, and I know he's a distinguished gentleman, and very rich, and that he has a son and a daughter, and since he was widowed there's no one in the entire village who can say he's seen the face of his daughter, for he keeps her so secluded not even the sun can see her; and, even so, the rumor is that she's extremely beautiful."

"That is true," responded the maiden, "and I'm that daughter, and you, Señores, can say now if the rumor about my beauty is false or not, for you have seen me."

And then she began to weep most piteously; seeing this, the secretary leaned toward the butler's ear and said very quietly:

"There can be no doubt that something important has happened to this poor maiden, because in these clothes, and at this hour, and being a gentlewoman, she's not in her house."

"No doubt about it," responded the butler, "and her tears confirm your suspicion."

Sancho consoled her with the best words he knew and asked her to have no fear and tell them what had happened to her, and all of them would attempt very earnestly to remedy it in every way possible.

"The fact is, Señores," she responded, "that my father has kept me secluded for ten years, the same amount of time my mother has been in the ground. At home Mass is said in a magnificent oratory, and in all this time I have not seen more than the sun in the sky during the day, and the moon and stars at night, and I don't know what streets or squares or temples or even men look like, except for my father and a brother of mine, and Pedro Pérez, the tax collector, and because he normally comes to my house, I had the idea of saying he was my father in order not to reveal who mine really is. This seclusion, and my father's refusal to allow me to leave the house, not even to go to church, have made me very unhappy for many long days and months; I would like to see the world, or, at least, the village where I was born, and it seemed to me that this desire did not go against the decorum that wellborn maidens ought to observe. When I heard that people had bullfights and cane fights[4] and put on plays, I asked my brother, who is a year younger than I am, to tell me what those things were, as well as many other things I had not seen; he told me in the best way he could, but this only inflamed my desire to see them. Finally, to shorten the tale of my perdition, I'll say that I begged

4. A battle game played on horseback with canes instead of lances.

and pleaded with my brother, and I wish I never had begged and pleaded
for anything. . . ."

And she began to cry again. The steward said to her:

"Your grace should continue, Señora, and finish telling us what has
happened, for your words and your tears have us all in suspense."

"I have few words left to say," responded the maiden, "but many tears
to weep, because badly placed desires cannot bring any reduction,[5] only
more of the same."

The maiden's beauty had left its mark in the butler's soul, and once
more he raised his lantern in order to see her again, and it seemed to him
she was shedding not tears but seed pearls or the dew on the meadows,
and he exalted them even higher and compared them to Oriental pearls,
and he hoped her misfortune was not as great as her tears and sighs
seemed to indicate. The governor was becoming impatient at the length
of time it took the girl to tell her history, and he told her not to keep
them in suspense any longer, for it was late and they still had a good part
of the town to patrol. She, between interrupted sobs and broken sighs,
said:

"My misfortune and my misery are simply that I asked my brother to
let me dress as a man in some of his clothes, and to take me out one night
to see the village while our father was sleeping; he, besieged by my pleas,
agreed, and he gave me these clothes, and dressed himself in some of
mine, which suited him as if he had been born to them because he
doesn't have a beard yet and looks exactly like a very beautiful maiden;
and tonight, about an hour ago, more or less, we left the house, and
guided by our young and foolish thoughts we walked all around the village; when we wanted to return home we saw a great crowd of people
coming toward us, and my brother said to me: 'Sister, this must be the
patrol: put wings on your feet and run with me so they won't recognize
us, for that will not be in our favor.' And saying this, he turned, and I
won't say he began to run, but to fly; before I had taken six steps I fell, I
was so frightened, and then the officer of the law came and brought me
before your graces, where, because I am wicked and capricious, I find myself shamed before so many people."

"And so, Señora," said Sancho, "no other misfortune has happened
to you, not even the jealousy you mentioned at the beginning of your
story, to bring you out of your house?"

5. It was a commonplace, when people suffered a misfortune, to say that it helped reduce the number of sins they would have to atone for.

"Nothing has happened to me, and jealousy didn't bring me out, but only my desire to see the world, which didn't go beyond seeing the streets of this town."

And the truth of what the maiden had said was confirmed by the arrival of constables holding her brother, whom one of them had overtaken when he ran from his sister. He wore a rich skirt and a shawl of blue damask with fine gold passementerie, and no headdress or any other adornment on his head except for his hair, which was so blond and curly it looked like rings of gold. The governor, the steward, and the butler moved to one side with him, and not letting his sister hear what they were saying, they asked him why he was wearing those clothes, and he, with no less shame and embarrassment, told the same story that his sister had told, which brought great joy to the enamored butler. But the governor said:

"Certainly, Señores, this has been a childish prank, and to tell about this foolishness and daring, there was no need for so many long tears and sighs; just saying, 'We're so-and-so and such-and-such, and we left our father's house in disguise to enjoy ourselves, just out of curiosity, for no other reason,' would have been the end of the story without all that sobbing and weeping and carrying on."

"That's true," responded the maiden, "but your graces should know I was so upset I could not be as brief as I should have been."

"Nothing's been lost," responded Sancho. "Let's go, and we'll leave your graces at your father's house; maybe he hasn't missed you. And from now on don't be so childish, or so eager to see the world; an honorable maiden and a broken leg stay in the house; and a woman and a hen are soon lost when they wander; and a woman who wants to see also wants to be seen. That's all I'll say."

The boy thanked the governor for his kindness in taking them to their house, and so they set out, for it was not very far. When they arrived, the brother tossed a pebble at a jalousied window, and a maid who had been waiting for them came down immediately and opened the door, and they went in, leaving everyone amazed by their gentility and beauty, and by their desire to see the world, at night, and without leaving the village; but they attributed it all to their youth.

The butler's heart had been pierced, and he resolved to go the next day and ask her father for her hand, certain he would not be denied since he was a servant to the duke; and even Sancho had a desire and a wish to marry the boy to his daughter, Sanchica, and he decided to do so when the time came, believing that no husband could be denied the daughter of a governor.

With this the night's patrol ended, and two days later the governorship and with it all his plans were wiped out and destroyed, as we shall see later.

CHAPTER L

Which declares the identities of the enchanters and tormentors who beat the duenna and pinched and scratched Don Quixote, and recounts what befell the page who carried the letter to Teresa Sancha,[1] *the wife of Sancho Panza*

Cide Hamete, that most punctilious observer of the smallest details in this true history, says that at the same time Doña Rodríguez left her room to go to Don Quixote's chamber, another duenna who slept in the same room heard her, and since all duennas are fond of knowing, understanding, and inquiring, she followed her so silently that Doña Rodríguez did not know she was there; and as soon as the duenna saw her go into Don Quixote's chamber, and in order not to fail in the widespread custom of all duennas to be gossips, she went immediately to tell her mistress the duchess that Doña Rodríguez was in Don Quixote's room.

The duchess told the duke and asked his leave to go with Altisidora to see what that duenna wanted with Don Quixote; the duke agreed, and the two women, with very cautious and silent steps, approached the door of his room, and stood so close they could hear everything that was said inside; and when the duchess heard Doña Rodríguez disclose the Aranjuez of her flowing issues,[2] she could not bear it, and neither could Altisidora; and so, filled with rage and longing for vengeance, they burst into the room, and riddled Don Quixote with wounds, and beat the duenna in the manner that has been recounted, because affronts directed against the beauty and vanity of women

---

1. Frequently, among the lower classes, a wife was called by the feminine form of her husband's given name.

2. Aranjuez is a royal palace famous for its fountains; *fuente* is the word for both "fountain" and "issue," which allows the wordplay.

awaken in them an immense anger and kindle their desire to take revenge.

The duchess told the duke what had happened, which he enjoyed hearing very much, and the duchess, moving ahead with her intention of deceiving Don Quixote and deriving pleasure from that, dispatched the page who had played the part of Dulcinea in the performance concerning her disenchantment—which Sancho Panza had forgotten in his preoccupation with governing—to Teresa Panza, his wife, with the letter from her husband, and another from her, as well as a long string of fine corals as a present.

The history tells us, then, that the page was very clever and witty, and, desiring to serve his master and mistress, he left very willingly for Sancho's village; before entering it, he saw a number of women washing clothes in a stream, and he asked them if they could tell him if a woman named Teresa Panza, the wife of a certain Sancho Panza, who was squire to a knight named Don Quixote of La Mancha, lived in that village; and when he had asked the question, a girl who was washing rose to her feet and said:

"Teresa Panza is my mother, and Sancho is my father, and that knight is our master."

"Then come along, my girl," said the page, "and take me to your mother, because I have a letter and a present for her from your father."

"I'll do that very gladly, Señor," responded the girl, who looked about fourteen years old.

And leaving the clothes she was washing with a friend, without covering her head or putting on shoes, though she was barefoot and disheveled, she jumped in front of the page's horse and said:

"Come, your grace, for our house is at the entrance to the village, and my mother is in it, filled with grief because she hasn't heard anything from my father for so many days."

"Well, I'm bringing her news so good," said the page, "that she'll have to give thanks to God for it."

Jumping, running, and leaping, the girl finally reached the village, and before entering her house, she called from the door:

"Come out, Teresa, come out, Mother, come out, come out, because here's a gentleman who's bringing letters and other things from my good father."

At her call, Teresa Panza, her mother, came out, spinning a bunch of flax and wearing a dun-colored skirt so short it looked as if it had been cut to shame her,[3] a bodice that was also dun colored, and a chemise. She was not very old, although she looked over forty, but she was strong, hard, vigorous, and as brown as a hazelnut; and seeing her daughter, and the page on horseback, she said:

"What's this, girl? Who's this gentleman?"

"A servant of my lady Doña Teresa Panza," responded the page.

And having said this, he leaped down from the horse and went very humbly to kneel before Señora Teresa, saying:

"Your grace, give me your hands, my lady Doña Teresa, which you are as the sole legitimate wife of Señor Don Sancho Panza, governor of the ínsula of Barataria."

"Oh, Señor, get up, don't do that," responded Teresa. "I have nothing to do with palaces, I'm a poor peasant, the daughter of a farmer and the wife of a squire errant, not of any governor!"

"Your grace," responded the page, "is most worthy of a most archworthy governor, and to prove this truth, here are a letter and a present for your grace."

And he immediately took from his pocket a string of corals with gold beads and put it around her neck, saying:

"This letter is from my lord the governor, and another letter and these corals are from my lady the duchess, who has sent me to your grace."

Teresa was stunned, and her daughter no less so, and the girl said:

"On my life, our lord and master, Don Quixote, has something to do with this, for he must have given my father the governorship or countship that he promised him so often."

"That's true," responded the page, "and out of respect for Señor Don Quixote, Señor Sancho is now the governor of the ínsula of Barataria, as can be seen in this letter."

"Your grace must read it to me, Señor," said Teresa, "because I know how to spin but can't read a thing."

"Neither can I," added Sanchica, "but wait for me here, and I'll go and find somebody to read it, whether it's the priest himself or Bachelor Sansón Carrasco, and they'll be very happy to come hear news about my father."

"You don't have to find anybody, because I don't know how to spin, but I do know how to read, and I'll read it to you."

3. This was a way of publicly insulting a woman.

And so he read her Sancho's entire letter, and since it has already been cited, it is not set down here, and then he took out another letter, the one from the duchess, and it said:

> *My friend Teresa: The qualities of goodness and wit in your husband, Sancho, moved and obliged me to ask my husband, the duke, to give him the governorship of one of the many ínsulas which he possesses. I have been told that he governs in grand style, which makes me very happy, and of course, the duke my lord, too, for which I give many thanks to heaven that I was not deceived when I chose him for the governorship, because I want Señora Teresa to know that it is difficult to find a good governor in the world, and may God treat me in just the way that Sancho governs.*
>
> *I am sending you, my dear, a string of corals with gold beads; I'd be happy if they were Oriental pearls, but the person who gives you a bone doesn't want to see you dead;*[4] *one day we shall meet and communicate with each other, God knows when that will be. Remember me to your daughter, Sanchica, and tell her for me that she should get ready, because I plan to arrange an excellent marriage for her when she least expects it.*
>
> *I am told that there are fat acorns in your village: send me about two dozen, and I shall esteem them greatly because they come from your hand; write me a long letter informing me of your health and well-being; if you happen to need anything, you only have to say the word, and your word will be heeded. May God keep you. From this place.*
>
> *Your friend who loves you,*
The Duchess

"O," said Teresa when she heard the letter, "what a good and straightforward and humble lady! Let them bury me with ladies like these and not the gentlewomen we have in this village who think that because they're wellborn the wind shouldn't touch them, and who go to church with all the airs of queens, and seem to think it's a dishonor to look at a peasant woman; and you can see here where this good lady, even though she's a duchess, calls me her friend and treats me like an equal, and may I see her equal to the highest belltower in all of La Mancha. And as for the acorns, Señor, I'll send her ladyship a *celemín*[5] of ones so fat that people will come just to look at them. And for now, Sanchica, look after this

---

4. A saying that seems to mean "A person cannot do more than give you what he has."

5. A Castilian dry measure, approximately 4.6 liters and roughly equivalent to a peck.

gentleman: take care of his horse, and get some eggs from the stable, and cut plenty of bacon, and let's feed him like a prince; he deserves it for the good news he's brought us and for that nice face of his; in the meantime, I'll go out and tell the news about our luck to my neighbors and to the reverend priest and Master Nicolás, the barber, who are and have been such good friends of your father's."

"I will, Mother," responded Sanchica, "but look, you have to give me half of that necklace, because I don't think my lady the duchess is so foolish as to send the whole thing to you."

"It's all for you, daughter," responded Teresa, "but let me wear it around my neck for a few days, because it really seems to bring joy to my heart."

"You'll both feel joy," said the page, "when you see the package that's in this portmanteau; it's a suit of very fine cloth that the governor wore to the hunt only once, and he's sent all of it for Señora Sanchica."

"May he live a thousand years," responded Sanchica, "and the man who brings it not a year less, even two thousand, if that's necessary."

Then Teresa left the house, carrying the letters and wearing the necklace around her neck, and she drummed on the letters with her fingers as if they were tambourines, and when she happened to meet the priest and Sansón Carrasco, she began to dance, saying:

"By my faith, we're not poor relations anymore! We have a nice little governorship! And if the proudest of the gentlewomen tries to snub me now, I'll know how to put her in her place!"

"What is this, Teresa Panza? What madness is this, and what papers are those?"

"The only madness is that these are letters from duchesses and governors, and these things I'm wearing around my neck are fine corals, and the Hail Marys and Our Fathers are of beaten gold, and I'm a governor's wife."

"As God's in heaven we don't understand you, Teresa, and we don't know what you are talking about."

"You can see it here," responded Teresa.

And she handed them the letters. The priest read them aloud so that Sansón Carrasco could hear, and Sansón and the priest looked at each other as if amazed at what they had read, and the bachelor asked who had brought the letters. Teresa responded that if they came home with her, they would see the messenger, a handsome, well-mannered boy who had brought another present that was worth a good deal. The priest took the corals from around her neck and looked at them, and looked at them again, and being convinced of their value, he was amazed all over again and said:

"By the habit I wear, I don't know what to say or think about these letters and these gifts: on the one hand, I can see and touch the fineness of these corals, and on the other, I read that a duchess sends a request for two dozen acorns."

"It's ludicrous!" said Carrasco. "Let's go and see the messenger; he'll explain the things that perplex us."

They did, and Teresa returned with them. They found the page sifting some barley for his horse, and Sanchica cutting slices of bacon that she would cover with eggs and give to the page, whose bearing and grace pleased both men very much; after they had exchanged courteous greetings, Sansón asked him for news of Don Quixote as well as Sancho Panza, for although they had read the letters from Sancho and my lady the duchess, they were still confused and could not really grasp Sancho's governorship, especially of an ínsula, since all or most of the islands in the Mediterranean belonged to His Majesty. To which the page responded:

"Señor Sancho Panza is a governor, of that there can be no doubt; whether what he governs is an ínsula or not does not concern me, but it's enough to know that it's a place with more than a thousand residents; as for the acorns, I can say that my lady the duchess is so straightforward and humble," he said, "that she not only would send a request to a peasant for some acorns, but has on occasion asked to borrow a comb from a neighbor. Because I want your graces to know that the ladies of Aragón are as highborn but not as punctilious and haughty as Castilian ladies; they are simpler in their dealings with people."

While they were engaged in this conversation, Sanchica interrupted, her skirt filled with eggs, and asked the page:

"Tell me, Señor: does my father happen to wear full-length breeches since he's been governor?"

"I haven't noticed," responded the page, "but he probably does."

"O, God!" replied Sanchica. "How I'd like to see my father wearing them! Can you believe that since I was born I've wanted to see my father in those full-length breeches?"

"Well, your grace will see him wearing those things if you live," responded the page. "By God, if his governorship lasts two months, he'll even be wearing a cap for cold weather."

The priest and the bachelor saw clearly enough that the page was speaking sarcastically, but the fine quality of the corals and the hunting outfit that Sancho sent had the opposite effect, for Teresa had already shown them the clothing. And they could not help laughing at Sanchica's desire, especially when Teresa said:

"Señor Priest, keep your eyes open and see if anybody's going to Madrid or Toledo who can buy me a hooped skirt, nice and round and just the way it should be, right in fashion and the best quality, because the real truth is I have to honor my husband's governorship as much as I can, and even if it's a bother I have to go to that court and get a carriage like all the other ladies, because a woman who has a governor for a husband can easily buy and keep one."

"That's right, Mother!" said Sanchica. "Please God, it'll be today and not tomorrow, even though people who see me sitting next to my lady mother in that carriage will say: 'Just look at her, daughter of a garlic eater, sitting and leaning back in the carriage as if she were the pope!' But they can walk in the mud, and I'll go in my carriage with my feet off the ground. A bad year and a bad month to all the gossips in the world, and as long as I'm warm, people can laugh all they want! Am I right, Mother?"

"O daughter, you certainly are right!" responded Teresa. "And all of this good fortune, and some even greater than this, my good Sancho predicted for me, and you'll see, daughter, how he doesn't stop until he makes me a countess; it's all a matter of starting to be lucky; and I've heard your good father say very often—and he loves proverbs as much as he loves you—that when they give you the calf, run over with the rope; when they give you a governorship, take it; when they give you a countship, hold on to it tight, and when they call you over with a nice present, pack it away. Or else just sleep and don't answer when fortune and good luck come knocking at your door!"

"And what difference does it make to me," added Sanchica, "if they say when they see me so proud and haughty: 'The dog in linen breeches . . .'[6] and all the rest?"

Hearing this, the priest said:

"I can't help thinking that everyone in the Panza family was born with a sack of proverbs inside; I've never seen one of them who isn't always scattering proverbs around in every conversation they have."

6. ". . . says how crude, how crude," a proverb aimed at the poor who prosper and then scorn their old friends.

"That's true," said the page, "for Señor Governor Sancho says them all the time, and even though many are not to the point, they still give pleasure, and my lady the duchess and my lord the duke praise them a good deal."

"Then, Señor, does your grace still affirm that Sancho's governorship is true, and that there is a duchess in the world who sends his wife presents and writes to her? Because we, although we touched the presents and read the letters, don't believe it, and we think this is one of those things that concern our compatriot Don Quixote, who thinks they are all done by enchantment; and so, I'm ready to say that I want to touch and feel your grace to see if you are an imagined emissary or a man of flesh and blood."

"Señores, all I know," responded the page, "is that I am a true emissary, and Señor Sancho Panza is a real governor, and my master and mistress the duke and duchess can give, and have given him, the governorship, and I've heard that in it Sancho Panza is performing valiantly; whether or not there's enchantment in this is something your graces can argue among yourselves, because I don't know any more than this, and I swear to that on the lives of my parents, who are still living and whom I love and cherish very much."

"That may well be true," replied the bachelor, "but *dubitat Augustinus*."[7]

"No matter who doubts it," responded the page, "the truth is what I have said, and truth will always rise above a lie, as oil rises above water; and if not, *operibus credite, et non verbis:*[8] one of your graces should come with me, and you'll see with your own eyes what your ears don't believe."

"I should be the one to go," said Sanchica. "Señor, your grace can let me ride on the horse's hindquarters, because I'd be very happy to see my father."

"The daughters of governors should not travel the roads unescorted but should be accompanied by coaches and litters and a large number of servants."

"By God," responded Sancha, "I can ride a donkey as well as a coach. You must think I'm very hard to please!"

"Be quiet, girl," said Teresa. "You don't know what you're saying, and this gentleman is right; time changes the rhyme: when it's Sancho, it's

7. "St. Augustine places that in doubt," a phrase used by students in doctrinal controversies.

8. A phrase quoted in chapter XXV; it is based on John 10:38: ". . . though ye believe not me, believe the works."

Sancha, and when it's governor, it's Señora, and I don't know if I'm saying something or not."

"Señora Teresa is saying more than she thinks," said the page. "Give
me something to eat and then send me away, because I plan to go back
this afternoon."

To which the priest said:

"Your grace will come and do penance with me,[9] for Señora Teresa
has more desire than provisions for serving so worthy a guest."

The page refused, but then he had to concede, to his own advantage,
and the priest took him home very gladly, for it meant he would have the
opportunity to ask at his leisure about Don Quixote and his exploits.

The bachelor offered to write replies to her letters, but Teresa did not
want the bachelor involved in her affairs because she thought he was
something of a trickster, and so she gave a roll and two eggs to an altar
boy who knew how to write, and he wrote two letters, one for her husband and the other for the duchess, which she herself dictated, and they
are not the worst letters that appear in this great history, as we shall see
further on.

CHAPTER LI

Regarding the progress of Sancho Panza's governorship, and other matters of
comparable interest

The day following the night of the governor's patrol dawned, and for the
butler it was a sleepless night because his thoughts were filled with the
face, elegance, and beauty of the maiden in disguise; the steward used
what remained of the night to write to his master and mistress regarding
what Sancho Panza had done and said, and he was astonished by his
deeds and speech because his words and actions indicated an extraordinary mixture of intelligence and foolishness.

Finally the governor awoke, and by order of Dr. Pedro Recio his
breakfast consisted of a small amount of preserves and four swallows of

9. A courteous formula for inviting someone to eat with you.

cold water, which Sancho would have exchanged for a piece of bread and a bunch of grapes; but seeing that this was more a matter of coercion than choice, he accepted it with a sorrowful heart and a troubled stomach, while Pedro Recio tried to persuade him that very small amounts of delicate food would enliven his wits, something that was necessary for persons occupying high positions of authority in which one must use the strength not so much of the body as of the mind.

Because of this sophistry, Sancho suffered so much hunger that he secretly cursed the governorship, and even the one who had given it to him, but with his hunger and his preserves he began to judge that day's cases, the steward and the rest of the acolytes being present, and the first was an enigma presented to him by a stranger, who said:

"Señor, a very large river divided a lord's lands into two parts (and your grace should pay close attention, because the case is important and somewhat complicated). I say, then, that a bridge crossed this river, and at the end of it was a gallows and a kind of tribunal hall in which there were ordinarily four judges who applied the law set down by the owner of the river, the bridge, and the lands, which was as follows: 'If anyone crosses this bridge from one side to the other, he must first take an oath as to where he is going and why; and if he swears the truth, let him pass; and if he tells a lie, let him die by hanging on the gallows displayed there, with no chance of pardon.' Knowing this law and its rigorous conditions, many people crossed the bridge, and then, when it was clear that what they swore was true, the judges let them pass freely. It so happened, then, that a man once took the oath, and he swore and said that because of the oath he was going to die on the gallows, and he swore to nothing else. The judges studied the oath and said: 'If we allow this man to pass freely, he lied in his oath, and according to the law he must die; and if we hang him, he swore that he was going to die on this gallows, and having sworn the truth, according to the same law he must go free.' Señor Governor, the question for your grace is what should the judges do with the man, for they are still doubtful and undecided. And having heard of your grace's acute and elevated understanding, I have been sent to entreat your grace on their behalf to give your opinion regarding a case that is so intricate and confusing."

To which Sancho responded:

"Certainly those judges who sent you to me could have saved themselves the trouble, because I'm more of a dullard than a shrewd man, but even so, tell me this business again so I understand it; then maybe I'll figure it out."

The questioner repeated what he had said earlier, and then Sancho said:

"It seems to me I can pass judgment on this case in the blink of an eye, and it's this: the man swears he's going to die on the gallows, and if he dies there, his oath was true and by law he deserves to be free and cross over the bridge; and if they don't hang him, his oath was false, and by the same law he deserves to be hanged."

"It is just as your grace says, Señor Governor," said the messenger, "and as for the completeness of your understanding, there can be no question or doubt about that."

"Well then, I'll say now," replied Sancho, "that they let the part of the man that swore the truth pass freely, and hang the part that told a lie, and in this way the conditions for passing will be satisfied to the letter."

"But, Señor Governor," replied the questioner, "it will be necessary for the man to be divided into two parts, the lying part and the truthful, and if he is divided, of necessity he will die, and then nothing that the law demands is fulfilled, and it is an express obligation that it be obeyed."

"Come here, my good man," responded Sancho. "This traveler you've described, either I'm a fool or there's as much reason for him to die as to live and cross over the bridge, because just as the truth saves him, the lie condemns him; if this is so, and it is, it's my opinion that you should tell those gentlemen who sent you to me that since the reasons for condemning him or sparing him are balanced perfectly, they should let him pass freely, for doing good is always more praiseworthy than doing evil, and I'd sign this with my own name if I knew how to write, and in this case I haven't said my own idea but a precept that came to mind, one of many that was given to me by my master, Don Quixote, the night before I came to be governor of this ínsula, and it was that when the law is in doubt, I should favor and embrace mercy; it was God's will that I remembered it now, since it fits this case exactly."

"That's true," responded the steward, "and in my opinion Lycurgus himself, who gave laws to the Lacedaemonians, could not have made a better judgment than the one the great Panza has given. And with this let the court close for the morning, and I will give orders for the governor to have food that he likes for dinner."

"That's all I ask, and no tricks," said Sancho. "Give me something to eat, and let cases and doubts rain down on me, and I'll take care of them in midair."

The steward kept his word, for it seemed to him a matter of conscience not to starve to death so intelligent a governor; besides, he intended to be finished with him that night, when he would play the final trick on him that he had been commissioned to perform.

So it happened that when the governor, having eaten that day in defiance of all the rules and aphorisms of Dr. Tirteafuera, stood up from the table, a courier came in with a letter from Don Quixote. Sancho ordered the secretary to read it to himself and, if there was nothing in it that had to be kept secret, to then read it aloud. The secretary did so, and having first examined it, he said:

"It can certainly be read aloud, for what Señor Don Quixote writes to your grace deserves to be inscribed and written in letters of gold, and this is what it says:

LETTER FROM DON QUIXOTE OF LA MANCHA TO SANCHO PANZA,
GOVERNOR OF THE ÍNSULA BARATARIA

When I expected to hear news of your negligence and impertinence, Sancho my friend, I have heard about your intelligence, for which I gave special thanks to heaven, which can raise the poor from the dungheap, and make wise men out of fools. They tell me that you govern as if you were a man, and that you are a man as if you were an animal, so humbly do you behave; and I want you to be aware, Sancho, that many times it is proper and necessary, because of the authority of one's position, to contravene the humility of one's heart, because the admirable qualities in the person who holds high office ought to conform to the demands of the office, not the measures to which his humble state inclines him. Dress well, for a neatly decorated stick does not seem to be a stick at all. I do not say that you should wear jewels and finery, or, being a judge, that you should dress as a soldier, but only that you should wear the clothing your office requires, as long as it is clean and neat.

To win the good will of the people you govern, you must do two things, among others: one is to be civil to everyone, although this is something I have already told you, and the other is to attempt to provide them with the necessities of life, for there is nothing that troubles the heart of the poor more than hunger and need.

Do not issue many edicts, and if you do, try to make them good ones, and, above all, ones that are carried out and obeyed; for edicts that are not carried out are as good as nonexistent, and they let it be known that the prince who had the intelligence and authority to issue them did not have the courage to enforce them; laws that intimidate but are not enforced become like the log that was king of the frogs: at first it frightened them, but in time they came to despise it and climbed up on it.

Be a father to virtues and a stepfather to vices. Do not always be severe, or always mild, but choose the middle way between those two extremes; this is the object of wisdom. Visit the prisons, the slaughterhouses, and the market squares, for the presence of the governor in these places is of great importance: it consoles the prisoners, who can hope for a quick release; it frightens the butchers, who then make their weights honest; it terrifies the marketwomen, and for the same reason. Do not show yourself to be, even if you are—which I do not believe—a greedy man, a womanizer, or a glutton, because if the people and those who deal with you learn your specific inclination, that is where they will attack until they throw you down to the depths of perdition.

Look at and examine, consider and review the advice and precepts I gave to you in writing before you left here for your governorship, and you will see that you can find in them, if you follow them, something to help you bear the trials and difficulties that governors constantly encounter. Write to your lord and lady and show them that you are grateful, for ingratitude is the daughter of pride and one of the greatest sins we know, while the person who is grateful to those who have granted him benefits indicates that he will also be grateful to God, who has granted and continues to grant him so many.

My lady the duchess dispatched a messenger with your hunting outfit and another present to your wife, Teresa Panza; we expect a reply at any moment.

I have been somewhat indisposed by a certain clawing that happened at the expense of my nose, but it was nothing, for if there are enchanters who mistreat me, there are also those who defend me.

Tell me if the steward who is with you had anything to do with the actions of Countess Trifaldi, as you suspected, and also tell me about everything that happens to you, for the distance is not very great; further, I intend to leave this life of leisure very soon, for I was not born to be idle.

A matter has been presented to me that I believe will discredit me with the duke and duchess, but although it concerns me a great deal, at the same time it does not concern me at all, for, in the end, I must comply with my profession rather than with their desires; as the saying goes: Amicus Plato, sed magis amica veritas.[1] *I say this to you in Latin because I assume you must have learned it after you became a governor. May God be with you so that no one need feel sorry for you.*

Your friend,
DON QUIXOTE OF LA MANCHA

Sancho listened very attentively to the letter, and it was considered and held to be very wise by all who heard it; then Sancho got up from the table, called the secretary, went with him to his room, and without further delay wished to respond immediately to his master Don Quixote; and he told the secretary that without adding or taking away anything, he was to write down what he dictated, and the secretary did; the letter of reply said the following:

LETTER FROM SANCHO PANZA TO DON QUIXOTE OF LA MANCHA

I've been so busy with my affairs that I don't have time to scratch my head or even to cut my nails, and so I'm wearing them too long, God help me. I say this, dear master of my soul, so that your grace won't be surprised that I haven't told you anything until now about whether I'm faring well or badly in this governorship, where I'm hungrier than when the two of us were wandering through the forests and the wild places.

My lord the duke wrote to me the other day, saying that certain spies had entered the ínsula to kill me, and so far I haven't discovered any except for a certain doctor who is in this place on salary to kill all the governors who come here: his name is Dr. Pedro Recio, and he comes from Tirteafuera, and now your grace can see what a name he has and whether or not I should be afraid of dying at his hands! And this doctor says about himself that he doesn't cure diseases when they've arrived but prevents them so they won't come, and the medicines he uses are diet and more diet until the person's nothing but skin and bones, as if being skinny weren't a worse ailment than having a fever. In short, he's starving me to death, and I'm dying of despair because I thought I'd come to this governorship and have hot food and cold drinks, and please my body with linen sheets and featherbeds, but I've come to do penance, like a hermit, and since I'm not doing it willingly, I think the devil will take me in the end.

So far I haven't touched a fee or taken a bribe, and I can't think what it

---

1. "Be a friend to Plato, but a better friend to the truth."

means because they've told me here that people give or lend a good deal of money to the governors who usually come to this ínsula, even before they arrive, and that this is common practice for everybody who takes a governorship, not only this one.

Last night, when I was on patrol, I came across a very beautiful maiden in a man's clothes, and her brother who was dressed as a woman; my butler fell in love with the girl and chose her in his mind to be his wife, according to what he has told me, and I chose the boy to be my son-in-law; today we'll put our thoughts into practice with their father, whose name is Diego de la Llana, a gentleman and as old a Christian as you could wish.

I visit the market squares, as your grace advises, and yesterday I found a marketwoman who was selling fresh hazelnuts, and I saw that she had mixed a fanega[2] of fresh hazelnuts with a fanega of ones that were old, worthless, and rotten; I took them all for the boys in catechism class, who'll know very well how to tell them apart, and I ordered her not to come to the market square for two weeks. People told me it was a good thing to do; what I can tell your grace is that in this village they say there are no people worse than marketwomen, because they're all shameless, hardhearted, and bold, and I believe it because I've seen them in other villages.

I'm very happy that my lady the duchess has written to Teresa Panza, my wife, and sent her the present your grace has mentioned, and I'll try to show my gratitude at the right time: your grace should kiss her hands on my behalf, saying that I say she hasn't thrown anything into a torn sack, as my actions will prove.

I wouldn't want your grace to have any unpleasant disputes with my lord and my lady, because if your grace argues with them, it will obviously harm me, and it wouldn't be right if after you advised me to show gratitude, your grace doesn't show it to those who have granted you so many favors and treated you so well in their castle.

I don't understand what you said about clawing, but I imagine it must be one of the evil villainies that wicked enchanters usually do to you; I'll find out when we see each other.

I'd like to send your grace something, but I don't know what to send, except some very curious tubing for syringes that they make on this ínsula to be used with bladders; though if my position lasts, I'll find something to send to you, one way or another.

If my wife, Teresa Panza, writes to me, would your grace please pay the

---

2. A dry measure roughly equivalent to 1.6 bushels in Spain.

cost and send me the letter, for I long to know the condition of my house, my
wife, and my children. And with this, may God free your grace from the evil
intentions of enchanters, and take me from this governorship safe and sound,
which I doubt, because according to how Dr. Pedro Recio treats me, I don't
think I'll get away with more than my life.

Your grace's servant,
SANCHO PANZA THE GOVERNOR

The secretary sealed the letter and dispatched the courier immediately, and then the men who were deceiving Sancho met and decided how to dispatch him from the governorship; Sancho spent the afternoon issuing some ordinances concerning the good government of what he imagined to be an ínsula, and he ordered that there were to be no speculators in provisions in the nation, and that wine could be imported from anywhere, as long as its place of origin was indicated, so that it could be priced according to its value, quality, and reputation, and whoever watered it or changed its name would lose his life.

He lowered the price of all footwear, especially shoes, because it seemed to him they were sold at an exorbitant price; he put a cap on the salaries of servants, which were galloping unchecked along the road of greed; he imposed very serious penalties on those who sang lewd and lascivious songs, either by night or by day. He ordered that no blind man could sing verses about miracles unless he carried authentic testimonies to their truth, because it seemed to him that most of the ones blind men sang about were false, bringing those that were true into disrepute.

He created and appointed a bailiff for the poor, not to persecute them but to examine them to see if they really were poor, because in the shadow of feigned cripples and false wounds come the strong arms of thieves and very healthy drunkards. In short, he ordained things so good that to this day they are obeyed in that village and are called *The Constitution of the Great Governor Sancho Panza.*

CHAPTER LII

Which recounts the adventure of the second Dolorous, or Anguished, Duenna, also called Doña Rodríguez

Cide Hamete recounts that when Don Quixote's claw marks had healed, it seemed to him that the life he was leading in the castle contradicted the entire order of chivalry that he professed, and so he resolved to ask the permission of the duke and duchess to leave for Zaragoza, whose tourney was fast approaching; there he intended to win the armor that is awarded at the festival.

One day, when he was sitting at the table with the duke and duchess and beginning to put his intention into effect and to ask for their permission, suddenly there came through the door of the great room two women, as they subsequently proved to be, covered in mourning from head to toe, and one of them came up to Don Quixote and threw herself flat on the floor before him, her mouth pressed to his feet, and lamenting with such sad, deep, and dolorous moans that everyone who heard and saw her was thrown into confusion; although the duke and duchess thought it was probably a trick their servants wanted to play on Don Quixote, still, when they saw how earnestly the woman sighed, moaned, and wept, they were uncertain and in suspense, until Don Quixote, filled with compassion, lifted her from the floor and asked her to disclose her identity by removing the veil that hid her weeping face.

She did so, and showed herself to be the last person anyone expected, because she revealed the countenance of the duenna Doña Rodríguez, and the other woman in mourning was her daughter, who had been deceived by the rich farmer's son. All those who knew the duenna were astounded, the duke and duchess more than anyone, for although they thought her a harmless fool, they did not think she would go so far as to commit acts of madness. Finally, Doña Rodríguez turned to her master and mistress and said:

"May it please Your Excellencies to give me permission to converse with this knight for a moment, that being necessary to the success of a matter in which I have become involved because of the audacity of an ill-intentioned villain."

The duke said that he gave it, and that she might converse with Señor Don Quixote for as long as she wished. She, directing her voice and turning her face toward Don Quixote, said:

"Some days ago, O valiant knight, I recounted to you the injustice and treachery committed by a wicked farmer against my dearly loved daughter, this unfortunate woman here present, and you promised to defend her, righting the wrong that has been done to her, and now it has come to my attention that you wish to leave this castle to wander in search of good fortune, and may God grant that to you; but before you slip away down those roads I would like you to challenge this uncouth rustic and force him to marry my daughter and fulfill the promise he made to be her husband before and prior to his lying with her, because to think that my lord the duke will execute justice is to ask the elm tree for pears, for the reason I have already mentioned to your grace in private. And so, may Our Lord grant your grace very good health, and may He not forsake us."

Don Quixote responded to these words with great solemnity and gravity, saying:

"Good duenna, moderate your tears, or, I should say, dry them, and hold back your sighs, for I take it as my responsibility to assist your daughter, who should not have been so ready to believe lovers' promises, which are simple to make and very difficult to keep; and so, with the permission of my lord the duke, I shall leave immediately to look for this heartless young man, and I shall find him, and challenge him, and kill him if and when he refuses to keep the promise he made, for the principal intention of my profession is to forgive the humble and punish the proud, I mean to say, to assist the unfortunate and destroy the cruel."

"There is no need," responded the duke, "for your grace to take the trouble to look for the rustic about whom this good duenna is complaining, nor is there any need for your grace to ask my permission to challenge him, for I consider him already challenged, and take responsibility for informing him of this challenge, and telling him to accept it and come to my castle to answer it for himself, and I shall give both of you a reliable field, satisfying all the conditions that generally ought to be satisfied in such actions, and satisfying the demands of justice for each of you, which is the obligation of all princes who provide an unencumbered field to those who do battle within the borders of their domains."

"Then with this assurance and the kind permission of your highness," replied Don Quixote, "I say here that for this occasion I renounce my status as gentleman, and lower myself to the level of the miscreant's base birth, and make myself his equal, thereby allowing him to do combat with me; and so, although he is absent, I challenge and defy him because of the wrong he committed in defrauding this poor woman who was a maiden, and no longer is, the fault being his; and he must fulfill the promise he made to her to be her legitimate husband, or die in the contest."

And then, removing a glove, he threw it into the middle of the room, and the duke picked it up, saying, as he had said before, that he accepted the challenge in the name of his vassal and set the time for their encounter as six days hence, and the field, the courtyard of the castle, and the weapons, those customarily used by knights: lance and shield and articulated armor, and all the other accoutrements, without deceit, fraud, or trickery of any kind, for they would be seen and examined by the judges in the field.

"But before anything else, it is necessary for this excellent duenna and this imperfect maiden to put their right to justice in the hands of Señor Don Quixote, for otherwise nothing will be accomplished, and the challenge will not be carried out as it should."

"I do," responded the duenna.

"And so do I," added her daughter, tearful, ashamed, and bad-tempered.

Then, having made this arrangement, and the duke having decided what needed to be done, the women in mourning left, and the duchess ordered that from then on they were to be treated not as her servants, but as enterprising ladies who had come to her house to ask for justice; and so they were given a private room and served as if they were strangers, not without consternation among the other serving women who did not know where the foolishness and audacity of Doña Rodríguez and her unfortunate daughter would end.

At this point, to give a final touch of joy to the festivities and bring the meal to a successful conclusion, into the room came the page who had carried the letters and presents to Teresa Panza, wife of the governor

Sancho Panza, and his arrival made the duke and duchess very happy, for they were longing to know what had happened to him on his journey; when they asked him, the page responded that he could not tell them publicly, or in only a few words, and if it pleased Their Excellencies, that should wait until they were alone, and in the meantime they could enjoy the letters. And he took out two letters and placed them in the hands of the duchess. One of them said in the address: *Letter for my lady the duchess so-and-so of I don't know where,* and the other said: *To my husband, Sancho Panza, governor of the ínsula of Barataria. God keep him more years than me.* The duchess could not wait for her bread to bake, as the saying goes, until she had read her letter, and she opened it and read it to herself, and seeing that she could read it aloud so that the duke and the others present could hear it, she read as follows:

LETTER FROM TERESA PANZA TO THE DUCHESS

Señora, the letter your highness wrote to me made me very happy, for the truth is it was something I had been wanting. The string of corals is very nice, and my husband's hunting outfit is just as good. Your ladyship making my spouse, Sancho, a governor has given a lot of pleasure to the whole village, even if nobody believes it, especially the priest, and Master Nicolás the barber, and Sansón Carrasco the bachelor, but that doesn't bother me; as long as it's true, which it is, each person can say whatever he wants, though to tell you the truth, if the corals and the outfit hadn't come I wouldn't believe it either, because in this village everybody takes my husband for a fool, and except for governing a herd of goats, they can't imagine what governorship he'd be good for. May God make him good and show him how to see what his children need.

Señora of my soul, I've decided, with your grace's permission, to put this good day in my house[1] by going to court and leaning back in a carriage and making their eyes pop, for there are thousands who are already envious of me; and so I beg Your Excellency to tell my husband to send me some money, and to make it enough, because at court expenses are high: bread sells for a real, and a pound of meat costs thirty maravedís, which is a judgment,[2] and if he doesn't want me to go, he should let me know soon, because my feet are itch-

---

1. The phrase is based on a proverb: "When you have a good day, put it in the house," which is roughly equivalent to "Make hay while the sun shines."

2. A phrase that alludes to the Final Judgment, suggesting punishment for sin; in English we would say, figuratively, that something we disapprove of is a "sin" or a "crime."

ing to get started; my friends and neighbors tell me that if my daughter and I look grand and important in court, my husband will be known through me and not me through him, because many people are bound to ask: 'Who are those ladies in that carriage?' And a servant of mine will respond: 'The wife and daughter of Sancho Panza, governor of the ínsula of Barataria,' and in this way Sancho will become known, and I'll be admired, so let's get to it, no matter what.

It makes me as sorry as I can be that this year they haven't picked acorns in this village; even so, I'm sending your highness about half a celemín; I went to the woods myself to pick them and pick them over one by one, and I couldn't find acorns any bigger; I wish they were like ostrich eggs.

Your magnificence mustn't forget to write to me, and I'll be sure to answer and tell you about my health and everything there is to tell about in this village, where I'm praying that Our Lord keeps your highness, and doesn't forget about me. My daughter, Sancha, and my son, kiss the hands of your grace.

Wishing to see your ladyship more than to write to you,

I am your servant,
TERESA PANZA

Everyone derived great pleasure from hearing Teresa Panza's letter, especially the duke and duchess, and the duchess asked Don Quixote if he thought it would be all right to open the letter that had come for the governor, for she imagined it to be very fine. Don Quixote said he would open it in order to give them pleasure, and he did so and saw that it said as follows:

LETTER FROM TERESA PANZA TO HER HUSBAND, SANCHO PANZA

I received your letter, Sancho of my soul, and I can tell you and swear to you as a Catholic Christian that I practically went crazy with happiness. Just think, my husband: when I heard that you were a governor, I thought I'd fall down dead from sheer joy, because you know, people say that sudden joy can kill just like great sorrow. Your daughter, Sanchica, wet herself without realizing it, she was so happy. I had the outfit you sent us in front of me, and the corals my lady the duchess sent around my neck, and both letters in my hands, and the man who brought them right there, and even so I believed and thought that what I saw and touched was all a dream, because who could ever imagine that a goatherd would become a governor of ínsulas? And you know, dear husband, my mother used to say you had to live a lot to see a lot: I say this because I plan to see more if I live more, because I don't plan to stop until I see you as a landlord or a tax collector, for these are trades, after all, in which you always have and handle money, though the devil carries off anyone who misuses them. My lady the duchess will tell you how much I want to go to court; think about it, and let me know if you like the idea, and I'll try to honor you there by riding in a carriage.

The priest, the barber, the bachelor, and even the sacristan can't believe you're a governor; they say it's all a fraud, or a question of enchantment, like everything that has to do with your master Don Quixote; Sansón says he'll go to look for you and get the governorship out of your head and Don Quixote's craziness out of his skull; I don't do anything but laugh, and look at my necklace, and plan the dress I'll make for our daughter out of your outfit.

I sent some acorns to my lady the duchess; I wish they were made of gold. Send me some pearl necklaces, if they wear them on that ínsula.

The news from the village is that Berrueca married her daughter to a painter without any talent who came here to paint whatever it turned out to be; the Council told him to paint His Majesty's coat of arms over the doors of the town hall, he asked for two ducados, they paid him in advance, he worked for a week, at the end of that time he hadn't painted anything, and he said he couldn't paint trifles; he gave back the money, and even so he got married claiming to be a skilled workman; the truth is he's put down the brush and picked up a hoe and goes to the fields like a gentleman. Pedro de Lobo's son has taken orders and has a tonsure and intends to become a priest; Minguilla, Mingo Silvato's granddaughter, found out and has made a complaint against him, saying he promised to marry her; gossips are saying she's pregnant by him, but he absolutely denies it.

There are no olives this year, and there's not a drop of vinegar to be found anywhere in the village. A company of soldiers came through here and took three village girls away with them; I don't want to tell you who they are: maybe they'll come back, and there's bound to be somebody who'll marry them, with their good or bad qualities.

Sanchica is making lace trimming; she earns eight maravedís a day free and clear, and she's putting them in a money box to help with her dowry, but now that she's the daughter of a governor, you'll give her a dowry and she won't have to work for it. The fountain in the square dried up; lightning hit the pillory, which doesn't bother me at all.

I'm waiting for your answer to this letter, and a decision about my going to court; and with this, may God grant you more years than He does me, or as many, because I wouldn't want to leave you without me in this world.

> Your wife,
> TERESA PANZA

The letters were celebrated, laughed at, approved, and admired; as a final touch, the courier arrived with the letter Sancho had sent to Don Quixote, which was also read publicly, casting doubt on the foolishness of the governor.

The duchess withdrew in order to learn from the page what had occurred in Sancho's village, which he recounted to her in great detail, not failing to relate every circumstance; he gave her the acorns, as well as a cheese that Teresa had given him because it was very good, even better than the ones from Tronchón.[3] The duchess received it with the greatest pleasure, and with that we shall leave her in order to recount the end of the governorship of the great Sancho Panza, the flower and model of all insular governors.

CHAPTER LIII

Regarding the troubled end and conclusion of the governorship of Sancho Panza

To believe that the things of this life will endure forever, unchanged, is to believe the impossible; it seems instead that everything goes around, I mean around in a circle: spring pursues summer, summer pursues *estío*,[1] *estío* pursues autumn, autumn pursues winter, and winter pursues spring, and in this way time turns around a continuous wheel; only human life races to its end more quickly than time, with no hope for renewal except in the next life, which has no boundaries that limit it. So says Cide Hamete, a Muslim philosopher, because an understanding of the fleeting

---

3. A village in the present-day province of Teruel.

1. Currently a literary term for "summer" (*verano*); when the year was divided into three seasons, *estío* was the season that began at the vernal equinox and ended at the autumnal equinox.

impermanence of our present life, and the everlasting nature of the eternal life that awaits us, has been grasped by many without the enlightenment of faith but with only the light of their natural intelligence; but here our author says this because of the speed with which the governorship of Sancho ended, evaporated, dissolved, and disappeared in shadow and smoke.

Sancho was in bed on the seventh night of the days of his governorship, full not of bread or wine, but of judging and giving opinions and issuing statutes and decrees, when sleep, notwithstanding and despite his hunger, began to close his eyes, and he heard such a great noise of bells ringing and voices shouting that it seemed as if the entire ínsula were being destroyed. He sat up in bed, listening attentively to see if he could learn what the cause might be of so much tumult; not only did he fail, but the sound of infinite trumpets and drums was added to the clamor of shouts and bells, leaving him more confused, and more full of fear and consternation; getting out of bed, he put on slippers because the floor was damp, and not bothering with a robe or anything resembling one, he went to the door of his room just in time to see more than twenty persons coming along the corridors, carrying burning torches and holding unsheathed swords in their hands, all of them shouting in loud voices:

"To arms, to arms, Señor Governor, to arms! Infinite enemies have entered the ínsula, and we are lost if your ingenuity and valor do not come to our aid!"

Clamorous, frenzied, in an uproar, they approached the place where Sancho was standing, astonished and stupefied at what he was hearing and seeing, and when they had reached him one of them said:

"Arm yourself immediately, your lordship, or else you will be lost along with the entire ínsula!"

"What do I have to do with arming?" responded Sancho. "And what do I know about arms or coming to anybody's aid? These things are better left to my master, Don Quixote, who in the wink of an eye would dispatch and see to them. But I, sinner that I am, I don't know anything about this kind of battle."

"Ah, Señor Governor!" said another. "What reluctance is this? Arm yourself, your grace, for we bring you both offensive and defensive weapons, and go out to the square, and be our guide and our captain, for by right that is your duty, being our governor."

"Then arm me, and may it be for the best," replied Sancho.

And they immediately brought two full-length shields that they had been carrying and placed them over his nightshirt, not allowing him to put on any other clothing, one shield in front and the other behind, and they pulled his arms through some space they had made, and tied the shields on very carefully with cords, leaving him walled in and boarded up, as straight as a spindle and unable to bend his knees or take a single step. In his hands they placed a lance, which he leaned on in order to keep his balance. When they had him in this state, they told him to walk, and lead them, and encourage them all, for with him as their polestar, their lighthouse, and their lamp, their affairs would have a happy conclusion.

"Wretch that I am, how can I walk," responded Sancho. "when I can't move my kneecaps because of these boards sewed up so tight against my body? What you'll have to do is carry me in your arms and lay me down or stand me up at some postern gate, and I'll guard it either with this lance or with my body."

"Go on, Señor Governor," said another man, "it's fear more than boards that keeps you from walking; put an end to this, and start to move, for it's late, our enemies are increasing, their shouts are becoming louder, and the danger is growing."

Their persuasion and insults prodded the poor governor into moving, and he fell to the ground with such force that he thought he had broken into pieces. He lay there like a giant turtle enclosed and covered by its shells, or like half a side of bacon held between two salting-boards, or even like a boat lying upside down in the sand, but not even when they saw that he had fallen did those mockers have any compassion for him; instead, they put out the torches and shouted even louder, repeating the call to arms with such urgency, and running over poor Sancho and stamping so hard on the shields, that if he had not retreated and pulled back, drawing his head inside the shields, things would have gone very badly for the poor governor who, enclosed in that narrow space, sweated and perspired and with all his heart commended himself to God, praying that He deliver him from that danger.

Some stumbled over him, others fell, and one even stood on top of him for a long while, and from there, as if from a watchtower, he commanded the armies and shouted in a loud voice, saying:

"Our men here, the enemy is pressing hard over here! Guard that opening, close that gate, down with those ladders! Bring the pitch-pots,[2]

2. Blazing pots filled with pitch and other flammable material, which were thrown at the enemy.

the tar and resin in cauldrons of burning oil! Barricade the streets with mattresses!"

In short, he named with great zeal all the implements and instruments and tools of war used to prevent an attack on a city, and the battered Sancho, who heard and suffered it all, said to himself:

"Oh, if only Our Lord would put an end to the loss of this ínsula, and I would find myself dead or free of this affliction!"

Heaven heard his prayer, and when he least expected it, he heard voices shouting:

"Victory, victory! The enemy is retreating! Oh, Señor Governor, your grace should get up and come enjoy the conquest and divide the spoils taken from the enemy by the valor of that invincible arm!"

"Pick me up," the dolorous Sancho said in a doleful voice.

They helped him to his feet, and when he was standing he said:

"The enemy that I've conquered I want you to nail to my forehead.[3] I don't want to divide the enemy's spoils, but I beg and implore some friend, if I have any, to give me a drink of wine and wipe away and dry this sweat, because I'm turning into water."

They dried him, brought him wine, and untied the shields, and he sat on his bed and fainted from fear, shock, and alarm. Those who had deceived him regretted having carried the joke so far, but Sancho's return to consciousness tempered the regret caused by his swoon. He asked the time; they responded that dawn had broken. He fell silent, and without saying another word he began to dress, deep in silence, and everyone watched him, waiting to see what the outcome would be of his dressing so urgently. Finally he was dressed, and very slowly, because he was bruised and could not move quickly, he went to the stable, followed by everyone present, and when he reached the gray he embraced him and gave him a kiss of peace on the forehead, and, not without tears in his eyes, he said:

"Come here, my companion and friend, comrade in all my sufferings and woes: when I spent time with you and had no other thoughts but mending your harness and feeding your body, then my hours, my days, and my years were happy, but after I left you and climbed the towers of ambition and pride, a thousand miseries, a thousand troubles, and four thousand worries have entered deep into my soul."

As he was saying these words, he was also saddling his donkey, and no one said anything to him. And when the donkey was saddled, with great

---

3. This indicates that what has just been said is either impossible or untrue.

sadness and sorrow he mounted him, and directing his words and thoughts to the steward, the secretary, the butler, the physician Pedro Recio, and the many others who were present, he said:

"Make way, Señores, and let me return to my old liberty; let me go and find my past life, so that I can come back from this present death. I was not born to be a governor, or to defend ínsulas or cities from enemies who want to attack them. I have a better understanding of plowing and digging, of pruning and layering the vines, than of making laws or defending provinces and kingdoms. St. Peter's fine in Rome: I mean, each man is fine doing the work he was born for. I'm better off with a scythe in my hand than a governor's scepter; I'd rather eat my fill of gazpacho than suffer the misery of a brazen doctor who starves me to death, and I'd rather lie down in the shade of an oak tree in summer and wrap myself in an old bald sheepskin in winter, in freedom, than lie between linen sheets and wear sables, subject to a governorship. God keep your graces, and tell my lord the duke that I was born naked, and I'm naked now: I haven't lost or gained a thing; I mean, I came into this governorship without a *blanca*, and I'm leaving without one, which is very different from how the governors of other ínsulas leave. Now move aside and let me go: I'll apply some poultices, because I think all my ribs are crushed, thanks to the enemies who ran over me tonight."

"It must not be like this, Señor Governor," said Dr. Recio, "for I shall give your grace a potion against falls and bruising, which will return you to your former well-being and vigor; as for food, I promise your grace to mend my ways and allow you to eat as much as you want of anything you like."

"You peeped too late!"[4] responded Sancho. "I'd sooner become a Turk than not leave. These aren't tricks you can play twice. By God, I'm as likely to stay here, or accept another governorship, even if they handed it to me on a platter, as I am to fly up to heaven without wings. I'm from the lineage of the Panzas, and they're all stubborn, and if they say odds once, odds it'll be, even if it's evens, no matter what anybody says. Here in this stable I'll leave the wings on the ant that carried me into the air where the martins and other birds could eat me, and I'll go back to walking on my feet on level ground, and if they're not adorned with cutout shoes[5] of Cordoban leather, they won't lack for sandals made

4. An allusion to the story of a man who sucked on an egg, and when the chick peeped in his throat, he said: "You peeped too late."

5. Shoes worn by the nobility were often decorated with holes and cutouts.

of hemp. Every sheep with its mate, and let no man stretch his leg farther than the length of the sheet, and now let me pass, it's getting late."

To which the steward said:

"Senor Governor, we would very gladly let your grace pass, though it saddens us greatly to lose you, for your wit and Christian behavior oblige us to want to keep you; but as everyone knows, every governor is obliged, before he abandons the place he has governed, to give an accounting of his governorship: your grace, give us one for the ten days in which you have held the governorship, and then go and God's peace go with you."

"No one can ask that of me," responded Sancho, "unless he is ordered to by my lord the duke; I'm going to see him, and I'll give an exact accounting to him; besides, leaving naked, as I am, no other proof is necessary to show that I governed like an angel."

"By God, the great Sancho is correct," said Dr. Recio, "and I am of the opinion that we should let him leave, because the duke will surely be overjoyed to see him."

They all agreed, and allowed him to go, first offering to accompany him and to give him everything he might want for the gratification of his person and the comfort of his journey. Sancho said he wanted no more than a little barley for his donkey, and half a cheese and half a loaf of bread for himself; since the way was so short, there was no need for more or better provisions. Everyone embraced him, and he, weeping, embraced all of them, and he left them marveling not only at his words but at his decision, which was so resolute and intelligent.

CHAPTER LIV

Which deals with matters related to this history and to no other

The duke and duchess resolved that Don Quixote's challenge to their vassal for the reason already recounted should go forward, and since the young man was in Flanders, where he had fled so as not to have Doña Rodríguez for a mother-in-law, they ordered a Gascon footman named Tosilos to appear in his place, first instructing him very carefully in everything he had to do.

Two days later, the duke told Don Quixote that in four days his opponent would come to present himself in the field, armed as a knight, to maintain that the maiden was lying through some, if not all, of her teeth[1] if she affirmed he had given her a promise of marriage. Don Quixote was very happy to hear the news, and he promised himself to perform miracles in this matter, and he considered it very fortunate that an opportunity had presented itself that would allow the duke and duchess to see the extent of the valor of his mighty arm; and so, with joy and delight, he waited for the four days to pass, although if reckoned by his desire, they had become four hundred centuries.

Let us allow them to pass, as we have allowed other things to pass, and accompany Sancho, who was both happy and sad as he came riding on the gray to find his master, whose companionship pleased him more than being governor of all the ínsulas in the world.

He had not gone very far from the ínsula of his governorship—he had never bothered to find out if it was an island, city, town, or village that he was governing—when he saw coming toward him along the road six pilgrims with their staffs,[2] the kind of foreign pilgrims who beg for alms by singing, and as they approached him they arranged themselves in a row, lifted their voices, and began to sing in their own language, which Sancho could not understand except for the one word *alms*, which was clearly pronounced, and then he understood that in their song they were asking for alms; since he, as Cide Hamete says, was excessively charitable, he took from his saddlebags his provisions of half a loaf of bread and half a cheese, which he offered to the pilgrims, indicating by signs that he had nothing else to give. They accepted the food very gladly and said:

"Geld! Geld!"[3]

"I don't understand," responded Sancho, "what you're asking of me, good people."

Then one of them took a purse from his shirt and showed it to Sancho, who then understood that they were asking for money, and he, placing his thumb on his throat and extending his hand upward, gave them to understand that he did not have any money at all; and

1. The equivalent phrases in Spanish, *mentir por mitad de la barba* and *mentir por toda la barba* ("to lie through half of one's beard" and "to lie through one's whole beard"), mean essentially the same thing; unfortunately, the contrast between "half" and "whole" makes little sense in English.

2. Martín de Riquer indicates that hoodlums and thieves frequently dressed as pilgrims.

3. "Money" in German.

spurring the donkey, he broke through the line, and as he passed, a pilgrim who had been looking at him very carefully rushed toward him, threw his arms around his waist, and said in a loud and very Castilian voice:

"God save me! What do I see? Is it possible that I have my arms around my dear friend and good neighbor Sancho Panza? I do, no doubt about it, because I'm not asleep or drunk now."

Sancho was amazed to hear himself called by name and to find himself embraced by a foreign pilgrim, and he looked at him very carefully, not saying a word, but did not recognize him; the pilgrim, however, seeing his bewilderment, said:

"How is it possible, my brother Sancho Panza, that you don't know your neighbor Ricote the Morisco,[4] a shopkeeper in your village?"

Then Sancho looked at him even more closely, and began to recognize his face, and finally knew exactly who he was, and without dismounting, Sancho threw his arms around the man's neck and said:

"Who the devil could recognize you, Ricote, in the ridiculous disguise you're wearing? Tell me, who turned you into a foreigner, and why did you risk coming back to Spain? It'll be very dangerous for you if they catch you and recognize you."

"If you don't give me away, Sancho," responded the pilgrim, "I'm sure nobody will know me in these clothes; let's move off the road to that grove of poplars where my companions want to eat and rest, and you can eat with them, for they're very peaceable people. I'll have a chance to tell you what happened to me after I left our village, obeying His Majesty's proclamation that threatened the unfortunate members of my race so severely, as you must have heard."[5]

Sancho agreed, and after Ricote spoke to the other pilgrims, they set out for the grove of poplars that could be seen at some distance from the king's highway. They threw down their staffs, took off their hooded cloaks or capes, and remained in their shirtsleeves; they were all young and good-looking except for Ricote, who was a man well on in years. All of them carried traveling bags, and all of these, it seemed, were well-

4. A person of Muslim descent, living in territory controlled by Christians, who had ostensibly, and often forcibly, been converted to Christianity.

5. Between 1609 and 1613, public proclamations ordered the immediate expulsion from Spain of the Moriscos, who were accused of continuing to practice Islam in secret and of having a pernicious influence on Spanish society.

provisioned, at least with things that call up and summon a thirst from two leagues away.

They stretched out on the ground, and with the grass as their table-cloth, they set out bread, salt, knives, nuts, pieces of cheese, and bare ham-bones that could not be gnawed but could still be sucked. They also set out a black food called *cabial*[6] that is made of fish eggs and is a great awakener of thirst. There was no lack of olives, dried without any brine but good-tasting and flavorful. What stood out most on the field of that banquet, however, were six wineskins, for each of them took one out of his bag; even the good Ricote, transformed from a Morisco into a German or Teu-ton, took out his own wineskin, comparable in size to the other five.

They began to eat with great pleasure, savoring each mouthful slowly, just a little of each thing, which they picked up with the tip of a knife, and then all at once, and all at the same time, they raised their arms and the wineskins into the air, their mouths pressed against the mouths of the wineskins and their eyes fixed on heaven, as if they were taking aim; they stayed this way for a long time, emptying the in-nermost contents of the skins into their stomachs, and moving their heads from one side to the other, signs that attested to the pleasure they were receiving.

Sancho watched everything, and not one thing caused him sorrow;[7] rather, in order to comply with a proverb that he knew very well—"When in Rome, do as the Romans do"—he asked Ricote for his wine-skin and took aim along with the rest and with no less pleasure than they enjoyed.

The skins were tilted four times, but a fifth time was not possible be-cause they were now as dry and parched as esparto grass, something that withered the joy the pilgrims had shown so far. From time to time one of them would take Sancho's right hand in his and say:

"*Español y tudesqui, tuto uno: bon compaño!*"

And Sancho would respond:

"*Bon compaño, jura Di!*"

And he burst into laughter that lasted for an hour, and then he did not remember anything that had happened to him in his governorship; for during the time and period when one eats and drinks, cares tend to be of little importance. Finally, the end of the wine was the beginning of a

---

6. In contemporary Spanish, the word is spelled *caviar*.

7. This phrase is taken from a ballad that begins: "Nero, on Tarpeian Rock, / watched as Rome went up in flames; / crying ancients, screaming infants, / and not one thing caused him sorrow."

fatigue that overcame everyone and left them asleep on their tables and cloths; only Ricote and Sancho were awake, because they had eaten more and drunk less than the others; Ricote moved away with Sancho to sit at the foot of a beech tree, leaving the pilgrims deep in their sweet sleep, and Ricote, without slipping at all into his Moorish language, said these words in pure Castilian:

"You know very well, O Sancho Panza, my neighbor and friend, how the proclamation and edict that His Majesty issued against those of my race brought terror and fear to all of us; at least, I was so affected, I think that even before the time granted to us for leaving Spain had expired, I was already imagining that the harsh penalty had been inflicted on me and my children. And so I arranged, as a prudent man, I think, and as one who knows that by a certain date the house where he lives will be taken away and he'll need to have another one to move into, I arranged, as I said, to leave the village alone, without my family, and find a place where I could take them in comfort and without the haste with which others were leaving; because I saw clearly, as did all our elders, that those proclamations were not mere threats, as some were saying, but real laws that would be put into effect at the appointed time; I was forced to believe this truth because I knew the hateful and foolish intentions of our people, and they were such that it seems to me it was divine inspiration that moved His Majesty to put into effect so noble a resolution, not because all of us were guilty, for some were firm and true Christians, though these were so few they could not oppose those who were not, but because it is not a good idea to nurture a snake in your bosom or shelter enemies in your house.

In short, it was just and reasonable for us to be chastised with the punishment of exile: lenient and mild, according to some, but for us it was the most terrible one we could have received. No matter where we are we weep for Spain, for, after all, we were born here and it is our native country; nowhere do we find the haven our misfortune longs for, and in Barbary and all the places in Africa where we hoped to be received, welcomed, and taken in, that is where they most offend and mistreat us. We did not know our good fortune until we lost it, and the greatest desire in almost all of us is to return to Spain; most of those, and there are many of them, who know the language as well as I do, abandon their wives and children and return, so great is the love they have for Spain; and now I know and feel the truth of the saying that it is sweet to love one's country.

As I was saying, I left our village, went to France, and though they made us welcome there, I wanted to see everything. I traveled to Italy, and came to Germany, and there it seemed to me I could live in greater freedom because the inhabitants don't worry about subtleties: each man lives as he chooses, because in most places there is freedom of conscience. I took a house in a village near Augsburg; I joined these pilgrims, for many travel to Spain every year to visit the shrines, which they think of as their Indies: as sure profit and certain gain. They travel through most of the country, and they leave every town well-fed and well-drunk, as they say, and with at least a *real* in money, and at the end of the trip they have more than a hundred *escudos* left over, which they change into gold coins and hide in the hollows of their staffs, or under the patches on their cloaks, or wherever else they can, and they take them out of this kingdom and into their own countries in spite of the guards at the posts and ports where there are inspections.

Now, Sancho, my intention is to take out the treasure I buried here, and since it's outside the village, I'll be able to do it without danger, and then I'll write to my daughter and wife, or leave from Valencia and go to Algiers, where I know they are, and find a way to take them to a French port, and from there to Germany, where we'll wait for whatever God has in store for us; in short, Sancho, I know for a fact that my daughter, Ricota, and my wife, Francisca Ricota, are true Catholic Christians, and though I'm less of one, I'm still more Christian than Moor, and I always pray that God will open the eyes of my understanding and let me know how I must serve Him. What amazes me is not knowing why my wife and daughter went to Barbary instead of France, where they could have lived as Christians."

To which Sancho responded:

"Look, Ricote, that probably wasn't their decision, because Juan Tiopieyo, your wife's brother, left with them, and since he's probably a shrewd Moor, he took them to the place he thought best, and I can tell you something else, too: I think it's useless for you to look for what you buried, because we heard that the pearls and gold coins your brother-in-law and your wife were carrying were taken at inspection."

"That might be, Sancho," replied Ricote, "but I know they didn't touch what I hid away: I didn't tell them where it was because I feared some calamity; and so, Sancho, if you want to come with me and help me to dig it up and hide it, I'll give you two hundred *escudos*, and with that you can meet all your needs, for you know that I know you have a good many of them."

"I'd do it," responded Sancho, "but I'm not a greedy man, because just this morning I left a post where I could have had gold walls in my house and been eating off silver plates in six months' time; and for this reason, and because I think it would be treason against my king if I helped his enemies, I wouldn't go with you even if you gave me four hundred *escudos* in cash right here and now instead of promising me two hundred later."

"And what post is it that you've left, Sancho?" asked Ricote.

"I've left the governorship of an ínsula," responded Sancho, "one so good that, by my faith, you'd have a hard time finding another like it."

"And where is this ínsula?" asked Ricote.

"Where?" responded Sancho. "Two leagues from here, and it's called Ínsula Barataria."

"That's amazing, Sancho," said Ricote. "Ínsulas are in the ocean; there are no ínsulas on terra firma."

"What do you mean?" replied Sancho. "I tell you, Ricote my friend, I left there this morning, and yesterday I was there governing to my heart's content, like an archer;[8] but even so, I left it because the post of governor seems like a dangerous one to me."

"What did you get from your governorship?" asked Ricote.

"I got," responded Sancho, "the lesson that I'm not good for governing unless it's a herd of livestock, and that the riches you can gain in governorships come at the cost of your rest and your sleep and even your food, because on ínsulas the governors have to eat very little, especially if they have doctors who are looking out for their health."

"I don't understand you, Sancho," said Ricote, "but it seems to me that everything you're saying is nonsense; who would give you ínsulas to govern? Was there a lack of men in the world more competent than you to be governors? Really, Sancho, come to your senses and decide if you want to come with me, as I said, and help me take out the treasure I hid; the truth is there's so much it can be called a treasure, and I'll give you enough to live on, as I said."

"I already told you, Ricote," replied Sancho, "that I don't want to; be satisfied that I won't betray you, and go on your way in peace, and let me continue on mine: I know that well-gotten gains can be lost, and ill-gotten ones can be lost, too, along with their owner."

"I don't want to insist, Sancho," said Ricote, "but tell me: did you

8. The word in Spanish is *sagitario*, which in underworld slang also meant a person who was whipped through the streets by the authorities. Martín de Riquer speculates that since this meaning seems out of place here, Sancho may simply be repeating a word he has heard Don Quixote use or is referring indirectly to the rigor of his governance by alluding to the archers of the Holy Brotherhood who executed criminals at Peralvillo.

happen to be in our village when my wife, my daughter, and my brother-in-law left?"

"Yes, I was," responded Sancho, "and I can tell you that your daughter looked so beautiful when she left that everybody in the village came out to see her, and they all said she was the fairest creature in the world. She was crying and embracing all her friends and companions, and all those who came out to see her, and asking them all to commend her to God and Our Lady, His Mother, and she did this with so much feeling it made me cry, though I'm not usually much of a weeper. By my faith, there were many who wanted to hide her and take her from those she was leaving with, but fear of defying the orders of the king stopped them. The one who seemed most affected was Don Pedro Gregorio, that rich young man who's going to inherit his father's estate, you know who I mean, they say he loved her very much, and after she left he's never been seen in our village again, and we all think he went after them to abduct her, but so far we haven't heard anything."

"I always suspected," said Ricote, "that he was wooing my daughter, but I trusted in the principles of my Ricota, and knowing he loved her never troubled me, because you must have heard, Sancho, that Moriscas rarely if ever become involved with Old Christians, and my daughter, who, I believe, cared more for being a better Christian than for being in love, would not pay attention to that young gentleman's entreaties."

"May it be God's will," replied Sancho, "because that would not be good for either one of them. And now let me leave here, Ricote my friend; tonight I want to reach the place where my master, Don Quixote, is."

"God go with you, Sancho my friend; my companions are beginning to stir, and it's time for us to leave, too."

Then the two of them embraced, and Sancho mounted his donkey, and Ricote grasped his staff, and they went their separate ways.

CHAPTER LV

Regarding certain things that befell Sancho on the road, and others that are really quite remarkable

Sancho's having stopped with Ricote did not permit him to reach the duke's castle that day, for although he had come to within half a league of it, night, which was somewhat dark and gloomy, overtook him; as it was summer, this did not trouble him very much, and so he moved off the road, intending to wait for morning, and it was his bad luck and misfortune that as he was looking for a spot where he would be comfortable, he and the gray fell into a deep and very dark pit that lay between some very old buildings, and as he fell he commended himself to God with all his heart, thinking he would not stop falling until he reached the depths of the abyss. But this was not the case, because after a little more than three *estados* the donkey hit bottom, and Sancho found himself on top of him, not having received any kind of wound or injury.

He felt his body and took a deep breath to see if he was whole or had been punctured anywhere; and seeing that he was safe and sound and in perfect health, he could not give enough thanks to Our Lord God for the mercy He had shown him, for he no doubt thought he had broken into a thousand pieces. He also felt the walls of the pit with his hands to see if it would be possible to climb out without anyone's help, but he found that all of them were smooth, without any kind of foothold, which greatly distressed Sancho, especially when he heard the donkey moaning woefully and grievously, and no wonder, for he was not lamenting capriciously; in truth, he was not in very good condition.

"Oh," said Sancho then, "what unexpected things can happen to those who live in this miserable world! Who could have said that the person who only yesterday sat on the governor's throne on an ínsula, giv-

ing orders to his servants and vassals, today would find himself buried in
a pit with no one to comfort him, and no servant or vassal to come and
help him? Here my donkey and I will starve to death, if we don't die first,
he because he's bruised and broken, and me because I'm full of grief. At
least I won't be as lucky as my master, Don Quixote of La Mancha, when
he went down and descended into the cave of the enchanted Montesinos, where he found somebody who treated him better than they do
in his own house, because it seems he found the table laid and the bed
made. There he saw beautiful and peaceable visions, and here, it seems,
I'll see frogs and snakes. Woe is me, just look where my madness and fantasy have brought me! They'll take my bones out of here, smooth, white,
and scraped bare, and those of my good donkey with them, and maybe
that, at least, will let them know who we are if they've heard that
Sancho Panza was never parted from his donkey, or his donkey from
Sancho Panza. I'll say it again: how wretched we are, for our bad luck
hasn't allowed us to die in our own land, with our own people, so that
even if there wasn't a remedy for our misfortune, there'd be no lack of
people to grieve over it, and to close our eyes at the final hour of our
passing! Oh, my companion and friend, how badly I've paid you for your
good service! Forgive me, and ask Fortune, in the best way you know
how, to take us out of this terrible trouble, and I promise to crown your
head with laurel so you'll look exactly like a poet laureate, and to give
you double rations."

Sancho lamented in this fashion, and his donkey listened without
saying a single word in response: such was the distress and anguish in
which the poor creature found himself. Finally, after an entire night
spent in wretched complaints and lamentations, day broke, and in its
clear, bright light Sancho saw that it was utterly impossible to get out of
the pit without help, and he began to lament and cry out, to see if anyone heard him, but all his shouts were cries in the wilderness, because
there was no one to hear him anywhere in the vicinity, and then he
began to think of himself as dead.

The gray was lying on his back, and Sancho Panza moved him
around until he had him on his feet, though he could barely stand; he
took a piece of bread out of the saddlebags, which had experienced the
same unfortunate fall, and gave it to his donkey, who thought it did not
taste bad, and Sancho said to him, as if he could understand:

"Griefs are better with bread."

And then Sancho discovered that on one side of the pit there was a hole big enough for a person to fit into if he stooped and bent over. Sancho Panza went over to it, crouched down, went in, and saw that on the other side it was spacious and long, and he could see this because through what could be called the roof a ray of sunlight came in and illuminated everything. He also saw that the space widened and lengthened into another large concavity; when he saw this he returned to the donkey and with a stone began to dig the earth away from the hole; in a short while he made it large enough for the donkey to pass through, which he did; and taking him by the halter, Sancho began to walk through the cave to see if he could find another way out. At times he walked in darkness, and at times without light, but at no time without fear.

"May Almighty God save me!" he murmured to himself. "What for me is a misadventure would seem like an adventure to my master, Don Quixote. He'd think these caverns and dungeons were gardens in flower and the palaces of Galiana,[1] and would expect to come out of this dark, narrow place into a flowering meadow; but I'm so unlucky, so in need of advice, and so lacking in courage, that at each step I think another pit deeper than the first one is suddenly going to open beneath my feet and swallow me up. Evil is welcome if it comes alone."

In this manner, and with these thoughts, it seemed to him he must have walked more than half a league when he saw a dim illumination that he thought was daylight, shining in somewhere and indicating an opening at the end of what seemed to him like the road to the next world.

Here Cide Hamete Benengeli leaves him and returns to Don Quixote, who, with joy and happiness, waited for the appointed time of the battle that he was to fight with the thief of the honor of Doña Rodríguez's daughter, for he intended to right the wrong and correct the outrage so wickedly committed against her.

It so happened that he rode out one morning to practice and rehearse what he was to do during the combat he would soon be engaged in, and after spurring Rocinante into a charge or short gallop, the horse's feet came so close to a cave that if he had not pulled hard on the reins, it would have been impossible not to fall in. In short, Don Quixote

---

1. A legendary Moorish princess whose father, Gadalfe, built gorgeous palaces for her in Toledo, on the banks of the Tajo. She later converted and became the first wife of Charlemagne. The story gave rise to an idiom: if people are not happy with their accommodations, they are often asked if they would prefer the palaces of Galiana. It was also the subject of *Maynet,* a French epic chanson about the youthful adventures of Charlemagne.

stopped Rocinante and did not fall, and coming a little closer, and without dismounting, he peered into that deep hole, and as he was looking in he heard someone shouting inside; he listened carefully and could understand and ascertain what was being said:

"You up there! Is there some Christian who can hear me, some charitable knight who'll take pity on a sinner buried alive, an unfortunate governor without a governorship?"

It seemed to Don Quixote that he was hearing the voice of Sancho Panza, which left him astonished and perplexed, and raising his voice as much as he could, he said:

"Who is down there? Who is crying out?"

"Who else would be here crying out," was the response, "but a wretched Sancho Panza, the governor, on account of his sins and bad luck, of the Ínsula Barataria, and at one time the squire of the famous knight Don Quixote of La Mancha?"

When Don Quixote heard this, his amazement doubled and his bewilderment increased, for it occurred to him that Sancho Panza might be dead and his soul suffering the torments of purgatory down there; carried away by this thought, he said:

"I conjure thee by all that I can conjure thee with as a Catholic Christian to tell me who thou art, and if thou art a soul in torment, tell me what thou wantest me to do for thee, for since it is my profession to favor and come to the aid of those in need in this world, I shall do the same and come to the aid and assistance of those in distress in the next world who cannot help themselves."

"From the way your grace talks," came the response, "it seems to me you must be my master, Don Quixote of La Mancha, and from the sound of your voice, you can be nobody else, no doubt about that."

"I am Don Quixote," replied Don Quixote, "whose profession it is to assist and help the living and the dead in their distress. Therefore tell me who you are, for you have astonished me; if you are my squire, Sancho Panza, and you have died, and the devils have not carried you off, and through God's mercy you are in purgatory, our Holy Mother Roman Catholic Church has enough prayers of intercession to deliver you from the torments you are suffering, and I, for my part, shall supplicate as far as my fortune will allow; therefore declare yourself once and for all and tell me who you are."

"By God," came the response, "and by the birth of whoever your grace loves, I swear, Señor Don Quixote of La Mancha, that I'm your

squire, Sancho Panza, and I've never died in all the days of my life, but I
left my governorship for causes and reasons that I need more time to tell
you about, and last night I fell into this pit where I'm lying now, and the
gray with me, and he won't let me tell a lie, to be specific, he's here with
me now."

And there is more: it seems as if the donkey understood exactly what
Sancho said, because he immediately began to bray, and so loudly that
the entire cave resonated.

"A famous witness!" said Don Quixote. "I recognize the bray as if it
were my own, and I hear your voice, friend Sancho. Wait for me: I shall
go to the duke's castle, which is close by, and bring someone who can rescue you from the pit where your sins must have brought you."

"Go, your grace," said Sancho, "and by the one God come back soon,
because I can't stand being buried alive here, and I'm dying of fear."

Don Quixote left him and went to the castle to recount to the duke
and duchess what had happened to Sancho Panza, which caused them
no small astonishment, although they knew very well where he must
have fallen because it corresponded to a cave that had been there from
time immemorial; they could not imagine, however, how he could have
abandoned his governorship without their being informed that he was
coming to the castle. Finally, thick ropes and stout cords, as they say,[2]
were brought in, and by dint of many people and a good amount of work,
they raised the gray and Sancho Panza out of that darkness into the light
of the sun. A student saw him and said:

"This is how all wicked governors should leave their governorships,
just as this sinner leaves the depths of the abyss: dying of hunger, pale,
and without a *blanca*, or so it seems."

Sancho heard him and said:

"It was eight or ten days ago, Brother Gossip, that I came to govern
the ínsula that they gave me, and in all that time I didn't even have
enough bread to eat; I've been persecuted by doctors and had my bones
trampled by enemies, and I haven't had time to take any bribes or collect
any fees, and this being true, which it is, in my opinion I didn't deserve
to leave in this way; but man proposes and God disposes, and God knows
what suits each man and what's best for him, and time changes the
rhyme, and nobody should say, 'That's water I won't drink,' because
you're in a place where you think there's bacon, and you don't even find

---

2. A reference to a ballad that begins, "Doña Urraca, that princess," in which one of the lines reads:
"Take up thick ropes and stout cords."

a nail; God understands me, and that's enough, and I'll say no more, though I could."

"Do not be angry, Sancho, or troubled by what you may hear, for there is no end to it: you keep your conscience clear, and let them say whatever they wish, for trying to restrain the tongues of slanderers is the same as trying to put doors in a field. If the governor leaves his governorship a wealthy man, they say he has been a thief, and if he leaves it poor, they say he has been a dullard and a fool."

"Then there's no doubt," responded Sancho, "that this time they'll have to take me for a fool and not a thief."

Conversing in this way, and surrounded by boys and by many other people, they arrived at the castle, where the duke and the duchess were already in a gallery waiting for Don Quixote and Sancho, who did not wish to go up to see the duke without first settling the gray in the stable, because he said the donkey had spent a very bad night in the cave; then he went up to see his lord and lady, before whom he kneeled and said:

"My lord and my lady, because it was the wish of your highnesses, and not because of any merit in me, I went to govern your ínsula of Barataria, which I entered naked, and I'm naked now: I haven't lost or gained a thing. As to whether I governed well or badly, I've had witnesses before me, and they'll say whatever they want. I decided questions and settled cases, always dying of hunger, for such was the desire of Dr. Pedro Recio, a native of Tirteafuera and a governoresque and insulano doctor. Enemies attacked us by night, placing us in great difficulties, and the people of the ínsula say we emerged free and victorious because of the valor of my arm, and if they're telling the truth, may God keep them safe. In short, in this time I've weighed the burdens and obligations that come with governing, and I've found, by my own reckoning, that my shoulders can't carry them; they're not the right load for my ribs, and not the right arrows for my quiver, and so, before the governorship could do away with me I decided to do away with the governorship, and yesterday morning I left the ínsula just as I found it, with the same streets, houses, and roofs that it had when I came in. I haven't borrowed money from anybody, or taken any profits, and though I planned to issue a few good laws, I didn't, because I was afraid nobody would obey them, and then it doesn't matter if you issue them or not. As I said, I left the ínsula with no other escort but my donkey; I fell into a pit and walked through it until this morning, when by the light of the sun I saw the way out, but it wasn't so easy to leave, and if heaven hadn't provided me with my master, Don Quixote, I would've been there until the end of the world. And so, my lord duke and my lady duchess, here's your governor Sancho Panza; in the ten short days he had the governorship, he learned that he wouldn't give anything to be a governor, not just of an ínsula but of the whole world; and knowing that, and kissing the feet of your graces, and imitating the children's game when they say, 'You jump out and give it to me,'[3] I'll jump out of the governorship and pass into the service of my master, Don Quixote, and there, though I eat my bread in fear, at least I eat my fill; and for me, if I have enough to eat, I don't care if it's carrots or partridges."

With this Sancho brought his long speech to an end, Don Quixote constantly fearing he would say thousands of nonsensical things, and when he saw him conclude having said so few, he gave thanks to heaven in his heart, and the duke embraced Sancho and said he was grieved to his very soul that he had left the governorship so soon, but he would arrange to give him another less burdensome and more profitable position on his estate. The duchess also embraced him and ordered that he be very well treated, for he showed signs of having been badly bruised and of having slept even worse.

CHAPTER LVI

Regarding the extraordinary and unprecedented battle that Don Quixote of La Mancha had with the footman Tosilos in defense of the daughter of the duenna Doña Rodríguez

The duke and duchess did not repent of the joke played on Sancho Panza with regard to the governorship they had given him, especially because on that same day their steward arrived and recounted point by point, and almost in their entirety, Sancho's words and actions during the days of his governorship, and finally he elaborated for them the attack on the ínsula, and Sancho's fear, and his departure, giving them no small pleasure.

After this, the history recounts that the appointed day of the battle

---

3. Martín de Riquer believes this may be a game called "four corners;" each of four positions is occupied by one player, a fifth is in the middle, the four change places, and "it" tries to take over a corner, forcing the original occupant into the center.

arrived, and the duke, having instructed his footman Tosilos over and over again how he was to confront Don Quixote and defeat him without killing or wounding him, ordered the iron tips removed from the lances, saying to Don Quixote that the Christianity on which he prided himself would not permit the encounter to put their lives at so much risk and danger, and Don Quixote should be content with the open field he was providing even though this contravened the decree of the Holy Council[1] that prohibits such challenges, and he did not wish their fierce combat to be carried to the extreme.

Don Quixote said that His Excellency should arrange the details of the matter however he chose, for he would obey him in everything. And when the fearful day arrived, the duke had ordered a large platform erected at the front of the castle square, for the judges as well as the claimants, mother and daughter; infinite numbers of people came from all the surrounding towns and villages to see the unusual battle, for those who lived in that land, and even those who had died there, had never seen or heard of anything like it.

The first to enter the field of battle was the master of ceremonies, who scrutinized the field and walked all around it to be sure there was no deception and nothing concealed where one might stumble and fall; then the duennas came in and took their seats, wrapped in their cloaks to their eyes, even to their breasts, showing signs of no small emotion. Don Quixote entered the field, and shortly after that, accompanied by many trumpets, the huge footman Tosilos appeared at one end of the square on a powerful horse, overshadowing everyone, his visor lowered and sitting erect in strong and shining armor. His large, dappled horse appeared to be a Frisian,[2] and from each fetlock there hung an *arroba* of hair.

The valorous combatant came in, well-instructed by the duke his lord regarding how he was to behave with the valiant Don Quixote of La Mancha, and warned that under no circumstances was he to kill him but should attempt to flee the first charge in order to avoid the risk of Don Quixote's death, which was certain if he was to meet him head-on. He crossed the square, reached the place where the duennas were sitting, and began to look at the one who wanted him for a husband. The master of the field summoned Don Quixote, who had come onto the square, and

1. An allusion to Law 19 of the Council of Trent prohibiting challenges and tourneys.
2. A breed of horses that are very strong, with broad hooves.

together with Tosilos he spoke to the duennas, asking if they consented to Don Quixote defending their cause. They said they did, and that everything decided in this matter they would consider correct, irrevocable, and binding.

By this time, the duke and duchess were seated in a gallery that overlooked the field, which was crowded with an infinite number of people waiting to see the fierce, unprecedented battle. It was stipulated by the combatants that if Don Quixote was victorious, his adversary would be obliged to marry the daughter of Doña Rodríguez, and if he was defeated, his opponent would be free of the promise demanded of him and need give no other satisfaction.

The master of ceremonies apportioned the sun[3] and directed each combatant to his place. The drums rolled, the air filled with the sound of trumpets, the earth trembled beneath their feet. The hearts of the crowd of onlookers were in suspense, some fearing and others hoping for the good or bad outcome of the matter. Finally, Don Quixote, commending himself with all his heart to God Our Lord and his lady Dulcinea of Toboso, waited to receive the precise signal to charge, but our footman had other ideas, for he was thinking only about what I shall tell you now:

It appears that when he looked at his enemy, Doña Rodríguez's daughter, she seemed the most beautiful woman he had ever seen in his entire life, and the little blind boy, ordinarily called Amor along these streets, did not wish to miss the opportunity that had been offered him to triumph over a footman's soul and place it on the list of his trophies, and so he approached him very cunningly, without anyone seeing him, and he pierced the poor footman on his left side with an arrow two *varas* long that passed right through his heart; Amor could do this with complete impunity because he is invisible and comes and goes as he pleases, without anyone demanding that he account for his actions.

And so, I say, when the signal was given for the charge, our footman was in ecstasy, thinking about the beauty of the woman whom he had already made mistress of his liberty, and he did not attend to the sound of the trumpet as Don Quixote did, for as soon as he heard it he charged, and galloping as fast as Rocinante would permit, he attacked his enemy, and seeing him attack, his good squire, Sancho, called in a loud voice:

"May God guide you, flower and jewel of knights errant! May God grant you victory, for right is on your side!"

3. As indicated earlier, this meant to divide the field in such a way that the sun would not be in one combatant's eyes more than in the other's.

And even though Tosilos saw Don Quixote coming toward him, he did not move a step away from his position; instead, he called for the master of the field, who came to see what he wanted, and he said:

"Señor, isn't this combat to decide if I marry or don't marry that lady?"

"It is," was the response.

"Well then," said the footman, "I fear for my conscience, and I would put too great a weight on it if I went forward with this combat, and so I say that I declare myself defeated, and wish to marry that lady immediately."

The master of the field was amazed at Tosilos's words, and since he was one of those privy to the scheme, he did not know how to respond. Don Quixote stopped in the middle of his charge when he saw that his enemy was not attacking him. The duke did not know why the combat did not go forward, but the master of the field went to tell him what Tosilos had said, which left the duke astonished and extremely irate.

While this was happening, Tosilos went up to where Doña Rodríguez was sitting and said in a very loud voice:

"I, Señora, wish to marry your daughter, and I do not want to attain through disputes and battles what I can attain peacefully and with no risk of death."

The valiant Don Quixote heard this and said:

"Since this is true, I am released and set free from my promise; let them marry, and good fortune to them, and since God Our Lord has granted the marriage, may St. Peter bless it."

The duke came down to the castle square, and approaching Tosilos, he said:

"Is it true, O knight, that you declare yourself defeated, and that pressed by your timorous conscience, you wish to marry this maiden?"

"Yes, Señor," responded Tosilos.

"He's doing the right thing," said Sancho Panza, "because if you give the cat what you were going to give to the mouse, your troubles will be over."

Tosilos was loosening his helmet and asked for help because he was having trouble catching his breath and could not bear to be confined for so long in so narrow a space. It was quickly removed, and the footman's face was uncovered and revealed, and seeing this, Doña Rodríguez and her daughter cried out, saying:

"Deception! This is a deception! They sent in Tosilos, a footman to my lord the duke, instead of my true husband! We demand the justice of God and the king against so much guile, not to say wickedness!"

"Do not grieve, Señoras," said Don Quixote, "for this is neither guile nor wickedness, and if it is, the duke has not been the cause but the evil enchanters who pursue me, and who, envious of my achieving the glory of this victory, have transformed the face of your husband into that of this man, whom you say is a footman of the duke. Take my advice, and despite the guile of my enemies marry him, for he undoubtedly is the one you desire for your husband."

The duke, who heard this, was about to turn all his anger into laughter, and he said:

"The things that befall Señor Don Quixote are so extraordinary that I am prepared to believe this man is not my footman, but let us make use of this stratagem and artifice: we shall delay the marriage for fifteen days, if you like, and keep this person, about whom we have our doubts, confined, and in that time he may return to his original appearance, for the rancor the enchanters feel toward Señor Don Quixote cannot last that long, especially since they derive so little profit from these tricks and transformations."

"Oh, Señor!" said Sancho Panza. "It's the habit and custom of these scoundrels to change the appearance of things that have to do with my master. They made a knight he defeated some days ago, who was called the Knight of the Mirrors, look like Bachelor Sansón Carrasco, who comes from our village and is a good friend of ours, and they turned my lady Dulcinea of Toboso into a rough peasant girl, and so I imagine that this footman will die and live a footman for all the days of his life."

To which the daughter of Doña Rodríguez responded:

"Whoever this man is who asks me to be his wife, I thank him for it; I'd rather be the legitimate wife of a footman than the deceived mistress of a gentleman, though the one who deceived me is no such thing."

In short, all these stories and events resulted in Tosilos being locked away until they could see the outcome of his transformation; all the spectators acclaimed Don Quixote as the victor, and most were sad and melancholy at seeing that the long-awaited combatants had not hacked each other to pieces, just as boys are sad when the hanged man they have been waiting for does not come out because he has been pardoned, either by the other party or by the court. The people left, the duke and Don Quixote returned to the castle, Tosilos was confined, Doña Rodríguez and her daughter were delighted to see that one way or the other, the matter would end in marriage, and Tosilos hoped for nothing less.

CHAPTER LVII

Which recounts how Don Quixote took his leave of the duke, and what befell him with the clever and bold Altisidora, the duchess's maiden

Now it seemed to Don Quixote that it would be good for him to abandon the extreme idleness in which he had been living in the castle, for he imagined it would be a great mistake for him to remain confined and inactive among the infinite luxuries and pleasures offered to him as a knight errant by the duke and duchess, and he thought he would have to give a strict accounting to heaven with regard to this confinement and inactivity; and so, one day he asked the duke and duchess for permission to leave. They granted it, indicating that it grieved them deeply that he was going. The duchess gave Sancho Panza the letters from his wife, and he wept over them, saying:

"Who would have thought that hopes as great as the ones born in the heart of my wife, Teresa Panza, at the news of my governorship would end in my returning to the miserable adventures of my master, Don Quixote of La Mancha? Even so, I'm happy to see that my Teresa behaved like the person she is and sent the acorns to the duchess, because if she hadn't sent them, I would have been very sorry to see her so ungrateful. What comforts me is that this gift can't be called a bribe, because I already had the governorship when she sent them, and it's only right that people who receive a benefit should show that they are grateful, even if it's with trifles. In fact, I came into the governorship naked, and I left it naked, and so I can say with a clear conscience, which is no small thing: 'Naked I was born, and I'm naked now: I haven't lost or gained a thing.'"

Sancho said this to himself on the day of their departure, and Don Quixote, having taken his leave of the duke and duchess the night before, came out in the morning and appeared in his armor on the castle square. All the people in the castle watched him from the passageways, and the duke and duchess also came out to see him. Sancho was on his gray, with his saddlebags, traveling case, and provisions, and he was very happy because the duke's steward, the one who had played Countess Trifaldi, had given him a purse with two hundred gold *escudos* for expenses on the road, and Don Quixote did not know about this yet.

While everyone was looking at Don Quixote, as has been said, suddenly, from among the duchess's duennas and maidens who were watching him, the bold and clever Altisidora raised her voice, and in woeful tones she said:

> "Oh listen, most wicked knight;
> pull up your reins for a while;
> do not belabor the flanks
> of your uncontrollable steed.
>   Consider, false one, no fearsome
> serpent pursues you, you flee
> nothing but a gentle lamb,
> one far from being a ewe.
>   O monster, you have deceived
> the fairest, most comely maid
> Diana saw in her forests,
> or Venus saw in her woods.
> *Vireno most cruel, O fugitive Aeneas,*[1]
> *may Barabbas go with you; you belong with him.*
>
>   You take with you, oh cruel taking,
> clutched in your bloodthirsty claws
> the loving heart of a damsel
> enamored, humble, and young.
>   You have taken her three nightcaps,
> and garters both black and white
> from legs that rival the purest
> marble in their smooth whiteness.
>   You have taken two thousand sighs
> that could, if they were of fire,
> burn and destroy two thousand Troys
> if there were two thousand Troys.

1. Vireno abandoned Olimpia in Ariosto's *Orlando furioso*; Aeneas abandoned Dido in Virgil's *Aeneid*.

Vireno most cruel, oh fugitive Aeneas,
may Barabbas go with you; you belong with him.

As for your squire named Sancho,
may his heart be as hard as stone,
as cold as ice: then Dulcinea
will ne'er be freed of enchantment.
    The fault is no one's but yours,
but let her pay for your crime;
perhaps in my land the just
must pay and suffer for sinners.
    May your most noble adventures
be nothing but misadventures,
your pleasures, nothing but dreams,
your courage, gone and forgotten.
Cruel Vireno, fugitive Aeneas,
May Barabbas go with you; you belong with him.

    May you be known as false-hearted
from Sevilla to Marchena,
from Granada to far Loja,
from fair London throughout England.
    If you ever play *reinado,*
los cientos, or *la primera,*[2]
may all the kings fly from you,
as well as aces and sevens.
    If you ever trim your corns,
may the blood spurt from the wounds,
and if you have your molars pulled
may they break off at the roots.
Cruel Vireno, fugitive Aeneas,
May Barabbas go with you; you belong with him."

While the piteous Altisidora lamented her aforementioned fate, Don Quixote stared fixedly at her, not saying a word, and then he turned to Sancho and said:

"By all the years of your forebears, Sancho my friend, I implore you to tell me the truth. Tell me, have you, by any chance, taken the

---

2. Three card games in which kings, aces, and sevens, respectively, are the most valuable cards.

three nightcaps and the garters that this enamored maiden has mentioned?"

To which Sancho responded:

"I do have the three nightcaps, but the garters—that's really crazy."

The duchess was amazed at the boldness of Altisidora, for although she considered her audacious, lively, and bold, she did not think she would dare carry things so far, and since she had not been told about this joke, her amazement grew even more. The duke wanted to go on with the clever deception, and he said:

"It does not seem right to me, Señor Knight, that after receiving in this castle the warm welcome that was offered to you, you have dared take away at least three nightcaps, not to mention garters, that belong to my maiden; these are indications of an ungrateful heart, signs that do not correspond to your fame. Return the garters to her; if not, I challenge you to mortal combat, with no fear that your roguish enchanters will change or alter my face, as they did to Tosilos, my footman, who entered into battle with you."

"God forbid," responded Don Quixote, "that I unsheathe my sword against your most illustrious person, from whom I have received so many kindnesses; I shall return the nightcaps, because Sancho says he has them; as for the garters, that is impossible, because I do not have them and neither does he; if this maiden of yours would look through her hiding places, I am sure she would find them. I, Señor Duke, have never been a thief, nor do I intend to be one for the rest of my life, unless God abandons me. This maiden speaks, as she has said, as one enamored, and for that I am not to blame; and so, I have no reason to beg her pardon, or yours, although I implore Your Excellency to have a better opinion of me, and to once again give me your permission to continue on my way."

"May God so favor you there," said the duchess, "Señor Don Quixote, that we always hear good reports of your deeds. And go with God, for the longer you tarry, the more you fan the flames in the hearts of the maidens who look upon you; as for this maiden, I shall punish her so that from now on she will not be insolent in her glances or her words."

"I want you to hear only one more word of mine, O valiant Don Quixote!" said Altisidora. "I beg your pardon for saying you stole my garters, because by God and my soul, I am wearing them, and I have fallen into the careless error of the man who went looking for the donkey he was riding on."

"Didn't I say so?" said Sancho. "I'm the right one to go around hiding stolen things! If I wanted to do that, I could've done it to my heart's content in my governorship."

Don Quixote bowed his head in deference to the duke and duchess and all the onlookers, and turning Rocinante's reins, and with Sancho riding after him on the gray, he left the castle and followed the road to Zaragoza.

CHAPTER LVIII

Which recounts how so many adventures rained down on Don Quixote that there was hardly room for all of them

When Don Quixote saw himself in the open countryside, free and clear of Altisidora's wooing, it seemed to him that he had returned to his own element, that his spirits had revived and were ready to resume his chivalric pursuits, and turning to Sancho, he said:

"Freedom, Sancho, is one of the most precious gifts heaven gave to men; the treasures under the earth and beneath the sea cannot compare to it; for freedom, as well as for honor, one can and should risk one's life, while captivity, on the other hand, is the greatest evil that can befall men. I say this, Sancho, because you have clearly seen the luxury and abundance we have enjoyed in this castle that we are leaving, but in the midst of those flavorful banquets and those drinks as cool as snow, it seemed as if I were suffering the pangs of hunger because I could not enjoy them with the freedom I would have had if they had been mine; the obligations to repay the benefits and kindnesses we have received are bonds that hobble a free spirit. Fortunate is the man to whom heaven has given a piece of bread with no obligation to thank anyone but heaven itself!"

"In spite of everything," said Sancho, "that your grace has said, it's not right for us to be ungrateful for the two hundred gold *escudos* in a purse that the duke's steward gave to me and that I wear as a cure and a comfort over my heart, in case of emergencies, for we aren't always going to find castles where they welcome us; we might come across some inns where they beat us instead."

The two errants, knight and squire, were engaged in conversations like these when, having traveled a little more than a league, they saw a

small green meadow where approximately a dozen men dressed as farmers were sitting and eating on their cloaks, which were spread on the
grass. Next to them were what seemed like white sheets covering several
objects that were placed at intervals, either standing up straight or lying
flat. Don Quixote approached the men who were eating, and after first
greeting them courteously, he asked what they had under those cloths.
One of them responded:

"Señor, under these cloths are wooden images carved in relief for an
altarpiece that we're erecting in our village; we carry them covered so
they won't be damaged, and on our shoulders so they won't break."

"If you would be so kind," responded Don Quixote, "I should like
very much to see them, for images that are carried with so much care undoubtedly are good."

"Well, of course they are!" said another. "They cost enough: the truth
is that every one of them costs more than fifty *ducados*; so that your grace
can see the truth of this, just wait, and your grace will see with your own
eyes."

And he stood up, stopped eating, and went to remove the covering of
the first image, which turned out to be St. George mounted on a horse, a
serpent lying coiled at his feet, its mouth run through by a lance, all of it
depicted with the customary ferocity. The entire image seemed to glitter
like gold, as they say. When he saw it, Don Quixote said:

"This was one of the best knights errant the divine militia ever had:
his name was Don St. George,[1] and he was also a protector of damsels.
Let us see this next one."

The man uncovered it, and it seemed to be St. Martin astride a horse
as he divided his cape with the poor man; and as soon as he saw it, Don
Quixote said:

"This knight was another Christian seeker of adventures, and I believe he was more generous than brave, as you can see, Sancho, for he is
dividing his cape with the poor man and giving him half, and no doubt it
must have been winter then; otherwise, he was so charitable he would
have given him the entire cape."

"That couldn't have been the reason," said Sancho, "but he must
have been paying attention to the proverb that says: 'For giving and
keeping you need some brains.'"

Don Quixote laughed and asked them to remove another cloth, and

---

1. Martín de Riquer points out that there is no ironic or comic intent involved in using the honorific *don* with St. George, the patron saint of the crown of Aragón: in medieval Catalonian texts,
he was referred to as *Monsenyer Sant Jordi*.

beneath it was revealed the image of the patron saint of Spain on horse-back, his sword stained with blood, riding down Moors and trampling on their heads; and when he saw it, Don Quixote said:

"This one certainly is a knight, a member of the squadrons of Christ; his name is St. James the Moorkiller, one of the most valiant saints and knights the world has ever had, and that heaven has now."

Then they removed another cloth, and it covered the fall of St. Paul from his horse, with all the details that are usually depicted in images of his conversion. It looked so lifelike that one would say that Christ was speaking and Paul responding.

"This," said Don Quixote, "was the greatest enemy the Church of God Our Lord had at the time, and the greatest defender it will ever have; a knight errant in life, and a steadfast saint in death, a tireless worker in the vineyard of the Lord, a teacher of peoples whose school was heaven and whose professor and master was Jesus Christ Himself."

There were no more images, and so Don Quixote said they should be covered again, and he told the men who were carrying them:

"Brothers, I take it as a good omen that I have seen what I have seen here, because these saints and knights professed what I profess, which is the practice of arms; the difference, however, between me and them is that they were saints and fought in the divine manner, and I am a sinner and fight in the human manner. They conquered heaven by force of arms, for 'the kingdom of heaven suffereth violence,'[2] and so far I do not know what I am conquering by the force of my labors, but if my Dulcinea of Toboso were to be free of the ills she is suffering, thereby improving my fortune and strengthening my judgment, it might be that my feet would travel a better road than the one I follow now."

"May God hear and sin be deaf," said Sancho.

The men were as baffled by Don Quixote's appearance as they were by his words, for they did not understand half of what he said. They fin-ished their meal, picked up their images, and, taking their leave of Don Quixote, continued on their way.

Sancho once again was so amazed at what his master knew, it was as if he had never known him, for it seemed there was no history or event in the world that Don Quixote did not have clearly in mind and fixed in his memory; and Sancho said:

"The truth is, Señor Master, that if what happened to us today can be

---

2. Matthew 11:12.

called an adventure, it has been one of the gentlest and sweetest that has happened to us in the course of our wanderings: we've come out of it with no beatings and no fear, and we haven't laid a hand on our swords, or battered the ground with our bodies, or been left hungry. God be praised for allowing me to see such a thing with my own eyes."

"What you say is correct, Sancho," said Don Quixote, "but you must realize that not all times are the same, nor do they always follow the same course, and what common people generally call omens, which are not founded on any natural cause, the wise man must consider and judge to be happy events. One of these superstitious men gets up in the morning, leaves his house, happens to meet a friar of the Order of the Blessed St. Francis, and as if he had met a gryphon,[3] he turns around and returns home. Another Mendoza[4] spills salt on the table, and melancholy spills in his heart, as if nature were obliged to give signs of impending misfortunes with things as trivial as those we have mentioned. A wise Christian should not try to guess what heaven intends to do. When Scipio arrived in Africa, he stumbled as he leaped ashore, and his soldiers considered it an evil omen, but he embraced the ground and said: 'You cannot escape me, Africa, because I am holding you tight in my arms.' And so, Sancho, having come across these images has been a very happy event for me."

"I believe that, too," responded Sancho, "and I'd like your grace to tell me why it is that Spaniards, when they're about to go into battle, invoke that St. James the Moorkiller and say: 'St. James, and close Spain!' By some chance is Spain open so that it's necessary to close her, or what ceremony is that?"[5]

"You are very simple, Sancho," responded Don Quixote. "Remember that God gave this great Knight of the Scarlet Cross to Spain to be her patron and protector, especially in the harsh conflicts that the Spaniards have had with the Moors, and so they invoke and call on him as their defender in every battle they fight, and they often have seen him throwing down, trampling, destroying, and killing the squadrons of Hagar,[6] and I

3. A mythical animal with the body and hind legs of a lion and the head, wings, and forelegs of an eagle.

4. It was traditional to attribute superstitious beliefs to people named Mendoza.

5. The phrase in Spanish is ¡*Santiago, y cierra España!* The verb *cerrar* usually means "to close," but Martín de Riquer points out that it could also mean "attack," so that the battle cry, with the addition of a comma, should be "St. James, and attack, Spain!" He also remarks on the fact that Don Quixote does not answer Sancho's very reasonable question.

6. Hagar, Abraham's concubine and the mother of Ishmael, is considered the mother of all Arab peoples and, by extension, of Muslims.

could give you many examples of this truth that are recounted in truthful Spanish histories."

Sancho changed the subject and said to his master:

"I'm amazed, Señor, at the boldness of Altisidora, the duchess's maiden: she must have been badly wounded and run through by the one they call Amor; they say he's a little blind boy, and his vision is dim, or, I should say, he's sightless, but if he takes aim at a heart, no matter how small, he hits it with his arrows and runs it through. I've also heard that a maiden's modesty and reserve can make those amorous arrows blunt and dull, but in Altisidora they seem to grow sharper, not duller."

"You should know, Sancho," said Don Quixote, "that love shows no restraint, and does not keep within the bounds of reason as it proceeds, and has the same character as death: it attacks the noble palaces of kings as well as the poor huts of shepherds, and when it takes full possession of a heart, the first thing it does is to take away fear and shame; lacking them, Altisidora declared her desires, which gave rise in my bosom to more confusion than compassion."

"What notable cruelty!" said Sancho. "What glaring ingratitude! For me, I can say that at her smallest word of love I'd surrender and submit. Whoreson, what a heart of marble you have, and a will of bronze, and a soul of mortar! But I can't think what this maiden saw in your grace that made her surrender and submit like that: what grace, what elegance, what charm, what face, each thing by itself or all of them together, made her fall in love? Because to tell you the truth, I often stop to look at your grace from the tips of your toes to the last hair on your head, and I see more things to drive her away than to make her fall in love; I've also heard that beauty is the first and principal quality that makes people love, and since your grace doesn't have any, I don't know what the poor maiden fell in love with."

"You should know, Sancho," responded Don Quixote, "that there are two kinds of beauty: one of the soul and the other of the body; that of the soul is found and seen in one's understanding, chastity, virtuous behavior, liberality, and good breeding, and all of these qualities can exist and reside in an ugly man; and when a person looks at this beauty, and not at that of the body, an intense and advantageous love is engendered. I see very clearly, Sancho, that I am not handsome, but I also know that I am not deformed; it is enough for a virtuous man not to be a monster to be well-loved, if he has the endowments of the soul which I have mentioned to you."

As they were having this conversation, they entered a forest that was to the side of the road, and suddenly, before he was aware of it, Don Quixote found himself caught in some nets of green string that were stretched from tree to tree; unable to imagine what this might be, he said to Sancho:

"It seems to me, Sancho, that the reason for these nets must be one of the strangest adventures anyone could imagine. By my soul, the enchanters who pursue me must want to entangle me in them and stop my journey in order to avenge the severity I showed Altisidora. Well, I can assure them that even if these nets were made not of green string but of the hardest diamonds, or were stronger than the net with which the jealous god of blacksmiths[7] trapped Venus and Mars, I would break them as if they were made of reeds or cotton threads."

And when he attempted to step forward and break the nets, suddenly there appeared before him, coming out from among the trees, two extremely beautiful shepherdesses: at least, they were dressed as shepherdesses, except that their jackets and skirts were made of fine brocade, I mean, their skirts were made of rich moiré shot with gold. Their hair, so blond it rivaled the rays of the sun, hung loose down their backs and was crowned with garlands woven of green laurel and red amaranth. Their age, apparently, was no less than fifteen and no more than eighteen.

This was a sight that amazed Sancho, astounded Don Quixote, made the sun stop in its course to see them, and held all four of them in stunned silence. Finally, the person who spoke first was one of the two shepherdesses, who said to Don Quixote:

"Step back, Señor Knight, and do not break the nets that are stretched there not to harm you but for our entertainment; and because I know you will ask why they are hung there and who we are, I want to tell you briefly. In a village about two leagues from here, where there are many wellborn people, and many rich nobles, it was agreed among a good number of friends and relatives that their sons, wives, daughters, neighbors, friends, and relatives would come to enjoy this spot, which is one of the most pleasant in the entire region, and that all of us would create a second pastoral Arcadia,[8] the girls dressing as shepherdesses and the boys as shepherds. We've studied two eclogues, one by the famous poet Garcilaso and the other by the excellent Camoes,[9] in his own Portuguese language, neither of which we have performed yet. Yesterday

---

7. Vulcan, married to Venus, threw a net over her and Mars while they were making love.

8. Originally a rural district in the Peloponnesus, Arcadia subsequently became the preferred setting in Renaissance pastoral literature.

9. Luiz Vaz de Camoes, the great Portuguese poet of the sixteenth century (1524?–1580).

was the first day we spent here: we put up some tents, they say they're called field tents, along the banks of a large stream that waters all these meadows; last night we stretched these nets between the trees to deceive the simple little birds that we frightened deliberately with our noise so they would fly into them. If, Señor, you would like to be our guest, you will be treated generously and courteously, for now no sorrow or melancholy must enter this place."

She stopped speaking and said no more, and Don Quixote responded:

"Certainly, most beautiful lady, Actaeon[10] could not have been more astonished or amazed when he suddenly saw Diana bathing in the waters than I am at the sight of your beauty. I praise the subject of your entertainments, and I am grateful for your offer; and if I can serve both of you, with the certainty that you will be obeyed you can command me, because my profession is none other than to show that I am grateful and a benefactor to all manner of people, especially the wellborn, which your persons represent; and if these nets, which occupy only a small space, were to occupy the entire globe, I would seek new worlds where I could pass through without breaking them; so that you will give some credence to my exaggeration, you should know that the promise, at least, is made by Don Quixote of La Mancha, in the event this name has reached your ears."

"O, my dear friend!" the other shepherdess said then. "What good fortune for us! Do you see this gentleman in front of us? Well, let me tell you that he is the most valiant, and most enamored, and most courteous knight in the world, if a history of his deeds which is in print, and which I have read, does not lie to us and deceive us. I'll wager that this man with him is a certain Sancho Panza, his squire, whose comical remarks no one can equal."

"It's true," said Sancho, "I'm the comical fellow and the squire, just as your grace has said, and this gentleman is my master, the historied Don Quixote of La Mancha you've mentioned."

"Oh!" said the other girl. "Dear friend, let's ask him to stay, for our parents and brothers and sisters will enjoy that so much; I've heard about his courage and grace, too, just as you've described them, and they say especially that he's the most steadfast and loyal lover who ever lived, and that his lady is a certain Dulcinea of Toboso, known to be the most beautiful woman in all of Spain."

10. A hunter who came upon Diana when she was bathing; she turned him into a stag, and he was then torn to pieces by his own dogs.

"And with reason," said Don Quixote, "unless your peerless beauty calls that into question. Do not weary yourselves, Señoras, in trying to detain me, because the obligatory demands of my profession do not allow me to rest very long in one place."

Just then a brother of one of the shepherdesses came to the spot where the four of them were, and he too was dressed as a shepherd, as richly and elegantly as the two girls, who told him that the man with them was the valiant Don Quixote of La Mancha and the other was his squire, Sancho, both of whom he already knew about because he had read their history. The charming shepherd paid his compliments and asked the knight to accompany him to his tents, and Don Quixote finally had to agree.

At this point the beaters arrived, and the nets were filled with a variety of small birds that were deceived by the color of the nets and fell into the very danger they were fleeing. More than thirty people gathered in that place, all of them splendidly dressed as shepherds and shepherdesses, and in a moment all of them knew who Don Quixote and his squire were, which pleased them a great deal because they already knew about the two of them from their history. They went to the tents and found the tables richly, abundantly, and immaculately laid; they honored Don Quixote by seating him at the head, and everyone looked at him and was amazed to see him.

Finally, when the tables had been cleared, Don Quixote very calmly raised his voice and said:

"Although some may say pride is the greatest sin men commit, I say it is ingratitude, for I am guided by the adage that says hell is filled with the ungrateful. This sin is one I have attempted to flee, as much as it was possible for me to do so, since I first reached the age of reason; if I cannot repay the good deeds done for me with other deeds, in their place I put the desire I have to perform them, and if that is not enough, I proclaim those good deeds far and wide, because the person who tells about and proclaims the good deeds that have been performed on his behalf would also recompense them with other deeds if he could, because most of the time those who receive are subordinate to those who give: therefore God is above us all, because He gives to us all, and the gifts of man cannot be compared to those of God, for they are separated by an infinite distance; this paucity and dearth, in a certain sense, can be made up for by gratitude. And I, grateful for the kindness shown to me here, and not being able to correspond in kind, for I am restrained by the narrow limitations of my means, offer what little I can and am able to do; and so I say that I shall maintain for two whole days, in the middle of the king's highway to Zaragoza, that these damsels, the feigned shepherdesses here present, are the most beautiful and courteous maidens in the world, excepting only the peerless Dulcinea of Toboso, the sole lady of my thoughts, with no offense intended to all the gentlemen and ladies who hear me."

Upon hearing this, Sancho, who had been listening very attentively, gave a great shout, saying:

"Is it possible that there are persons in the world who dare to say and swear that my master is crazy? Your graces, Señores Shepherds, tell me: is there a village priest, no matter how intelligent and educated, who can say what my master has said, or a knight errant, no matter how famous for courage, who can offer what my master has offered here?"

Don Quixote turned to Sancho, his face ablaze with anger, and said:

"Is it possible, O Sancho, that there is anyone in the whole wide world who can say you are not a dolt, lined with doltishness and trimmed with a certain wickedness and malice? Who has asked you to mind my business or determine if I am intelligent or a fool? Be quiet, and do not answer me, but saddle Rocinante if he is unsaddled, and let us go to put my offer into effect, for with the rightness of my cause, you can consider all who might wish to contradict it as already vanquished."

And with great fury and signs of anger, he rose from his seat, leaving the onlookers perplexed, wondering if they should consider him as mad or sane. Finally, they attempted to persuade him not to issue the challenge, for they considered his gratitude well-known, and there was no need for further proofs of his valiant spirit since the ones alluded to in the history of his deeds were more than enough; yet despite all this, Don Quixote carried out his intention, and sitting on Rocinante, his shield on his arm and his lance in his hand, he placed himself in the middle of a king's highway not far from the green meadow. Sancho followed him on his gray, along with all the people in the pastoral flock, for they wished to see how far his arrogant and unparalleled offer would go.

When Don Quixote was situated in the middle of the road—as I have already told you—he pierced the air with these words:

"O you travelers and wayfarers, knights and squires, those on foot and those on horseback who pass or will pass along this road during the next two days! Know that Don Quixote of La Mancha, knight errant, is here to maintain that of all the beauty and courtesy in the world, none is greater than that found in the nymphs who inhabit these meadows and forests, putting to one side the lady of my soul, Dulcinea of Toboso. Therefore whoever holds a contrary opinion, let him come forward: I wait for him here."

Twice he repeated these same words, and twice they were not heard by any seeker of adventures; but Fortune, who was directing his affairs from one success to another, ordained that in a little while there would appear on the road a crowd of men on horseback, many of them with lances in their hands, riding very close together, in some confusion and in great haste. As soon as those who were with Don Quixote saw them, they turned and moved a good distance from the road, knowing that if they waited, they could be in danger; only Don Quixote, with an intrepid heart, stayed where he was, and Sancho Panza took cover behind Rocinante's hindquarters.

The troop of lancers approached, and one of them, who was riding at their head, began to shout at Don Quixote, saying:

"Move aside, you devil, or these bulls will trample you to death!"

"Hah, you rabble!" responded Don Quixote. "What do I care for bulls, even if they are the fiercest bred on the banks of the Jarama! Confess, you villains, that what I have proclaimed here is true, without knowing what it is, and if you do not, you will have to contend with me."

The herder had no time to respond, and Don Quixote had no time to move away, even if he had wanted to, and the crowd of fierce bulls and tame lead oxen, and the multitude of herders and other people who were taking them to a town where they would fight the next day, passed over Don Quixote, and over Sancho, Rocinante, and the gray, knocking them all down and sending them rolling along the ground. Sancho was left bruised, Don Quixote stunned, the donkey battered, and Rocinante none too sound; but, finally, they all got to their feet, and Don Quixote, stumbling here and falling there, began to run as fast as he could after the herd of bulls, shouting:

"Stop, wait, you villainous rabble! A single knight awaits you, one who does not concur or agree with those who say that one should build a silver bridge for the enemy who flees!"

But not even this could stop the speeding runners, and they paid no more attention to his threats than to the clouds of yesteryear. Exhaustion stopped Don Quixote, and more vexed than avenged, he sat down by the side of the road, waiting for Sancho, Rocinante, and the gray to reach him. They did, and master and servant remounted, and without returning to take their leave of the feigned or counterfeit Arcadia, and with more shame than pleasure, they continued on their way.

CHAPTER LIX

Which recounts an extraordinary incident that befell Don Quixote and can be considered an adventure

The dust and weariness that Don Quixote and Sancho took away with them from their encounter with the discourteous bulls was alleviated by a clear, fresh spring that they found in a cool grove of trees, and the two of them, the fatigued master and servant, sat at its edge, leaving the gray and Rocinante free, without bridle or bit. Sancho turned to the provisions in his saddlebags and took out what he liked to call his feed; he rinsed his mouth, and Don Quixote washed his face, and this refreshment helped to revive their discouraged spirits. Don Quixote did not eat out of pure sorrow, and Sancho did not dare to touch the food before him out of pure courtesy, for he was waiting for his master to take the first mouthful; but seeing him so lost in thought that he forgot to raise the bread to his mouth, Sancho did not open his to speak, and violating every rule of good manners, he began to pack his stomach with the bread and cheese that were in front of him.

"Eat, Sancho my friend," said Don Quixote, "sustain life, which matters to you more than to me, and let me die at the hands of my thoughts and by means of my misfortunes. I, Sancho, was born to live by dying, and you to die by eating; so you can see that I am telling you the truth in this regard, consider me, printed in histories, famous in the practice of arms, courteous in my actions, respected by princes, wooed by maidens; and when I expected the palms, triumphs, and crowns that were earned and deserved by my valorous deeds, I have seen myself this morning trampled and kicked and bruised by the feet of filthy and unclean animals. This thought dulls my teeth, blunts my molars, numbs my hands, and completely takes away my desire for food, and so I think I shall let myself die of hunger, the cruelest of all deaths."

"That means," said Sancho, not stopping his rapid chewing, "that your grace doesn't agree with the proverb that says, 'Let Marta die but keep her belly full.' I, at least, don't plan to kill myself; instead, I plan to do what the shoemaker does when he pulls on the leather with his teeth and stretches it until it reaches as far as he wants: I'll stretch my life by eating until it reaches the end that heaven has arranged for it; you should know, Señor, that there's no greater madness than wanting to despair, the way your grace does; believe me, after you eat something, you should sleep a little on the green featherbed of this grass, and you'll see that when you wake up you'll feel much relieved."

Don Quixote complied, thinking that Sancho's words were those of a philosopher, not a fool, and he said to him:

"If you, O Sancho, would do for me what I shall tell you now, my relief will be more certain and my sorrows not as great; and it is that while I sleep, following your advice, you ought to move a little distance from here, and expose your flesh, and with Rocinante's reins give yourself three or four hundred of the three thousand–odd lashes you must give yourself in order to disenchant Dulcinea, for it is no small shame that the poor lady is still enchanted because of your thoughtlessness and neglect."

"There is a good deal to say about that," said Sancho. "For now, let's both sleep, and later God will decide what will happen. Your grace should know that a man whipping himself in cold blood is a very harsh matter, especially if the lashes fall on a body that is badly nourished and underfed; let my lady Dulcinea be patient, and when she least expects it she'll see me riddled with lashes; everything's life until we die; I mean, I still have mine, along with the desire to keep my promise."

Don Quixote thanked him and ate something, and Sancho ate a great deal, and both of them lay down to sleep, leaving Rocinante and the gray, the two constant companions and friends, free to wander wherever they chose to graze on the plentiful grass that abounded in the meadow. They awoke rather late and remounted and continued on their way, riding quickly in order to reach an inn that seemed to be about a league away. I say it was an inn because that is what Don Quixote called it, in contrast with his usual custom of calling all inns castles.

And so they reached the inn and asked the landlord if there was lodging. The answer was yes, with all the comfort and luxury that one could find in Zaragoza. They dismounted, and Sancho put his provisions away in a room to which the landlord gave him the key; he led the animals to the stable, gave them their fodder, went out to see what orders Don Quixote, who was sitting on a stone bench built into the wall, might have for him, and gave particular thanks to heaven because the inn had not seemed like a castle to his master.

The time for supper arrived, and they withdrew to their room; Sancho asked the landlord what he had for supper. The landlord responded that he could have anything and could ask for whatever he wanted: the inn was stocked with the birds of the air, the fowl of the earth, and the fish of the sea.

"There's no need for so much," responded Sancho. "If you roast a couple of chickens for us, we'll have enough, because my master is delicate and doesn't eat a lot, and I'm not much of a glutton."

The landlord responded that he did not have any chickens because the hawks had devoured them all.

"Well, Señor Landlord," said Sancho, "have them roast a pullet, if it's tender."

"A pullet? Good Lord!" responded the landord. "The truth of the matter is that yesterday I sent fifty to be sold in the city; but, except for pullets, your grace can order whatever you want."

"Then that means," said Sancho, "that you have plenty of veal or goat."

"For the moment, there's none in the house," responded the landlord, "because it's all gone, but next week there'll be plenty."

"That does us a lot of good!" responded Sancho. "I'll wager that everything you don't have can be made up for by all the eggs and bacon you do have."

"By God," responded the landlord, "that's a nice sense of humor my guest has. I already told you I don't have pullets or chickens, and now you want me to have eggs? Talk about some other delicacies, if you like, and stop asking for chickens."

"Let's settle this, for God's sake," said Sancho, "and tell me once and for all what you do have, and enough talking, Señor Landlord."

"What I really and truly have are two cows' heels that seem like calves' feet, or two calves' feet that seem like cows' heels; they're stewed with chickpeas, onions, and bacon, and right now they're saying, 'Eat me! Eat me!' "

"Right now I mark them as mine," said Sancho, "and don't let anybody touch them; I'll pay a better price for them than anybody else, because as far as I'm concerned nothing could taste any better, and it's all the same to me whether they're calves' feet or cows' heels."

"Nobody will touch them," said the innkeeper, "because the other guests I have are so highborn they brought their own cook and steward, and their own provisions."

"If it's highborn you want," said Sancho, "there's nobody better than my master, but his profession doesn't allow any butlers or wine stewards; we just lie down in the middle of a meadow and eat our fill of acorns and medlar fruit."

This was the conversation that Sancho had with the innkeeper; Sancho did not want to answer any of his questions, for he had already asked about his master's profession or office.

The time for supper arrived, Don Quixote returned to his room, the landlord brought in the *olla* full of stew, and Don Quixote sat down to eat very deliberately. It seems that in the next room, which was separated from his only by a thin partition, Don Quixote heard someone say:

"By heaven, Señor Don Jerónimo, while they bring in our supper, let us read another chapter of the second part of *Don Quixote of La Mancha*."

As soon as Don Quixote heard his name, he stood and listened very carefully to what they were saying about him, and he heard the man called Don Jerónimo respond:

"Señor Don Juan, why does your grace want us to read this nonsense? Whoever has read the first part of the history of Don Quixote of La Mancha cannot possibly derive any pleasure from reading this second part."

"Even so," said Don Juan, "it would be nice to read it because there's no book so bad that it doesn't have something good in it. What I dislike the most in this one is that it depicts Don Quixote as having fallen out of love with Dulcinea of Toboso."[1]

When he heard this, Don Quixote, full of wrath and fury, raised his voice and said:

"If anyone says that Don Quixote of La Mancha has forgotten or ever can forget Dulcinea of Toboso, I shall make him understand with the most steadfast arms that he is very far from the truth, because the peerless Dulcinea of Toboso cannot be forgotten, nor does forgetting have any place in Don Quixote, for his coat of arms is constancy and his profession is to preserve it gently, and without force of any kind."

"Who is answering us?" came the response from the next room.

"Who can it be," responded Sancho, "but Don Quixote of La Mancha

---

1. In the *Don Quixote* by Avellaneda, which is the book the two travelers are discussing, Don Quixote renounces his love for Dulcinea and is then called the Disenamored Knight.

himself, who'll carry out everything he's said, and even what he might say? For the man who pays his debts doesn't worry about guaranties."

As soon as Sancho said this, two gentlemen, for that is what they seemed to be, came in through the door of the room, and one of them threw his arms around Don Quixote's neck and said:

"Your presence cannot give the lie to your name, nor can your name not vouch for your presence: there is no doubt, Señor, that you are the true Don Quixote of La Mancha, the polestar and guiding light of knight errantry, notwithstanding and despite one who has wanted to usurp your name and annihilate your deeds, as the author of this book, which I give to you now, has done."

And he placed a book in his hands, which his companion had been carrying; Don Quixote accepted it and without saying a word began to leaf through it, and in a little while he returned it, saying:

"In this short perusal I have found three things in this author that are worthy of reprimand. The first is some words that I have read in the prologue;[2] the second is that the language is Aragonese, because sometimes he writes without articles;[3] the third, which confirms his ignorance, is that he strays and deviates from the truth in the most important part of the history, because he says that the wife of my squire, Sancho Panza, is named Mari Gutiérrez, which is incorrect, for her name is Teresa Panza;[4] if he errs in something so important, it is reasonable to fear that he will err in everything else."

To which Sancho said:

"That's a nice thing in a historian! He must certainly know all about us if he calls my wife Mari Gutiérrez instead of Teresa Panza! Look at the book again, Señor, and see if I'm in it, and if he's changed my name."

"From what I have heard you say, my friend," said Don Jerónimo, "you undoubtedly are Sancho Panza, the squire to Señor Don Quixote."

"Yes, I am," responded Sancho, "and proud of it."

---

2. According to Martín de Riquer, these are the insults directed at Cervantes that are mentioned in the prologue to the authentic part II.

3. Many critics have attempted to prove that Avellaneda was Aragonese on the basis of this statement, but Martín de Riquer states that it cannot be proved. He points out that the omission of articles has never been a characteristic of the Aragonese dialect or of writers from Aragón; further, in Avellaneda's book there are only four cases of missing articles, something that could just as easily be found in texts by Cervantes. If Cervantes uses "articles" to mean "particles" (as some contemporary grammarians did), there are more instances of this kind of omission in the "False *Quixote*," but it is still not a characteristic of Aragonese writing.

4. As Martín de Riquer points out, the error is less Avellaneda's than Cervantes's; in part I, Sancho's wife had four different names, one of which was Mari Gutiérrez.

"Well, by my faith," said the gentleman, "this modern author does not treat you with the decency you demonstrate in your person: he depicts you as gluttonous, and simpleminded, and not at all amusing, and very different from the Sancho described in the first part of the history of your master."[5]

"May God forgive him," said Sancho. "He should have left me in my corner and forgotten about me, because you shouldn't play music unless you know how, and St. Peter's just fine in Rome."

The two gentlemen asked Don Quixote to come into their room and have supper with them, for they knew very well that the inn did not have food worthy of his person. Don Quixote, who was always courteous, agreed to their request and had supper with them, and Sancho was left with the power of life and death and absolute jurisdiction over the *olla;* he sat at the head of the table, along with the innkeeper, who was no less fond than Sancho of feet and heels.

In the course of their supper, Don Juan asked Don Quixote if he had news of Señora Dulcinea of Toboso: if she had married, or given birth, or was pregnant, or if she was still a virgin and remembered—within the bounds of her modesty and decorum—the amorous thoughts of Señor Don Quixote. To which he responded:

"Dulcinea is a virgin, and my thoughts are more constant than ever; our communications, as barren as always; her beauty, transformed into that of a crude peasant."

And then he recounted, point by point, the enchantment of Señora Dulcinea and what had happened to him in the Cave of Montesinos, along with the instructions the wise Merlin had given him on how to disenchant her, which had to do with Sancho's lashes.

The two gentlemen were exceedingly happy to hear Don Quixote relate the strange events of his history, and they were as amazed by the nonsensical things he said as by the elegant manner in which he said them. Here they considered him intelligent, and there he seemed to slip into foolishness, and they could not determine where precisely to place him between intelligence and madness.

Sancho finished eating, and leaving the innkeeper looking like an X,[6] he went to the room where his master was having supper, and when he entered he said:

5. According to Martín de Riquer, Avellaneda's Sancho, unlike the original, is stupid, slovenly, and coarse.

6. The idiom (*hecho equis*) means "staggering drunk" and is based on the image of the shape an inebriated person's legs assume when he stumbles and struggles to keep his balance.

"By my soul, Señores, I don't think the author of this book that your graces have wants to get along with me; since he calls me a glutton, as your graces say, I wouldn't want him to call me a drunkard, too."

"He does say that," said Don Jerónimo, "but I don't remember precisely how, although I do know that his words are offensive, and false as well, as I can see by the physiognomy of the good Sancho here present."

"Believe me, your graces," said Sancho, "the Sancho and the Don Quixote in that history are not the ones who appear in the history composed by Cide Hamete Benengeli, the ones who are us: my master is valiant, intelligent, and in love, and I'm simple, amusing, and not a glutton or a drunkard."

"I believe that," said Don Juan, "and if it were possible, I would order that no one could dare to deal with the affairs of the great Don Quixote except Cide Hamete, the first author, just as Alexander the Great ordered that no one could dare paint his portrait except Apelles."

"Let anyone who wishes to," said Don Quixote, "portray me, but not mistreat me, for patience often falters when it is loaded down with injuries."

"No injury," said Don Juan, "can be done to Señor Don Quixote that he cannot avenge, if he does not ward it off with the shield of his patience, which, in my opinion, is strong and great."

They spent a good part of the night in these and other similar conversations, and although Don Juan wanted Don Quixote to read more of the book in order to hear his comments, he would not be persuaded, saying he considered that he had read it, and confirmed that all of it was foolish, and if it happened to come to the attention of the author that he had held it in his hands, he did not want him to celebrate the idea that Don Quixote had read it, for one's thoughts must eschew obscene and indecent things, as must one's eyes. They asked him where he had decided to travel. He responded to Zaragoza, to take part in the jousts for the suit of armor that are held in the city every year. Don Juan told him that in the new history, the account of how Don Quixote, or whoever he was, ran at the ring[7] was lacking in invention, poor in letters,[8] and very poor in liveries,[9] though rich in stupidities.

---

7. A chivalric activity in which men on horseback would gallop past a ring hanging from a cord and attempt to catch it on the tip of their lance.

8. The verses and epigrams, normally alluding to their ladies, on the shields carried by knights in jousts.

9. Martín de Riquer indicates that this objection is not justified, since Avellaneda's descriptions of the liveries worn at the Zaragozan jousts are adequate.

"For this very reason," responded Don Quixote, "I shall not set foot in Zaragoza, and in this way I shall proclaim the lies of this modern historian to the world, and then people will see that I am not the Don Quixote he says I am."

"That would be very wise," said Don Jerónimo. "There are other jousts in Barcelona, where Señor Don Quixote will be able to prove his valor."

"I intend to do that," said Don Quixote, "and if your graces will permit me, it is time for me to go to bed, and I hope you will consider and count me among your greatest friends and servants."

"And me too," said Sancho. "Maybe I'll be good for something."

With this they took their leave, and Don Quixote and Sancho withdrew to their room, leaving Don Juan and Don Jerónimo astonished by the mixture of intelligence and madness they had seen and convinced that these were the true Don Quixote and Sancho, not the ones described by the Aragonese author.

Don Quixote awoke at dawn, and knocking on the wall of their room, he said goodbye to his supper hosts. Sancho paid the innkeeper very generously and advised him to praise the provisions of his inn a little less or to keep it better supplied.

CHAPTER LX

Concerning what befell Don Quixote on his way to Barcelona

The morning was cool, and it showed signs of remaining cool for the rest of the day when Don Quixote left the inn, first having learned the most direct road to Barcelona that avoided Zaragoza, so great was his desire to prove that the new historian, who, they said, had so maligned him, was a liar.

As it happened, in more than six days nothing occurred that was worth recording, but then, at the end of that time, when he had wandered away from the road, night overtook him in a thick stand of oak or cork trees; in this instance, Cide Hamete does not honor the exactitude he usually observes in such matters.

Master and servant climbed down from their mounts, and leaning against the tree trunks, Sancho, who had eaten that afternoon, allowed himself to rush headlong through the doors of sleep, but Don Quixote, whose imagination kept him awake much more than hunger did, could not close his eyes; instead, his thoughts wandered back and forth through a thousand different places. Now he seemed to find himself in the Cave of Montesinos; then he saw Dulcinea, transformed into a peasant, leaping onto the back of her donkey; next the words of the wise Merlin resounded in his ears, telling him the conditions that had to be met and the tasks that had to be completed in order to disenchant Dulcinea. He despaired to see the carelessness and lack of charity in Sancho his squire, who, he believed, had given himself only five lashes, a painfully small quantity considering the infinite number he still had to administer, and this caused him so much grief and anger that he reasoned in this fashion:

"If Alexander the Great cut the Gordian knot, saying: 'It does not matter if it is cut or untied,' and that did not keep him from being the universal lord of all Asia, then in the disenchantment of Dulcinea it might not matter if I whip Sancho against his will, for if the condition of this remedy is that Sancho receive some three thousand lashes, what difference does it make to me if he administers them himself or if another does, since the essence of the matter is that he receive them regardless of where they come from?"

With this thought in mind he approached Sancho, having first taken Rocinante's reins and arranged them so that he could use them as a whip, and began to remove the cords that held up Sancho's breeches, although it is believed he had them only in front; but no sooner had Don Quixote come up to him than Sancho started, fully awake, and said:

"What is it? Who's touching me and untying my cords?"

"I am," responded Don Quixote. "I have come to make up for your failings and to put an end to my travails: I have come to whip you, Sancho, and to discharge, in part, the debt you have assumed. Dulcinea perishes; you live in negligence; I die of desire; and so, expose yourself of your own free will, for mine is to give you at least two thousand lashes in this solitary place."

"Oh, no," said Sancho, "your grace had better stand still; if not, by the true God, even the deaf will hear us. The lashes I promised to give myself must be voluntary, not given by force, and now I don't feel like lashing myself; it's enough for me to give your grace my word to flog and thrash myself as soon as I feel that desire."

"It must not be left to your courtesy, Sancho," said Don Quixote, "because you have a hard heart, and although you are a peasant, your flesh is tender."

And so he attempted and struggled to untie the cords, seeing which

Sancho Panza got to his feet, rushed at his master in a fury, and tripped him so that he fell to the ground and lay there faceup; Sancho placed his right knee on his chest, and with his hands he held down his master's hands, not allowing him to move and barely permitting him to breathe. Don Quixote said to him:

"What, you traitor? You dare to raise your hand against your natural lord and master? You presume to defy the person who gives you your bread?"

"I depose no king, I impose no king," responded Sancho, "but I'll help myself, for I'm my own lord.[1] Promise me, your grace, that you'll stay where you are, and won't try to whip me now, and I'll let you go and set you free; if not,

> Oh, here you will die, you traitor
> enemy of Doña Sancha."[2]

Don Quixote promised and swore by his life and thoughts not to touch a thread of Sancho's clothing and to leave the administering of the lashes entirely to his free will and desire.

Sancho got up and moved a good distance away, and as he was about to lean against another tree, he felt something graze his head, and he raised his hands and touched two feet in shoes and stockings. He trembled with fear and hurried to another tree, where the same thing happened. He shouted, calling for Don Quixote to help him. Don Quixote approached, asking what had happened and why he was afraid, and Sancho responded that all the trees were filled with human feet and legs. Don Quixote touched them and soon realized what they might be, and he said to Sancho:

"There is no need for you to be afraid, because these feet and legs that you touch but do not see undoubtedly belong to outlaws and bandits who have been hanged from these trees, for in this region the law usually hangs them when it catches them, in groups of twenty or thirty, which leads me to think I must be close to Barcelona."[3]

And the truth was just as he had imagined it.

They looked up, apparently, and saw the bodies of bandits hanging

---

1. This parodies a celebrated statement attributed to Duguesclin (also known as Beltrán del Claquín), a French knight of the fourteenth century who came to Spain with an army of mercenaries to assist Enrique de Trastámara in his war with Pedro el Cruel: "I depose no king, I impose no king, but I shall help my lord."

2. These are lines from one of the ballads about the Infantes of Lara.

3. In Cervantes's time, banditry was an especially severe problem in Cataluña.

from the branches of those trees. Just then dawn broke, and if the dead men had startled them, they were no less distressed by the more than forty live bandits who suddenly surrounded them, telling them in Catalan to stand still and be quiet until their captain arrived.

Don Quixote found himself on foot, his horse unbridled, his lance leaning against a tree, in short, with no defenses at all, and so he considered it the wisest course to fold his hands, bow his head, and wait for a better occasion and opportunity.

The bandits quickly looked over the gray and left nothing in the saddlebags and traveling case; it was Sancho's good fortune that he carried the duke's *escudos* and the ones he had brought from home tightly bound in a sash he wore around his stomach, and even so, those good people would have searched and dug down to what he had hidden between his skin and his flesh if their captain had not arrived at that point; he seemed to be about thirty-four years old and was robust, of more than medium height, with a solemn gaze and a dark complexion. He was riding a powerful horse, wearing a halberk,[4] and carrying four pistols, which in that country are called *pedreñales*,[5] at his sides. He saw that his squires—the name given to those who engage in this practice—were about to strip Sancho Panza; he ordered them to stop and was obeyed instantly, and so the sash escaped. He was surprised to see a lance leaning against a tree, a shield on the ground, and a pensive Don Quixote in armor, with a face sadder and more melancholy than anything sadness itself could fashion. He went up to him, saying:

"Do not be so sad, my good man, for you have not fallen into the hands of some cruel Osiris,[6] but into those of Roque Guinart,[7] and his are more compassionate than severe."

4. A short, high-necked jacket of mail that was usually sleeveless.

5. A kind of short harquebus favored by the bandits of Cataluña; they were usually worn on a leather bandolier called a *charpa*.

6. Martín de Riquer points out that this is a mistake: the reference should be to Busiris, an Egyptian king who killed foreigners as sacrifices to the gods.

7. Perot Roca Guinarda was a historical figure whom Cervantes had already praised in his dramatic interlude *La cueva de Salamanca* (*The Cave of Salamanca*). Born in 1582, he fought constantly in factional wars, and although his adversaries favored the nobility, he received support from members of the aristocracy and the Church hierarchy, including Don Antonio Moreno, who plays a part in Don Quixote's adventures in Barcelona. Roca Guinarda was known for his chivalric nature, and like other Catalan bandits, or *bandoleros*, he eventually abandoned his former life of crime and fought for the Spanish crown in Italy and Flanders. In 1611, he was granted a pardon and left for Naples as a captain in the Spanish army. The date of his death is unknown. As Martín de Riquer indicates, the topic of the Catalan bandit became a romantic theme in the literature of the sixteenth and seventeenth centuries, as exemplified by these passages in *Don Quixote*.

"My sadness," responded Don Quixote, "is not that I have fallen into your hands, O valorous Roque, whose fame reaches far beyond the borders of your land, but because my negligence was so great that your soldiers found me unprepared, when I am obliged, according to the order of knight errantry which I profess, to be constantly on the alert, and at all hours to serve as my own sentinel; because I assure you, O great Roque, that if they had found me on my horse, with my lance and shield, it would not have been very easy for them to defeat me, for I am Don Quixote of La Mancha, he whose exploits are known all over the world."

Then Roque Guinart realized that Don Quixote's infirmity was closer to madness than to valor, and although he had heard about him on occasion, he never had considered his deeds to be true, for he could not convince himself that this kind of humor could control the heart of a man; he was extremely pleased to have encountered him and therefore touch in proximity what he had heard about at a distance, and so he said:

"Valorous knight, do not be indignant or consider the circumstance in which you find yourself sinister; it may be that by means of these difficulties your tortuous fortunes will be set straight, for heaven, by strange, inconceivable turnings which men cannot imagine, tends to raise the fallen and enrich the poor."

Don Quixote was about to thank him when at their backs they heard a noise that sounded like a troop of horses, but it was only one, ridden in a fury by a young man who seemed to be about twenty years old and was dressed in green damask breeches and coat, both trimmed in gold, a plumed hat worn at an angle, close-fitting waxed boots, spurs, a golden dagger and a sword, a small flintlock in his hand, and two pistols at his sides. At the sound Roque turned his head and saw this beautiful figure, who rode up to him and said:

"I have come looking for you, O valorous Roque, to find in you if not a remedy, at least relief for my misfortune; and so as not to keep you in suspense, because I know you have not recognized me, I want to tell you who I am: I am Claudia Jerónima, daughter of Simón Forte, your dear friend and the particular enemy of Clauquel Torrellas, who is also your enemy because he belongs to the faction that opposes you;[8] and you already know that this Torrellas has a son named Don Vicente Torrellas, or, at least, that was his name two hours ago. To make the story of my misfortune short, I shall tell you briefly the grief he has caused me. He

---

8. The factions, or *bandos*, gave rise to the word *bandolero* (cf. "band" and "bandit" in English).

saw me and flattered me, I listened to him and fell in love, behind my father's back, because there is no woman, no matter how secluded her life and no matter how modest her nature, who does not have more than enough time to execute and put into effect her transgressive desires. In short, he promised to be my husband, and I gave him my word that I would be his wife, though we did not pass beyond that into actions. I learned yesterday that he had forgotten what he owed me and was marrying another; the wedding was to take place this morning, a piece of news that troubled my judgment and put an end to my patience; since my father was away, I put on these clothes that you see, and rode this horse at a gallop until I overtook Don Vicente about a league from here, and not bothering to complain, or to listen to excuses, I fired this flint-lock at him, and these two pistols as well, and I believe I must have put more than two bullets in his body, opening doors through which my honor, mixed with his blood, could pour out. I left him there with his servants, who did not dare to, or could not, defend him. I have come to find you so that you can get me across the border into France, where I have kinfolk with whom to live, and also to implore you to defend my father so that Don Vicente's many supporters will not dare wreak a terrible vengeance on him."

Roque, marveling at the lovely Claudia's gallantry, courage, beautiful appearance, and remarkable story, said:

"Come, Señora, and let us see if your enemy is dead, and then we shall see what it is best for you to do."

Don Quixote, who had been listening attentively to what Claudia said and how Roque Guinart responded, said:

"No one need bother to defend this lady, for I take that responsibility as mine; give me my horse and my arms, and wait for me here, and I shall find this knight and, whether he is dead or alive, I shall oblige him to keep the promise he made to such great beauty."

"Nobody should doubt that," said Sancho, "because my master is a very good hand at matchmaking: not many days ago he obliged another man to marry who had also denied his promise to another maiden, and if it wasn't because the enchanters who pursue him changed that man's real face into a footman's, by now that maiden would no longer be one."

Roque, who was more concerned with thinking about what had happened to the beautiful Claudia than with the words of master and servant, did not hear them, and after ordering his squires to return to Sancho everything they had taken from the gray, he also ordered them to withdraw to the place where they had spent the night, and then he galloped away with Claudia to find the wounded or dead Don Vicente. They reached the place where Claudia had met him and found nothing there except recently spilled blood, but they looked all around and saw some people climbing a hill, and they assumed, which was the truth, that it must be Don Vicente, dead or alive, carried by his servants to be healed or buried; they hurried to reach them, and since they were climbing slowly, this was an easy matter.

They found Don Vicente in the arms of his servants, imploring in a faint and feeble voice that they leave him there to die, because the pain of his wounds would not permit him to go any farther.

Claudia and Roque leaped from their horses and approached him; the servants were frightened at the presence of Roque, and Claudia was disquieted at the sight of Don Vicente, and with a mixture of compassion and harshness she went up to him, grasped his hands, and said:

"If you had given me these and abided by our agreement, this never would have happened to you."

The wounded gentleman opened his half-closed eyes, and recognizing Claudia, he said:

"I see clearly, beautiful and deceived lady, that you were the one who killed me, a punishment I did not deserve or merit, for neither with my desires nor my actions did I ever wish or intend to offend you."

"Then, isn't it true," said Claudia, "that this morning you were going to marry Leonora, the daughter of the wealthy Balvastro?"

"No, certainly not," responded Don Vicente. "My ill fortune must have brought you that news so that you, in jealousy, would take my life, but since I leave it in your hands and arms, I consider my luck to be good. And in order to assure yourself that this is true, press my hand and accept me as your husband, if you like, for I have no greater satisfaction to give you for the injury you think you have received from me."

Claudia pressed his hand, and her own heart felt pressed, causing her to faint onto the bloody bosom of Don Vicente, who was shaken by a mortal paroxysm. Roque was bewildered and did not know what to do. The servants hurried to find water to sprinkle on the lovers' faces, and they brought some and bathed their faces with it. Claudia recovered from her swoon, but not Don Vicente from his paroxysm, because his life had ended. Seeing this, Claudia realized that her sweet husband was no longer alive, and she pierced the air with sighs, wounded the heavens with lamentations, tore her hair and threw it into the wind, scratched her face with her own hands, and showed all the signs of sorrow and grief that could be imagined in a wounded heart.

"O cruel and thoughtless woman," she said, "how easily you were moved to act upon so evil a thought! O raging power of jealousy, to what a desperate end you led one who sheltered you in her bosom! O husband of mine, because you were loved by me, your unfortunate fate has brought you from the nuptial bed to the grave!"

Claudia's lamentations were so sad that they brought tears to Roque's eyes, which were not accustomed to shed them under any circumstances. The servants wept, Claudia fainted over and over again, and the area around them seemed to be a field of sorrow and a place of misfortune. Finally Roque Guinart ordered the servants to carry Don Vicente's body to his father's house, which was nearby, for burial. Claudia told Roque that she wanted to go to a convent where an aunt of hers was abbess, and there she intended to end her days in the company of a better, and an eternal, husband. Roque praised her good intention and offered to accompany her wherever she wished and to defend her father against Don Vicente's kin, and anyone else, if they tried to injure him. On no account did Claudia wish his company, and after thanking him for his offers with the best words she knew, she took her leave of him in tears. Don Vicente's servants carried away his body, and Roque returned to his people, and so ended the love story of Claudia Jerónima. But what other ending could it have if the threads of her pitiable tale were woven by the invincible and cruel forces of jealousy?

Roque Guinart found his squires in the place where he had ordered them to wait; Don Quixote was with them, mounted on Rocinante and speaking to them in an attempt to persuade them to abandon a mode of life so dangerous for both the soul and the body, but since most of them were Gascons,[9] a crude and unruly people, they were not particularly influenced by Don Quixote's discourse. When Roque arrived, he asked Sancho Panza if his men had returned and restored to him the gems and jewels they had taken from the gray. Sancho responded that they had, but he was missing three nightcaps that were worth three cities.

"Man, what are you saying?" said one of the outlaws. "I have them, and they're not worth three *reales*."

"That is true," said Don Quixote, "but my squire values them in the manner he has said because of the person who gave them to me."

9. Martín de Riquer states that many of the Catalan *bandoleros* were in fact from Gascony and may have been Huguenot fugitives from France.

Roque Guinart commanded that they be returned immediately, and after ordering his men into a line, he said that all the clothing, jewels, and money, everything they had stolen since the last distribution, should be placed in front of them; and after quickly making an estimate and set-ting aside what could not be divided and reducing it to money,[10] he dis-tributed goods to his entire company with so much equity and prudence that he adhered absolutely to distributive justice and gave no one too much or too little. When this had been concluded, and everyone was content, satisfied, and well-paid, Roque said to Don Quixote:

"If one were not scrupulous with these men, there would be no way to live with them."

To which Sancho said:

"According to what I've seen here, justice is so great a good that it's necessary to use it even among thieves."

One of the squires heard this, and he raised the butt of a harquebus and undoubtedly would have used it to crack open Sancho's skull if Roque Guinart had not shouted at him to stop. Sancho was terrified, and he resolved not to open his mouth again for as long as he was among those people.

Just then, one or some of the squires who had been posted as sen-tinels along the roads to watch the travelers and to inform their leader about everything that happened, came up to Roque and said:

"Señor, not far from here there's a large group of people traveling along the Barcelona road."

To which Roque responded:

"Could you see if they're the kind who come looking for us, or the kind we go looking for?"

"They're the kind we go looking for," responded the squire.

"Then all of you go," replied Roque, "and bring them here to me, and don't let a single one escape."

They did as he said, and Don Quixote, Sancho, and Roque were left alone, waiting to see what the squires would bring back; and while they were waiting, Roque said to Don Quixote:

"Our manner of life must seem unprecedented to Señor Don Quixote: singular adventures, singular events, and all of them dangerous; I don't wonder that it seems this way to you, because really, I confess there is no mode of life more unsettling and surprising than ours. Certain

10. According to Martín de Riquer, Roque kept what could not be divided and gave his men their share of its equivalent value in money.

desires for revenge brought me to it, and they have the power to trouble the most serene heart; by nature I am compassionate and well-intentioned, but, as I have said, my wish to take revenge for an injury that was done to me threw all my good inclinations to the ground, and I continue in this state in spite of and despite my understanding; as one abyss calls to another abyss, and one sin to another sin, vengeance has linked with vengeance so that I bear responsibility not only for mine but for those of others, but it is God's will that although I find myself in the midst of a labyrinth of my own confusions, I do not lose the hope of coming out of it and into a safe harbor."

Don Quixote was amazed to hear Roque speak so well and so reasonably, because he had thought that among those whose profession it was to rob, kill, and steal, there could be no one who was well-spoken, and he responded:

"Señor Roque, the beginning of health lies in knowing the disease, and in the patient's willingness to take the medicines the doctor prescribes; your grace is ill, you know your ailment, and heaven, or I should say God, who is our physician, will treat you with the medicines that will cure you, and which tend to cure gradually, not suddenly and miraculously; furthermore, intelligent sinners are closer to reforming than simpleminded ones, and since your grace has demonstrated prudence in your speech, you need only be brave and wait for the illness of your conscience to be healed; if your grace wishes to save time and put yourself without difficulty on the road to salvation, come with me, and I shall teach you how to be a knight errant, a profession in which one undergoes so many trials and misfortunes that, if deemed to be penance, they would bring you to heaven in the wink of an eye."

Roque laughed at the advice of Don Quixote and then, changing the subject, recounted the tragic story of Claudia Jerónima, which caused Sancho great sorrow, for he had liked the girl's beauty, confidence, and spirit.

Then the squires arrived with their prey, bringing with them two gentlemen on horseback, and two pilgrims on foot, and a carriage of women with six servants who accompanied them, mounted and on foot, and two muledrivers who were with the gentlemen. The squires kept them surrounded, and both the vanquished and the victors maintained a deep silence, waiting for the great Roque Guinart to speak, and he asked the gentlemen who they were and where they were going and how much money they were carrying. One of them responded:

"Señor, we are two captains of the Spanish infantry: our companies are in Naples and we are going to embark on four galleys that, we are told, are in Barcelona under orders to sail to Sicily; we are carrying two or three hundred *escudos*, which, in our opinion, makes us rich and content, for the ordinary poverty of soldiers does not allow greater treasure."

Roque asked the pilgrims the same questions he had asked the captains; they responded that they were going to embark for Rome and that between the two of them they might have some sixty *reales*. He also wanted to know who was riding in the carriage, and where they were going, and how much money they were carrying, and one of the men on horseback said:

"My lady Doña Guiomar de Quiñones, the wife of the chief magistrate of the vicariate of Naples, with her little daughter, a maid, and a duenna, are riding in the carriage; we are six servants who are accompanying her, and the money amounts to six hundred *escudos*."

"That means," said Roque Guinart, "that we have here nine hundred *escudos* and sixty *reales*; my soldiers number about sixty; see how much is owed to each of them, because I don't count very well."

When they heard this, the robbers raised their voices, shouting:

"Long live Roque Guinart in spite of the *lladres*[11] who are trying to ruin him!"

The captains showed their grief, the magistrate's wife grew sad, and the pilgrims were not at all happy at the confiscation of their goods. Roque kept them in suspense for a while, but he did not want their sorrow to continue, for by now it could be seen a harquebus's shot away, and turning to the captains, he said:

"Señores, would your graces please be so kind as to lend me sixty *escudos*, and the lady eighty, to keep this squadron of mine happy, for the abbot eats if the tithes are paid, and then you can go on your way free and unimpeded, and with a safe conduct that I'll give you, and if you happen to meet other squadrons of mine in the vicinity, no harm will be done to you, for it is not my intention to injure soldiers or women, especially those who are highborn."

Infinite and well-spoken words were used by the captains to thank Roque for his courtesy and liberality, for that is what they considered his leaving them their money. Señora Doña Guiomar de Quiñones wanted

---

11. This is the Catalan word for "thieves," used here as an insult.

to leap out of her carriage to kiss the feet and hands of the great Roque, but he would not consent on any account; instead, he begged her pardon for the injury he had done to her, forced on him by the strict obligations of his evil profession. The chief magistrate's wife ordered one of her servants to immediately give him the eighty *escudos* that were her share, and the captains had already taken their sixty out of the purse. The pilgrims were about to offer all of their paltry wealth, but Roque told them to be still, and turning to his men, he said:

"Of these *escudos*, two go to each man, and that leaves twenty; ten should go to these pilgrims, and the other ten to this good squire so that he can speak well of this adventure."

His men brought him the writing materials that he always carried with him, and Roque wrote out a safe conduct addressed to the chiefs of his squadrons, and then he said goodbye to the travelers and let them go, and they were astonished at his nobility, his gallant disposition, and unusual behavior, thinking of him more as an Alexander the Great than as a well-known thief. One of his squires said in his Gascon and Catalan language:

"This captain of ours is more of a *frade*[12] than a bandit: if he wants to be generous from now on, let it be with his goods, not ours."

The unfortunate man did not speak quietly enough, and Roque heard him, drew his sword, and split his head almost in two, saying:

"This is how I punish insolent men who talk too much."

Everyone was terrified, and no one dared say a word: that was the obedience they showed him.

Roque moved to one side and wrote a letter to a friend of his in Barcelona, informing him that the famous Don Quixote of La Mancha, the knight errant about whom so many things had been said, was with him, and telling his friend that the knight was the most amusing and best-informed man in the world, and that in four days' time, which was the feast of St. John the Baptist,[13] he would present himself along the shore of the city, armed with all his armor and weapons, mounted on his horse, Rocinante, with his squire, Sancho, riding a donkey; Roque asked his friend to inform his friends the Niarros so that they could derive

---

12. Martín de Riquer points out that, given the similarities between the languages of Gascony and Cataluña, the *bandoleros* probably spoke a mixture of the two; *frade*, however, is Portuguese (the word for "friar" is *frare* in Catalan, *frayre* in Gascon). Riquer assumes that either Cervantes mistakenly attributed a Portuguese word to the bandits or the typesetter made an error.

13. It is Martín de Riquer's opinion that the reference is to the commemoration of John the Baptist's beheading (August 29), not to the celebration of his birth (June 24).

pleasure from this, but he wished to deprive his enemies the Cadells[14] of this amusement; it was impossible, however, because the madness and intelligence of Don Quixote, and the wit of his squire, Sancho Panza, could not help but give pleasure to everyone. He dispatched the letter with one of his squires, who changed his bandit's clothes for those of a peasant, and entered Barcelona, and delivered it to the person to whom it was addressed.

CHAPTER LXI

Regarding what befell Don Quixote when he entered Barcelona, along with other matters that have more truth in them than wit

Don Quixote spent three days and three nights with Roque, and if it had been three hundred years, there would have been no lack of things to observe and marvel at in the way he lived: they awoke here and ate there; at times they fled, not knowing from whom, and at other times they waited, not knowing for whom. They slept on their feet, interrupting their slumber and moving from one place to another. It was always a matter of posting spies, listening to scouts, blowing on the locks of their harquebuses, although they had few of those since everyone used flint-locks. Roque spent the nights away from his men, in locations and places they did not know, because the many edicts issued by the viceroy of Barcelona[1] against his life made him uneasy and apprehensive, and he did not dare trust anyone, fearing his own men might kill him or turn him in to the authorities: a life, certainly, that was disquieting and troublesome.

Finally, using abandoned roads, shortcuts, and hidden paths, Roque, Don Quixote, Sancho, and another six squires set out for Barcelona. They reached the shore on the night of St. John's Eve, and Roque embraced Don Quixote and Sancho, presented the squire with the ten *escu-*

---

14. The Niarros (Nyerros in Catalan) and the Cadells were the factions in whose wars the historic Roque had been involved.

1. More accurately, the viceroy of Cataluña.

dos he had promised but had not yet given him, and took his leave, with a thousand services offered on both sides.

Roque returned to the countryside, and Don Quixote remained mounted on his horse, waiting for daybreak, and it was not long before the pale face of dawn began to appear along the balconies of the east, bringing joy to the grass and flowers rather than to the ear, for at that very moment ears were made joyous by the sound of many flageolets and timbrels, the jingling of bells, the "make way, make way, stand aside, stand aside!" of runners who, apparently, were coming from the city. Dawn made way for the sun, whose face, larger than a shield, gradually rose from below the horizon.

Don Quixote and Sancho turned their eyes in all directions; they saw the ocean, which they had not seen before: it seemed broad and vast to them, much larger than the Lakes of Ruidera that they had seen in La Mancha; they saw the galleys near the shore, and when the canopies were raised, their pennants and streamers were revealed, fluttering in the wind and kissing and sweeping the water; from the galleys came the sound of bugles, trumpets, and flageolets, and the breeze carried the sweetly martial tones near and far. The ships began to move, performing a mock skirmish on the quiet waters, and, corresponding in almost the same fashion, an infinite number of knights on beautiful horses and in splendid livery rode out from the city. The soldiers on the galleys fired countless pieces of artillery, to which those who were on the walls and in the forts of the city responded, and the heavy artillery shook the air with a fearsome clamor and was answered by the midship cannon on the galleys. The joyful sea, the jocund land, the transparent air, perhaps clouded only by the smoke from the artillery, seemed to create and engender a sudden delight in all the people.

Sancho could not imagine how those shapes moving on the ocean could have so many feet. And then, the knights in livery, with shouts, *lelelíes*, and cries, came galloping up to a stupefied and astounded Don Quixote, and one of them, who had been advised by Roque, called in a loud voice to Don Quixote:

"May the model, beacon, light, and polestar of all knight errantry be welcome to our city, world without end. Welcome, I say, to the valorous Don Quixote of La Mancha: not the false, the fictitious, the apocryphal one we have seen recently in false histories, but the true, the legitimate, the faithful one described for us by Cide Hamete Benengeli, the flower of all historians."

Don Quixote did not say a word, and the knights did not wait for him to respond, but wheeling and turning with all their entourage behind them, they began to move in caracoles around Don Quixote, who turned to Sancho and said:

"These men know us very well: I would wager that they have read our history, and even the one recently published by the Aragonese."

The knight who had spoken to Don Quixote returned, saying:

"Your grace, Señor Don Quixote, come with us, for we are all your servants and great friends of Roque Guinart's."

To which Don Quixote responded:

"If courtesy engenders courtesy, yours, Señor Knight, is the daughter or close relative of the great Roque's. Take me wherever you wish, for I shall have no will but yours, above all if you desire to employ mine in your service."

The knight responded with words no less courtly, and the others encircled Don Quixote, and to the sound of flageolets and timbrels they rode with him to the city, and as they entered it, there were the Evil One, who ordains all wickedness, and boys, who are more evil than the Evil One; two of them who were particularly mischievous and impudent made their way through all the people, and one lifted the gray's tail and the other lifted Rocinante's, and there they placed and inserted branches of furze[2] in each one. The poor animals felt these new spurs, and when they pressed down their tails, they increased their discomfort to such an extent that they reared and bucked a thousand times and threw their riders to the ground. Don Quixote, enraged and affronted, hurried to remove the plumage from the tail of his nag, and Sancho did the same for his gray. Those who were escorting Don Quixote wanted to punish the insolence of the boys, but it was not possible because they hid among the thousand others who were following them.

Don Quixote and Sancho remounted; accompanied by the same acclamation and music, they arrived at the house of their guide, which was large and imposing, as befitted a wealthy gentleman, and there we shall leave them for now, since this is the wish of Cide Hamete.

---

2. A prickly evergreen shrub native to European wastelands.

CHAPTER LXII

Which relates the adventure of the enchanted head, as well as other foolishness that must be recounted

Don Antonio Moreno was the name of Don Quixote's host, a wealthy and discerning gentleman, very fond of seemly and benign amusements, who, finding Don Quixote in his house, sought ways to make his madness public without harming him; for jests that cause pain are not jests, and entertainments are not worthwhile if they injure another. The first thing he did was to have Don Quixote remove his armor and to take him, dressed in the tight-fitting chamois clothes we have already described and depicted, out to a balcony that overlooked one of the principal streets in the city, in plain view of passersby and boys, who looked at him as if he were a monkey. Once again the horsemen in livery galloped before him, as if they had put on finery for him alone and not to celebrate the feast day, and Sancho was extremely happy because it seemed to him that without knowing how or why, he found himself at another Camacho's wedding, another house like Don Diego de Miranda's, another castle like the duke's.

Some of Don Antonio's friends ate dinner with him that day, and they all honored Don Quixote and treated him as if he were a knight errant, which so filled him with pride and vanity that he could hardly contain his joy. Sancho made so many comical remarks that all the servants in the house, and everyone else who heard him, hung on his every word. When they were at the table, Don Antonio said to Sancho:

"We have heard, good Sancho, that you are so fond of white morsels,[1] and of rissoles, that if any are left over, you keep them in your shirt for the next day."[2]

1. *Manjar blanco:* a dish made of chicken breasts, rice flour, milk, and sugar.

2. In Avellaneda's book, Sancho is said to be extremely fond of rissoles.

"No, Señor, that isn't so," responded Sancho, "because I'm more clean than gluttonous, and my master, Don Quixote, here before you, knows very well that we both can go a week on a handful of acorns or nuts. It's true that if somebody happens to give me a calf, I come running with the rope; I mean, I eat what I'm given, and take advantage of the opportunities I find, and anybody who says I'm dirty and stuff myself when I eat doesn't know what he's talking about, and I'd say it another way if I didn't see so many honorable beards at this table."

"There is no doubt," said Don Quixote, "that the moderation and cleanliness with which Sancho eats could be written and engraved on bronze plates and remembered forever in times to come. True, when he is hungry, he seems something of a glutton because he eats quickly and chews voraciously, but he is always perfectly clean, and during the time he was governor he learned to eat so fastidiously that he ate grapes, and even the seeds of a pomegranate, with a fork."

"What?" said Don Antonio. "Sancho was a governor?"

"Yes," responded Sancho, "of an ínsula called Barataria. For ten days I governed it as nicely as you please, and during that time I lost my peace of mind and learned to look down on all the governorships in the world; I left there in a hurry, and fell into a pit where I thought I was going to die, and by a miracle I came out of it alive."

Don Quixote recounted in detail the story of Sancho's governorship, affording great pleasure to those who heard him.

When the table had been cleared, Don Antonio took Don Quixote by the hand and led him to a side room where the only furnishing was a table, apparently of jasper, on a base of the same material, and on it there was a head, made in the fashion of the busts of Roman emperors, which seemed to be of bronze. Don Antonio walked with Don Quixote around the chamber, circling the table many times, and then he said:

"Now that I am certain, Señor Don Quixote, that no one is listening, and no one can hear us, and the door is closed, I want to tell your grace about one of the strangest adventures, or I should say marvels, that anyone could imagine, on the condition that whatever I tell your grace must be buried in the deepest recesses of secrecy."

"I swear to that," responded Don Quixote, "and I shall even place a stone over it for greater security, because I want your grace to know, Señor Don Antonio"—for by now Don Quixote knew his name—"that you are speaking to one who has ears to hear but no tongue with which to speak; therefore your grace can safely transfer what is in your heart to mine and be certain it has been thrown into the abysses of silence."

"Trusting in that promise," responded Don Antonio, "I am going to astound your grace with what you will see and hear, and alleviate some of the sorrow I feel at not having anyone to whom I can communicate my secrets, for they are not the sort that can be entrusted to everyone."

Don Quixote was perplexed, waiting to see where so many precautions would lead. At this point, Don Antonio took his hand and passed it over the bronze head, and around the entire table, and along the jasper base on which it rested, and then he said:

"This head, Señor Don Quixote, has been fabricated and made by one of the greatest enchanters and wizards the world has ever seen, a Pole, I believe, and a disciple of the famous Escotillo,[3] about whom so many marvels are told; he was here in my house, and for a thousand *escudos*, which I paid him, he fashioned this head, which has the property and virtue of responding to any question spoken into its ear. He determined the bearings, painted the characters, observed the stars, looked at the degrees, and finally completed this with all the perfection that we shall see tomorrow, because the head is mute on Fridays, and since today is Friday, we shall have to wait until tomorrow. During this time, your grace will be able to prepare the questions you wish to ask; through experience I know it is truthful in all its responses."

Don Quixote, astonished at the head's virtue and property, was inclined not to believe Don Antonio, but seeing how little time he would have to wait to experience it for himself, he said nothing except to thank him for having disclosed so great a secret to him. They left the room, Don Antonio locked the door with a key, and they went to the large room where the other gentlemen were waiting. During this time, Sancho had recounted to them many of the adventures and incidents that had befallen his master.

That afternoon the gentlemen took Don Quixote out riding, dressed not in armor but in ordinary street clothes, a long, caped cassock of tawny woolen cloth that would have made ice itself perspire at that time of year. The servants were told to keep Sancho entertained and not to let him leave the house. Don Quixote did not ride Rocinante but was mounted on a large, smooth-gaited mule with very fine trappings. They gave him the cassock to put on, and on the back, which he did not see, they had attached

---

3. Martín de Riquer is certain the reference is to Michael Scot (d. ca. 1232), who studied at Oxford, Bologna, Paris, and eventually Toledo, where he learned Arabic, the language from which he translated (or supervised the translation of) many of Aristotle's writings into Latin. *Escotillo* is the diminutive of *Escoto*, his name in Spanish. For a variety of reasons, including his interests in astrology, alchemy, and the occult sciences, he was widely known as a magician and soothsayer.

a sign that read, in large letters: *This is Don Quixote of La Mancha*. As they were starting out, the announcement caught the eye of all the passersby, and since they read "This is Don Quixote of La Mancha," Don Quixote was surprised to see that everyone who looked at him recognized him and knew his name; turning to Don Antonio, who was at his side, he said:

"Great is the prerogative contained within knight errantry, rendering the man who professes it well-known and famous everywhere on earth, for your grace will observe, Señor Don Antonio, that even the boys in this city, who have never seen me before, know who I am."

"That is so, Señor Don Quixote," responded Don Antonio, "for just as fire cannot be hidden and enclosed, virtue cannot fail to be recognized, and that which is achieved through the profession of arms exceeds and outshines all others."

It so happened that while Don Quixote was receiving the acclaim that has been mentioned, a Castilian who read the sign on his back raised his voice and said:

"The devil take Don Quixote of La Mancha! How did you get this far without dying from all the beatings you've received? You're a madman, and if you were a madman in private, behind the doors of your madness, it wouldn't be so bad, but you have the attribute of turning everyone who deals with you or talks to you into madmen and fools, too; if you don't believe me, just look at these gentlemen who are accompanying you. Return, fool, to your house, and look after your estate, your wife, and your children, and stop this nonsense that is rotting your brain and ruining your mind."

"Brother," said Don Antonio, "go on your way, and don't give advice to people who don't ask for it. Señor Don Quixote of La Mancha is a very prudent man, and we who accompany him are not dolts; virtue must be honored wherever it is found; go now, and bad luck to you, and stop minding other people's business."

"By God, your grace is right," responded the Castilian. "Giving this good man advice is like kicking at thorns; even so, it makes me very sad that the good sense everyone says this fool has in other matters should run out into the gutter of his knight errantry; as for the bad luck your grace mentioned, let it be for me and all my descendants if after today, though I live longer than Methuselah, I ever give advice to anybody again, even if he asks for it."

The dispenser of advice left, and the excursion continued, but there was such a crush of boys and other people reading the sign that Don

Antonio had to remove it, under the pretext that he was removing something else.

Night fell; they returned home, where there was a soirée of ladies, for Don Antonio's wife, who was wellborn, good-natured, beautiful, and clever, had invited her friends to come and honor their guest and enjoy his incomparable madness. A number of ladies attended, a splendid supper was served, and the soirée began when it was almost ten o'clock. Among the ladies there were two with mischievous and jocund tastes, and although very respectable, they were somewhat brash in devising amusing but harmless jokes. They were so insistent on Don Quixote's dancing with them that they exhausted him, not only in body but in spirit. Don Quixote was a remarkable sight: tall, scrawny, lean, sallow, wearing tight-fitting clothes, awkward, and not at all graceful. The young ladies entreated him on the sly, and he, also on the sly, rejected them, but finding himself hard-pressed by their entreaties, he raised his voice and said:

"*Fugite, partes adversae!*[4] Leave me in peace, unwelcome thoughts. Señoras, control your desires, for she who is queen of mine, the peerless Dulcinea of Toboso, does not allow any but her own to subdue and defeat me."

And having said this, he sat down on the floor in the middle of the room, exhausted and wearied by so much dancing. Don Antonio ordered him picked up and carried to his bed, and the first to lay hands on him was Sancho, saying:

"Unlucky for you, Señor Master, when you started dancing! Do you think all brave men are dancers and all knights errant spin around? I say that if you think so, you're mistaken; there are men who'd dare to kill a giant before they'd prance around. If you'd been stamping your heels and toes, I'd have taken your place, because I'm a wonderful stamper, but as for dancing, I don't know anything about it."

With these and other words like them, Sancho gave those at the soirée reason for laughter, and he put his master to bed, wrapping him in blankets so that he would sweat out the chill he felt because of his dancing.

The next day, Don Antonio thought it would be a good idea to try the enchanted head, and with Don Quixote, Sancho, and another two friends, along with the two ladies who had exhausted Don Quixote with

---

4. "Flee, enemies," a formula used in exorcisms.

their dancing, for they had spent the night with Don Antonio's wife, he went into the room with the head and closed the door. He told them about its properties, charged them to keep the secret, and said that this was the first day the virtue of the enchanted head would be tested; except for Don Antonio's two friends, no one else knew the secret of the enchantment, and if Don Antonio had not revealed it to them earlier, they too would have been as astounded as the others: it was so carefully planned and designed.

The first to go up to the ear of the head was Don Antonio himself, and he said in a quiet voice, but not so quiet that the others could not hear him:

"Tell me, head, by the virtue contained within you: what are my thoughts now?"

And the head responded, not moving its lips, in a clear and distinct voice, so that it was heard by everyone:

"I do not consider thoughts."

When they heard this everyone was stunned, especially since nowhere in the room or near the table was there a human being who could have responded.

"How many people are here?" Don Antonio asked.

And in the same tone came the response:

"There are you and your wife, two friends of yours and two of hers, a famous knight called Don Quixote of La Mancha, and his squire, whose name is Sancho Panza."

At this everyone certainly was stunned; at this everyone's hair certainly stood on end from sheer terror! And Don Antonio, moving away from the head, said:

"This is enough for me to know I was not deceived by the one who sold you to me, O wise head, speaking head, responding head, admirable head! Let others come up and ask whatever they wish."

And since women are ordinarily very hasty and fond of knowing, the first to approach was one of the two friends of Don Antonio's wife, and the question she asked was:

"Tell me, head, what should I do to be very beautiful?"

And the response to her was:

"Be very virtuous."

"I won't ask you anything else," said the questioner.

Then her friend approached and said:

"I'd like to know, head, if my husband really loves me."

And the answer was:

"Think about what he does for you, and then you will know."

The married woman moved away, saying:

"This answer didn't need a question, because it is a fact that a man's actions declare his feelings."

Then one of Don Antonio's two friends came up and asked:

"Who am I?"

And the response was:

"You know who you are."

"I'm not asking you that," responded the gentleman, "I'm asking you to tell me if you know me."

"Yes, I know you," was the response. "You are Don Pedro Noriz."

"I don't want to know more, for this is enough for me to realize, O head, that you know everything."

When he moved away, the other friend approached and asked:

"Tell me, head, what does my son and heir desire?"

"I have already said," came the response, "that I do not consider desires, but despite this, I can tell you that what your son desires is to bury you."

"That's right," said the gentleman. "What I see with my eyes I can touch with my finger."

And he asked nothing more. Don Antonio's wife came up and said:

"Head, I don't know what to ask you; I only wanted to know if I'll enjoy many more years with my good husband."

And the response was:

"You will, because his health and temperate living promise many years of life, which many people tend to cut short by their intemperance."

Then Don Quixote approached and said:

"Tell me, you who respond: was my account of what happened to me in the Cave of Montesinos the truth or a dream? Will the lashes of my squire Sancho be completed? Will the disenchantment of Dulcinea take place?"

"As for the cave," was the response, "there is much to say, for it has something of both: Sancho's lashes will go slowly, and the disenchantment of Dulcinea will be duly effected."

"I do not wish to know more," said Don Quixote, "for when I see Dulcinea disenchanted, I shall think that all the good fortune I could wish for has come all at once."

The final questioner was Sancho, and what he asked was:

"By any chance, head, will I have another governorship? Will I ever escape a squire's poverty? Will I see my wife and children again?"

The response was:

"You will govern in your house, and if you return there, you will see your wife and children, and when you stop serving, you will stop being a squire."

"By God, that's good!" said Sancho Panza. "I could have told myself that: the prophet Old Chestnut couldn't have said more."

"Animal," said Don Quixote, "what response do you want? Is it not enough that this head has given answers that correspond to what is asked of it?"

"Yes, it's enough," responded Sancho, "but I'd like it to declare more and tell me more."

With this the questions and answers came to an end, but not the amazement felt by everyone except the two friends of Don Antonio, who were privy to the secret. Cide Hamete Benengeli wished to explain the matter immediately in order to curb the astonishment of those who might think that some magical and extraordinary mystery was contained in the head, and so he tells us that Don Antonio Moreno, in imitation of another head he had seen in Madrid, which had been fabricated by an engraver, had this one made in his own house for his own entertainment and to astound the ignorant; it was constructed in this fashion: the table-top was of wood painted and varnished to look like jasper, and the base on which it rested was made of the same material, with four eagle's talons projecting from it for greater stability. The head, which resembled a carved portrait bust of a Roman emperor cast in bronze, was completely hollow, as was the tabletop into which it fit so perfectly that there was no sign of their joining. The base of the table was also hollow, correspon-ding to the throat and chest of the head, and all this connected to an-other chamber beneath the room where the head was located. Through the entire hollow of the base, tabletop, throat, and chest of the portrait bust ran a tube of tinplate that was very precisely fitted and could not be seen by anyone. Posted in the corresponding chamber below was the man who would respond, his mouth up against the tube, so that, as if the tube were an ear trumpet, one voice would travel down and the other would travel up in clear, well-articulated words, and in this way it was not possible to discover the deception. Don Antonio's nephew, an astute and clever student, was the responder; having been told by his uncle who would come into the room with him to question the head that day, it was easy for him to respond quickly and accurately to the first question; he responded to the others by conjecture and, since he was clever, with cleverness.

Cide Hamete goes on to say that this marvelous device lasted ten or twelve days, but word spread throughout the city that Don Antonio had an enchanted head in his house that would answer every question asked of it, and fearing that the rumors would reach the ears of the alert guardians of our Faith, he informed the inquisitors of the matter and was ordered to dismantle it and not to use it in the future lest it cause turmoil among the ignorant common people; but in the opinion of Don Quixote and Sancho Panza, the head was still enchanted and responsive, more to the satisfaction of Don Quixote than of Sancho.

The gentlemen of the city, in order to please Don Antonio and to entertain Don Quixote and give him the opportunity to reveal his madness, arranged to hold a tilting of the ring in six days' time, but it did not take place because of an accident that will be recounted later. Don Quixote wanted to go out into the city in a simple manner, and on foot, fearing that if he went on horseback, he would be pursued by boys, and so he and Sancho, and two servants offered to him by Don Antonio, went out for a walk.

As he was going down a street, Don Quixote happened to look up, and over a door he saw written, in very large letters: *Books Printed Here*,[5] which made him very happy because he had never visited a print shop, and he wished to know what it was like. He went in with his entourage, and he saw them printing in one place, correcting in another, typesetting here, revising there, in short, all of the procedures that can be seen in large printing houses. Don Quixote approached one section and asked what they were doing there; the workmen told him, he marveled, and moved on. He went up to another workman and asked him what he was doing. He responded:

"Señor, this gentleman here"—and he pointed to a rather serious man of fine appearance and figure—"has translated a Tuscan book into our Castilian language, and I'm setting the type so that it can be printed."

"What is the title of the book?" asked Don Quixote.

5. According to Martín de Riquer, Cervantes is describing the printing house of Sebastián de Cormellas, on Calle del Call, which brought out a good number of the classic works of the Spanish Golden Age.

To which the translator replied:

"Señor, in Tuscan the book is called *Le Bagatele*."[6]

"And what does *le bagatele* mean in our Castilian?" asked Don Quixote.

"*Le bagatele*," said the translator, "would be like our saying *the playthings*, and though this book has a humble name, it contains and includes very good and substantive things."

"I," said Don Quixote, "know a little Tuscan, and take pride in singing some stanzas by Ariosto. But tell me, Señor—and I do not say this because I wish to test your grace's abilities but simply out of curiosity—in your translating, has your grace ever come across the word *pignata?*"

"Yes, many times," responded the translator.

"And how does your grace translate it into Castilian?" asked Don Quixote.

"How would I translate it," replied the translator, "except by saying *stew pot?*"

"By God," said Don Quixote, "how well your grace knows the Tuscan language! I would wager a good sum that where the Tuscan says *piace*, your grace says *please* in Castilian, and where it says *piu*, you say *more*, and *su* you render as *above*, and *giu* as *below*."

"Yes, I do, certainly," said the translator, "because those are the corresponding words."

"And I shall be so bold as to swear," said Don Quixote, "that your grace is not well-known in the world, which is always unwilling to reward rare talents and praiseworthy efforts. What abilities are lost there! What talents ignored! What virtues scorned! But despite all this, it seems to me that translating from one language to another, unless it is from Greek and Latin, the queens of all languages, is like looking at Flemish tapestries from the wrong side, for although the figures are visible, they are covered by threads that obscure them, and cannot be seen with the smoothness and color of the right side; translating easy languages does not argue for either talent or eloquence, just as transcribing or copying from one paper to another does not argue for those qualities. And I do not wish to infer from this that the practice of translating is not

6. Martín de Riquer points out that the book has not been identified and that in Italian the title would be *Le Bagattelle*, not *Le Bagatele*. There has been speculation that this might be an anagram for *Le Galatee*, by Giovanni della Casa, which was translated into Spanish in 1585 by Dr. Domingo Becerra, who was a prisoner in Algiers at the same time as Cervantes.

deserving of praise, because a man might engage in worse things that bring him even less benefit. From this reckoning I except two famous translators: one is Dr. Cristóbal de Figueroa, for his *Pastor Fido*, and the other is Don Juan de Jáurigui, for his *Aminta*,[7] where they happily bring into question which is the translation and which the original. But tell me, your grace: is this book being printed at your expense or have the rights already been sold to a bookseller?"

"I am printing it at my own expense," responded the translator, "and expect to earn at least a thousand *ducados* with this first printing, which will consist of two thousand copies that can easily be sold for six *reales* each."

"Your grace is certainly good at calculations!" responded Don Quixote. "But it seems you do not know how printers collude or the favors they do for one another. I promise that when you find yourself burdened with two thousand copies of the book, your body will be so exhausted it will disconcert you, especially if the book is slightly out of the ordinary and not at all risqué."

"And?" said the translator. "Would your grace prefer that I give it to a bookseller, who'll pay me three *maravedís* for the rights and think he's doing me a favor? I don't print my books to achieve fame in the world, because I'm already well-known for my work; I want profit: without it, fame isn't worth a thing."

"God grant your grace good fortune," responded Don Quixote.

And he moved to another section, where he saw that they were correcting sheets from a book entitled *Light of the Soul*,[8] and when he saw it he said:

"These are the kinds of books, although there are a good number of them, which ought to be printed, because there are countless sinners, and infinite illumination is needed for so many who are unenlightened."

He moved on and saw that they were also correcting another book, and when he asked its title, they responded that it was called the *Second Part of the Ingenious Gentleman Don Quixote of La Mancha*, written by somebody from Tordesillas.[9]

---

7. Cristóbal Suárez de Figueroa's translation of *Il pastor Fido*, by Battista Guarini, was published in Naples in 1602; Juan de Jáuregui's translation of Torquato Tasso's *L'Aminta* was published in Rome in 1607.

8. *Luz del alma* . . . (Valladolid, 1554), by the Dominican friar Felipe de Meneses, was heavily influenced by Erasmus. For a time it was widely read and had several printings, though none in Barcelona, as far as anyone knows.

9. Avellaneda called himself "a native of the town of Tordesillas." Apparently there was no Barcelona edition of the "false *Quixote*" in the seventeenth century; the second printing appeared in Madrid in 1732.

"I have already heard of this book," said Don Quixote, "and by my conscience, the truth is I thought it had already been burned and turned to ashes for its insolence; but its day of reckoning will come, as it does to every pig,[10] for feigned histories are good and enjoyable the closer they are to the truth or the appearance of truth, and as for true ones, the truer they are, the better."

And having said this, and showing some signs of displeasure, he left the printing house. And that same day, Don Antonio arranged for him to be taken to see the galleys along the coast, which made Sancho very happy because he had never seen any before. Don Antonio informed the *cuatralbo*[11] that he would be bringing his famous guest, Don Quixote of La Mancha, about whom the *cuatralbo* and all the residents of the city had heard, to see the galleys that afternoon; and what happened to him on board will be recounted in the following chapter.

CHAPTER LXIII

Regarding the evil that befell Sancho Panza on his visit to the galleys, and the remarkable adventure of the beautiful Morisca

Don Quixote meditated at length on the response of the enchanted head, never realizing the deception, and always concluding with the promise, which he regarded as certain, of Dulcinea's disenchantment. He returned to it again and again and rejoiced, believing he would soon see the promise fulfilled; and Sancho, although he had despised being governor, as has already been said, still wished to give orders and be obeyed, for command, even mock command, brings this misfortune with it.

In short, that afternoon their host, Don Antonio Moreno, and his two friends, along with Don Quixote and Sancho, went to see the galleys. The *cuatralbo* had been advised of their most welcome visit, since it meant seeing the famous pair, Don Quixote and Sancho, and as soon as they reached the harbor all the galleys took down their canopies, and fla-

---

10. The phrase in Spanish is . . . *su San Martín se le llegará, como a cada puerco.* "Having your St. Martin's Day come" is roughly equivalent to "paying the piper" in English, since St. Martin's Day also refers to the time when animals were slaughtered.

11. An officer in command of four galleys.

geolets began to sound; then a skiff covered with rich tapestries and pillows of scarlet velvet was lowered into the water, and as soon as Don Quixote set foot in it the flagship fired its midship cannon, and the other galleys did the same, and when Don Quixote climbed the starboard ladder, the oarsmen and the entire crew cheered him, as was customary when a distinguished person boarded a galley, repeating, "Hurrah, hurrah, hurrah!" three times. The admiral general, which is what we shall call him, for he was a distinguished gentleman from Valencia, gave him his hand, then embraced Don Quixote, saying:

"I shall mark this day with a white stone because it is one of the best I think I shall ever have in my life, for on it I have seen Señor Don Quixote of La Mancha, who demonstrates that all the valor of knight errantry is epitomized and exemplified in his person."

Don Quixote responded with words no less courteous, delighted beyond measure to find himself treated so nobly. They all went to the stern, which was beautifully adorned, and they sat on the side benches; the boatswain passed along the midship gangway and signaled on his whistle for the oarsmen to strip to the waist,[1] which they did instantly. Sancho was stunned to see so many people undressed, especially when he saw the canopy lowered so quickly it seemed to him that all the devils were working there, but this was mere child's play compared to what I shall tell you now. Sancho was sitting on the pole that held the canopy, next to the stern rower[2] on the starboard side, who had already received his instructions, and he seized Sancho and lifted him up in his arms, while all the oarsmen stood ready, and beginning on the starboard side, the arms of the rowers passed him and tossed him from bench to bench with so much speed that poor Sancho's eyes could no longer see, and he undoubtedly thought the demons were carrying him off, and the oarsmen did not stop until they had returned him along the port side back to the stern. The poor man was bruised, breathless, perspiring, and unable to imagine what had happened to him.

Don Quixote, who saw Sancho's wingless flight, asked the admiral general if these were ceremonies used with those who boarded galleys for the first time, because if they were, he, who had no intention of adhering to them, did not wish to engage in the practice, and he made a vow to God that if anyone attempted to seize him and toss him, he

---

1. This meant that they were prepared to row.
2. One of the oarsmen who sat with his back to the stern.

would tear the soul out of his body, and saying this, he stood and grasped his sword.

At that moment they raised the canopy, and with an extremely loud noise they dropped the lateen yard. Sancho thought the sky had come loose from its frame and was about to fall on his head, and filled with fear, he lowered his head and put it between his legs. Don Quixote was frightened as well, and he trembled and hunched his shoulders, and the color drained from his face. The crew hoisted the yard as quickly and noisily as they had lowered it, and they did it all without a word, as if they had neither voice nor breath. The boatswain signaled that they should weigh anchor, and jumping onto the middle of the gangway with his whip or scourge, he began to flog the backs of the oarsmen, and the ship slowly put out to sea. When Sancho saw the movement of so many red feet, for that is what he thought the oars were, he said to himself:

"These are the things that really are enchanted, not the ones my master says. What have these unfortunate men done to be whipped in this way, and how does one man, who walks around here whistling, dare to flog so many people? I say this must be hell, or purgatory at least."

Don Quixote, who saw how attentively Sancho observed what was going on, said to him:

"Ah, Sancho, my friend, how quickly and at how little cost you could, if you wished, strip down to your waist, and sit among these gentlemen, and conclude the disenchantment of Dulcinea! For surrounded by the misery and suffering of so many, you would not feel your own so much; moreover, it might be that the wise Merlin would count each of these lashes, since they are administered by an able hand, as ten of those you must finally give yourself."

The admiral general wanted to ask about the lashes and the disenchantment of Dulcinea, but just then a sailor called out:

"Montjuich[3] is signaling that there's an oared vessel along the coast to the west."

When he heard this, the admiral general jumped onto the gangway and said:

"Ho, my boys, don't let it get away! The watchtower must be signaling us about a pirate brigantine out of Algiers!"

The other three galleys approached the flagship to learn their orders. The admiral general commanded that two of them head out to sea while

---

3. The castle of Montjuich, which overlooks Barcelona.

he and the other ship sailed close to shore, and in this way the brigantine would not escape. The oarsmen pulled on their oars, propelling the galleys with so much fury that they seemed to fly. When the galleys heading out to sea had gone about two miles, they caught sight of a brigantine that they judged to have about fourteen or fifteen rowers' benches, which was true; when the brigantine sighted the galleys, it tried to escape, intending and hoping to get away on account of its speed, but things went badly for her because the flagship was one of the fastest vessels sailing the sea, and as it was overtaking the brigantine, it became clear to her captain that she could not escape, and he wanted the crew to lower their oars and surrender in order not to anger the captain in command of our galleys. But fate, having something else in store, ordained that when the flagship had come so close that those on the brigantine could hear the voices telling them to surrender, two drunken *Toraquis*, which is to say, two Turks out of the fourteen on board the brigantine, fired their muskets and killed two soldiers who were on our foredecks. Seeing this, the admiral general swore not to leave anyone on the other vessel alive, but as he began a furious assault, the brigantine slipped away under the flagship's oars. The galley moved a good distance forward; those in the brigantine saw that they had escaped and set sail as the galley was turning, and again, with sails and oars, they attempted to flee, but their diligence did not help them as much as their audacity had hurt them, because the flagship overtook them in little more than half a mile, then lowered its oars onto the brigantine and captured everyone on board alive.

At this point the other two galleys approached, and all four of them, with their prize, returned to shore, where an infinite number of people were waiting, impatient to know what they were bringing in. The admiral general dropped anchor close to land and learned that the viceroy of the city was on shore. He sent the skiff for him and ordered the lateen yard lowered so that he could immediately hang the pirate captain and the rest of the Turks he had captured, who numbered some thirty-six persons, all of them valiant and most of them Turkish musketeers. The admiral general asked which of them was the captain of the brigantine, and the response came in the Castilian tongue from one of the captives, a Spanish renegade, as it turned out:

"Señor, this young man whom you see here is our captain."

And he pointed to one of the handsomest and most gallant boys the human mind could imagine. His age seemed less than twenty. The admiral general asked him:

"Tell me, ill-advised dog, who urged you to kill my soldiers when you saw it was impossible to escape? Is that the respect you show to flagships? Don't you know that temerity is not valor? Doubtful outcomes should make men bold, not rash."

The captain wanted to respond, but for the moment the admiral general could not hear his response because he went to receive the viceroy who was boarding the galley, along with some of his servants and several people from the city.

"It was a fine chase, Señor Admiral General," said the viceroy.

"Your Excellency will soon see how fine, when they are hanged from this lateen yard."

"Why hanged?" replied the viceroy.

"Because," responded the admiral general, "contrary to the law and all the rights and customs of war, they have killed two of the best soldiers sailing on these galleys, and I have sworn to hang everyone I captured, and principally this boy, who is the captain of the brigantine."

And he showed him the captain, with his hands tied and a noose around his neck, waiting for death.

The viceroy looked at him and saw him so handsome and so gallant and so humble that the boy's good looks provided him with an immediate letter of recommendation, and the viceroy felt a desire to pardon his death, and so he asked:

"Tell me, Captain, are you of Turkish nationality, or a Moor, or a renegade?"

To which the boy responded, also in the Castilian tongue:

"I am not of Turkish nationality, or a Moor, or a renegade."

"Then what are you?" replied the viceroy.

"A Christian woman," responded the young man.

"A woman, and a Christian, in those clothes, in these circumstances? It is more to be wondered at than believed."

"Oh, Señores!" said the boy. "Suspend my execution for a little while; not much will be lost if you delay your revenge while I recount to you my life."

Whose heart was so hard that these words would not soften it, at least enough to hear those that the sad and sorrowful boy wished to say? The admiral general told him to say whatever he wished, but not to expect a pardon for his infamous crime. With this permission, the boy began to speak in this manner:

"I was born to Morisco parents and am of that nation, more unhappy than wise, upon whom a sea of afflictions has lately poured down. In the current of their misfortunes, I was taken to Barbary by two of my uncles, and it did me no good to say that I was a Christian, as in fact I am, and not one of the false or apparent ones but a true Catholic Christian. In vain did I tell this truth to those responsible for our wretched banishment, and my uncles did not wish to believe it, either; instead, they considered it a lie and an invention that I had devised in order to remain in the land where I had been born, and so by force rather than by my will, they took me with them. I had a Christian mother and a wise, Christian father; I drank in the Catholic faith with my mother's milk; I was brought up with good morals; neither in my speech nor in my behavior did I ever give a sign of being Morisca. Along with these virtues, which is what I think they are, grew whatever beauty I have, and although I lived in great modesty and seclusion, it could not have been enough because a young gentleman had the opportunity to see me; his name was Don Gaspar Gregorio, the oldest son of a gentleman whose village is next to ours. How he saw me, how we spoke, how he lost his heart to me and I could not keep mine from him, would be a long story, especially now, when I fear that the merciless noose threatening me will tighten between my tongue and my throat; and so, I shall say only that Don Gaspar Gregorio wanted to accompany me into our exile. He mingled with the Moriscos who had come from other villages, for he knew the language very well, and on the journey he became friends with the two uncles who were taking me with them; as soon as my prudent and farsighted father heard the first proclamation of our banishment, he left our village to find a place in foreign kingdoms that would take us in. He left many pearls and precious stones, along with coins of gold and silver and gold *doblones*, buried and hidden in a place that I alone knew about. He told me that in the event we were banished before he returned, under no circumstances was I to touch the treasure he had left behind.

I did as he told me, and with my uncles, as I have said, and other relatives and friends, we crossed to Barbary, and the place where we settled was Algiers, and it was as if we had settled in hell itself. The king heard of my beauty, and rumors of my wealth, and this was, in some ways, to my advantage. He summoned me, asked me what part of Spain I came from, and what money and jewels I had brought with me. I told him the name of our village and said that my jewels and money were buried there but could easily be recovered if I went back for them. I said this yet feared he would be blinded not by my beauty but by his own greed. While we were having this conversation, he was told that one of the most gallant and

handsome young men imaginable had accompanied me. I realized immediately that they were speaking of Don Gaspar Gregorio, whose beauty
far surpasses any other, no matter how praiseworthy. I was troubled when
I considered the danger to him, because among those barbarous Turks a
handsome boy or youth is more highly esteemed than a woman, no matter how beautiful she may be.

The king immediately ordered the young man brought before him so
that he could see him, and he asked me if what had been said about the
boy was true. Then I, almost as if forewarned by heaven, said that it was,
but I told him the boy wasn't a man but a woman like me, and I begged
him to let me dress her in her rightful clothes so that her beauty could be
fully displayed, and she might appear before him without awkwardness.
He told me I could leave, and said we would talk the next day about how
I could return to Spain and bring back the hidden treasure. I spoke to
Don Gaspar, I told him of the danger he was in if he appeared as a man, I
dressed him as a Moorish girl, and that same afternoon I brought him before the king, who, when he saw him, was stunned, and decided to keep
her and make a present of her to his great lord; to avoid the danger she
might face in his seraglio, and fearing what he himself might do, he ordered her placed in the home of some wellborn Moorish women who
would protect and serve her. Don Gaspar was taken there at once.

What the two of us felt, for I cannot deny that I love him, I leave to
the consideration of those who love and must part. Then the king devised a plan in which I would return to Spain on this brigantine, accompanied by two Turks, who were the ones who killed your soldiers. This
Spanish renegade also came with me"—and she pointed to the man who
had spoken first—"and I know very well that he is a secret Christian and
has more desire to remain in Spain than to return to Barbary; the rest of
the crew on the brigantine are Moors and Turks who serve only as oarsmen. The two Turks, who are greedy and insolent, did not obey their orders, which were that as soon as we reached Spain they were to put me
and this renegade ashore, in Christian clothes, which we have brought
with us; instead, they wanted to sail along this coast and take a prize, if
they could, for they feared that if they put us ashore first, through unforeseen circumstances we might reveal that the brigantine was at sea, and if
there were galleys along this coast, their vessel would be captured. Last
night we saw this coastline, and not knowing about the four galleys, we
were discovered, and you have witnessed what has befallen us.

In short, Don Gaspar Gregorio remains dressed as a woman among women, in clear danger of being lost, and I find myself with my hands tied, waiting, or I should say fearing, to lose my life, which already wearies me. This is, Señores, the end of my lamentable history, as true as it is unfortunate; what I beg of you is that you allow me to die as a Christian, for as I have said, in no way have I been guilty of the offense into which those of my nation have fallen."

And then she fell silent, her eyes brimming with heartfelt tears that were accompanied by the many shed by those present. The viceroy, tenderhearted and compassionate, did not say a word but went up to her and with his own hands removed the rope that bound the beautiful hands of the Morisca.

As the Christian Morisca was recounting her strange history, an ancient pilgrim who had boarded the galley with the viceroy had not taken his eyes off her, and as soon as she finished speaking, he threw himself at her feet and embraced them, and in words interrupted by a thousand sobs and sighs, he said:

"O Ana Félix, my unfortunate daughter! I am your father, Ricote, who came back to find you because I cannot live without you, for you are my soul."

At these words, Sancho opened his eyes and raised his head—he had lowered it, thinking about the evil that had befallen him—and, looking at the pilgrim, he recognized the same Ricote whom he had met on the day he left his governorship, and he confirmed that the girl was Ricote's daughter, for when she was untied she embraced her father, mixing her tears with his, and Ricote said to the admiral general and the viceroy:

"Señores, this is my daughter, more unfortunate in what has happened to her than in her name.[4] She is called Ana Félix, and her surname is Ricote, and she is as famous for her beauty as she is for my wealth. I left my country to look in foreign lands for a place that would welcome and shelter us, and having found it in Germany, I came back dressed as a pilgrim, in the company of other Germans, to find my daughter and retrieve the great riches I left hidden here. I did not find my daughter but I did find my treasure, which I have with me, and now, through the strange twist of fate that you have witnessed, I have found the treasure that enriches me most, which is my beloved daughter. If in the integrity of your justice our small guilt, and her tears and mine, can open the doors to mercy, then show us mercy, for we never thought of of-

---

4. *Félix* (*feliz* in contemporary Spanish) means "happy" or "fortunate."

fending you, nor did we ever agree in any way with the intentions of our people, who have so justly been expelled."

Then Sancho said:

"I know Ricote very well, and I know that what he says about Ana Félix being his daughter is true; as for this other business of coming and going and having good or bad intentions, I have nothing to say about that."

Everyone present was astonished at this strange matter, and the admiral general said:

"Drop by drop, your tears will not permit me to keep my vow; live, beautiful Ana Félix, the years of life that heaven has granted you, and let the insolent and rash men who committed the crime bear the penalty."

And then he ordered the two Turks who had killed his two soldiers hung from the lateen yard, but the viceroy begged him very earnestly not to hang them, for theirs was more a crime of madness than of audacity. The admiral general did as the viceroy requested, for revenge in cold blood is not easily carried out. Then they attempted to devise a plan to free Don Gaspar Gregorio from danger; to that end, Ricote offered the more than two thousand *ducados* he had in pearls and precious stones. They thought of many schemes, but none was as good as the one proposed by the Spanish renegade we have mentioned, who offered to return to Algiers in a small vessel, with some six rowers' benches, manned by Christian oarsmen, because he knew where, how, and when he could and should disembark, and by the same token he knew the house where Don Gaspar was being kept. The admiral general and the viceroy doubted if they could trust the renegade or be certain about the safety of the Christians who would man the oars, but Ana Félix vouched for him, and her father Ricote said he would pay the ransom for the Christians if they happened to be captured.

Having decided, then, on this plan, the viceroy disembarked, and Don Antonio Moreno took the Morisca and her father home with him, the viceroy having charged him to welcome and treat them as hospitably as possible, and he himself offering whatever was in his house for their entertainment, for Ana Félix's beauty had inspired great benevolence and charity in his heart.

CHAPTER LXIV

Which deals with the adventure that caused Don Quixote more sorrow than any others that had befallen him so far

The history recounts that the wife of Don Antonio Moreno was very pleased to see Ana Félix in her house. She welcomed her with great amiability, as charmed by her beauty as by her intelligence, for the Morisca was exceptionally endowed with both, and all the people in the city, as if summoned by a pealing bell, came to see her.

Don Quixote told Don Antonio that the plan they had devised to free Don Gaspar Gregorio was not a good one because it was more dangerous than feasible, and it would be better to put him ashore in Barbary with his arms and his horse, and he would set the young man free despite the entire host of Moors, just as Don Gaiferos had done for his wife, Melisendra.

"Your grace should remember," said Sancho when he heard this, "that Señor Don Gaiferos rescued his wife on dry land and took her to France on dry land, but here, if we do release Don Gregorio, we have no way to bring him to Spain because there's an ocean in the middle."

"There is a remedy for everything except death," responded Don Quixote, "for if we have a ship along the coast, we can embark on that even if the whole world attempts to prevent it."

"Your grace paints a very nice picture and makes it seem very easy," said Sancho, "but there's many a slip 'tween cup and lip, and I'll depend on the renegade, who looks to me like an honest and good-hearted man."

Don Antonio said that if the renegade failed in the enterprise, he would arrange for the great Don Quixote to go to Barbary.

Two days later, the renegade sailed in a light vessel with six oars on each side, manned by a very valiant crew of oarsmen, and two days after that the galleys departed for the Levant, the admiral general first having asked the viceroy to please keep him informed regarding the rescue of Don Gaspar Gregorio, and the matter of Ana Félix, and the viceroy having agreed.

One morning, when Don Quixote went out to ride along the shore armed and in his armor because, as he often said, they were his adornment and combat was his ease, and he was never without them, he saw a knight approaching in full armor, and on his shield was depicted a resplendent moon; and coming close enough to be heard, and addressing his words to Don Quixote, he cried out in a loud voice, saying:

"Renowned knight and never sufficiently praised Don Quixote of La Mancha, I am the Knight of the White Moon, whose extraordinary deeds perhaps have come to your attention; I am here to do battle with you and to test the strength of your mighty arms, obliging you to recognize and confess that my lady, whoever she may be, is incomparably more beautiful than your Dulcinea of Toboso; and if you confess this truth clearly and plainly, you will save yourself from death, and save me the trouble of killing you; and if you do battle and I conquer you, I want no other satisfaction than that you abandon your arms, abstain from seeking adventures, and withdraw and retire to your home for a period of one year, where you must live without laying a hand on your sword, in peaceful tranquility and profitable serenity, for such is required for the increase of your fortune and the salvation of your soul; and if you should conquer me, my life will be at your mercy, and my arms and horse will be yours, as spoils, and the fame of my deeds will be added to yours. Consider what you should do, and respond immediately, for I have only this day to settle this matter."

Don Quixote was amazed and astonished, not only by the arrogance of the Knight of the White Moon, but by the cause for which he was challenging him, and with great calm and a severe bearing, he responded:

"Knight of the White Moon, whose deeds have not yet come to my attention, I should dare to swear that you have never seen the illustrious Dulcinea, for if you had, I know you would not attempt to undertake this enterprise, because the sight of her would cause you to accept this truth: there never has been nor can there ever be a beauty that compares to hers; and so, not saying that you lie, but only that you are not correct in what you propound, I accept your challenge with the conditions you have mentioned, and I do so immediately, so that the one day you have set aside does not slip away; but I do not accept the condition that your deeds be added to my fame, because I do not know what they are or what kind they may be; I am content with mine, such as they are. Take, then, whichever part of the field you wish, and I shall do the same, and whomever God favors may St. Peter bless."

People in the city who had seen the Knight of the White Moon told the viceroy that he was speaking with Don Quixote of La Mancha. The viceroy, believing it was probably a new adventure devised by Don Antonio Moreno or by some other gentleman of the city, immediately rode out to the shore with Don Antonio, accompanied by many other gentlemen, and they arrived just as Don Quixote was turning the reins of Rocinante in order to take the distance needed for his charge.

Seeing that the two knights were showing signs of engaging in combat, the viceroy placed himself between them, asking what reason moved them to so unexpected a battle. The Knight of the White Moon responded that it was a question of precedence in beauty, and briefly repeated the same words he had said to Don Quixote, and stated that the conditions of the challenge had been accepted by both parties. The viceroy approached Don Antonio and asked him quietly if he knew the identity of the Knight of the White Moon or if this was a trick they wanted to play on Don Quixote. Don Antonio responded that he did not know who the knight was or if the challenge was in jest or in earnest. The viceroy was perplexed by this reply, for he did not know if he should allow them to continue with the battle; however, unable to persuade himself that it was anything but a joke, he moved aside, saying:

"Señores, if the only remedy is to confess or die, and Señor Don Quixote is adamant, and the Knight of the White Moon is obdurate, then the matter is in the hands of God. Set to!"

The Knight of the White Moon thanked the viceroy with appropriate and courteous words for the permission he had granted them, and Don Quixote did the same, and commending himself with all his heart to heaven and to his Dulcinea—which was his custom at the beginning of the battles that presented themselves to him—he took a little more ground, because he saw that his adversary was doing the same, and without the playing of a trumpet or any other martial instrument that would signal to them to charge, they both turned their horses at the same time; since the mount of the Knight of the White Moon was faster, he reached Don Quixote when he had gone two-thirds of the way, meeting his adversary with such power and force that without touching him with his lance—which he had raised, it seemed, intentionally—he toppled both Rocinante and Don Quixote in a dangerous fall. He rushed at him immediately, and putting his lance to Don Quixote's visor, he said:

"You are vanquished, knight, and dead if you do not confess the conditions of our challenge."

Don Quixote, battered and stunned, not raising his visor, and as if speaking from the tomb, said in a weak and feeble voice:

"Dulcinea of Toboso is the most beautiful woman in the world, and I am the most unfortunate knight on earth, and it is not right that my weakness should give the lie to this truth. Wield your lance, knight, and take my life, for you have already taken my honor."

"That I certainly shall not do," said the Knight of the White Moon. "Let the fame of Señora Dulcinea of Toboso's beauty live in its entirety; let it live, I say, for the satisfaction I ask is that the great Don Quixote retire to his village for a year, or for as long as I shall determine, as we agreed before entering into this battle."

All this was heard by the viceroy and Don Antonio, as well as by many others who were present, and they also heard Don Quixote respond that as long as he asked nothing that was to the detriment of Dulcinea, he would comply with all the rest like a true and honorable knight.

When this confession was made, the Knight of the White Moon turned his horse, bowed his head respectfully to the viceroy, and entered the city at a canter.

The viceroy ordered Don Antonio to go after him and learn without fail who he was. They picked up Don Quixote, uncovered his face, and found him pale and perspiring. Rocinante had been so badly hurt that he could not move. Sancho, utterly sad and utterly grief-stricken, did not know what to say or do: it seemed to him that the entire episode was a dream and everything that had happened a matter of enchantment. He saw his master defeated and obliged to not take up arms for a year; he imagined the light of his glorious deeds dimmed and the hopes of his latest promises to Sancho dissipated, as the wind dissipates smoke. He feared that Rocinante would be left crippled and his master's bones dislocated, though it would be no misfortune if he had been made sane.[1] Finally, the viceroy sent for a sedan chair and Don Quixote was carried back to the city, and the viceroy returned as well, desiring to know the identity of the Knight of the White Moon who had left Don Quixote in so terrible a state.

1. Cervantes creates a wordplay that cannot be duplicated in English. It is based on *loco* ("crazy" or "mad") and the possibilities of "dislocated" (*deslocado*).

CHAPTER LXV

Which reveals the identity of the Knight of the White Moon, and recounts the release of Don Gaspar Gregorio, as well as other matters

Don Antonio Moreno followed the Knight of the White Moon, who was also followed, even pursued, by a good number of boys, until he entered an inn inside the city. Don Antonio went in as well, desiring to meet him; a squire came out to greet him and remove his armor; the knight withdrew to a room on the ground floor, and Don Antonio went after him, for he could barely wait to find out who he might be. The Knight of the White Moon, seeing that this gentleman would not leave him alone, said:

"I know very well, Señor, why you have come: you want to know who I am, and since there is no reason not to tell you, while my servant removes my armor I shall tell you the truth of the matter, omitting nothing. Know then, Señor, that my name is Bachelor Sansón Carrasco; I am from the same village as Don Quixote of La Mancha, whose madness and foolishness move all of us who know him to pity; I have been one of those who pitied him most, and believing that his health depends on his remaining peacefully in his own village and in his own house, I devised a way to oblige him to do that, and so some three months ago I took to the road as a knight errant, calling myself the Knight of the Mirrors, and intending to do combat with him and defeat him without doing him harm, and setting as a condition of our combat that the vanquished would have to obey the victor; what I planned to ask of him, because I already considered him defeated, was that he return to his village and not leave it again for a year, for in that time he could be cured; but fate ordained otherwise, because he defeated me and toppled me from my horse, and so my idea did not succeed; he continued on his way, and I returned home, defeated, chagrined, and bruised from my fall, which was a dangerous one, yet not even this could diminish my desire to find him again and defeat him, as you have witnessed today. And since he is so punctilious in complying with the rules of knight errantry, he undoubtedly will comply with the conditions I have set, and keep his word. This, Señor, is what has happened, and I have nothing more to tell you, and I implore you not to reveal my identity or tell Don Quixote who I am, so that my good intentions can be put into effect and a man can regain his reason, for his is fine when free of the absurdities of chivalry."

"Oh, Señor," said Don Antonio, "may God forgive you for the harm you have done to the entire world in wishing to restore the sanity of the most amusing madman in it! Don't you see, Señor, that the benefit caused by the sanity of Don Quixote cannot be as great as the pleasure produced by his madness? But I imagine that all the good bachelor's efforts will not suffice to restore sanity to a man so hopelessly mad; and if it were not contrary to charity, I would say that Don Quixote should never be cured, because when he regains his health we lose not only his amusing words and actions, but those of his squire, Sancho Panza, any one of which could cheer melancholy itself. Even so, I shall be silent and tell him nothing, if only to see if I am correct in supposing that Señor Carrasco's endeavors will have no effect."

The bachelor responded that the matter was well under way, and he expected a successful outcome. When Don Antonio offered to do whatever he might require, Sansón Carrasco took his leave, had his armor tied on to a mule, mounted the same horse he had ridden into battle, left the city that same day, and returned home without anything happening to him that needs to be recounted in this true history.

Don Antonio told the viceroy everything Carrasco had told him, which did not give the viceroy much pleasure: Don Quixote's retirement meant that all who knew of his madness would lose the pleasure that might have been theirs.

Don Quixote spent six days in bed, sick at heart, sad, melancholy, and morose as he went over and over again in his imagination the misfortune of his defeat. Sancho consoled him, and among other things, he said:

"Señor, your grace should lift up your head and be glad, if you can, and give thanks to heaven that even though you were toppled to the ground, you didn't break any ribs; and since you know there are always wins and losses, and you may have the hook but not the bacon, forget about the doctor because you don't need him to be cured of what's ailing you, and let's go back home and stop going around looking for adventures in places and countries we don't know; if you think about it, I'm the one who's lost the most, though your grace has been hurt more. When I gave up the governorship I also gave up any desire to be a governor again, but I didn't give up wanting to be a count, which will never happen if your grace gives up being a king by giving up the practice of your chivalry, which means all my hopes going up in smoke."

"Be quiet, Sancho, for my retirement and withdrawal do not need to last longer than a year, and then I shall return to my honorable practice, and there will be no lack of kingdoms for me to win and countships to give to you."

"May God hear you," said Sancho, "and sin be deaf, for I've always heard that virtuous hope is better than wicked possession."

Just then Don Antonio came in and said, with indications of great joy:

"Good news, Señor Don Quixote! Don Gaspar Gregorio and the renegade who went to rescue him are ashore! What do I mean ashore? They are already in the house of the viceroy, and will be here at any moment."

Don Quixote was cheered somewhat and said:

"The truth is I was about to say that I should be pleased if everything had turned out otherwise, because then I would be obliged to go to Barbary, where, by the strength of my arm, I would free not only Don Gaspar Gregorio, but all the Christian captives in Barbary. But what am I saying, wretch that I am? Am I not the vanquished one? Am I not the defeated one? Am I not the one who cannot take up arms for a year? Then what am I promising? Why do I praise myself when it would be more appropriate for me to use a distaff and not a sword?"

"Enough of that, Señor," said Sancho. "Long live the hen, even with the pip; today it's your turn and tomorrow it's mine; these matters of clashes and blows shouldn't be taken too seriously, because the man who falls today can pick himself up tomorrow, unless he decides to stay in bed, I mean if he lets himself lose heart and doesn't find new spirit for new fights. And your grace should get up now to receive Don Gaspar Gregorio, because it seems to me that everybody's in an uproar, and he must be in the house by now."

And this was true, because Don Gaspar Gregorio and the renegade had already given an account to the viceroy of the journey there and back, and since Don Gaspar Gregorio was longing to see Ana Félix, he came with the renegade to the house of Don Antonio; although he had been dressed in women's clothes when they took him out of Algiers, on the boat he had exchanged them for the clothes of a captive who had been rescued along with him, but no matter what he wore he would have been sought after, served, and esteemed because he was extraordinarily handsome, and his age, apparently, was seventeen or eighteen years old. Ricote and his daughter came out to receive him, the father with tears in his eyes and the daughter with modesty. They did not embrace each other, because where there is great love, generally there is not excessive boldness. The beauty of Don Gaspar Gregorio and Ana Félix, seen together, astounded everyone present. Silence spoke for the two lovers, and their eyes were the tongues that revealed their chaste and joyful thoughts.

The renegade recounted the ingenious means he had used to rescue Don Gaspar Gregorio; Don Gaspar Gregorio recounted the dangers and difficulties he had undergone with the women in whose house he had been living, not at length but in a few words, showing that he had intelligence far beyond his years. In the end, Ricote paid and liberally compensated the renegade as well as the oarsmen. The renegade was reconciled with and reintegrated into the Church, a rotting limb who became cleansed and healthy again through penance and repentance.

Two days later, the viceroy discussed with Don Antonio what means to employ so that Ana Félix and her father could stay in Spain, for it seemed to them there was no good reason that so Christian a daughter and, apparently, so well-intentioned a father should not remain. Don Antonio offered to go to court to negotiate the matter, for he had to go there in any event to tend to other affairs, letting it be known that by means of favors and gifts, many difficult issues can be resolved.

"One must not place hope," said Ricote, who was present at this conversation, "in favors or gifts, because with the great Don Bernardino de Velasco, Count of Salazar,[1] whom His Majesty made responsible for our expulsion, prayers are in vain, as are promises, gifts, and lamentations, for although it is true that he mixes mercy with justice, he sees that the entire body of our nation is contaminated and rotten, and he burns it with a cautery rather than soothing it with an ointment; and so, with prudence, sagacity, diligence, and the fear he imposes, he has borne on his strong shoulders the weight of this great plan, and put it into effect, and our schemes, strategies, pleas, and deceptions have not been able to blind his eyes of Argus, which are always alert so that none of our people can stay behind or be concealed, like a hidden root that in times to come

---

1. He was in charge of the expulsion of the Moriscos from Castilla.

will send out shoots and bear poisonous fruits in Spain, which is clean now, and rid of the fears caused by our numbers. What a heroic decision by the great Felipe III,[2] and what unparalleled wisdom to have entrusted its execution to Don Bernardino de Velasco!"

"When I am there at court, I shall undertake all possible measures, one by one, and may heaven's will be done," said Don Antonio. "Don Gaspar Gregorio will come with me and alleviate the sorrow his parents must feel on account of his absence; Ana Félix will stay with my wife in my house, or in a convent, and I know the viceroy would like the good Ricote to stay with him until we see the outcome of my negotiations."

The viceroy consented to everything that was proposed, but Don Gaspar Gregorio, when he learned their plans, said that under no circumstances could he or would he leave Doña Ana Félix, but because he intended to see his parents and then arrange to come back for her, he finally agreed. Ana Félix stayed with Don Antonio's wife, and Ricote stayed with the viceroy.

The day of Don Antonio's departure arrived, and two days later that of Don Quixote and Sancho, for his fall did not allow him to set out any sooner. There were tears, sighs, swoons, and sobs when Don Gaspar Gregorio took his leave of Ana Félix. Ricote offered him a thousand *escudos*, if he wanted them, but he would not take any, though he did borrow five *escudos* from Don Antonio, promising to repay them at court. With this they left, and subsequently Don Quixote and Sancho departed, as has been said, Don Quixote unarmed and in traveling clothes and Sancho on foot, since the gray was carrying the armor.

2. Felipe III (1578–1621) became king in 1598 and ruled until his death.

CHAPTER LXVI

Which recounts what will be seen by whoever reads it, or heard by whoever listens to it being read

As he left Barcelona, Don Quixote turned to look at the place where he had fallen, saying:

"Here was Troy! Here my misfortune, not my cowardice, did away with the glories I had achieved; here Fortune turned her changes and reverses against me; here my deeds were obscured; here, in short, my happiness fell, never to rise again!"

When Sancho heard this, he said:

"Señor, it is as fitting for valiant hearts to endure misfortune as it is for them to rejoice in prosperity; and I judge this on the basis of my own experience, for if I was happy when I was governor, now that I'm a squire on foot, I'm not sad, because I've heard that the woman they call Fortune is drunken, and fickle, and most of all blind, so she doesn't see what she's doing and doesn't know who she's throwing down or raising up."

"You sound very philosophical, Sancho," responded Don Quixote, "and you speak very wisely; I do not know who taught that to you. What I can say is that there is no fortune in the world, and the things that happen in it, whether good or bad, do not happen by chance but by the particular providence of heaven, which is why people say that each man is the architect of his own fortune. I have done that with mine, but without the necessary prudence, and so my assumptions have turned out badly, for I should have realized that Rocinante's weakness could not resist the power and size of the horse belonging to the Knight of the White Moon. In short, I took a risk, I did what I could, I was toppled, and although I lost my honor, I did not lose, nor can I lose, the virtue of keeping my word. When I was a knight errant, daring and brave, my acts and my hands brought credit to my deeds, and now, when I am an ordinary gentleman, I shall bring credit to my words by keeping the promise I made. Walk on, then, Sancho my friend, and let us go home to spend the year of our novitiate, and in that seclusion we shall gather new strength to return to the practice of arms, which will never be forgotten by me."

"Señor," responded Sancho, "traveling on foot is not so pleasant a thing that it leads or moves me to travel a great distance each day. Let's leave this armor hanging from some tree instead of a hanged man, and if I can sit on my gray, with my feet off the ground, we'll travel whatever distances your grace asks for and decides, but if you think I'll walk great distances on foot, you'd better think again."

"You have spoken well, Sancho," responded Don Quixote. "Let my armor be hung as a trophy, and beneath it, or all around it, we shall carve on the trees what was written on the trophy of Roland's arms:

> Let no one move them
> who cannot test his own against Roland."[1]

"That all seems like pearls to me," responded Sancho, "and if we weren't going to need Rocinante on the road, it would be a good idea to leave him hanging, too."

"Well," replied Don Quixote, "I do not want either him or my arms hanged, so that no one can say this is a bad reward for good service!"

"Your grace is right," responded Sancho, "because according to wise men, you shouldn't blame the packsaddle for the donkey's mistake, and since your grace is to blame for what happened, you should punish yourself and not turn your anger against your battered and bloody arms, or the gentle Rocinante, or my tender feet by wanting them to walk more than is fair."

They spent all that day in this kind of talk and conversation, and another four as well, and nothing happened to interfere with their journey, but on the fifth day, at the entrance to a village, they discovered a crowd of people at the door of an inn, for it was a holiday and they were there enjoying themselves. When Don Quixote reached them, a peasant raised his voice, saying:

"One of these two gentlemen, who don't know the parties, can decide our wager."

1. These lines by Ariosto are also cited in chapter XIII of the first part.

"I shall, certainly," responded Don Quixote, "and with complete rectitude, if I can understand it."

"Well then, Señor," said the peasant, "the fact is that a man from this village, so fat he weighs eleven *arrobas*, challenged a neighbor of his, who doesn't weigh more than five, to a race. The condition was that they had to run a hundred paces carrying equal weight, and when the challenger was asked how they would equal the weight he said that the other man, who weighs five *arrobas*, should add another six *arrobas* of iron on his back, and in this way the thin man's eleven *arrobas* would match the eleven of the fat man."

"Oh no," said Sancho before Don Quixote could respond. "Just a few days ago I stopped being a governor, and it's up to the judge, as everybody knows, to decide questions and give an opinion in every case."

"You are welcome to respond," said Don Quixote, "Sancho my friend; I would not be competent to do so, my judgment is so shaken and confused."

With this permission, Sancho said to the peasants, who stood around him with their mouths open, waiting for his verdict:

"Brothers, what the fat man asks for is not fair and doesn't have a shred of justice in it, because if what they say is true, and the one who's challenged can choose his weapons, it isn't right for him to choose ones that would keep him or stop him from being victorious, and so it's my opinion that the fat challenger should prune, trim, peel away, scrape, pare off, and lose six *arrobas* of his flesh, here and there on his body, wherever he thinks best, and in this way, when he weighs five *arrobas*, he'll match and be equal to the five of his adversary, and so they'll be able to run carrying equal weight."[2]

"By my soul!" said a peasant who had listened to Sancho's decision. "This gentleman has spoken like a saint and given a verdict like a canon! But I'll bet the fat man won't want to lose an ounce of his flesh, let alone six *arrobas* of it."

"The best thing would be if they don't run," responded another, "because then the thin man won't be worn out carrying that weight, and the fat man won't have to lose any; let half the wager be in wine, and let's take these gentlemen to the tavern that has the good wine, and let it be on me . . . and wear a cape when it rains."

"Señores," responded Don Quixote, "I thank you, but I cannot stop

---

2. This story is taken from the *Floresta general* (*General Anthology*) by Melchor de Santa Cruz, a sixteenth-century student and collector of proverbs.

even for a moment; melancholy thoughts and events make me seem discourteous and oblige me to travel quickly."

And so, spurring Rocinante, he rode forward, leaving them all amazed at having seen and observed both his strange figure and the intelligence of his servant, for that is what they judged Sancho to be. And another of the peasants said:

"If the servant is this intelligent, what must the master be like! I'll bet if they went to study in Salamanca, in the wink of an eye they'd be magistrates; everything's deceit except studying and more studying, and having favor and good luck; when a man least expects it, he finds himself with a staff in his hand or a mitre on his head."

Master and servant spent that night in the middle of a field, in the open air; the next day, as they continued their journey, they saw a man walking toward them, with saddlebags around his neck and a pike or javelin in his hand, looking exactly like a courier on foot; as he approached Don Quixote, he quickened his pace until he was almost running, and he came up to him and embraced his right thigh, which was as high as he could reach, and said with displays of great joy:

"Oh, Señor Don Quixote of La Mancha, what happiness will fill the heart of my lord the duke when he knows that your grace is returning to his castle, for he is still there with my lady the duchess!"

"I do not recognize you, friend," responded Don Quixote, "and I shall not know who you are if you do not tell me."

"I, Señor Don Quixote," responded the courier, "am Tosilos, the footman of my lord the duke who refused to fight with your grace over marrying the daughter of Doña Rodríguez."

"God save me!" said Don Quixote. "Is it possible that you are the one whom the enchanters, my enemies, transformed into the footman you mention in order to cheat me of the honor of that combat?"

"Be quiet, Señor," replied the letter carrier. "There was no enchantment at all, and no change in anybody's face: I entered the field as much Tosilos the footman as I was when I left it. I wanted to marry without fighting, because I liked the girl's looks, but things turned out just the opposite of my intention, because as soon as your grace left our castle, my lord the duke had me lashed a hundred times for going against the orders he had given me before I went into combat, and the upshot is that the girl is a nun, and Doña Rodríguez has gone back to Castilla, and I'm going now to Barcelona to bring a packet of letters to the viceroy that my master has sent him. If your grace would like a drink that's pure, though warm, I have a gourd filled with good wine, and a few slices of Tronchón cheese that will call upon and wake your thirst if it happens to be sleeping."

"I'll see this bet," said Sancho, "and stake it all on courtesy, and let good Tosilos pour in spite of and despite all the enchanters in the Indies."

"Well, well," said Don Quixote, "you are, Sancho, the greatest glutton in the world, and the most ignorant man on earth, for you cannot be persuaded that this courier is enchanted and this Tosilos a counterfeit. Stay with him, and drink your fill, and I shall go ahead slowly and wait for you until you come."

The footman laughed, uncovered his gourd, and took his cheese and a small loaf of bread out of a saddlebag, and he and Sancho sat on the green grass and in companionable peace quickly dispatched and finished the contents of the saddlebags with so much spirit that they licked the packet of letters simply because it smelled of cheese. Tosilos said to Sancho:

"There's no doubt that your master, Sancho my friend, must be a madman."

"What do you mean, 'must be'?" responded Sancho. "He doesn't owe anybody anything;[3] he pays for everything, and more, when madness is the coin. I see it clearly, and I tell him so clearly, but what good does it do? Especially now, when he's really hopeless because he was defeated by the Knight of the White Moon."

Tosilos begged him to tell him what had happened, but Sancho responded that it was discourteous to allow his master to wait for him, and on another day, if they were to meet, there would be time for that. And having stood after he had shaken his tunic and brushed the crumbs from his beard, he walked behind the gray, said goodbye, left Tosilos, and overtook his master, who was waiting for him in the shade of a tree.

---

3. The untranslatable wordplay is based on the verb *deber*, which is the equivalent of "must" as well as of "owe."

CHAPTER LXVII

Regarding the decision Don Quixote made to become a shepherd and lead a pastoral life until the year of his promise had passed, along with other incidents that are truly pleasurable and entertaining

If many thoughts had troubled Don Quixote before his fall, many more troubled him after he was toppled. As has been said, he was in the shade of the tree, and there, like flies swarming around honey, thoughts came to him and stung him: some had to do with the disenchantment of Dulcinea and others with the life he would have to live in his forced retirement. Then Sancho arrived and praised the liberality of the footman Tosilos.

"Is it possible," said Don Quixote, "Oh, Sancho, that you still think he is the real footman? It seems you have forgotten that you saw Dulcinea changed and transformed into a peasant, and the Knight of the Mirrors into Bachelor Carrasco, the work, in both cases, of the enchanters who pursue me. But tell me now: did you ask the man you call Tosilos what God has done with Altisidora? Did she weep over my absence, or has she already placed in the hands of oblivion the amorous thoughts that so troubled her in my presence?"

"Mine were not the kind," responded Sancho, "that would let me ask about nonsense. By God, Señor, is your grace interested now in asking about other people's thoughts, especially amorous ones?"

"Look, Sancho," said Don Quixote, "there is a great difference between the actions one takes because of love and those taken because of gratitude. A knight may well be unenamored, but strictly speaking, he can never be ungrateful. Altisidora, it seems, loved me dearly; she gave me the three nightcaps, which you know about, she wept at my departure, she cursed me, she reviled me, she complained, despite all modesty, publicly; all of these were signs that she adored me, for the anger of lovers often ends in curses. I had no hopes to offer her or treasures to present to her, because all of mine I have given to Dulcinea, and the treasures of knights errant are, like those of goblins,[1] apparent and false, and I can give her only the innocent memories I have of her; as for those I have of Dulcinea, you offend her with your slackness in administering the lashes and in punishing that flesh—may I see it devoured by wolves—which you would rather preserve for the worms than use for the relief of that poor lady."

"Señor," responded Sancho, "if you want to know the truth, I'm not convinced that lashing my backside has anything to do with disenchanting the enchanted, because it would be like saying, 'If you have a headache, put some ointment on your knees.' I'd swear, at least, that in all the histories about knight errantry that your grace has read, you've never seen a disenchantment by flogging; but, whether that's true or not, I'll give myself the lashes when I feel like it and it's a convenient time for me to punish myself."

"May it be God's will," responded Don Quixote, "and may the heavens grant you the grace to realize the obligation you have to help my lady, who is yours as well, since you are my servant."

They were conversing as they continued on their way, until they reached the same place and spot where they had been trampled by the bulls. Don Quixote recognized it and said to Sancho:

"This is the meadow where we encountered the beautiful shepherdesses and gallant shepherds who wanted to restore and imitate pastoral Arcadia here, a thought as original as it is intelligent, and like them, if you think it is a good idea, I should like, O Sancho, for us to become shepherds, at least for the time I must be retired. I shall buy some sheep, and all the other things needed for the pastoral exercise, and my name will be *Shepherd Quixotiz* and yours *Shepherd Pancino,* and we shall roam the mountains, the woods, and the meadows, singing here, lamenting there, drinking the liquid crystal of the fountains, or the limpid streams, or the rushing rivers. With a copious hand the oaks will give us their sweetest fruit; the hard cork trees, their trunks as seats; the willows, their shade; the roses, their fragrance; the broad meadows, carpets of a thousand shades and colors; the clear, pure air, our breath; the moon and stars, our light in spite of night's darkness; pleasure will give us our songs;

---

1. It was believed that goblins turned buried treasure into coal, which is the origin of the phrase *tesoro de duende* ("goblin's treasure") to describe wealth that is squandered.

joy, our weeping; Apollo, our verses; love, our conceits; and with these we shall make ourselves eternal and famous, not only in the present but in times to come."[2]

"By God," said Sancho, "that sort of life squares so well with me it even corners; besides, as soon as Bachelor Sansón Carrasco and the barber Master Nicolás see it, they'll want to lead that life and become shepherds along with us; God willing, the priest will decide to join the fold, too, he's so good-natured and fond of enjoying himself."

"You have spoken very well," said Don Quixote, "and Bachelor Sansón Carrasco, if he enters the pastoral fraternity, as he undoubtedly will, can call himself *Shepherd Sansonino*, or even *Shepherd Carrascón*; Barber Nicolás can be *Miculoso*,[3] as old Boscán was called *Nemoroso*;[4] I do not know what name we could give the priest, unless it is one derived from his profession, and we call him *Shepherd Curiambro*.[5] As for the shepherdesses whose lovers we shall be, we can choose their names as if we were picking pears, and since my lady's fits a shepherdess as well as a princess, there is no reason for me to try to find another that would be more suitable; you, Sancho, can call yours whatever you like."

"I don't plan," responded Sancho, "to give her any name but *Teresona*, which will suit her plumpness[6] and the name she already has, which is Teresa; besides, I'll celebrate her in my verses and reveal my chaste desires, for I don't plan to go looking for trouble in other men's houses. It won't be good for the priest to have a shepherdess, because he ought to set a good example, but if the bachelor wants to have one, his soul is his own business."

"God save me!" said Don Quixote. "What a life we shall lead, Sancho my friend! What flageolets will reach our ears, what Zamoran pipes, what timbrels, what tambourines, and what rebecs! Well, and what if in the midst of all this music albogues should resound! Then we would have all the pastoral instruments."

"What are albogues?" asked Sancho. "I've never heard of them or seen them in my life."

2. Martín de Riquer points out that despite this essentially satiric depiction of the pastoral novel, Cervantes was very pleased with his pastoral *Galatea* and was working on its second part at approximately the same time that he wrote this passage.

3. This name is based on a pastoral version of Micolás for Nicolás.

4. At one time it was thought that Nemoroso, in Garcilaso's first eclogue, was the poet's friend and fellow poet Boscán (a name related to *bosque*, or "forest"): *Nemus* has the same meaning in Latin.

5. The Spanish word for "priest" that is used here is *cura*.

6. *Ona* is an augmentative ending, so that *Teresona* is roughly equivalent to "Big Teresa."

"Albogues," responded Don Quixote, "are something like brass candlesticks, and when you hit one with the other along the empty or hollow side, it makes a sound that is not unpleasant, though it may not be very beautiful or harmonious, and it goes well with the rustic nature of pipes and timbrels; this word *albogues* is Moorish, as are all those in our Castilian tongue that begin with *al*, for example: *almohaza, almorzar, alhombra, alguacil, alhucema, almacén, alcancía,*[7] and other similar words; our language has only three that are Moorish and end in the letter *i*, and they are *borceguí, zaquizamí*, and *maravedí*.[8] *Alhelí* and *alfaquí*,[9] as much for their initial *al* as for the final *i*, are known to be Arabic. I have told you this in passing because it came to mind when I happened to mention albogues; one thing that will help us a great deal to achieve perfection in this endeavor is that I am something of a poet, as you know, and Bachelor Sansón Carrasco is even better. I say nothing about the priest, but I would wager that he has a touch of the poet, and Master Nicolás as well, I have no doubt about that, because all barbers, or most of them, are guitarists and rhymers. I shall complain of absence; you will praise yourself as a steadfast lover; Shepherd Carrascón will lament being scorned; the priest Curiambro, whatever he chooses; and so things will go so well that no one could ask for more."

To which Sancho responded:

"I am, Señor, so unfortunate, that I fear the day will never come when I can join this exercise. Oh, how polished I'll keep the spoons when I'm a shepherd. What soft bread, what cream, what garlands, what pastoral odds and ends that, if they don't earn me fame as a wise man, can't help but earn me fame as a clever one! Sanchica, my daughter, will bring food up to our flocks. But wait! She's a good-looking girl, and there are shepherds more wicked than simple, and I wouldn't want her to go for wool and come back shorn; love and unchaste desires are as likely in the countryside as in the cities, in shepherd's huts as in royal palaces, and if you take away the cause, you take away the sin, and if your eyes don't see, your heart doesn't break, and a jump over the thicket is better than the prayers of good men."

"No more proverbs, Sancho," said Don Quixote, "for any one of those you have said is enough to explain your thoughts; I have often ad-

---

7. The words mean "curry comb," "to eat lunch," "carpet," "bailiff," "lavender," "storehouse," "money box." Despite the general correctness of this oddly placed lesson in etymology, Martín de Riquer points out that Cervantes is not entirely accurate in the examples he chooses, although he agrees generally with the linguists of his day.

8. The words mean "Moorish half-boot," "hovel," "ancient Spanish coin."

9. The words mean "gillyflower," "teacher of the Koran."

vised you not to be so prodigal in your proverbs and to restrain yourself from saying them, but it seems that is like preaching in the desert, and 'My mother punishes me, and I deceive her.' "

"It seems to me," responded Sancho, "that your grace is like the pot calling the kettle black. You reprove me for saying proverbs, and your grace strings them together two at a time."

"Look, Sancho," responded Don Quixote, "I say proverbs when they are appropriate, and when I say them they fit like the rings on your fingers, but you drag them in by the hair, and pull them along, and do not guide them, and if I remember correctly, I have already told you that proverbs are brief maxims derived from the experience and speculation of wise men in the past, and if the proverb is not to the point, it is not a maxim, it is nonsense. But let us leave this for now, and since night is approaching, let us withdraw some distance from the king's highway, and spend the night there, and God alone knows what tomorrow will bring."

They withdrew and had a scant, late supper, much against the will of Sancho, to whom it seemed that the austerities of knight errantry were common in the forests and mountains, while abundance was displayed in castles and houses, as much in the house of Don Diego de Miranda or Don Antonio Moreno as at the wedding of the wealthy Camacho, but he considered that it could not always be day, and it could not always be night, and so he spent that night sleeping, while his master kept watch.

CHAPTER LXVIII

Regarding the porcine adventure that befell Don Quixote

The night was somewhat dark although the moon was in the sky, but not in a place where she could be seen: perhaps the lady Diana had taken a trip to the Antipodes and left the mountains black and the valleys dark. Don Quixote fulfilled his obligations to nature by sleeping his first sleep,[1] but not giving way to his second, unlike Sancho, who never had a second sleep because his sleep lasted from nightfall until morning, prov-

---

1. In Spanish, *primer sueño*, or "first sleep," is the equivalent of "beauty sleep"—that is, sleep before midnight, generally considered the most restful.

ing he had a strong constitution and few cares. Those of Don Quixote kept him awake until he woke Sancho and said:

"I am astounded, Sancho, at your carefree disposition: I imagine that you are made of marble or hard bronze, and that feeling or sentiment has no place in you. I keep vigil while you sleep, I weep while you sing, I swoon from fasting while you are lazy and sluggish from sheer satiety. It is in the nature of good servants to share the griefs of their masters and to feel what they are feeling, if only for appearance's sake. Look at the serenity of this night and the solitude of this place, inviting us to mingle some wakefulness with our sleep. Get up, for the love of God, and go a little distance from here, and with good courage and the boldness of gratitude give yourself three or four hundred of the lashes you owe for the disenchantment of Dulcinea; I plead with you to do this; I do not wish to come to blows with you, as we did last time, because I know you have a heavy hand. After you have flogged yourself, we shall spend what remains of the night singing, I of my absent love, and you of your valor, thereby beginning the pastoral life we shall practice in our village."

"Señor," responded Sancho, "I'm not a monk who wakes up in the middle of the night to discipline myself, and I also don't think anybody can feel the extreme pain of a whipping and then start singing music. Your grace should let me sleep and stop pressing me about the lashes, or you'll force me to swear that I'll never even touch a thread of my tunic, let alone my flesh."

"O unfeeling soul! O pitiless squire! O undeserved bread and unthinking favors that I have given to you and intend to give to you in the future! Because of me you found yourself a governor, and because of me you have hopes of becoming a count or receiving another equivalent title, and the fulfillment of those hopes will take no longer than the time it takes for this year to pass, for *Post tenebras spero lucem*.[2]

"I don't understand that," replied Sancho. "I only understand that while I'm sleeping I have no fear, or hope, or trouble, or glory; blessed be whoever invented sleep, the mantle that covers all human thought, the food that satisfies hunger, the water that quenches thirst, the fire that warms the cold, the cold that cools down ardor, and, finally, the general coin with which all things are bought, the scale and balance that make

2. "After the darkness I hope for the light," cited by Martín de Riquer as Job 17:12, although in the King James Bible that line reads, "They change the night into day: the light is short because of darkness." Perhaps more important than the biblical source is the fact that the phrase was the motto of the printer Juan de la Cuesta and therefore appears on the frontispiece of the earliest editions of both parts of *Don Quixote*.

the shepherd equal to the king, and the simple man equal to the wise. There is only one defect in sleep, or so I've heard, and it is that it resembles death, for there is very little difference between a man who is sleeping and a man who is dead."

"I have never heard you speak, Sancho," said Don Quixote, "as elegantly as now, which leads me to recognize the truth of the proverb that you like to quote: 'It is not where you were born but who your friends are now that counts.' "

"Ah, confound it, Señor!" replied Sancho. "Now I'm not the one stringing proverbs together; they also drop two by two from your grace's mouth better than they do from mine, but between my proverbs and yours there must be this difference: your grace's come at the right time, while mine are out of place, but in fact they're all proverbs."

They were engaged in this conversation when they heard a deafening sound and a harsh noise that extended through all the valleys. Don Quixote rose to his feet and put his hand to his sword, and Sancho crouched under the gray, pulling the armor down on one side and his donkey's packsaddle down on the other, trembling from fear as much as Don Quixote trembled from excitement. Gradually the noise grew louder as it came closer to the two fearful men: to one of them, at least; as for the other, his courage is already well-known.

The fact is, at that early hour, some swineherds were taking more than six hundred pigs to a fair to sell them, and the animals made so much noise grunting and snorting that it deafened Don Quixote and Sancho, who could not imagine what the sound could be. The large grunting herd came running in great haste and confusion, and without showing respect for the authority of either Don Quixote or Sancho, they ran over them both, destroying Sancho's stockade and knocking down not only Don Quixote but Rocinante for good measure. The herd, the grunting, the speed with which the unclean animals ran past, threw into confusion and to the ground the packsaddle, the armor, the gray, Rocinante, Sancho, and Don Quixote.

Sancho struggled to his feet and asked his master for his sword, saying that he wanted to kill half a dozen of those stout and discourteous pigs, for he had realized what they were. Don Quixote said:

"Let them be, my friend, for this affront is chastisement for my sin, and heaven's just punishment is that a defeated knight errant will be devoured by jackals, and stung by wasps, and trampled by pigs."

"It must also be heaven's punishment," responded Sancho, "that the squires of defeated knights will be bitten by flies, eaten by lice, and attacked by hunger. If we squires were the children of the knights we serve, or close relatives of theirs, it wouldn't be surprising if the punishment for their faults reached us all the way to the fourth generation, but what do the Panzas have to do with the Quixotes? Well then, let's get comfortable again and sleep for the rest of the night, and God will send the dawn, and we'll be fine."

"You sleep, Sancho," responded Don Quixote, "for you were born to sleep, but I, born to stand watch, shall give free rein to my thoughts in the time that remains until daylight, and proclaim them in a madrigal I composed in my mind last night without your knowledge."

"It seems to me," responded Sancho, "that thoughts that move you to write verses can't be very troublesome. Your grace should versify all you want, and I'll sleep all I can."

And then, taking all the ground he wished, he curled up and fell fast asleep, undisturbed by guaranties or debts or any sorrow. Don Quixote, leaning against the trunk of a beech or a cork tree—for Cide Hamete Benengeli does not specify what kind of tree it was—sang to the sound of his own sighs:

> O Love, when my thoughts turn
> to the suffering, dread and fierce, you bring,
> I swiftly run toward death,
> hoping to end forever the pain I feel;
>   but when I reach that place,
> the port in this rough ocean of my torment,
> I feel such joy and gladness
> that life grows strong and does not let me pass.
>   And so my living kills me,
> and death insists and gives me back my life.
> Mine is a novel state:
> I go on living, and constantly die.[3]

Each of these verses was accompanied by many sighs and no few tears, befitting one whose heart was pierced by the pain of defeat and the absence of Dulcinea.

Then day arrived, the sun shone its rays into Sancho's eyes, he awoke and stretched, shaking and extending his sluggish limbs; he looked at

3. The madrigal is a translation from the Italian of a poem by Pietro Bembo (1470–1547).

the destruction wreaked on his provisions by the pigs, and cursed the herd, and even more than that. Finally the pair resumed their journey, and as the afternoon drew to a close, they saw some ten men on horseback and four or five men on foot coming toward them. Don Quixote's heart beat faster, and Sancho's was alarmed, because the men approaching carried lances and shields and seemed very warlike. Don Quixote turned to Sancho and said:

"If I could wield my weapons, Sancho, and the promise I gave had not tied my arms, I would deem this group coming toward us as nothing more than mere child's play, but perhaps it is not what we fear."

By then the men on horseback had reached them, and raising their lances, and not saying a word, they surrounded Don Quixote and held their weapons to his back and chest, threatening him with death. One of those on foot brought his finger to his mouth to indicate silence, seized Rocinante's bridle, and led him off the road; the rest of the men on foot, driving Sancho and the gray before them, and maintaining the most astonishing silence, followed in the footsteps of those who had taken Don Quixote, who tried to ask two or three times where they were taking him or what they wanted, but as soon as he began to move his lips they were closed by the points of the lances; the same thing happened to Sancho, because as soon as he gave signs of wanting to speak, one of the men on foot goaded him with a barb, and the donkey, too, as if he wanted to speak as well. Night fell, they hurried their pace, and the two prisoners felt a growing fear, especially when they heard their captors say from time to time:

"Move, troglodytes!"

"Silence, barbarians!"

"Atone, anthropophagi!"

"No complaints, Scythians,[4] don't even open your eyes, murdering Polyphemuses,[5] bloodthirsty lions!"

And many other similar names with which they tormented the ears of the wretched master and servant. As Sancho walked, he said to himself:

"They call us tortoise-tykes? Barbers and ant puffs? Pollies that can be called like pissants? I don't like these names at all; it's an ill wind blowing on this pile of grain; all this wickedness comes down on us at once,

4. A nomadic and fierce people from southeastern Europe; their territory, Scythia, lay between the Carpathians and the Don.

5. One of the Cyclopes, he was blinded by Ulysses.

like blows on a dog, and may it please God that what this misadventurous adventure threatens goes no further than blows!"

Don Quixote was dazed, unable to guess, no matter how he tried, the purpose of the insulting names, but certain, at least, that from those words nothing good could be hoped for and a good deal of harm could be feared. And then, almost an hour after nightfall, they arrived at what Don Quixote recognized as the castle of the duke, where they had been only a short while before.

"God save me!" he said as soon as he recognized the estate. "What can this mean? In this house all is courtesy and good manners, but for those who have been defeated, good becomes bad, and bad becomes even worse."

They entered the principal courtyard of the castle, and they saw that it was adorned and decorated in a manner that increased their bewilderment and doubled their fear, as will be seen in the next chapter.

CHAPTER LXIX

Concerning the strangest and most remarkable event to befall Don Quixote in the entire course of this great history

The horsemen dismounted, and together with those on foot, they seized Sancho and Don Quixote, lifted them up, and carried them into the courtyard, around which almost a hundred torches set in sconces were burning; more than five hundred lamps had been placed along the passages in the courtyard, so that despite the night, which proved to be somewhat dark, the lack of daylight went unnoticed. In the middle of the courtyard a catafalque rose some two *varas* off the ground, entirely covered by a very large canopy of black velvet; around it, on its steps, candles of white wax burned in more than a hundred silver candelabras; displayed on the catafalque was the dead body of a damsel so beautiful that her beauty made death itself beautiful. Her head, crowned with a garland of fragrant flowers, lay on a brocade pillow, and her hands, crossed on her bosom, held a branch of yellow triumphant palm.

To one side of the courtyard a stage had been erected, and on it were two seats, upon which two persons were sitting, and the crowns on their heads and the scepters in their hands indicated that they were kings, either real or feigned. To the side of the stage, on the steps leading up to it, two other seats were placed, and on these the men carrying the prisoners seated Don Quixote and Sancho; they did all this in silence, and signaled to the pair that they should be silent as well, but even without the signals they would have been silent because the astonishment they felt at what they were seeing had tied their tongues.

At that moment, two distinguished personages mounted the stage, followed by a large retinue; they were recognized immediately by Don Quixote as the duke and duchess, his hosts, and they sat in two richly decorated chairs beside the two men who seemed to be kings. Who would not have been astounded at this, especially when Don Quixote realized that the dead body on the catalfaque was the beauteous Altisidora?

When the duke and duchess mounted the stage, Don Quixote and Sancho rose and made deep obeisances, and the duke and duchess responded with a slight bow of their heads.

Then one of their officials crossed the courtyard, came up to Sancho, and placed on him a garment of black buckram decorated with flames of fire; he removed his cap and put on his head a cone-shaped hat, of the sort given to penitents to wear by the Holy Office, and he said into his ear that if he opened his mouth, they would gag him or take his life. Sancho looked at himself and saw himself in flames, but since they did not burn he did not care at all about them. He removed the hat, saw that it was decorated with devils, and put it back on, saying to himself:

"It'll be fine if the flames don't burn me and the devils don't carry me off."

Don Quixote looked at him as well, and although fear had stunned his senses he could not help laughing at Sancho's appearance. At this point the soft, pleasant music of flutes began to be heard, coming, apparently, from beneath the catafalque, and, unconstrained by any human voice, because in that place silence imposed silence on itself, the music sounded gentle and amorous. Then suddenly, next to the pillow of what was, apparently, a corpse, there appeared a handsome youth dressed in Roman fashion, and to the sound of a harp that he played himself, in a soft, clear voice he sang these two stanzas:

Until Altisidora 'turns to life,
killed by the cruelty of Don Quixote;
until, in the enchanting court, the ladies
begin to wear cloth made of rough goat's hair;
until my mistress dresses all her duennas
in clothes of heavy flannel and wool serge,
I shall sing of her beauty and affliction
more sweetly than that famed singer of Thrace.[1]

And yet I do not think that this sad duty
ends for me on the day that my life ends,
but with a cold, dead tongue, a lifeless mouth,
I shall lift my voice in sweetest song to you.
And when my soul, freed of its mortal shell,
is led across the dark infernal Styx,
it will celebrate you still, and with that song
it will halt the waters of oblivion.[2]

"No more," said one of the two who seemed to be monarchs, "no more, divine singer, for it would mean continuing into infinity if you were to represent for us now the death and charms of the peerless Altisidora, who is not dead, as the ignorant world thinks, but alive on the tongues of Fame, and in the punishment that Sancho Panza, here present, must undergo in order to return her to the light she has lost; and so you, Rhadamanthus,[3] who judges with me in the gloomy caverns of Dis,[4] and who knows everything that has been determined by the inscrutable Fates regarding the return of this maiden to life, speak and declare it now so that the good we expect from her return to a new life is no longer delayed."

As soon as Minos, judge and companion of Rhadamanthus, had spoken, Rhadamanthus rose to his feet and said:

"Ho, officials of this house, both high and low, great and small, come one after the other and mark the face of Sancho with twenty-four slaps to the nose, and twelve pinches and six pinpricks on his arms and back, for the welfare of Altisidora depends on this ceremony!"

1. The earliest Greek poets, including Orpheus, were allegedly from Thrace.

2. This second stanza is from Garcilaso's third eclogue.

3. With his brother, Minos, he was a judge of the shades in Hades.

4. Martín de Riquer points out that the first edition had *Lite* rather than *Dite* (Spanish for "Dis"), which he thinks resulted from some confusion with *Leteo* (Lethe), the mythical river of oblivion. In any case, Dis is another name for Pluto, or Hades, the god of the underworld.

Hearing this, Sancho Panza broke the silence and said:

"By God, I'm as likely to become a Moor as to let anybody mark my face or slap my nose! By my faith! What does slapping my face have to do with the resurrection of this maiden? The old woman liked the greens so much . . .[5] They enchant Dulcinea, and whip me to disenchant her; Altisidora dies of ills that God sent her, and they'll bring her back by slapping me twenty-four times and riddling my body with pinpricks, and pinching my arms black and blue! Try those tricks on your brother-in-law! I'm an old dog, and you don't have to call me twice!"

"You will die!" said Rhadamanthus in a loud voice. "Soften your heart, tiger; humble yourself, proud Nimrod, and suffer and be silent, for you are not being asked to do the impossible. And do not become involved in determining the difficulties of this business: slapped you must be, riddled with holes you must be, and pinched until you moan. Ho, I say, officials, obey my commands, or by the faith of a virtuous man, you will find out why you were born!"

At that moment some six duennas appeared, crossing the courtyard in procession, one after the other, four of them wearing spectacles, and all of them holding up their right hands, with four finger widths of wrist exposed to make their hands seem longer, following the current fashion. As soon as Sancho saw them, he bellowed like a bull, saying:

"I might let myself be handled by the whole world, but consenting to being touched by duennas, never! Let cats claw my face, as they did to my master in this very castle; let them run my body through with sharpened daggers; let them tear at the flesh of my arms with red hot pincers, and I'll bear it all patiently to serve these gentlemen, but I won't consent to duennas touching me even if the devil carries me off."

Don Quixote broke the silence, too, saying to Sancho:

"Be patient, my friend, and oblige these gentlemen, and give many thanks to heaven for having placed such virtue in your person that through its martyrdom you can disenchant the enchanted and resuscitate the dead."

By now the duennas were close to Sancho, and he, more docile and convinced, settled himself in his chair and held up his face and beard to the first duenna, who gave him a very sharp slap, followed by a very deep curtsy.

"Less courtesy, and less face paint, Señora Duenna," said Sancho, "because, by God, your hands smell of *vinagrillo!*"[6]

---

5. The second part of the proverb is: ". . . that she didn't leave any, green or dry."

6. A cosmetic lotion made of vinegar, alcohol, and aromatic essences.

Finally, all the duennas marked him, and many other people from the house pinched him, but what he could not endure were the pinpricks, and so he got out of his chair, apparently angry, and grasping one of the burning torches that was near him, he chased after the duennas, and all his other tormentors, saying:

"Away, ministers of hell! I'm not made of bronze! I feel your awful tortures!"

At this point Altisidora, who must have been tired after spending so much time supine, turned to one side, and when the onlookers saw this, almost all of them cried out in unison:

"Altisidora is alive! Altisidora lives!"

Rhadamanthus ordered Sancho to set aside his wrath, for their intended purpose had been achieved.

As soon as Don Quixote saw Altisidora begin to move, he fell to his knees before Sancho, saying:

"Now it is time, friend of my soul rather than my squire, to give yourself some of the lashes to which you are obliged in order to disenchant Dulcinea. Now, I say, is the time when your virtue is ripe and ready to perform the good deed that is expected of you."

To which Sancho responded:

"This seems like one dirty trick on top of another, and not honey on hotcakes. How nice it would be after pinches, slaps, and pinpricks to have a few lashes. Why not just take a big stone and tie it around my neck and put me in a well, and I won't mind it too much since I have to be a laughing-stock in order to solve other people's problems. Let me alone; if not, I swear I'll knock down and destroy everything, and I don't care what happens."

By this time Altisidora had sat up on the catalfaque, and at the same instant flageolets began to play, accompanied by flutes and the sound of everyone's voices, crying:

"Long live Altisidora! Altisidora, long may she live!"

The duke and duchess rose to their feet, as did Kings Minos and Rhadamanthus, and all of them together, along with Don Quixote and Sancho, went to greet Altisidora and take her down from the catafalque, and she, pretending to be faint, curtsied to the duke and duchess and to the kings, and looking at Don Quixote out of the corner of her eye, she said to him:

"God forgive you, coldhearted knight, for because of your cruelty I have been in the next world for more than a thousand years, it seems to me; and you, the most compassionate squire on earth, I thank you for the life I possess! Today, friend Sancho, I promise you will have six chemises of mine to use to make six shirts for yourself, and if some are torn, at least they are all clean."

Sancho kissed her hands in gratitude for the present, with his knees on the ground and the cone-shaped hat in his hand. The duke ordered that it be taken from him and his own cap returned, and they put on his tunic and took off the garment with the flames. Sancho asked the duke to allow him to keep the robe and mitre, for he wanted to take them back to his own village as a keepsake and memento of that incomparable event. The duchess responded that he could, for he already knew what a great friend of his she was. The duke ordered the courtyard cleared, and everyone to withdraw to their own quarters, and Don Quixote and Sancho to be taken to the rooms they already knew from their previous visit.

CHAPTER LXX

Which follows chapter LXIX, and deals with matters necessary to the clarity of this history

That night Sancho slept on a low, small bed in the same room as Don Quixote, something that Sancho would have avoided if he could because he knew very well that with all his questions and answers, his master would not let him sleep, and he was not inclined to speak a great deal because the pains of his recent torments were very present and had done nothing to loosen his tongue, and he would have preferred to sleep in a hovel alone than in that rich chamber in the company of another. What he feared was so real and what he suspected so true, that as soon as his master climbed into his bed, he heard his master say:

"What do you think, Sancho, of what happened tonight? Great and powerful is the strength of love scorned, for with your own eyes you saw Altisidora dead, not by arrows or sword or any other instrument of war, or by deadly poison, but because of the harshness and disdain with which I have always treated her."

"She was welcome to die as much as she wanted and however she wanted," responded Sancho, "and to leave me alone, because I never fell in love with her or scorned her in my life. As I've said before, I don't know how it can be that Altisidora's well-being, a maiden who's more willful than wise, has anything to do with the sufferings of Sancho Panza. Now at last I see, clearly and distinctly, that there are enchanters and enchantments in the world, and may God save me from them because I don't know how to save myself; even so, I beg your grace to let me sleep and not ask me anything else, unless you want me to throw myself out a window."

"Then sleep, Sancho my friend," responded Don Quixote, "if the pinpricks and pinches and slaps you have received allow you to sleep."

"No pain," replied Sancho, "was as great an insult as the slaps, simply because they were given to me by duennas, confound them; and again I beg your grace to let me sleep, because it relieves the miseries we feel when we're awake."

"Then sleep," said Don Quixote, "and God be with you."

Both of them fell asleep, and during this time Cide Hamete, author of this great history, wished to write and give an account of what moved the duke and duchess to devise the elaborate scheme that has just been narrated; he says that Bachelor Sansón Carrasco, not having forgotten when the Knight of the Mirrors was vanquished and overthrown by Don Quixote, a defeat and a fall that ruined and destroyed all his plans, wanted to try his hand again, hoping for better success than before; and so, learning from the page who carried the letter and gift to Teresa Panza, Sancho's wife, where Don Quixote was, he found new arms and another horse, and on his shield he put the white moon and had all of it carried by a mule led by a peasant and not Tomé Cecial, his former squire, so that he would not be recognized by Sancho or Don Quixote.

And so he came to the castle of the duke, who informed him of the direction and route Don Quixote had taken and of his intention to appear in the jousts at Zaragoza. He also told him of the tricks that had been played on Don Quixote and of the scheme for disenchanting Dulcinea that would have to take place at the expense of Sancho's hindquarters. Finally, he recounted the trick that Sancho had played on his master, leading him to believe that Dulcinea had been enchanted and transformed into a peasant girl, and how his wife, the duchess, led Sancho to believe that he was the one deceived because Dulcinea really was enchanted; the bachelor laughed a good deal and marveled as he considered Sancho's shrewdness and simplicity, and the extremes of Don Quixote's madness.

The duke asked if he found Don Quixote, and regardless of whether he defeated him or not, that he return and tell him what had occurred.

The bachelor agreed and set out to look for him; he did not find him in Zaragoza and continued on his way, and what has already been related happened to him.

He returned to the castle of the duke and told him everything, including the conditions of their combat, and he said that Don Quixote was already returning home to keep, like a good knight errant, his promise to withdraw to his village for a year, in which time it might be, said the bachelor, that his madness would be cured; for this was the purpose that had moved him to assume those disguises, since it was a sad thing for a gentleman as intelligent as Don Quixote to be mad. With this, he took his leave of the duke and returned to his village and waited there for Don Quixote, who was riding behind him.

This gave the duke the opportunity to arrange the deception: such was the pleasure he derived from matters concerning Sancho and Don Quixote; he sent out many of his servants on foot and on horseback to search roads close to and far from the castle, all the ones he imagined Don Quixote might use to return home, so that either willingly or by force they could bring him back to the castle if they found him. They did find him, and they so informed the duke, who had already arranged what was to be done, and as soon as he had been informed of their arrival, he ordered the torches lit, and the lamps placed in the courtyard, and Altisidora to climb the catafalque, and all the devices that have been recounted performed so vividly and realistically that there was very little difference between them and the truth.

Cide Hamete goes on to say that in his opinion the deceivers are as mad as the deceived, and that the duke and duchess came very close to seeming like fools since they went to such lengths to deceive two fools, who, one sleeping soundly and the other keeping watch over his unrestrained thoughts, were overtaken by daylight and filled with the desire to arise, for the featherbeds of idleness never gave pleasure to Don Quixote, whether he was the vanquished or the victor.

Altisidora—restored to life, in Don Quixote's opinion—followed the whim of her master and mistress, and crowned with the same garland she had worn on the catafalque, and dressed in a tunic of white taffeta sown with gold flowers, and with her hair hanging loose down her back, and leaning on a staff of fine black ebony, she entered Don Quixote's room; her presence disquieted and confused him, and he covered and concealed himself almost completely under the sheets and blankets on the bed, his tongue silenced, unable to utter a single courtesy. Altisidora sat on a chair near the head of his bed, and after heaving a great sigh, in a faint and piteous voice she said:

"When highborn women and secluded maidens trample on their honor, and give permission to their tongues to break free of all restraints and proclaim in public the secrets hidden in their hearts, they find themselves in desperate circumstances. I, Señor Don Quixote of La Mancha, am one of these, afflicted, vanquished, enamored, but with it all longsuffering and modest, so much so, and so much of each, that my silence made my heart burst and I lost my life. For two days, on account of the harshness with which you have treated me, O unfeeling knight,

Oh, harder than marble to my complaints![1]

I was dead, or, at least, judged to be so by those who saw me; and if it had not been that Love took pity on me and placed the remedy in the sufferings of this good squire, I would have remained in the next world."

"Love could just as well have placed them in the sufferings of my donkey, and I would have thanked him for that. But tell me, Señora, and may heaven find you another lover more tenderhearted than my master, what did you see in the next world? What's it like in hell? Because whoever dies in despair is bound to go there."

"To tell the truth," responded Altisidora, "I probably didn't die completely because I didn't enter hell, and if I had, I really couldn't have left even if I'd wanted to. The truth is I reached the gate, where about a dozen devils were playing pelota, all of them in tights and doublets, their collars trimmed with borders of Flemish lace and cuffs of the same material, exposing four fingers' width of arm so that their hands appeared longer, and in them they were holding bats of fire, and what amazed me most was that instead of balls they were using books, apparently full of wind and trash, which was something marvelous and novel; but this did not amaze me as much as seeing that, although it is natural for players to be happy when they win and sad when they lose, in that game everybody was grumbling, everybody was quarreling, and everybody was cursing."

"That's not surprising," responded Sancho, "because devils, whether they play or not, can never be happy, whether they win or not."

"That must be true," responded Altisidora, "but there's something else that also surprises me, I mean, surprised me then, and it was that at

1. The line is by Garcilaso.

the first volley there wasn't a ball left in play that was in condition to be used again, and so they went through books, new and old, which was a remarkable thing to see. One of them, brand new and nicely bound, was hit so hard that its innards spilled out and its pages were scattered. One devil said to another:

'See what book that is.'

And the other devil responded:

'This is the second part of the history of Don Quixote of La Mancha, composed not by Cide Hamete, its first author, but by an Aragonese who is, he says, a native of Tordesillas.'

'Take it away from here,' responded the other devil, 'and throw it into the pit of hell so that my eyes never see it again.'

'Is it so bad?' responded the other one.

'So bad,' replied the first, 'that if I myself set out to make it worse, I would fail.' And they continued with their game, hitting other books, and I, because I had heard the name of Don Quixote, whom I love and adore so passionately, did my best to keep this vision in my memory."

"It must have been a vision, no doubt about it," said Don Quixote, "because there is no other I in the world, and that history is already being passed from hand to hand but stops in none, because everyone's foot is kicking it along. I have not been perturbed to hear that I wander like a shade in the darkness of the abyss or in the light of the world, because I am not the one told about in that history. If it is good, faithful, and true, it will have centuries of life, but if it is bad, the road will not be long between its birth and its grave."

Altisidora was going to continue her complaints about Don Quixote, when the knight said to her:

"As I have often told you, Señora, I am grieved that you have turned your thoughts to me, for they can sooner be thanked than remedied by mine; I was born to belong to Dulcinea of Toboso, and the Fates, if there are any, have dedicated me to her, and to think that any other beauty can occupy the place she has in my soul is to think the impossible. This is sufficient discouragement for you to withdraw inside the borders of your modesty, for no one can be obliged to do the impossible."

Hearing which, Altisidora, showing signs of anger and vexation, said:

"Good Lord! Don Codfish, with a soul of metal, like the pit of a date, harder and more stubborn than a peasant when he has his mind set on something, if I get near you I'll scratch out your eyes! Do you think by any chance, Don Defeated, Don Battered, that I died for you? Everything you saw tonight was pretense; I'm not the kind of woman who would let herself suffer as much as the dirt under her fingernail, much less die, on account of nonsense like that."

"I believe it," said Sancho, "because all this about lovers dying makes me laugh: they can say it easily enough, but doing it is a story only Judas would believe."

While they were having this conversation, the musician, singer, and poet, who had sung the two stanzas already described, came in, and making a deep bow to Don Quixote, he said:

"Señor Knight, your grace should consider and count me in the number of your greatest admirers, for I have been devoted to you for some time now, as much for your fame as for your exploits."

Don Quixote responded:

"Your grace should tell me who you are so that my courtesy may respond to your merits."

The youth responded that he was the musician and panegyrist of the previous night.

"Certainly," replied Don Quixote, "your grace has an excellent voice, but what you sang did not seem very appropriate to me. What do stanzas by Garcilaso have to do with the death of this lady?"

"Your grace should not be surprised at that," responded the musician, "for among the untutored poets of our day, the custom is for each to write however he wishes and steal from whomever he wishes regardless of whether or not it suits his intention, and there is no foolishness, either sung or written, that is not attributed to poetic license."

Don Quixote wished to respond but was prevented from doing so by the duke and duchess, who came in to see him, and they had a long and pleasant conversation in which Sancho said so many amusing things and so many clever things that the duke and duchess were once again astounded by his simplicity and his shrewdness. Don Quixote asked them to give him permission to depart that very day, because it is more seemly for defeated knights like him to sleep in pigsties rather than in royal palaces. They gave it willingly, and the duchess asked if Altisidora remained in his good graces. He responded:

"Señora, your ladyship should know that all the problems afflicting this maiden are born of idleness, and the remedy lies in honest and constant labor. She has told me that they use lace trimmings in hell, and since she must know how to make them, she should never let them out of her hands; if she is occupied in moving the bobbins, the image or images of what she desires will not move through her imagination, and this is the truth, this is my opinion, and this is my advice."

"And mine," added Sancho, "for I've never seen in all my life a lace-maker who's died for love; maidens who are occupied think more about finishing their tasks than about love. At least that's true for me, because when I'm busy digging I never think about my better half, I mean my Teresa Panza, and I love her more than my eyelashes."

"Well said, Sancho," said the duchess, "and from now on I shall keep my Altisidora busy doing needlework, which she does extremely well."

"There's no reason, Señora," responded Altisidora, "to make use of this remedy, for consideration of the cruelties this wicked vagrant has inflicted on me will wipe him from my memory with no need for other measures. And with the permission of your highness, I should like to leave now in order not to have before my eyes not only his sorrowful face, but his hideous and hateful features."

"That seems to me," said the duke, "like the old saying:

> Because the one who says insults
> is very close to forgiving."[2]

Altisidora made a show of drying her tears with a handkerchief, and after curtsying to her master and mistress, she left the room.

"Go in peace," said Sancho, "poor maiden, go in peace, I mean, you have bad luck because you fell in love with a soul of esparto grass and a heart of oak. By my faith, if you'd fallen in love with me, you'd be singing a different tune!"

The conversation came to an end, and Don Quixote dressed, dined with the duke and duchess, and departed that afternoon.

2. The lines are from a ballad.

CHAPTER LXXI

What befell Don Quixote and his squire, Sancho, as they were traveling to their village

The vanquished and exhausted Don Quixote was extremely melancholy on the one hand and very happy on the other. His sadness was caused by his defeat and his happiness by his consideration of Sancho's virtue and how it had been demonstrated in the resurrection of Altisidora, even though he had felt certain reservations when he persuaded himself that the enamored maiden had in fact been dead. Sancho was not at all happy, because it made him sad to see that Altisidora had not kept her promise to give him the chemises, and going back and forth over this, he said to his master:

"The truth is, Señor, that I'm the most unfortunate doctor one could find anywhere in the world, where a physician can kill the sick person he's treating and wants to be paid for his work, which is nothing but signing a piece of paper for some medicines that are made not by him but by the apothecary, and that's the whole swindle; but when other people's well-being costs me drops of blood, slaps, pinches, pinpricks, and lashes, they don't give me an *ardite*. Well, I swear that if they bring me another patient, before I cure anybody they'll have to grease my palm, because if the abbot sings he eats his supper, and I don't want to believe that heaven gave me this virtue to use for others at no charge."

"You are right, Sancho my friend," responded Don Quixote, "and it was very wrong of Altisidora not to give you the chemises she promised, although your virtue is *gratis data*[1] and has not cost you any study at all, for suffering torments on your person is more than study. As for me, I can tell

---

1. Latin for "given free of charge."

you that if you wanted payment for the lashes of Dulcinea's disenchantment, I should have given it to you gladly, but I do not know if payment would suit the cure, and I would not want rewards to interfere with the treatment. Even so, it seems to me that nothing would be lost if we tried it: decide, Sancho, how much you want, and then flog yourself and pay yourself in cash and by your own hand, for you are carrying my money."

At this offer Sancho opened his eyes and ears at least a span and consented in his heart to flog himself willingly, and he said to his master:

"Well now, Señor, I'm getting ready to do what your grace desires, and to make a little profit, too, because the love I have for my children and my wife makes me seem greedy. Tell me, your grace: how much will you pay me for each lash I give myself?"

"If I were to pay you, Sancho," responded Don Quixote, "according to what the greatness and nobility of this remedy deserve, the treasure of Venice and the mines of Potosí would not be enough; estimate how much of my money you are carrying, and then set a price for each lash."

"The lashes," responded Sancho, "amount to three thousand, three hundred, and a few; of those I've given myself five: that leaves the rest; let the five count as those few, and we come to the three thousand and three hundred, which at a *cuartillo* each, and I won't do it for less even if the whole world ordered me to, comes to three thousand and three hundred *cuartillos*, and that three thousand comes to fifteen hundred half-*reales*, and that's seven hundred fifty *reales*; and the three hundred comes to one hundred fifty half-*reales*, which is seventy-five *reales*, and add that to the seven hundred fifty, it comes to a total of eight hundred twenty-five *reales*. I'll take that out of your grace's money, and I'll walk into my house a rich and happy man, though badly whipped; because trout aren't caught . . . ,[2] and that's all I'll say."

"O blessed Sancho! O kind and courteous Sancho!" responded Don Quixote. "Dulcinea and I shall be obliged to serve you for all the days of life that heaven grants us! If she returns to the state that was lost, and it is impossible that she will not, her misfortune will have been fortune, and my defeat a glorious triumph. Decide, Sancho, when you want to begin the flogging; if you do it soon, I shall add another hundred *reales*."

"When?" replied Sancho. "Tonight, without fail. Your grace should

_____

2. The rest of the proverb is: "with a bare line."

arrange for us to spend it in the countryside, out of doors, and I'll lay open my flesh."

Night fell, anticipated by Don Quixote with the deepest longing in the world, for it seemed to him that the wheels on Apollo's carriage[3] had broken and that the day lasted longer than usual, which is what lovers generally feel, for they can never account for their desire. At last they entered a pleasant wood a short distance from the road, and leaving Rocinante's saddle and the gray's packsaddle unoccupied, they lay on the green grass and ate their supper from Sancho's provisions; then, making a powerful and flexible whip from the donkey's halter and headstall, Sancho withdrew some twenty paces from his master into a stand of beeches. Don Quixote, who saw him go with boldness and spirit, said:

"Be careful, my friend, not to tear yourself to pieces; pause between lashes; do not try to race so quickly that you lose your breath in the middle of the course; I mean, you should not hit yourself so hard that you lose your life before you reach the desired number. And to keep you from losing by a card too many or too few, I shall stand to one side and count the lashes you administer on my rosary. May heaven favor you as your good intentions deserve."

"A man who pays his debts doesn't care about guaranties," responded Sancho. "I plan to lash myself so that it hurts but doesn't kill me: that must be the point of this miracle."

Then he stripped down to his waist, and seizing the whip he had fashioned, he began to flog himself, and Don Quixote began to count the lashes.

Sancho must have given himself six or eight lashes when the joke began to seem onerous and the price very low, and he stopped for a while and said to his master that he withdrew from the contract because each of those lashes should be worth a half-*real*, not a *cuartillo*.

"Continue, Sancho my friend, and do not lose heart," said Don Quixote, "for I shall double the stakes on the price."

"In that case," said Sancho, "let it be in God's hands, and rain down the lashes!"

But the crafty scoundrel stopped lashing his back and began to whip the trees, from time to time heaving sighs that seemed to be torn from his heart. Don Quixote's was tender, and fearing that Sancho might end

3. The sun, in Greek mythology.

his life and because of that imprudence not achieve the knight's desire, he said:

"On your life, friend, let the matter stop here, for this remedy seems very harsh to me, and it would be a good idea to take more time: Zamora was not won in an hour. You have given yourself more than a thousand lashes, if I have counted correctly: that is enough for now, for the donkey, speaking coarsely, will endure the load, but not an extra load."

"No, no, Señor," responded Sancho, "let no one say of me: 'Money was paid and his arms grew weak.' Your grace should move a little farther away, and let me give myself another thousand lashes at least: two more rounds of these and we'll finish the game and even have something left over."

"Since you are so well-disposed," said Don Quixote, "then may heaven help you; go on with your whipping, and I shall move away."

Sancho returned to his task with so much enthusiasm that he had soon stripped the bark from a number of trees, such was the rigor with which he flogged himself; and once, raising his voice as he administered a furious blow to a beech, he said:

"Here you will die, Samson, and all those with you!"

Don Quixote immediately hurried to the sound of the doleful voice and the pitiless flogging, and seizing the twisted halter that served as a whip, he said to Sancho:

"Fate must not allow, Sancho my friend, that in order to please me you lose your life, which must serve to support your wife and children: let Dulcinea wait for another occasion, and I shall keep myself within the bounds of proximate hope, waiting for you to gain new strength so that this matter may be concluded to everyone's satisfaction."

"Señor, since that is your grace's wish, may it be for the best, and toss your cape over my shoulders because I'm sweating and don't want to catch a chill: new penitents run that risk."

Don Quixote did so, and in his shirtsleeves he covered Sancho, who slept until he was awakened by the sun, and then they continued their journey, which they brought to a halt, for the time being, in a village three leagues away. They dismounted at an inn, which Don Quixote took to be an inn and not a castle with a deep moat, towers, portcullises, and drawbridges, for after he was defeated he thought with sounder judgment about everything, as will be recounted now. He was lodged in a room on the ground floor, and hanging on its walls were the kind of old painted tapestries still used in villages. On one of them was painted, very badly, the abduction of Helen, at the moment the audacious guest stole her away from Menelaus,[4] and the other showed the history of Dido and Aeneas: she stood on a high tower and signaled with a large cloth to her fugitive guest, who fled by sea on a frigate or brigantine.

He noted in the two histories that Helen did not go very unwillingly, for she was laughing, slyly and cunningly, but the beautiful Dido seemed to shed tears the size of walnuts, and seeing this, Don Quixote said:

"These two ladies were extremely unfortunate because they were not born in this age, and I am the most unfortunate of men because I was not born in theirs: if I had encountered these gentlemen, Troy would not have been burned, nor Carthage destroyed, for simply by my killing Paris, so many misfortunes would have been avoided."[5]

"I'll wager," said Sancho, "that before long there won't be a tavern, an inn, a hostelry, or a barbershop where the history of our deeds isn't painted. But I'd like it done by the hands of a painter better than the one who did these."

"You are right, Sancho," said Don Quixote, "because this painter is like Orbaneja, a painter in Úbeda, who, when asked what he was painting, would respond: 'Whatever comes out.' And if he happened to be painting a rooster, he would write beneath it: 'This is a rooster,' so that no one would think it was a fox. And that, it seems to me, Sancho, is how the painter or writer—for it amounts to the same thing—must be who brought out the history of this new Don Quixote: he painted or wrote whatever came out; or he may have been like a poet who was at court some years ago, whose name was Mauleón; when asked a question, he would say the first thing that came into his head, and once when asked the meaning of *Deum de Deo*, he responded: 'Dim down the drummer.'[6] But leaving that aside, tell me, Sancho, if you intend to administer another set of lashes tonight, and if you wish it to take place under a roof or out of doors."

"By God, Señor," responded Sancho, "considering how I plan to whip myself, a house would be as good as a field, but even so, I'd like it to be under the trees, because they seem like companions and help me to bear this burden wonderfully well."

"It should not be like this, Sancho my friend," responded Don

---

4. The reference is to Paris abducting Helen, who was married to Menelaus; this incident sparked the Trojan War.

5. In Virgil's recounting of the legend, Dido, the founder of Carthage, had a love affair with Aeneas, a hero of the Trojan War and the founder of Rome. When he abandoned Dido, she killed herself on a funeral pyre.

6. The joke is based on the repetition of the initial *d* in both Latin and Spanish (*Dé donde diere*: "Give wherever you choose") and on the duplication of rhythm in the two phrases, which actually have no other connection.

Quixote. "Instead, so that you can regain your strength, we should save this for our village, where we shall arrive the day after tomorrow at the latest."

Sancho responded that he would do as his master wished but would like to conclude this matter quickly, while his blood was hot and the grindstone rough, because in delay there is often danger, and pray to God and use the hammer, and one "here you are" was worth more than two "I'll give it to you," and a bird in hand was worth two in the bush.

"By the one God, Sancho, no more proverbs," said Don Quixote. "It seems you are going back to *sicut erat*;[7] speak plainly, and simply, and without complications, as I have often told you, and you will see how one loaf will be the same as a hundred for you."

"I don't know why I'm so unlucky," responded Sancho, "that I can't say a word without a proverb, and every proverb seems exactly right to me, but I'll change, if I can."

And with this their conversation came to an end.

CHAPTER LXXII

Concerning how Don Quixote and Sancho arrived in their village

Don Quixote and Sancho spent the entire day in that village and in that inn, waiting for nightfall, the latter, to conclude a round of whipping in the open air, and the former, to see it completed, for this was all his desire. In the meantime, a traveler on horseback arrived at the inn, along with three or four servants, one of whom said to the one who seemed to be their master:

"Señor Don Álvaro Tarfe, your grace can spend the hottest part of the day here: the inn seems clean and cool."

Hearing this, Don Quixote said to Sancho:

"Look, Sancho: when I leafed through that book about the second part of my history, it seems to me I happened to run across this name of Don Álvaro Tarfe."[1]

7. The phrase is equivalent to "as it was before"—that is, "up to your old tricks."
1. Don Álvaro Tarfe is a character in Avellaneda's *Don Quixote*.

"That might be," responded Sancho. "We'll let him dismount, and then we can ask him about it."

The gentleman dismounted, and the innkeeper gave him a room on the ground floor, across from Don Quixote's lodging, which was hung with other tapestries like the ones in Don Quixote's room. The newcomer, dressed in summer clothes, came out to the portico of the inn, which was spacious and cool, and seeing Don Quixote walking there, he asked:

"Señor, may I ask where your grace is traveling?"

And Don Quixote responded:

"To a nearby village, which is where I live. And your grace, where are you going?"

"I, Señor," responded the gentleman, "am going to Granada, which is my home."

"A fine home!" replied Don Quixote. "But would your grace please be so kind as to tell me your name, because I believe it will be more important for me to know it than I can ever tell you."

"My name is Don Álvaro Tarfe," responded the guest at the inn.

To which Don Quixote replied:

"I think beyond any doubt that your grace must be the Don Álvaro Tarfe whose name appears in the second part of the *History of Don Quixote of La Mancha*, recently published and brought into the light of the world by a modern author."

"I am," responded the gentleman, "and Don Quixote, the principal subject of this history, was a great friend of mine; I was the one who took him from his home, or, at least, persuaded him to come with me to the jousts being held in Zaragoza; and the truth of the matter is that I became very friendly with him and saved him more than once from tasting a whip on his back because of his insolence."

"And, Señor Don Álvaro, can your grace tell me if I resemble in any way the Don Quixote you have mentioned?"

"No, certainly not," responded the guest, "not at all."

"And that Don Quixote," said our Don Quixote, "did he have with him a squire named Sancho Panza?"

"He did," responded Don Álvaro, "and though he was famous for being very amusing, I never heard him say any witticism that was."

"I can believe that," said Sancho at this point, "because saying amusing things is not for everybody, and the Sancho your grace is talking about, Señor, must be a great scoundrel, a dullard, and a thief all at the same time, because I'm the real Sancho Panza, and I have more amusing things to say than there are rainstorms; and if you don't think so, your grace can put it to the test, and follow after me for at least a year, and then you'll see whether or not amusing things drop off me at every step, so many of them that without my knowing what I've said most of the time, I make everybody who hears me laugh; and the real Don Quixote of La Mancha, the one who's famous, valiant, intelligent, and enamored, the righter of wrongs, the defender of wards and orphans, the protector of widows, a ladykiller with maidens, the one whose only lady is the peerless Dulcinea of Toboso, he is this gentleman here present, my master; every other Don Quixote and any other Sancho Panza are a trick and a dream."

"By God, I believe it!" responded Don Álvaro. "You have said more amusing things, my friend, in the few sentences you have spoken than the other Sancho Panza did in all the ones I heard him speak, and there were many! He was more gluttonous than well-spoken, and more foolish than amusing, and I believe beyond any doubt that the enchanters who pursue the good Don Quixote have wanted to pursue me along with the bad Don Quixote. But I don't know what to say, because I would swear I left him in the House of the Nuncio[2] in Toledo to be cured, and now suddenly here's another Don Quixote, though one very different from mine."

"I," said Don Quixote, "do not know if I am good, but I can say I am not the bad one, and as proof of this I want your grace to know, Señor Don Álvaro Tarfe, that in all the days of my life I have never been in Zaragoza; rather, because I had been told that this imaginary Don Quixote had gone to the jousts there, I refused to enter the city, thereby revealing the lie to everyone; instead, I went directly to Barcelona: fountain of courtesy, shelter of strangers, hospice to the poor, land of the valiant, avenger of the offended, reciprocator of firm friendship, a city unique in its location and beauty. And although the events that befell me there are not pleasing, but very grievous, I bear them better simply for having seen Barcelona. In short, Señor Don Álvaro Tarfe, I am Don Quixote of La Mancha, the same one who is on the lips of Fame, and not that unfortunate man who has wanted to usurp my name and bring honor to himself with my thoughts. I implore your grace, for the sake of what you owe to your being a gentleman, to please make a statement to the magistrate of this village, saying that your grace has not seen me in

---

2. The madhouse in Toledo, where Avellaneda's Don Quixote is confined.

all the days of your life until now, and that I am not the Don Quixote published in the second part, nor is this Sancho Panza, my squire, the one known by your grace."

"I shall do that very gladly," responded Don Álvaro, "although it astounds me to see two Don Quixotes and two Sanchos at the same time, as alike in their names as they are different in their actions; and I say again and affirm again that I have not seen what I have seen or experienced what I have experienced."

"No doubt," said Sancho, "your grace must be enchanted, like my lady Dulcinea of Toboso, and if it please heaven, I could disenchant your grace by giving myself another three thousand or so lashes the way I'm doing for her, and I would do it without charging interest."

"I don't understand what you mean by lashes," said Don Álvaro.

And Sancho responded that it was a long story, but he would tell it to him if they were traveling in the same direction.

At this point it was time to eat, and Don Quixote and Don Álvaro dined together. The magistrate of the village happened to come into the inn, along with a scribe, and Don Quixote submitted a petition to him saying that under the law it would be a good idea if Don Álvaro Tarfe, the gentleman here present, should declare before his grace that he did not know Don Quixote of La Mancha, also present, and that he, Don Quixote, was not the one who had appeared in a history entitled *Second Part of Don Quixote of La Mancha*, written by someone named Avellaneda, a native of Tordesillas. In brief, the magistrate gave his legal decision; the statement was made with all the juridical force that could be brought to bear in such cases, which made Don Quixote and Sancho very happy, as if such a statement mattered a great deal, and as if the difference between the two Don Quixotes and the two Sanchos could not be clearly seen in their actions and words. Many courtesies and offers of service were exchanged by Don Álvaro and Don Quixote, and in them the great Manchegan showed so much intelligence and sense that Don Álvaro was convinced he had been in error, and even came to believe he must have been enchanted, for he had touched two such antithetical Don Quixotes with his own hand.

As evening approached they left the village, and after about half a league their ways diverged, one leading to Don Quixote's village, the other the road that Don Álvaro had to follow. In this short period of time, Don Quixote recounted the misfortune of his defeat, and the enchantment of Dulcinea and its remedy, all of which caused renewed astonishment in Don Álvaro, who embraced Don Quixote and Sancho and continued on his way, while Don Quixote continued on his, planning to spend the night in another wood in order to give Sancho a chance to complete his penance, which he did in the same manner as the previous night, more at the expense of the bark on the beeches than his back, which he protected so carefully that the lashes could not have removed a fly if one had been there.

The deceived Don Quixote did not miss a single blow as he kept count, and he discovered that with those administered the night before, they amounted to three thousand twenty-nine. It seems the sun rose early in order to witness the sacrifice, and in its light they resumed their journey, the two of them discussing the deception of Don Álvaro and how wise it had been to take his statement legally, before a magistrate.

They traveled that day and night, and nothing occurred worthy of recording except that Sancho completed his task, which made Don Quixote extraordinarily happy, and he longed for daylight to see if he would meet on the road his disenchanted lady Dulcinea; but as he traveled, he encountered no woman whom he recognized as Dulcinea of Toboso, for he considered it incontrovertible that the promises of Merlin could not lie.

With these thoughts and desires they climbed a hill, and from there they could see their village, and when he saw it, Sancho dropped to his knees and said:

"Open your eyes, my beloved country, and see that your son Sancho Panza has come back to you, if not very rich, at least well-flogged. Open your arms and receive as well your son Don Quixote, who, though he returns conquered by another, returns the conqueror of himself; and, as he has told me, that is the greatest conquest anyone can desire. I'm bringing money, because if I've had a good lashing, at least I left riding a horse."[3]

"Enough of your foolishness," said Don Quixote, "and let us get off to a good start in our village, where we shall exercise our imaginations and plan the pastoral life we intend to lead."

With this they descended the hill and went toward their village.

---

3. Martín de Riquer observes that this statement probably alludes to a comic anecdote regarding the fate of a man who had been whipped.

CHAPTER LXXIII

Regarding the omens Don Quixote encountered as he entered his village, along with other events that adorn and lend credit to this great history

And at the entrance, according to Cide Hamete, Don Quixote saw two boys arguing on the threshing floor of the town, and one said to the other:

"Don't worry, Periquillo, you won't see it[1] in all the days of your life."

Don Quixote heard this and said to Sancho:

"Friend, did you notice that the boy said: 'You won't see her in all the days of your life'?"

"Well, why does it matter," responded Sancho, "what the boy said?"

"Why?" replied Don Quixote. "Do you not see that if you apply those words to my intention, it signifies that I am not to see Dulcinea again?"

Sancho was about to respond but was prevented from doing so when he saw a hare racing across the field, followed by a good number of greyhounds and hunters, and the terrified animal took refuge and shelter between the feet of the gray. Sancho picked it up, keeping it from harm, and handed it to Don Quixote, who was saying:

"*Malum signum! Malum signum!*[2] A hare flees, with greyhounds in pursuit: Dulcinea will not appear!"

"Your grace is a puzzle," said Sancho. "Let's suppose that this hare is Dulcinea of Toboso and these greyhounds chasing her are the wicked enchanters who changed her into a peasant; she flees, I catch her and turn her over to your grace, who holds her and cares for her: what kind of bad sign is that? What kind of evil omen can you find here?"

1. Don Quixote's misunderstanding is based on the fact that in Spanish, the objective pronoun *la* is the equivalent of both "it" and "her" in English.

2. Latin for "a bad sign" or "an evil omen."

The two boys who had been quarreling came over to see the hare, and Sancho asked one of them why they were arguing. And the one who had said 'You won't see it again in your whole life' responded that he had taken a cricket cage from the other boy and never intended to give it back to him. Sancho took four *cuartos* from his pocket and gave them to the boy in exchange for the cage, and he placed it in Don Quixote's hands, saying:

"Here, Señor, are your omens, broken and wrecked, and as far as I'm concerned, though I may be a fool, they have no more to do with our affairs than the clouds of yesteryear. And if I remember correctly, I've heard the priest in our village say that it isn't right for sensible Christians to heed this kind of nonsense, and even your grace has told me the same thing, letting me know that Christians who paid attention to omens were fools. But there's no need to spend any more time on this; let's go on into our village."

The hunters rode up, asked for their hare, and Don Quixote gave it to them; he and Sancho went on, and at the entrance to the village they encountered the priest and Bachelor Carrasco praying in a small meadow. And it should be noted here that Sancho Panza had draped the buckram tunic painted with flames, which they had placed on him in the duke's castle on the night Altisidora was resuscitated, over the bundle of armor on the gray to serve as his *repostero*.[3] He had also set the cone-shaped hat on the gray's head, which was the oddest transformation and adornment ever seen on any donkey in the world.

The priest and the bachelor recognized them immediately and came toward them with open arms. Don Quixote dismounted and embraced them warmly, and some boys, who are as sharp-eyed as lynxes, caught sight of the donkey's hat and hurried over to see it, saying to one another:

"Come on, boys, and you'll see Sancho Panza's donkey all dressed up and Don Quixote's animal skinnier today than he ever was."

In short, surrounded by boys and accompanied by the priest and the bachelor, they entered the village and went to Don Quixote's house, and at the door they saw his housekeeper and his niece, who had already heard the news of their return. Teresa Panza, Sancho's wife, had heard exactly the same news, and disheveled and half-dressed and pulling her daughter, Sanchica, along by the hand, she hurried to see her husband,

3. An embroidered cloth or tapestry, bearing a knight's coat of arms, that was draped over pack mules.

and when she saw him not as elegantly dressed as she thought a governor should be, she said:

"Husband, why are you traveling like this, on foot and footsore and, it seems to me, looking more like a misgoverned fool than like a governor?"

"Be quiet, Teresa," responded Sancho, "because often you can have hooks and no bacon;[4] let's go home, and there you will hear wonderful things. I have money, which is what matters, that I earned by my own labor, and with no harm to anybody."

"Bring the money, my good husband," said Teresa, "no matter if you earned it here or there; no matter how you did it, you won't have thought up any new ways of earning it."

Sanchica embraced her father and asked if he had brought her anything, for she had been waiting for him like the showers of May, and she held him on one side by his belt; and with his wife holding his hand and his daughter leading the gray, they went to their house, leaving Don Quixote in his, in the hands of his niece and his housekeeper, and in the company of the priest and the bachelor.

Don Quixote, at that very moment, without regard for the time or the hour, withdrew with the bachelor and the priest, and when they were alone he told them briefly about his defeat and the obligation he was under not to leave his village for a year, which he intended to obey to the letter and not violate in the slightest, as befitted a knight errant bound by the order and demands of knight errantry, and that he had thought of becoming a shepherd for the year and spending his time in the solitude of the countryside, where he could freely express his amorous thoughts and devote himself to the virtuous pastoral occupation; and he implored them, if they did not have too much to do and were not prevented by more important matters, to be his companions, and he would buy enough sheep and livestock to give them the name of shepherds; and he told them that the most important part of the business had already been taken care of, because he had given them names that would fit them like a glove. The priest asked him to say what they were. Don Quixote responded that he would be called *Shepherd Quixotiz,* and the bachelor would be *Shepherd Carrascón,* and the priest, *Shepherd Curambro,* and Sancho Panza, *Shepherd Pancino.*

They were stunned by Don Quixote's new madness, but in order to

---

4. As Martín de Riquer observes, Sancho seems to be citing an inappropriate proverb, since he means to say that despite his wretched appearance, he has brought home money.

keep him from leaving the village again on chivalric exploits, and hoping he might be cured during that year, they acquiesced to his new intentions, and approved his madness as sensible, and offered to be his companions in his occupations.

"Moreover," said Sansón Carrasco, "as everyone already knows, I am a celebrated poet and shall constantly compose pastoral verses, or courtly ones, or whatever seems most appropriate, to entertain us as we wander those out-of-the-way places; and what is most necessary, Señores, is for each to choose the name of the shepherdess to be celebrated in his verses, the name he will carve and inscribe on every tree, no matter how hard, as is the usage and custom of enamored shepherds."

"That is quite fitting," responded Don Quixote, "although I do not need to find the name of a feigned shepherdess, for there is the peerless Dulcinea of Toboso, glory of these fields, ornament of these meadows, mainstay of beauty, flower of all graces, and, in short, a subject on whom all praise sits well, no matter how hyperbolic."

"That is true," said the priest, "but we shall have to find some well-mannered shepherdesses, and if their names don't suit us, we can trim them to fit."

To which Sansón Carrasco added:

"And if our invention fails, we can give them the names that have been published and printed and that fill the world: Phyllida, Amaryllis, Diana, Flerida, Galatea, and Belisarda; since they're sold on every square, we can certainly buy them and keep them for our own. If my lady, or I should say my shepherdess, happens to be named Ana, I shall celebrate her under the name *Anarda*, and if her name is Francisca, I shall call her *Francenia*, and if Lucia, *Lucinda*, for that's all it amounts to; and Sancho Panza, if he joins our fraternity, can celebrate his wife, Teresa Panza, with the name *Teresaina*."

Don Quixote laughed at the aptness of the name, and the priest praised to the skies his honest and honorable resolution and once again offered to accompany him in the time he was not occupied in attending to his obligations. And with this they took their leave of Don Quixote and implored him and advised him to take care of his health and to eat well.

It so happened that the niece and the housekeeper heard the conversation of the three men, and as soon as the visitors left, the two women entered the room to see Don Quixote, and his niece said:

"What is this, Uncle? We thought your grace would stay at home again and lead a quiet and honorable life, and now you want to go into new labyrinths and become

> Little shepherd, now you're coming,
> little shepherd, now you're going?[5]

Well, the truth is that the stem's too hard for making flutes.[6]

To which the housekeeper added:

"And there in the countryside will your grace be able to endure the heat of summer, the night air of winter, the howling of the wolves? No, certainly not; this is work for strong, hard men who've been brought up to the life almost from the time they're in swaddling clothes. No matter how bad it is, it's better to be a knight errant than a shepherd. Look, Señor, take my advice; I'm giving it to you not when I'm full of bread and wine, but when I'm fasting, and based on what I've learned in my fifty years: stay in your house, tend to your estate, go to confession often, favor the poor, and let it be on my soul if that does you any harm."

"Be quiet, my dears," responded Don Quixote, "for I know what I must do. Take me to my bed, because I think I am not well, and you can be certain that regardless of whether I am a knight errant or a shepherd on the verge of wandering, I shall always provide for you, as my actions will prove."

And the two good women, which the housekeeper and niece undoubtedly were, took him to his bed, where they fed him and pampered him as much as possible.

---

5. The lines are from a Christmas carol.

6. The origin of the proverb was the tradition of forming flutes or pipes out of green barley stems; it is used when a mature and sensible person does not wish to engage in childish activities.

CHAPTER LXXIV

Which deals with how Don Quixote fell ill, and the will he made, and his death

Since human affairs, particularly the lives of men, are not eternal and are always in a state of decline from their beginnings until they reach their final end, and since the life of Don Quixote had no privilege from heaven to stop its natural course, it reached its end and conclusion when he least expected it, for whether it was due to the melancholy caused by his defeat or simply the will of heaven, he succumbed to a fever that kept him in bed for six days, during which time he was often visited by his friends the priest, the bachelor, and the barber, while Sancho Panza, his good squire, never left his side.

They believed that his grief at being defeated, and his unsatisfied longing to see Dulcinea free and disenchanted, were responsible for his condition, and they did everything they could think of to lift his spirits; the bachelor told him to be of good cheer and to get out of bed so that they could begin the pastoral life, for which he had already composed an eclogue that would put all those written by Sannazaro[1] to shame, and he said he had bought with his own money two famous dogs to guard the flocks, one named Barcino and the other Butrón, which had been sold to him by a herder from Quintanar. But not even this could bring Don Quixote out of his sorrow.

His friends called the physician, who took his pulse and did not give them good news, and said there was no doubt that he should attend to the health of his soul because the health of his body was in peril. Don Quixote heard him with a tranquil spirit, but not his housekeeper, his

1. The Italian Jacopo Sannazaro (1458–1530) was the author of *La Arcadia*, the first pastoral novel of the Renaissance.

niece, and his squire, who began to weep piteously, as if he were already lying dead before them. It was the physician's opinion that melancholy and low spirits were bringing his life to an end. Don Quixote asked to be left alone because he wanted to sleep for a while. They did as he asked, and he slept more than six hours at a stretch, as they say, so long that his housekeeper and his niece thought he would never open his eyes again. He awoke after the length of time that has been mentioned, and giving a great shout, he said:

"Blessed be Almighty God who has done such great good for me! His mercies have no limit, and the sins of men do not curtail or hinder them."

His niece listened carefully to her uncle's words, and they seemed more sensible than the ones he usually said, at least during his illness, and she asked him:

"What is your grace saying, Señor? Is there news? Which mercies are these, and which sins of men?"

"The mercies, Niece," responded Don Quixote, "are those that God has shown to me at this very instant, and as I said, my sins do not hinder them. My judgment is restored, free and clear of the dark shadows of ignorance imposed on it by my grievous and constant reading of detestable books of chivalry. I now recognize their absurdities and deceptions, and my sole regret is that this realization has come so late it does not leave me time to compensate by reading other books that can be a light to the soul. I feel, Niece, that I am about to die; I should like to do so in a manner that would make it clear that my life was not so wicked that I left behind a reputation for being a madman, for although I have been one, I should not like to confirm this truth in my death. Dear girl, call my good friends for me: the priest, the bachelor Sansón Carrasco, and the barber Master Nicolás, for I wish to confess and make my will."

But the niece was excused from this task by the entrance of the three men. As soon as Don Quixote saw them, he said:

"Good news, Señores! I am no longer Don Quixote of La Mancha but Alonso Quixano, once called *the Good* because of my virtuous life. Now I am the enemy of Amadís of Gaul and all the infinite horde of his lineage; now all the profane histories of knight errantry are hateful to me; now I recognize my foolishness and the danger I was in because I read them; now, by God's mercy, I have learned from my experience and I despise them."

When the three men heard him say this, they undoubtedly believed that some new madness had taken hold of him, and Sansón said:

"Now, Señor Don Quixote, you say this now, when we have news of the disenchantment of Señora Dulcinea? And now that we are on the point of becoming shepherds and spending our lives in song, like princes, now your grace wishes to be a hermit? For God's sake, be quiet, come to your senses, and tell us no more tales."

"Those that until now," replied Don Quixote, "have been real, to my detriment, will, with the help of heaven, be turned to my benefit by my death. Señores, I feel that I am dying very rapidly; let us put all jokes aside, and bring me a confessor to hear my confession, and a scribe to write my will, for at critical moments like these a man cannot play games with his soul; and so, while the priest hears my confession, I beg you to bring the scribe."

They exchanged glances, astonished by Don Quixote's words, and although they had their doubts, they tended to believe him; one of the signs that led them to think he really was dying was how easily he had moved from madness to sanity, because to the words already cited he added many others that were so well-spoken, so Christian, and so reasonable that their doubts were completely dispelled and they believed he was sane.

The priest had everyone leave, and was alone with him, and heard his confession.

The bachelor went for the scribe and returned a short time later with him and with Sancho Panza, and Sancho—who had already been told by the bachelor about his master's condition—found the housekeeper and the niece weeping, and he began to sob and shed tears. When the confession had ended the priest came out and said:

"Alonso Quixano the Good is truly dying, and he has truly recovered his reason; we ought to go in so that he can make his will."

This news put terrible pressure on the already full eyes of his housekeeper, his niece, and his good squire, Sancho Panza, forcing tears from their eyes and a thousand deep sighs from their bosoms, because the truth is, as has already been said, that whether Don Quixote was simply Alonso Quixano the Good, or whether he was Don Quixote of La Mancha, he always had a gentle disposition and was kind in his treatment of others, and for this reason he was dearly loved not only by those in his household, but by everyone who knew him.

The scribe came in with the others, and after Don Quixote had completed the preface to the will and tended to his soul with all the Christian particulars that are required, he came to the bequests and said:

"Item: it is my will that with regard to certain monies held by Sancho Panza, whom, in my madness, I made my squire, because between him and me there were certain accounts and debts and payments, and I do not want him held responsible for them, nor should any accounting be demanded of him, but if anything is left over after he has taken what I owe him, the remainder, which will not amount to much, should be his, and may it do him good; and if, when I was mad, I was party to giving him the governorship of the ínsula, now, when I am sane, if I could give him the governorship of a kingdom, I would, because the simplicity of his nature and the fidelity of his actions deserve it."

And turning to Sancho, he said:

"Forgive me, my friend, for the opportunity I gave you to seem as mad as I, making you fall into the error into which I fell, thinking that there were and are knights errant in the world."

"Oh!" responded Sancho, weeping. "Don't die, Señor; your grace should take my advice and live for many years, because the greatest madness a man can commit in this life is to let himself die, just like that, without anybody killing him or any other hands ending his life except those of melancholy. Look, don't be lazy, but get up from that bed and let's go to the countryside dressed as shepherds, just like we arranged: maybe behind some bush we'll find Señora Doña Dulcinea disenchanted, as pretty as you please. If you're dying of sorrow over being defeated, blame me for that and say you were toppled because I didn't tighten Rocinante's cinches; besides, your grace must have seen in your books of chivalry that it's a very common thing for one knight to topple another, and for the one who's vanquished today to be the victor tomorrow."

"That's right," said Sansón, "and our good Sancho Panza knows the truth of these cases."

"Señores," said Don Quixote, "let us go slowly, for there are no birds today in yesterday's nests. I was mad, and now I am sane; I was Don Quixote of La Mancha, and now I am, as I have said, Alonso Quixano the Good. May my repentance and sincerity return me to the esteem your graces once had for me, and let the scribe continue.

Item: I bequeath my entire estate to Antonia Quixana, my niece, who is present, having first taken out, in the most convenient way, what is necessary to fulfill the other bequests I have made; and the first that I want to make is to pay the salary owed to my housekeeper for the time she has served me, plus another twenty *ducados* for a dress. As executors I appoint the priest and Bachelor Sansón Carrasco, who are both present.

Item: it is my will that if Antonia Quixana, my niece, wishes to marry, she marry a man regarding whom it has first been determined that he does not know anything about books of chivalry; and in the event it is discovered that he does know about them, and despite this my niece still wishes to marry him, she must lose all that I have left her, which can then be distributed by my executors in pious works, as they see fit.

Item: I implore the aforementioned executors that if they are fortunate enough to meet the author who, they say, composed a history entitled *The Second Part of the Exploits of Don Quixote of La Mancha,* that they ask him for me, as courteously as possible, to forgive the occasion I unwittingly gave him for writing so many and such great absurdities as he wrote therein, because I depart this life with qualms that I have been the reason he wrote them."

With this he brought his will to a close, and falling into a swoon, he collapsed on his bed. Everyone was alarmed and hurried to assist him, and in the three days he lived after making his will, he fainted very often. The house was in an uproar, but even so the niece ate, the housekeeper drank, and Sancho Panza was content, for the fact of inheriting something wipes away or tempers in the heir the memory of the grief that is reasonably felt for the deceased.

In brief, Don Quixote's end came after he had received all the sacraments and had execrated books of chivalry with many effective words. The scribe happened to be present, and he said he had never read in any book of chivalry of a knight errant dying in his bed in so tranquil and Christian a manner as Don Quixote, who, surrounded by the sympathy and tears of those present, gave up the ghost, I mean to say, he died.

When he saw this, the priest asked the scribe to draw up a document to the effect that Alonso Quixano the Good, commonly called Don Quixote of La Mancha, had passed from this life and had died a natural death; he said he was requesting this document in order to remove the possibility that any author other than Cide Hamete Benengeli would falsely resurrect him and write endless histories of his deeds.

This was the end of the Ingenious Gentleman of La Mancha, whose village Cide Hamete did not wish to name precisely, so that all the towns and villages of La Mancha might contend among themselves to claim him as their own, as the seven cities in Greece contended to claim Homer.

The tears of Sancho and of Don Quixote's niece and housekeeper, new epitaphs for his grave, are not recorded here, although Sansón Carrasco did write this one for him:

Here lies the mighty Gentleman
who rose to such heights of valor
that death itself did not triumph
over his life with his death.
He did not esteem the world;
he was the frightening threat
to the world, in this respect,
for it was his great good fortune
to live a madman, and die sane.

And a most prudent Cide Hamete said to his pen:

"Here you will remain, hanging from this rack on a copper wire, and I do not know if you, my quill pen, are well or badly cut, but there you will live, down through the ages, unless presumptuous and unscrupulous historians take you down to profane you. But before they reach you, you can warn them and tell them as well as you are able:

Careful, careful, worthless idlers!
Let no one lay a hand on me;
for this enterprise, O king,
is reserved only for me.

For me alone was Don Quixote born, and I for him; he knew how to act, and I to write; the two of us alone are one, despite and regardless of the false Tordesillan writer who dared, or will dare, to write with a coarse and badly designed ostrich feather about the exploits of my valorous knight, for it is not a burden for his shoulders or a subject for his cold creativity; and you will warn him, if you ever happen to meet him, to let the weary and crumbling bones of Don Quixote rest in the grave, and not attempt, contrary to all the statutes of death, to carry them off to Castilla la Vieja,[2] removing him from the tomb where he really and truly lies, incapable of undertaking a third journey or a new sally; for to mock the many undertaken by so many knights errant, the two he made were enough, and they have brought delight and pleasure to everyone who knows of them, in these kingdoms as well as those abroad. And with this you will fulfill your Christian duty, by giving good counsel to those who do not wish you well, and I shall be pleased and proud to have been the

2. This was recounted by Avellaneda at the end of his book; he also expresses his confidence that another author will take up the task of writing the new adventures of Don Quixote.

first who completely enjoyed the fruits of his writing, just as he wished, for my only desire has been to have people reject and despise the false and nonsensical histories of the books of chivalry, which are already stumbling over the history of my true Don Quixote, and will undoubtedly fall to the ground. *Vale*."

Don Quixote